ROBERT MUSIL

THE MAN
WITHOUT QUALITIES

Robert Musil was born in Klagenfurt, Austria, in 1880. Trained in science and philosophy, he left a career in the military to turn to writing. The publication of his novel *Young Törless* in 1906 brought him international recognition; to this day it remains a classic parable on the misuse of power. After serving in the First World War, Musil lived alternately in Vienna and Berlin, with much of his time being dedicated to the slow writing of his masterwork, *The Man Without Qualities*. In 1938, when Hitler's rise to power threatened Musil's work with being banned in both Austria and Germany, he emigrated to Switzerland, where he and his wife lived until his death in 1942. The first complete German edition of *The Man Without Qualities* finally appeared in 1978.

INTERNATIONAL

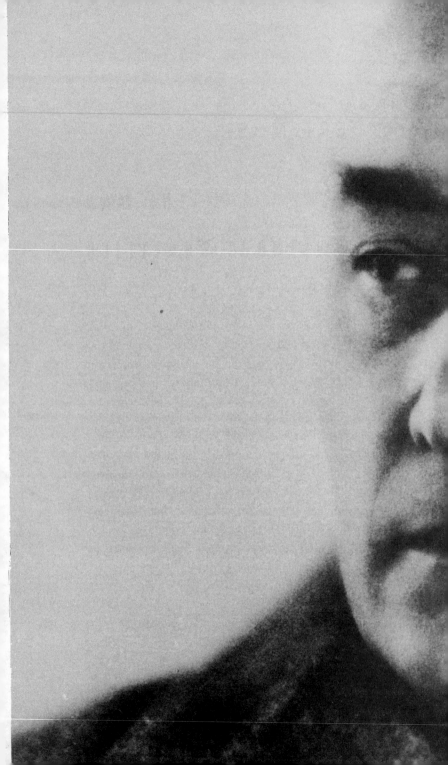

ROBERT MUSIL

INTO THE MILLENNIUM

TRANSLATED FROM THE GERMAN BY **SOPHIE WILKINS**

EDITORIAL CONSULTANT: **BURTON PIKE**

FROM THE POSTHUMOUS PAPERS

TRANSLATED FROM THE GERMAN BY

BURTON PIKE

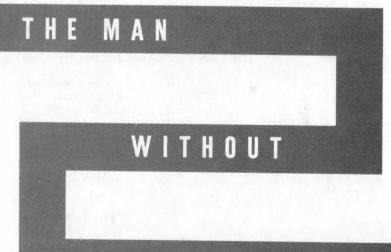

THE MAN WITHOUT QUALITIES

VINTAGE INTERNATIONAL

VINTAGE BOOKS   A DIVISION OF RANDOM HOUSE, INC.   NEW YORK

II

FIRST VINTAGE INTERNATIONAL EDITION, DECEMBER 1996

Copyright © 1995 by Alfred A. Knopf, Inc.

The Library of Congress has cataloged
the Knopf edition as follows:
Musil, Robert, 1880–1942.
[Mann ohne Eigenschaften. English]
The man without qualities / Robert Musil ;
translated from the German by Sophie Wilkins and Burton Pike.
p. cm.
ISBN 0-394-51052-6
(boxed set)
I. Title
PT2625.U8M313 1995
833'.912—DC20 92-37943
CIP
Vintage ISBN: 0-679-76802-5

Random House Web address: http://www.randomhouse.com/

Printed in the United States of America
10 9

CONTENTS

PART III: INTO THE MILLENNIUM (THE CRIMINALS)

FROM THE POSTHUMOUS PAPERS

A table of contents for this section
follows page 1131.

PART III

INTO THE MILLENNIUM

(THE CRIMINALS)

1

The forgotten sister

On his arrival in ——— toward evening of the same day, as Ulrich came out of the station he saw before him a wide, shallow square that opened into streets at both ends and jolted his memory almost painfully, as happens with a landscape one has seen often and then forgotten again.

"Believe me, income has dropped by twenty percent and prices have gone up twenty percent, that's a total of forty percent!" "Believe *me*, a six-day bike race promotes international goodwill like nothing else!" These voices were still coming out of his ear: train voices. Then he distinctly heard someone saying: "Still, for me, there's nothing to beat opera!" "Is that your hobby?" "It's my passion."

He tilted his head as though to shake water out of his ear. The train had been crowded, the journey long. Driblets of the general conversation around him that had seeped into him during the trip were oozing out again. Ulrich had waited for the joyfulness and bustle of arrival—which had poured into the quiet square from the station exit as from the mouth of a drainpipe—to subside to a trickle; now he was standing in the vacuum of silence left behind by such noise. But even as his hearing was still disturbed from the abrupt change, he was struck by an unaccustomed peace that met his eyes. Everything visible was more intensely so than usual, and when he looked across the square the crossbars of perfectly ordinary windows stood as black against the pale sheen of glass in the dimming light as if they were the crosses of Golgotha. And everything that moved seemed to detach itself from the calm of the street in a way that never happens in very large cities. Whether passing or standing still, things evidently had the space here in which to make their importance felt. He could see this with the curiosity of reacquaintance as he gazed out on the large provincial town where he had spent some brief, not very pleasant, parts of his life. It had, as he well knew, an air of someplace colonial, a place of exile: here a nucleus of ancient German burgher stock, transplanted centuries ago to Slavic soil, had withered away so that hardly anything was left, apart from a few churches and family names, to remind one of it; nor, except for a fine old palace that had been preserved, was there evidence of its having become, later on, the old seat of the Provincial Diet. But in the era of absolute rule this past had been overlaid by a vast apparatus of imperial administration, with its provincial headquarters, schools and universities, barracks, courthouses, prisons, bishop's palace, assembly rooms, and theater, together with the people needed to run them and the merchants and artisans who came in their wake, until finally an industry of entrepreneurs moved in, filling the suburbs with their factories one after the other, with a greater influence on the fate of this piece of earth in the past few generations than anything else had had. This town had a past, and it even had a face, but the eyes did not go with the mouth, or the chin with the hair; over everything lay the traces of a hectic life that is inwardly empty. This could possibly, under special personal circumstances, foster great originality.

To sum it up in a phrase perhaps equally arguable, Ulrich had the sense of something "spiritually insubstantial" in which one lost oneself so entirely as to awaken unbridled imaginings. In his pocket he carried his father's eccentric telegram, which he knew by heart: "This is to inform you that I am deceased" was the old gentleman's message for him—or was it to him? as indicated by the signature at the end: "Your father." His Excellency the Privy Councillor never went in for levity at serious moments. The weird information of the message was consequently infernally logical, since he was himself notifying his son when, in expectation of his end, he wrote or dictated word for word the message that was to be dispatched the instant he had drawn his last breath; the facts could really not be more correctly stated, and yet this act by which the present tried to dominate a future it could not live to see emitted from the grave an uncanny whiff of an angrily decayed will!

This manifestation, which somehow reminded Ulrich of the meticulously undiscriminating taste of small towns, made him think with some misgiving of his sister, who had married in the provinces and whom he was about to meet, in the next few minutes. He had been wondering about her already on the train, for he did not know much about her. From time to time standard items of family news reached him through his father's letters; for example: "Your sister Agathe is married," adding some of the details, since at the time Ulrich had not been able to come home for the wedding. Only about a year later he received notice of the young husband's death; then, three years or so after that, if he was not mistaken, word came that "Your sister Agathe, I am glad to say, has decided to marry again." At this second wedding, five years ago, Ulrich had been present and had seen his sister for a few days, but all he remembered was a ceaseless whirl, like a giant wheel of white cambric and lace. He also remembered the bridegroom, who made a poor impression on him. Agathe must have been twenty-two then, while he was twenty-seven, for he had just received his doctorate, so that his sister had to be twenty-seven now; but he had not seen her since that time, nor exchanged letters with her. He recalled only that his father had later written more than once: "It pains me to report that all does not seem to be going as well as it might in your sister's marriage, although her husband is a capital fellow" and "The latest successes of your sister Agathe's husband have been most gratifying": Such, more or less, were his father's comments in letters to which Ulrich had, regrettably, never paid any attention; but once, as he now remembered quite clearly, in connection with a disapproving comment on his sister's childlessness, their father expressed the hope that she was nevertheless contented in her marriage, although it was not in her character ever to admit it.

"I wonder what she looks like now," he thought.

It had been one of the old gentleman's eccentricities to keep them conscientiously informed about each other after he had sent them away from home at a tender age, right after their mother's death, to be educated in different schools. Ulrich, who got into scrapes, was often not allowed home for school holidays; so that since their childhood, when they had in fact been inseparable, he had hardly seen his sister again, with the exception of one longish visit when Agathe was ten.

In the circumstances, Ulrich had thought it only natural that they did not write. What would they have had to say to each other? At the time of Agathe's first marriage he was, as he now remembered, a lieutenant in the army, and in the hospital recovering from a bullet wound received in a duel: Lord, what an ass he had been! In fact, he had made every kind of ass of himself. For he remembered now that the memory of the wounded lieutenant belonged someplace else. He had been about to qualify as an engineer and had something "important" to do that had kept him from the family ceremony. Later he learned that his sister had been very much in love with her first husband; he could not remember who had told him, but what does "very much in love" mean anyway? It's what people say. She had married again, and Ulrich could not stand her second husband; that was the one thing he was sure of. He disliked him not only for the bad impression he made personally but also for that made by some of his books, which Ulrich had read, so that Ulrich's subsequent forgetting of his sister might not have been quite unintentional. It was nothing to be proud of, but he had to admit that even during this last year, when he had thought of so many things, he had never given her a thought, not even when he had received the news of their father's death. But he did ask the old manservant who came to meet him at the station whether his brother-in-law had arrived yet, and was relieved to hear that Professor Hagauer was not expected until the day of the funeral. Even though it could be no more than two or three days till then, it seemed to him like a respite of indefinite duration, which he would spend alone with his sister as though they were the closest people in the world. There would have been no point in trying to see any logic in this; the thought of "my unknown sister" was evidently one of those roomy abstractions in which many feelings that are not quite at home anywhere could find a place.

Thus preoccupied, Ulrich had walked slowly into the town that opened up before him, at once strange and familiar. He had sent on his luggage, into which he had stuffed quite a number of books at the last minute, in a cab with the old servant, a part of his childhood memories, who had come to combine the functions of caretaker, butler, and clerk in a fashion that over the years made them hard to distinguish from one another. It was probably this self-effacing, taciturn man to whom Ulrich's father had dictated his death notice, and Ulrich's feet led him homeward in pleasurable wonder as his now alert senses curiously took in the fresh impressions that every growing city springs on someone who has not seen it for a long time. At a certain point, which they remembered before he did, Ulrich's feet turned off the main street, and he soon found himself in a narrow lane formed by two garden walls. Diagonally across his path stood the house of barely two stories, the main building higher than the wings, with the old stable to one side and, still pressed against the garden wall, the little house where the servant and his wife lived; it looked as though for all his confidence in them the aged master had wished to keep them as far as possible from him while still embracing them within his walls. Ulrich had absently walked up to the locked garden gate and dropped the big ring-shaped knocker that hung there in lieu of a bell against the low door, black with age, before the servant came running up to correct his error. They had to go back around the wall to the main entrance, where the cab had drawn up, and it was only at this moment, seeing the shuttered façade of the house before him, that it occurred to Ulrich that his sister had not come to meet him at the station. The servant reported that Madame had a migraine and had retired after lunch, ordering them to wake her when the Herr Doktor arrived. Did his sister suffer from migraine often? Ulrich went on to ask, then instantly regretted his slip in drawing the old servant's attention to family matters that were better passed over in silence.

"The young Madame gave orders for tea to be served in half an hour," the well-trained old man replied, with a servant's politely blank expression giving discreet assurance that he understood nothing beyond his duty.

Spontaneously Ulrich glanced up at the windows, supposing that Agathe might be standing there observing his arrival. He wondered whether she would be agreeable, becoming uneasily aware how awkward the visit would be if he happened not to like her. That she had neither come to meet his train nor met him at the house door was distinctly in her favor, however, showing a certain rapport of feeling: rushing to meet him, after all, would have been as uncalled for as it would have been for him on arrival to rush to his father's coffin. He left word for her that he would be down in half an hour, and went to his room to get himself in order. The room he was to stay in was in the mansard-roofed second story of the main house and had been his childhood room, now curiously supplemented by the addition of a few random pieces for an adult's comfort. "It was probably the best they could do as long as the body is still in the house," Ulrich thought, settling in among the ruins of his childhood a little awkwardly, yet also with a rather warm feeling that seemed to rise like mist from the floor. As he started to change it occurred to him to put on a pajama-like lounging suit he came across while unpacking. "She might at least have come down to say hello when I got here," he thought, and there was a hint of rebuke in his casual choice of dress, even as he continued to feel that his sister's reason for acting as she did was likely to be a congenial one, so that he was also complimenting her by his unforced expression of ease.

The loose lounging suit of soft wool he put on was patterned in black and gray squares, almost a Pierrot costume, gathered at the waist, wrists, and ankles; he liked its comfort, which felt pleasant after that sleepless night and the long train journey, as he came down the stairs. But when he entered the room where his sister was waiting, he was amazed at his costume, for by some mysterious directive of chance he found his appearance echoed in that of a tall, blond Pierrot in a pattern of delicate gray and rust stripes and lozenges, who at first glance looked quite like himself.

"I had no idea we were twins!" Agathe said, her face lighting up with a smile.

2

CONFIDENCES

They did not greet each other with a kiss but merely stood amicably facing each other, then moved apart, and Ulrich was able to take a good look at his sister. They were of matching height. Agathe's hair was fairer than his and had the same dry fragrance as her skin, the fragrance that was the only thing he liked about his own body. Instead of being all bosom she had small, firm breasts, and her limbs seemed to have the long, slender spindle shape that combines natural athletic ability and beauty.

"I hope you're over your migraine," Ulrich said. "It doesn't show."

"I never had migraine; it was just the simplest thing to say," Agathe explained. "I couldn't very well send you a long and complicated message through the servants. I was lazy, that's all. I took a nap. In this house I've got into the habit of sleeping every chance I get. I'm basically lazy—out of desperation, I think. And when I heard you were coming I thought, 'Let's hope this is the last time I feel sleepy,' and I gave myself up to a sort of sleep cure. I thought it over carefully and then, for the butler's convenience, decided to call it migraine."

"Don't you go in for any sports?" Ulrich asked.

"Some tennis. But I detest sports."

As she spoke, he studied her face again. It did not seem very like his own, but perhaps he was mistaken; maybe it was like the same face done in pastels and in a woodcut, the difference in the medium obscuring the congruence of line and plane. There was something in this face he found disturbing. After a while, he realized that he simply could not read its expression; what was missing was whatever it is that enables one to draw the usual inferences about the person. It was an expressive face, but nothing in it was emphasized, nothing combined in the way that normally suggests traits of character.

"How did you happen to dress like that?" Ulrich asked.

"No special reason. I thought it would be nice."

"It's very nice!" Ulrich laughed. "But positively a conjuring trick of chance! And Father's death doesn't seem to have greatly upset you either?"

Agathe rose slowly on her toes and then just as slowly sank back on her heels.

"Is your husband here yet?" her brother asked, just to say something.

"Professor Hagauer is coming for the funeral." She seemed to relish the occasion to pronounce that name so formally and to dissociate herself from it as if it were some strange object.

Ulrich was at a loss how to respond. "Oh yes, so I was told," he said.

Again they looked at each other, and then they went, as the proper next step, into the little room where the body lay.

The room had been kept artificially dark for a whole day; it was drenched in black. Flowers and lighted candles glowed and scented the air. The two Pierrots stood straight as they faced the dead man, as if watching him.

"I'll never go back to Hagauer," Agathe said, just to get it out. One could almost think she wanted the dead man to hear it too.

There he lay on his bier, as he had directed: in full evening dress, the pall drawn halfway down his chest to expose the stiff shirtfront with all his decorations, his hands folded without a crucifix. Small, hard-ridged brows, sunken cheeks and lips. Stitched into the horrible, eyeless corpse's skin, which is still a part of the personality and yet already something apart: life's traveling bag. In spite of himself, Ulrich felt shaken at his very core, deep beneath any feeling or thought; but nowhere else. If he had had to put it into words, he would only have been able to say that a tiresome, loveless relationship had come to an end. Just as a bad marriage debases the people who cannot get free of it, so does every burdensome bond meant to last forever when the mortal substance shrivels away from under it.

"I would have liked you to come sooner," Agathe went on, "but Papa wouldn't have it. He made all the arrangements for his death himself. I think he would have been embarrassed to die with you looking on. I've been living here for two weeks now; it's been horrible."

"Did he love *you*, at least?" Ulrich asked.

"Whatever he wanted done he told old Franz to take care of, and from then on he gave the impression of someone who has nothing to do and has no purpose in life. But every fifteen minutes or so he'd lift up his head to check whether I was still in the room. For the first few days, that is. Then it was only every half hour, then every hour, and during that frightful last day it happened only two or three times. And all that time he never said a word to me except when I asked him something."

As she spoke, Ulrich was thinking: "She's really hard. Even as a child she could be incredibly stubborn, in her quiet way. And yet she seems to be amenable enough. . . ." And suddenly he thought of an avalanche. He had once almost lost his life in a forest that was being devastated by an avalanche. It had been no more than a soft cloud of powdery snow, and yet the irresistible force behind it gave it the impact of a toppling mountain.

"Was it you who sent me the telegram?" he asked.

"That was old Franz, of course. It was all settled beforehand. He wouldn't let me take care of him, either. He certainly never loved me, and I don't know why he sent for me. I felt miserable and shut myself up in my room as often as I could. It was during one of those times that he died."

"He probably did it to prove that you were in the wrong," Ulrich said bitterly. "Come on!" He drew her toward the door. "But maybe he wanted you to stroke his forehead? Or kneel by his bedside? Even if it was only because he had always read that it's the proper way to take leave of a father for the last time. Only he couldn't bring himself to ask you."

"Maybe," she said.

They had stopped for another look at him.

"How horrible it is, all of it!" Agathe said.

"Yes," Ulrich said. "And we know so little about it."

As they were leaving the room Agathe stopped again and said to Ulrich: "I'm springing something on you that can't be of any concern to you, of course, but it was during Father's illness that I decided not to go back to my husband under any circumstances."

Her brother could not help smiling at the stubbornness with which she said this, for Agathe had a vertical furrow between her brows and spoke vehemently; she seemed to fear that he would not be on her side, and reminded him of a terrified cat whose fright makes it leap bravely to the attack.

"Does he consent?" Ulrich asked.

"He knows nothing about it yet," Agathe said. "But he won't consent!"

Her brother gave her a questioning look. She shook her head impatiently. "Oh no, it's not what you think. There's no third person involved," she said.

With this, their conversation came to an end for the time being. Agathe apologized for having been so unmindful of Ulrich's hunger and fatigue, led him to a room where tea had been laid out, then went herself to fetch something that was missing from the tray. Left to himself, Ulrich used the opportunity to concentrate on whatever he could recollect about her husband, the better to understand her. Professor Hagauer was a man of medium height with a ramrod bearing and plump legs in baggy trousers, rather fleshy lips under a bristly mustache, and a fondness for florid neckties, probably as a sign that he was no common schoolmaster but one who was future-oriented. Ulrich felt his cold misgivings about Agathe's choice reawaken, but that Gottlieb Hagauer, with candor shining from his brow and eyes, would harbor secret vices was entirely out of the question. "He's the very model of the industrious, capable person, doing his best for humanity in his own field without meddling in matters beyond his scope," Ulrich decided, remembering Hagauer's writings, as well, and falling into not entirely agreeable thoughts.

Such people can first be recognized for what they are even in their school days. They study not so much conscientiously—as it is called, confusing the effect with the cause—as in an orderly and practical fashion. They lay out every task beforehand, just as one has to lay out every piece of tomorrow's clothing, down to the last collar button, the night before if one wants to dress quickly and without a hitch in the morning. There is no chain of thought they cannot fix in their minds by using half a dozen such laid-out studs, and there is no denying that the results do them credit and stand up to scrutiny. This takes them to the head of the class without their being perceived as prigs by their classmates, while people like Ulrich, who may be far more gifted but are given to overdoing a bit here and falling a bit short there, get gradually left behind in some imperceptibly fated way. It occurred to him that he was secretly somewhat in awe of these favored types, because the precision with which their minds worked made his own romantic enthusiasm for precision seem a bit windy. "They haven't a trace of soul," he thought, "and they're good-natured fellows. After the age of sixteen, when adolescents get worked up about intellectual problems, they seem to fall behind a little, not quite able to catch on to new ideas and feelings, but here, too, they work with their ten studs, and the day comes when they're able to prove that they have always understood everything, of course without going to any untenable extremes, and in the end they are the ones who introduce the new ideas into practical life when for everyone else those ideas have faded away with their long-past adolescence, or have become lonely eccentricities." And so, by the time Agathe came back into the room, Ulrich could still not imagine what had actually happened to her, but he felt that entering the lists against her husband, even if it was unfair, was likely to offer him a most reprehensible pleasure.

Agathe seemed to see no point in trying to explain her decision rationally. Outwardly her marriage was in the most perfect order, as was only to be expected in the case of a man of Hagauer's character. No quarrels, hardly any differences of opinion; if only because Agathe, as she told Ulrich, never confided her opinion to him on any subject. Of course no vices: no drink, no gambling, not even bachelor habits. Income fairly apportioned. Orderly household. Smooth social life as well as unsocial life, when they were alone.

"So if you simply leave him for no reason at all," Ulrich said, "the divorce will be decided in his favor, provided he sues."

"Let him sue!" Agathe said defiantly.

"Wouldn't it be a good idea to offer him a small financial compensation if he'll agree to a friendly settlement?"

"All I took away with me," she replied, "was what I would need during an absence of three weeks, except for a few childish things and mementos from the time before Hagauer. He can keep all the rest; I don't want it. But for the future he's to get nothing more out of me—absolutely nothing!"

Again she had spoken with surprising vehemence. One could perhaps explain it by saying that Agathe wanted to revenge herself on this man for having let him take too much advantage of her in the past. Ulrich's fighting spirit, his sportsmanship, his inventiveness in surmounting obstacles, were now aroused, although he was not especially pleased to feel it; it was too much like the effect of a stimulant that moves the superficial emotions while the deeper ones remain quite untouched. Groping for an overview, he gave the conversation a different turn:

"I've read some of his work, and I've heard of him too," he said. "As far as I can gather, he's regarded as a coming man in pedagogy and education."

"Yes," Agatha said. "So he is."

"Judging by what I know of his work, he's not only a sound educator but a pioneer of reform in higher education. I remember one book of his in which he discussed the unique value of history and the humanities for a moral education on the one hand, and on the other the equally unique value of science and mathematics as intellectual discipline, and then, thirdly, the unique value of that brimming sense of life in sports and military exercise that makes one fit for action. Is that it?"

"I suppose so," Agatha said, "but did you notice his way with quotations?"

"Quotations? Let me see: I dimly remember noticing something there. He uses lots of quotations. He quotes the classics. Of course, he quotes the moderns too. . . . Now I've got it: He does something positively revolutionary for a schoolmaster—he quotes not merely academic sources but even aircraft designers, political figures, and artists of today. . . . But I've already said that, haven't I?" He ended on that uncertain note with which recollection runs into a dead end.

"What he does," Agatha added, "with music, for instance, is to go recklessly as far as Richard Strauss, or with painting as far as Picasso, but he will never, even if only to illustrate something that's wrong, cite a name that hasn't become more or less established currency in the newspapers, even if it's only treated negatively."

That was it. Just what he had been groping for in his memory. He looked up. He was pleased by the taste and the acuity shown in Agathe's reply.

"So he's become a leader, over time, by being among the first to follow in time's train," he commented with a laugh. "All those who come after him see him already ahead of them! But do you like our leading figures yourself?"

"I don't know. In any case, I don't quote them."

"Still, we ought to give him his due," Ulrich said. "Your husband's name stands for a program that many people today regard as the most advanced. His achievement represents a solid small step forward. His rise cannot be long in coming. Sooner or later he will have at least a university chair, even though he has had to toil for his living as a schoolteacher, while as for me, all I ever had to do was go straight along the course laid out for me—and today I've come so far that I probably wouldn't even get a lectureship."

Agathe was disappointed, which was probably why her face took on a blank, porcelain-smooth, ladylike mask as she sweetly said: "Oh, I don't know; perhaps you ought to keep on his good side."

"When do you expect him?" Ulrich asked.

"Not before the funeral; he has no time to spare. But under no circumstances is he to stay in this house—I won't have it!"

"As you like," Ulrich decided unexpectedly. "I shall meet him at the station and drop him off at some hotel. And if you want, I'll tell him, 'This is where you stay.'"

Agathe was surprised and suddenly elated.

"That will make him furious, because he'll have to pay; he was of course counting on staying here with us!" Her expression had instantly changed and regained the look of a wild and mischievous child.

"What is the situation, actually?" her brother asked. "Does the house belong to you, me, or both of us? Is there a will?"

"Papa left a big package for me that's supposed to contain all we need to know." They went to the study, which lay beyond the deceased.

Again they moved through candlelight and the scent of flowers, through the field of vision of those two eyes that no longer saw. In the flickering half-darkness Agathe was for the space of a second a shimmering haze of gold, gray, and pink. They found the package holding the will and took it back with them to the tea table, where they then forgot to open it.

For as they sat down again Agathe told her brother that, to all intents and purposes, she had been living apart from her husband, though under the same roof; she didn't say how long this had been going on.

It made a bad impression on Ulrich at first. When a married woman sees a man as a possible lover, she is likely to treat him to this kind of confidence, and although his sister had come out with it in embarrassment, indeed with defiance, in a clumsy and palpable effort to throw down a challenge, he was annoyed with her for not coming up with something more original; he thought she was making too much of it.

"Frankly," he said, "I have never understood how you could have lived with such a man at all."

Agathe told him that it was their father's idea, and what could she have done to stop it?

"But you were a widow by then, not an underage virgin!"

"That's just it. I had come back to Papa. Everyone was saying that I was still too young to live on my own; even if I was a widow, I was only nineteen. And then I just couldn't stand it here."

"Then why couldn't you have looked for another man? Or studied something and made yourself independent that way?" Ulrich demanded relentlessly.

Agathe merely shook her head. There was a pause before she answered: "I've told you already: I'm lazy."

Ulrich felt that this was no answer. "So you had some special reason for marrying Hagauer?"

"Yes."

"You were in love with someone you couldn't have?"

Agathe hesitated. "I loved my first husband."

Ulrich regretted he had used the word "love" so glibly, as though he regarded the importance of the social arrangement it refers to as inviolable. "Trying to comfort the grieving is no better than handing a dry crust to a beggar," he thought. Nevertheless, he felt tempted to go on in the same vein. "And then you realized what you'd let yourself in for, and you started to make trouble for Hagauer?" he suggested.

"Yes," she admitted, "but not right away—quite late," she added. "Very late, in fact."

At this point they got into a little argument.

These confessions were visibly costing Agathe an effort, even though she was making them of her own accord and evidently, as was to be expected at her age, saw in her sex life an important subject of general conversation. From the first she seemed ready to take her chances on his sympathy or lack of it; she wanted his trust and was determined, not without candor and passion, to win her brother over. But Ulrich, still in the mood to dispense moral guidance, could not yet meet her halfway. For all his strong-mindedness he was by no means always free of those same prejudices he rejected intellectually, having too often let his life go one way and his mind another. For he had more than once exploited and misused his power over women, with a hunter's delight in catching and observing his quarry, so he had almost always seen the woman as the prey struck down by the amorous male spear. The lust of humiliation to which the woman in love subjects herself was fixed in his mind, while the man is very far from feeling a comparable surrender. This masculine notion of female weakness before male power is still quite common today, although with the successive waves of new generations more modern concepts have arisen, and the naturalness with which Agathe treated her dependence on Hagauer offended her brother. It seemed to him that his sister had suffered defilement without being quite aware of it when she subjected herself to the influence of a man he disliked and went on enduring it for years. He did not say so, but Agathe must have read something of the kind in his face, for she suddenly said:

"After all, I couldn't simply bolt the moment I had married him; that would have been hysteria!"

Ulrich was suddenly jerked out of his role as elder brother and dispenser of edifying narrow-mindedness.

"Would it really be hysteria to feel disgusted and draw all the necessary conclusions?" He tried to soften this by following it up with a smile and looking at his sister in the friendliest possible manner.

Agathe looked back at him, her face somehow rendered defenseless with the effort of deciphering the expression on his.

"Surely a normal healthy person is not so sensitive to distasteful circumstances?" she persisted. "What does it matter, after all?"

Ulrich reacted by pulling himself together, not wanting to let his mind be ruled by one part of himself. He was once more all objective intelligence. "You're quite right," he said. "What happens doesn't really matter. What counts is the system of ideas by which we understand it, and the way it fits into our personal outlook."

"How do you mean?" Agathe asked dubiously.

Ulrich apologized for putting it so abstractly, but while he was searching for a more easily accessible formulation, his brotherly jealousy reasserted itself and influenced his choice of terms.

"Suppose that a woman we care about has been raped," he offered. "From a heroic perspective, we would have to be prepared for vengeance or suicide; from a cynical-empirical standpoint, we would expect her to shake it off like a duck shedding water; and what would actually happen nowadays would probably be a mixture of these two. But this lack of a touchstone within ourselves is more sordid than all the rest."

However, Agathe did not accept this way of putting it either. "Does it really seem so horrible to you?" she asked simply.

"I don't know. I thought it must be humiliating to live with a person one doesn't love. But now . . . just as you like."

"Is it worse than a woman who wants to marry less than three months after a divorce having to submit to an examination by an officially appointed gynecologist to see whether she's pregnant, because of the laws of inheritance? I read that somewhere." Agathe's forehead seemed to bulge with defensive anger, and the little vertical furrow between her eyebrows appeared again. "And they all put up with it, if they have to!" she said disdainfully.

"I don't deny it," Ulrich responded. "Everything that actually happens passes over us like rain and sunshine. You're probably being much more sensible than I in regarding that as natural. But a man's nature isn't natural; it wants to change nature, so it sometimes goes to extremes." His smile was a plea for friendship, and his eyes saw how young she looked. When she got excited her face did not pucker up but smoothed out even more under the stress going on behind it, like a glove within which the hand clenches into a fist.

"I've never thought about it in such general terms," she now said. "But after listening to you, I am again reminded that I've been leading a dreadfully wrong kind of life."

"It's only because you've already told me so much, of your own accord, without coming to the point," said her brother, lightly acknowledging this concession in response to his own. "How am I to judge the situation properly when you won't let me know anything about the man for whom you are, after all, really leaving Hagauer?"

Agathe stared at him like a child or a pupil whose teacher is being unfair. "Does there have to be a man? Can't it happen of itself? Did I do something wrong by leaving him without having a lover? I would be lying if I said that I've never had one; I don't want to be so absurd; but I haven't got a lover now, and I'd resent it very much if you thought I'd really need one in order to leave Hagauer!"

Her brother had no choice but to assure her that passionate

women were known to leave their husbands even without having a lover, and that he even regarded this as the more dignified course.

The tea they had come together to share merged into an informal and haphazard supper, at Ulrich's suggestion, because he was very tired and wanted to go to bed early to get a good night's sleep on account of the next day, which was likely to be busy with bothersome details. They smoked their final cigarettes before parting, and Ulrich still did not know what to make of his sister. She did not have anything either emancipated or bohemian about her, even if she was sitting there in those wide trousers in which she had received her unknown brother. It was more something hermaphroditic, as it now seemed to him; as she moved and gestured in talking, the light masculine outfit suggested the tender form beneath with the semitransparency of water, and in contrast to the independent freedom of her legs, she wore her beautiful hair up, in true feminine style. But the center of this ambivalence was still her face, so rich in feminine charm yet with something missing, something held in reserve, whose nature he could not quite make out.

And that he knew so little about her and was sitting with her so intimately, though not at all as he would with a woman for whom he would count as a man, was something very pleasant in his present state of fatigue, to which he was now beginning to succumb.

"What a change from yesterday!" he thought.

He was grateful for it and tried to think of something affectionately brotherly to say to Agathe as they said goodnight, but as all this was something new to him, he could think of nothing to say. So he merely put his arm around her and kissed her.

3

Start of a New Day in a
House of Mourning

The next morning Ulrich woke early as smoothly as a fish leaping out of water, from a dreamless sound sleep that had wiped out every trace of the previous day's fatigue. He prowled through the house looking for breakfast. The ritual of mourning had not yet fully resumed; only a scent of it hung in all the rooms; it made him think of a shop that had opened its shutters early in the day, while the street is still empty of people. Then he got his scientific work out of his suitcase and took it into his father's study. As he sat there, with a fire in the grate, the room looked more human than on the previous evening: Even though a pedantic mind, always weighing all pros and cons, had created it, right up to the plaster busts facing each other symmetrically on the top bookshelves, the many little personal things left lying about—pencils, eyeglass, thermometer, an open book, boxes of pen nibs, and the like—gave the room the touching emptiness of a habitat that had just been abandoned. Ulrich sat, not too far from the window, in the midst of it, at the desk, the room's nerve center, and felt a peculiar listlessness. The walls were hung with portraits of his forebears, and some of the furniture dated from their time. The man who had lived here had formed the egg of his life from the shells of theirs; now he was dead, and his belongings stood as sharply there as if he had been chiseled out of the space; yet already the order of things was about to crumble, adapt itself to his successor, and one sensed all these objects that had outlasted him quickening with a new life as yet almost imperceptible behind their fixedly mournful air.

In this mood Ulrich spread out his work, which he had interrupted weeks and months ago, and his eyes immediately alighted on the equations in hydrodynamics where he had stopped. He dimly remembered having thought of Clarisse as he used the three basic states of water to exemplify a new mathematical operation, and Clarisse having distracted him from it. There is a kind of recollection that evokes not the word itself but the atmosphere in which it was spoken, and so Ulrich suddenly thought: "Carbon . . ." and got the feeling, as if from nowhere, that at this instant all he needed to continue was to know all the various states in which carbon occurred; but he could not remember, and thought instead: "The human being comes in twos. As man and as woman." He paused at this for quite a while, evidently stunned with amazement, as if he had just made some earthshaking discovery. But beneath this stalling of his mind something different was concealed. For one can be hard, selfish, eager, sharply profiled against the world, as it were, and can suddenly feel oneself, the same Ulrich What's-his-name, quite the opposite: deeply absorbed, a selfless, happy creature at one with an ineffably tender and somehow also selfless condition of everything around him. And he asked himself: "How long is it since I last felt like this?" To his surprise it turned out to be hardly more than twenty-four hours. The silence surrounding Ulrich was refreshing, and the condition he was reminded of did not seem as uncommon as he ordinarily thought. "We're all organisms, after all," he thought, relaxing, "who have to strain all their energies and appetites in an unkind world to prevail against each other. But together with his enemies and victims each one of us is also a particle and an offspring of this world, not at all as detached from the others and as independent as he imagines." In which case it was surely not incomprehensible that at times an intimation of oneness and love arises from the world, almost a certainty that the normal exigencies of life keep us from seeing more than half of the great pattern of the interrelationships of being. There was nothing objectionable in this for a man of mathematical-scientific bent and precise feelings; on the contrary, it reminded Ulrich of a study by a psychologist whom he happened to know personally, which dealt with two main opposing groups of concepts, one based on a sense of being enveloped by the content of one's experiences, the other on one's enveloping them, and advanced the connection that such a "being on the inside" and "looking at something from the outside," a feeling of "concavity" and "convexity," a "spatiality" as well as a "corporeality," an "introspection" and an "observation," occurred in so many other pairs of opposites of experience and in their linguistic tropes that one might assume a primal dual form of human consciousness behind it all. It was not one of those strictly factual academic studies but one of the imaginative kind, a speculative groping into the future, that are prompted by some stimulus outside the scope of everyday scientific activity; but it was well grounded and its deductions were persuasive, moving toward a unity of feeling back in the mists of creation, whose tangled wreckage, Ulrich thought, might be the origin of the present-day attitude that vaguely organizes our experience around the contrast between a male and a female mode of experience but is secretly and mysteriously shadowed by ancient dreams.

Here Ulrich tried to secure his footing—literally, as one uses ropes and crampons for a descent down a dangerous rock face—and began to reflect further:

"The most ancient philosophies, obscure and almost incomprehensible as they are to us, often speak of a male and a female principle," he thought.

"The goddesses that existed alongside the gods in primitive religions are in fact no longer within our emotional range," he thought. "Any relationship we might have to such superhuman women would be masochistic!

"But nature," he thought, "provides men with nipples and women with rudimentary male sex organs, which shouldn't lead us to conclude that our ancestors were hermaphrodites. Nor need they have been psychological hybrids either. And so it must have been from outside that they received the double possibility of a giving and a receiving vision, as a dual aspect of nature, and somehow all this is far older than the difference of gender, on which the sexes later drew to fill out their psychological wardrobe. . . ."

As he thought along these lines he remembered a detail from his childhood that distracted him, because—this had not happened for a long time—it gave him pleasure to remember. Here it must be mentioned that his father had in earlier days been a horseman and had even kept riding horses, to which the empty stable by the garden wall, the first sight Ulrich had seen on his arrival, bore witness. Riding was evidently the only aristocratic inclination his father had presumed to adopt, out of admiration for his feudal friends' way of life. But Ulrich had been a little boy; now, in his musings, he experienced anew the sense of the infinite or at least something immeasurable that the horse's high, muscular body aroused in the marveling child, like some awesome legendary mountain range covered with slopes of hair, across which the twitchings of the skin ran like the waves of a great wind. It was the kind of recollection, he realized, that owes its glamour to the child's powerlessness to make its wishes come true; but that hardly counts compared with the greatness of that splendor, which was no less than supernatural, or with the no less miraculous splendor little Ulrich touched shortly afterward with his fingertips in his quest for the first one. For at that time the town was placarded with circus posters showing not only horses but lions and tigers, too, and huge, splendid dogs that lived on good terms with the wild beasts. He had stared at these posters for a long time before he managed to get one of the richly colored pieces of paper for himself, cut the animals out, and stiffen them with little wooden supports so that they could stand up. What happened next can only be compared to drinking that never quenches one's thirst no matter how long one drinks, for there was no end to it, nor, stretching on for weeks, did it get anywhere; he was constantly being drawn to and into these adored creatures with the unutterable joy of the lonely child, who had the feeling every time he looked at them that he owned them, with the same intensity that he felt something ultimate was missing, some unattainable fulfillment the very lack of which gave his yearning the boundless radiance that seemed to flood his whole being. Along with this peculiarly boundless memory there arose unbidden from the oblivion of that early time another, slightly later experience, which now, despite its childish futility, took possession of the grown body dreaming with open eyes. It was the little girl who had only two qualities: one, that she had to belong to him, and the other, the fights with other boys this got him into. And of these two things only the fights were real, because there was no little girl. Strange time, when he used to go out like a knight errant to leap at some boy's throat, preferably when the boy was bigger than he, in some deserted street that might harbor a mystery, and wrestle with the surprised enemy! He had collected quite a few beatings, and sometimes won great victories too, but no matter how it turned out he felt cheated of his satisfaction. Nor would his feelings accept any connection, obvious as it was, between the little girls he actually knew and the secret child he fought for, because, like all boys his age, he froze and became

tongue-tied in the presence of girls until, one day, an exception occurred. And now Ulrich remembered as clearly as if the circular
image in the field of a telescope were trained across the years on that
evening when Agathe was dressed up for a children's party. She wore
a velvet dress, and her hair flowed over it like waves of bright velvet,
so that the sight of her, even though he was himself encased in a
terrifying knight's costume, suddenly filled him, in the same indescribable way as he had longed for the animals on the circus posters,
with the longing to be a girl. At that age he still knew so little about
men and women that he did not regard this as entirely impossible,
but he knew enough not to try immediately, as children usually do, to
force his wish to come true; rather, if he tried to define it now, it had
been as if he were groping in darkness for a door and suddenly came
up against some blood-warm or warmly sweet resistance, pressing
against it time and again as it yielded tenderly to his urge to penetrate it without actually giving way. Perhaps it also resembled some
harmless form of vampire passion, which sucks the desired being
into itself, except that this infant male did not want to draw that infant female into himself but wanted to take her place entirely, and
this happened with that dazzling tenderness present only in the first
intimations of sexuality.

Ulrich stood up and stretched his arms, astonished at his daydreaming. Not ten steps away, on the other side of the wall, his father's body was laid out, and he now noticed for the first time that
around them both the place had been for some time swarming with
people, as though they had shot up out of the ground, bustling about
this dead house that went on living. Old women were laying down
carpets and lighting fresh candles, there was hammering on the staircase, floors were being waxed, flowers delivered, and now he was
about to be drawn into these goings-on. People had come to see him
who were up and about at this early hour because they wanted something, or needed to know something, and from this moment the
chain of people never stopped. There were inquiries from the university about the funeral, a peddler came and shyly asked for clothing, a German firm had commissioned a dealer in local antiquities,
who with profuse apologies made on the firm's behalf an offer for a
rare legal tome that the library of the deceased might contain; a
chaplain needed to see Ulrich about some point that had to be

cleared up in the parish register, a man from the insurance company came with long and complicated questions, someone wanted a piano cheap, a real estate agent left his card in case the house might be for sale, a retired government clerk offered to address envelopes; and so they incessantly came, went, asked, and wanted all through the precious morning hours: at the front door, where the old servant shook off as many as he could, and upstairs, where Ulrich had to see those that managed to slip through, each beginning with a matter-of-fact reference to the death, and each asserting, vocally or in writing, his own claim to life. Ulrich had never before realized how many people were politely waiting for someone to die, and how many hearts are set throbbing the moment one's own stops. It took him somewhat aback, and he saw a dead beetle lying in the woods, and other beetles, birds, and flapping butterflies gathering around.

For all this commotion of profit-seeking was shot through with the flickerings and flutterings of the forest-deep darkness. Through the lenses of eyes veiled with emotion the profit motive gleamed like a lantern left burning in bright daylight, as a man with black crêpe on the black sleeve of something between mourner's garb and business suit entered, stopping at the door; he seemed to expect either Ulrich or himself to burst into tears. When neither happened, after a few seconds he seemed satisfied, for he came forward and like any other businessman introduced himself as the funeral director, come to make sure that Ulrich was satisfied with the arrangements thus far. He assured Ulrich that everything else would be conducted in a manner that even the late lamented, who everyone knew had been a gentleman none too easy to please, was bound to have approved. He pressed into Ulrich's hand a form covered with fine print and rectangles and made him read through what turned out to be a contract drawn to cover all possible classes of funerals, such as: eight horses or two horses . . . wreath carriage . . . number of . . . harness, style of . . . with outrider, silver-plated . . . attendants, style of . . . torches à la Marienburg . . . à la Admont . . . number of attendants . . . style of lighting . . . for how long . . . coffin, kind of wood . . . potted plants . . . name, date of birth, gender, occupation . . . disclaimer of liability . . . Ulrich had no idea where these terms, some of them archaic, came from; he inquired; the funeral director looked at him in surprise; he had no idea either. He stood there facing Ulrich like a synapse in the brain of mankind, linking stimulus and response while failing to generate any consciousness whatever. This merchant of mourning, who had been entrusted with centuries-old traditions which he could use as his stock-in-trade, felt that Ulrich had loosened the wrong screw, and quickly tried to cover this up with a remark intended to expedite the business in hand. He explained that all this terminology was unfortunately required by the statutes of the national association of undertakers, but that it really didn't matter if they were ignored in practice, as indeed they always were, and if Ulrich would just be good enough to sign the form—Madame, his sister, had refused to do so yesterday without consulting her brother—it would simply indicate that the client was in accord with the instructions left by his father, and he would be assured of a first-rate execution of the order.

While Ulrich signed, he asked the man whether he had already seen here in town one of those electrically powered sausage machines with a picture of Saint Luke as patron of the guild of butchers and sausage makers; he himself had seen some once in Brussels—but there was no answer to wait for, because in the place of the funeral director stood another man who wanted something from him, a journalist from the leading local newspaper seeking information for the obituary. Ulrich gave it, dismissing the undertaker with the form; but as soon as he tried to provide an account of the most important aspects of his father's life, he realized that he did not know what was important and what was not, and the reporter had to come to his aid. Only then, in the grip of the forceps of a professional curiosity trained to extract what was worth knowing, did the interview proceed, and Ulrich felt as if he were present at the Creation. The journalist, a young man, asked whether the old gentleman had died after a long illness or unexpectedly, and when Ulrich said that his father had continued lecturing right up to the last week of his life, this was framed as: ". . . working to the very end in the vigorous exercise of all his powers." Then the chips began to fly off the old man's life until nothing was left but a few ribs and joints: Born in Protivin in 1844 . . . educated at . . . and the University of . . . appointed to the post of . . . on [date] . . . until, with the listing of five such appointments and honorary degrees, the basic facts were almost exhausted. Marriage at some point. A few books. Once nearly became Minister of Justice, but someone's opposition prevailed. The reporter took notes, Ulrich checked them, they were in order. The reporter was pleased; he had the necessary number of lines. Ulrich was astonished at the little heap of ashes that remains of a human life. For every piece of information he had received, the reporter had had in readiness some six- or eight-cylinder phrase: distinguished scholar, wide sympathies, forward-looking but statesmanlike, mind of truly universal scope, and so on, as if no one had died for a long time and the phrases had been unemployed for quite a while and were hungering to be used. Ulrich tried to think; he would have liked to add something worth saying about his father, but the chronicler had his facts and was putting his notebook away; what remained was like trying to pick up the contents of a glass of water without the glass.

The comings and goings had meanwhile slackened. All the flood of people who had, the day before, been told by Agathe to see him had now passed; so when the reporter took his leave, Ulrich found himself alone. Something or other had put him in an embittered mood. Hadn't his father been right to drag along his sacks of knowledge, turning the piled grain of that knowledge now and then, and for the rest simply submitting to those powers of life that he regarded as the strongest? Ulrich thought of his own work, lying untouched in a desk drawer. Probably no one would even be able to say of him, someday, as they could of his father, that he had turned the grain pile over! Ulrich stepped into the little room where the dead man lay on his bier. This rigid, geometric cell surrounded by the ceaseless bustle to which it gave rise was incredibly eerie. The body floated stiff as a little wooden stick amid the floods of activity; but now and then for an instant the image would be reversed, and then all the life around him seemed petrified and the body seemed to be gliding along with a peculiarly quiet motion. "What does the traveler care," it said at such moments, "for the cities he has left behind at the landings? Here I once lived, and I did what was expected of me, and now I'm on my way again." Ulrich's heart constricted with the self-doubt of a man who in the midst of others wants something different than they do. He looked his father in the face. What if everything he regarded as his own personality was no more than a reaction against that face, originating in some childish antagonism? He looked around for a mirror, but there was none, only this blank face to reflect the light.

He scrutinized it for resemblances. Perhaps there were some. Perhaps it was all there: their race, their ties with the past, the impersonal element, the stream of heredity in which the individual is only a ripple, the limitations, disillusionments, the endless repetitiveness of the mind going around in circles, which he hated with every fiber of his deepest will to live.

In a sudden fit of discouragement he thought of packing up and leaving even before the funeral. If there really was something he could still achieve in life, what was he doing here?

But in the doorway he bumped into his sister, who had come looking for him.

4

OLD ACQUAINTANCE

For the first time Ulrich saw her dressed as a woman, and after his impression of her yesterday she seemed to be in disguise. Through the open door artificial light mingled with the tremulous gray of midmorning, and this black apparition with blond hair seemed to be standing in an ethereal grotto through which radiant splendor flowed. Agathe's hair was drawn back closer to her head, making her face look more feminine than it had yesterday. Her delicate womanly breasts were embedded in the black of the severe dress in that perfect balance between yielding and resistance characteristic of the feather-light hardness of a pearl; the slim long legs he had seen yesterday as so like his own were now curtained by a skirt. Now that her appearance as a whole was less like his own, he could see how alike their faces were. He felt as if it were his own self that had entered through a door and was coming to meet him, though it was a more beautiful self, with an aura in which he never saw himself. For the first time it flashed on him that his sister was a dreamlike repetition and variant of himself, but as the impression lasted only a moment he forgot it again.

Agathe had come to remind her brother of certain duties that were on the point of being delayed too long, for she had overslept. She held their father's will in her hands and drew Ulrich's attention to some dispositions in it that must be dealt with at once. Most urgent was a rather odd stipulation about the old man's decorations, which was also known to the servant Franz. Agathe had zealously, if somewhat irreverently, underlined this point in the will in red pencil. The deceased had wanted to be buried with his decorations on his chest, and he had quite a few of them, but since it was not from vanity that he wanted this done he had added a long and ruminative justification of this wish. His daughter had read only the beginning, leaving it to her brother to explain the rest to her.

"Now, how shall I put it?" Ulrich said after he had read the passage. "Papa wants to be buried with all his decorations because he considers the individualistic theory of the state to be false! He favors the universalist view: It is only through the creative community of the state that the individual gains a purpose that transcends the merely personal, a sense of value and justice. Alone he is nothing, which is why the monarch personifies a spiritual symbol. In short, when a man dies he should wrap himself in his decorations as a dead sailor is wrapped in the flag when his body is consigned to the sea!"

"But didn't I read somewhere that these medals have to be given back?"

"The heirs are obliged to return the medals to the Chamberlain's Office. So Papa had duplicates made. Still, he seems to feel that the ones he bought are not quite the real thing, so he wants us to substitute them for the originals only when they close the coffin; that's the trouble. Who knows, perhaps that's his silent protest against the regulation, which he wouldn't express any other way."

"But by that time there'll be hundreds of people here, and we'll forget!" Agathe worried.

"We might just as well do it now."

"There's no time now. You'd better read the next part, what he writes about Professor Schwung. Professor Schwung may be here at any moment; I was expecting him all day yesterday."

"Then let's do it after Schwung leaves."

"But it's not very nice," Agathe objected, "not to let him have his wish."

"He'll never know it."

She looked at him doubtfully. "Are you sure of that?"

"Oh?" Ulrich laughed. "Are *you* not quite sure, by any chance?"

"I'm not sure about anything," Agathe answered.

"Even if it weren't sure, he was never satisfied with us anyway."

"That's true," Agathe said. "All right, let's do it later. But tell me something," she added. "Don't you ever bother about what's expected of you?"

Ulrich hesitated. "She has a good dressmaker," he thought. "I needn't have worried that she might be provincial!" But because these words somehow brought back all yesterday evening, he tried to think of an answer that would really be appropriate and helpful to her; but he could not find a way to put it that would not cause misunderstanding, so he ended up with involuntarily youthful brashness:

"It's not only Father who's dead; all the ceremonials around him are dead too. His will is dead. The people who turn up here are dead. I'm not trying to be nasty; God knows we probably ought to be grateful to all those who shore up the world we live in: but all that is the limestone of life, not its oceans!" He noticed a puzzled glance from his sister and realized how obscurely he was talking. "Society's virtues are vices to the saint," he ended with a laugh.

He put his hands on her shoulders, in a gesture that could have been construed as either patronizing or high-spirited but sprang only from embarrassment. Yet Agathe stepped back with a serious face and would not go along.

"Did you make that up yourself?" she asked.

"No; a man whom I love said it."

She had the sullenness of a child forcing itself to think hard as she tried to sum up his responses in one statement: "So you would hardly call a man who is honest out of habit a good man? But a thief who steals for the first time, with his heart pounding, you'll call a good man?"

These odd words took Ulrich aback, and he became more serious.

"I really don't know," he said abruptly. "In some situations I personally don't very much care whether something is considered right or wrong, but I can't give you any rules you could go by."

Agathe slowly turned her questioning gaze away from him and

picked up the will again. "We must get on with this; here's another marked passage," she admonished herself.

Before taking to his bed for the last time the old gentleman had written a number of letters, and his will contained explanations elucidating them and directions for sending them. The marked passage referred to Professor Schwung, one of his old colleagues, who after a lifelong friendship had so galled the last year of his life by opposing his view on the statute relating to diminished responsibility. Ulrich immediately recognized the familiar long-drawn-out arguments about illusion and will, the sharpness of law and the ambiguity of nature, which his father had summarized for him again before his death. Indeed, nothing seemed to have been so much on his mind in his final days as Schwung's denunciation of the social school of thought, which his father had joined, as an emanation of Prussian influence. He had just begun to outline a pamphlet that was to have been titled "The State and the Law; or, Consistency and Denunciation," when he felt his strength beginning to fail and saw with bitterness the enemy left in sole possession of the field. In solemn words such as are inspired only by the imminence of death and the struggle to preserve that sacred possession, one's reputation, he enjoined his children not to let his work fall into oblivion, and most particularly charged his son to cultivate the influential connections he owed to his father's tireless efforts, in order to crush totally all Professor Schwung's hopes of realizing his aims.

Once one has expressed oneself in this fashion, then after one's task is done, or at least the way is paved for its completion, it by no means precludes one's feeling the urge to forgive a former friend such errors as have arisen from gross vanity. When a man is seriously ill and feels his mortal coil quietly uncoiling, he is inclined to forgive and ask forgiveness; but when he feels better he takes it all back, because the healthy body is by nature implacable. The old gentleman must have experienced both these states of mind as his condition fluctuated during his last illness, and the one must have seemed as justified as the other. But such a situation is unbearable for a distinguished jurist, and so his logically trained mind had devised a means of leaving his last will unassailably valid, impervious to the influence of any last-minute emotional waverings: He wrote a letter of forgiveness but left it unsigned and undated, with instructions for Ulrich to date it at the hour of his father's death, then sign it together with his sister Agathe as proxies, as can be done with an oral will when a dying man no longer has the strength to sign his name. Actually, he was, without wanting to admit it, an odd fish, this little old man who had always submitted to the hierarchies of existence and defended them as their most zealous servant while stifling within himself all sorts of rebellious impulses, for which, in his chosen course of life, he could never find an outlet. Ulrich was reminded of the death notice he had received, which had probably been dictated in the same frame of mind; he even almost recognized a certain kinship with himself in it, though not resentfully this time but with compassion, at least in the sense that he could see how the old man's lifelong frustration at not being able to express his feelings must have led to his being infuriated to the point of hatred by this son who made life easy for himself by taking unpardonable liberties. For this is how the ways of sons always appear to fathers, and Ulrich felt a twinge of filial sympathy as he thought of all that was still unresolved inside himself. But he no longer had time to find some appropriate expression for all this that Agathe would also understand; he had just begun when a man swung with great energy into the twilit room. He strode in, hurled forward by his own energy right into the shimmer of the candlelight, before the derailed old servant could catch up to announce him. He lifted his arm in another wide sweep to shield his eyes with his hand, one step from the bier.

"My revered friend!" the visitor intoned sonorously. And the little old man lay with clenched jaws in the presence of his enemy Schwung.

"Ah, my dear young friends," Professor Schwung continued: "Above us the majesty of the starry firmament, within us the majesty of the moral law!" With veiled eyes he gazed down upon his faculty colleague. "Within this breast now cold there lived the majesty of the moral law!" Only then did he turn around to shake hands with the brother and sister.

Ulrich took this first opportunity to acquit himself of his charge.

"You and my father were unfortunately at odds with each other lately, sir?" he opened cautiously.

For a moment the graybeard did not seem to catch his meaning.

"Differences of opinion, hardly worth mentioning!" he replied magnanimously, gazing earnestly at the deceased. But when Ulrich politely persisted, hinting that a last will was involved, the situation in the room suddenly became tense, the way it does in a low-down dive when everyone knows someone has just drawn a knife under the table and in a moment all hell will break loose. So even with his last gasp the old boy had managed to gall his colleague Schwung! Enmity of such long standing had of course long since ceased to be a feeling and become a habit; provided something or other did not happen to stir up the hostility afresh, it simply ceased to exist. There was only the accumulated experience of countless grating episodes in the past, which had coagulated into a contemptuous opinion each held of the other, an opinion as unaffected by the flux of emotion as any unbiased truth would be. Professor Schwung felt this just as his antagonist, now dead, had felt it. Forgiveness seemed to him quite childish and beside the point, for that one relenting impulse before the end—merely a feeling at that, not a professional admission of error—naturally counted for nothing against the experiences of years of controversy and, as Schwung saw it, could only serve, and rather brazenly, to put him in the wrong if he should take advantage of his victory. But this had nothing to do with Professor Schwung's need to take leave of his dead friend. Good Lord, they had known each other back at the start of their academic careers, before either of them was married! Do you remember that evening in the Burggarten, how we drank to the setting sun and argued about Hegel? However many sunsets there may have been since then, that's the one I always remember. And do you remember our first professional disagreement, which almost made enemies of us way back then? Those were the days! Now you are dead, and I'm still on my feet, I'm glad to say, even though I'm standing by your coffin.

Such are the feelings, as everyone knows, of elderly people faced with the death of their contemporaries. When we come into the sere and yellow leaf, poetry breaks out. Many people who have not turned a verse since their seventeenth year suddenly write a poem at seventy-seven, when drawing up their last will. Just as at the Last Judgment the dead shall be called forth one by one, even though they have long been at rest at the bottom of time together with their centuries, like the cargoes of foundered ships, so too, in the last will, things are summoned by name and have their personalities, worn away by use, restored to them: "The Bokhara rug with the cigar burn, in my study . . ." is the sort of thing one reads in such final disposi-tions, or "The umbrella with the rhinoceros-horn handle that I bought at Sunshine & Winter's in May 1887 . . ." Even the bundles of securities are named and invoked individually by number.

Nor is it chance that, as each object lights up again for the last time, the longing should arise to attach to it a moral, an admonition, a blessing, a principle, to cast one last spell on so many unreckoned things that rise up once more as one feels oneself sinking. And so, together with the poetry of testament-making time, philosophy too awakens; usually an ancient and dusty philosophy, understandably enough, hauled out from where it had been forgotten fifty years ear-lier. Ulrich suddenly realized that neither of these two old men could possibly have given way. "Let life take care of itself, as long as princi-ples remain intact!" is an appropriate sentiment when a person knows that in a few months or years he will be outlived by those very principles. And it was plain to see how the two impulses were still contending with each other in the old academician: His romanticism, his youth, his poetic side, demanded a fine, sweeping gesture and a noble statement; his philosophy, on the other hand, insisted on keep-ing the law of reason untainted by sudden eruptions of feeling and sentimental lapses such as his dead opponent had placed on his path like a snare. For the last two days Schwung had been thinking: "Well, now he's dead, and there'll no longer be anything to interfere with the Schwungian view of diminished responsibility"; his feelings flowed in great waves toward his old friend, and he had worked out his scene of farewell like a carefully regulated plan of mobilization, waiting only for the signal to be put into operation. But a drop of vinegar had fallen into his scenario, with sobering effect. Schwung had begun on a great wave of sentiment, but now he felt like some-one suddenly coming to his senses in the middle of a poem, and the last lines won't come. And so they confronted each other, a white stubby beard and white beard stubble, each with jaws implacably clenched.

"What's he going to do now?" Ulrich wondered, intent on the scene before him. But finally Hofrat Schwung's happy certainty that Paragraph 318 of the Penal Code would now be formulated in accordance with his own proposals prevailed over his irritation, and freed from angry thoughts, he would most have liked to start singing "Should auld acquaintance be forgot . . ." so as to give vent to his now entirely benevolent and undivided feelings. But since this was out of the question, he turned to Ulrich and said: "Listen to me, my friend's young son: It is the moral crisis that comes first; social decay is its consequence!" Then, turning to Agathe, he added: "It was the mark of greatness in your father that he was always ready to support an idealistic view struggling to prevail in the foundation of our laws."

Then he seized one of Agathe's hands and one of Ulrich's, pressed them both, and exclaimed:

"Your father attached far too much importance to minor differences of opinion, which are sometimes unavoidable in long years of collaboration. I was always convinced that he did so in order not to expose his delicate sense of justice to the slightest reproach. Many eminent scholars will be coming tomorrow to take their leave of him, but none of them will be the man he was!"

And so the encounter ended on a conciliatory note. When he left, Schwung even assured Ulrich that he might count on his father's friends in case he should still decide to take up an academic career.

Agathe had listened wide-eyed, contemplating the uncanny final form life gives to human beings. "It was like being in a forest of plaster trees!" she said to her brother afterward.

Ulrich smiled and said: "I'm feeling as sentimental as a dog in moonlight."

5

THEY DO WRONG

"Do you remember," Agathe asked him after a while, "how once when I was still very small, you were playing with some boys and fell into the water right up to your waist and tried to hide it? You sat at lunch, with your visible top half dry, but your bottom half made your teeth start chattering!"

When he had been a boy home from boarding school on vacation—this had actually been the only instance over a long period—and when the small shriveled corpse here had still been an almost all-powerful man for both of them, it was not uncommon for Ulrich to balk at admitting some fault, and he resisted showing remorse even when he could not deny what he had done. As a result, he had, on one occasion, caught a chill and had to be packed off to bed with an impressive fever.

"And all you got to eat was soup," Agathe said.

"That's true," her brother confirmed with a smile. At this moment the memory of his punishment, something of no concern to him now, seemed no different than if he were seeing on the floor his tiny baby shoes, also of no concern to him now.

"Soup was all you would have got anyway, on account of your fever," Agathe said. "Still, it was also prescribed for you as a punishment."

"That's true," Ulrich agreed again. "But of course it was done not in anger but in fulfillment of some idea of duty." He didn't know what his sister was getting at. He was still seeing those baby shoes. Or not seeing them: he merely saw them *as if* he were seeing them. Feeling likewise the humiliations he had outgrown. And he thought: "This having-nothing-to-do-with-me-anymore somehow expresses the fact that all our lives, we're somehow only half integrated with ourselves!"

"But you wouldn't have been allowed to eat anything but soup anyway!" Agathe reiterated, and added: "I think I've spent my whole life being afraid I might be the only person in the world who couldn't understand that sort of thing."

Can the memories of two people talking of a past familiar to both not only supplement each other but coalesce even before they are uttered? Something of the kind was happening at this moment. A shared state of mind surprised and confused both brother and sister, like hands that come out of coats in places one would never expect and suddenly grasp each other. All at once they both knew more of the past than they had supposed they knew, and Ulrich was again seeing the fever light creeping up the walls like the glittering of the candles in this room where they were now standing. And then his father had come in, waded through the cone of light cast by the table lamp, and sat down by his bed.

"If you did it without realizing the full extent of the consequences, your deed might well appear in a milder light. But in that case you would first have had to admit to yourself that it was so." Perhaps these were phrases from the will or from those letters about Paragraph 318 foisted back onto that memory. Normally he could not remember details or the way things were put, so there was something quite unusual in this recollection of whole sentences in formal array; it had something to do with his sister standing there before him, as though it were her proximity that was bringing about this change in him.

" 'If you were capable, spontaneously and independent of any outward necessity, of choosing to do something wrong, then you must also realize that you have behaved culpably,' " he continued, quoting his father aloud. "He must have talked that way to you too."

"Perhaps not quite the same way," Agathe qualified this. "With me, he usually allowed for mitigating circumstances arising from my psychological constitution. He was always instructing me that an act of the will is linked with a thought, that it is not a matter of acting on instinct."

" 'It is the will,' " Ulrich quoted, " 'that, in the process of the gradual development of the understanding and the reason, must dominate the desires and, relative to them, the instincts, by means of reflection and the resolves consequent thereon.' "

"Is that true?" his sister asked.

"Why do you ask?"

"Because I'm stupid, I suppose."

"You're not stupid!"

"Learning always came hard to me, and I never quite understand."

"That hardly proves anything."

"Then there must be something wrong with me, because I don't assimilate what I do understand."

They were close together, face-to-face, leaning against the jamb of the doorway that had been left open when Professor Schwung took his departure. Daylight and candlelight played over their faces, and their voices intertwined as in a responsory. Ulrich went on intoning his sentences like a liturgy, and Agathe's lips moved quietly in response. The old ordeal of those admonitions, which consisted in imprinting a hard, alien pattern on the tender, uncomprehending mind of childhood, gave them pleasure now, and they played with it.

And then, without having been prompted by anything preceding, Agathe exclaimed: "Just imagine this applied to the whole thing, and you have Gottlieb Hagauer." And she proceeded to mimic her husband like a schoolgirl: " 'You mean to say you really don't know that *Lamium album* is the white dead nettle?' 'But how else can we make progress except through the same hard process of induction that has brought our human race step by step through thousands of years, by painful labor full of error, to our present level of understanding, as at the hand of a faithful guide?' 'Can't you see, my dear Agathe, that thinking is also a moral obligation? To concentrate is a constant struggle against one's indolence.' 'Mental discipline is that training of the mind by means of which a man becomes steadily more capable of working out a growing series of concepts rationally, always consistently questioning his own ideas, that is by means of flawless syllogisms categorical, hypothetical, or disjunctive, or by induction, and finally of submitting the conclusions gained to verification for as long as is necessary to bring all the concepts into agreement!' "

Ulrich marveled at his sister's feat of memory. Agathe seemed to revel in the impeccable recitation of these pedantic dicta she had appropriated from God knew where, some book perhaps. She claimed that this was how Hagauer talked.

Ulrich did not believe it. "How could you remember such long, complicated sentences from only hearing them in conversation?"

"They stuck in my mind," Agathe replied. "That's how I am."

"Do you have any idea," Ulrich asked, astonished, "what a categorical syllogism is, or a verification?"

"Not the slightest!" Agathe admitted with a laugh. "Maybe he only read that somewhere himself. But that's the way he talks. I learned it by heart as a series of meaningless words by listening to him. I think it was out of anger because he talks like that. You're different from me; things lie inert in my mind because I don't know what to do with them—so much for my good memory. Because I'm stupid, I have a terrific memory!" She acted as though this contained a sad truth she would have to shake off in order to go on in her exuberant vein: "It's the same even when he's playing tennis. 'When, in learning to play tennis, I deliberately for the first time place my racket in a certain position in order to give a specific new direction to the ball, which up to that point had been following the precise course I intended, then I intervene in the flow of phenomena: I am experimenting!' "

"Is he a good tennis player?"

"I beat him six–love."

They laughed.

"Do you realize," Ulrich said, "that with all the things you're making Hagauer say, he's actually quite right? It just sounds funny."

"He may be right, for all I know," Agathe replied. "I don't understand any of it. But do you know that a boy in his class once translated a passage from Shakespeare quite literally, and the effect was touching, beginning with 'Cowards die many times before their deaths,' and without any feeling for what the boy had done, Hagauer simply crossed it out and replaced it, word for word, with the old Schlegel version!

"And I remember another instance, a passage from Pindar, I think: 'The law of nature, King of all mortals and immortals, reigns supreme, approving extreme violence, with almighty hand,' and Hagauer polished it: 'The law of nature, that reigns over all mortals and immortals, rules with almighty hand, even approving violence.'

"And wasn't it lovely," she urged, "the way that little boy, whom he criticized, translated the words so literally it gave one the shivers, just the way he found them lying there like a collapsed heap of stones." And she recited: " 'Cowards die so much before they die, / The brave ones just die once. / Among all the miracles, why should men fear death / Because it happens to everyone whenever it comes.' " With her hand high around the doorpost as though it were a tree trunk, she flung out the boy's roughhewn version of Caesar's lines with a splendid wildness, quite oblivious of the poor shriveled body lying there under her youthful gaze alight with pride.

Frowning, Ulrich stared at his sister. "The person who won't try to 'restore' an old poem but leaves it in its decayed state, with half its meaning lost, is the same as the person who will never put a new marble nose on an old statue that has lost its own," he thought. "One could call it a sense of style, but that's not what it is. Nor is it the person whose imagination is so vivid that he doesn't mind when something's missing. It's rather the person who cares nothing for perfection and accordingly doesn't demand that his feelings be 'whole' either. She's capable of kissing," he concluded with a sudden twist, "without her body going all to pieces over it."

At this moment it seemed to him that he need know nothing more of his sister than her passionate declamation to realize that she, too, was only ever "half integrated" with herself, that she, like himself, was a person of "piecemeal passions." This even made him forget the other side of his nature, which yearned for moderation and control. He could now have told his sister with certainty that nothing she did ever fitted in with her surroundings, but that all was dependent on some highly problematic vaster world, a world that begins nowhere and has no limits. This would satisfactorily explain the contradictory impressions of their first evening together. But his habitual reserve was stronger, and so he waited, curious and even slightly skeptical, to see how she would get herself down from the high limb she had got herself out on. She was still standing, with her arm raised against the doorpost, and one instant too many could spoil the whole effect. He detested women who behaved as though they had been brought into the world by a painter or a director, or who do an artful fade-out after such a moment of high excitement as Agathe's. "She could come down," he thought, "from this peak of enthusiasm with the dim-witted look of a sleepwalker, like a medium coming out of a trance. She doesn't have much choice, and it's bound to be awkward." But Agathe seemed to be aware of this herself, or possibly something in her brother's eye had put her on guard. She leapt gaily from her high limb, landed on both feet, and stuck out her tongue at him.

But then she was grave and quiet again, and without saying a word went to fetch the medals. And so brother and sister set about acting in defiance of their father's last will.

It was Agathe who did it. Ulrich felt shy about touching the defenseless old man lying there, but Agathe had a way of doing wrong that undercut any awareness of wrongdoing. Her movements of hand and eye were those of a woman tending a patient, and they had at times the spontaneous and appealing air of young animals who suddenly pause in their romping to make sure that their master is watching. The master took from her the decorations that had been removed and handed her the replicas. He was reminded of a thief whose heart is in his mouth. And if he had the impression that the stars and crosses shone more brightly in his sister's hand than in his own, indeed as if they would turn into magical objects, it might really have been true in the greenish darkness in the room, filled with glimmerings of light reflected off the leaves of the big potted plants; or it might have been that he felt his sister's will, hesitantly taking the lead and youthfully seizing his. But since no conscious motive was to be recognized in this, there again arose in these moments of unalloyed contact an almost dimensionless and therefore intangibly powerful sense of their joint existence.

Now Agathe stopped; it was done. Yet something or other still remained, and after thinking about it for a while she said with a smile: "How about each of us writing something nice on a piece of paper and putting it in his pocket?"

This time, Ulrich instantly knew what she meant, for they did not have many such shared memories, and he recalled how, at a certain age, they had loved sad verses and stories in which someone died and was forgotten by everyone. It might perhaps have been the loneliness of their childhood that had brought this about, and they often made up such stories between them, but even then Agathe had been inclined to act them out, while Ulrich took the lead only in the more manly undertakings, which called for being bold and hard. And so it had been Agathe's idea, one day, that they each should cut off a fingernail to bury in the garden, and she even slipped a small lock of her blond hair in with the parings. Ulrich proudly declared that in a hundred years someone might stumble across these relics and wonder who it might have been, since he was concerned with making an appearance in posterity; but for little Agathe the burial had been an end in itself. She had the feeling that she was hiding a part of herself, permanently removing it from the supervision of a world whose pedagogical demands always intimidated her even though she never thought very highly of them. And because that was when the cottage for the servants was being built at the bottom of the garden, they decided to do something special for it. They would write wonderful poems on two slips of paper, adding their names, to be bricked up in the walls. But when they began writing these poems that were supposed to be so splendid, they couldn't think of anything to say, day after day, and the walls were already rising out of the foundations.

Finally, when it was almost too late, Agathe copied a sentence out of her arithmetic book, and Ulrich wrote: "I am . . ." and added his name. Nevertheless, their hearts were pounding furiously when they sneaked up on the two bricklayers at work in the garden, and Agathe simply threw her piece of paper in the ditch where they were standing and ran off. But Ulrich, as the bigger and as a man even more frightened of being stopped and questioned by the astonished bricklayers, could move neither hand nor foot from excitement; so that Agathe, emboldened because nothing had happened to her, finally came back and took his slip from him. She then sauntered along with it innocently, inspected a brick at the end of a freshly laid row, lifted it, and slipped Ulrich's name into the wall before anyone could turn her away. Ulrich himself had hesitantly followed her and felt at the moment she did it the vise in which in his fright he had been gripped turning into a wheel of sharp knives whirling so rapidly in his chest that it threw off sparks like a flaming catherine wheel.

It was this incident to which Agathe was alluding now, and Ulrich gave no answer for the longest while, but smiled in a way that was meant to deter her, for repeating such a game with the dead man seemed taboo to him. But Agathe had already bent down, slid from her leg a wide silk garter that she wore to relieve the pull on her girdle, lifted the pall, and slipped it into her father's pocket.

And Ulrich? He could hardly believe his eyes to see this childhood memory restored to life. He almost leapt forward to stop her, just because it was so completely out of order. But he caught in his sister's eyes a flash of the dewy fresh innocence of early morning that is still untainted by any of the drab routines of the day, and it held him back.

"What do you think you're doing?" he admonished her softly. He did not know whether she was trying to propitiate the deceased because he had been wronged, or doing him one last kindness because of all the wrong he had done himself. He could have asked, but the barbaric notion of sending the frosty dead man on his way with a garter still warm from his daughter's thigh tightened his throat and muddled his brain.

6

THE OLD GENTLEMAN IS FINALLY
LEFT IN PEACE

The short time left before the funeral was filled with any number of unaccustomed small chores and passed quickly; in the last half hour before the departure of the deceased, the number of callers in black whose coming had run through all the hours like a black thread finally became a black festival. The undertaker's men had intensified their hammering and scraping—with the gravity of a surgeon to whom one has entrusted one's life and from that moment on surrendered any right to interfere—and had laid, through the untouched normality in the rest of the house, a gangway of ceremonial feeling, which ran from the entrance past the stairs into the room that held the coffin. The flowers and potted plants, the black cloth and crêpe hangings, and the silver candelabra with trembling little golden tongues of flame, which received the visitors, knew their responsibility better than Ulrich and Agathe, who had to represent the family and were obliged to welcome all who had come to pay their last respects, though they hardly knew who any of them were and would have been lost without their father's old servant, who unobtrusively prompted them whenever especially eminent guests appeared. All those who appeared glided up to them, glided past, and dropped anchor somewhere in the room, alone or in little groups, motionlessly observing the brother and sister, whose expressions grew stiff with solemn restraint, until at last the funeral director—the same man who had given Ulrich the printed forms to sign and in this last half hour had dashed up and down the steps at least twenty times—bounded up to Ulrich from the side and, with the studiously modulated self-importance of an adjutant reporting to his general on parade, told him that all was ready.

To conduct the funeral cortège ceremoniously through the town—the mourners would only later be seated in their carriages—Ulrich had to take the lead on foot, flanked on one side by His Imperial and Royal Majesty's representative, the Governor of the province, who had come in person to honor the final sleep of a member of the Upper House, and on the other by an equally high-ranking gentleman, the senior member of three from the Upper House, followed by the two other noblemen of that delegation, then by the Rector and Senate of the University. Only after these, though ahead of the interminable stream of silk hats topping off public figures of slowly diminishing importance and dignity, came Agathe, hemmed in by women in black and personifying the point where, among the peaks of officialdom, the sanctioned private grief had its place. For the unregulated participation of those who had come "merely to show their sympathy" had its place only after those officially in attendance, and it is even possible that it may have consisted solely of the old serving couple trudging along by themselves behind the procession. Thus it was a procession composed mainly of men, and it was not Ulrich who walked at Agathe's side but her husband, Professor Hagauer, whose apple-cheeked face with the bristly caterpillar mustache above the upper lip had been rendered unfamiliar to her by its curious dark-blue cast, produced by the thick black veil that allowed her to observe him unseen. As for Ulrich, who had been spending the many preceding hours with his sister, he could not help feeling that the ancient protocol of funeral precedence, dating back to the medieval beginnings of the University, had torn her from his side, and he missed her without daring to turn around to look for her. He tried to think of something funny to make her laugh when they met again, but his thoughts were distracted by the Governor, pacing along silently beside him with his lordly bearing and occasionally addressing a quiet word to Ulrich, who had to catch it, along with the many other attentions being shown him by all the Excellencies, Lordships, and Worships, for he was looked upon as Count Leinsdorf's shadow, so that even the mistrust with which His Grace's patriotic campaign was gradually coming to be regarded added to Ulrich's prestige.

The curbs and the windows were filled with clusters of the curious, and even though he knew it would all be over in an hour, like a theater performance, he nevertheless experienced everything happening that day with a special vividness, and the universal concern with his personal fate weighed on his shoulders like a heavily braided cape. For the first time he felt the upright attitude of tradition. The involvement that ran like a wave ahead of the procession, among the chatting crowds that lined the pavements, who fell silent and then breathed freely again; the spell cast by the clergy; the thudding of clods of earth on wood that one knew was coming; the dammed-up silence of the procession—all this plucked at the spinal cord as if it were some primordial musical instrument, and Ulrich was amazed to sense within himself an indescribable resonance whose vibrations buoyed up his whole body as though he were actually being borne along by the waves of ceremony around him. And as he was feeling closer to the others on this day, he imagined how it would be if at this moment he were really striding forward in the original sense—half forgotten in the pomp it assumed in its present-day form—as the real heir of a great power. The thought banished the sadness, and death was transmuted from a horrible private affair to a transition that was completed as a public ceremony. Gone was the gaping hole, stared at in dread, that every man whose presence one is accustomed to leaves behind in the first days after his disappearance, for his successor was already striding along in his place, the crowd breathing in homage to him, the funeral being at the same time a coming of age for him who now took up the sword and, for the first time without someone ahead of him, and alone, now walked toward his own end.

"I should have been the one," Ulrich surprised himself by thinking, "to close my father's eyes! Not for his sake, or my own, but . . ." He did not know how to complete the thought. That he had neither liked his father, nor his father him, seemed a petty overestimation of personal importance in the face of this order of things; in the face of death, anyway, personal concerns had the stale taste of meaninglessness, while everything that was of significance now seemed to emanate from the gigantic body of the cortège moving slowly through the streets lined with people, no matter how much idleness, curiosity, and mindless conformity were intermingled with it.

Still, the music played on, it was a light, clear, dazzling day, and Ulrich's feelings wavered this way and that, like the canopy carried in procession above the Holy of Holies. Now and then he would see his own reflection in the glass panes of the hearse in front of him, his head with its hat, his shoulders, and from time to time he glimpsed on the floor of the hearse, beside the armorially resplendent coffin, little droppings of candle wax, never quite cleaned away from previous funerals, and he simply and without thinking felt sorry for his father, as one feels sorry for a dog run over in the street. Then his eyes grew moist, and when he gazed over all the blackness at the onlookers on the curb they looked like colorful sprinkled flowers, and the thought that it was he, Ulrich, who was seeing this, and not the man who had always lived here and who, moreover, loved ceremony so much more than he did, was so peculiar that it seemed downright impossible that his father should miss seeing himself leaving the world, which he had, on the whole, regarded as a good world. Deeply moved as he was, however, Ulrich could not help noticing that the director or undertaker who was leading this Catholic funeral procession to the cemetery and keeping it in good order was a tall, muscular Jew in his thirties: graced with a long blond mustache, carrying papers in his pocket like a courier, he dashed up and down, now straightening a horse's harness, now whispering some instruction to the band. This reminded Ulrich further that his father's body had not been in the house on the last day but had been brought back to it only just before the funeral, in accordance with the old gentleman's testamentary last wish, inspired by the free spirit of humanistic inquiry, to put his body at the disposal of science; after which anatomical intervention it was only natural to assume that the old gentleman had been hurriedly sewn up again. Behind those shiny glass panes that reflected Ulrich's image, then, at the center of this great, beautiful, solemn pageantry, was an untidily recobbled object. "With or without his decorations?" Ulrich wondered in dismay. He had forgotten about it and had no idea whether his father had been dressed again in the lab before the closed coffin was returned to the house. And what about Agathe's garter? It could have been found—and he could imagine the jokes of the medical students. It was all extremely embarrassing, and so the protestations of the present again fragmented his feeling into myriad details, after it had for a moment almost rounded itself out into the smooth shell of a living dream. All he could feel now was the absurdity, the confused wavering nature of human order, and of himself.

"Now I'm all alone in the world," he thought. "A mooring rope has snapped—up I go!" This echo of his first sensation on receiving the news of his father's death now once more expressed his feelings as he walked on between the walls of people.

7

A LETTER FROM CLARISSE ARRIVES

Ulrich had not left his address with anyone, but Clarisse had it from
Walter, who knew it as well as he knew his own childhood.
She wrote:

My dar*ling*—my duck*ling*—my *ling!*
Do you know what a *ling* is? I can't work it out. Could Walter
be a weak*ling?* [All the "lings" were heavily underlined.]
Do you think I was drunk when I came to you? I *can't* get
drunk. (Men get drunk before I do. An *amaz*ing fact.)
But I don't know what I said to you; I can't remember. I'm
afraid you imagine I said things I never said. I never said them.
But this is supposed to be a letter—in a minute! But first: You
know how dreams open up. You know how, when you're
dreaming, sometimes: you've been there before, you've talked
with that person already, or—it's like finding your memory again.
Being awake means knowing I've been awake.
(I have sleepmates.)
Do you still remember who Moosbrugger is? There's
something I have to tell you:
Suddenly, there was his name again.
Those three musical syllables.
But music is fakery. I mean, when it's by itself. Music by itself
is for aesthetes or something like that; no vitality. But music
combined with vision, that makes the walls shake and the life of
those to come rise up out of the grave of the present. Those three
musical syllables, I didn't just hear them, I saw them. They
loomed up in my memory! Then suddenly you know: Where
these appear, there's something more. Why, I once wrote your
Count a letter about Moosbrugger—how could I possibly have
forgotten that! Now I hear-see a world in which the things stand
still and the people move around, just as you've always known it,

but in sound that's visible! I don't know how to describe it exactly, because only three syllables have shown up so far. Can you understand that? It may be too soon to talk about it.

I told Walter: "I must meet Moosbrugger!"

Walter asked: "Who's Moosbrugger?"

I told him: "Ulo's friend the murderer."

We were reading the paper; it was morning, time for Walter to go to the office. Remember how we used to read the paper together, the three of us? (You have a *poor* memory, you *won't* remember!) So I had just unfolded the part of the paper Walter had handed me, one arm left, one right: suddenly I feel hard wood, I'm nailed to the Cross. I ask Walter: "Wasn't it only yesterday that there was something in the paper about a train wreck near Budweis?"

"Yes," he says. "Why do you ask? A minor accident, one person killed, or two."

After a while I say: "Because there's been an accident in America too. Where's Pennsylvania?"

He doesn't know. "In America," he says.

I say: "Those engineers never have a head-on collision on purpose!"

He looks at me. I could tell he didn't understand. "Of course not," he says.

I ask him when Siegmund's coming. He's not sure.

So there you are: of course the engineers don't deliberately drive their locomotives into each other head-on; *but why else do they do it?* I'll tell you why. That monstrous network of tracks, switches, and signals that covers the whole globe drains our conscience of all its power. Because if we had the strength to check ourselves just once more, to go over everything we had to do once more, we would do what was necessary every time and avoid the disaster. *The disaster is that we halt before the next-to-last step!*

Of course we can't expect Walter to realize this at once. I think that I'm capable of achieving this immense power of conscience, and I had to shut my eyes so Walter wouldn't see the lightning flash in them.

For all these reasons I regard it as my duty to get to know Moosbrugger.

You know my brother Siegmund is a doctor. He'll help me.

I was waiting for him.

Last Sunday he came.

When he's introduced to someone he says: "But I'm neither . . . nor musical." That's his sort of joke. Just because his name is Siegmund he doesn't want to be thought to be either a Jew or musical. *He was conceived in a Wagnerian ecstasy.* You can't get him to give a sensible answer to anything. All the time I was talking to him he only muttered some nonsense or other. He threw a rock at a bird, he bored holes in the snow with his stick. He wanted to shovel out a path too; he often comes to work in our garden, because, as he says, he doesn't like staying home with his wife and children. Funny that you've never met him. "You two have the *Fleurs du mal* and a vegetable garden!" he says. I pulled his ears and punched him in the ribs, but it did no good whatsoever.

Then we went indoors to Walter, who of course was sitting at the piano, and Siegmund had his jacket under his arm and his hands were all dirty.

"Siegmund," I said to him in front of Walter, "when do you understand a piece of music?"

He grinned and answered: "Absolutely never."

"When you *play it inside yourself,*" I said. "When do you understand another human being? When you feel with him. *Feel with him.*" That's a great mystery, Ulrich! You have to be like him: not by putting yourself *into him* but by taking him *out* into yourself! We redeem *outward:* that's the *strong* way! We fall *in* with people's actions, but *we* fill them *out* and rise above them.

Sorry to be writing so much about this. But the trains collide because our conscience doesn't take that final step. Worlds don't materialize unless we pull them. More of this another time. *The man of genius is duty bound to attack!* He has the mysterious power required. But Siegmund, the coward, looked at his watch and mentioned supper, because he had to go home. You know, Siegmund always tries to find the balance between the blasé

attitude of the seasoned physician who has no very high opinion
of the ability of his profession, and the blasé attitude of the
contemporary person who has transcended the intellectual and
already rediscovered the hygiene of the simple life and
gardening. But Walter shouted: "Oh, for God's sake, why are you
two talking such nonsense? What do you want with this
Moosbrugger anyway?" And that was a help.

Because then Siegmund said: "He's neither insane nor a
criminal, that's true. But what if Clarisse has a notion that she can
do something for him? I'm a doctor, and I have to let the hospital
chaplain imagine the same sort of thing! Redeem him, she says!
Well, why not let her at least see him?"

He brushed off his trousers, adopted an air of serenity, and
washed his hands; we worked it all out over supper.

Now we've already been to see Dr. Friedenthal; he's the
deputy medical officer Siegmund knows. Siegmund said straight
out that he'd take the responsibility for bringing me in under
some sort of false pretenses, as a writer who would like to see
the man.

But that was a mistake, because when it was put to him so
openly, Dr. Friedenthal could only refuse. "Even if you were
Selma Lagerlöf I'd be delighted to see you, of course, as I am in
any case, but here we recognize only a scientific interest."

It was rather fun to be called a writer. I looked him straight in
the eye and said: "In this situation I count for more than Selma
Lagerlöf, because I'm not doing it for 'research.'"

He looked at me, and then he said: "The only thing I can
suggest is for you to bring a letter of introduction from your
embassy to the superintendent of the clinic." He took me for a
foreign writer, not realizing that I was Siegmund's sister.

We finally agreed that I would not be coming to see
Moosbrugger the psychiatric patient but Moosbrugger the
prisoner. Siegmund got me a letter of introduction from a
charitable organization and a permit from the District Court.
Afterward Siegmund told me that Dr. Friedenthal regards
psychiatry as a science that's half art, and called him the
ringmaster of a demons' circus. I rather liked that.

What I liked best was that the clinic is housed in an old

monastery. We had to wait in the corridor, and the lecture hall is in a chapel. It has huge Gothic windows, and I could see inside from across the courtyard. The patients are dressed in white, and they sit up on the dais with the professor. And the professor bends over their chairs in a friendly way. I thought: "Maybe they'll bring Moosbrugger in now." I felt like flying into the lecture hall through that tall window. You'll say I can't fly: jump through the window, then? But I'd never have jumped; that was not how I felt at all.

I hope you'll be coming back soon. One can *never* express things. Least of all in a letter.

This was signed, heavily underlined, *"Clarisse."*

8

A FAMILY OF TWO

Ulrich says: "When two men or women have to share a room for any length of time when traveling—in a sleeping car or a crowded hotel—they're often apt to strike up an odd sort of friendship. Everyone has his own way of using mouthwash or bending over to take off his shoes or bending his leg when he gets into bed. Clothes and underwear are basically the same, yet they reveal to the eye innumerable little individual differences. At first—probably because of the hypertensive individualism of our current way of life—there's a resistance like a faint revulsion that keeps the other person at arm's length, guarding against any invasion into one's own personality. Once that is overcome a communal life develops, which reveals its unusual origin like a scar. At this point many people behave more cheerfully than usual; most become more innocuous; many more talkative; almost all more friendly. The personality is changed; one might almost say that under the skin it has been exchanged for a less idiosyncratic one: the Me is displaced by the beginnings—clearly uneasy and perceived as a diminution, and yet irresistible—of a We."

Agathe replies: "This revulsion from closeness affects women especially. I've never learned to feel at ease with women myself."

"You'll find it between a man and a woman too," Ulrich says. "But there it's covered up by the obligatory rituals of love, which immediately claim all attention. But more often than you might think, those involved wake suddenly from their trance and find—with amazement, irony, or panic, depending on their individual temperament—some totally alien being ensconced at their side; indeed, some people experience this even after many years. Then they can't tell which is more natural: their bond with others or the self's bruised recoil from that bond into the illusion of its uniqueness—both impulses are in our nature, after all. And they're both entangled with the idea of the family. Life within the family is not a full life: Young people feel robbed, diminished, not fully at home with themselves within the circle of the family. Look at elderly, unmarried daughters: they've been sucked dry by the family, drained of their blood; they've become quite peculiar hybrids of the Me and the We."

Clarisse's letter came as a disturbance to Ulrich. The manic outbursts in it bother him much less than the steady and quasi-rational working out of some obviously demented scheme deep within her. He has told himself that after his return he will have to talk to Walter about it, and since then he has deliberately been speaking of other things.

Agathe, stretched out on the couch with one knee drawn up, eagerly picks up what he has just said: "You yourself are explaining, with what you're saying, why I had to marry again!"

"And yet there is also something in the so-called sanctity of the family, in the entering into one another, serving one another, the selfless movement within a closed circle . . . ," Ulrich continues, taking no notice, and Agathe wonders at the way his words so often move away from her again just when they have been so close. "Usually this collective self is only a collective egotist, and then a strong family feeling is the most insufferable thing imaginable. Still, I can also imagine this unconditional leaping into the breach for one another, this fighting shoulder-to-shoulder and licking each other's wounds, as an instinctual feeling of satisfaction rooted deep in the

beginnings of the human race, and even marked in herd animals . . . ,"
she hears him say, without being able to make much of it. Nor can
she do more with his next statement: "This condition is subject to
rapid degeneration, as it happens, like all ancient conditions whose
origin has been lost," and it is only when he ends by saying, "and
would presumably have to require that the individuals involved be
something quite special if the group they form is not to become some
pointless caricature!" that she again feels comfortable with him and
tries, as she looks at him, to keep her eyes from blinking so that he
won't meanwhile disappear, because it's so amazing that he is sitting
there saying things that vanish high into the air and then suddenly
drop down again like a rubber ball caught in the branches of a tree.

Brother and sister had met in the late afternoon in the drawing
room; many days had already passed since the funeral.

This long room was not only decorated in the Biedermeier taste, it
was furnished with genuine pieces of the period. Between the windows hung tall rectangular mirrors in plain gilt frames, and the stiff,
sober chairs were ranged along the walls, so that the empty floor
seemed to have flooded the room with the darkened gleam of its parquet and filled a shallow basin, into which one hesitantly set foot. At
the edge of this salon's elegant barrenness—for the study where Ulrich had settled down on the first morning was set aside for him—
about where in a quarried-out niche the tiled stove stood like a
severe pillar, wearing a vase on its head (and also a lone candlestick,
precisely in the middle of its front, on a shelf running around the
stove at waist height), Agathe had created a very personal peninsula
for herself. She had had a couch moved here, with a rug beside it,
whose ancient reddish blue, in common with the couch's Turkish
pattern that repeated itself in infinite meaninglessness, constituted a
voluptuous challenge to the subtle grays and sober, unassertive linea-
ments that were at home in this room by ancestral decree. She had
further outraged that chaste and well-bred decree by rescuing a
large-leaved man-sized plant complete with tub from the funeral
decorations and installing it at the head of the couch, as a "grove," on
the other side from the tall, bright floor lamp that would enable her
to read in comfort while lying down, and which, in that classicizing
setting, had the effect of a searchlight or an antenna pole. This salon,
with its coffered ceiling, pilasters, and slender glass cabinets, had not

changed much in a hundred years, for it was seldom used and had never really been drawn into the lives of its more recent owners. In their forefathers' day the walls now painted a pale gray might have been covered in fine fabrics, and the upholstery on the chairs had probably looked different too; but Agathe had known this salon as it now was since childhood, without even knowing whether it was her great-grandparents who had furnished it like this or strangers. She had grown up in this house, and the only association she had was the memory that she had always entered this room with the awe that is instilled into children about something they might easily damage or dirty.

But now she had laid aside the last symbol of the past, the mourning she had worn, and put on her lounging pajamas again, and was lying on the rebelliously intruding couch, where since early morning she had been reading all kinds of books, good and bad, whatever she could get her hands on, interrupting herself from time to time to eat or fall asleep; now that the day spent in this fashion was fading into evening, she gazed through the darkening room at the pale curtains that, already quite immersed in twilight, ballooned at the windows like sails, which made her feel that she was voyaging through that stiffly dainty room within the harsh corona of her lamp and had only just come to a halt. So her brother had found her, taking in her well-lit encampment at a glance, for he, too, remembered this salon and could even tell her that the original owner was supposed to have been a rich merchant whose fortunes declined, so that their great-grandfather, an imperial notary, had been in a position to acquire the attractive property at a price well within his means. Ulrich knew all sorts of other things as well about this room, which he had looked over thoroughly; his sister was especially impressed to hear that in their grandparents' day such formal décor had been seen as particularly natural. This was not easy for her to comprehend, since it looked to her like something spawned in a geometry class, and it took a while before she could begin to grasp the outlook of a time so over-saturated with the swirling aggressiveness of the Baroque that its own leaning toward symmetry and somewhat unbending forms was veiled by the tender illusion of being truer to nature in being pure, unadorned, and rational. But when she finally succeeded in grasping this shift of ideas, with the help of all the details Ulrich could supply, she was delighted to know so much about things that every experience in her life up until then had taught her to despise; and when her brother wanted to know what she was reading, she quickly rolled over on top of her supply of books, even though she defiantly said that she enjoyed trashy reading just as much as good.

Ulrich had worked all morning and then gone out. His hope of concentrating, of gaining the new impetus he had expected from the interruption of his customary life, had up to now not been fulfilled; it was outweighed by the distractions resulting from his new circumstances. Only after the funeral had there been a change, when his relations with the outside world, which had begun so actively, had been cut off at a stroke. The brother and sister had been the center of sympathetic attention for a few days, if only as a kind of representation of their father, and had felt the connections attendant upon their position; but apart from Walter's old father they knew no one in town they would have felt like visiting, and in consideration of their mourning no one invited them. Only Professor Schwung had appeared not only at the funeral but again the following day to inquire whether his late friend had not left a manuscript on the problem of diminished responsibility, which one might hope to see published posthumously.

The brusque transition from a constantly seething commotion to the leaden stillness that had followed produced something like a physical shock. Besides, they were still sleeping on camp beds up in the attic, in the rooms they had occupied as children—there were no guest rooms in the house—surrounded by the sparse odds and ends left over from the nursery, their bareness suggesting that of a padded cell, a bareness that, with the insipid sheen of the oilcloth on the tables or the linoleum on the floor—on whose desert the box of building blocks had once spewed forth its rigid ideas of architecture—invaded their dreams. These memories, as senseless and as endless as the life for which they were supposed to have been a preparation, made it a relief that their bedrooms were at least adjacent, separated only by a clothes and storage room; and because the bathroom was on the floor below, they were much in each other's company soon after they got up, meeting on the empty stairs and throughout the empty house, having to show consideration for one another and deal together with all the problems of that unfamiliar household with which they had suddenly been entrusted. In this way they also felt the inevitable comedy of this coexistence, as intimate as it was unexpected: it resembled the adventurous comedy of a shipwreck that had stranded them back on the lonely island of their childhood, and so, after those first few days, over the course of which they had had no control, they strove for independence, although both did so out of altruism more than selfishness.

This was why Ulrich had been up before Agathe had built her peninsula in the drawing room, and had slipped quietly into the study to take up his interrupted mathematical investigation, really more as a way of passing time than with the intention of getting it done. But to his considerable astonishment he all but finished in one morning—except for insignificant details—the work he had left lying untouched for months. He had been helped in this unexpected solution by one of those random ideas of which one might say, not that they turn up only when one has stopped expecting them, but rather that the startling way they flash into the mind is like another sudden recognition—that of the beloved who had always been just another girl among one's friends until the moment when the lover is suddenly amazed that he could ever have put her on the same level as the rest. Such insights are never purely intellectual, but involve an element of passion as well, and Ulrich felt as though he should at this moment have been finished with it and free; indeed, since he could see neither reason nor purpose in it, he had the impression of having finished prematurely, and the leftover energy swept him off into a reverie. He glimpsed the possibility of applying the idea that had solved his problem to other, far more complex problems, and playfully let his imagination stretch the outlines of such a theory. In these moments of happy relaxation he was even tempted to consider Professor Schwung's insinuation that he should return to his career and find the path that leads to success and influence. But when, after a few minutes of intellectual pleasure, he soberly considered what the consequences would be if he were to yield to his ambition and now, as a straggler, take up an academic career, he felt for the first time that he was too old to start anything like that. Since his boyhood he had never felt that the half-impersonal concept of "age" had any independent meaning, any more than he had known the thought: This is something you are no longer able to do!

When Ulrich was telling this to his sister afterward, late that afternoon, he happened to use the word "destiny," and it caught her attention. She wanted to know what "destiny" was.

"Something halfway between 'my toothache' and 'King Lear's daughters,' " Ulrich answered. "I'm not the sort of person who goes in for that word too much."

"But for young people it is part of the song of life; they want to have a destiny but don't know what it is."

"In times to come, when more is known, the word 'destiny' will probably have acquired a statistical meaning," Ulrich responded.

Agathe was twenty-seven. Young enough to have retained some of those hollow, sentimental concepts young people develop first; old enough to already have intimations of the other content that reality pours into them.

"Growing old is probably a destiny in itself!" she answered, but was far from pleased with her answer, which expressed her youthful sadness in a way that seemed to her inane.

But her brother did not notice this, and offered an example: "When I became a mathematician," he said, "I wanted to achieve something in my field and gave it all I had, even though I regarded it only as preliminary to something else. And my first papers—imperfect beginner's work though they were—really did contain ideas that were new at the time, but either remained unnoticed or even met with resistance, though everything else I did was well received. Well, I suppose you could call it destiny that I soon lost patience with having to keep hammering at that wedge."

"Wedge?" Agathe interrupted, as though the mere sound of such a masculine, workmanlike term could mean nothing but trouble. "Why do you call it a wedge?"

"Because it was only my first move; I wanted to drive the wedge further, but then I lost patience. And today, as I completed what may well be the last piece of work that reaches back to that time, I realized that I might actually have had some justification in seeing myself as the leader of a new school of thought, if I'd had better luck then, or shown more persistence."

"You could still make up for it!" Agathe said. "After all, a man doesn't get too old to do things, the way a woman does."

"No," Ulrich replied. "I don't want to go back to that! It's surprising, but true, that objectively—historically, or in the development of science itself—it would have made no difference. I may have been ten years ahead of my time, but others got there without me, even if more slowly or by other means. The most I could have done was to lead them there more quickly, but it remains a question whether such a change in my life would have been enough to give me a fresh impetus that would take me beyond that goal. So there you have a bit of what one calls personal destiny, but what it finally amounts to is something remarkably impersonal.

"Anyway," he went on, "it happens that the older I get, the more often I see something I used to hate that subsequently and in round-about ways takes the same direction as my own road, so that I suddenly can no longer dismiss its right to exist; or it happens that I begin to see what's wrong with ideas or events I used to get excited about. So in the long run it hardly seems to matter whether one gets excited or to what cause one commits one's existence. It all arrives at the same goal; everything serves an evolution that is both unfathomable and inescapable."

"That used to be ascribed to God's working in mysterious ways," Agathe remarked, frowning, with the tone of one speaking from her own experience and not exactly impressed. Ulrich remembered that she had been educated in a convent. She lay on her sofa, as he sat at its foot; she wore her pajama trousers tied at the ankle, and the floor lamp shone on them both in such a way that a large leaf of light formed on the floor, on which they floated in darkness.

"Nowadays," he said, "destiny gives rather the impression of being some overarching movement of a mass; one is engulfed by it and rolled along." He remembered having been struck once before by the idea that these days every truth enters the world divided into its half-truths, and yet this nebulous and slippery process might yield a greater total achievement than if everyone had gone about earnestly trying to accomplish the whole task by himself. He had once even come out with this idea, which lay like a barb in his self-esteem and yet was not without the possibility of greatness, and concluded, tongue-in-cheek, that it meant one could do anything one pleased! Actually, nothing could have been further from his intention than this conclusion, especially now, when his destiny seemed to have set him down and left him with nothing more to do; and at this moment so dangerous to his ambition, when he had been so curiously driven to end, with this belated piece of work, the last thing that had still tied him to his past—precisely at this moment when he felt personally quite bare, what he felt instead of a falling off was this new tension that had begun when he had left his home. He had no name for it, but for the present one could say that a younger person, akin to him, was looking to him for guidance; one could also just as well call it something else. He saw with amazing clarity the radiant mat of bright gold against the black-green of the room, with the delicate lozenges of Agathe's clown costume on it, and himself, and the superlucidly outlined happenstance, cut from the darkness, of their being together.

"Can you say that again?" Agathe asked.

"What we still refer to as a personal destiny," Ulrich said, "is being displaced by collective processes that can finally be expressed in statistical terms."

Agathe thought this over and had to laugh. "I don't understand it, of course, but wouldn't it be lovely to be dissolved by statistics?" she said. "It's been such a long time since love could do it!"

This suddenly led Ulrich to tell his sister what had happened to him when, after finishing his work, he had left the house and walked to the center of town, in order to somehow fill the void left in him by the completion of his paper. He had not intended to speak of it; it seemed too personal a matter. For whenever his travels took him to cities to which he was not connected by business of any kind, he particularly enjoyed the feeling of solitude this gave him, and he had rarely felt this so keenly as he did now. He noticed the colors of the streetcars, the automobiles, shop windows, and archways, the shapes of church towers, the faces and the façades, and even though they all had the usual European resemblances, his gaze flew over them like an insect that has strayed into a field bright with unfamiliar colors and cannot, try as it will, find a place to settle on. Such aimless, purposeless strolling through a town vitally absorbed in itself, the keenness of perception increasing in proportion as the strangeness of the surroundings intensifies, heightened still further by the connection that it is not oneself that matters but only this mass of faces, these movements wrenched loose from the body to become armies of arms, legs, or teeth, to all of which the future belongs—all this can evoke the feeling that being a whole and inviolate strolling human being is positively antisocial and criminal. But if one lets oneself go even further in this fashion, this feeling may also unexpectedly produce a physical well-being and irresponsibility amounting to folly, as if the body were no longer part of a world where the sensual self is enclosed in strands of nerves and blood vessels but belongs to a world bathed in somnolent sweetness. These were the words that Ulrich used to describe to his sister what might perhaps have been the result of a state of mind without goal or ambition, or the result of a diminished ability to maintain an illusory individuality, or perhaps nothing more than that "primal myth of the gods," that "double face of nature," that "giving" and "taking vision," which he was after all pursuing like a hunter.

Now he was waiting curiously to see if Agathe would show by some sign that she understood, that she, too, was familiar with such impressions, but when this did not happen he explained it again: "It's like a slight split in one's consciousness. One feels enfolded, embraced, pierced to the heart by a sense of involuntary dependence; but at the same time one is still alert and capable of making critical judgments, and even ready to start a fight with these people and their stuffy presumptuousness. It's as though there were two relatively independent strata of life within us that normally keep each other profoundly in balance. And we were speaking of destiny: it's as if we had two destinies—one that's all superficial bustle, which takes life over, and one that's motionless and meaningful, which we never find out about."

Now Agathe, who had been listening for a long time without stirring, said out of the blue: "That's like kissing Hagauer!"

Laughing, she had propped herself up on one elbow, her legs still stretched out full length on the couch. And she added: "Of course, it wasn't as beautiful as the way you describe it!"

Ulrich was laughing too. It was not really clear why they were laughing. Somehow this laughter had come upon them from the air, or from the house, or from the traces of bewilderment and uneasiness left behind by the solemnities of the last few days, which had touched so uselessly on the Beyond; or from the uncommon pleasure they found in their conversation. For every human custom that has reached an extreme of cultivation already bears within itself the seeds of change, and every excitement that surpasses the ordinary soon mists over with a breath of sorrow, absurdity, and satiety.

In this fashion and in such a roundabout way they finally end up, as if for relaxation, talking about less demanding matters, about Me and Us and Family, and arriving at the discovery, fluctuating between mockery and astonishment, that the two of them constitute a family. And while Ulrich speaks of the desire for community—once more with the zeal of a man out to mortify his own nature, without knowing whether it is directed against his true nature or his assumed nature—Agathe is listening as his words come close to her and retreat again, and what he notices, looking at her lying quite defenseless in that bright island of light and in her whimsical costume, is that for some time now he has been searching for something about her that would repel him, as he regrettably tends to do, but he has not found anything, and for this he is thankful with a pure and simple affection that he otherwise never feels. And he is thoroughly delighted by the conversation. But when it is over, Agathe asks him casually: "Now, are you actually *for* what you call the family or are you against it?"

Ulrich answers that this is beside the point, because he was talking about an indecision on the part of the world, not his personal indecision.

Agathe thinks it over.

Finally, she says abruptly: "I have no way of judging that. But I wish I could be entirely at one and at peace with myself, and also . . . well, somehow be able to live accordingly. Wouldn't you like to try that too?"

9

AGATHE WHEN SHE CAN'T TALK TO ULRICH

The moment Agathe got on the train and began the unexpected journey to her father something had happened that bore every resemblance to a sudden rupture, and the two fragments into which the
moment of departure exploded flew as far apart as if they had never
belonged together. Her husband had seen her off, had raised his hat
and held it, that stiff, round, black hat that grew visibly smaller and
smaller, in the gesture appropriate to leave-taking, aslant in the air,
as her train began to move, so that it seemed to Agathe that the station was rolling backward as fast as the train was rolling forward. At
this moment, though an instant earlier she had still been expecting to
be away from home no longer than circumstances absolutely required, she made the decision never to return, and her mind became
agitated like a heart that realizes suddenly that it has escaped a danger of which it had been wholly unaware.

When Agathe thought it over afterward, she was by no means
completely satisfied. What troubled her about her attitude was that
its form reminded her of a curious illness she had had as a child, soon
after she had begun going to school. For more than a year she had
suffered from a not inconsiderable fever that neither rose nor sub-
sided, and she had grown so thin and frail that it worried the doctors,
who could not determine the cause. Nor was this illness ever explained later. Actually, Agathe had rather enjoyed seeing the great
physicians from the University, who at first entered her room so full
of dignity and wisdom, visibly lose some of their confidence from
week to week; and although she obediently swallowed all the medicines prescribed for her and really would have liked to get well, because it was expected of her, she was still pleased to see that the
doctors could not bring this about with their remedies and felt herself in an unearthly or at least an extraordinary condition, as her
physical self diminished. That the grownups' world had no power
over her as long as she was sick made her feel proud, though she had

no idea how her little body had brought this about. But in the end it recovered of its own accord, and just as mysteriously, too.

Almost all she knew about it today was what the servants had told her later: they maintained that she had been bewitched by a beggar woman who came often to the house but had once been rudely turned away from the door. Agathe had never been able to find out how much truth there was in this story, for although the servants freely dropped hints, they could never be pinned down to explanations and were obviously frightened of violating a strict ban her father was supposed to have issued. Her own memory of that time held only a single, though indeed remarkably lively, image, in which she saw her father in front of her, lashing out in a raging fury at a suspicious-looking woman, the flat of his hand repeatedly making contact with her cheek. It was the only time in her life she had seen that small, usually painfully proper man of reason so utterly changed and beside himself; but to the best of her recollection this had happened not before but during her illness, for she thought she remembered lying in bed, and this bed was not in her nursery but on the floor below, "with the grownups," in one of the rooms where the servants would not have been allowed to let the beggar woman in, even if she had been no stranger to the kitchen and below stairs. Actually, Agathe believed this incident must have occurred rather toward the end of her illness and that she had suddenly recovered a few days later, roused from her bed by a remarkable impatience that ended this illness as unexpectedly as it had begun.

Of course, she could not tell how far these memories stemmed from facts or whether they were fantasies born of the fever. "Probably the only curious thing about it is the way these images have stayed floating in my mind somewhere between reality and illusion," she thought moodily, "without my finding anything unusual about it."

The jolting of the taxi that was driving them over badly paved streets prevented a conversation. Ulrich had suggested taking advantage of the dry winter weather for an outing, and even had an idea where to go, though it was not a specific destination so much as an advance into a half-remembered country of the mind. Now they found themselves in a car that was to take them to the edge of town. "I'm sure that's the only odd thing about it!" Agathe kept saying to herself. This was how she had learned her lessons in school, so that she never knew whether she was stupid or bright, willing or unwilling: she had a facility for coming up with the answers that were demanded of her without ever seeing the point of the questions, from which she felt protected by a deep-seated indifference. After she recovered from her illness she liked going to school as much as before, and because one of the doctors had hit upon the idea that it might help to remove her from the solitary life in her father's house and give her more company of her own age, she had been placed in a convent school. There, and in the secondary school she was sent on to, she was regarded as cheerful and docile. Whenever she was told that something was necessary or true she accommodated herself to it, and she willingly accepted everything required of her, because it seemed the least trouble and it would have seemed foolish to her to do anything against an established system that had no relevance to herself but obviously belonged to a world ordained by fathers and teachers. However, she did not believe a word of what she was learning, and since despite her apparent docility she was no model pupil and, wherever her desires ran counter to her convictions, calmly did as she pleased, she enjoyed the respect of her schoolmates and even that admiring affection won in school by those who know how to make things easy for themselves. It could even be that her mysterious illness had been such an arrangement, for with this one exception she had really always been in good health and hardly ever high-strung. "In short, an idle, good-for-nothing character!" she concluded uncertainly. She remembered how much more vigorously than herself her friends had often mutinied against the strict discipline of the convent, and with what moral indignation they had justified their offenses against the regulations; yet as far as she had been in a position to observe, the very girls who had been most passionate in rebelling against details had eventually succeeded admirably in coming to terms with the whole; they developed into well-situated women who brought up their children not very differently from the way they had been brought up themselves. And so, although dissatisfied with herself as she was, she was not convinced that it was better to have an active and a good character.

Agathe despised the emancipation of women just as she disdained the female's need for a brood in a nest supplied by the male. She remembered with pleasure the time when she had first felt her breasts tightening her dress and had borne her burning lips through the cooling air of the streets. But the fussy erotic busyness of the female sex, which emerges from the guise of girlhood like a round knee from pink tulle, had aroused scorn in her for as long as she could remember. When she asked herself what her real convictions were, a feeling told her that she was destined to experience something extraordinary and of a rare order—even then, when she knew as good as nothing of the world and did not believe the little she had been taught. And it had always seemed to her like a mysterious but active response, corresponding to this impression, to let things go as they had to, without overestimating their importance.

Out of the corner of her eye Agathe glanced at Ulrich, sitting gravely upright, rocking to and fro in the jolting cab, and recalled how hard it had been on their first evening together to make him see why she had not simply run away from her husband on their wedding night, although she didn't like him. She had been so tremendously in awe of her big brother while she was awaiting his arrival, but now she smiled as she secretly recalled her impression of Hagauer's thick lips in those first months, every time they rounded amorously under the bristles of his mustache; his entire face would be drawn in thick-skinned folds toward the corners of his mouth, and she would feel, as if satiated: Oh, what an ugly man he is! She had even suffered his mild pedagogic vanity and kindliness as a merely physical disgust, more outward than inward. After the first surprise was over, she had now and then been unfaithful to him. "If you can call it that," she thought, "when an inexperienced young thing whose sensuality is dormant instantly responds to the advances of a man who is not her husband as if they were thunderclaps rattling her door!" But she had shown little talent for unfaithfulness; lovers, once she had got to know them a little, were no more masterful to her than husbands, and it soon seemed to her that she could take the ritual masks of African tribal dancers as seriously as the love masks put on by European men. Not that she never lost her head; but even in the first attempts to repeat the experience the magic was gone. The world of acted-out fantasies, the theatricality of love, left her unenchanted. These stage directions for the soul, mostly formulated by men, which all came to the conclusion that the rigors of life now and then entitled one to an hour of weakness—with some subcategories of weakening: letting go, going faint, being taken, giving oneself, surrendering, going crazy, and so on—all struck her as smarmy exaggeration, since she had at no time ever felt herself other than weak in a world so superbly constructed by the strength of men.

The philosophy Agathe acquired in this way was simply that of the female person who refuses to be taken in but who automatically observes what the male person is trying to put over on her. Of course, it was no philosophy at all, only a defiantly hidden disappointment, still mingled with a restrained readiness for some unknown release that possibly increased even as her outward defiance lessened. Since Agathe was well-read but not by nature given to theorizing, she often had occasion to wonder, in comparing her own experiences with the ideals in books and plays, that she had never fallen prey to the snares of her seducers, like a wild animal in a trap (which would have accorded with the Don Juanish self-image a man in those days assumed when he and a woman had an affair); nor had her married life, in accord with another fashion, turned into a Strindbergian battle of the sexes in which the imprisoned woman used her cunning and powerlessness to torment her despotic but inept overlord to death. In fact, her relations with Hagauer, in contrast with her deeper feelings about him, had always remained quite good. On their first evening together Ulrich had used strong terms for these relations, such as panic, shock, rape, which completely missed the mark. She was sorry, Agathe thought, rebellious even as she remembered this, but she could not pretend to be an angel; the fact was that everything about the marriage had taken a perfectly natural course. Her father had supported the man's suit with sensible reasons, she herself had decided to marry again; all right, then, it was done, one had to put up with whatever was involved. It was neither especially wonderful nor overly unpleasant! Even now she was sorry to be hurting Hagauer deliberately, though she absolutely wanted to do just that! She had not wanted love, she had thought it would work out somehow, he was after all a good man.

Well, perhaps it was rather that he was one of those people who always do the good thing; they themselves have no goodness in them, Agathe thought. It seems that goodness disappears from the human being to the same extent that it is embodied in goodwill or good deeds! How had Ulrich put it? A stream that turns factory wheels loses its gradient. Yes, he had said that too, but that wasn't what she was looking for. Now she had it: "It seems really that it's only the people who don't do much good who are able to preserve their goodness intact!" But the instant she recalled this sentence, which must have sounded so illuminating when Ulrich said it, it sounded to her like total nonsense. One could not detach it from its now-forgotten context. She tried to reshuffle the words and replace them with similar ones, but that only proved that the first version was the right one, for the others were like words spoken into the wind: nothing was left of them. So that was the way Ulrich had said it. "But how can one call people good who behave badly?" she thought. "That's really nonsense!" But she knew: while Ulrich was saying this, though it had no more real substance when he did so, it had been wonderful! Wonderful wasn't the word for it: she had felt almost ill with joy when she heard him say it. Such sayings illuminated her entire life. This one, for instance, had come up during their last long talk, after the funeral and after Hagauer had left; suddenly she had realized how carelessly she had always behaved, like the time she had simply thought things would "somehow" work out with Hagauer, because he was "a good person." Ulrich often said things that filled her momentarily with joy or misery, although one could not "preserve" those moments. When was it, for example, that Ulrich had said that under certain circumstances it might be possible for him to love a thief but never a person who was honest from habit? At the moment she couldn't quite recall, but then realized with delight that it hadn't been Ulrich but she herself who had said it. As a matter of fact, much of what he said she had been thinking herself, only without words; all on her own, the way she used to be, she would never have made such bold assertions.

Up to now Agathe had been feeling perfectly comfortable between the joggings and joltings as the cab drove over bumpy suburban streets, leaving them incapable of speech, wrapped as they were in a network of mechanical vibrations, and whenever she had used her husband's name in her thoughts, it was as a mere term of reference to a period and its events. But now, for no particular reason, an infinite horror slowly came over her: Hagauer had actually been there with her, in the flesh! The way in which she had tried up to now to be fair to him disappeared, and her throat tightened with bitterness.

He had arrived on the morning of the funeral and had affectionately insisted, late as he was, on seeing his father-in-law, had gone to the autopsy lab and delayed the closing of the coffin. In a tactful, honorable, undemonstrative fashion, he had been truly moved. After the funeral Agathe had excused herself on grounds of fatigue, and Ulrich had to take his brother-in-law out to lunch. As he told her afterward, Hagauer's constant company had made Ulrich as frantic as a tight collar, and for that reason he had done everything to get him to leave as soon as possible. Hagauer had intended to go to the capital for an educators' conference and there devote another day to calling on people at the Ministry and some sightseeing, but he had reserved the two days prior to this to spend with his wife as an attentive husband and to go into the matter of her inheritance. But Ulrich, in collusion with his sister, had made up a story that made it seem impossible for Hagauer to stay at the house, and told him he had booked a room for him at the best hotel in town. As expected, this made Hagauer hesitant: the hotel would be inconvenient and expensive, and he would in all decency have to pay for it himself; instead, he could allot two days to his calls and sightseeing in the capital, and if he traveled at night save the cost of the hotel. So Hagauer expressed fulsome regrets at being unable to take advantage of Ulrich's thoughtfulness, and finally revealed his plan, unalterable by now, to leave that very evening. All that was left to discuss was the question of the inheritance, and this made Agathe smile again, because at her instigation Ulrich had told her husband that the will could not be read for a few days yet. Agathe would be here, after all, he was told, to look after his interests, and he would also receive a proper legal statement. As for whatever concerned furniture, mementos, and the like, Ulrich, as a bachelor, would make no claims to anything his sister might happen to want. Finally, he had asked Hagauer whether he would agree in case they decided to sell the house, which was of no use to them, without committing himself, of course, since none of them had yet seen the will; and Hagauer had agreed, without committing himself, of course, that he could see no objection for the moment, though he must of course reserve the right to determine his position in the light of the actual conditions. Agathe had suggested all this to her brother, and he had passed it on because it meant nothing to him one way or the other, and he wanted to be rid of Hagauer.

Suddenly Agathe felt miserable again, for after they had managed this so well, her husband had after all come to her room, together with her brother, to say goodbye to her. Agathe had behaved as coldly as she could and said that there was no way of telling when she would be returning home. Knowing him as she did, she could tell at once that he had not been prepared for this and resented the fact that his decision to leave right away was now casting him in the role of the unfeeling husband; in retrospect he was suddenly offended at having been expected to stay at a hotel and by the cool reception accorded him. But since he was a man who did everything according to plan he said nothing, decided to have it out with his wife when the time came, and kissed her, after he had picked up his hat, dutifully on the lips.

And this kiss, which Ulrich had seen, now seemed to demolish Agathe. "How could it happen," she asked herself in consternation, "that I stood this man for so long? But then, haven't I put up with things all my life without resisting?" She furiously reproached herself: "If I were any good at all, things could never have gone this far!"

Agathe turned her face away from Ulrich, whom she had been watching, and stared out the window. Low suburban buildings, icy streets, muffled-up people—images of an ugly wilderness rolling past, holding up to her the wasteland of the life into which she felt she had fecklessly allowed herself to drift. She was no longer sitting upright but had let herself slide down into the cab's musty-smelling upholstery; it was easier to look out the window in this position, and she remained in this ungraceful posture, in which she was rudely jolted and shaken to the very bowels. This body of hers, being tossed about like a bundle of rags, gave her an uncanny feeling, for it was the only thing she owned. Sometimes, when as a schoolgirl she awakened in the gray light of dawn, she had felt as though she were drifting into the future inside her body as if inside the hull of a wooden skiff. Now she was just about twice as old as she had been then, and the light in the cab was equally dim. But she still could not picture her life, had no idea what it ought to be. Men were a complement to one's body, but they were no spiritual fulfillment; one took them as they took oneself. Her body told her that in only a few years it would begin to lose its beauty, which meant losing the feelings that, because they arise directly out of its self-assurance, can only barely be expressed in words or thoughts. Then it would be all over, without anything having ever been there. It occurred to her that Ulrich had spoken in a similar vein about the futility of his athletics, and while she doggedly kept her face turned away to the window, she planned to make him talk about it.

10

FURTHER COURSE OF THE EXCURSION TO THE SWEDISH RAMPARTS. THE MORALITY OF THE NEXT STEP

Brother and sister had left the cab at the last, low, and already quite rural-looking houses on the edge of the town and set off along a wide, furrowed country road that rose steadily uphill. The frozen earth of the wheel tracks crumbled beneath their tread. Their shoes were soon covered with the miserable gray of this parquet for carters and peasants, in sharp contrast with their smart city clothes, and although it was not cold, a cutting wind blowing toward them from the top of the hill made their cheeks glow, and the glazed brittleness of their lips made it hard to talk.

The memory of Hagauer drove Agathe to explain herself to her brother. She was convinced that he could not possibly understand her bad marriage from any point of view, not even in the simplest of social terms. The words were already there within her, but she could not make up her mind to overcome the resistance of the climb, the cold, and the wind lashing her face. Ulrich was striding ahead, in a broad track left by a dragging brake, which they were using as their path; looking at his lean, broad-shouldered form, she hesitated. She had always imagined him hard, unyielding, a bit wild, perhaps only because of the critical remarks she had heard from her father and occasionally also from Hagauer; thinking of her brother, estranged and escaped from the family, had made her ashamed of her own subservience. "He was right not to bother about me!" she thought, and her dismay at having continually submitted to demeaning situations returned. But in fact she was full of those same tempestuous, conflicting feelings that had made her break out with those wild lines of poetry between the doorposts of her father's death chamber. She caught up with Ulrich, which left her out of breath, and suddenly questions such as this workaday road had probably never heard before rang out, and the wind was torn to ribbons by words whose sounds no other wind had ever carried in these rural hills.

"You surely remember . . . ," she exclaimed, and named several well-known instances from literature: "You didn't tell me whether you could forgive a thief, but do you mean you'd regard these murderers as good people?"

"Of course!" Ulrich shouted back. "No—wait. Perhaps they're just potentially good people, valuable people. They still are, even afterward, as criminals. But they don't stay good!"

"Then why do you still like them after their crime? Surely not because of their earlier potentiality but because you still find them attractive?"

"But that's always the way it is," Ulrich said. "It's the person who gives character to the deed; it doesn't happen the other way round. We separate good and evil, but in our hearts we know they're a whole!"

Agathe's wind-whipped cheeks flushed an even brighter red because the passion of her questions, which words both revealed and hid, had forced her to resort to books for examples. The misuse of "cultural problems" is so extreme that one could feel them out of place wherever the wind blows and trees stand, as though human culture did not include all of nature's manifestations! But she had struggled bravely, linked her arm through her brother's, and now replied, close to his ear so as not to have to raise her voice anymore and with a flicker of bravado in her face: "I suppose that's why we execute bad men but cordially serve them a hearty breakfast first."

Ulrich, sensing some of the agitation at his side, leaned down to speak in his sister's ear, though in a normal voice: "Everyone likes to think that he couldn't do anything evil, because he himself is good."

With these words they had reached the top, where the road no longer climbed but cut across a rolling, treeless plateau. The wind had suddenly dropped and it was no longer cold, but in this pleasant stillness the conversation stopped as if severed, and would not start up again.

"What on earth got you onto Dostoyevsky and Stendhal in the middle of that gale?" Ulrich asked a while later. "If anybody had seen us they'd have thought we were crazy."

Agathe laughed. "They wouldn't have understood us anymore than the cries of the birds. . . . Anyway, you were talking to me the other day about Moosbrugger."

They walked on.

After a while, Agathe said: "I don't like him at all!"

"And I'd nearly forgotten him," Ulrich replied.

After they had again walked on in silence, Agathe stopped. "Tell me," she asked. "You've surely done some irresponsible things yourself. I remember, for instance, that you were in the hospital once with a bullet wound. You certainly don't always look before you leap . . . ?"

"What a lot of questions you're asking today!" Ulrich said. "What do you expect me to say to that?"

"Are you never sorry for anything you do?" Agathe asked quickly. "I have the impression that you never regret anything. You even said something like that once."

"Good God," Ulrich answered, beginning to walk on again. "There's a plus in every minus. Maybe I did say something like that, but you don't have to take it so literally."

"A plus in every minus?"

"Some good in everything bad. Or at least in much of the bad. A human minus-variant is likely to contain an unrecognized plus-variant—that's probably what I meant to say. Having something to regret may be just the thing to give you the strength to do something far better than you might ever have done otherwise. It's never what one does that counts, but only what one does next!"

"Suppose you've killed someone: what can you do next?"

Ulrich shrugged his shoulders. He was tempted to answer, for the sake of the argument: "It might enable me to write a poem that would enrich the inner life of thousands of people, or to come up with a great invention!" But he checked himself. "That would never happen," he thought. "Only a lunatic could imagine it. Or an eighteen-year-old aesthete. God knows why, but those are ideas that contradict the laws of nature. On the other hand," he conceded, "it did work that way for primitive man. He killed because human sacrifice was a great religious poem!"

He said neither the one thing nor the other aloud, but Agathe went on: "You may regard my objections as silly, but the first time I heard you say that what matters isn't the step one takes but always the next step after that, I thought: So if a person could fly inwardly, fly morally, as it were, and could keep flying at high speed from one improvement to the next, then he would know no remorse! I was madly envious of you!"

"That's nonsense!" Ulrich said emphatically. "What I said was that one false step doesn't matter, only the next step after that. But then what matters after the next step? Evidently the one that follows after *that*. And after the *n*th step, the *n*-plus-one step! Such a person would have to live without ever coming to an end or to a decision, indeed without achieving reality. And yet it is still true that what counts is always only the next step. The truth is, we have no proper method of dealing with this unending series. Dear Agathe," he said abruptly, "I sometimes regret my entire life."

"But that's just what you can't do!" his sister said.

"And why not? Why not that in particular?"

"I have never really done anything," Agathe replied, "and so I've always had time to regret the little I have done. I'm sure you don't know what that's like: such a dim state of mind! The shadows come, and what was has power over me. It's present in the smallest detail, and I can forget nothing and understand nothing. It's an unpleasant state of mind. . . ." Her tone was unemotional, quite unassuming. Ulrich had in fact never known this backwash of life, since his own had always been oriented toward expansion, and it merely reminded him that his sister had several times already expressed dissatisfaction with herself in strong terms. But he failed to question her because they had meanwhile reached a hilltop that he had chosen as their destination and stepped toward its edge. It was a huge mound associated by legend with a Swedish siege in the Thirty Years' War because it looked like a fortification, even though it was far too big for that: a green rampart of nature, without bush or tree, that broke off to a high, bright rock face on the side overlooking the town. A low, empty world of hills surrounded this mound; no village, no house was to be seen, only the shadows of clouds and gray pastures. Once again Ulrich felt the spell of this place, which he remembered from his youth: the town was still lying there, far below in the distance, anxiously huddled around a few churches that looked like hens herding their chicks, so that one suddenly felt like leaping into their midst with one bound and laying about one, or scooping them up in the grip of a giant hand.

"What a glorious feeling it must have been for those Swedish adventurers to reach such a place after trotting relentlessly for weeks, and then from their saddles catch sight of their quarry," he said to his sister after telling her the story of the place. "It is only at such moments that the weight of life, the burden of our secret grievance—that we must all die, that it's all been so brief and probably for nothing—is ever really lifted from us."

"What moments do you mean?"

Ulrich did not know what to answer. He did not want to answer at all. He remembered that as a young man he had always felt the need in this place to clench his teeth and keep silent. Finally, he replied: "Those romantic moments when events run away with us—the senseless moments!" He felt as if his head were a hollow nut on his neck, full of old saws like "Death be not proud" or "I care for nobody, no, not I," and with them the faded fortissimo of those years when there was not yet a boundary between life's expectations and life itself. He thought: "What single-minded and happy experiences have I had since then? None."

Agathe responded: "I've always acted senselessly, and it only makes one unhappy."

She had walked ahead, to the very edge. Her ears were deaf to her brother's words; she did not understand them, and saw a somber, barren landscape before her whose sadness harmonized with her own. When she turned around she said: "It's a place to kill oneself," and smiled. "The emptiness in my head could melt with sweet peace into the emptiness of this view!" She took a few steps back to Ulrich. "All my life," she went on, "I've been reproached with having no willpower, with loving nothing, respecting nothing; in short, for being a person with no real will to live. Papa used to scold me for it, and Hagauer blamed me for it. So now I wish you would tell me, for God's sake, tell me at long last, in which moments does something in life strike us as necessary?"

"When one turns over in bed!" Ulrich said gruffly.

"What does that mean?"

"Excuse the mundane example," he said. "But it's a fact: You're in an uncomfortable position; you incessantly think of changing it and decide on one move and then another, without doing anything; finally, you give up; and then all at once you've turned over! One really should say you've been turned over. That's the one pattern we act on, whether in a fit of passion or after long reflection." He did not look at her as he spoke; he was answering himself. He still had the feeling: Here I stood and longed for something that has never been satisfied.

Agathe smiled again, but the smile twisted her mouth as if in pain. She returned to where she had been standing and stared silently into the romantic distance. Her fur coat made a dark outline against the sky, and her slender form presented a sharp contrast to the broad silence of the landscape and the shadows of the clouds flying over it. Looking at her, Ulrich had an indescribably strong sense that something was happening. He was almost ashamed to be standing there in the company of a woman instead of beside a saddled horse. And although he was perfectly aware that the cause of this was the tranquil image emanating at this moment from his sister, he had the impression that something was happening, not to him, but somewhere in the world, and he was missing it. He felt he was being ridiculous. And yet there had been something true in his blurting out that he regretted the way he had lived his life. He sometimes longed to be wholly involved in events as in a wrestling match, even if they were meaningless or criminal, as long as they were valid, absolute, without the everlasting tentativeness they have when a person is superior to his experiences. "Something an end in itself, authentic," Ulrich thought, seriously looking for the right expression, and, unawares, his thoughts stopped pursuing imaginary events and focused on the sight that Agathe herself now presented, as nothing but the mirror of her self. So brother and sister stood for quite a while, apart and solitary, immobilized by a hesitancy filled with conflicting feelings. Most curious of all, perhaps, was that it never occurred to Ulrich that something had indeed already happened when, at Agathe's behest and in his own desire to get rid of him, he had palmed off on his unsuspecting brother-in-law the lie that there was a sealed testament that could not be opened for several days, and had assured him, also against his better knowledge, that Agathe would look after his interests: something Hagauer would subsequently refer to as "aiding and abetting."

Eventually they did move away from this spot, where each had been sunk in thought, and walked on together without having talked things out. The wind had freshened again, and because Agathe seemed fatigued, Ulrich suggested stopping to rest at a shepherd's cottage he knew of nearby. They soon found the stone cabin, and they had to duck their heads as they went in, while the shepherd's wife, staring, fended them off in embarrassment. In the mixture of German and Slavic that prevailed in this part of the country and that he still vaguely remembered, Ulrich asked if they might come in for a while to warm themselves and eat their provisions indoors, and supported this request with a tip so generous that the involuntary hostess broke out into horrified lamentations that her wretched poverty did not enable her to offer better hospitality to such "fine gentry." She wiped off the greasy table by the window, fanned a fire of twigs on the hearth, and put on some goat's milk to heat. Agathe had immediately squeezed past the table to the window without paying any attention to these efforts, as if it were a matter of course that one would find shelter somewhere, no matter where. She looked out through the dim little square of four panes at the landscape here, on the far side of the rampart, which without the wide extent of the view they had had from the top was more reminiscent of what a swimmer sees, surrounded by green crests. Though it was not yet evening, the day had passed its zenith and the light was fading.

Suddenly Agathe asked: "Why don't you ever talk to me seriously?"

How could Ulrich have found a better answer to this other than to glance up at her with an air of innocence and surprise? He was busy laying out ham, sausage, and boiled eggs on a piece of paper between himself and his sister.

But Agathe continued: "If one accidentally bumps into you it hurts, and one feels a shock at the terrific difference. But when I try to ask you something crucial you dissolve into thin air!"

She did not touch the food he pushed toward her—indeed, in her aversion to winding up the day with a rural picnic, her back was so straight that she was not even touching the table. And now something recurred that was like their climb up the country road. Ulrich shoved aside the mugs of goat's milk that had just been brought to the table from the stove and were emitting a very disagreeable smell to noses unaccustomed to it; the faint nausea it produced in him had a sobering, stimulating effect such as comes from a sudden rush of bitterness.

"I've always spoken seriously to you," he retorted. "If you don't like what I say, it's not my fault; what you don't like in my responses is the morality of our time." He suddenly realized that he wanted to explain to his sister as completely as possible all she would have to know in order to understand herself, and to some extent her brother as well. And with the firmness of a man who will brook no idle interruptions, he launched on a lengthy speech.

"The morality of our time, whatever else may be claimed, is that of achievement. Five more or less fraudulent bankruptcies are acceptable provided the fifth leads to a time of prosperity and patronage. Success can cause everything else to be forgotten. When you reach the point where your money helps win elections and buys paintings, the State is prepared to look the other way too. There are unwritten rules: if you donate to church, charities, and political parties, it needs to be no more than one tenth of the outlay required for someone to demonstrate his goodwill by patronizing the arts. And even success still has its limits; one cannot yet acquire everything in every way; some principles of the Crown, the aristocracy, and society can still to some extent restrain the social climber. On the other hand, the State, for its own suprapersonal person, quite openly countenances the principle that one may rob, steal, and murder if it will provide power, civilization, and glory. Of course, I'm not saying that all this is acknowledged even in theory; on the contrary, the theory of it is quite obscure. I just wanted to sum up the most mundane facts for you. The moral argumentation is just one more means to an end, a weapon used in much the same way as lies. This is the world that men have made, and it would make me want to be a woman—if only women did not love men!

"Nowadays we call good whatever gives us the illusion that it will get us somewhere, but this is precisely what you just called the flying man without remorse, and what I've called a problem we have no method for solving. As a scientifically trained person I feel in every situation that my knowledge is incomplete, no more than a pointer, and that perhaps tomorrow I will have new knowledge that will cause me to think differently. On the other hand, even a person wholly governed by his feelings, 'a person on the way up,' as you have depicted him, will see everything he does as a step upward, from which he is raised to the next step. So there is something in our minds and in our souls, a morality of the 'next-step'—but is that simply the morality of the five bankruptcies, is the entrepreneurial morality of our time so deeply rooted in our inner life? Or is there only the illusion of a connection? Or is the morality of the careerists a monstrosity prematurely born from deeper currents? At this point I really don't know the answer!"

Ulrich's short pause for breath was only rhetorical, for he intended to develop his views further. Agathe, however, who had so far been listening with the curiously passive alertness that was sometimes characteristic of her, switched the conversation onto a totally different track with the simple remark that she wasn't interested in this answer because all she wanted to know was where Ulrich himself stood; she was not in a position to grasp what everyone might think.

"But if you expect me to accomplish anything in any form whatsoever, I'd rather have no principles at all," she added.

"Thank God for that!" Ulrich said. "It's always a pleasure for me, every time I look at your youth, beauty, and strength, to hear from you that you have no energy at all! Our era is dripping with the energy of action. It's not interested in ideas, only in deeds. This fearful activity stems from the single fact that people have nothing to do. Inwardly, I mean. But even outwardly, in the last analysis, everyone spends his whole life repeating the same thing over and over: he gets into some occupation and then goes on with it. I think this brings us back to the question you raised before, out there in the open air. It's so simple to have the energy to act, and so hard to make any sense of it! Almost nobody understands that these days. That's why our men of action look like men bowling; they manage to knock down their nine pins with all the gestures of a Napoleon. It wouldn't even surprise me to see them ending up by assaulting each other in a frenzy, because of their inability to comprehend why all action is inadequate. . . ." He had spoken energetically at first but lapsed again, first into pensiveness, then into silence for a while. At last he just glanced up with a smile and contented himself with saying: "You say that if I expect any moral effort from you, you are bound to disappoint me. I say that if you expect any moral counsel from me, I am bound to disappoint you. I think that we have nothing definite to demand of one another—all of us, I mean; we really shouldn't demand action from one another; we should create the conditions that make action possible; that's how I feel about it."

"But how is that to be done?" Agathe said. She realized that Ulrich had abandoned the big pronouncements he had begun with and had drifted into something closer to himself, but even this was too general for her taste. She had, as we know, no use for general analysis and regarded every effort that extended beyond her own skin, as it were, as more or less hopeless; she was sure of this for her own part, and believed it was probably true of the general assertions of others too. Still, she understood Ulrich quite well. She noticed that as he sat there with his head down, speaking softly against the energy of action, her brother kept absentmindedly carving notches and lines into the table with his pocketknife, and all the sinews of his hand were tense. The unthinking but almost impassioned motion of his hand, and the frank way he had spoken of Agathe's youth and beauty, made for an absurd duet above the orchestra of the other words; nor did she try to give it a meaning other than that she was sitting here watching.

"What's to be done?" Ulrich replied in the same tone as before. "At our cousin's I once proposed to Count Leinsdorf that he should found a World Secretariat for Precision and Soul, so that even the people who don't go to church would know what they had to do. Naturally, I only said it in fun, for while we created science a long time ago for truth, asking for something similar to cope with everything else would still appear so foolish today as to be embarrassing. And yet everything the two of us have been talking about so far would logically call for such a secretariat!" He had dropped the speech and leaned back against his bench. "I suppose I'm dissolving into thin air again if I add: But how would that turn out today?"

Since Agathe did not reply, there was a silence. After a while Ulrich said: "Anyway, I sometimes think that I can't really stand believing that myself! When I saw you before, standing on the rampart," he added in an undertone, "I suddenly had a wild urge to *do* something! I don't know why. I really have done some rash things sometimes. The magic lay in the fact that when it was over, there was something more besides me. Sometimes I'm inclined to think that a person could be happy even as a result of a crime, because it gives him a certain ballast and perhaps keeps him on a steadier course."

This time, too, his sister did not answer right away. He looked at her quietly, perhaps even expectantly, but without reexperiencing the surge he had just described, indeed without thinking of anything at all. After a little while, she asked him: "Would you be angry with me if I committed a crime?"

"What do you expect me to say to that?" Ulrich said; he had bent over his knife again.

"Is there no answer?"

"No; nowadays there is no real answer."

At this point Agathe said: "I'd like to kill Hagauer."

Ulrich forced himself not to look up. The words had entered his ear lightly and softly, but when they had passed they left behind something like broad wheel marks in his mind. He had instantly forgotten her tone; he would have had to see her face to know how to take her words, but he did not want to accord them even that much importance.

"Fine," he said. "Why shouldn't you? Is there anyone left today who hasn't wanted to do something of the kind? Do it, if you really can! It's just as if you had said: 'I would like to love him for his faults!'" Now he straightened up again and looked his sister in the face. It was stubborn and surprisingly excited. Keeping his eyes on her, he said slowly:

"There's something wrong here, you see; on this frontier between what goes on inside us and what goes on outside, some kind of communication is missing these days, and they adapt to each other only with tremendous losses. One might almost say that our evil desires are the dark side of the life we lead in reality, and the life we lead in reality is the dark side of our good desires. Imagine if you actually did it: it wouldn't at all be what you meant, and you'd be horribly disappointed, to say the least. . . ."

"Perhaps I could suddenly be a different person—you admitted that yourself!" Agathe interrupted him.

As Ulrich at this moment looked around, he was reminded that they were not alone; two people were listening to their conversation. The old woman—hardly over forty, perhaps, but her rags and the traces of her humble life made her look older—had sat down sociably near the stove, and sitting beside her was the shepherd, who had come home to his hut during their conversation without their noticing him, absorbed in themselves as they were. The two old people sat with their hands on their knees and listened, or so it appeared, in wonder and with pride to the conversation that filled their hut, greatly pleased even though they did not understand a single word. They saw that the milk went undrunk, the sausage uneaten; it was all a spectacle and, for all anyone knew, an edifying one. They were not even whispering to each other. Ulrich's glance dipped into their wide-open eyes, and he smiled at them in embarrassment, but of the two only the woman smiled back, while the man maintained his serious, reverential propriety.

"We must eat," Ulrich said to his sister in English. *"They're wondering about us."*

She obediently toyed with some bread and meat, and he for his part ate resolutely and even drank a little of the milk. Meanwhile Agathe went on, aloud and unembarrassed: "The idea of actually hurting him is repugnant to me when I come to think of it. So maybe I don't want to kill him. But I do want to wipe him out! Tear him into little pieces, pound them in a mortar, flush it down the drain; that's what I'd like to do! Root out everything that's happened!"

"This is a funny way for us to be talking," Ulrich remarked.

Agathe was silent for a while. But then she said: "But you promised me the first day you'd stand by me against Hagauer!"

"Of course I will. But not like that."

Again she was silent. Then she said suddenly: "If you bought or rented a car we could drive to my house by way of Iglau and come back the longer way around, through Tabor, I think. It would never occur to anyone that we'd been there in the night."

"And the servants? Fortunately, I can't drive!" Ulrich laughed, but then he shook his head in annoyance. "Such up-to-date ideas!"

"So you say," Agathe answered. Pensively, she pushed a bit of bacon back and forth on her plate with a fingernail, and it looked as though the fingernail, which had a greasy spot from the bacon, was doing it on its own. "But you've also said that the virtues of society are vices to the saint!"

"But I didn't say that the vices of society are virtues to the saint!" Ulrich pointed out. He laughed, caught hold of Agathe's hand, and cleaned it with his handkerchief.

"You always take everything back!" Agathe scolded him with a dissatisfied smile, the blood rushing to her face as she tried to free her finger.

The two old people by the stove, still watching exactly as before, now smiled broadly in echo.

"When you talk with me first one way, then another," Agathe said in a low but impassioned voice, "it's as if I were seeing myself in a splintered mirror. With you, one never sees oneself from head to toe!"

"No," Ulrich answered without letting go of her hand. "One never sees oneself as a whole nowadays, and one never moves as a whole—that's just it!"

Agathe gave in and suddenly stopped withdrawing her hand. "I'm certainly the opposite of holy," she said softly. "I may have been worse than a kept woman with my indifference. And I'm certainly not spoiling for action, and maybe I'll never be able to kill anyone. But when you first said that about the saint—and it was quite a while ago—it made me see something 'as a whole.' " She bowed her head, in thought or possibly to hide her face. "I saw a saint—maybe a figure on a fountain. To tell the truth, maybe I didn't see anything at all, but I felt something that has to be expressed this way. The water flowed, and what the saint did also came flowing over the rim, as if he were a fountain gently brimming over in all directions. That's how one ought to be, I think; then one would always be doing what was right and yet it wouldn't matter at all what one did."

"Agathe sees herself standing in the world overflowing with holiness and trembling for her sins, and sees with incredulity how the snakes and rhinoceroses, mountains and ravines, silent and even smaller than she is, lie down at her feet," he said, gently teasing her. "But what of Hagauer?"

"That's just it. He doesn't fit in. He has to go."

"Now I have something to tell you," her brother said. "Every time I've had to take part in anything with other people, something of genuine social concern, I've been like a man who steps outside the theater before the final act for a breath of fresh air, sees the great dark void with all those stars, and walks away, abandoning hat, coat, and play."

Agathe gave him a searching look. It was and wasn't an adequate answer.

Ulrich met her gaze. "You, too, are often plagued by a sense that there's always a 'dislike' before there's a 'like,' " he said, and thought: "Is she really like me?" Again he thought: "Perhaps the way a pastel resembles a woodcut." He regarded himself as the more stable. And she was more beautiful than he. Such a pleasing beauty! He shifted his grip from her finger to her whole hand, a warm, long hand full of life, which up to now he had held in his own only long enough for a greeting. His young sister was upset, and while there were no actual tears in her eyes, he saw a moist shimmer there.

"In a few days you'll be leaving me too," she said, "and how can I cope with everything then?"

"We can stay together; you can follow me."

"How do you suppose that would work?" Agathe asked, with the little thoughtful furrow on her forehead.

"I don't suppose at all; it's the first I've thought of it."

He stood up and gave the sheepherders some more money, "for the carved-up table."

Through a haze Agathe saw the country folk grinning, bobbing, and saying something about how glad they were, in short, incomprehensible words. As she went past them, she felt their four hospitable eyes, staring with naked emotion at her face, and realized that she and Ulrich had been taken for lovers who had quarreled and made up.

"They took us for lovers!" she said. Impetuously she slid her arm in his, and a wave of joy welled up in her. "You must give me a kiss!" she demanded, laughing, and pressed her arm in her brother's as they stood on the threshold of the hut and the low door opened into the darkness of evening.

11

HOLY DISCOURSE: BEGINNING

For the rest of Ulrich's stay little more was said about Hagauer; nor for a long time did they again refer to the idea that they should make their reunion permanent and take up life together. Nevertheless, the fire that had flamed up in Agathe's unrestrained desire to do away with her husband still smoldered under the ashes. It spread out in conversations that reached no end and yet burst out again; perhaps one should say: Agathe's feelings were seeking another possibility of burning freely.

She usually began such conversations with a definite, personal question, the inner form of which was: "May I, or may I not . . . ?" The lawlessness of her nature had until now rested on the sad and dispirited principle that "I'm allowed to do anything, but I don't want to anyway," and so his young sister's questions sometimes seemed to Ulrich, not inappropriately, like the questions of a child, which are as warm as the little hands of these helpless beings.

His own answers were different in kind, though no less characteristic: he always enjoyed sharing the yield of his experience and his reflections, and as was his custom expressed himself in a fashion as frank as it was intellectually enterprising. He always arrived quickly at the "moral of the story" his sister was talking about, summed things up in formulas, liked to use himself for illustration, and managed in this fashion to tell Agathe a great deal about himself, especially about his earlier, more eventful life. Agathe told him nothing about herself, but she admired his ability to speak about his own life like that, and his way of subjecting every point she raised to moral scrutiny suited her very well. For morality is nothing more than an ordering that embraces both the soul and things, so it is not strange that young people, whose zeal for life has not yet been blunted on every side, talk about it a good deal. But with a man of Ulrich's age and experience some explanation is called for, because men talk of morality only in their working lives, if it happens to be part of their professional jargon; otherwise, the word has been swallowed by the business of living and never manages to regain its freedom. So when Ulrich spoke of morality it was a sign of some profound disorder, which attracted Agathe because it corresponded to something in herself. She was ashamed, now that she heard what complicated preconditions would have to be met, of her naïve proclamation that she intended to live "in complete harmony" with herself, and yet she was impatient for her brother to come more quickly to a conclusion; for it often seemed to her that everything he said brought him closer to it, and with greater precision the further he went, but he always stopped at the last step, just at the threshold, where, every time, he gave up the attempt.

The locus of this deflection and of these last steps—and their paralyzing effect did not escape Ulrich—can most generally be indicated by noting that every proposition in European morality leads to such a point, which one cannot get beyond, so that a person taking stock of himself has first the gestures of wading in shallows, as long as he feels firm convictions underfoot, succeeded by the sudden gestures of horribly drowning when he goes a little farther, as though the solid ground of life had abruptly fallen off from the shallows into a completely imponderable abyss. This had a particular way of manifesting itself as well when brother and sister were talking: Ulrich could speak calmly and clearly on any subject he brought up, so long as his reason was involved, and Agathe felt a similar eagerness in listening; but when they stopped and fell silent, a much greater tension came over their faces. And so it happened once that they were carried across the frontier they had hitherto unconsciously respected. Ulrich had maintained that "the only basic characteristic of our morality is that its commandments contradict each other. The most moral of all propositions is: The exception proves the rule!" He had apparently been moved to this assertion only by his distaste for a system that claims to be unyielding, but in practice must yield to every deflection, which makes it the opposite of a precise procedure that first bases itself on experience and then derives the general law from these observations. He was of course aware of the distinction between natural and moral laws, that the first are derived from observing amoral nature, while the second have to be imposed on less stubborn human nature; but being of the opinion that something about this opposition was today no longer accurate, he had been just about to say that the moral system was intellectually a hundred years behind the times, which was why it was so hard to adapt it to changed conditions. But before he could get that far with his explanation Agathe interrupted him with an answer that seemed very simple, but for the moment took him aback.

"Isn't it good to be good?" she asked her brother, with a gleam in her eye like the one she'd had when she was fiddling with her father's medals, which presumably not everybody would have considered good.

"You're right," he replied eagerly. "One really has to formulate some such proposition if one wants to feel the original meaning again! But children still like being 'good' as if it were some tidbit. . . ."

"And being 'bad' as well," Agathe added.

"But does being good have any part in the passions of adults?" Ulrich asked. "It certainly is part of their principles. Not that they *are* good—they would regard that as childish—but that their behavior is good. A good person is one who has good principles and who does good things: it's an open secret that he can be quite disgusting as well."

"See Hagauer," Agathe volunteered.

"There's an absurd paradox inherent in those good people," Ulrich said. "They turn a condition into an imperative, a state of grace into a norm, a state of being into a purpose! In a whole lifetime this household of good people never serves up anything but leftovers, while keeping up a rumor that these are the scraps from a great feast day that was celebrated once. It's true that from time to time a few virtues come back into fashion, but as soon as that happens they lose their freshness again."

"Didn't you once say that the same act may be either good or bad, depending on circumstances?" Agathe asked.

Ulrich agreed. That was his theory, that moral values were not absolutes but functional concepts. But when we moralize or generalize we separate them out from their natural context: "And that is presumably the point where something goes wrong on the path to virtue."

"Otherwise, how could virtuous people be so dreary," Agathe added, "when their intention to be good ought to be the most delightful, challenging, and enjoyable thing anyone could imagine!"

Her brother hesitated, but suddenly he let slip a remark that was soon to bring them into a most unusual relationship.

"Our morality," he declared, "is the crystallization of an inner movement that is completely different from it. Not one thing we say is right! Take any statement, like the one that just occurred to me: 'Prison is a place for repentance.' It's something we can say with the best conscience in the world, but no one takes it literally, because it would mean hellfire for the prisoners! So how is one to take it? Surely few people know what repentance is, but everybody can tell you where it should reign. Or imagine that something is uplifting—how did that ever get to be part of our morals? When did we ever lie with our faces in the dust, so that it was bliss to be uplifted? Or try to imagine literally being seized by an idea—the moment you were to feel such a thing physically you'd have crossed the border into insanity! Every word demands to be taken literally, otherwise it decays into a lie; but one can't take words literally, or the world would turn into a madhouse! Some kind of grand intoxication rises out of this as a dim memory, and one sometimes wonders whether everything we experience may not be fragmented pieces torn from some ancient entity that was once put together wrong."

The conversation in which this remark occurred took place in the library-study, and while Ulrich sat over several books he had taken along on his trip, his sister was rummaging through the legal and philosophical books, a bequest of which she was the co-inheritor and out of which she picked the notions that led to her questions. Since their outing the pair had rarely left the house. This was how they spent most of their time. Sometimes they strolled in the garden, where winter had peeled the leaves from the bare shrubbery, exposing the earth beneath, swollen with rain. The sight was agonizing. The air was pallid, like something left too long under water. The garden was not large. The paths soon turned back upon themselves. The state of mind induced in both of them by walking on these paths eddied in circles, as a rising current does behind a dam. When they returned to the house the rooms were dark and sheltered, and the windows resembled deep lighting shafts through which the day arrived with all the brittle delicacy of thinnest ivory.

Now, after Ulrich's last, vehement words, Agathe descended from the library ladder on which she had been sitting and put her arms around his shoulders without a word. It was an unaccustomed show of tenderness, for apart from the two kisses, the first on the evening of their first encounter and the other a few days ago when they had set out on their way home from the shepherd's hut, the siblings' natural reserve had released itself in nothing more than words or little acts of attentiveness, and on both those occasions, too, the effect of the intimate contact had been concealed by its unexpectedness and exuberance. But this time Ulrich was instantly reminded of the still-warm garter that his sister had given the deceased as a parting gift instead of a flood of words. The thought shot through his head: "She certainly must have a lover; but she doesn't seem too attached to him, otherwise she wouldn't be staying on here so calmly." Clearly, she was a woman, who had led her life as a woman independently of him and would go on doing so. His shoulder felt the beauty of her arm from the distribution of its resting weight, and on the side turned toward his sister he had a shadowy sense of the nearness of her blond armpit and the outline of her breast. So as not to go on sitting there in mute surrender to that quiet embrace, he placed his hand over her fingers close to his neck, with this contact drowning out the other.

"You know, it's rather childish, talking the way we do," he said, not without some ill humor. "The world is full of energetic resolution, and here we sit in luxuriant idleness, talking about the sweetness of being good and the theoretical pots we could fill with it."

Agathe freed her fingers but let her hand go back to its place. "What's that you've been reading all this time?" she asked.

"You know what it is," he said. "You've been looking at the book behind my back often enough!"

"But I don't know what to make of it."

He could not bring himself to talk about it. Agathe, who had drawn up a chair, was crouching behind him and had simply nestled her face peacefully in his hair as though she were napping. Ulrich was strangely reminded of the moment when his enemy Arnheim had thrown an arm around him and the unregulated current of physical contact with another being had invaded him as through a breach. But this time his own nature did not repel the alien one; on the contrary, something in him advanced toward her, something that had been buried under the rubble of mistrust and resentment that fills the heart of a man who has lived a fairly long time. Agathe's relationship to him, which hovered between sister and wife, stranger and friend, without being equatable to any one of them, was not even based on a far-reaching accord between their thoughts or feelings, as he had often told himself, yet it was in complete accord—as he was now almost astonished to note—with the fact, which had crystallized after relatively few days full of countless impressions not easy to review in a moment, that Agathe's mouth was bedded on his hair with no further claim, and that his hair was becoming warm and moist from her breath. This was as spiritual as it was physical, for when Agathe repeated her question Ulrich was overcome with a seriousness such as he had not felt since the credulous days of his youth; and before this cloud of imponderable seriousness fled again, a cloud that extended from the space behind his back to the book before him, on which his thoughts were resting, he had given an answer that astonished him more for the total absence of irony in its tone than for its meaning:

"I'm instructing myself about the ways of the holy life."

He stood up; not to move away from his sister but in order to be able to see her better from a few steps away.

"You needn't laugh," he said. "I'm not religious; I'm studying the road to holiness to see if it might also be possible to drive a car on it!"

"I only laughed," she replied, "because I'm so curious to hear what you're going to say. The books you brought along are new to me, but I have a feeling that I would find them not entirely incomprehensible."

"You understand that?" her brother asked, already convinced that she did understand. "One may be caught up in the most intense feeling, when suddenly one's eye is seized by the play of some godforsaken, man-forsaken thing and one simply can't tear oneself away. Suddenly one feels borne up by its puny existence like a feather floating weightlessly and powerlessly on the wind."

"Except for the intense feeling you make such a point of, I think I know what you mean," Agathe said, and could not help smiling at the almost ferocious glare of embarrassment on her brother's face, not at all in keeping with the tenderness of his words. "One sometimes forgets to see and to hear, and is struck completely dumb. And yet it's precisely in minutes like these that one feels one has come to oneself for a moment."

"I would say," Ulrich went on eagerly, "that it's like looking out over a wide shimmering sheet of water—so bright it seems like darkness to the eye, and on the far bank things don't seem to be standing on solid ground but float in the air with a delicately exaggerated distinctness that's almost painful and hallucinatory. The impression one gets is as much of intensification as of loss. One feels linked with everything but can't get close to anything. You stand here, and the world stands there, overly subjective and overly objective, but both almost painfully clear, and what separates and unites these normally fused elements is a blazing darkness, an overflowing and extinction, a swinging in and out. You swim like a fish in water or a bird in air, but there's no riverbank and no branch, only this floating!" Ulrich had slipped into poetry, but the fire and firmness of his language stood out in relief against its tender and airy meaning like metal. He seemed to have cast off the caution that usually controlled him, and Agathe looked at him astonished, but also with an uneasy gladness.

"So you think," she asked, "that there's something behind it? More than a 'fit,' or whatever hateful, placating words are used?"

"I should say I do!" He sat down again at his earlier place and leafed through the books that lay there, while Agathe got up to make room for him. Then he opened one of them, with the words: "This is how the saints describe it," and read aloud:

" 'During those days I was exceeding restless. Now I sat awhile, now I wandered back and forth through the house. It was like a torment, and yet it can be called more a sweetness than a torment, for there was no vexation in it, only a strange, quite supernatural contentment. I had transcended all my faculties and reached the obscure power. There I heard without sound, there I saw without light.

And my heart became bottomless, my spirit formless, and my nature immaterial.' "

It seemed to them both that this description resembled the restlessness with which they themselves had been driven through house and garden, and Agathe in particular was surprised that the saints also called their hearts bottomless and their spirits formless. But Ulrich seemed to be caught up again in his irony.

He explained: "The saints say: Once I was imprisoned, then I was drawn out of myself and immersed in God without knowledge. The emperors out hunting, as we read about them in our storybooks, describe it differently: They tell how a stag appeared to them with a cross between its antlers, causing the murderous spear to drop from their hands; and then they built a chapel on the spot so they could get on with their hunting. The rich, clever ladies in whose circles I move will answer immediately, if you should ask them about it, that the last artist who painted such experiences was van Gogh. Or perhaps instead of a painter they might mention Rilke's poetry, but in general they prefer van Gogh, who is a superb investment and who cut his ear off because his painting didn't do enough when measured against the rapture of things. But the great majority of our people will say, on the contrary, that cutting your ear off is not a *German* way of expressing deep feelings; a German way is that unmistakable vacuousness of the elevated gaze one experiences on a mountaintop. For them the essence of human sublimity lies in solitude, pretty little flowers, and murmuring little brooks; and yet even in that bovine exaltation, with its undigested delight in nature, there lurks the misunderstood last echo of a mysterious other life. So when all is said and done, there must be something of the sort, or it must have existed at some time!"

"Then you shouldn't make fun of it," Agathe objected, grim with curiosity and radiant with impatience.

"I only make fun of it because I love it," Ulrich said curtly.

12

Holy discourse: Erratic progress

In the following days there were always many books on the table, some of which he had brought from home, others that he had bought since, and he would either talk extemporaneously or cite a passage, one of many he had marked with little slips of paper, to prove a point or quote the exact wording. The books before him were mostly lives of the mystics, their writings, or scholarly works about them, and he usually deflected the conversation from them by saying: "Now let's take a good hard look and see what's really going on here." This was a cautious attitude he was not prepared to give up easily, and so he said to her once:

"If you could read right through all these accounts that men and women of past centuries have left us, describing their state of divine rapture, you would find much truth and reality in among the printed words, and yet the statements made of these words would go wholly against the grain of your present-day mind." And he went on: "They speak of an overflowing radiance. Of an infinite expanse, a boundless opulence of light. Of an overarching oneness of all things and all the soul's energies. Of an awesome and indescribable uplifting of the heart. Of insights coming so swiftly that it's all simultaneous and like drops of fire falling into the world. And then again they speak of a forgetting and no longer understanding, even of everything falling utterly away. They speak of an immense serenity far removed from all passion. Of growing mute. A vanishing of thoughts and intentions. A blindness in which they see clearly, a clarity in which they are dead and supernaturally alive. They call it a shedding of their being, and yet they claim to be more fully alive than ever. Aren't these the same sensations, however veiled by the difficulty of expressing them, still experienced today when the heart—'greedy and gorged,' as they say!—stumbles by chance into those utopian regions situated somewhere and nowhere between infinite tenderness and infinite loneliness?"

As he paused briefly to think, Agathe's voice joined in: "It's what you once called two layers that overlie each other within us."

"I did? When?"

"When you walked aimlessly into town and felt as though you were dissolving into it, although at the same time you didn't like the place. I told you that this happens to me often."

"Oh yes! You even said 'Hagauer!' " Ulrich exclaimed. "And we laughed—now I remember. But we didn't really mean it. Anyway, it's not the only time I talked to you about the kind of vision that gives and the kind that receives, about the male and female principles, the hermaphroditism of the primal imagination and so on—I can say a lot about these things. As if my mouth were as far away from me as the moon, which is also always on hand for confidential chats in the night! But what these believers have to say about their souls' adventures," he went on, mingling the bitterness of his words with objectivity and even admiration, "is sometimes written with the force and the ruthless analytic conviction of a Stendhal. But only"—he limited this—"as long as they stick to the phenomena and their judgment doesn't enter in, which is corrupted by their flattering conviction that they've been singled out by God to have direct experience of Him. For from that moment on, of course, they no longer speak of their perceptions, which are so hard to describe and have no nouns or verbs, but begin to speak in sentences with subject and object, because they believe in their soul and in God as in the two doorposts between which the miraculous will blossom. And so they arrive at these statements about the soul being drawn out of the body and absorbed into the Lord, or say that the Lord penetrates them like a lover. They are caught, engulfed, dazzled, swept away, raped by God, or else their soul opens to Him, enters into Him, tastes of Him, embraces Him with love and hears Him speak. The earthly model for this is unmistakable, and these descriptions no longer resemble tremendous discoveries but rather a series of fairly predictable images with which an erotic poet decks out his subject, about which only one opinion is permissible. For a person like me, anyway, brought up to maintain reserve, these accounts stretch me on the rack, for the elect, even as they assure me that God has spoken to them, or that they have understood the speech of trees and animals, neglect to tell me what it was that was imparted to them; or if they do, it comes out as purely personal details, or a rehash of the *Clerical News*. It's an everlasting pity that no trained scientists have visions!" he ended his lengthy reply.

"Do you think they could?" Agathe was testing him.

Ulrich hesitated for an instant. Then he answered like a believer: "I don't know; maybe it could happen to me!" When he heard himself saying these words he smiled, as if to mitigate them.

Agathe smiled too; she now seemed to have the answer she had been hankering after, and her face reflected the small moment of letdown that follows the sudden cessation of a tension. Perhaps she now raised an objection only because she wanted to spur her brother on.

"You know," she said, "that I was raised in a very strict convent school. So I have the most scandalous urge to caricature anyone I hear talking about pious ideals. Our teachers wore a habit whose two colors formed a cross, as a sort of enforced reminder of one of the sublimest thoughts we were supposed to have before us all day long; but we never once thought it; we just called the good sisters the cross-spiders, because of the way they looked and their silky way of talking. That's why, while you were reading aloud, I didn't know whether to laugh or cry."

"Do you know what that proves?" Ulrich exclaimed. "Just that the power for good which is somehow present in us eats its way instantly through the walls if it gets locked into solid form, and immediately uses that as a bolt hole to evil! It reminds me of the time I was in the army and upheld throne and altar with my brother officers; never in my life have I heard such loose talk about both as I did in our circle! All emotions refuse to be chained, and some refuse absolutely. I'm convinced your good nuns believed what they preached to you, but faith mustn't ever be more than an hour old! That's the point!"

Although in his haste Ulrich had not expressed himself to his satisfaction, Agathe understood that the faith of those nuns who had taken away the pleasure of faith for her was merely a "bottled" variety, preserved in glass jars, so to speak, in its natural condition and not deprived of any of its qualities of faith but still not fresh; indeed, in some imponderable way it had changed into a different condition from its original one, which now hovered momentarily before this truant and rebellious pupil of holiness as a kind of intimation.

This, with everything else they had been saying about morality, was one of the gripping doubts her brother had implanted in her mind, and also part of that inner reawakening she had been feeling ever since, without rightly knowing what it was. For the attitude of indifference she made such a point of displaying outwardly and encouraging inwardly had not always ruled her life. Something had once happened that had caused her need for self-punishment to spring directly out of a deep depression, which made her appear to herself as unworthy because she believed she had not been granted the ability to keep faith with lofty emotions, and she had despised herself for her heart's sloth ever since.

This episode lay between her life as a young girl in her father's house and her incomprehensible marriage to Hagauer, and was so narrowly circumscribed that even Ulrich, for all his sympathy, had forgotten to ask about it. What had happened is soon told: At the age of eighteen Agathe had married a man only slightly older than herself, and on a trip that began with their wedding and ended in his death, he was snatched away from her within a few weeks, before they had even had time to think about choosing a place to live, by a fatal disease he had caught on their travels. The doctors called it typhus, and Agathe repeated the word after them, finding in it a semblance of order, for that was the side of the event polished smooth for the uses of the world; but on the unpolished side, it was different: until then Agathe had lived with her father, whom everyone respected, so that she reluctantly regarded herself as to blame for not loving him; and the uncertain waiting at school to become herself, through the mistrust it awakened in her mind, had not helped to stabilize her relationship to the world either. Later, on the other hand, when with suddenly aroused vivacity she had united with her childhood playmate to overcome in a matter of months all the obstacles put in the way of such a youthful marriage (even though their families had no objections to each other), she had all at once no longer been isolated and had thereby become herself. This could well be called love; but there are lovers who stare at love as into the sun and merely become blinded by it, and there are lovers who seem to discover life for the first time with astonishment when it is illuminated by love. Agathe was one of the latter kind; she had not even had time to find out whether it was her husband she loved or something else, when something struck that was called, in the language of the unilluminated world, an infectious disease. With primal suddenness horror irrupted upon them from the alien regions of life—a struggle, a flickering, an extinction; a visitation upon two human beings clinging to each other and the disappearance of an innocent world in vomiting, excrement, and fear.

Agathe had never faced up to this event that had annihilated her feelings. Bewildered with despair, she had lain on her knees at the dying man's bedside and persuaded herself that she could conjure up the power that had enabled her as a child to overcome her own illness. When his decline continued nevertheless, and his consciousness was already gone, she kept staring into the vacant face, in that hotel room far from home, unable to understand; she had held the dying body in her arms without considering the danger and without considering the realities being attended to by an indignant nurse. She had done nothing but murmur for hours into his fading ear: "You can't, you can't, you can't!" But when it was all over she had stood up in amazement, and without thinking or believing anything in particular, acting simply from a solitary nature's stubbornness and capacity to dream, she had from that moment on inwardly treated this empty astonishment at what had happened as though it were not final. We see the onset of something similar in everyone who cannot bring himself to believe bad news, or finds a way to soften the irrevocable, but Agathe's attitude was unique in the force and extent of this reaction, which marked the sudden outburst of her disdain for the world. Since then she had conscientiously assimilated anything new as something less actual than extremely uncertain, an attitude greatly facilitated by the mistrust with which she had always confronted reality; the past, on the other hand, was petrified by the blow she had suffered, and eroded by time much more slowly than usually happens with memories. But it had none of the swirl of dreams, the onesidedness or the skewed sense of proportion that brings the doctor on the scene. On the contrary, Agathe went on living in perfect lucidity, quietly virtuous and merely a little bored, slightly inclined to that reluctance about life that was really like the fever she had suffered so willingly as a child. In her memory, which in any case never let its impressions dissolve into generalizations, every hour of what had been and still was fearful remained vivid, like a corpse under a white sheet; despite all the anguish of remembering so exactly, it made her happy, for it had the effect of a secret, belated indication that all was not yet over, and it preserved in her, despite the decay of her emotional life, a vague but high-minded tension. In truth, all it meant was that she had again lost the sense of meaning in her life and had consciously put herself in a state of mind that did not suit her years; for only old people live by dwelling on the experiences and achievements of a time that is gone and remain untouched by the present. But at the age Agathe was then, fortunately, while resolves are made for eternity a single year feels like half an eternity, and so it was only to be expected that after a time a repressed nature and a fettered imagination would violently free themselves. The details of how it happened are of no consequence in themselves; a man whose advances would in other circumstances never have succeeded in disturbing her equilibrium succeeded, and became her lover, but this attempt at reliving something ended, after a brief period of manic hope, in passionate disenchantment. Agathe now felt herself cast out by both her real life and her unreal life, and unworthy of her own high hopes. She was one of those intense people who can keep themselves motionless and in reserve for a long time, until at some point they suddenly fall prey to total confusion; and so, in her disappointment, she soon took another rash step, which was, in short, to punish herself in a way opposite to the way she had sinned, condemning herself to share her life with a man who inspired in her a mild aversion. And this man whom she had picked out as a penance was Gottlieb Hagauer.

"It was certainly both unfair to him and inconsiderate," Agathe admitted to herself—and it must be admitted that this was the first time she had ever faced up to it, because fairness and consideration are not virtues in high favor with the young. Still, her self-punishment in this marriage was not inconsiderable either, and Agathe now gave it some more thought. She had strayed far from their conversation, and Ulrich, too, was leafing through his books for something and seemed to have forgotten the conversation. "In earlier centuries," she thought, "a person in my state of mind would have entered a convent," and the fact that she had got married instead was not without an innocently comical side, which had previously escaped her. This comedy, which she had then been too young to notice, was simply that of the present day, which satisfies its need for a refuge from the world at worst in some tourist accommodation but usually in an Alpine hotel, and even strives to furnish its prisons tastefully. It expresses the profound European need not to overdo anything. No European any longer scourges himself, smears himself with ashes, cuts out his tongue, really takes part in things or totally withdraws from society, swoons with passion, breaks people on the wheel or impales them, but everyone sometimes feels the need to do so, so that it's hard to say which is more to be avoided: wanting to do it or not doing it. Why should an ascetic, of all people, starve himself? It only gives him disturbing fantasies. A sensible asceticism consists of an aversion to eating while being constantly well nourished. Such an asceticism promises longevity and offers the mind a freedom that is unattainable so long as it remains enslaved to the body in passionate rebellion. Such bitterly humorous reflections, which she had learned from her brother, were now doing Agathe a world of good, for they dissected the "tragic"—a rigid belief that in her inexperience she had long assumed to be a duty—into irony and a passion that had neither name nor aim, and for that reason alone were not bracketed with what she had experienced previously.

It was in this way above all that she had begun to realize, ever since being with her brother, that something was happening to the great split she had suffered between irresponsible living and a spectral fantasy life; there was a movement of release and of recombining what had been released. Now, for instance, in this silence between herself and her brother, which was deepened by the presence of books and memories, she thought of the description Ulrich had given her of his wandering aimlessly into town, and of how the town had entered him as he entered it. It reminded her very exactly of the few weeks of her happiness. And it had also been right for her to laugh, wildly and for no reason, when he told her about it, because it struck her that there was something of this turning of the world inside out, this delicious and funny inversion he was speaking of, even in Hagauer's thick lips when they pursed for a kiss. It made her shudder, of course, but there is a shudder, she thought, even in the bright light of noon, and it made her feel that somehow there was still hope for her. Some mere nothing, some break that had always lain between past and present, had recently vanished. She glanced around covertly. The room she was in had formed part of the space in which her fate had taken shape: it was the first time since her arrival that this had occurred to her. For it was here that she had met with her childhood friend when her father was out, and they made the great decision to love each other; here, too, she had sometimes received her "unworthy" suitor, standing at the window hiding tears of rage or desperation, and here, finally, Hagauer's courting had run its course, with her father's blessing. After having been for so long merely the unnoticed other side of events, the furniture and walls, the peculiarly confined light, now became in this moment of recognition strangely tangible, and the quixotic things that had occurred here assumed a physical and completely unambiguous pastness, as if they were ashes or burned charcoal. What remained, and became almost unbearably powerful, was that funny, shadowy sense of things done with—that strange tickling one feels when confronted with old traces, dried to dust, of one's self—which, the moment one feels it, one can neither grasp nor banish.

Agathe made sure that Ulrich was not paying attention, and carefully opened the top of her dress, where she kept next to her skin the locket with the tiny picture that she had never taken off through the years. She went to the window and pretended to look out. Cautiously, she snapped open the sharp edge of the tiny golden scallop and gazed furtively at her dead love. He had full lips and soft, thick hair, and the cocky expression of the twenty-one-year-old flashed out at her from a face still half in its eggshell. For a long time she did not know what she thought, but then suddenly the thought came: "My God, a twenty-one-year-old!"

What do such youngsters talk about with each other? What meaning do they give to their concerns? How funny and arrogant they often are! How the intensity of their ideas misleads them about the worth of those ideas! Curious, Agathe unwrapped from the tissue paper of memory some sayings that she—thank goodness for her cleverness—had preserved in it. My God, that was almost worth saying, she thought, but she could not really be sure of even that unless she also recalled the garden in which it had been spoken, with the strange flowers whose names she did not know, the butterflies that settled on them like weary drunkards, and the light that flowed over their faces as if heaven and earth were dissolved in it. By that measure she was today an old, experienced woman, even though not that many years had passed. With some confusion she noted the incongruity that she, at twenty-seven, still loved the boy of twenty-one: he had grown much too young for her! She asked herself: "What feelings would I have to have if, at my age, this boyish man were really to be the most important thing in the world to me?" They would certainly have been odd feelings, but she was not even able to imagine them clearly. It all dissolved into nothing.

Agathe recognized in a great upsurge of feeling that the one proud passion of her life had been a mistake, and the heart of this error consisted of a fiery mist she could neither touch nor grasp, no matter whether one were to say that faith could not live more than an hour, or something else. It was always this that her brother had been talking about since they had been together, and it was always herself he was speaking of, even though he hedged it about in his intellectual fashion and his diplomacy was much too slow for her impatience. They kept coming back to the same conversation, and Agathe herself blazed with desire that his flame should not diminish.

When she now spoke to Ulrich he had not even noticed how long the interruption had lasted. But whoever has not already picked up the clues to what was going on between this brother and sister should lay this account aside, for it depicts an adventure of which he will never be able to approve: a journey to the edge of the possible, which led past—and perhaps not always past—the dangers of the impossible and unnatural, even of the repugnant: a "borderline case," as Ulrich later called it, of limited and special validity, reminiscent of the freedom with which mathematics sometimes resorts to the absurd in order to arrive at the truth. He and Agathe happened upon a path that had much in common with the business of those possessed by God, but they walked it without piety, without believing in God or the soul, nor even in the beyond or in reincarnation. They had come upon it as people of this world, and pursued it as such—this was what was remarkable about it. Though at the moment Agathe spoke again Ulrich was still absorbed in his books and the problems they set him, he had not for an instant forgotten their conversation, which had broken off at the moment of her resistance to the devoutness of her teachers and his own insistence on "precise visions," and he immediately answered:

"There's no need to be a saint to experience something of the kind! You could be sitting on a fallen tree or a bench in the mountains, watching a herd of grazing cows, and experience something amounting to being transported into another life! You lose yourself and at the same time suddenly find yourself—you talked about it yourself!"

"But what actually happens?" Agathe asked.

"To know that, you first have to decide what is normal, sister human," Ulrich joked, trying to brake the much too rapid rush of the idea. "What's normal is that a herd of cattle means nothing to us but grazing beef. Or else a subject for a painting, with background. Or it hardly registers at all. Herds of cattle beside mountain paths are part of the mountain paths, and we would only notice what we experience when we see them if a big electric clock or an apartment house were to stand there in their place. For the rest, we wonder whether to get up or stay put; we're bothered by the flies swarming around the cattle; we wonder whether there's a bull in the herd; we wonder where the path goes from here—there are any number of minor deliberations, worries, calculations, and observations that make up the paper, as it were, that has the picture of the cows on it. We have no awareness of the paper, only of the cows!"

"And suddenly the paper tears!" Agathe broke in.

"Right. That is, some tissue of habit in us tears. There's no longer something edible grazing out there, or something paintable; nothing blocks your way. You can't even form the word 'grazing,' because a host of purposeful, practical connotations go along with it, which you have suddenly lost. What is left on the pictorial plane might best be called an ocean swell of sensations that rises and falls, breathes and shimmers, as though it filled your whole field of view without a horizon. Of course, there are still countless individual perceptions contained within it: colors, horns, movements, smells, and all the details of reality; but none of them are acknowledged any longer, even if they should still be recognized. Let me put it this way: the details no longer have their egoism, which they use to capture our attention, but they're all linked with each other in a familiar, literally 'inward' way. And of course the 'pictorial plane' is no longer there either; but everything somehow flows over into you, all boundaries gone."

Again Agathe picked up the description eagerly. "So instead of the

egoism of the details, you only need to say the egoism of human beings," she exclaimed, "and you've got what is so hard to put into
words. 'Love thy neighbor!' doesn't mean love him on the basis of
what you both are; it characterizes a dream state!"

"All moral propositions," Ulrich agreed, "characterize a sort of
dream state that has already flown the coop of rules in which we
tether it."

"Then there's really no such thing as good and evil, but only
faith—or doubt!" cried Agathe, to whom a self-supporting primal
condition of faith now seemed so close, as did its disappearance from
the morality her brother had spoken of when he said that faith could
not live past the hour.

"Yes, the moment one slips away from a life of inessentials, everything enters into a new relationship with everything else," Ulrich
agreed. "I would almost go so far as to say into a nonrelationship. For
it's an entirely unknown one, of which we have no experience, and all
other relationships are blotted out. But despite its obscurity, this one
is so distinct that its existence is undeniable. It's strong, but impalpa-
bly strong. One might put it this way: ordinarily, we look at something, and our gaze is like a fine wire or a taut thread with two
supports—one being the eye and the other what it sees, and there's
some such great support structure for every second that passes; but
at this particular second, on the contrary, it is rather as though something painfully sweet were pulling our eye beams apart.

"One possesses nothing in the world, one holds on to nothing, one
is not held by anything," Agathe said. "It's all like a tall tree on which
not a leaf is stirring. And in that condition one could not do anything
mean."

"They say that nothing can happen in that condition which is not
in harmony with it," Ulrich added. "A desire to 'belong to' it is the
only basis, the loving vocation, and the sole form of all acting and
thinking that have their place in it. It is something infinitely serene
and all-encompassing, and everything that happens in it adds to its
quietly growing significance; or it doesn't add to it, in which case it's a
bad thing, but nothing bad can happen, because if it did the stillness
and clarity would be torn and the marvelous condition would end."
Ulrich gave his sister a probing look she was not meant to notice; he

had a nagging feeling that it was about time to stop. But Agathe's face was impassive; she was thinking of things long past.

"It makes me wonder at myself," she answered, "but there really was a brief period when I was untouched by envy, malice, vanity, greed, and things like that. It seems incredible now, but it seems to me that they had all suddenly disappeared, not only out of my heart but out of the world! In that state it isn't only oneself who can't behave badly; the others can't either. A good person makes everything that touches him good, no matter what others may do to him; the instant it enters his sphere it becomes transformed."

"No," Ulrich cut in, "not quite. On the contrary, put that way, this would be one of the oldest misconceptions. A good person doesn't make the world good in any way; he has no effect on it whatsoever; all he does is separate himself from it."

"But he stays right in the midst of it, doesn't he?"

"He stays right in its midst, but he feels as if the space were being drawn out of things, or something or other imaginary were happening; it's hard to say."

"All the same, I have the idea that a 'highhearted' person—the word just occurred to me!—never comes in contact with anything base. It may be nonsense, but it does happen."

"It may happen," Ulrich replied, "but the opposite happens too! Or do you suppose that the soldiers who crucified Jesus didn't feel they were doing something base? And they were God's instrument! Incidentally, the mystics themselves testify to the existence of bad feelings—they complain about falling from the state of grace and then enduring unspeakable misery, knowing fear, pain, shame, and perhaps even hatred. Only when the quiet burning begins again do remorse, anger, fear, and misery turn into bliss. It's so hard to know what to make of all this!"

"When were *you* that much in love?" Agathe asked abruptly.

"Me? Oh . . . I've already told you about that: I fled a thousand miles away from the woman I loved, and once I felt safe from any possibility of really embracing her, I howled for her like a dog at the moon!"

Now Agathe confided to him the story of her love. She was excited. Her last question had snapped from her like an overly tightened violin string, and the rest followed in the same vein. She was trembling inwardly as she revealed what had been concealed for many years.

But her brother was not particularly moved. "Memories usually age along with people," he pointed out, "and with time the most passionate experiences take on a comic perspective, as though one were seeing them at the end of ninety-nine doors opened in succession. Still, sometimes certain memories that were tied to strong emotions don't age, but keep a tight grip on whole layers of one's being. That was your case. There are such points in almost everyone, which distort the psychic balance a little. One's behavior flows over them like a river over an invisible boulder—in your case this was very strong, so that it almost amounted to a dam. But you've freed yourself after all; you're moving again!"

He said this with the calm of an almost professional opinion; how easily he was diverted! Agathe was unhappy. Stubbornly she said: "Of course I'm in motion, but that's not what I'm talking about! I want to know where I almost got to back then." She was irritated too, without meaning to be, but simply because her excitement had to express itself somehow. She went on talking, nevertheless, in her original direction and was quite dizzy between the tenderness of her words and the irritation behind them. She was talking about that peculiar condition of heightened receptivity and sensitivity that brings about a rising and falling tide of impressions and creates the feeling of being connected with all things as in the gentle mirror of a sheet of water, giving and receiving without will: that miraculous feeling of the lifting of all bounds, the boundlessness of the outer and inner that love and mysticism have in common. Agathe did not, of course, put it in such terms, which already contain an explanation; she was merely making passionate fragments of her memories into a sequence. But even Ulrich, although he had often thought about it, could not offer any explanation of these experiences; indeed, he did not even know whether he should attempt to deal with such an experience in its own way or according to the usual procedures of rationality; both came naturally to him, but not to the obvious passion of his sister. And so what he said in reply was merely a mediation, a kind of testing of the possibilities. He pointed out how in the exalted state they were speaking of, thought and the moral sense went hand in hand, so that each thought was felt as happiness, event, and gift, and neither lost itself in the storerooms of the brain nor formed attachments to feelings of appropriation and power, of retention and observation; thus in the head no less than in the heart the delight of self-possession is replaced by a boundless self-giving and bonding.

"Once in a lifetime," Agathe replied with passionate decisiveness, "everything one does is done for someone else. One sees the sun shining for him. He is everywhere, oneself nowhere. But there is no egoism à deux, because the same thing must be happening with the other person. In the end, they hardly exist for each other anymore, and what's left is a world for nothing but couples, a world consisting of appreciation, devotion, friendship, and selflessness!"

In the darkness of the room her face glowed with eagerness like a rose standing in the shade.

"Let's be a little more sober again," Ulrich gently proposed. "There can be too much fakery in these matters." There was nothing wrong with that either, she thought. Perhaps it was the irritation, still not quite gone, that somewhat dampened her delight over the reality he was invoking. But this vague trembling of the borderline was a not unpleasant feeling.

Ulrich began by speaking of the mischief of interpreting the kind of experiences they were talking about not as if what was going on in them was merely a peculiar change in thinking, but as if superhuman thinking was taking the place of the ordinary kind. Whether one called it divine illumination or, in the modern fashion, merely intuition, he considered it the main hindrance to real understanding. In his opinion, nothing was to be gained by yielding to notions that would not stand up under careful investigation. That would only be like Icarus's wax wings, which melted with the altitude, he exclaimed. If one wished to fly other than in dreams, one must master it on metal wings.

He paused for a moment, then went on, pointing to his books: "Here you have testimony, Christian, Judaic, Indian, Chinese, some separated by more than a thousand years. Yet one recognizes in all of them the same uniform structure of inner movement, divergent from the ordinary. Almost the only way they differ from each other comes from the various didactic superstructures of theology and cosmic wisdom under whose protective roof they have taken shelter. We therefore may assume the existence of a certain alternative and uncommon condition of great importance, which man is capable of achieving and which has deeper origins than religions.

"On the other hand," he added, qualifying what he had said, "the churches, that is, civilized communities of religious people, have always treated this condition with the kind of mistrust a bureaucrat feels for the spirit of private enterprise. They've never accepted this riotous experience without reservations; on the contrary, they've directed great and apparently justified efforts toward replacing it with a properly regulated and intelligible morality. So the history of this alternative condition resembles a progressive denial and dilution, something like the draining of a swamp.

"And when confessional authority over the spirit and its vocabulary became outmoded, our condition understandably came to be regarded as nothing more than a chimera. Why should bourgeois culture, in replacing the old religious culture, be more religious than its predecessor? Bourgeois culture has reduced this other condition to the status of a dog fetching intuitions. There are hordes of people today who find fault with rationality and would like us to believe that in their wisest moments they were doing their thinking with the help of some special, suprarational faculty. That's the final public vestige of it all, itself totally rationalistic. What's left of the drained swamp is rubbish! And so, except for its uses in poetry, this old condition is excusable only in uneducated people in the first weeks of a love affair, as a temporary aberration, like green leaves that every so often sprout posthumously from the wood of beds and lecterns; but if it threatens to revert to its original luxuriant growth, it is unmercifully dug up and rooted out!"

Ulrich had been talking for about as long as it takes a surgeon to wash his arms and hands so as not to carry any germs into the field of operation, and also with all the patience, concentration, and even-handedness it paradoxically takes to cope with the excitement attendant on the task ahead. But after he had completely disinfected himself he almost yearned for a little fever or infection—after all, he did not love sobriety for its own sake. Agathe was sitting on the library ladder, and even when her brother fell silent she gave no sign of participation. She gazed out into the endless oceanic gray of the sky and listened to the silence just as she had been listening to the words. So Ulrich took up the thread again, with a slight obstinacy that he barely managed to mask by his lighthearted tone.

"Let's get back to our bench on the mountain, with that herd of cows," he suggested. "Imagine some high bureaucrat sitting there in his brand-new leather shorts with 'Grüss Gott' embroidered on his green suspenders. He represents 'real life' on vacation. Of course, this temporarily alters his consciousness of his existence. When he looks at the herd of cows he neither counts them, classifies them, nor estimates the weight on the hoof of the animals grazing before him; he forgives his enemies and thinks indulgently of his family. For him the herd has been transformed from a practical object into a moral one, as it were. He may also, of course, be estimating and counting a little and not forgiving a whole lot, but then at least it is bathed in woodland murmurs, purling brooks, and sunshine. In a word, what otherwise forms the content of his life seems 'far away' and 'not all that important.' "

"It's a holiday mood," Agathe agreed mechanically.

"Exactly! If he regards his nonvacation life as 'not all that important,' it means only as long as his vacation lasts. So that is the truth today: a man has two modes of existence, of consciousness, and of thought, and saves himself from being frightened to death by ghosts—which this prospect would of necessity induce—by regarding one condition as a vacation from the other, an interruption, a rest, or anything else he thinks he can recognize. Mysticism, on the other hand, would be connected with the intention of going on vacation permanently. Our high official is bound to regard such an idea as disgraceful and instantly feel—as in fact he always does toward the end of his vacation—that *real* life lies in his tidy office. And do we feel any differently? Whether something needs to be straightened out or not will always eventually decide whether one takes it completely seriously, and here these experiences have not had much luck, for over thousands of years they have never got beyond their primordial disorder and incompleteness. And for this we have the ready label of Mania—religious mania, erotomania, take your choice. You can be assured that in our day even most religious people are so infected with the scientific way of thinking that they don't trust themselves to look into what is burning in their inmost hearts but are always ready to speak of this ardor in medical terms as a mania, even though officially they take a different line!"

Agathe gave her brother a look in which something crackled like fire in the rain. "So now you've managed to maneuver us out of it!" she accused him, when he didn't go on.

"You're right," he admitted. "But what's peculiar is that though we've covered it all up like a suspect well, some remaining drop of this unholy holy water burns a hole in all our ideals. None of our ideals is quite right, none of them makes us happy: they all point to something that's not there—we've said enough about that today. Our civilization is a temple of what would be called unsecured mania, but it is also its asylum, and we don't know if we are suffering from an excess or a deficiency."

"Perhaps you've never dared surrender yourself to it all the way," Agathe said wistfully, and climbed down from her ladder; for they were supposed to be busy sorting their father's papers and had let themselves be distracted from what had gradually become a pressing task, first by the books and then by their conversation. Now they went back to checking the dispositions and notes referring to the division of their inheritance, for the day of reckoning with Hagauer was imminent. But before they had seriously settled down to this, Agathe straightened up from her papers and asked him once more: "Just how much do you yourself believe everything you've been telling me?"

Ulrich answered without looking up. "Suppose that while your heart had turned away from the world, there was a dangerous bull among the herd. Try to believe absolutely that the deadly disease you were telling me about would have taken another course if you had not allowed your feelings to slacken for a single instant." Then he raised his head and pointed to the papers he had been sorting: "And law, justice, fair play? Do you really think they're entirely superfluous?"

"So just how much do you believe?" Agathe reiterated.

"Yes and no," Ulrich said.

"That means no," Agathe concluded.

Here chance intervened in their talk. As Ulrich, who neither felt inclined to resume the discussion nor was calm enough to get on with the business at hand, rounded up the scattered papers, something fell to the floor. It was a loose bundle of all kinds of things that had inadvertently been pulled out with the will from a corner of the desk drawer where it might have lain for decades without its owner knowing. Ulrich looked at it distractedly as he picked it up and recognized his father's handwriting on several pages; but it was not the script of his old age but that of his prime. Ulrich took a closer look and saw that in addition to written pages there were playing cards, snapshots, and all sorts of odds and ends, and quickly realized what he had found. It was the desk's "poison drawer." Here were painstakingly recorded jokes, mostly dirty; nude photographs; postcards, to be sent sealed, of buxom dairy maids whose panties could be opened behind; packs of cards that looked quite normal but showed some awful things when held up to the light; mannequins that voided all sorts of stuff when pressed on the belly; and more of the same. The old gentleman had undoubtedly long since forgotten the things lying in that drawer, or he would certainly have destroyed them in good time. They obviously dated from those mid-life years when quite a few aging bachelors and widowers warm themselves with such obscenities, but Ulrich blushed at this exposure of his father's unguarded fantasies, now released from the flesh by death. Their relevance to the discussion just broken off was instantly clear to him. Nevertheless, his first impulse was to destroy this evidence before Agathe could see it. But she had already noticed that something unusual had fallen into his hands, so he changed his mind and asked her to come over.

He was going to wait and hear what she would say. Suddenly the realization possessed him again that she was, after all, a woman who must have had her experiences, a point he had totally lost sight of while they were deep in conversation. But her face gave no sign of what she was thinking; she looked at her father's illicit relics seriously and calmly, at times smiling openly, though not animatedly. So Ulrich, despite his resolve, began.

"Those are the dregs of mysticism!" he said wryly. "The strict moral admonitions of the will in the same drawer as this swill!"

He had stood up and was pacing back and forth in the room. And once he had begun to talk, his sister's silence spurred him on.

"You asked me what I believe," he began. "I believe that all our moral injunctions are concessions to a society of savages.

"I believe none of them are right.

"There's a different meaning glimmering behind them. An alchemist's fire.

"I believe that nothing is ever done with.

"I believe that nothing is in balance but that everything is trying to raise itself on the fulcrum of everything else.

"That's what I believe. It was born with me, or I with it."

He had stood still after each of these sentences, for he spoke softly and had somehow or other to give emphasis to his credo. Now his eye was caught by the classical busts atop the bookshelves; he saw a plaster Minerva, a Socrates; he remembered that Goethe had kept an over-lifesize plaster head of Juno in his study. This predilection seemed alarmingly distant to him; what had once been an idea in full bloom had since withered into a dead classicism. Turned into the rearguard dogmatism of rights and duties of his father's contemporaries. All in vain.

"The morality that has been handed down to us," he said, "is like being sent out on a swaying high wire over an abyss, with no other advice than: 'Hold yourself as stiff as you can!'

"I seem, without having had a say in the matter, to have been born with another kind of morality.

"You asked me what I believe. I believe there are valid reasons you can use to prove to me a thousand times that something is good or beautiful, and it will leave me indifferent; the only mark I shall go by is whether its presence makes me rise or sink.

"Whether it rouses me to life or not.

"Whether it's only my tongue and my brain that speak of it, or the radiant shiver in my fingertips.

"But I can't prove anything, either.

"And I'm even convinced that a person who yields to this is lost. He stumbles into twilight. Into fog and nonsense. Into unarticulated boredom.

"If you take the unequivocal out of our life, what's left is a sheepfold without a wolf.

"I believe that bottomless vulgarity can even be the good angel that protects us.

"And so, I don't believe!

"And above all, I don't believe in the domestication of evil by good as the characteristic of our hodgepodge civilization. I find that repugnant.

"So I believe and don't believe!

"But maybe I believe that the time is coming when people will on the one hand be very intelligent, and on the other hand be mystics. Maybe our morality is already splitting into these two components. I might also say into mathematics and mysticism. Into practical improvements and unknown adventure!"

He had not been so openly excited about anything in years. The "maybe"s in his speech did not trouble him; they seemed only natural.

Agathe had meanwhile knelt down before the stove; she had the bundle of pictures and papers on the floor beside her. She looked at everything once more, piece by piece, before pushing it into the fire. She was not entirely unsusceptible to the vulgar sensuality of the obscenities she was looking at. She felt her body being aroused by them. This seemed to her to have as little to do with her self as the feeling of being on a deserted heath and somewhere a rabbit scutters past. She did not know whether she would be ashamed to tell her brother this, but she was profoundly fatigued and did not want to talk anymore. Nor did she listen to what he was saying; her heart had by now been too shaken by these ups and downs, and could no longer keep up. Others had always known better than she what was right; she thought about this, but she did so, perhaps because she was ashamed, with a secret defiance. To walk a forbidden or secret path: in that she felt superior to Ulrich. She heard him time and again cautiously taking back everything he had let himself be carried away into saying, and his words beat like big drops of joy and sadness against her ear.

13

ULRICH RETURNS AND LEARNS FROM THE
GENERAL WHAT HE HAS MISSED

Forty-eight hours later Ulrich was standing in his abandoned house. It was early in the morning. The house was meticulously tidy, dusted and polished; his books and papers lay on the tables precisely as he had left them at his hasty departure, carefully preserved by his servant, open or bristling with markers that had become incomprehensible, this or that paper still with a pencil stuck between the pages. But everything had cooled off and hardened like the contents of a melting pot under which one has forgotten to stoke the fire. Painfully disillusioned, Ulrich stared blankly at these traces of a vanished hour, matrix of the intense excitement and ideas that had filled it. He felt repelled beyond words at this encounter with his own debris. "It spreads through the doors and the rest of the house all the way down to those idiotic antlers in the hall. What a life I've been leading this last year!" He shut his eyes where he stood, so as not to have to see it. "What a good thing she'll soon be following me," he thought. "We'll change everything!" Then he was tempted after all to visualize the last hours he had spent here; it seemed to him that he had been away for a very long time, and he wanted to compare.

Clarisse: that was nothing. But before and after: the strange turmoil in which he had hurried home, and then that nocturnal melting of the world! "Like iron softening under some great pressure," he mused. "It begins to flow, and yet it is still iron. A man forces his way into the world," he thought, "but it suddenly closes in around him, and everything looks different. No more connections. No road on which he came and which he must pursue. Something shimmering enveloping him on the spot where a moment ago he had seen a goal, or actually the sober void that lies before every goal." Ulrich kept his eyes closed. Slowly, as a shadow, his feeling returned. It happened as if it were returning to the spot where he had stood then and was again standing now, this feeling that was more out there in the room than in his consciousness—it was really neither a feeling nor a thought, but some uncanny process. If one were as overstimulated and lonely as he had been then, one could indeed believe that the essence of the world was turning itself inside out; and suddenly it dawned on him—how was it possible that it was happening only now?—and lay there like a peaceful backward glance, that even then his feelings had announced the encounter with his sister, because from that moment on his spirit had been guided by strange forces, until . . . but before he could think "yesterday," Ulrich turned away, awakened as abruptly and palpably from his memories as if he had bumped against some solid edge. There was something here he was not yet ready to think about.

He went over to his desk and without taking off his coat looked through the mail lying there. He was disappointed not to find a telegram from his sister, although he had no reason to expect one. A huge pile of condolence mail lay intermingled with scientific communications and booksellers' catalogs. Two letters had come from Bonadea; both so thick that he did not bother to open them. There was also an urgent request from Count Leinsdorf that he come to see him, and two fluting notes from Diotima, also inviting him to put in an appearance immediately upon his return; perused more closely, one of them, the later one, revealed unofficial overtones of a very warm, wistful, almost tender cast. Ulrich turned to the telephone messages that had come during his absence: General Stumm von Bordwehr, Section Chief Tuzzi, Count Leinsdorf's private secretary (twice), several calls from a lady who would not leave her name, probably Bonadea; Bank Director Leo Fischel; and, for the rest, business calls. While Ulrich was reading all this, still standing at his desk, the phone rang, and when he lifted the receiver a voice said: "War Ministry, Culture and Education, Corporal Hirsch," clearly taken aback at finding itself unexpectedly ricocheting off Ulrich's own voice, but hastening to explain that His Excellency the General had given orders to ring Ulrich every morning at ten, and that His Excellency would speak to him right away.

Five minutes later Stumm was assuring him that he had to attend some "supremely important meetings" that very morning, but absolutely had to speak to Ulrich first. When Ulrich asked what about, and why it could not be taken care of over the phone, Stumm sighed into the receiver and proclaimed "news, worries, problems," but could not be made to say anything more specific. Twenty minutes later a War Ministry carriage drew up at the gate and General Stumm entered the house, followed by an orderly with a large leather briefcase slung from his shoulder. Ulrich, who well remembered this receptacle for the General's intellectual problems from the battle plans and ledger pages of Great Ideas, raised his eyebrows interrogatively. Stumm von Bordwehr smiled, sent the orderly back to the carriage, unbuttoned his tunic to get out the little key for the security lock, which he wore on a fine chain around his neck, unlocked the case, and wordlessly exhumed its sole contents, two loaves of regulation army bread.

"Our new bread," he declared after a dramatic pause. "I've brought you some for a taste!"

"How nice of you," Ulrich said, "bringing me bread after I've spent a night traveling, instead of letting me get some sleep."

"If you have some schnapps in the house, which one may assume," the General retorted, "then there's no better breakfast than bread and schnapps after a sleepless night. You once told me that our regulation bread was the only thing you liked about the Emperor's service, and I'll go so far as to say that the Austrian Army beats any other army in the world at making bread, especially since our Commissariat brought out this new loaf, Model 1914! So I brought you one, though that's not the only reason. The other is that I always do this now on principle. Not that I have to spend every minute at my desk, or account for every step I take out of the room, you understand, but you know that our General Staff isn't called the Jesuit Corps for nothing, and there's always talk when a man is out of the office a lot; also my chief, His Excellency von Frost, may not, perhaps, have a completely accurate idea of the scope of the mind—the civilian mind, I mean—and that's why for some time now I've been taking along this official bag and an orderly whenever I want to go out for a bit; and since I don't want the orderly to think that the bag is empty, I always put two loaves of bread in it."

Ulrich could not help laughing, and the General cheerfully joined in.

"You seem to be less enchanted with the great ideas of mankind than you were?" Ulrich asked.

"Everyone is less enchanted with them," Stumm declared while he sliced the bread with his pocketknife. "The new slogan that's been handed out is 'Action!' "

"You'll have to explain that to me."

"That's what I came for. You're not the true man of action."

"I'm not?"

"No."

"Well, I don't know about that."

"Maybe I don't either. But that's what they say."

"Who's 'they'?"

"Arnheim, for one."

"You're on good terms with Arnheim?"

"Well, of course. We get along famously. If he weren't such a high-brow we could be on a first-name basis by now!"

"Are you involved with the oil fields too?"

To gain time, the General drank some of the schnapps Ulrich had had brought in and chewed on the bread. "Great taste," he brought out laboriously, and kept on chewing.

"Of course you're involved with the oil fields!" Ulrich burst out, suddenly seeing the light. "It's a problem that concerns your naval branch because it needs fuel for its ships, and if Arnheim wants the drilling fields he'll have to concede a favorable price for you. Besides, Galicia is deployment territory and a buffer against Russia, so you have to provide special safeguards in case of war for the oil supply he wants to develop there. So his munitions works will supply you with the cannons you want! Why didn't I see this before? You're positively born for each other!"

The General had taken the precaution of munching on a second piece of bread, but now he could contain himself no longer, and making strenuous efforts to gulp down the whole mouthful at once, he said: "It's easy for you to talk so glibly about an accommodation; you've no idea what a skinflint he is! Sorry—I mean, you have no idea," he amended himself, "what moral dignity he brings to a business deal like this. I never dreamed, for example, that ten pennies per ton per railway mile is an ethical problem you have to read up on in Goethe or the history of philosophy."

"You're conducting these negotiations?"

The General took another gulp of schnapps. "I never said that negotiations were going on! You could call it an exchange of views, if you like."

"And you're empowered to conduct them?"

"Nobody's empowered! We're talking, that's all. Surely one can talk now and then about something besides the Parallel Campaign? And if anyone were empowered, it certainly wouldn't be me; that's no job for the Culture and Education Department, it's a matter for the higher-ups, even the Chiefs of Staff. If I had anything at all to do with it, it would be only as a kind of technical adviser on civilian intellectual questions, an interpreter, so to speak, because of Arnheim being so educated."

"And because you're always running into him, thanks to me and Diotima! My dear Stumm, if you want me to go on being your stalking horse, you'll have to tell me the truth!"

But Stumm had had time to prepare himself for this. "Why are you asking, if you know it already?" he countered indignantly. "Do you think you can nail me down and that I don't know that Arnheim takes you into his confidence?"

"I don't know a thing!"

"But you've just been telling me that you do know."

"I know about the oil fields."

"And then you said that we have a common interest with Arnheim in those oil fields. Give me your word of honor that you know this, then I can tell you everything." Stumm von Bordwehr seized Ulrich's reluctant hand, looked him in the eye, and then said slyly:

"All right, since you're giving me your word of honor that you knew everything already, I give you mine that you know all there is. Agreed? There isn't anything more. Arnheim is trying to use us, and we him. I sometimes have the most complicated spiritual conflicts over Diotima!" he exclaimed. "But you mustn't say a word to anyone; it's a military secret!" The General waxed cheerful. "Do you know, incidentally, what a military secret is?" he went on. "A few years ago, when they were mobilizing in Bosnia, the War Ministry wanted to ax me. I was still a colonel then, and they gave me the command of a territorial battalion; of course, I could have been given a brigade, but since I'm supposed to be Cavalry, and since they wanted to ax me, they sent me to a battalion. And since you need money to fight a war, once I got there they sent me the battalion cashbox too. Did you ever see one of those in your time in the army? It looks like a cross between a coffin and a corn crib; it's made of heavy wood with iron bands all around, like the gate to a fortress. It has three locks, and three officers carry the keys to them, one each, so that no one can unlock it by himself: the commander and his two co-cashbox-key-unlockers. Well, when I got there we congregated as if for a prayer meeting, and one after the other we each opened a lock and reverently took out the bundles of banknotes. I felt like a high priest with two acolytes, only instead of reading the Gospel we read out the figures from the official ledger. When we were done we closed up the box, put the iron bands back on, and locked the locks, the whole thing over again, except in reverse order. I had to say something I can't remember now, and that was the end of the ceremony. Or so I thought, and so you'd have thought, and I was full of respect for the unflagging foresight of the military administration in wartime! But I had a fox terrier in those days, the predecessor to the one I have now; there was no regulation against it. He was a clever little beast, but he couldn't see a hole without starting to dig like mad. So as I was going out I noticed that Spot—that was his name; he was English—was busying himself with the cashbox, and there was no getting him away from it. Well, you keep hearing stories about faithful dogs uncovering the darkest conspiracies, and war was almost upon us too, so I thought to myself, Let's see what's up with Spot. And what do you suppose was the matter with Spot? You must remember that Ordnance doesn't provide the field battalions with the very latest supplies, so our cashbox was a venerable antique, but who would ever have thought that while the three of us were locking up in front, it had a hole in the back, near the bottom, wide enough to put your arm through? There'd been a knot in the wood there, which had fallen out in some previous war. But what was to be done? The whole Bosnian scare was just over when the relief troops we had applied for came, and until then we could go through our ceremony every week, except that I had to leave Spot home so he wouldn't give our secret away. So you see, that's what a military secret sometimes looks like!"

"Hmm . . . it seems to me you're still not quite so open as that cashbox of yours," Ulrich commented. "Are you fellows really closing the deal or not?"

"I don't know. I give you my word of honor as an officer on the General Staff: it hasn't come to that yet."

"And Leinsdorf?"

"He hasn't the faintest idea, of course. Besides, he wouldn't have anything to do with Arnheim. I hear he's still terribly angry about the demonstration—you remember, you were there too. He's now dead set against the Germans."

"Tuzzi?" Ulrich asked, continuing the cross-examination.

"He's the last man we'd want to find out anything! He would ruin the scheme at once. Of course we all want peace, but we military men have a different way of serving it than the bureaucrats."

"And Diotima?"

"Oh, my dear fellow, please! This is altogether a man's affair; she couldn't think of such things even with gloves on! I certainly can't bring myself to burden her with the truth. And I can see why Arnheim wouldn't tell her anything about it. He talks such a lot and so beautifully, it might well be a pleasure for him to hold his tongue about something for once. Like taking a dose of bitters for the stomach, I imagine."

"Do you realize that you've turned into a rogue?" Ulrich asked, and raised his glass. "Here's to your health!"

"No, not a rogue," the General defended himself. "I'm a member of a ministerial council. At a meeting everyone proposes what he would like and thinks right, and in the end something comes out that no one really wanted, the so-called outcome. I don't know if you follow me—I can't express it any better."

"Of course I follow you. But the way you're all treating Diotima is disgraceful, just the same."

"I'd be sorry to think so," Stumm said. "But a hangman, you know, is a disreputable fellow, no question about it; yet the rope manufacturer who supplies the prison with the rope can be a member of the Ethical Society. You don't take that sufficiently into account."

"You got that from Arnheim!"

"Could be. I don't know. One's mind gets so complicated nowadays," the General complained sincerely.

"And where do I come in?"

"Well, you see, I was thinking, here you are, a former army officer . . ."

"Never mind. But what has this to do with being, or not being, a 'man of action'?" Ulrich asked, affronted.

"Man of action?" the General echoed, mystified.

"You began everything by saying I wasn't a man of action."

"Oh, that. That's got nothing at all to do with it; I just happened to start with it. I mean, Arnheim doesn't exactly think of you as a man of action; he once said so. You have nothing to do, he says, and that puts ideas into your head. Or words to that effect."

"Idle ideas, you mean? Ideas that can't be 'introduced in spheres of power'? Ideas for their own sake? In short, true and independent ideas! Is that it? Or possibly the ideas of an 'unworldly aesthete'?"

"Well," Stumm von Bordwehr agreed diplomatically, "something like that."

"Like what? What do you think is more dangerous to the life of the mind—dreams or oil fields? There's no need to stuff your mouth with bread; stop it! I couldn't care less what Arnheim thinks of me. But you started off by saying, 'Arnheim, for one.' So who else is there who doesn't see me as enough of a man of action?"

"Well, you know," Stumm affirmed, "quite a few. I told you that 'Action!' is now the great rallying cry."

"What does that mean?"

"I don't really know either. Old man Leinsdorf said: 'Something has to be done!' That's how it started."

"And Diotima?"

"Diotima calls it a New Spririt. So now lots of people on the Council are saying that. I wonder if you know what it's like, that dizzy feeling in your stomach when a beautiful woman has such a head on her shoulders?"

"I'll take your word for it," Ulrich conceded, refusing to let Stumm wriggle out of it. "But now I'd like to hear what Diotima has to say about this New Spirit."

"It's what people are saying," Stumm answered. "The people on the Council are saying that the times are getting a New Spirit. Not right away, but in a few years; unless something unexpected happens sooner. And this New Spirit won't have many ideas in it. Nor is it a time for feelings. Ideas and feelings—they're more for people who have nothing to do. In short, it's a spirit of action, that's really all I know about it. But it has sometimes occurred to me," the General added pensively, "to wonder if, in the end, that isn't simply the military spirit?"

"An action has to make sense!" Ulrich claimed, and in all serious-ness, far beyond this jesters' motley conversation, his conscience re-minded him of the first conversation he had had on that subject with Agathe, on the Swedish rampart.

But the General agreed. "That's what I just said. If someone doesn't have anything to do, and doesn't know what to do with him-self, he becomes energetic. Then he starts boozing, bawling, brawl-ing, and bullying man and beast. On the other hand, you'll have to admit that someone who knows exactly what he wants can be an intri-guer. Just look at any of our youngsters on the General Staff, silently pressing his lips together and making a face like Moltke: In ten years he'll have a general's paunch under his tunic buttons—not a benign one, like mine, but a bellyful of poison. So it's hard to decide how much sense any action can make." He thought it over, and added: "If you know how to get hold of it, there's a great deal to be learned in the army—I'm more and more convinced of it as time goes on—but don't you think the simplest thing would be if we could still find the Great Idea?"

"No," Ulrich retorted. "That was nonsense."

"All right, but in that case there's really nothing left but action." Stumm sighed. "It's almost what I've been saying myself. Do you re-member, by the way, my warning you once that all these excessive ideas only end up in homicide? That's what we've got to prevent! But," he wheedled, "what we need is someone to take over the lead-ership."

"And what part have you had the kindness to assign to me in the matter?" Ulrich asked, yawning openly.

"Very well, I'm leaving," Stumm assured him. "But now that we've had this heart-to-heart talk, if you wanted to be a true comrade there *is* something important you could do. Things are not going too well between Diotima and Arnheim."

"You don't say!" His host showed some small signs of life.

"You'll see for yourself; no need to take it from me. Besides, she confides in you more than in me."

"She confides in you? Since when?"

"She seems to have got used to me a little," the General said proudly.

"Congratulations."

"Thanks. And you ought to look in on Leinsdorf again soon. On account of his antipathy to the Prussians."

"I won't do it."

"Now look, I know you don't like Arnheim. But you'll have to do it anyway."

"That's not why. I have no intention of going back to Leinsdorf."

"But why not? He's such a fine old gentleman. Arrogant, and I can't stand him, but he's been splendid to you."

"I'm getting out of this whole affair."

"But Leinsdorf won't let you go. Nor Diotima either. And I certainly won't! You wouldn't leave me all alone . . .?"

"I'm fed up with the whole stupid business."

"You are, as always, supremely right. But what isn't stupid? Look, without you, I'm pretty dumb. So will you go to Leinsdorf for my sake?"

"But what's this about Diotima and Arnheim?"

"I won't tell you; otherwise you won't go to Diotima either!" Suddenly the General had an inspiration. "If you like, Leinsdorf can get you an assistant to take care of whatever you don't like. Or I can get you one from the War Ministry. Pull out as far as you like, but keep a guiding hand over me!"

"Let me get some sleep first," Ulrich pleaded.

"I won't go till you promise."

"All right, I'll sleep on it," Ulrich conceded. "Don't forget to put the bread of military science back in your bag."

14

What's new with Walter and Clarisse. A showman and his spectators

Toward evening his restlessness drove Ulrich to go out to Walter and Clarisse's. On the way he tried to remember Clarisse's letter, which he had either stowed away irretrievably in his luggage or lost, but he could recall nothing in detail except for a final sentence, "I hope you'll be coming back soon," and his general impression that he would really have to talk with Walter, a feeling tinged not only with regret and uneasiness but also with a certain malice. It was this fleeting and involuntary feeling, of no significance, that he now dwelled on instead of brushing it aside, feeling rather like someone with vertigo who finds relief by getting himself down as low as he can.

When he turned the corner to the house, he saw Clarisse standing in the sun by the side wall where the espaliered peach tree was. She had her hands behind her and was leaning back against the yielding branches, gazing into the distance, oblivious to his approach. There was something self-forgetful and rigid in her attitude, but also something faintly theatrical, apparent only to the friend who knew her ways so well; she looked as if she were acting out a part in the significant drama of her own ideas and one of those ideas had taken hold of her, refusing to let go. He remembered her saying to him: "I want the child from you!" The words did not affect him as disagreeably now as they had at the time; he called out to her softly and waited.

But Clarisse was thinking: "This time Meingast is going through his transformation in our house." He had undergone several rather remarkable transformations in his lifetime, and without reacting to Walter's lengthy answer to his letter, he had, one day, turned the announcement of his coming into reality. Clarisse was convinced that the work he then immediately plunged into in their house had to do with a transformation. The thought of some Indian god who takes up his abode somewhere before each new purification mingled in her mind with the memory of creatures that choose a specific place to change into a pupa, and from this notion, which struck her as tremendously healthy and down-to-earth, she went on to take in the sensuous fragrance of peaches ripening on a sunny wall. The logical result of all this was that she was standing under the window in the glow of the sinking sun, while the prophet had withdrawn into the shadowy cavern behind it. The day before, he had explained to her and Walter that in its original sense "knight" had meant boy, servant, squire, man-at-arms, and hero. Now she said to herself, "I am his knight!" and served him and safeguarded his labors: There was no need to say a word; she simply stood still, dazzled, and faced down the rays of the sun.

When Ulrich spoke to her she slowly turned her face toward the unexpected voice, and he discovered that something had changed. The eyes that looked toward him contained a chill such as the colors of a landscape radiate after the dying of day, and he instantly realized: She no longer wants anything from you! There was no trace anymore in her look of how she had wanted to "force him out of his block of stone," of his having been a great devil or god, of wanting to escape with him through the hole in the music, of wanting to kill him if he would not love her. Not that he cared; it was doubtless a quite ordinary little experience, this extinguished glow of self-interest in a gaze; still, it was like a small rent in the veil of life through which the indifferent void stares out, and it laid the basis for much that was to happen later.

Ulrich was told that Meingast was there, and understood.

They went quietly into the house to fetch Walter, and the three of them just as quietly came back out of doors again so as not to disturb the great man working. Through an open door Ulrich twice caught a glimpse of Meingast's back. Meingast was housed in an empty room detached from the rest of the apartment but belonging to it; Clarisse and Walter had dug up an iron bedstead somewhere for him; a kitchen stool and a tin basin served as a washstand and bath, and in addition to these the room, with its uncurtained window, held only an old kitchen cupboard containing books, and a small, unpainted deal table. Meingast sat at this table writing, and did not turn his head when they passed his door. All this Ulrich either saw for himself or found out from his friends, who had no scruples about providing much more primitive accommodations for the Master than they had themselves; on the contrary, for some reason, they seemed to take pride in his being content with it. It was touching, and it made things easy for them. Walter declared that if one went into this room in Meingast's absence one felt the indescribable aura of a threadbare old glove that had been worn on a noble and forceful hand.

And in fact Meingast greatly enjoyed working in these surroundings, whose spartan simplicity flattered him. It made him feel his will forming the words on paper. And when in addition Clarisse was standing under his window, as she had been just then, or on the landing, or even if she was merely sitting in her room—"wrapped in the cloak of invisible northern lights," as she had confided to him—his pleasure was enhanced by this ambitious disciple on whom he had such a paralyzing effect. Then ideas simply flowed from his pen, and his huge dark eyes above the sharp, quivering nose began to glow. What he intended to complete under these circumstances would be one of the most important sections of his new book, and one ought to be allowed to call it not a book but a call to arms for the spirit of a new breed of men! When he heard an unfamiliar male voice coming from where Clarisse was standing, he had broken off and cautiously peered out; he did not recognize Ulrich, though he dimly remembered him, but he found no reason in the footsteps coming up the stairs to shut his door or turn his head from his work. He wore a heavy wool cardigan under his jacket, showing his imperviousness to weather and people.

Ulrich was taken out for a walk and treated to ecstatic praise of the Master, who was meanwhile devoting himself to his work.

Walter said: "Being friends with a man like Meingast makes one realize how much one has suffered from antipathy to others! Associating with him, one feels . . . let me put it this way: everything seems painted in pure colors, without any grays at all!"

Clarisse said: "Being with him, one feels one has a destiny. There one stands, entirely oneself, fully illuminated."

Walter added: "Today everything splits into hundreds of layers and becomes opaque and blurred—*his* mind is like glass!"

Ulrich's reply to them was: "There are always scapegoats and bellwethers; and then there are sheep who need them!"

Walter flung back at him: "It was to be expected that such a man wouldn't suit you!"

Clarisse cried out: "You once maintained that no one can live by ideas, remember? Well, Meingast can!"

Walter said more soberly: "Not that I always see eye-to-eye with him, of course . . ."

Clarisse broke in: "Listening to him, one feels shudders of light inside."

Ulrich retorted: "A particularly fine head on a man usually means that he's stupid; particularly deep philosophers are usually shallow thinkers; in literature, talents not much above average are usually regarded by their contemporaries as geniuses."

What a curious phenomenon admiration is! In the life of individuals it occurs only in spasms, but it is firmly institutionalized in collective life. Walter would actually have found it more satisfying if he himself could have occupied Meingast's place in his own and Clarisse's esteem, and could not at all understand why this was not so; and yet there was a certain slight advantage in it too. The emotion he was spared in this way was likewise credited to Meingast's account, as when one adopts someone else's child as one's own. On the other hand, it was for this very reason that his admiration for Meingast was not really a pure and wholesome feeling, as Walter himself realized; it was rather an overcharged need to surrender himself to believing in him. There was something assiduous in this admiration; it was a "keyboard emotion," raging without real conviction. Ulrich sensed this too. One of the elementary needs for passion, which life today breaks into fragments and jumbles to the point where they are unrecognizable, was here seeking a way back, for Walter praised Meingast with the ferocity of a theater audience that applauds far beyond the limits of its real opinion the commonplaces that are designed to arouse its need to applaud. He praised him out of one of those desperate urges to admire, which normally find their outlet in festivals and celebrations, in great contemporaries or ideas and the honors bestowed on them, in situations where everyone involved joins in without anybody really knowing for whom or for what, while being inwardly prepared to be twice as mean as usual the next day in order to have nothing to reproach oneself for. This was how Ulrich thought about his friends, and he kept them on their toes by aiming barbed remarks at Meingast from time to time; for like everyone who knows better, he had been annoyed countless times by his contemporaries' capacity for enthusiasms, which almost invariably fasten on the wrong object and so end up destroying even what indifference has let survive.

Dusk had already fallen by the time they had returned, still talking, to the house.

"This Meingast lives on our current confusion of intuition and faith," Ulrich finally said. "Almost everything that isn't science can only be intuited, and for that you need passion and prudence. So a methodology for dealing with what we don't know is almost the same as a methodology for life. But you two 'believe' the minute someone like Meingast comes along! And so does everyone. But this 'belief' is almost as much of a disaster as if you decided to plump your esteemed bodies down on a basket of eggs to hatch their unknown contents!"

They were standing at the foot of the stairs. And suddenly Ulrich realized why he had come here and was talking with them the way he used to. It did not surprise him when Walter answered:

"And the world is supposed to stand still until you've worked out your methodology?"

They evidently did not take him seriously because they did not realize how desolate this area of faith was that stretches between the certainty of knowledge and the mists of intuition! Old ideas swarmed in his head, crowding so thickly they almost suffocated thought. But now he knew that it was no longer necessary to start all over again, like a carpet weaver whose mind has been blinded by a dream, and that this was the only reason he was here again. Everything had become so much simpler lately. The last two weeks had annulled everything that had gone before and had tied up the lines of his inner motions with a powerful knot.

Walter was expecting Ulrich to give him an answer that he could resent. He wanted to pay him back with interest! He had made up his mind to tell Ulrich that people like Meingast were saviors. "Salvation, after all, means the same thing as making one whole," he thought. And: "Saviors may be wrong, but they make us whole again!" he intended to say. And he was going to add: "I don't suppose you have any idea what that means?" The resentment he felt toward Ulrich was like what he felt when he had to go to the dentist.

But Ulrich merely asked him distractedly just what Meingast had actually been writing and doing in the past few years.

"You see!" Walter said, disappointed. "You see, you don't even know that much, but you disparage him!"

"Well," Ulrich said lightly, "I don't have to know; a few lines are sufficient!" He set his foot on the stairs. But Clarisse held him by the jacket and whispered: "Meingast isn't even his real name!"

"Of course it isn't; but is that a secret?"

"He turned into Meingast once, and now that he's here with us he's changing again!" Clarisse whispered intensely and mysteriously, and this whisper had something in common with a blowtorch. Walter flung himself on it to put it out. "Clarisse!" he implored her. "Clarisse, stop this nonsense!"

Clarisse kept quiet and smiled. Ulrich went ahead up the stairs; he wanted at long last to see this messenger who had descended upon Walter and Clarisse's domestic life from Zarathustra's mountains. By the time they got upstairs, Walter was in a temper not only at him but at Meingast as well.

Meingast received his admirers in their dark apartment. He had seen them coming, and Clarisse immediately walked over to him where he stood against the gray windowpane, becoming a small pointed shadow beside his tall gaunt one. There was no introduction, or only a one-sided one in that Ulrich's name was mentioned in order to refresh the Master's memory. Then they were all silent. Ulrich, being curious to see how the situation would develop, positioned himself at the other, unoccupied, window, and Walter made the surprising move of joining him there, probably for no better reason than, being subject to momentarily equal forces of repulsion, he was attracted by the stimulus of the brightness filtering into the room through the less obstructed window.

The calendar said March, but meteorology is not always dependable; it sometimes produces a premature June evening or a belated one, Clarisse thought. The darkness outside the window seemed to her like a summer night. Where the light of the gas lamps fell, the night was lacquered a bright yellow. The bushes nearby were a surging mass of black. Where they hung into the light they became green or whitish—there was no right word for it—scalloped into leaves and floating in the lamplight like laundry spread out in a gently running stream. A narrow iron ribbon on dwarflike posts—a mere reminder and admonition to think of order—ran for a while along the edge of the lawn where the bushes stood, and then vanished in the darkness: Clarisse knew it came to an end there. There might at some time have been a plan to embellish the area with the suggestion of a garden, but it had soon been abandoned.

Clarisse moved close to Meingast, to see as far as possible up the road from his angle; her nose was flat against the windowpane, and their two bodies were touching hard and at as many points as if Clarisse had stretched out full length on the stairs, as she occasionally did. Her right arm had to give way, and was clasped at the elbow by Meingast's long fingers as by the sinewy talons of an extremely absentminded eagle crumpling something like a silk handkerchief in its claws. Clarisse had for a while been watching a man who had something wrong with him, but she couldn't make out what it was. His gait was by turns hesitant and negligent; he gave the impression that something was wrapping itself around his will to walk, and every time he had torn through this he walked for a bit like anyone who was not hurrying but not stopping either. The rhythm of this irregular movement had caught Clarisse's attention; as the man passed a streetlamp she tried to make out his features, which struck her as hollow and numb. When he passed the next-to-last streetlamp she decided that it was an insignificant, unpleasant, and furtive face, but as he approached the nearest lamppost, the one almost beneath her window, his face looked extremely pale, and it floated around on the light as the light floated around on the darkness, so that the thin iron post of the streetlamp looked very straight and aroused beside it, striking the eye with a more penetrating vivid green than it really warranted.

All four had gradually begun to observe this man, who thought himself unseen. He now noticed the bushes bathed in light, and they made him think of the scalloping of a woman's petticoat, more luxurious than any he had ever seen, but one he would like to see. At this moment he was seized by his resolve. He stepped over the low railing, stood on the grass, which reminded him of the green wood shavings in a box of toy trees, stared for a while in bewilderment at his feet, was roused by his head as it cautiously looked around, and concealed himself in the shadows, as was his habit. People lured outdoors by the warm weather were returning home; their noise and their pleasure could be heard from far off. It filled the man with fear, and he sought comfort under the petticoat of leaves. Clarisse still had no idea what was the matter with him. He emerged whenever a group of people had passed by, their eyes blinded to the darkness by the gaslight. Without lifting his feet, he shuffled toward the circle of light, like someone on a shallow bank who will not go into water over the soles of his shoes. Clarisse was struck by how pale the man was; his face was distorted into a white disk. She was overcome with pity for him. But he was making strange little movements that puzzled her for a long time, until, suddenly horrified, she had to grab hold of something; and since Meingast still had a grip on her arm, so that she could not move freely, she grabbed his wide trousers in her search for protection, pulling them taut over the Master's leg like a flag in a gale. So the two of them stood, without letting go.

Ulrich, thinking he was the first to have realized that the man under the windows was one of those sick people who through the abnormality of their sex lives attract the lively curiosity of the sexually normal, worried needlessly for a while about the effect this discovery might have on Clarisse, since she was so unstable. Then he forgot about it, and would have been glad to know for himself what might actually be going on in such a person. The change, he thought, must have been so complete at the moment of stepping over the rail as to defy any attempt to describe it in detail. And as naturally as if it were an appropriate comparison, he was reminded of a singer who has just finished eating and drinking and then steps up to the piano, folds his hands over his stomach, and, opening his mouth to sing, is partly someone else and partly not. Ulrich also thought of His Grace Count Leinsdorf, who was able to switch into a religious-ethical circuit and into a banker's imperial man-of-the-world circuit. He was fascinated by the completeness of this transformation, which takes place inwardly but is confirmed outwardly by the world's acceptance. He did not care how this man down there had got where he was in psychological terms, but he could not help imagining his head gradually filling with tension, like a balloon filling with gas, probably, slowly and for days, but still swaying on the ropes that anchor it to terra firma until there is an inaudible command or some chance occurrence, or simply the set time finally runs its course, at which point anything at all would serve to let the ropes go, and the head, with no connection to the human world, floats off into the emptiness of the abnormal. And there the man actually stood in the shelter of the bushes with his sunken, ordinary face, lurking like a beast of prey. To carry out his purpose he really should have waited for the merrymakers to thin out so that the area might be safer for him. But the moment women passed by, alone in the interval between groups, or sometimes even protected within a group, dancing along and laughing gaily, they were no longer people to him but dolls playing some grotesque part in his consciousness. He was filled with the utter ruthlessness of a killer, immune to their mortal fear; but at the same time he was himself suffering some minor torment at the thought that they might discover him and chase him off like a dog before he could reach the climax of insensibility, and his tongue quivered in his mouth with anxiety. He waited in a stupor, and gradually the last glimmer of twilight faded. Now a solitary woman neared his hiding place, but when he was still separated from her by the streetlamps, he could already see her detached from all her surroundings, bobbing up and down on the waves of light and darkness, a black lump dripping with light before she came closer. Ulrich, too, saw her, a shapeless middle-aged woman approaching. She had a body like a sack filled with gravel, and her expression was not congenial but domineering and cantankerous. But the gaunt pale man in the bushes knew how to get at her without her noticing until it was too late. The dull motions of her eyes and her legs were probably already twitching in his flesh, and he was getting ready to assault her before she had a chance to defend herself, to assault her with the sight of him, which would take her by surprise and enter into her forever, however she might twist and turn. This excitement was whirling and turning in his knees, hands, and larynx, or so it seemed at least to Ulrich as he observed the man groping his way through the bushes where they were already in the half-light, getting ready to step out at the right moment and expose himself. Dazed, the miserable man, leaning into the last slight resistance of the twigs, glued his eyes on the ugly face now pitching up and down toward him in the full light, his breath panting obediently in time with the rhythm of the stranger. "Will she scream?" Ulrich thought. This coarse person was perfectly capable of flying into a rage instead of a panic, and going over to the attack; in which case the demented coward would have to take to his heels, and his frustrated lust would plunge its knife into his own flesh, the squat handle first! But at this tense moment Ulrich heard the casual voices of two men coming down the road, and since he could hear them through the glass they must have penetrated the hissing excitement down below, for the man beneath the window cautiously dropped the nearly opened veil of twigs and withdrew soundlessly back into the midst of the darkness.

"What a swine!" Clarisse whispered to the friend beside her, energetically but not at all indignantly. Back before Meingast's transformation he had often heard her use such terms, provoked by his free-and-easy ways with her, so the word might be considered historical. Clarisse assumed that Meingast would still remember it, despite his transformation, and it really did seem to her that his fingers stirred very faintly on her arm in answer. There was nothing at all accidental about this evening; it was not even by chance that the man had chosen Clarisse's window to stand under. She was firmly convinced that she had a baneful attraction for men who had something wrong with them; it had often proved to be so! Taken all in all, it was not so much that her ideas were confused as that they left out connections, or that they were saturated with affect in many places where other people have no such inner wellspring. Her conviction that she had been the one who had made it possible at the time for Meingast to remake himself was in itself not improbable; if one also considered how independently this change had taken its own course, because there had been no contact over distance and for years, and further how great a change it was—for it had made a prophet out of a superficial worldling—and finally how it was soon after Meingast's departure that the love between Walter and Clarisse had risen to that height of discord where it still remained, then even Clarisse's notion that she and Walter would have had to take on the sins of the still untransformed Meingast to make his rise possible was no worse reasoning than any number of respected ideas people believe in today. This had given rise, however, to the relationship of knightly servitude that Clarisse felt toward the returned Master, and whenever she now spoke of his new "transformation," instead of simply a change, she was only giving fitting expression to the elevated state in which she had since found herself. The awareness of finding herself in a significant relationship could uplift Clarisse in the literal sense. One doesn't quite know whether to paint saints with a cloud under their feet or whether they should be standing on nothing a finger's breadth above the ground, and this was exactly how it now stood with her, since Meingast had chosen her house in which to accomplish his great work, which apparently was grounded in something quite profound. Clarisse was not in love with him as a woman; it was rather like a boy who admires a man: ecstatic when he manages to set his hat at the same angle as his idol, and filled with a secret ambition even to outdo him eventually.

Walter knew this. He could not hear what Clarisse was whispering to Meingast, nor could his eye make out any more of the pair than a heavily fused mass of shadow in the dim light of the window, but he could see through everything. He, too, had recognized what was wrong with the man in the bushes, and the silence that reigned in the room lay most heavily upon him. He managed to make out that Ulrich, who stood motionless beside him, was staring intently out the window, and he assumed that the two at the other window were doing the same. "Why doesn't anyone break this silence?" he thought. "Why doesn't someone open the window and scare this monster off?" It occurred to him that they were obligated to call the police, but there was no telephone in the house, and he lacked the courage to undertake something that might make his companions look down on him. He had no desire whatever to be an "outraged bourgeois," but he was just so exasperated! He could understand very well the "chivalric relationship" in which his wife stood to Meingast, for even in lovemaking it was impossible for her to imagine exaltation without effort: she derived her exaltation not from sensuality, only from ambition. He remembered how incredibly alive she could sometimes be in his arms, at a time when he had still been preoccupied with art; but except by such detours it was impossible to arouse her. "Perhaps ambition is all that really takes people out of themselves," he reflected dubiously. It had not escaped him that Clarisse "stood watch" while Meingast was working, in order to protect his ideas with her body, although she did not even know what these ideas were. Painfully, Walter regarded the lonely egotist in his bush; this wretch offered a warning example for the devastation that can be created in an all-too-isolated mind. That he knew exactly what

Clarisse was feeling as she stood there watching tormented him. "She will be slightly excited, as if she had just run up a flight of stairs," he thought. He himself felt a pressure in the scene that was before his eyes, as if something had been wrapped in a cocoon and was trying to break its envelope, and he felt how within this mysterious pressure, which Clarisse, too, was feeling, the will was aroused not merely to watch but right away, soon, somehow, to do something, to intervene in what was happening in order to set it free. Other people got their ideas from life, but whatever Clarisse experienced came, every time, from ideas: such an enviable madness! And Walter was more inclined to the exaggerations of his wife, even if she was perhaps mentally ill, than to the way of thinking of his friend Ulrich, who fancied himself cautious and cool: somehow the more irrational was closer to him; perhaps it left him personally untouched, it appealed to his sympathy. In any event, many people prefer crazy ideas to difficult ones, and he even derived a certain satisfaction from Clarisse's whispering with Meingast in the dark, while Ulrich was condemned to stand beside him as a mute shadow; it served Ulrich right to be beaten by Meingast. But from time to time Walter was tormented by the expectation that Clarisse would fling open the window or rush down the stairs to the bushes: then he detested both male shadows and their obscene silent watching, which made the situation for the poor little Prometheus he was shielding, who was so vulnerable to every temptation of the spirit, more problematic from one minute to the next.

During this time the afflicted man's shame and frustrated lust had fused into an all-pervasive disappointment that filled his gaunt body with its massive bitterness as he withdrew into his bushes. When he had reached the innermost darkness he collapsed, letting himself fall to the ground, and his head hung from his neck like a leaf. The world stood ready to punish him, and he saw his situation much as it would have appeared to the two passersby had they discovered him. But after this man had wept for himself for a while, dry-eyed, the original change came over him once again, this time mixed with even more vengefulness and spite. And again it miscarried. A girl passed by who might have been around fifteen and was obviously late coming from somewhere; she seemed lovely to him, a small, hastening ideal: the depraved man felt that he now really ought to step out and speak to her in a friendly way, but this plunged him instantly into wild terror. His imagination, ready to conjure up anything that could even be suggested by a woman, became fearful and awkward when confronted with the natural possibility of admiring this defenseless little creature approaching in her beauty. The more she was suited to please his daylight self, the less pleasure she provided his shadow self, and he vainly tried to hate her, since he could not love her. So he stood uneasily at the borderline between shadow and light and exposed himself. When the child noticed his secret she had already passed by him and was about eight paces away; at first she had merely looked at the leaves moving without realizing what was going on, and when she did she could already feel secure enough not to be scared to death: her mouth did stay open for a while, but then she gave a loud scream and began to run; the scamp even seemed to enjoy looking back, and the man felt himself humiliatingly abandoned. He wrathfully hoped that a drop of poison might somehow have fallen into her eyes and would later eat its way through her heart.

This relatively harmless and comical outcome relieved the spectators' sense of humanity; this time they would indeed have intervened if the scene had not resolved itself as it did; and preoccupied with this, they hardly noticed how the business below did come to an end; they could only confirm that it had done so when they observed that the male "hyena," as Walter put it, had suddenly disappeared. The man finally realized his intentions when a perfectly ordinary woman came along who looked at him aghast and with loathing, involuntarily shocked into stopping for a moment, and then tried to pretend that she had not seen anything. During this instant he felt himself, together with his roof of leaves and the whole topsy-turvy world he had come from, sliding deep into the defenseless woman's resisting gaze. That may have been how it happened, or perhaps it was some other way. Clarisse had not been paying attention. With a deep breath she raised herself from her half-crouching position; she and Meingast had let go of each other some time before. It seemed to her that she was suddenly landing on the wooden floor with the soles of her feet, and a whirlpool of inexpressible, horrible desire stilled itself in her body. She was firmly convinced that everything that had just occurred had a special meaning, minted just for her; and strange as it may sound, the repulsive scene left her with the impression that she was a bride who had just been serenaded. In her head, intentions were dancing helter-skelter, some ready to be carried out and others, new ones, just occurring to her.

"Funny!" Ulrich suddenly said into the darkness, the first of the four to break the silence. "What an absurdly twisted notion it is to think how this fellow's fun would have been spoiled if he only knew he was being watched the whole time!"

Meingast's shadow detached itself from the nothingness and stood, a slender compression of darkness, facing in the direction of Ulrich's voice.

"We attach far too much importance to sex," the Master said. "These are in fact the goatlike caperings of our era's will." He said nothing further. But Clarisse, who had winced with annoyance at Ulrich's words, felt borne forward by what Meingast said, although in this darkness there was no telling in what direction.

15

THE TESTAMENT

When Ulrich returned home from what he had experienced, even more dissatisfied than he had been before, he decided that he must not avoid a decision any longer, and tried to recall as best he could the "incident," as he euphemistically called what had happened in his last few hours with Agathe, only a few days after their deep discussion.

He was all packed and ready to leave on a sleeper that came through the town late, and so he and Agathe met for a final meal. They had agreed earlier that she would join him soon, and they somewhat uncertainly estimated this separation at from five days to two weeks.

At dinner Agathe said: "There's something more we have to do before you leave."

"What?" Ulrich asked.

"We have to change the will!"

Ulrich remembered looking at his sister without surprise; despite all their earlier talk he had assumed she was leading up to a joke. But Agathe was gazing down at her plate, with the familiar meditative wrinkle between her eyebrows. Slowly she said:

"He won't keep as much of me between his fingers as would be left if a woolen thread had been burned away between them!"

Something must have been intensely at work in her in the last few days. Ulrich was about to tell her that he regarded such deliberations about how Hagauer's interests could be injured as impermissible and did not want to hear any more about it. But at that moment their father's old servant came in with the next course, and they could only go on talking in veiled allusions.

"Aunt Malvina . . . ," Agathe said, smiling at her brother. "Do you remember Aunt Malvina? She had intended to leave everything she owned to our cousin; it was all arranged and everyone knew about it! Accordingly, all she was left in her parents' will was the legal minimum she was entitled to, all the rest going to her brother, so that neither of the children, whose father was equally devoted to both of them, should inherit more than the other. You remember that, surely? The annuity that Agathe—Alexandra, our cousin, that is"—she corrected herself with a laugh—"had been receiving since her marriage was, for the time being, discounted against her legal share; it was a complicated arrangement, to give Aunt Malvina time to die. . . ."

"I don't understand you," Ulrich muttered.

"Oh, but it's perfectly simple! Aunt Malvina is dead, but before she died she lost all her money; she even had to be supported. Now, if Papa should for some reason have forgotten to revoke that provision in his will, Alexandra gets nothing at all, even if her marriage contract had stipulated joint ownership of property!"

"I don't know about that; it seems very doubtful!" Ulrich said impulsively. "Besides, Father must have given certain assurances. He can't possibly have made such provisions without talking it over with his son-in-law!"

He remembered saying this only too well, because he could not possibly keep silent while listening to his sister's dangerous error. He could still see vividly in his mind the smile with which she had looked at him. "Isn't it just like him?" she seemed to be thinking. "One only has to present a case to him as if it weren't flesh and blood but some abstraction, and one can lead him around by the nose." And then she had asked curtly: "Is there any written evidence of such arrangements?" and answered herself: "I never heard anything about it, and if anyone knew about it, it would certainly be me. But of course Papa was strange about everything."

Now the servant was back at the table, and she took advantage of Ulrich's helplessness to add: "Verbal agreements can always be contested. But if the will was changed again after Aunt Malvina lost everything, then all signs point to this new codicil having been lost."

Again Ulrich let himself be tempted to steer her right: "That still leaves the sizable automatic inheritance that can't be taken away from children of one's body."

"But I've just told you that all of that was paid out during the father's lifetime! After all, Alexandra was married twice." They were alone for a moment, and Agathe hastened to add: "I've looked at that passage very carefully. Only a few words need to be changed to make it look as if my share had already been paid out to me in full. Who knows anything about it now? When Papa went back to leaving us equal shares after Aunt Malvina's losses, he put it in a codicil that can be destroyed. Anyway, there's nothing to have prevented me from having renounced my legal share in your favor for one reason or another."

Ulrich looked at her dumbfounded and missed his opportunity to respond to her inventions as he felt obliged to do; by the time he was ready, they were no longer alone, and he had to resort to circumlocutions.

"One really shouldn't," he began hesitantly, "even think such things!"

"Why not?" Agatha retorted.

Such questions are simple as long as they are left alone, but the moment they rear their heads they are a monstrous serpent that had been curled up into a harmless blob. Ulrich remembered answering: "Even Nietzsche asks the 'free spirits' to observe certain external rules for the sake of a greater internal freedom!" He had said this with a smile, although he felt it was rather cowardly to hide behind someone else's words.

"That's a lame principle!" Agathe said, dismissing it out of hand. "That's the principle behind my marriage!"

And Ulrich thought: "It really is a lame principle." It seems that people who have new and revolutionary answers to particular problems make up for it by compromising on everything else, which enables them to lead highly moral lives in carpet slippers; all the more so as the attempt to keep everything constant except what they are trying to change corresponds totally to the creative economy of thinking in which they feel at home. Even Ulrich had always regarded this more as a strict than as a slack procedure, but when he was having this talk with his sister he felt that she had struck home; he could no longer bear the indecision he had loved, and it seemed to him that it was precisely Agathe who had been given the mission of bringing him to this point. And while he was nevertheless propounding the "rule of the free spirits" to her, she laughed and asked him whether he didn't notice that the moment he tried to formulate general principles a different man appeared in his place.

"And even though you are surely right to admire him, basically he doesn't mean a thing to you!" she declared, giving her brother a willful and challenging look. Again he had no ready answer and said nothing, expecting an interruption at any moment, yet he could not bring himself to drop the subject. This situation emboldened her.

"In the short time we've been together," she went on, "you've given me such wonderful guidelines for my life, things I would never have dared think out for myself, but then you always end up wondering whether they're really true! It seems to me that the truth the way you use it is only a way of mistreating people!"

She was amazed at her own daring in making such reproaches; her own life seemed so worthless to her that she surely ought to have kept quiet. But she drew her courage from Ulrich himself, and there was something so curiously feminine in her way of leaning on him while she attacked him that he felt it too.

"You don't understand the desire to organize ideas in large, articulated masses," Ulrich said. "The battle experiences of the intellect are alien to you; all you see in them is columns marching in some kind of formation, the impersonality of many feet stirring up the truth like a cloud of dust!"

"But didn't you yourself describe to me, far more precisely and clearly than I ever could, the two states of mind in which you can live?" she answered.

A glowing cloud, with ever-changing outlines, flew across her face. She felt the desire to bring her brother to the point where he could no longer retreat. The thought made her feverish, but she did not yet know whether she would have enough courage to carry it through, and so she put off ending the meal.

Ulrich knew all this, he guessed it, but he had pulled himself together and taken up his position. He sat facing her, his eyes focused, absent, his mouth forced to utterance, and had the impression that he was not really there but had remained somewhere behind himself, calling out to himself what he was saying:

"Suppose that, on a trip somewhere, I wanted to steal some stranger's golden cigarette case—I ask you, isn't that simply unthinkable? I don't want to go into the question right now of whether a move such as you're contemplating is or isn't justifiable on grounds of intellectual freedom. For all I know, it may be in order to do Hagauer some injury. But imagine me in a hotel, neither penniless nor a professional thief, nor a mental defective with deformed head or body, nor the offspring of a hysterical mother or a drunkard father, nor confused or stigmatized by anything else in any way at all: yet I steal, nevertheless. I repeat: This couldn't happen anywhere in the world! It's simply impossible! It can be ruled out with absolute scientific certainty!"

Agathe burst out laughing. "But Ulo, what if one does it all the same?"

Ulrich himself had to laugh at this answer, which he had not anticipated. He leapt to his feet and pushed his chair back hastily in order not to encourage her by his concurrence. Agathe got up from the table.

"You cannot do this!" he pleaded with her.

"But Ulo," she said, "do you think even in your dreams, or do you dream something that's happening?"

This question reminded him of his argument, a few days before, that all moral demands pointed to a kind of dream state that had fled from them by the time they were fully postulated. But Agathe had already gone, after her last remark, into her father's study, which now could be seen lamplit beyond two open doors; and Ulrich, who had not followed her, saw her standing in this frame. She was holding a sheet of paper in the light, reading something. "Doesn't she have any idea what it is she's taking on herself?" he wondered. But on that whole key ring of contemporary notions, such as neurotic inferiority, mental deficiency, arrested development, and the like, none fit, and in the lovely picture she made while committing her crime there was no trace of greed or vengefulness or any other inner ugliness. And although with the aid of such concepts Ulrich could have seen even the actions of a criminal or a near psychotic as relatively controlled and civilized, because the distorted and displaced motives of ordinary life shimmer in their depths, his sister's gently fierce determination, an inextricable blend of purity and criminality, left him momentarily speechless. He could not accept the idea that this person, quite openly engaged in committing a bad act, could be a bad person, while at the same time he had to watch how Agathe took one paper after another out of the desk, read it, and laid it aside, seriously searching for a specific document. Her determination gave the impression of having descended from some other planet to the plane of everyday decision.

As he watched, Ulrich was also troubled by the question of why he had talked Hagauer into leaving in good faith. It seemed to him that he had behaved all along as the tool of his sister's will, and to the very last his responses, even when he was disagreeing with her, had only encouraged her. Truth dealt cruelly with people, she had said. "Well put, but she has no idea what truth means!" Ulrich mused. "With the passing of the years it leaves one stiff and gouty, but in one's youth it's a life of hunting and sailing!" He had sat down again. Now he suddenly realized not only that Agathe had somehow got from him what she had said about truth, but that he had sketched out for her in advance what she was doing next door. Had he not said that in the highest state of human awareness there was no such thing as good and evil, but only faith or doubt; that strict rules were contrary to the innermost nature of morality and that faith can never be more than an hour old; that in a state of faith one could never do anything base; that intuition was a more passionate state than truth? And Agathe was now on the point of abandoning the safe enclosure of morality and venturing out upon those boundless deeps where there is no decision other than whether one will rise or fall. She was doing this just as she had the other day when she took her father's medals from his reluctant hand to exchange them for the imitations, and at this moment he loved her in spite of her lack of principle, with the remarkable feeling that it was his own thoughts that had gone from him to her and were now returning from her to him, poorer in deliberation but with that balsamic scent of freedom about them like a creation of the wild. And while he was trembling with the strain of controlling himself, he cautiously made a suggestion:

"I'll put off leaving for a day and sound out a notary or lawyer. Perhaps what you're doing is terribly obvious!"

But Agathe had already ascertained that the notary her father had used was no longer alive. "There's not a soul left who knows anything about this business," she said. "Let it be!"

Ulrich saw that she had taken a piece of paper and was practicing imitating her father's handwriting.

Fascinated, he had drawn closer and stood behind her. There in piles lay the papers on which his father's hand had lived—one could still almost feel its movements—and here Agathe, with an actress's mimicry, conjured up almost the same thing. It was strange to see this happening. The purpose it was serving, the thought that it was a forgery, disappeared. And in truth Agathe had not given this any thought at all. An aura of justice with flames, not with logic, hovered about her. Goodness, decency, abiding by the law, as she had come to know it in people she knew, notably Professor Hagauer, had always seemed to her like removing a spot from a dress; while the wrongdoing that enveloped her at this moment was like the world drowning in the light of a rising sun. It seemed to her that right and wrong no longer constituted a general notion, a compromise devised to serve millions of people, but were a magical encounter between Me and You, the madness of original creation before there was anything to compare it to or anything to measure it by. She was really making Ulrich the present of a crime by putting herself in his hands, trusting him wholeheartedly to understand her rashness, as children do who come up with the most unexpected ideas when they want to give someone a present and have nothing to give. And Ulrich guessed most of this. As his eyes followed her movements he felt a pleasure he had never known before, for it had in it something of the magical absurdity of yielding totally and without remonstrance, for once, to what another being was doing. Even when the thought intervened that this was causing harm to a third person, it flashed only for an instant, like an ax, and he quickly put his mind at rest, since what his sister was doing here was really not anyone else's business; it was not at all certain that these attempts at copying someone's handwriting would actually be used, and what Agathe was doing inside her own four walls was her own affair as long as it had no effect beyond them.

She now called out to her brother, turned around, and was surprised to find him standing behind her. She awoke. She had written all she wanted to write and resolutely singed it over a candle flame in order to make the handwriting look old. She held out her free hand to Ulrich, who did not take it, but he was not able to withdraw entirely behind a somber frown either. She responded by saying: "Listen! If something is a contradiction, and you love both sides of it—really love it!—doesn't that cancel it out, willy-nilly?"

"That's much too frivolous a way of putting it," Ulrich muttered. But Agathe knew how he would judge it in his "second thinking." She took a clean sheet of paper and lightheartedly wrote, in the old-fashioned hand she was so good at imitating: "My bad daughter Agathe proffers no reason to change the above-ordained instructions to the disadvantage of my good son Ulo!" Not yet satisfied, she wrote on the second sheet: "My daughter Agathe is for some time longer to be educated by my good son Uli."

So that was how it had happened, but now that Ulrich had reawakened it down to the last detail, he ended up with just as little knowledge of what to do about it as before.

He ought not to have left without first straightening things out, no doubt about that! And clearly the fashionable superstition that one shouldn't take anything too seriously had played him a trick when it whispered to him to quit the field for a time and not give too much weight to the issue between them by emotional resistance. Heat can't pass from the cooler to the hotter; the most violent extremes, left to themselves, eventually give rise to a new mediocrity; one could hardly take a train or walk in the street without a cocked gun if one could not trust the law of averages, which automatically reduces extreme possibilities to improbability. It was this European faith in empiricism that Ulrich was obeying when, despite all his scruples, he returned home. Deep down he was even glad that Agathe had shown herself to be different.

Nevertheless, the matter could not be properly resolved other than by Ulrich's now taking action, and as soon as possible, to make up for his negligence. He should have sent his sister an immediate special delivery letter or telegram, which should have stated in effect: "I won't have anything to do with you unless you . . . !" But he had absolutely no intention of writing anything of the kind; at the moment he simply could not do it.

Besides, they had decided before that fateful incident that in the next few weeks they would try to live together or at least move in together, and this was what they had mainly talked about in the brief time remaining before his departure. They had agreed that for the moment it would be for "the time it will take to get the divorce," so that Agathe would have a refuge and counsel. But now, in thinking about it, Ulrich also remembered an earlier remark of his sister's about wanting "to kill Hagauer"; this "scheme" had evidently been working in her and taken on a new form. She had insisted vehemently on selling the family property at once, possibly also in the interest of making the inheritance evaporate, although it might seem advisable on other grounds as well. In any case, they had agreed to put the sale in the hands of a broker and had set their terms. And so Ulrich now had to give some thought as well to what was to become of his sister after he returned to his casually interim life, which he did not himself regard as real. It was impossible for her present situation to continue. Amazingly close though they had grown in so short a time—as though their fates were linked, even though this had arisen from all sorts of unconnected details; Agathe probably had a more quixotic view of it—they knew hardly anything of each other in the many and various superficialities on which a shared life depends. When he thought of his sister objectively Ulrich could even perceive numerous unsolved problems, nor could he form a very clear idea of her past; his best guess was that she dealt most casually with everything that happened to her or through her, and that she lived rather vaguely and perhaps with fantasies that ran alongside her actual life;

such an explanation would plausibly account for her having stayed so long with Hagauer and then broken with him so suddenly. And even the carelessness with which she treated the future fitted in with this view: she had left home, and that seemed to satisfy her for the present; and when questions arose about what should happen now, she avoided them. Nor was Ulrich himself capable of either picturing a life for her without a husband, in which she would hover around in vague expectations like a young girl, or imagining what the man would look like who would be right for his sister; he had even told her so shortly before he left.

She had given him a startled look—perhaps she was clowning a bit, pretending to be startled—and then calmly countered with the question: "Can't I just stay with you for the time being, without our having to decide everything?"

It was in this fashion, without anything more definite, that the idea of their moving in together had been ratified. But Ulrich realized that this experiment meant the end of the experiment of his "life on leave." He did not want to think about the possible consequences, but that his life would henceforth be subject to certain restrictions was not unwelcome, and for the first time he again thought of the circle and especially the women of the Parallel Campaign. The idea of cutting himself off from everything, as part of his new life, seemed delightful. Just as it often takes only a trifling alteration in a room to change its dull acoustics to a glorious resonance, so now in his imagination his little house was transformed into a shell within which one heard the roar of the city as a distant river.

And then, toward the end of that conversation, this other special little conversation had taken place:

"We'll live like hermits," Agathe had said with a bright smile, "but of course we'll each be free to pursue any love affairs. For you, at any rate, there's no obstacle!" she assured him.

"Do you realize," Ulrich said by way of an answer, "that we shall be entering into the Millennium?"

"What's that?"

"We've talked so much about the love that isn't a stream flowing toward its goal but a state of being like the ocean. Now tell me honestly: When they told you in school that the angels in heaven did nothing but bask in the presence of the Lord and sing His praises, were you able to imagine this blissful state of doing nothing and thinking nothing?"

"I always thought it must be rather boring, which is certainly due to my imperfection," was Agathe's answer.

"But after everything we've agreed on," Ulrich explained, "you must now imagine this ocean as a state of motionlessness and detachment, filled with everlasting, crystal-clear events. In ages past, people tried to imagine such a life on earth. That is the Millennium, formed in our own image and yet like no world we know. That's how we'll live now! We shall cast off all self-seeking, we shall collect neither goods, nor knowledge, nor lovers, nor friends, nor principles, nor even ourselves! Our spirit will open up, dissolving boundaries toward man and beast, spreading open in such a way that we can no longer remain 'us' but will maintain our identities only by merging with all the world!"

This little interlude had been a joke. He had been sitting with paper and pencil, making notes and talking meanwhile with his sister about what she could expect from the sale of the house and the furniture. He was also still cross, and he himself did not know whether he was blaspheming or dreaming. And with all this they had not got around to talking seriously about the will.

It was probably because of these ambiguities in the way it had happened that Ulrich even now was far from feeling any active regret. There was much about his sister's bold stroke that pleased him, though he was himself the defeated one; he had to admit that it suddenly brought the person living by the "rule of the free spirits," to whom he had given far too much ease within himself, into grave conflict with that deep, undefined person from whom real seriousness emanates. Nor did he want to dodge the consequences of this act by quickly making it good in the usual way; but then, there was no norm, and events had to be allowed to take their course.

16

REUNION WITH DIOTIMA'S DIPLOMATIC HUSBAND

Next morning Ulrich's mind was no clearer, and late that afternoon he decided to lighten the serious mood that was oppressing him by looking up his cousin who was occupied with liberating the soul from civilization.

To his surprise he was received by Section Chief Tuzzi, who came to greet him even before Rachel had returned from Diotima's room.

"My wife's not feeling well today," the seasoned husband said, with that unconscious tone of tenderness in his voice which regular monthly use has made into a formula that exposes the domestic secret to the world. "I don't know whether she'll be up to a visit." Though dressed to go out, he was quite willing to stay and keep Ulrich company.

Ulrich took the opportunity of inquiring about Arnheim.

"Arnheim's been in England and is now in St. Petersburg," Tuzzi told him. The effect of this trivial and predictable news on Ulrich, depressed as he was by his own experiences, was to make him feel as though world, fullness, and motion were rushing in upon him.

"A good thing too," the diplomat added. "Let him travel here and there as much as he likes. It gives one a chance to make one's observations and pick up some information."

"So you still believe," said Ulrich, amused, "that he's on some pacifist mission for the Czar?"

"I believe it more than ever," was the plain answer from the man who bore official responsibility for carrying out Austro-Hungarian policy. But suddenly Ulrich doubted whether Tuzzi was really so unsuspecting or was only pretending to be and pulling his leg; somewhat annoyed, he dropped Arnheim and asked: "I hear that 'Action!' has become the watchword since I left."

As always when the Parallel Campaign came up, Tuzzi seemed

to relish playing both the innocent and the shrewd insider. He shrugged and grinned.

"I'll let my wife fill you in on that—you'll hear all about it from her as soon as she's able to see you!" But a moment later his little mustache began to twitch and the large dark eyes in the tanned face glistened with a vague distress. "You're a man who has read all the books," he said hesitantly. "Could you perhaps tell me what is meant by a man having soul?"

This was apparently something Tuzzi really wanted to talk about, and it was obviously his insecurity that was responsible for the impression that he was distressed. When Ulrich failed to respond immediately, he went on: "When we speak of someone as 'a good soul,' we mean an honest, conscientious, dependable fellow—I have an administrator in my office like that—but what that amounts to, surely, is the virtues of an underling. Or there's soul as a quality of women, meaning more or less that they cry more easily, or blush more easily, than men do. . . ."

"Your wife has soul," Ulrich corrected him, as gravely as if he were stating that she had raven-black hair.

A faint pallor rushed across Tuzzi's face. "My wife has a mind," he said slowly. "She is rightly regarded as a woman of some intellect. I like to tease her about it and tell her she's an aesthete. That galls her. But that isn't soul. . . ." He thought for a moment. "Have you ever been to a fortune-teller?" he asked. "They read the future in your palm, or from a hair of your head, sometimes amazingly on target. They have a gift for it, or tricks. But can you make any sense of somebody telling you, for instance, that there are signs that a time is coming when our souls will behold each other directly, so to speak, without the mediation of the senses? Let me say at once," he added quickly, "that this is not to be understood only as a figure of speech, but if you're not a good person, then no matter what you do, people today can feel it much more clearly than in earlier centuries, because this is an age of the awakening soul. Do you believe that?"

With Tuzzi, one never knew if his barbs were directed against himself or his listener, so Ulrich answered: "If I were you I'd just let it come to the test."

"Don't make jokes, my dear friend," Tuzzi said plaintively. "It's not decent when you're safely on the sidelines. My wife expects me to take such propositions seriously even if I can't subscribe to them, and I have to surrender without having a chance to defend myself. So in my hour of need I remembered that you're one of those bookish people. . . ."

"Both of these assertions come from Maeterlinck, if I'm not mistaken," Ulrich said helpfully.

"Really? From . . . ? Yes, I can see that. That's the . . . ? I see, that's good; then perhaps he's also the one who claims that there's no such thing as truth—except for people in love! he says. If I am in love with a person, according to him, I participate directly in a secret truth more profound than the common kind. On the other hand, if we say something based on observation and a thorough knowledge of human nature, that's supposed to be worthless, of course. Is that another of this Mae—this man's ideas?"

"I really don't know. It might be. It's what you would expect from him."

"I imagined it came from Arnheim."

"Arnheim has taken a lot from him, as he has from others—they're both gifted eclectics."

"Really? Then it's all old stuff? But in that case can you tell me, for heaven's sake, how it is possible to let that sort of thing be published nowadays?" Tuzzi asked. "When my wife says things like: 'Reason doesn't prove a thing; ideas don't reach as far as the soul!' or 'There's a realm of wisdom and love far beyond your world of facts, and one only desecrates it with considered statements!' I can understand what makes her talk like that: she's a woman, that's all, and this is her way of defending herself against a man's logic! But how can a man say such things?" Tuzzi edged his chair closer and laid a hand on Ulrich's knee. " 'The truth swims like a fish in an invisible principle; the moment you lift it out, it's dead.' What do you make of *that*? Could it maybe have something to do with the difference between an 'eroticist' and a 'sexualist'?"

Ulrich smiled. "Do you really want me to tell you?"

"I can't wait to hear!"

"I don't know how to begin."

"There it is, you see! Men can't bring themselves to utter such things. But if you had a soul, you would now simply be contemplating my soul and marveling at it. We would reach heights where there are no thoughts, no words, no deeds. Nothing but mysterious forces and a shattering silence! May a soul smoke?" he asked, and lit a cigarette, only then recalling his duty as host and offering one to Ulrich. At bottom he was rather proud of now having read Arnheim's books, and precisely because he still found them insufferable he was pleased with himself for having privately discovered the possible usefulness of their puffed-up style for the inscrutable workings of diplomacy. Nor would anyone else have wanted to do such hard labor for nothing, and anyone in his place would have continued making fun of it to his heart's content, only to yield after a while to the temptation of trying out one quotation or another, or dressing up something that could not be stated clearly in any case in one of those annoyingly fuzzy new ideas. This is done reluctantly, because one still considers the new "costume" ridiculous, but one quickly gets used to it, and so the spirit of the times is imperceptibly transformed by its new terminology, and in specific cases Arnheim might in fact have gained a new admirer. Even Tuzzi was ready to concede that the call to unite soul and commerce, despite any hostility to it on principle, could be thought of as a new psychology of economics, and all that kept him unshakably immune from Arnheim's influence was actually Diotima herself. For between her and Arnheim at that time—unknown to anyone—a certain coolness had begun to gain ground, burdening everything Arnheim had ever said about the soul with the suspicion of being a mere evasion; with the result that his sayings were flung in Tuzzi's face with more irritation than ever. Under these circumstances Tuzzi could be forgiven for assuming that his wife's attachment to the stranger was still in the ascendant, though it was not the kind of love against which a husband could take steps, but a "state of love" or "loving state of mind" so far above all base suspicion that Diotima herself spoke openly of the ideas with which it inspired her, and had lately been insisting rather unrelentingly that Tuzzi take spiritual part in them.

He felt inordinately bewildered and vulnerable, surrounded as he was by this state that blinded him like sunlight coming from all sides at once without the sun itself having any fixed position to orient oneself by, so as to find shade and relief.

He heard Ulrich saying: "But let me offer this for your consideration: Within us there is usually a steady inflow and outflow of experiences. The states of excitation that form in us are aroused from outside and flow out of us again as actions or words. Think of it as a mechanical game. But then think of it being disturbed: The flow gets dammed up. The banks are flooded in some fashion. Occasionally it may be no more than a certain gassiness. . . ."

"At least you talk sensibly, even if it's all nonsense . . . ," Tuzzi noted with approval. He could not quite grasp how all this was supposed to explain matters to him, but he had kept his poise, and even though he was inwardly lost in misery, the tiny malicious smile still lingered proudly on his lips, ready for him to slip right back into it.

"What the physiologists say, I think," Ulrich continued, "is that what we call conscious action is the result of the stimulus not just flowing in and out through a reflex arc but being forced into a detour. That makes the world we experience and the world in which we act, which seem to us one and the same, actually more like the water above and below a mill wheel, connected by a sort of dammed-up reservoir of consciousness, with the inflow and the outflow dependent on regulation of level, pressure, and so forth. Or in other words, if something goes wrong on one of the two levels—an estrangement from the world, say, or a disinclination to action—we could reasonably assume that a second, or higher, consciousness might be formed in this fashion. Or don't you think so?"

"Me?" Tuzzi said. "I'd have to say it's all the same to me. Let the professors work that out among themselves, if they think it important. But practically speaking"—he moodily stubbed out his cigarette in the ashtray, then looked up in exasperation—"is it the people with two reservoirs or only one reservoir who run the world?"

"I thought you only wanted to know how I imagine such ideas might arise. . . ."

"If that's what you've been telling me, I'm afraid I don't follow you," Tuzzi said.

"But it's very simple. You have no second reservoir—so you haven't got the principle of wisdom and you don't understand a word of what the people who have a soul are talking about. Do accept my congratulations!"

Ulrich had gradually become aware that he was expressing, in ig-nominious form and in curious company, ideas that might be not at all unsuited to explain the feelings that obscurely stirred his own heart. The surmise that in a state of enhanced receptivity an overflowing and receding of experiences might arise that would connect the senses boundlessly and gently as a sheet of water with all creation called to mind his long talks with Agathe, and his face involuntarily took on an expression that was partly obdurate, partly forlorn. Tuzzi studied him from under his indolently raised eyelids and gathered from the form of Ulrich's sarcasm that he himself was not the only person present who was "dammed up" in a manner not of his own choice.

Both of them hardly noticed how long Rachel was taking. She had been detained by Diotima, who had needed her help in quickly putting herself and her sickroom into an ordered state of suffering that would be informal, yet proper for receiving Ulrich. Now the maid brought a message that Ulrich should not leave but be patient just a bit longer, and then hurried back to her mistress.

"All those quotations you cited are of course allegories," Ulrich continued after this interruption, to make up to his host for having to keep him company. "A kind of butterfly language! And people like Arnheim give me the impression that they can guzzle themselves potbellied with this vaporous nectar of theirs! I mean . . . ," he hastened to add, remembering just in time that he must not include Diotima in the insult, "I have this impression about Arnheim in particular, just as he also paradoxically gives the impression that he carries his soul in his breast pocket like a wallet!"

Tuzzi put down his briefcase and gloves, which he had picked up when Rachel appeared, and said with some force: "Do you realize what this is? I mean, what you've explained to me so well. It's nothing but the spirit of pacifism!" He paused to let this revelation sink in. "In the hand of amateurs, pacifism can be extremely dangerous!" he added portentously.

Ulrich would have laughed, but Tuzzi was being dead serious; he had, in fact, linked two things that actually were distantly related, funny as it might be to see how love and pacifism were connected for him in an impression of dilettantish debauchery. At a loss for an answer, Ulrich took the occasion to fall back on the Parallel Campaign and its chosen watchword, "Action!"

"That's a Leinsdorf idea," Tuzzi said disdainfully. "Do you recall the last discussion here before you went away? Leinsdorf said: 'Something's got to be done!' That's all there was to it, and that's what they mean by their new watchword, 'Action!' And Arnheim is of course trying to foist his Russian pacifism on it. Do you remember how I warned them about it? I'm afraid they'll have cause to remember me! Nowhere in the world is foreign policy as difficult as it is here, and I said even then: 'Whoever takes it upon himself these days to put fundamental political ideas into practice has to be part gambler and part criminal.'" This time, Tuzzi was really opening up, probably because Ulrich might be called by his wife at any moment, or because in this conversation he did not want to be the only one to have things explained to him.

"The Parallel Campaign is arousing suspicion all over the world," he reported, "and at home, where it's being viewed as both anti-German and anti-Slav, it's also having repercussions in our foreign relations. But if you want to know the difference between amateur and professional pacifism, let me tell you something: Austria could prevent a war for at least thirty years by joining the Entente Cordiale! And this could of course be done on the Emperor's Jubilee with a matchless pacifist flourish, while at the same time we assure Germany of our brotherly love whether or not she follows suit. The majority of our nationalities would be overjoyed. With easy French and English credit we could make our army so strong that Germany couldn't bully us. We'd be rid of Italy altogether. France wouldn't be able to do a thing without us. In short, we would be the key to peace and war, we'd make the big political deals. I'm not giving away any secrets; this is a simple diplomatic calculation that any commercial attaché could work out. So why can't it be done? Imponderables at Court. Where they dislike the Emperor so heartily that they'd consider it almost indecent to let it happen. Monarchies are at a disadvantage today because they're weighed down by decency! Then there are imponderables of so-called public opinion—which brings me to the Parallel Campaign. Why doesn't it educate public opinion? Why doesn't it teach the public to see things objectively? You see"— but at this point Tuzzi's statements lost some of their plausibility and began to sound more like concealed affliction—"this fellow Arnheim really amuses me with those books he writes! He didn't invent writing, and the other night, when I couldn't fall asleep, I had time to

think about it a little. There have always been politicians who wrote
novels or plays, like Clemenceau, for instance, or Disraeli; not Bismarck, but Bismarck was a destroyer. And now look at those French
lawyers who are at the helm today: enviable! Political profiteers, but
with a first-rate diplomatic corps to advise them, to give them guidelines, and all of them have at one time or another dashed off plays or
novels without the slightest embarrassment, at least when they were
young, and even today they're still writing books. Do you think these
books are worth anything? I don't. But I give you my word that last
night I was thinking that our own diplomats are missing out on something because they're not writing books too. And I'll tell you why:
First of all, it's as true for a diplomat as for an athlete that he has to
sweat off his excess water. Secondly, it's good for public security. Do
you know what the European balance of power is?"

They were interrupted by Rachel, who came to tell Ulrich that Diotima was expecting him. Tuzzi let her hand him his hat and coat. "If
you were a patriot . . . ," he said, slipping into the sleeves as Rachel
held his coat for him.

"What would I do then?" Ulrich asked him, looking at the black
pupils of Rachel's eyes.

"If you were a patriot, you'd alert my wife or Count Leinsdorf to
some of these problems. I can't do it myself—coming from a husband it could easily seem narrow-minded."

"But nobody here takes me seriously," Ulrich said calmly.

"Oh, don't say that!" Tuzzi cried out. "They may not take you seriously the way they take other people seriously, but for a long time
now they've all been quite afraid of you. They're afraid that you're
liable to put Leinsdorf up to something crazy. Do you know what the
European balance of power is?" the diplomat probed intently.

"I suppose so; more or less," Ulrich said.

"Then I must congratulate you!" Tuzzi flared up bitterly. "We professional diplomats have no idea—none of us do. It is what mustn't
be disturbed if people are not to be at each other's throats. But what
it is that mustn't be disturbed, no one knows exactly. Just cast your
mind back a little over what's been going on around you these last
few years and is still going on: the Italo-Turkish war, Poincaré in
Moscow, the Baghdad question, armed intervention in Libya, Aus-
tro-Serbian tensions, the Adriatic problem . . . Is that a balance? Our

never-to-be-forgotten Baron Ährenthal— But I mustn't keep you any longer!"

"Too bad," Ulrich said. "If that's what the European balance of power comes to, then it's the best possible expression of the European spirit!"

"Yes, that's what makes it so interesting," Tuzzi replied from the door, with an indulgent smile. "And from that point of view the spiritual achievement of our Parallel Campaign is not to be underestimated!"

"Why don't you put a stop to it?"

Tuzzi shrugged his shoulders. "In this country, if a man in His Grace's position wants something, one can't come out against it. All one can do is just keep one's eyes open."

"And how have you been getting on?" Ulrich asked the little black-and-white sentry who was now taking him to Diotima.

17

DIOTIMA HAS CHANGED THE BOOKS
SHE READS

"My dear friend," Diotima said when Ulrich came in, "I didn't want to let you leave without having a word with you, but to have to receive you in this state . . . !" She was wearing a negligee in which her majestic form, through its accidental position, looked slightly pregnant; this lent the proud body, which had never given birth, something of the lovely abandon of the travail of motherhood. Beside her on the sofa lay a fur collar, which she had obviously been using to keep herself warm, and on her forehead a compress against migraine had been allowed to stay in place because she knew it was decorative, like a Greek headband. Though it was late, no lamp had been lit, and the mingled scent of medications and fresheners for some unknown malaise hung in the air, mixed with a powerful fragrance that had been tossed over all the individual odors like a blanket.

Ulrich bent his face low to kiss Diotima's hand, as if he were trying to make out from the scent of her arm what changes had taken place during his absence. But her skin exuded only the same rich, well-fed, well-bathed aroma it always did.

"Ah, my friend, how good it is to have you back! Oh!" she suddenly moaned, but with a smile. "I'm having the most awful cramps!"

Such information, from a straightforward person as neutral as a weather report, on Diotima's lips took on all the emphasis of a breakdown and a confession.

"Dear cousin!" Ulrich exclaimed, and leaned forward with a smile to look into her face. For an instant Ulrich confused Tuzzi's delicate hint about his wife's indisposition with a conjecture that Diotima had become pregnant, which would have been a momentous turn of events for the household.

Half guessing what was in his mind, she made a languid gesture of denial. What she had was only menstrual cramps, which were, however, something new in her experience; she had begun having them only in the last few months, suggesting an obscure connection with her wavering between Arnheim and her husband. When she heard of Ulrich's return it gave her some comfort, and she welcomed him as the confidant of her struggles, which is why she had received him. She lay there, with only a token pretense of sitting up, abandoned to the pains that raged within her, and was in his company a piece of untrammeled nature, without fences or No Trespassing signs, a rare enough condition with her. She had assumed she could convincingly plead a nervous stomachache, no more than a sign of a sensitive constitution; otherwise, she would not have let him see her.

"Why don't you take something for it?" Ulrich asked her.

"Ah," Diotima sighed, "it's only this excitement. My nerves can't take it much longer!"

There was a little pause, because this was really Ulrich's cue to inquire after Arnheim, but he was more interested in finding out about the things that directly concerned himself, and he could not immediately find a way. Finally, he asked:

"Liberating the soul from civilization is not so easy, I suppose?" and added: "I'm afraid I can flatter myself that I predicted long since that your efforts to blaze a trail for the spirit into the world would come to a painful end!"

Diotima remembered how she had escaped from the reception and sat with Ulrich on the shoe bench in her foyer: she had been almost as depressed then as she was today, and yet there had been countless risings and ebbings of hope since then.

"Wasn't it glorious, dear friend," she said, "when we still believed in the great idea! Today I can say that the world listened, but how deeply disappointed I am myself!"

"But why, actually?" Ulrich asked.

"I don't know. It must be my fault."

She was about to add something about Arnheim, but Ulrich wanted to know what people had made of the great demonstration; the last he remembered of it was not finding Diotima at home after Count Leinsdorf had sent him to prepare her for some firm intervention, while making sure she would not worry.

Diotima made a disdainful gesture. "The police arrested a few young people, and then they let them go; Leinsdorf was very annoyed, but what else could they do? Now he's backing Wisnieczky more than ever, and insists that something must be done. But Wisnieczky can't organize any propaganda if no one knows what it's supposed to be for!"

"I hear it's supposed to be 'Watchword: Action!'" Ulrich interjected. The name of Baron Wisnieczky, who as Cabinet Minister had been wrecked by the opposition of the German nationalist parties—so that putting him at the head of the committee to drum up support for the undefined great patriotic idea of the Parallel Campaign could only arouse intense suspicion—vividly reminded Ulrich of His Grace's political ministrations, whose fruit this was. It seemed that the casual course of Count Leinsdorf's thinking—perhaps confirmed by the predictable failure of all attempts to electrify the spirit of the homeland, and beyond that of all Europe, by a concerted effort of its leading intellects—had now led him to the realization that it would be best to give this spirit a push, no matter from what direction. In His Grace's deliberations this might also have been supported by experiences with cases of possession, whose victims were sometimes supposed to be helped by being ruthlessly screamed at or shaken. But this speculation, which had rushed through Ulrich's mind before Diotima could reply, was now interrupted by her answer. This time, the invalid again addressed him as "dear friend."

"My dear friend," she said, "there is some truth in that! Our century is thirsting for action. An action—"

"But what action? What kind of action?" Ulrich broke in.

"It doesn't matter! In action there is a magnificent pessimism about words. We can't deny that in the past all we have done is talk. We have lived for great and eternal words and ideals; for a heightening of human values; for being true to our inmost selves; for an ever-increasing enrichment of life. We have striven for a synthesis, we have lived for new aesthetic joys and new standards of happiness, and I won't deny that the quest for truth is child's play compared with the immense responsibility of becoming a truth oneself. But we overreached, considering the meager sense of reality the human soul has in our time, and we have lived in a dream of yearning, but for nothing!"

Diotima had urgently risen on one elbow. "It's a healthy sign these days to renounce the search for the buried entrance to the soul and try instead to come to terms with life as it is!" she concluded.

Now Ulrich had a second, authorized version of the slogan "Action!" to set beside the conjectural Leinsdorfian one. Diotima seemed to have changed her library books. He remembered seeing her, as he came in, surrounded by piles of books, but it had grown too dark to make out the titles; besides, some were covered by the meditative young woman's body as by a great serpent that had now reared up higher and was eagerly watching his face. Since girlhood Diotima had been inclined to nourish herself on very sentimental and subjective books, but now, as Ulrich gathered from what she said, she had been seized by that spiritual urge for renewal which is constantly at work, striving to find what it has failed to find in the ideas of the last twenty years in the ideas of the next twenty years. This may turn out to be the root of those great changes of mood in history, which seesaw between humanitarianism and ruthlessness, rage and indifference, or other such contradictions for which there seems to be no adequate explanation. It passed through Ulrich's mind that the little residue of uncertainty left over from every moral experience, about which he had talked so much with Agathe, must really be the cause of this human instability; but because he shied away from the pleasure with which he remembered those conversations, he forced his thoughts to turn aside and focus instead on the General, who had been the first to tell him that the age was receiving a new spirit, and had done so in a tone of healthy irritation that left no room for beguiling oneself with bewitching doubts. And because he was now thinking of the General, the latter's request that Ulrich might look into the ruffled relationship between his cousin and Arnheim came to mind, so that he ended by responding bluntly to Diotima's speech of farewell to the soul:

" 'Boundless love' doesn't seem to have quite agreed with you!"

"Oh, you're incorrigible!" His cousin sighed, letting herself fall back into her pillows, where she closed her eyes; unaccustomed to such straightforward language in Ulrich's absence, she needed time to recollect just how much she had confided in him. But suddenly his nearness brought it back. She dimly remembered a talk with Ulrich about "love beyond measure," which had been continued at their last or penultimate meeting: a conversation in which she had sworn that souls could step outside the prison of the body, or at least lean out of it halfway, as it were, and Ulrich had retorted that these were the delirious ravings of starved love, and that she should concede her "concession" to Arnheim, or himself, or anyone at all; he had even named Tuzzi in that connection, as she now recalled—suggestions of this kind were probably easier to remember than the rest of the things a man like Ulrich talks about. At the time, she had probably been justified in feeling this as impudent, but since past pain is a harmless old friend compared with present pain, it now enjoyed the advantage of being a memory of frankness between friends. So Diotima opened her eyes again and said: "There's probably no perfect love on this earth!"

She said it with a smile, but beneath her compress her brow was sadly furrowed, which gave her face a curiously twisted expression in the dim light. In whatever concerned her personally Diotima was not averse to believing in supernatural possibilities. Even General Stumm's unexpected appearance at the Council meeting had startled her as though it were the doing of spirits, and as a child she had prayed that she might never die. This made it easier for her to believe in a supernatural way in her relationship with Arnheim, or more accurately, to believe with that not quite complete disbelief, that something-that-cannot-be-ruled-out, which today has become the basic attitude in matters of faith. Had Arnheim been capable of doing more than drawing something invisible from her soul and his own, something that touched in midair when they were five yards apart, or had their eyes been able to meet in such a way that something tangible would come of it—a coffee bean, a barleycorn, an ink stain—some trace of some kind of real use or even just a suggestion of progress, then the next thing Diotima would have expected was that someday this connection would go higher still, turning into one of those otherworldly connections that it is just as hard to form an exact idea of as it is of most worldly ones. She could even put up with Arnheim's lately being away more often and for longer periods than before, and his being immersed to a surprising degree in his business affairs even on days when he was present. She permitted herself no doubt that his love for her was still the great event in his life, and whenever they came together again alone, the level of their souls instantly rose so high, and their sense of contact was so powerful, that their feelings were struck dumb, and if they could not find anything impersonal to talk about, a vacuum developed that left a bitter exhaustion in its wake. However little the possibility could be excluded that this was passion, she could just as little bring herself—accustomed as she was by the times she lived in to regard everything not practical as merely a matter of belief, or rather of unsettled unbelief—to exclude the possibility that something more would come of it, which would be contrary to all reasonable expectations. But at this moment, when she had opened her eyes to look straight at Ulrich, of whom she could make out only a dark outline, and who stood there in silence, she asked herself: "What *am* I waiting for? What am I really expecting to happen?"

At length Ulrich said: "But Arnheim wanted to marry you!"

Diotima again propped herself up on her arm, and she said: "Can one solve the problem of love by getting divorced or married?"

"So I was mistaken about the pregnancy," Ulrich noted mentally, unable to think of anything to say in response to his cousin's outburst. Then he said abruptly: "I warned you about Arnheim!" Perhaps he now felt obligated to tell her what he knew about the tycoon's mixing up both their souls in his business deals; but he instantly dropped the idea, for he felt that in this conversation every word had its allotted place, like the objects in his study that he had found carefully dusted on his return, as though he had been dead for the space of a minute.

Diotima chided him: "You shouldn't take it so lightly. There's a deep friendship between Arnheim and me; and if at times there's also something else between us, something I might call a great anxiety, it only comes from our frankness. I don't know whether you've ever experienced this, or whether you can: between two people who reach a certain level of emotional rapport any lie becomes so impossible that they can hardly speak to each other at all anymore!"

In this reproof Ulrich's finely tuned ear heard that his cousin's soul was more accessible to him than usual, and because he was highly amused by her unintended confession that she could not talk with Arnheim without lying, he demonstrated his own openness for a while by not saying anything either. Then, when she had lain back again, he bent over her arm and kissed its hand in a gentle gesture of friendship. Light as the marrow of elder twigs it rested in his own, and remained lying there even after the kiss. Her pulse throbbed on his fingertips. The powder-fine scent of her nearness clung to his face like a puff of cloud. And although this gallant kiss on the hand had been only in jest, it was like infidelity in leaving behind a certain bitter aftertaste of desire, of having leaned so closely over a person that one drank from her like an animal, and no longer saw one's own image rising back up out of the water.

"What are you thinking?" Diotima asked. Ulrich merely shook his head and so gave her a fresh opportunity—in the darkness that was brightened only by a last velvety glimmering—to make comparative studies of silence. She was reminded of a wonderful saying: "There are people with whom not even the greatest hero would trust himself to remain silent." Or it was something like that. She seemed to remember that it was a quotation; Arnheim had used it, and she had applied it to herself. Other than Arnheim's, she had since the first weeks of her marriage never held a man's hand in hers for longer than two seconds; but it was happening now with Ulrich's hand. Wrapped up in herself as she was, she overlooked what the next step might be, but found herself a moment later pleasantly convinced that she had been quite right not to wait idly for the hour of supreme love—perhaps yet to come, perhaps not—but to use the time of temporizing indecision to devote herself somewhat more to her husband. Married people have it easy; where others would be breaking faith with a lover, they can say that they are remembering their duty.

And because Diotima told herself that, come what might, she must do her duty for now at the post where fate had placed her, she had undertaken to improve her husband's shortcomings and infuse him with a little more soul. Again a poet's words came to mind, roughly to the effect that there was no deeper despair than to be entwined in a common fate with a person one did not love; and that also proved that she must make an effort to feel something for Tuzzi as long as their fate had not separated them. In sensible contrast to the incalculable events of the soul, from which she had made him suffer long enough, she set about it systematically; she felt pride in the books on which she was lying, for they concerned themselves with the physiology and psychology of marriage, and somehow everything harmonized: that it was dark, that she had these books by her, that Ulrich was holding her hand, that she had conveyed to him the magnificent pessimism that she might soon be expressing in her public role by renouncing her ideals. So thinking, Diotima pressed Ulrich's hand from time to time as if her suitcases were standing packed for her to take leave of everything that had been. She moaned softly, and the faintest wave of pain ran through her body by way of excuse; but Ulrich reassured her with the pressure of his fingertips. After this had happened several times, Diotima thought it really might be too much, yet she no longer dared to withdraw her hand, because it lay so light and dry in his, even trembling at times, as she herself recognized, like an inadmissible indication of the physiology of love, which she had not the slightest intention of betraying by some awkward movement of flight.

It was "Rachelle," busying herself in the adjoining room—she had been acting in an oddly impertinent fashion lately—who put an end to this scene by suddenly turning on the light on the other side of the open door. Diotima hastily pulled her hand away from Ulrich's, in which a space that had been filled with weightlessness remained lying for a moment longer.

"Rachelle," Diotima called in a hushed voice, "turn the light on in here too!"

When this was done their illumined heads had the look of something just emerged from the depths, as though the darkness had not quite dried off them. Shadows lay around Diotima's mouth, giving it moistness and fullness; the little mother-of-pearl bulges on her neck and under her cheeks, which ordinarily seemed to have been created for the delectation of lovers, were hard as a linocut and shaded with slashes of ink. Ulrich's head, too, loomed up in the unaccustomed light, painted in black and white like that of a savage on the warpath. Blinking, he tried to make out the titles on the books surrounding Diotima, and saw with amazement what his cousin's choice of reading matter revealed about her desire to learn the hygiene of body and soul. "Someday he's going to hurt me!" she suddenly thought, following his glance and troubled by it, but it did not enter her consciousness in the form of that sentence: she merely felt much too defenseless as she lay there in the light under his gaze and struggled to recover her poise. With a gesture meant to be thoroughly superior, as befitted a woman "independent" of everything, she waved her hand over her reading and said in the most matter-of-fact tone: "Would you believe that adultery sometimes strikes me as far too simple a solution for marital conflict?"

"At all events it's the most sparing," Ulrich replied, irritating her with his mocking tone. "I'd say it can do no harm at all."

Diotima gave him a reproachful look and made a sign to warn him that Rachel could hear what they were saying from the next room. Then she said aloud: "That's certainly not what I meant!" and called her maid, who appeared sullenly and accepted with bitter jealousy her being sent out.

This interlude had, however, given their feelings time to put themselves to rights. The illusion, favored by the darkness, that they were committing a tiny infidelity together, though rather indefinably and toward no one in particular, evaporated in the light, and Ulrich now turned to the business that had to be attended to before he could leave.

"I haven't yet told you that I'm resigning as Secretary," he began.

Diotima, however, had heard of it, and told him that he would have to stay on; there was no way out of it. "There's such an immense amount of work still to be done," she pleaded. "Be patient a while longer; we're bound to find a solution soon! A real secretary will be found to place at your disposal."

This impersonal "will be found" aroused Ulrich's curiosity, and he asked for details.

"Arnheim has offered to lend you his own secretary."

"No, thanks," Ulrich replied. "I have the feeling that might not be quite disinterested." Again he was more than strongly tempted to let Diotima in on the simple connection with the oil fields, but she had not even noticed the ambiguity of his answer, and simply continued:

"Apart from that, my husband has also offered to let you have one of the clerks in his office."

"Wouldn't you mind?"

"To be frank, I wouldn't be entirely happy about that," Diotima said more energetically. "Especially as there's no dearth of possibilities. Even your friend the General has given me to understand that he'd be delighted to send you an aide from his department."

"And Leinsdorf?"

"These three offers were made to me spontaneously, so I had no reason to ask Leinsdorf; but I'm sure he wouldn't shrink from making a sacrifice."

"Everyone's spoiling me," Ulrich commented, summing up with these words the amazing readiness of Arnheim, Tuzzi, and Stumm to plant a man of their own inside the Parallel Campaign at such low cost. "But perhaps it would be most advisable for me to take on your husband's clerk."

"My dear friend—" Diotima said, still protesting, but she did not really know how to go on, which was probably why something quite tangled came out. Again she propped herself up on an elbow and said with feeling: "I reject adultery as too crude a solution of marital conflicts—I've told you that! But even so, there's nothing so hard as being linked for life in a single destiny with a person one doesn't love enough!"

This was a most unnatural cry of nature. But Ulrich, unmoved, would not be shaken from his resolve. "No doubt Section Chief Tuzzi would like this way of having a hand in your operation; but so would the others," he pointed out. "All three are in love with you, and each of them has to reconcile this somehow with his duty." How odd, he thought, that Diotima did not understand either the language of facts or that of the comments he made on them, and rising to take his leave, he added with even heavier irony: "The only one who loves you unselfishly is myself—because I have no duties of any kind and no commitments. But feelings without distraction are destructive; you've meanwhile found that out for yourself, and you have always regarded me with a justifiable, even if only instinctive, mistrust."

Although Diotima did not know why, this was precisely and endearingly the reason that she was pleased to see Ulrich siding with her own house in this matter of the secretary, and she did not let go of the hand he offered her.

"And how does this fit in with your affair with 'that' woman?" she asked, playfully taking her cue from his remark—insofar as Diotima could be playful; the effect was rather that of a shot-putter playing with a feather.

Ulrich did not know whom she could mean.

"That judge's wife you introduced to me!"

"You noticed that, cousin?"

"Dr. Arnheim drew my attention to it."

"Oh, did he? How flattering that he should think he can hurt my standing with you in this fashion. But of course my relations with the lady are entirely innocent!" Ulrich stated, defending Bonadea's honor in the conventional fashion.

"She was in your house twice during your absence," Diotima said with a laugh. "The first time, we happened to be passing by, and we heard about the second time some other way. So there's no point in trying to be discreet. But on the other hand, I wish I could understand *you*! I simply *can't!*"

"How on earth could I explain this to you, of all people!"

"Try!" Diotima commanded. She had put on her expression of "official immorality," a sort of bespectacled look she donned whenever her mind commanded her to speak or hear things that were out of bounds for her soul as a lady. But Ulrich declined and repeated that his understanding of Bonadea could only be guesswork.

"All right," Diotima gave in, "even though your lady friend herself was not sparing with her hints! She seems to feel called upon to justify some wrong or other in my eyes. But do speak of this, if you'd rather, as if you were merely guessing!"

Now Ulrich felt a thirst for knowledge, and he learned that Bonadea had been to see Diotima several times, and not only in matters connected with the Parallel Campaign and her husband's position.

"I must admit I find her a beautiful woman," Diotima conceded, "and she is extraordinarily high-minded. I'm really upset that you're always eliciting confidences from me but always withholding yours!"

At this moment Ulrich's attitude was approximately "the devil take both of you!" He felt like giving Diotima a scare and paying Bonadea back for her intrusiveness, or else he was suddenly feeling the full distance between himself and the life in which he had been indulging.

"All right," he told her, summoning up a gloomy expression: "The woman is a nymphomaniac and I find that irresistible!"

Diotima knew "academically" what nymphomania was. There was a pause, and then she drawled: "The poor woman! And you find *that* attractive?"

"Isn't it idiotic?" Ulrich said.

Diotima wanted to know "the details"—would he explain this "lamentable phenomenon" and enable her to understand it in "human terms"? He did so without exactly going into detail, but she was nevertheless overcome by a feeling of satisfaction that doubtless rested on that well-known gratitude to God that she was not like the other woman; but at its apex this feeling faded into dismay and curiosity, which was not to be without influence on her subsequent relations with Ulrich. Pensively she said: "But it must be simply awful to embrace a person who doesn't mean anything to you!"

"You think so?" her cousin asked candidly. At this insinuation Diotima felt hurt and indignant to the marrow, but she could not let herself show it; she contented herself with letting go of his hand and sinking back into her pillows with a dismissive gesture. "You never should have told me this!" she said from where she lay. "You treated that poor woman very badly just now, and you've been most indiscreet!"

"I'm never indiscreet!" Ulrich objected, and could not help laughing at his cousin. "You're really being unfair. You are the first woman to whom I've ever confided anything about another woman, and it was you who made me do it!"

Diotima was flattered. She wanted to say something of the same kind, to the effect that without a spiritual transformation one cheated oneself of the best in life; but she could not come out with it because it suddenly seemed too personal. Finally, something from one of the books surrounding her prompted her to answer noncommittally, from within the protection of her official persona: "Like all men," she chided him, "you make the mistake of treating your love partner not as an equal but merely as a complement to yourself, and then you're disappointed. Has it never occurred to you that the only way to a transcendent, harmonious eroticism may lie through stricter self-discipline?"

Ulrich's jaw nearly dropped, but he answered in spontaneous self-defense: "Do you know that Section Chief Tuzzi has already grilled me today on the possibilities of the origin and training of the soul?"

Diotima sat up straight: "What? Tuzzi talks with you about soul?" she asked in amazement.

"Of course he does; he's trying to find out what it is," Ulrich assured her, but he could not be induced to stay any longer. He merely promised to betray a confidence some other time and tell her all about that too.

18

PROBLEMS OF A MORALIST WITH
A LETTER TO WRITE

With this visit to Diotima the restless state Ulrich had been in since his return came to an end. On the afternoon of the very next day he sat down at his desk, and in doing so felt at home again, and began writing a letter to Agathe.

It was clear to him—as simple and clear as a windless day sometimes is—that her rash scheme was extremely dangerous. What had happened so far could still be taken as a risky prank, of no concern to anyone but themselves, but that depended entirely on its being rescinded before it acquired connections with reality, and the danger was growing with every passing day. Ulrich had written this much when he stopped, uneasy at the thought of entrusting to the mails a letter in which this was so openly discussed. He told himself that it would be better in every way to take the next train back, in place of the letter; but of course this made no sense to him either, since he had let days go by without doing anything about it. He knew he would not go.

He realized that there was something behind this tantamount to a choice: he simply felt like letting things take their course and seeing what came of this incident. So his problem was just how far he actually, definitely *could* want to risk it, and all sorts of wide-ranging thoughts went through his mind.

It occurred to him right at the start, for instance, that whenever he had taken a "moral" stance so far, he had always been psychologically worse off than when he was doing or thinking something that might usually be considered "immoral." This is a common occurrence, for in situations that are in conflict with their surroundings these ideas and actions develop all their energies, while in the mere doing of what is right and proper they understandably behave as if they were paying taxes. This suggests that all evil is carried out with zest and imagination, while good is distinguished by an unmistakable dreariness and dearth of feeling. Ulrich recalled that his sister had expressed this moral dilemma quite casually by asking him whether being good was no longer a good thing. It ought to be difficult and breathtaking, she had maintained, and wondered why, nevertheless, moral people were almost always bores.

He smiled contentedly, spinning this thought out with the realization that Agathe and he were as one in their particular opposition to Hagauer, which could be roughly characterized as that of people who were bad in a good way to a man who was good in a bad way. Leaving out of account the broad middle of life's spectrum, which is, reasonably enough, occupied by people whose minds have not been troubled by the general terms good and evil since they let go of their mother's apron strings, there remain the two extremes where purposeful moral efforts are still made. Today these are left to just such bad/good and good/bad people, the first kind never having seen good fly or heard it sing, thus expecting their fellowmen to enthuse with them about a moral landscape where stuffed birds perch on dummy trees, while the second kind, the good/bad mortals, exasperated by their competitors, industriously show a penchant for evil, at least in theory, as if they were convinced that only wrongdoing, which is emotionally not quite as threadbare as doing good, still twitches with a bit of moral vitality. And so Ulrich's world—not, of course, that he was fully aware of this—had at that time the option of letting itself be ruined by either its lame morality or its lively immoralists, and to this day it probably does not know which of those two choices it finally embraced with stunning success, unless that majority who can never spare the time to concern themselves with morality in general did pay attention to one case in particular because they had lost confidence in their own situation and, as a result, had of course lost a number of other things as well. For bad/bad people, who can so easily be blamed for everything, were even then as rare as they are today, and the good/good ones represent a mission as far removed as a distant nebula. Still, it was precisely of them that Ulrich was thinking, while everything else he appeared to be thinking about left him cold.

And he gave his thoughts an even more general and impersonal form by setting the relationship that exists between the demands "Do!" and "Don't!" in the place of good and evil. For as long as a particular morality is in the ascendant—and this is just as valid for the spirit of "Love thy neighbor" as it is for a horde of Vandals— "Don't!" is still only the negative and natural corollary of "Do!" Doing and leaving undone are red hot, and the flaws they contain don't count because they are the flaws of heroes and martyrs. In this condition good and evil are identical with the happiness and unhappiness of the whole person. But as soon as the contested system has achieved dominance and spread itself out, and its fulfillment no longer faces any special hurdles, the relationship between imperative and taboo perforce passes through a decisive phase where duty is not born anew and alive each day but is leached and drained and cut up into ifs and buts, ready to serve all sorts of uses. Here a process begins, in the further course of which virtue and vice, because of their common root in the same rules, laws, exceptions, and limitations, come to look more and more alike, until that curious and ultimately unbearable self-contradiction arises which was Ulrich's point of departure: namely, that the distinction between good and evil loses all meaning when weighed against the pleasure of a pure, deep, spontaneous mode of action, a pleasure that can leap like a spark from permissible as well as from forbidden activities. Indeed, whoever takes an unbiased view is likely to find that the negative aspect of

morality is more highly charged with this tension than the positive:
While it seems relatively natural that certain actions called "bad"
must not be allowed to happen, actions such as taking what belongs
to others or overindulgence in sensual gratification, or, if they are
committed, at least *ought* not to be committed, the corresponding
affirmative moral traditions, such as unlimited generosity in giving or
the urge to mortify the flesh, have already almost entirely disappeared; and where they are still practiced they are practiced by fools,
cranks, or bloodless prigs. In such a condition, where virtue is de-
crepit and moral conduct consists chiefly in the restraint of immoral
conduct, it can easily happen that immoral conduct appears to be not
only more spontaneous and vital than its opposite, but actually more
moral, if one may use the term not in the sense of law and justice but
with regard to whatever passion may still be aroused by matters of
conscience. But could anything possibly be more perverse than to
incline inwardly toward evil because, with all one has left of a soul,
one is seeking good?

Ulrich had never felt this perversity more keenly than at this moment, when the rising arc his reflections had followed led him back
to Agathe again. Her innate readiness to act in the good/bad mode—
to resort once more to the term they had coined in passing—as so
notably exemplified in her tampering with their father's will, offended the same innate readiness in his own nature, which had
merely taken on an abstract theoretical form, something like a
priest's admiration of the Devil, while as a person he was not only
able to lead his life more or less according to the rules but even, as he
could see, did not wish to be disturbed in so doing. With as much
melancholy satisfaction as ironic clear-sightedness, he noted that
all his theoretical preoccupation with evil basically amounted to
this, that he wanted to protect the bad things that happened from
the bad people who undertook them, and he was suddenly overcome
by a longing for goodness, like a man who has been wasting his time
in foreign parts dreaming of coming home one day and going straight
to the well in his native village for a drink of water. If he had not
been caught up in this comparison, he might have noticed that his
whole effort to see Agathe as a morally confused person, such as the
present age produces in profusion, was only a pretext to screen out a
prospect that frightened him a good deal more. For his sister's con-

duct, which certainly did not pass muster objectively, exerted a remarkable fascination as soon as one dreamed along with it; for then all the controversies and indecisions vanished, and one was left with the impression of a passionate, affirmative virtue lusting for action, which could easily seem, compared with its lifeless daily counterpart, to be some kind of ancient vice.

Ulrich was not the man to indulge himself lightly in such exaltations of his feelings, least of all with this letter to write, so he redirected his mind into general reflections. These would have been incomplete had he not remembered how easily and often, in the times he had lived through, the longing for some duty rooted in completeness had led to first one virtue, then another, being singled out from among the available supply, to be made the focus of noisy glorification. National, Christian, humanistic virtues had all taken their turn; once, it was the virtue of chromium steel, another time, the virtue of kindness; then it was individuality, and then fellowship; today it is the fraction of a second, and yesterday it was historical equilibrium. The changing moods of public life basically depend on the exchange of one such ideal for another: it had always left Ulrich unmoved, and only made him feel that he was standing on the sidelines. Even now all it meant for him was a filling in of the general picture, for only incomplete insight can lead one to believe that one can get at life's moral inexplicability, whose complications have become overwhelming, by means of one of the interpretations already embedded within it. Such efforts merely resemble the movements of a sick person restlessly changing his position, while the paralysis that felled him progresses inexorably. Ulrich was convinced that the state of affairs that gave rise to these efforts was inescapable and characterized the level from which every civilization goes into decline, because no civilization has so far been capable of replacing its lost inner elasticity. He was also convinced that the same thing that had happened to every past moral system would happen to every future one. For the slackening of moral energy has nothing to do with the province of the Commandments or the keeping of them: it is independent of their distinctions; it cannot be affected by any outer discipline but is an entirely inner process, synonymous with the weakening of the significance of all actions and of faith in the unity of responsibility for them.

And so Ulrich's thoughts, without his having intended it, found their way back to the idea he had ironically characterized to Count Leinsdorf as the "General Secretariat for Precision and Soul," and although he had never spoken of it other than flippantly and in jest, he now realized that all his adult life he had consistently behaved as though such a General Secretariat lay within the realm of possibility. Perhaps, he could say by way of excuse, every thoughtful person harbors in himself some such idea of order, just as grown men may still wear next to their skin the picture of a saint that their mother hung around their necks when they were small. And this image of order, which no one dares either to take seriously or to put away, must be more or less something like this: On one hand, it vaguely stands for the longing for some law of right living, a natural, iron law that allows no exceptions and excludes no objections: that is, as liberating as intoxication and sober as the truth. On the other hand, however, it evinces the conviction that one will never behold such a law with one's own eyes, never think it out with one's own thoughts, that no one person's mission or power can bring it about but only an effort by everyone—unless it is only a delusion.

Ulrich hesitated for an instant. He was doubtless a believing person who just didn't believe in anything. Even in his greatest dedication to science he had never managed to forget that people's goodness and beauty come from what they believe, not from what they know. But faith had always been bound up with knowledge, even if that knowledge was illusory, ever since those primordial days of its magic beginnings. That ancient knowledge has long since rotted away, dragging belief down with it into the same decay, so that today the connection must be established anew. Not, of course, by raising faith "to the level of knowledge," but by still in some way making it take flight from that height. The art of transcending knowledge must again be practiced. And since no one man can do this, all men must turn their minds to it, whatever else their minds might be on. When Ulrich at this moment thought about the ten-year plan, or the hundred- or thousand-year plan that mankind would have to devise in order to work toward a goal it can have no way of knowing, he soon realized that this was what he had long imagined, under all sorts of names, as the truly experimental life. For what he meant by the term "faith" was not so much that stunted desire to know, the credulous ignorance that is what most people take it to be, but rather a knowledgeable intuition, something that is neither knowledge nor fantasy, but is not faith either; it is just that "something else" which eludes all these concepts.

He suddenly pulled the letter toward him, but immediately pushed it away again.

The stern glow on his face went out, and his dangerous favorite idea struck him as ridiculous. As though with one glance through a suddenly opened window, he felt what was really around him: cannons and business deals. The notion that people who lived in this fashion could ever join in a planned navigation of their spiritual destiny was simply inconceivable, and Ulrich had to admit that historical development had never come about by means of any such coherent combination of ideas as the mind of the individual may just manage in a pinch; the course of history was always wasteful and dissipated, as if it had been flung on the table by the fist of some low-life gambler. He actually felt a little ashamed. Everything he had thought during the last hour was suspiciously reminiscent of a certain "Inquiry for the Drafting of a Guiding Resolution to Ascertain the Desires of the Concerned Sections of the Population"; even the fact that he was moralizing at all, this thinking theoretically that surveyed Nature by candlelight, seemed completely unnatural, while the simple man, accustomed to the clarity of the sun, goes straight for the next item, unbothered by any problem beyond the very definite one of whether he can risk this move and make it work.

At this point Ulrich's thoughts flowed back again from these general considerations to himself, and he felt what his sister meant to him. It was to her he had revealed that curious and unlimited, incredible, and unforgettable state of mind in which everything is an affirmation: the condition in which one is incapable of any spiritual movement except a moral one, therefore the only state in which there exists a morality without interruption, even though it may only consist in all actions floating ungrounded within it. And all Agathe had done was to stretch out her hand toward it. She was the person who stretched out her hand and made Ulrich's reflections give way to the bodies and forms of the real world. All his thoughts now appeared to him a mere delaying and transition. He decided to "take a chance" on what might come of Agathe's idea, and at this moment he could not care less that the mysterious promise it held out had started with what was commonly viewed as a reprehensible act. One could only wait and see whether the morality of "rising or sinking" would show itself as applicable here as the simple morality of honesty. He remembered his sister's passionate question as to whether he himself believed what he was saying, but he could affirm this even now as little as he could then. He admitted to himself that he was waiting for Agathe to be able to answer this question.

The phone rang shrilly, and Walter was suddenly rushing at him with flustered explanations and hasty snatches of words. Ulrich listened indifferently but readily, and when he put down the receiver and straightened up he still felt the ringing of its bell, now finally stopping. Depth and darkness came flooding back into his surroundings to soothe him, though he could not have said whether it happened as sounds or colors; it was a deepening of all his senses. Smiling, he picked up the sheet of paper on which he had begun writing to his sister and, before he left the room, slowly tore it into tiny pieces.

19

Onward to Moosbrugger

Meanwhile Walter, Clarisse, and the prophet Meingast were sitting around a platter loaded with radishes, tangerines, almonds, big Turkish prunes, and cream cheese, consuming this delicious and wholesome supper. The prophet, again wearing only his wool cardigan over his rather bony torso, made a point now and again of praising the natural refreshments offered to him, while Clarisse's brother, Siegmund, sat apart, with his hat and gloves on, reporting on yet another conversation he had "cultivated" with Dr. Friedenthal, the assistant medical officer at the psychiatric clinic, to make arrangements for his "completely crazy" sister Clarisse to see Moosbrugger.

"Friedenthal insists that he can do it only with a permit from the District Court," he wound up dispassionately, "and the District Court is not satisfied with the application I obtained for all of you from the Final Hour Welfare Society but requires a recommendation from the Embassy, because we lied, unfortunately, about Clarisse's being a foreigner. So there's nothing else to be done: Tomorrow Dr. Meingast will have to go to the Swiss Embassy!"

Siegmund, who was the elder, resembled his sister, except that his face was unexpressive. If one looked at them side by side, the nose, mouth, and eyes in Clarisse's pallid face suggested cracks in parched soil, while the same features in Siegmund's face had the soft, slightly blurred contours of rolling grassland, although he was clean-shaven except for a small mustache. He had not shed his middle-class appearance nearly as much as his sister, and it gave him an ingenuous naturalness even at the moment when he was so brazenly disposing of a philosopher's precious time. No one would have been surprised if thunder and lightning had burst from the plate of radishes at this imposition, but the great man took it amiably—which his admirers regarded as an event that would make a great anecdote—and blinked an assenting eye toward Siegmund like an eagle that tolerates a sparrow on the perch beside him.

Nonetheless, the sudden and insufficiently discharged tension made it impossible for Walter to contain himself any longer. He pushed back his plate, reddened like a little cloud at sunrise, and stated emphatically that no sane person who was neither a doctor nor an attendant had any business inside an insane asylum. On him, too, the sage bestowed a barely perceptible nod. Siegmund, who in the course of his life had appropriated quite a few opinions, articulated this assent with the hygienic words: "It is, no doubt, a revolting habit of the affluent middle class to see something demonic in mental cases and criminals."

"But in that case," Walter exclaimed, "please tell me why you all want to help Clarisse do something you don't approve of and that can only make her more nervous than ever?"

His wife did not dignify this with an answer. She made an unpleasant face, whose expression was so remote from reality as to be frightening; two long, arrogant lines ran down alongside her nose, and her chin came to a hard point. Siegmund did not feel himself obliged or authorized to speak for the others, so Walter's question was followed by a short silence, until Meingast said quietly and equably: "Clarisse has suffered too strong an impression. It can't be left at that."

"When?" Walter demanded.

"Just the other day—that evening at the window."

Walter turned pale, because he was the only one who had not been told before—Clarisse had evidently told Meingast and even her brother. Isn't that just like her! he thought.

And although it was not exactly called for, he suddenly had the feeling, across the plate of produce, that they were all about ten years younger. That was the time when Meingast—still the old, untransformed Meingast—was bowing out and Clarisse had opted for Walter. Later she confessed to him that Meingast had still, even though he had already given her up, sometimes kissed and fondled her. The memory was like the large arc of a swing. Walter had been swung higher and higher: he succeeded in everything he did then, even though there were lots of downswings too. Yet even then Clarisse had been unable to speak with Walter when Meingast was present; he had often had to find out from others what she was thinking and doing. With him she froze up. "When *you* touch me, I freeze up!" she had said to him. "My body goes solemn—that's quite different from the way it is with Meingast!" And when he kissed her for the first time she said to him: "I promised Mother never to do anything like this." Later on, though, she admitted to him that in those days Meingast was always secretly playing footsie with her under the dining room table. It was all Walter's doing! The richness of the inner development he had called forth in her had hindered her freedom of movement, as he explained it to himself.

Now he thought of the letters he and Clarisse had written to each other in those days; he still believed that if one were to search through all of literature it would be hard to find anything to match them for passion and originality. In those stormy days he would punish Clarisse, when she was keeping company with Meingast, by running off—and then he would write her a letter; and she wrote him letters, swearing that she was faithful, while candidly reporting that Meingast had kissed her once again on her knee, through her stocking. Walter had wanted to publish these letters as a book, and still thought, off and on, that he would do so someday. So far, unfortunately, nothing had come of it except for a fateful misunderstanding with Clarisse's governess. One day Walter had said to her: "You'll see, soon I shall make up for everything!" He had only meant it in his sense: namely, how splendidly he would be justified in the family's eyes once publication of the letters brought him fame and success; for strictly speaking, things between him and Clarisse at that time were not what they should be. Clarisse's governess—a family heirloom, pensioned off in the honorable guise of serving as an assistant mother, misunderstood him, however, in her sense, and a rumor promptly arose in the family that Walter was about to put himself in a position to ask for Clarisse's hand in marriage; once the word was out, it led to very particular joys and restraints. "Real life" instantly awakened: Walter's father announced that he would no longer pay his son's bills unless Walter began to earn his keep. Walter's prospective father-in-law invited him to his studio, where he spoke to him of the hardships and disillusionments awaiting the practitioner of pure, disinterested art, whether in the visual arts, music, or literature. And finally both Walter and Clarisse began to itch with the suddenly tangible thought of having their own house, children, openly sharing a bedroom: like a crack in the skin that cannot heal because one unconsciously keeps scratching at it. And so it came to pass that Walter, only a few weeks after his impulsive words, actually became engaged to Clarisse, which made both of them very happy but also very tense, because it was the beginning of that search for an established place in life that burdens life with all the problems of Western civilization, since the position Walter was sporadically seeking had to pass muster not only as to income but as to how it would affect six major aspects of his life: Clarisse, himself, their love life, literature, music, and painting. Actually, they had only recently emerged from the whirlwind of complications unleashed as soon as he let his tongue run off with him in the elderly mademoiselle's company, when he accepted his present position in the Department of Works and Monuments and moved with Clarisse into this modest little house, where the rest was up to fate.

In his heart Walter felt it would be quite pleasant if fate were now to call it a day: though the end would not be precisely what the beginning had promised—but then, when apples are ripe they don't fall up the tree, but to the ground. That was what Walter was thinking, and

meanwhile, across the table from him, above the diametrically opposite end of the colorful tray of wholesome vegetarian food, his wife's
small head hovered; Clarisse was trying to supplement Meingast's
explanation with the utmost objectivity, indeed as objectively as
Meingast himself: "I must do something to pulverize the shock. The
shock was too much for me, Meingast says," she specified, and added
on her own: "It was certainly no coincidence that that man stopped
in the bushes right under my window."

"Nonsense!" Walter waved this away as a sleeper waves off a fly.
"It was just as much my window as yours!"

"Our window, then," Clarisse corrected herself, her thin-lipped
smile so pointed that one could not decide whether it expressed bitterness or scorn. "*We* attracted him. But would you like me to tell
you what that man was doing? He was *stealing* sexual pleasure!"

It made Walter's head ache, crammed full as it was of the past, and
now the present was wedging itself in, leaving no clear difference
between past and present. There were still bushes with their bright
patches of foliage in Walter's head, with bicycle paths winding
among them. Their adventurous long trips and walks could have happened only this morning. Girls' skirts were swinging again just as
they had in those years when ankles had been boldly exposed for the
first time and the hems of white petticoats had frothed with the new
movements of a sports-loving generation. In those days, Walter
thought—to put it mildly—that what was going on between him and
Clarisse was not all it should be, because what happened on these
bike trips in the spring of the year they became engaged was in fact
everything that can happen and leave a girl technically still a virgin.
"Almost incredible, for such a nice girl!" Walter thought, reveling in
his memories. Clarisse had called it "taking Meingast's sins upon
ourselves"—he had just gone abroad and was not yet known as Meingast. "It would be cowardly not to be sensual because he was!" was
the way Clarisse phrased it, adding: "But with you and me I want it to
be spiritual!" Walter did at times worry about the fact that these goings-on were too closely connected with the man who had been gone
such a little while, but Clarisse replied: "People who aim at greatness, as we do in art, for instance, can't be bothered with worrying
about this and that." Walter could remember the zeal with which
they set about annihilating the past by repeating it in a new spirit,

and the relish with which they found out how to excuse illicit physical pleasures by magically attributing to them some transcendent purpose. At that time, Clarisse had been as energetic in her lustfulness as she was later in refusing herself to him, Walter admitted, letting his mind wander for a moment to dwell on the refractory thought that her breasts were still as taut today as they had been then. Everyone could see that, even through her clothes. Meingast happened to be staring at her breasts just then; perhaps he didn't realize it. "Her breasts are mute!" Walter declaimed inwardly with all the richness of association of a dream or a poem; and in almost the same way, while this was happening, the reality of the present forced itself through the padding of emotions:

"Come, Clarisse, tell us what you're thinking," he heard Meingast prompting her, like a doctor or a teacher, in that polite, formal tone he sometimes took with her since his return.

Walter also noticed that Clarisse was looking questioningly at Meingast.

"You were telling me about a certain Moosbrugger, that he was a carpenter. . . ."

Clarisse kept her eyes on him.

"Who else was a carpenter? The Savior! Wasn't that what you said? In fact, you even told me that you had written a letter about it to some influential person, didn't you?"

"Stop it!" Walter burst out. His head was spinning. But he had no sooner expressed his protest than it occurred to him that the letter was something else he had not heard about, and growing weak, he asked: "What letter?"

He got no answer from anyone. Meingast, passing over his question, said: "It's one of the most timely ideas. We're incapable of liberating ourselves by our own efforts, no doubt about it; we call it democracy, but that's merely the political term for our psychological state, our 'you can do it this way, but you can also do it another way.' Ours is the era of the ballot. Each year we determine our sexual ideal, the beauty queen, by ballot, and all we have done by making empirical science our intellectual ideal is to let the facts do the voting for us. We are living in an unphilosophical, dispirited age; it doesn't have the courage to decide what is valuable and what isn't, and democracy means, expressed most succinctly: Do whatever is happening! Incidentally, this is one of the most disgraceful vicious circles in all the history of our race."

While he spoke, the prophet had irritably cracked and peeled a nut, the pieces of which he was now shoving into his mouth. Nobody had understood what he was saying. He broke off his speech in favor of a slow chewing motion of his jaws, in which the turned-up tip of his nose also participated, while the rest of his face remained ascetically still, but he did not take his eyes off Clarisse. They remained fixed somewhere in the region of her breast. The eyes of both the other men involuntarily left the master's face to follow his abstracted gaze. Clarisse felt a suction, as though these six eyes might lift her right out of her chair if they remained fastened on her much longer. But the master vigorously gulped down the last of his nut and went on with his lecture:

"Clarisse has found out that Christian legend has decreed that the Savior was a carpenter. That's not quite correct: his foster father was. Nor is she in the least justified in trying to make something of the fact that some criminal she's heard of happens to be a carpenter too. Intellectually that's simply beneath criticism. Morally it is frivolous. But it shows courage! It really does!" Here Meingast paused, to let the force with which he had said "courage" take effect. Then he quietly continued: "She recently saw, as we did also, a psychopath exposing himself. She makes too much of it; there is in general far too much emphasis on sexuality these days. But Clarisse says: 'It is not by chance that this man stopped under my window. . . .' Now, let us try to understand her rightly. She's wrong, for causally the incident is, of course, a coincidence. But what Clarisse is really saying is: If I regard everything as explained, then a person will never be able to change the world. She regards it as inexplicable that a murderer whose name, if I am not mistaken, is Moosbrugger happens to be a carpenter; she regards it as inexplicable that an unknown sufferer from sexual disturbances should have stopped just under her window; and so she has fallen into the habit of regarding all sorts of other things that happen to her as inexplicable and . . ." Again Meingast kept his listeners waiting awhile; his voice had become reminiscent of a man with a resolve who is firmly but warily tiptoeing up to something, and now he pounced: "And so she will do something!" Meingast ended on a strong note.

It gave Clarisse goose pimples.

"I repeat," Meingast said, "this is not subject to intellectual criticism. But intellectuality is, as we know, only the expression or the tool of a life that has dried out, while the point Clarisse is making may arise from another sphere: that of the will. Clarisse may never be able to explain what is happening to her, but she may well be able to solve it, resolve it. So she is quite right to call it 'salvation'—she is instinctively using the right term for it. It would be easy for one of us to speak of delusional thinking, or to say that Clarisse is a person with weak nerves, but what would be the point? The world is currently so undeluded that it doesn't know when to hate or to love anything, and since we're all of two minds about everything, all of us are neurasthenics and weaklings. In short," the prophet concluded abruptly, "although it is not easy for a philosopher to renounce insight, it is probably the great, growing insight of the twentieth century that this is what must be done. For me, in Geneva, it is today of greater spiritual importance that we have a French boxing coach than that the dissector Rousseau did his thinking there!"

Meingast could have continued talking, now that he had hit his stride: To begin with, the idea of salvation had always been anti-intellectual. "What the world today needs more than anything else is a strong, healthy delusion" was what he had been on the point of saying, but he had swallowed it in favor of the other ending. Second, there was the concomitant physical meaning implied in the etymology of *salvation*, its link with "salve" carrying an inference that deeds alone could save, or at least experiences involving the whole person, neck and crop. Third, he had been prepared to say that the overintellectualization of the male could under certain conditions bring woman to the fore as the instinctive leader in action, of which Clarisse was one of the first examples. Finally, there were all the transformations of the salvation idea in the history of peoples, and the present movement from salvation as a purely religious concept, which had been dominant for centuries, toward the realization that salvation must be brought about by resoluteness of will and even, if necessary, by force. Saving the world by force happened to be his central idea at the moment.

Meanwhile, however, the suction of all those eyes on her was becoming more than Clarisse could stand, and she cut off the master's discourse by turning to Siegmund, as the point of least resistance, saying to him rather too loudly:

"That's what I told you: we have to experience something ourselves to understand it. That's why we have to go to the asylum ourselves!"

Walter, who had been peeling a tangerine as a way of keeping steady, at this moment cut too deeply; an acid jet spurted into his eyes, making him start back and grope for his handkerchief. Siegmund, as always well dressed, first contemplated with an expert's concern the acid's effect on his brother-in-law's eye, then moved his gaze to that still life of respectability, the pigskin gloves and bowler hat resting on his knee. It was only when he could not shake off his sister's relentless stare, and no one spoke to save him the trouble, that he looked up with a grave nod and murmured serenely: "I have never doubted that we all belong in an asylum."

Clarisse then turned to Meingast and said: "I've told you about the Parallel Campaign. That could be another tremendous opportunity and obligation for us to do away with all the 'you can do it this way . . . and another way' that is the great evil of our century."

The master waved this off with a smile.

Clarisse, overcome with a heady sense of her own importance, cried out obstinately and somewhat incoherently: "A woman who lets a man have his way with her when it's only going to weaken his mind is a sex murderer too!"

Here Meingast issued a gentle warning: "Let's keep this on a general plane! Incidentally, I can set your mind at rest on one point: As regards those absurd committee meetings where a dying democracy is trying to give birth to one more great mission, I've had my observers and confidential agents for a long time now."

Clarisse simply felt ice at the roots of her hair.

Walter made another vain stab at stemming developments. Deferentially, he took his stand against Meingast, his tone very different from that which he might have used with Ulrich, for example: "What you say probably amounts to much the same thing I've been saying for a long time, that one ought to paint only in pure colors. It's high time to finish with the broken and blurred, with our concessions to the inane, to the fainthearted vision that no longer dares see that each thing has a true outline, true colors. I put it in pictorial terms, you in philosophic terms. But even though we share a point of view . . ." He suddenly became embarrassed, feeling that he could not talk openly in front of the others about why he dreaded Clarisse's involvement with the insane.

"No, I won't have Clarisse doing it!" he exclaimed. "It won't happen with my consent."

The master had listened amiably, and he answered Walter just as pleasantly as if not one of these emphatic words had reached his ear. "Incidentally, there's something Clarisse has expressed beautifully: She claimed that besides the 'sinful form' we inhabit, we all have an 'innocent form.' We could take this in the lovely sense that, apart from the miserable world of experience, our mind has access to a glorious realm where in lucid moments we feel our image moved by dynamics of an infinitely different kind. How did you put it, Clarisse?" he asked her in an encouraging tone. "Didn't you say that if you could stand up for this wretch without disgust, go into his cell and play the piano for him day and night, without tiring, you would draw his sins, as it were, out of him, take them upon yourself, and ascend with them? Naturally," he said, turning back to Walter, "this is to be taken not literally but as a subliminal process in the soul of the age, a process that here assumes the form of a parable about this man, inspiring her will. . . ."

He was at this point uncertain whether to add something about Clarisse's relation to the history of the idea of salvation, or whether it might be more attractive to explain her mission of leadership to her all over again in private. But Clarisse leapt from her chair like an overexcited child, raised her arm, with fist clenched, high above her head, and with a shyly ferocious smile cut short all further praise of herself with the shrill cry: "Onward to Moosbrugger!"

"But we still have nobody who can get us admitted . . . ," Siegmund was heard to say.

"I am not going along with this!" Walter said firmly.

"I cannot accept favors from a state where freedom and equality are to be had at every price and in every quality," Meingast declared.

"Then Ulrich must get us permission!" Clarisse exclaimed.

Meingast and Siegmund, having gone to enough trouble already, gladly agreed to a solution that relieved them, at least temporarily, of the responsibility, and even Walter finally had to give in, in spite of his protest, and take on the mission of going down to the nearby grocery to phone their chosen emissary.

This was the call that made Ulrich break off writing his letter to Agathe. Walter's voice took him by surprise, and so did his proposal. There was certainly room for a difference of opinion about Clarisse's scheme, Walter freely conceded, but it could not be entirely discounted as a whim. Perhaps it was time to somehow make a start somewhere, it didn't matter so much where. Of course, it was only a coincidence that Moosbrugger was involved; but Clarisse was so startlingly direct: her mind looked like those modern paintings in unmixed primary colors, harsh and unwieldy, but if one went along with it, often amazingly right. He couldn't really explain it all on the phone, but he hoped Ulrich wouldn't let him down. . . .

Ulrich was happy to drop what he was doing and agreed to come, although it was a disproportionately long way to go for the sake of talking with Clarisse for a mere fifteen minutes; for Clarisse had been invited for supper at her parents', along with Walter and Siegmund. On the way, Ulrich had time to wonder at his not having given a thought to Moosbrugger in so long and always having to be reminded of him by Clarisse, though the man had been almost constantly on his mind before. Even in the darkness of late evening through which Ulrich had to walk from the last trolley stop to his friends' house, there was no room for such a haunting apparition; a void in which he had occurred had closed. Ulrich noted this with satisfaction and also with that faint self-questioning which is a consequence of changes whose extent is clearer than their cause. He was enjoying the sensation of cutting through the permeable darkness with the solider black of his own body, when Walter came uncertainly toward him, nervous at night in this lonely vicinity but anxious to say a few words to Ulrich before they joined the others. He eagerly took up his explanations from the point where he had broken off. He appeared to be trying to defend himself, and Clarisse as well, from being misunderstood. Even when her notions seemed to be incoherent, he said, one could always detect behind them an element of pathology that was part of the ferment of the times; it was her most curious faculty. She was like a dowsing rod pointing to hidden springs—in this case, the necessity of replacing modern man's passive, merely intellectual, rational attitude with "values." The form of intelligence of the time had destroyed all firm ground, so it was only the will—indeed, if it couldn't be done otherwise, then it was only violence—that could create a new hierarchy of values in which a person could find beginning and end for his inner life. . . . He was repeating, reluctantly and yet with enthusiasm, what he had heard from Meingast.

Guessing this, Ulrich asked him impatiently: "Why are you talking so pompously? Is it that prophet of yours? It used to be you couldn't have enough simplicity and naturalness!"

Walter put up with this for Clarisse's sake, lest his friend decline to help, but had there been just one ray of light in that moonless gloom, the flash of his teeth would have been visible as he bared them in frustration. He said nothing, but his suppressed rage made him weak, and the presence of his muscular friend shielding him from the eerie loneliness of the place made him soft. Suddenly he said: "Imagine loving a woman and then meeting a man you admire and realizing that your wife admires and loves him, too, and that both of you feel, in love, jealousy, and admiration, this man's hopeless superiority—"

"I'd rather not imagine it!" Ulrich should have heard him out, but he squared his shoulders with a laugh and interrupted him.

Walter shot him a venomous glance. He had meant to ask: "What would you do in such a case?" But it was the same game they had been playing since their school days. As they entered the dimly lit hall he said:

"Drop that act of yours! You're not as conceited and thick-skinned as all that!" Then he had to run to catch up with Ulrich on the stairs, where he hastily whispered the rest of what Ulrich needed to know.

"What has Walter been telling you?" Clarisse asked when they got upstairs.

"I can do it, all right," Ulrich said, going straight to the point, "but I don't think it would be sensible."

"Did you hear that? His very first word was 'sensible,'" Clarisse called out to Meingast, laughing. She was rushing back and forth between the clothes closet, the washstand, the mirror, and the half-open door between her room and the one where the men were. They could catch glimpses of her now and then: with a wet face and her hair hanging down; with her hair brushed up; still bare-legged; in stocking feet; in her long-skirted dinner dress below with a dressing jacket above that looked like a white institutional uniform. She enjoyed this appearing and disappearing. Since she had got her way, all her feelings were submerged in an easy sensuality. "I'm dancing on light-ropes!" she shouted into the room. The men smiled, but Siegmund glanced at his watch and dryly asked her to hurry up. He was treating the whole thing as a gymnastic exercise.

Then Clarisse glided on a "light-rope" to the far corner of her room, for a pin, and shut the drawer of her night table with a bang.

"I can change faster than a man," she called back to Siegmund in the other room, but suddenly paused over the double meaning of "change," which right now could mean for her both "dressing for dinner" and "being transformed by mysterious destinies." She quickly finished dressing, stuck her head through the door, and gravely regarded her friends one after the other. Anyone who did not think of it as a game might have been alarmed that something in this solemn countenance had been extinguished that should have been part of a natural, healthy face. She bowed to her friends and said ceremonially: "So now I have put on my destiny!" But when she straightened up again she looked quite normal, even rather charming, and her brother Siegmund cried: "Forward—march! Papa doesn't like people to be late for dinner!"

When the four of them walked to the streetcar—Meingast had disappeared before they left the house—Ulrich fell back a few steps with Siegmund and asked him whether he had not been a bit worried about his sister of late. The glow of Siegmund's cigarette sketched a flatly rising arc in the darkness.

"No doubt she's abnormal," he replied. "But is Meingast normal? Or even Walter? Is playing the piano normal? It's an unusual state of excitement associated with tremors in the wrists and ankles. For a physician, there's no such thing as normal. Still, if you want my serious opinion, my sister is somewhat overwrought, and I think it will pass once the great panjandrum has left. What do you make of him?" There was a hint of malice in "the great panjandrum."

"He's a gasbag," Ulrich said.

"Isn't he, though!" Siegmund was delighted. "Repulsive, repulsive.

"But his ideas are interesting, I wouldn't deny that altogether," he added after a pause.

20

COUNT LEINSDORF HAS QUALMS ABOUT "CAPITAL AND CULTURE"

And so it happened that Ulrich again appeared before Count Leins-dorf.

He found His Grace, enveloped in tranquillity, dedication, solemnity, and beauty, at his desk, reading a newspaper that was lying spread out over a high pile of documents. The Imperial Liege-Count sadly shook his head after once more expressing his condolences to Ulrich.

"Your father was one of the last true representatives of capital and culture," he said. "How well I remember the days when we both sat in the Bohemian Diet. He well deserved the confidence we always placed in him!"

Ulrich inquired out of politeness how the Parallel Campaign had fared in his absence.

"Well, because of that hullabaloo in the street outside my house that afternoon, which you observed, we've set up a Commission to Ascertain the Desires of the Concerned Sections of the Population in Reference to Administrative Reform," Count Leinsdorf told him. "The Prime Minister himself asked us to take this off his shoulders for the time being, because as a patriotic enterprise we enjoy, so to speak, the public's confidence."

With a straight face Ulrich assured him that at any rate the Commission's name had been well chosen and was likely to have a certain effect.

"Yes, a good deal depends on finding the right words," His Grace said pensively, and suddenly asked: "What do you make of this business of the municipal employees in Trieste? I should think it would be high time for the government to pull itself together and take a firm stand." He made as if to hand over the paper he had folded up when Ulrich came in, but at the last moment chose to open it again and read aloud to his visitor, with vivid feeling, from a long-winded article. "Can you imagine this sort of thing happening in any other country in the world?" he asked, when he had finished. "For years the Austrian city of Trieste has been hiring only Italians, subjects of the King of Italy, in its civil service, to make a point that their allegiance is to Italy, not to us. I was there once on His Majesty's birthday: not a single flag in all Trieste except on the administration building, the tax office, the prison, and the roofs of a few barracks! But if you should have any business in some municipal office in Trieste on the King of Italy's birthday, you wouldn't find a clerk anywhere without a flower in his buttonhole!"

"But why has this been tolerated till now?" Ulrich inquired.

"Why shouldn't it be tolerated?" Count Leinsdorf said in a disgruntled tone. "If our government forces the city to discharge its foreign staff, we will immediately be accused of Germanizing. That is just the reproach every government fears. Even His Majesty doesn't like it. After all, we're not Prussians!"

Ulrich seemed to remember that the coastal and port city of Trieste had been founded on Slavic soil by the imperialistic Venetian Republic and today embraced a large Slavic population, so that even if one were to view it as merely the private concern of its inhabitants—without regard to its also being the gateway to the Empire's eastern trade and in every way dependent on the Empire for its prosperity—there was no getting around the fact that its large Slavic lower middle class passionately contested the favored Italian upper class's right to consider the city as its own property. Ulrich said as much to the Count.

"True enough," Count Leinsdorf instructed him, "but once the word is out that we're Germanizing, the Slovenes immediately side with the Italians, even though they have to take time off from tearing each other's hair out, and all the other minorities rally to support them as well! We've been through this often enough. In terms of practical politics, it's the Germans we have to regard as a threat to peace within the Empire, whether we want to or not." This conclusion left Count Leinsdorf deep in thought for a while, for he had touched on the great political scheme that weighed on his mind, though it had not come clearly into focus for him until this moment. But suddenly he livened up again, and continued cheerfully: "Anyway, the others have been told off properly this time." With a tremor of impatience, he replaced his pince-nez and again read aloud to Ulrich with relish all those satisfying passages in the edict issued by His Imperial and Royal Majesty's Governor in Trieste.

" 'Repeated warnings issued by the governmental institutions of public safety to no avail . . . harm done to our people . . . In view of this obstinate resistance to the prescribed official orders, the Governor of Trieste finds himself obliged to take steps toward enforcing the observance of the existing lawful regulations . . .' " He interrupted himself to ask: "Spoken with dignity, don't you think?" He raised his head but immediately lowered it again, eager to get to the final bit, whose official urbane authority underlined his voice with great aesthetic satisfaction:

" 'Furthermore,' " he read, " 'it is reserved to the administration at any time to give careful and sympathetic consideration to each individual case of application for citizenship made by such public functionaries, insofar as these are officially deemed worthy of exceptional regard through long years of public service and an unblemished record, and in such cases the Imperial and Royal Administration is inclined to avoid immediate enforcement of these regulations, while reserving its right to enforce them at such time and in such circumstances as it may think fit.' Now, that's the tone our government should have taken all along!" Count Leinsdorf exclaimed.

"Don't you think, sir, on the basis of this last point, that in the last analysis this leaves things pretty much where they have always been?" Ulrich asked a little later, when the tail end of this long snake of an official sentence had finally vanished inside his ear.

"Yes, that's just it!" His Grace replied, twiddling his thumbs for a while, as he always did when some hard thinking was going on inside. Then he gave Ulrich a searching look and opened his heart to him.

"Do you remember how, when we were at the police exhibition, the Interior Minister announced that there was a new spirit of 'mutual support and strictness' in the offing? Well, I wouldn't expect them to immediately lock up all the troublemakers who were raising such a rumpus on my doorstep, but the Minister could at least have said a few dignified words of repudiation in Parliament!" His feelings were hurt.

"I assumed it was done during my absence," Ulrich cried with feigned astonishment, aware that a genuine distress was roiling the mind of his benevolent friend.

"Not a thing was done!" His Grace said. Again he fixed his worried, protuberant eyes on Ulrich's face with a searching look, and he opened his heart further: "But something will be done!" He straightened up and leaned back in his chair, shutting his eyes as he lapsed into silence.

When he opened them again he began to explain in a calmer tone: "You see, my dear fellow, our Constitution of 1861 entrusted the undisputed leadership in the new experimental governmental scheme to the German element in the population, and in particular to those within that element who represented capital and culture. That was a munificent gift of His Majesty's, a proof of his generosity and his confidence, perhaps not quite in keeping with the times; for what has become of capital and culture since then?" Count Leinsdorf raised one hand and then dropped it in resignation on the other. "When His Majesty ascended the throne in 1848, at Olmütz, that is to say, practically in exile . . . ," he went on slowly, but suddenly becoming impatient or uncertain, he fished a few notes out of his pocket with trembling fingers, struggled in some agitation to set his pince-nez firmly on his nose, and read aloud, his voice sometimes quavering with emotion, as he strained to decipher his own handwriting:

" '. . . he was surrounded by the uproar of the nationalities' wild urge for freedom. He succeeded in quenching the extreme manifestations of this upsurge. Finally, even if after granting some concessions to the demands of his peoples, he stood triumphant as the victor, and a gracious and magnanimous victor, moreover, who forgave his subjects the errors of their ways and held out his hand to them with the offer of a peace honorable for them as well. Although the Constitution and the other liberties had been granted by him under the press of circumstances, it was nevertheless an act of His Majesty's free will, the fruit of his wisdom and compassion, and of hope in the progressive civilization of his peoples. But in recent years this model relationship between the Emperor and his peoples has been tarnished by the work of agitators, demagogues—' " Here Count Leinsdorf broke off reading his exposition of political history, in which every word had been scrupulously weighed and polished, and gazed pensively at the portrait of his ancestor the Grand Marshal and Knight of the Order of Maria Theresa, hanging on the wall facing him. When Ulrich's expectant gaze finally drew his attention, he said: "That's as far as I've come.

"But you can see that I have been giving these problems a great deal of thought lately," he went on. "What I have just read to you is the beginning of the response which the Minister should have presented to Parliament in the matter of the demonstration against me, if he had been doing his job! I've gradually worked it out for myself, and I don't mind telling you that I shall have occasion to present it to His Majesty as soon as I have finished it. You see, it was not without purpose that the Constitution of 1861 entrusted the leadership of our country to capital and culture. It was meant to secure our future. But where are capital and culture today?"

He seemed really put out with the Minister of the Interior, and to divert him Ulrich remarked innocently that one could at least say about capital that it was nowadays not only in the hands of the bankers but also in the time-tested hands of the landed aristocracy.

"I've nothing at all against the Jews," Count Leinsdorf assured Ulrich out of the blue, as though Ulrich had said something that required such a disclaimer. "They are intelligent, hardworking, and reliable. But it was a great mistake to give them those unsuitable names. Rosenberg and Rosenthal, for instance, are aristocratic names; Baer and Wolf and all such creatures are originally heraldic beasts; Meyer derives from landed property; Silver and Gold are armorial colors. All those Jewish names," His Grace disclosed, to Ulrich's surprise, "are nothing but the insolence of our bureaucrats aimed at our nobility. It was the noble families, not the Jews, who were the butt of these officials, which is why the Jews were given other names as well, like Abrahams, Jewison, or Schmucker. You cannot infrequently observe this animus of our bureaucracy against the old nobility surfacing even today, if you know how to look for it," he said oracularly, with a gloomy, obstinate air, as though the struggle of the central administration against feudalism had not long since been overtaken by history and vanished completely from sight. In fact, there was nothing His Grace could resent so pureheartedly as the social privileges enjoyed by important bureaucrats by virtue of their position even when their names might be plain Fuchsenbauer or

Schlosser. Count Leinsdorf was no diehard country *Junker;* he wanted to move with the times, and did not mind such a name when it was that of a Member of Parliament or even a cabinet minister or an influential private citizen, nor did he at all object to the political or economic influence of the middle class; what provoked him, with a passion that was the last vestige of venerable traditions, was the social status of high-ranking administrative officials with middle-class names. Ulrich wondered whether Leinsdorf's remarks might have been prompted by his own cousin's husband. It was not out of the question, but Count Leinsdorf continued talking and was, as always happened, soon lifted above all personal concerns by an idea that had apparently been working inside him for a long time.

"The whole so-called Jewish Question would disappear without a trace if the Jews would only make up their minds to speak Hebrew, go back to their old names, and wear Eastern dress," he explained. "Frankly, a Galician Jew who has just recently made his fortune in Vienna doesn't look right on the Esplanade at Ischl, wearing Tyrolean costume with a chamois tuft on his hat. But put him in a long, flowing robe, as rich as you like so long as it covers his legs, and you'll see how admirably his face and his grand sweeping gestures go with his costume! All those things people tend to joke about would then be in their proper place—even the showy rings they like to wear. I am against assimilation the way the English nobility practice it; it's a tedious and uncertain process. But give the Jews back their true character and watch them become a veritable ornament, a genuine aristocracy of a rare and special kind among the nations gratefully thronging around His Majesty's throne—or, if you'd prefer to see it in everyday terms, imagine them strolling along on our Ringstrasse, the only place in the world where you can see, in the midst of Western European elegance at its finest, a Mohammedan with his red fez, a Slovak in sheepskins, or a bare-legged Tyrolean!"

At this point Ulrich could not do otherwise than express his admiration for His Grace's acumen, which had now also enabled him to uncover the "real Jew."

"Well, you know, the true Catholic faith teaches us to see things as they really are," Count Leinsdorf explained benevolently. "But you would never guess what it was that put me on the right track. It wasn't Arnheim—I'm not speaking of the Prussians right now. But I

have a banker, a man of the Mosaic faith, of course, whom I've had to
see regularly for years now, and at first his intonation always used to
bother me a bit, so that I couldn't keep my mind on the business at
hand. He speaks exactly as if he wanted me to think he was my
uncle—I mean, as if he'd just got out of the saddle, or back from a
day's grouse shooting; exactly the way our own kind of people talk, I
must say. Well and good; but then, when he gets carried away, he
can't keep it up and, to make no bones about it, slips into a kind of
Yiddish singsong. It used to bother me considerably, as I believe I've
told you already, because it always happened when some important
business matter was at stake, so that I was always unconsciously
primed for it, and it got so that I couldn't pay attention to what he
was talking about, or else I imagined I was listening to something
important the whole time. But then I found a way around it: Every
time he began to talk like that I imagined he was speaking Hebrew,
and you ought to have heard how attractive it sounded then! Positively enchanting—it is, after all, a liturgical language; such a melodi-
ous chanting: I'm very musical, I should add. In short, from then on
he had me lapping up the most complicated calculations of com-
pound interest or discount positively as if he were at the piano!" As
he said this, Count Leinsdorf had for some reason a melancholy
smile.

Ulrich took the liberty of pointing out that the people so favored
by His Grace's sympathetic interest would be more than likely to
turn down his suggestion.

"Oh, of course they won't want to!" the Count said. "But they
would have to be forced to for their own good. It would amount to a
world mission for the Empire, and it's not a question of whether they
want to or not. You see, many people at the beginning have had to be
made to do what's best for them. But think, too, what it would mean
if we ended up allied with a grateful Jewish State instead of with the
Germans and Prussia! Seeing that our Trieste happens to be the
Hamburg of the Mediterranean, as it were, apart from the fact that it
would make us diplomatically invincible to have not only the Pope on
our side but the Jews as well!"

Abruptly, he added: "You must remember that I have to concern
myself with problems of the currency, too, these days." And again he
smiled in that strangely sad, absentminded way.

It was astonishing that His Grace, who had repeatedly sent out urgent calls for Ulrich, did not discuss the problems of the day now that he had finally come, but lavished his ideas on him. Apparently ideas had come to him in abundance while he had had to do without his confidant, ideas as restless as bees that stream out for miles but are sure to return in their own good time, laden with honey.

"You might perhaps object," Count Leinsdorf resumed, although Ulrich had not said anything, "that I have on earlier occasions often expressed a decidedly low opinion of the financial world. I don't deny it: too much is too much, and we have too much finance in modern life. But that's precisely why we must deal with it! Look, culture has not been pulling its weight alongside capital—there you have the whole secret of developments since 1861. And that's why we must concern ourselves with capital."

His Grace made an almost imperceptible pause, just long enough to let his listener know that now he was coming to the secret of capital, but then went on in his gloomily confidential tone:

"You see, what's most important in a culture is what it forbids people: whatever doesn't belong is out. For instance, a well-bred man will never eat gravy with his knife, only God knows why; they don't teach you these things in school. That's so-called tact, it's based on a privileged class for culture to look up to, a cultural model; in short, if I may say so, an aristocracy. Granted that our aristocracy has not always lived up to that ideal. That's exactly the point, the downright revolutionary experiment, of our 1861 Constitution: Capital and culture were meant to make common cause with the aristocracy. Have they done so? Were they up to taking advantage of the great opportunity His Majesty had so graciously made available to them? I'm sure you'd never claim that the results of your cousin's great efforts that we see every week are in keeping with such hopes." His voice grew more animated as he exclaimed: "You know, it's really most interesting, what sorts of things claim to be 'mind' these days! I was telling His Eminence the Cardinal about it recently, when we were out hunting in Mürzsteg—no, it was Mürzbruck, at the Hostnitz girl's wedding—and he laughed and clapped his hands together: 'Something new every year,' he said. 'Now you can see how modest we are; we've been telling people the same old thing for almost two thousand years.' And that's so true. The main thing about faith is that it keeps believing the same old thing, even if it's heresy to say so. 'You know,' he said, 'I always go out hunting because my predecessor in the days of Leopold von Babanberg did too. But I never kill,' he said—he happens to be known for never firing a shot on the hunt—'because it goes against my grain, something tells me it's not in keeping with my cloth. I can talk about this to you, old friend, because we were boys in dancing class together. But I'd never stand up in public and say: "You shall not shoot while hunting!" Good Lord, who knows whether that would be true, and besides, it's no part of the Church's teaching. But the people who meet at your friend's house make a public issue of things like that the minute it occurs to them! There you have what's called "intelligence" nowadays!' It's easy for him to laugh," Count Leinsdorf went on, speaking for himself again. "He holds that job in perpetuity, but we laymen have the hard task of finding the right path amid perpetual change. I told him as much. I asked him: 'Why did God let literature and painting and all that come into the world anyway, when they're really such a bore?' And he came up with a very interesting explanation. 'You've heard about psychoanalysis, haven't you?' he asked me. I didn't know quite what I was supposed to say. 'Well,' he said, 'you'll probably say it's just a lot of filth. We won't argue about it, it's what everyone says; and yet they all run to these newfangled doctors more than to our Catholic confessional. Take it from me, they rush to them in droves because the flesh is weak! They let their secret sins be discussed because they enjoy it, and if they disparage it, take it from me, we always pick holes in the things we mean to buy! But I could also prove to you that what their atheistic doctors imagine they invented is nothing but what the Church has been doing from the beginning: exorcising the Devil and healing the possessed. It's identical step for step with the ritual of exorcism, for instance, when they try with their own methods to make the person who's possessed talk about what's inside him; according to Church teaching, that's precisely the turning point, where the Devil is getting ready to break out! We merely missed adapting ourselves in time to changing conditions by talking of psychosis, the unconscious, and all that current claptrap instead of filth and the Devil.' Isn't that interesting?" Count Leinsdorf asked. "But what comes next may be even more so. 'Never mind the weakness of the flesh,' the Cardinal said. 'What we need to talk about is that the spirit is weak too. And that's where the Church has kept its wits and not let anything slip by. People aren't nearly so scared of the Devil in the flesh, even if they make a great show of fighting him, as they are of the illumination that comes from the spirit. You never studied theology,' he said to me, 'but at least you respect it, and that's more than a secular philosopher in his blindness ever does. Let me tell you, theology is so difficult that a man can devote himself to studying it and nothing else for fifteen years before he realizes that he hasn't really understood a word of it! If people knew how difficult it is, none of them would have any faith at all; they'd only run us down! They'd run us down exactly the way they run people down—you understand?' he said slyly, '—who are writing their books and painting their pictures and trotting out their theories. And today we're only too glad to let them have plenty of rope to hang themselves with, because, let me tell you, the more earnestly one of those fellows sets about it, the less he's a mere entertainer, or working for his own pocket; the more, in other words, he serves God in his mistaken way, the more he bores people, and the more they run him down. "That's not what life is like!" they say. But we know very well what it's like, and we'll show them too, and because we can also wait, you may yet live to see them come running back to us, full of fury about the time they wasted on all that clever talk. You can see it happening in our own families, even now. And in our fathers' day, God knows, they thought they were going to turn heaven itself into a university.'

"I wouldn't go so far," Count Leinsdorf rounded out this part of his discourse to start on a new topic, "as to say he meant all that literally. The Hostnitzes in Mürzbruck happen to have a celebrated Rhine wine that General Marmont left behind and forgot in 1805 because he had to march on Vienna in such a hurry, and they brought some of it out for the wedding. But in the main I'm sure the Cardinal was right on target. So if I ask myself now what to make of it, all I can say is, I'm sure it's true, but it doesn't work. I mean, there can be no doubt that the people we brought in because we were told they represent the spirit of the times have nothing to do with real life, and the Church can well afford to wait them out. But we civilian politicians can't wait; we must squeeze what good we can out of life as we find it. After all, man doesn't live by bread alone, but by the soul as well. The soul is that which enables him to digest his bread, so to speak. And that's why it's necessary . . ." Count Leinsdorf was of the opinion that politics should be a spur to the soul. "In short, something has to happen," he said, "that's what the times demand. Everyone has that feeling, as it were, not just the politically minded. The times have a sort of interim character that nobody can stand indefinitely." He had the idea that the trembling balance of ideas upon which the no less trembling balance of power in Europe rested must be given a push.

"It hardly matters what kind of push," he assured Ulrich, who made a show of being stunned by His Grace's having turned, in the period since they had last seen each other, into a veritable revolutionary.

"Well, why not?" Count Leinsdorf retorted, flattered. "His Eminence of course also thought that it might be a small step in the right direction if His Majesty could be persuaded to replace the present Minister of the Interior, but such petty reforms don't do the trick in the long run, however necessary they may be. Do you know that as I mull this over I actually find my thoughts turning to the Socialists?" He gave his interlocutor time to recover from the amazement he assumed this was bound to cause, and then continued firmly: "You can take it from me, real socialism wouldn't be nearly as terrible as people seem to think. You may perhaps object that the Socialists are republicans; that's true, you simply can't listen when they're talking, but if you consider them in terms of practical politics, you might well reach the conclusion that a social-democratic republic with a strong ruler at the helm would not be an impossible solution at all. For my own part, I'm convinced that if we were to go just a little way to meet them, they'd be glad to give up the idea of using brute force and they'd recoil from the rest of their objectionable principles. As it is, they're already inclined to modify their notion of the class struggle and their hostility to private property. And there really are people among them who still place country before party, as compared with the middle-class parties who've gone radical since the last elections in putting their conflicting national-minority interests above everything else. Which brings us to the Emperor." He lowered his voice confidentially. "As I've said already, we must learn to think in economic terms. The one-sided policy of encouraging national minorities has led the Empire into the desert. Now, to the Emperor, all this Czech-Polish-German-Italian ranting about autonomy . . . I don't know how to put it: let's just say His Majesty couldn't care less. What His Majesty does care about, deeply, is our getting the defense budget through without any cuts so that the Empire may be strong, and apart from that he feels a hearty distaste for all the pretensions of the middle-class idea-mongers, a distaste he probably acquired in 1848. But these two priorities simply make His Majesty the First Socialist in the land, as it were. You can now see, I think, the magnificent vista I was speaking of? Which leaves only the problem of religiosity, in which there is still an unbridgeable gap between opposing camps, and that's something I'd have to talk over with His Eminence again."

His Grace fell silent, absorbed in his conviction that history, in particular that of his own country, bogged down as it was in fruitless nationalist dissensions, would shortly be called upon to take a step into the future—whereby he perceived the spirit of history as being more or less two-legged, but otherwise a philosophical necessity. Hence it was understandable that he surfaced suddenly with sore eyes, like a diver who had gone too far down. "In any case, we must get ready to do our duty!" he said.

"But where does our duty lie, Your Grace?"

"Why, in doing our duty, of course! It's the only thing we can always do! But to change the subject . . ." It was only now that Count Leinsdorf seemed to remember the pile of newspapers and files on which his fist rested. "Look here, what the people want today is a strong hand. But today a strong hand needs fine words, or the people won't put up with it. And you, and I mean you personally, are eminently qualified in this respect. What you said, for instance, the last time we all met at your cousin's before you left town, was that what we actually need—if you recall—is a central committee for eternal happiness, to bring it in step with our earthly precision in ratiocination. . . . Well, it wouldn't work out quite so easily, but His Eminence laughed heartily when I told him about it; actually, I rubbed it in a bit, as they say, and even though he's always making fun of everything, I can tell pretty well whether his laugh comes from the spleen or from the heart. The fact is, my dear man, we simply can't do without you. . . ."

While all of Count Leinsdorf's other pronouncements that day had had the character of complicated dreams, the wish he now expressed—that Ulrich should give up "definitively, at least for now," any idea of resigning his post as Honorary Secretary of the Parallel Campaign—was so definite and so pointedly fledged, and his hand had come down on Ulrich's arm with such an effect of a surprise maneuver, that Ulrich almost had the not entirely pleasing impression that all the elaborate harangues he had been listening to had only been calculated, far more slyly than he had anticipated, to put him off his guard. At this moment he was quite annoyed with Clarisse, who had got him into this fix. But since he had appealed on her behalf to Count Leinsdorf's kindness the very first time there had been an opening in the conversation, and the request had been granted instantly by the obliging high official, who wanted only to go on talking without interruption, he had no choice now but reluctantly to square the account.

"I've heard from Tuzzi," Count Leinsdorf said, pleased with his success, "that you might decide on a man from his office to take the routine business off your hands. 'Splendid,' I told him, 'if he stays on.' After all, his man has taken his oath of office, which we'll give you too, and my own secretary, whom I'd gladly have put at your disposal, is unfortunately an idiot. All you perhaps shouldn't let him see is the strictly confidential stuff, because he's Tuzzi's man, and that has certain drawbacks; but otherwise, do arrange matters to suit your own convenience," His Grace said, concluding this successful interview with the utmost cordiality.

21

CAST ALL THOU HAST INTO THE FIRE, EVEN UNTO THY SHOES

During this time and from the moment she had stayed behind alone, Agathe had been living in a state of utter release from all ties to the world, in a sweetly wistful suspension of will; a condition that was like a great height, where only the wide blue sky is to be seen. Once a day she treated herself to a short stroll in town; at home, she read, attended to her affairs, and experienced this mild, trivial business of living with grateful enjoyment. Nothing troubled her state: no clinging to the past, no straining for the future; if her eye lit upon some nearby object, it was like coaxing a baby lamb to her: either it came gently closer or it took no notice of her at all—but at no time did her mind deliberately take hold of it with that motion of inner grasping which gives to every act of cold understanding a certain violence as well as a certain futility, for it drives away the joy that is in things. In this fashion everything around her seemed far more intelligible to Agathe than ordinarily, but in the main she was still preoccupied with her conversations with her brother. In keeping with the peculiarity of her unusually exact memory, which did not distort its material with any bias or prejudice, there rose up in her mind more or less at random the living words, the subtle surprises of cadence and gestures, in these conversations, much as they were before she had quite understood them and realized where they were tending. Nevertheless, it all held the utmost significance for her; her memory, so often dominated by remorse, was now suffused with a quiet devotion, and the time just past clung like a caress to the warmth of her body, instead of drifting off as it usually did into the frost and darkness that awaits life lived in vain.

And so, veiled in an invisible light, Agathe also dealt with the lawyers, notaries, brokers, and agents she now had to see. No one refused her; everyone was glad to oblige the attractive young woman—whose father's name was sufficient recommendation—in every way. She conducted herself with as much self-assurance as detachment; she was sure of what she wanted, but it was detached from herself, as it were, and the experience she had acquired in life—also something that can be seen as detached from the personality—went on working in pursuit of that purpose like a shrewd laborer calmly taking advantage for his commission of whatever opportunities presented themselves. That she was engaged in preparing a felony—the significance of her action that would have been strikingly apparent to an outsider—simply did not enter her state of mind during this time. The unity of her conscience excluded it. The pure light of this conscience outshone this dark point, which nevertheless, like the core of a flame, formed its center. Agathe herself did not know how to express it; by virtue of her intention she found herself in a state that was a world away from this same ugly intention.

On the morning after her brother had left, Agathe was already considering her appearance with great care: it had begun by accident with her face, when her gaze had landed on it and not come back out of the mirror. She was held fast, much as one who sometimes has absolutely no desire to walk keeps walking a hundred steps, and then another hundred, all the way toward something one catches sight of only at the end, at which point one definitely intends to turn back and yet does not. In this way she was held captive, without vanity, by this landscape of her self, which confronted her behind the shimmer of glass. She looked at her hair, still like bright velvet; she opened the collar of her reflection's dress and slipped the dress off its shoulders; then she undressed the image altogether and studied it down to the rosy nails, to where the body tapers off into fingers and toes and hardly belongs to itself anymore. Everything was still like the sparkling day approaching its zenith: ascendant, pure, exact, and infused with that forenoon growth that manifests itself in a human being or a young animal as ineffably as in a bouncing ball that has not yet reached its highest point in the air, but is just about to. "Perhaps it is passing through that point this very moment," Agathe thought. The idea frightened her. Still, she was only twenty-seven; it might take a while yet. Her body, as untouched by athletic coaches and masseurs as it was by childbearing and maternal toil, had been formed by nothing but its own growth. If it could have been set down naked in one of those grand and lonely landscapes that mountain ranges form on the side turned toward the sky, the vast, infertile, billowing swell of such heights would have borne it upward like some pagan goddess. In a nature of this kind, noon does not pour down exhalations of light and heat; it merely seems for a while longer to rise above its zenith and then to pass imperceptibly into the sinking, floating beauty of the afternoon. From the mirror came the eerie sense of that undefinable hour.

It occurred to her at this moment that Ulrich, too, was letting his life go by as though it would last forever. "Perhaps it is a mistake that we didn't first meet when we were old," she said to herself, conjuring up the melancholy image of two banks of fog drifting earthward in the evening. "They're not as fine as the blaze of noon, but what do those formless gray shapes care what people make of them? Their hour has come, and it is just as tender as the most glowing hour!"

She had now almost turned her back on the mirror, but was provoked by a certain extravagance in her mood to turn around again before she knew it, and had to laugh at the memory of two fat people taking the waters at Marienbad years ago; she had watched them as they sat on one of those green benches, doting on each other with the sweetest and tenderest feelings. "Their beating hearts are slim under all that fat, and being lost in their vision of each other, they have no idea how funny they look to the world," Agathe reminded herself, and made an ecstatic face while trying to puff up her body with imaginary rolls of fat. When this fit of exuberance had passed, it looked as if some tiny tears of rage had risen to her eyes, and pulling herself together, she coolly resumed the point-by-point scrutiny of her appearance. Although she was considered slender, she observed in her body with some concern a possibility that she could become heavy. Perhaps she was too broad-chested. In her face, its very white skin dimmed by her golden hair as if by candles burning in the daytime, the nose was a bit too wide, and its almost classical line a bit dented on one side at the tip. It could be that everywhere inside her flame-like given form a second was lurking, broader and more melancholy, like a linden leaf that has fallen among twigs of laurel. Agathe felt a curiosity about herself, as though she were really seeing herself for the first time. This was how she might well have been perceived by the men she had become involved with, without her having known anything about it. It was a rather uncanny feeling. But by some trick of the imagination, before she could call her memories to account for it, she kept hearing behind everything she had experienced the ardent, long-drawn-out mating cry of donkeys, which had always curiously aroused her: a hopelessly foolish and ugly sound, which for that very reason makes no other heroism of love seem so desperately sweet as theirs. She shrugged her shoulders at her life and resolutely turned back to her image to discover a place where her appearance might already be yielding to age. There were those small areas near the eyes and ears that are the first to change, beginning by looking as though something had slept on them, or the inner curve under the breasts, which so easily loses its definition. At this moment it would have been a satisfaction to her and a promise of peace to come had she seen such a change, but there was none yet to be seen, and the loveliness of her body floated almost eerily in the depths of the mirror.

It now seemed odd to her that she was actually Frau Hagauer, and the difference between the clear and close relationship that implied and the vagueness with which the fact reached deep into her being was so great that she seemed to herself to be standing there without a body while the body in the mirror belonged to Frau Hagauer, who was the one who would have to learn to cope with its having committed itself to a situation beneath its dignity. Even in this there was some of that elusive pleasure in living that sometimes startles, and it made Agathe, once she had hastily dressed again, go straight to her bedroom to look for a capsule that must be in her luggage. This small airtight capsule, which had been in her possession almost as long as she had been married to Hagauer, and which she always kept within reach, contained a tiny quantity of a drab powder she had been assured was a deadly poison. Agathe recalled certain sacrifices it had cost her to obtain this forbidden stuff, about which she knew only what she had been told of its effect and one of those chemical names the uninitiated must memorize, like a magic formula, without knowing what they mean. But evidently all those means by which the end may be brought a little closer, such as poison or guns, or seeking out survivable dangers, are part of the romantic love of life; and it may be that most people's lives are so oppressed, so fluctuating, with so much darkness in their brightness, and altogether so perverse, that life's inherent joy can be released only by the distant possibility of putting an end to it. Agathe felt better when her eyes lit on the tiny metal object, which she regarded, amid the uncertainty that lay ahead of her, as a bringer of luck, a talisman.

So this did not at all mean that Agathe at this time already intended to kill herself. On the contrary, she feared death just as every young person does to whom, for instance, before falling asleep in bed at night, after a well-spent day, it suddenly occurs that "It's inevitable: sometime, on another fine day just like this, I'll be dead." Nor does one acquire an appetite for dying by having to watch someone else die; her father's death had tormented her with impressions whose horrors had returned since she had been left alone in the house after her brother's departure. But "I'm sort of dead, in a way" was something Agathe felt often; and especially in moments like this, when she had just been conscious of her young body's shapeliness and good health, its taut beauty, equally unfathomable in the mystery of what held it together and what made its elements decompose in death, she tended to fall from her condition of happy confidence into one of anxiety, amazement, and silence: it was like stepping from a noisy, crowded room and suddenly standing under the shimmering stars. Regardless of her awakening intentions and her satisfaction at having extricated herself from a bungled life, she now felt rather detached from herself and only obscurely linked to her own existence. Coolly she thought of death as a state in which one is released from all efforts and illusions, imagined it as a tender inward rocking to sleep: one lies in God's hand, and this hand is like a cradle or a hammock slung between two tall trees swaying faintly in the wind. She thought of death as a great tranquillity and fatigue, the end of all wanting and striving, of all paying attention and having to think, like the pleasant slackening of the fingers one feels when sleep cautiously loosens their hold on whatever last thing of this world they have still been clutching. No doubt she was indulging herself in a rather easy and casual notion of death, typical of someone disinclined to take on the exertions of living; and in the end she was amused to think how this was all of a piece with her moving the couch into her father's austere drawing room to lounge on, reading—the only change she had made in the house on her own initiative.

Still, the thought of giving up life was anything but a game for Agathe. It seemed profoundly believable to her that all this frustrating turmoil must be followed by a state of blissful repose, which she could not help imagining in physical terms. She felt it this way because she had no need of the suspenseful illusion that the world could be improved, and she was always ready to surrender her share in it completely, as long as it could be done in a pleasant fashion. Besides, she had already had a special encounter with death in that extraordinary illness that had befallen her on the borderline between childhood and girlhood. That was when—in an almost imperceptibly gradual loss of energy that seemed to infiltrate each tiniest particle of time, though as a whole it happened with an irresistible rush—more and more parts of her body seemed to dissolve away from her day by day and be destroyed; yet, keeping pace with this decline and this slipping away from life there was an unforgettable fresh striving toward a goal that banished all the unrest and anxiety of her illness, a curiously substantive state that even enabled her to exert a certain domination over the adults around her, who were becoming more and more unsure of themselves. It is not out of the question that this sense of power, gained under such impressive circumstances, could later have been at the heart of her spiritual readiness to withdraw in similar fashion from a life whose allurements for some reason fell short of her expectations. But more probably it was the other way around: that that illness, which enabled her to escape the demands of school and home, was the first manifestation of her attitude to the world, an attitude that was transparent and permeated by the light of an emotion unknown to her. For Agathe felt herself to be a person of a spontaneous, simple temperament, warm, lively, even gay and easy to please; she had in fact adapted herself good-naturedly to a great variety of circumstances, nor had she ever suffered that collapse into indifference that befalls women who can no longer bear their disillusionment. But in the midst of her laughter or the tumult of some sensual adventure that continued nonetheless, there lived a disenchantment that made every fiber of her body tired and nostalgic for something else, something best described as nothingness.

This nothingness had a definite, if indefinable, content. For a long time she had been in the habit of repeating to herself, on all sorts of occasions, words of Novalis: "What then can I do for my soul, that lives within me like an unsolved riddle, even while it grants the visible man the utmost license, because there is no way it can control him?" But the flickering light of this utterance always went out again, like a flash of lightning that only left her in darkness, for she did not believe in a soul, as it was something too presumptuous and in any case much too definite for her own person. On the other hand, she could not believe in the earthly here and now either. To understand this rightly, one need only realize that this turning away from an earthly order when there is no faith in a supernatural order is a profoundly natural response, because in every head, alongside the process of logical thought, with its austere and simple orderliness reflecting the conditions of our external world, there is an affective world, whose logic, insofar as it can be spoken of at all, corresponds to feelings, passions, moods. The laws governing these two bear roughly the same relation to each other as those of a lumberyard, where chunks of wood are hewn into rectangular shapes and stacked ready for transport, bear to the dark tangled laws of the forest, with its mysterious workings and rustlings. And since the objects of our thought are in no way quite independent of its conditions, these two modes of thinking not only mingle in each person but can, to a certain extent, even present him with two worlds, at least immediately before and after that "first mysterious and indescribable moment" of which a famous religious thinker has said that it occurs in every sensory perception before vision and feeling separate and fall into the places in which one is accustomed to find them: one of them an object in space and the other a mental process enclosed within the observer.

And so, whatever the relationship may be between objects and feeling in the civilized person's mature view of the world, everyone surely knows those ecstatic moments in which a split has not yet occurred, as though water and land had not yet been divided and the waves of feeling still shared the same horizon as the hills and valleys that form the shape of things. There is even no need to assume that Agathe experienced such moments unusually often or with unusual intensity; she merely perceived them more vividly or, if you like, more superstitiously, for she was always willing to trust the world and then again not really trust it, just as she had done ever since her school days, and she had not unlearned it even later, when she had come in closer contact with masculine logic. In this sense, which is not to be confused with whim and willfulness, Agathe could have claimed—given more self-confidence than she had—to be the most illogical of women. But it had never occurred to her to regard the alienated feelings she experienced as more than a personal eccentricity. It was only through the encounter with her brother that a transformation occurred within her. In these empty rooms, all hollowed out in the shadows of solitude, rooms so recently filled with talk and a fellowship that reached to the innermost soul, the distinction between physical separation and mental presence unwittingly lost itself; and as the days glided by without a trace, Agathe felt with a hitherto unknown intensity the curious charm of that sense of omnipresence and omnipotence which occurs when the felt world makes the transition to perceptions. Her attention now seemed to be not with the senses but already opened wide deep inside her emotions, where no light could enter that did not already glow like the light in her heart, and it seemed to her, remembering her brother's words, that regardless of the ignorance she normally complained of she could understand everything that mattered without having to reflect on it. And as in this way her spirit was so filled with itself that even the liveliest idea had something of the soundless floating quality of a memory about it, everything that came her way spread out into a limitless present. Even when she did something, only a dividing line melted between herself, the doer, and the thing done, and her movements seemed to be the path by which things came to her when she stretched out her arms to them. This gentle power, this knowledge, and the world's speaking presence were, however, whenever she wondered with a smile what she *was* doing after all, hardly distinguishable from absence, helplessness, and a profound muteness of the spirit. With only a slight exaggeration of what she was feeling, Agathe could have said that she no longer knew where she was. On all sides she was in a state of suspension in which she felt both lifted up and lost to sight. She might have said: I am in love, but I don't know with whom. She was filled with a clear will, something she had always felt the lack of, but she did not know what she should undertake in its clarity, since all that her life had ever held of good and evil was now meaningless.

So it was not only when she looked at the poison capsule but every day that Agathe thought she would like to die, or that the happiness of death must be like the happiness in which she was spending her days while she was waiting to go and join her brother, meanwhile doing exactly what he had pleaded with her to stop doing. She could not imagine what would happen after she was with her brother in the capital. She remembered almost reproachfully that he had sometimes nonchalantly given signs of assuming that she would be successful there and would soon find a new husband or at least a lover; it would be nothing like that, that much she knew. Love, children, fine days, gay social gatherings, travel, a little art—the good life was so easy; she understood its appeal and was not immune to it. But ready as she was to regard herself as useless, Agathe felt the total contempt of the born rebel for this easy way out. She recognized it as a fake. The life supposedly lived to the full is in truth a life "without rhyme or reason"; in the end—and truly at the real end, death—something is always missing. It is—how should she put it?—like things piled up without being ordered by some guiding principle; unfulfilled in its fullness, the opposite of easy or simple, a jumble one accepts with the cheerfulness of habit! And suddenly going off at a tangent, she thought: "It's like a bunch of strange children you look at with conventional friendliness, with growing anxiety because you can't find your own child among them!"

She took some comfort in her resolve to put an end to her life if the new turn it was about to take should prove to have changed nothing. Like fermenting wine, she felt hope streaming in her that death and terror would not be the final word of truth. She felt no need to think about it. Actually, she feared this need, which Ulrich was always so glad to indulge, and she feared it aggressively. For she did feel that everything that moved her so strongly was not entirely free of a persistent hint that it was merely illusion. But it was just as true that every illusion contained a reality, however fluid and dissolved: perhaps a reality not yet solidified into earth, she thought; and in one of those wonderful moments when the place where she was standing seemed to melt away, she was able to believe that behind her, in that space into which one could never see, God might be standing. This was too much, and she recoiled from it. An awesome immensity and emptiness suddenly flooded through her, a shoreless radiance darkened her mind and overwhelmed her heart with fear. Her youth, easily prone to such anxieties as come with a lack of experience, whispered to her that she might be in danger of allowing an incipient madness to grow in her; she struggled to back away. Fiercely, she reminded herself that she did not believe in God at all. And she really did not believe, ever since she had been taught belief; it was part of her mistrust of everything she was taught. She was anything but religious if it meant faith in the supernatural, or at least some moral conviction. But after a while, exhausted and trembling, she still had to admit to herself that she had felt "God" as distinctly as if he were a man standing behind her and putting a coat on her shoulders.

When she had thought this over and recovered her nerve, she discovered that the meaning of her experience did not lie in that "solar eclipse" of her physical sensations, but was mainly a moral matter. A sudden change of her inmost condition, and hence of all her relations with the world, had for a moment given her that "unity of the conscience with the senses" which she had so far experienced so fleetingly that it was barely sufficient to impart to her ordinary life a tinge of something disconsolate and murkily passionate, whether Agathe tried to behave well or badly. This change seemed to her an incomparable outpouring that emanated as much from her surroundings toward her as from herself toward them, a oneness of the highest significance through the smallest mental motion, a motion that was barely distinguishable from the objects themselves. The objects were perfused by her sensations and the sensations by the objects in a way so convincing that Agathe felt she had never before been remotely touched by anything for which she had formerly used the word "convincing." And this had happened in circumstances that would normally be expected to rule out the possibility of her being convinced.

So the meaning of what she experienced in her solitude did not lie in its possible psychological import, as an indication of a high-strung or overly fragile personality, for it did not lie in the person at all but in something general, or perhaps in the link between his generality and the person, something Agathe not unjustly regarded as a moral conclusion in the sense that it seemed to the young woman—disappointed as she was in herself—that if she could always live as she did in such exceptional moments, and if she was not too weak to keep it up, she could love the world and willingly accommodate herself to it—something she would never be able to do otherwise! Now she was filled with a fierce longing to recover that mood, but such moments of highest intensity cannot be willed by force. It was only when her furious efforts proved useless that she realized, with the clarity which a pale day takes on after sunset, that the only thing she could hope for, and what in fact she was waiting for, with an impatience merely masked by her solitude, was the strange prospect that her brother had once half-humorously called the Millennium. He could just as well have chosen another word for it, for what it meant to Agathe was the convincing and confident ring of something that was coming. She would never have dared make this assertion. Even now she did not know whether it was truly possible. She had no idea what it could be. She had at the moment again forgotten all the words with which her brother had proved to her that beyond what filled her spirit with nebulous light, possibility stretched onward into

the uncharted. As long as she had been in his company she had simply felt that a country was crystallizing out of his words, crystallizing
not in her head but actually under her feet. The very fact that he
often spoke of it only ironically, and his usual way of alternating between coolness and emotion, which had so often confused her in the
beginning, now gladdened her in her loneliness, and she took it as a
kind of guarantee that he meant it—antagonistic states of soul being
more convincing than rapturous ones. "I was apparently thinking of
death only because I was afraid he was not being serious enough,"
she confessed to herself.

The last day she had to spend in absentia took her by surprise. All
at once everything in the house was cleared out and tidied up; nothing was left to do but hand the keys over to the old couple who were
being pensioned off under the provisions of the will and were to go
on living in the servants' lodge until the property found a new owner.
Agathe refused to go to a hotel, intending to stay at her post until her
train left in the small hours. The house was packed up and shrouded.
One naked bulb was lit. Some crates, pushed together, served as
table and chair. She had them set her table for supper on the edge of
a ravine on a terrace of crates. Her father's old factotum juggled a
loaded tray through light and shadow; he and his wife had insisted on
cooking a dinner in their own kitchen, so that, as they expressed it,
"the young lady" should be properly taken care of for her last meal at
home. Suddenly Agathe thought, completely outside the state of
mind in which she had spent the last few days: "Can they possibly
have noticed anything?" She could easily have neglected to destroy
every last scrap of paper on which she had practiced changing the
will. She felt cold terror, a nightmarish weight that hung on all her
limbs: the miserly dread of reality that holds no nourishment for the
spirit but only consumes it. Now she perceived with fierce intensity
her newly awakened desire to live; it furiously resisted the possibility
of anything getting in her way. When the old servant returned, she
scrutinized his face intently. But the old man, with his discreet smile,
went about his business unsuspecting, seeming to feel something or
other that was mute and ceremonious. She could not see into him
any more than she could see into a wall, and did not know what else
there might be in him behind his blank polish. Now she, too, felt
something muted, ceremonious, and sad. He had always been her

father's confidant, unfailingly ready to betray to him his children's every secret as soon as he had discovered it. But Agathe had been born in this house, and everything that had happened since was coming to an end this day: Agathe was moved to find herself and him here now, solemnly alone. She made up her mind to give him a special little gift of money, and in a fit of sudden weakness she planned to tell him that it came from Professor Hagauer; not from some calculating motive but as an act of atonement, with the intention of leaving nothing undone, even though she realized this was as unnecessary as it was superstitious. Before the old man returned again, she also took out her locket and capsule. The locket with the portrait of her never-forgotten beloved she slipped, after one last frowning look at his face, under the loosely nailed lid of a crate destined to go into storage indefinitely; it appeared to contain kitchen utensils or lamps, for she heard the clink of metal on metal, like branches falling from a tree. Then she placed the capsule with the poison where she had formerly worn the portrait.

"How old-fashioned of me!" she thought with a smile as she did this. "I'm sure there are things more important than one's love life!" But she did not believe it.

At this moment it would have been as untrue to say that she was disinclined to enter into illicit relations with her brother as that she desired to. That might depend on how things turned out; but in her present state of mind nothing corresponded to the clarity of such a problem.

The light painted the bare boards of the crates between which she was sitting a glaring white and deep black. And a similar tragic mask gave an eerie touch to the otherwise simple thought that she was now spending her last evening in the house where she had been born of a woman she had never been able to remember, who had also given birth to Ulrich. An old impression came to her of clowns with dead-serious faces and strange instruments standing around her. They began to play. Agathe recognized it as a childhood daydream of hers. She could not hear the music, but all the clowns were looking at her. She told herself that at this moment her death would be no loss to anyone or anything, and for herself it would mean no more than the outward end of an inner dying. So she thought while the clowns were sending their music up to the ceiling and she seemed to be sitting on a circus floor strewn with sawdust, tears dropping on her finger. It was a feeling of utter futility she had known often as a girl, and she thought: "I suppose I've remained childish to this day," which did not prevent her from thinking at the same time of something that loomed vastly magnified by her tears: how, in the first hour of their reunion, she and her brother had come face-to-face in just such clown costumes. "What does it mean that it is my brother, of all people, who seems to hold the key to what's inside me?" she wondered. And suddenly she was really weeping. It seemed to be happening for no other reason she knew of but sheer pleasure, and she shook her head hard, as though there were something here she could neither undo nor put together.

At the same time she was thinking with a native ingenuousness that Ulrich would find the answers to all problems . . . until the old man came back again and was moved at seeing her so moved. "Oh my, the dear young lady!" he said, also shaking his head.

Agathe looked at him in confusion, but when she realized the misunderstanding behind this compassion, that it had been aroused by her appearance of childlike grief, her youthful high spirits rose again.

"Cast all thou hast into the fire, even unto thy shoes. When thou has nothing left, think not even on thy shroud, but cast thyself naked into the fire!" she said to him.

It was an ancient saying that Ulrich had read to her delightedly, and the old man showed the stumps of his teeth in a smile at the grave and mellow lilt of the words she recited to him, her eyes aglow with tears; with his eyes he followed her hand pointing at the high-piled crates—she was trying to help his understanding by misleading it—suggesting something like a pyre. He had nodded at the word "shroud," eager to follow even though the path of the words was none too smooth, but he'd stiffened from the word "naked" on, and when she repeated her maxim, his face had reverted to the mask of the well-trained servant whose expression gives assurance that he can be trusted not to hear, see, or judge his betters.

In all his years with his old master that word had never once been uttered in his hearing; "undressed" would have been the closest permissible. But young people were different nowadays, and he would probably not be able to give them satisfaction in any case. Serenely, as one who has earned his retirement, he felt that his career was over.

But Agathe's last thought before she left was: "Would Ulrich really cast everything into the fire?"

22

FROM KONIATOWSKI'S CRITIQUE OF DANIELLI'S THEOREM TO THE FALL OF MAN. FROM THE FALL OF MAN TO THE EMOTIONAL RIDDLE POSED BY A MAN'S SISTER

The state in which Ulrich emerged into the street on leaving the Palais Leinsdorf was rather like the down-to-earth sensation of hunger. He stopped in front of a billboard and stilled his hunger for bourgeois normality by taking in the announcements and advertisements. The billboard was several yards wide and covered with words.

"Actually," it occurred to him, "one might assume that these particular words, which are met with in every corner of the city, have a great deal to tell us." The language seemed to him akin to the clichés uttered by the characters in popular novels at important points in their lives. He read: "Have you ever worn anything so flattering yet so durable as Topinam silk stockings?" "His Excellency Goes Out on the Town!" "*Saint Bartholomew's Night*—A Brand-New Production!" "For Fun and Food Come to the Black Pony!" "Hot Sex Show & Dancing at the Red Pony!" Next to this he noticed a political poster: "Criminal Intrigues!" but it referred to the price of bread, not to the Parallel Campaign. He turned away and, a few steps farther along, looked into the window of a bookshop. "The Great Author's Latest Work," said a cardboard sign beside a row of fifteen copies of the same book. In the opposite corner of the display window, a sign accompanying another book read: "*Love's Tower of Babel* by ——— makes gripping reading for men and women."

"The Great Author?" Ulrich thought. He remembered having read one book by him and resolved never to read another; but since then the man had nevertheless become famous. Considering the window display of German intellect, Ulrich was reminded of an old army joke: "Mortadella!" During Ulrich's military service this had been the nickname of an unpopular general, after the popular Italian sausage, and if anyone wondered why, the answer was: "Part pig, part donkey." He was prevented from pursuing this stimulating analogy by the voice of a woman asking him:

"Are you waiting for the streetcar too?" Only then did he realize that he was no longer standing in front of the bookshop. He also had not realized that he was now standing immobile at a streetcar stop. The woman who had called this to his attention wore a knapsack and glasses, and turned out to be an acquaintance from the staff of the Astronomical Institute, one of the few women of accomplishment in this man's profession. He looked at her nose and the bags under her eyes, which the strain of unremitting intellectual effort had turned into something resembling underarm dress shields made of gutta-percha. Then he glanced down and noticed her short tweed skirt, then up and saw a black rooster feather in a green mountaineer's hat that floated over her learned features, and he smiled.

"Are you off to the mountains?" he asked.

Dr. Strastil was going to the mountains for three days to "relax." "What do you think of Koniatowski's paper?" she asked Ulrich. Ulrich had nothing to say. "Kneppler will be furious," she said, "but Koniatowski's critique of Kneppler's deduction from Danielli's theorem is interesting, don't you agree? Do *you* think Kneppler's deduction is possible?"

Ulrich shrugged his shoulders.

He was one of those mathematicians called logicians, for whom nothing was ever "correct" and who were working out new theoretical principles. But he was not entirely satisfied with the logic of the logicians either. Had he continued his work, he would have gone right back to Aristotle; he had his own views of all that.

"For my part, I don't think Kneppler's deduction is mistaken, it's just that it's wrong," Dr. Strastil confessed. She might have said with the same firmness that she did consider the deduction mistaken but nevertheless not essentially wrong. She knew what she meant, but in ordinary language, where the terms are undefined, one cannot express oneself unequivocally. Using this holiday language under her tourist hat made her feel something of the timid haughtiness that might be aroused in a cloistered monk who was rash enough to let himself come in contact with the sensual world of the laity.

Ulrich got into the streetcar with Fräulein Strastil; he didn't know why. Perhaps it was because she cared so much about Koniatowski's criticism of Kneppler. Perhaps he felt like talking to her about literature, about which she knew nothing.

"What will you do in the mountains?" he asked.

She was going up to the Hochschwab.

"There'll still be too much snow up there." He knew the mountains. "It's too late for skis, and too early to go up there without them."

"Then I'll stay down," Fräulein Strastil declared. "I once spent three days in a cabin at the foot of the Farsenalm. I only want to get back to nature for a bit!"

The expression on the worthy astronomer's face as she uttered the word "nature" provoked Ulrich to ask her what she needed nature for.

Dr. Strastil was sincerely indignant. She could lie on the mountain meadow for three whole days without stirring—"just like a boulder!" she declared.

"That's because you're a scientist," Ulrich pointed out. "A peasant would be bored."

Dr. Strastil did not see it that way. She spoke of the thousands who sought nature every holiday, on foot, on wheels, or by boat.

Ulrich spoke of the peasants deserting the countryside in droves for the attractions of the city.

Fräulein Strastil doubted that he was feeling on a sufficiently elementary level.

Ulrich claimed that the only elementary level, besides eating and love, was to make oneself comfortable, not to seek out an alpine meadow. The natural feeling that was supposed to drive people to do such things was actually a modern Rousseauism, a complicated and sentimental attitude.

He was not at all pleased with the way he was expressing himself, but he did not care what he said, and merely kept on talking because he had not yet come to what he wanted to get out of his system. Fräulein Strastil gave him a mistrustful look. She could not make him out. Here her considerable experience in abstract thinking was of no use to her; she could neither keep separate nor fit together the ideas he seemed merely to be juggling so nimbly; she guessed that he was talking without thinking. She took some comfort in listening to him with a rooster feather on her hat, and it reinforced her joy in the solitude she was heading for.

At this point Ulrich's eye happened to light on the newspaper of the man opposite him, and he read the opening line of an advertisement, in heavy type: "Our time asks questions—Our time gives answers." It could have been the announcement of a new arch support or of a forthcoming lecture—who could tell these days?—but his mind suddenly leapt onto the track he had been seeking.

His companion struggled to be objective. "I'm afraid," she admitted with some hesitation, "that I don't know much about literature; people like us never have time. Perhaps I don't know the right things, either. But ————"—she mentioned a popular name— "means a great deal to me. A writer who can make us feel things so intensely is surely what we mean by a great writer!"

However, since Ulrich felt he had now profited enough from Dr. Strastil's combination of an exceptionally developed capacity for abstract thought and a notably retarded understanding of the soul, he stood up cheerfully, treated his colleague to a bit of outrageous flattery, and hastily got off, excusing himself on the grounds that he had gone two stops past his destination. When he stood on the street, raising his hat to her once more, Fräulein Strastil remembered that she had recently heard some disparaging remarks about his own work; but she also felt herself blushing in response to his charming parting words to her, which, to her way of thinking, was not exactly to his credit. But he now knew, without yet being fully conscious of it, why his thoughts were revolving on the subject of literature and what it was they were after, from the interrupted "Mortadella" comparison to his unintentionally leading the good Strastil on to those confidences. After all, literature had been no concern of his since he had written his last poem, at twenty; still, before that, writing secretly had been a fairly regular habit, which he had given up not because he had grown older or had realized he didn't have enough talent, but for reasons that now, with his current impressions, he would have liked to define by some kind of word suggesting much effort culminating in a void.

For Ulrich was one of those book-lovers who do not want to go on reading because they feel that the whole business of reading and writing is a nuisance. "If the sensible Strastil wants to be 'made to feel,' " he thought ("Quite right too! If I had objected she'd have brought up music as her trump card!")—and as one so often does, he was partly thinking in words, partly carrying on a wordless argument in his head—so if this reasonable Dr. Strastil wants to be made to feel, it only amounts to what everyone wants from art, to be moved, overwhelmed, entertained, surprised, to be allowed a sniff of noble ideas; in short, to be made to experience something "alive," have a "living" experience. Ulrich was certainly not against it. Somewhere at the back of his mind he was thinking something that ended in a mingling of a touch of sentiment and ironic resistance: "Feeling is rare enough. To keep feeling at a certain temperature, to keep it from cooling down, probably means preserving the body warmth from which all intellectual development arises. And whenever a person is momentarily lifted out of his tangle of rational intentions, which involve him with countless alien objects, whenever he is raised to a state wholly without purpose, such as listening to music, for instance, he is almost in the biological condition of a flower on which the rain and the sunshine fall." He was willing to admit that there is a more eternal eternity in the mind's pauses and quiescence than in its activity; but he had been thinking first "feeling" and then "experiencing": a contradiction was implied here. For there were experiences of the will! There were experiences of action at its peak! Though one could probably assume that by the time each experience had reached its acme of radiant bitterness it was sheer feeling; which would bring up an even greater contradiction: that in its greatest purity the state of feeling is a quiescence, a dying away of all activity. Or was it not a contradiction, after all? Was there some curious connection by which the most intense activity was motionless at the core? At this point he realized that this sequence of ideas had begun not so much as a thought at the back of his mind as one that was unwelcome, for with a sudden stiffening of resistance against the sentimental turn it had taken, Ulrich repudiated the whole train of thought into which he had slipped. He had absolutely no intention of brooding over certain states of mind and, when he was thinking about feeling, succumbing to feelings.

He suddenly realized that what he was getting at could best be defined, without much ado, as the futile actuality or the eternal momentariness of literature. Does it lead to anything? Literature is either a tremendous detour from experience to experience, ending back where it came from, or an epitome of sensations that leads to nothing at all definite. "A puddle," he now thought, "has often made a stronger impression of depth on someone than the ocean, for the simple reason that we have more occasion to experience puddles than oceans." It seemed to him that it was the same with feelings, which was the only reason commonplace feelings are regarded as the deepest. Putting the ability to feel above the feeling itself—the characteristic of all sensitive people—like the wanting to make others feel and be made to feel that is the common impulse behind all our arrangements concerning the emotional life, amounts to downgrading the importance and nature of the feelings compared with their fleeting presence as a subjective state, and so leads to that shallowness, stunted development, and utter irrelevance, for which there is no lack of examples. "Of course," Ulrich added mentally, "this view will repel all those people who feel as cozy in their feelings as a rooster in his feathers and who even preen themselves on the idea that eternity starts all over again with every separate 'personality'!" He had a clear mental image of an immense perversity of a scope involving all mankind, but he could not find a way to express it that would satisfy him, probably because its ramifications were too intricate.

While busy with all this he was watching the passing trolley cars, waiting for the one that would take him back as close as possible to the center of town. He saw people climbing in and out of the cars, and his technically trained eye toyed distractedly with the interplay of welding and casting, rolling and bolting, of engineering and hand finishing, of historical development and the present state of the art, which combined to make up these barracks-on-wheels that these people were using.

"As a last step, a committee from the municipal transportation department comes to the factory and decides what kind of wood to use as veneer, the color of the paint, upholstery, arms on the seats and straps for standees, ashtrays, and the like," he thought idly, "and it is precisely these trivial details, along with the red or green color of the exterior, and how they swing themselves up the steps and inside, that for tens of thousands of people make up what they remember, all they experience, of all the genius that went into it. This is what forms their character, endows it with speed or comfort; it's what makes them perceive red cars as home and blue ones as foreign, and adds up to that unmistakable odor of countless details that clings to the clothing of the centuries." So there was no denying—and this suddenly rounded out Ulrich's main line of thought—that life itself largely peters out into trivial realities or, to put it technically, that the power of its spiritual coefficient is extremely small.

And suddenly, as he felt himself swinging aboard the trolley, he said to himself: "I shall have to make Agathe see that morality is the subordination of every momentary state in our life to one enduring one!" This principle had come to him all at once in the form of a definition. But this highly polished concept had been preceded and was followed by others which, though not so fully developed and articulated, rounded out its meaning. The innocuous business of feeling was here set in an austere conceptual framework, it was given a job to do, with a strict hierarchy of values, vaguely foreshortened, in the offing: feelings must either be functional or refer to a still-undefined condition as immense as the open sea. Should it be called an idea or a longing? Ulrich had to leave it at that, for from the moment his sister's name had occurred to him her shadow had darkened his thoughts. As always when he thought of her, he felt that he had shown himself in her company in a different frame of mind than usual. And he knew, too, that he was longing passionately to get back into that frame of mind. But the same memory overcame him with humiliation when he thought of himself carrying on in a presumptuous, ludicrous, and drunken fashion, no better than a man who sinks to his knees in a frenzy in front of people he won't be able to look in the face the next day. Considering how balanced and controlled the intellectual exchange between brother and sister had been this was a wild exaggeration, and if it was not completely unfounded, it was probably no more than a reaction to feelings that had not yet taken shape. He knew Agathe was bound to arrive in a few days, and he had done nothing to stop her. Had she actually done anything wrong? One might suppose that as she cooled off she had gone back on it all. But a lively premonition assured him that Agathe had not abandoned her scheme. He could have tried to find out by asking her. Again he felt duty bound to write and warn her against it. But instead of giving this even a moment's serious consideration, he tried to imagine what could have prompted Agathe to do something so irregular: he saw it as an incredibly vehement gesture meant to show her trust in him and to put herself entirely in his hands. "She has very little sense of reality," he thought, "but a wonderful way of doing what she wants. Rash, I suppose, but just for that reason spontaneous! When she's angry, she sees red with a vengeance." He smiled indulgently and looked around at the other passengers. Every one of them had evil thoughts, of course, and every one suppressed them, and nobody blamed himself overmuch; but no one else had these thoughts outside himself, in another person, who would give them the enchanting inaccessibility of an experience in a dream.

Since Ulrich had left his letter unfinished, he realized for the first time that he no longer had a choice but was already in the state he was still hesitating to enter. According to its laws—he indulged himself in the overweening ambiguity of calling them "holy"—Agathe's misstep could not be undone by repentance but only be made *good* by actions that followed it, which incidentally was doubtless in keeping with the original meaning of repentance as a state of purifying fire, not a state of being impaired. To repair the damage done to Agathe's inconvenient husband, or indemnify him, would have meant only to undo the damage done, that is, it would only have been that double and crippling negation of which ordinary good conduct consists, which inwardly cancels out to zero. But what should be done for Hagauer, how a looming burden should be "lifted," was possible only if one could marshal a great sympathy for him, a prospect Ulrich could not face without dismay. Keeping within the framework of this logic that Ulrich was trying to adapt to, all that could ever be made good was something other than the damage done, and he did not doubt for an instant that this would have to be his and his sister's whole life.

"Putting it presumptuously," he thought, "this means: Saul did not make good each single consequence of his previous sins; he turned into Paul!" Against this curious logic, however, both feeling and judgment raised the customary objection that it would nevertheless be more decent—and no deterrent to more romantic future possibilities—to straighten out accounts with one's brother-in-law first, and only then to plan one's new life. The kind of morality to which he was so attracted was not, after all, suited in the least to dealing with money matters and business and the resulting conflicts. So insoluble and conflicting situations were bound to arise on the borderline between that other life and everyday life, which it would be better not to allow to develop into borderline cases; they should be dispatched at the outset, in the normal, unemotional way of simple decency. But here again Ulrich felt it was impossible to take one's bearings from the normal conditions of goodness if one wanted to press on into the realm of unconditional goodness. The mission laid upon him, to take the first step into uncharted territory, would apparently suffer no abatement.

His last line of defense was his strong aversion to the terms he had been using so lavishly, such as "self," "feeling," "goodness," "alternative goodness," "evil," for being so subjective and at the same time presumptuous, gauzy abstractions, which really corresponded to the moral ponderings of very much younger people. He found himself doing what any number of those who are following his story are likely to do, irritably picking out individual words and phrases, asking himself such questions as: " 'Production and results of feelings?' What a machinelike, rationalistic, humanly unrealistic notion! 'Morality as the problem of a permanent state to which all individual states are subordinate'—and that's all? The inhumanity of it!" Looked at through a rational person's eyes, it all seemed extraordinarily perverse. "The essence of morality virtually hinges on the important feelings remaining constant," Ulrich thought, "and all the individual has to do is act in accord with them!"

But just at this point the rolling locale that enclosed him and that had been created with T-square and compass came to a halt, at a spot where his eye, peering out from the body of modern transportation and still an involuntary part of it, lit on a stone column that had been standing beside this roadway since the period of the Baroque, so that the engineered comfort of this calculated artifact, unconsciously taken for granted, suddenly clashed with the passion erupting from the statue's antiquated pose, which suggested something not unlike a petrified bellyache. The effect of this optical collision was to powerfully confirm the ideas from which Ulrich had just been trying to escape. Could anything have illustrated life's confusion more clearly than this chance spectacle? Without taking sides with either the Now or the Then in matters of taste, as one usually does when faced with such a juxtaposition, he felt his mind abandoned by both sides without an instant's hesitation, and saw in it only the great demonstration of a problem that is at bottom a moral problem. He could not doubt that the transience of what is regarded as style, culture, the will of the time, or the spirit of an era, for which it is admired, was a moral weakness. For in the great scale of the ages this instability means exactly what it would mean on the smaller scale of personal life: to have developed one's potential one-sidedly, to have dissipated it in extravagant exaggerations, never taking the measure of one's own will, never achieving a complete form, and in disjointed passions doing now this, now that. Even the so-called succession or progress of the ages seemed to him to be only another term for the fact that none of these experiments ever reach the point where they would all meet and move on together toward a comprehensive understanding that would at last offer a basis for a coherent development, a lasting enjoyment, and that seriousness of great beauty of which nowadays hardly more than a shadow occasionally drifts across our life.

Ulrich of course saw the preposterous arrogance of assuming that everything had in effect come to nothing. And yet it was nothing. Immeasurable as existence; confusion as meaning. At least, judging by the results, it was no more than the stuff of which the soul of the present is made, which is not much. While Ulrich was thinking this he was nevertheless savoring the "not much," as if it were the last meal at the table of life his outlook would permit him to have. He had left the streetcar and taken a route that would bring him quickly to the city's center. He felt as if he were coming out of a cellar. The streets were screeching with gaiety and filled with unseasonable warmth like a summer day. The sweet poisonous taste of talking to oneself had left his mouth: everything was expansive and out in the sun. Ulrich stopped at almost every shop window. Those tiny bottles in so many colors, stoppered scents, countless variants of nail scissors—what quantities of genius there were even in a hairdresser's window! A glove shop: what connections, what inventions, before a goat's skin is drawn up on a lady's hand and the animal's pelt has become more refined than her own! He was astonished at the luxuries one took for granted, the countless cozy trappings of the good life, as though he were seeing them for the first time. Trap-pings! What a charming word, he felt. And what a boon, this tremendous contract to get along together! Here there was no reminder of life's earth crust, of the unpaved roads of passion, of—he truly felt this— the *uncivilized* nature of the soul! One's attention, a bright and narrow beam, glided over a flower garden of fruits, gemstones, fabrics, forms and allurements whose gently persuasive eyes were opened in all the colors of the rainbow. Since at that time a white skin was prized and guarded from the sun, a few colorful parasols were already floating above the crowd, laying silky shadows on women's pale faces. Ulrich's glance was even enchanted by the pale-golden beer seen in passing through the plate-glass windows of a restaurant, on tablecloths so white that they formed blue patches at the edges of shadows. Then the Archbishop's carriage drove by, a gently rocking, heavy carriage, whose dark interior showed red and purple. It had to be the Archbishop's carriage, for this horse-drawn vehicle that Ulrich followed with his eyes had a wholly ecclesiastical air, and two policemen sprang to attention and saluted this follower of Christ without thinking of their predecessors who had run a lance into *his* predecessor's side.

He gave himself up with such zest to these impressions, which he had just been calling "life's futile actuality," that little by little, as he sated himself with the world, his earlier revulsion against it began to reassert itself. Ulrich now knew exactly where his speculations fell short. "What's the point, in the face of all this vainglory, of looking for some result beyond, behind, beneath it all? Would that be a philosophy? An all-embracing conviction, a law? Or the finger of God? Or, instead of that, the assumption that morality has up to now lacked an 'inductive stance,' that it is much harder to be good than we had believed, and that it will require an endless cooperative effort, like every other science? I think there is no morality, because it cannot be deduced from anything constant; all there are are rules for uselessly maintaining transitory conditions. I also assume that there can be no profound happiness without a profound morality; yet my thinking about it strikes me as an unnatural, bloodless state, and it is absolutely not what I want!" Indeed, he might well have asked himself much more simply, "What is this I have taken upon myself?" which is what he now did. However, this question touched his sensibility more than his intellect; in fact, the question stopped his thinking and diminished bit by bit his always keen delight in strategic planning before he had even formulated it. It began as a dark tone close to his ear, accompanying him; then it sounded inside him, an octave lower than everything else; finally, Ulrich had merged with his question and felt as though he himself were a strangely deep sound in the bright, hard world, surrounded by a wide interval. So what was it he had really taken on himself, what had he promised?

He thought hard. He knew that he had not merely been joking when he used the expression "the Millennium," even if it was only a figure of speech. If one took this promise seriously, it meant the desire to live, with the aid of mutual love, in a secular condition so transcendent that one could only feel and do whatever heightened and maintained that condition. He had always been certain that human beings showed hints of such a disposition. It had begun with the "affair of the major's wife," and though his subsequent experiences had not amounted to much, they had always been of the same kind. In sum, what it more or less came to was that Ulrich believed in the "Fall of Man" and in "Original Sin." That is, he was inclined to think that at some time in the past, man's basic attitude had undergone a fundamental change that must have been roughly comparable to the moment when a lover regains his sobriety; he may then see the whole truth, but something greater has been torn to shreds, and the truth appears everywhere as a mere fragment left over and patched up again. Perhaps it was even the apple of "knowledge" that had caused this spiritual change and expelled mankind from a primal state to which it might find its way back only after becoming wise through countless experiences and through sin. But Ulrich believed in such myths not in their traditional form, but only in the way he had discovered them; he believed in them like an arithmetician who, with the system of his feelings spread out before him, concludes, from the fact that none of them could be justified, that he would have to introduce a fantastic hypothesis whose nature could be arrived at only intuitively. That was no trifle! He had turned over such thoughts in his mind often enough, but he had never yet been in the situation of having to decide within a few days whether to stake his life on it. A faint sweat broke out under his hat and collar, and he was bothered by the proximity of all the people jostling by him. What he was thinking amounted to taking leave of most of his living relationships; he had no illusions about that. For today our lives are divided, and parts are entangled with other people; what we dream has to do with dreaming and also with what other people dream; what we do has sense, but more sense in relation with what others do; and what we believe is tied in with beliefs only a fraction of which are our own. It is therefore quite unrealistic to insist upon acting out of the fullness of one's own personal reality. Especially for a man like himself, who had been imbued all his life with the thought that one's beliefs had to be shared, that one must have the courage to live in the midst of moral contradictions, because that was the price of great achievement. Was he at least convinced of what he had just been thinking about the possibility and significance of another kind of life? Not at all! Nevertheless, he could not help being emotionally drawn to it, as though his feelings were facing the unmistakable signs of a reality they had been looking forward to for years.

At this point he did have to ask himself what, if anything, entitled him, like a veritable Narcissus, to wish not to do ever again anything that left his soul unmoved. Such a resolve runs counter to the principles of the active life with which everyone is today imbued, and even if God-fearing times could have fostered such ambitions, they have melted away like the half-light of dawn as the sun grows stronger. There was an odor of something reclusive and syrupy clinging to him that Ulrich found increasingly distasteful. He tried to rein in his unruly thoughts as quickly as possible, and told himself—if not quite sincerely—that the promise of a Millennium he had so oddly given his sister, rationally considered, boiled down to no more than a kind of social work: living with Agathe would probably call for all the delicacy and selflessness he could muster—qualities that had been all too lacking in him. He recalled, the way one recalls an unusually transparent cloud flitting across the sky, certain moments of their recent time together that had already been of this kind. "Perhaps the content of the Millennium is merely the burgeoning of this energy, which at first shows itself in two people, until it grows into a resounding universal communion," he wondered in some embarrassment. Again he resorted to his own "affair of the major's wife" for more light on the subject. Leaving aside the delusions of love, since immaturity had been at the root of that aberration, he focused all his attention on the feelings of tender care and adoration of which he had been capable in his solitude at the time, and it seemed to him that feeling trust and affection, or living for another person, must be a happiness that could move one to tears, as lovely as the lambent sinking of day into the peace of evening and also, just a little, an impoverishing of spirit and intellect to the point of tears. For there was also a funny side to their project, as of two elderly bachelors setting up house together, and such twitchings of his imagination warned him how little the notion of a life of service in brotherly love was likely to offer him fulfillment. With some detachment he could see that from the first there had been a large measure of the asocial intermingled in his relationship with Agathe. Not only the business with Hagauer and the will, but the whole emotional tone of their association, pointed to something impetuous, and there was no doubt that what brought them together was not so much love for each other as a repelling of the rest of the world.

"No!" Ulrich thought. "Wanting to live for another person is no more than egoism going bankrupt and then opening a new shop next door, with a partner!"

Actually, his inner concentration, despite this brilliantly honed insight, had already passed its peak at the moment when he had been tempted to confine the diffuse illumination that filled him inside an earthly lamp, and now that this had shown itself to be a mistake, his thinking had lost the urge to press for a decision and was eager for some distraction. Not far from him two men had just collided and were shouting unpleasant remarks at each other as if getting ready to fight; Ulrich watched with a renewed interest, and had hardly turned away when his glance struck that of a woman giving him a look like a fat flower nodding on its stem. In that pleasant mood which is an equal blend of feeling and extroverted attention, he noted that real people pursue the ideal commandment to love one another in two parts, the first consisting in their detesting one another and the second in making up for it by entering into sexual relations with the half that is excepted. Without stopping to think he too turned, after a few steps, to follow the woman; it was a quite mechanical consequence of their eye contact. He could see her body beneath her dress like a big white fish just under the surface of the water. He felt the male urge to harpoon the fish and watch it flap and struggle, and there was in this as much repugnance as desire. Some hardly perceptible signs made him certain this woman knew he was prowling after her and was interested. He tried to work out her place on the social scale and decided on "upper-middle class," where it is hard to pinpoint the position with precision. "Business family? Government service?" he speculated. Various random images came to him, even including that of a pharmacy: he could feel the pungently sweet smell of the husband coming home, the compact atmosphere of the household betraying no sign of the shifting beam from the burglar's flashlight that had just recently moved through it. It was vile, no doubt, but shamefully exciting.

As Ulrich kept following the woman, actually afraid that she might stop at some shop window and so force him either to stumble foolishly past her or to pick her up, something in him was still undistracted and wide awake. "What exactly might Agathe want from *me?*" he asked himself for the first time. He did not know. He assumed that it would be something like what he wanted of her, but he had nothing to base this on but intuition. Wasn't it amazing how quickly and unexpectedly it had all happened? Other than a few childhood memories he had known nothing about her, and the little he had heard, such as her connection of some years with Hagauer, he found rather distasteful. He now recalled the curious hesitancy, almost reluctance, with which he had approached his father's house on his arrival. Suddenly the idea took hold of him: "My feeling for Agathe is just imagination!" In a man who continually wanted something other than what those around him wanted—he was thinking seriously again—in such a man, who always felt strong dislikes and never got as far as liking, the usual kindliness and lukewarm human goodness can easily separate and turn into a cold hardness with a mist of impersonal love floating above it. Seraphic love, he had once named it. It could also, he thought, be called love without a partner. Or, just as well, love without sex. Sexual love was all the love there was nowadays: those alike in gender repelled each other, and in the sexual crossover people loved with a growing resentment of the overestimation of this compulsion. But seraphic love was free of both these defects. It was love cleansed of the crosscurrents of social and sexual aversions. This love, which makes itself felt everywhere in company with the cruelty of modern life, could truly be called the sisterly love of an age that has no room for brotherly love, he said to himself, wincing in irritation.

Yet having finally arrived at this conclusion, alongside it and alternately with it he went on dreaming of a woman who could not be attained at all. He had a vision of her like late-autumn days in the mountains, when the air is as if drained of its lifeblood to the point of death, while the colors are aflame with fierce passion. He saw the blue vistas, without end in their mysterious gradations. He completely forgot the woman who was actually walking ahead of him; he was far from desire and perhaps close to love.

He was distracted only by the lingering gaze of another woman, like that of the first, yet not so brazen and obvious; this one was well-bred and delicate as a pastel stroke that leaves its stamp in a fraction of a second. He looked up and in a state of utmost emotional exhaustion beheld a very beautiful lady in whom he recognized Bonadea.

The glorious day had lured her out for a walk. Ulrich glanced at his watch: he had been strolling along only fifteen minutes, and no more than forty-five had passed since he left the Palais Leinsdorf.

Bonadea said: "I'm not free today."

Ulrich thought: "How long, by comparison, is a whole day, a year, not to mention a resolution for a lifetime!" It was beyond calculation.

23

BONADEA; OR, THE RELAPSE

And so it happened that Ulrich received a visit soon afterward from his abandoned mistress. Their encounter on the street had not provided him with an opportunity to call her to account for misusing his name to win Diotima's friendship, nor had it given Bonadea enough time to reproach him for his long silence and not only defend herself from the charge of indiscretion and call Diotima "an ignoble snake" but even make up a story to prove it. Hence she and her retired lover had hurriedly agreed that they must meet once again and have it all out.

The visitor who appeared was no longer the Bonadea who coiled her hair until it gave her head something of a Grecian look when she studied it in the mirror with eyes narrowed, intending to be just as pure and noble as Diotima, nor was she the one who raved in the night, maddened by the withdrawal pains of such a cure for her addiction, cursing her exemplar shamelessly and with a woman's instinct for the lethal thrust; she was once again the dear old Bonadea whose curls hung down over her none-too-wise brow or were swept back from it, depending on the dictates of fashion, and in whose eyes there was always something reminiscent of the air rising above a fire. While Ulrich started to reprove her for having betrayed their relationship to his cousin, she was carefully removing her hat before the mirror, and when he wanted to know exactly how much she had said, she smugly and in great detail told him a story she claimed to have made up for Diotima about having had a letter from him in which he asked her to see that Moosbrugger was not overlooked entirely, whereupon she had thought the best thing to do was to turn to the woman of whose high-mindedness the writer of the letter had so often spoken to her. Then she perched on the arm of Ulrich's chair, kissed his forehead, and meekly insisted that it was all perfectly true, except for the letter.

Her bosom emitted a great warmth.

"Then why did you call my cousin a snake? You were one yourself!" Ulrich said.

Bonadea pensively shifted her gaze from him to the wall. "Oh, I don't know," she answered. "She's so nice to me. She takes so much interest in me!"

"What is that supposed to mean?" Ulrich asked. "Are you participating in her efforts for the Good, the True, and the Beautiful?"

Bonadea replied: "She explained to me that no woman can live for her love with all her might, she no more than I. And that is why every woman must do her duty in the place appointed to her by fate. She really is so very decent," Bonadea went on, even more thoughtfully. "She keeps telling me to be more patient with my husband, and she insists that a superior woman can find considerable happiness in making the most of her marriage; she puts far more value in that than in adultery. And after all, it's exactly what I've always thought myself!"

It happened to be true, in fact; for Bonadea had never thought otherwise, she had merely always acted otherwise, and so she could agree with a good conscience. When Ulrich said as much to her, it earned him another kiss, this time somewhat lower than the forehead. "You happen to upset my polygamous balance," she said with a little sigh of apology for the discrepancy that had arisen between her principles and her conduct.

It turned out, after some cross-examination, that she had meant to say "polyglandular balance"—a new physiological term at that time comprehensible only to initiates, which might be translated as balance of secretions, on the assumption that certain glands which affected the blood had a stimulating or inhibiting effect, thereby influencing character and, more specifically, a person's temperament, especially the kind of temperament Bonadea had to a degree that caused her much suffering in certain circumstances.

Ulrich raised his eyebrows in curiosity.

"Well, something to do with glands," Bonadea said. "It's rather a relief to know one can't help it!" She gave the lover she had lost a wistful smile. "A person who loses her balance easily is liable to have unsuccessful sexual experiences."

"My dear Bonadea," Ulrich marveled, "what kind of talk is this?"

"It's what I've been learning to say. You are an unsuccessful sexual experience, your cousin says. But she also says that a person can escape the shattering physical and emotional effects by bearing in mind that nothing we do is merely our own personal affair. She's very nice to me. She says that *my* mistake is that I make too much of a single aspect of love instead of taking in the whole spectrum of the experience. You see, what she means by a single aspect is what she also calls 'the crude mechanics': it's often very interesting to see things in her light. But there's one thing about her I don't like. She may say that a strong woman sees her life's work in monogamy and should love it like an artist, but she does have three men, and, counting you, possibly four, on her string, and I have none at all now to make me happy!"

The gaze with which she scrutinized her AWOL reservist was warm and questioning. Ulrich did his best to ignore it.

"So the two of you talk about me?" he asked with some foreboding.

"Oh, only on and off," Bonadea replied. "When your cousin needs to exemplify something, or when your friend the General is present."

"I suppose Arnheim is in on this too?"

"He lends a dignified ear to what the gracious ladies have to say." Bonadea made fun of him, not without talent for unobtrusive mimicry, but she added seriously: "I don't like the way he treats your cousin at all. Most of the time he's off on some trip or other, and when he's present he talks too much to everyone, and when she is quoting Frau von Stern, for example—"

"Frau von Stein?" Ulrich corrected her by asking.

"Of course, I meant Stein: it isn't as if Diotima didn't talk about her often enough. Well, when she talks about Frau von Stein and Goethe's other woman, the Vul . . . What's her name? It sounds a little obscene, I think. . . ."

"Vulpius."

"Oh yes. You know, I get to hear so many foreign words there that I'm beginning to forget the simplest ones! So when she's making her comparisons between Frau von Stein and the other, Arnheim keeps staring at me as if, compared with his idol, I was no better than the kind you just said."

Now Ulrich insisted on an explanation of these new developments. It turned out that since Bonadea had claimed the status of Ulrich's confidante she had made great strides in her intimacy with Diotima.

Her alleged nymphomania, which Ulrich had carelessly mentioned to Diotima in a moment of pique, had had a far-reaching effect on his cousin. She had begun by inviting the newcomer to her gatherings, in the role of a lady vaguely active in social welfare, and watched her covertly. This intruder, soaking up Diotima's domestic interiors with eyes soft as blotting paper, not only had been downright uncanny but had also aroused in her as much feminine curiosity as dread. To tell the truth, when Diotima pronounced the term "venereal disease" she felt the same vague sensations as when she tried to imagine what her new acquaintance actually did, and from one occasion to the next she was expecting, with an uneasy conscience, some impossible behavior, outrage, or scandal from her. Bonadea succeeded, however, in calming these suspicions by cloaking her ambition in the kind of especially well-bred behavior that naughty children affect when their moral zeal is aroused by the tone of their surroundings. In the process she even managed to forget that she was jealous of Diotima, who was surprised to find that her disturbing protégée was just as much given over to "ideals" as she was herself. For the "fallen sister," as she thought of her, had soon become a protégée, in whom Diotima was moved to take an especially active interest because her own situation made her see the ignoble mystery of nymphomania as a kind of female sword of Damocles which, she said, might hang by a thin thread even over the head of a vestal virgin. "I know, my child," she consolingly instructed Bonadea, who was about her own age, "there is nothing so tragic as embracing a man of whom one is not entirely convinced!" and kissed her on that unchaste mouth with a heroic effort that would have been enough to make her press her lips on the blood-dripping bristles of a lion's beard.

Diotima's position at that time was midway between Arnheim and Tuzzi: a seesaw position, metaphorically speaking, one end of which was weighted down too much, the other not enough. Even Ulrich had found her, on his return, with hot towels around her head and stomach; but these female complaints, the intensity of which she sensed to be her body's protest against the contradictory orders it was receiving from her soul, had also awakened in Diotima that noble resolve that was characteristic of her as soon as she refused to be just like every other woman. It was of course hard to decide, at first, whether it was her soul or her body that was called upon to take action, or whether a change in her attitude toward Arnheim or toward Tuzzi would be the better response; but this was settled with the world's help, for while her soul with its enigmas eluded her like a fish one tries to hold bare-handed, the suffering seeker was surprised to find plenty of advice in the books of the *zeitgeist*, once she had decided to deal with her fate from the physical angle, as represented by her husband. She had not known that our time, which has presumably distanced itself from the concept of passionate love because it is more of a religious than a sexual concept, regards love contemptuously as being too childish to still bother about, devoting all its energies instead to marriage, the bodily operations of which in all their variants it investigates with zestful specificity. There was already at that time a spate of books that discussed the "sexual revolution" with the clean-mindedness of a gym teacher, and whose aim was to help people be happy though married. In these books man or wife were referred to only as "male and female procreators," and the boredom they were supposed to exorcise by all manner of mental and physical diversions was labeled "the sexual problem." When Diotima first immersed herself in this literature she furrowed her brow, but it soon smoothed out again; for it was a spur to her ambition to discover that a great new movement of the *zeitgeist* was under way, which had so far escaped her notice. Transported, she finally clapped hands to brow in amazement that she who had it in her to set the world a great goal (though it was not yet clear what) had never before realized that even the unnerving discomfitures of marriage could be dealt with by using one's intellectual resources. This possibility coincided with her inclinations and suddenly opened the prospect of treating her relationship with her husband, which she had so far regarded as something to be endured, as a science and an art.

"Wherever we may roam, there's no place like home," Bonadea said, with her characteristic taste for platitudes and quotations. For it came about that Diotima, in the role of guardian angel, soon took on Bonadea as a pupil in these matters, in accordance with the pedagogical principle that one learns best by teaching. This enabled Diotima to go on extracting, from the still undirected and unclear impressions she gained from her new reading, points she could really believe in—guided as she was by the happy secret of "intuition," that you are sure to hit the bull's-eye if you talk about anything long enough. At the same time it worked to Bonadea's advantage that she could bring to the dialogue that response without which the student remains barren soil for even the best teacher: her rich practical experience, doled out with restraint, had served the theoretician Diotima as an anxiously studied source of information ever since she had set out to put her marriage in order with the aid of textbooks.

"Look, I'm sure I'm not nearly as bright as she is," Bonadea explained, "but often there are things in her books that even I never dreamed of, and that makes her so discouraged sometimes, and then she'll say things like: This can't be decided at the council table of the marriage bed, I'm afraid; it would, unfortunately, take an immense amount of trained sexual experience, a lot of real physical practice on living material!"

"But for heaven's sake," Ulrich exclaimed, convulsed with laughter at the mere idea of his chaste cousin's straying into "sexology," "what on earth is she after?"

Bonadea gathered her memories of the happy conjunction between the scientific interests of the time and unthinking utterance. "It's a question of how best to develop and manage her sex instinct," she finally responded, in the spirit of her teacher. "And she stands for the principle that a joyous and harmonious sex life has to be achieved through the most severe self-discipline."

"So you two are in training? Endurance training, at that? I'm impressed, I must say," Ulrich exclaimed. "But now will you kindly explain just what it is Diotima is training for?"

"To begin with, she's training her husband, of course," Bonadea corrected him.

"The poor devil!" Ulrich could not help thinking. "In that case," he said, "I'd like to know how she does it. Please don't turn prudish on me all of a sudden."

Under this grilling Bonadea did, in fact, feel inhibited by her ambition to shine, like a prize pupil in an exam.

"Her sexual atmosphere is poisoned," she explained cautiously. "The only way to save it is for her and Tuzzi to make a most careful study of their behavior. There are no general rules for this. Each of them has to observe how the other reacts to life. To be a good observer, a person has to have some insight into sexual life. One has to be able to compare one's practical experience with the results of theoretical research, Diotima says. Woman today happens to have a new and different attitude to the sex problem; she expects a man not only to act but to act with a real understanding of the feminine!" And for Ulrich's entertainment or even just to amuse herself, she gaily added: "Just imagine what it must be like for her husband, who hasn't the faintest inkling of all this new stuff and gets to hear about it mostly at bedtime while they're undressing—let's say when Diotima is taking her hair down and fishing for hairpins, with her petticoats tucked between her knees, and then suddenly she starts talking about all that. I tried it out on my husband, and it drove him almost to apoplexy. One thing you must admit: If marriage is to be for a lifetime, at least there's the advantage that you have the opportunity of getting all the erotic possibilities in it out of your spouse. Which is what Diotima is trying to do with Tuzzi, who happens to be a bit crude!"

"Sounds like hard times for your husbands!" Ulrich teased.

Bonadea laughed, and he could tell how glad she would be to occasionally play truant from the oppressive earnestness of her school of love.

But Ulrich's probing instincts would not let go; he sensed that his greatly changed friend was keeping quiet about something she would much rather have talked about. He professed to be mystified because, from what he had heard, the two husbands involved had so far rather erred in overdoing the "erotic possibilities."

"Of course, that's all you ever think!" Bonadea said reproachfully, giving him a long, pointed glance with a little hook at its end that could easily be interpreted as regret for the innocence she had acquired. "You take advantage of a woman's physiological feeblemindedness yourself!"

"What do I take advantage of? You've found a splendid expression for the history of our love!"

Bonadea slapped his face lightly and, nervously, patted her hair in front of the mirror. Glancing at him out of the mirror, she said: "That's from a book."

"Of course. A very well known book."

"But Diotima disputes it. She found something in another book that speaks of 'the physiological inferiority of the male.' The author is a woman. Do you think it really makes much difference?"

"How can I tell, since I've no idea what we're talking about?"

"Well then, listen! Diotima's starting point is the discovery that she calls 'a woman's constant readiness for sex.' Can you see that?"

"Not in Diotima!"

"Don't be so crude!" she rebuked him. "It's a delicate theory, and it's hard for me to explain it to you so that you don't draw false conclusions from the fact that I happen to be here alone with you in your house while I'm talking about it. So this theory has it that a woman can be made love to even when she doesn't feel like it. Now do you see?"

"I do."

"Unfortunately, it can't be denied either. On the other hand, they say that quite often a man can't make love even when he wants to. Diotima says this has been scientifically established. Do you believe that?"

"It's been known to happen."

"Oh, I don't know," Bonadea said doubtfully. "But Diotima says that if you regard it in the light of science, it's obvious. For in contrast with a woman's constant readiness for sex, a man—well, in a word, a man's manliest part is easily discouraged." Her face was the color of bronze as she now turned it away from the mirror.

"I never would have guessed it about Tuzzi," Ulrich said tactfully.

"I don't think it used to be the case, either," Bonadea said. "It's only happening now, as a belated confirmation of the theory, because she lectures him on it day in, day out. She calls it the theory of the 'fiasco.' Because the male procreator is so prone to this fiasco, he only feels sexually secure if he doesn't have to be afraid of a woman's being in some way or other spiritually superior, and that's why men hardly ever have the courage to try a relationship with a woman who's their equal as a human being. At least, they try right away to put them down. Diotima says that the guiding principle of all male love transactions, and especially of male arrogance, is fear. Great men show it—she means Arnheim, of course. Lesser men hide it behind brutal physical aggression and abusing a woman's soul—I mean you! And she means Tuzzi. That sort of 'Now or never!' you men so often use to make us give in is only a kind of overcomp—" She was about to say "compress"; "overcompensation," Ulrich said, coming to the rescue.

"Right. That's how you men manage to overcome the impression of your physiological inferiority!"

"What have you two decided to do, then?" Ulrich said meekly.

"We have to make an effort to be nice to men! That's why I've come to see you. We'll see how you take it."

"And Diotima?"

"Heavens, what do you care about Diotima? Arnheim's eyes pop out like a snail's when she tells him that the most intellectually superior men unfortunately seem to find full satisfaction only with inferior women and fail with women who are their equals, as attested scientifically by the case of Frau von Stein and the Vulpius woman. You see, now I've got her name right, but of course I've always known she was the noted sex partner of the aging Olympian!"

Ulrich tried to steer the conversation away from himself and back to Tuzzi. Bonadea began to laugh; she was not without sympathy for the sorry predicament of the diplomat, whom she found quite attractive as a man, and felt a certain malicious and conspiratorial glee about his having to suffer under the castigations of the soul. She reported that Diotima was basing her treatment of Tuzzi on the assumption that she must cure him of his fear of her, which had also enabled her to come to terms somewhat with his "sexual brutality." The great blunder of her life, she admitted, was in achieving an eminence too great for her male marriage partner's naïve need to feel superior, so she had set about toning it down by hiding her spiritual superiority behind a more suitable erotic coquetry.

Ulrich broke in to ask, with lively interest, what she understood by that.

Bonadea's glance bored deeply into his face. "She might say to him, for instance, 'Up to now our life has been spoiled by our competing for status.' And then she admits to him that the poisonous effect of the male struggle for power dominates all of public life as well. . . ."

"But that's neither coquettish nor sexy!" Ulrich objected.

"Oh, but it is! You have to remember that a man in the grip of passion will behave toward a woman like an executioner toward his victim. That's part of his struggle for self-assertion, as it's now called. On the other hand, you won't deny that the sex drive is important to a woman too?"

"Certainly not!"

"Good. But a happy sexual relationship demands an equal give-and-take. To get a really rapturous response from the love partner, the partner must be respected as an equal and not just as a will-less extension of oneself," she went on, caught up in her mentor's mode of expression like someone sliding helplessly and anxiously across a polished surface, carried along by his own momentum. "If no other

human relationship is able to endure unremitting pressure and coun-
terpressure, how much less can a sexual—"

"Oho!" Ulrich disagreed.

Bonadea pressed his arm, and her eye glittered like a falling star.
"Hold your tongue!" she cried. "None of you have any firsthand experience of the feminine psyche! And if you want me to go on telling
you about your cousin . . ." But her energy was spent, and her eyes
now had the glitter of a tigress's as she watches fresh meat being carried past her cage. "No, I can't listen to any more of this myself!" she
cried.

"Does she really talk like that?" Ulrich asked. "Did she actually say
these things?"

"But it's all I hear every day, nothing but sexual practice, successful embraces, key principles of eroticism, glands, secretions, repressed urges, erotic training, and regulation of the sex drive!
Apparently everyone has the sexuality he deserves, at least that's
what your cousin claims, but do I deserve to be so overloaded with
it?"

Her gaze firmly held his.

"I don't think so," Ulrich said slowly.

"After all, couldn't one just as easily say that my strong capacity for
experiencing represents a physiological superiority?" Bonadea asked
with a gaily suggestive burst of laughter.

There was no more discussion. When, some considerable time
later, Ulrich became aware of a certain resistance in himself, living
daylight was spraying through the chinks in the curtains, and if one
glanced in that direction the darkened room resembled the sepul-
cher of an emotion that had shriveled past the point of recognition.
Bonadea lay there with her eyes closed, giving no sign of life. The
feeling she now had of her body was not unlike that of a child whose
defiance had been broken by a whipping. Every inch of that body,
which was both completely satiated and battered, cried out for the
tenderness of moral forgiveness. From whom? Certainly not from
the man in whose bed she lay and whom she had implored to kill her,
because her lust could not be appeased by any repetition or intensification. She kept her eyes shut to avoid having to see him. She tried
thinking: "I'm in his bed." This—and "I'll never let myself be driven
out of it again!"—was what she had been shouting inwardly just a

short time before; now it merely expressed a situation she could not get out of without having to go through an embarrassing performance, which was still ahead of her. Bonadea slowly and indolently picked up her thoughts where she had dropped them.

She thought of Diotima. Gradually, words came to mind, then whole sentences and fragments of sentences, but mainly only a sense of satisfaction at being where she was while words as incomprehensible and hard to remember as hormones, lymphatic glands, chromosomes, zygotes, and inner secretions thundered past her ear in a cascade of talk. For her mentor's chastity recognized no boundaries as soon as they were effaced by the glare of scientific illumination. Diotima was capable of saying to her listeners: "One's sex life is not a craft that is to be learned; it should always be the highest art we may acquire in life!" while feeling as little unscientific emotion as when in her zeal she spoke of a "point of reference" or "a central point." Her disciple now recalled these expressions exactly. Critical analysis of the embrace, clarification of the physical elements, erogenous zones, the way to highest fulfillment for the woman, men who have themselves well under control and are considerate of their partner . . . Just an hour ago Bonadea, who normally admired these scientific, intellectual, and highly refined terms, had felt grossly deceived by them. To her surprise she had just now realized with returning consciousness that this jargon was meaningful not only for science but for the emotions too, when the flames were already licking out from the unsupervised emotional side. At that point she hated Diotima. "Talking that way about such things, it's enough to kill your appetite!" she had thought, feeling horribly vindictive toward Diotima, who evidently, with four men of her own, begrudged Bonadea anything at all and was deliberately hoodwinking her in this fashion. Indeed, Bonadea had actually considered the enlightenment with whose help sexual science cleans up the occult ways of the sexual process as a plot of Diotima's. Now she could not understand that any more than she could understand her passionate longing for Ulrich. She tried to remember the moments in which all her thoughts and feelings had gone wild; it was as incomprehensible as if a man bleeding to death were to try to think back on the impatience that had led him to tear off his protective bandages. Bonadea thought of Count Leinsdorf, who had called marriage a high office and had compared Diotima's

books on the subject with a manual for organizing official procedures. She thought of Arnheim, who was a multimillionaire and who
had called the revival of marital fidelity, based on the idea of the
body, a true necessity of the times. And she thought of all the other
famous men she had recently met, without even remembering
whether they had short legs or long ones, were fat or lean, for all she
saw in them was the radiance of their celebrity rounded out by a
vague physical mass, much as the delicate frame of a young roast pi-
geon is given substance by a solid mass of herb stuffing. Sunk in
these memories, Bonadea vowed that she would never again let herself be prey to one of those sudden hurricanes that mix up above and
below, and she swore this to herself so fervently that she could already see herself—if only she could hold firmly enough to her resolve—in fantasy and without physical particulars, as the mistress of
the finest of all her great friend's admirers, hers for the choosing. But
since for the present there was no getting around the fact that she
was still lying in Ulrich's bed with very little on, reluctant to open her
eyes, this rich sense of eager contrition, instead of developing further
into a comfort to her, turned into a wretched state of exasperation.

The passion whose workings split Bonadea's life into such opposing elements had its deepest roots not in sensuality but in ambition.
Ulrich, who knew her well, thought about this but said nothing, to
avoid bringing on her complaints, as he studied her face, while her
eyes hid from him. The root of all her desires seemed to him a desire
for distinction that had got on the wrong track, quite literally the
wrong nerve track. And why shouldn't, really, an ambition to break
social records that can be celebrated with triumph, such as drinking
the most beer or hanging the most diamonds on one's neck, sometimes manifest itself, as in Bonadea's case, as nymphomania? Now
that it was over, she regretted this form of expression and wished she
could undo it, he could see that; and he could also appreciate the fact
that Diotima's elaborate artificiality must impress Bonadea, whom
the devil had always ridden bareback, as divine. He looked at her
lidded eyeballs resting exhausted and heavy in their sockets; he saw
before him her tawny nose, turned decidedly upward at the tip, with
its pink, pointed nostrils; he noticed in some bewilderment the various lines of her body, its large round breasts spreading on the
straight corset of her ribs, the bulbous curve of hips, the hollow

sweep of the back rising from them, the hard pointed nails shielding the soft tips of the fingers. And finally, as he gazed for some time in revulsion at a few tiny hairs sprouting before his eyes from his mistress's nostrils, he, too, wondered at recalling how his desires had been aroused only a short while ago by this person's seductive charms. The bright, mischievous smile with which Bonadea had arrived for their "talk," the natural ease with which she had fended off any rebukes or told the latest story about Arnheim, indeed her new, almost witty keenness of observation: she really had changed for the better; she seemed to have grown more independent, to have achieved a finer balance between the forces in her nature that pulled her up and those that pulled her down, and Ulrich found this lack of moral ponderousness particularly refreshing after his own recent bouts of seriousness. He still could feel the pleasure with which he had listened to her and watched the play of expression on her face, like sun and waves. Suddenly, while his gaze was still on Bonadea's now sulky face, it struck him that only serious people could really be evil. "One might safely say," he thought, "that lighthearted people are proof against wickedness. On the same principle that the villain in opera is always a bass!" Somehow this also implied an uncomfortable link in his own case between "deep" and "dark." Guilt is certainly mitigated when incurred "lightly" by a cheerful person, but on the other hand this may apply only to love, where impassioned seducers seem to act far more destructively and unforgivably than frivolous ones, even when they are doing the same thing. So his thoughts went this way and that, and if this hour of love, so lightly begun, left him a little downhearted, it had also unexpectedly stimulated him.

So thinking, he forgot, without quite knowing how, the Bonadea who was there; resting his head on his arm, he had pensively turned his back to Bonadea and was gazing through the walls at distant things, when his total silence moved her to open her eyes. All unaware, he was at this moment remembering how he had once on a journey got off a train before reaching his destination; a translucent day that had mysteriously, seductively, swept the veils from the landscape had lured him away from the station for a walk, only to desert him at nightfall, when he found himself without his luggage in a hamlet hours away. Indeed, he seemed to recall that he had always had the quality of staying out for unpredictable lengths of time and never returning by the same road; and this suddenly brought back a far distant memory, from a period in his childhood that he normally could not recall, which cast a light on his life. Through a tiny chink in time he seemed to feel again the mysterious yearning by which a child is drawn toward some object it sees, to touch it or even put it in its mouth, at which point the magic comes to a stop as in a blind alley. Just as briefly, he regarded it as possible that the longing of adults, which drives them toward any distance merely to transform it into nearness, is no better or worse—the same sort of longing that dominated him, a compulsion, to judge by a certain aimlessness that was merely masked by curiosity; and finally, this basic image changed to a third, emerging as this hasty and disappointing episode with Bonadea, which neither of them had wanted to turn out as it had. Lying side by side in bed seemed utterly childish to him. "But what does its opposite mean, that motionless, hushed love at a great distance, as incorporeal as an early autumn day?" he wondered. "Probably only another version of child's play," he thought skeptically, and remembered the colorful animal prints he had loved more rapturously as a child than he had loved his mistress today.

Bonadea at this point had seen just about enough of his back to gauge her unhappiness, and she spoke up: "It was your fault!"

Ulrich turned to her with a smile and said spontaneously: "My sister is coming here in a few days to stay with me—did I tell you? We'll hardly be able to see each other then."

"For how long?" Bonadea asked.

"To stay," Ulrich answered, smiling again.

"Well?" Bonadea said. "What difference will it make? Unless you're trying to tell me that your sister won't let you have a lover?"

"That's just what I am trying to tell you," Ulrich said.

Bonadea laughed. "Here I came to see you today in all innocence, and you never even let me finish my story!" she complained.

"I seem to have been designed as a machine for the relentless devaluation of life! I want to be different for once," Ulrich retorted. This was quite beyond her, but it made her remember defiantly that she loved Ulrich. All at once she stopped being the helpless victim of her nerves and found a convincing naturalness; she said, simply: "You've started an affair with her!"

Ulrich warned her not to say such things; a little more grimly than he had meant to. "I intend for a long time to love no woman otherwise than if she were my sister," he said, and stopped. The length of his silence impressed Bonadea with a greater sense of his determination than was perhaps justified by his words.

"You're really perverse!" she cried in a tone of prophetic warning, and leapt out of bed in order to hurry back to Diotima's academy of love, whose unsuspecting portals stood wide open to receive its repentant and refreshed disciple.

24

AGATHE ACTUALLY ARRIVES

That evening there was a telegram, and the next afternoon Agathe arrived.

Ulrich's sister brought only a few suitcases, in accordance with her plan to leave everything behind—not that the quantity of her luggage was wholly in keeping with the precept "Cast all thou hast into the fire, even unto thy shoes." When he heard about the precept, Ulrich laughed; there were even two hatboxes that had escaped the fire.

Agathe's forehead showed the charming furrow denoting hurt feelings and futile brooding over them.

Whether it was fair of Ulrich to find fault with the imperfect expression of a grand and sweeping emotion was left undetermined, for Agathe did not raise the question. The cheerful fuss and upheaval that of necessity attended her arrival made an uproar in her ears and eyes like a dance swaying around a brass band. She was in fine spirits but faintly disappointed, although she had not been expecting anything in particular and had even made a point during her journey of not forming any expectations. It was only that when she remembered that she had stayed up all the previous night she was suddenly overcome with fatigue. She didn't mind when Ulrich had to tell her, after a while, that her telegram had come too late for him to postpone an appointment he had for the afternoon. He promised to be back in an hour, and settled his sister on the sofa in his study with such elaborate care that they both had to laugh.

When Agathe woke up, the hour was long gone, and Ulrich was not there. The room was sunk in deep twilight and was so alien that she felt suddenly dismayed at finding herself in the midst of the new life to which she had been looking forward. As far as she could make out, the walls were lined with books just as her father's had been, and the tables covered with papers. Curiosity led her to open a door and enter the adjacent room: here she found clothes closets, shoe boxes, the punching bag, barbells, and parallel bars. Beyond these were more books, the bathroom with its eau de cologne, bath salts, brushes, and combs, her brother's bedroom, and the hall, with its hunting trophies. Her passage was marked by lights flashing on and off, but as chance would have it, Ulrich noticed none of this, even though he was home by now. He had put off waking her to let her rest a while longer, and now he ran into her on the landing as he was coming up from the little-used basement kitchen. He had gone there to look around for a snack to bring her; since he had not planned ahead, there was no one to wait on them that day. It was only when they stood side by side that Agathe's random impressions began to coalesce into a perception that left her so disconcerted and disheartened that she felt it would be best to bolt as soon as she could. There was something so impersonal, so indifferent about the spirit in which things had been thrown together here that it frightened her.

Ulrich noticed this and apologized, explaining the situation lightheartedly. He told her how he had come to acquire his house and gave its history in detail, beginning with the antlers he had come to own without ever going hunting and ending with the punching bag, which he set bobbing for her benefit. Agathe looked at everything again with disquieting seriousness, and even turned her head for another look whenever they left a room. Ulrich tried to make this examination entertaining, but as it went on he began to feel embarrassed about his house. It turned out—something habit had made him overlook—that he had used only the few rooms he needed, leaving the rest dangling from them like a neglected decoration. When they sat down together after this survey Agathe asked: "But why did you do it, if you don't like it?"

Her brother provided her with tea and every refreshment he could find in the house, and insisted on giving a hospitable welcome, belated though it was, so that their second reunion should not be inferior to the first in material comforts. Dashing back and forth on these errands, he confessed: "I've done everything so carelessly and wrong that the place doesn't have anything at all to do with me."

"But it's all really very attractive," Agathe now consoled him.

Ulrich responded that it would probably have been even worse if he had done it differently. "I can't stand houses with interiors tailored to express one's personality," he declared. "It would make me feel that I had ordered myself from an interior decorator too."

And Agathe said: "I shy away from that kind of house also."

"Even so, it can't be left the way it is," Ulrich rectified. He was sitting at the table with her, and the very fact that they would now be having their meals together raised a number of problems. The realization that all sorts of things would have to be changed took him by surprise; it would take a quite unprecedented effort on his part, and he reacted to this at first with the zeal of a beginner.

"A person living alone," he said, when his sister seemed considerately willing to leave everything as it was, "can afford to have a weakness; it will merge with his other qualities and hardly be noticeable. But when two people share a weakness it becomes twice as conspicuous in comparison with the qualities they don't share, and approaches a public confession."

Agathe could not see it.

"In other words, as brother and sister there are things that each of us could indulge in on our own but we cannot do together; that's exactly why we have come together."

This appealed to Agathe. Still, his negative formulation, that they had come together in order *not* to do something, left something to be desired, and after a while she asked, returning to the way his furnishings had been assembled by the best firms: "I'm afraid I still don't understand. Why did you let the place be done like this if you didn't think it was right?"

Ulrich met her cheerful gaze and let his eyes rest on her face, which, above the slightly crumpled traveling dress she was still wearing, now looked smooth as silver and so amazingly *present* that it felt equally near and far from him; or perhaps the closeness and the remoteness in his presence canceled each other out, just as, out of the infinity of sky, the moon suddenly appears behind the neighboring roof.

"Why did I do it?" he answered, smiling. "I forget now. Probably because I could just as well have done it some other way. I felt no responsibility. I'd be less sure of myself if I were to tell you that the irresponsible way in which we're conducting ourselves now may well be the first step toward a new responsibility."

"How so?"

"Oh, in all sorts of ways. You know: the life of an individual person may be only a slight variant of the most probable average value in the series, and so on."

All Agathe took in of this was what made sense to her. She said: "Which comes to: 'Quite nice' and 'Very nice indeed.' Soon one stops realizing what a revolting life one is leading. But sometimes it gives one the creeps, like waking up to find oneself on a slab in the mortuary!"

"What was your place like?" Ulrich asked.

"Middle-class respectable, à la Hagauer. 'Quite nice.' Just as counterfeit as yours!"

Ulrich had meanwhile found a pencil and was sketching the plan of his house on the tablecloth, reallotting the rooms. That was easy, and so quickly done that Agathe's housewifely gesture of protecting the tablecloth came too late and ended uselessly with her hand resting on his. Problems arose again only over the principles of how the place should be furnished.

"We happen to have a house," Ulrich argued, "and we do have to make some changes to accommodate the two of us. But by and large it's an outdated and idle question these days. 'Setting up house' is putting up a façade with nothing behind it: social and personal relations are no longer solid enough for homes; no one takes any real pleasure now in keeping up a show of durability and permanence. In the old days people did that, to show who they were by the number of rooms and servants and guests they had. Today almost everyone feels that only a formless life corresponds to the variety of purposes and possibilities life is filled with, and young people either prefer stark simplicity, which is like a bare stage, or else they dream of wardrobe trunks and bobsled championships, tennis cups and luxury hotels along great highways, with golf course scenery and music on tap in every room."

He spoke in a light conversational tone, as if playing host to a stranger, but was actually talking himself up to the surface because he was self-conscious about their being together in a situation that combined finality with a new beginning.

After she had let him have his say, his sister asked:

"Are you suggesting that we ought to live in a hotel?"

"Not at all!" Ulrich hastened to assure her. "Except now and then when traveling."

"And for the rest of the time, should we build ourselves a bower on an island or a log cabin in the mountains?"

"We'll be settling in here, of course," Ulrich answered, more seriously than the nature of their conversation warranted. There was a brief lull in the exchange. He had stood up and was pacing up and down the room. Agathe pretended to be picking at a thread on the hem of her dress, bending her head below the line on which their eyes had been meeting. Suddenly Ulrich stopped and said, with some effort in his voice but going straight to the point:

"My dear Agathe, there's a whole circle of questions here, which has a large circumference and no center, and all these questions are: 'How should I live?' "

Agathe had risen, too, but still did not look at him. She shrugged her shoulders.

"We'll have to try!" she said. Her face was flushed from bending over, but when she lifted her head, her eyes were alight with high spirits, the flush only lingering on her cheek like a passing cloud. "If we're going to stay together," she declared, "you'll have to start by helping me unpack and put my things away and change, because I haven't seen a maid anywhere!"

His bad conscience traveled into his arms and legs and made them galvanically mobile, under Agathe's direction and with her help, to make up for his negligence. He cleared out closets like a hunter disemboweling an animal, abandoning his bedroom to Agathe, swearing to her that it was hers and that he would find a sofa somewhere. Eagerly he moved to and fro all objects of daily use that had hitherto lived in their places like flowers in a flower bed, waiting to be picked one at a time by a selecting hand. Suits were piled up on chairs; on the glass shelves in the bathroom, cosmetics were carefully separated into men's and women's departments. By the time order had more or less been transformed into disorder, only Ulrich's gleaming leather slippers remained, abandoned on the floor like an offended lapdog evicted from its basket: a pitiful symbol of disrupted comfort in all its pleasant triviality. But there was no time to take this to heart, for Agathe's suitcases were next, and however few there seemed to be, they were inexhaustibly crammed with exquisitely folded things that spread open as they were lifted out, blossoming in the air just like the hundreds of roses a magician pulls from his hat. These things had to be hung up or laid down, shaken out and put in piles, and because Ulrich was helping, it proceeded with slip-ups and laughter.

But in the midst of all this activity, he could only think, incessantly, that for his whole life, and up to a few hours ago, he had lived alone. And now Agathe was here. This little sentence, "Agathe is here now," repeated itself in waves, like the astonishment of a boy who has received a new plaything; there was something mind-numbing about it and, on the other hand, a quite overwhelming sense of presence too, all of which expressed itself again and again in the words: Agathe is here now.

"So she's tall and slender?" Ulrich thought as he watched her covertly. But she wasn't at all; she was shorter than he, and had broad, athletic shoulders. "Is she attractive?" he mused. That was hard to say too. Her proud nose, for instance, was slightly tilted up from one side; there was far more potent charm in this than attractiveness. "Could she be a beauty?" Ulrich wondered in a rather strange way, for he was not quite at ease with this question even though, leaving aside all convention, Agathe was a stranger to him. There is, after all, no such thing as a natural inhibition against looking at a blood relation with sexual interest; it is only a matter of custom, or to be explained by the detours of morality or eugenics. Also, the circumstance that they had not grown up together had prevented the sterilized brother-sister relationship that is prevalent in European families. Even so, their origin and their feeling toward each other were enough to take the edge off even the harmless question of how beautiful she might be, a missing excitement Ulrich now noticed with distinct surprise. To find something beautiful surely means, first of all, to *find* it: whether it is a landscape or a lover, there it is, looking at the pleased finder, and it seems to have been waiting for him alone. And so, delighted that she was now his and ready to be discovered by him, he was hugely pleased with his sister. But he still thought: "One can't regard one's own sister as truly beautiful; at most one can be pleased by the admiration she evokes in others." But then he was hearing her voice for minutes at a time, where no voice had been before, and what was her voice like? Waves of scent accompanied the movement of her clothing, and what was this scent like? Her movements were now knee, now delicate finger, now rebelliousness of a curl. All one could say about it was: it was there. It was there where before there had been nothing. The difference in intensity between the most vivid moment of thinking about the sister he had left behind and the emptiest present moment was still so great and distinct a pleasure that it was like a shady spot filling up with the warmth of the sun and the scent of wild herbs unfurling.

Agathe was aware of her brother's watching her, but she did not let him know it. During the pauses, when she felt his eyes following her movements while the interval between a response and the next remark was not so much a complete stop as like a car coasting over some deep and risky patch of road with its motor switched off, she, too, enjoyed the supercharged air and the calm intensity that surrounded their reunion. When they had finished unpacking and putting things away and Agathe was alone in her bath, an adventure threatened to break into these peaceful pastures like a wolf, for she had undressed down to her underclothes in the room where Ulrich, smoking a cigarette, was now keeping watch over her abandoned things. Soaking in the water, she wondered what she should do. There was no maid, so ringing was as pointless as calling out; there was evidently nothing to be done but to wrap herself in Ulrich's bathrobe, which was hanging on the wall, knock on the door, and send him out of the room. But considering the serious intimacy that, if not already flourishing, had just been born between them, Agathe cheerfully doubted whether it was appropriate to play the young lady and beg Ulrich to withdraw, so she decided to ignore the ambivalence of femininity and simply appear before him as the natural, familiar companion he should see in her, dressed or not.

Yet when she resolutely entered the room again, both felt an unexpected quickening of the heart. They each tried not to feel embarrassed. For an instant they could not shake off the conventional inconsistency that permits virtual nakedness on the beach while indoors the hem of a chemise or a panty becomes the smuggler's path to romantic intimacy. Ulrich smiled awkwardly as Agathe, with the light of the anteroom behind her, stood in the open door like a silver statue lightly veiled in a haze of batiste and, in a voice much too emphatically casual, asked for her dress and stockings, which turned out to be in the next room. Ulrich showed her the way, and saw to his secret delight that she strode off in a manner that was a little too boyish, taking a sort of defiant pleasure in it, as women tend to do when they don't feel themselves protected by their skirts. Then something new came up, when a little later Agathe found herself stuck midway getting into her dress and had to call Ulrich for help. While he was busy at her back she sensed, without sisterly jealousy but rather, if anything, with pleasure, that he clearly knew his way around women's clothing, and she moved with agility to make it easier for him when the nature of the procedure made it necessary.

Bending over close to the moving, delicate, yet full and fresh skin of her shoulders, intent upon the unaccustomed task, which raised a flush on his brow, Ulrich felt himself lapped by a pleasing sensation not easily put into words, unless one might say that his body was equally affected by having a woman and yet not having a woman so close to him; or one could just as easily have said that though he was unquestionably standing there in his own shoes, he nevertheless felt drawn out of himself and over to her as though he had been given a second, far more beautiful, body for his own.

This was why the first thing he said to his sister when he had straightened up again was: "Now I know what you are: you are my self-love!" It may have sounded odd, but it really expressed what it was that moved him so. "In a sense," he explained, "I've always lacked the right sort of love for myself that others seem to have in abundance. And now," he added, "by some mistake or by fate, it has been embodied in you instead of myself!"

It was his first attempt that evening to pass a verdict on the meaning of his sister's arrival.

25

THE SIAMESE TWINS

Later that evening he came back to this.

"You should know," he started to tell his sister, "that there's a kind of self-love that's foreign to me, a certain tenderness toward oneself that seems to come naturally to most other people. I don't know how best to describe it. I could say, for instance, that I've always had lovers with whom I've had a skewed relationship. They've been illustrations of some sudden idea, caricatures of my mood—in effect, just instances of my inability to be on easy terms with other people. That in itself reveals something about one's relationship to oneself. Basically, lovers I have chosen were always women I didn't like. . . ."

"There's nothing wrong with that!" Agathe interrupted. "If I were a man, I wouldn't have any qualms about trifling with women in the most irresponsible way. And I'd desire them only out of absentmindedness and wonder."

"Oh? Would you really? How nice of you!"

"They're such absurd parasites. Women share a man's life on the same level as his dog!" There was no hint of moral indignation in Agathe's statement. She was pleasantly tired and kept her eyes closed, for she had gone to bed early and Ulrich, who had come to say good night, saw her lying in his place in his bed. But it was also the bed in which Bonadea had lain thirty-six hours earlier, which was probably why Ulrich reverted to the subject of his mistresses.

"All I was trying to describe was my own incapacity for a reasonably forgiving relationship to myself," he repeated, smiling. "For me to take a real interest in something it must be part of some context, it must be controlled by an idea. The experience itself I'd really prefer to have behind me, as a memory; the emotional effort it exacts strikes me as unpleasant and absurdly beside the point. That's how it is with me, to describe myself to you bluntly. Now, the simplest, most instinctive idea one can have, at least when one is young, is that one's a hell of a fellow, the new man the world's been waiting for. But that doesn't last beyond thirty!" He reflected for a moment and then said: "That's not it. It's so hard to talk about oneself. What I would have to say is that I have never subjected myself to an idea with staying power. One never turned up. One should love an idea like a woman; be overjoyed to get back to it. And one always has it inside oneself! And always looks for it in everything outside! I never formed such ideas. My relationship to the so-called great ideas, and perhaps even to those that really are great, has always been man-to-man: I never felt I was born to submit to them; they always provoked me to overthrow them and put others in their place. Perhaps it was precisely this jealousy that drove me to science, whose laws are established by teamwork and never regarded as immutable!" Again he paused and laughed, at either himself or his argument. "But however that may be," he went on seriously, "by connecting no idea or every idea with myself, I got out of the habit of taking life seriously. I get much more out of it when I read about it in a novel, where it's wrapped up in some point of view, but when I'm supposed to experience it in all its fullness it always seems already obsolete, overdone in an old-fashioned way, and intellectually outdated. And I don't think that's peculiar to me. Most people today feel much the same. Lots of people feign an urgent love of life, the way schoolchildren are taught to hop about merrily among the daisies, but there's always a certain premeditation about it, and they feel it. Actually, they're as capable of killing each other in cold blood as they are of being the best of friends. Our time certainly does not take all the adventures and goings-on it's full of at all seriously. When they happen, there's a fuss. They immediately set off more happenings, a kind of vendetta of happenings, a whole compulsive alphabet of sequels, from *B* to *Z*, and all because someone said *A*. But these happenings in our lives have less life than a book, because they have no coherent meaning."

So Ulrich talked, loosely, his moods changing. Agathe offered no response; she still had her eyes closed but was smiling.

Ulrich said: "Now I've forgotten what I'm telling you. I don't think I know my way back to the beginning."

They were silent for a while. He was able to scrutinize his sister's face at leisure, since it was not defended by the gaze of her eyes. It lay there, a piece of naked body, the way women are when they're together in a women's public bath. The feminine, unguarded, natural cynicism of this sight, not intended for men's eyes, still had an unusual effect on Ulrich, though no longer quite as powerful as in their first days together, when Agathe had from the start claimed her right as a sister to talk to him without any mental beating around the bush, since for her he was not a man like others. He remembered the mixture of surprise and horror he had experienced as a boy when he saw a pregnant woman on the street, or a woman nursing her child; secrets from which the boy had been carefully shielded suddenly bulged out full-blown and unembarrassed in the light of day. Perhaps he had long been carrying vestiges of such reactions about with him, for all at once he seemed to feel entirely free of them. That Agathe was a woman with many experiences behind her was a pleasant and comfortable thought; there was no need to be on his guard in talking with her, as he would be with a young girl; indeed, it was touchingly natural that everything was morally relaxed with a mature woman. It also made him feel protective toward her, to make up to her for something by being good to her in some way. He decided to do all he could for her. He even decided to look for another husband for her. This need to be kind restored to him, although he barely noticed, the lost thread of his discourse.

"Our self-love probably undergoes a change during adolescence," he said without transition. "That's when a whole meadow of tenderness in which one had been playing gets mowed down to provide the fodder for one particular instinct."

"So that the cow can give milk!" Agathe added, after the slightest pause, pertly and with dignity but without opening her eyes.

"Yes, it's all connected, I suppose," Ulrich agreed, and went on: "So there's a moment when the tenderness goes out of our lives and concentrates on that one particular operation, which then remains overcharged with it. It's as though there were a terrible drought everywhere on earth except for one place where it never stops raining, don't you think?"

Agathe said: "I think that as a child I loved my dolls more fiercely than I have ever loved a man. After you'd gone I found a whole trunkful of my old dolls in the attic."

"What did you do with them?" Ulrich asked. "Did you give them away?"

"Who was there to give them to? I gave them a funeral in the kitchen stove," she said.

Ulrich responded with animation: "When I remember as far back as I can, I'd say that there was hardly any separation between inside and outside. When I crawled toward something, it came on wings to meet me; when something important happened, the excitement was not just in us, but the things themselves came to a boil. I won't claim that we were happier then than we were later on. After all, we hadn't yet taken charge of ourselves. In fact, we didn't really yet exist; our personal condition was not yet separated from the world's. It sounds strange, but it's true: our feelings, our desires, our very selves, were not yet quite inside ourselves. What's even stranger is that I might as easily say: they were not yet quite taken away from us. If you should sometime happen to ask yourself today, when you think you're entirely in possession of yourself, who you really are, you will discover that you always see yourself from the outside, as an object. You'll notice that one time you get angry, another time you get sad, just as your coat will sometimes be wet and sometimes too warm. No matter how intensely you try to look at yourself, you may at most find out something about the outside, but you'll never get inside yourself. Whatever you do, you remain outside yourself, with the possible exception of those rare moments when a friend might say that you're beside yourself. It's true that as adults we've made up for this by being able to think at any time that 'I am'—if you think that's fun. You see a car, and somehow in a shadowy way you also see: 'I am seeing a car.' You're in love, or sad, and see that it's you. But neither the car, nor your sadness, nor your love, nor even yourself, is quite fully there. Nothing is as completely there as it once was in childhood; everything you touch, including your inmost self, is more or less congealed from the moment you have achieved your 'personality,' and what's left is a ghostly hanging thread of self-awareness and murky self-regard, wrapped up in a wholly external existence. What's gone wrong? There's a feeling that something might still be salvaged. Surely you can't claim that a child's experience is all that different from a man's? I don't know any real answer, even if there may be this or that idea about it. But for a long time I've responded by having lost my love for this kind of 'being myself' and for this kind of world."

Ulrich was glad that Agathe listened to him without interrupting, for he was not expecting an answer from her any more than he was from himself, and was convinced that for the present, nobody could give him the kind of answer he had in mind. Yet he did not fear for an instant that anything he was talking about might be above her head. He did not see it as philosophizing, nor even as an unusual subject for a conversation, any more than a young man—and he was behaving like one, in this situation—will let the difficulty of groping for the right words keep him from finding everything simple when he is exchanging views on the eternal problems of "Who are you? This is who I am" with someone else. He derived the assurance that his sister was able to follow him word for word not from having reflected on it but from her inner being. His eyes rested on her face, and there was something in it that made him happy. This face, its eyes closed, did not thrust back at him. The attraction it held for him was bottomless, even in the sense that it seemed to draw him into never-ending depths. Submerging himself in contemplation of this face, he nowhere found that muddy bottom of dissolved resistances from which the diver into love kicks off, to rebound to the surface and reach dry ground again. But since he was accustomed to experience every inclination toward a woman as a forcibly reversed disinclination against human beings, which—even though he found it regrettable—did offer some guarantee against losing himself in her, the pure inclination as he bent even deeper toward her in curiosity alarmed him almost as if he were losing his balance, so that he soon drew back from this state, and from pure happiness took refuge in a boy's trick for recalling Agathe to everyday reality: with the most delicate touch he could manage, he tried to open her eyes. Agathe opened them wide with a laugh and cried: "Isn't this pretty rough treatment for someone who's supposed to be your self-love?"

This response was as boyish as his attack, and their looks collided hard, like two little boys who want to tussle but are laughing too much to begin. Suddenly Agathe dropped this and asked seriously: "You know that myth Plato tells, following some ancient source, that the gods divided the original human being into two halves, male and female?" She had propped herself up on one elbow and unexpectedly blushed, feeling awkward at having asked Ulrich if he knew so familiar a story; then she resolutely charged ahead: "Now those two pathetic halves do all kinds of silly things to come together again. It's in all the schoolbooks for older children; unfortunately, they never tell you why it doesn't work!"

"I can tell you that," Ulrich broke in, glad to see how well she had understood him. "Nobody knows which of so many halves running around in the world is his missing half. He grabs one that seems to be his, vainly trying to become one with her, until the futility of it becomes hopelessly clear. If a child results, both halves believe for a few youthful years that they've at least become one in the child. But the child is merely a third half, which soon shows signs of trying to get as far away from the other two as it possibly can and look for a fourth half. In this way human beings keep 'halving' themselves physiologically, while the ideal of oneness remains as far away as the moon outside the bedroom window."

"You'd think that siblings might have succeeded halfway already!" Agathe interjected in a voice that had become husky.

"Twins, possibly."

"Aren't we twins?"

"Certainly!" Ulrich suddenly became evasive. "Twins are rare; twins of different gender especially so. But when, into the bargain, they differ in age and have hardly known each other for the longest time, it's quite a phenomenon—one really worthy of us!" he declared, struggling to get back into a shallower cheeriness.

"But we met as twins!" Agathe challenged him, ignoring his tone.

"Because we unwittingly dressed alike?"

"Maybe. And in all sorts of ways! You may say it was chance; but what is chance? *I* think it's fate or destiny or providence, or whatever you want to call it. Haven't you ever thought it was by chance that you were born as yourself? Our being brother and sister doubles that chance!" That was how Agathe put it, and Ulrich submitted to this wisdom.

"So we declare ourselves to be twins," he agreed. "Symmetrical creatures of a whim of nature, henceforth we shall be the same age, the same height, with the same hair, walking the highways and byways of the world in identical striped clothes with the same bow tied under our chins. But I warn you that people will turn around and look after us, half touched and half scornful, as always happens when something reminds them of the mysteries of their own beginnings."

"Why can't we dress for contrast?" Agathe said lightly. "One in yellow when the other is in blue, or red alongside green, and we can dye our hair violet or purple, and I can affect a hump and you a paunch: yet we'd still be twins!"

But the joke had gone stale, the pretext worn out, and they fell silent for a while.

"Do you realize," Ulrich then said suddenly, "that this is something very serious we're talking about?"

No sooner had he said this than his sister again dropped the fan of her lashes over her eyes and, veiling her consent, let him talk alone. Or perhaps it only looked as if she had shut her eyes. The room was dark; what light there was did not so much clarify outlines as pour over them in bright patches. Ulrich had said: "It's not only the myth of the human being divided in two; we could also mention Pygmalion, the Hermaphrodite, or Isis and Osiris—all different forms of the same theme. It's the ancient longing for a doppelgänger of the opposite sex, for a lover who will be the same as yourself and yet someone else, a magical figure that is oneself and yet remains magical, with the advantage over something we merely imagine of having the breath of autonomy and independence. This dream of a quintessential love, unhampered by the body's limitations, coming face-to-face in two identical yet different forms, has been concocted countless times in solitary alchemy in the alembic of the human skull. . . ."

Here he broke off; evidently something disturbing had occurred to him, and he ended with the almost unfriendly words: "There are traces of this in even the most commonplace situations of love: the charm of every change of clothing, every disguise, the meaning two people find in what they have in common, the way they see themselves repeated in the other. This little magic is always the same, whether one's seeing an elegant lady naked for the first time or a naked girl formally dressed for the first time in a dress buttoned up to the neck, and great reckless passions all have something to do with the fact that everyone thinks it's his own secret self peering out at him from behind the curtains of a stranger's eyes."

It sounded as though he were asking her not to attach too much importance to what they were saying. But Agathe was again thinking of the lightning flash of surprise she had felt when they first met, disguised, as it were, in their lounging suits. And she answered:

"So this has been going on for thousands of years. Is it any easier to understand as a case of shared self-delusion?"

Ulrich was silent.

And after a while, Agathe said delightedly: "But it does happen in one's sleep! There you do sometimes see yourself transformed into something else. Or meet yourself as a man. And then you're much kinder to him than you are to yourself. You'll probably say that these are sexual dreams, but I think they are much older."

"Do you often have that sort of dream?" Ulrich asked.

"Sometimes. Not often."

"I almost never do," he confessed. "It must be ages since I had such a dream."

"And yet you once explained to me," Agathe now said, "—it must have been at the very beginning, back in our old house—that people really did experience life differently thousands of years ago."

"Oh, you mean the 'giving' and the 'receiving' vision?" Ulrich replied, smiling at her although she could not see him. "The 'embracing' and 'being embraced' of the spirit? Yes, of course I should have talked about this mysterious dual sexuality of the soul too. And how much else besides! There's a hint of it wherever you look. Every analogy contains a remnant of that magic of being identical and not identical. But haven't you noticed? In all these cases we've been talking about, in dream, in myth, poem, childhood, even in love, feeling more comes at the cost of understanding less, and that means: through a loss of reality."

"Then you don't really believe in it?" Agathe asked.

Ulrich did not answer. But after a while he said: "Translated into the ghastly jargon of our times, we could call this faculty we all lack to such a frightening degree nowadays 'the percentual share' of an individual's experiences and actions. In dreams it's apparently a hundred percent, in our waking life not even half as much. You noticed it today at once in my house; but it's exactly the same with my relations to the people you'll meet. I also once called it—if I'm not mistaken, in conversation with a woman where it was truly relevant, I must admit—the acoustics of the void. If a pin drops in an empty room, the sound it makes is somehow disproportionate, even incommensurable; but it's the same when there's a void between people. There's no way to tell: is one screaming, or is there a deathly silence? For everything out of place and askew acquires the magnetic attraction of a tremendous temptation when there's nothing with which to counteract it. Don't you agree? . . . But I'm sorry," he interrupted himself, "you must be tired, and I'm not letting you have your rest. It seems there are many things in my surroundings and my social life that won't be much to your liking, I'm afraid."

Agathe had opened her eyes. After coming out of hiding at last, her glance contained something uncommonly hard to define, which Ulrich felt coursing sympathetically through his whole body. He suddenly started to talk again: "When I was younger I tried to see just that as a source of strength. And if one doesn't have anything to pit against life? Fine, then life flees from man into his works! That's more or less what I thought. And I suppose there's something daunting about the lovelessness and irresponsibility of today's world. At the very least there's something in it of adolescence, which centuries can go through as well as teenagers, years of rapid, uneven growth. And like every young man I began by plunging into work, adventures, amusements; what difference did it make what one did, as long as one did it wholeheartedly? Do you remember that we once spoke of 'the morality of achievement'? We're born with that image, and orient ourselves by it. But the older one gets, the more clearly one finds out that this apparent exuberance, this independence and mobility in everything, this sovereignty of the driving parts and the partial drives—both your own against yourself and yours against the world—in short, everything that we 'people of the present' have regarded as a strength and a special distinction of our species, is basically nothing but a weakness of the whole as against its parts. Passion and willpower can do nothing about it. The moment you're ready to go all out into the middle of something, you find yourself washed back to the periphery. Today this is the experience in all experiences!"

Agathe, with her eyes now open, was waiting for something to happen in his voice; when nothing changed and her brother's words simply came to an end like a path turning off a road into a dead end, she said: "So your experience tells you that one can never really act with conviction and will never be able to. By conviction," she explained, "I don't mean whatever knowledge or moral training have been drilled into us, but simply feeling entirely at home with oneself and with everything, feeling replete now where there's emptiness, something one starts out from and returns to—" She broke off. "Oh, I don't really know *what* I mean! I was hoping you'd explain it to me."

"You mean just what we were talking about," Ulrich answered gently. "And you're also the only person I can talk to about these things. But there'd be no point in starting over just to add a few more seductive words. I'd have to say, rather, that being 'at the inner core' of things, in a state of unmarred 'inwardness'—using the word not in any sentimental sense but with the meaning we just gave it—is apparently not a demand that can be satisfied by rational thinking." He had leaned forward and was touching her arm and gazing steadily into her eyes. "Human nature is probably averse to it," he said in a low voice. "All we really know is that we feel a painful need for it! Perhaps it's connected with the need for sibling love, an addition to ordinary love, moving in an imaginary direction toward a love unmixed with otherness and not-loving." And after a pause he added: "You know how popular those babes-in-the-wood games are in bed: people who could murder their real siblings fool around as brother-and-sister babies under the same blanket."

In the dim light his face twitched in self-mockery. But Agathe put her trust in his face and not in his confused words. She had seen faces quivering like this a moment before they plunged; this one did not come nearer; it seemed to be moving at infinitely great speed over an immense distance. Tersely she answered: "Being brother and sister isn't really enough, that's all."

"Well, we've already spoken of being twins," Ulrich responded, getting noiselessly to his feet, because he thought that she was finally being overwhelmed by fatigue.

"We'd have to be Siamese twins," Agathe managed to say.

"Right, Siamese twins!" her brother echoed, gently disengaging her hand from his and carefully placing it on the coverlet. His words had a weightless sound, light and volatile, expanding in widening circles even after he had left the room.

Agathe smiled and gradually sank into a lonely sadness, whose darkness imperceptibly turned into that of sleep. Ulrich meanwhile tiptoed into his study and stayed there, unable to work, for another two hours, until he, too, grew tired, learning for the first time what it was like to be cramped out of considerateness. He was amazed at how much he would have wanted to do during this time that would involve making noise and so had to be suppressed. This was new for him. And it almost irritated him a little, although he did his best to imagine sympathetically what it would be like to be really physically attached to another person. He knew hardly anything about how such nervous systems worked in tandem, like two leaves on a single stalk, united not only through a single bloodstream but still more by the effect of their total interdependence. He assumed that every agitation in one soul would also be felt by the other, even though whatever evoked it was going on in a body that was not, in the main, one's own. "An embrace, for instance—you are embraced by way of the other body," he thought. "You may not even want it, but your other self floods you with an overwhelming wave of acceptance! What do you care who's kissing your sister? But her excitement is something you must love jointly. Or suppose it's you who are making love, and you have to find a way to 'ensure' her participation; you can't just let her be flooded with senseless physiological processes . . . !" Ulrich felt a strong arousal and a great uneasiness at this idea; it was hard for him to draw the line between a new way of looking at something and a distortion of the ordinary way.

26

Spring in the Vegetable Garden

The praise Meingast bestowed on her and the new ideas she was getting from him had deeply impressed Clarisse.

Her mental unrest and excitability, which sometimes worried even her, had eased, but they did not give way this time, as they so often did, to dejection, frustration, and hopelessness; they were succeeded instead by an extraordinary taut lucidity and a transparent inner atmosphere. Once again she took stock of herself and arrived at a critical estimate. Without questioning it, and even with a certain satisfaction, she noted that she was not overly bright; she had not been educated enough. Ulrich, on the other hand, whenever she thought of him by comparison, was like a skater gliding to and fro at will on a surface of intellectual ice. There was no telling where it came from when he said something, or when he laughed, when he was irritable, when his eyes flashed, when he was there and with his broad shoulders preempting Walter's space in the room. Even when he merely turned his head in curiosity, the sinews of his neck tautened like the rigging of a sailboat taking off with the wind into the blue. There was always more to him than she could grasp, which acted as a spur to her desire to fling herself on him bodily to catch hold of it. But the tumult in which this sometimes happened, so that once nothing in the world had mattered except that she wanted to bear Ulrich's child, had now receded far into the distance, leaving behind not even that flotsam and jetsam that incomprehensibly keeps bobbing up in the memory after the tide of passion has ebbed. When she thought of her failure at Ulrich's house, insofar as she ever still did, Clarisse felt cross, at most, but her self-confidence was hale and hearty thanks to the new ideas supplied by her philosophic guest, not to mention the sheer excitement of again seeing this old friend who had been transported into the sublime. Thus many days passed in all kinds of suspense while everyone in the little house, now bathed in spring sunshine, waited to see whether Ulrich would or would not bring the permit to visit Moosbrugger in his eerie domicile.

There was one idea in particular that seemed important to Clarisse in this connection: The Master had called the world "so thoroughly stripped of illusions" that people could no longer say about anything whether they ought to love it or hate it. Since then Clarisse felt that one was obliged to surrender oneself to an illusion if one received the grace of having one. For an illusion is a mercy. How was anyone at that time to know whether to turn right or left on leaving the house, unless he had a job, like Walter, which then cramped him, or, like herself, had a visit to pay to her parents or brothers and sisters, who bored her! It's different in an illusion! There life is arranged as efficiently as a modern kitchen: you sit in the middle and hardly need stir to set all the gadgets going. That had always been Clarisse's sort of thing. Besides, she understood "illusion" to mean nothing other than what was called "the will," only with added intensity. Up to now Clarisse had felt intimidated by being able to understand so little of what was going on in the world. But since Meingast's return she saw this as a veritable advantage that freed her to love, hate, and act as she pleased. For according to the Master's word mankind needed nothing so much as willpower, and when it came to wanting something with a will, Clarisse had always had that inner power! When Clarisse thought about it she was chilled with joy and hot with responsibility. Of course, what was meant by will here was not the grim effort it took to learn a piano piece or win an argument; it meant being powerfully steered by life itself, being deeply moved within oneself, being swept away with happiness!

Eventually she could not help telling Walter something about it. She informed him that her conscience was growing stronger day by day. But despite his admiration for Meingast, the suspected instigator of this deed, Walter answered angrily: "It's probably lucky for us that Ulrich doesn't seem able to get the permit!"

Clarisse's lips merely quivered slightly, betraying sympathy for his ignorance and stubbornness.

"What is it you want from this criminal, anyway, who has nothing whatever to do with any of us?" Walter demanded manfully.

"It'll come to me when I get there!" she said.

"I should think you ought to know it already," Walter asserted.

His little wife smiled the way she always did when she was about to hurt him to the quick. But then she merely said: "I'm going to do something."

"Clarisse!" Walter remonstrated firmly. "You may not do anything without my permission. I am your lawful husband and guardian."

This tone was new to her. She turned away and took a few steps in confusion.

"Clarisse!" Walter called after her, getting up to follow her. "I intend to take steps to deal with the insanity that's going around in this house!"

Now she realized that the healing power of her resolve was already manifesting itself, even in the strengthening of Walter's character. She turned on her heel: "What steps?" she asked, and a flash of lightning from her narrowed eyes struck into the moist, wide-open brown of his.

"Now look," he said to mollify her, backing away a little, in surprise at her demanding such a concrete response. "We've all got this in our system, this intellectual taste for the unhealthy, the problematic, for making our flesh creep; every thinking person has it; but—"

"But we let the philistines have their way!" Clarisse interrupted triumphantly. Now she advanced on him without taking her eyes off him; felt how a sense of her own healing power held him in its strong embrace and overpowered him. Her heart was filled with an odd and inexpressible joy.

"But we won't make such a to-do over it," Walter muttered sulkily, finishing his sentence. Behind him, at the hem of his jacket, he felt an obstacle; reaching backward, he identified it as the edge of one of those light, thin-legged little tables they had, which suddenly seemed spooky to him; realized that if he kept backing away he would make it slide backward, which would be ludicrous. So he resisted the sudden desire to get far away from this struggle, to some dark-green meadow under blossoming fruit trees, among people whose healthy cheerfulness would wash his wounds clean. It was a quiet, stout wish, graced with women hanging on his words and paying their toll of grateful admiration. At the moment Clarisse came up close he actually felt rudely molested, in a nightmarish way. But to his surprise Clarisse did not say: "You're a coward!" Instead, she said: "Walter? Why are we unhappy?"

At the sound of her appealing, clairvoyant voice he felt that happiness with any other woman could never take the place of his unhappiness with Clarisse. "We have to be!" he answered with an equally noble upsurge.

"No, we shouldn't have to be," she said obligingly. She let her head droop to one side, trying to find a way to convince him. It didn't matter what it was: They stood there facing each other like a day without an evening, pouring out its fire hour after hour without lessening.

"You'll have to admit," she said finally, at once shyly and stubbornly, "that really great crimes come about not because somebody commits them but because we let them happen."

Now Walter knew, of course, what was coming, and felt a shock of disappointment.

"Oh God!" he cried out impatiently. "I know as well as you do that far more people's lives are ruined by indifference and by the ease with which most of us today can square our conscience than by the evil intentions of isolated individuals. And of course it's admirable that you're now going to say that this is why we must all quicken our conscience and carefully weigh in advance every step we take."

Clarisse interrupted him by opening her mouth, but thought better of it and did not respond.

"Of course I think about poverty too, and hunger, and all the corruption that's allowed to go on in this world, or mines caving in because the management economized on safety measures," Walter went on in a deflated tone, "and I've agreed with you about it already."

"But in that case two lovers mustn't love each other either, as long as they're not in a state of 'pure happiness,' " Clarisse said. "And the world will never improve until there are such lovers!"

Walter struck his hands together. "Don't you understand how unfair to life such great, dazzling, uncompromising demands are?" he exclaimed. "And it's the same with this Moosbrugger, who keeps popping into your head like something on a turntable. Of course you're right to claim that no stone should be left unturned as long as such miserable human creatures are simply killed off because society doesn't know what to do with them. But of course it's even more right that the healthy, normal conscience is justified in simply refusing to bother with such overrefined scruples. A healthy way of thinking is recognizable, in fact, by certain signs; one can't prove it but has to have it in one's blood."

"In *your* blood," Clarisse replied, " 'of course' always means 'of course not.' "

Nettled, Walter shook his head to show that he would not answer this. He was fed up with always being the one to warn that a diet of one-sided ideas was unhealthy; in the long run, it was probably also making him unsure of himself.

But Clarisse read his thoughts with that nervous sensitivity that never failed to amaze him. With her head high, she jumped over all the intermediate stages and landed on his main point with the subdued but intense question: "Can you imagine Jesus as boss of a coal mine?" He could see in her face that by "Jesus" she really meant him, through one of those exaggerations in which love is indistinguishable from madness. He waved this off with a gesture at once indignant and discouraged. "Not so direct, Clarisse!" he pleaded. "Such things mustn't be said so directly!"

"Yes, they must," she answered. "It's the only way! If we don't have the strength to save him, we will never have the strength to save ourselves!"

"And what difference will it make if they do string him up?" Walter burst out. The brutality of it made him believe he felt the liberating taste of life itself on his tongue, gloriously blended with the taste of death and the doom of their entanglement with it that Clarisse was conjuring up with her hints.

Clarisse looked at him expectantly. But Walter said nothing more, either from relief after his outburst or from indecision. And like someone forced to play an unbeatable final trump card, she said: "I've had a sign!"

"But that's just one of your fantasies!" Walter shouted at the ceiling, which represented heaven. But with those last airy words Clarisse had ended their tête-à-tête, giving him no chance to say anything more.

Yet he saw her only a short while later talking eagerly with Meingast, who was rightly troubled by a feeling that they were being watched but was too nearsighted to be sure of it. Walter was not really participating in the gardening being done so zestfully by his visiting brother-in-law, Siegmund, who with rolled-up shirtsleeves was kneeling in a furrow doing something or other that Walter had insisted must be done in the spring if one wanted to be a human being and not a bookmark in the pages of a gardening book. Instead of gardening, Walter was sneaking glances at the pair talking in the far corner of the open kitchen garden.

Not that he suspected anything untoward in the corner he was observing. Still, his hands felt unnaturally cold in the spring air; his legs were cold too, what with the wet places on his trousers from occasionally kneeling to give Siegmund instructions. He took a high tone with his brother-in-law, the way weak, downtrodden people will whenever they get a chance to work off their frustrations on someone. He knew that Siegmund, who had taken it into his head to revere Walter, would not be easily shaken in his loyalty. But this did not prevent him from feeling a veritable after-sunset loneliness, a graveyard chill, as he watched Clarisse; she never cast a glance in his direction but was all eyes for Meingast, hanging on the Master's words. Moreover, Walter actually took a certain pride in this. Ever since Meingast had come to stay in his house, he was just as proud of the chasms that suddenly opened up in it as he was anxious to cover them up again. From his standing height he had dispatched to the kneeling Siegmund the words: "Of course we all feel and are familiar with a certain hankering for the morbid and problematic!" He was no sneaking coward. In the short time since Clarisse had called him a philistine for saying the same thing to her, he had formulated a new phrase: "life's petty dishonesty."

"A little dishonesty is good, like sweet or sour," he now instructed his brother-in-law, "but we are obligated to refine it in ourselves to the point where it would do credit to a healthy life! What I mean by a little dishonesty," he went on, "is as much the nostalgic flirting with death that seizes us when we listen to *Tristan* as the secret fascination that's in most sex crimes, even though we don't succumb to it. For there's something dishonest and antihuman, you see, both in elemental life when it overpowers us with want and disease, and in exaggerated scruples of mind and conscience trying to do violence to life. Everything that tries to overstep the limits set for us is dishonest! Mysticism is just as dishonest as the conceit that nature can be reduced to a mathematical formula! And the plan to visit Moosbrugger is just as dishonest as"—here Walter paused for a moment—"as if you were to invoke God at a patient's bedside!"

There was certainly something in what he had said, and he had even managed to take Siegmund by surprise with his appeal to the physician's professional and spontaneous humanitarianism, to make him see Clarisse's scheme and her overwrought motivation as an impermissible overstepping of bounds. However, Walter was a genius compared with Siegmund, as may be seen in Walter's healthy outlook having led him to confess such ideas as these, while his brother-in-law's even healthier outlook manifested itself in his dogged silence in the face of such dubious subject matter. Siegmund patted the soil with his fingers while tilting his head now to one side, now to the other, without opening his lips, as if he were trying to pour something out of a test tube, or then again, as if he had just heard enough with that ear. And when Walter had finished there was a fearfully profound silence, in which Walter now heard a statement that Clarisse must have called out to him once, for without being as vivid as a hallucination, it was as if the hollow space were punctuated by these words: "Nietzsche and Christ both perished of their incompleteness!" Somehow, in some uncanny fashion reminiscent of the "coal mine boss," he felt flattered. It was a strange position that he, health personified, should be standing here in the cool garden between a man he regarded condescendingly and two unnaturally overheated people just out of earshot, whose mute gesticulations he watched with a superior air and yet with longing. For Clarisse was the slightly dishonest element his own health needed to keep from flagging, and a secret voice told him that Meingast was at this very moment engaged in immeasurably increasing the permissible limits of this dishonesty. He admired Meingast as an obscure relation admires a famous one, and seeing Clarisse whispering conspiratorially with him aroused his envy more than his jealousy—a feeling, that is, that ate into him even more deeply than jealousy would have, and yet it was also somehow uplifting; the consciousness of his own dignity forbade him to get angry or to go over there and disturb them; in view of their agitation he felt himself superior, and from all this arose, he did not know how, some vague, mongrel notion, spawned outside all logic, that the two of them over there were in some reckless and reprehensible fashion invoking God.

If such a curiously mixed state of mind must be called thinking, it was of a kind that cannot possibly be put into words, because the chemistry of its darkness is instantly ruined by the luminous influence of language. Besides, as his remark to Siegmund had shown, Walter did not associate belief of any sort with the word "God," and when the word occurred to him it generated an abashed void around itself. And so it happened that the first thing Walter said to his brother-in-law, after a long silence, had nothing to do with this. "You're an idiot to think you have no right to talk her out of this visit in the strongest possible terms," he said bitterly. "What are you a doctor for?"

Siegmund wasn't in the least offended. "You're the one who will have to have it out with her," he replied, glancing up calmly before turning back to what he was doing.

Walter sighed, then started over again. "Clarisse is an extraordinary person, of course. I can understand her very well. I'll even admit that she's not all wrong to be as austere in her views as she is. Just thinking of the poverty, hunger, misery of every kind the world is so full of, the disasters in coal mines, for instance, because the management wouldn't spend enough on timbering . . ."

Siegmund gave no sign that he was giving it any thought.

"Well, *she* does!" Walter continued sternly. "And I think it's wonderful of her. The rest of us get ourselves a good conscience much too easily. And she's better than we are for insisting that we all ought to change and have a more active conscience, the kind with no limit to it, ever. But what I'm asking you is whether this isn't bound to lead to a pathological state of moral scrupulousness, if it isn't something like that already. You must have an opinion!"

Siegmund responded to this pressing challenge by propping himself up on one knee and giving his brother-in-law a searching look. "Crazy!" he said. "But not, strictly speaking, in a medical sense."

"And what do you say," Walter continued, forgetting his superior stance, "to her claim that she's being sent signs?"

"She says she's being sent signs?" Siegmund said dubiously.

"Signs, I tell you. That crazy killer, for instance. And that crazy swine outside our window the other day!"

"A swine?"

"No, a kind of exhibitionist."

"I see," Siegmund said, turning it over in his mind. "You're sent signs too, when you find something to paint. She just expresses herself in a more high-strung way than you," he concluded.

"And what about her claim that she has to take these people's sins on herself, and yours and mine as well, and I don't know whose else's?" Walter pressed him.

Siegmund had risen to his feet and was brushing the dirt from his hands. "She feels oppressed by sin, does she?" he asked, again superfluously, politely agreeing as if glad to be able at last to support his brother-in-law. "That's a symptom!"

"That's a symptom?" Walter echoed, crushed.

"Fixed ideas about sin are a symptom," Siegmund affirmed with the detachment of a professional.

"But it's like this," Walter added, instantly appealing against the judgment he had just been suing for: "You must first ask yourself: Does sin exist? Of course it does. But in that case there's also a fixed idea of sin that is no delusion. You might not understand that, because it's beyond empiricism! It's a human being's aggrieved sense of responsibility toward a higher life!"

"But she insists she's receiving signs?" Siegmund persisted.

"But you just said that signs are sent to me too!" Walter cried. "And I can tell you there are times when I would like to go down on my knees and beg fate to leave me in peace; but it keeps sending signs, and it sends the most inspiring signs through Clarisse!" Then he continued more calmly: "She now claims, for instance, that this man Moosbrugger represents her and me in our 'sinful body' and has been sent to us as a warning; but it can be understood as a symbol of our neglecting the higher possibilities of our lives, our 'astral body,' as it were. Years ago, when Meingast left us—"

"But an obsession with sin *is* a symptom of specific disorders," Siegmund reminded him, with the relentless equanimity of the expert.

"Symptoms, that's all you know!" Walter said in animated defense of his Clarisse. "Anything beyond that is outside your experience! But perhaps this superstition, which regards everything that doesn't accord with the most pedestrian experience as a disorder, is itself the true sin and sinful form of our life. Clarisse demands spiritual action against this! Many years ago, when Meingast left and we . . ." He thought of how he and Clarisse had "taken Meingast's sins upon themselves," but realized it was hopeless to try telling Siegmund the process of a spiritual awakening, so he ended vaguely by saying: "Anyway, I don't suppose you'll deny that there have always been people who have, so to speak, drawn humanity's sins on themselves or even concentrated them in themselves."

His brother-in-law looked at him complacently. "There you are!"

he said amiably. "You yourself prove just what I've been saying. That she regards herself as oppressed by sin is a characteristic attitude of certain disorders. But there are also untypical modes of behavior in life: I never claimed anything more."

"And the exaggerated stringency with which she carries things out?" Walter asked after a while, with a sigh. "Surely to be so rigorous can hardly be called normal?"

Clarisse, meanwhile, was having an important conversation with Meingast.

"You've said," she reminded him, "that the kind of people who pride themselves on understanding and explaining the world will never change anything in it, isn't that so?"

"Yes," the Master replied. " 'True' and 'false' are the evasions of people who never want to arrive at a decision. Truth is something without end."

"So that's why you said one must have the courage to choose between 'worth' and 'worthless'?" she pressed on.

"Right," the Master said, somewhat bored.

"And then there's your marvelously contemptuous formulation," Clarisse cried, "that in modern life people only do what is happening anyway."

Meingast stopped and looked down; one might have said that he was either inclining an ear or studying a pebble lying before him on the path, slightly to the right. But Clarisse did not go on proffering honeyed praises; she, too, had now bent her head, so that her chin almost rested in the hollow of her neck, and her gaze bored into the ground between the tips of Meingast's boots. A gentle flush rose to her pale cheeks as, cautiously lowering her voice, she continued:

"You said all sexuality was nothing but goatish caperings."

"Yes, I did say that in a particular context. Whatever our age lacks in willpower it expends, apart from its so-called scientific endeavors, in sexuality."

After some hesitation, Clarisse said: "I have plenty of willpower myself, but Walter is for capering."

"What's really the matter between you two?" the Master asked with some curiosity, but almost immediately added in a tone of disgust: "I can guess, I suppose."

They were standing in a corner of the treeless garden that lay under the full spring sun, almost diametrically opposite the corner where Siegmund was squatting on the ground with Walter standing over and haranguing him. The garden formed a rectangle parallel with and against the long wall of the house, with a gravel path running around its vegetable and flower beds, and two others forming a bright cross on the still-bare ground in the middle. Warily glancing in the direction of the two men, Clarisse replied: "Perhaps he can't help it; you see, I attract Walter in a way that's not quite right."

"I can imagine," the Master answered, this time with a sympathetic look. "There is something boyish about you."

At this praise Clarisse felt happiness bouncing through her veins like hailstones. "Did you notice *before*," she eagerly asked him, "that I can change clothes faster than a man?"

A blank expression came over the philosopher's benevolently seamed face. Clarisse giggled. "That's a double word," she explained. "There are others too: sex murder, for instance."

The Master probably thought it would be wise not to show surprise at anything. "Oh yes, I know," he replied. "You did say once that to satisfy desire in the usual embrace is a kind of sex murder." But what did she mean by "changing," he wanted to know.

"To offer no resistance is murder," Clarisse explained with the speed of someone going through one's paces on slippery ground and losing one's footing through overagility.

"Now you've really lost me," Meingast admitted. "You must be talking about that fellow the carpenter again. What is it you want from him?"

Clarisse moodily scraped the gravel with the tip of her shoe. "It's all part of the same thing," she said. And suddenly she looked up at the Master. "I think Walter should learn to deny me," she said in an abruptly cut-off sentence.

"I can't judge that," Meingast remarked, after waiting in vain for her to go on. "But certainly radical solutions are always best."

He said this only to cover all contingencies. But Clarisse dropped her head again so that her gaze burrowed somewhere in Meingast's suit, and after a while her hand reached slowly for his forearm. She suddenly had an uncontrollable impulse to take hold of that hard, lean arm under the broad sleeve and touch the Master, who was pretending to have forgotten all those illuminating things he had said about the carpenter. While this was happening she was dominated by the feeling that she was pushing a part of herself over to him, and in the slowness with which her hand disappeared inside his sleeve, in this flooding slowness, there eddied fragments of a mysterious lust, which derived from her perception that the Master was keeping still and letting her touch him.

But Meingast for some reason stared aghast at the hand clutching his arm this way and creeping up it like some many-legged creature mounting its female. Under the little woman's lowered eyelids he caught a flash of something peculiar and realized the dubious character of what was taking place, although he was moved by her doing it so publicly.

"Come!" he said gently, removing her hand from his arm. "We're too conspicuous, standing here like this; let's go on walking."

As they strolled up and down the path, Clarisse said: "I can dress quickly, faster than a man if I have to. Clothes come flying onto my body when I'm—what shall I call it?—when I'm like that! Maybe it's a kind of electricity. I attract things that belong to me. But it's usually a sinister attraction."

Meingast smiled at her puns, which he still did not understand, and fished haphazardly in his mind for an impressive retort. "So you put on your clothes like a hero his destiny?" he responded.

To his surprise, Clarisse stopped short and cried: "Yes, that's it exactly! Whoever lives like this feels it even in a dress, shoes, knife and fork!"

"There's some truth in that," the Master confirmed her obscurely credible assertion. Then he asked point-blank: "But how do you do it with Walter, actually?"

Clarisse failed to understand. She looked at him, and suddenly saw in his eyes yellow clouds that seemed to be driven on a desert wind.

"You said," Meingast went on with some reluctance, "that you attract him in a way that 'isn't right.' You mean, I suppose, not right for a woman? How do you mean? Are you frigid with men?"

Clarisse did not know the word.

"Being frigid," the Master explained, "is when a woman is unable to enjoy the act of love with men."

"But I only know Walter," Clarisse objected timidly.

"Even so, it does seem a fair assumption, after what you've been telling me."

Clarisse was nonplussed. She had to think about it. She didn't know. "Me? But I'm not supposed to—I'm the one who must put a stop to it!" she said. "I can't permit it to happen!"

"You don't say?" The Master's laugh was vulgar. "You have to prevent yourself from feeling anything? Or prevent Walter from getting satisfaction?"

Clarisse blushed. But now she understood more clearly what she had to say. "When you give in, everything gets swamped in lust," she replied seriously. "I won't let a man's lust leave him and become my lust. That's why I've attracted men ever since I was a little girl. There's something wrong with the lust of men."

For various reasons Meingast preferred not to go into that.

"Do you have that much self-control?" he asked.

"Well, yes and no," Clarisse said candidly. "But I told you, if I let him have his way, I'd be a sex murderer!" Warming to her subject, she went on: "My woman friends say they 'pass out' in the arms of a man. I don't know what that is. I've never passed out in a man's arms. But I do know what it's like to 'pass out' *without* being in a man's arms. You must know about that too; after all, you did say that the world is too devoid of illusions . . . !"

Meingast waved this off with a gesture, as if to say she had misunderstood him. But now it was all too clear to her.

"When you say, for instance, that one must decide against the lesser value for the sake of the higher value," she cried, "it means that there's a life in an immense and boundless ecstasy! Not sexual ecstasy but the ecstasy of genius! Against which Walter would commit treason if I don't prevent him!"

Meingast shook his head. Denial filled him on hearing this altered and impassioned version of his words; it was a startled, almost frightened denial, but of all the things it prompted him to say, he chose the most superficial: "But who knows whether he could do anything else?"

Clarisse stopped, as if rooted to the ground by a bolt of lightning. "He must!" she cried. "You yourself taught us that!"

"So I did," the Master granted reluctantly, trying in vain to get her to keep walking by setting an example. "But what do you really want?"

"There was nothing I wanted before you came, don't you see?" Clarisse said softly. "But it's such an awful life, to take nothing more than the little bit of sexual pleasure out of the vast ocean of the possible joys in life! So now I want something."

"That's just what I am asking you about," Meingast prompted.

"One has to be here for a purpose. One has to be 'good' for something. Otherwise everything is horribly confused," Clarisse answered.

"Is what you want connected with Moosbrugger?" Meingast probed.

"That's hard to say. We'll have to see what comes of it," Clarisse replied. Then she said thoughtfully: "I'm going to abduct him. I'm going to create a scandal!" As she said this, her expression took on an air of mystery. "I've been watching you!" she said suddenly. "You have strange people coming to see you. You invite them when you think we're not home. Boys and young men! You don't talk about what they want!" Meingast stared at her, speechless. "You're working up to something," Clarisse went on, "you're getting something going! But I," she uttered in a forceful whisper, "I'm also strong enough to have several different friends at the same time. I've gained a man's character and a man's responsibilities. Living with Walter, I've learned masculine feelings!" Again her hand groped for Meingast's arm; it was evident she was unaware of what she was doing. Her fingers came out of her sleeve curved like claws. "I'm two people in one," she whispered, "you must know that! But it's not easy. You're right that one mustn't be afraid to use force in a case like this!"

Meingast was still staring at her in embarrassment. He had never known her in such a state. The import of her words was incomprehensible. For Clarisse herself at the moment, the concept of being two people in one was self-evident, but Meingast wondered whether she had guessed something of his secret life and was alluding to that. There was nothing much to guess at yet; he had only recently begun to perceive a shift in his feelings that accorded with his male-oriented philosophy, and begun to surround himself with young men who meant more to him than disciples. But that might have been why he had changed his residence and come here, where he felt safe from observation; he had never thought of such a possibility, and this little person, who had turned uncanny, was apparently capable of guessing what was going on in him. Somehow more and more of her arm was emerging from the sleeve of her dress without reducing the distance between the two bodies it connected, and this bare, skinny forearm, together with its attached hand, which was clutching Meingast, seemed at this moment to have such an unusual shape that everything in the man's imagination that had hitherto been distinct became wildly muddled.

But Clarisse no longer came out with what she had been just about to say, even though it was perfectly clear inside her. The double words were signs, scattered throughout the language like snapped-off twigs or leaves strewn on the ground, to mark a secret path. "Sex murder" and "changing" and even "quick" and many other words— perhaps all others—exhibited double meanings, one of which was secret and private. But a double language means a double life. Ordinary language is evidently that of sin, the secret one that of the astral body. "Quick," for instance, in its sinful form meant ordinary, everyday, tiring haste, while in its joyous form everything flew off it in joyful leaps and bounds. But then the joyous form can also be called the form of energy or of innocence, while the sinful form can be called all the names having to do with the depression, dullness, and irresolution of ordinary life. There were these amazing connections between the self and things, so that something one did had an effect where one would never have expected it; and the less Clarisse could express all this, the more intensely the words kept coming inside her, too fast for her to gather them in. But for quite some time she had been convinced of one thing: the duty, the privilege, the mission of whatever it is we call conscience, illusion, will, is to find the vital form, the light form. This is the one where nothing is accidental, where there is no room for wavering, where happiness and compulsion coincide. Other people have called this "living authentically" and spoken of the "intelligible character"; they have referred to instinct as innocence and to the intellect as sin. Clarisse could not think in these terms, but she had made the discovery that one could set something in motion, and then sometimes parts of the astral body would attach themselves to it of their own accord and in this fashion become embodied in it. For reasons primarily rooted in Walter's hypersensitive inaction, but also because of heroic aspirations she never had the means of satisfying, she had been led to think that by taking forceful action one could set up a memorial to oneself in advance, and the memorial would then draw one into itself. So she was not at all clear about what she intended to do with Moosbrugger, and could not answer Meingast's question.

Nor did she want to. While Walter had forbidden her to say that the Master was about to undergo another transformation, there was no doubt that his spirit was moving toward secret preparations for some action, she did not know what, but one which could be as magnificent as his spirit was. He was therefore bound to understand her, even if he pretended not to. The less she said, the more she showed him how much she knew. She also had a right to take hold of him, and he could not forbid it. Thus he accorded recognition to her undertaking and she entered into his and took part in it. This, too, was a kind of being-two-people-in-one, and so forceful that she could hardly grasp it. All her strength, more than she could know she had, was flowing through her arm in an inexhaustible stream from her to her mysterious friend, draining the very marrow from her bones and leaving her faint with sensations surpassing any of those from making love. She could do nothing but look at her hand, smiling, or alternately look into his face. Meingast, too, was doing nothing but gaze now at her, now at her hand.

All at once, something happened that at first took Clarisse by surprise and then threw her into a whirl of bacchantic ecstasy:

Meingast had been trying to keep a superior smile fixed on his face in order not to betray his uncertainty. But this uncertainty was growing from moment to moment, constantly reborn from something apparently incomprehensible. For every act undertaken with doubts is preceded by a brief span of weakness, corresponding to the moments of remorse after the thing is done, though in the normal course of events it may barely be apparent. The convictions and vivid illusions that protect and justify the completed act have not yet been fully formed and are still wavering in the mounting tide of passion, vague and formless as they will probably be when they tremble and collapse afterward in the outgoing tide of passionate remorse. It was in just this state of his intentions that Meingast had been surprised. It was doubly painful for him because of the past and because of the regard in which he was now held by Walter and Clarisse, and then, every intense excitement changes the sense of one's image of reality so that it can rise to new heights. His own frightened state made Clarisse frightening to Meingast, and the failure of his efforts to get back to sober reality only increased his dismay. So instead of projecting superior strength, the smile on his face stiffened from one minute to the next; indeed, it became a sort of floating stiffness, which ended by floating away stiffly, as if on stilts. At this moment the Master was behaving no differently than a large dog facing some much smaller creature he does not dare to attack, like a caterpillar, toad, or snake; he reared up higher and higher on his long legs, drew back his lips and arched his back, and found himself suddenly swept away by the currents of discomfort from the place where they had their source, without being able to conceal his flight by any word or gesture.

Clarisse did not let go of him. As he took his first, hesitant steps, her clinging might have been taken for ingenuous eagerness, but after that he was dragging her along with him while barely finding the necessary words to explain that he was in a hurry to get back to his room and work. It was only in the front hall that he managed to shake her off completely; up till then he had been driven only by his urge to escape, paying no attention to what Clarisse was saying and choked by his caution not to attract the attention of Walter and Siegmund. Walter had actually been able to guess at the general pattern of what was going on. He could see that Clarisse was passionately demanding something that Meingast was refusing her, and jealousy bored into his breast like a double-threaded screw. For although he suffered agonies at the thought that Clarisse was offering her favors to their friend, he was even more furious at the insult of seeing her apparently disdained. If that feeling were taken to its logical conclusion, he would have to force Meingast to take Clarisse, only to be plunged into despair by the sweep of that same impulse. He felt deeply sad and heroically excited. It was insufferable, with Clarisse poised on the razor's edge of her destiny, that he should have to listen to Siegmund asking whether the seedlings should be planted loosely in the soil or if it had to be patted firmly around them. He had to say something, and felt like a piano in the fraction of a second between the moment when the ten-fingered crash of an incredible blow hits it and the cry of pain. Light was in his throat, words that would surely put a wholly new and different face on everything. Yet all he managed to say was something quite different from what he expected. "I won't have it!" he said, again and again, more to the garden than to Siegmund.

But it turned out that Siegmund, intent as he had seemed to be on the seedlings and on pushing the soil this way and that, had also noticed what was going on and even given it some thought. For now he rose to his feet, brushed the dirt from his knees, and gave his brother-in-law some advice.

"If you feel she's going too far, you'll have to give her something else to think about," he said in a tone that implied he had of course been thinking all this time, with a doctor's sense of responsibility, about everything Walter had confided in him.

"And how am I to do that?" Walter asked, disconcerted.

"Like any man!" Siegmund said. "All a woman's fuss and fury is to be cured in one place, to quote Mephistopheles more or less!"

Siegmund put up with a great deal from Walter. Life is full of such relationships, in which one partner keeps the upper hand and constantly suppresses the other, who never rebels. In fact, and in accordance with Siegmund's own convictions, this is the way normal, healthy life is. The world would probably have come to an end in the Bronze Age if everyone had stood up for himself to the last drop of his blood. Instead, the weaker have always moved away and looked around for neighbors they in their turn could push around; the majority of human relationships follow this model to this day, and with time these things take care of themselves.

In his family circle, where Walter passed for a genius, Siegmund had always been treated as a bit of a blockhead; he had accepted it, and even today would have been the one who yielded and did homage wherever it was a matter of precedence in the family hierarchy. That old hierarchical structure had ceased to matter years ago, compared with the new status each of them had acquired, and precisely for that reason it could be left undisturbed. Siegmund not only had a very respectable practice as a physician—and the doctor's power, unlike that of the bureaucrat, is not imposed from above but is owed to his personal ability; people come to him for help and submit to him willingly—but also had a wealthy wife, who had presented him within a brief period with herself and three children, and to whom he was unfaithful with other women, not often but regularly, whenever it pleased him. So he was certainly in a position, if he chose, to give Walter confident and reliable advice.

At this moment Clarisse came back out of the house. She no longer remembered what had been said during their tempestuous rush indoors. She realized that the Master had been trying to get away from her, but the memory of it had lost its details, had folded up and closed. Something had happened! With this one notion in her head, Clarisse felt like someone emerging from a thunderstorm, still charged from head to toe with sensual energy. In front of her, a few yards beyond the bottom of the small flight of stone steps she had come out by, she saw a shiny blackbird with a flame-colored beak, dining on a fat caterpillar. There was an immense energy in the creature, or in the two contrasting colors. One could not say that Clarisse was thinking anything about it; it was more like a response coming from behind and all around her. The blackbird was a sinful body in the act of committing violence. The caterpillar the sinful form of a butterfly. Fate had placed the two creatures in her path, as a sign that she must act. One could see how the blackbird assumed the caterpillar's sins through its flaming orange-red beak. Wasn't the bird a "black genie"? Just as the dove is the "white spirit"? Weren't these signs linked in a chain? The exhibitionist with the carpenter, with the Master's flight . . . ? Not one of these notions was clearly formed in her; they lodged invisibly in the walls of the house, summoned but still keeping their answer to themselves. But what Clarisse really felt as she stepped out on the stairs and saw the bird that was eating the caterpillar was an ineffable correspondence of inner and outer happenings.

She conveyed it in some curious way to Walter. The impression he received instantly corresponded with what he had called "invoking God"; there was no mistaking it this time. He could not make out what was going on inside Clarisse, she was too far away, but there was something in her bearing that was not happenstance, as she stood facing the world into which the little flight of stairs descended like steps leading down to a swimming pool. It was something exalted. It was not the attitude of ordinary life. And suddenly he understood; this was what Clarisse meant when she said: "It's not by chance that this man is under my window!" Gazing at his wife, he himself felt how the pressure of strange forces came flooding in to fill appearances. In the fact that he was standing here and Clarisse there, at such an angle to him that he had to turn his eyes away from the direction they had automatically taken, along the length of the garden, in order to see her clearly—even in this simple juxtaposition, the mute emphasis of life suddenly outweighed natural contingency. Out of the fullness of images thrusting themselves upon the eye something geometrically linear and extraordinary reared up. This must be how it could happen that Clarisse found a meaning in almost empty correlations, such as the circumstance of one man stopping under her window while another was a carpenter. Events seemed to have a way of arranging themselves that was different from the usual pattern, as elements in some strange entity that revealed them in unexpected aspects, and because it brought these aspects out from their obscure hiding places, it justified Clarisse's claim that it was she herself who was attracting events toward herself. It was hard to express this without sounding fanciful, but then it occurred to Walter that it came closest to something he knew very well—what happens when you paint a picture. A painting, too, has its own inexplicable way of excluding every color or line not in accord with its basic form, style, and palette of colors, while on the other hand it extracts from the painter's hand whatever it needs, thanks to the laws of genius, which are not the same as the usual laws of nature. At this point he no longer had in him any of that easy, healthy self-assurance which scrutinizes life's excrescences for anything that might come in handy and which he had been extolling only a little while ago; what he felt was more the misery of a little boy too timid to join in a game.

But Siegmund was not the man to let go of something so easily once he had taken it up. "Clarisse is high-strung," he declared. "She's always been ready to run her head through a wall, and now she's got it stuck in one. You'll have to get a good grip on her, even if she resists you."

"You doctors don't have a clue about human psychology!" Walter cried. He looked for a second point of attack and found it. "You talk of 'signs,' " he went on, his irritation overlaid by his pleasure in being able to speak about Clarisse, "and you carefully examine when signs indicate a disorder and when they don't, but I tell you this: the true human condition is the one in which everything is a sign! But everything! You may be able to look truth in the eye, but truth will never look you in the eye; this divine, uncertain feeling is something you'll never know!"

"You're obviously both crazy," Siegmund remarked dryly.

"Yes, of course we are!" Walter cried out. "You're not a creative man, after all; you've never learned what it means to 'express oneself,' which means first of all, for an artist, to *understand* something. The expression we impart to things is what develops our ability to perceive them aright. I can only understand what I want, or someone else wants, by carrying it out! This is our living experience, as distinct from your dead experience! Of course you'll say it's paradoxical, a confusion of cause and effect; you and your medical causality!"

But Siegmund did not say this; he merely reiterated doggedly: "It will definitely be for her own good if you won't put up with too much. Excitable people need a certain amount of strictness."

"And when I play the piano at the open window," Walter asked, as if he had not heard his brother-in-law's warning, "what am I doing? People are passing by, some of them young girls, perhaps anyone who feels like it stops to listen; I play for young lovers and lonely old people. Clever people, stupid people. I'm not giving them something to *think* about. What I'm playing isn't rational information. I'm giving them myself. I sit invisible in my room and give them signs: just a few notes, and it's their life, and it's my life. You could certainly call this crazy too . . . !" Suddenly he fell silent. That feeling: "Oh, I could tell all of you a thing or two!"—that basic ambitious urge of every inhabitant of earth who feels the need to communicate something but has no more than an average creative capacity—had fallen to pieces. Every time Walter sat in the soft emptiness of the room behind his open window and released his music into the air with the proud awareness of the artist giving happiness to unknown thousands, this feeling was like an open umbrella, and the instant he stopped playing, it was like a sloppily closed one. All the airiness was gone, it was as if everything that had happened had not happened, and all he could say was that art had lost its connection to the people and everything was no good. He thought of this and felt dejected. He tried to fight it off. After all, Clarisse had said: music must be played "through to the end." Clarisse had said: "We understand something only as long as we ourselves are part of it!" But Clarisse had also said: "That's why we have to go to the madhouse ourselves!" Walter's "inner umbrella" flapped halfway closed in irregular stormy gusts.

Siegmund said: "Excitable people need a certain amount of guidance, for their own good. You yourself said you wouldn't put up with it anymore. Professionally and personally, I can only give you the same advice: Show her that you're a man. I know she balks at that, but she'll come around." Siegmund was like a dependable machine tirelessly reiterating the "answer" he had come up with.

Walter, in a "stormy gust," replied: "This medical exaggeration of a well-adjusted sex life is old hat! When I make music or paint or think, I am affecting both an immediate and a distant audience, without depriving the ones of what I give to the others. On the contrary! Take it from me, there's probably no sphere of life in which one remains justified in living only for oneself, thinking of life as a private matter! Not even marriage!"

But the heavier pressure was on Siegmund's side, and Walter sailed before the wind across to Clarisse, of whom he had not lost sight during this conversation. He did not relish anyone's being able to say of him that he was not a man; he turned his back on this suggestion by letting it drive him over to Clarisse. And halfway there he felt the certainty, between nervously bared teeth, that he would have to begin with the question: "What do you mean, talking about signs?"

But Clarisse saw him coming. She had already seen him wavering while he was still standing there. Then his feet were pulled from the ground and bore him toward her. She participated in this with wild elation. The blackbird, startled, flew off, hastily taking its caterpillar with it. The way was now clear for her power of attraction. Yet she suddenly thought better of it and eluded the encounter for the time being by slowly slipping along the side of the house into the open, not turning away from Walter but moving faster than he, hesitant as he was, could move out of the realm of telepathic effect into that of statement and response.

27

AGATHE IS QUICKLY DISCOVERED AS A SOCIAL ASSET BY GENERAL STUMM

Since Agathe had joined forces with him, Ulrich's relations with the extensive social circle of the Tuzzis had been making great demands on his time. For although it was late in the year the winter's busy social season was not yet over, and the least he could do in return for the great show of sympathy he had received upon his father's death was not hide Agathe away, even though their being in mourning relieved them of having to attend large affairs. Had Ulrich chosen to take full advantage of it, their mourning would actually have allowed them to avoid attending all social functions for a long time, so that he could have dropped out of a circle of acquaintances that he had fallen into only through curious circumstances. However, since Agathe had put her life into his charge Ulrich acted against his own inclination, and assigned to a part of himself labeled with the traditional concept "duties of an elder brother" many decisions that his whole person was undecided about, even when he did not actually disapprove of them. The first of these duties of an elder brother was to see that Agathe's flight from her husband's house should end only in the house of a better husband.

"If things continue this way," he would say, whenever they touched on the subject of what arrangements needed to be made in setting up house together, "you will soon be getting some offers of marriage, or at least of love," and if Agathe planned something for more than a few weeks ahead he would say: "By that time everything will be different." This would have wounded her even more had she not perceived the conflict in her brother, so that for the present she refrained from making an issue of it when he chose to widen their social circle to the limit. And so after Agathe's arrival they became far more involved in social obligations than Ulrich would have been on his own.

Their constant appearances together, when for a long time Ulrich had always been seen alone and without ever uttering a word about a sister, caused no slight sensation. One day General Stumm von Bordwehr had shown up at Ulrich's with his orderly, his briefcase, and his loaf of bread, and started to sniff the air suspiciously. Then Stumm discovered a lady's stocking hanging over a chair, and said reproachfully: "Oh, you young fellows!"

"My sister," Ulrich declared.

"Oh, come on—you haven't got a sister!" the General protested. "Here we are, tormented by the most serious problems, and you're hiding out with a little playmate!"

Just then Agathe came in, and the General lost his composure. He saw the family resemblance, and could tell by the casual air with which Agathe wandered in that Ulrich had told the truth, yet he could not shake off the feeling that he was looking at one of Ulrich's girlfriends, who incomprehensibly and misleadingly happened to look like him.

"I really don't know what came over me, dear lady," he told Diotima later, "but I couldn't have been more amazed if he'd suddenly stood before me as a cadet again!" For at the sight of Agathe, to whom he was instantly attracted, Stumm had been overcome by that stupor he had learned to recognize as a sign of being deeply moved. His tender plumpness and sensitive nature inclined the General to hasty retreat from such a tricky situation, and despite all Ulrich's efforts to make him stay, he did not learn much more about the serious problems that had brought the educated General to him.

"No!" Stumm blamed himself. "Nothing is so important as to justify my disturbing you like this."

"But you haven't disturbed us at all," Ulrich assured him with a smile. "What's there to be disturbed?"

"No, of course not," Stumm assured him, now completely confused. "Of course not, in a sense. But all the same . . . look, why don't I come back another time?"

"You might at least tell me what brought you here, before you dash off again," Ulrich demanded.

"Nothing, not a thing! A trifle!" the General cried in his eagerness to take to his heels. "I think the Great Event is about to start!"

"A horse! A horse! Take ship for France!" Ulrich threw in in fun.

Agathe looked at him in surprise.

"I do apologize," the General said, turning to her. "You can't have any idea what this is all about."

"The Parallel Campaign has found its crowning idea!" Ulrich filled her in.

"No, I never said that," the General demurred. "All I meant was that the great event everyone was waiting for is now on its way."

"I see," Ulrich said. "Well, it's been on its way from the start."

"No, not quite like this," the General earnestly assured him. "There is now a quite definite nobody-knows-what in the air. There's soon to be a decisive gathering at your cousin's. Frau Drangsal—"

"Who's she?" Ulrich had never heard of her.

"That only shows how much you've been out of touch," the General said reproachfully, and turned immediately to Agathe to mend matters. "Frau Drangsal is the lady who has taken the poet Feuermaul under her wing. I suppose," he said, turning his round body back again to the silent Ulrich, "you don't know him either?"

"Yes, I do. The lyric poet."

"Writes verses," the General said, mistrustfully avoiding the unaccustomed word.

"Good verse, in fact. And all sorts of plays."

"I don't know about plays. And I haven't got my notes with me. But he's the one who says: Man is good. In short, Frau Drangsal is backing the hypothesis that man is good, and they say it is a great European idea and that Feuermaul has a great future. She was married to a man who was a world-famous doctor, and she means to make Feuermaul world-famous too. Anyway, there's a danger that your cousin may lose the leadership to Frau Drangsal, whose salon has also been attracting all the celebrities."

The General mopped the sweat from his brow, though Ulrich did not find the prospect at all alarming.

"You surprise me!" Stumm scolded him. "As an admirer of your cousin like everyone else, how can you say such things? Don't you agree, dear lady," he appealed to Agathe, "that your brother is being incredibly disloyal and ungrateful toward an inspiring woman?"

"I've never met my cousin," Agathe admitted.

"Oh!" said Stumm, and in words that turned a chivalrous intention into a rather backhanded compliment which involved an obscure concession to Agathe, he added: "Though she hasn't been at her best lately!"

Neither Ulrich nor Agathe had anything to say to this, so the General felt he had to elucidate. "And you know why, too," he said meaningfully to Ulrich. He disapproved of Diotima's current absorption in sexology, which was distracting her mind from the Parallel Campaign, and he was worried because her relationship with Arnheim was not improving, but he did not know how far he might go in speaking of such matters in the presence of Agathe, whose expression was now growing steadily cooler. But Ulrich answered calmly: "I suppose you're not making any progress with your oil affair if our Diotima no longer has her old influence on Arnheim?"

Stumm made a pathetically pleading gesture, as if to stop Ulrich from making a joke not fit for a lady's ear, but at the same time threw him a sharp glance of warning. He even found the energy, despite his weight, to bounce to his feet like a young man, and tugged his tunic straight. Enough of his original suspicion about Agathe's background lingered to keep him from exposing the secrets of the War Ministry in her presence. It was only when Ulrich had escorted him out to the hall that he clutched his arm and whispered hoarsely, through a smile: "For God's sake, man, don't talk open treason!" and enjoined Ulrich from uttering a word about the oil fields in front of any third person, even one's own sister. "Oh, all right," Ulrich promised. "But she's my *twin* sister."

"Not even in front of a twin sister!" the General asseverated, still so incredulous about the sister that he could take the addition of "twin" in stride. "Give me your word!"

"But it's no use making me promise such a thing." Ulrich was even more outrageous. "We're Siamese twins, don't you see?" Stumm finally caught on that Ulrich, whose manner was never to give a straight answer to anything, was making fun of him. "Your jokes used to be better," he protested, "than to suggest the unappetizing notion that such a delightful person, even if she's ten times your sister, is fused together with you!" But this had reawakened his lively mistrust of the reclusiveness in which he had found Ulrich, and so he appended a few more questions to find out what he had been up to. Has the new secretary turned up yet? Have you been to see Diotima? Have you kept your promise to visit Leinsdorf? Have you found out how things are between your cousin and Arnheim? Since the plump skeptic was of course already informed on all these points, he was merely testing Ulrich's truthfulness, and was satisfied with the result.

"In that case, do me a favor and don't be late for this crucial session," he pleaded while buttoning up his greatcoat, slightly out of breath from mastering the traversal through the sleeves. "I'll call you again beforehand and fetch you in my carriage, agreed?"

"And when will this boredom take place?" Ulrich asked, not exactly with enthusiasm.

"In a couple of weeks or so, I think," the General said. "We want to bring the rival party to Diotima's, but we want Arnheim to be there too, and he's still abroad." With one finger he tapped the golden sword knot dangling from his coat pocket. "Without him, it's not much fun for *us*, as you can understand. But believe me"—he sighed—"there's nothing I personally desire more than that our spiritual leadership should stay with your cousin; it would be horrible for me, if I had to adapt to an entirely new situation!"

Thus it was this visit that brought Ulrich, now accompanied by his sister, back into the fold he had deserted when he was still alone. He would have had to resume his social obligations even if he had not wanted to, as he could not possibly stay in hiding with Agathe a day longer and expect Stumm to keep to himself a discovery so ripe for gossip. When "the Siamese" called on Diotima, she had apparently already heard of this curious and dubious epithet, if she was not yet charmed with it. For the divine Diotima, famed for the distinguished and remarkable people always to be met under her roof, had at first taken Agathe's unheralded debut very badly; a kinswoman who might not be a social success could be far more damaging to her own position than a male cousin, and she knew just as little about this new cousin as she had previously known about Ulrich, which in itself caused the all-knowing Diotima some annoyance when she had to admit her ignorance to the General. So she had decided to refer to Agathe as "the orphan sister," partly to help reconcile herself to the situation and partly to prepare wider circles for it. It was in this spirit that she received the cousins.

She was agreeably surprised by the socially impeccable manners

Agathe was able to produce, while Agathe, mindful of her good education in a pious boarding school and always ready, with a mixture of irony and wonder, to take life as it came—an attitude she deplored to Ulrich—from the first managed almost unconsciously to win the gracious sympathies of the stupendous young woman whose ambition for "greatness" left Agathe quite cold and indifferent. She marveled at Diotima with the same guilelessness with which she would have marveled at a gigantic power station in whose mysterious function of spreading light one did not meddle. Once Diotima had been won over, especially as she could soon see that Agathe was generally liked, she laid herself out to extend Agathe's social success, which she arranged to throw greater credit on herself. The "orphan sister" aroused much sympathetic interest, which among Diotima's intimates began on a note of frank amazement that nobody had ever heard of her before, and in wider circles was transformed into that vague pleasure at everything new and surprising which is shared by princes and the press alike.

And so it happened that Diotima, with her dilettante's knack for choosing instinctively, among several options, that which was both the worst and the most promising of public success, made the move that assured Ulrich and Agathe of their permanent place in the memory of that distinguished circle by promptly passing on the delightful story—as she now suddenly found it to be—that the cousins, reunited under romantic circumstances after an almost lifelong separation, called themselves Siamese twins, even though they had been blindly fated thus far to be almost the opposite. It would be hard to say why Diotima first, and then everyone else, was so taken with this circumstance, and why it made the "twins" ' resolve to live together appear both extraordinary and natural; such was Diotima's gift for leadership; and this outcome—for both things happened—proved that she still exerted her gentle sway despite all her rivals' maneuvers. Arnheim, when he heard of it on his return from abroad, delivered an elaborate address to a select circle, rounding it off with a homage to aristocratic-popular forces. Somehow the rumor arose that Agathe had taken refuge with her brother from an unhappy marriage with a celebrated foreign savant. And since the arbiters of good form at that time had the landowners' antipathy to divorce and made do with adultery, many older persons perceived Agathe's choice in that double halo of the higher life composed of willpower and piety which Count Leinsdorf, who looked upon the "twins" with special favor, at one point characterized with the words: "Our theaters are always treating us to displays of the most awful excesses of passion. Now here's a story the Burgtheater could use as a good example!"

Diotima, in whose presence this was uttered, responded: "It's become fashionable for many people to say that man is good. But anyone who knows, as I have learned in my studies, the confusions of our sex life will know how rare such examples are!"

Did she mean to qualify His Grace's praise or reinforce it? She had not yet forgiven Ulrich what she called his lack of confidence in her, since he had not given her advance notice of his sister's arrival; but she was proud of the success in which she had a part, and this entered into her reply.

28

TOO MUCH GAIETY

Agathe proved naturally adept at making use of the advantages social life offered, and her brother was pleased to see her moving with so much poise in these demanding social circles. The years she had spent as the wife of a secondary-school principal in the provinces seemed to have fallen from her without leaving a trace. For the present, however, Ulrich summed it all up with a shrug, saying: "Our high nobility find it amusing that we should be called the Siamese twins. They've always gone in more for menageries than, say, for art."

By tacit agreement they treated all that was happening as a mere interlude. There was much that needed changing or rearranging in their household, as they had seen from the very first day; but they did nothing about it, because they shied away from another discussion whose limits could not be foreseen. Ulrich had given up his bedroom to Agathe and settled himself in the dressing room, with the bathroom between them, and had gradually given up most of his closet space to her. He declined her offer of sympathy for these hardships with an allusion to Saint Lawrence and his grille; and anyway it did not occur to Agathe that she might be interfering with her brother's bachelor life, because he assured her that he was very happy and because she could have only the vaguest idea of the degrees of happiness he might have enjoyed previously. She had come to like this house with its unconventional arrangements, its useless extravagance of anterooms and reception rooms around the few habitable rooms, which were now overcrowded; there was about it something of the elaborate civilities of a bygone age left defenseless against the self-indulgent and churlish high-handedness of the present. Sometimes the mute protest of the handsome rooms against the disorderly invasion seemed mournful, like broken, tangled strings hanging from the exquisitely carved frame of an old instrument. Agathe now saw that her brother had not really chosen this secluded house without interest or feeling, as he pretended, and from its ancient walls emerged a language of passion that was not quite mute, but yet not quite audible. But neither she nor Ulrich admitted to anything more than enjoying its casualness. They lived in some disarray, had their meals sent in from a hotel, and derived from everything a sort of wild fun that comes with eating a meal more awkwardly on the grass at a picnic than one would have had to do at one's table.

In these circumstances they also did not have the right domestic help. The well-trained servant Ulrich had taken on temporarily when he moved in—an old man about to retire and only waiting for some technicality to be settled first—could not be expected to do more than the minimum Ulrich expected of him; the part of lady's maid fell to Ulrich himself, since the room where a regular maid might be lodged was, like everything else, still in the realm of good intentions, and a few efforts in that direction had not brought good results. Instead, Ulrich was making great strides as a squire arming his lady knight to set forth on her social conquests. In addition, Agathe had done some shopping to supplement her wardrobe, and her acquisitions were strewn all over the house, which was nowhere equipped for the demands of a lady. She had acquired the habit of using the entire house as a dressing room, so that Ulrich willy-nilly took part in her new purchases. The doors between rooms were left open, his gymnastic apparatus served as clotheshorse and coatrack, and he would be called away from his desk for conferences like Cincinnatus from his plow. This interference with his latent but at least potential will to work was something he put up with not merely because he thought it would pass but because he enjoyed it; it was something new and made him feel young again. His sister's vivacity, idle as it might appear to be, crackled in his loneliness like a small fire in a long-unused stove. Bright waves of charming gaiety, dark waves of warm trustfulness, filled the space in which he lived, taking from it the nature of a space in which he up till then had moved only at the dictates of his own will. But what was most amazing about this inexhaustible fountain of another presence was that the sum of the countless trifles of which it consisted added up to a non-sum that was of a quite different kind: his impatience with wasting his time, that unquenchable feeling that had never left him since he could remember, no matter what he had taken up that was supposed to be great and important, was to his astonishment totally gone, and for the first time he loved his day-to-day life without thinking.

He even overdid it a little, gasping in delight when Agathe, with the seriousness women feel in these matters, offered for his admiration the thousand charming things she had been buying. He acted as if the quaint workings of a woman's nature—which, on the same level of intelligence, is more sensitive than the male and therefore more susceptible to the suggestion of dressing up to a point of crass self-display that is even further removed from the ideal of a cultivated humanity than the man's nature—irresistibly compelled his participation. And perhaps it really was so. For the many small, tender, absurd notions he became involved with—tricking oneself out with glass beads, crimping the hair, the mindless arrangements of lace and embroidery, the ruthless seductive colors: charms so akin to the tinfoil stars at the fairgrounds that every intelligent woman sees right through them without in the least losing her taste for them—began to entangle him in the network of their glittering madness. For the moment one begins to take anything, no matter how foolish or tasteless, seriously and puts oneself on its level, it begins to reveal a rationale of its own, the intoxicating scent of its love for itself, its innate urge to play and to please. This was what happened to Ulrich when he helped equip Agathe with her new outfits. He fetched and carried, admired, appraised, was asked for advice, helped with trying on. He stood with Agathe in front of the mirror. Nowadays, when a woman's appearance suggests that of a well-plucked fowl ready for the oven, it is hard to imagine her predecessor's appearance in all its charm of endlessly titillated desire, which has meanwhile become ridiculous: the long skirt, to all appearances sewn to the floor by the dressmaker and yet miraculously in motion, enclosing other, secret gossamer skirts beneath it, pastel-shaded silk flower petals whose softly fluttering movements suddenly turned into even finer tissues of white, which were the first to touch the body itself with their soft foam. And if these clothes resembled waves in that they drew the eye seductively and yet repulsed it, they were also an ingenious contrivance of way stations and intermediate fortifications around expertly guarded marvels and, for all their unnaturalness, a cleverly curtained theater of the erotic, whose breathtaking darkness was lit only by the feeble light of the imagination. It was these quintessential preliminaries that Ulrich now saw removed daily, taken apart, as it were from the inside. Even though a woman's secrets had long since lost their mystery for him, or just because he had always only rushed through them as anterooms or outer gardens, they had quite a different effect on him now that there was no gateway or goal for him. The tension that lies in all these things struck back. Ulrich could hardly have said what changes it wrought. He rightly regarded himself as a man of masculine temperament, and he could understand being attracted by seeing what he so often desired from its other side, for once, but at times it was almost uncanny, and he warded it off with a laugh.

"As if the walls of a girls' boarding school had sprouted all around me in the night, completely locking me in!" he protested.

"Is that so terrible?" Agathe asked.

"I don't know," he replied.

Then he called her a flesh-eating plant and himself a miserable insect that had crawled into her shimmering calyx. "You've closed it around me," he said, "and now I'm sitting surrounded by colors, perfume, and radiance, already a part of you in spite of myself, waiting for the males we're going to attract!"

And it really was uncanny for him to witness the effect his sister had on men, considering his concern to "get her a husband." He was

not jealous—in what capacity could he have been?—and put her interests ahead of his, hoping that the right man would soon come
along to release her from this interim phase in which leaving
Hagauer had placed her; and yet, when he saw her surrounded by
men paying her attentions, or when a man on the street, attracted by
her beauty and ignoring her escort, gave her a bold stare, Ulrich did
not know what to make of his feelings. Here too, natural male jealousy being forbidden him, he often felt somehow caught up in a
world he had never entered before. He knew from experience all
about the male mating dance as well as the female's warier technique
in love, and when he saw Agathe being treated to the one and responding with the other, it pained him; he felt as if he were watching
the courtship of horses or mice, the sniffing and whinnying, the pouting and baring of teeth, with which strangers parade their self-regard
and regard of the opposite sex; to Ulrich, observing this without empathy, it was nauseating, like some stupefaction welling up from
within the body. And if he nevertheless tried to put himself in his
sister's place, prompted by some deep-seated emotional need, it
sometimes would not have taken much afterward for him to feel, not
just bewilderment at such tolerance, but the sort of shame a normal
man feels when deviously approached by one who is not. When he
let Agathe in on this, she laughed.

"There are also several women among our friends who take an interest in you," she said.

What was going on here?

Ulrich said: "Basically it's a protest against the world!" And then
he said: "You know Walter: It's been a long time since we've liked
each other. But even when I'm annoyed with him and know that I
irritate him too, I nevertheless often feel, at the mere sight of him, a
certain warmth as if we understood each other perfectly, as in fact we
don't. Look, there's so much in life we understand without agreeing
with it; that's why accepting someone from the beginning, before understanding him, is pure mindless magic, like water in spring running
down all the hillsides to the valley!"

What he felt was: "That's the way it is now!" And what he thought
was: "Whenever I succeed in shedding all my selfish and egocentric
feelings toward Agathe, and every single hateful feeling of indifference too, she draws all the qualities out of me the way the Magnetic

Mountain draws the nails out of a ship! She leaves me morally dissolved into a primary atomic state, one in which I am neither myself nor her. Could this be bliss?"

But all he said was: "Watching you is so much fun!"

Agathe blushed deeply and said: "Why is that 'fun'?"

"Oh, I don't know. Sometimes you're self-conscious with me in the room," Ulrich said. "But then you remember that, after all, I'm 'only your brother.' And at other times you don't seem to mind at all when I catch you in circumstances that would be most interesting for a stranger, but then it suddenly occurs to you that I shouldn't be looking at you, and you make me look the other way. . . ."

"And why is *that* fun?" Agathe asked.

"Maybe it's a form of happiness to follow another person with one's eyes for no reason at all," Ulrich said. "It's like a child's love for its possessions, without the child's intellectual helplessness. . . ."

"Maybe it's fun for you to play at brother-and-sister only because you've had more than enough of playing at man-and-woman?"

"That too," Ulrich said, watching her. "Love is basically a simple urge to come close, to grab at something that has been split into two poles, lady and gentleman, with incredible tensions, frustrations, spasms, and perversions arising in between. We've now had enough of this inflated ideology; it's become nearly as ridiculous as a science of eating. I'm convinced most people would be glad if this connection between an epidermic itch and the entire personality could be revoked. And sooner or later there will be an era of simple sexual companionship in which boy and girl will stand in perfectly tuned incomprehension, staring at an old heap of broken springs that used to be Man and Woman."

"But if I were to tell you that Hagauer and I were pioneers of that era you would hold it against me!" Agathe retorted, with a smile as astringent as good dry wine.

"I no longer hold things against people," Ulrich said. He smiled. "A warrior unbuckled from his armor. For the first time since God knows when, he feels nature's air instead of hammered iron on his skin and sees his body growing so lax and frail that the birds might carry him off," he assured her.

And still smiling, simply forgetting to stop smiling, he contemplated his sister as she sat on the edge of a table, swinging one leg in its black silk stocking; aside from her chemise, she was wearing only short panties. But these were somehow fragmentary impressions, detached, solitary images, as it were. "She's my friend, in the delightful guise of a woman," Ulrich thought. "Though this *is* complicated by her really being a woman!"

And Agathe asked him: "Is there really no such thing as love?"

"Yes, there is," Ulrich said. "But it's the exception. You have to make distinctions. There is first of all a physical experience, to be classed with other irritations of the skin, a purely sensory indulgence without any requisite moral or emotional accessories. Second, emotions are usually involved, which become intensely associated with the physical experience, but in such a way that with slight variations they are the same for everyone; so that even the compulsory sameness of love's climax belongs on the physical-mechanical level rather than on that of the soul. Finally, there is also the real spiritual experience of love, which doesn't necessarily have anything to do with the other two. One can love God, one can love the world; perhaps one can *only* love God and the world. Anyway, it's not necessary to love a person. But if one does, the physical element takes over the whole world, so that it turns everything upside down, as it were. . . ." Ulrich broke off.

Agathe had flushed a dark red. If Ulrich had deliberately chosen and ordered his words with the hypocritical intention of suggesting to Agathe's imagination the physical act of love inevitably associated with them, he could not have succeeded better.

He looked around for a match, simply to undo the unintended effect of his speech by some diversion. "Anyway," he said, "love, if that is love, is an exceptional case, and can't serve as a model for everyday action."

Agathe had reached for the corners of the tablecloth and wrapped them around her legs. "Wouldn't strangers, who saw and heard us, talk about a perverse feeling?" she asked suddenly.

"Nonsense!" Ulrich maintained. "What each of us feels is the shadowy doubling of his own self in the other's opposite nature. I'm a man, you're a woman; it's widely believed that every person bears within him the shadowy or repressed opposite inclination; at least each of us has this longing, unless he's disgustingly self-satisfied. So my counterpart has come to light and slipped into you, and yours into me, and they feel marvelous in their exchanged bodies, simply because they don't have much respect for their previous environment and the view from it!"

Agathe thought: "He's gone into all that more deeply before. Why is he attenuating it now?"

What Ulrich was saying did, of course, fit quite well with the life they were leading as two companions who occasionally, when the company of others leaves them free, take time to marvel at the fact that they are man and woman but at the same time twins. Once two people find themselves in such an accord their relations with the world as individuals take on the charm of an invisible game of hide-and-seek, each switching bodies and costumes with the other, practicing their carefree two-in-one deception for an unsuspecting world behind two kinds of masks. But this playful and overemphatic fun— as children sometimes make noise instead of being noisy—was not in keeping with the gravity that sometimes, from a great height, laid its shadow on the hearts of this brother and sister, making them fall unexpectedly silent. So it happened one evening, as they exchanged a few chance words more before going to bed, that Ulrich saw his sister in her long nightgown and tried to joke about it, saying: "A hundred years ago I would have cried out: 'My angel!' Too bad the term has become obsolete!" He fell silent, disconcerted by the thought: "Isn't that the only word I should be using for her? Not friend, not wife! 'Heavenly creature!' was another term they used. Ridiculously high-flown, of course, but nevertheless better than not having the courage of one's convictions."

Agathe was thinking: "A man in pajamas doesn't look like an angel!" But he did look fierce and broad-shouldered, and she suddenly felt ashamed of her wish that this strong face framed in tousled hair might cast its shadow over her eyes. In some physically innocent way she was sensually aroused; her blood was pulsing through her body in wild waves, spreading over her skin while leaving her drained and weak inside. Since she was not such a fanatical person as her brother, she simply felt what she felt. When she was tender, she was tender, not lit up with ideas or moral impulses, even though this was something she loved in him as much as she shrank from it.

Again and again, day after day, Ulrich summed it all up in the idea: Basically, it's a protest against life! They walked arm in arm through the city: well matched in height, well matched in age, well matched in their attitude to things. Strolling along side by side, they could not see much of each other. Tall figures, pleasing to one another, they walked together for the sheer enjoyment of it, feeling at every step the breath of their contact in the midst of all the strangeness surrounding them. We belong together! This feeling, far from uncommon, made them happy, and half within it, half in resistance to it, Ulrich said: "It's funny we should be so content to be brother and sister. The world in general regards it as a commonplace relationship, but we're making something special of it!"

Perhaps he had hurt her feelings in saying this. He added: "But it's what I've always wished for. When I was a boy I made up my mind to marry only a woman I'd have adopted as a child and brought up myself. I think plenty of men have such fantasies; they're pretty banal, I suppose. But as an adult I actually once fell in love with such a child, though it was only for two or three hours!" And he went on to tell her about it:

"It happened on a streetcar. A little girl of about twelve got on, with her very young father or her older brother. The way she got on, sat down, and casually handed the fare to the conductor for both of them, she was every inch a lady, without a trace of childish affectation. It was the same when she talked to her companion, or quietly listened to him. She was extraordinarily beautiful: brunette, with full lips, strong eyebrows, a slightly turned-up nose; perhaps a dark-haired Polish girl, or a southern Slav. As I recall, the dress she was wearing suggested some national costume: long jacket, tight waist, laced bodice, and frills at the throat and wrists, all in its way as perfect as the little person herself. Perhaps she was Albanian. I was sitting too far away to be able to hear what she was saying. It struck me that the features of her grave little face were mature beyond her years, so that she seemed fully adult; yet it was not the face of a dwarfishly tiny woman, but unquestionably that of a child. On the other hand, it was not at all the immature stage of an adult's face. It seems that a woman's face may sometimes be complete at the age of twelve, formed even spiritually like a perfect first sketch from the hand of a master, so that everything added later to develop the picture only spoils its original greatness. One can fall passionately in love with such a phenomenon, mortally so, and really without any physical desire. I remember I glanced around nervously at the other passengers, because I felt as if I were falling apart. When she got off, I got off, too, but lost her in the crowded street," he ended his little story.

After giving it a moment or two, Agathe asked with a smile: "And how does that fit in with the time for love being over, leaving only sex and companionship?"

"It doesn't fit in at all!" Ulrich laughed.

His sister thought about it, and remarked with a noticeable harshness—it seemed to be an intentional repetition of the words he had used the evening of her arrival: "All men like to play at little-brother-and-little-sister. There must really be some stupid idea behind it. These little brothers and sisters call each other 'father' and 'mother' when they're not quite sober."

Ulrich was taken aback. It was not merely that Agathe was right, for gifted women are merciless observers of the men they love in their lives; but not being inclined to theorize, they make no use of their discoveries except when provoked. He felt somewhat affronted.

"Of course they've got a psychological explanation for it," he said hesitantly. "It's pretty obvious that the two of us are psychologically suspect. Incestuous tendencies, demonstrable in early childhood, together with antisocial dispositions and a rebellious attitude toward life. Possibly even a not sufficiently rooted gender identification, although I—"

"Nor I, either!" Agathe broke in, laughing, if possibly somewhat against her will. "I have no use for women at all!"

"It really doesn't matter anyway," Ulrich said. "Psychic entrails, in any case. You might also say that there's a sultanesque need to be the only one who adores and is adored, to the exclusion of the rest of the world. In the ancient Orient it produced the harem, and today we have family, love, and the dog. And I don't mind saying that the mania to possess another person so entirely that no one else can come anywhere near is a sign of personal loneliness within the human community, which even the socialists rarely deny. If you'd like to see it that way, we represent nothing but a bourgeois extravagance! Oh, look at that! How splendid!" He broke off, pulling on her arm.

They were standing at the edge of a small marketplace surrounded by old houses. Around the neoclassical statue of some intellectual giant, colorful vegetables were spread out, the big canvas umbrellas of the market stands had been set up, fruits tumbled, baskets were being dragged along, dogs chased away from the outspread treasures, and one saw the red faces of rough men and women. The air throbbed and pounded with industriously loud voices and smelled of the sun that shines on the earthly hodgepodge.

"Can we help loving the world when we simply see it and smell it?" Ulrich asked spiritedly. "Yet we can't love it, because we don't agree with what's inside people's heads," he added.

This did not happen to be a reservation entirely to Agathe's taste, and she did not reply. But she pressed her brother's arm, and both of them understood that this was as if she had gently laid her hand over his mouth.

Ulrich laughed, saying: "Not that I like myself either! That's what happens when one is always finding fault with other people. But even I have to be able to love something, and a Siamese sister who's neither me nor herself, but just as much me as herself, is clearly the only point where everything comes together for me!"

He had cheered up again. And Agathe usually went along with his mood. But they never again talked as they had on the first night of their reunion, or before. That was gone, like castles in the clouds, which, when they hover over city streets teeming with life instead of over the deserted countryside, are hard to believe in. Perhaps the cause of this was only that Ulrich did not know what degree of substantiality he should ascribe to the experiences that moved him, while Agathe often thought that he regarded them solely as excesses of fantasy. And she could not prove to him that it was not so; she always spoke less than he did, she could not hit the right note, and did not feel confident enough to try. She merely felt that he was avoiding coming to grips with it, and that he should not be doing that. So they were actually both hiding in their lighthearted happiness, which had no depth or weight, and Agathe became sadder day by day, although she laughed quite as often as her brother.

29

PROFESSOR HAGAUER TAKES PEN IN HAND

But thanks to Agathe's disregarded husband, this changed.

On a morning that brought these joyful days to an end, Agathe received a fat, official-looking letter with a great round yellow seal imprinted with the white insignia of the Imperial and Royal Rudolfs-gymnasium in ———. Instantly, while she was still holding the letter unopened in her hand, there arose out of nothing two-story houses with the mute mirrors of well-polished windows; with white thermometers on the outside of their brown frames, one for each story, to tell what the weather was; with classical pediments and Baroque scallops above the windows, heads projecting from the walls, and other such mythological sentinels, which looked as if they had been produced in a wood-carving shop and painted as stone. The streets ran through the town brown and wet, just like the country roads they were on the way in, with deep ruts, and lined on both sides by shops with their brand-new display windows, looking for all that like gentlewomen of thirty years earlier who have lifted up their long skirts but cannot make up their mind to step from the sidewalk into the muddy street: the provinces in Agathe's head! Apparition in Agathe's head! Something incomprehensible still inside her, which she had been so sure of having shaken off forever! Even more incomprehensible: that she had ever been tied to it! She saw the way from her front door, past familiar housefronts, to the school, the way taken four times daily by her husband, Hagauer, which in the beginning she had often taken with him, accompanying him from his home to his work, in those days when she conscientiously did not let a drop of her bitter medicine escape. "Is Hagauer taking his lunches at the hotel these days?" she wondered. "Does he tear a page off the calender each morning, which I used to do?" It had all suddenly come back to life, so surreally vivid as if it could never die, and with a mute shudder she recognized that familiar craven feeling awakening in her that consisted of indifference, of lost courage, of saturation with ugliness, and of her own insecure volatility. With a kind of avidity, she opened the thick letter her husband had addressed to her.

When Professor Hagauer had returned to his home and workplace from his father-in-law's funeral and a brief visit to the capital, his surroundings welcomed him exactly as they always did after one of his short trips: with the agreeable awareness of his having properly accomplished his mission; and changing from his shoes into the house slippers in which a man works twice as well, he turned his attention to his environment. He went off to his school, was respectfully greeted by the porter, felt welcomed back when he met the teachers who were under him. In the administration office the files and problems no one had dared to deal with in his absence awaited him. When he hastened through the corridors he was accompanied by the feeling that his steps lent wings to the whole building: Gottlieb Hagauer was somebody, and he knew it. Encouragement and good cheer beamed from his brow throughout the educational establishment under his wing, and when anyone outside school inquired after the health and whereabouts of his wife, he replied with the serenity of a man conscious of having married creditably. Everyone knows that the male of the species, so long as he is still capable of procreation, reacts to brief interruptions of his married life as if an easy yoke has been lifted from his shoulders, even when he does not think of illicit associations in connection with it and at the end of this interlude, refreshed, resumes his happy lot. In this manner Hagauer at first accepted his wife's absence, and for a while did not even notice how long she was staying away.

What actually first drew his attention to it was that same wall calendar that had figured in Agathe's memory as such a hateful symbol of life by its needing to have a page torn off every morning. It hung in the dining room as a spot that did not belong on the wall, stranded there as a New Year's greeting from a stationery shop brought home from school by Hagauer, and because of its dreariness not only tolerated but actually cultivated by Agathe. It would have been quite true to form for Hagauer to have taken over the chore of ripping off the daily page in Agathe's absence, for it was not in keeping with his habits to let that part of the wall run wild, as it were. On the other hand, he was also a man who always knew precisely on what latitude of the week or month he found himself upon the ocean of infinity; moreover, he of course had a proper calendar in his office at school; and lastly, just as he was nevertheless about to lift his hand so as to properly regulate the time in his household, and inwardly smiling, he felt something peculiar stop him—one of those impulses through which, as it would later turn out, fate declares itself, but which at the time he merely took for a tender, chivalrous sentiment that surprised him and made him feel pleased with himself: he decided to leave untouched the page marking the day on which Agathe had left the house as a token of homage and a reminder, until her return.

So the wall calendar became in time a festering wound, reminding Hagauer at every glance how long his wife was avoiding her home. A man thrifty with his emotions as with his household, he wrote her postcards to let her know how he was and to ask her, with gradually increasing urgency, when she would be coming back. He received no answer. Now he no longer beamed in answer to sympathetic inquiries whether his wife would be away much longer in fulfillment of her sad duties. But luckily he always had a great deal to keep him busy, apart from his duties at school and the various clubs to which he belonged, since the mail daily brought him a pile of invitations, inquiries, letters from admiring readers, attacks, proofs, periodicals, and important books. Hagauer's human self might be living in the provinces, as an element in the unendearing impressions these might make on a stranger passing through, but his spirit called Europe its home, and this kept him for a long time from grasping the full significance of Agathe's prolonged absence. There came a day, however, when the mail brought him a letter from Ulrich, curtly informing him that Agathe no longer intended to return to him and asking him to agree to a divorce. Politely worded as it was, this letter was so laconic and was written with such a lack of consideration as to make Hagauer feel indignantly that Ulrich cared about his, the recipient's, feelings about as much as if he were an insect to be flicked off a leaf. His first reaction of inner defense was: Don't take it seriously, a whim! There the letter lay, like a grinning specter in the bright daylight of pressing correspondence and showers of professional recognition.

It was not until evening, when Hagauer entered his empty house again, that he sat down at his desk and in dignified brevity wrote to Ulrich that it would be best to pretend his communication had never been written. But he soon received a new letter from Ulrich, rejecting this view of the matter, reiterating Agathe's request (without her knowledge), and merely asking Hagauer in somewhat more courteous detail to do all he could toward keeping the necessary legal steps simple as befitted a man of his high moral principles, and as was also desirable if the deplorable concomitants of a public dispute were to be avoided. Hagauer now grasped the seriousness of the situation, and allowed himself three days' time to compose an answer that would leave nothing to be either desired or regretted afterward.

For the first two days he felt as though someone had struck him a blow in the solar plexus. "A bad dream!" he said plaintively to himself several times, and it took great self-discipline not to let himself forget that he had really received such a request. He felt a deep discomfort in his breast very much like injured love, and an indefinable jealousy as well, which was directed not so much against a lover—which he assumed to be the cause of Agathe's behavior—as against some incomprehensible Something that had shunted him aside. It was a kind of humiliation, similar to that of an extremely orderly man when he has broken or forgotten something; something that had had its fixed place in his mind since time immemorial and that he no longer noticed, but on which much depended, was suddenly smashed. Pale and distraught, in real anguish—not to be underestimated merely because it was lacking in beauty—Hagauer made his rounds, avoiding people, shrinking from the explanations he would have to give and the humiliations to be borne. It was only on the third day that his condition finally stabilized. Hagauer's natural dislike for Ulrich was just as great as Ulrich's for him, and while this had never before come out into the open it did so now, all at once, when he intuitively imputed all the blame for Agathe's conduct to her will-o'-the-wisp gypsy brother, who must have turned her head. He sat down at his desk and demanded in a few words the immediate return of his wife, resolutely declaring that as her husband he would only discuss anything further with her.

From Ulrich came a refusal, equally terse and resolute.

Now Hagauer decided to work on Agathe herself; he made copies of his correspondence with Ulrich and added a long, carefully considered letter; all of this was what Agathe saw before her when she opened the large envelope with the official seal.

Hagauer himself was unable to believe that these things were really happening. Back from his daily obligations, he had sat that evening in his "deserted home," facing a blank sheet of paper much as Ulrich had faced one, not knowing how to begin. But in Hagauer's experience the tried and true "buttons method" had worked more than once, and he resorted to it again in this case. It consists in taking a systematic approach to one's problems, even problems that cause great agitation, on the same principle on which a man has buttons sewn on his clothes to save the time that would be lost if he acted on the assumption that he could get out of his clothes faster without buttons. The English writer Surway, for example, whose work on the subject Hagauer now consulted, for even in his depressed state it was important for him to compare Surway's work with his own views, distinguishes five such buttons in the process of successful reasoning: (*a*) close observation of an event, in which the observation immediately reveals problems of interpretation; (*b*) establishing such problems and defining them more narrowly; (*c*) hypothesis of a possible solution; (*d*) logically developing the consequences of this hypothesis; and (*e*) further observations, leading to acceptance or rejection of the hypothesis and thereby to a successful outcome of the thinking process. Hagauer had already profitably applied a similar method to so worldly an enterprise as lawn tennis when he was learning the game at the Civil Service Club, and it had lent considerable intellectual charm to the game for him; but he had never yet resorted to this method for purely emotional matters, since his ordinary inner life consisted mainly of professional concerns, and for personal events he relied on that "sound instinct" which is a mix of all the possible feelings acceptable and customary to the Caucasian race in any given situation, with a certain bias toward the most proximate local, professional, or class feelings. Applying the buttons to so extraordinary a situation as his wife's extraordinary demand was not going to be easy given his lack of practice, and in cases of personal problems even the "sound instinct" shows a tendency to split in two: It told Hagauer on the one hand that much obliges a man who moved with the times as he did to put no obstacles in the way of a proposal to dissolve a relationship based on trust; but on the other hand, if this goes against the grain, much also absolves him of such an obligation, for the widespread irresponsibility in such matters nowadays should in no way be encouraged. In such a case, as Hagauer had learned, it behooves a modern man to "relax," i.e., disperse his attention, loosen up physically, and listen intently for whatever may be audible of his deepest inner self. So he cautiously stopped thinking, stared at the orphaned wall calendar, and hearkened to his inner voice; after a while it answered, coming from a depth beneath his conscious mind, and told him what he had already thought: the voice said that he had no reason whatsoever to put up with anything so unjustifiable as Agathe's preposterous demand.

But at this point Professor Hagauer's mind found itself set down willy-nilly in front of Surway's buttons *a* to *e*, or some equivalent series of buttons, and he felt afresh all the difficulties of interpreting the event under his observation. "Can I, Gottlieb Hagauer, possibly be to blame for this embarrassing business?" he asked himself. He examined himself and could not find a single point on which he could be faulted. "Is the cause another man she is in love with?" was his second hypothesis toward a possible solution. It was an assumption he had difficulty accepting, for if he forced himself to look at the matter objectively, he could not really see what another man could offer Agathe that was better than what he did. Still, this problem was especially susceptible to being muddied by personal vanity, so he studied it in exacting detail; and here he found vistas opening up that he had never even thought of. Suddenly, from Surway's point *c*, Hagauer found himself on the track of a possible solution via *d* and *e*: for the first time since his marriage, he was struck by a complex of phenomena reported, as far as he knew, only in women whose erotic response to the opposite sex was never deep or passionate. It pained him to find nowhere in his memories any indication of that completely openhearted, dreamy surrender he had experienced earlier, in his bachelor years, with females about whose sensual bent there could be no doubt; but this offered the advantage of enabling him to rule out, with absolute scientific detachment, the destruction of his marital bliss by a third party. Agathe's conduct was reduced, in consequence, to a purely idiosyncratic rebellion against their happiness, all the more so because she had left without giving the slightest hint of such intentions, and there simply had not been enough time since then for her to develop a rational basis for changing her mind! Hagauer had to conclude, and this conviction never left him, that

Agathe's incomprehensible behavior could only be understood as one of those slowly building temptations to turn one's back on life, known to occur in characters who do not know what they want.

But was Agathe really that sort of person? That still remained to be investigated, and Hagauer pensively weeded his whiskers with the end of his pen. Though she usually seemed companionable enough, easy to live with, as he put it, still, when it came to what most preoccupied him, she tended to show a marked indifference, not to say apathy! There was in fact something in her that did not fit in with himself or other people and their interests; not that she set herself up against them. She laughed along with them and looked serious in the right places, but she had always, now that he came to think of it, made a somewhat distracted impression through all these years. She seemed to be listening attentively to what she was told, yet never to believe it. There was something downright unhealthy about her indifference, the more he thought about it. Sometimes one got the impression that she was not taking in what was going on around her at all. . . . And all at once, before he was aware of it himself, his pen had begun to race over the paper with his purposeful motion. "Who can guess what may be going on in your mind," he wrote, "if you think yourself too good to love the life I am in a position to offer you, which I can say in all modesty is a pure and full life; you've always handled it as if with fire tongs, as it now seems to me. You have shut yourself off from the riches of human and moral values that even an unassuming life has to offer, and even if I had to believe that you could somehow have felt justified in doing this, there is still your lack of the moral will to change; instead, you have chosen an artificial way out, a fantasy!"

He mulled it over once more. He mustered the schoolboys who had passed through his guiding hands, searching for a case that might be instructive. But even before he had got into this, there popped into his mind the missing bit that had been uneasily hovering in the back of his mind. At this point Agathe ceased to be a completely personal problem for him, without any clues to its general nature, for when he thought how much she was ready to give up in life without being blinded by any specific passion he was led inescapably, to his joy, to that basic assumption so familiar to modern pedagogy, that she lacked the capacity for objective thought and for keeping in firm intellectual touch with the world of reality! Swiftly he wrote: "Probably you are even at this moment far from being aware of what it is, exactly, that you are about to do; but I warn you, before you come to a decisive conclusion! You are perhaps the absolute opposite of the kind of person, such as I represent, who knows life and knows how to face it, but that is precisely why you should not lightly divest yourself of the support I offer you!"

Actually, Hagauer had meant to write something else. For human intelligence is not a self-contained and unrelated faculty; its flaws involve moral flaws—we speak of moral idiocy—just as moral flaws, though so much less attention is paid to them, often misdirect or totally confuse the rational power in whatever direction they choose. And so Hagauer had formed in his mind an image of a fixed type that he was now inclined, in the course of these reflections, to define as "an adequately intelligent variant of moral idiocy that expresses itself only in certain irregular forms of behavior." But he could not bring himself to use this illuminating phrase, partly to avoid provoking his runaway wife even more, and partly because a layperson usually misunderstands such terms when applied to himself. Objectively, however, it was now established that the forms of behavior that Hagauer deprecated came under the great inclusive genus of the "subnormal," and in the end Hagauer hit upon a way out of this conflict between conscience and chivalry: the irregularities in his wife's conduct could be classified with a fairly general pattern of female behavior and termed "socially deficient."

In this spirit he concluded his letter in words charged with feeling. With the prophetic ire of the scorned lover and pedagogue, he depicted Agathe's asocial, solipsistic, and morbid temperament as a "minus factor" that never permitted her to grapple vigorously and creatively with life's problems, as "our era" demands of "its people," but "shielded her instead from reality behind a pane of glass," mired in deliberate isolation and always on the edge of pathological peril. "If there was something about me you didn't like, you ought to have done something about it," he wrote, "but the truth is that your mind is not equipped to cope with the energies of our time, and evades its demands! Now that I have warned you about your character," he concluded, "I repeat: You, more urgently than most people, need someone strong to lean on. In your own interest I urge you to come back immediately, and I assure you that the responsibility I bear as your husband forbids me to accede to your wish."

Before signing this letter Hagauer read it through once more. Although not satisfied with his description of the psychological type under discussion, he made no changes except at the end—expelling as a gusty sigh through his mustache the unaccustomed, proudly mastered strain of thinking hard about his wife as he pondered how much more still needed to be said about "our modern age"—where he inserted beside the word "responsibility" a chivalrous phrase about his venerated late father-in-law's precious bequest to him.

When Agathe had read all this, a strange thing happened: the content of these arguments did not fail to make an impression on her. After reading it word for word a second time, where she stood, without bothering to sit down, she slowly lowered the letter and handed it to Ulrich, who had been observing his sister's agitation with astonishment.

30

ULRICH AND AGATHE LOOK FOR A REASON AFTER THE FACT

While Ulrich was reading, Agathe dispiritedly watched his face. It was bent over the letter, and its expression seemed to be irresolute, as though he could not decide between ridicule, gravity, sadness, or contempt. Now a heavy weight descended on Agathe from all sides, as if the air that had been so unnaturally light and delicious were becoming unbearably dense and sultry; what she had done to her father's will oppressed her conscience for the first time. To say that she suddenly realized the full measure of her culpability would not be sufficient; what she realized rather was her guilt toward everything, even her brother, and she was overcome with an indescribable disillusionment. Everything she had done seemed incomprehensible to her. She had talked of killing her husband, she had falsified a will, and she had imposed herself on her brother without asking whether she would be disrupting his life: she had done this in a state of being drunk on her own fantasies. What she was most ashamed of at this moment was that it had never occurred to her to do the obvious, the most natural thing: any other woman who wanted to leave a husband she did not like would either look for a better man or arrange for something else, something equally natural. Ulrich himself had pointed this out often enough, but she had paid no attention. And now here she stood and did not know what he would say. Her behavior seemed to her so much that of a being who was not entirely mentally competent that she thought Hagauer was right; he was only holding up the mirror to her in his own way. Seeing his letter in Ulrich's hand struck her dumb in the same way a person might be struck dumb who had been charged with a crime and on top of that receives a letter from a former teacher excoriating him. She had of course never allowed Hagauer to have any influence over her; nevertheless, it now looked as if he had the right to say: "I'm disappointed in you!" or else: "I'm afraid I've never been disappointed in you but always had the feeling you'd come to a bad end!" In her need to shake off this absurd and distressing feeling she impatiently interrupted Ulrich, who was still absorbed in reading the letter without giving any sign of coming to the end, by saying: "His description of me is really quite accurate." She spoke in an apparently casual tone but with a note of defiance, clearly betraying some hope of hearing the opposite. "And even if he doesn't say it in so many words, it's true; either I was not mentally competent when I married him for no compelling reason, or I am not so now, when I'm leaving him for just as little reason."

Ulrich, who was rereading for the third time those passages that made his vivid imagination an involuntary witness of her close relations with Hagauer, absently muttered something she did not catch.

"Do please listen to me!" Agathe pleaded. "Am I the up-to-date woman, active somehow either economically or intellectually? No. Am I a woman in love? No again. Am I the good, nest-building wife and mother who simplifies things and smooths over the rough spots? That least of all. What else is there? Then what in the world am I good for? The social life we're caught up in, I can tell you frankly, basically means nothing at all to me. And I almost think I could get along without whatever it is in music, art, and literature that sends the cognoscenti into raptures. Hagauer, for instance, is different: he needs all that, if only for his quotations and allusions. He at least has the pleasure and satisfaction of a collector. So isn't he right when he accuses me of doing nothing at all, of rejecting the 'wealth of the beautiful and moral,' and tells me that it's only with Professor Hagauer that I can find any sympathy and tolerance?"

Ulrich handed the letter back to her and replied with composure. "Let's face it, the term for you is 'socially retarded,' isn't it?" He smiled, but there was in his tone a hint of irritation left from his having been made privy to this intimate letter.

But her brother's answer did not sit well with Agathe. It made her feel worse. Shyly she tried to turn the tables on him: "In that case why did you insist, if that is what you did, without telling me anything, that I must get a divorce and lose my only protector?"

"Well," he said evasively, "probably because it is so delightfully easy to adopt a firm, manly tone in our exchanges. I bang *my* fist on the table, he bangs *his* fist on the table; so of course I have to bang mine twice as hard the next time around. That's why I think I did it."

Up to now—although her dejection kept her from realizing it herself—Agathe had been really glad, overjoyed in fact, at her brother's secretly doing the opposite of what he had outwardly advocated during the time of their humorous brother-sister flirtation, since offending Hagauer could only have the effect of erecting a barrier to her ever returning to him. Yet even in the place of that secret joy there was now only a hollow sense of loss, and Agathe fell silent.

"We mustn't overlook," Ulrich went on, "how well Hagauer succeeds in misunderstanding you so accurately, if I may say so. Just wait, you'll see that in his own way—without hiring detectives, just by cogitating over the weaknesses of your attachment to the human race—he'll find out what you did to Father's will. How are we going to defend you then?"

So it happened that for the first time since they had been together again the subject came up of the blissful but horrible prank Agathe had played on Hagauer. She fiercely shrugged her shoulders, with a vague gesture of waving it aside.

"Hagauer is in the right, of course," Ulrich offered, with gentle emphasis, for her consideration.

"He's not in the right!" she answered vehemently.

"He's partly right," Ulrich compromised. "In so risky a situation we must start off by facing things openly, including ourselves. What you've done can put us both in jail."

Agathe stared at him with startled eyes. She had known this, of course, but it had never been so straightforwardly stated.

Ulrich responded with a reassuring gesture. "But that's not the worst of it," he continued. "How do we keep what you've done, and the way you did it, from being perceived as"—he groped for the right word and failed to find it—"well, let's just say that to some extent it's the way Hagauer sees it, that it's all a bit on the shadowy side, the side of abnormality and the kind of flaw that comes from something already flawed. Hagauer voices what the world thinks, even though it sounds ridiculous coming from him."

"Now we're getting to the cigarette case," Agathe said in a small voice.

"Right, here it comes," Ulrich said firmly. "I have to tell you something that's been on my mind for a long time."

Agathe tried to stop him. "Wouldn't it be better to undo the whole thing?" she asked. "Suppose I have a friendly talk with him and make some sort of apology?"

"It's already too late for that. He might use it to blackmail you into coming back to him," Ulrich declared.

Agathe was silent.

Ulrich returned to his hypothetical cigarette case, stolen on a whim by a man who is well off. He had worked out a theory that there could be only three basic motivations for such a theft of property: poverty, profession, or, if it was neither of these, a damaged psyche. "You pointed out when we talked about it once that it might be done out of conviction too," he added.

"I said one might just do it!" Agathe interjected.

"Right, on principle."

"No, not on principle!"

"But that's just it!" Ulrich said. "If one does such a thing at all, there has to be at least some conviction behind it! There's no getting away from that. Nobody 'just does' anything; there has to be a reason, either an external or an internal one. It may be hard to know one from the other, but we won't philosophize about that now. I'm only saying that if one feels one is doing the right thing with absolutely no basis for it, or some decision arises out of the blue, then there's good reason to suspect some sickness, something constitutionally wrong."

This was certainly far more and much worse than Ulrich had meant to say; it merely converged with the drift of his qualms.

"Is that all you have to say to me about it?" Agathe asked very quietly.

"No, it's not all," Ulrich replied grimly. "When one has no reason, one must look for one!"

Neither of them was in any doubt where to look for it. But Ulrich was after something else, and after a slight pause he continued thoughtfully: "The moment you fall out of step with the rest of the world, you can never ever know what's good and what's evil. If you want to be good you have to be convinced that the world is good. And neither one of us is. We're living at a time when morality is either dissolving or in convulsions. But for the sake of a world yet to come, one should keep oneself pure."

"Do you really think that will have any effect on whether it comes or not?" Agathe asked skeptically.

"No, I'm afraid I don't think that. Or at most I think like this: If even those people who understand don't act as they should, it certainly won't come at all, and there's no way to stop everything from falling apart!"

"And what do you care whether it's any different five hundred years from now or not?"

Ulrich hesitated. "I'm doing my duty, don't you see? Maybe like a soldier."

Probably because on that miserable morning Agathe needed a more comforting, more affectionate kind of answer than Ulrich was giving, she said: "No different from your General, then?"

Ulrich said nothing.

Agathe was not inclined to stop. "You don't even know for sure whether it's your duty," she went on. "You do it because that's how you are and because you enjoy it. And that's all I did!"

Suddenly she lost her self-control. Something was terribly sad.

Tears sprang to her eyes, and a violent sob rose in her throat. To hide it from her brother's eyes, she threw her arms around his neck and hid her face against his shoulder. Ulrich felt her crying and the trembling of her back. A burdensome embarrassment came over him: he was aware of turning cold. At this moment, when he should have been sympathetic, all the tender and happy feelings he thought he had for his sister deserted him; his sensibility was disturbed and wouldn't function. He stroked Agathe's back and whispered some comforting words, but it went against his grain. Since he did not share her agitation, the contact of their two bodies seemed to him like that of two wisps of straw. He put an end to it by leading Agathe to a chair and himself sitting down in another, some distance away. Then he gave her his answer: "You're not enjoying this business with the will at all. And you never shall, because it's all been a disorderly mess!"

"Order?" Agathe exclaimed through her tears. "Duty?"

She was really quite beside herself because Ulrich had behaved so coldly. But she was already smiling again. She realized that she would have to work things out for herself. She felt that the smile she had forced seemed to be hovering somewhere out there, far from her icy lips. Ulrich meanwhile had shaken off his embarrassment; he was even pleased not to have felt the usual physical stirring; he realized that this, too, would have to be different between them. But he did not have time to think about that now, because he could see that Agathe was deeply troubled, and so he began to talk.

"Don't be upset by the words I used," he pleaded, "and don't hold them against me. I suppose I'm wrong to use words such as 'order' and 'duty'—they sound too much like preaching. But why"—he now went off at a tangent—"why the devil is preaching contemptible? It really ought to be our greatest joy!"

Agathe had no desire to answer this.

Ulrich let it drop.

"Please don't think I'm trying to set myself up as morally superior!" he begged. "I didn't mean to say that I never do anything bad. What I don't like is having to do it in secret. I like the good highway robbers of morality, not the sneak thieves. I'd like to make a moral robber out of you," he joked, "and not let you err out of weakness."

"It's not a point of honor with me," his sister said from behind her distantly hovering smile.

"It's really extremely funny that there are times like ours, when all young people are infatuated with whatever's bad," he said with a laugh, to distance the conversation from the personal level. "This current preference for the morally gruesome is a weakness, of course. Probably middle-class gorging on goodness; being all sucked dry. I myself originally thought one had to say no to everything; everyone thinks so who is between twenty-five and forty-five today; but of course it was only a kind of fashion. I can imagine a reaction setting in soon, and with it a new generation that will again stick morality instead of immorality in its buttonhole. The oldest donkeys, who never in their lives felt any moral fervor, who merely uttered moral platitudes when the occasion called for them, will then suddenly be hailed as precursors and pioneers of a new character!"

Ulrich had risen to his feet and was restlessly pacing the room.

"We might put it this way," he suggested. "Good has become a cliché almost by its very nature, while evil remains criticism. The immoral achieves its divine right by being a drastic critique of the moral! It shows us that life has other possibilities. It shows us up for liars. For this we show our gratitude by a certain forbearance. That there are truly delightful people who forge wills should prove that there is something amiss with the sanctity of private property. Even if this doesn't need proving, it is where our task begins: for every kind of crime, we must be able to conceive of criminals who can be excused, even including infanticide or whatever other horrors there may be. . . ."

He had been trying in vain to catch his sister's eye, even though he was teasing her by bringing up the will. Now she made an involuntary gesture of protest. She was no theoretician; the only crime she regarded as excusable was her own, and she was insulted all over again by his comparison.

Ulrich laughed. "It looks like an intellectual game, but this kind of juggling does mean something," he assured her. "It goes to show that there's something amiss in the way we judge our conduct. And there really is, you know. In a company of will-forgers you would certainly stand up for the inviolability of the legal regulations; it's only in the company of the righteous that it all gets blurred and perverted. If only Hagauer were a rogue, you would be flamingly just; it's too bad he's such a decent fellow! That's the seesaw we're on."

He waited for a response but none came, so he shrugged his shoulders and came back to the point:

"We're looking to justify what you did. We have established that respectable people are deeply attracted to crime, though of course only in their imagination. We might add that criminals, to hear them talk, would almost without exception like to be regarded as respectable people. So we might arrive at a definition: Crimes are the concentrated form, within sinners, of everything other people work off in little irregularities, in their imagination and in innumerable petty everyday acts and attitudes of spite and viciousness. We could also say: Crimes are in the air and simply seek the path of least resistance, which leads them to certain individuals. We could even say that while they are the acts of individuals who are incapable of behaving morally, in the main they're the condensed expression of some kind of general human maladjustment where the distinction between good and evil is concerned. This is what has imbued us from our youth with the critical spirit our contemporaries have never been able to get beyond!"

"But what is good and evil?" Agathe tossed off the question, while Ulrich remained oblivious to the pain his banter was causing her.

"Well, how would I know?" he answered with a laugh. "I've only just noticed for the first time that I loathe evil. Until today I really didn't know how much. My dear Agathe, you have no idea what it's like," he complained moodily. "Take science, for instance! For a mathematician, to put it very simply, minus five is no worse than plus five. A scientist researching a problem mustn't recoil in horror from anything, and under certain conditions he might get more excited by a lovely cancer than a lovely woman. A man of knowledge knows that nothing is true and that the whole truth will be revealed only at the end of time. Science is amoral. All our glorious thrusting of ourselves into the Unknown gets us out of the habit of being personally concerned with our conscience; in fact, it doesn't even give us the satisfaction of taking our conscience entirely seriously. And art? Doesn't it amount to a creation of images that don't correspond to the realities of life? I'm not talking about bogus idealism, or the paintings of voluptuous nudes in a period when everyone goes around covered up to the eyeballs," he joked again. "But think of a real work of art: have you never had the feeling that something about it is reminiscent of the smell of burning metal you get from a knife you're whetting on a grindstone? It's a cosmic, meteoric, lightning-and-thunder smell, something divinely uncanny!"

This was the only point at which Agathe interrupted him with real interest: "Didn't you once write poetry yourself?" she asked him.

"You still remember that? When did I let you in on it?" Ulrich asked. "Yes; we all write verses at one time or another. I even went on doing it when I was a mathematician," he admitted. "But the older I got, the worse they became; not so much because of lack of talent, I think, as from a growing aversion to the disorderly and bohemian romanticism of that sort of emotional excess. . . ."

His sister shook her head almost imperceptibly, but Ulrich noticed it. "Yes," he insisted, "a poem should be no more of an exceptional phenomenon than an act of goodness! But what, if I may ask, becomes of the moment of inspiration the moment after? You love poetry, I know; but what I'm saying is that it isn't enough to breathe out one great puff of fire and let it fade away. This kind of sporadic performance is the counterpart of the kind of morality that exhausts itself in half-baked criticism." And abruptly returning to his main subject, he said to his sister: "If I were to behave in this Hagauer matter the way you're expecting me to today, I would have to be skeptical, casual, and ironic. The exemplary children you or I might yet have would then be able to say truthfully of us that we belonged to a very secure period of middle-class values that was never plagued by doubts, or plagued at most by superficial doubts. But in fact you and I have already gone to such trouble over our philosophy . . . !"

Ulrich probably wanted to say a great deal more; he was actually only leading up to some way of coming down on his sister's side, which he had already worked out, and it would have been good if he had revealed it to her. For she suddenly stood up and on some vague pretext got her outdoor things.

"So we're leaving it that I'm morally retarded?" she asked with a forced attempt at humor. "I can't keep up with all you've been saying to the contrary!"

"We're both morally retarded!" Ulrich gallantly assured her. "Both of us!" And he was rather proud of the haste with which his sister left him without saying when she would return.

31

AGATHE WANTS TO COMMIT SUICIDE AND MAKES A GENTLEMAN'S ACQUAINTANCE

In truth she had rushed off to spare her brother the sight of the tears she could barely hold back. She was as sad as a person who has lost everything. She did not know why. It had come over her while Ulrich was talking. Why? She didn't know that either. He should have done something other than talk. What? She didn't know. He was right, of course, not to take seriously the "stupid coincidence" of her being upset and the arrival of that letter, and to go on talking as he always did. But Agathe had to get away.

At first she felt only the need to walk. She rushed headlong from their house. Where the layout of the streets forced her to detour, she always kept to the same general direction. She fled, in the way people and animals flee from a catastrophe. Why, she did not ask herself. It was only when she grew tired that she realized what she intended to do: never go back!

She would keep walking until dusk. Farther from home with every step. She assumed that by the time she came up against the barricade of evening her decision would be made. The decision was to kill herself. It was not an actual decision to kill herself, but the expectation that by evening it would be. Behind this expectation was a desperate seething and whirling inside her head. She did not even have anything with her to kill herself with. Her little poison capsule lay somewhere in a drawer or in a suitcase. The only clear thing about her death was the longing never to have to go back again. She wanted to walk out of life. That was where the walking came from. It was as if every step she took was already a step out of life.

As she tired she began to long for green fields and woods, for walking in silence and the open air. She could not get there on foot. She took a streetcar. She had been brought up to control herself in public. So her voice betrayed no emotion when she bought her ticket and asked for directions. She sat straight-backed and impassive, with not a finger twitching. And as she sat there the thoughts started coming. She would of course have felt better had she been able to let herself go; with her limbs fettered as they were, these thoughts came in large bundles that she vainly tried to force through an opening. She bore Ulrich a grudge for what he had said. She didn't want to hold it against him. She gave up her right to. What had she done for him? She was only taking up his time, and doing nothing for him in return; she was in the way of his work and his habits. When she thought of his habits she felt a pang. It seemed that no woman had entered his house in all the time she'd been there. Agathe was convinced that her brother always had to have a woman in his life. So he was depriving himself for her sake. At this moment she would have liked to turn back and tenderly beg his forgiveness. As there was no way she could make it up to him, she was being selfish and bad. But then she remembered again how cold he had been. He was obviously sorry he had taken her in. To think of all he had planned and said before he got tired of her! Now he no longer mentioned any of it. Agathe's heart was again tormented with the great disillusionment her husband's letter had brought her. She was jealous. Senselessly and commonly jealous. She would have liked to force herself on her brother; she felt the passionate and helpless friendship of the person throwing himself against his own rejection. "I could steal or walk the streets for him!" she thought, knowing this was ridiculous but not able to help it. Ulrich's conversations, with their humor and sovereign air of being above the battle, made a mockery of this idea. She admired his superiority and all his intellectual needs, which surpassed her own. But she didn't see why every idea always had to be equally true for everyone! In her humbled state she needed some personal comforting, not edifying sermons! She did not want to be brave! And after a while, she reproached herself for being the way she was, and enlarged her pain by imagining that she deserved nothing better than Ulrich's indifference.

This self-denigration, for which neither Ulrich's conduct nor even Hagauer's upsetting letter was sufficient cause, was a temperamental outburst. Ever since Agathe had outgrown her childhood, not so very long ago, everything she regarded as her failure in the face of society's demands had had to do with her sense of not living in accord with her own deepest inclinations, or even in opposition to them. She inclined to devotion and trustfulness, for she had never become so much at home in solitude as her brother; and if she had found it impossible to yield herself heart and soul to a person or a cause, it was because she had the capacity for some greater devotion, whether it reached out to the whole world or to God. There is the well-known path of devotion to all mankind that begins with an inability to get along with one's neighbor, and just so may a deep latent yearning for God arise in an antisocial character equipped with a great capacity for love; in that sense, the religious criminal is no greater paradox than the religious old woman who never found a husband. Agathe's behavior toward Hagauer, which had the absurd appearance of a selfish action, was as much the outburst of an impatient will as was the intensity with which she accused herself of losing life by her own weakness just when she had been awakened to it by her brother.

She soon lost patience with the slow, rumbling streetcar. When the buildings along the way grew lower and more rural, she got off and continued the rest of the way on foot. The courtyards were open; through archways and over low fences came glimpses of handymen at their chores, animals, children at play. The air was filled with a peace in whose distances voices sounded and tools banged; sounds moved in the bright air with the irregular, gentle motions of a butterfly, while Agathe felt herself gliding like a shadow past them toward the rising ground of vineyards and woodland. Just once she paused, in front of a yard where coopers were at work and there was the good noise of mallets hammering on barrel staves. She had always liked watching such honest work and taken pleasure in the modest, sensible, well-considered labor of the workmen. This time, too, she could not get enough of the rhythm of the mallets and the men's moving round and round the barrel. For a few moments it made her forget her misery and plunged her into a pleasant, unthinking oneness with the world. She always admired people who could do this kind of task, with skills developed so variously and naturally out of a generally acknowledged need. But there was nothing she wanted to do herself, although she had all kinds of mental and practical aptitudes. Life was complete without her. And suddenly, before she saw the connection, she heard church bells ringing, and could barely restrain herself from bursting into tears again. Both bells of the little local church had probably been chiming the whole time, but Agathe just now noticed it and was instantly overcome by how these useless chimes, excluded from the good, lavish earth and flying passionately through the air, were related to her own existence.

She hastily resumed walking, and accompanied by the chimes, which now would not leave her ears, she passed swiftly between the last of the houses and emerged where the road climbed the hillside with its vineyards and scattered bushes lining the paths below, while above, the bright green of the woods beckoned. Now she knew where she was going, and it was a beautiful feeling, as though with every step she were sinking more deeply into nature. Her heart pounded with joy and effort when she sometimes stopped and found the bells still accompanying her, though now hidden high in the air and scarcely audible. It seemed to her she had never heard bells chiming like this in the midst of an ordinary day, for no apparent festive reason, mingling democratically with the natural and self-sufficient affairs of men. But of all the tongues of this thousand-voiced city, this was the last to speak to her, and something in it seized hold of her as if to lift her high and swing her up the hill, only to drop her again as it faded into a slight metallic sound no better than all the chirping, rumbling, and rustling sounds of the countryside. So Agathe climbed and walked upward for perhaps another hour, until she suddenly found herself facing the little shrubby wilderness she had carried in her memory. It enclosed a neglected grave at the edge of the woods, where nearly a hundred years before a poet had killed himself and where, in accordance with his last wish, he had also been laid to rest. Ulrich had said that he was not a good poet, even if he was famous. Ulrich was sharply critical of the rather shortsighted poetics that expressed a longing to be *buried high up with a view*. But Agathe had loved the inscription on the big stone slab since the day they had come this way and together deciphered the beautiful, rain-worn Biedermeier lettering, and she leaned over the black chain fence with its great angular links, which marked off the rectangle of death from life.

"I meant nothing to all of you" were the words the disgruntled poet had had inscribed on his gravestone, and Agathe thought that this could equally well be said of herself. This thought, here on the edge of the wooded pulpit above the greening vineyards and the alien, immeasurable city that was slowly waving its trails of smoke in the morning sun, moved her afresh. Impulsively she knelt down to press her forehead against one of the stone posts that held the chains; the unaccustomed position and the cool touch of the stone feigned the rather stiff and passive tranquillity of the death that was awaiting her. She tried to pull herself together, but was not immediately successful; bird calls intruded on her ear, so many and such various bird calls that it surprised her; branches stirred, and since she did not feel the wind she had the impression that the trees were waving their branches of their own accord. In a sudden hush, a faint pattering could be heard; the stone she was resting against, touching, was so smooth that she felt that a piece of ice between it and her forehead was keeping her from quite touching it. Only after a while did she realize that what distracted her was precisely what she was trying to hold on to, that fundamental sense of being superfluous which, reduced to its simplest terms, could be expressed only in the words that life was so complete without her that she had no business being in it. This cruel feeling contained, at bottom, neither despair nor offense, but was rather a listening and looking on that Agathe had always known; it was just that she had no impulse, indeed no possibility, of taking a hand in her own fate. This state of exclusion was almost a shelter, just as there is a kind of astonishment that forgets to ask questions. She could just as well go away. Where to? There really must be a Somewhere. Agathe was not one of those people who can find satisfaction in their conviction of the emptiness of all illusions, which, as a way of accepting a disappointing fate, is equivalent to a militant and spiteful asceticism. She was generous and uncritical in such matters, unlike Ulrich, who subjected all his feelings to the most relentless scrutiny in order to outlaw any that did not pass the test. She was simply stupid! That's what she told herself. She didn't want to think things over! Defiantly she pressed her forehead against the iron chains, which gave a little and then stiffened in resistance. During these last weeks she had somehow begun to believe in God again, but without thinking of Him. Certain states of mind, in which she perceived the world differently from what it appeared to be, in such a way that even she lived no longer shut out but completely enveloped in a radiant certainty, had been brought, under Ulrich's influence, to something akin to an inward metamorphosis, a total transformation.

She would have been willing to imagine a God who opens up His world like a hiding place. But Ulrich said that this was not necessary, it could only do harm to imagine more than one could experience. And it was for him to decide in these matters. But then, it was also for him to guide her without abandoning her. He was the threshold between two lives, and all her longing for the one and all her flight from the other led first to him. She loved him as shamelessly as one loves life. When she opened her eyes in the morning, he awoke in every limb of her body. He was looking at her even now, from the dark mirror of her anguish: which made Agathe remember that she wanted to kill herself. She had a feeling that it was to spite him that she had run away to God when she had left home to kill herself. But that intention now seemed exhausted, to have sunk back to its source, which was that Ulrich had hurt her feelings. She was angry with him, she still felt that, but the birds were singing, and now she heard them again. She was just as confused as before, but it was now a joyful confusion. She wanted to do something, but it should strike out at Ulrich, not just at herself. The endless stupor in which she had been kneeling gave way to the warmth of the blood streaming back into her limbs as she rose to her feet.

When she looked up, a man was standing beside her. She was embarrassed, not knowing how long he had been watching her. As her glance, still dark with agitation, met his, she saw that he was looking at her with unconcealed sympathy, manifestly hoping to inspire her with wholehearted confidence. The man was tall and lean and wore dark clothes, and a short blond beard covered his cheeks and chin. Beneath his mustache one could easily make out full, soft lips, which were in remarkably youthful contrast to the many gray hairs already scattered among the blond ones, as if age had forgotten them in the growth of hair. It was altogether not an easy face to read. The first impression led one to think of a secondary-school teacher; the severity in this face was not carved in hardwood but rather resembled something soft that had hardened under petty daily frustrations. But if one started with this softness, on which the manly beard seemed to have been planted in order to adjust it to a system with which the wearer concurred, then one realized that this originally rather effeminate face showed hard, almost ascetic details, clearly the work of a relentlessly active will upon the soft basic material.

Agathe did not know what to make of this face, which left her suspended between attraction and repulsion; all she understood was
that this man wanted to help her.

"Life offers us just as much opportunity to strengthen the will as to
weaken it," the stranger said, wiping his glasses, which had been
misted over, in order to see her better. "One should never run away
from problems, but try to master them!" Agathe stared at him in surprise. He had obviously been watching her for quite some time, because his words were emerging from the middle of some interior
monologue. Startled by his own voice, he raised his hat, his manners
belatedly catching up with this essential gesture of courtesy, then
quickly regained his composure and went straight on: "Do forgive
my asking whether I may be of some help," he said. "It seems to me
that it is truly easier to speak of one's pain to a stranger, even concerning a grave shock to the self, such as I believe I am witnessing
here?"

Evidently it was not without effort that the stranger spoke to her;
apparently he had felt called upon to do so out of duty, as an act of
charity; and now that he found himself walking beside this beautiful
woman, he was literally struggling for words. For Agathe had simply
stood up and begun slowly to walk with him away from the grave and
out from under the trees into the open space at the edge of the hills,
neither of them deciding whether they wanted to choose one of the
paths leading downward, or which one. Instead, they walked along
the hilltop for quite a distance, talking, then turned back, and then
turned back to walk in the original direction once more; neither of
them knew where the other had meant to go originally, and neither
wanted to interfere with the other's plans.

"Won't you tell me why you were crying?" the stranger persisted,
in the mild tones of a physician asking where it hurts.

Agathe shook her head. "It wouldn't be easy to explain," she said,
and suddenly asked him: "But tell me something else: What makes
you so sure you can help me without knowing me? I'd be inclined to
think that one can't help anyone!"

Her companion did not answer right away. He opened his mouth
to speak several times, but seemed to force himself to hold back. Finally, he said: "One can probably only help someone who is suffering
from something one has experienced oneself."

He fell silent. Agathe laughed at the thought that this man could suppose himself to have been through what she was suffering, which would have been repellent to him had he known what it was. But her companion seemed not to hear this laugh, or to regard it as a rudeness born of nerves. After a pause, he said calmly: "Of course, I don't mean that anyone has a right to imagine that he can tell anyone else what to do. But you see, fear in a catastrophe is infectious—and successful escape is also infectious! I mean just having escaped as from a fire, when everyone has lost his head and run into the flames: what an immense help when a single person stands outside, waving, does nothing but wave and shout incomprehensibly that there is a way out. . . ."

Agathe nearly laughed again at the horrible ideas this kindly man harbored; but just because they seemed so out of character, they molded his wax-soft face almost uncannily.

"You talk like a fireman!" she retorted, deliberately adopting the teasing, frivolous tone of high society to hide her curiosity. "Still, you must have formed some notion of the kind of catastrophe I'm involved in, surely?" Unintentionally, the seriousness of her scorn showed through, for the simple idea that this man presumed to offer her help aroused her indignation by the equally simple gratitude that welled up in her. The stranger looked at her in astonishment, then collected himself and said almost in rebuke: "You are probably still too young to know how simple life is. It only becomes hopelessly confused when one is thinking of oneself; but as soon as one stops thinking of oneself and asks oneself how to help someone else, it's quite simple!"

Agathe thought it over in silence. And whether it was her silence or the inviting distance into which his words took wing, the stranger went on, without looking at her:

"It's a modern superstition to overestimate the personal. There's so much talk today about cultivating one's personality, living one's life to the full, and affirming life. But all this fuzzy and ambiguous verbiage only betrays the user's need to befog the real meaning of his protest. What, exactly, is to be affirmed? Anything and everything, higgledy-piggledy? Evolution is always associated with resistance, an American thinker has said. We cannot develop one side of our nature without stunting another. Then what's to be lived to the full? The mind or the instincts? Every passing whim or one's character? Selfishness or love? If our higher nature is to fulfill itself, the lower must learn renunciation and obedience!"

Agathe was considering why it should be simpler to take care of others than of oneself. She was one of those completely nonegotistical characters who may always be thinking about themselves, but not for their own benefit, which differs far more from the usual selfishness, which is always on the lookout for its own advantage, than does the complacent unselfishness of those who are always worrying about their fellow human beings. So what her companion was saying was at bottom foreign to her nature, and yet it somehow moved her, and the words he seized hold of so forcefully sailed alarmingly before her eyes as though their meaning were more to be seen in the air than heard. Also, they happened to be walking along a ridge that gave Agathe a marvelous view of the deep curving valley below, a position that evidently gave her companion the sense of being in a pulpit or on a lecture platform. She stopped and with her hat, which all this time she had been swinging carelessly in her hand, she drew a line through the stranger's argument: "So you *have* formed your own picture of me," she said. "I can see it shining through your words, and it isn't flattering."

The tall gentleman seemed dismayed, for he hadn't meant to hurt her, and Agathe looked at him with a friendly laugh. "You seem to be confusing me with the cause of the liberated personality, and a rather neurotic and unpleasant personality at that!" she maintained.

"I was only speaking of the underlying principle of the personal life," he said apologetically. "I must confess that the situation in which I found you suggested to me that you might want some helpful advice. The underlying principle of life is so widely misunderstood nowadays. Our entire modern neurosis, with all its excesses, arises solely from a flabby inner state in which the will is lacking, for without a special effort of will no one can achieve the integrity and stability that lifts a person above the obscure confusion of the organism!"

Here again were two words, "integrity" and "stability," that echoed her old longings and self-accusations. "Do tell me what you mean by that," she asked him. "Surely there can only really be a will when one has a goal?"

"What I mean doesn't matter," was the answer she received, in a tone both mild and brusque. "Don't all the great ancient scriptures of mankind tell us with utmost clarity what to do and not to do?"

Agathe was disconcerted.

"To set up fundamental ideals of life," her companion explained, "requires such a penetrating knowledge of life and of people, and such a heroic mastery of the passions and egotism, as has been granted to only very few individuals in the course of thousands of years. And these teachers of mankind have throughout the ages always taught the same truths."

Agathe instinctively resisted, as would anyone who considers her young flesh and blood better than the bones of dead sages.

"But precepts formulated thousands of years ago can't possibly apply to conditions today!" she cried.

"Those precepts are not nearly as foreign as is claimed by skeptics, who are out of touch with living experience and self-knowledge," her chance companion answered, with bitter satisfaction. "Life's deepest truths are not arrived at in debate, as Plato already said. Man hears them as the living meaning and fulfillment of his self. Believe me, what makes the human being truly free, and what takes away his freedom, what gives him true bliss and what destroys it, isn't subject to 'progress'—it is something every genuinely alive person knows perfectly well in his own heart, if he will just listen to it!"

Agathe liked the expression "living meaning," but then something suddenly occurred to her: "Are you religious?" she asked him. She looked at her companion with curiosity. He gave no answer.

"You're not a priest, by any chance . . . ?" she continued, but was reassured by his beard, for the rest of his appearance suddenly suggested that surprising possibility. It must be said to her credit that she would not have been more astounded had he casually referred to "our sublime ruler, the divine Augustus." She knew that religion plays a great role in politics, but one is so used to not taking ideas bandied about in public life seriously that to expect the "Christian" parties to be composed of true believers is the same kind of exaggeration as expecting every postal clerk to be a philatelist.

After a lengthy, somewhat wavering pause, the stranger replied: "I would prefer not to answer your question; you are too remote from all that."

But Agathe was seized with a lively curiosity.

"I'd like to know who you are!" she demanded to be told, and this was, after all, a feminine privilege that was not to be denied. He showed the same, slightly comical hesitation as before, when he had belatedly raised his hat to her. His arm seemed to twitch as if he were thinking of thus saluting her again, but then something in him stiffened, as though one army of thoughts had battled another and won, instead of a trifling gesture being playfully performed.

"My name is Lindner, and I teach at the Franz Ferdinand Gymnasium," he said, adding after a moment's thought: "I also lecture at the University."

"Then you might know my brother?" Agathe asked in relief, adding Ulrich's name. "He read a paper there recently, if I'm not mistaken, at the Pedagogical Society, on Mathematics and the Humanities, or something like that."

"Only by name. We've never met. Oh yes, I did attend that lecture," Lindner admitted. He seemed to say it with a certain reserve, but Agathe's attention was caught by his next question:

"Your father must have been the distinguished jurist?"

"Yes. He died recently, and I'm now staying with my brother," Agathe said freely. "Won't you come and see us?"

"I'm afraid I have no time for social calls," Lindner replied brusquely, his eyes cast down in uncertainty.

"In that case I hope you won't have any objections if I come to see you sometime," Agathe said, paying no attention to his reluctance. "I do need your advice." And since he had been calling her "Fräulein," she said: "I'm married; Hagauer is my name."

"Then you're the wife of the noted Professor of Education Hagauer . . . !" Lindner cried. He had begun the sentence on a note of high enthusiasm, but it wavered and became hesitant. For Hagauer was two things: he was in education and he was a progressive in education. Lindner was actually opposed to his ideas, but how bracing it was to recognize, through the uncertain mists of a female psyche, which has just proposed the impossible notion of inviting herself to a man's house, the familiar form of an enemy; it was the drop from the second to the first of these sentiments that was reflected in his change of tone.

Agathe had noticed it. She did not know whether to tell Lindner of the situation between her husband and herself. If she told him, it might put an immediate end to everything between herself and this new friend, that much was clear. And she would have been sorry; precisely because there was so much about Lindner that made her laugh at him, he also made her feel that she could trust him. The impression, borne out by his appearance, that this man seemed to want nothing for himself oddly moved her to be forthright with him: he quieted all longing, and that made frankness quite natural.

"I'm about to get a divorce," she finally admitted.

A silence followed. Lindner now had a downcast look. It put Agathe out of all patience with him. Finally, Lindner said with an offended smile: "I thought it must be something like that when I first caught sight of you!"

"Does that mean you're opposed to divorce too?" Agathe cried, giving free rein to her irritation with him. "Of course, you're bound to be against it. But it really does put you rather behind the times!"

"At least I can't regard it as matter-of-factly as you do." Lindner defended himself pensively, took off his glasses, polished them, put them on again, and contemplated Agathe. "It seemed to me you have too little willpower," he stated.

"Willpower? My will, for what it's worth, is to get a divorce!" Agathe cried, knowing it was not a very sensible answer.

"Please don't misunderstand me," Lindner gently corrected her. "I am of course willing to believe that you have good reasons. It's only that I see things in a different light. The free and easy morals prevailing nowadays amount, in effect, to nothing more than a sign that the individual is chained hand and foot to his own ego and incapable of living and acting from any wider perspective. Our esteemed poets," he added jealously, with an attempt at humor about Agathe's perfervid pilgrimage to the poet's grave, an attempt that only turned sour on his lips, "who play up to the sentiments of young ladies, and are therefore overestimated by them, have a far easier role to play than I, when I tell you that marriage is an institution of responsibility and the mastery of the human being over its passions! Before anyone dissociates himself from the external safeguards that mankind has wisely set up against its own undependability, he should recognize that isolation from and disobedience to the greater whole do far more harm than the physical disappointments we so fear!"

"That sounds like a military code for archangels," Agathe said, "but I'm not inclined to agree with you. Let me walk with you part-way. You must explain how it is possible to think as you do. Which way are you going now?"

"I must get home," Lindner answered.

"Would your wife mind very much if I walked home with you? When we get back down to town we can take a taxi. I have plenty of time."

"My son will be coming home from school," Lindner said with de-fensive dignity. "Mealtimes are on a strict schedule with us, which is why I must be home on time. My wife died suddenly, some years ago," he added, correcting Agathe's mistaken assumption, and with a glance at his watch he said with nervous impatience: "I must hurry!"

"Then you must explain it to me some other time. It is important to me!" Agathe insisted with feeling. "If you won't come to see us, I shall look you up."

Lindner caught his breath, but nothing came of it. Finally, he said: "But as a lady you can't come calling on a man!"

"Oh, yes I can!" Agathe assured him. "I shall simply arrive one day, you'll see. Though I can't say when. There is no harm in it!"

With this, she said good-bye and took a path diverging from his.

"You have no willpower!" she said under her breath, trying to imi-tate Lindner, but the word "willpower" tasted fresh and cool in her mouth. It had overtones of pride, toughness, and confidence; her heart beat higher; the man had done her good.

32

THE GENERAL MEANWHILE TAKES ULRICH
AND CLARISSE TO THE MADHOUSE

While Ulrich was alone at home, the War Ministry telephoned to ask whether His Excellency the Chief of the Department for Military, Educational, and Cultural Affairs could see him privately in half an hour, and thirty-five minutes later General Stumm von Bordwehr's official carriage came dashing up the little drive.

"A fine kettle of fish!" the General cried out to his friend, who instantly noticed that this time the orderly with the intellectual bread was absent. The General was in full dress, decorations and all. "A fine mess you've got me into!" he reiterated. "There's a plenary session at your cousin's this evening. I haven't even had a chance to see my chief about it. And now suddenly the bombshell bursts—we have to be at the madhouse within an hour!"

"But why?" Ulrich asked, not unnaturally. "Usually that sort of thing is arranged ahead of time!"

"Don't ask so many questions!" the General implored him. "Just go and telephone your little friend or cousin or whatever she is, and tell her we're coming to call for her!"

Ulrich telephoned the grocery store where Clarisse was in the habit of doing her local shopping, and while he was waiting for her to come to the phone he heard about the misfortune the General was bemoaning. To make the arrangements for Clarisse to visit Moosbrugger, as a favor to Ulrich, Stumm had turned to the Chief of the Medical Corps, who then got in touch with his celebrated colleague the head of the University Clinic, where Moosbrugger was awaiting a top-level opinion on his psychiatric status. However, through a misunderstanding by both these gentlemen, the appointment for the date and time of Clarisse's visit had been made on the spot, as Stumm had been told with many apologies at the last minute, along with the error that he himself had been named as one of the visiting party that the famous psychiatrist was expecting with great pleasure.

"I feel quite ill!" he declared. This was a time-honored formula for his needing a schnapps. After he had tossed it off, he relaxed a little. "What's a madhouse to me! It's only because of you that I have to go!" he lamented. "Whatever will I say to that idiot professor when he asks me why I came along?"

At this moment a jubilant war whoop sounded at the other end of the line.

"Fine!" the General said fretfully. "But I also must absolutely talk to you about tonight. And I still have to report to my chief about it too. And he leaves the office at four!" He glanced at his watch and out of sheer hopelessness did not budge from his chair.

"Well, I'm ready," Ulrich said.

"Your lovely sister isn't coming?" Stumm asked in surprise.

"My sister is out."

"Too bad." The General sighed. "Your sister is the most remarkable woman I have ever met."

"I thought that was Diotima," Ulrich said.

"She's another," Stumm replied. "Diotima is admirable too. But since she's been going in for sex education I feel like a schoolboy. I'm happy to look up to her—God knows, a soldier's trade is a simple and crude kind of manual labor, as I always say, but precisely in the realm of sex it goes against one's honor as an officer to let oneself be treated as a novice!"

By now they were in the carriage and being driven off at a brisk trot.

"Is your young lady pretty, at least?" Stumm inquired suspiciously.

"She's quite an original, as you'll see," Ulrich replied.

"Now, as regards tonight"—the General sighed—"something is brewing. I expect something to happen."

"That's what you say every time you come to see me," Ulrich protested, smiling.

"Maybe, but it's true just the same. And tonight you'll be present at the encounter between your cousin and Frau Professor Drangsal. I hope you haven't forgotten everything I've told you about that. The Drangsal pest—that's what your cousin and I call her between ourselves—has been pestering your cousin for such a long time that she's got what she wanted: she's been haranguing everyone, and tonight will be the showdown between them. We were only waiting for Arnheim, so that he can form an opinion too."

"Oh?" Ulrich had not seen Arnheim for a long time, and had not known that he was back.

"Of course. Just for a few days," Stumm said. "So we had to set it up—" He broke off suddenly, bounding up from the swaying upholstery toward the driver's box with an agility no one would have expected of him. "Idiot!" he barked into the ear of the orderly disguised as a civilian coachman who was driving the ministerial horses, and he rocked helplessly back and forth with the carriage as he clung to the back of the man he was insulting, shouting: "You're taking the long way round!" The soldier in civvies held his back stiff as a board, numb to the General's extramilitary use of his body to save himself from falling, turned his head exactly ninety degrees, so that he could not see either his general or his horses, and smartly reported to a vertical that ended in the air that the shortest route was blocked off by street repairs, but he would soon be back on it. "There you are—so I was right!" Stumm cried as he fell back, glossing over his futile outburst of impatience, partly for the orderly's benefit and partly for Ulrich's. "So now the fellow has to take a detour, when I'm supposed to report to my chief this very afternoon, and he wants to go home at four o'clock, by which time he should have briefed the Minister himself! . . . His Excellency the Minister has sent word to the Tuzzis to expect him in person tonight," he added in a low voice, just for Ulrich's ear.

"You don't say!" Ulrich showed himself properly impressed by this news.

"I've been telling you for a long time there's something in the air."

Now Ulrich wanted to know what was in the air. "Come out with it, then," he demanded. "What does the Minister want?"

"He doesn't know himself," Stumm answered genially. "His Excellency has a feeling that the time has come. Old Leinsdorf also has a feeling that the time has come. The Chief of the General Staff likewise has a feeling that the time has come. When a lot of people have such a feeling, there may be something in it."

"But the time for what?" Ulrich persisted.

"Well, we don't need to know that yet," the General instructed him. "These are simply reliable indications! By the way," he asked abstractedly, or perhaps thoughtfully, "how many of us will there be today?"

"How would I know?" Ulrich asked in surprise.

"All I meant," Stumm explained, "is how many of us are going to the madhouse? Excuse me! Funny, isn't it, that kind of misunderstanding? There are days when there's too much coming at one from all sides. So: how many are coming?"

"I don't know who else will be coming—somewhere between three and six people."

"What I meant," the General said earnestly, "was that if there are more than three of us, we'll have to get another cab—you understand, because I'm in uniform."

"Oh, of course," Ulrich reassured him.

"I can't very well drive in a sardine can."

"Of course not. But tell me, what's this about reliable indications?"

"But will we be able to get a cab out there?" Stumm worried. "It's so far out you can hear the animals snoring."

"We'll pick one up on the way," Ulrich said firmly. "Now will you please tell me how you have reliable indications that it's time for something to happen?"

"There's nothing to tell," Stumm replied. "When I say about something that that's the way it is and it can't be otherwise, what I'm really saying is that I can't explain it! At most one might add that this Drangsal is one of those pacifists, probably because Feuermaul, who's her protégé, writes poems about 'Man is good.' Lots of people believe that sort of thing now."

Ulrich was not convinced. "Didn't you tell me the opposite just a little while ago? That they're now all in favor of taking action, taking a strong line, and all that?"

"True too," the General granted. "And influential circles are backing Drangsal; she has a great knack for that sort of thing. They expect the patriotic campaign to come up with a humanitarian action."

"Really?" Ulrich said.

"You know, you really don't seem to care about anything anymore! The rest of us are worried. Let me remind you, for instance, that the fratricidal Austro-German war of 1866 only happened because all the Germans in the Frankfurt Parliament declared themselves to be brothers. Not, of course, that I'm suggesting that the War Minister or the Chief of the General Staff might be worrying along those lines; that would be nonsense. But one thing does lead to another. That's how it is! See what I mean?"

It was not clear, but it made sense. And the General went on to make a very wise observation:

"Look, you're always wanting things to be clear and logical," he remonstrated with his seatmate. "And I do admire you for it, but you must for once try to think in historical terms. How can those directly involved in what's happening know beforehand whether it will turn out to be a great event? All they can do is pretend to themselves that it is! If I may indulge in a paradox, I'd say that the history of the world is written before it happens; it always starts off as a kind of gossip. So that people who have the energy to act are faced with a very serious problem."

"You have a point," Ulrich said appreciatively. "But now tell me all about it."

Although the General wanted to expand on it, there was so much on his mind in these moments, when the horse's hooves had begun to hit softer ground, that he was suddenly seized by other anxieties.

"Here I am, decked out like a Christmas tree in case the Minister calls for me," he cried, underlining it by pointing to his light-blue tunic and the medals hanging from it. "Don't you think it could lead to awkward incidents if I appear like this, in full dress, in front of loonies? What do I do, for instance, if one of them decides to insult the Emperor's uniform? I can hardly draw my sword, but it would be really dangerous for me *not* to say anything, either!"

Ulrich calmed him down by pointing out that he would be likely to wear a doctor's white coat over his uniform. But before Stumm had time to declare himself fully satisfied with this solution they met Clarisse, impatiently coming to meet them in a smart summer dress, escorted by Siegmund. She told Ulrich that Walter and Meingast had refused to join them. And after they had managed to find a second carriage, the General was pleased to say to Clarisse: "As you were coming down the road toward us, my dear young lady, you looked positively like an angel!"

But by the time he left the carriage at the hospital gate, Stumm von Bordwehr appeared rather flushed and ill at ease.

33

THE LUNATICS GREET CLARISSE

Clarisse was twisting her gloves in her hands, looking up at the windows, and fidgeting constantly while Ulrich paid for the cab. Stumm von Bordwehr protested Ulrich's doing this, and the cabbie sat on his box with a flattered smile as the two gentlemen kept each other back. Siegmund brushed specks off his coat with his fingertips, as usual, or stared into space.

In a low voice, the General said to Ulrich: "There's something odd about your lady friend. She lectured me the whole way about what will is. I didn't understand a word!"

"That's the way she is," Ulrich said.

"Pretty, though," the General whispered. "Like a fourteen-year-old ballerina. But why does she say that we came here in order to follow our 'hallucination'? The world is 'too free of hallucinations,' she says. D'you know anything about that? It was so distressing, I simply couldn't think of a word to say."

The General was obviously holding up the departure of the cab only because he wanted to ask these questions, but before Ulrich could answer he was relieved of the responsibility by an emissary who welcomed the visitors in the name of the director of the clinic, and apologizing to the General for having to keep them waiting because of some urgent business, he led the company upstairs to a waiting room. Clarisse took in every inch of the staircase and the corridors with her eyes, and even in the little waiting room, with its chairs upholstered in threadbare green velvet so reminiscent of an old-fashioned first-class waiting room in a railway station, her gaze roved about slowly almost the whole time. There the four of them sat, after the emissary had left, and found nothing to say until Ulrich, to break the silence, teased Clarisse by asking her whether the thought of meeting Moosbrugger face-to-face wasn't making her blood run cold.

"Bah!" Clarisse said. "He's only known ersatz women; it had to come to this."

The General had come up with a face-saving idea, something having belatedly occurred to him: "The will is now very up-to-date," he said. "We're very much concerned with this problem in our patriotic action too!"

Clarisse gave him a smile and stretched her arms to ease the tension in them. "Having to wait like this, one can feel what's coming in one's arms and legs, as if one were looking through a telescope," she replied.

Stumm von Bordwehr gave it some thought, careful not to put a foot wrong again. "That's true!" he said. "It may have something to do with the current cult of exercise and bodybuilding. We're concerned with that also."

At this point the Medical Director swept in with his cavalcade of assistants and nurses and a gracious word for everyone, especially Stumm; mumbled about something pressing, which would, regrettably, prevent him from taking them around himself, as he had intended; and introduced Dr. Friedenthal, who would take good care of them in his stead.

Dr. Friedenthal was a tall, slender man with a somewhat effeminate body and a thick mop of hair, who smiled at them, as he was introduced, like an acrobat climbing a ladder for a death-defying performance. When the director had gone, the white lab coats were brought in. "We don't want to get the patients excited," Dr. Friedenthal explained.

As Clarisse slipped into hers she experienced a strange surge of power. She stood there like a little doctor. She felt very much a man, and very white.

The General looked around for a mirror. It was hard to find a lab coat to fit his idiosyncratic proportion of girth to height; when they finally managed to get him into something that covered him completely, he looked like a child in an adult's nightshirt. "Don't you think I should take my spurs off?" he asked Dr. Friedenthal.

"Army doctors wear spurs too," Ulrich pointed out.

Stumm made one last feeble and laborious effort to see what he looked like from behind, where the medical coverall was caught up in heavy folds above his spurs. Then they set out. Dr. Friedenthal enjoined them to keep calm no matter what they might see.

"So far so good!" Stumm whispered to his friend. "But I'm not really interested in any of this. Could use the time much better to talk with you about tonight's meeting. Now look, you said you wanted me to tell you frankly what's going on. It's quite simple: the whole world is arming. The Russians have a brand-new field artillery. Are you listening? The French are using their two-year conscription law to build up an enormous army. The Italians . . ."

They had descended the same old-fashioned princely staircase they had climbed before and, after somehow turning off the main corridor, found themselves in a maze of small rooms and twisting passages with whitewashed beams protruding from the ceiling. These were mostly utility rooms and offices, cramped and dreary because of a shortage of space in the ancient building. Sinister figures, only some of whom wore institutional uniforms, populated them. One door bore the inscription "Reception"; another, "Men." The General's talk dried up. He had a premonition that things could happen at any moment, requiring by their unprecedented nature great presence of mind. He could not help wondering what he would do if an irresistible need forced him to leave the group and he were to stumble, alone and without an expert guide in a place where all men are equal, upon a madman.

Clarisse, on the other hand, was walking a step ahead of Dr. Friedenthal. His having said that they had to wear these white coats so as not to alarm the patients buoyed her up like a life vest on the current of her impressions. She was mulling over some of her pet ideas. Nietzsche: "Is there a pessimism of strength? An intellectual predisposition to whatever is hard, sinister, evil, problematic in life? A yearning for the terrible as a worthy foe? Perhaps madness is not necessarily a symptom of degeneracy." She was not thinking this in so many words, but she remembered it as a whole; her thoughts had compressed it all into a tiny packet, admirably fitted to the smallest space, like a burglar's tool. For her this excursion was half philosophy and half adultery.

Dr. Friedenthal stopped in front of an iron door and took a flat key from his pants pocket. When he opened the door they stepped out from the shelter of the building and were blinded by the brightness. At the same moment Clarisse heard a frightful shriek such as she had never heard before in her life. For all her pluckiness, she winced.

"Just a horse!" Dr. Friedenthal said, smiling.

And in fact they were on a road that led from the front gate, along the side of the administration building, and around to the kitchen yard of the institution. It was no different from other such roads, with old wheel tracks and homely weeds on which the sun was blazing hotly. And yet all the others too, with the exception of Dr. Friedenthal, felt oddly disconcerted and—in a startled, confused fashion—almost indignant, to find themselves on a wholesome and ordinary road after having already survived a long, arduous passage. Freedom, at first blush, had something disconcerting about it, even though it was incredibly comforting; it actually took some getting used to again. With Clarisse, who was more vulnerable to the clash of contrasts, the tension shattered in a loud giggle.

Still smiling, Dr. Friedenthal strode ahead across the road and on the other side opened a small but heavy iron door in the high wall of a park. "This is where it begins," he said gently.

And now they really found themselves inside that world to which Clarisse had felt herself inexplicably attracted for weeks, not only with the shudder at something incommensurable and impenetrable, but as though she were fated to experience something there that she could not imagine beforehand. At first there was nothing to differentiate this world from any other big old park, with the greensward sloping up in one direction toward groups of tall trees, among which small white villa-like buildings could be seen. The sweep of the sky behind them gave promise of a lovely view, and from one such lookout point Clarisse saw patients with attendants standing and sitting in groups, looking like white angels.

General Stumm took this as the right moment to resume his conversation with Ulrich. "Now, let me prime you a bit more for this evening," he began. "The Italians, the Russians, the French, and the English too, you know, are all arming, and we—"

"You want your artillery; I know that already," Ulrich interrupted.

"Among other things!" the General continued. "But if you don't ever let me finish, we'll soon be among the loonies and won't be able to talk in peace. So, as I was saying, we're in the middle of all this, in a very risky position from the military point of view. And in this fix we're being badgered—I'm referring to the Parallel Campaign—to think of nothing but the goodness of man!"

"And your people are against it! I understand."

"Not at all, on the contrary!" Stumm protested. "We're not against it! We take pacifism very seriously! But we must get our artillery budget through. And if we could do that hand in hand with pacifism, so to speak, it would be the best safeguard against all those imperialistic misunderstandings that are so quick to assert that we're endangering world peace! It's true, if you like, that we're in bed with La Drangsal, just a little. But we also have to proceed with caution because her opposition, the nationalist movements, who now have their people inside the Campaign too, are against pacifism and in favor of getting our army up to scratch!"

The General had to cut himself short, with an expression of bitterness, for they had almost reached the top of the incline, where Dr. Friedenthal was awaiting his troop. The angels' gathering place turned out to be lightly fenced in; their guide crossed it without paying it much attention, as a mere prelude. "A 'quiet' ward," he explained.

They were all women; their hair hung loose down to their shoulders, and their faces were repellent, with fat, blurred, puffy features. One of them came rushing up to the doctor and forced a letter on him. "It's always the same thing," Dr. Friedenthal explained to his visitors and read aloud: " 'Adolf, my love! When are you coming to see me? Have you forgotten me?' " The woman, about sixty, stood there with an apathetic face and listened. "You'll send it out right away, won't you?" she begged. "Of course!" Dr. Friedenthal promised, then he tore the letter into pieces in front of her eyes and smiled at the nurse. Clarisse instantly challenged him: "How could you do this?" she asked. "These patients must be taken seriously!"

"Come along," Dr. Friedenthal said. "There's no point in wasting our time here. If you like, I'll show you hundreds of such letters later. You must have noticed that the old woman didn't react at all when I tore it up?"

Clarisse was disconcerted, because what Dr. Friedenthal said was true, but it confused her thoughts. And before she could straighten them out again, they were further disturbed when, on their way out, another old woman, who had been lying in wait for them, lifted up her skirt and exposed to the passing gentlemen her ugly old-woman's thighs up to her belly, above coarse woolen stockings.

"The old sow," Stumm von Bordwehr muttered, sufficiently outraged and disgusted to forget politics for a while.

But Clarisse had discovered a resemblance between the thigh and the face. The thigh probably showed the same stigmata of fatty physical degeneration as the face, but this gave Clarisse for the first time an impression of strange correspondences and a world that worked differently from what one could grasp with the usual categories. She also now realized that she had not noticed the transformation of the white angels into these women, and indeed that even while walking through their midst she had not been able to distinguish the patients from the nurses. She turned around and looked back, but because the path had curved behind a building, she could no longer see anything and stumbled after the others like a child that turns its head away. From this point on, her impressions no longer formed the transparent flow of events that one accepts life to be, but became a foaming torrent with only occasional smooth patches that stuck in the memory.

"Another quiet ward, this time for men," Dr. Friedenthal announced, gathering his flock at the entrance to a building, and when they paused at the first bed he presented its occupant to them in a considerately lowered voice as a case of "depressive dementia paralytica."

"An old syphilitic. Delusions of sin and nihilistic obsessions," Siegmund whispered, translating the terms for his sister. Clarisse found herself face-to-face with an old gentleman who, to all appearances, had once belonged to the upper reaches of society. He sat upright in bed, was perhaps in his late fifties, and had a very white skin. His well-cared-for and highly intelligent face was framed in thick white hair and looked as improbably distinguished as the faces one finds described only in the cheapest novels.

"Couldn't one do a portrait of him?" Stumm von Bordwehr asked. "The very model of intellectual beauty! I'd love to give the portrait to your cousin!" he said to Ulrich.

Dr. Friedenthal gave a sad smile and commented: "The noble expression is caused by a slackening of tension in the facial muscles."

He demonstrated with a quick movement the unresponsive fixity of the man's pupils, then led them onward. There was not enough time for all the available material. The old gentleman, who had nodded mournfully to everything said at his bedside, was still muttering in a low, troubled voice when the five of them stopped again, several beds farther on, to consider the next case Dr. Friedenthal had chosen for them.

This time it was someone who was himself engaged in art, a cheerful, fat painter whose bed stood close to a sunny window. He had paper and many pencils on his blanket, and busied himself with them all day long. Clarisse was immediately struck by the happy restlessness of his movements. "That's the way Walter should be painting!" she thought. Friedenthal, seeing her interest, quickly snatched a sheet of paper from the fat man and handed it to Clarisse; the painter snickered and behaved like a serving girl who'd just been pinched. But Clarisse was amazed to see a sketch for a large composition, drawn with sure, accomplished strokes, entirely sensible to the point of banality, with many figures woven together in accurate perspective and a large hall, everything executed in meticulous detail, so that the whole effect was of something so salutary and professorial that it could have come from the National Academy. "What amazing craftsmanship!" she cried impulsively.

Dr. Friedenthal responded with a flattered smile.

The artist gleefully made a rude noise at him.

"You see, that gentleman likes it! Show him some more, go on! Amazing how good it is, he said! Go on, show him! I know you're only laughing at me, but he likes it!" He spoke good-humoredly, holding out the rest of his drawings to the doctor, with whom he seemed to be on easy terms although the doctor didn't appreciate his work.

"We don't have time for you today," Dr. Friedenthal told him and, turning to Clarisse, summed up the case by saying: "He's not schizophrenic; sorry he's the only one we have here at the moment. Schizophrenics are often fine artists, quite modern."

"And insane?" Clarisse said dubiously.

"Why not?" Dr. Friedenthal answered sadly.

Clarisse bit her lip.

Meanwhile Stumm and Ulrich were already on the threshold to the next ward, and the General was saying: "Looking at this, I'm really sorry I called my orderly an idiot this morning. I'll never do it again!" For the ward they were facing was a room with extreme cases of idiocy.

Clarisse had not yet seen this and was thinking: "So even academic art, so respectably and widely recognized, has a sister in Bedlam—a sister denied, deprived, and yet so much a twin one can barely tell the difference!" This almost impressed her more than Friedenthal's remark that another time he might be able to show her expressionist artists. She made up her mind to take him up on it. Her head was down, and she was still biting her lip. There was something wrong with all this. It seemed to her clearly wrong to lock up such gifted people; the doctors might know about diseases, she thought, but probably did not understand art and all it stood for. Something would have to be done, she felt. But it was not clear to her what. Yet she did not lose heart, for the fat painter had immediately called her "that gentleman"—it seemed to her a good omen.

Friedenthal scrutinized her with curiosity.

When she felt his gaze she looked up with her thin-lipped smile and moved toward him, but before she could say anything an appalling sight made her mind a blank. In this new ward a series of horrible apparitions crouched and sat in their beds, everything about their bodies crooked, unclean, twisted, or paralyzed. Decayed teeth. Waggling heads. Heads too big, too small, totally misshapen. Slack, drooping jaws from which saliva was dribbling, or brutish grinding motions of the mouth, without food or words. Yard-wide leaden barriers seemed to lie between these souls and the world, and after the low chuckling and buzzing in the other room, the silence here, broken only by obscure grunting and muttering sounds, was oppressive. Such wards for severe mental deficiency are among the most horrifying sights to be found in the hideousness of a mental institution, and Clarisse felt herself plunged headlong into a ghastly darkness that blotted out all distinctions.

But their guide, Friedenthal, could see even in the dark, and pointing to various beds, he explained: "That's idiocy over there, and over here you have cretinism."

Stumm von Bordwehr pricked up his ears. "A cretin is not the same as an idiot?" he asked.

"No," the doctor said, "there's a medical distinction."

"Interesting," Stumm said. "In ordinary life one would never think of such a thing."

Clarisse moved from bed to bed. Her eyes bored into the patients, as she tried with all her might to understand, without succeeding in the least in gleaning anything from these faces that took no cognizance of her. All thought in them was extinguished. Dr. Friedenthal followed her softly and explained: "congenital amaurotic idiocy"; "tubercular hypertrophic sclerosis"; "idiotia thymica . . ."

The General, who meanwhile felt that he had seen enough of these "morons" and assumed that Ulrich felt the same way, glanced at his watch and said: "Now, where were we? We mustn't waste time!" And rather unexpectedly he resumed: "So, if you'll bear in mind: the War Ministry finds itself flanked by the pacifists on one side and the nationalists on the other. . . ."

Ulrich, not so quick to tear his mind away from his surroundings, gave him a blank stare.

"This is no joke, my friend!" Stumm explained. "I'm talking politics! Something's got to be done. We've come to a stop once before already. If we don't do something soon, the Emperor's birthday will be upon us before we know it, and we'll look like fools. But *what* is to be done? It's a logical question, isn't it? And summing up rather bluntly what I told you, we're being pushed by one crowd to help them love mankind, and by the other to let them bully the rest of the world so that the nobler blood will prevail, or however you want to call it. There's something to be said for both sides. Which is why, in a word, you should somehow bring them together so there'll be no damage!"

"Me?" Ulrich protested at his friend's bombshell, and would have burst out laughing in other circumstances.

"Certainly you—who else?" the General replied decisively. "I'll do all I can to help, but you're the campaign's secretary and Leinsdorf's right hand!"

"I can get you admitted here!" Ulrich announced firmly.

"Fine!" The General knew from the art of war that it was best to avoid unexpected resistance in the most unruffled manner possible. "If you get me in here I might meet someone who has found the Greatest Idea in the world. Outside they seem to have lost their taste for great ideas anyway." He glanced at his watch again. "I hear they've got some people here who are the Pope, or the universe. We haven't met a single one, and they're the ones I was most looking forward to getting acquainted with. Your little friend's terribly conscientious," he complained.

Dr. Friedenthal gently eased Clarisse away from the defectives.

Hell is not interesting, it is terrifying. If it has not been humanized—as by Dante, who populated it with writers and other prominent figures, thereby distracting attention from the technicalities of punishment—but an attempt has been made to represent it in some original fashion, even the most fertile minds never get beyond childish tortures and unimaginative distortions of physical realities. But it is precisely the bare idea of an unimaginable and therefore inescapable everlasting punishment and agony, the premise of an inexorable change for the worse, impervious to any attempt to reverse it, that has the fascination of an abyss. Insane asylums are also like that. They are poorhouses. They have something of hell's lack of imagination. But many people who have no idea of the causes of mental illness are afraid of nothing so much, next to losing their money, as that they might one day lose their minds; an amazing number of people are plagued by the notion that they could suddenly lose themselves. It is apparently an overestimation of their self-worth that leads to the overestimation of the horror with which the sane imagine mental institutions to be imbued. Even Clarisse suffered a faint disappointment, which stemmed from some vague expectation implanted by her upbringing. It was quite the contrary with Dr. Friedenthal. He was used to these rounds. Order as in a military barracks or another mass institution, alleviation of conspicuous pains or complaints, prevention of avoidable deterioration, a slight improvement or a cure: these were the elements of his daily activity. Observing a good deal, knowing a good deal, without having a sufficient explanation for the overall problems, was his intellectual portion. These rounds through the wards, prescribing a few sedatives besides the usual medications for coughs, colds, constipation, and bedsores, were his daily work of healing. He felt the ghostly horror of the world he lived in only when the contrast was awakened through contact with the normal world, which did not happen every day, but visits are such occasions, and that was why what Clarisse got to see had been prepared not without a certain sense of theatrical production, so that no sooner had he aroused her from her absorption with one phenomenon that he immediately went on to something new and even more dramatic.

They had hardly left this ward when they were joined by several large men in crisp white uniforms, with hulking shoulders and jovial corporals' faces. It happened so silently that it had the effect of a drum roll.

"Now we're coming to a disturbed ward," Dr. Friedenthal announced, and they approached a screaming and squawking that seemed to issue from an immense birdcage. They stood in front of a door that had no handle, which had to be opened with a special key by one of the attendants. Clarisse started to enter first, as she had done up until now, but Dr. Friedenthal pulled her back roughly.

"Wait!" he said with emphasis, wearily, without apology.

The attendant who had opened the door had opened it only a crack, while covering the open space with his powerful body; after first listening and then peering inside, he hastily slipped in, followed by a second attendant, who took up a position at the other side of the entrance. Clarisse's heart started to pound.

"Advance guard, rear guard, cover flank!" the General said appreciatively. And thus covered, they walked in and were escorted from bed to bed by the two attending giants. What were sitting in the beds thrashed about, agitated and screaming, with arms and eyes, as if each of them was shouting into some private space that was for himself alone, and yet they all seemed to be caught up in a raging conversation, like alien birds locked in the same cage, each speaking the dialect of its own island. Some of them sat without restraints, while others were tied down to their beds with straps that allowed only limited movement of the hands.

"To keep them from attempting suicide," the doctor explained, and listed the diseases: paralysis, paranoia, manic depression, were the species to which these strange birds belonged.

Clarisse again felt intimidated at first by her confused impressions and could not get her bearings. And so it came as a friendly sign when she saw someone waving to her excitedly from a distance, calling out something to her while she was still many beds away. He was moving back and forth in his bed as if desperately trying to free himself in order to dash over to her, outshouting the chorus with his complaints and fits of rage, and succeeding in concentrating Clarisse's attention on himself. The closer she came to him, the more she was troubled by her sense of his addressing himself only to her, while she was completely unable to understand a word of what he was trying to say. When they finally reached his bed, the senior attendant told the doctor something so softly that Clarisse could not hear, and Friedenthal, looking very grave, gave some instructions. But then he said something in a light vein to the patient, who was slow to react but then suddenly asked: "Who's that man?" with a gesture indicating Clarisse.

Friedenthal nodded toward Siegmund and answered that it was a doctor from Stockholm.

"No, that one!" The patient insisted on Clarisse. Friedenthal smiled and said she was a woman doctor from Vienna.

"No. That's a man," the patient contradicted him, and fell silent. Clarisse felt her heart thudding. Here was another who took her for a man!

Then the patient intoned slowly: "It is the seventh son of our Emperor."

Stumm von Bordwehr nudged Ulrich.

"That is not so," Friedenthal told him, and continued the game by turning to Clarisse, saying: "Do tell him yourself that he's mistaken."

"It's not true, my friend," Clarisse said in a low voice to the patient, so moved she could barely speak.

"You *are* the seventh son," the patient replied stubbornly.

"No, no," Clarisse assured him, smiling at him in her excitement as if she were playing a love scene, her lips stiff with stage fright.

"Yes you are!" the patient repeated, and looked at her in a way she could not find words for. She could not think of another thing to say, and just kept gazing helplessly with a fixed smile into the eyes of the lunatic who took her for a prince. Something remarkable was happening in her mind: the possibility was forming that he might be right. The force of his repeated assertion dissolved some resistance in her; in some way she lost control over her thoughts, new patterns took shape, their outlines looming from mist: he was not the first who wanted to know who she was and to take her for a "gentleman." But while she was still gazing at his face, caught up in this strange bond, taking no account of his age or of any other vestiges of a normal life still left in his countenance, something quite incomprehensible was beginning to happen in that face and in the whole person. It looked as though her gaze was too heavy for the eyes on which it rested; they began to slide away and fall. His lips, too, began to quiver, and like heavy drops merging more and more quickly, audible obscenities mixed themselves with a rush of jabbering. Clarisse was as stunned by this slithering transformation as if something were slipping away from her; she impulsively reached out to the miserable creature with both arms, and before anyone could interfere, the patient leapt to meet her: he cast off his bedclothes, knelt at the foot of the bed, and began to masturbate like a caged monkey.

"Don't be such a pig!" the doctor said quickly and sternly, while the attendants instantly grabbed the man and his bedclothes and in a flash reduced both to a lifeless bundle on the bed. Clarisse had turned dark red. She felt as dizzy as when the floor of an elevator all at once seems to drop away from under one's feet. Suddenly it seemed to her that all the patients they had already passed were shouting at her back and the others, whom they had not yet seen, were shouting at her from in front. And as chance would have it, or the infectious power of excitement, a friendly old man in the next bed, who had been making good-natured little jokes while the visitors stood nearby, leapt up the instant Clarisse hurried past him, and began raving at them in foul language that formed a disgusting foam on his lips. On him, too, the attendants' fists descended like a heavy press, crushing all resistance.

But the magician Friedenthal had even more tricks to conjure up. Under guard at the exit as they had been at the entrance, the visitors left this ward at the far end, and suddenly their ears seemed plunged into healing silence. They found themselves in a clean, cheerful corridor with a linoleum floor, and encountered people in their Sunday best and attractive children, all greeting the doctor confidently and politely. They were visitors, waiting to get to see their relatives, and once again the impact of this healthy world was disconcerting; for a moment all these discreet and well-behaved people in their best clothes seemed like dolls, or extremely well-made artificial flowers. But Friedenthal passed through them hurriedly and announced to his friends that he was now about to take them to the ward for murderers and others of the criminally insane. The watchful looks and behavior of the attendants at the next iron gate did not bode at all well. They entered a cloistered courtyard surrounded by a gallery, resembling one of those gardens of modern design that have many stones and few plants. The empty air first seemed like a cube of silence; it was only after a while that one noticed figures sitting mutely along the walls. Near the entrance some retarded boys were squatting, runny-nosed, dirty, motionless, as if a sculptor had had the grotesque idea of attaching them to the pillars flanking the gate. Near them, the first figure by the wall, sitting apart from the others, was an ordinary-looking man still in his dark Sunday suit, but without a collar; he must have just been admitted, and was indescribably moving in his impression of not belonging anywhere. Clarisse suddenly imagined the anguish she would cause Walter if she left him, and almost burst into tears. It was the first time this had ever happened, but she quickly suppressed it, for the other men past whom she was being escorted merely gave the impression of habitual submission to be expected in prisons: They greeted the doctor with shy politeness and made minor requests. Only one made a nuisance of himself with his complaints, a young man who emerged from heaven knew what oblivion. He demanded to be released at once, and why was he here in the first place? When Dr. Friedenthal replied evasively that such requests were handled by the superintendent, not by him, the young man persisted; his pleas became repetitive, like links in a chain rattling past faster and faster; gradually, a note of urgency came into his voice and grew threatening, finally turning into brutish, mindless danger. At that point the giants pushed him back down on the bench, and he crept back into his silence like a dog, without having received an answer. By now Clarisse was used to this, and it merely became part of her general excitement.

There would have been no time for anything else, since they had reached the armored door at the far end of the courtyard, and the guards were banging on it. This was something new, for up to this point they had used great caution in opening doors but had not announced themselves. On this door they banged their fists four times, and listened to the stirrings from the other side.

"That's the signal for everyone inside to line up against the walls," Dr. Friedenthal explained, "or sit on the benches along the walls."

And indeed, as the door turned slowly, inch by inch, they could see that all the men who had been milling around quietly or noisily were behaving obediently, like well-drilled prisoners. Even so, the guards were so cautious as they entered that Clarisse suddenly clutched at Dr. Friedenthal's sleeve and asked excitedly whether Moosbrugger was here. Friedenthal only shook his head. He had no time. He hastily admonished the visitors to stay at least two paces away from every prisoner. His responsibilities in this situation seemed to cause him some anxiety. They were seven against thirty, in a remote, walled courtyard full of insane men almost all of whom had committed a murder.

Those who are accustomed to carrying a weapon feel more exposed without it than others, so one could not hold it against the General, who had left his saber in the waiting room, that he asked the doctor: "Don't you have a weapon on you?" "Alertness and experience!" Dr. Friedenthal replied, pleased at the flattering question. "It's all a matter of nipping any potential disturbance in the bud."

And in fact at the slightest move among the inmates to break ranks, the guards rushed in and thrust the offender back into place so swiftly that these attacks seemed to be the only acts of violence occurring. Clarisse did not approve of them. "What the doctors don't seem to understand," she thought, "is that although these men are shut in here together all day long without supervision, they don't do anything to each other; it's only we, coming from the world that is foreign to them, who may be in danger." She wanted to speak to one of them, suddenly imagining that she could certainly find a way to communicate properly with him. In a corner right near the entrance was a sturdy-looking man of medium height, with a full brown beard and piercing eyes; he was leaning against the wall with his arms folded, silently surveying the visitors' activity with an angry expression. Clarisse stepped toward him, but Dr. Friedenthal instantly restrained her with a hand on her arm. "Not this one," he said in a low voice. He chose another murderer for Clarisse and spoke to him. This was a short, squat fellow with a pointy head, shaved convict fashion, apparently known to the doctor as tractable, who instantly stood at attention and, answering smartly, showed two rows of teeth that dubiously suggested two rows of gravestones.

"Ask him why he's here," Dr. Friedenthal whispered to Clarisse's brother, and Siegmund asked the broad-shouldered man with the pointy head: "Why are you here?"

"You know that very well!" was the curt reply.

"No, I don't know," Siegmund—who did not like to give up too easily—said rather foolishly. "So tell me why you're here."

"You know that very well!" The response was repeated with a stronger emphasis.

"Why are you being rude to me?" Siegmund asked. "I honestly don't know why!"

"This lying!" Clarisse thought, and she was glad when the patient simply answered: "Because I choose! I can do as I like!" he insisted, and bared his teeth at them.

"Well, there's no need to be rude for no reason," the hapless Siegmund persisted, just as unable as the insane man to come up with anything new.

Clarisse was furious with him for playing the stupid role of someone teasing a caged animal in a zoo.

"It's none of your business! I do as I like, get it? Whatever I like!" The mental patient barked like a sergeant and produced a laugh from somewhere in his face, but not his mouth or eyes, which were both charged with uncanny anger.

Even Ulrich was thinking: "I wouldn't care to be alone with this fellow just now." Siegmund was having a hard time standing his ground, since the madman had stepped up close to him, and Clarisse was wishing he would seize her brother by the throat and bite him in the face. Friedenthal complacently let the scene take its course, for after all, as a medical colleague Siegmund ought to be able to handle it, and Friedenthal was rather enjoying the other's discomfiture. With his sense of theater, he waited for the scene to reach a climax, and only when Siegmund was beyond uttering another word did he give the signal to break it off. But the desire to meddle was back in Clarisse; it had somehow grown stronger and stronger as the man drummed out his answers. Suddenly she could no longer hold back and, walking up to the man, said:

"I'm from Vienna!"

It made as little sense as a random sound one might entice from a bugle. She neither knew what she meant by saying it nor where the idea had come from, nor had she stopped to wonder whether the man knew what town he was in, and if he did know, her remark would be even more pointless. But she felt tremendously sure of herself as she said it. And in fact miracles still do happen, occasionally, and they have a partiality for insane asylums. As she spoke, flaming with excitement, a glow came over him; his rock-grinder teeth withdrew behind his lips, and benevolence spread over the glare in his eyes.

"Ah, Vienna, city of dreams! A beautiful place!" he said with the smugness of the former petit bourgeois who has his clichés in order.

"Congratulations!" Dr. Friedenthal laughed.

But for Clarisse the episode had become an event.

"Now let's go on to Moosbrugger!" Friedenthal said.

But this was not to be. They moved cautiously back through the two courtyards and were walking up an incline toward what appeared to be a distant isolated pavilion, when a guard who seemed to have been looking for them everywhere came running up to them. He whispered to Friedenthal at some length, something important and disagreeable, to judge by the doctor's expression as he listened and asked an occasional question. Finally, Dr. Friedenthal turned back to the others with a grave, apologetic air and told them that he had to go to another ward, to deal with an incident that would take some time, so that he would, regretfully, have to curtail their tour. He addressed himself primarily to the official personage in the General's uniform beneath the lab coat; Stumm von Bordwehr gratefully assured him that he had seen enough of the outstanding organization and discipline of this institution, and that after what they had been through, one murderer more or less did not matter. Clarisse, however, had such a disappointed, stricken face that Friedenthal proposed to make up the visit to Moosbrugger, along with some other interesting cases, some other time; he would give Siegmund a call as soon as a date could be arranged.

"Very kind of you"—the General thanked him on behalf of the group—"though for my part, I really can't say whether other obligations will allow me to be present."

With this reservation, a future visit was agreed upon, and Friedenthal set off along a path that soon took him over the rise and out of sight, while the others, accompanied by the attendant Friedenthal had left with them, headed back to the gate. They left the path and took a shortcut across the grassy slope between fine beeches and plane trees. The General had slipped out of his lab coat and carried it jauntily over his arm, as one might carry a raincoat on an outing, but nobody seemed to feel like talking. Ulrich showed no interest in being coached further for the evening's reception, and Stumm was himself too preoccupied with what was awaiting him at his office, though he felt called upon to make some amusing remarks to Clarisse, whom he was gallantly escorting. But Clarisse was absent-minded and quiet. "Perhaps she's still embarrassed over that filthy pig," he mused, feeling the need to apologize somehow for not having been in a position to offer his chivalric protection, but on the other hand, it was probably best to say no more about it. So the walk back passed in silence and constraint.

It was only when Stumm von Bordwehr had entered his carriage, leaving it to Ulrich to see Clarisse and her brother home, that his good spirits returned, and with them an idea that gave a certain shape to the whole depressing episode. He had taken a cigarette out of the big leather case in his pocket, and leaning back in the cushions and blowing the first little blue clouds into the sunny air, he thought comfortably: "Terrible thing, to be out of one's mind like that. Come to think of it, all the time we were there I didn't see a single one of them having a smoke! People don't realize how well off they are as long as they're still in their right mind!"

34

A GREAT EVENT IS IN THE MAKING. COUNT LEINSDORF AND THE INN RIVER

This eventful day culminated in a gala reception at the Tuzzis'.

The Parallel Campaign was on parade, in glory and brilliance: eyes blazed, jewels blazed, prominence blazed, wit blazed. A lunatic might conceivably conclude from this that on such a social occasion eyes, jewels, prominent names, and wit amount to the same thing, and he would not be far off the mark: everyone who did not happen to be on the Riviera or the north Italian lakes was there, except for those few who refused on principle to recognize any "events" so late in the season.

In their place were quite a number of people whom no one had ever seen before. A long respite had torn holes in the guest list, and to fill it up again new people had been invited more hastily than was consonant with Diotima's circumspect ways: Count Leinsdorf himself had turned over to her a list of people he wanted invited for political reasons, and once the principle of her salon's exclusiveness had thus been sacrificed to higher considerations, she had no longer attached the same importance to it. His Grace was, in fact, the sole begetter of this festive gathering: Diotima was of the opinion that humanity could be helped only in pairs. But Count Leinsdorf held firmly to his assertion that "capital and culture have not done their duty by our historical development; we must give them one last chance!"

Count Leinsdorf was always coming back to this point.

"Tell me, my dear, haven't you come to a decision yet?" he would ask. "It's high time. All sorts of people are coming to the fore with destructive tendencies. We must give the cultural sector one last opportunity to restore the balance." But Diotima, deflected by the wealth of variation in the forms of human coupling, was deaf to all else.

Finally, Count Leinsdorf had to call her to order.

"You know, my dear, I hardly seem to know you anymore! We've given out the password 'Action!' to all and sundry; I myself had a hand—surely I may tell you in confidence that it was I who was behind the Minister of the Interior's resignation. It had to be done on a high level, you understand; a very high level! But it had really become a scandal, and nobody had the courage to put a stop to it. So this is just for your own ears," he continued, "and now the Premier has asked us to bestir ourselves a bit with our Inquiry Concerning the Desires of the Concerned Sections of the Population with Respect to the Conduct of Home Affairs, because the new Minister naturally can't be expected to have it at his fingertips; and now you want to leave me in the lurch, you who have always been the last to give up? We *must* give capital and culture a last chance! You know, it's either that or . . ."

This somewhat incomplete final sentence was uttered so menacingly that there was no mistaking that he knew what he wanted, and

Diotima obediently promised to hurry; but then she forgot again and did nothing.

And then one day Count Leinsdorf was seized by his well-known energy and drove straight to her door, propelled by forty horse-power.

"Has anything happened yet?" he asked, and Diotima had to admit that nothing had.

"Do you know the Inn River, my dear?" he asked.

Of course Diotima knew the Inn, second only to the Danube as Kakania's most famous river, richly interwoven with the country's geography and history. She observed her visitor rather dubiously, while doing her best to smile.

But Count Leinsdorf was in deadly earnest. "Apart from Innsbruck," he said, "what ridiculous backwoods places all those little towns in the Inn Valley are, and what an imposing river the Inn is in our culture! And to think I never realized it before!" He shook his head. "You see, I happened by chance to look at a highway map today," he said, finally coming to the point, "and I noticed that the Inn rises in Switzerland. I must have known it before, of course, we all know it, but we never give it a thought. It rises at Majola, I've seen it there myself; a ridiculous little creek no wider than the Kamp or the Morava in our country. But what have the Swiss made of it? The Engadine! The world-famous Engadine! The Engad-Inn, my dear! Has it ever occurred to you that the whole Engadine comes from the name Inn? That's what I hit upon today. While we, with our insufferable Austrian modesty, of course never make anything out of what belongs to us!"

After this chat Diotima hastened to arrange for the desired reception, partly because she realized that she had to stand by Count Leinsdorf, and partly because she was afraid of driving her high-ranking friend to some extreme if she continued to refuse.

But when she gave him her promise, Leinsdorf said:

"And this time, I beg of you, dearest lady, don't fail to invite—er—that x you call Drangsal. Her friend Frau Wayden has been pestering me about this person for weeks, and won't leave me in peace!"

Diotima promised this too, although at other times she would have regarded putting up with her rival as a dereliction of duty to her country.

35

A GREAT EVENT IS IN THE MAKING. PRIVY COUNCILLOR MESERITSCHER

When the rooms were filled with the radiance of festive illumination and the assembled company, an observer could note among those present not only His Excellency, together with other leading members of the high aristocracy for whose appearance he had arranged, but also His Excellency the Minister of War, and in the latter's entourage the intensely intellectual, somewhat overworked head of General Stumm von Bordwehr. One observed Paul Arnheim (without the "Dr.": simple and most effective; the observer had thought it over carefully—it's called "litotes," an artful understatement, like removing some trifle from one's body, as when a king removes a ring from his finger to place it on someone else's). Then one observed everyone worth mentioning from the various ministries (the Minister of Education and Culture had apologized to His Excellency in the Upper House for not coming in person; he had to go to Linz for the consecration of a great altar screen). Then one noted that the foreign embassies and legations had sent an "elite." There were well-known names "from industry, art, and science," and a time-honored allegory of diligence lay in this invariable combination of three bourgeois activities, a combination that seized hold of the scribbling pen all by itself. That same adept pen then presented the ladies: beige, pink, cherry, cream . . . ; embroidered, draped, triple-tiered, or dropped from the waist. . . . Between Countess Adlitz and Frau Generaldirektor Weghuber was listed the well-known Frau Melanie Drangsal, widow of the world-famous surgeon, "in her own right a charming hostess, who provides in her house a hearth for the leading lights of our times." Finally, listed separately at the end of this section, was the name of Ulrich von So-and-so and sister. The observer had hesitated about adding "whose name is widely associated with his selfless service on behalf of that high-minded and patriotic undertaking," or even "a coming man." Word had gone around long since that one of these days this protégé of Count Leinsdorf was widely expected to involve his patron in some rash misstep, and the temptation to go on record early as someone in the know was great. However, the deepest satisfaction for those in the know is always silence, especially when it proceeds from caution. It was to this that Ulrich and Agathe owed the mere mention of their names as stragglers, immediately preceding those leaders of society and the intelligentsia who are not named individually but simply destined for the mass grave of "all those of rank and station." Many people fell into this category, among them the well-known professor of jurisprudence Councillor Herr Professor Schwung, who happened to be in the capital as a member of a government commission of inquiry, and also the young poet Friedel Feuermaul, for although his was known to be among the moving spirits behind this evening's gathering, that was a far cry from the more substantial significance of a title or the triumphs of haute couture. People such as Acting Bank Director Leo Fischel and family—who had won admittance thanks to Gerda's grueling efforts, without any help from Ulrich, in other words because of Diotima's momentarily flagging attention—were simply buried in the corner of one's eye. And the wife of an eminent jurist (who was well known but on such an occasion still below the threshold of public notice), a lady whose name, Bonadea, was unknown even to the observer, was later exhumed for listing among the wearers of noteworthy gowns because her sensational looks aroused great admiration.

This impersonal seeing eye, the surveying curiosity of the public, was of course a person. There are usually quite a lot of them, but in the Kakanian metropolis at that time there was one who overtopped all the rest: Privy Councillor Meseritscher. Born in the Wallachian town of Meseritsch, whence his name, this publisher, editor, and news correspondent of the *Parliamentary and Social Gazette*, which he had founded in the sixties of the last century, had come to the capital as a young man, sacrificing his expectation of taking over his parents' tavern in his native town in order to become a journalist, having been attracted by the political promise of liberalism that was then at its zenith. And before long he had made his contribution to that era by founding a news agency, which began by supplying small local items of a police nature to the newspapers. Thanks to the industry, reliability, and thoroughness of its owner, this rudimentary agency not only earned the esteem of the papers and the police but was soon noticed by other high authorities as well, and used by them for placing items they wanted to publicize without taking responsibility, so that the agency soon found itself in a privileged position for tapping unofficial information from official sources. A man of great enterprise and a tireless worker, Meseritscher, as he saw this success developing, extended his activity to include news from the Court and Society; indeed, he would probably never have left Meseritsch for the capital if this had not been his guiding vision. Flawless reporting of "those present" was regarded as his specialty. His memory for people and what was said about them was extraordinary, and this assured him of the same splendid relationship with the salon that he had with the prison. He knew Society better than it knew itself, and his unflagging devotion enabled him to make people who had met at a gathering properly acquainted with each other the very next morning, like some old cavalier in whom everyone has for decades been confiding all their marriage plans and the problems they were having with their dressmakers. And so, on every sort of great occasion, the zealous, nimble, ever-obliging, affable little man was a familiar institution, and in his later years it was only he and his presence that conferred indisputable prestige to such occasions.

Meseritscher's career had reached a peak when the title Privy Councillor was bestowed upon him, and this involves an interesting peculiarity. Kakania was the most peace-loving of countries, but at some time or other it had decided, in the profound innocence of its convictions, that, wars being a thing of the past, its civil service should be organized as a hierarchy corresponding to military ranks, complete with similar uniforms and insignia. Since then the rank of Privy Councillor corresponded to that of a lieutenant colonel in His Majesty's Imperial and Royal Army. But even though this was not in itself an exalted rank, the peculiarity was that according to an immutable tradition, which, like everything immutable in Kakania, was modified only in exceptional cases, Meseritscher should really have been named an Imperial Councillor. An Imperial Councillor was not, as one might suppose from the term, superior to a Privy Councillor, but inferior: it only corresponded to the rank of captain. Meseritscher should have been an Imperial Councillor because that title was given, other than to certain civil servants, only to those engaged in independent professions such as, for example, court barber or coach builder, and, by the same token, writers and artists; while Privy Councillor was at the time an actual high-ranking title in the civil service. That Meseritscher was nevertheless the first and only member of his profession to be so honored expressed something more than the high honor of the title itself—indeed, even more than the daily reminder not to take too seriously whatever happens in this country of ours; the unjustified title was a subtle and discreet way of assuring the indefatigable chronicler his close association with Court, State, and Society.

Meseritscher had been a model for many journalists in his time, and was on the boards of leading literary associations. The story also went around that he had had made for himself a uniform with a gold collar, but only put it on, sometimes, at home. Chances are the rumor was untrue, because deep down Meseritscher had always preserved certain memories of the tavern trade in Meseritsch, and a good tavernkeeper also knows the secrets of all his guests but doesn't make use of everything he knows; he never brings his own opinions into a discussion but enjoys noting and telling everything in the way of fact, anecdote, or joke. And so Meseritscher, whom one met on every social occasion as the acknowledged memorializer of beautiful women and distinguished men, had himself never even thought of going to a good tailor; he knew all the behind-the-scenes intricacies of politics, yet had never dabbled in politics in even a single line of print; he knew about all the discoveries and inventions of his time without understanding any of them. He was perfectly satisfied to know that they existed and were "present." He honestly loved his time, and his time reciprocated his affection to a certain degree, because he daily reported its presence to the world.

When Diotima caught sight of him as he entered, she immediately beckoned him to her side.

"My dear Meseritscher," she said, as sweetly as she knew how. "You surely didn't take His Excellency's speech in the Upper House today as an expression of our position—you couldn't have taken it literally?"

His Excellency, in the context of the Minister's downfall and exasperated by his cares, had made a widely noticed speech in the Upper House in which he not only charged his victim with having failed to show the true constructive spirit of cooperation and strictness of principle, but also let his zeal carry him to making general observations that in some inexplicable fashion culminated in a recognition of the importance of the press, in which he reproached this "institution risen to the status of a world power" with pretty much everything with which a feudal-minded, independent, nonpartisan, Christian gentleman could charge an institution that in his view is the dead opposite of himself. It was this that Diotima was diplomatically trying to smooth over, and Meseritscher listened pensively as she found increasingly fine and unintelligible language for Count Leinsdorf's real point of view. Then suddenly he laid a hand on her arm and magnanimously interrupted her:

"My dear lady, how can you upset yourself like this?" he summed up. "His Excellency is a good friend to us, isn't he? What if he did exaggerate? Why shouldn't he, a gallant gentleman like him?" And to prove that his relationship to the Count was unruffled, he added: "I'll just go and greet him now!"

That was Meseritscher! But before he moved off he turned to Diotima once more and asked confidentially:

"What about Feuermaul, dear lady?"

Smiling, Diotima shrugged her beautiful shoulders. "Nothing so very earthshaking, my dear Councillor. We wouldn't like it to be said that we rebuffed anyone who came to us in good faith!"

"Good faith—that's rich," Meseritscher thought on his way to Count Leinsdorf. But before he reached him, indeed even before his thoughts had reached a conclusion, his host stepped amicably into his path.

"My dear Meseritscher, my official sources have let me down again," Section Chief Tuzzi began with a smile. "So I'm turning to you as our semi-official source of information. Can *you* tell me anything about this Feuermaul who's here this evening?"

"What would I have to tell you, Herr Section Chief?" Meseritscher deprecated.

"I'm told he's a genius."

"Glad to hear it!" Meseritscher answered.

If the news is to be reported with speed and confidence, today's news should not be too different from yesterday's, or what one knows already. Even genius is no exception: real, acknowledged genius, that is, whose significance can be readily assessed in its own time. Not so the genius that is not instantly recognized by all and sundry! This sort of genius has something distinctly ungenial about it, a quality, moreover, that is not even solely its own, so that it is possible to misjudge it in every respect. Privy Councillor Meseritscher had a solid inventory of geniuses, which he tended with care and attention, but he was not keen on adding new items. The older and more experienced he grew, in fact, the more he had even formed the habit of regarding any rising artistic genius, especially in his neighboring field of literature, merely as a frivolous interference with his own work of reportage, and he hated it in all righteousness until it became ripe for inclusion in his lists of "those present." At that time Feuermaul still had a long way to go, and his way had yet to be smoothed for him. Privy Councillor Meseritscher was not quite sure he was in favor.

"They say he's supposed to be a great poet," Tuzzi repeated hesitantly, and Meseritscher retorted firmly: "Who says so? The critics on the book page? I ask you, Section Chief, what difference does that make? The specialists say these things, and what of it? Many of them say the opposite. We've even known the same experts to say one thing one day and something else the next. Does it really matter what they say? A real literary reputation has to have reached the illiterates; only then can you depend on it! Would you like to know what I think? What a great man does, apart from his arriving and leaving, is nobody's business!"

He had worked himself up into a gloomy fervor, and his eyes were glued to Tuzzi's. Tuzzi gave up and said nothing.

"What's really going on here this evening, Section Chief?" Meseritscher asked him.

Tuzzi smiled absently and shrugged his shoulders. "Nothing. Nothing, really. A little ambition. Have you ever read any of Feuermaul's books?"

"I know what he writes about: peace, friendship, goodness, et cetera."

"So you don't think too much of him?" Tuzzi said.

"Good Lord!" Meseritscher started wriggling. "Who am I to say . . . ?" At this point Frau Drangsal came bearing down on them, and Tuzzi had to take a courteous step or two in her direction. Meseritscher saw the chance to slip into a breach he had espied in the circle around Count Leinsdorf, and seizing it before anyone else could waylay him, he dropped anchor beside His Grace.

Count Leinsdorf was talking with the Minister and some other men, but as soon as Meseritscher had paid them all his devout respects, His Grace turned slightly and drew him aside.

"Meseritscher," he said intently. "Promise me that there will be no misunderstandings; the gentlemen of the press never seem to know what to write. Now then: Nothing whatsoever has changed in our position since the last time. Something may change. We don't know about that. For the time being there must be no interference. So please, even if one of your colleagues should ask you, remember that this whole evening here is nothing more than a private party given by Frau Tuzzi."

Meseritscher's eyelids slowly and solicitously conveyed that he had understood these top-level commands. And since one confidence deserves another, he moistened his lips, which then gleamed as his eyes should have done, and asked: "And what about Feuermaul, Your Excellency, if I may be permitted to ask?"

"Why on earth shouldn't you?" Count Leinsdorf replied in surprise. "There's nothing whatever to be said about Feuermaul! He was invited because Baroness Wayden wouldn't leave us in peace until he was! What else should there be? Perhaps you know something?"

Up to this point Privy Councillor Meseritscher had not been inclined to take the Feuermaul question too seriously, but regarded it as one of the many social rivalries he ran into every day. But now that even Count Leinsdorf denied so energetically that there was anything in it, Meseritscher had to think again, and came to the conclusion that something important was in the wind. "What can they be up to now?" he brooded as he wandered through the throng, pondering one by one the most daring possibilities of domestic and foreign policy. But after a while he decided abruptly: "There's probably nothing to it," and refused to let himself be distracted any longer from his job of reporting the news.

For however much it appeared to be in conflict with his mission in life, Meseritscher did not believe in great events; indeed, he did not hold with them. When one believes that one is living in a very important, very splendid, and very great period, one does not welcome the idea that anything especially important, splendid, and great has yet to happen in it. Meseritscher was no alpinist, but if he had been he would have said that his attitude was as correct as it was to put lookout towers on middling-high mountains but never on the really high peaks. Since such analogies did not occur to him, it was enough to register a certain uneasiness and make up his mind that he would not mention Feuermaul in his column at all, not even by name.

36

A GREAT EVENT IS IN THE MAKING. MEETING SOME OLD ACQUAINTANCES

Ulrich, who had been standing beside his cousin while she was speaking with Meseritscher, asked her as soon as they were alone for a moment:

"I'm sorry I arrived too late; how was your first encounter with La Drangsal?"

Diotima raised her heavy eyelashes to give him a single world-weary glance and dropped them again.

"Delightful, of course. She'd been to see me. We'll arrange something or other this evening. As if it made any difference!"

"You see!" Ulrich said, in the tone of their old conversations, as if to draw a final line under all that.

Diotima turned her head and gave her cousin a quizzical look.

"I told you already," Ulrich said. "Now it's almost all over, as if nothing had happened." He needed to talk: when he had got home that afternoon, Agathe had been there but soon left again; they had spoken only a few brief words before they came to Diotima's; Agathe had dressed with the aid of the gardener's wife. "I did warn you!" Ulrich said.

"Against what?" Diotima asked slowly.

"Oh, I don't know. Against everything!"

In fact, he no longer knew himself what he had *not* warned her against: her ideas, her ambition, the Parallel Campaign, love, intellect, the Jubilee Year, the world of business, her salon, her passions; against the dangers of sensibility and of casually letting things take their course, against letting herself go too far and holding herself too much in check, against adultery and marriage. There was nothing he had not warned her against. "That's how she is," he thought. Everything she did looked ridiculous to him, yet she was so beautiful it made him sad.

"I warned you," Ulrich repeated. "I hear that you're no longer interested in anything but the scientific approach to sexual problems."

Diotima ignored this. "Do you think this Drangsal's protégé is really gifted?" she asked.

"Certainly," Ulrich replied. "Gifted, young, undeveloped. His success and this woman will be the ruin of him. In this country newborn babies are ruined by being told that they are people with fabulous instincts that intellectual development would only rob them of. He sometimes comes up with good ideas, but can't let ten minutes go by without making an ass of himself." He leaned over to say in her ear: "Do you know anything specific about that woman?"

Diotima shook her head almost imperceptibly.

"She's dangerously ambitious," Ulrich said. "But not uninteresting from the point of view of your current researches. Where beautiful women used to wear a fig leaf, she wears a laurel leaf! I hate women like that!"

Diotima did not laugh, nor even smile; she merely inclined her head toward the "cousin."

"And how do you find him as a man?" he asked.

"Pathetic," Diotima whispered. "Like a lambkin running to premature fat."

"What of it? The beauty of the male is only a secondary sexual characteristic," Ulrich said. "What's primarily exciting about him is the expectation of his success. Ten years from now Feuermaul will be an international celebrity; Drangsal's connections will take care of that, and then she'll marry him. If he remains a celebrity, it'll be a happy marriage."

Diotima bethought herself and gravely corrected him: "Happiness in marriage depends on factors one cannot judge without first subjecting oneself to a certain discipline!" Then she abandoned him as a proud ship abandons the quay alongside which it has lain. Her duties as hostess bore her away from him with the barest nod, not even a glance, as she cast off her moorings. But she did not mean it unkindly; on the contrary, Ulrich's voice had affected her like an old tune from her youth. She even wondered privately what she might learn about him by subjecting his sexuality to the illumination of a scientific study. Oddly enough, in all her detailed research into these problems, she had never thought of connecting them with him.

Ulrich looked up, and through a gap in the festive tumult—a kind of optical channel through which Diotima's gaze might have preceded his own just before she had taken her somewhat abrupt departure—he saw, in the room beyond the next, Paul Arnheim in conversation with Feuermaul, with Frau Drangsal standing benignly by. She had brought the two men together. Arnheim was holding the hand with the cigar raised, as though in an unconscious gesture of self-defense, but he was smiling most engagingly; Feuermaul was talking vivaciously, holding his cigar with two fingers and sucking at it between sentences with the greed of a calf butting its muzzle at the maternal udder. Ulrich could have imagined what they were talking about, but he didn't bother; he stayed where he was, in happy isolation, looking around for his sister. He discovered her in a group of men who were mostly strangers to him, and a cool chill ran through him despite his distractedness. But just then Stumm von Bordwehr poked him gently in the ribs with a fingertip, and at the same moment Hofrat Professor Schwung approached him on the other side but was stopped a few steps away by the intervention of one of his colleagues from the capital.

"So there you are at last!" the General murmured in relief. "The Minister wants to know what an 'ethos' is."

"Why an ethos?"

"I don't know. What's an ethos?"

"An eternal truth," Ulrich defined, "that is neither eternal nor true, but valid for a time to serve as a standard for people to go by. It's a philosophical and sociological term, and not often used."

"Aha, that'll be it," the General said. "Arnheim, you see, was claiming that the proposition 'Man is good' is only an ethos. Feuermaul replied that he didn't know what an ethos was, but man is good, and that's an eternal truth! Then Leinsdorf said, 'Quite right. There can't really be any evil people, since no one can possibly will evil; these people are only misguided. People are rather nervous these days because in times like these we have so many skeptics who won't believe in anything solid.' I couldn't help thinking he should have been with us this afternoon. Anyway, he also thinks that people who won't realize what's good for them have to be forced to. And so the Minister wants to know what an ethos is. I'll just dash over to him and come right back. Don't budge, so I can find you again! There's something else I must talk with you about, urgently, and then I'll take you to the Minister."

Before Ulrich could ask for particulars, Tuzzi slipped a hand around his arm in passing, saying: "We haven't seen you here in ages!" Then he went on: "Do you remember my prediction that we'd have a pacifist invasion to deal with?" So saying, he gazed cordially into the General's eyes, but Stumm was in a hurry and merely said that though his ethos as an officer was of another kind, any sincere conviction . . . The rest of this sentence vanished with him, because he always found Tuzzi irritating, which is not conducive to good thinking.

The Section Chief blinked gaily at the General's retreating form and then turned back to the "cousin." "That business with the oil fields is only a blind, of course," he said.

Ulrich looked at him in surprise.

"You don't mean to say you haven't heard about the oil fields?" Tuzzi asked.

"I have," Ulrich answered. "I was merely surprised that you knew about them," and, not to be impolite, added, "You really understood how to keep quiet about it!"

"I've known about them for quite some time," Tuzzi said, flattered. "That this fellow Feuermaul is here this evening is of course Arnheim's doing, by way of Leinsdorf. Have you read his books, incidentally?"

Ulrich admitted that he had.

"A dyed-in-the-wool pacifist!" Tuzzi said. "And La Drangsal, as my wife calls her, mothers him so ambitiously that she'll kill for pacifism if she has to, even though it's not really her line—artists are her line." Tuzzi paused to consider, then revealed to Ulrich: "Pacifism is the main thing, of course; the oil fields are only a red herring; that's why they're pushing Feuermaul, with his pacifism, to make everyone think: 'Aha, that's the red herring!' and believe that what's behind it is the oil fields! Neatly done, but much too clever to fool anybody. For if Arnheim has the Galician oil fields and a contract to supply the Army, we naturally have to protect our frontier. We also have to install oil bases for the Navy on the Adriatic, which will upset the Italians. But if we provoke our neighbors this way, the outcry for peace goes up, and so does the peace propaganda, and then when the Czar steps forward with some idea about Perpetual Peace, he'll find the ground psychologically prepared for it. That's Arnheim's real objective!"

"And you've something against it?"

"Of course we have nothing against it," Tuzzi said. "But as you may remember, I've already explained to you why there's nothing so dangerous as peace at any price. We must defend ourselves against the dilettantes!"

"But Arnheim is a munitions maker!" Ulrich objected, smiling.

"Of course he is!" Tuzzi murmured with some exasperation. "For heaven's sake, how can you be so naïve about these things? He'll have his contract in his pocket. At most, our neighbors will arm too. Mark my words: at the crucial moment, he'll show his hand as a pacifist! Pacifism is a safe, dependable business for munitions makers; war is a risk!"

"It seems to me the military doesn't really mean any harm," Ulrich said, trying to mollify him. "They're only using the business with Arnheim to bring their artillery up-to-date, nothing more. Today the whole world is only arming for peace, after all, so it only seems right to let the pacifists help."

"And how do these people imagine that's to be done?" Tuzzi inquired, ignoring the joke.

"I don't think they've got that far yet; for the present they're still searching their hearts."

"Naturally!" Tuzzi agreed crossly, as though this were just what he had expected. "The military ought to stick to thinking about war and leave everything else to the department responsible. But before doing that, these gentlemen with their dilettantism would rather endanger the whole world! I tell you again: Nothing is so dangerous in diplomacy as loose talk about peace! Every time the demand for peace has reached a certain pitch and was no longer to be contained, it's led straight to war! I can document that for you!"

Now Hofrat Professor Schwung had rid himself of his colleague and turned with great warmth to Ulrich for an introduction to their host. Ulrich obliged with the remark that one might say that this distinguished jurist condemned pacifism in the sphere of the penal code as ardently as the authoritative Section Chief did in the political arena.

"But good gracious," Tuzzi protested, laughing, "you've misunderstood me entirely!"

And Schwung too, after a moment's hesitation, was sufficiently reassured to join forces with him, saying that he would not like his view of diminished responsibility to be regarded as in any way bloodthirsty or inhumane.

"Quite the opposite!" he said, spreading his voice in place of his arms like an old actor on the lecture platform. "It is precisely the pacification of the human being that requires us to be strict! May I assume that the Herr Section Chief has heard something about my most recent current efforts in this matter?" And he now turned directly to his host, who had heard nothing about the dispute as to whether the diminished responsibility of an insane criminal is based exclusively in his ideas or exclusively in his will, and thus hastened all the more politely to agree with everything Schwung said. Schwung, well satisfied with the effect he had produced, then began to praise the serious view of life to which this evening's gathering gave witness, and reported that he had often overheard in conversations here and there such expressions as "manly severity" and "moral soundness." "Our culture is far too infested with inferior types and moral imbeciles," he added by way of his own contribution, and asked: "But what is the real purpose of this evening? As I passed some of the groups, I've been struck by how often I've heard positively Rousseauistic sentiments about the innate goodness of man."

Tuzzi, to whom this question was principally addressed, merely smiled, but just then the General came back to Ulrich, and Ulrich, who wanted to give him the slip, introduced him to Schwung and called him the man best qualified among all those present to answer the question. Stumm von Bordwehr vehemently denied this, but neither Schwung nor even Tuzzi would let him go. Ulrich was already beating a jubilant retreat, when he was grabbed by an old acquaintance, who said:

"My wife and daughter are also here." It was Bank Director Leo Fischel.

"Hans Sepp has passed his State Exam," he said. "What do you say to that? All he has to do now is pass one more exam for his doctorate! We're all sitting in that corner over there...." He pointed toward the farthest room. "We know too few people here. Nor have we seen anything of you for a long time! Your father, wasn't it...? Hans Sepp got us the invitation for this evening—my wife was dead set on it—so you see the fellow isn't entirely hopeless. They're semi-officially engaged now, he and Gerda. You probably didn't know that, did you? But Gerda, you see, that girl, I don't even know whether she's in love with him or has just got it into her head that she is. Won't you come over and join us for a bit?"

"I'll be along later," Ulrich promised.

"Please do," Fischel urged, and fell silent. Then he whispered: "Isn't that our host? Won't you introduce me? We haven't had the opportunity. We don't know either him or her."

But when Ulrich made a move in that direction, Fischel held him back. "And how is the great philosopher? What's he up to?" he asked. "My wife and Gerda are of course mad about him. But what's this about the oil fields? The word now is that it was a false rumor, but I don't believe it. They always deny it! You know, it's the same as when my wife is annoyed with a maid, then I keep hearing that the maid is untruthful, immoral, impertinent—nothing but defects of character, you see? But when I quietly promise the girl a raise, just to have peace in the house, then her character suddenly disappears. No more talk about character, everything's suddenly in order, and my wife doesn't know why. Isn't it always like that? There's too much economic probability in those oil fields for the denials to be believed."

And because Ulrich held his peace, while Fischel wanted to return to his wife as the glorious bearer of inside information, he began once more:

"One has to admit it's very nice here. But my wife would like to know what all the strange talk is about. And who is this Feuermaul anyway?" he added. "Gerda says he's a great poet; Hans Sepp says he's nothing but a careerist who's taken everyone in!"

Ulrich allowed that the truth probably lay somewhere in between.

"Now, that's well put!" Fischel said gratefully. "The truth always lies somewhere in between, which everyone forgets nowadays, they're all so extreme! I keep telling Hans Sepp that everyone's entitled to his opinions, but the only opinions that count are the ones that enable you to earn a living, because that means that other people appreciate your opinions too!"

There had been an impalpable but important change in Leo Fischel, but Ulrich unfortunately passed up the opportunity to look into it and merely hastened to leave Gerda's father with the group around Section Chief Tuzzi. Here Stumm von Bordwehr had meanwhile grown eloquent, frustrated at his inability to pin Ulrich down, and so highly charged with things to say that they burst out by the shortest path.

"How to account for this gathering tonight?" he cried, reiterating Hofrat Schwung's question. "I would assert, in the same judicious spirit in which it was asked: Not at all! I'm not joking, gentlemen," he went on, not without a touch of pride. "This very afternoon I happened to ask a young lady whom I had to show around the psychiatric clinic of our University what it was she was actually interested in seeing, so we could explain it properly, and she gave me a very witty answer, exceptionally thought-provoking. What she said was: 'If we stop to explain everything, we will never change anything in the world.' "

Schwung shook his head in disapproval.

"What she meant by that I don't really know"—Stumm defended himself—"and I won't take responsibility for it, but you can't help feeling there is some truth in it. You see, I am, for instance, indebted to my friend here"—he gave a polite nod in Ulrich's direction—"who has so often given His Grace, and thereby the Parallel Campaign too, the benefit of his thoughts, for a great deal of instruction. But what is taking shape here tonight is a certain distaste for instruction. Which brings me back to my first assertion."

"But isn't what you want . . . ?" Tuzzi said. "I mean, the word is that colleagues from the War Ministry hope to stimulate a patriotic decision here, a collection of public funds or some such thing, in order to bring our artillery up to strength. Naturally, a mere token demonstration, just to put some pressure on Parliament through public opinion."

"That is certainly my understanding of some things I've heard tonight!" Hofrat Schwung concurred.

"It's much more complicated, Herr Section Chief," the General said.

"And what about Dr. Arnheim?" Tuzzi said bluntly. "If I may be quite candid: Are you sure that Arnheim wants nothing more than the Galician oil fields, which are tied up, as it were, with the artillery problem?"

"I can only speak of myself and my part in it, Section Chief," Stumm said, warding him off, then repeated: "And it's all much more complicated!"

"Naturally it's more complicated," Tuzzi said, smiling.

"Of course we need the guns," the General said, warming to the subject, "and it may indeed be advantageous to work with Arnheim along the lines you suggest. But I repeat that I can only speak from my point of view as a cultural officer, and as such I put it to you: 'What's the use of cannons without the spirit to go with them?' "

"And why, in that case, was so much importance attached to bringing in Herr Feuermaul?" Tuzzi asked ironically. "That is defeatism pure and simple!"

"Permit me to disagree," the General said firmly, "but that is the spirit of the times! Nowadays the spirit of the times has two separate currents. His Grace—he's standing over there with the Minister; I've just come from talking with them—His Grace, for instance, says that the call has to go out for action, that's what the times demand. And in fact people are much less enchanted with the great idea of humanity than they were, say, a hundred years ago. On the other hand, there is of course something to be said for the point of view of loving mankind, but about that His Grace says that those who do not want what is good for them must in certain circumstances be forced to accept it! So His Grace is in favor of the one current, but without turning his back on the other."

"I don't quite follow that," Professor Schwung demurred.

"It's not easy to follow," Stumm readily admitted. "Suppose we go back to the point that I see two currents at work in the mind of our period. The one states that man is good by nature, when he is left to himself, as it were—"

"How do you mean good?" Schwung interrupted. "Who can possibly think in such naïve terms nowadays? We're not living in the world of eighteenth-century idealism!"

"Well, I don't know about that." The General sounded rather nettled. "Just think of the pacifists, the vegetarians, the enemies of violence, the back-to-nature people, the anti-intellectuals, the conscientious objectors—I can't call them all to mind offhand—and all the people who put their faith in mankind, as it were; they all form one big current. But if you prefer," he added in that obliging way he had that made him so likable, "we can just as easily start out from the opposite point of view. Suppose we start with the fact that people must be regimented because they never do the right thing of their own accord; we might find it easier to agree on that. The masses need a strong hand, they need leaders who can be tough with them and don't just talk; in a word, they need to be guided by the spirit of action. Human society consists, as it were, of only a small number of volunteers, who also have the necessary training, and of millions without any higher ambitions, who serve only because they must. Isn't that so, roughly speaking? And because experience has gradually forced us to recognize this fact even here in our campaign, the first current—for what I've just been talking about is the second current—the first current, I say, is alarmed at the possibility that the great idea of love and faith in mankind might get lost altogether. Hence there were forces at work, you see, that have sent Feuermaul into our midst to save what can still be saved at the eleventh hour. Which makes it all much easier to understand than we first thought, no?"

"And what's going to happen then?" Tuzzi wanted to know.

"Nothing, I imagine," Stumm replied. "We've had lots of currents in the campaign by now."

"But there's an intolerable contradiction between your two currents," protested Professor Schwung, who as a jurist could not bear such ambiguity.

"Not if you look at it closely," Stumm countered. "The one current is of course also in favor of loving mankind, provided you change it first by force. They differ on a technicality, you might say."

Now Director Fischel spoke up: "As a latecomer to the discussion, I'm afraid I don't have a complete picture. But if I may say so, it seems to me that respect for humanity is basically on a higher level than its opposite. This evening I've heard some incredible sentiments—not representative of this gathering, I'm sure, but still—incredible sentiments about people of different convictions and above all of differing nationalities." With his chin clean-shaven between muttonchop whiskers and his tilted pince-nez, he looked like an English lord upholding the freedom of humanity and free trade; he did not mention that the disreputable sentiments in question were those of Hans Sepp, his prospective son-in-law, who was in his element in "the second current" of our times.

"Savage sentiments?" the General asked helpfully.

"Extraordinarily savage," Fischel confirmed.

"Could they have been talking about 'toughening up'? It's easy to misconstrue that kind of talk," Stumm said.

"No, no," Fischel exclaimed. "Utterly nihilistic, positively revolutionary views! Perhaps you're out of touch with our rebellious younger generation, Herr Major General. I'm surprised that such people are admitted here at all."

"Revolutionary views?" Stumm asked, not at all pleased, and smiling in as chilly a manner as his plump face would allow. "I'm afraid I must admit, Herr Direktor, that I'm by no means an out-and-out opponent of revolutionary views. Short of an actual revolution, of course. There's often a good deal of idealism in that sort of thing. And as for admitting them here, our campaign, which is intended to draw the whole country together, has no right to turn away constructive forces, in whatever mode they may express themselves!"

Leo Fischel was silent. Professor Schwung was not much interested in the views of a dignitary who was outside the ranks of the civilian bureaucracy. Tuzzi had been dreaming: "first current . . . second current." It reminded him of two similar expressions, "first reservoir . . . second reservoir," but he could not remember them precisely, or the conversation with Ulrich in which they had come up; yet it stirred in him an incomprehensible jealousy of his wife, which was connected to this harmless General by intangible links he could not begin to disentangle. Awakened to reality by the silence, he wanted to show the representative of the military that he was not to be sidetracked by digressions.

"All in all, General," he began, "the military party wants—"

"But, my dear Section Chief, there *is* no military party!" Stumm immediately broke in. "People are always talking about a military party, but by its very nature the military is above party!"

"Let's say the military hierarchy, then," Tuzzi replied, chafing at the interruption. "You were saying that what the army needs is not just guns but the spirit to go with them; by what spirit will you be pleased to have your guns loaded?"

"That's going too far, Section Chief!" Stumm protested. "It all started with my being asked to explain tonight's gathering to these gentlemen, and I said one really couldn't explain anything; that's all I'm taking my stand on! If the spirit of the times really has two such currents as I have described, neither of them favors 'explanation'; today we favor instinctual energies, dark forces in the blood, and the like. I certainly don't go along with that, but there's something in it!"

At these words Fischel began to fume again, finding it immoral for the military to even consider making terms with the anti-Semites in order to get their guns.

"Come now, Herr Director," Stumm tried to pacify him. "In the first place, a little anti-Semitism more or less hardly matters when people are already so anti to begin with: the Germans anti the Czechs and the Magyars, the Czechs anti the Magyars and the Germans, and so on, everybody against everybody else. Second, if anyone has always been international, it has been the Austrian Army Officers Corps: you need only look at the many Italian, French, Scottish, and Lord knows what other names; we even have an Infantry General von Kohn, he's a corps commandant in Olmütz!"

"All the same, I'm afraid you've bitten off more than you can chew," Tuzzi broke in on this diversion. "You're both internationalist and war-minded, but you want to deal with the nationalist movements and the pacifists as well: that's almost more than a professional diplomat could manage. Conducting military politics with pacifism is the task confronting the greatest diplomatic experts in Europe at this moment!"

"But we're not at all the ones who are playing politics!" Stumm protested again, in a tone of weary complaint over so much misunderstanding. "His Grace simply wanted to give capital and culture one last chance to join forces—that's the whole reason for this evening. Of course, if the civilian sector can't come to some kind of accord, we would find ourselves in a position—"

"In what position? That would be interesting to hear, indeed!" Tuzzi cried, a bit too eager to fan the flame.

"Well, in a difficult position, of course," Stumm said with caution and modesty.

While the four gentlemen were engaged in this discussion, Ulrich had long since unobtrusively slipped away to find Gerda, giving a wide berth to the group around His Grace and the Minister to avoid a summons from that quarter.

He caught sight of her from some way off, sitting by the wall beside her mother, who was gazing stiffly into the salon. Hans Sepp was standing at her other side, with an uneasy, defiant look. Since her last miserable encounter with Ulrich, Gerda had grown even thinner, looking more barren of feminine charms the closer he came, and yet, by the same measure, more banefully attractive, her head on those slack shoulders standing out against the room. When she caught sight of Ulrich her face flushed scarlet, only to turn paler than ever, and she made an involuntary movement with her upper body like someone with a sharp pain in the heart who is somehow unable to press a hand to the spot. He had a fleeting vision of the scene when, wildly intent on his animal advantage in having aroused her physically, he had abused her confusion. There that body was sitting, visible to him beneath her dress, receiving orders from her humiliated will to hold itself proudly high, but trembling the while. Gerda was not angry at him, he could see, but she wanted to be done with him at all costs. He unobtrusively slowed down, trying to savor this to the full, and this sensuous tarrying seemed in keeping with the relationship between these two people, who could never quite come together. When Ulrich was very close to her, aware of nothing now but the quivering in the uplifted face awaiting him, he felt in passing something weightless, like a shadow or a gust of warmth; and he perceived Bonadea, who had passed by him in silence but hardly without intent, and in all probability had been following him. He bowed to her. The world is beautiful if one takes it as it is: For a second the naïve contrast between the voluptuous and the meager, as expressed in these two women, loomed as large to him as that between pasture and rock at the timberline, and he felt himself stepping down from the Parallel Campaign, even though with a guilty smile. When Gerda saw this smile slowly sinking down toward her outstretched hand, her eyelids quivered.

At this moment Diotima noticed that Arnheim was taking young Feuermaul to meet His Grace and the War Minister, and, skilled tactician that she was, she thwarted all encounters by ordering the servants in with trays of refreshments.

37

A COMPARISON

Such conversations as those just reported went on by the dozen, and they all had something in common, which is not easy to describe but that cannot be passed over if one lacks Privy Councillor Meseritscher's flair for giving a dazzling account of a party just by making lists: who was there, wearing what, and saying this and that—all those things that are, in fact, considered by many to be the truest narrative art. So Friedel Feuermaul was not really being a miserable toady, which he never was, but merely finding the right word for the time and place when he said of Meseritscher, while standing in front of him: "He's really the Homer of our era! No, I mean it," he added, when Meseritscher tried to brush it off. "That epic, imperturbable 'and' with which you link all persons and events strikes me as having real greatness!" He had got hold of Meseritscher because the editor of the *Parliamentary and Social Gazette* had been reluctant to leave without paying his respects to Arnheim; but this still did not get Feuermaul's name into print "among those present."

Without going into the finer distinctions between idiots and cretins, suffice it to say that an idiot of a certain degree is not up to forming the concept "parents," even though he has no trouble with the idea of "father and mother." This same simple additive, "and," was Meseritscher's device for relating social phenomena to one another. Another point about idiots is that in the basic concreteness of their thinking they have something that is generally agreed to appeal to the emotions in a mysterious way; and poets appeal directly to the emotions in very much the same way, insofar as their minds run to palpable realities. And so, when Friedel Feuermaul addressed Meseritscher as a poet, he could just as well—that is, out of the same obscure, hovering feeling, which, in his case, was also tantamount to a sudden illumination—have called him an idiot, in a way that would have had considerable significance for all mankind. For the element common to both is a mental condition that cannot be spanned by far-reaching concepts, or refined by distinctions and abstractions, a mental state of the crudest pattern, expressed most clearly in the way it limits itself to the simplest of coordinating conjunctions, the helplessly additive "and," which for those of meager mental capacity replaces more intricate relationships; and it may be said that our world, regardless of all its intellectual riches, is in a mental condition akin to idiocy; indeed, there is no avoiding this conclusion if one tries to grasp as a totality what is going on in the world.

Not that those who are the first to propound or who come to share such a view have a monopoly on intelligence! It simply doesn't depend in the least on the individual, or on the pursuits he is engaged in—and which were indeed being engaged in, with more or with less shrewdness, by all those who had come to Diotima's on this evening. For when General Stumm von Bordwehr, for instance, during the pause caused by the arrival of refreshments, got into a conversation with His Grace in the course of which he argued in a genially obstinate and respectfully daring tone: "With all due respect, Your Grace, permit me to disagree most strongly; there is more than mere presumption in people who are proud of their race; there is also something appealingly aristocratic!" he knew precisely what he meant by these words, but not so precisely what he conveyed by them, for such civilities are wrapped in an extra something that is like a pair of thick gloves in which one must struggle to pick up a single match out of a full box. And Leo Fischel, who had not budged from Stumm's side after he noticed that the General was moving impatiently toward His Grace, added:

"People must be judged not by their race but on their merit!"

What His Grace replied was logical; disregarding Director Fischel, who had only just been introduced to him, he answered Stumm:

"What does the middle class need race for? They've always been up in arms about a court chamberlain needing sixteen noble ancestors, and now what are they doing themselves? Trying to ape it, and exaggerating it to boot! More than sixteen ancestors is sheer snobbery!" For His Grace was upset, and therefore it was quite logical for him to express himself in this fashion. Man is indisputably endowed with reason; the problem is only how he uses his reason in the company of others.

His Grace was vexed by the intrusion of "national" elements into the Parallel Campaign, although he himself had brought it about. Various political and social considerations had driven him to it; he himself recognized only "the national populace." His political friends had advised him: "There's no harm in listening to what they have to say about race and purity and blood—who takes what anyone says seriously anyway?"

"But they're talking about human beings as if they were beasts!" Count Leinsdorf had objected; he had a Catholic view of human dignity, which prevented him from seeing that the principles of the chicken farm and of horse breeding could be equally well applied to God's children, even though he was a great landowner. To this his friends had replied: "Come now, you've no need to brood about it. And anyhow it's probably better than their talking about the good of mankind and all that revolutionary drivel from abroad, as they've been doing." His Grace had finally seen the light on this point. But His Grace was also vexed because this fellow Feuermaul, whom he had forced Diotima to invite, was merely bringing fresh confusion into the Parallel Campaign and was a disappointment to him. Baroness Wayden had praised Feuermaul to the skies, and he had finally yielded to her insistence. "You're quite right," Leinsdorf had conceded. "The way things are going just now, we can easily be accused of Germanizing. And there may be no harm, as you say, in inviting a poet who says that we *have* to love all mankind. But don't you see, I can't really spring that on Frau Tuzzi!" But the Baroness would not give an inch and must have found new and effective arguments, for at the end of their conversation Leinsdorf had promised to make Diotima invite Feuermaul. "Not that I like doing it," he had said, "but a strong hand does need the right word to get its message across; I must agree with you there. And it's also true that things have been moving too slowly recently; we haven't had the right spirit!"

But now he was dissatisfied. His Grace was far from thinking that other people were stupid, even if he did think himself more intelligent than they were, and he could not comprehend why all these intelligent people taken together made such a poor impression on him. Indeed, life as a whole made this impression on him, as though all the intelligence in individuals and in official institutions—among which he was known to count religion and science—somehow added up to a state of total unaccountability. New ideas that one had not heard of before kept popping up, aroused passions, and then vanished again after running their course; people were always chasing after some leader or another, and stumbling from one superstition to the next, cheering His Majesty one day and giving the most disgusting incendiary speeches in Parliament the next, and none of it ever amounted to anything in the end! If this could be miniaturized by a factor of a million and reduced, as it were, to the dimensions of a single head, the result would be precisely the image of the unaccountable, forgetful, ignorant conduct and the demented hopping around that had always been Count Leinsdorf's image of a lunatic, although he had hitherto had little occasion to think about it. Glumly he stood here now, in the midst of the men surrounding him, and reflected that the whole idea of the Parallel Campaign had been to bring out the truth behind all this, and he found himself unable to formulate some vague idea about faith that was there in his mind; all he could feel was something as pleasantly soothing as the shade of a high wall—a church wall, presumably.

"Funny," he said to Ulrich, giving up his thought after a while. "If you look at all this with some detachment, it somehow reminds you of starlings—you know, the way they flock together in autumn in the fruit trees."

Ulrich had come back after seeing Gerda. Their conversation had not lived up to its promising beginning; Gerda had not managed to utter more than brief, laborious answers hacked off from something that stuck like a hard wedge in her breast, while Hans Sepp talked all the more; he had set himself up as her watchdog and let it be known at once that he was not to be intimidated by his decadent surroundings.

"You don't know the great racial theorist Bremshuber?" he had asked Ulrich.

"Where does he live?" Ulrich had asked.

"In Schärding on the Laa," Hans Sepp had told him.

"What does he do?" Ulrich had asked.

"What difference does that make?" Hans had said. "New people are coming to the top! He's a druggist."

Ulrich had said to Gerda: "I hear you're now formally engaged."

And Gerda had replied: "Bremshuber demands the ruthless suppression of all alien races; that's surely less cruel than toleration and contempt!" Her lip had trembled again as she forced out this sentence that was so badly patched together from broken bits of thought.

Ulrich had merely looked at her and shaken his head. "I don't understand that," he had said, holding out his hand to say good-bye, and now, standing beside Leinsdorf, he felt as innocent as a star in the infinity of space.

"But if you don't regard it with detachment"—Count Leinsdorf slowly continued his new thought, after a pause—"then it keeps circling around in your head like a dog trying to catch its tail! Now I've let my friends have their way with me," he added, "and I've let the Baroness Wayden have her way, and if you go around listening to what we're saying here, each separate bit sounds quite sensible, but in the nobler spiritual context we're looking for, it sounds really rambling and incoherent!"

Around the War Minister and Feuermaul, whom Arnheim had brought over, a group had formed in which Feuermaul was holding forth, loving all mankind, while a second, more distant group was collecting around Arnheim, who had moved away; in it Ulrich saw Hans Sepp and Gerda some while later. Feuermaul could be heard proclaiming: "We don't learn about life by studying it in books, but through kindness. We must believe in life!" Frau Professor Drangsal stood ramrod straight behind him and pressed his point home by saying:

"After all, Goethe was no Ph.D.!"

In her eyes, Feuermaul bore a strong resemblance to Goethe. The War Minister also held himself very straight and smiled tenaciously, as he was accustomed to doing when graciously acknowledging the salute of parading troops.

Count Leinsdorf asked Ulrich: "Tell me, who is this Feuermaul?"

"His father owns some factories in Hungary," Ulrich answered. "I think it has something to do with phosphorus, since none of the workers lives past forty. Occupational disease: necrosis of the bone."

"Hmm, I see, but the son?" Leinsdorf was unmoved by the factory workers' fate.

"He was slated to go to the university; law, I believe. The father is a self-made man, and he took it hard that his son was not interested in studying."

"Why wasn't he interested in studying?" Count Leinsdorf persisted; he was being very thorough today.

"Who knows?" Ulrich shrugged. "Probably *Fathers and Sons*. When the father is poor, the sons love money; when Papa has money, the sons love mankind. Hasn't Your Grace heard about the father-son problem in our day?"

"Yes, I've heard about it. But why is Arnheim playing the patron to this young man? Has it anything to do with those oil fields?"

"Your Grace knows about that?" Ulrich exclaimed.

"Of course; I know everything," Leinsdorf said patiently. "But what I still don't understand is this: That people should love each other, and that it takes a firm hand in government to make them do it, is nothing new. So why should it suddenly be a case of either/or?"

Ulrich answered: "Your Grace has always wanted a spontaneous rallying cry arising from the entire nation; this is the form it's bound to take!"

"Oh, that's not true!" Count Leinsdorf disagreed spiritedly, but before he could go on they were interrupted by Stumm von Bordwehr, coming from the Arnheim group with a burning question for Ulrich.

"Excuse me for interrupting, Your Grace," he said. "But tell me," he turned to Ulrich, "can one really claim that people are motivated entirely by their feelings and never by their reason?"

Ulrich stared at him blankly.

"There's one of those Marxists over there," Stumm explained, "who seems to be claiming that a person's economic substructure entirely determines his ideological superstructure. And there's a psychoanalyst denying it and insisting that the ideological superstructure is entirely the product of man's instinctual substructure."

"It's not that simple," Ulrich said, hoping to wriggle out of it.

"That's just what I always say! It didn't do me a bit of good, though," the General answered promptly, keeping his eyes fixed on Ulrich. But now Leinsdorf entered the discussion.

"Now there, you see," he said to Ulrich, "is something rather like the question I was about to raise myself. No matter whether the substructure is economic or sexual, well, what I wanted to say before is: Why are people so unreliable in their superstructure? You know the common saying that the world is crazy; it is getting all too easy to believe it's true!"

"That's the psychology of the masses, Your Grace," the learned General interposed again. "So far as it applies to the masses it makes sense to me. The masses are moved only by their instincts, and of course that means by those instincts most individuals have in common; that's logical. That's to say, it's illogical, of course. The masses are illogical; they only use logic for window dressing. What they really let themselves be guided by is simply and solely *suggestion!* Give me the newspapers, the radio, the film industry, and maybe a few other avenues of cultural communication, and within a few years—as my friend Ulrich once said—I promise I'll turn people into cannibals! That's precisely why mankind needs strong leadership, as Your Grace knows far better than I do. But that even highly cultivated individuals are not motivated by logic in some circumstances is something I find it hard to believe, though Arnheim says so."

What on earth could Ulrich have offered his friend by way of support in this scattered debate? Like a bunch of weeds an angler catches on his hook instead of a fish, the General's question was baited with a tangled bunch of theories. Does a man follow only his feelings, doing, feeling, even thinking only that to which he is moved by unconscious currents of desire, or even by the milder breeze of pleasure, as we now assume? Or does he not rather act on the basis of reasoned thought and will, as we also widely assume? Does he primarily follow certain instincts, such as the sexual instinct, as we assume? Or is it above all not the sexual instinct that dominates, but rather the psychological effect of economic conditions, as we also assume today? A creature as complicated as man can be seen from many different angles, and whatever one chooses as the axis in the theoretical picture one gets only partial truths, from whose interpretation the level of truth slowly rises higher—or does it? Whenever a partial truth has been regarded as the only valid one, there has been a high price to pay. On the other hand, this partial truth would hardly have been discovered if it had not been overestimated. In this fashion the history of truth and the history of feeling are variously linked, but that of feeling remains obscure. Indeed, to Ulrich's way of thinking it was no history at all, but a wild jumble. Funny, for instance, that the religious ideas, meaning the passionate ideas, of the Middle Ages about the nature of man were based on a strong faith in man's reason and his will, while today many scholars, whose only passion is smoking too much, consider the emotions as the basis for all human activity. Such were the thoughts going through Ulrich's head, and he naturally did not feel like saying anything in response to the oratory of Stumm, who was in any case not waiting for an answer but only cooling off a bit before returning to Arnheim's group.

"Count Leinsdorf," Ulrich said mildly. "Do you remember my old suggestion to establish a General Secretariat for all those problems that need the soul as much as the mind for a solution?"

"Indeed I do," Leinsdorf replied. "I remember telling His Eminence about it, and his hearty laugh. But he did say that you had come too late!"

"And yet it's the very thing you were feeling the lack of, Your Grace," Ulrich continued. "You notice that the world no longer remembers today what it wanted yesterday, that its mood keeps changing for no perceptible reason, that it's in a constant uproar and never resolves anything, and if we imagined all this chaos of humanity brought together in a single head, we'd have a really unmistakable case of recognizable pathological symptoms that one would count as mental insufficiency. . . ."

"Absolutely right!" cried Stumm von Bordwehr, whose pride in everything he had learned that afternoon had welled up again. "That's precisely the configuration of . . . well, I can't think of the name of that mental disease at the moment, but that's it exactly!"

"No," Ulrich said with a smile. "It's surely not the description of any specific disease; the difference between a normal person and an insane one is precisely that the normal person has all the diseases of the mind, while the madman has only one!"

"Brilliantly put!" Stumm and Leinsdorf cried as with one voice, though in slightly different words, and then added in the same way: "But what does that mean exactly?"

"It means this," Ulrich stated. "If I understand by morality the ordering of all those interrelations that include feeling, imagination, and the like, each of these takes its relative position from the others and in that way attains some sort of stability; but all of them together, in moral terms, don't get beyond the state of delusion!"

"Come, that's going too far," Count Leinsdorf said good-naturedly. And the General said: "But surely every man has to have his own morals; you can't order anyone to prefer a cat to a dog . . . ?"

"Can one prescribe it, Your Grace?" Ulrich asked intently.

"Well, in the old days," Count Leinsdorf said diplomatically, although he had been challenged in his religious conviction that "the truth" existed in every sphere. "It was easier in the old days. But today . . . ?"

"Then that leaves us in a permanent state of religious war," Ulrich pointed out.

"You call that a religious war?"

"What else?"

"Hmm . . . not bad. Quite a good characterization of modern life. Incidentally, I always knew that there's not such a bad Catholic secretly tucked away inside you."

"I'm a very bad one," Ulrich said. "I don't believe that God has been here yet, but that He is still to come. But only if we pave the way for Him more than we have so far!"

His Grace rejected this with the dignified words: "That's over my head."

38

A GREAT EVENT IS IN THE MAKING. BUT NO ONE HAS NOTICED

The General, however, cried: "I'm afraid I must get back to His Excellency the Minister at once, but you absolutely will have to explain all that to me—I won't let you off! I'll join you gentlemen again soon, if I may."

Leinsdorf gave the impression of wanting to say something—his mind was clearly hard at work—but he and Ulrich had hardly been left alone for a moment when they found themselves surrounded by people borne toward them by the constant circulation of the guests and the charisma of His Grace. There could, of course, be no more talk about what Ulrich had just said, and no one besides him was giving it a thought, when an arm slipped into his from behind; it was Agathe.

"Have you found grounds for my defense yet?" she asked in a maliciously caressing tone.

Ulrich took a grip on her arm and drew her aside from the crowd around them.

"Can't we go home?" Agathe asked.

"No," Ulrich said. "I can't leave yet."

"I suppose," she teased him, "that times to come, for whose sake you're keeping yourself pure here, won't let you go?"

Ulrich pressed her arm.

"Isn't it greatly in my favor that I don't belong here but in jail?" she whispered in his ear.

They looked for a place where they could be alone. The party had reached the boiling point and was impelling the guests to constantly circulate. On the whole, however, the twofold grouping was still distinguishable: around the Minister of War the talk was of peace and love, and around Arnheim, at the moment, about how the German love of peace flourished best in the shadow of German power.

Arnheim lent a benevolent ear to this, because he never snubbed an honest opinion and was especially interested in new ones. He was worried that the deal for the oil fields might run into opposition in Parliament. He was certain of the unavoidable opposition of the Slavic contingent, and hoped he could count on the pro-German faction to support him. On the Ministry level all seemed to be going well, except for a certain antagonism in the Ministry of Foreign Affairs, but he did not regard this as particularly significant. Tomorrow he was going to Budapest.

There were plenty of hostile "observers" around him and other leading personages. They were easily spotted in that they always said yes to everything and were unfailingly polite, while the others tended to have different opinions.

Tuzzi was trying to win one of them over by asserting: "What they're saying doesn't mean a thing. It never means anything!" His listener, a member of Parliament, believed him. But this did not change his mind, made up before he had come, that something fishy was going on here.

His Grace, on the other hand, spoke up on behalf of the evening's seriousness by saying to another skeptic: "My dear sir, ever since 1848 even the revolutions have been brought about by nothing more than a lot of talk!"

It would be wrong to regard such differences as no more than acceptable variants on the otherwise usual monotony of life; and yet this error, with all its grave consequences, occurs almost as frequently as the expression "It's a matter of feeling," without which our mental economy would be unthinkable. This indispensable phrase divides what *must* be in life from what *can* be.

"It sets apart," Ulrich said to Agathe, "the given order of things from a private, personal preserve. It separates what has been rationalized from what is held to be irrational. As commonly used, it is an admission that we are forced to be humane on major counts, but being humane on minor counts is suspiciously arbitrary. We think life would be a prison if we were not free to choose between wine or water, religion or atheism, but nobody believes in the least that we have any real option in matters of feeling; on the contrary, we draw a line, ambiguous though it may be, between legitimate and illegitimate feelings."

The feelings between Ulrich and Agathe were of the illegitimate kind, although they did no more than talk about the party as, still arm in arm, they looked in vain for a private corner, while experiencing a wild and unacknowledged joy in being reunited after their estrangement. By contrast, the choice between loving all one's fellow human beings, or first annihilating some of them, obviously involved doubly legitimate feelings, or it would not have been so eagerly debated in Diotima's house and in the presence of His Grace, even though it also split the company into two spiteful parties. Ulrich maintained that invention of "a matter of feeling" had rendered the worst possible service to the cause of feeling, and as he undertook to describe to his sister the curious impression this evening's affair had awakened in him, he soon found himself saying things that unintentionally took up where their talk of the morning had broken off and were apparently intended to justify it.

"I hardly know where to start," he said, "without boring you. May I tell you what I understand by 'morality'?"

"Please do," Agathe said.

"Morality is regulation of conduct within a society, beginning with regulation of its inner impulses, that is, feelings and thoughts."

"That's a lot of progress in a few hours!" Agathe replied with a laugh. "This morning you were still saying you didn't know what morality was!"

"Of course I don't. That doesn't stop me from giving you a dozen explanations. The oldest reason for it is that God revealed the order of life to us in all its details. . . ."

"That would be the best," Agathe said.

"But the most probable," Ulrich said emphatically, "is that morality, like every other form of order, arises through force and violence! A group of people that has seized power simply imposes on the rest those rules and principles that will secure their power. Morality thereby tends to favor those who brought it to power. At the same time, it sets an example in so doing. And at the same time reactions set in that cause it to change—this is of course too complicated to be described briefly, and while it by no means happens without thought, but then again not by means of thought, either, but rather empirically, what you get in the end is an infinite network that seems to span everything as independently as God's firmament. Now, everything relates to this self-contained circle, but this circle relates to nothing. In other words: Everything is moral, but morality itself is not!"

"How charming of morality," Agathe said. "But do you know that I encountered a good person today?"

The change of subject took Ulrich by surprise, but when Agathe began telling him of her meeting with Lindner, he first tried to find a place for it in his train of thought. "You can find good people here by the dozen too," he said, "but I'll tell you why the bad people are here as well, if you'll let me go on."

As they talked they gradually edged their way out of the throng and reached the anteroom, and Ulrich had to think where they might turn for refuge: Diotima's bedroom occurred to him, and also Rachel's little room, but he did not want to set foot in either of them again, so he and Agathe remained for the time being among the unpeopled coats that were hanging there. Ulrich could not find a way to pick up the thread. "I really ought to start again from the beginning," he said, with an impatient, helpless gesture. Then suddenly he said:

"You don't want to know whether you've done something good or bad; you're uneasy because you do both without a solid reason!"

Agathe nodded.

He had taken both her hands in his.

The matte sheen of his sister's skin, with its fragrance of plants unknown to him, rising before his eyes from the low neckline of her gown, lost for a moment all earthly connection. The motion of the blood pulsed from one hand into the other. A deep moat from some other world seemed to enclose them both in a nowhere world of their own.

He suddenly could not find the ideas to characterize it; he could not even get hold of those that had often served him before: "Let's not act on the impulse of the moment but act out of the condition that lasts to the end." "In such a way that it takes us to the center from which one cannot return to take anything back." "Not from the periphery and its constantly changing conditions, but out of the one, immutable happiness." Such phrases did come to mind, and he might well have used them if it had only been as conversation. But in the direct immediacy with which they were to be applied to this very moment between him and his sister, it was suddenly impossible. It left him helplessly agitated. But Agathe understood him clearly. And she should have been happy that for the first time the shell encasing her "hard brother" had cracked, exposing what was inside, like an egg that has fallen to the floor. To her surprise, however, her feelings this time were not quite ready to fall into step with his. Between morning and evening lay her curious encounter with Lindner, and although this man had merely aroused her wonder and curiosity, even this tiny grain sufficed to keep the unending mirroring of reclusive love from coming into play.

Ulrich felt it in her hands even before she said anything—and Agathe made no answer.

He guessed that this unexpected self-denial had something to do with the experience he had just had to listen to her describing. Abashed and confused by the rejection of his unanswered feelings, he said, shaking his head:

"It's annoying how much you seem to expect from the goodness of such a man!"

"I suppose it is," Agathe admitted.

He looked at her. He realized that this encounter meant more to his sister than the attentions paid to her by other men since she had been under his protection. He even knew this man slightly. Lindner was a public figure of sorts; he was the man who, at the very first session of the Parallel Campaign, had made the brief speech, received with embarrassing silence, hailing the "historical moment" or something similar: awkward, sincere, and pointless. . . . On impulse Ulrich glanced around, but he did not recall seeing the man tonight, for he had not been asked again, as Ulrich knew. He must have come across him elsewhere from time to time, probably at some learned society, and have read one or another of his publications, for as he concentrated his memory, ultramicroscopic traces of images from the past condensed like a repulsive viscous drop into his verdict: "That dreary ass! The more anyone wants to be taken seriously, the less one can take such a man seriously, any more than Professor Hagauer!" So he said to Agathe.

Agathe met it with silence. She even pressed his hand.

He felt: There is something quite contradictory here, but there's no stopping it.

At this point people came into the anteroom, and the siblings drew slightly apart.

"Shall I take you back in?" Ulrich asked.

Agathe said no and looked around for an escape.

It suddenly occurred to Ulrich that the only way they could get away from the other guests was by retreating to the kitchen. Three batteries of glasses were being filled and trays loaded with cakes. The cook was bustling about with great zeal; Rachel and Soliman were waiting to be loaded up, standing apart and motionless and not whispering to each other as they used to do on such occasions. Little Rachel dropped a curtsy as they came in, Soliman merely saluted with his dark eyes, and Ulrich said: "It's too stuffy in there; can we get something to drink here?"

He sat down with Agathe on the window seat and put a glass and a plate down for show so that in case anyone should see them it would look as if two old friends of the family were having a private chat. When they were seated, he said with a little sigh: "So it's merely a matter of feeling whether one finds such a Professor Lindner good or insufferable?"

Agathe was concentrating on unwrapping a piece of candy.

"Which is to say," Ulrich went on, "that the feeling is neither true nor false. Feeling has remained a private matter! It remains at the mercy of suggestion, fantasy, or persuasion. You and I are no different from those people in there. Do you know what these people want?"

"No. But does it matter?"

"Perhaps it does. They are forming two parties, each of which is as right or as wrong as the other."

Agathe said she could not help thinking that it was better to believe in human goodness than only in guns and politics, even if the manner of the belief was absurd.

"What's he like, this man you met?"

"Oh, that's impossible to say. He's good!" his sister answered with a laugh.

"You can no more depend on what looks good to you than on what looks good to Leinsdorf," Ulrich responded testily.

Both their faces were tense with excitement and laughter; the easy flow of humorous civility blocked deeper countercurrents. Rachel sensed it at the roots of her hair, under her little cap, but she was feeling so miserable herself that her perception was much dimmer than it used to be, like a memory of better days. The lovely curve of her cheeks was a shade hollow, the black blaze of her eyes dulled with discouragement. Had Ulrich been in a mood to compare her beauty with that of his sister, he would have been bound to notice that Rachel's former dark brilliance had crumbled like a piece of coal that had been run over by a heavy truck. But he had no eyes for her now. She was pregnant, and no one knew it except Soliman, who showed no understanding of the disastrous reality and responded with nothing but childish romantic schemes.

"For centuries now," Ulrich went on, "the world has known truth in thinking and accordingly, to a certain degree, rational freedom of thought. But during this same time the emotional life has had neither the strict discipline of truth nor any freedom of movement. For every moral system has, in its time, regulated the feelings, and rigidly too, but only insofar as certain basic principles and feelings were needed for whatever action it favored; the rest was left to individual whim, to the private play of emotions, to the random efforts of art, and to academic debate. So morality has adapted our feelings to the needs of moral systems and meanwhile neglected to develop them, even though it depends on feelings: morality is, after all, the order and integrity of the emotional life." Here he broke off. He felt Rachel's fascinated stare on his animated face, even if she could no longer quite muster her former enthusiasm for the concerns of important people.

"I suppose it's funny how I go on talking about morality even here in the kitchen," he said in embarrassment.

Agathe was gazing at him intently and thoughtfully. He leaned over closer to his sister and added softly, with a flickering smile: "But it's only another way of expressing an impassioned state that takes up arms against the whole world!"

Without intending to, he was reenacting their confrontation of the morning, in which he had played the unpleasant role of the lecturing schoolmaster. He could not help it. For him morality was neither conformism nor philosophic wisdom, but living the infinite fullness of possibilities. He believed in morality's capacity for intensification, in stages of moral experience, and not merely, as most people do, in stages of moral understanding, as if it were something cut-and-dried for which people were just not pure enough. He believed in morality without believing in any specific moral system. Morality is generally understood to be a sort of police regulations for keeping life in order, and since life does not obey even these, they come to look as if they were really impossible to live up to and accordingly, in this sorry way, not really an ideal either. But morality must not be reduced to this level. Morality is imagination. This was what he wanted to make Agathe see. And his second point was: Imagination is not arbitrary. Once the imagination is left to caprice, there is a price to pay.

The words twitched in his mouth. He was on the verge of bringing up the neglected difference between the way in which various historical periods have developed the rational mind in their own fashion and the way they have kept the moral imagination static and closed off, also in their own fashion. He was on the verge of talking about this because it results in a line that rises, despite all skepticism, more or less steadily through all of history's transformations, representing the rational mind and its patterns, and contrasting with a mound of broken shards of feelings, ideas, and potentials of life that were heaped up in layers just the way they were when they came into being, as eternal side issues, and that were always discarded. And also because a further result is that this finally adds up to any number of possibilities for forming an opinion one way or another, as soon as they are extended into the realm of principles; but that there is never a possibility of bringing them together. And because it follows that the various opinions lash out at each other since they have no way of communicating. And because it follows, finally, that the emotional life of mankind slops back and forth like water in an unsteady tub. Ulrich had an idea that had been haunting him all evening, an old idea of his, incidentally, but everything that had happened this evening had somehow simply confirmed it, and he wanted to show Agathe where her error lay and how it could be put right, if everyone agreed. Actually, it was only his painful intention to prove that one could not, on the whole, even trust the discoveries of one's own imagination.

Agathe now said, with a little sigh, as a hard-pressed woman gets in one last, quick defensive move before surrendering:

"So one has to do everything 'on principle,' is that it?"

And she looked at him, responding to his smile.

But he answered: "Yes, but only on *one* principle!"

This was something quite different from what he had meant to say. It again came from the realm of the Siamese twins and the Millennium, where life grows in magical stillness like a flower, and even if it were not a mere flight of fancy, it pointed to the frontiers of thought, which are solitary and treacherous. Agathe's eyes were like split agate. If at this instant he had said only a little more, or touched her with his hand, something would have happened—something that was gone a moment later, before she even knew what it was. For Ulrich did not want to say any more. He took a knife and a piece of fruit and began to peel. He was happy because the distance that had separated him from his sister shortly before had melted into an immeasurable closeness; but he was also glad that at this moment they were interrupted.

It was the General, who came peering into the kitchen with the sly glance of a patrol leader surprising the enemy encampment. "Please forgive the intrusion," he called out as he entered, "but as it's only a tête-à-tête with your brother, dear lady, it can't be too great a crime!" And turning to Ulrich, he said: "They're looking for you high and low."

And Ulrich told the General what he had meant to say to Agathe. But first he asked: "Who are *they*?"

"I was supposed to bring you to the Minister!" Stumm said reproachfully.

Ulrich waved that aside.

"Well, it's too late anyway," the good-natured General said. "The old boy just left. But on my own account, as soon as Madame has chosen some better company than yours, I shall have to interrogate you about what you meant with that 'religious war'—if you'll be so kind as to remember your own words."

"We were just talking about that," Ulrich said.

"How very interesting!" the General exclaimed. "Your sister is also interested in moral systems?"

"It's all my brother talks about," Agathe corrected him, smiling.

"That was virtually the whole agenda this evening!" Stumm sighed. "Leinsdorf, for instance, said only a few minutes ago that morality is just as important as eating. I can't see it myself." So saying, he bent with relish over the candies Agathe handed him. It was supposed to be a joke. Agathe said, to comfort him: "Neither can I."

"An officer and a woman must have morals, but they don't like to talk about it," the General went on improvising. "Don't you agree, dear lady?"

Rachel had brought him a kitchen chair, which she was zealously dusting off with her apron when these words of his stabbed her to the heart; she nearly broke into tears.

Stumm was prompting Ulrich again: "Now then, what's this about the religious war?" But before Ulrich could say anything, he forestalled him, saying: "Actually, I have the feeling that your cousin is also prowling around looking for you, and I have my military training to thank for finding you first. So I must make the most of my time. Things are not going well in there! It's supposed to be our fault. And your cousin—how shall I put it? She's simply let go of the reins. Do you know what they've decided?"

"Who decided?"

"A lot of people have already left. Some have stayed and are paying very close attention," the General described the situation. "There's no telling who is deciding."

"In that case it might be better if you told me first what they've decided," Ulrich said.

Stumm von Bordwehr shrugged his shoulders. "All right. But luckily it's not a resolution in the sense of committee business," he elucidated. "Since all the responsible people had left in time, thank heaven. So it's only what you might call a special-interest proposal, a suggestion, or a minority vote. I shall take the line that we have no official knowledge of it. But you'd better tell your secretary to watch the minutes so none of this gets into the record. Do forgive me," he said to Agathe, "for talking business like this!"

"But what happened?" she urged him on.

Stumm made a wide, sweeping gesture. "Feuermaul . . . if you remember the young man we really only invited because—how shall I put it?—because he is an exponent of the spirit of the times, and because we had to invite the opposing exponents anyway. We had hoped that nevertheless, and with the added stimulus of intellectual debate, we'd be able to get down to talking about the things that, unfortunately, really matter. Your brother knows about it, dear lady; the idea was to get the Minister together with Leinsdorf and Arnheim, to see whether Leinsdorf has any objections to . . . certain patriotic views. And all in all I'm not really dissatisfied." He turned confidentially to Ulrich. "So far so good. But while this was going on, Feuermaul and the others . . ." Here Stumm felt obliged to add for Agathe's benefit: ". . . that is, the exponent of the view that man is basically a good and peace-loving creature who responds best to kindness, and those who expound approximately the opposite view, that it takes a strong hand and all that to keep order in the world. This Feuermaul got into an argument with these others, and before anyone could stop them they had agreed on a joint proposal!"

"A joint proposal?" Ulrich was incredulous.

"That's right. Perhaps I seem to be making light of it"—Stumm sounded rather pleased with himself at the unintended comic effect of his story—"but nobody could have predicted anything of the sort. And if I tell you what their resolution was, you won't believe it! Since I was supposed to visit Moosbrugger this afternoon in a semi-official capacity, the whole Ministry will refuse to believe that I wasn't the one who put them up to it!"

Here Ulrich burst out laughing, and he interrupted him the same way from time to time as Stumm went on with his story; only Agathe understood why, while his friend commented somewhat huffily each time that he seemed to be wrought up. But what had happened corresponded far too much to the pattern Ulrich had just laid out for his sister for him not to find it hilarious.

The Feuermaul group had appeared on the scene at the very last moment to save what could still be saved. In such cases the object tends to be less clear than the intention. The young poet Friedel Feuermaul—who was called Pepi by his intimates, and who went about trying to look like the young Schubert, for he doted on everything having to do with Old Vienna, though he had been born in a small provincial town in Hungary—happened to believe in Austria's mission, and he believed besides in mankind. It was obvious that an undertaking like the Parallel Campaign that did not include him would from the beginning have made him uneasy. How could a humanitarian project in an Austrian key, or an Austrian project in a humanitarian key, flourish without him? It is true that he had said this, with a shrug, only in private to his friend Frau Drangsal, but she, the widow of a celebrity and a credit to her country, as the hostess presiding over a spiritual beauty salon overshadowed only during the last year by Diotima's, had repeated it to every influential person with whom she came in contact. Hence a rumor had begun to make the rounds that the Parallel Campaign was in peril, unless . . . This "unless" and the peril naturally enough remained rather undefined, for first Diotima had to be made to invite Feuermaul, and after that one would see. But the news of some danger apparently connected with the patriotic campaign was noted by those alert politicians who acknowledged no fatherland, but only an ethnic motherfolk living in enforced wedlock with the State as an abused wife; they had long suspected that the Parallel Campaign would only produce some new form of oppression. And even though they were civil enough to conceal this suspicion, they attached far less importance to the intention of diverting it—for there had always been despairing humanists among the Germans, but as a whole they would always be oppressors and bureaucratic parasites!—than to the useful hint that even Germans admitted how dangerous their people's nationalism was. Consequently Frau Drangsal and the poet Feuermaul felt buoyed up by sympathies for their aims, which they accepted without bothering to investigate, and Feuermaul, who was a recognized man of feeling, was obsessed with the notion that something compelling about love and peace had to be said to the Minister of War in person. Why the Minister of War, and what he was expected to do about it, remained unclear; but the idea itself was so dazzlingly original and dramatic that it really needed no additional support. On this point they had even won the approval of Stumm von Bordwehr, the fickle General, whose devotion to culture sometimes took him to Frau Drangsal's salon, unbeknownst to Diotima; it was his doing, moreover, that the original perception of Arnheim the munitions maker as part of the danger gave way to the view of Arnheim the thinker as an important element of everything good.

So far all had gone as befitted the participants, even including the fact that, despite Frau Drangsal's help, the Minister's encounter with Feuermaul unfolded as is usual in the course of human events, producing nothing more than some flashes of Feuermaulian brilliance, to which His Excellency lent a tolerant ear. But Feuermaul was far from spent, and because the troops he could summon to arms consisted of literary men young and old, councillors, Hofräte, librarians, and some pacifists, in short, people of all ages and in all sorts of positions, united in their feeling for their old Fatherland and its mission in the world—a sentiment as readily marshaled in the cause of bringing back the historic three-horse omnibus as in that of Viennese porcelain—and because all these faithful had in the course of the evening made many diverse contacts with their opponents, who also did not go around showing their claws, many discussions had sprung up in which opinions crisscrossed wildly in all directions. Such was the temptation facing Feuermaul when the Minister of War had finished with him and Frau Drangsal's attention had been distracted for a while through some unknown occurrence. Stumm von Bordwehr could only report that Feuermaul had got into an extremely lively exchange with a young man who, from his description, might well have been Hans Sepp. The young man was in any case one of those who find a scapegoat on which to blame all the evils they cannot cope with themselves; nationalist arrogance is only that special case of it in which honest conviction makes one choose a scapegoat not of one's own breed and as unlike oneself as possible. Now, everyone knows what a great relief it is when one is upset to work off one's anger on someone, even if it has nothing to do with him; but it is less well known that this also applies to love. For love, too, must often be worked off in the same way on someone not really involved, for lack of a more suitable outlet. Feuermaul, for instance, was an industrious young man who could be quite unpleasant in the struggle for his own advantage, but his lovegoat happened to be "Man," and the moment he thought of Man in general, there was no restraining his unsatisfied benevolence. Hans Sepp, on the other hand, was basically a decent fellow who could not even bring himself to deceive Director Fischel, and so his scapegoat was "non-German man," on whom he blamed everything beyond his power to change. Lord knows what they had started to talk to each other about; they must have instantly mounted their respective goats and charged at each other, for as Stumm put it:

"I've really no idea how it happened; suddenly they were surrounded, and the next minute there was a real crowd, and finally everyone still here was standing around them."

"Do you know what they were arguing about?" Ulrich asked him.

Stumm shrugged his shoulders. "Feuermaul shouted at the other fellow: 'You want to hate, but you can't do it! Because we're all born with love inside!' or something like that. And the other one shouted back at him: 'And you want to love? But that's something you're even less capable of, you—you—' Well, I can't really say exactly; I had to hold myself a bit apart, because of my uniform."

"Oh," Ulrich said. "I see the point." He turned to Agathe, trying to catch her eye.

"No—the point was the resolution!" Stumm reminded him. "There they were, ready to bite each other's heads off, and then, as if nothing had happened, they agreed to make common cause, and I do mean common!"

With his rounded figure, Stumm gave the impression of unwavering gravity. "The Minister left on the spot," he reported.

"But what was it they agreed on?" Ulrich and Agathe asked.

"I can't exactly say," Stumm replied, "because of course I took off myself before they were finished. Besides, it's always hard to remember that sort of thing clearly. It's something in favor of Moosbrugger and against the army."

"Moosbrugger? How on earth . . ." Ulrich laughed again.

"How on earth?" the General echoed venomously. "It's easy for you to laugh, but I'm the one who's going to be called on the carpet for it! At the very least it'll mean days of paperwork! How does anyone know 'how on earth' with such people? Maybe it was that old professor's fault, the one who was talking to everyone in favor of hanging and against leniency. Or it could have been because the papers have been making such a fuss again lately about the problem of that monster. Anyway, they were suddenly talking about him. This has got to be undone again!" he declared with unwonted severity.

At this moment the kitchen was invaded in quick succession by Arnheim, Diotima, and even Tuzzi and Count Leinsdorf. Arnheim had heard voices in the foyer. He had been on the point of slipping away quietly, hoping that the disturbance would enable him to escape another heart-to-heart talk with Diotima; and tomorrow he would be leaving town again for some time. But his curiosity made him glance into the kitchen, and since Agathe had seen him, politeness prevented him from withdrawing. Stumm instantly besieged him with questions about how things stood.

"I can even give it to you verbatim," Arnheim replied with a smile. "Some of it was so quaint that I simply had to write it down on the sly."

He drew a small card from his wallet and slowly read, deciphering his shorthand, the contents of the proposed manifesto:

" 'The patriotic campaign has passed the following resolution, as proposed by Herr Feuermaul and Herr—' I didn't catch the other name. 'Any man may choose to die for his own ideas, but whoever induces men to die for ideas not their own is a murderer!' That was the proposal," he added, "and my impression was that it was final."

"That's it!" the General exclaimed. "That's the way I heard it too! They're enough to make you sick, these intellectual debates!"

Arnheim said gently: "It's the desire of young people today for stability and leadership."

"But it wasn't only young people," Stumm said in disgust. "Even baldheads were agreeing!"

"Then it's a need for leadership in general," Arnheim said with a friendly nod. "It's widespread these days. Incidentally, the resolution was borrowed from a recent book, if I remember rightly."

"Indeed?" Stumm said.

"Yes," Arnheim said. "And of course we'll pretend it never happened. But if we could find a way to direct the sentiment it expresses into some useful channel, it would certainly be of help."

The General appeared somewhat relieved and, turning to Ulrich, asked:

"Do you have any idea what could be done?"

"Of course!" Ulrich said.

Arnheim's attention was diverted by Diotima.

"In that case," the General said in a low voice, "fire away! I would prefer it if we could remain in control."

"You have to focus on what actually happened," Ulrich said, taking his time. "These people aren't so far wrong, you know, when one of them accuses the other of wanting to love if he only could, and the other retorts that it's the same with wanting to hate. It's true of all the feelings. Hatred today has something companionable about it, and on the other hand, in order to feel what would really be love for another human being—I maintain," Ulrich said abruptly, "that two such people have never yet existed!"

"That's certainly most interesting," the General interrupted quickly, "especially as I completely fail to understand how you can assert such a thing. But I have to write a protocol tomorrow about everything that happened here tonight, and I implore you to bear this in mind! In the army, what counts most is being able to report progress; a certain optimism is indispensable even in defeat—that's part of the profession. So how can I report what happened here as a step forward?"

"Write," Ulrich advised him with a wink, "that the moral imagination has taken its revenge!"

"But you can't write that sort of thing in the military!" Stumm replied indignantly.

"Then let's put it another way," Ulrich said seriously, "and write: All creative periods have been serious. There is no profound happiness without a profound ethos. There is no morality that is not derived from a firm basis. There is no happiness that does not rest on a strong belief. Not even animals live without morality. But today human beings no longer know on what—"

Stumm broke in on this calmly flowing dictation too: "My dear friend, I can speak of a troop's morale, or morale in battle, or a woman's morals; but always only in specific instances. I cannot discuss morality without such a restriction in a military report, any more than I could imagination or God Almighty. You know that as well as I do!"

Diotima saw Arnheim standing at the window of her kitchen, an oddly domestic sight after they had exchanged only a few circumspect words during the entire evening. Paradoxically, it only made her suddenly wish to continue her unfinished chat with Ulrich. Her mind was dominated by that comforting despair which, breaking in from several directions at once, had almost become sublimated into an amiable and serene state of expectation. The long-foreseen collapse of her Council left her cold. Arnheim's faithlessness also left her, as she thought, almost equally indifferent. He looked at her as she came in, and for a moment it brought back the old feeling of a living space in which they were united. But she remembered that he had been avoiding her for weeks, and the thought "Sexual coward!" stiffened her knees again so that she could move toward him regally.

Arnheim saw it: her seeing him, her faltering, the distance between them melting; over frozen roads connecting them in innumerable ways hovered an intimation that they might thaw out again. He had moved away from the others, but at the last moment both he and Diotima made a turn that brought them together with Ulrich, General Stumm, and the rest, who were on the other side.

In all its manifestations, from the inspired ideas of original thinkers to the kitsch that unites all peoples, what Ulrich called the moral imagination, or, more simply, feeling, has for centuries been in a state of ferment without turning into wine. Man is a being who cannot survive without enthusiasm. And enthusiasm is that state of mind in which all his feelings and thoughts have the same spirit. You think it is rather the opposite, that it is a condition in which one overpowering feeling—of being carried away!—sweeps all the others along with it? You weren't going to say anything at all? Anyway, that's how it is. Or one way it is. But there is nothing to sustain such an enthusiasm. Feelings and thoughts become lasting only with each other's help, in their totality; they must somehow be aligned with each other and carry each other onward. And by every available means, through drugs, liquor, fantasies, hypnosis, faith, conviction, often even through the simplifying effect of stupidity, man is always trying to achieve a condition like it. He believes in ideas not because they are sometimes true but because he needs to believe; because he has to keep his feelings in order. Because he must have an illusion to stop up the gap between the walls of his life, through which his feelings would otherwise fly off in every direction. The answer is probably at least to seek the conditions of an authentic enthusiasm, instead of giving oneself up to transient delusory states. But although, all in all, the number of choices based on feeling is infinitely greater than those based on clear logic, and every event that moves mankind arises from the imagination, only the purely rational problems have achieved an objective order, while nothing deserving the name of a joint effort, or even hinting at any insight into the desperate need for it, has been done for the world of feeling and imagination.

This was more or less what Ulrich said, interspersed with understandable protests from the General.

All Ulrich saw in the events of the evening, even though they had been impetuous enough and were destined through malicious misrepresentation to have grave consequences, was the example of an infinite disorder. Feuermaul seemed at this moment to matter to him as little as the love of mankind, nationalism as little as Feuermaul, and Stumm was asking him in vain how to distill a sense of some tangible progress out of an attitude so very personal.

"Why don't you simply report," Ulrich responded, "that it's the Millennial War of Religion. And that people have never been as unprepared to fight it as now, when the rubble of 'ineffectual feelings,' which every period bequeaths to the next, has grown into mountains without anything being done about it. So the War Ministry can sit back and serenely await the next mass catastrophe."

Ulrich was foretelling the future, with no inkling of it. His concern was not with real events at all; he was struggling for his salvation. He was trying to throw in everything that could get in its way, and it was for that reason that he laughed so much and tried to mislead them into thinking he was joking and exaggerating. He was exaggerating for Agathe's benefit, carrying on his long-standing dialogue with her, not just this most recent one. Actually, he was throwing up a bulwark of ideas against her, knowing that in a certain place there was a little bolt, and that if this bolt were drawn back, everything would be flooded and buried by feeling. In truth he was thinking incessantly of this bolt.

Diotima was standing near him and smiling. She sensed something of Ulrich's efforts on behalf of his sister, and was sadly moved; she forgot sexual enlightenment, and something in her opened up: it was doubtless the future, but in any case, her lips were slightly open too.

Arnheim asked Ulrich: "And you think . . . that something might be done about it?" The tone of his question suggested that he had caught the seriousness behind the exaggeration, but that he regarded even the seriousness as an exaggeration.

Tuzzi said to Diotima: "Something must in any case be done to prevent this affair from leaking out."

"Isn't it obvious?" Ulrich said in reply to Arnheim. "Today we are facing too many possibilities of feeling, too many possible ways of living. But isn't it like the kind of problem our intellect deals with whenever it is confronted with a vast number of facts and a history of the relevant theories? And for the intellect we have developed an open-ended but precise procedure, which I don't need to describe to you. Now tell me whether something of the kind isn't equally possible for the feelings. We certainly need to find out what we're here for; it's one of the main sources of all violence in the world. Earlier centuries tried to answer it with their own inadequate means, but the great age of empiricism has done nothing of its own, so far. . . ."

Arnheim, who caught on quickly and liked to interrupt, laid his hand on Ulrich's shoulder as if to restrain him. "This implies an increasing relationship with God!" he said in a low tone of warning.

"Would that be so terrible?" Ulrich asked, not without a hint of mockery at such premature alarm. "But I haven't gone that far yet!"

Arnheim promptly checked himself and smiled. "How delightful after a long absence to find someone unchanged. Such a rarity, these days!" he said. He was genuinely glad, in fact, once he felt safe again behind his defensive front of benevolence. Ulrich might, after all, have very well taken him up on that rash offer of a position, and Arnheim was grateful that Ulrich, in his irresponsible intransigence, disdained touching the earth with his feet. "We must have a talk about this sometime," he added cordially. "It's not clear to me how you conceive of applying our theoretical attitude to practical affairs."

Ulrich knew very well that it was still unclear. What he meant was not a life of "research," or a life "in the light of science," but a "quest for feeling" similar to a quest for truth, except that truth was not the issue here. He watched Arnheim moving over to Agathe. Diotima was standing there too; Tuzzi and Count Leinsdorf came and went. Agathe was chatting with everyone and thinking: "Why is he talking with all these people? He ought to have left with me! He's cheapening what he said to me!" She liked many of the things she heard him say from across the room, and yet they hurt her. Everything that came from Ulrich was hurting her again, and for the second time that day she suddenly felt the need to get away from him. She despaired of ever being able, with her limitations, to be what he wanted, and the prospect that they would soon be going home like any other couple, gossiping about the evening behind them, was intolerable.

Meanwhile Ulrich was thinking: "Arnheim will never understand that." And he added: "It is precisely in his feelings that the scientist is limited, and the practical man even more so. It's as necessary as having your legs firmly planted if you intend to lift something with your arms." In ordinary circumstances he was that way himself; the moment he began thinking about anything, even if it was about feeling itself, he was very cautious about letting any feeling into it. Agathe called this coldness, but he knew that in order to be wholly otherwise one has to be prepared to renounce life, as if on a mortal adventure, for one has no idea what its course will be! He was in the mood for it, and for the moment no longer feared it. He gazed for a long time at his sister: the lively play of conversation on the deeper, untouched face. He was about to ask her to leave with him, but before he could move, Stumm had come back and was intent on talking with him.

The good General was fond of Ulrich. He had already forgiven him his witticisms about the War Ministry, and was actually rather taken with the phrase "religious war": it had such a festively military air, like oak leaves on a helmet, or shouts of hurrah on the Emperor's birthday. With his arm pressed to Ulrich's, he steered him out of earshot of the others. "You know, I like what you said about all events originating in the imagination," he said. "Of course, that's more my private opinion than my official attitude," and he offered Ulrich a cigarette.

"I've got to go home," Ulrich said.

"Your sister is having a fine time; don't disturb her," Stumm said. "Arnheim's outdoing himself to pay court to her. But what I was going to say: the joy seems to have gone out of mankind's great ideas. You ought to put some life back into them. I mean, there's a new spirit in the air, and you're the man to take charge!"

"What gives you that idea?" Ulrich asked guardedly.

"That's how it strikes me." Stumm passed over it and went on intently: "You're for order too; everything you say shows it. And so then I ask myself: which is more to the point—that man is good, or that he needs a firm hand? It's all tied in with our present-day need to take a stand. I've already told you it would put my mind at rest if you would take charge of the campaign again. With all this talk, there's simply no knowing what may happen otherwise!"

Ulrich laughed. "Do you know what I'm going to do now? I'm not coming here anymore!" he said happily.

"But why?" Stumm protested hotly. "All those people will be right who've been saying that you've never been a real power!"

"If I told them what I really think, they would *really* say so." Ulrich answered, laughing, and disengaged himself from his friend.

Stumm was vexed, but then his good humor prevailed, and he said in parting: "These things are so damned complicated. Sometimes I've actually thought it would be best if a real idiot came along to tackle all these insoluble problems—I mean some sort of Joan of Arc. A person like that might be able to help!"

Ulrich's eyes searched for his sister but did not find her. While he was asking Diotima about her, Leinsdorf and Tuzzi returned from the salon and announced that everyone was leaving.

"I said all along," His Grace remarked cheerfully to the lady of the house, "that what those people were saying was not what they really meant. And Frau Drangsal has come up with a really saving idea; we've decided to continue this evening's meeting another time. Feuermaul, or whatever his name is, will read us some long poem he has written, so things will be much quieter. I of course took it upon myself, on account of the urgency, to say I was sure you'd agree!"

It was only then that Ulrich learned that Agathe had suddenly said good-bye and left the house without him. She had left word that she had not wanted to disturb him.

FROM THE
POSTHUMOUS PAPERS

TRANSLATED FROM THE GERMAN BY

BURTON PIKE

CONTENTS

PART 2

Drafts of Character and Incident

Ulrich / Ulrich and Agathe / Agathe

Musil did not finish *The Man Without Qualities*, although he often said he intended to. There is no way of telling from either the parts published in his lifetime or his posthumous papers how he would have done so, or indeed whether he could have done so to his own satisfaction. This is because of the novel's rigorously experimental structure, consisting of an "open architecture" that could be developed in many directions from any given point. The novel does contain coherent individual threads and incidents, but Musil firmly rejected the idea of a plotted narrative whole. Therefore, while the drafts of the twenty chapters in Part 1 of "From the Posthumous Papers" carry on from where "Into the Millennium" left off, the material in Part 2 is not preliminary to a final version in the usual sense, but consists rather of notes, sketches, and drafts that Musil was keeping in suspension for possible use in some form at some place in the ultimate text, a version he never decided upon and that must forever remain the object of tantalizing speculation.

We have a fortuitous, if unhappy, benchmark for this posthumous material: When Musil had to leave Vienna in 1938, he took with him into exile in Switzerland material that he considered most useful for his further work on *The Man Without Qualities*. Everything left behind in Vienna was destroyed during the war. (A further loss was suffered when two of Musil's surviving notebooks were stolen from an editor's car in Italy in 1970, before they could be transcribed.)

The extent to which Musil regarded this novel as experimental was extraordinary. He had begun work on it in earnest in 1924 and was most reluctant when the urging of publishers and worsening external conditions forced him to publish parts of it in 1931 and 1933 (pages 1–1130 in this edition). From his point of view, the entire text ought to have remained "open" from the beginning until it had all been written and he could then revise the text as a whole. He complained that partial publication removed those parts of the novel from the possibility of further alteration, as well as distorting the shape (again, a never defined, "open" shape) he had in mind for the whole work. As it was, in 1938, in less than robust health and apparently apprehensive that he would again be forced into premature publication, he withdrew the first twenty chapters that appear in "From the Posthumous Papers" when they were already set in galleys, in order to rework them still further. These chapters were intended not to conclude the novel but to continue "Into the Millennium." Like Goethe, Musil had a strange sense of having infinite time stretching out before him in which to complete his task. One is tempted to see in his solitary and stubborn pursuit of his ideal more than a little of Kafka's Hunger Artist.

Musil's purpose in writing *The Man Without Qualities* was a moral one. He had set out to explore possibilities for the right life in a culture that had lost both its center and its bearings but could not tear itself away from its outworn forms and habits of thought, even while they were dissolving. Musil equated ethics and aesthetics, and was convinced that a union of "precision and soul," the language and discoveries of science with one's inner life of perceptions and feelings, could be, and must be, achieved. He meant this novel to be experienced as a moral lever to move the world, as Emerson and Nietzsche intended their writing to be experienced, in such a way that (in Rilke's words) "you must change your life." Musil's anguish becomes palpable as he pursues this search for the right life using the tools of scientific skepticism, while remaining all too aware of the apparently inherent limitations of human societies and, especially, of human nature. Fortunately, this anguish is leavened by a sparkling wit of language and situation, as when a character is described as wearing "a wig of split hairs."

The search for the right life leads to an increasing inwardness in the novel. Musil intended to have Ulrich and Agathe somehow rejoin the world after the failure of their attempt to achieve a *unio mystica*, but as the reader will see, this was left completely up in the air among a welter of conflicting possibilities. Much of the material in Part 2 consists of startlingly dramatic or even melodramatic nuclei that Musil weighed using at some point. He frequently inserts identical or slightly varied material in different places, obviously to try it out in alternative contexts, but without committing himself. Always an analytical thinker and a methodical worker, Musil used an elaborate and cryptic system of referencing and cross-referencing codes and notations, some of them still undeciphered, to remind himself of the many interconnections. These markings are ubiquitous, indicating how thoroughly the different parts of the work were simultaneously present in his mind. These codes are to be found in the German edition but have been suppressed here in the interest of readability.

Among the experiments Musil tries out, for example, are the possibilities of Ulrich having sexual relations, sometimes aggressive and perverse, with his sister, Agathe, his cousin Diotima, and Clarisse, his friend Walter's wife. Moosbrugger, the sex murderer who haunts the entire novel, is somehow freed by Clarisse in one version, while Ulrich's attempt to free him himself, together with some hired criminals, fails in another. Moosbrugger is executed, and Hans Sepp commits suicide (under a train in one place, by gunshot in another). Ulrich's escape to the idyllic Italian island is now with Agathe, now with Clarisse; the idyll fails with Agathe, fails with Clarisse. Clarisse looms much larger in these drafts than in the main text; here the stages of her growing insanity are carefully detailed. Ulrich appears crueler, more morally indolent, as his successive failures are recorded. (Musil should not be identified with Ulrich; as is made quite clear here, in his role as narrator Musil is usually critical of Ulrich.) These posthumous papers also shed a great deal of light on Musil's concept of mysticism and the "Other Condition."

Musil had suffered a stroke in 1936, and the tone of Part 1 of "From the Posthumous Papers," written after that, is markedly different from the earlier sections of the novel; quieter, strikingly inward, more difficult, the writing often of a rare beauty. In the selection of drafts, notes, and sketches presented in Part 2, which cover the span of time between 1920 and 1942, Musil makes clear how the faults of his characters are intended to mirror the larger faults of the age; as he says, these figures live on an arc without being able to close the circle. As the age comes unglued and spirals toward war, so do the characters spiral more clearly toward failure, helplessness, madness, and suicide, even as they press forward in their firm belief in a better future, if only they could find the key. *The Man Without Qualities* is not a pessimistic work.

The contents of "From the Posthumous Papers" have not been previously translated into English. Much of what is presented here became available in German for the first time only with the publication of the 1978 German edition of Musil's collected works. This new German edition is not definitive, but it completely supersedes the edition of the 1950s on which the first, incomplete, English translation was based. The guiding principle in selecting the material for translation in "From the Posthumous Papers" was to present to the English-speaking public in readable form the major narrative portions of the posthumous material in the 1978 German edition, as well as selections that illuminate Musil's methods of thinking and working. Scholarly completeness could not be the goal in any case, since the 1978 German edition offers only a major selection from the extant posthumous papers, together with some scholarly apparatus. There exists in manuscript even more material relating to *The Man Without Qualities* than is in the German edition: The various Musil research centers finished the painstaking process of transcribing these papers only in 1990, and this transcription, 34 megabytes of data (not all of it relating to the novel), has been made available in German on a CD-ROM disk. Omitted in what follows, aside from the cross-referencing codes, are (1) longer repetitive variations of chapters or sections in which the changes are slight—Musil was an obsessive rewriter and polisher; and (2) many brief notes, jottings, and indications that are too sketchy to be informative except to the specialist.

Except for the galley drafts of the first twenty chapters, this material is for the most part not polished or "written up" in final form; some of it is quite sketchy, some merely jotted notes. Over the years, Musil changed the names of some of his characters and switched others, and this can be confusing. The essence of the characters, however, seems to have been fixed from the early stages, so these name changes are purely verbal. Ulrich was originally called "Anders," then called "Achilles"; the names, but not the characters, of

Lindner and Meingast were reversed. Clarisse's brother is called Siegmund in the main text, Siegfried and Wotan here. In the interest of readability the names, with one or two obvious exceptions, have been changed to be consistent with those used previously in the novel and are spelled out—Musil usually refers to them by their initials—as are most of the numerous other abbreviations. Given the fragmentary nature of the texts in Part 2, and for the sake of readability, elisions have not been indicated; with very minor exceptions they are between selections, not within selections. Items between slashes or in parentheses are Musil's; material in square brackets is mine. Double and triple ellipsis points in the text reproduce those in the German edition.

The only major departure from the 1978 German edition in how this material appears has to do with the ordering of the contents of Part 2. The German edition presents this material in reverse chronology, beginning with what Musil was working on at his death and proceeding backward to the earliest sketches. It seemed to me that since Musil was thinking about this material experimentally and not chronologically, such an ordering is not necessarily indicated, especially in the absence of the author's ultimate intentions about the work as a whole.

A further problem was that in chronological order, whether forward or backward, the random mixture of elements in Part 2 of "From the Posthumous Papers" would put off the general reader, for whom this edition is intended. That would be unfortunate, since these pages contain some of Musil's most powerful and evocative writing. Rearranging the contents of Part 2 according to character groupings, narrative sections, and Musil's notes about the novel makes this material much more accessible, and given the author's experimental attitude toward these fragments this rearrangement seems not unreasonable. Readers who wish to see this material presented in roughly chronological reverse order—some of it can be dated only approximately—should consult the German edition.

The original choice of material to include here was made in extensive consultation with Professor Philip Payne of the University of Lancaster, England, to whom I would like to express my appreciation. I owe a profound debt of gratitude to Professor Adolf Frisé, editor of the German edition, for his constant friendly encouragement and advice. Without his work, and without the unflagging patience and skill with which he and the various Musil research teams in Vienna, Klagenfurt, Saarbrücken, and Reading deciphered Musil's difficult manuscripts, no Musil edition would have been possible. And without the determination, persistence, fine German, and ear and eye for quality of Carol Janeway, Sophie Wilkins's and my editor at Knopf, this translation would never have come to fruition.

Burton Pike

PART 1

Musil had given chapters 39 through 58 to the printer. He re-
vised them in galley proofs in 1937–1938, then withdrew them
to work on them further. They were intended to continue "Into
the Millennium," of 1932–1933, but not conclude it.

39

AFTER THE ENCOUNTER

As the man who had entered Agathe's life at the poet's grave, Professor August Lindner, climbed down toward the valley, what he saw
opening before him were visions of salvation.

If she had looked around at him after they parted she would have
been struck by the man's ramrod-stiff walk dancing down the stony
path, for it was a peculiarly cheerful, assertive, and yet nervous walk.
Lindner carried his hat in one hand and occasionally passed the
other hand through his hair, so free and happy did he feel.

"How few people," he said to himself, "have a truly empathic
soul!" He depicted to himself a soul able to immerse itself completely in a fellow human being, feeling his inmost sorrows and lowering itself to his innermost weaknesses. "What a prospect!" he
exclaimed to himself. "What a miraculous proximity of divine mercy,
what consolation, and what a day for celebration!" But then he recalled how few people were even able to listen attentively to their
fellow creatures; for he was one of those right-minded people who
descend from the unimportant to the trivial without noticing the difference. "How rarely, for instance, is the question 'How are you?'
meant seriously," he thought. "You need only answer in detail how
you really feel, and soon enough you find yourself looking into a
bored and distracted face!"

Well, *he* had not been guilty of this error! According to his principles the particular and indispensable doctrine of health for the

strong was to protect the weak; without such a benevolent, self-imposed limitation, the strong were all too easily susceptible to brutality; and culture, too, needed its acts of charity against the dangers inherent within itself. "Whoever tries to tell us what 'universal education' is supposed to be," he affirmed for himself through inner exclamation, mightily refreshed by a sudden lightning bolt loosed against his fellow pedagogue Hagauer, "should truly first be advised: experience what another person feels like! Knowing through empathy means a thousand times more than knowing through books!" He was evidently giving vent to an old difference of opinion, aimed on the one hand at the liberal concept of education and on the other at the wife of his professional brother, for Lindner's glasses gazed around like two shields of a doubly potent warrior. He had been self-conscious in Agathe's presence, but if she were to see him now he would have seemed to her like a commander, but a commander of troops that were by no means frivolous. For a truly manly soul is ready to assist, and it is ready to assist because it is manly. He raised the question whether he had acted correctly toward the lovely woman, and answered himself: "It would be a mistake if the proud demand for subordination to the law were to be left to those who are too weak for it; and it would be a depressing prospect if only mindless pedants were permitted to be the shapers and protectors of manners and morals; that is why the obligation is imposed upon the vital and strong to require discipline and limits from their instincts of energy and health: they must support the weak, shake up the thoughtless, and rein in the licentious!" He had the impression he had done so.

As the pious soul of the Salvation Army employs military uniform and customs, so had Lindner taken certain soldierly ways of thinking into his service; indeed, he did not even flinch from concessions to the "man of power" Nietzsche, who was for middle-class minds of that time still a stumbling block, but for Lindner a whetstone as well. He was accustomed to say of Nietzsche that it could not be maintained that he was a bad person, but his doctrines were surely exaggerated and ill equipped for life, the reason for this being that he rejected empathy; for Nietzsche had not recognized the marvelous counterbalancing gift of the weak person, which was to make the strong person gentle. And opposing to this his own experience, he thought with joyful purpose: "Truly great people do not pay homage to a sterile cult of the self, but call forth in others the feeling of their sublimity by bending down to them and indeed, if it comes to that, sacrificing themselves for them!" Sure of victory and with an expression of amicable censure that was meant to encourage them, he looked into the eyes of a pair of young lovers who, intricately intertwined, were coming up toward him. But it was a quite ordinary couple, and the young idler who formed its male component squeezed his eyelids shut as he responded to this look of Lindner's, abruptly stuck out his tongue, and said: "Nyaa!" Lindner, unprepared for this mockery and vulgar menace, was taken aback; but he acted as if he did not notice. He loved action, and his glance sought a policeman, who ought to have been in the vicinity to guarantee honor's public safety; but as he did so his foot struck a stone, and the sudden stumbling motion scared off a swarm of sparrows that had been regaling themselves at God's table over a pile of horse manure. The explosion of wings was like a warning shot, and he was just able at the last moment, before falling ignominiously, to hop over the double obstacle with a balletically disguised jump. He did not look back, and after a while was quite satisfied with himself. "One must be hard as a diamond and tender as a mother!" he thought, using an old precept from the seventeenth century.

Since he also esteemed the virtue of modesty, at no other time would he have asserted anything like this in regard to himself; but there was something in Agathe that so excited his blood! Then again, it formed the negative pole of his emotions that this divinely tender female whom he had found in tears, as the angel had found the maiden in the dew . . . oh, he did not want to be presumptuous, and yet how presumptuous yielding to the spirit of poetry does make one! And so he continued in a more restrained manner: that this wretched woman was on the point of breaking an oath placed in the hands of God—for that is how he regarded her desire for a divorce. Unfortunately, he had not made this forcefully clear when they had stood face-to-face—God, what nearness again in these words!—unfortunately, he had not presented this idea with sufficient firmness; he merely remembered having spoken to her in general about loose morals and ways of protecting oneself against them. Besides, the name of God had certainly not passed his lips, unless as a rhetorical flourish; and the spontaneity, the dispassionate, one might even say the irreverent, seriousness with which Agathe had asked him whether he believed in God offended him even now as he remembered it. For the truly pious soul does not permit himself to simply follow a whim and think of God with crude directness. Indeed, the moment Lindner thought of this unreasonable question he despised Agathe as if he had stepped on a snake. He resolved that if he should ever be in the situation of repeating his admonitions to her, he would follow only the dictates of that powerful logic which is in keeping with earthly matters and which has been placed on earth for that purpose, because not every ill-bred person can be permitted to ask God to trouble Himself on behalf of his long-established confusions; and so he began to make use of this logic straightaway, and many expressions occurred to him that it would be appropriate to use to a person who has stumbled. For instance, that marriage is not a private affair but a public institution; that it has the sublime mission of evolving feelings of responsibility and empathy, and the task (which hardens a people) of exercising mankind in the bearing of difficult burdens; perhaps indeed, although it could only be adduced with the greatest tact, that precisely by lasting over a fairly long period of time, marriage constituted the best protection against the excesses of desire. He had an image of the human being, perhaps not wrongly, as a sack full of devils that had to be kept firmly tied shut, and he saw unshakable principles as the tie.

How this dutiful man, whose corporeal part could not be said to project in any direction but height, had acquired the conviction that one had to rein oneself in at every step was indeed a riddle, which could only be solved, though then quite easily, when one knew its benefit. When he had reached the foot of the hill a procession of soldiers crossed his path, and he looked with tender compassion at the sweaty young men, who had shoved their caps back on their heads, and with faces dulled from exhaustion looked like a procession of dusty caterpillars. At the sight of these soldiers, his horror at the frivolity with which Agathe had dealt with the problem of divorce was dreamily softened by a joyful feeling that such a thing should be happening to his free-thinking colleague Hagauer; and this stirring in any event served to remind him again of how indispensable it was to mistrust human nature. He therefore resolved to make ruthlessly plain to Agathe—should the occasion actually, and through no fault of his own, arise—that selfish energies could in the last analysis have only a destructive effect, and that she should subordinate her personal despair, however great it might be, to moral insight, and that the true basic touchstone of life is living together.

But whether the occasion was once again to offer itself was evidently just the point toward which Lindner's mental powers were so excitedly urging him. "There are many people with noble qualities, which are just not yet gathered into an unshakable conviction," he thought of saying to Agathe; but how should he do so if he did not see her again; and yet the thought that she might pay him a visit offended all his ideas about tender and chaste femininity. "It simply has to be put before her as strongly as possible, and immediately!" he resolved, and because he had arrived at this resolution he also no longer doubted that she really would appear. He strongly admonished himself to selflessly work through with her the reasons she would advance to excuse her behavior before he went on to convince her of her errors. With unwavering patience he would strike her to the heart, and after he had imagined that to himself too, a noble feeling of fraternal attention and solicitude came over his own heart, a consecration as between brother and sister, which, he noted, was to rest entirely on those relations that the sexes maintain with each other. "Hardly any men," he cried out, edified, "have the slightest notion how deep a need noble feminine natures have for the noble man, who simply deals with the human being in the woman without being immediately distracted by her exaggerated desire to please him sexually!" These ideas must have given him wings, for he had no idea how he had got to the terminus of the trolley line, but suddenly there he was; and before getting in he took off his glasses in order to wipe them free of the condensation with which his heated inner processes had coated them. Then he swung himself into a corner, glanced around in the empty car, got his fare ready, looked into the conductor's face, and felt himself entirely at his post, ready to begin the return journey in that admirable communal institution called the municipal trolley. He discharged the fatigue of his walk with a contented yawn, in order to stiffen himself for new duties, and summed up the astonishing digressions to which he had surrendered himself in the sentence: "Forgetting oneself is the healthiest thing a human being can do!"

40

THE DO-GOODER

Against the unpredictable stirrings of a passionate heart there is only one reliable remedy: strict and absolutely unremitting planning; and it was to this, which he had acquired early, that Lindner owed the successes of his life as well as the belief that he was by nature a man of strong passions and hard to discipline. He got up early in the morning, at the same hour summer and winter, and at a washbasin on a small iron table washed his face, neck, hands, and one seventh of his body—every day a different seventh, of course—after which he rubbed the rest with a wet towel, so that the bath, that time-consuming and voluptuous procedure, could be limited to one evening every two weeks. There was in this a clever victory over matter, and whoever has had occasion to consider the inadequate washing facilities and uncomfortable beds that famous people who have entered history have had to endure will hardly be able to dismiss the conjecture that there must be a connection between iron beds and iron people, even if we ought not exaggerate it, since otherwise we might soon be sleeping on beds of nails. So here, moreover, was an additional task for reflection, and after Lindner had washed himself in the glow of stimulating examples he also took advantage of drying himself off to do a few exercises by skillful manipulation of his towel, but only in moderation. It is, after all, a fateful mistake to base health on the animal part of one's person; it is, rather, intellectual and moral nobility that produce the body's capacity for resistance; and even if this does not always apply to the individual, it most certainly applies on a larger scale, for the power of a people is the consequence of the proper spirit, and not the other way around. Therefore Lindner had also bestowed upon his rubbings-down a special and careful training, which avoided all the uncouth grabbing that constitutes the usual male idolatry but on the contrary involved the whole personality, by combining the movements of his body with uplifting inner tasks. He especially abhorred the perilous worship of smartness that, coming from abroad, was already hovering as an ideal before many in his fatherland; and distancing himself from this was an integral part of his morning exercises. He substituted for it, with great care, a statesmanlike attitude in the calisthenic application of his limbs, combining the tensing of his willpower with timely yielding, the overcoming of pain with commonsense humanity, and if perchance, in a concluding burst of courage, he jumped over an upside-down chair, he did so with as much reserve as self-confidence. Such an unfolding of the whole wealth of human talents made his calisthenics, in the few years since he had taken them up, true exercises in virtue for him.

That much can also be said in passing against the bane of transitory self-assertion that, under the slogan of body care, has taken possession of the healthy idea of sports, and there is even more to be said against the peculiarly feminine form of this bane, beauty care. Lindner flattered himself that in this, too, he was one of the few who knew how to properly apportion light and shadow, and thus, as he was ever ready to remove from the spirit of the times an unblemished kernel, he also recognized the moral obligation of appearing as healthy and agreeable as he possibly could. For his part, he carefully groomed his beard and hair every morning, kept his nails short and meticulously clean, put lotion on his skin and a little protective ointment on the feet that in the course of the day had to endure so much: given all this, who would care to deny that it is lavishing too much attention on the body when a worldly woman spends her whole day at it? But if it really could not be otherwise—he gladly approached women tenderly, because among them might be wives of very wealthy men—than that bathwaters and facials, ointments and packs, ingenious treatments of hands and feet, masseurs and friseurs, succeed one another in almost unbroken sequence, he advocated as a counterweight to such one-sided care of the body the concept of inner beauty care—inner care, for short—which he had formulated in a public speech. May cleanliness thus serve as an example to remind us of inner purity; rubbing with ointment, of obligations toward the soul; hand massage, of that fate by which we are bound; and pedicure, that even in that which is more deeply concealed we should offer a fair aspect. Thus he transferred his image to women, but left it to them to adapt the details to the needs of their sex.

Of course it might have happened that someone who was unpre-

pared for the sight Lindner offered during his health and beauty
worship and, even more, while he was washing and drying himself,
might have been moved to laughter: for seen merely as physical gestures, his movements evoked the image of a multifariously turning
and twisting swan's neck, which, moreover, consisted not of curves
but of the sharp element of knees and elbows; the shortsighted eyes,
freed from their spectacles, looked with a martyred expression into
the distance, as if their gaze had been snipped off close to the eye,
and beneath his beard his soft lips pouted with the pain of exertion.
But whoever understood how to see spiritually might well experience
the spectacle of seeing inner and outer forces begetting each other in
ripely considered counterpoint; and if Lindner was thinking meanwhile of those poor women who spend hours in their bathrooms and
dressing rooms and solipsistically inflame their imaginations through
a cult of the body, he could seldom refrain from reflecting on how
much good it would do them if they could once watch him. Harmless
and pure, they welcome the modern care of the body and go along
with it because in their ignorance they do not suspect that such exaggerated attention devoted to their animal part might all too easily
awaken in it claims that could destroy life unless strictly reined in!

Indeed, Lindner transformed absolutely everything he came in
contact with into a moral imperative; and whether he was in clothes
or not, every hour of the day until he entered dreamless sleep was
filled with some momentous content for which that hour had been
permanently reserved. He slept for seven hours; his teaching obligations, which the Ministry had limited in consideration of his well-
regarded writing activity, claimed three to five hours a day, in which
was included the lecture on pedagogy he held twice weekly at the
university; five consecutive hours—almost twenty thousand in a dec-
ade!—were reserved for reading; two and a half served for the setting down on paper of his own articles, which flowed without pause
like a clear spring from the inner rocks of his personality; mealtimes
claimed an hour every day; an hour was dedicated to a walk and
simultaneously to the elucidation of major questions of life and profession, while another was dedicated to the traveling back and forth
determined by his profession and consecrated also to what Lindner
called his "little musings," concentrating the mind on the content of
an activity that had recently transpired or that was to come; while

other fragments of time were reserved, in part permanently, in part alternating within the framework of the week, for dressing and undressing, gymnastics, letters, household affairs, official business, and profitable socializing. And it was only natural that this planning of his life not only was carried out along its more general disciplinary lines but also involved all sorts of particular anomalies, such as Sunday with its nondaily obligations, the longer cross-country hike that took place every two weeks, or the bathtub soak, and it was natural, too, for the plan to contain the doubling of daily activities that there has not yet been room to mention, to which belonged, by way of example, Lindner's association with his son at mealtimes, or the character training involved in patiently surmounting unforeseen difficulties while getting dressed at speed.

Such calisthenics for the character are not only possible but also extremely useful, and Lindner had a spontaneous preference for them. "In the small things I do right I see an image of all the big things that are done right in the world" could already be read in Goethe, and in this sense a mealtime can serve as well as a task set by fate as the place for the fostering of self-control and for the victory over covetousness; indeed, in the resistance of a collar button, inaccessible to all reflection, the mind that probes more deeply could even learn how to handle children. Lindner of course did not by any means regard Goethe as a model in everything; but what exquisite humility had he not derived from driving a nail into a wall with hammer blows, undertaking to mend a torn glove himself, or repair a bell that was out of order: if in doing these things he smashed his fingers or stuck himself, the resulting pain was outweighed, if not immediately then after a few horrible seconds, by joy at the industrious spirit of mankind that resides even in such trifling dexterities and their acquisition, although the cultivated person today imagines himself (to his general disadvantage) as above all that. He felt with pleasure the Goethean spirit resurrected in him, and enjoyed it all the more in that thanks to the methods of a more advanced age he also felt superior to the great classic master's practical dilettantism and his occasional delight in discreet dexterity. Lindner was in fact free of idolatry of the old writer, who had lived in a world that was only halfway enlightened and therefore overestimated the Enlightenment, and he took Goethe as a model more in charming small things than in serious and great things, quite apart from the seductive Minister's notorious sensuality.

His admiration was therefore carefully meted out. There had nevertheless been evident in it for some time a remarkable peevishness that often stimulated Lindner to reflection. He had always believed that his view of what was heroic was more proper than Goethe's. Lindner did not think much of Scaevolas who stick their hands in the fire, Lucretias who run themselves through, or Judiths who chop the heads off the oppressors of their honor—themes that Goethe would have found meaningful anytime, although he had never treated them; indeed, Lindner was convinced, in spite of the authority of the classics, that those men and women, who had committed crimes for their personal convictions, would nowadays belong not on a pedestal but rather in the courtroom. To their inclination to inflict severe bodily injury he opposed an "internalized and social" concept of courage. In thought and discourse he even went so far as to place a duly pondered entry on the subject into his classbook, or the responsible reflection on how his housekeeper was to be blamed for precipitate eagerness, because in that state one should not be permitted to follow one's own passions only, but also had to take the other person's motives into account. And when he said such things he had the impression of looking back, in the well-fitting plain clothes of a later century, on the bombastic moral costume of an earlier one.

He was by no means oblivious to the aura of absurdity that hovered around such examples, but he called it the laughter of the spiritual rabble, and he had two solid reasons for this. First, not only did he maintain that *every* occasion could be equally well exploited for the strengthening or weakening of human nature, but it seemed to him that occasions of the smaller kind were better suited for strengthening it than the large ones, since the human inclination to arrogance and vanity is involuntarily encouraged by the shining exercise of virtue, while its inconspicuous everyday exercise consists simply of pure, unsalted virtue. And second, systematic management of the people's moral good (an expression Lindner loved, along with the military expression "breeding and discipline," with its overtones of both peasantry and being fresh from the factory) would also not despise the "small occasions," for the reason that the godless belief advanced by "liberals and Freemasons" that great human accomplishments arise so to speak out of nothing, even if it is called Genius, was already at that time going out of fashion. The sharpened focus of public attention had already caused the "hero," whom earlier times had made into a phenomenon of arrogance, to be recognized as a tireless toiler over details who prepares himself to be a discoverer through unremitting diligence in learning, as an athlete who must handle his body as cautiously as an opera singer his voice, and who as political rejuvenator of the people must always repeat the same thing at countless meetings. And of this Goethe, who all his life had remained a comfortable citizen-aristocrat, had had no idea, while he, Lindner, saw it coming! So it was comprehensible, too, that Lindner thought he was protecting Goethe's better part against the ephemeral part when he preferred the considerate and companionable, which Goethe had possessed in such gratifying measure, to the tragic Goethe; it might also be argued that it did not happen without reflection when, for no other reason than that he was a pedant, he considered himself a person threatened by dangerous passions.

Truly, it shortly afterward became one of the most popular human possibilities to subject oneself to a "regimen," which may be applied with the same success to overweight as it is to politics and intellectual life. In a regimen, patience, obedience, regularity, equanimity, and other highly respectable qualities become the major components of the individual in his private, personal capacity, while everything that is unbridled, violent, addictive, and dangerous, which he, as a crazy romantic, cannot dispense with either, has its admirable center in the "regimen." Apparently this remarkable inclination to submit oneself to a regimen, or lead a fatiguing, unpleasant, and sorry life according to the prescription of a doctor, athletic coach, or some other tyrant (although one could just as well ignore it with the same failure rate), is a result of the movement toward the worker-warrior-anthill state toward which the world is moving: but here lay the boundary that Lindner was not able to cross, nor could he see that far, because his Goethean heritage blocked it.

To be sure, his piety was not of a sort that could not have been reconciled to this movement; he did leave the divine to God, and undiluted saintliness to the saints; but he could not grasp the thought of renouncing his personality, and there hovered before him as an ideal for the world a community of fully responsible moral personalities, which as God's civil army would certainly have to struggle against the inconstancy of baser nature and make everyday life a shrine, but would also decorate this shrine with the masterpieces of art and science. Had someone counted Lindner's division of the day, it would have struck him that whatever the version, it added up to only twenty-three hours; sixty minutes of a full day were lacking, and of these sixty minutes, forty were invariably set aside for conversation and kindly investigation into the striving and nature of other people, as part of which he also counted visits to art exhibitions, concerts, and entertainments. He hated these events. Almost every time, their content affronted his mind; as he saw it, it was the infamous over-wrought nerves of the age that were letting off steam in these over-blown and aimless constructions, with their superfluous stimulants and genuine suffering, with their insatiability and inconstancy, their inquisitiveness and unavoidable moral decay. He even smiled dis-concertedly into his scanty beard when on such occasions he saw "or-dinary men and women" idolize culture with flushed cheeks. They did not know that the life force is enhanced by being circumscribed, not by being fragmented. They all suffered from the fear of not hav-ing time for *every*thing, not knowing that having time means nothing more than *not* having any time for everything. Lindner had realized that the bad nerves did not come from work and its pressure, which in our age are blamed for them, but that on the contrary they came from culture and humanitarianism, from breaks in routine, the inter-ruption of work, the free minutes in which the individual would like to live for himself and seek out something he can regard as beautiful, or fun, or important: these are the moments out of which the mias-mas of impatience, unhappiness, and meaninglessness arise. This was what he felt, and if he had had his way—that is, according to the visions he had at such moments—he would sweep away all these art workshops with an iron broom, and festivals of labor and edification, tightly tied to daily activity, would take the place of such so-called spiritual events; it really would require no more than excising from an entire age those few minutes a day that owed their pathological existence to a falsely understood liberality. But beyond making a few allusions, he had never summoned up the decisiveness to stand up for this seriously and in public.

Lindner suddenly looked up, for during these dreamy thoughts he had still been riding in the trolley; he felt irritated and depressed, as one does from being irresolute and blocked, and for a moment he had the confused impression that he had been thinking about Agathe the entire time. She was accorded the additional honor that an annoyance that had begun innocently as pleasure in Goethe now fused with her, although no reason for this could be discerned. From habit, Lindner now admonished himself. "Dedicate part of your isolation to quiet reflection about your fellowman, especially if you should not be in accord with him; perhaps you will then learn to better understand and utilize what repels you, and will know how to be indulgent toward his weaknesses and encourage his virtue, which may simply be overawed," he whispered with mute lips. This was one of the formulas he had coined against the dubious activities of so-called culture and in which he usually found the composure to bear them; but this did not happen, and this time it was apparently not righteousness that was missing. He pulled out his watch, which confirmed that he had accorded Agathe more time than was allotted. But he would not have been able to do so if in his daily schedule there had not been those twenty leftover minutes set aside for unavoidable slippage. He discovered that this Loss Account, this emergency supply of time, whose precious drops were the oil that lubricated his daily works, even on this unusual day, would still hold ten spare minutes when he walked into his house. Did this cause his courage to grow? Another of his bits of wisdom occurred to him, for the second time this day: "The more unshakable your patience becomes," said Lindner to Lindner, "the more surely you will strike your opponent to the heart!" And to strike to the heart was a pleasurable sensation, which also corresponded to the heroic in his nature; that those so struck never strike back was of no importance.

41

BROTHER AND SISTER THE NEXT MORNING

Ulrich and his sister came to speak of this man once more when they saw each other again the morning after Agathe's sudden disappearance from their cousin's party. On the previous day Ulrich had left the excited and quarrelsome gathering soon after she had, but had not got around to asking her why she had up and left him; for she had locked herself in, and was either already sleeping or purposely ignoring the listener with his soft inquiry as to whether she was still awake. Thus the day she had met the curious stranger had closed just as capriciously as it had begun. Nor was any information to be had from her this morning. She herself did not know what her real feelings were. When she thought of her husband's letter, which had forced its way to her and which she had not been able to bring herself to read again, although from time to time she noticed it lying beside her, it seemed to her incredible that not even a day had passed since she had received it; so often had her condition changed in the meantime. Sometimes she thought the letter deserved the horror tag "ghosts from the past"; still, it really frightened her, too. And at times it aroused in her merely a slight unease of the kind that can be aroused by the unexpected sight of a clock that has stopped; at other times, she was plunged into futile brooding that the world from which this letter came was claiming to be the real world for her. That which inwardly did not so much as touch her surrounded her outwardly in an invisible web that was not yet broken. She involuntarily compared this with the things that had happened between her and her brother since the arrival of this letter. Above all they had been conversations, and despite the fact that one of them had even brought her to think of suicide, its contents had been forgotten, though they were evidently still ready to reawaken, and not surmounted. So it really did not matter much what the subject of a conversation was, and pondering her heart-stopping present life against the letter, she had the impression of a profound, constant, incomparable, but powerless movement. From all this she felt this morning partly exhausted and disillusioned, and partly tender and restless, like a fever patient after his temperature has gone down.

In this state of animated helplessness she said suddenly: "To empathize in such a way that one truly experiences another person's mood must be indescribably difficult!" To her surprise, Ulrich replied immediately: "There are people who imagine they can do it." He said this ill-humoredly and offensively, having only half understood her. Her words caused something to move aside and make room for an annoyance that had been left behind the day before, although he ought to find it contemptible. And so this conversation came to an end for the time being.

The morning had brought a day of rain and confined brother and sister to their house. The leaves of the trees in front of the windows glistened desolately, like wet linoleum; the roadway behind the gaps in the foliage was as shiny as a rubber boot. The eyes could hardly get a hold on the wet view. Agathe was sorry for her remark, and no longer knew why she had made it. She sighed and began again: "Today the world reminds me of our nursery." She was alluding to the bare upper rooms in their father's house and the astonishing reunion they had both celebrated with them. That might be farfetched; but she added: "It's a person's first sadness, surrounded by his toys, that always keeps coming back!" After the recent stretch of good weather, expectations had automatically been directed toward a lovely day, and this filled the mind with frustrated desire and impatient melancholy. Ulrich, too, now looked out the window. Behind the gray, streaming wall of water, will-o'-the-wisps of outings never taken, open green, and an endless world beckoned; and perhaps, too, the ghost of a desire to be alone once more and free again to move in any direction, the sweet pain of which is the story of the Passion and also the Resurrection of love. He turned to his sister with something of this still in the expression on his face, and asked her almost vehemently: "I'm surely *not* one of those people who can respond empathically to others?"

"No, you really aren't!" she responded, and smiled at him.

"But just what such people presume," he went on, for it was only now that he understood how seriously her words had been meant "namely, that people can suffer together, is as impossible for them a* it is for anyone else. At most they have a nursing skill in guessing what someone in need likes to hear—"

"In which case they must know what would help him," Agathe objected.

"Not at all!" Ulrich asserted more stubbornly. "Apparently the only comfort they give is by talking: whoever talks a lot discharges another person's sorrow drop by drop, the way rain discharges the electricity in a cloud. That's the well-known alleviation of every grief through talking!"

Agathe was silent.

"People like your new friend," Ulrich now said provocatively, "perhaps work the way many cough remedies do: they don't get rid of the sore throat but soothe its irritation, and then it often heals by itself!"

In any other situation he could have expected his sister's assent, but Agathe, who since yesterday had been in a peculiar frame of mind because of her sudden weakness for a man whose worth Ulrich doubted, smiled unyieldingly and played with her fingers. Ulrich jumped up and said urgently: "But I know him, even if only fleetingly; I've heard him speak several times!"

"You even called him a 'vacuous fool,' " Agathe interjected.

"And why not?" Ulrich defended it. "People like him know less than anyone about how to empathize with another person! They don't even know what it means. They simply don't feel the difficulty, the terrible equivocation, of this demand!"

Agathe then asked: "Why do you think the demand is equivocal?"

Now Ulrich was silent. He even lit a cigarette to underline that he was not going to answer; they had, after all, talked about it enough yesterday. Agathe knew this too. She did not want to provoke any new explanations. These explanations were as enchanting and as devastating as looking at the sky when it forms gray, pink, and yellow cities of marble cloud. She thought, "How fine it would be if he would only say: 'I want to love you as myself, and I can love you that way better than any other woman because you are my sister!' " But because he was not about to say it, she took a small pair of scissors and carefully cut off a thread that was sticking out somewhere, as if this were at that moment the only thing in the entire world that deserved her full attention. Ulrich observed this with the same attention. She was at this instant more seductively present to all his senses than ever, and he guessed something of what she was hiding, even if not everything. For she meanwhile had had time to resolve: if Ulrich could forget that she herself was laughing at the stranger who presumed he could be of help here, he was not going to find it out from her now. Moreover, she had a happy presentiment about Lindner. She did not know him. But that he had offered his assistance selflessly and wholeheartedly must have inspired confidence in her, for a joyous melody of the heart, a hard trumpet blast of will, confidence, and pride, which were in salutary opposition to her own state, now seemed to be playing for her and refreshing her beyond all the comedy of the situation. "No matter how great difficulties may be, they mean nothing if one seriously wills oneself to deal with them!" she thought, and was unexpectedly overcome by remorse, so that she now broke the silence in something of the way a flower is broken off so that two heads can bend over it, and added as a second question to her first: "Do you still remember that you always said that 'love thy neighbor' is as different from an obligation as a cloudburst of bliss is from a drop of satisfaction?"

She was astonished at the vehemence with which Ulrich answered her: "I'm not unaware of the irony of my situation. Since yesterday, and apparently always, I have done nothing but raise an army of reasons why this love for one's neighbor is no joy but a terribly magnificent, half-impossible task! So nothing could be more understandable than that you're seeking protection with a person who has no idea about any of this, and in your position I'd do the same!"

"But it's not true at all that I'm doing that!" Agathe replied curtly.

Ulrich could not keep himself from throwing her a glance that held as much gratitude as mistrust. "It's hardly worth the bother of talking about," he assured her. "I really didn't want to either." He hesitated a moment and then went on: "But look, if you do have to love someone else the way you love yourself, however much you love him it really remains a self-deceiving lie, because you simply can't feel along with him how his head or his finger hurts. It is absolutely unbearable that one really can't be part of a person one loves, and it's an absolutely simple thing. That's the way the world is organized. We wear our animal skin with the hair inside and cannot shake it out. And this horror within the tenderness, this nightmare of coming to a standstill in getting close to one another, is something that the people who are conventionally correct, the 'let's be precise' people, never experience. What they call their empathy is actually a substitute for it, which they use to make sure they didn't miss anything!"

Agathe forgot that she had just said something that was as close to a lie as a non-lie. She saw illuminated in Ulrich's words the disillusion over the vision of sharing in each other, before which the usual proofs of love, goodness, and sympathy lost their meaning; and she understood that this was the reason he spoke of the world more often than of himself, for if it was to be more than idle dreaming, one must remove oneself along with reality like a door from its hinges. At this moment she was far away from the man with the sparse beard and timid severity who wanted to do her good. But she couldn't say it. She merely looked at Ulrich and then looked away, without speaking. Then she did something or other, then they looked at each other again. After the shortest time the silence gave the impression of having lasted for hours.

The dream of being two people and one: in truth the effect of this fabrication was at many moments not unlike that of a dream that has stepped outside the boundaries of night, and now it was hovering in such a state of feeling between faith and denial, in which reason had nothing more to say. It was precisely the body's unalterable constitution by which feeling was referred back to reality. These bodies, since they loved each other, displayed their existence before the inquiring gaze, for surprises and delights that renewed themselves like a peacock's tail sweeping back and forth in currents of desire; but as soon as one's glance no longer lingered on the hundred eyes of the spectacle that love offers to love, but attempted to penetrate into the thinking and feeling being behind it, these bodies transformed themselves into horrible prisons. One found oneself again separated from the other, as so often before, not knowing what to say, because for everything that desire still had to say or repeat a far too remote, protective, covering gesture was needed, for which there was no solid foundation.

And it was not long before the bodily motions, too, involuntarily grew slower and congealed. The rain beyond the windows was still filling the air with its twitching curtain of drops and the lullaby of sounds through whose monotony the sky-high desolation flowed downward. It seemed to Agathe that her body had been alone for centuries, and time flowed as if it were flowing with the water from the sky. The light in the room now was like that of a hollowed-out silver die. Blue, sweetish scarves of smoke from heedlessly burning cigarettes coiled around the two of them. She no longer knew whether she was tender and sensitive to the core of her being or impatient and out of sorts with her brother, whose stamina she admired. She sought out his eyes and found them hovering in this uncertain atmosphere like two dead moons. At the same instant something happened to her that seemed to come not from her will but from outside: the surging water beyond the windows suddenly became fleshy, like a fruit that has been sliced, and its swelling softness pressed between herself and Ulrich. Perhaps she was ashamed or even hated herself a little for it, but a completely sensual wantonness—and not at all only what one calls an unleashing of the senses but also, and far more, a voluntary and unconstrained draining of the senses away from the world—began to gain control over her; she was just able to anticipate it and even hide it from Ulrich by telling him with the speediest of all excuses that she had forgotten to take care of something, jumped up, and left the room.

42

UP JACOB'S LADDER INTO A STRANGER'S DWELLING

Hardly had that been done when she resolved to look up the odd man who had offered her his help, and immediately carried out her resolution. She wanted to confess to him that she no longer had any idea what to do with herself. She had no clear picture of him; a person one has seen through tears that dried up in his company will not easily appear to someone the way he actually is. So on the way, she thought about him. She thought she was thinking clearheadedly, but actually it was fantasy. She hastened through the streets, bearing before her eyes the light from her brother's room. It had not been a proper kind of light at all, she considered; she should rather say that all the objects in the room had suddenly lost their composure, or a kind of understanding that they must certainly have otherwise had. But if it were the case that it was only she herself who had lost her composure, or her understanding, it would not have been limited just to her, for there had also been awakened in the objects a liberation that was astir with miracles. "The next moment it would have peeled us out of our clothes like a silver knife, without our having moved a finger!" she thought.

She gradually let herself be calmed by the rain, whose harmless gray water bounced off her hat and down her coat, and her thoughts became more measured. This was perhaps helped, too, by the simple clothes she had hastily thrown on, for they directed her memory back to schoolgirl walks without an umbrella, and to guiltless states. As she walked she even thought unexpectedly of an innocent summer she had spent with a girlfriend and the friend's parents on a small island in the north: there, between the harsh splendors of sea and sky, she had discovered a seabirds' nesting place, a hollow filled with white, soft bird feathers. And now she knew: the man to whom she was being drawn reminded her of this nesting place. The idea cheered her. At that time, to be sure, in view of the strict sincerity that is part of youth's need for experience, she would have hardly let it pass that at the thought of the softness and whiteness she would be abandoning herself to an unearthly shudder, as illogically, indeed as youthfully and immaturely, as she was now allowing to happen with such assiduity. This shudder was for Professor Lindner; but the unearthly was also for him.

The intimation, amounting to certainty, that everything that happened to her was connected as in a fairy tale with something hidden was familiar to her from all the agitated periods of her life; she sensed it as a nearness, felt it behind her, and was inclined to wait for the hour of the miracle, when she would have nothing to do but close her eyes and lean back. But Ulrich did not see any help in unearthly dreaminess, and his attention seemed claimed mostly by transforming, with infinite slowness, unearthly content into an earthly one. In this Agathe recognized the reason why she had now left him for the third time within twenty-four hours, fleeing in the confused expectation of something that she had to take into her keeping and allow to rest from the afflictions, or perhaps just from the impatience, of her passions. But then as soon as she calmed down she was herself again, standing by his side and seeing in what he was teaching her all the possibilities for healing; and even now this lasted for a while. But as the memory of what had "almost" happened at home—and yet not happened!—reasserted itself more vividly, she was again profoundly at a loss. First she wanted to convince herself that the infinite realm of the unimaginable would have come to their aid if they had stuck it out for another instant; then she reproached herself that she had not waited to see what Ulrich would do; finally, however, she dreamed that the truest thing would have been simply to yield to love and make room for a place for overtaxed nature to rest on the dizzying Jacob's ladder they were climbing. But hardly had she made this concession than she thought of herself as one of those incompetent fairytale creatures who cannot restrain themselves, and in their womanly weakness prematurely break silence or some other oath, causing everything to collapse amid thunderclaps.

If her expectation now directed itself again toward the man who was to help her find counsel, he not only enjoyed the great advantage bestowed on order, certainty, kindly strictness, and composed behavior by an undisciplined and desperate mode of conduct, but this stranger also had the particular quality of speaking about God with certainty and without feeling, as if he visited God's house daily and could announce that everything there that was mere passion and imagining was despised. So what might be awaiting her at Lindner's? While she was asking herself this she set her feet more firmly on the ground as she walked, and breathed in the coldness of the rain so that she would become quite clearheaded; and then it started to seem highly probable to her that Ulrich, even though he judged Lindner one-sidedly, still judged him more correctly than she did, for before her conversations with Ulrich, when her impression of Lindner was still vivid, she herself had thought quite scornfully of this good man. She was amazed at her feet, which were taking her to him anyway, and she even took a bus going in the same direction so she would get there sooner.

Shaken about among people who were like rough, wet pieces of laundry, she found it hard to hold on to her inner fantasy completely, but with an exasperated expression on her face she persevered, and protected it from being torn to shreds. She wanted to bring it whole to Lindner. She even disparaged it. Her whole relation to God, if that name was to be applied to such adventurousness at all, was limited to a twilight that opened up before her every time life became too oppressive and repulsive or, which was new, too beautiful. Then she ran into it, seeking. That was all she could honestly say about it. And it had never led to anything, as she told herself with a sigh. But she noticed that she was now really curious about how her unknown man would extricate himself from this affair that was being confided to him, so to speak, as God's representative; for such a purpose, after all, some omniscience must have rubbed off on him from the great Inaccessible One, because she had meanwhile firmly resolved, squeezed between all kinds of people, on no account to deliver a complete confession to him right away. But as she got out she discovered in herself, remarkably enough, the deeply concealed conviction that this time it would be different from before, and that she had also made up her mind to bring this whole incomprehensible fantasy out of the twilight and into the light on her own. Perhaps she would have quickly extinguished this overblown expression again if it had entered her consciousness at all; but all that was present there was not a word, but merely a surprised feeling that whirled her blood around as if it were fire.

The man toward whom such passionate emotions and fantasies were en route was meanwhile sitting in the company of his son, Peter, at lunch, which he still ate, following a good rule of former times, at the actual hour of noon. There was no luxury in his surroundings, or, as it would be better to say in the German tongue, no *excess;*° for the German word reveals the sense that the alien word obscures. "Luxury" also has the meaning of the superfluous and dispensable that idle wealth might accumulate; "excess," on the other hand, is not so much superfluous—to which extent it is synonymous with luxury—as it is overflowing, thus signifying a padding of existence that gently swells beyond its frame, or that surplus ease and

---

°*Überfluss,* literally, "overflow."—Trans.

magnanimity of European life which is lacking only for the extremely poor. Lindner discriminated between these two senses of luxury, and just as luxury in the first sense was absent from his home, it was present in the second. One already had this peculiar impression, although it could not be said where it came from, when the entry door opened and revealed the moderately large foyer. If one then looked around, none of the arrangements created to serve mankind through useful invention was lacking: an umbrella stand, soldered from sheet metal and painted with enamel, took care of umbrellas. A runner with a coarse weave removed from shoes the dirt that the mud brush might not have caught. Two clothes brushes hung in a pouch on the wall, and the stand for hanging up outer garments was not missing either. A bulb illuminated the space; even a mirror was present, and all these utensils were lovingly maintained and promptly replaced when they were damaged. But the lamp had the lowest wattage by which one could just barely make things out; the clothes stand had only three hooks; the mirror encompassed only four fifths of an adult face; and the thickness as well as the quality of the carpet was just great enough that one could feel the floor through it without sinking into softness: even if it was futile to describe the spirit of the place through such details, one only needed to enter to feel overcome by a peculiar general atmosphere that was not strict and not lax, not prosperous and not poor, not spiced and not bland, but just something like a positive produced by two negatives, which might best be expressed in the term "absence of prodigality." This by no means excluded, upon one's entering the inner rooms, a feeling for beauty, or indeed of coziness, which was everywhere in evidence. Choice prints hung framed on the walls; the window beside Lindner's desk was adorned with a colorful showpiece of glass representing a knight who, with a prim gesture, was liberating a maiden from a dragon; and in the choice of several painted vases that held lovely paper flowers, in the provision of an ashtray by the nonsmoker, as well as in the many trifling details through which, as it were, a ray of sunshine falls into the serious circle of duty represented by the preservation and care of a household, Lindner had gladly allowed a liberal taste to prevail. Still, the twelve-edged severity of the room's shape emerged everywhere as a reminder of the hardness of life, which one should not forget even in amenity; and wherever something stemming from earlier times that was undisciplined in a feminine way managed to break through this unity—a little cross-stitch table scarf, a pillow with roses, or the petticoat of a lampshade—the unity was strong enough to prevent the voluptuous element from being excessively obtrusive.

Nevertheless, on this day, and not for the first time since the day before, Lindner appeared at mealtime nearly a quarter of an hour late. The table was set; the plates, three high at each place, looked at him with the frank glance of reproach; the little glass knife rests, from which knife, spoon, and fork stared like barrels from gun carriages, and the rolled-up napkins in their rings, were deployed like an army left in the lurch by its general. Lindner had hastily stuffed the mail, which he usually opened before the meal, in his pocket, and with a bad conscience hastened into the dining room, not knowing in his confusion what he was meeting with there—it might well have been something like mistrust, since at the same moment, from the other side, and just as hastily as he, his son, Peter, entered as if he had only been waiting for his father to come in.

43

THE DO-GOODER AND THE DO-NO-GOODER; BUT AGATHE TOO

Peter was a quite presentable fellow of about seventeen, in whom Lindner's precipitous height had been infused and curtailed by a broadened body; he came up only as far as his father's shoulders, but his head, which was like a large, squarish-round bowling ball, sat on a neck of taut flesh whose circumference would have served for one of Papa's thighs. Peter had tarried on the soccer field instead of in school and had on the way home unfortunately got into conversation with a girl, from whom his manly beauty had wrung a half-promise to see him again: thus late, he had secretly slunk into the house and to the door of the dining room, uncertain to the last minute how he was going to excuse himself; but to his surprise he had heard no one in the room, had rushed in, and, just on the point of assuming the bored expression of long waiting, was extremely embarrassed when he collided with his father. His red face flushed with still redder spots, and he immediately let loose an enormous flood of words, casting sidelong glances at his father when he thought he wasn't noticing, while looking him fearlessly in the eye when he felt his father's eyes on him. This was calculated behavior, and often called upon: its purpose was to fulfill the mission of arousing the impression of a young man who was vacant and slack to the point of idiocy and who would be capable of anything with the one exception of hiding something. But if that wasn't enough, Peter did not recoil from letting slip, apparently inadvertently, words disrespectful of his father or otherwise displeasing to him, which then had the effect of lightning rods attracting electricity and diverting it from dangerous paths. For Peter feared his father the way hell fears heaven, with the awe of stewing flesh upon which the spirit gazes down. He loved soccer, but even there he preferred to watch it with an expert expression and make portentous comments than to strain himself by playing. He wanted to become a pilot and achieve heroic feats someday; he did not, however, imagine this as a goal to be worked toward but as a personal disposition, like creatures whose natural attribute it is that they will one day be able to fly. Nor did it influence him that his lack of inclination for work was in contradiction to the teachings of school: this son of a well-known pedagogue was not in the least interested in being respected by his teachers; it was enough for him to be physically the strongest in his class, and if one of his fellow pupils seemed to him too clever, he was ready to restore the balance of the relationship by a punch in the nose or stomach. As we know, one can lead a respected existence this way; but his behavior had the one disadvantage that he could not use it at home against his father; indeed, that his father should find out as little about it as possible. For faced with this spiritual authority that had brought him up and held him in gentle embrace, Peter's vehemence collapsed into wailing attempts at rebellion, which Lindner senior called the pitiable cries of the desires. Intimately exposed since childhood to the best principles, Peter had a hard time denying their truth to himself and was able to satisfy his honor and valor only with the cunning of an Indian in avoiding open verbal warfare. He too, of course, used lots of words in order to adapt to his opponent, but he never descended to the need to speak the truth, which in his view was unmanly and garrulous.

So this time, too, his assurances and grimaces bubbled forth at once, but they met with no reaction from his master. Professor Lindner had hastily made the sign of the cross over the soup and begun to eat, silent and rushed. At times, his eye rested briefly and distractedly on the part in his son's hair. On this day the part had been drawn through the thick, reddish-brown hair with comb, water, and a good deal of pomade, like a narrow-gauge railroad track through a reluctantly yielding forest thicket. Whenever Peter felt his father's glance resting on it he lowered his head so as to cover with his chin the red, screamingly beautiful tie with which his tutor was not yet acquainted. For an instant later the eye could gently widen upon making such a discovery and the mouth follow it, and words would emerge about "subjection to the slogans of clowns and fops" or "social toadiness and servile vanity," which offended Peter. But this time nothing happened, and it was only a while later, when the plates were being changed, that Lindner said kindly and vaguely—it was not even at all certain whether he was referring to the tie or whether his admonition was brought about by some unconsciously perceived sight—"People who still have to struggle a lot with their vanity should avoid anything striking in their outward appearance."

Peter took advantage of his father's unexpected absentmindedness of character to produce a story about a poor grade he was chivalrously supposed to have received because, tested after a fellow pupil, he had deliberately made himself look unprepared in order not to outshine his comrade by demonstrating the incredible demands that were simply beyond the grasp of weaker pupils.

Professor Lindner merely shook his head at this.

But when the middle course had been taken away and dessert came on the table, he began cautiously and ruminatively: "Look, it's precisely in those years when the appetites are greatest that one can win the most momentous victories over oneself, not for instance by starving oneself in an unhealthy way but through occasionally renouncing a favorite dish *after* one has eaten enough."

Peter was silent and showed no understanding of this, but his head was again vividly suffused with red up to his ears.

"It would be wrong," his father continued, troubled, "if I wanted to punish you for this poor grade, because aside from the fact that you are lying childishly, you demonstrate such a lack of the concept of moral honor that one must first make the soil tillable in order for the punishment to have an effect on it. So I'm not asking anything of you except that you understand this yourself, and I'm sure that then you'll punish yourself!"

This was the moment for Peter to point animatedly to his weak health and also to the overwork that could have caused his recent failures in school and that rendered it impossible for him to steel his character by renouncing dessert.

"The French philosopher Comte," Professor Lindner replied calmly, "was accustomed after dining, without particular inducement, to chew on a crust of dry bread instead of dessert, just to remember those who do not have even dry bread. It is an admirable trait, which reminds us that *every* exercise of abstemiousness and plainness has profound social significance!"

Peter had long had a most unfavorable impression of philosophy, but now his father added literature to his bad associations by continuing: "The writer Tolstoy, too, says that abstemiousness is the first step toward freedom. Man has many slavish desires, and in order for the struggle against all of them to be successful, one must begin with the most elemental: the craving for food, idleness, and sensual desires." Professor Lindner was accustomed to pronounce any of these three terms, which occurred often in his admonitions, as impersonally as the others; and long before Peter had been able to connect anything specific with the expression "sensual desires" he had already been introduced to the struggle against them, alongside the struggles against idleness and the craving for food, without thinking about them any more than his father, who had no need to think further about them because he was certain that basic instruction in these struggles begins with self-determination. In this fashion it came about that on a day when Peter did not yet know sensual longing in its most desired form but was already slinking about its skirts, he was surprised for the first time by a sudden feeling of angry revulsion against the loveless connection between it and idleness and the craving for food that his father was accustomed to make; he was not allowed to come straight out with this but had to lie, and cried: "I'm a plain and simple person and can't compare myself with writers and philosophers!"—whereby, in spite of his agitation, he did not choose his words without reflection.

His tutor did not respond.

"I'm hungry!" Peter added, still more passionately.

Lindner put on a pained and scornful smile.

"I'll die if I don't get enough to eat!" Peter was almost blubbering.

"The first response of the individual to all interventions and attacks from without occurs through the instrument of the voice!" his father instructed him.

And the "pitiable cries of the desires," as Lindner called them, died away. On this particularly manly day Peter did not want to cry, but the necessity of developing the spirit for voluble verbal defense was a terrible burden to him. He could not think of anything more at all to say, and at this moment he even hated the lie because one had to speak in order to use it. Eagerness for murder alternated in his eyes with howls of complaint. When it had got to this point, Professor Lindner said to him kindly: "You must impose on yourself serious exercises in being silent, so that it is not the careless and ignorant person in you who speaks but the reflective and well-brought-up one, who utters words that bring joy and firmness!" And then, with a friendly expression, he lapsed into reflection. "I have no better advice, if one wants to make others good"—he finally revealed to his son the conclusion he had come to—"than to be good oneself; Matthias Claudius says too: 'I can't think of any other way except by being oneself the way one wants children to be'!" And with these words Professor Lindner amiably but decisively pushed away the dessert, although it was his favorite—rice pudding with sugar and chocolate—without touching it, through such loving inexorability forcing his son, who was gnashing his teeth, to do the same.

At this moment the housekeeper came in to report that Agathe was there. August Lindner straightened up in confusion. "So she did come!" a horribly distinct mute voice said to him. He was prepared to feel indignant, but he was also ready to feel a fraternal gentleness that combined in sympathetic understanding with a delicate sense of moral action, and these two countercurrents, with an enormous train of principles, staged a wild chase through his entire body before he was able to utter the simple command to show the lady into the living room. "You wait for me here!" he said to Peter severely, and hastily left. But Peter had noticed something unusual about his father's behavior, he just didn't know what; in any event, it gave him so much rash courage that after the latter's departure, and a brief hesitation, he scooped into his mouth a spoonful of the chocolate that was standing ready to be sprinkled, then a spoonful of sugar, and finally a big spoonful of pudding, chocolate, and sugar, a procedure he repeated several times before smoothing out all the dishes to cover his tracks.

And Agathe sat for a while alone in the strange house and waited for Professor Lindner; for he was pacing back and forth in another room, collecting his thoughts before going to encounter the lovely and perilous female. She looked around and suddenly felt anxious, as if she had lost her way climbing among the branches of a dream tree and had to fear not being able to escape in one piece from its world of contorted wood and myriad leaves. A profusion of details confused her, and in the paltry taste they evinced there was a repellent acerbity intertwined in the most remarkable way with an opposite quality, for which, in her agitation, she could not immediately find words. The repulsion was perhaps reminiscent of the frozen stiffness of chalk drawings, but the room also looked as if it might smell in a grandmotherly, cloying way of medicines and ointments; and old-fashioned and unmanly ghosts, fixated with unpleasant maliciousness upon human suffering, were hovering within its walls. Agathe sniffed. And although the air held nothing more than her imaginings, she gradually found herself being led further and further backward by her feelings, until she remembered the rather anxious "smell of heaven," that aroma of incense half aired and emptied of its spices which clung to the scarves of the habits her teachers had once worn when she was a girl being brought up together with little friends in a pious convent school without at all succumbing to piety herself. For as edifying as this odor may be for people who associate it with what is right, its effect on the hearts of growing, worldly-oriented, and resistant girls consisted in a vivid memory of smells of protest, just as ideas and first experiences were associated with a man's mustache or with his energetic cheeks, pungent with cologne and dusted with talc. God knows, even that odor does not deliver what it promises! And as Agathe sat on one of Lindner's renunciative upholstered chairs and waited, the empty smell of the world closed inescapably about her with the empty smell of heaven like two hollow hemi-spheres, and an intimation came over her that she was about to make up for a negligently endured class in the school of life.

She knew now where she was. Afraid yet ready, she tried to adapt to these surroundings and think of the teachings from which she had perhaps let herself be diverted too soon. But her heart reared up at this docility like a horse that refuses to respond to encouragement, and began to run wild with terror, as happens in the presence of feelings that would like to warn the understanding but can't find any words. Nevertheless, after a while she tried again, and in support thought of her father, who had been a liberal man and had always exhibited a somewhat superficial Enlightenment style and yet, in total contradiction, had made up his mind to send her to a convent school for her education. She was inclined to regard this as a kind of conciliatory sacrifice, an attempt, propelled by a secret insecurity, to do for once the opposite of what one thinks is one's firm conviction: and because she felt a kinship with any kind of inconsistency, the situation into which she had got herself seemed to her for an instant like a daughter's secret, unconscious act of repetition. But even this second, voluntarily encouraged shudder of piety did not last; apparently she had definitively lost her ability to anchor her animated imaginings in a creed when she had been placed under that all-too-clerical care: for all she had to do was inspect her present surroundings again, and with that cruel instinct youth has for the distance separating the infinitude of a teaching from the finiteness of the teacher, which indeed easily leads one to deduce the master from the servant, the sight of the home surrounding her, in which she had imprisoned herself and settled full of expectation, suddenly and irre-sistibly impelled her to laughter.

Yet she unconsciously dug her nails into the wood of the chair, for she was ashamed of her lack of resolution. What she most wanted to do was suddenly and as quickly as possible fling into the face of this unknown man everything that was oppressing her, if he would only finally deign to show himself: The criminal trafficking with her father's will—absolutely unpardonable, if one regarded it undefiantly. Hagauer's letters, distorting her image as horribly as a bad mirror without her being quite able to deny the likeness. Then, too, that she wanted to destroy this husband without actually killing him; that she had indeed once married him, but not really, only blinded by self-contempt. There were in her life nothing but unusual incompletions; and finally, bringing everything together, she would also have to talk about the presentiment that hovered between herself and Ulrich, and this she could never betray, under any circumstances! She felt as churlish as a child who is constantly expected to perform a task that is too difficult. Why was the light she sometimes glimpsed always immediately extinguished again, like a lantern bobbing through a vast darkness, its gleam alternately swallowed up and exposed? She was robbed of all resolution, and superfluously remembered that Ulrich had once said that whoever seeks this light has to cross an abyss that has no bottom and no bridge. Did he himself, therefore, in his inmost soul, not believe in the possibility of what it was they were seeking together? This was what she was thinking, and although she did not really dare to doubt, she still felt herself deeply shaken. So no one could help her except the abyss itself! This abyss was God: oh, what did she know! With aversion and contempt she examined the tiny bridge that was supposed to lead across, the humility of the room, the pictures hung piously on the walls, everything feigning a confidential relationship with Him. She was just as close to abasing herself as she was to turning away in horror. What she would probably most have liked to do was run away once more; but when she remembered that she always ran away she thought of Ulrich again and seemed to herself "a terrible coward." The silence at home had been like the calm before a storm, and the pressure of what was approaching had catapulted her here. This was the way she saw it now, not without quite suppressing a smile; and it was also natural that something else Ulrich had said should occur to her, for he had said at some time or other: "A person never finds himself a total coward, because if something frightens him he runs just far enough away to consider himself a hero again!" And so here she sat!

44

A MIGHTY DISCUSSION

At this moment Lindner entered, having made up his mind to say as much as his visitor would; but once they found themselves face-to-face, things turned out differently. Agathe immediately went on the verbal attack, which to her surprise turned out to be far more ordinary than what led up to it would have indicated.

"You will of course recall that I asked you to explain some things to me," she began. "Now I'm here. I still remember quite well what you said against my getting a divorce. Perhaps I've understood it even better since!"

They were sitting at a large round table, separated from each other by the entire span of its diameter. In relation to her final moments alone Agathe first felt herself, at the very beginning of this encounter, deep under water, but then on solid ground; she laid out the word "divorce" like a bait, although her curiosity to learn Lindner's opinion was genuine too.

And Lindner actually answered at almost the same instant: "I know quite well why you are asking me for this explanation. People will have been murmuring to you your whole life long that a belief in the suprahuman, and obeying commandments that have their origin in this belief, belong to the Middle Ages! You have discovered that such fairy tales have been disposed of by science! But are you certain that's really the way it is?"

Agathe noticed to her astonishment that at every third word or so, his lips puffed out like two assailants beneath his scanty beard. She gave no answer.

"Have you thought about it?" Lindner continued severely. "Do you know the vast number of problems it involves? It's clear you don't! But you have a magnificent way of dismissing this with a wave of your hand, and you apparently don't even realize that you're simply acting under the influence of an external compulsion!"

He had plunged into danger. It was not clear what murmurers he had in mind. He felt himself carried away. His speech was a long tunnel he had bored right through a mountain in order to fall upon an idea, "lies of freethinking men," which was sparkling on the other side in a cocksure light. He was not thinking of either Ulrich or Hagauer but meant both of them, meant everyone. "And even if you had thought about it"—he exclaimed in an assertively rising voice— "and were to be convinced of these mistaken doctrines that the body is nothing but a system of dead corpuscles, and the soul an interplay of glands, and society a ragbag of mechano-economic laws; and even if that were correct—which it is far from being—I would still deny that such a way of thinking knows anything about the truth of life! For what calls itself science doesn't have the slightest qualification to explicate by externals what lives within a human being as spiritual inner certainty. Life's truth is a knowledge with no beginning, and the facts of true life are not communicated by rational proof: who-ever lives and suffers has them within himself as the secret power of higher claims and as the living explanation of his self!"

Lindner had stood up. His eyes sparkled like two preachers in the high pulpit formed by his long legs. He looked down on Agathe om-nipotently.

"Why is he talking so much right away?" she thought. "And what does he have against Ulrich? He hardly knows him, and yet he speaks against him openly." Then her feminine experience in the arousal of feelings told her more quickly and certainly than reflection would have done that Lindner was speaking this way only because, in some ridiculous fashion, he was jealous. She looked up at him with an en-chanting smile.

He stood before her tall, waveringly supple, and armed, and seemed to her like a bellicose giant grasshopper from some past geo-logic age. "Good heavens!" she thought. "Now I'm going to say something that will annoy him all over again, and he'll chase after me again with his Where am I? What game am I playing?" It confused her that Lindner irritated her to the point of laughter and yet that she was not able to shrug off some of his individual expressions, like "knowledge with no beginning" or "living explanation"; such strange terms at present, but secretly familiar to her, as if she had always used them herself without being able to remember ever having heard them before. She thought: "It's gruesome, but he's already planted some of his words in my heart like children!"

Lindner was aware of having made an impression on her, and this satisfaction conciliated him somewhat. He saw before him a young woman in whom agitation seemed to alternate precariously with feigned indifference, even boldness; since he took himself for a scrupulous expert on the female soul, he did not allow himself to be put off by this, knowing as he did that in beautiful women there was an inordinately great temptation to be arrogant and vain. He could hardly ever observe a beautiful face without an admixture of pity. People so marked were, he was convinced, almost always martyrs to their shining outward aspect, which seduced them to self-conceit and its dragging train of coldheartedness and superficiality. Still, it can also happen that a soul dwells behind a beautiful countenance, and how often has insecurity not taken refuge behind arrogance, or despair beneath frivolity! Often, indeed, this is true of particularly noble people, who are merely lacking the support of proper and unshakable convictions. And now Lindner was gradually and completely overcome once more with how the successful person has to put himself in the frame of mind of the slighted one; and as he did this he became aware that the form of Agathe's face and body possessed that delightful repose unique to the great and noble; even her knee seemed to him, in the folds of its covering envelope, like the knee of Niobe. He was astonished that this specific image should force itself on him, since so far as he knew there was nothing in the least appropriate about it; but apparently the nobility of his moral pain had unilaterally come together in this image with the suspiciousness many children have, for he felt no less attracted than alarmed. He now noticed her breast too, which was breathing in small, rapid waves. He felt hot and bothered, and if his knowledge of the world had not come to his aid again he would even have felt at a loss; but at this moment of greatest captiousness it whispered to him that this bosom must enclose something unspoken, and that according to all he knew, this secret might well be connected with the divorce from his colleague Hagauer; and this saved him from embarrassing foolishness by instantaneously offering the possibility of desiring the revelation of this secret instead of the bosom. He desired this with all his might, while the union of sin with the chivalric slaying of the dragon of sin hovered before his eyes in glowing colors, much as they glowed in the stained glass in his study.

Agathe interrupted this rumination with a question she addressed to him in a temperate, even restrained tone, after she had regained her composure. "You claimed that I was acting on insinuations, on external compulsion; what did you mean by that?"

Disconcerted, Lindner raised the glance that had been resting on her heart to her eyes. This had never happened to him before: he could no longer remember the last thing he had said. He had seen in this young woman a victim of the free-minded spirit that was confusing the age, and in his victorious joy had forgotten it.

Agathe repeated her question slightly differently: "I confided to you that I want a divorce from Professor Hagauer, and you replied that I was acting under insinuating influences. It might be useful to me to find out what you understand by them. I repeat, none of the customary reasons is entirely apt; even my aversion has not been insurmountable, as the standards of the world go. I am merely convinced that they may not be surmounted but are to be immeasurably enlarged!"

"By whom?"

"That's just the problem you're supposed to help me solve." She again looked at him with a gentle smile that was a kind of horribly deep décolleté and that exposed her inner bosom as if it were covered by a mere wisp of black lace.

Lindner involuntarily protected his eyes from the sight with a motion of his hand feigning some adjustment to his glasses. The truth was that courage played the same timid role in his view of the world as it did in the feelings he harbored toward Agathe. He was one of those people who have recognized that it greatly facilitates the victory of humility if one first flattens arrogance with a blow of one's fist, and his learned nature bade him fear no arrogance so bitterly as that of open-minded science, which reproaches faith with being unscientific. Had someone told him that the saints, with their empty and beseeching raised hands, were outmoded and in today's world would have to be portrayed grasping sabers, pistols, or even newer instruments in their fists, he would no doubt have been appalled; but he did not want to see the arms of knowledge withheld from faith. This was almost entirely an error, but he was not alone in committing it; and that was why he had assailed Agathe with words that would have merited an honorable place in his writings—and presumably did—but were out of place directed to the woman who was confiding in him. Since he now saw sitting modestly and reflectively before him the emissary of quarters of the world hostile to him, delivered into his hands by a benevolent or demonic fate, he felt this himself and was embarrassed how to respond. "Ah!" he said, as generally and disparagingly as possible, and accidentally hitting not far from the mark: "I meant the spirit that runs everything today and makes young people afraid they might look stupid, even unscientific, if they don't go along with every modern superstition. How should I know what slogans are in their minds: 'Live life to the full!' 'Say yes to life!' 'Cultivate your personality!' 'Freedom of thought and art!' In any case, everything but the commandments of simple and eternal morality."

The happy intensification "stupid, even unscientific" gladdened him with its subtlety and reinvigorated his combative spirit. "You will be surprised," he continued, "that in conversing with you I am placing such emphasis on science, without knowing whether you have occupied yourself with it a little or a lot—"

"Not at all!" Agathe interrupted him. "I'm just an ignorant woman." She emphasized it and seemed to be pleased with it, perhaps with a kind of nonsanctimoniousness.

"But it's the world you move in!" Lindner corrected her emphatically. "And whether it's freedom in values or freedom in science, they both express the same thing: spirit that has been detached from morality."

Agathe again felt these words as sober shadows that were, however, cast by something still darker in their vicinity. She was not minded to conceal her disappointment, but revealed it with a laugh: "Last time, you advised me not to think about myself, and now you're the one who is talking about me incessantly," she mockingly offered for the man standing before her to think about.

He repeated: "You're afraid of seeming old-fashioned to yourself!"

Something in Agathe's eyes twitched angrily. "You leave me speechless: this certainly doesn't apply to me!"

"And I say to you: 'You have been bought dear; do not become the servants of man!' " The way he said this, which was in total contrast to his entire physical appearance, like a too-heavy blossom on a weak stem, made Agathe brighten. She asked urgently and almost coarsely: "So what should I do? I was hoping you would give me a definite answer!"

Lindner swallowed and turned gloomy with earnestness. "Do what is your duty!"

"I don't know what my duty is!"

"Then you must seek duties out!"

"I don't know what duties are!"

Lindner smiled grimly. "There we have it! That's the liberation of the personality!" he exclaimed. "Vain reflection! You can see it in yourself: when a person is free he is unhappy! When a person is free he's a phantom!" he added, raising his voice somewhat more, out of embarrassment. But then he lowered it again, and concluded with conviction: "Duty is what mankind in proper self-awareness has erected against its own weakness. Duty is one and the same truth that all great personalities have acknowledged or pointed to. Duty is the work of the experience of centuries and the result of the visionary glance of the blessed. But what even the simplest person knows with precision in his inmost being, if only he lives an upright life, is duty too!"

"That was a hymn with quivering candles!" Agathe noted appreciatively.

It was disagreeable that Lindner, too, felt that he had sung falsely. He ought to have said something else but didn't trust himself to recognize in what the deviation from the genuine voice of his heart consisted. He merely allowed himself the thought that this young creature must be deeply disappointed by her husband, since she was raging so impudently and bitterly against herself, and that in spite of all the censure she provoked, she would have been worthy of a stronger man; but he had the impression that a far more dangerous idea was on the point of succeeding this one. Agathe, meanwhile, slowly and very decisively shook her head; and with the spontaneous assurance with which an excited person is seduced by another into doing something that unbalances an already precarious situation completely, she continued: "But we're talking about my divorce! And why aren't you saying anything more about God today? Why don't you simply say to me: 'God orders you to stay with Professor Hagauer!' I can't honestly imagine that He would command such a thing!"

Lindner shrugged his tall shoulders indignantly; indeed, as they rose he himself actually seemed to hover in the air. "I have never said a word to you about it; you're the only one who has tried to!" He defended himself gruffly. "And for the rest, don't believe for a minute that God bothers Himself with the tiny egoistic antics of our emotions! That's what His law is for, which we must follow! Or doesn't that seem heroic enough for you, since people today are always looking for what's 'personal'? Well, in that case I'll set a higher heroism against your claims: heroic submission!"

Every word of this carried significantly more weight than a layperson really ought to permit himself, were it only in his thoughts; Agathe, in return, could only go on smiling in the face of such coarse derision if she did not want to be forced to stand up and break off the visit; and she smiled, of course, with such assured adroitness that Lindner felt himself goaded into ever-greater confusion. He became aware that his inspirations were ominously rising and increasingly reinforcing a glowing intoxication that was robbing him of reflection and resounded with the will to break the obstinate mind and perhaps save the soul he saw facing him. "Our duty is painful!" he exclaimed. "Our duty may be repulsive and disgusting! Don't think I have any intention of becoming your husband's lawyer, or that my nature is to stand by his side. But you must obey the law, because it is the only thing that bestows lasting peace on us and protects us from ourselves!"

Agathe now laughed at him; she had guessed at the weapon, stemming from her divorce, that these effects put in her hand, and she turned the knife in the wound. "I understand so little about all that," she said. "But may I honestly confess an impression I have? When you're angry you get a little slippery!"

"Oh, come on!" Lindner retorted. He recoiled, his one desire not to concede such a thing at any price. He raised his voice defensively and entreated the sinning phantom sitting before him: "The spirit must not submit itself to the flesh and all its charms and horrors! Not even in the form of disgust! And I say to you: Even though you might find it painful to control the reluctance of the flesh, as the school of marriage has apparently asked of you, you are not simply permitted to run away from it. For there lives in man a desire for liberation, and we can no more be the slaves of our fleshly disgust than the slaves of our lust! This is obviously what you wanted to hear, since otherwise you would not have come to me!" he concluded, no less grandiloquently than spitefully. He stood towering before Agathe; the strands of his beard moved around his lips. He had never spoken such words to a woman before, with the exception of his own deceased wife, and his feelings toward her had been different. But now these feelings were intermingled with desire, as if he were swinging a whip in his fist to chastise the whole earth; yet they were simultaneously timid, as if he were being lofted like an escaped hat on the crest of the tornado of the sermon of repentance that had taken hold of him.

"There you go again, saying such remarkable things!" Agathe noted without passion, intending to shut off his insolence with a few dry words; but then she measured the enormous crash looming up before him and preferred to humble herself gently by holding back, so she continued, in a voice that had apparently suddenly been darkened by repentance: "I came only because I wanted you to lead me."

Lindner went on swinging his whip of words with confused zeal; he had some sense that Agathe was deliberately leading him on, but he could not find a way out, and entrusted himself to the future. "To be chained to a man for a lifetime without feeling any physical attraction is certainly a heavy sentence," he exclaimed. "But hasn't one brought this on oneself, especially if the partner is unworthy, by not having paid enough attention to the signs of the inner life? There are many women who allow themselves to be deluded by external circumstances, and who knows if one is not being punished in order to be shaken up?" Suddenly his voice cracked. Agathe had been accompanying his words with assenting nods of her head; but imagining Hagauer as a bewitching seducer was too much for her, and her merry eyes betrayed it. Lindner, driven crazy by this, blared in falsetto: " 'For he that spares the rod hates his child, but whosoever loves it chastises it!' "

His victim's resistance had now transformed this philosopher of life, dwelling in his lofty watchtower, into a poet of chastisement and the exciting conditions that went with it. He was intoxicated by a feeling he did not recognize, which emanated from an inner fusion of the moral reprimand with which he was goading his visitor and a provocation of all his manliness, a fusion that one might symbolically characterize, as he himself now saw, as lustful.

But the "arrogant conquering female," who was finally to have been driven from the empty vanity of her worldly beauty to despair, matter-of-factly picked up on his threats about the rod and quietly asked: "Who is going to punish me? Whom are you thinking of? Are you thinking of God?"

But it was unthinkable to say such a thing! Lindner suddenly lost his courage. His scalp prickled with sweat. It was absolutely impossible that the name of God should be uttered in such a context. His glance, extended like a two-tined fork, slowly withdrew from Agathe. Agathe felt it. "So he can't do it either!" she thought. She felt a reckless desire to go on tugging at this man until she heard from his mouth what he did not want to yield to her. But for now it was enough: the conversation had reached its outer limit. Agathe understood that it had only been a passionate rhetorical subterfuge, heated to the point where it became transparent, and all to avoid mentioning the decisive point. Besides, Lindner, too, now knew that everything he had said, indeed everything that had got him worked up, even the excess itself, was only the product of his fear of excesses; the most dissolute aspect of which he considered to be the approach with the prying tools of mind and feeling to what ought to remain veiled in lofty abstractions, toward which this excessive young woman was obviously pushing him. He now named this to himself as "an offense against the decency of faith." For in these moments the blood drained back out of Lindner's head and resumed its normal course; he awoke like a person who finds himself standing naked far from his front door, and remembered that he could not send Agathe away without consolation and instruction. Breathing deeply, he stood back from her, stroked his beard, and said reproachfully: "You have a restless and overimaginative nature!"

"And you have a peculiar idea of gallantry!" Agathe responded coolly, for she had no desire to go on any longer.

Lindner found it necessary to repair his standing by saying something more: "You should learn in the school of reality to take your subjectivity mercilessly in hand, for whoever is incapable of it will be overtaken by imagination and fantasy, and dragged to the ground . . . !" He paused, for this strange woman was still drawing the voice from his breast quite against his will. "Woe to him who abandons morality; he is abandoning reality!" he added softly.

Agathe shrugged her shoulders. "I hope next time you will come to us!" she proposed.

"To that I must respond: Never!" Lindner protested, suddenly and now totally down to earth. "Your brother and I have differences of opinion about life that make it preferable for us to avoid contact," he added as excuse.

"So I'm the one who will have to come studiously to the school of reality," Agathe replied quietly.

"No!" Lindner insisted, but then in a remarkable fashion, almost menacingly, he blocked her path; for with those words she had got up to go. "That cannot be! You cannot put me in the ambiguous position toward my colleague Hagauer of receiving your visits without his knowledge!"

"Are you always as passionate as you are today?" Agathe asked mockingly, thereby forcing him to make way for her. She now felt, at the end, spiritless but strengthened. The fear Lindner had betrayed drew her toward actions alien to her true condition; but while the demands her brother made demoralized her easily, this man gave her back the freedom to animate her inner self however she wanted, and it comforted her to confuse him.

"Did I perhaps compromise myself a little?" Lindner asked himself after she had left. He stiffened his shoulders and marched up and down the room a few times. Finally he decided to continue seeing her, containing his malaise, which was quite pronounced, in the soldierly words: "One must set oneself to remain gallant in the face of every embarrassment!"

When Agathe got up to leave, Peter had slipped hurriedly away from the keyhole, where he had been listening, not without astonishment, to what his father had been up to with the "big goose."

45

BEGINNING OF A SERIES OF
WONDROUS EXPERIENCES

Shortly after this visit there was a repetition of the "impossible" that was already hovering almost physically around Agathe and Ulrich, and it truly came to pass without anything at all actually happening.

Brother and sister were changing to go out for the evening. There was no one in the house to help Agathe aside from Ulrich; they had started late and had thus been in the greatest haste for a quarter of an hour, when a short pause intervened. Piece by piece, nearly all the ornaments of war a woman puts on for such occasions were strewn on the chair backs and surfaces of the room, and Agathe was in the act of bending over her foot with all the concentration that pulling on a thin silk stocking demands. Ulrich was standing at her back. He saw her head, her neck, her shoulders, and this nearly naked back; her body was curved over her raised knee, slightly to one side, and the tension of this process rounded three folds on her neck, which shot slender and merry through her clear skin like three arrows: the charming physicality of this painting, born of the momentarily spreading stillness, seemed to have lost its frame and passed so abruptly and directly into Ulrich's body that he moved from the spot and, neither with the involuntariness of a banner being unfurled by the wind nor exactly with deliberate reflection, crept closer on tiptoe, surprised the bent-over figure, and with gentle ferocity bit into one of these arrows, while his arm closed tightly around his sister. Then Ulrich's teeth just as cautiously released his overpowered victim; his right hand had grabbed her knee, and while with his left arm he pressed her body to his, he pulled her upright with him on upward-bounding tendons. Agathe cried out in fright.

Up to this point everything had taken place as playfully and jokingly as much that had gone on before, and even if it was tinged with the colors of love, it was only with the actually shy intention of concealing love's unwonted dangerous nature beneath such cheerfully intimate dress. But when Agathe got over her fright, and felt herself not so much flying through the air as rather resting in it, suddenly liberated into weightlessness and directed instead by the gentle force of the gradually decelerating motion, it brought about one of those accidents beyond human control, in which she seemed to herself strangely soothed, indeed carried away from all earthly unrest; with a movement changing the balance of her body that she could never have repeated, she also brushed away the last silken thread of compulsion, turned in falling to her brother, continued, so to speak, her rise as she fell, until she lay, sinking down, as a cloud of happiness in his arms. Ulrich bore her, gently pressing her body to his, through the darkening room to the window and placed her beside him in the mellow light of the evening, which flowed over her face like tears. Despite the energy everything demanded, and the force Ulrich had exercised on his sister, what they were doing seemed to them remarkably remote from energy and force; one might perhaps have been able, again, to compare it with the wondrous ardor of a painting, which for the hand that invades the frame to grasp it is nothing but a ridiculous painted surface. So, too, they had nothing in mind beyond what was taking place physically, which totally filled their consciousness; and yet, alongside its nature as a harmless, indeed, at the beginning, even coarse joke, which called all their muscles into play, this physical action possessed a second nature, which, with the greatest tenderness, paralyzed their limbs and at the same time ensnared them with an inexpressible sensitivity. Questioningly they flung their arms around each other's shoulders. The fraternal stature of their bodies communicated itself to them as if they were rising up from a single root. They looked into each other's eyes with as much curiosity as if they were seeing such things for the first time. And although they would not have been able to articulate what had really happened, since their part in it had been too pressing, they still believed they knew that they had just unexpectedly found themselves for an instant in the midst of that shared condition at whose border they had long been hesitating, which they had already described to each other so often but had so far only gazed at from outside.

If they tested it soberly (and surreptitiously they both did), it signified hardly more than a bewitching accident and ought to have dissolved the next moment, or at least with the return of activity, into nothingness; and yet this did not happen. On the contrary, they left the window, turned on the lights, and resumed their preparations, only soon to relinquish them again, and without their having to say anything to each other, Ulrich went to the telephone and informed the house where they were expected that they were not coming. He was already dressed for the evening, but Agathe's gown was still hanging unfastened around her shoulders and she was just striving to impart some well-bred order to her hair. The technical resonance of his voice in the instrument and the connection to the world that had been established had not sobered Ulrich in the slightest: he sat down opposite his sister, who paused in what she was doing, and when their glances met, nothing was so certain as that the decision had been made and all prohibitions were now a matter of indifference to them. Their understanding announced itself to them with every breath; it was a defiantly endured agreement to finally redeem themselves from the ill humor of longing, and it was an agreement so sweetly suffered that the notions of making it a reality nearly tore themselves loose from them and united them already in imagination, as a storm whips a veil of foam on ahead of the waves: but a still greater desire bade them be calm, and they were incapable of touching each other again. They wanted to begin, but the gestures of the flesh had become impossible for them, and they felt an ineffable warning that had nothing to do with the commandments of morality. It seemed that from a more perfect, if still shadowy, union, of which they had already had a foretaste as in an ecstatic metaphor, a higher commandment had marked them out, a higher intimation, curiosity, or expectation had breathed upon them.

Brother and sister now remained perplexed and thoughtful, and after they had calmed their feelings they hesitantly began to speak.

Ulrich said, without thinking, the way one talks into thin air: "You are the moon—"

Agathe understood.

Ulrich said: "You have flown to the moon and it has given you back to me again—"

Agathe said nothing: moon conversations so consume one's whole heart.

Ulrich said: "It's a figure of speech. 'We were beside ourselves,' 'We exchanged bodies without even touching each other,' are metaphors too! But what does a metaphor signify? A little something true with a good deal of exaggeration. And yet I was about to swear, impossible as it may be, that the exaggeration was quite small and the reality was becoming quite large!"

He said no more. He was thinking: "What reality am I talking about? Is there a second one?"

If one here leaves the conversation between brother and sister in order to follow the possibilities of a comparison that had at least some part in determining their talk, it might well be said that this reality was truly most closely related to the quixotically altered reality of moonlit nights. But if one does not comprehend this reality either, if one sees in it merely an opportunity for some ecstatic foolishness that by day were better suppressed, then if one wanted to picture accurately what was actually happening one would have to summon up the totally incredible idea that there's a piece of earth where all feelings really do change like magic as soon as the empty busyness of day plunges into the all-experiencing corporeality of night! Not only do external relationships melt away and re-form in the whispering enclosures of light and shadow, but the inner relationships, too, move closer together in a new way: the spoken word loses its self-will and acquires fraternal will. All affirmations express only a single surging experience. The night embraces all contradictions in its shimmering maternal arms, and in its bosom no word is false and no word true, but each is that incomparable birth of the spirit out of darkness that a person experiences in a new thought. In this way, every process on moonlit nights partakes of the nature of the unrepeatable. Of the nature of the intensified. Of the nature of selfless generosity and a stripping away of the self. Every imparting is a parting without envy. Every giving a receiving. Every conception multifariously interwoven in the excitement of the night. To be this way is the only access to the knowledge of what is unfolding. For in these nights the self holds nothing back; there is no condensation of possession on the self's surface, hardly a memory; the intensified self radiates into an unbounded selflessness. And these nights are filled with the insane feeling that something is about to happen that has never happened before, indeed that the impoverished reason of day can not even conceive of. And it is not the mouth that pours out its adoration but the body, which, from head to foot, is stretched taut in exaltation above the darkness of the earth and beneath the light of the heavens, oscillating between two stars. And the whispering with one's companion is full of a quite unknown sensuality, which is not the sensuality of an individual human being but of all that is earthly, of all that penetrates perception and sensation, the suddenly revealed tenderness of the world that incessantly touches all our senses and is touched by them.

Ulrich had indeed never been aware in himself of a particular preference for mouthing adorations in the moonlight; but as one ordinarily gulps life down without feeling, one sometimes has, much later, its ghostly taste on one's tongue: and in this way he suddenly felt everything he had missed in that effusiveness, all those nights he had spent heedless and lonely before he had known his sister, as silver poured over an endless thicket, as moon flecks in the grass, as laden apple trees, singing frost, and gilded black waters. These were only details, which did not coalesce and had never found an association, but which now arose like the commingled fragrance of many herbs from an intoxicating potion. And when he said this to Agathe she felt it too.

Ulrich finally summed up everything he had said with the assertion: "What made us turn to each other from the very beginning can really be called a life of moonlit nights!" And Agathe breathed a deep sigh of relief. It did not matter what it meant; evidently it meant: and why don't you know a magic charm against its separating us at the last moment? She sighed so naturally and confidingly that she was not even aware of it herself.

And this again led to a movement that inclined them toward each other and kept them apart. Every strong excitement that two people have shared to the end leaves behind in them the naked intimacy of exhaustion; if even arguing does this, then it is infinitely more true of tender feelings that ream out the very marrow to form a flute! So Ulrich, touched, would have almost embraced Agathe when he heard her wordless complaint, as enchanted as a lover on the morning after the first tempests. His hand was already touching her shoulder, which was still bare, and at this touch she started, smiling; but in her eyes there reappeared immediately the unwished-for dissuasion. Strange images now arose in his mind: Agathe behind bars. Or fearfully motioning to him from a growing distance, torn from him by the sundering power of alien fists. Then again he was not only the one

who was powerless and dismissed, but also the one who did this.
. . . Perhaps these were the eternal images of the doubts of love,
merely consumed in the average life; then again, perhaps not. He
would have liked to speak to her about this, but Agathe now looked
away from him and toward the open window, and hesitantly stood
up. The fever of love was in their bodies, but their bodies dared no
repetition, and what was beyond the window, whose drapes stood
almost open, had stolen away their imagination, without which the
flesh is only brutal or despondent. When Agathe took the first steps
in this direction, Ulrich, guessing her assent, turned out the light in
order to free their gaze into the night. The moon had come up behind the tops of the spruce trees, whose greenly glimmering black
stood out phlegmatically against the blue-gold heights and the palely
twinkling distance. Agathe resentfully inspected this meaningful
sliver of the world.

"So nothing more than moonshine?" she asked.

Ulrich looked at her without answering. Her blond hair flamed in
the semidarkness against the whitish night, her lips were parted by
shadows, her beauty was painful and irresistible.

But evidently he was standing there in similar fashion before her
gaze, with blue eye sockets in his white face, for she went on: "Do
you know what you look like now? Like 'Pierrot Lunaire'! It calls for
prudence!" She wanted to wrong him a little in her excitement,
which almost made her weep. Ages ago, all useless young people had
appeared to each other, painfully and peevishly, in the pale mask of
the lunarly lonely Pierrot, powdered chalk-white except for the drop-
of-blood-red lips and abandoned by a Columbine they had never
possessed; this trivialized rather considerably the love for moonlit
nights. But to his sister's initially growing grief, Ulrich willingly
joined in. "Even 'Laugh, clown, laugh' has already sent a chill of total
recognition down the spines of thousands of philistines when they
hear it sung," he affirmed bitterly. But then he added softly, whispering: "This whole area of feeling really *is* highly questionable! And yet
I would give all the memories of my life for the way you look right
now." Agathe's hand had found Ulrich's. Ulrich continued softly and
passionately: "To our time, the bliss of feeling means only the glut-
tony of feelings and has profaned being swept away by the moon into
a sentimental debauch. It does not even begin to understand that this

bliss must be either an incomprehensible mental disturbance or the fragment of another life!"

These words—precisely because they were perhaps an exaggeration—had the faith, and with it the wings, of adventure. "Good night!" Agathe said unexpectedly, and took them with her. She had released herself and closed the drapes so hastily that the picture of the two of them standing in the moonlight disappeared as if at one blow; and before Ulrich could turn on the light she succeeded in finding her way out of the room.

And Ulrich gave her yet more time. "Tonight you'll sleep as impatiently as before the start of a great outing!" he called after her.

"I hope so too!" was what resounded by way of an answer in the closing of the door.

46

MOONBEAMS BY SUNLIGHT

When they saw each other again the next morning it was, from a distance, the way one stumbles on an out-of-the-ordinary picture in an ordinary house, or even the way one catches sight of an important outdoor sculpture in the full haphazardness of nature: an island of meaning unexpectedly materializes in the senses, an elevation and condensing of the spirit from the watery fens of existence! But when they came up to each other they were embarrassed, and all that was to be felt in their glances, shading them with tender warmth, was the exhaustion of the previous night.

Who knows, besides, whether love would be so admired if it did not cause fatigue! When they became aware of the unpleasant after-effects of the previous day's excitement it made them happy again, as lovers are proud of having almost died from desire. Still, the joy they found in each other was not only such a feeling but also an arousal of the eye. Colors and shapes presented themselves as dissolved and unfathomable, and yet were sharply displayed, like a bouquet of flowers drifting on dark water: their boundaries were more emphatically marked than usual, but in a way that made it impossible to say whether this lay in the clarity of their appearance or in the underlying agitation. The impression was as much part of the concise sphere of perception and attention as it was of the imprecise sphere of emotion; and this is just what caused this impression to hover between the internal and the external, the way a held breath hovers between inhalation and exhalation, and made it hard to discern, in peculiar opposition to its strength, whether it was part of the physical world or merely owed its origin to the heightening of inner empathy. Nor did either of them wish to make this distinction, for a kind of shame of reason held them back; and through the longish period that followed it also still forced them to keep their distance from each other, although their sensitivity was lasting and might well give rise to the belief that suddenly the course of the boundaries between them, as well as those between them and the world, had changed slightly.

The weather had turned summery again, and they spent a lot of time outdoors: flowers and shrubs were blooming in the garden. When Ulrich looked at a blossom—which was not exactly an ingrained habit of this once-impatient man—he now sometimes found no end to contemplation and, to say it all, no beginning either. If by chance he could name it, it was a redemption from the sea of infinity. Then the little golden stars on a bare cane signified "forsythia," and those early leaves and umbels "lilacs." But if he did not know the name he would call the gardener over, for then this old man would name an unknown name and everything was all right again, and the primordial magic by which possession of the correct name bestows protection from the untamed wildness of things demonstrated its calming power as it had ten thousand years ago. Still, it could happen differently: Ulrich could find himself abandoned and without a helper as he confronted such a little twig or flower, without even Agathe around to share his ignorance: then it suddenly seemed to him quite impossible to understand the bright green of a young leaf, and the mysteriously outlined fullness of the form of a tiny flower cup became a circle of infinite diversion that nothing could interrupt. In addition, it was hardly possible for a man like him, unless he were lying to himself, which on Agathe's account could not be allowed to happen, to believe in an abashed rendezvous with nature, whose whisperings and upward glances, piety and mute music making, are more the privilege of a special simplicity which imagines that hardly has it laid its head in the grass than God is already tickling its neck, although it has nothing against nature being bought and sold on the fruit exchange on weekdays. Ulrich despised this cut-rate mysticism of the cheapest price and praise, whose constant preoccupation with God is at bottom exceedingly immoral; he preferred instead to continue abandoning himself to the dizziness of finding the words to characterize a color distinct enough to reach out and take hold of, or to describe one of the shapes that had taken to speaking for themselves with such mindless compellingness. For in such a condition the word does not cut and the fruit remains on the branch, although one thinks it already in one's mouth: that is probably the first mystery of day-bright mysticism. And Ulrich tried to explain this to his sister, even if his ulterior motive was that it should not, someday, disappear like a delusion.

But as he did so, the passionate condition was succeeded by another—of a calmer, indeed sometimes almost absentminded conversation—which came to permeate their exchange and served each of them as a screen from the other, although they both saw through it completely. They usually lay in the garden on two large deck chairs, which they were constantly dragging around to follow the sun; this early-summer sun was shining for the millionth time on the magic it works every year; and Ulrich said many things that just happened to pass through his mind and rounded themselves off cautiously like the moon, which was now quite pale and a little dirty, or like a soap bubble: and so it happened, and quite soon, that he came round to speaking of the confounded and frequently cursed absurdity that all understanding presupposes a kind of superficiality, a penchant for the surface, which is, moreover, expressed in the root of the word "comprehend," to lay hold of, and has to do with primordial experiences having been understood not singly but one by the next and thereby unavoidably connected with one another more on the surface than in depth. He then continued: "So if I maintain that this grass in front of us is green, it sounds quite definite, but I haven't actually said much. In truth no more than if I'd told you that some man passing by was a member of the Green family. And for heaven's sake, there's no end of greens! It would be a lot better if I contented myself with recognizing that this grass is grass-green, or even green like a lawn on which it has just rained a little. . . ." He squinted languidly across the fresh plot of grass illuminated by the sun and thought: "At least this is how *you* would probably describe it, since you're good at making visual distinctions from judging dress materials. But I, on the other hand, could perhaps measure the color as well: I might guess it had a wavelength of five hundred forty millionths of a millimeter; and then this green would apparently be captured and nailed to a specific point! But then it gets away from me again, because this ground color also has something material about it that can't be expressed in words of color at all, since it's different from the same green in silk or wool. And now we're back at the profound discovery that green grass is just grass green!"

Called as a witness, Agathe found it quite understandable that one could not understand anything, and responded: "I suggest you try looking at a mirror in the night: it's dark, it's black, you see almost nothing at all; and yet this nothing is something quite distinctly different from the nothing of the rest of the darkness. You sense the glass, the doubling of depth, some kind of remnant of the ability to shimmer—and yet you perceive nothing at all!"

Ulrich laughed at his sister's immediate readiness to cut knowledge's reputation down to size; he was far from thinking that concepts have no value, and knew quite well what they accomplish, even if he did not act accordingly. What he wanted to bring out was the inability to get hold of individual experiences, those experiences that for obvious reasons one has to go through alone and lonely, even when one is with another person. He repeated: "The self never grasps its impressions and utterances singly, but always in context, in real or imagined, similar or dissimilar, harmony with something else; and so everything that has a name leans on everything else in regular rows, as a link in large and incalculable unities, one relying on another and all penetrated by a common tension. But for that reason," he suddenly went on, differently, "if for some reason these associations fail and none of them addresses the internal series of orders, one is immediately left again to face an indescribable and inhuman creation, indeed a disavowed and formless one." With this they were back at their point of departure; but Agathe felt the dark creation above it, the abyss that was the "universe," the God who was to help her!

Her brother said: "Understanding gives way to irrepressible astonishment, and the smallest experience—of this tiny blade of grass, or the gentle sounds when your lips over there utter a word—becomes something incomparable, lonely as the world, possessed of an unfathomable selfishness and radiating a profound narcosis . . . !"

He fell silent, irresolutely twisting a blade of grass in his hand, and at first listened with pleasure as Agathe, apparently as unplagued by introspection as she was by an intellectual education, restored some concreteness to the conversation. For she now responded: "If it weren't so damp, I'd love to lie on the grass! Let's go away! It would be so nice to lie on a meadow and get back to nature as simply as a discarded shoe!"

"But all that means is being released from all feelings," Ulrich objected. "And God alone knows what would become of us if feelings did not appear in swarms, these loves and hates and sufferings and goodnesses that give the illusion of being unique to every individual. We would be bereft of all capacity to think and act, because our soul was created for whatever repeats itself over and over, and not for what lies outside the order of things. . . ." He was oppressed, thought he had stumbled into emptiness, and with an uneasy frown looked questioningly at his sister's face.

But Agathe's face was even clearer than the air that enveloped it and played with her hair, as she gave a response from memory. " 'I know not where I am, nor do I seek myself, nor do I want to know of it, nor will I have tidings. I am as immersed in the flowing spring of His love as if I were under the surface of the sea and could not feel or see from any side any thing except water.' "

"Where's that from?" Ulrich asked curiously, and only then discovered that she was holding in her hands a book she had taken from his own library.

Agathe opened it for him and read aloud, without answering: " 'I have transcended all my faculties up to the dark power. There I heard without sound, saw without light. Then my heart became bottomless, my soul loveless, my mind formless, and my nature without being.' "

Ulrich now recognized the volume and smiled, and only then did

Agathe say: "It's one of your books." Then, closing the book, she concluded from memory: " 'Are you yourself, or are you not? I know nothing of this, I am unaware of it, and I am unaware of myself. I am in love, but I know not with whom; I am neither faithful nor unfaithful. Therefore what am I? I am even unaware of my love; my heart is at the same time full of love and empty of love!' "

Even in ordinary circumstances her excellent memory did not easily rework its recollections into ideas but preserved them in sensory isolation, the way one memorizes poems; for which reason there was always in her words an indescribable blending of body and soul, no matter how unobtrusively she uttered them. Ulrich called to mind the scene before his father's funeral, when she had spoken the incredibly beautiful lines of Shakespeare to him. "How wild her nature is compared to mine!" he thought. "I haven't let myself say much today." He thought over the explanation of "day-bright mysticism" he had given her: All things considered, it was nothing more than his having conceded the possibility of transitory deviations from the accustomed and verified order of experience; and looked at this way, her experiences were merely following a basic principle somewhat richer in feelings than that of ordinary experience and resembled small middle-class children who have stumbled into a troupe of actors. So he had not dared say any more, although for days every bit of space between himself and his sister had been filled with uncompleted happenings! And he slowly began to concern himself with the problem of whether there might not be more things that could be believed than he had admitted to himself.

After the lively climax of their dialogue he and Agathe had let themselves fall back into their chairs, and the stillness of the garden closed over their fading words. Insofar as it has been said that Ulrich had begun to be preoccupied by a question, the correction must be made that many answers precede their questions, the way a person hastening along precedes his open, fluttering coat. What preoccupied Ulrich was a surprising notion, one that did not require belief but whose very appearance created astonishment and the impression that such an inspiration must never be allowed to be forgotten, which, considering the claims it asserted, was rather disquieting. Ulrich was accustomed to thinking not so much godlessly as God-free, which in the manner of science means to leave every possible turning to God to the emotions, because such a turning is not capable of furthering knowledge but can only seduce it into the impracticable. And even at this moment he did not in the least doubt that the way of science was the only correct way, since the most palpable successes of the human spirit had managed to come into being only since this spirit had got out of God's way. But the notion that had come upon him said: "What if this selfsame ungodliness turned out to be nothing but the contemporary path to God? Every age has had its own pathway of thought to Him, corresponding to the energies of its most powerful minds; would it not also be our destiny, the fate of an age of clever and entrepreneurial experience, to deny all dreams, legends, and ingeniously reasoned notions only because we, at the pinnacle of exploring and discovering the world, again turn to Him and will begin to derive a relationship to Him from a kind of experience that is just beginning?"

This conclusion was quite undemonstrable, Ulrich knew that; indeed, to most people it would appear as perverse, but that did not bother him. He himself really ought not to have thought it either: the scientific procedure—which he had just finished explaining as legitimate—consists, aside from logic, in immersing the concepts it has gained from the surface, from "experience," into the depths of phenomena and explaining the phenomena by the concepts, the depths by the surface; everything on earth is laid waste and leveled in order to gain mastery over it, and the objection came to mind that one ought not extend this to the metaphysical. But Ulrich now contested this objection: the desert is not an objection, it has always been the birthplace of heavenly visions; and besides, prospects that have not yet been attained cannot be predicted either! But it escaped him that he perhaps found himself in a second kind of opposition to himself, or had stumbled on a direction leading away from his own: Paul calls faith the expectation of things hoped for and belief in things not seen, a statement thought out to the point of radiant clarity; and Ulrich's opposition to the Pauline statement, which is one of the basic tenets of the educated person, was among the strongest he bore in his heart. Faith as a diminished form of knowing was abhorrent to his being, it is always "against one's better knowledge"; on the other hand, it had been given to him to recognize in the "intimation 'to the best of' one's knowledge" a special condition and an area in which exploring minds could roam. That his opposition had now weakened was later to cost him much effort, but for the moment he did not even notice it, for he was preoccupied and charmed by a swarm of incidental considerations.

He singled out examples. Life was becoming more and more homogeneous and impersonal. Something mechanical, stereotypical, statistical, and serial was insinuating itself into every entertainment, excitement, recreation, even into the passions. The life will was spreading out and becoming shallow, like a river hesitating before its delta. The will to art had already become more or less suspicious, even to itself. It seemed as though the age was beginning to devalue individual life without being able to make up the loss through new collective achievements. This was the face it wore. And this face, which was so hard to understand; which he had once loved and had attempted to remold in the muddy crater of a deeply rumbling volcano, because he felt himself young, like a thousand others; and from which he had turned away like these thousands because he could not gain control over this horribly contorted sight—this face was transfigured, becoming peaceful, deceptively beautiful, and radiant, by a single thought! For what if it were God Himself who was devaluing the world? Would it not then again suddenly acquire meaning and desire? And would He not be forced to devalue it, if He were to come closer to it by the tiniest step? And would not perceiving even the anticipatory shadow of this already be the one real adventure? These considerations had the unreasonable consistency of a series of adventures and were so exotic in Ulrich's head that he thought he was dreaming. Now and then he cast a cautiously reconnoitering glance at his sister, as if apprehensive that she would perceive what he was up to, and several times he caught sight of her blond head like light on light against the sky, and saw the air that was toying with her hair also playing with the clouds.

When that happened, she too, raising herself up slightly, looked around in astonishment. She tried to imagine how it would be to be set free from all life's emotions. Even space, she thought, this always uniform, empty cube, now seemed changed. If she kept her eyes closed for a while and then opened them again, so that the garden met her glance untouched, as if it had just that moment been created, she noticed as clearly and disembodiedly as in a vision that the course that bound her to her brother was marked out among all the others: the garden "stood" around this line, and without anything having changed about the trees, walks, and other elements of the actual environment—about this she could easily reassure herself—everything had been related to this connection to make an axis and was thereby invisibly changed in a visible way. It may sound paradoxical; but she could just as well have said that the world was sweeter here; perhaps, too, more sorrowful: what was remarkable was that one thought one was seeing it with one's eyes. There was, moreover, something striking in the way all the surrounding shapes stood there eerily abandoned but also, in an eerily ravishing way, full of life, so that they were like a gentle death, or a passionate swoon, as if something unnameable had just left them, and this lent them a distinctly human sensuality and openness. And as with this impression of space, something similar had happened with the feelings of time: that flowing ribbon, the rolling staircase with its uncanny incidental association with death, seemed at many moments to stand still and at many others to flow on without any associations at all. In the space of one single outward instant it might have disappeared into itself, without a trace of whether it had stopped for an hour or a minute.

Once, Ulrich surprised his sister during these experiments, and probably had an inkling of them, for he said softly, smiling: "There is a prophecy that a millennium is to the gods no longer than a blink of the eye!" Then they both leaned back and continued listening to the dream discourse of the silence.

Agathe was thinking: "Having brought all this about is all his doing; and yet he doubts every time he smiles!" But the sun was falling in a constant stream of warmth as tenderly as a sleeping potion on his parted lips. Agathe felt it falling on her own, and knew herself at one with him. She tried to put herself in his place and guess his thoughts, which they had really decided they would not do because it was something that came from outside and not from their own creative participation; but as a deviation it was that much more secret. "He doesn't want this to become just another love story," she thought, and added: "That's not my inclination either." And immediately thereafter she thought: "He will love no other woman after me, for this is no longer a love story; it is the very last love story there can be!" And she added: "We will be something like the Last Mohicans of love!" At the moment she was also capable of this tone toward herself, for if she summed things up quite honestly, this enchanted garden in which she found herself together with Ulrich was also, of course, more desire than reality. She did not really believe that the Millennium could have begun, in spite of this name Ulrich had once bestowed on it, which had the sound of standing on solid ground. She even felt quite deserted by her powers of desire, and, wherever her dreams might have sprung from, she didn't know where it was, bitterly sobered. She remembered that before Ulrich, she really had more easily been able to imagine a waking sleep, like the one in which her soul was now rocking, which was able to conduct her behind life, into a wakefulness after death, into the nearness of God, to powers that came to fetch her, or merely alongside life to a cessation of ideas and a transition into forests and meadows of imaginings: it had never become clear what that was! So now she made an effort to call up these old representations. But all she could remember was a hammock, stretched between two enormous fingers and rocked with an infinite patience; then a calm feeling of being towered over, as if by high trees, between which she felt raised up and removed from sight; and finally a nothingness, which in some incomprehensible way had a tangible content: All these were probably transitory images of suggestion and imagination in which her longing had found solace. But had they really been only passing and half formed? To her astonishment, something quite remarkable slowly began to occur to Agathe. "Truly," she thought, "it's as one says: a light dawns! And it spreads the longer it lasts!" For what she had once imagined seemed to be in almost everything that was now standing around her, calm and enduring, as often as she dispatched her glance to look! What she had imagined had soundlessly entered the world. God, to be sure—differently from the way a literally credulous person might have experienced it—stayed away from her adventure, but to make up for this she was, in this adventure, no longer alone: these were the only two changes that distinguished the fulfillment from the presentiment, and they were changes in favor of earthly naturalness.

47

WANDERINGS AMONG PEOPLE

In the time that followed they withdrew from their circle of acquaintances, astonishing them by turning down every invitation and not allowing themselves to be contacted in any way. They stayed at home a great deal, and when they went out they avoided places in which they might meet people of their social set, visiting places of entertainment and small theaters where they felt secure from such encounters; and whenever they left the house they generally simply followed the currents of the metropolis, which are an image of people's needs and, with the precision of tide tables, pile them up in specific places or suck them away, depending on the hour. It amused them to participate in a style of living that differed from their own and relieved them for a time of responsibility for their usual way of life. Never had the city in which they lived seemed to them at once so lovely and so strange. In their totality the houses presented a grand picture, even if singly or in particular they were not handsome at all; diluted by the heat, noise streamed through the air like a river reaching to the rooftops; in the strong light, attenuated by the depths of the streets, people looked more passionate and mysterious than they presumably deserved. Everything sounded, looked, and smelled irreplaceable and unforgettable, as if it were signaling how it appeared to itself in all its momentariness; and brother and sister not unwillingly accepted this invitation to turn toward the world.

In doing so, they came upon an extraordinary discord. The experiences that they had not shared openly with each other separated them from other people; but the same problematic passion, which they continued to feel undiminished and which had come to grief not because of a taboo but because of some higher promise, had also transported them to a state that shared a similarity with the sultry intermissions of a physical union. The desire that could not find expression had again sunk back within the body, filling it with a tenderness as indefinable as one of the last days of autumn or first days of spring. It was, nonetheless, not at all as if they loved every person they saw, or everything that was going on: they merely felt the lovely shadow of "how it would be" falling on their hearts, and their hearts could neither fully believe in the mild delusion nor quite escape its pull. It seemed that through their conversations and their continence, through their expectation and its provisional limits, they had become sensitive to the barriers reality places before the emotions, and now perceived together the peculiarly double-sided nature of life, which dampens every higher aspiration with a lower one. This two-sided nature combines a retreat with every advance, a weakness with every strength, and gives no one a right that it does not take away from others, straightens out no tangle without creating new disorder, and even appears to evoke the sublime only in order to mistake it, an hour later, for the stale and trite. An absolutely indissoluble and profoundly necessary connection apparently combines all happy and cheerful human endeavors with the materialization of their opposites and makes life for intellectual people, beyond all dissension, hard to bear.

The way the plus and minus sides of life adhere to each other has been judged in quite different ways. Pious misanthropists see in it an effluence of earthly decrepitude, bulldog types life's juiciest filet; the man in the street feels as comfortable within this contradiction as he does between his left and right hands, and people who are proper say that the world was not created in order to correspond to human expectations but it is the other way round: these ideas were created in order to correspond to the world, and why is it that they never bring it to pass in the sphere of the just and the beautiful? As mentioned, Ulrich was of the opinion that this state of affairs served the production and preservation of a middling condition of life, which more or less leaves it up to chance to mix human genius with human stupidity, as this condition itself also emerges from such a mixture; a long time ago he had expressed this by saying that the mind has no mind, and just recently, at Diotima's soiree, he had again talked about it at length as the great confusion of the emotions. But whether it had been recently or long ago, and no matter how obvious it might have been to continue the same thought, as soon as Ulrich began to do so he had the feeling that such words were coming from his mouth a few days too late. This time, he frequently found himself lacking in desire to occupy himself with things that did not directly concern him, for his soul was prepared to submit to the world with all its senses, however this might turn out. His judgment was as good as disconnected from this altogether. Even whether something pleased him or not hardly mattered, for everything simply seized hold of him in a way that surpassed his capacity for understanding. This was as true for every general state of mind as for every particular and individual one; indeed, at times it was entirely without thought, and corporeal; but when it had lasted awhile and reached full measure, it became unpleasant or seemed ridiculous to him, and he was then ready, in a manner just as unfounded as the one in which he had first submitted, to retract that submission.

And Agathe in her fashion was experiencing pretty much the same thing. At times, her conscience was oppressed, and expected or made for itself new oppressions from the world she had left behind but that nonetheless proclaimed itself in all its power all around her. In the manifold bustle that fills day and night there was probably not a single task in which she could participate with all her heart, and her failure to venture into anything should not be regarded with the certainty of blame or disdain, or even contempt. There was in this a remarkable peace! It might perhaps be said, to alter a proverb, that a bad conscience, as long as it is bad enough, may almost provide a better pillow on which to rest than a good one: the incessant ancillary activity in which the mind engages with a view to acquiring a good individual conscience as the final outcome of all the injustice in which it is embroiled is then abolished, leaving behind in mind and emotions a hectic independence. A tender loneliness, a sky-high arrogance, sometimes poured their splendor over these holidays from the world. Alongside one's own feelings the world could then appear clumsily bloated, like a captive balloon circled by swallows, or, *mutatis mutandis*, humbled to a background as small as a forest at the periphery of one's field of vision. The offended civic obligations echoed like a distant and crudely intrusive noise; they were insignificant, if not unreal. A monstrous order, which is in the last analysis nothing but a monstrous absurdity: that was the world. And yet every detail Agathe encountered also had the tensed, high-wire-act nature of the once-and-never-again, the nature of discovery, which is magical and admits of no repetition; and whenever she wanted to speak of this, she did so in the awareness that no word can be uttered twice without changing its meaning.

So the attitude of brother and sister toward the world at this time was a not entirely irreproachable expression of confident benevolence, containing its own brand of parallel attraction and repulsion in a state of feeling that hovered like a rainbow, instead of these opposites combining in the stasis that corresponds to the self-confident state of every day. And something else was connected with this: in the days following that strange night, the tone of their conversations changed too; the echo of destiny faded, and the progression became freer and looser; indeed, it sometimes volatilized in a playful fluttering of words. Still, this did not indicate a temporizing born of despondency as much as it indicated an unregulated broadening of the living foundations of their own adventure. They sought support in observing the ordinary ways in which life was carried on, and were secretly convinced that the equilibrium of this usual form of living was also a pretense. In this way it happened one day that their conversation took a direction in which, despite some fluctuation, it persisted. Ulrich asked: "What does the commandment 'Love thy neighbor as thyself' really mean?"

"Love the person farthest away like thyself is what it means!" Agathe responded with the tenderest forbearance, to which her brother had a right in questions of loving one's fellowmen.

But Ulrich was not satisfied. "And what does it mean to say 'Love what you do not know'? To love someone you don't know, although you might well be convinced that after you got acquainted you wouldn't like each other? So, in the last analysis: to love him although you know him?" he insisted more explicitly.

"That's clearly the situation most people are in, but they don't let it bother them!" Agathe replied. "They put doubt and confidence inside each other!"

"They foresee nothing more in the commandment of love than the reasonable prohibition against hurting each other so long as it serves no purpose," Ulrich offered.

But Agathe said that that would be the insipid rule of thumb "What you don't want someone to do to you, don't do to anyone else," and it was impossible that the entire purpose of this high-mindedly passionate, cheerfully generous task could be to love a stranger without even asking who he was!

"Perhaps the word 'love' here is only an expression that has taken far too great a swing to overcome the obstacles?" Ulrich reflected. But Agathe insisted that it really did mean "love him!" and "without any particular reason," and that it was not to be haggled over, so Ulrich yielded. "What it means is: Love him in spite of what you know!" he objected. "And before you know him!" Agathe repeated and underlined it once again: "At least, without knowing him!"

But she stopped abruptly and looked at her brother, bewildered. "But what is it you really love in a person if you don't know him at all?" she asked impatiently.

Thus the playful questions took on various forms as they sped back and forth. But Ulrich did not hasten to his sister's aid. He was of the opinion that to love something means to prefer it over other things, and that surely assumed a certain knowing.

"Almost everybody loves himself best, and knows himself least!" Agathe threw in.

"True love is independent of merit and reward," Ulrich confirmed, mimicking a moralizing tone and shrugging his shoulders.

"Something's wrong here!"

"A lot's wrong!" he ventured.

"And if you love everything? If you're supposed to love the whole world, the way you are today? What is it then that you're loving? You would say: 'Nothing special'!" Agathe laughed.

"Haven't you noticed, too, that today it's downright disturbing if you happen to meet a person who is so beautiful that you have to say something personal about it?" he asked her.

"Then it's not a feeling about the real world and the real person!" she said firmly.

"So then we have to tackle the question as to what part of this person it's true of, or what metamorphosis and transformation of the real person and the real world," Ulrich said, softly but emphatically.

After a short pause, Agathe answered, with a timid conscience: "Perhaps that *is* the real person?" But Ulrich hesitantly resisted this, shaking his head.

Shining through the content of this inquiring assertion there was, no doubt, a profound obviousness. The breezes and delights of these days were so tender and merry that the impression arose spontaneously that man and world must be showing themselves as they really were: this transparency harbored a small, odd, suprasensory shudder, such as is glimpsed in the flowing transparency of a brook, a transparency that allows the glance to see to the bottom but, when it arrives there, wavering, makes the mysterious colored stones look like fish scales, and beneath them what the glance had thought it was experiencing is truly concealed, without possibility of access. Agathe, surrounded by sunshine, needed only to disengage her glance a little to have the feeling of having stumbled into a supernatural domain; for the shortest interval she could easily imagine that she had come in contact with a higher truth and reality, or at least had come upon an aspect of existence where a little door behind the earth mysteriously indicated the way from the earthly garden into the beyond. But when she again limited the range of her glance to an ordinary span and let life's glare stream in on her once more, she saw whatever might actually happen to be there: perhaps a little flag being waved to and fro by a child's hand, merrily and without any kind of puzzled thought; a police wagon with prisoners, its black-green paint sparkling in the light; or a man with a colorful cap contentedly turning a pile of manure; or finally a company of soldiers, whose shouldered rifles were pointing their barrels at the sky. All this seemed to have had poured over it something related to love, and everyone also seemed more ready to open themselves to this feeling than usual: but to believe that the empire of love was now really happening would be just as difficult, Ulrich said, as imagining that at this moment no dog could bite or no person do anything evil.

The same happened with all the other attempts at explanation, which had in common with this one that they opposed some kind of person who was far off and true to people who were everyday, earthbound, and bad and good, but at all events people as we know them. Brother and sister examined these ideal types one after the other, and could not believe in any of them. There was the feeling that on such festive days nature brought forth in her creatures all their hidden goodness and beauty. Then there were the more psychological explanations, that people in this transparent, nuptial air did not show themselves as different in some magical way, but still displayed themselves so as to be as lovable as they would like to be and saw themselves as being: sweating their egotism and inward-turned indulgence, as it were, out through their pores. And finally there is also the variation that people were showing their goodwill; to be sure, this cannot prevent them from doing evil, but emerges miraculously and unscathed on days like these from the evil will that usually governs them, like Jonah from the belly of the whale. But the most succinct explanation one heard was that this is the immortal part of man, which shimmers through the mortal part. All these imputations had in common that they located the real person in a part of him that, among the insubstantial remainder, does not come into play; and if the promising contact with this real self was a process clearly directed upward, there was also a second, no less abundant group of explanations, which directed this process just as clearly downward: these were all those according to which man is supposed to have lost his natural innocence through intellectual arrogance and all kinds of misfortune brought upon him by civilization. There are, therefore, two genuine people, who appear to the mind with the greatest punctuality in the same, constantly recurring situations, yet both these types—the one a divine superman, the other an animal-like infra-man—were on opposite sides of the person as he really is. Finally, Ulrich remarked dryly: "The only trait that remains as common, and also very characteristic, is that even when he is being good, a person does not seek the true person in himself but takes himself to be something else 'plus or minus'!"

But here brother and sister had arrived at a borderline case of that love for another that is so problematic and so gently entwines everything within it, and Agathe sighed in vexation, but not without charm. "Then all that remains of all this is just a 'mood'!" she said, disappointed. "The sun is shining. You get into a frame of mind!"

Ulrich added to this: "The social instincts stretch themselves out in the sun like mercury in the thermometer tube, at the expense of the egotistic instincts, which otherwise hold them more or less in balance. Perhaps nothing else."

"So an 'unconscious craving' like a schoolgirl's or schoolboy's!" Agathe continued. "They would like to kiss the whole world and have no idea why! So we can't say any more than that either?"

They had suddenly become tired of feeling; and it sometimes happened that in such a conversation, dealing only with their capacity for feeling, they neglected to use it. Also, because the surfeit of emotions that could nowhere find an outlet actually hurt, they sometimes got back at it with a little ingratitude. But when they had both spoken in this fashion, Agathe quickly looked sidelong at her brother. "That would," she protested, "be saying too little!"

The moment she said this, they both felt once more that they were not just relying on some subjective fantasy but were facing an invisible reality. Truth was hovering in the mood inundating them, reality was under the appearance, transformation of the world gazed out of the world like a shadow! The reality about which they felt so expectant was, to be sure, remarkably lacking a nucleus and only half comprehensible, and it was a long-intimate half-truth, familiar and unfulfillable, that wooed credibility: not an everyday reality and truth for everyone, but a secret one for lovers. Obviously, it was not just caprice or delusion either, and its most mysterious insinuation whispered: "Just leave yourself to me without mistrust, and you'll discover the whole truth!" Giving an account of this was so difficult because the language of love is a secret language and in its highest perfection is as silent as an embrace.

The thought "secret language" had the effect of making Agathe dimly recall that it was written somewhere: "Whosoever abides in love abides in God, and God in him. He who has not love does not know God." She did not know where.

Ulrich on the other hand, because she had said before that it was "just a mood," was considering an idea as sweetly temperate as the sound of a flute. One had only to assume that such a mood of being in love was not always just a transitory special state but was also, beyond its immediate occasion, capable of enduring and spreading; in other words, all you had to assume was that a person could be a lover alone and in accordance with his enduring being, in exactly the same way that he can be indifferent, and this would lead him to a totally changed way of life: indeed, presumably it would take him to an entirely unfamiliar world that would be present in his mind without his having to be considered mentally ill. This thought, that everything could be made different by one small step, indeed just by a movement that the mind merely had to let happen, was extremely seductive. And suddenly Ulrich asked his sister with curiosity: "What do you think would happen if we were to stop one of these people and say to him: 'Brother, stay with us!' or 'Stop, O hastening soul'?"

"He would look at us flabbergasted," Agathe replied.

"And then unobtrusively double his pace, or call a policeman," Ulrich finished.

"He would probably think he'd fallen in with good-natured madmen," Agathe added.

"But if we were to yell at him: 'You criminal, you piece of nothing!' he probably wouldn't consider us crazy," Ulrich noted with amusement, "but would merely take us to be 'people who think differently,' or 'members of a different party,' who had turned angry at him."

Agathe frowned, smiling, and then they both again gazed into the human current that was pulling them along and flowing against them. Together they felt again the self-forgetfulness and power, the happiness and goodness, the deep and elevated constraint, that predominate inside a vital human community, even if it is only the contingent community of a busy street, so that one does not believe that there could also be anything bad or divisive; and their own sense of existence, that sharply bounded and difficult having-been-placed-here, that basic happiness and basic hostility, stood in marvelous contrast to this communal scene. They both thought the same; but they also thought differently, without its being obvious. They guessed each other's meaning; but sometimes they guessed wrongly. And gradually an indolence, indeed a paralysis of thinking, emanated from this double-pearled juxtaposition on the oyster shell of the world, as Ulrich called it rather scornfully, and they then parried it by laughing at each other, or about something.

But when this happened again Agathe said: "It always makes me so sad when we're forced to laugh at ourselves; and I don't know why I have to."

Ulrich replied: "Nothing is funnier than opening one's eyes to reality when they're still filled with the inner soul!"

But Agathe did not pick up on this; she repeated: "Everything remains so uncertain. It seems to draw itself together and then extend itself again, without any shape. It permits no activity, and the inactivity becomes unbearable. I can't even say that I really love these people, or that I love these real people, as they are when we look at them. I'm afraid our own feelings are pretty unreal!"

"But these people respond to each other in exactly the same way!" Ulrich retorted. "They want to love each other, yet at the decisive moment they think antipathy is more natural and healthier! So it's the same for everyone: We feel that real life has snapped off a possible life!"

"But then tell me," Agathe retorted angrily, "why love always needs a church or a bed!"

"For heaven's sake"—Ulrich soothed his companion with a laugh—"don't speak so openly!" He touched her hand with his fingertips and went on, joking mysteriously: "All these people can also be called in public what you and I are in private: the unseparated but not united!"

It was not an assertion, merely a cajoling constellation of words, a joke, a candid little cloud of words; and they knew that feeling oneself chosen was the cheapest of all magic formulas and quite adolescent. Nevertheless, Ulrich's fraternal words slowly rose from the ground to a position above their heads. Agathe, too, now whispered jokingly: "Sometimes you feel your breath blow back from your veil still hot, like a pair of strange lips: that's how it sometimes seems to me—call it illusion or reality—that I'm you!" was her response, and her gentle smile drew silence closed like a curtain after it as it died away.

In such back-and-forth fashion they came to reproach the millions of loving couples who in their serious desire for certainty ask themselves a hundred times a day whether they really and truly love each other, and how long it can last: who, however, don't have to fear conjuring up similar oddities.

48

LOVE BLINDS. OR DIFFICULTIES WHERE
THEY ARE NOT LOOKED FOR

Another of these world-oriented discussions went like this: "Then how would things stand when a love occurs between two so-called persons of different gender, which is as famous as it is gladly experienced?" Ulrich objected. "You probably are really partly in love with the person you think you're loving."

"But what you're mostly doing is simply making a puppet of him!" Agathe interjected resentfully.

"In any event, what he says and thinks in the process also has its charm!"

"As long as you love him! Because you love him! But not the other way round! If you've once understood how the other person means it, it's not only anger that's disarmed, as one always says, but for the most part love as well!"

Again it was Agathe who gave this passionate answer. Ulrich smiled. She must have banged her head pretty hard against this wall more than once.

"But at first you can like the other person's opinions, that's often involved in the beginning: the well-known marvelous 'agreeing about everything'; later, of course, you no longer understand it at all," he said placatingly, and asked: "But deeds? Does love depend on deeds?"

"Only insofar as they embody a person's sentiments. Or turn the imagination into a sort of monument!"

"But didn't we just decide it wasn't so much a matter of sentiments?" Ulrich recalled teasingly.

"It doesn't depend on anything at all!" Agathe cried. "Not on what the other person is, not on what he thinks, not on what he wants, and not on what he does! There are times when you despise a person but love him all the same. And there are times when you love a person and have the secret feeling that this person with the beard (or breasts), whom you think you've known for a long time and . . . treasure, and who talks about himself incessantly, is really only visiting love. You could leave aside his sentiments and merits, you could change his destiny, you could give him a new beard or different legs—you could leave aside almost the whole person, and still love him! As far as you happen to love him at all," she added, mitigating her statement.

Her voice had a deep ring, with a restless glitter buried in its depths like a flame. She sat down guiltily, having involuntarily jumped up from her chair in her zeal.

Ulrich summed up the result in balanced fashion: "Both contradictions are always present and form a team of four horses: you love a person because you know him and because you don't know him; and you know him because you love him and don't know him because you love him. And sometimes that grows strong enough to become quite palpable. Those are the well-known moments when Venus gazes through Apollo and Apollo through Venus at an empty scarecrow, and each is mightily surprised at having seen something there before. If, furthermore, love is stronger than astonishment, it comes to a struggle between them, and sometimes out of this struggle love emerges—even if it is despairing, exhausted, and mortally wounded—as the victor. But if love is not that strong, it leads to a battle between the people involved, to insults intended to make up for having been played for a simpleton . . . to terrible incursions of reality . . . to utter degradation. . . ." He had participated in this stormy weather of love often enough to be at ease describing it.

Agathe interrupted him. "But I find that these marital and extramarital affairs of honor are usually greatly overrated!" she objected.

"Love as a whole is overrated! The maniac who in his delusion pulls a knife and stabs some innocent person who just happens to be standing in for his hallucination—in love he's the normal one!" Ulrich said, and laughed.

Agathe, too, smiled as she looked at him.

Ulrich became serious. "It's odd enough to have to think that there really are no two people who can agree spontaneously, without their opinions and convictions being more or less powerfully influenced," he noted thoughtfully, and for a while this gave the conversation a somewhat different turn.

Brother and sister were sitting in Ulrich's room, on either side of the long, darkly shining desk of heavy wood, whose center was now empty because apparently Ulrich was not working on anything. Each of them had lazily posed an arm on the desk and was looking at a small papier-mâché horse standing in the vacant middle ground between them.

"Even in rational thinking, where everything has logical and objective connections," Ulrich went on, "it's usually the case that you unreservedly recognize the superior conviction of someone else only if you have submitted to him in some way, whether as a model and guide, or as a friend or teacher. But without such a feeling, which has nothing to do with the case, every time you make someone else's opinion your own, it will only be with the silent reservation that you can do more with it than its originator; if indeed you weren't already out to show this fellow what unsuspected importance his idea really contained! Especially in art, most of us certainly know it would be impossible for us to do ourselves what we read, see, and hear; but we still have the patronizing awareness that if we *were* able to do any of these things, we could of course do them better! And perhaps it has to be that way, and lies in the active nature of the mind, which doesn't allow itself be filled up like an empty pot," Ulrich concluded, "but actively appropriates everything, and literally has to make it part of itself."

He would gladly have added something more that occurred to him, and it would not let him rest, so he was already giving vent to his scruple before Agathe had any chance to respond. "But we should also ask ourselves," he suggested, "what sort of life would arise if all this were not so unfavorable. Our feelings ultimately want to be handled quite roughly, it appears, but in the other borderline case— when we assimilate someone else's sentiments without resistance, when we submit completely to someone else's feelings, indeed, when we reach a pure agreement with a second understanding—is there not a happiness that is pathologically tender, in fact almost anti-intellectual? And how could this light be produced without the shadow?" This thought made him want to linger over the conversation; but although the idea was not entirely alien to Agathe either, she was occupied at the moment with smaller concerns. She looked at her brother for a while without speaking, struggling against what was coming over her, but then made up her mind to ask the offensive question, as casually as possible, whether that meant he had arrived at the considered conviction that "even only two people" could never be of one mind, and lovers under no circumstances whatever?

Ulrich was almost at the point of expressing through a gesture that this was neither to be taken as real nor worth talking about, when he was struck by his sister's misplaced warmth; he had to suppress a smile at this suspicious inquisitiveness, but in doing so lost his own more serious inquisitiveness and fell back again into the interrupted merry flow of his initial joking way of talking. "You yourself began by belittling love!" he replied.

"Let's leave it at that!" Agathe decreed magnanimously. "Let's leave it at people not agreeing, when they're in love. But in ordinary life, which is certainly nothing less than loving, you must admit that all kinds of people have similar convictions and that that plays an enormous role!"

"They only think they have them!" Ulrich broke in.

"They agree with each other!"

"The agreement is imposed on them! People are like a fire that immediately shoots out in all directions unless there's a stone on top!"

"But aren't there, for instance, generally prevailing opinions?" Agathe asked, intending to keep up with her brother.

"Now you're saying it yourself!" he countered. " 'Prevailing!' Since it's necessary that we agree, innumerable arrangements of course exist to take care of the externals and delude us inwardly into thinking it so. In making us people of one mind, these arrangements aren't exactly subtle. Hypnotic suggestion, violence, intimidation, thoughtlessness, cowardice, and such things play a not inconsiderable role. The exercise of these arrangements is mostly alloyed with something base and corrupting. But if their influence stops for just a single moment, allowing reason to take over their affairs, you will very shortly see mankind start gabbling and fall to quarreling, the way the insane start running around when their warders aren't looking!"

Agathe recalled the walks in lovely weather where everything had been in unqualified harmony with everything else, and the people, even if they were apparently mistaken in believing that they loved each other, were at least very attentive to one another and filled with an almost solemn amiability and curiosity. It seemed appropriate to mention that love was, after all, the only thing in the world that made people of one mind, and that in every one of its varieties it did so from both sides voluntarily.

"But love is precisely one of the agreement machines. It has the lucky effect of making people blind!" Ulrich objected. "Love *blinds:* half the riddles about loving one's neighbor we've been trying to solve are already contained in this proposition!"

"The most one might add is that love also enables one to see what isn't there," Agathe maintained, concluding reflectively: "So really these two propositions contain everything you need in the world, in order to be happy despite it!"

In direct connection with this point, however, it was the tiny papier-mâché horse, standing between them all alone in the middle of the desk, that bore the sole responsibility for their conversation. It was hardly a hand's breadth high; its neck was daintily curved; the brown of its coat was as tender and full as the stomach of a fifteen-year-old girl who has almost, but not yet quite, eaten too much cake, and its mane and tail, its hooves and reins, were of one single, deepest black. It was a horse belonging to a court carriage, but as in legend two gods often grow into one, it was also a candy box in the form of a horse. Ulrich had discovered this little horse in a suburban confectioner's window and had immediately acquired it, for he knew it from his childhood and had loved it so intensely back then that he could hardly recall whether he had ever owned it. Fortunately, such mercantile poems are sometimes preserved over several generations and merely wander with time from the centers of commerce to display windows in more modest parts of the city. So Ulrich had reverently installed this find on his desk, having already explained the significance of the species to his sister. The candy horse was a close relative of those circus animals—lions, tigers, horses, and dogs—that had lived at the same time, the time of Ulrich's childhood, on the posters of traveling circuses, and could no more be summoned from the raging expressions of their palpable but one-dimensional existence into fully developed life than this little horse could jump through the glass pane of the shop window. Agathe had quickly understood this, for the confectioner's horse constituted part of the large family of children's fancies which are always chasing their desires with the zigzag flight of a butterfly, until at last they reach their goal only to find a lifeless object. And wandering back along childhood's paths of love, brother and sister had even opened the horse and, with the mixed feelings attending the unsealing of a crypt, found inside a variety of round, flat little tents strewn with grains of sugar, which they thought they had not seen for decades, and which they enjoyed with the cautious courage of explorers.

In a distracted and pensive way, during the pause that had followed the last exchange with Ulrich, Agathe had been observing this small object with the magnetic soul that stood before them. In the far distances of this daydreaming, perhaps there also emerged from the river of words about similarities and differences in thinking, that idea of the unseparated but not united, and now this joined in a peculiar way with their companionship as children. Agathe finally landed on time's other shore of silence without knowing how long the interruption had lasted, and she picked up the conversation where it had left off by asking with direct vehemence, as if something had been forgotten: "But not *every* love has to blind!"

Ulrich, too, was immediately ready to be pressed into service again in pursuit of the exchange of words that had rushed away, as if he were not sure how long he had been standing there distracted. "Let's go on!" he suggested, and led with a random example: "Maternal love!"

"Doting, it's called," Agathe replied.

"In any case, it loves blindly, loves in advance. Won't let anything distract it," Ulrich stated, immediately continuing: "And its opposite, a child's love?"

"Is that love at all?" Agathe asked.

"There's a lot of selfishness and instinctive need for protection and such things in it," Ulrich ventured, but added that it could also be, at least at certain stages, a real passion. Next, he asked about the love of friends.

They were again agreed: youth was the only time for passionate friendships.

"Love of honor?" Ulrich asked.

Agathe shrugged her shoulders.

"Love of virtue?"

She repeated the gesture, then thought it over and said: "Saints or martyrs might call it love."

"But then it's obviously a passion for overcoming the world, or something like that, as well," Ulrich interjected. "An oppositional passion, but in any case something containing a lot of complications."

"But there can also be a lot of complications in love of honor," Agathe added.

"Love of power?" Ulrich went on, assenting to her objection with only a nod of his head.

"That's probably a contradiction in terms."

"Perhaps," Ulrich agreed. "You might think that force and love are mutually exclusive."

"But they *aren't!*" Agathe exclaimed, having changed her mind in the meantime. "Look: to be compelled! For women especially, being loved and being compelled is no contradiction at all!"

Ulrich responded in contradictory ways to this reminder of the possibility of such experiences in his sister's past; on the one hand he desired an informed explanation; on the other, the primordial ignorance of the gods. Frowning, he thought over what his response should be, and finally said, clearly but hesitating involuntarily: "In that case the association of the words is indeed ambivalent. All power is laid low before love, and if it humiliates love, then—"

"Let's not dwell on it," Agathe interrupted, and offered a new question: "Love of truth?"

Since he hesitated, "You should know all about that!" she added in jesting reproach; his long-drawn-out efforts to be accurate sometimes made her impatient.

But the conversation was already inhibited, and slowly it became diffuse. "There, too, it's not easy to separate out the right concepts," Ulrich decided. "You can love truth in many different ways: as honor, as power, as virtue, or also like pure spring water and the air you breathe, or like—"

"Is that love?" Agathe interrupted him again. "That way you could love spinach too!"

"And why not? Even being partial to something is a form of love.

There are many transitions," Ulrich countered. "And 'love of truth' especially is one of the most contradictory terms: If the concept of truth is stronger, love is correspondingly less, and in the last analysis you can hardly call the honorable or even the utilitarian need for truth 'love'; but if the concept of love is strong, what you might call the purest, highest love, then truth ceases to exist."

"Truth, unfortunately, arises in cold blood," Agathe remarked pointedly.

"To demand truth from love is just as mistaken as demanding justice from anger," Ulrich agreed. "Emotion is injurious there."

"Oh perhaps that's only men's talk!" Agathe protested.

"That's the way it is: Love tolerates truth, but truth does not tolerate love," Ulrich confirmed. "Love dissolves truth."

"But if it dissolves the truth, then it has no truth?" Agathe asked this with the seriousness of the ignorant child who knows by heart the story it wants to hear repeated for the twentieth time.

"A new truth begins," Ulrich said. "As soon as a person encounters love not as some kind of experience but as life itself, or at least as a kind of life, he knows a swarm of truths. Whoever judges without love calls this opinions, personal views, subjectivity, whim; and for him that's all it is. But the one who loves knows about himself that he is not insensitive to truth, but oversensitive. He finds himself in a kind of ecstasy of thinking, where the words open up to their very centers. He understands in every way more than is necessary. He can hardly save himself from an inexhaustible flood. And he feels that every rational desire to understand can only banish it. I don't want to claim that this really is a different truth—for there is only one and the same truth—but it is a hundred possibilities that are more important than truth; it is, to say it more clearly, something by means of which all truth loses the importance attributed to it. Perhaps one might say: truth is the unequivocal result of an attitude to life which we by no means feel unequivocally to be the true attitude!" Ulrich, happy because he had finally achieved a more exact description, drew the conclusion: "So apparently to be surrounded by a swarm of truths means nothing other than that the lover is open to everything that has been loved, and also willed, thought, and put down in words; open to all contradictions, which are after all those of sentient beings; open even to every shared experience, if a word exists that can lift it tenderly to the point of articulation. The distinctive signs of truth and morality have been suppressed for him by the gentle power of life stirring all around him; they remain present, but fruitfulness and fullness have out- and overgrown them. For the lover, truth and deception are equally trivial, and yet this does not strike him as caprice: Now, this is probably no more than a changed personal attitude, but I would say that it still finally depends on countless possibilities underlying whatever reality has conquered them, possibilities that could also have become realities. The lover awakens them. Everything suddenly appears different to him from what you think. Instead of a citizen of this world, he becomes a creature of countless worlds—"

"But that *is* another reality!" Agathe exclaimed.

"No!" said Ulrich hesitantly. "At least *I* don't know. It's merely the age-old opposition between knowledge and love, which has always been supposed to exist."

Agathe gave him a confused but encouraging smile.

"No!" Ulrich repeated. "That's still not the right one."

Her smile disappeared. "So we have to pick up our business once again, otherwise we won't get to the end this way either," Agathe suggested with comic distress, and with a sigh she began anew: "What is love of money?"

"You said things like that weren't love at all," Ulrich interjected.

"But *you* said there were transitions," Agathe countered.

"Love of beauty?" Ulrich asked, ignoring this.

"Love is also supposed to make an ugly person beautiful," Agathe replied, following a sudden inspiration. "Do you love something because it's beautiful or is it beautiful because it's loved?"

Ulrich found this question important but unpleasant. So he responded: "Perhaps beauty is nothing other than having been loved. If something was once loved, its ability to be beautiful is directed outward. And beauty presumably arises in no other way but this: that something pleases a person who also has the power to give other people a kind of set of directions for repetition." Then he added sharply: "Nevertheless, men who, like friend Lindner, waylay beauty are simply funny!"

"Love one's enemy?" Agathe asked, smiling.

"Difficult!" said Ulrich. "Perhaps a leftover from magical-religious cannibalism."

"Compared to that, loving life is simple," Agathe stated. "No idea at all is connected with it; it's simply a blind instinct."

"Passion for hunting?"

"Love of fatherland? Love of home? Necrophilia? Love of nature? Love of ponies? Idolatry? Puppy love? Hate-love?" Agathe shook them all out together, raising her arms in a circle and letting them fall to her lap with a gesture of discouragement.

Ulrich answered with a shrug of the shoulders and a smile. "Love becomes real in many ways and in the most varied connections. But what is the common denominator? What in all these loves is the essential fluid and what merely its crystallization? And what, especially, is that 'love!' that can also occur spontaneously and fill the whole world?" he asked, showing little hope of an answer. "Even if someone were to compare the various forms more seriously," he went on, "he would presumably find only as many emotions as there are external conditions and attitudes. Under all these circumstances one can love; but only because one can also despise or remain indifferent: in this way whatever is shared in common surfaces as something vaguely like love."

"But doesn't that just mean that full love doesn't correspond to experience?" Agathe interrupted. "But who questions that? That's the decisive point! If love exists, in order to become manifest it will be entirely different from everything it is alloyed with!"

Now Ulrich interrupted. "What would that prove? As feeling and action, this love would have no limits, and therefore there is no attitude or behavior that would correspond to it."

Agathe listened eagerly. She was waiting for a final word. "And what do you do if there is no attitude or behavior?" she asked.

Ulrich understood her artless question. But he showed himself prepared for these reconnaissance expeditions to last even longer; he merely shrugged his shoulders resignedly and answered with a jest: "It doesn't seem nearly so simple to love as nature would have us believe, just because she's provided every bungler with the tools!"

49

General von Stumm drops a bomb.
Congress for World Peace

A soldier must not let anything deter him. So General Stumm von Bordwehr was the only person to push his way through to Ulrich and Agathe; but then he was perhaps the only person for whom they did not make it absolutely impossible, since even refugees from the world can see to it that their mail is forwarded to them periodically. And as he burst in to interrupt their continuing their conversation, he crowed: "It wasn't easy to penetrate all the perimeter defenses and fight my way into the fortress!", gallantly kissed Agathe's hand, and, addressing himself to her in particular, said: "I'll be a famous man, just because I've seen you! Everyone is asking what event could have swallowed up the Inseparables, and is asking after you; and in a certain sense I am the emissary of society, indeed of the Fatherland, sent to discover the cause of your disappearance! Please excuse me if I appear importunate!"

Agathe bade him a polite welcome, but neither she nor her brother was immediately able to conceal their distractedness from their visitor, who stood before them as the embodiment of the weakness and imperfection of their dreams; and as General Stumm again stepped back from Agathe, a remarkable silence ensued. Agathe was standing on one long side of the desk, Ulrich on the other, and the General, like a suddenly becalmed sailing vessel, was at a point approximately halfway between them. Ulrich meant to come forward to meet his visitor, but could not stir from the spot. Stumm now noticed that he really had butted in, and considered how he might save the situation. The twisted beginnings of a friendly smile lay on all three faces. This stiff silence lasted barely a fraction of a second; it was just then that Stumm's glance fell on the small papier-mâché horse standing isolated among them, like a monument, in the center of the empty desk.

Clicking his heels together, he pointed to it solemnly with the flat of his hand and exclaimed with relief: "But what's this? Do I perceive in this house the great animal idol, the holy animal, the revered deity of the cavalry?"

At Stumm's remark, Ulrich's inhibition, too, dissolved, and moving quickly over to Stumm but at the same time turning toward his sister, he said animatedly: "Admittedly it's just a coach horse, but you have wonderfully guessed the rest! We were really just talking about idols and how they originate. Now tell me: What is it one loves, which part, what reshaping and transformation does one love, when one loves one's neighbor without knowing him? In other words, to what extent is love dependent on the world and reality, and to what extent is it the other way round?"

Stumm von Bordwehr had directed his glance questioningly to Agathe.

"Ulrich is talking about this little thing," she assured him, somewhat disconcerted, pointing to the candy horse. "He used to have a passion for it."

"That was, I hope, quite a long time ago," Stumm said in astonishment. "For if I'm not mistaken, it's a candy jar?"

"It is *not* a candy jar! Friend Stumm!" Ulrich implored, seized by the disgraceful desire to chat with him about it. "If you fall in love with a saddle and harness that are too expensive for you, or a uniform or a pair of riding boots you see in a shop window: what are you in love with?"

"You're being outrageous! I don't *love* things like that!" the General protested.

"Don't deny it!" Ulrich replied. "There are people who can dream day and night of a suit fabric or a piece of luggage they have seen in a shop; everyone's known something like that; and the same thing will have happened to you, at least with your first lieutenant's uniform! And you'll have to admit that you might have no use for this material or this suitcase, and that you don't even have to be in the position of being able to really desire it: so nothing is easier than loving something before you know it and without knowing it. May I, moreover, remind you that you loved Diotima at first sight?"

This time, the General looked up cunningly. Agathe had in the meantime asked him to sit down and also procured a cigar for him, since her brother had forgotten his duty. Stumm, fringed with blue clouds, said innocently: "Since then she's become a textbook of love, and I didn't much like textbooks in school, either. But I still admire and respect this woman," he added with a dignified composure that was new to him.

Ulrich, unfortunately, didn't notice it immediately. "All those things are idols," he went on, pursuing the questions he had directed at Stumm. "And now you see where they came from. The instincts embedded in our nature need only a minimum of external motivation and justification; they are enormous machines set in motion by a tiny switch. But they equip the object they are applied to with only as many ideas that can bear investigation as perhaps correspond to the flickering of light and shadow in the light of an emergency lamp—"

"Stop!" Stumm begged from his cloud of smoke. "What is 'object'? Are you talking about the boots and that suitcase again?"

"I'm speaking of passion. Of longing for Diotima, just as much as longing for a forbidden cigarette. I want to make clear to you that every emotional relationship had the groundwork laid for it by preliminary perceptions and ideas that belong to reality; but that such a relationship also immediately conjures up perceptions and ideas that it fits out in its own way. In short, affect sets up the object the way it needs it to be, indeed it creates it so that the affect finally applies to an object that, having come about in such a way, is no longer recognizable. But affect isn't destined for knowledge, either, but really for passion! This object that is born of passion and hovers in it," Ulrich concluded, returning to his starting point, "is of course something different from the object on which it is outwardly fastened and which it can reach out to grasp, and this is therefore also true of love. 'I love you' is mistaken; for 'you,' this person who has evoked the passion and whom you can seize in your arms, is the one you think you love; the person evoked *by* passion, this wildly religious invention, is the one you really love, but it is a different person."

"Listening to you"—Agathe interrupted her brother with a reproach that betrayed her inner sympathies—"you might think you don't really love the *real* person, but *really* love an unreal person!"

"That's precisely what I meant to say, and I've also heard you saying much the same."

"But in reality both are ultimately one person!"

"That's exactly the major complication, that the hovering image of the person you love has to be represented in every outward connection by the person himself and is indeed one and the same. That's what leads to all the confusions that give the simple business of love such an excitingly ghostly quality!"

"But perhaps it's only love that makes the real person entirely real? Perhaps he's not complete before then?"

"But the boot or the suitcase you dream about is in reality none other than the one you could actually buy!"

"Perhaps the suitcase only becomes completely real if you love it!"

"In a word, we come to the question of what is real. Love's old question!" Ulrich exclaimed impatiently, yet somehow satisfied.

"Oh, let's forget the suitcase!" To the astonishment of both, it was the General's voice that interrupted their sparring. Stumm had comfortably squeezed one leg over the other, which, once achieved, lent him great security. "Let's stay with the person," he went on, and praised Ulrich: "So far you've said some things terrifically well! People always believe that nothing is easier than loving each other, and then you have to remind them every day: 'Dearest, it's not as easy as it is for the apple woman!' " In explanation of this more military than civilian expression, he turned politely to Agathe. "The 'apple woman,' dear lady, is an army expression for when someone thinks something is easier than it is: in higher mathematics, for example, when you're doing short division so short that, willy-nilly, you come up with a false result! Then the appple woman is held up to you, and it's applied the same way in other places as well, where an ordinary person might just say: that's not so simple!" Now he turned back to Ulrich and continued: "Your doctrine of the two persons interests me a good deal, because I'm also always telling people that you can love people only in two parts: in theory, or, as you put it, as a hovering person, is the way you ought to love someone, as I see it; but in practice, you have to treat a person strictly and, in the last analysis, harshly too! That's the way it is between man and woman, and that's the way it is in life in general! The pacifists, for instance, with their love that has no soles on its shoes, haven't the slightest notion of this; a lieutenant knows ten times as much about love as these dilettantes!"

Through his earnestness, through his carefully weighed manner of speaking, and not least through the boldness with which, despite

Agathe's presence, he had condemned woman to obedience, Stumm von Bordwehr gave the impression of a man to whom something important had happened and who had striven, not without success, to master it. But Ulrich still had not grasped this, and proposed: "Well, you decide which person is truly worth loving and which has the walk-on part!"

"That's too deep for me!" Stumm stated calmly, and, inhaling from his cigar, added with the same composure: "It's a pleasure to hear again how well you speak; but on the whole you speak in such a way that one really must ask oneself whether it's your only occupation. I must confess that after you disappeared I expected to find you, God knows, busy with more important matters!"

"Stumm, this *is* important!" Ulrich exclaimed. "Because at least half the history of the world is a love story! Of course you have to take all the varieties of love together!"

The General nodded his resistance. "That may well be." He barricaded himself behind the busyness of cutting and lighting a fresh cigar, and grumbled: "But then the other half is a story of anger. And one shouldn't underestimate anger! I have been a specialist in love for some time, and I know!"

Now at last Ulrich understood that his friend had changed and, curious, asked him to tell what had befallen him.

Stumm von Bordwehr looked at him for a while without answering, then looked at Agathe, and finally replied in a way that made it impossible to distinguish whether he was hesitating from irritation or enjoyment: "Oh, it will hardly seem worth mentioning in comparison with your occupations. Just one thing has happened: the Parallel Campaign has found a goal!"

This news about something to which so much sympathy, even if counterfeit, had been accorded would have broken through even a fully guarded state of seclusion, and when Stumm saw the effect he had achieved he was reconciled with fortune, and found again for quite a while his old, guileless joy in spreading news. "If you'd rather, I could just as well say: the Parallel Campaign has come to an end!" he offered obligingly.

It had happened quite incidentally: "We all of us had got so used to nothing happening, while thinking that something ought to happen," Stumm related. "And then all of a sudden, instead of a new proposal, someone brought the news that this coming autumn a Congress for World Peace is to meet, and here in Austria!"

"That's odd!" Ulrich said.

"What's odd? We didn't know the least thing about it!"

"That's just what I mean."

"Well, there you're not entirely off the track," Stumm von Bordwehr agreed. "It's even being asserted that the news was a plant from abroad. Leinsdorf and Tuzzi went so far as to suspect that it might be a Russian plot against our patriotic campaign, if not ultimately even a German plot. For you must consider that we have four years before we have to be ready, so it's entirely possible that someone wants to rush us into something we hadn't planned. Beyond that, the different versions part company; but it's no longer possible to find out what the truth of the matter is, although of course we immediately wrote off everywhere to learn more. Remarkably enough, it seems that people all over already knew about this pacifistic Congress—I assure you: in the whole world! And private individuals as well as newspaper and government offices! But it was assumed, or bandied about, that it emanated from us and was part of our great world campaign, and people were merely surprised because they couldn't get any kind of rational response from us to their questions and queries. Maybe someone was playing a joke on us; Tuzzi was discreetly able to get hold of a few invitations to this Peace Congress; the signatures were quite naïve forgeries, but the letter paper and the style were good as gold! Of course we then called in the police, who quickly discovered that the whole manner of execution pointed to a domestic origin, and in the course of this it emerged that there really are people here who would like to convene a World Peace Congress here in the autumn—because some woman who has written a pacifist novel is going to celebrate her umpteenth birthday or, in case she's died, would have: But it quickly became clear that these people quite evidently had not the least connection with disseminating the material that was aimed at us, and so the origin of the affair has remained in the dark," Stumm said resignedly, but with the satisfaction that every well-told tale provides. The effortful exposition of the difficulties had drawn shadows over his face, but now the sun of his smile burst through this perplexity, and with a trace of scorn that was as unconstrained as it was candid, he added: "What's most remarkable is that everyone agreed that there *should* be such a congress, or at least no one wanted to say no! And now I ask you: what are we to do, especially since we have already announced that we are undertaking something meant to serve as a model for the whole world and have constantly been spreading the slogan 'Action!' around? For two weeks we've simply had to work like savages, so that retroactively at least it looks the way it would have looked prospectively, so to speak, under other circumstances. And so we showed ourselves equal to the organizational superiority of the Prussians—assuming that it *was* the Prussians! We're now calling it a preliminary celebration. The government is keeping an eye on the political part, and those of us in the campaign are working more on the ceremonial and cultural-human aspects, because that is simply too burdensome for a ministry—"

"But what a strange story it is!" Ulrich asserted seriously, although he had to laugh at this development.

"A real accident of history," the General said with satisfaction. "Such mystifications have often been important."

"And Diotima?" Ulrich inquired cautiously.

"Well, she has speedily had to jettison Amor and Psyche and is now, together with a painter, designing the parade of regional costumes. It will be called: 'The clans of Austria and Hungary pay homage to internal and external peace,'" Stumm reported, and now turned pleadingly toward Agathe as he noticed that she, too, was parting her lips to smile. "I entreat you, dear lady, please don't say anything against it, and don't permit any objection to it either!" he begged. "For the parade of regional costumes, and apparently a military parade, are all that is definite so far about the festivities. The Tyrolean militia will march down the Ringstrasse, because they always look picturesque with their green suspenders, the rooster feathers in their hats, and their long beards; and then the beers and wines of the Monarchy are to pay tribute to the beers and wines of the rest of the world. But even here there is still no unanimity on whether, for instance, only Austro-Hungarian beers and wines shall pay tribute to those of the rest of the world, which would allow the charming Austrian character to stand out more hospitably by renouncing a tribute from the other side, or whether the foreign beers and wines should be allowed to march along as well so that they can pay homage to ours, and whether they have to pay customs duties on them or not. At any rate, one thing is certain: that there never has been and never can be a parade in this country without people in Old Germanic costumes sitting on carts with casks and on beer wagons drawn by horses; and I just can't imagine what it must have been like in the actual Middle Ages, when the Germanic costumes weren't yet old and wouldn't even have looked any older than a tuxedo does today!"

But after this question had been sufficiently appreciated, Ulrich asked a more delicate one. "I'd like to know what our non-German nationalities will say to the whole thing!"

"That's simple: they'll be in the parade!" Stumm assured him cheerfully. "Because if they won't, we'll commandeer a regiment of Bohemian dragoons into the parade and make Hussite warriors out of them, and we'll drag in a regiment of Ulans as the Polish liberators of Vienna from the Turks."

"And what does Leinsdorf say to these plans?" Ulrich asked hesitantly.

Stumm placed his crossed leg beside the other and turned serious. "He's not exactly delighted," he conceded, relating that Count Leinsdorf never used the word "parade" but, in the most stubborn way possible, insisted on calling it a "demonstration." "He's apparently still thinking of the demonstrations he experienced," Ulrich said, and Stumm agreed. "He has often said to me," he reported, " 'Whoever brings the masses into the street is taking a heavy responsibility upon himself, General!' As if I could do anything for or against it! But you should also know that for some time we've been getting together fairly often, he and I. . . ."

Stumm paused, as if he wanted to leave space for a question, but when neither Agathe nor Ulrich asked it, he went on cautiously: "You see, His Excellency ran into another demonstration. Quite recently, on a trip, he was nearly beaten up in B—— by the Czechs as well as the Germans."

"But why?" Agathe exclaimed, intrigued, and Ulrich, too, showed his curiosity.

"Because he is known as the bringer of peace!" Stumm proclaimed. "Loving peace and people is not so simple in reality—"

"Like with the apple woman!" Agathe broke in, laughing.

"I really wanted to say, like with a candy jar," Stumm corrected her, adding to this discreet reproach for Ulrich the observation on

Leinsdorf: "Still, a man like him, once he has made up his mind, will totally and completely exercise the office he has been given."

"What office?" Ulrich asked.

"Every office!" the General stated. "On the festival reviewing stand he will sit beside the Emperor, only in the event, of course, that His Majesty sits on the reviewing stand; and, moreover, he is drafting the address of homage from our peoples, which he will hand to the All-Highest Ruler. But even if that should be all for the time being, I'm convinced it won't stay that way, because if he doesn't have any other worries, he creates some: such an active nature! By the way, he would like to speak with you," Stumm injected tentatively.

Ulrich seemed not to have heard this, but had become alert. "Leinsdorf is not 'given' an office!" he said mistrustfully. "He's been the knob on top of the flagstaff all his life!"

"Well," the General said reservedly. "I really didn't mean to say anything; of course he is and always was a high aristocrat. But look, for example, not long ago Tuzzi took me aside and said to me confidentially: 'General! If a man brushes past me in a dark alley, I step aside; but if in the same situation he asks me in a friendly way what time it is, then I not only reach for my watch but grope for my gun too!' What do you say to that?"

"What should I say to that? I don't see the connection."

"That's just the government's caution," Stumm explained. "In relation to a World Peace Congress it thinks of all the possibilities, while Leinsdorf has always been one to have his own ideas."

Ulrich suddenly understood. "So in a word: Leinsdorf is to be removed from leadership because people are afraid of him?"

The General did not answer this directly. "He asks you through me to please resume your friendly relations with your cousin Tuzzi, in order to find out what's going on. I'm saying it straight out; he, of course, expressed it in a more reserved fashion," Stumm reported. And after a brief hesitation, he added by way of excuse: "They're not telling him everything! But then that's the habit of ministries: we don't tell each other everything among ourselves either!"

"What relationship did my brother really have with our cousin?" Agathe wanted to know.

Stumm, snared in the friendly delusion that he was pleasantly joking, unsuspectingly assured her: "He's one of her secret loves!" adding immediately to encourage Ulrich: "I have no idea what happened between you, but she certainly regrets it! She says that you are such an indispensable bad patriot that all the enemies of the Fatherland, whom we are trying to make feel at home here, must really love you. Isn't that nice of her? But of course she can't take the first step after you withdrew so willfully!"

From then on the leave-taking became rather monosyllabic, and Stumm was mightily oppressed at such a dim sunset after he had stood at the zenith.

Thus it was that Ulrich and Agathe got to hear something that brightened their faces again and also brought a friendly blush to the General's cheeks. "We've got rid of Feuermaul!" he reported, happy that he had remembered it in time and adding, full of scorn for that poet's love of mankind: "In any event, it's become meaningless." Even the "nauseating" resolution from the last session, that no one should be forced to die for other people's ideas, whereas on the other hand everyone should die for his own—even this resolution, which would fundamentally ensure peace, had, as was now apparent, been dropped, along with everything belonging to the past, and at the General's instigation was no longer even on the agenda. "We suppressed a journal that printed it; no one believes such exaggerated rumors anymore!" Stumm added to this news, which seemed not quite clear in view of the preparations under way for a pacifistic congress. Agathe then intervened a little on behalf of the young people, and even Ulrich finally reminded his friend that the incident had not been Feuermaul's fault. Stumm made no difficulties about this, and admitted that Feuermaul, whom he had met at the house of his patroness, was a charming person. "So full of sympathy with everything! And so spontaneously, absolutely, really good!" he exclaimed appreciatively.

"But then he would most certainly be an estimable addition to this Congress!" Ulrich again threw in.

But Stumm, who had meanwhile been making serious preparations to leave, shook his head animatedly. "No! I can't explain so briefly what's involved," he said resolutely, "but this Congress ought not to be blown out of proportion!"

50

AGATHE FINDS ULRICH'S DIARY

While Ulrich was personally escorting the parting guest to the door, Agathe, defying an inner self-reproach, carried out something she had decided on with lightning speed. Even before Stumm's intrusion, and again a second time in his presence, her eye had been caught by a pile of loose papers lying in one of the drawers of the desk, on both occasions through a suppressed motion of her brother's, which had given the impression that he would have liked to refer to these papers during the conversation but could not make up his mind—indeed, deliberately refrained from doing so. Her intimacy with him had allowed her to sense this more than guess it on any substantive basis, and in the same way she also understood that this concealment must be connected with the two of them. So when he was barely out of the room she opened the drawer, doing so, whether it was justified or not, with that feeling which furthers quick decisions and does not admit moral scruples. But the notes that she took up in her hands, with many things crossed out, loosely connected and not always easily decipherable, immediately imposed a slower tempo on her passionate curiosity.

"Is love an emotion? This question may at first glance seem nonsensical, since it appears so certain that the entire nature of love is a process of feeling; the correct answer is the more surprising: for emotion is really the least part of love! Looked at merely as emotion, love is hardly as intense and overwhelming, and in any event not as strongly marked, as a toothache."

The second, equally odd note ran: "A man may love his dog and his wife. A child may love a dog more dearly than a man his wife. One person loves his profession, another politics. Mostly, we seem to love general conditions; I mean—if we don't happen to hate them—their inscrutable way of working in concert, which I might call their 'horse-stall feeling': we are contentedly at home in our life the way a horse is in its stall!

"But what does it mean to bring all these things that are so disparate together under the same word, 'love'? A primordial idea has settled in my mind, alongside doubt and derision: Everything in the world is love! Love is the gentle, divine nature of the world, covered by ashes but inextinguishable! I wouldn't know how to express what I understand by 'nature'; but if I abandon myself to the idea as a whole without worrying about it, I feel it with a remarkably natural certainty. At least at moments."

Agathe blushed, for the following entries began with her name. "Agathe once showed me places in the Bible; I still vaguely remember how they ran and have decided to write them down: 'Everything that happens in love happens in God, for God is love.' And a second says: 'Love is from God, and whosoever loves God is born of God.' Both these places stand in obvious contradiction to each other: in one, love comes from God; in the other, it is God!

"Therefore the attempts to express the relationship of 'love' to the world seem fraught with difficulty even for the enlightened person; how should the uninstructed understanding not fail to grasp it? That I called love the nature of the world was nothing but an excuse; it leaves the choice entirely open to say that the pen and inkpot I am writing with consist of love in the moral realm of truth, or in the empirical realm of reality. But then *how* in reality? Would they then consist of love or would they be its consequences, the embodying phenomenon or intimation? Are they already themselves love, or is love only what they would be in their totality? Are they love by nature, or are we talking about a supranatural reality? And what about this 'in truth'? Is it a truth for the more heightened understanding, or for the blessedly ignorant? Is it the truth of thinking, or an incomplete symbolic connection that will reveal its meaning completely only in the universality of mental events assembled around God? What of this have I expressed? More or less everything and nothing!

"I could also just as well have said about love that it is divine reason, the Neoplatonic *logos*. Or just as well something else: Love is the lap of the world: the gentle lap of unselfconscious happening. Or, again differently: O sea of love, about which only the drowning man, not the ship-borne traveler, knows! All these allusive exclamations can transmit their meaning only because one is as untrustworthy as another.

"Most honest is the feeling: how tiny the earth is in space, and how man, mere nothing compared with the merest child, is thrown on the resources of love! But that is nothing more than the naked cry for love, without a trace of an answer!

"Yet I might perhaps speak in this way without exaggerating my words into emptiness: There is a condition in the world the sight of which is barred to us, but that things sometimes expose here or there when we find ourselves in a state that is excited in a particular way. And only in this state do we glimpse that things are 'made of love.' And only in it, too, do we grasp what it signifies. And only this state is then real, and we would only then be true.

"That would be a description I would not have to retract in any part. But then, I also have nothing to add to it!"

Agathe was astonished. In these secret entries Ulrich was holding himself back much less than usual. And although she understood that he allowed himself to do this, even for himself, only under the reservation of secrecy, she still imagined she could see him before her, stirred and irresolute, in the act of opening his arms toward something.

The notes went on: "That, too, is a notion reason itself might almost chance upon, although to be sure only reason that has to some extent managed to get out of its passive position: imagining the All-Loving as the Eternal Artist. He loves creation as long as he is creating it, but his love turns away from the finished portions. For the artist must also love what is most hateful in order to shape it, but what he has already shaped, even if it is good, cools him off; it becomes so bereft of love that he hardly still understands himself in it, and the moments when his love returns to delight in what it has done are rare and unpredictable. And so one could also think: What lords over us loves what it creates; but this love approaches and withdraws from the finished part of creation in a long ebbing flow and a short returning swell. This idea fits the fact that souls and things of the world are like dead people who are sometimes reawakened for seconds."

Then came a few other quick entries, which looked as if they were only tentative.

"A lion under the morning sky! A unicorn in the moonlight! You have the choice between love's fire and rifle fire. Therefore there are at least two basic conditions: love and violence. And without doubt it is violence, not love, that keeps the world moving and from going to sleep!

"Here the assumption might also, of course, be woven in that the world has become sinful. Before, love and paradise. That means: the world as it is, sin! The possible world, love!

"Another dubious question: The philosophers imagine God as a philosopher, as pure spirit; wouldn't it make sense, then, for officers to imagine Him as an officer? But I, a mathematician, imagine the divine being as love? How did I arrive at that?

"And how are we to participate without more ado in one of the Eternal Artist's most intimate experiences?"

The writing broke off. But then Agathe's face was again suffused with a blush when, without raising her eyes, she took up the next page and read on:

"Lately Agathe and I have frequently had a remarkable experience! When we undertook our expeditions into town. When the weather is especially fine the world looks quite cheerful and harmonious, so that you really don't pay attention to how different all its component parts are, according to their age and nature. Everything stands and moves with the greatest naturalness. And yet, remarkably, there is in such an apparently incontrovertible condition of the present something that leads into a desert; something like an unsuccessful proposal of love, or some similar exposure, the moment one does not unreservedly participate in it.

"Along our way we find ourselves walking through the narrow violet-blue streets of the city, which above, where they open to the light, burn like fire. Or we step out of this tactile blue into a square over which the sun freely pours its light; then the houses around the square stand there looking taken back and, as it were, placed against the wall, but no less expressively, and as if someone had scratched them with the fine lines of an engraving tool, lines that make everything too distinct. And at such a moment we do not know whether all this self-fulfilled beauty excites us profoundly or has nothing at all to do with us. Both are the case. This beauty stands on a razor's edge between desire and grief.

"But does not the sight of beauty always have this effect of brightening the grief of ordinary life and darkening its gaiety? It seems that beauty belongs to a world whose depths hold neither grief nor gaiety. Perhaps in that world even beauty itself does not exist, but merely some kind of almost indescribable, cheerful gravity, and its name arises only through the refraction of its nameless splendor in our ordinary atmosphere. We are both seeking this world, Agathe and I, without yet being able to make up our minds; we move along its borders and cautiously enjoy the profound emanation at those points where it is still mingled with the powerful lights of every day and is almost invisible!"

It seemed as if Ulrich, through his sudden idea of speaking of an Eternal Artist, had been led to bring the question of beauty into his observations, especially since, for its part, beauty also expressed the oversensitivity that had arisen between brother and sister. But at the same time he had changed his manner of thinking. In this new sequence of entries he proceeded no longer from his dominant ideas as they faded down to the vanishing point of his experiences, but from the foreground, which was clearer but, in a few places that he noted, really too clear, and again almost permeable by the background.

Thus Ulrich went on. "I said to Agathe: 'Apparently beauty is nothing other than having been loved.' For to love something and beautify it is one and the same. And to propagate its love and make others see its beauty is also one and the same. That's why everything can appear beautiful, and everything beautiful, ugly; in both cases it will depend on us no less than it compels us from outside, because love has no causality and knows no fixed sequence. I'm not certain how much I've said about that, but it also explains this other impression that we have so vividly on our walks: We look at people and want to share in the joy that is in their faces; but these faces also radiate a discomfiture and an almost uncanny repulsion. It emanates, too, from the houses, clothes, and everything that they have created for themselves. When I considered what the explanation for this might be, I was led to a further group of ideas, and through that back to my first notes, which were apparently so fantastic.

"A city such as ours, lovely and old, with its superb architectural stamp, which over the course of ages has arisen from changing taste, is a single great witness to the capacity for loving and the incapacity for loving long. The proud sequence of this city's structures represents not only a great history but also a constant change in the direction of thought. Looked at in this manner, the city is a mutability that has become a chain of stone and that surveys itself differently every quarter century in order to be right, in the end, for eternal ages. Its mute eloquence is that of dead lips, and the more enchantingly seductive it is, the more violently it must evoke, in its most profound moment of pleasing and of expropriation, blind resistance and horror."

"It's ridiculous, but tempting," Agathe responded to that. "In that case the swallowtail coats of these dawdlers, or the funny caps officers wear on their heads like pots, would have to be beautiful, for they are most decidedly loved by their owners and displayed for love, and enjoy the favor of women!"

"We made a game of it too. In a kind of merry bad temper we enjoyed it to the utmost and for a while asked ourselves at every step, in opposition to life: What, for example, does the red on that dress over there mean by being so red? Or what are these blues and yellows and whites really doing on the collars of those uniforms? And why in God's name are the ladies' parasols round and not square? We asked ourselves what the Greek pediment of the Parliament building was after, with its legs astraddle? Either 'doing a split,' as only a dancer or a pair of compasses can, or disseminating classical beauty? If you put yourself back that way into a preliminary state in which you are not touched by feelings, and where you do not infuse things with the emotions that they complacently expect, you destroy the faith and loyalty of existence. It's like watching someone eat silently, without sharing his appetite: You suddenly perceive only swallowing movements, which look in no way enviable.

"I call that cutting oneself off from the 'meaning' of life. To clarify this, I might begin with how we unquestionably seek the firm and solid in life as urgently as a land animal that has fallen into the water. This makes us overestimate the significance of knowledge, justice, and reason, as well as the necessity of compulsion and violence. Perhaps I shouldn't say overestimate; but in any case, by far the greatest number of manifestations of our life rest on the mind's insecurity. Faith, supposition, assumption, intimation, wish, doubt, inclination, demand, prejudice, persuasion, exemplification, personal views, and other conditions of semi-certainty predominate among them. And because meaning, on this scale, lies roughly halfway between reasoning and capriciousness, I am applying its name to the whole. If what we express with words, no matter how magnificent they are, is mostly just a meaning, an opinion, then what we express without words is always one.

"Therefore I say: Our reality, as far as it is dependent on us, is for the most part only an expression of opinion, although we ascribe every imaginable kind of importance to it. We may give our lives a specific manifestation in the stones of buildings: it is always done for the sake of a meaning we impute to it. We may kill or sacrifice ourselves: we are acting only on the basis of a supposition. I might even say that all our passions are mere suppositions; how often we err in them; we can fall into them merely out of a longing for decisiveness! And also, doing something out of 'free' will really assumes that it is merely being done at the instigation of an opinion. For some time Agathe and I have been sensitive to a certain hauntedness in the empirical world. Every detail in which our surroundings manifest themselves 'speaks to us.' It means something. It shows that it has come into being with a purpose that is by no means fleeting. It is, to be sure, only an opinion, but it appears as a conviction. It is merely a sudden idea, but acts as if it were an unshakable will. Ages and centuries stand upright with legs firmly planted, but behind them a voice whispers: Rubbish! Never has the Hour Struck, never has the Time Come!

"It seems to be willfulness, but it enables me to understand what I see if I note in addition: This opposition between the self-obsession that puffs out the chest of everything we have created in all its splendor, and the secret trait of being given up and abandoned, which likewise begins with the first minute, is wholly and completely in agreement with my calling everything merely an opinion. By this means we recognize that we are in a peculiar situation. For every attribution of meaning shows the same double peculiarity: as long as it is new it makes us impatient with every opposing meaning (when red parasols are having their day, blue ones are 'impossible'—but something similar is also true of our convictions); yet it is the second peculiarity of every meaning that it is nevertheless given up with time, entirely of its own accord and just as surely, when it is no longer new. I once said that reality does away with itself. It could now be put like this: If man is for the most part only proclaiming meanings, he is never entirely and enduringly proclaiming himself; but even if he can never completely express himself, he will try it in the most various ways, and in doing so acquires a history. So he has a history only out of weakness, it seems to me, although the historians understandably enough consider the ability to make history a particular badge of distinction!"

Here Ulrich seemed to have embarked on a digression, but he continued in this direction: "And this is apparently the reason why I have to take note of this today: History happens, events happen—even art happens—from a lack of happiness. But such a lack does not lie in circumstances—in other words, in their not allowing happiness to reach us—but in our emotions. Our feeling bears the cross of this double aspect: it suffers no other beside itself and itself does not endure. By this means everything connected with it acquires the aspect of being valid for eternity, but we all nonetheless strive to abandon the creations of our feelings and change the meanings that are expressed in them. For a feeling changes in the instant of its existence; it has no duration or identity; it must be consummated anew. Emotions are not only changeable and inconstant—as they are well taken to be—but the instant they weren't, they would become so. They are not genuine when they last. They must always arise anew if they are to endure, and even in doing this they become different emotions. An anger that lasted five days would no longer be anger but be a mental disorder; it transforms itself into either forgiveness or preparations for revenge, and something similar goes on with all the emotions.

"Our emotions always seek a foothold in what they form and shape, and always find it for a while. But Agathe and I feel an imprisoned ghostliness in our surroundings, the reverse magnetism of two connected poles, the recall in the call, the mobility of supposedly fixed walls; we see and hear it suddenly. To have stumbled 'into a time' seems to us like an adventure, and dubious company. We find ourselves in the enchanted forest. And although we cannot encompass 'our own,' differently constituted feeling, indeed hardly know what it is, we suffer anxiety about it and would like to hold it fast. But how do you hold a feeling fast? How could one linger at the highest stage of rapture, if indeed there were any way of getting there at all? Basically this is the only question that preoccupies us. We have intimations of an emotion removed from the entropy of the other emotions. It stands like a miraculous, motionless shadow in the flow before us. But would it not have to arrest the world in its course in order to exist? I arrive at the conclusion that it cannot be a feeling in the same sense as the other feelings."

And suddenly Ulrich concluded: "So I come back to the question: Is love an emotion? I think not. Love is an ecstasy. And God Himself, in order to be able to lastingly love the world and, with the love of God-the-Artist, also embrace what has already happened, must be in a constant state of ecstasy. This is the only form in which he may be imagined—"

Here he had broken off this entry.

51

GREAT CHANGES

Ulrich had personally escorted the General out with the intention of discovering what he might have to say in confidence. As he accompanied him down the stairs, he sought at first to offer a harmless explanation for having distanced himself from Diotima and the others, so that the real reason would remain unstated. But Stumm was not satisfied, and asked: "Were you insulted?"

"Not in the least."

"Then you had no right to!" Stumm replied firmly.

But the changes in the Parallel Campaign, about which in his withdrawal from the world Ulrich had not had the least inkling, now had an invigorating effect on him, as if a window had suddenly been thrown open in a stuffy hall, and he continued: "I would still like to find out what's really going on. Since you've decided to open my eyes halfway, please finish the job!"

Stumm stopped, supporting his sword on the stone of the step, and raised his glance to his friend's face; a broad gesture, which lasted the longer in that Ulrich was standing one step higher: "Nothing I'd like better," he said. "That's the reason I came."

Ulrich calmly began to interrogate him. "Who's working against Leinsdorf? Tuzzi and Diotima? Or the Ministry of War with you and Arnheim—?"

"My dear friend, you're stumbling through abysses!" Stumm interrupted him. "And blindly walking past the simple truth, the way all intellectuals seem to do! Above all, I beg you to be convinced that I have passed on Leinsdorf's wish to have you visit him and Diotima only as the most selfless favor—"

"Your officer's word of honor?"

The General's mood turned sunny. "If you're going to remind me of the spartan honor of my profession, you conjure up the danger that I really will start lying to you; for there might be an order from above that would obligate me to do so. So I'd rather give you my private word of honor," he said with dignity, and continued by way of explanation: "I was even intending to confide to you that recently I have seen myself at times compelled to reflect upon such difficulties; I find myself lying often these days, with the ease of a hog wallowing in garbage." Suddenly he turned completely toward his more elevated friend and added the question: "How does it happen that lying is so agreeable, assuming you have an excuse? Just speaking the truth seems absolutely unproductive and frivolous by comparison! If you could tell me that, it would be, straight out, one of the reasons I came to hunt you up."

"Then tell me honestly what's going on," Ulrich asked, unyielding.

"In total honesty, and also quite simply: I don't know!" Stumm protested.

"But you have a mission!" Ulrich probed.

The General answered: "In spite of your truly unfriendly disappearance, I have stepped over the corpse of my self-respect to confide this mission to you. But it is a partial mission. A teeny commission. I am now a little wheel. A tiny thread. A little Cupid who has been left with only a single arrow in his quiver!" Ulrich observed the portly figure with the gold buttons. Stumm had definitely become more self-reliant; he did not wait for Ulrich's response but set himself in motion toward the door, his sword clanking on every step. And as the entry hall, whose noble furnishings would otherwise have instilled in him a reverence for the master of the house, arched up over the two of them as they came down, he said over his shoulder to this master: "It's clear you still have not quite grasped that the Parallel Campaign is now no longer a private or family undertaking but a political process of international stature!"

"So now it's being run by the Foreign Minister?" Ulrich volleyed.

"Apparently."

"And consequently Tuzzi?"

"Presumably; but I don't know," Stumm quickly added. "And of course he acts as if he knows nothing at all! You know what he's like: these diplomats pretend to be ignorant even when they really are!"

They walked through the front door, and the carriage drove up. Suddenly Stumm turned, confidingly and comically pleading, to Ulrich: "But that's why you should really start frequenting the house again, so that we have a quasi-confidant there!"

Ulrich smiled at this scheming, and laid his arm around the General's shoulder; he felt reminded of Diotima. "What is she up to?" he asked. "Does she now recognize the man in Tuzzi?"

"What she's up to?" the General responded, vexed. "She gives the impression of being irritated." And he added good-naturedly: "To the discriminating glance, perhaps even a moving impression. The Ministry of Education gives her hardly any other assignments than deciding whether the patriotic association Wiener Schnitzel should be allowed to march in the parade, or a group called Roast Beef with Dumplings as well—"

Ulrich interrupted him suspiciously. "Now you're talking about the Ministry of Education? Weren't you just saying that the Foreign Ministry had appropriated the campaign?"

"But look, maybe the Schnitzels are really the affair of the Interior Ministry. Or the Ministry of Trade. Who can predict?" Stumm instructed him. "But in any case, the Congress for World Peace as a whole belongs to the Ministry of Foreign Affairs, to the extent that it's not already owned by the two Ministerial Presidiums."

Ulrich interrupted him again. "And the War Ministry is nowhere in your thoughts at all?"

"Don't be so suspicious!" Stumm said calmly. "Of course the War Ministry takes the most active interest in a congress for world peace; I would say no less an interest than police headquarters would take in

an international congress of anarchists. But you know what these civilian ministries are like: they won't grant even a toehold to the likes
of us!"

"And—?" Ulrich asked, for Stumm's innocence still made him
suspicious.

"There's no 'and'!" Stumm assured him. "You're rushing things! If
a dangerous business involves several ministries, then one of them
wants to either shove it off on, or take it away from, one of the others;
in both cases the result of these efforts is the creation of an interministerial commission. You only need to remind yourself how many
committees and subcommittees the Parallel Campaign had to create
at the beginning, when Diotima was still in full command of its energies; and I can assure you that our blessed council was a still life compared with what's being worked up today!" The carriage was waiting,
the coachman sitting bolt upright on his coach box, but Stumm gazed
irresolutely through the open vehicle into the bright-green garden
that opened beyond. "Perhaps you can give me a little-known word
with 'inter' in it?" he asked, and toted up with prompting nods of his
head: "Interesting, interministerial, international, intercurrent, intermediate, interpellation, interdicted, internal, and a few more; because now you hear them at the General Staff mess more often than
the word 'sausage.' But if I were to come up with an entirely new
word, I could create a sensation!"

Ulrich steered the General's thoughts back to Diotima. It made
sense to him that the highest mandate came from the Ministry of
Foreign Affairs, from which it in all probability followed that the
reins were in Tuzzi's hands: but then, how could another ministry
offend this powerful man's wife? At this question Stumm disconsolately shrugged his shoulders. "You still haven't got it through your
head that the Parallel Campaign is an affair of state!" he responded,
adding spontaneously: "Tuzzi is slyer than we thought. He himself
would never have been able to ascribe such a thing to it, but interministerial technology has allowed him to hand over his wife to another ministry!"

Ulrich began to laugh softly. From the message clothed in these
rather odd words he could vividly imagine both people: magnificent
Diotima—the power station, as Agathe called her—and the smaller,
spare Section Chief, for whom he had an absolutely inexplicable

sympathy, although he knew Tuzzi looked down on him. It was fear of the moon-nights of the soul that drew him to this man's rational feelings, which were as dryly masculine as an empty cigarette case. And yet, when they had broken over the head of this diplomat, the sufferings of the soul had brought him to the point of seeing in everyone and everything only pacifist intrigues; for pacifism was for Tuzzi the most intelligible representation of soulful tenderness! Ulrich recalled that Tuzzi had finally come to regard Arnheim's increasingly open efforts concerning the Galician oil fields—indeed, his efforts concerning his own wife—as merely a divertissement whose purpose was to deflect attention from a secret enterprise of a pacifistic nature: so greatly had the events in his house confused Tuzzi! He must have suffered unbearably, and it was understandable: the spiritual passion that he found himself unexpectedly confronting not only offended his concept of honor, just as physical adultery would have done, but struck directly and contemptuously at his very ability to form concepts, which in older men is the true retirement home of manly dignity.

And Ulrich cheerfully continued his thought aloud: "Apparently the moment his wife's patriotic campaign became the object of public teasing, Tuzzi completely regained control over his lost mental faculties, as befits a high official. It must have been then at the latest that he recognized all over again that more things are going on in the lap of world history than would find room in a woman's lap, and your Congress for World Peace, which turned up like a foundling, will have woken him with a start!" With coarse satisfaction, Ulrich depicted to himself the murky, ghost-ridden state that must have come first, and then this awakening, which perhaps did not even have to be associated with a feeling of awakening; for the moment the souls of Arnheim and Diotima, wandering around in veils, started to touch down in reality, Tuzzi, freed from every haunting spirit, again found himself in that realm of necessity in which he had spent almost his entire life. "So now he's getting rid of all those friends of his wife's who are saving the world and uplifting the Fatherland? They always were a thorn in his side!" Ulrich exclaimed with great satisfaction, and turned queryingly to his companion.

Stumm, portly and lost in thought, was still standing in the doorway. "So far as I know, he told his wife that she owed it to him and his position, especially under these changed conditions, to bring the Parallel Campaign to an honorable conclusion. She would get a decoration. But she had to entrust herself to the protection and insights of the ministry he had selected for that purpose," he reported conscientiously.

"And so he's made peace with you—I mean, with the Ministry of War and Arnheim?"

"It looks that way. Because of the Peace Congress, he seems to have argued with the government for support of the rapid modernization of our artillery, and with the Minister of War concerning the political consequences. It is said that he wants to push the necessary laws through Parliament with the help of the German parties, and for that reason is now counseling a German line in domestic politics. Diotima told me that herself."

"Wait a minute!" Ulrich interrupted. "German line? I've forgotten everything!"

"Quite simple! He always said that everything German was a misfortune for us; and now he's saying the opposite."

Ulrich objected that Section Chief Tuzzi never expressed himself so unambiguously.

"But he does to his wife," Stumm replied. "And between her and me there's a kind of bond ordained by fate."

"Well, how do things stand between her and Arnheim?" asked Ulrich, who was at the moment more interested in Diotima than in the concerns of the government. "He no longer needs her; and I suppose that's making his soul suffer!"

Stumm shook his head. "That's apparently not so simple either!" he declared with a sigh.

Up to now he had answered Ulrich's questions conscientiously but without emotion, and perhaps for that very reason relatively sensibly. But since the mention of Diotima and Arnheim, he looked as if he wanted to come out with a quite different story, which seemed to him more important than Tuzzi's finding himself. "You might have long thought that Arnheim had had enough of her," he now began. "But they're Great Souls! It may be that you can understand something about such souls, but they *are* them! You can't say, was there something between them or was there nothing between them? Today they still talk the way they used to, except that you have the feeling: now there definitely *isn't* anything between them: They're always talking in what you might call 'last words'!"

Ulrich, remembering what Bonadea, the practitioner of love, had told him about its theoretician, Diotima, held up to Stumm Stumm's own, more measured statement that Diotima was a manual of love. The General smiled thoughtfully at this. "Perhaps we aren't judging it from a broad enough perspective," he generalized discreetly. "Let me preface this by saying that before her I never heard a woman talk that way; and when she starts talking, it's like having ice bags all over me. Besides, she's doing this less often now; but when it occurs to her even today she speaks, for instance, of this World Peace Congress as a 'pan-erotic human experience,' and then I feel myself all of a sudden unmanned by her cleverness. But"—and he intensified the significance of his words by a brief pause—"there must be something in it—some need, some so-called characteristic of the age—because even in the War Ministry they're beginning to talk that way now. Since this Congress has turned up, you can hear officers of the General Staff talking about love of peace and love of mankind the way they talk about the Model 7 machine gun or the Model 82 medical supply wagon! It's absolutely nauseating!"

"Is that why you called yourself a disappointed specialist in love just now?" Ulrich interjected.

"Yes, my friend. You have to excuse me: I couldn't stand hearing you talk so one-sidedly! But officially I derive great profit from all these things."

"And you no longer have any enthusiasm for the Parallel Campaign, for the celebration of great ideas, and such things?" Ulrich probed out of curiosity.

"Even such an experienced woman as your cousin has had enough of culture," the General replied. "I mean culture for its own sake. Besides, even the greatest idea can't stop your ears from getting boxed!"

"But it can cause someone else's getting his ears boxed next time."

"That's right," Stumm conceded. "But only if you use the spirit *for* something, not if you serve it selflessly!" Then he looked up at Ulrich, curious to enjoy along with him the effect of his next words, and lowering his voice expectantly, certain of success, he added: "But even if I would like to, I can't anymore: I've been removed!"

"I'm impressed!" Ulrich exclaimed, instinctively acknowledging the insight of the military authorities. But then he followed another sudden idea and said quickly: "Tuzzi got you into this mess!"

"Not a bit of it!" Stumm protested, sure of himself.

Up to this point the conversation had taken place in the vicinity of the door, and besides the two men there was a third participant who was waiting for them to finish, staring straight ahead so motionlessly that for him the world stopped between the ears of two pairs of horses. Only his fists in their white cotton gloves, through which the reins ran, surreptitiously moved in irregular, soothing rhythms, because the horses, not quite so accessible to military discipline as people, were getting more and more bored with waiting, and were pulling impatiently at their harnesses. At last the General commanded this man to take the carriage to the gate and exercise the horses there until he got in; he then invited Ulrich to walk through the garden on foot, so that he could fill him in properly about what had gone on, without being overheard.

But Ulrich thought he saw vividly what it was all about, and at first didn't let Stumm get a word in. "It makes no difference whether Tuzzi took you out of the game or not," he said, "for in this matter you are, if you will excuse me, only a minor figure. What's important is that almost at the very moment when he began to get suspicious on account of the Congress and began to face a difficult and onerous test, he simplified his political as well as his personal situation the quickest way he could. He went to work like a sea captain who hears of a big storm coming and doesn't let himself be influenced by the still-dreaming ocean. Tuzzi has now allied himself with what repelled him before—Arnheim, your military policies, the German line—and he would also have allied himself with the efforts of his wife if, in the circumstances, it had not been more useful to wreck them. I don't know how I should put it. Is it that life becomes easy if one doesn't bother with emotions but merely keeps to one's goal; or is it a murderous enjoyment to calculate with the emotions instead of suffering from them? It seems to me I know what the devil felt when he threw a fistful of salt into life's ambrosia!"

The General was all fired up. "But that's what I told you at the beginning!" he exclaimed. "I only happened to be talking about lies, but genuine malice is, in all its forms, an extraordinarily exciting thing! Even Leinsdorf, for instance, has rediscovered a predilection for *realpolitik* and says: *Realpolitik* is the opposite of what you would like to do!"

Ulrich went on: "What makes the difference is that before, Tuzzi was always confused by what Diotima and Arnheim were talking about together; but now it can only make him happy, because the loquacity of people who aren't able to seal off their feelings always gives a third person all sorts of footholds. He no longer needs to listen to it with his inner ear, which he was never good at, but only with the outer, and that's roughly the difference between swallowing a disgusting snake or beating it to death!"

"What?" Stumm asked.

"Swallowing it or beating it to death!"

"No, that bit about the ears!"

"I meant to say: it was fortunate for him that he retreated from the inward side of feeling to the outward side. But perhaps that might still not make sense to you; it's just an idea I have."

"No, you put it very well!" Stumm protested. "But why are we using others as examples? Diotima and Arnheim are Great Souls, and for that reason alone it'll never work right!" They were strolling along a path but had not got very far; the General stopped. "And what happened to me isn't just an army story!" he informed his admired friend.

Ulrich realized he hadn't given him a chance to speak, and apologized. "So you didn't fall on account of Tuzzi?" he asked politely.

"A general may perhaps stumble over a civilian minister, but not over a civilian section chief," Stumm reported proudly and matter-of-factly. "I believe I stumbled over an idea!" And he began to tell his story.

52

TO HER DISPLEASURE, AGATHE IS CONFRONTED WITH A HISTORICAL SYNOPSIS OF THE PSYCHOLOGY OF THE EMOTIONS

Agathe, meanwhile, had come upon a new group of pages, in which her brother's notes continued in a quite different manner. It appeared that he had suddenly made up his mind to ascertain what an emotion was, and to do this conceptually and in a dry fashion. He also must have called up all manner of things from his memory, or read them specifically for this purpose, for the papers were covered with notes relating in part to the history and in part to the analysis of the concept of the emotions; altogether, it formed a collection of fragments whose inner coherence was not immediately apparent.

Agathe first found a hint about what had moved him to do this in the phrase "a matter of emotion!" which was written in the margin at the beginning; for she now remembered the conversation, with its profound oscillations that bared the foundations of the soul, which she and her brother had had on this subject in their cousin's house. And she could see that if one wanted to find out what a matter of emotions was, one had to ask oneself, whether one liked it or not, what emotion was.

This served her as a guide, for the entries began by saying that everything that happens among people has its origin either in feelings or in the privation of feelings; but without regard to that, an answer to the question of what an emotion was could not be gained with certainty from the entire immense literature that had grappled with the issue, for even the most recent accomplishments, which Ulrich really did think were advances, called for an act of trust of no small degree. As far as Agathe could see, he had not taken psychoanalysis into account, and this surprised her at first, for like all people stimulated by literature, she had heard it spoken of more than other kinds of psychology. Ulrich said he was leaving it out not because he didn't recognize the considerable merits of this significant theory, which was full of new concepts and had been the first to teach how many things could be brought together that in all earlier periods had been anarchic private experience, but because its method was not really appropriate to his present purpose in a way that would be worthy of its quite demanding self-awareness. He laid out as his task, first, to compare the existing major answers to the question of what emotion is, and went on to note that on the whole, only three answers could be ascertained, none of which stood out so clearly as to entirely negate the others.

Then followed sketches that were meant to work this out: "The oldest but today still quite prevalent way of representing feeling proceeds from the conviction that clear distinctions can be made among the state of feeling, its causes, and its effects. This method understands by the emotions a variety of inner experiences that are fundamentally distinct from other kinds—and these are, according to this view, sensation, thinking, and willing. This view is popular and has long been traditional, and it is natural for it to regard emotion as a state. This is not necessary, but it comes about under the vague impression of the perception that at every moment of an emotion, and in the middle of its dynamic changes, we can not only distinguish *that* we are feeling but also experience, as something apparently static, that we are persisting in a state of feeling.

"The more modern way of representing emotion, on the other hand, proceeds from the observation that it is most intimately associated with action and expression; and it follows both that this view is inclined to consider emotion as a process and that it does not direct its attention to emotion alone but sees it as a whole, together with its origin and forms of expression. This approach originated in physiology and biology, and its efforts were first directed at a physiological explanation of spiritual processes or, more emphatically, at the physical totality in which spiritual manifestations are also involved. The results of this can be summarized as the second main answer to the problem of the nature of emotion.

"But directing the thirst for knowledge toward the whole instead of its constituent elements, and toward reality instead of a preconceived notion, also distinguishes the more recent psychological investigations of emotion from the older kinds, except that its aims and leading ideas are naturally derived from its own discipline. This leads these recent investigations to yield a third answer to the problem of what emotion is, an answer that builds on the others as well as standing on its own. This third answer, however, is no longer in any way part of a retrospective view, because it marks the beginning of insight into the concept formation currently under way or regarded as possible.

"I wish to add, since I mentioned earlier the question of whether emotion is a state or a process, that this question actually plays just about no role at all in the developments I have outlined, unless it be that of a weakness common to all views, which is perhaps not entirely unfounded. If I imagine an emotion, as seems natural in the older manner, as something constant that has an effect both inwardly and outwardly, and also receives input from both directions, then I am obviously faced with not just one emotion but an indeterminate number of alternating emotions. For these subcategories of emotion, language rarely has a plural at its disposal: it knows no envies, angers, or spites. For language these are internal variations of an emotion, or emotion in various stages of development; but without question a sequence of stages points just as much toward a process as does a sequence of emotions. If, on the other hand—which would accord with this and also seem to be closer to the contemporary view—one believes that one is looking at a process, then the doubt as to what emotion 'really' is, and where something stops belonging to itself and becomes part of its causes, consequences, or accompanying circumstances, is not to be solved so easily. In a later place I shall come back to this, for such a divided answer customarily indicates a fault in the way the question is put; and it will, I think, become clear that the question of whether emotion is a state or a process is really an illusory one, behind which another question is lurking. For the sake of this possibility, about which I can't make up my mind, I will let this question stand."

"I will now continue following the original doctrine of emotion, which distinguishes four major actions or basic states of the soul. It goes back to classical antiquity and is presumably a dignified remnant of antiquity's belief that the world consists of the four elements earth, air, fire, and water. In any event, one often hears mention even today of four particular classes of elements of consciousness that cannot be reduced to each other, and in the class of 'emotion' the two feelings 'pleasure' and 'lack of pleasure' usually occupy a privileged position; for they are supposed to be either the only ones, or at least the only ones involving emotions that are not in any way alloyed with anything else. In truth they are perhaps not emotions at all but only a coloration and shading of feelings in which have been preserved the original distinction between attraction and flight, and probably also the opposition between succeeding and failing, and other contrasts of the originally so symmetrical conduct of life as well. Life, when it succeeds, is pleasurable: Aristotle said it long before Nietzsche and our time. Kant, too, said that 'pleasure is the feeling of furthering life, pain that of hindering it.' And Spinoza called pleasure the 'transition in man from lesser to greater perfection.' Pleasure has always had this somewhat exaggerated reputation of being an ultimate explanation (not least on the part of those who have suspected it of deception!).

"But it can really arouse laughter in the case of thinkers who are not quite major and yet are suspiciously passionate. Here let me cite from a contemporary manual a lovely passage of which I would not like to lose a single word: 'What appears to be more different in kind than, for example, joy over an elegant solution to a mathematical problem and joy over a good lunch! And yet both are, as pure emotion, one and the same, namely pleasure!' Also let me add a passage from a court decision that was actually handed down just a few days ago: 'The purpose of compensation is to bestow upon the injured party the possibility of acquiring the feelings of pleasure corresponding to his usual circumstances, which balance the absence of pleasure caused by the injury and its consequences. Applied to the present case, it already follows from the limited choice of feelings of pleasure that correspond to the age of two and a quarter years, and the ease of providing means for them, that the compensation sought is too high.' The penetrating clarity expressed in both these examples permits the respectful observation that pleasure and the absence of pleasure will long remain as the hee and the haw of the doctrine of feeling."

. . .

"If I look around further, I discover that this doctrine that carefully weighs pleasure and the absence of pleasure understands by 'mixed feelings' the 'connection of the elements of pleasure and lack of pleasure with the other elements of consciousness,' meaning by these grief, composure, anger, and other things upon which lay people place such high value that they would gladly find out more about them beyond the mere name. 'General states of feeling' such as liveliness or depression, in which mixed feelings of the same kind predominate, are called 'unity of an emotional situation.' 'Affect' is what this connection calls an emotional situation that occurs 'suddenly and violently,' and such a situation that is, moreover, 'chronic' it calls 'passion.' Were theories to have a moral, the moral of this doctrine would be more or less contained in the words: If you take small steps at the beginning, you can take big leaps later on!"

"But in distinctions such as these, whether there is just one pleasure and lack of pleasure or perhaps several; whether beside pleasure and the absence of pleasure there are not also other basic oppositions, for instance whether relaxation and tension are not such (this bears the majestic title of singularistic and pluralistic theory); whether an emotion might change and whether, if it changes, it then becomes a different emotion; whether an emotion, should it consist of a sequence of feelings, stands in relation to these the way genus stands in relation to species, or the caused to its causes; whether the stages an emotion passes through, assuming it is itself a state, are conditions of a single state or different states, and therefore different emotions; whether an emotion can bring about a change in itself through the actions and thoughts it produces, or whether in this talk about the 'effect' of an emotion something as figurative and barely real is meant as if one were to say that the rolling out of a sheet of steel 'effects' its thinning, or a spreading out of clouds the overcasting of the sky: in such distinctions traditional psychology has achieved much that ought not to be underestimated. Of course one might then ask whether love is a 'substance' or a 'quality,' and what is

1244 · THE MAN WITHOUT QUALITIES

involved with regard to love in terms of 'haeccity' and 'quiddity'; but is one ever certain of not having to raise this question yet again?"

"All such questions contain a highly useful sense of ordering, although considering the unconstrained nature of emotions, this seems slightly ridiculous and is not able to help us much with regard to how emotions determine our actions. This logical-grammatical sense of order, like a pharmacy equipped with its hundred little drawers and labels, is a remnant of the medieval, Aristotelian-scholastic observation of nature, whose magnificent logic came to grief not so much on account of the experiences people had with it as on account of those they had without it. It is particularly the fault of the developing natural sciences and their new kind of understanding, which placed the question of what is real ahead of the question of what is logical; yet no less, too, the misfortune that nature appears to have been waiting for just such a lack of philosophy in order to let itself be discovered, and responded with an alacrity that is by no means yet exhausted. Nevertheless, so long as this development has not brought forth the new cosmic philosophical egg, it is still useful even today to feed it occasionally from the old bowl, as one does with laying hens. And this is especially true for the psychology of the emotions. For in its buttoned-up logical investiture it was, ultimately, completely unproductive, but the opposite is only too true for the psychologists of emotion who came after; for in regard to this relation between logical raiment and productivity, they have been, at least in the fine years of their youth, well-nigh sans-culottes!"

"What should I call to mind from these beginnings for more general advantage? Above all that this more recent psychology began with the beneficent sympathy that the medical faculty has always had for the philosophical faculty, and it cleared away the older psychology of emotion by totally ceasing to speak of emotions and beginning to talk instead about 'instincts,' 'instinctive acts,' and 'affects.' (Not that talk of man as a being ruled by his instincts and affects was new; it became the new medicine because from then on man was *exclusively* to be so regarded.)

"The advantage consisted in the prospect of reducing the higher human attitude of inspiration to the general invigorated attitude constructed on the basis of the powerful natural constraints of hunger, sex, persecution, and other fundamental conditions of life to which the soul is adapted. The sequences of actions these determine are called 'instinctive drives,' and these arise without thinking or purpose whenever a stimulus brings the relevant group of stimuli into play, and these are similarly activated in all animals of the same species; often, too, in both animal and man. The individual but almost invariable hereditary dispositions for this are called 'drives'; and the term 'affect' is usually associated in this connection with a rather vague notion according to which the 'affect' is supposed to be the experience or the experienced aspect of the instinctive action and of drives stimulated to action.

"This also mostly assumes, either emphatically or discreetly, that all human actions are instinctive actions, or combinations from among such actions, and that all our emotions are affects or parts or combinations of affects. Today I leafed through several textbooks of medical psychology in order to refresh my memory, but not one of their thematic indexes had a mention of the word 'emotion,' and it is really no mean accomplishment for a psychology of the emotions not to contain any emotions!"

"This is the extent to which, even now, a more or less emphatic intention dominates in many circles to substitute scientific concepts meant to be as concrete as possible for the useless spiritual observation of the soul. And however one would originally have liked emotions to be nothing more than sensations in the bowels or wrists (which led to such assertions as that fear consists of an accelerated heartbeat and shallow breathing, or that thinking is an inner speaking and thus really a stimulation of the larynx), what is honored and esteemed today is the purified concept that reduces all inner life to chains of reflexes and the like, and this serves a large and successful school by way of example as the only permissible task of explaining the soul.

"So if the scientific goal may be said to be a broad and wherever possible ironclad anchoring in the realm of nature, there is still blended with it a peculiar exuberance, which can be roughly expressed in the proposition: What stands low stands firm. In the overcoming of a theological philosophy of nature, this was once an exuberance of denial, a 'bearish speculation in human values.' Man preferred to see himself as a thread in the weave of the world's carpet rather than as someone standing on this carpet; and it is easy to understand how a devilish, degrading desire for soullessness also rubbed off on the emptiness of the soul when it straggled noisily into its materialistic adolescence. This was later held against it in religiously straitlaced fashion by all the pious enemies of scientific thinking, but its innermost essence was nothing more than a good-natured gloomy romanticism, an offended child's love for God, and therefore also for his image, a love that in the abuse of this image still has unconscious aftereffects today."

"But it is always dangerous when a source of ideas is forgotten without this being noticed, and thus many things that had merely derived their unabashed certainty from it were preserved in just as unabashed a state in medical psychology. This gave rise in places to a condition of neglect involving precisely the basic concepts, and not least the concepts of instinct, affect, and instinctive action. Even the question of what a drive is, and which or how many there are, is answered not only quite disparately but without any kind of trepidation. I had an exposition before me that distinguished among the 'drive groups' of taking in food, sexuality, and protection against danger; another, which I compared with it, adduced a life drive, an assertion drive, and five more. For a long time psychoanalysis, which incidentally is also a psychology of drives, seemed to recognize only a single drive. And so it continues: Even the relationship between instinctive action and affect has been determined with equally great disparities: everybody does seem to be in agreement that affect is the 'experience' of instinctive action, but as to whether in this process the entire instinctive action is experienced as affect, including external behavior, or only the internal event, or parts of it, or parts of the external and internal process in a particular combination: sometimes one of these claims is advanced, sometimes the other, and sometimes both simultaneously. Not even what I wrote before from memory without protest, that an instinctive action happens 'without intention or reflection,' is correct all the time."

"Is it then surprising if what comes to light behind the physiological explanations of our behavior is ultimately, quite often, nothing but the familiar idea that we let our behavior be steered by chain reflexes, secretions, and the mysteries of the body simply because we were seeking pleasure and avoiding its opposite? And not only in psychology, also in biology and even in political economy—in short, wherever a basis is sought for an attitude or a behavior—pleasure and its lack are still playing this role; in other words, two feelings so paltry that it is hard to think of anything more simpleminded. The far more diversified idea of satisfying a drive would indeed be capable of offering a more colorful picture, but the old habit is so strong that one can sometimes even read that the drives strive for satisfaction because this fulfillment is pleasure, which is about the same as considering the exhaust pipe the operative part of a motor!"

And so at the end Ulrich had also come to mention the problem of simplicity, although it was doubtless a digression.

"What is so attractive, so specially tempting to the mind, that it finds it necessary to reduce the world of emotions to pleasure and its lack, or to the simplest psychological processes? Why does it grant a higher explanatory value to something psychological, the simpler it is? Why a greater value to something physiological-chemical than to something psychological, and finally, why does it assign the highest value of all to reducing things to the movement of physical atoms? This seldom happens for logical reasons, rather it happens half consciously, but in some way or other this prejudice is usually operating. Upon what, in other words, rests this faith that nature's mystery has to be simple?

"There are, first, two distinctions to be made. The splitting up of the complex into the simple and the minuscule is a habit in everyday life justified by utilitarian experience: it teaches us to dance by imparting the steps, and it teaches that we understand a thing better after we have taken it apart and screwed it together again. Science, on the other hand, uses simplicity really only as an intermediate step; even what appears as an exception subordinates itself to this. For ultimately science does not reduce the complex to the simple but reduces the particularity of the individual case to the generally valid laws that are its goal, and which are not so much simple as they are general and summarizing. It is only through their application, that is to say at second hand, that they simplify the variety of events.

"And so everywhere in life two simplicities contrast with each other: what it is beforehand and what it becomes afterward are simple in different senses. What it is beforehand, whatever that may be, is mostly simple because it lacks content and form, and therefore is generally foolish, or it has not yet been grasped. But what becomes simple, whether it be an idea or a knack or even will, both entails and participates in the power of truth and capability that compel what is confusingly varied. These simplicities are usually confused with each other: it happens in the pious talk of the simplicity and innocence of nature; it happens in the belief that a simple morality is closer in all circumstances to the eternal than a complicated one; it happens, too, in the confusion between raw will and a strong will."

When Agathe had read this far she thought she heard Ulrich's returning steps on the garden gravel and hastily shoved all the papers back into the drawer. But when she was sure that her hearing had deceived her, and ascertained that her brother was still lingering in the garden, she took the papers out again and read on a bit further.

53

THE D AND L REPORTS

When General Stumm von Bordwehr began expounding in the garden why he thought he had stumbled over an idea, it soon became evident that he was talking with the joy that a well-rehearsed subject provides. It began, he reported, with his receiving the expected rebuke on account of the hasty resolution that had forced the Minister of War to flee Diotima's house. "I predicted the whole thing!" Stumm protested confidently, adding more modestly: "except for what came afterward." For in spite of all countermeasures, a whiff of the distressing incident had got through to the newspapers, and had surfaced again during the riots of which Leinsdorf became the sacrificial lamb. But on Count Leinsdorf's way back from his Bohemian landholdings, in a city where he was trying to catch the train— Stumm now spelled out what he had already indicated in Agathe's presence—his carriage had happened to get caught between the two fronts of a political encounter, and Stumm described what happened next in the following manner: "Of course their demonstrations were about something entirely different: some regulation or other concerning the use of local national languages in the state agencies, or an issue like that, something people have got so upset about so often that it's hard to get excited about it anymore. So all that was going on was that the German-speaking inhabitants were standing on one side of the street shouting "Shame!" at those across the way, who wanted other languages and were shouting "Disgrace!" at the Germans, and nothing further might have happened. But Leinsdorf is famous as a peacemaker; he wants the national minorities living under the Monarchy to be a national people, as he's always saying. And you know, too, if I may say so here where no one can hear us, that two dogs often growl around each other in a general way, but the moment someone tries to calm them they jump at each other's throats. So as soon as Leinsdorf was recognized, it gave a tremendous impetus to everyone's emotions. They began asking in chorus, in two languages: 'What's going on with the Commission to Establish the Desires of the Concerned Sections of the Populace, Your Excellency?' And then they shouted: 'You fake peace abroad, and in your own house you're a murderer!' Do you remember the story that's told about him that once, a hundred years ago, when he was much younger, a coquette he was with died during the night? This was what they were alluding to, people are saying now. And all this happened on account of that stupid resolution that you should let yourself be killed for your own ideas but not for other people's, a stupid resolution that doesn't even exist because I kept it out of the minutes! But obviously word got around, and because we had refused to allow it, now all of

us are suspected of being murderers of the people! It's totally irrational, but ultimately logical!"

Ulrich was struck by this distinction.

The General shrugged his shoulders. "It originated with the Minister of War himself. Because when he had me called in after the row
at Tuzzi's, he said to me: 'My dear Stumm, you shouldn't have let it
get so far!' I responded as well as I could about the spirit of the times,
and that this spirit needs a form of expression and, on the other hand,
a footing too: in a word, I tried to prove to him how important it is to
look for an idea in the times and get excited about it, even if just now
it happens to be two ideas that contradict each other and give each
other apoplexy, so that at any given moment it's impossible to know
what's going to develop. But he said to me: 'My dear Stumm, you're a
philosopher! But it's a general's job to *know!* If you lead a brigade
into a skirmish, the enemy doesn't confide in you what his intentions
are and how strong he is!' Whereupon he ordered me once and for
all to keep my mouth shut." Stumm interrupted his tale to draw
breath, and went on: "That's why, as soon as the Leinsdorf business
came up on top of that, I immediately asked to speak to the Minister;
because I could see that the Parallel Campaign would be blamed
again, and I wanted to forestall it. 'Your Excellency!' I began. 'What
the populace did was irrational, but that might have been expected,
because it always is. That's why in such cases I never regard it as
reason, but as passion, fantasies, slogans, and the like. But aside from
this, even that wouldn't have helped, because Count Leinsdorf is a
stubborn old fellow who won't listen to anything!' This is more or less
what I said, and the Minister of War listened the whole time, nodding but not saying anything. But then he either forgot what he had
just been chewing me out about or must have been in a really bad
temper, because he suddenly said: 'You are indeed a philosopher,
Stumm! I'm not in the least interested in either His Excellency or the
people; but you say reason here and logic there as if they were one
and the same, and I must point out to you that they are *not* one and
the same! Reason is something a civilian can have but can get along
without. But what you have to confront reason with—which I must
demand from my generals—is logic. Ordinary people have no logic,
but they have to be made to feel it over them!' And that was the end
of the discussion," Stumm von Bordwehr concluded.

"I can't say I understand that at all," Ulrich remarked, "but it seems to me that on the whole, your Second-Highest Generalissimo was treating you not ungraciously."

They were strolling up and down the garden paths, and Stumm now walked a few paces without replying, but then stopped so violently that the gravel crunched beneath his boots. "You don't understand?" he exclaimed, and added: "At first I didn't understand either. But little by little the whole range of just how right His Excellency the Minister of War was dawned on me! And why is he right? Because the Minister of War is always right! If there should be a scandal at Diotima's, I can't leave before he does, and I can't divine the future of Mars either; it's an unreasonable thing to ask of me. Nor can I fall into disgrace, as in Leinsdorf's case, for something with which I have as little connection as I do with the birth of my blessed grandmother! But still, the Minister of War is right when he imputes all that to me, because one's superior is always right: that both is and isn't a banality! Now do you understand?"

"No," Ulrich said.

"But look," Stumm implored. "You're just trying to make things difficult for me because you don't feel involved, or because you have a feeling for justice, or for some such reason, and you won't admit that this is something a lot more serious! But really you remember quite well, because when you were in the army, people said to you all the time that an officer must be able to think logically! In our eyes, logic is what distinguishes the military from the civilian mind. But does logic mean reason? No. Reason is what the army rabbi or chaplain or the fellow from the military archives has. But logic is not reason. Logic means acting honorably in all circumstances, but consistently, ruthlessly, and without emotion; and don't let anything confuse you! Because the world isn't ruled by reason but must be dominated by iron logic, even if the world has been full of idle chatter since it began! That's what the Minister of War was giving me to understand. You will object that in me it didn't fall upon the most barren ground, because it's nothing more than the old tried-and-true mentality of the military mind. Since then I've got more of that back, and you can't deny it: we must be prepared to strike before we all start talking about eternal peace; we must first repair our omissions and weaknesses so as not to be at a disadvantage when we join the universal brotherhood. And our spirit is *not* ready to strike! It's never ready! The civilian mind is a highly significant back-and-forth, an up-and-down, and you once called it the millennial war of faith: but we can't let that destroy us! Somebody has to be there who, as we say in the military, has initiative and takes over the leadership, and that's the vocation of one's superior. I see that now myself, and I'm not entirely certain whether before, in my sympathy for every spiritual endeavor, I wasn't sometimes carried away."

Ulrich asked: "And what would have happened if you hadn't realized that? Would you have been discharged?"

"No, *that* wouldn't have happened," Stumm corrected him. "Presuming, of course, that I still showed no deficiency in military feeling toward power relationships. But they would have given me an infantry brigade in Wladisschmirschowitz or Knobljoluka, instead of letting me continue at the crossroads of military power and civilian enlightenment and still be of some use to the culture we all share!"

They had now gone back and forth several times on the path between the house and the gate, near which the carriage was waiting, and this time, too, the General turned around before they reached the gate. "You mistrust me," he complained. "You haven't even asked me what actually happened when the Peace Congress suddenly materialized!"

"Well, what did happen? The Minister of War called you in again, and what did he say?"

"No! He didn't say anything! I waited a week, but he said nothing more," Stumm replied. And after a moment of silence he couldn't restrain himself any longer and proclaimed: "But they took 'Report D' away from me!"

"What is 'Report D'?" Ulrich asked, although he had some idea.

"'Report Diotima,' of course," Stumm responded with pained pleasure. "In a ministry, a report is prepared for every important question, and that had to be done when Diotima began to use the gatherings at her house for a patriotic notion and after we found out about Arnheim's active involvement. This report was assigned to me, as you will doubtless have noticed, and so I was asked what name it should be given, because you can't just stick such a thing in a row like something in medical supplies or when you do a commissary course, and the name Tuzzi couldn't be mentioned for interministerial reasons. But I couldn't think of anything appropriate either, so finally, in order not to say either too much or too little, I proposed calling it 'Report D': for me, 'D' was Diotima, but no one knew that, and for the others it sounded really terrific, like the name of a directory, or maybe even like a secret to which only the General Staff has access. It was one of my best ideas," Stumm concluded, adding with a sigh: "At that time I was still allowed to have ideas."

But he did not seem entirely cheered up, and when Ulrich— whose mood of falling back into the world was almost used up, or at least its oral supply of talkativeness was pretty well consumed—now fell into silence after an appreciative smile, Stumm began to complain anew. "You don't trust me. After what I've said, you think I'm a militarist. But on my honor, I fight against it, and I don't want to simply drop all those things I believed in for so long. It's these magnificent ideas that really make people out of soldiers. I tell you, my friend, when I think about it I feel like a widower whose better half has died first!" He warmed up again. "The Republic of Minds is of course just as disorderly as any other republic; but what a blessing is the superb idea that no person is in sole possession of the truth and that there are a host of ideas that haven't yet even been discovered, perhaps because of the very lack of order that prevails among them! This makes me an innovator in the military. Of course, in the General Staff they called me and my 'Report D' the 'mobile searchlight battery,' on account of the variety of my suggestions, but they really liked the cornucopia I was emptying!"

"And all that's over?"

"Not unconditionally; but I've lost a lot of my confidence in the mind," Stumm grumbled, seeking consolation.

"You're right about that," Ulrich said dryly.

"Now you're saying that too?"

"I've always said it. I always warned you, even before the Minister did. Mind is only moderately suited to governing."

Stumm wanted to avoid a lecture, so he said: "That's what I've always thought too."

Ulrich went on: "The mind is geared into life like a wheel, which it drives and by which it is also driven."

But Stumm let him go no further. "If you should suspect," he interrupted, "that such external circumstances were decisive for me,

you would be humiliating me! It's also a matter of a spiritual purification! 'Report D' was, moreover, taken from me with great respect.
The Minister called me in to tell me himself that it was necessary
because the Chief of the General Staff wanted a personal report on
the Congress for World Peace, and so they immediately took the
whole business out of the Office for Military Development and attached it to the Information Offices of the *Evidenzbüro*—"

"The Espionage Department?" Ulrich interjected, suddenly animated again.

"Who else? Whoever doesn't know what he wants himself at least
has to know what everyone else wants! And I ask you, what business
does the General Staff have at a Congress for World Peace? To interfere with it would be barbarous, and to encourage it in a pacifist way
would be unmilitary! So they observe it. Who was it who said 'Readiness is all'? Well, whoever it was knew something about the military."
Stumm had forgotten his sorrow. He twisted his legs from side to
side, trying to cut off a flower with the scabbard of his sword. "I'm
just afraid it will be too hard for them and they'll beg me on their
knees to come back and take over my report," he said. "After all, you
and I know from having been at it for nearly a year how such a congress of ideas splits up into proofs and counterproofs! Do you really
believe—disregarding for the moment the special difficulties of governing—that it's only the mind that can produce order, so to speak?"

He had now given up his preoccupation with the flower and,
frowning and holding the scabbard in his hand, gazed urgently into
his friend's face.

Ulrich smiled at him and said nothing.

Stumm let the saber drop because he needed the fingertips of
both white-gloved hands for the delicate determination of an idea.
"You must understand what I mean when I make a distinction between mind and logic. Logic is order. And there must be order! That
is the officer's basic principle, and I bow down to it! But on what
basis order is established doesn't make the slightest bit of difference:
that's mind—or, as the Minister of War put it in a rather old-fashioned way, reason—and that's not the officer's business. But the officer mistrusts the ability of civilian life to become reasonable by itself,
no matter what the ideas are by which it's always trying to do so. Be-

cause whatever mind there has ever been at any time, in the end it's always led to war!"

Thus Stumm explained his new insights and scruples, and Ulrich summarized them involuntarily in an allusion to a well-known saying when he asked: "So you really mean to say that war is an element of God's ordained ordering of the world?"

"That's talking on too high a plane!" Stumm agreed, with some reservation. "I ask myself straight out whether mind isn't simply dispensable. For if I'm to handle a person with spurs and bridle, like an animal, then I also have to have a part of the animal in me, because a really good rider stands closer to his steed than he does, for example, to the philosophy of law! The Prussians call this the scoundrel everyone carries inside himself, and constrain it with a Spartan spirit. But speaking as an Austrian general, I'd rather put it that the better, finer, and more ordered a nation is, the less it needs the mind, and in a perfect state it wouldn't be needed at all! I take this to be a really tough paradox! And by the way, who said what you just said? Who's it from?"

"Moltke. He said that man's noblest virtues—courage, renunciation, conscientiousness, and readiness to sacrifice—really develop only in war, and that without war the world would bog down in apathetic materialism."

"Well!" Stumm exclaimed. "That's interesting too! He's said something I sometimes think myself!"

"But Moltke says in another letter to the same person, and therefore almost in the same breath, that even a victorious war is a misfortune for the nation," Ulrich offered for consideration.

"You see, mind pinched him!" Stumm replied, convinced. "I've never read a line of him; he always seemed much too militaristic for me. And you can really take my word for it that I've always been an antimilitarist. All my life I've believed that today no one believes in war anymore, you only make yourself look ridiculous if you say you do. And I don't want you to think I've changed because I'm different now!" He had motioned the carriage over and already set his foot on the running board, but hesitated and looked at Ulrich entreatingly. "I have remained true to myself," he went on. "But if before I loved the civilian mind with the feelings of a young girl, I now love it, if I may put it this way, more like a mature woman: it's not ideal, it won't even let itself be made coherent, all of a piece. That's why I've told you, and not just today but for a long time, that one has to treat people with kindness as well as with a firm hand, one has to both love them *and* treat them shabbily, in order for things to come out properly. And that's ultimately no more than the military state of mind that rises above parties and is supposed to distinguish the soldier. I'm not claiming any personal merit here, but I want to show you that this conviction was what was speaking out of me before."

"Now you're going to repeat that the civil war of '66 came about because all Germans declared themselves brothers," Ulrich said, smiling.

"Yes, of course!" Stumm confirmed. "And now on top of that everybody is declaring themselves brothers! That makes me ask, what's going to come of it? What really comes happens so unexpectedly. Here we brooded for almost a whole year, and then it turned out quite differently. And so it seems to be my fate that while I was busily investigating the mind, the mind led me back to the military. Still, if you consider everything I've said, you'll find that I don't identify myself with anything but find something true in everything; *that's* the essence, more or less, of what we've been talking about."

After looking at his watch, Stumm started to give the sign to leave, for his pleasure at having unburdened himself was so intense that he hàd forgotten everything else. But Ulrich amicably laid his hand on him and said: "You still haven't told me what your newest 'little job' is."

Stumm held back. "Today there's no more time. I have to go."

But Ulrich held him by one of the gold buttons gleaming on his stomach, and wouldn't let go until Stumm gave in. Stumm fished for Ulrich's head and pulled his ear to his mouth. "Well, in strictest confidence," he whispered, "Leinsdorf."

"I take it he's to be done away with, you political assassin!" Ulrich whispered back, but so openly that Stumm, offended, pointed to the coachman. They decided to speak aloud but avoid naming names. "Let me think about it," Ulrich proposed, "and see for myself whether I still know something about the world you move in. *He* brought down the last Minister of Culture, and after the recent insult he received, one has to assume that he will bring down the current one as well. But that would be, momentarily, an unpleasant disturbance, and this has to be precluded. And, for whatever reason, *he* still clings firmly to the conviction that the Germans are the biggest threat to the nation, that Baron Wisnieczky, whom the Germans can't stand, is the man best suited to beat the drum among them that the government ought not to have changed course, and so on. . . ."

Stumm could have interrupted Ulrich but had been content to listen, only now intervening. "But it was under *him* in the campaign that the slogan 'Action!' came about; while everyone else was just saying 'It's a new spirit,' *he* was saying to everyone who didn't like to hear it: 'Something must be done!' "

"And he can't be brought down, he's not in the government. And the Parallel Campaign has been, so to speak, shot out from under him," Ulrich said.

"So now the danger is that he'll start something else," the General went on.

"But what can *you* do about it?" Ulrich asked, curious.

"Well! I've been assigned the mission of diverting him a little and, if you like, also watching over him a bit—"

"Ah! A 'Report L,' you coy deceiver!"

"That's what you can call it between us, but of course it doesn't have an official name. My mission is simply to sit on Leinsdorf's neck"—this time Stumm wanted to enjoy the name too, but again he whispered it—"like a tick. Those were the Minister's own gracious words."

"But he must have also given you a goal to aim for?"

The General laughed. "Talk! I'm to talk with him! Go along with everything he's thinking, and talk so much about it that he will, we hope, wear himself out and not do anything rash. 'Suck him dry,' the Minister told me, and called it an honorable mission and a demonstration of his confidence. And if you were to ask me whether that's all, I can only respond: it's a lot! Our old Excellency is a person of enormous culture, and tremendously interesting!" He had given the coachman the sign to start, and called back: "The rest next time. I'm counting on you!"

It was only as the coach was rolling away that the idea occurred

to Ulrich that Stumm might also have had the intention of rendering *him* innocuous, since he had once been suspected of being able
to lead Count Leinsdorf's mind off on some quite extravagant
fancy.

54

NAÏVE DESCRIPTION OF HOW AN EMOTION
ORIGINATES

Agathe had gone on to read a large part of the pages that followed.

They did not, at first, contain anything of the promised exposition
of the current development of the concept of emotion, for before
Ulrich gave a summary of these views, from which he hoped to derive the greatest benefit, he had, in his own words, sought to "present
the origin and growth of an emotion as naïvely, clumsily spelling it
out with his finger, as it might appear to a layman not unpracticed in
matters of the intellect."

This entry went on: "We are accustomed to regard emotion as
something that has causes and consequences, and I want to limit myself to saying that the cause is an external stimulus. But of course
appropriate circumstances are part of this stimulus as well, which is
to say appropriate external, but also internal, circumstances, an inner
readiness, and it is this trinity that actually decides whether and how
this stimulus will be responded to. For whether an emotion occurs all
at once or protractedly, how it expands and runs its course, what
ideas it entails, and indeed what emotion it is, ordinarily depend no
less on the previous state of the person experiencing the emotion and
his environment than they do on the stimulus. This is no doubt self-
evident in the case of the condition of the person experiencing the
emotion: in other words, his temperament, character, age, education, predispositions, principles, prior experience, and present tensions, although these states have no definite boundaries and lose

themselves in the person's being and destiny. But the external environment too, indeed simply knowing about it or implicitly assuming it, can also suppress or favor an emotion. Social life offers innumerable examples of this, for in every situation there are appropriate and inappropriate emotions, and emotions also change with time and region, with what groups of emotions predominate in public and in private life, or at least which ones are favored and which suppressed; it is even the case that periods rich in emotion and poor in emotion have succeeded one another.

"Add to all this that external and internal circumstances, along with the stimulus—this can easily be measured—are not independent of each other. For the internal state has been adapted to the external state and its emotional stimuli, and is therefore dependent on them as well; and the external state must have been assimilated in some fashion or other, in such a way that its manifestation depends on the inner state before a disturbance of this equilibrium evokes a new emotion, and this new emotion either paves the way for a new equalization or is one itself. But in the same way, the 'stimulus,' too, does not ordinarily work directly but works only by virtue of being assimilated, and the inner state again only carries out this assimilation on the basis of perceptions with which the beginnings of the excitation must already have been associated.

"Aside from that, the stimulus capable of arousing an emotion is connected with the emotion insofar as what stimulates, for instance, a starving person is a matter of indifference to a person who has been insulted, and vice versa."

"Similar complications result when the subsequent process is to be described *seriatim.* Thus even the question of *when* an emotion is present cannot be answered, although according to the basic view by which it is to be effected and then produce an effect itself, it must be assumed that there is such a point in time. But the arousing stimulus does not actually strike an existing state, like the ball in the mechanical contraption that sets off a sequence of consequences like falling dominoes, but continues in time, calling forth a fresh supply of inner forces that both work according to its sense and vary its effect. And just as little does the emotion, once present, dissipate immediately in its effects, nor does it itself remain the same even for an instant, resting, as it were, in the middle between the processes it assimilates and transmits; it is connected with a constant changing in everything to which it has connection internally and externally, and also receives reactions from both directions.

"It is a characteristic endeavor of the emotions to actively, often passionately, vary the stimuli to which they owe their origin, and to eliminate or abet them; and the major directions of life are those toward the outside and from the outside. That is why anger already contains the counterattack, desire the approach, and fear the transition to flight, to paralysis, or something between both in the scream. But an emotion also receives more than a little of its particularity and content through the retroactive effect of this active behavior; the well-known statement of an American psychologist that 'we do not weep because we are sad, but are sad because we weep' might be an exaggeration, yet it is certain that we don't just act the way we feel, but we also soon learn to feel the way we act, for whatever reasons.

"A familiar example of this back-and-forth pathway is a pair of dogs who begin to romp playfully but end up in a bloody fight; a similar phenomenon can be observed in children and simple people. And is not, ultimately, the entire lovely theatricality of life such an example writ large, with its half-momentous, half-empty gestures of honor and being honored, of menacing, civility, strictness, and everything else: all gestures of wanting-to-represent-something and of the representation that sets judgment aside and influences the emotions directly. Even the military 'drill' is part of this, based as it is on the effect that a behavior imposed for a long time finally produces the emotions from which it was supposed to have sprung."

"More important than this reacting to an action, in this and other examples, is that an experience changes its meaning if its course happens to veer from the sphere of the particular forces that steered it at the beginning into the sphere of other mental connections. For what is going on internally is similar to what is happening externally. The emotion pushes inside; it 'grabs hold of the whole person,' as colloquial language not inappropriately has it; it suppresses what doesn't suit it and supports whatever can offer it nourishment. In a psychiatric textbook, I came across strange names for this: 'switching energy' and 'switching work.' But in this process the emotion also stimulates the inner sphere to turn toward *it*. The inner readiness not already expended in the first instant gradually pushes toward the emotion; and the emotion will be completely taken over from within as soon as it gets hold of the stronger energies in ideas, memories, or principles, or in other stored-up energy, and these will change it in such a way that it becomes hard to decide whether one should speak of a moving or of a being moved.

"But if, through such processes, an emotion has reached its high point, the same processes must weaken and dilute it again as well. For emotions and experiences will then crisscross the region of this climax, but no longer subordinate themselves to it completely; indeed, they will finally displace it. This countercurrent of satiety and erosion really begins when the emotion first arises; the fact that the emotion spreads indicates not only an expansion of its power but, at the same time, a relaxation of the needs from which it arose or of which it makes use.

"This can also be observed in relation to the action; for emotion not only intensifies in the action, but also relaxes in it; and its satiety, if it is not disturbed by another emotion, can proceed to the point of excess, that is to say, to the point where a new emotion occurs."

"One thing deserves special mention. So long as an emotion subjugates the internal aspect, it comes in contact with activities that contribute to experiencing and understanding the external world; and thus the emotion will be able to partly pattern the world as we understand it according to its own pattern and sense, in order to be reinforced within itself through the reactive aspect. Examples of this are well known: A violent feeling blinds one toward something that uninvolved observers perceive and causes one to see things others don't. For the melancholy person, everything is gloomy; he punishes with disregard anything that might cheer him up; the cheerful person sees the world in bright colors and is not capable of perceiving anything that might disturb this. The lover meets the most evil natures with trusting confidence, and the suspicious person not only finds his mistrust confirmed on every side, but these confirmations also seek him out to plague him. In this way every emotion, if it attains a certain strength and duration, creates its own world, a selective and personal world, and this plays no small role in human relations! Here, too, is where our notorious inconsistency and our changeable opinions belong."

Here Ulrich had drawn a line and briefly reverted to the question of whether an emotion was a state or a process. The question's peculiarity now clearly emerged as illusory. What followed took up, in summary and continuing fashion, where the previous description had left off:

"Proceeding from the customary idea that emotion is a state that emanates from a cause and produces consequences, I was led in my exposition to a description that doubtless does represent a process if the result is observed over a fairly long stretch. But if I then proceed from the total impression of a process and try to grasp this idea, I see just as clearly that the sequence between neighboring elements, the one-after-another that is an essential part of a process, is everywhere missing. Indeed, every indication of a sequence in a particular direction is missing. On the contrary, it points to a mutual dependence and presupposition between the individual steps, and even to the image of effects that appear to precede their causes. Nor do any temporal relationships appear anywhere in the description, and all this points, for a variety of reasons, to emotion being a state.

"So strictly speaking I can merely say of an emotion that it seems to be a state as much as it is a process, or that it appears to be neither a state nor a process; one statement can be justified as easily as the other.

"But even that depends, as can easily be shown, at least as much on the manner of description as on what is described. For it is not a particular idiosyncrasy of mental activity, let alone that of emotion, but occurs also in other areas in describing nature; for instance, everywhere where there is talk of a system and its elements, or of a whole and its parts, that in one person's view can appear as a state while another person sees it as a process. Even the duration of a process is associated for us with the concept of a state. I could probably not say that the logic of this double idea-formation is clear, but apparently it has more to do with the distinction between states and processes belonging to the way thinking expresses itself in language than it does with the scientific picture presented by facts, a picture that states and processes might improve but might also, perhaps, allow to disappear behind something else."

"The German language says: Anger is in me, and it says: I am in anger [*Ich bin in Zorn*]. It says: I am angry, I feel angry [*Ich fühle mich zornig*]. It says: I am in love [*Ich bin verliebt*], and I have fallen in love [*Ich habe mich verliebt*]. The names the language has given to the emotions probably point back frequently, in its history, to language's having been affected by the impression of actions and through dangerous or obvious attitudes toward actions; nevertheless, language talks of an emotion as, in one case, a state embracing various processes, in another as of a process consisting of a series of states. As the examples show, it also includes quite directly in its forms of expression, various though these may be, the idea-formations of the individual and of external and internal, and in all this the language behaves as capriciously and unpredictably as if it had always intended to substantiate the disorder of German emotions.

"This heterogeneity of the linguistic picture of our emotions, which arose from impressive but incomplete experiences, is still reflected today in the idea-formation of science, especially when these ideas are taken more in breadth than in depth. There are psychological theories in which the 'I' appears as the most certain element, present in every movement of the mind, but especially in the emotion of what is capable of being experienced, and there are other theories that completely ignore the 'I' and regard only the relationships between expressions as capable of being experienced, describing them as if they were phenomena in a force field, whose origin is left out of account. There are also ego psychologies and psychologies without the ego. But other distinctions, too, are occasionally formulated: thus emotion may appear in one place as a process that runs through the relation of an 'I' to the external world, in another as a special case and state of connectedness, and so forth: distinctions that, given a more conceptual orientation of the thirst for knowledge, easily press to the fore so long as the truth is not clear.

"Much is here still left to opinion, even if one takes the greatest care to distinguish opinion from the facts. It seems clear to us that an emotion takes shape not just anywhere in the world but within a living being, and that it is 'I' who feels, or feels stimulation within itself. Something is clearly going on within me when I feel, and I am also changing my state. Also, though the emotion brings about a more intense relation to the external world than does a sense perception, it seems to me to be more 'inward' than a sense perception. That is one group of impressions. On the other hand, a stand taken by the entire person is associated with the emotion as well, and that is another group. I know about emotion, in distinction to sense perception, that it concerns 'all of me' more than sense perception does. Also, it is only by means of an individual person that an emotion brings something about externally, whether it is because the person acts or because he begins to see the world differently. Indeed, it cannot even be maintained that an emotion is an internal change in a person without the addition that it causes changes in his relation to the external world."

"So does the being and becoming of an emotion take place 'in' us, or to us, or by means of us? This leads me back to my own description. And if I may give credence to its disinterestedness, the relationships it discreetly illuminates once again reinforce the same thing: My emotion arises inside me and outside me; it changes from the inside and the outside; it changes the world directly from inside and indirectly, that is through my behavior, from outside; and it is therefore, even if this contradicts our prejudice, simultaneously inside and outside, or at least so entangled with both that the question as to what in an emotion is internal and what external, and what in it is 'I' and what the world, becomes almost meaningless.

"This must somehow furnish the basic facts, and can do so expeditiously, for, expressed in rather measured words, it merely states that in every act of feeling a double direction is experienced that imparts to it the nature of a transitory phenomenon: inward, or back to the individual, and outward, or toward the object with which it is concerned. What, on the other hand, inward and outward are, and even more what it means to belong to the 'I' or the world, in other words what stands at the end of both directions and would therefore be necessary to permit us to understand their presence completely: this is of course not to be clearly grasped in the first experience of it, and its origin is no clearer than anything else one experiences without knowing how. It is only through continuing experience and investigation that a genuine concept for this can be developed.

"That is why a psychology that considers it important that it be a real science of experience will treat these concepts and proceed no differently from the way such a science does with the concepts of state and process; and the closely related ideas of the individual person, the mind, and the 'I,' but also complete ideas of inward and outward, will appear in it as something to be explained, and not as something by whose aid one immediately explains something else."

"The everyday wisdom of psychology agrees with this remarkably well, for we usually assume in advance, without thinking about it much, that a person who shows himself in a way that corresponds to a specific emotion really feels that way. So it not seldom happens, perhaps it even happens quite often, that an external behavior, together with the emotions it embraces, will be comprehended directly as being all of a piece, and with great certainty.

"We first experience directly, as a whole, whether the attitude of a being approaching us is friendly or hostile, and the consideration whether this impression is correct comes, at best, afterward. What approaches us in the first impression is not something that might perhaps prove to be awful; what we feel is the awfulness itself, even if an instant later the impression should turn out to be mistaken. And if we succeed in reconstituting the first impression, this apparent reversal permits us to also discern a rational sequence of experiences, such as that something is beautiful and charming, or shameful or nauseating.

"This has even been preserved in a double usage of language we meet with every day, when we say that we consider something awful, delightful, or the like, emphasizing thereby that the emotions depend on the person, just as much as we say that something is awful, delightful, and the like, emphasizing that the origin of our emotions is rooted as a quality in objects and events. This doubleness or even amphibian ambiguity of the emotions supports the idea that they are to be observed not only within us, but also in the external world."

With these last observations Ulrich had already arrived at the third answer to the question of how the concept of emotion is to be determined; or, more reservedly, at the opinion on this question that prevails today.

55

FEELING AND BEHAVIOR.
THE PRECARIOUSNESS OF EMOTION

"The school of theoretical psychology most successful at the moment treats emotions and the actions associated with emotions as an indissoluble entity. What we feel when we act is for this psychology one aspect, and how we act with feeling the other aspect, of one and the same process. Contemporary psychology investigates both as a unit. For theories in this category, emotion is—in their terms—an internal and external behavior, event, and action; and because this bringing together of emotion and behavior has proved itself quite well, the question of how the two sides are to be ultimately separated again and distinguished from each other has become for the time being almost secondary. That is why instead of a single answer there is a whole bundle of answers, and this bundle is rather untidy."

"We are sometimes told that emotion is simply identical with the internal and external events, but we are usually merely told that these events are to be considered equivalent to the emotion. Sometimes emotion is called, rather vaguely, 'the total process,' sometimes merely internal action, behavior, course, or event. Sometimes it also seems that two concepts of emotion are being used side by side: one in which emotion would be in a broader sense the 'whole,' the other in which it would be, in a narrower sense, a partial experience that in some rather hazy way stamps its name, indeed its nature, on the whole. And sometimes people seem to follow the conjecture that one and the same thing, which presents itself to observation as a complex process, becomes an emotion when it is experienced; in other words, the emotion would then be the experience, the result, and, so to speak, what the process yields in consciousness.

"The origin of these contradictions is no doubt always the same. For every such description of an emotion exhibits components, preponderantly in the plural, that are obviously not emotions, because they are actually known and equally respected as sensation, comprehension, idea, will, or an external process, such as can be experienced at any time, and which also participate exactly as they are in the total experience. But in and above all this there is also just as clearly something that seems in and of itself to be emotion in the simplest and most unmistakable sense, and nothing else: neither acting, nor a process of thinking, nor anything else.

"That's why all these explanations can be summarized in two categories. They characterize the emotion either as an 'aspect,' a 'component,' or a 'force' of the total process, or else as the 'becoming aware' of this process, its 'inner result,' or something similar; expressions in which one can see clearly enough the embarrassment for want of better ones!"

"The most peculiar idea in these theories is that at first they leave vague the relation of the emotion to everything it is not, but with which it is filled; but they make it appear quite probable that this connection is in any case, and however it might be thought of otherwise, so constituted that it admits of no discontinuous changes, and that everything changes, so to speak, in the same breath.

"It can be thought of in terms of the example of melody. In melody the notes have their independent existence and can be recognized individually, and their propinquity, their simultaneity, their sequence, and whatever else can be heard are not abstract concepts but an overflowing sensory exposition. But although all these elements can be heard singly in spite of their connectedness, they can also be heard connectedly, for that is precisely what melody is; and if the melody is heard, it is not that there is something new in addition to the notes, intervals, and rhythms, but something *with* them. The melody is not a supplement but a second-order phenomenon, a special form of existence, under which the form of the individual existences can just barely be discerned; and this is also true of emotion in relation to ideas, movements, sensations, intentions, and mute forces that unite in it. And as sensitive as a melody is to any change in its 'components,' so that it immediately takes on another form or is destroyed entirely, so can an emotion be sensitive to an action or an interfering idea.

"In whatever relationship the emotion may therefore stand to 'internal and external behavior,' this demonstrates how any change in this behavior could correspond to a change in the emotion, and vice versa, as if they were the two sides of a page."

"(There are many model and experimental examples that confirm the broad extent of this theoretical idea, and other examples outside science that this idea fitfully illuminates, whether apparently or actually. I would like to retain one of these. The fervor of many portraits—and there are portraits, not just pictures, even of things—consists not least in that in them the individual existence opens up toward itself inwardly and closes itself off from the rest of the world. For the independent forms of life, even if they represent themselves as relatively hermetic, always have common links with the dispersive circle of a constantly changing environment. So when I took Agathe on my arm and we both took ourselves out of the frame of our lives and felt united in another frame, perhaps something similar was happening with our emotions. I didn't know what hers were, nor she mine, but they were only there for each other, hanging open and clinging to each other while all other dependency disappeared; and that is why we said we were outside the world and in ourselves, and used the odd comparison with a picture for this animated holding back and stopping short, this true homecoming and this becoming a unity of alien parts.)"

"So the peculiar thought I am talking about teaches that the alterations and modulations of the emotion, and those of the internal and external behavior, can correspond to each other point for point without the emotion having to be equated with the behavior or with part of it, or without anything else having to be maintained about the emotion beyond its possessing qualities that also have their civic rights elsewhere in nature. This result has the advantage of not interfering with the natural distinction between an emotion and an event, and yet bridges them in such a way that the distinction loses its significance. It demonstrates in the most general fashion how the spheres of two actions, which can remain totally unlike one another, may yet be delineated in each other.

"This obviously gives the question of how, then, an emotion is supposed to 'consist' of other mental, indeed even of physical processes, an entirely new and remarkable turn; but this only explains how every change in the behavior corresponds to a change in the emotion, and vice versa, and not what really leads to such changes as take place during the entire duration of the emotion. In that case, the emotion would appear to be merely the echo of its accompanying action, and this action would be the mirror image of the emotion, so it would be hard to understand their reciprocally changing each other.

"Here, consequently, the second major idea that can be derived from the newly opened up science of the emotions begins. I would like to call it the idea of shaping and consolidating."

"This idea is based on several notions and considerations. Since I would like to clarify it for myself, let me first go back to our saying that an emotion brings about a behavior, and the behavior reacts on the emotion; for this crude observation easily allows a better one to counter it, that between both there is, rather, a relationship of mutual reinforcement and resonance, a rampant swelling into each other, which also, to be sure, brings about mutual change in both components. The emotion is translated into the language of the action, and the action into the language of the emotion. As with every translation, something new is added and some things are lost in the process.

"Among the simplest relationships, the familiar expression that one's limbs are paralyzed with fear already speaks of this; for it could just as well be maintained that the fear is paralyzed by the limbs: a distinction such as the one between 'rigid with terror' and 'trembling with fear' rests entirely on this second case. And what is claimed by the simplest movement of expression is also true of the comprehensive emotional action: in other words, an emotion changes not just as a consequence of the action it evokes, but already within the action by which it is assimilated in a particular way, repeated, and changed, in the course of which both the emotion and the action mutually shape and consolidate themselves. Ideas, desires, and impulses of all sorts also enter into an emotion in this way, and the emotion enters them."

"But such a relationship of course presupposes a differentiation in the interaction in which the lead should alternate sequentially, so that now feeling, now acting, dominates, now a resolve, scruple, or idea becomes dominant and makes a contribution that carries all the components forward in a common direction. So this relationship is contained in the idea of a mutual shaping and consolidation, and it is this idea that really makes it complete.

"On the other side, the unity described previously must at the same time be able to assimilate changes and yet still have the ability to maintain its identity as a more or less defined emotional action; but it must also be able to exclude, for it assimilates influences from within and without or fends them off. Up to now, all I know of this unity is the law of its completed state. Therefore the origins of these influences must also be able to be adduced and ultimately explained, thanks to which providence or arrangement it happens that they enter into what is going on in the sense of a common development."

"Now, in all probability a particular ability to endure and be resuscitated, a solidity and degree of solidity, and thus finally also a particular 'energy,' cannot be ascribed to the unity alone, to the structure as such, the mere shape of the event; nor is it very likely that there exist other internal participatory energies that focus specifically on this. On the other hand, it is probable that these energies play nothing more than a secondary role; for our emotions and ideas probably also control the same numerous, instantaneous internal relationships and the same enduring dispositions, inclinations, principles, intentions, and needs that produce our actions as well as our emotions and ideas. Our emotions and ideas are the storage batteries of these elements, and it is to be assumed that the energies to which they give rise somehow bring about the shaping and consolidation of the emotions."

"How that happens I will try to make clear by means of a widely held prejudice. The opinion is often voiced that there is some kind of 'inner relation' among an emotion, the object to which it is directed, and the action that connects them. The idea is that it would then be more comprehensible that these form a unified whole, that they succeed one another, and so on. The heart of the matter is that a particular drive or a particular emotion—for example, hunger and the instinct for food—are directed not at random objects and actions but primarily, of course, at those that promise satisfaction. A sonata is of no help to a starving person, but food is: that is to say, something belonging to a more or less specific category of objects and events; and this gives rise to the appearance of this category and this state of stimulation always being connected. There is some truth in this, but no more mysterious a truth than that to eat soup we use a spoon and not a fork.

"We do so because it seems to us appropriate; and it is nothing but this commonplace appearing-to-be-appropriate that fulfills the task of mediating among an emotion, its object, the concomitant actions, ideas, decisions, and those deeper impulses that for the most part elude observation. If we act with an intention, or from a desire, or for a purpose—for instance, to help or hurt someone—it seems natural to us that our action is determined by the demand that it be appropriate; but beyond that it can turn out in many different ways. The same is true for every emotion. An emotion, too, longs for everything that seems suited to satisfying it, in which process this characteristic will be sometimes more tightly, sometimes more loosely, related; and precisely this looser connection is the natural path to shaping and consolidation.

"For it occasionally happens even to the drives that they go astray, and wherever an emotion is at its peak, it then happens that an action is merely attempted, that an intention or an idea is thrown in that later turns out to be inappropriate and is dropped, and that the emotion enters the sphere of a source of energy, or this sphere enters that of the emotion, from which it frees itself again. So in the course of the event not everything is shaped and consolidated; a great deal is also abandoned. In other words, there is also a shaping without consolidation, and this constitutes an indispensable part of the consolidating arrangement. For since everything that seems appropriate to serve the directing energies can be absorbed by the unity of the emotional behavior, but only so much of this is retained as is really appropriate, there enter of themselves into the feeling, acting, and thinking the common trait, succession, and duration which make it comprehensible that the feeling, acting, and thinking mutually and increasingly consolidate and shape themselves."

"The weak point of this explanation lies where the precisely described unity that arises at the end is supposed to be connected to the unknown and vaguely bounded sphere of the impulses that lies at the beginning. This sphere is hardly anything other than what is embraced by the essences 'person' and 'I' according to the proportion of their involvement, about which we know little. But if one considers that in the moment of an emotion even what is most inward can be recast, then it will not seem unthinkable that in such a moment the shaped unity of the action, too, can reach that point. If one considers, on the other hand, how much has to happen beforehand in order to prepare such a success as a person giving up principles and habits, one will have to desist from every idea that concentrates on the momentary effect. And if one were, finally, to be satisfied by saying that other laws and connections are valid for the area of the source than for the outlet, where the emotion becomes perceivable as internal and external action, then one would again come up against the insufficiency that we have no idea at all according to what law the transition from the causative forces to the resulting product could come about. Perhaps the postulation of a loose, general unity that embraces the entire process can be combined with this, in that it would ultimately enable a specific and solid unity to emerge: but this question extends beyond psychology, and for the time being extends beyond our abilities too."

"This knowledge, that in the process of an emotion from its source to its appearance a unity is indicated, but that it cannot be said when and how this unity assumes the closed form that is supposed to characterize the emotion's completely developed behavior (and in analyzing which I used the articulation of a melody as example)—this quite negative knowledge permits, remarkably, an idea to be brought in by means of which the deferred answer to the question of how the concept of the emotion appears in more recent research comes to a singular conclusion. This is the admission that the actual event corresponds neither in its entirety nor in its final form to the mental image that has been made of it. This is usefully demonstrated by a kind of double negative: One says to oneself: perhaps the pure unity that theoretically represents the law of the completed emotion never exists; indeed, it may not even be at all possible for it *to* exist, because it would be so completely cut off inside its own compass that it would not be able to assimilate any more influences of any other kind. But, one now says to oneself, there never is such a completely circumscribed emotion! In other words: emotions never occur purely, but always only in an approximating actualization. And in still other words: the process of shaping and consolidating never ends."

"But this is nothing other than what presently characterizes psychological thinking everywhere. Moreover, one sees in the basic mental concepts only ideational patterns according to which the internal action can be ordered, but one no longer expects that it is really constructed out of such elements, like a picture printed by the four-color process. In truth, according to this view, the pure nature of the emotion, of the idea, of sensation, and of the will are as little to be met with in the internal world as are the thread of a current or a difficult point in the outer world: There is merely an interwoven whole, which sometimes seems to will and sometimes to think because this or that quality predominates.

"The names of the individual emotions therefore characterize only types, which approximate real experiences without corresponding to them entirely; and with this, a guiding principle with the following content—even if this is rather crudely put—takes the place of the axiom of the older psychology by which the emotion, as one of the elemental experiences, was supposed to have an unalterable nature, or to be experienced in a way that distinguished it once and for all from other experiences: There are no experiences that are from the beginning distinct emotions, or even emotions at all; there are merely experiences that are destined to become emotion and to become a distinct emotion.

"This also gives the idea of arrangement and consolidation the significance that in this process emotion and behavior not only form, consolidate, and, as far as it is given them, determine; it is in this process that the emotion originates in the first place: so that it is never this or that specific emotion that is present at the beginning—say, in a weak state—together with its mode of action, but only something that is appropriate and has been destined to *become* such an emotion and action, which, however, it never becomes in a pure state."

"But of course this 'something' is not completely random, since it is understood to be something that from the start and by disposition is intended or appropriate to becoming an emotion, and, moreover, a specific emotion. For in the final analysis anger is not fatigue, and apparently not in the first analysis either; and just as little are satiety and hunger to be confused, even in their early stages. Therefore at the beginning something unfinished, a start, a nucleus, something like an emotion and things associated with that emotion, will already be present. I would like to call it a feeling that is not yet an emotion; but it is better to present an example, and for that I will take the relatively simple one of physical pain inflicted externally.

"This pain can be a locally restricted sensation that penetrates or burns in one spot and is unpleasant but alien. But this sensation can also flare up and overwhelm the entire person with affliction. Often, too, at the beginning there is merely an empty spot at the place, from which it is only in the following moments that sensation or emotion wells up: it is not only children who at the beginning often do not know whether something hurts. Earlier, one assumed that in these cases an emotion is superimposed on the sensation, but today one prefers to suppose that a nucleus of experience, originally as little a sensation as it is an emotion, can develop equally well into the one as the other.

"Also already part of this original stability of experience is the beginning of an instinctive or reflex action, a shrinking back, collapsing, fending off, or a spontaneous counterattack; and because this more or less involves the entire person, it will also involve an internal 'flight or fight' condition, in other words a coloration of the emotion by the kind of fear or attack. This proceeds of course even more strongly from the drives triggered, for not only are these dispositions for a purposive action but, once aroused, they also produce nonspecific mental states, which we characterize as moods of fearfulness or irritability, or in other cases of being in love, of sensitivity, and so forth. Even not acting and not being able to do anything has such an emotional coloration; but the drives are for the most part connected with a more or less definite will formation, and this leads to an inquiry into the situation that is in itself a confrontation and therefore has an aggressive coloration. But this inquiry can also have the effect of coolness and calm; or if the pain is quite severe, it does not take place, and one suddenly avoids its source. So even this example goes back and forth from the very beginning between sensation, emotion, automatic response, will, flight, defense, attack, pain, anger, curiosity, and being coolly collected, and thereby demonstrates that what is present is not so much the original state of a single emotion as rather varying beginnings of several, succeeding or complementing one another.

"This gives to the assertion that a feeling is present, but not yet an emotion, the sense that the disposition to an emotion is always present but that it does not need to be realized, and that a beginning is always present but it can turn out later to have served as the beginning of a different emotion."

"The peculiar manner in which the emotion is from the beginning both present and not present can be expressed in the comparison that one must imagine its development as the image of a forest, and not as the image of a tree. A birch, for example, remains itself from its germination to its death; but on the other hand, a birch forest can begin as a mixed forest; it becomes a birch forest as soon as birch trees—as the result of causes that can be quite varied—predominate in it and the departures from the pure stamp of the birch type are no longer significant.

"It is the same with the emotion and (this is always open to misunderstanding) with the action connected to the emotion. They always have their particular characteristics, but these change with everything that adheres to them until, with growing certitude, they take on the marks of a familiar emotion and 'deserve' its name, which always retains a trace of free judgment. But emotion and the action of emotion can also depart from this type and approximate another; this is not unusual, because an emotion can waver and, in any event, goes through various stages. What distinguishes this from the ordinary view is that in the ordinary view the emotion has validity as a specific experience, which we do not always recognize with certainty. On the other hand, the more recently established view ascribes the lack of certainty to the emotion and tries to understand it from its nature and to limit it concisely."

There followed in an appendix individual examples that really ought to have been marginal notations but had been suppressed at the places they had been intended for in order not to interrupt the exposition. And so these stragglers that had dropped out of their context no longer belonged to a specific place, although they did belong to the whole and retained ideas that might possibly have some useful application for the whole:

"In the relation 'to love something,' what carries such enormous distinctions as that between love of God and loving to go fishing is not the love but the 'something.' The emotion itself: the devotion, anxiousness, desire, hurt, gnawing—in other words, loving—does not admit a distinction."

. . .

"But it is just as certain that loving one's walking stick or honor is not 'apples and oranges' only for the reason that these two things do not resemble each other, but also because the use we make of them, the circumstances in which they assume importance—in short, the entire group of experiences—are different. It is from the noninter-changeability of a group of experiences that we derive the certainty of knowing our emotion. That is why we only truly recognize it after it has had some effect in the world and has been shaped by the world; we do not know what we feel before our action has made that decision."

"And where we say that our emotion is divided, we should rather say that it is not yet complete, or that we have not yet settled down."

"And where it appears as paradox or paradoxical combination, what we have is often something else. We say that the courageous person ignores pain; but in truth it is the bitter salt of pain that overflows in courageousness. And in the martyr it rises in flames to heaven. In the coward, on the contrary, the pain becomes unbearably concentrated through the anticipatory fear. The example of loathing is even clearer; those feelings inflicted with violence are associated with it, which, if received voluntarily, are the most intense desire.

"Of course there are differing sources here, and also varying combinations, but what comes into being most particularly are various directions in which the predominant emotion develops."

"Because they are constantly fluid, emotions cannot be stopped; nor can they be looked at 'under the microscope.' This means that the more closely we observe them, the less we know what it is we feel. Attention is already a change in the emotion. But if emotions were a 'mixture,' this should really be most apparent at the moment when it is stopped, even if attention intervenes."

· · ·

"Because the external action has no independent significance for the mind, emotions cannot be distinguished by it alone. Innumerable times we do not know what we feel, although we act vigorously and decisively. The enormous ambiguity of what a person does who is being observed mistrustfully or jealously rests on this lack of clarity."

"The emotion's lack of clarity does not, however, demonstrate its weakness, for emotions vanish precisely when feeling is at its height. Even at high degrees of intensity, emotions are extremely labile; see for instance the 'courage of despair,' or happiness suddenly changing into pain. At this level they also bring about contradictory actions, like paralysis instead of flight, or 'being suffocated' by one's own anger. But in quite violent excitation they lose, so to speak, their color, so that all that remains is a dead sensation of the accompanying physical manifestations, contraction of the skin, surging of the blood, blotting out of the senses. And what appears fully in these most intense stages is an absolute bedazzlement, so that it can be said that the shaping of the emotion, and with it the entire world of our emotions, is valid only in intermediate stages."

"In these average stages we of course recognize and name an emotion no differently from the way we do other phenomena that are in flux, to repeat this once again. To determine the distinction between hate and anger is as easy and as difficult as ascertaining the distinction between premeditated and unpremeditated murder, or between a basin and a bowl. Not that what is at work here is capriciousness in naming, but every aspect and deflection can be useful for comparison and concept formation. And so in this way the hundred and one kinds of love about which Agathe and I joked, not entirely without sorrow, are connected. The question of how it happens that such quite different things are characterized by the single word 'love' has the same answer as the question of why we unhesitatingly talk of dinner forks, manure forks, tree-branch forks, rifle forks, road forks, and other forks. Underlying all these fork impressions is a common 'forkness': it is not in them as a common nucleus, but it might almost be said that it is nothing more than a comparison possible for each of them. For they do not all even need to be similar to one another: it is already sufficient if one leads to another, if you go from one to the next, as long as the neighboring members are similar to one another. The more remote ones are then similar through the mediation of these proximate members. Indeed, even what constitutes the similarity, that which associates the neighboring members, can change in such a chain; and so one travels excitedly from one end of the path to the other, hardly knowing oneself how one has traversed it."

"But if we wished to regard, as we are inclined to do, the similarity existing among all kinds of love for its similarity to a kind of 'ur-love,' which so to speak would sit as an armless and legless torso in the middle of them all, it would most likely be the same error as believing in an 'ur-fork.' And yet we have living witness for there really being such an emotion. It is merely difficult to determine the degree of this 'really.' It is different from that of the real world. An emotion that is not an emotion *for* something; an emotion without desire, without preferment, without movement, without knowledge, without limits; an emotion to which no distinct behavior and action belongs, at least no behavior that is quite real: as truly as this emotion is not served with arms and legs, so truly have we encountered it again and again, and it has seemed to us more alive than life itself! Love is already too particular a name for this, even if it most intimately related to a love for which tenderness or inclination are expressions that are too obvious. It realizes itself in many different ways and in many connections, but it can never let itself be detached from this actualization, which always contaminates it. Thus has it appeared to us and vanished, an intimation that always remained the same. Apparently the dry reflections with which I have filled these pages have little to do with this, and yet I am almost certain that they have brought me to the right path to it!"

56

THE DO-GOODER SINGS

Professor August Lindner sang. He was waiting for Agathe.

> Ah, the boy's eyes seem to me
> So crystal clear and lovely,
> And a something shines in them
> That captivates my heart.
>
> Ah, those sweet eyes glance at me,
> Shining into mine!
> Were he to see his image there
> He would greet me tenderly.
>
> And this is why I yield myself
> To serve his eyes alone,
> For a something shines in them
> That captivates my heart.

It had originally been a Spanish song. There was a small piano in the house, dating from Frau Lindner's time; it was occasionally devoted to the mission of rounding out the education and culture of son Peter, which had already led Peter to remove several strings. Lindner himself never used it, except possibly to strike a few solemn chords now and then; and although he had been pacing up and down in front of this sound machine for quite some time, it was only after cautiously making sure that the housekeeper as well as Peter was out of the house that he had let himself be carried away by this unwonted impulse. He was quite pleased with his voice, a high baritone obviously well suited to expressing emotion; and now Lindner had not closed the piano but was standing there thinking, leaning on it with his arm, his weightless leg crossed over his supporting leg. Agathe, who had already visited him several times, was over an hour late. The emptiness of the house, stemming in part from that fact and in part from the arrangements he had made, welled up in his consciousness as a culpable plan.

He had found a soul of bedazzling richness, which he was making great efforts to save and which evoked the impression of confiding itself to his charge; and what man would not be charmed at finding something he had hardly expected to find, a tender female creature he could train according to his principles? But mixed in with this were deep notes of discontent. Lindner considered punctuality an obligation of conscience, placing it no lower than honesty and contractual obligations; people who made no punctual division of their time seemed to him pathologically scatterbrained, forcing their more serious fellow men, moreover, to lose parcels of *their* time along with them; and so he regarded them as worse than muggers. In such cases he took it as his duty to bring it to the attention of such beings, politely but unrelentingly, that his time did not belong to him but to his activity; and because white lies injure one's own mind, while people are not all equal, some being influential and some not, he had derived numerous character exercises from this; a host of their most powerful and malleable maxims now came to his mind and interfered with the gentle arousal brought on by the song.

But no matter: he had not sung any religious songs since his student days, and enjoyed it with a circumspect *frisson*. "What southern naïveté, and what charm," he thought, "emanate from such worldly lines! How delightfully and tenderly they relate to the boy Jesus!" He tried to imitate the poem's artlessness in his mind, and arrived at the result: "If I didn't know better, I'd be capable of believing that I feel a girl's chaste stirrings for her boy!" So one might well say that a woman able to evoke such homage was reaching all that was noblest in man and must herself be a noble being. But here Lindner smiled with dissatisfaction and decided to close the lid of the piano. Then he did one of his arm exercises that further the harmony of the personality, and stopped again. An unpleasant thought had crossed his mind. "She is unfeeling!" he sighed behind gritted teeth. "She would be laughing!"

He had in his face at this moment something that would have reminded his dear departed mother of the little boy under whose chin every morning she tied a big lovely bow before sending him off to school; this something might be called the complete absence of rough-hewn maleness. On this tall, slack, pipestem-legged apparition, the head sat as if speared on a lance over the roaring arena of his schoolmates, who jeered at the bow tie made by his mother's hand; and in anxiety dreams Professor Lindner even now sometimes saw himself standing that way and suffering for the good, the true, and the beautiful. But for this very reason he never conceded that roughness is an indispensable male characteristic, like gravel, which has to be mixed into mortar to give it strength; and especially since he had become the man he flattered himself to be, he saw in that early defect merely a confirmation of the fact that he had been born to improve the world, even if in modest measure. Today we are quite accustomed to the explanation that great orators arise from speech defects and heroes from weakness, in other words the explanation that our nature always first digs a ditch if it wants us to erect a mountain above it; and because the half-knowledgeable and half-savage people who chiefly determine the course of life are quick to proclaim nearly every stutterer a Demosthenes, it is that much easier, as a sign of intellectual good taste, to recognize that the only important thing about a Demosthenes was his original stuttering. But we have not yet succeeded in reducing the deeds of Hercules to his having been a sickly child, or the greatest achievements in the sprint and broad jump to flat-footedness, or courage to timidity; and so it must be conceded that there is something more to an exceptional talent than its omission.

Thus Professor Lindner was by no means restricted to acknowledging that the raillery and blows he had feared as a child could be a cause of his intellectual development. Nevertheless, the current disposition of his principles and emotions did him the service of transforming every such impression that reached him from the bustle of the world into an intellectual triumph; even his habit of weaving martial and sportive expressions into his speech, as well as his tendency to set the stamp of a strict and inflexible will on everything he said and did, had begun to develop to the degree that, as he grew up and lived among more mature companions, he was correspondingly removed from direct physical attacks. At the university, he had even joined one of the fraternities whose members wore their jackets, caps, boots, insignia, and sword just as picturesquely as the rowdies whom they despised, but made only peaceful use of them because their outlook forbade dueling. In this, Lindner's pleasure in a bravery for which no blood need be spilled had achieved its definitive form; but at the same time it gave witness that one can combine a noble temperament with the overflowing pulse of life or, of course in other terms, that God enters man more easily when he imitates the devil who was there before him.

So whenever Lindner reproached his more compact son, Peter, as he was unfortunately often called upon to do, that yielding to the very idea of force made a person effeminate, or that the power of humility and the courage of renunciation are of greater value than physical strength and courage, he was not talking as a layman in questions of courage but enjoying the excitement of a conjurer who has succeeded in yoking demons to the service of the good. For although there was really nothing that could disturb his equilibrium at the height of well-being he had attained, he was marked by a disinclination to jokes and laughter bordering almost on anxiety—as an injury that has healed leaves behind a limp—even when he merely suspected their bare possibility. "The tickling of jokes and humor," he was accustomed to instruct his son on the subject, "originate in the sated comfort of life, in malice, and in idle fantasies, and they easily induce people to say things their better selves would condemn! On the other hand, the discipline that comes from stifling 'witty' ripostes and ideas is an admirable test of strength and an annealing test of will, and the more you use the silence you have struggled to master in order to look into your joke more closely, the better it turns out for the whole man. "We usually see first," this standing admonition concluded, "how many impulses to elevate oneself and demean others it conceals, how much coquetry and frivolity lie behind most jokes, how much refinement of sympathy they stifle in ourselves and others, indeed how much horrifying coarseness and mockery comes to light in the laughter we try to coax from an audience!"

As a result, Peter had to hide carefully from his father his youthful inclination to mockery and joking; but he was so inclined, and Professor Lindner often felt the breath of the evil spirit in his surroundings without being able to spot the poisonous phantom. It could go so far that the father would instill fear in the son with a subduing glance, while secretly fearing him himself, and when this happened he was reminded of something ineffable between his wife and himself while his plump spouse was still on earth. Being lord and master in his own house, establishing its atmosphere and knowing that his family surrounded him like a peaceful garden in which he had planted his principles, belonged for Lindner to the indispensable preconditions of happiness. But Frau Lindner, whom he had married shortly after he finished his studies, during which time he had been a lodger at her mother's, had unfortunately soon thereafter ceased to share his principles and put on an air of being reluctant to contradict him that irritated him more than contradiction itself. He could not forget having sometimes caught a glance from the corner of her eye while her mouth was obediently silent, and every time this happened he subsequently found himself in a situation that was not exactly proof against adverse comment: for instance, in a nightshirt that was too short, preaching that her dignity as a woman should preclude her finding any pleasure in the rough, loose young men who with their drunkenness and scrapes still dominated student life at that time and who accordingly were not as undesirable as lodgers as they ought to be.

Woman's secret mockery is a chapter in itself, with the most intimate connections to her lack of understanding for those preoccupations of greatest importance to the male; and the moment Lindner remembered this, the mental processes that had until then been churning indistinctly within him uncorked the idea of Agathe. What would she be like to live with intimately? "There is no question of her being what one might comfortably call a good person. She doesn't even try to hide it!" he told himself, and a remark of hers that occurred to him in this connection, her laughing assertion that today the good people were no less responsible for the corruption of life than the bad ones, made his hair stand on end. But on the whole he had already "extracted the abscessed teeth" of these "horrible views," even if every time they came up they upset him all over again, by once and for all declaring to himself: "She has no conception of reality!" For he thought of Agathe as a noble being, even though she was, for a "daughter of Eve," full of venomous unrest. The proper attitude, however certain it may be for the believer, seemed to her the most intellectually unascertainable object, the solution of life's most extreme and difficult task. She seemed to have a dreamily confused idea of what was good and right, an idea inimical to order, with no more coherence than an accidental grouping of poems. "Reality is alien to her!" he repeated. "If, for example, she knows something about love, how can she make such cynical statements about it as that it's impossible, and the like?" Therefore she must be shown what real love is.

But here Agathe presented new difficulties. Let him admit it fearlessly and courageously: she was offensive! She all too gladly tore down from its pedestal whatever you cautiously raised up; and if you found fault with her, her criticism knew no bounds and she made it clear that she was out to wound. There are such natures that rage against themselves and strike the hand bringing them succor; but a determined man will never allow his behavior to depend on the behavior of others, and at this moment what Lindner saw was the image of a peaceful man with a long beard, bending over a sick woman anxiously fending him off, and seeing in the depths of her heart a profound wound. The moment was far removed from logic, and so this did not mean that he was this man; but Lindner straightened up— this he actually did—and reached for his beard, which in the meantime had lost a good deal of its fullness, and a nervous blush raced across his face. He had remembered that Agathe had the objectionable habit of instilling in him the belief, more than any other human being ever could have done, that she would like to share his most sublime and most secret feelings; indeed, that in her own constrained situation she was even waiting for a special effort of these feelings in order, once he had exposed the innermost treasures of his mind, to pour scorn on him. She was egging him on! Lindner admitted this to himself and could not have done otherwise, for there was a strange, restless feeling in his breast that one might have hardheartedly compared, although he was far from thinking this, with hens milling about in a chicken coop. But then she could suddenly laugh in the most mysterious way, or say something profane and hard that cut him to the quick, as if she had been building him up only in order to cut him down! And had she not already done this today too, even before her arrival, Lindner asked himself, bringing him to such a pass with this piano? He looked at it; it stood there beside him like a housemaid with whom the master of the house had transgressed!

He could not know what motivated Agathe to play this game

with him, and she herself would not have been able to discuss it with anyone—not even, and especially, Ulrich. She was behaving capriciously; but to the extent that this means with changeable emotions, it was done intentionally and signified a shaking and loosening up of the emotions, the way a person weighed down by a delicious burden stretches his limbs. So the strange attraction that several times had secretly led her to Lindner had contained from the beginning an insubordination against Ulrich, or at least against complete dependence on him; the stranger distracted her thoughts a little and reminded her of the diversity of the world and of men. But this happened only so that she might feel her dependence on her brother that much more warmly, and was, moreover, the same as Ulrich's secretiveness with his diary, which he kept locked away from her; indeed, it was even the same as his general resolve to let reason stand beside emotion as well as above it, and also to judge. But while this took up *his* time, her impatience and stored-up tension was seeking an outlet, an adventure, about which it could not yet be said what path it would take; and to the degree that Ulrich inspired or depressed her, Lindner, to whom she felt superior, caused her to be forbearing or high-spirited. She won mastery over herself by misusing the influence she exercised over him, and she needed this.

But something else was also at work here. For there was between her and Ulrich at this time no talk either of her divorce and Hagauer's letters or of the rash or actually superstitious altering of the will in a moment of disorientation, an act that demanded restitution, either civic or miraculous. Agathe was sometimes oppressed by what she had done, and she knew, too, that in the disorder one leaves behind in a lower circle of life Ulrich did not see any favorable sign of the order one strives for in a higher sense. He had told her so openly enough, and even if she no longer remembered every detail of the conversation that had followed on the suspicions Hagauer had recently raised against her, she still found herself banished to a position of waiting between good and ill. Something, to be sure, was lifting all her qualities upward to a miraculous vindication, but she could not yet allow herself to believe in this; and so it was her offended, recalcitrant feeling of justice that also found expression in the quarrel with Lindner. She was very grateful to him for seeming to impute to her all the bad qualities that Hagauer, too, had discovered in her and for unintentionally calming her by the very way he looked while doing it.

Lindner, who thus, in Agathe's judgment, had never come to terms with himself, had now begun to pace restlessly back and forth in his room, subjecting the visits she was paying him to a severe and detailed examination. She seemed to like being here; she asked about many details of his house and his life, about his educational principles and his books. He was surely not mistaken in assuming that one would express so much interest in someone's life only if one were drawn to share it; of course, the way she had of expressing herself in the process would just have to be accepted as her idiosyncrasy! In this vein he recalled that she had once told him about a woman—unpardonably a former mistress of her brother's—whose head always became "like a coconut, with the hair inside" when she fell in love with a man; and Agathe had added the observation that that was the way she felt about his house. It was all so much of a piece that it really made one "afraid for oneself!" But the fear seemed to give her pleasure, and Lindner thought he recognized in this paradoxical trait the feminine psyche's anxious readiness to yield, the more so as she indicated to him that she remembered similar impressions from the beginning of her marriage.

Now, it is only natural that a man like Lindner would more readily have thoughts of marriage than sinful ones. And so, both during and outside the periods he set aside for the problems of life, he had sometimes secretly allowed the idea to creep in that it would perhaps be good if the child Peter had a mother again; and now it also happened that instead of analyzing Agathe's behavior further, he stopped at one of its manifestations that secretly appealed to him. For in a profound anticipation of his destiny, Agathe had, from the beginning of their acquaintance, spoken of nothing with more passion than her divorce. There was no way he could sanction this sin, but he could also not prevent its advantages from emerging more clearly with every passing day; and in spite of his customary opinions about the nature of the tragic, he was inclined to find tragic the lot that compelled him to express bitter antipathy toward what he himself almost wished would happen. In addition, it happened that Agathe exploited this resistance mostly in order to indicate in her offensive way that she did not believe the truth of his conviction. He might trot out morality, place the Church in front of it, pronounce all the principles that had been so ready to hand all his life; she smiled when she answered, and this smile reminded him of Frau Lindner's smile in the later years of their marriage, with the advantage that Agathe's possessed the unsettling power of the new and mysterious. "It's Mona Lisa's smile!" Lindner exclaimed to himself. "Mockery in a pious face!" and he was so dismayed and flattered by what he took to be a meaningful discovery that for the moment he was less able than usual to reject the arrogance ordinarily associated with this smile when she interrogated him on his belief in God. This unbeliever had no desire for missionary instruction; she wanted to stick her hand in the bubbling spring; and perhaps this was precisely the task reserved for him; once again to lift the stone covering the spring to permit her a little insight, with no one to protect him if it should turn out otherwise, no matter how unpleasant, even alarming, this idea was to himself! And suddenly Lindner, although he was alone in the room, stamped his foot and said aloud: "Don't think for a minute that I don't understand you! And don't believe that the subjugation you detect in me comes from a creature subjugated from the beginning!"

As a matter of fact, the story of how Lindner had become what he was was far more commonplace than he thought. It began with the possibility that he, too, might have become a different person; for he still remembered precisely the love he had had as a child for geometry, for the way its beautiful, cleverly worked out proofs finally closed around the truth with a soft snap, delighting him as if he had caught a giant in a mousetrap. There had been no indication that he was particularly religious; even today he was of the opinion that faith had to be "worked for," and not received as a gift in the cradle. What had made him a shining pupil in religion class was the same joy in knowing and in showing off his knowledge that he demonstrated in his other subjects. His inner being, of course, had already absorbed the ways in which religious tradition expressed itself, to which the only resistance was the civic sense he had developed early. This had once found unexpected expression in the single extraordinary hour his life had ever known. It had happened while he was preparing himself for his final school examinations. For weeks he had been driving himself, sitting evenings in his room studying, when all at once an incomprehensible change came over him. His body seemed to become as light toward the world as delicate paper ash, and he was filled with an unutterable joy, as if in the dark vault of his breast a candle had been lit and was diffusing its gentle glow into all his limbs; and before he could come to terms with such a notion, this light surrounded his head with a condition of radiance. It frightened him a lot; but it was nevertheless true that his head was emitting light. Then a marvelous intellectual clarity overwhelmed all his senses, and in it the world was reflected in broad horizons such as no natural eye could encompass. He glanced up and saw nothing but his half-lit room, so it was not a vision; but the impetus remained, even if it was in contradiction to his surroundings. He comforted himself that he was apparently experiencing this somehow only as a "mental person," while his "physical person" was sitting somber and distinct on its chair and fully occupying its accustomed space; and so he remained for a while, having already got half accustomed to his dubious state, since one quickly grows used to the extraordinary as long as there is hope that it will be revealed as the product, even if a diabolical product, of order. But then something new happened, for he suddenly heard a voice, speaking quite clearly but moderately, as if it had already been speaking for some time, saying to him: "Lindner, where are you seeking me? *Sis tu tuus et ego ero tuus,*" which can be roughly translated: Just become Lindner, and I will be with you. But it was not so much the content of this speech that dismayed the ambitious student, for it was possible that he had already heard or read it, or at least some of it, and then forgotten it, but rather its sensuous resonance; for this came so independently and surprisingly from the outside, and was of such an immediately convincing fullness and solidity, and had such a different sound from the dry sound of grim industriousness to which the night was tuned, that every attempt to reduce the phenomenon to inner exhaustion or inner overstimulation was uprooted in advance. That this explanation was so obvious, and yet its path blocked, of course increased his confusion; and when it also happened that with this confusion the condition in Lindner's head and heart rose ever more gloriously and soon began to flow through his entire body, it got to be too much. He seized his head, shook it between his fists, jumped up from his chair, shouted "No!" three times, and, almost screaming, managed to speak the first prayer he could think of, upon which the spell finally vanished and the future professor, mortally frightened, took refuge in bed.

Soon afterward he passed his examinations with distinction and enrolled at the university. He did not feel in himself the inner calling to the clerical class—nor, to answer Agathe's foolish questions, had he felt it at any time in his life—and was at that time not even entirely and unimpeachably a believer, for he, too, was visited by those doubts that any developing intellect cannot escape. But the mortal terror at the religious powers hiding within him did not leave him for the rest of his life. The longer ago it had been, the less, of course, he believed that God had really spoken to him, and he therefore began to fear the imagination as an unbridled power that can easily lead to mental derangement. His pessimism, too, to which man appeared in general as a threatened being, took on depth, and so his decision to become a pedagogue was in part probably the beginning of an as it were posthumous educating of those schoolmates who had tormented him, and in part, too, an educating of that evil spirit or irregular God who might possibly still be lurking in his thoracic cavity. But if it was not clear to him to what degree he was a believer, it quickly became clear that he was an opponent of unbelievers, and he trained himself to think with conviction that he was convinced, and that it was one's responsibility to be convinced. At the university, it was also easier for him to learn to recognize the weaknesses of a mind that is abandoned to freedom, in that he had only a rudimentary notion of the extent to which the condition of freedom is an innate part of the creative powers.

It is difficult to summarize in a few words what was most characteristic of these weaknesses. It might be seen, for instance, in the ways that changes in living, but especially the results of thinking and experience itself, undermined those great edifices of thought aimed at a freestanding philosophical explanation of the world, whose last constructions were erected between the middle of the eighteenth and the middle of the nineteenth centuries: without the fullness of new knowledge the sciences brought to light almost every day having led to a new, solid, even if tentative way of thinking, indeed without the will to do so stirring seriously or publicly enough, so that the wealth of knowledge has become almost as oppressive as it is exhilarating. But one can also proceed quite generally from the premise that an extraordinary flourishing of property and culture had risen by insidious degrees to a creeping state of crisis, which, not long after this day—when Lindner, recuperating from the more stressful parts of his personal reminiscences, was thinking about the errors of the world—was to be interrupted by the first devastating blow. For assuming that someone came into the world in 1871, the year Germany was born, he would already have been able to perceive around the age of thirty that during his lifetime the length of railroads in Europe had tripled and in the whole world more than quadrupled; that postal service had tripled in extent and telegraph lines grown sevenfold; and much else had developed in the same way. The degree of efficiency of engines had risen from 50 to 90 percent; the kerosene lamp had been successively replaced by gaslight, gas mantle lamps, and electricity, producing ever newer forms of illumination; the horse team, which had maintained its position for millennia, was replaced by the motorcar; and airplanes not only had appeared on the scene but were already out of their baby shoes. The average length of life, too, had markedly increased, thanks to progress in medicine and hygiene, and relations among peoples had become, since the last warring skirmishes, noticeably more gentle and confiding. The person experiencing all this might well believe that at last the long-awaited progress of mankind had arrived, and who would not like to think that proper for an age in which he himself is alive!

But it appears that this civic and spiritual prosperity rested on assumptions that were quite specific and by no means everlasting, and today we are told that in those days there had been enormous new areas for farming and other natural riches that had just been appropriated; that there were defenseless colored peoples who had not yet been exploited (the reproach of exploitation was excused by the idea that it was a means of bestowing civilization upon them); and that there were also millions of white people living who, defenseless, were forced to pay the costs of industrial and mercantile progress (but one salved one's conscience with the firm and not even entirely unjustified faith that the dispossessed would be better off than before their dispossession). At any rate, the cornucopia from which physical and spiritual prosperity poured forth was so large and unbounded that its effects were invisible, and all one could see was the impression of increase with every achievement; and today it is simply impossible to conceive how natural it was at that time to believe in the permanence of this progress and to consider prosperity and intellect something that, like grass, springs up wherever it is not deliberately rooted out.

Toward this confident bliss, this madness of growth, this fatefully exultant broad-mindedness, the pale, scrawny student Lindner, tormented even physically by his height, had a natural aversion, which expressed itself in an instinctive sensing of any error and an alert receptivity for any sign of life that gave evidence of this aversion. Of course, economics was not his field of specialization, and it was only later that he learned to evaluate these facts properly; but this made him all the more clairvoyant about the other aspect of this development, and the rot going on in a state of mind that initially had placed free trade, in the name of a free spirit, at the summit of human activities and then abandoned the free spirit to the free trade, and Lindner sniffed out the spiritual collapse that then indeed followed. This belief in doom, in the midst of a world comfortably ensconced in its own progress, was the most powerful of all his qualities; but this meant that he might also possibly have become a socialist, or one of those lonely and fatalistic people who meddle in politics with the greatest reluctance, even if they are full of bitterness toward everything, and who assure the propagation of the intellect by keeping to the right path within their own narrow circle and personally do what is meaningful, while leaving the therapeutics of culture to the quacks. So when Lindner now asked himself how he had become the person he was, he could give the comforting answer that it had happened exactly the way one ordinarily enters a profession. Already in his last year at school he had belonged to a group whose agenda had been to criticize coolly and discreetly both the "classical paganism" that was half officially admired in the school and the "modern spirit" that was circulating in the world outside. Subsequently, repelled by the carefree student antics at the university, he had joined a fraternity in whose circles the influences of the political struggle were already beginning to displace the harmless conversations of youth, as a beard displaces a baby face. And when he got to be an upperclassman, the memorable occurrence applicable to every kind of thinking had dictatorially asserted itself: that the best support of faith is lack of faith, since lack of faith, observed and struggled against in others, always gives the believer occasion to feel himself zealous.

From the hour when Lindner had resolutely told himself that religion, too, was a contrivance, chiefly for people and not for saints, peace had come over him. Between the desires to be a child and a servant of God, his choice had been made. There was, to be sure, in the enormous palace in which he wished to serve, an innermost sanctum where the miracles reposed and were preserved, and everyone thought of them occasionally; but none of His servants tarried long in this sanctum: they all lived just in front of it; indeed, it was anxiously protected from the importunity of the uninitiated, which had involved experiences not of the happiest sort. This exerted a powerful appeal on Lindner. He made a distinction between arrogance and exaltation. The activity in the antechamber, with its dignified forms and myriad degrees of goings-on and subordinates, filled him with admiration and ambition; and the outside work he now undertook himself, the exercise of influence on moral, political, and pedagogic organizations and the imbuing of science with religious principles, contained tasks on which he could spend not one but a thousand lives, but rewarded him with that enduring dynamism harnessed to inner unchangeability which is the happiness of blessed minds: at least that is what he thought in contented hours, but perhaps he was confusing it with the happiness of political minds. And so from then on he joined associations, wrote pamphlets, delivered lectures, visited collections, made connections, and before he had left the university the recruit in the movement of the faithful had become a young man with a prominent place on the officers' list and influential patrons.

So there was truly no need for a personality with such a broad base and such a clarified summit to allow itself to be intimidated by the saucy criticism of a young woman, and on returning to the present, Lindner drew out his watch and confirmed that Agathe had still not come, although it was almost time when Peter could return home. Nevertheless, he opened the piano again and, if he did not expose himself to the unfathomableness of the song, he did let his eyes roam again over its words, accompanying them with a soft whisper. In doing this he became aware for the first time that he was giving them a false emphasis that was far too emotional and not at all in accord

with the music, which for all its charm was rather austere. He saw
before him a Jesus child that was "somehow by Murillo," which is to
say that in some quite vague way, besides the black cherry eyes of
that master's older beggar boys, it had their picturesque beggar's
rags, so that all this child had in common with the Son of God and the
Savior was the touchingly humanized quality, but in a quite obviously
overdone and really tasteless way. This made an unpleasant impression on him and again wove Agathe into his thoughts, for he recalled
that she had once exclaimed that there was really nothing so peculiar
as that the taste which had produced Gothic cathedrals and passionate devotion should have been succeeded by a taste that found pleasure in paper flowers, beading, little serrated covers, and simpering
language, so that faith had become tasteless, and the faculty for giving a taste and smell to the ineffable was kept alive almost solely by
nonbelievers or dubious people! Lindner told himself that Agathe
was "an aesthetic nature," meaning something that could not attain
the seriousness of economics or morality but in certain cases could
be quite stimulating, and this was one of them. Up to now Lindner
had found the invention of paper flowers beautiful and sensible, but
he suddenly decided to remove a bouquet of them that was standing
on the table, hiding it for the time being behind his back.

This happened almost spontaneously, and he was slightly dismayed by this action, but was under the impression that he probably
knew how to provide an explanation for the "peculiarity" remarked
on by Agathe, which she had let take its course, an explanation she
would not have expected of him. A saying of the Apostles occurred to
him: "Though I speak with the tongues of men and of angels, and
have not charity, I am become as sounding brass, or a tinkling cym-
bal!" And glancing at the floor with puckered forehead, he considered that for many years everything he had done stood in
relationship to eternal love. He belonged to a wondrous community
of love—and it was this that distinguished him from the ordinary intellectual—in which nothing happened for which an allegorical connection to the Eternal could not have been given, no matter how
contingent and yoked to things earthly: indeed, nothing in which this
connection would not have taken root as its inmost meaning, even if
this did not always result in one's consciousness always being polished to a shine. But there is a powerful difference between the love

one possesses as conviction and the love that possesses one: a distinction in freshness, he might say, even if, of course, the difference between purified knowledge and muddy turbulence was certainly just as justified. Lindner did not doubt that purified conviction deserved to be placed higher; but the older it is, the more it purifies itself, which is to say that it frees itself from the irregularities of the emotions that produced it; and gradually there remains not even the conviction of these passions but only the readiness to remember and be able to use them whenever they might be needed. This might explain why the works of the emotions wither away unless they are freshened once again by the immediate experience of love.

Lindner was preoccupied with such almost heretical considerations when suddenly the bell shrilled.

He shrugged his shoulders, closed the piano again, and excused himself to himself with the words: "Life needs not only worshipers but workers!"

57

TRUTH AND ECSTASY

Agathe had not finished reading the entries in her brother's diaries when for the second time she heard his steps on the gravel-strewn path beneath the windows, this time with unmistakable clarity. She made up her mind to penetrate his lair again, without his knowledge, at the first opportunity that presented itself. For however alien this way of viewing things was to her nature, she did want to get to know and understand it. Mixed in with this, too, was a little revenge, and she wanted to pay back secret with secret, and so did not want to be surprised. She hastily put the papers in order, replaced them, and erased every trace that might have betrayed her new knowledge. Moreover, a glance at the time told her that she really ought to have left the house long since and was no doubt being awaited with some irritation elsewhere, something Ulrich might not know about. The double standard she was applying suddenly made her smile. She knew that her own lack of candor was not really prejudicial to loyalty, and that this lack was, moreover, much worse than Ulrich's. This was a spontaneous satisfaction that enabled her to part from her discovery notably reconciled.

When her brother entered his study again he no longer found her there, but this did not surprise him. He had finally wandered back in, the people and circumstances he had been discussing with Stumm having so filled his mind that after the General left he had strolled about in the garden for some time. After long abstinence, a hastily drunk glass of wine can bring about a similar, merely alcoholic vivacity, behind whose colorful scene changes one remains gloomy and untouched; and so it had not even crossed his mind that the people in whose destinies he was again apparently so interested lived no great distance from him and could easily have been contacted. The actual connection with them had remained as paralyzed as a cut muscle.

Still, several memories formed an exception to this and had aroused thoughts to which there were even now bridges of feeling, although only quite fragmentary ones. For instance, what he had characterized as "the return of Section Chief Tuzzi from the inwardness of emotion to its external manipulation" gave him the deeper pleasure of reminding himself that his diaries aimed at a distinction between these two aspects of emotion. But he also saw before him Diotima in her beauty, which was different from Agathe's; and it flattered him that Diotima was still thinking of him, although with all his heart he did not begrudge her her chastisement at the hands of her husband in those moments when this heart again, so to speak, transformed itself into flesh. Of all the conversations he had had with her, he remembered the one in which she had postulated the possibility of occult powers arising in love; this insight had been vouchsafed her by her love for the rich man who also wanted to have Soul, and this now led him to think of Arnheim as well. Ulrich still owed him an answer to the emotional offer that was to have brought him influence on the world of action, and this led him to wonder what could have become of the equally magniloquent and no less vague offer of marriage that had once enraptured Diotima. Presumably the same thing: Arnheim would keep his word if you reminded him of it, but would have no objection if you forgot. The scornful tension that had emerged on his face at the memory of Diotima's moment of glory relaxed again. It really would be quite decent of her not to keep a hold on Arnheim, he thought. A voice speaking reasonably in her overpopulated mind. At times, she had fits of sobriety and felt herself abandoned by the higher things, and then she would be quite nice. Ulrich had always harbored some small inclination for her in the midst of all his disinclination, and did not want to exclude the possibility that she herself might finally have realized what a ridiculous pair she and Arnheim made: she prepared to commit the sacrifice of adultery, Arnheim the sacrifice of marriage, so that again they would not come together, finally convincing themselves of something heavenly and unattainable in order to elevate themselves above the attainable. But when Bonadea's story about Diotima's school of love occurred to him, he finally said to himself that there was still something unpleasant about her, and there was nothing to exclude her throwing her entire energy of love at *him* at some point.

This was, more or less, how Ulrich let his thoughts run on after his conversation with Stumm, and it had seemed to him that this was how upstanding people had to think whenever they concerned themselves with one another in the traditional way; but he himself had got quite out of the habit.

And when he entered the house all this had disappeared into nothingness. He hesitated a moment, again standing in front of his desk, took his diaries in his hands, and put them down again. He ruminated. In his papers a few observations about ecstatic conditions followed immediately after the exposition of the concept of the emotions, and he found this passage correct. An attitude entirely under the domination of a single emotion was indeed, as he had occasionally mentioned, already an ecstatic attitude. To fall under the sway of anger or fear is an ecstasy. The world as it looks to the eyes of a person who sees only red or only menace does not indeed last long, and that is why one does not speak of a world but speaks only of suggestions and illusions; but when masses succumb to this ecstasy, hallucinations of terrifying power and extent arise.

A different kind of ecstasy, which he had also pointed out previously, was the ecstasy of the uttermost degree of feeling. When this is attained, action is no longer purposeful but on the contrary becomes uncertain, indeed often absurd: the world loses its colors in a kind of cold incandescence, and the self disappears except for its empty shell. This vanishing of hearing and seeing is doubtless, too, an impoverishing ecstasy—and incidentally, all enraptured states of soul are poorer in diversity than the everyday one—and becomes significant only through its link with orgiastic ecstasy or the transports of madness, with the state of unbearable physical exertions, dogged expressions of will, or intense suffering, for all of which it can become the final component. For the sake of brevity, Ulrich had, in these examples, telescoped the overflowing and desiccating forms of losing oneself, and not unjustly so, for if from another point of view the distinction is indeed a quite significant one, yet in consideration of the ultimate manifestations, the two forms come close to merging. The orgiastically enraptured person leaps to his ruin as into a light, and tearing or being torn to pieces are for him blazing acts of love and deeds of freedom in the same way that, for all the differences, the person who is deeply exhausted and embittered allows himself to fall to his catastrophe, receiving salvation in this final act; in other words, he too receives something that is sweetened by freedom and love. Thus action and suffering blend on the highest plane on which they can still be experienced.

But this ecstasy of undivided sovereignty and of the crisis of an emotion are, of course, to a greater or lesser degree merely mental constructs, and true ecstasies—whether mystical, martial, or those of love groups or other transported communities—always presuppose a cluster of interrelated emotions and arise from a circle of ideas that reflects them. In less consolidated form, occasionally rigidifying and occasionally loosening up again, such unreal images of the world, formed in the sense of being particular groupings of ideas and feelings (as Weltanschauung, as personal tic), are so frequent in everyday life that most of them are not even regarded as ecstasies, although they are the preliminary stage of ecstasies in about the same way that a safety match in its box signifies the preliminary stage of a burning match. In his last entry, Ulrich had noted that a picture of the world whose nature is ecstatic also arises whenever the emotions and their subservient ideas are simply given priority over sobriety and reflection: it is the rapturous, emotional picture of the world, ecstatic life, that is periodically encountered in literature and to some extent also in reality, in larger or smaller social communes; but what was missing in this enumeration was precisely what for Ulrich was most important, the adducing of the one and only condition of soul and world which he considered an ecstasy that would be a worthy coequal of reality. But his thoughts now digressed from the subject, for if he wanted to make up his mind about evaluating this most seductive of exceptions, it was absolutely necessary—and this was also brought home to him in that he had hesitatingly alternated between an ecstatic world and a mere picture of an ecstatic world—to first become acquainted with the link that exists between our emotions and what is real: that is to say, the world to which we, as opposed to the illusions of ecstasy, impart this value.

But the standards by which we measure this world are those of the understanding, and the conditions under which this happens are likewise those of the understanding. But understanding—even if increasingly greater discrimination of its limits and rights places great obstacles in the path of the intellect—possesses a peculiarity in specific relation to the emotions that is easily perceived and characterized: in order to understand, we must put aside our emotions to the greatest extent possible. We block them out in order to be "objective," or we place ourselves in a state in which the abiding emotions neutralize each other, or we abandon ourselves to a group of cool feelings that, handled carefully, are themselves conducive to understanding. We draw upon what we apprehend in this clearheaded condition for comparison when in other cases we speak of "delusions" through the emotions; and then we have a zero condition, a neutralized state: in short, a specific situation of the emotions, the silent presupposition of experience and thought processes with whose aid we consider merely as subjective whatever other emotional states used to delude us. A millennium's experience has confirmed that we are most qualified to consistently satisfy reality if we place ourselves in this condition again and again, and that whoever wants not merely to understand but also to act also has need of this condition. Not even a boxer can do without objectivity, which in his case means "staying cool," and inside the ropes he can as little afford to be angry as he can to lose his courage if he does not want to come out the loser. So our emotional attitude too, if it is to be adapted to reality, does not depend solely on the emotions governing us at the moment or on their submerged instinctual levels, but depends simultaneously on the enduring and recurrent emotional state that guarantees an understanding of reality and is usually as little visible as the air within which we breathe.

This personal discovery of a connection that is usually not often taken into account had enticed Ulrich to thinking further about the relation of the emotions to reality. Here a distinction must be made between the sense perceptions and the emotions. The former also "deceive," and clearly neither the sensuous image of the world that sense perceptions represent to us is the reality itself, nor is the mental image we infer from it independent of the human way of thinking, though it is independent of the subjective way of thinking. But although there is no tangible similarity between reality and even the most exact representation of it that we have—indeed, there is, rather, an unbridgeable abyss of dissimilarity—and though we never get to see the original, yet we are able in some complex way to decide whether and under what conditions this image is correct. It is different with the emotions: for these present even the image falsely, to maintain the metaphor, and yet in so doing fulfill just as adequately the task of keeping us in harmony with reality, except that they do it in a different way. Perhaps this challenge of remaining in harmony with reality had a particular attraction for Ulrich, but aside from that, it is also the characteristic sign of everything that asserts itself in life; and there can thus be derived from it an excellent shorthand formula and demonstration of whether the image that perception and reason give us of something is correct and true, even though this formula is not all-inclusive. We require that the consequences of the mental picture of reality we have constructed agree with the ideational image of the consequences that actually ensue in reality, and only then do we consider the understanding's image to be correct. In contrast to this, it can be said of the emotions that they have taken over the task of keeping us constantly in errors that constantly cancel one another out.

And yet this is only the consequence of a division of labor in which the emotion that is served by the tools of the senses, and the thought processes that are heavily influenced by this emotion, develop and, briefly stated, have developed into sources of understanding, while the realm of the emotions themselves has been relegated to the role of more or less blind instigator; for in primeval times, our emotions as well as our sense sensations sprang from the same root, an attitude that involved the entire creature when it came into contact with a stimulus. The division of labor that arose later can even now be expressed by the statement that the emotions do *without* understanding what we would do *with* understanding if we were ever to do anything without some instigation other than understanding! If one could only project an image of this feeling attitude, it would have to be this: we assume about the emotions that they color the correct picture of the world and distort and falsely represent it. Science as well as everyday attitudes number the emotions among the "subjectivities"; they assume that these attitudes merely alter "the world we see," for they presume that an emotion dissipates after a short time and that the changes it has caused in a perception of the world will disappear, so that "reality" will, over a shorter or longer time, "reassert" itself.

It seemed to Ulrich quite remarkable that this sometimes paralyzed condition of the emotions, which forms the basis of both scientific investigation and everyday behavior, has a subsidiary counterpoint in that the canceling of emotions is also encountered as a characteristic of earthly life. For the influence our emotions exercise on the mind's impartial representations, those things that maintain their validity as being true and indispensable, cancels itself out more or less completely over a long enough period of time, as well as over the breadth of matter that gets piled up; and the influence of the emotions on the mind's non-impartial representations, on those unsteady ideas and ideologies, thoughts, views, and mental attitudes born out of changeable emotions, which dominate historical life both sequentially and in juxtaposition, also cancels itself out, even if it does so in opposition to certainty, even if it cancels itself out to worse than nothing, to contingency, to impotent disorder and vacillation—in short, to what Ulrich exasperatedly called the "business of the emotions."

Now that he read it again, he would have liked to work out this point more precisely but couldn't, because the written train of thought that ended here, trailing off in a few further catchwords, required that he bring more important things to a conclusion. For if we project the intellectual image of the world, the one that corresponds to reality (even if it is always just an image, it is the right image), on the assumption of a specific state of the emotions, the question arises of what would happen if we were to be just as effectively controlled not by it but by other emotional states. That this question is not entirely nonsensical can be seen in that every strong affect distorts our image of the world in its own way, and a deeply melancholy person, or one who is constitutionally cheerful, could object to the "fancies" of a neutral and evenhanded person, saying that it is not so much because of their blood that they are gloomy or cheerful as on account of their experiences in a world that is full of heavy gloom or heavenly frivolity. And so, however an image of the world may be imagined based on the predominance of an emotion or a group of emotions, including for instance the orgiastic, it can also be based on bringing emotions in general to the fore, as in the ecstatic and emotional frame of mind of an individual or a community; it is a normal everyday experience that the world is depicted differently on the basis of specific groups of ideas and that life is lived in different ways up to the point of obvious insanity.

Ulrich was not in the least minded to consider that understanding was an error, or the world an illusion, and yet it seemed to him admissible to speak not only of an altered picture of the world but also of another world, if instead of the tangible emotion that serves adaptation to the world some other emotion predominates. This other world would be "unreal" in the sense that it would be deprived of almost all objectivity: it would contain no ideas, computations, decisions, and actions that were adapted to nature, and dissension among people would perhaps fail to appear for quite some time but, once present, would be almost impossible to heal. Ultimately, however, that would differ from our world only in degree, and about that possibility only the question can decide whether a humanity living under such conditions would still be capable of carrying on with its life, and whether it could achieve a certain stability in the coming and going of attacks from the outer world and in its own behavior. And there are many things that can be imagined as subtracted from reality or replaced by other things, without people being unable to live in a world so constituted. Many things are capable of reality and the world that do not occur in a particular reality or world.

Ulrich was not exactly satisfied with this after he had written it down, for he did not want it to appear as if all these possible realities were equally justified. He stood up and paced back and forth in his study. Something was still missing, some kind of distinction between "reality" and "full reality," or the distinction between "reality for someone" and "real reality," or in other terms, an exposition of the distinctions of rank was missing between the claim to the validity of reality and world, and a motivation for our claiming a priority dependent on conditions impossible to fulfill for what seems to us to be real and true under all conditions, a priority that is true only under certain conditions. For on the one hand an animal, too, adapts splendidly to the world, and because it certainly does not do so in complete darkness of soul, there must be even in the animal something that corresponds to human ideas of world and reality without it having to be, on *that* account, even remotely similar; and on the other hand we don't possess true reality but can merely refine our ideas about it in an infinite, ongoing process, while in the hurly-burly of life we even use juxtaposed ideas of quite varying degrees of profundity, such as Ulrich himself had encountered in the course of this very hour in the example of a table and a lovely woman. But after having thought it over in approximately this fashion, Ulrich was rid of his restlessness and decided that it was enough; for what might still be said about this subject was not reserved for him, and not for this hour, either. He merely convinced himself once more that there was presumably nothing in his formulation that would be expected to impede a more precise exposition, and for honor's sake he wrote a few words to indicate what was missing.

And when he had done this he completely interrupted his activity, looked out the window into the garden lying there in the late-afternoon light, and even went down for a while in order to expose his head to the fresh air. He was almost afraid that he could now assert either too much or too little; for what was still waiting to be written down by him seemed to him more important than anything else.

58

Ulrich and the Two Worlds of Emotion

"Where would be the best place to begin?" Ulrich asked himself as he wandered around the garden, the sun burning his face and hands in one place, and the shadow of cooling leaves falling on them in another. "Should I begin right away with every emotion existing in the world in binary fashion and bearing within itself the origin of two worlds as different from each other as day and night? Or would I do better to mention the significance that sobered feeling has for our image of the world, and then come conversely to the influence that the image of the world born from our actions and knowledge exercises on the picture of our emotions that we create for ourselves? Or should I say that there have already been states of ecstasy, which I have sketchily described as worlds in which emotions do not mutually cancel each other out?" But even while he was asking himself these questions, he had already made up his mind to begin with everything at the same time; for the thought that made him so anxious that he had interrupted his writing had as many associations as an old friendship, and there was no longer any way of saying how or when it had arisen. While he was trying to put things in order, Ulrich had moved closer and closer to this thought—and it was only on his own account that he had taken it up—but now that he had come to the end, either clarity or emptiness would have to emerge behind the dispersing mists. The moment when he found the first decisive words was not a pleasant one: "In every feeling there are two fundamentally opposed possibilities for development, which usually fuse into one; but they can also come into play individually, and that chiefly happens in a state of ecstasy!"

He proposed to call them, for the time being, the outer and the inner development, and to consider them from the most harmless side. He had a crowd of examples at his disposal: liking, love, anger, mistrust, generosity, disgust, envy, despair, fear, desire . . . , and he mentally ordered them into a series. Then he set up a second series:

affability, tenderness, irritation, suspicion, high-spiritedness, anxiety, and longing, lacking only those links for which he could not find any name, and then he compared the two series. One contained specific emotions, chiefly as they are aroused in us by a specific encounter; the second contained nonspecific emotions, which are strongest when aroused by some unknown cause. And yet in both cases it was the same emotions, in one case in a general, in the other in a specific state. "So I would say," Ulrich thought, "that in every emotion there is a distinction to be made between a development toward specificity and a development toward nonspecificity. But before doing that, it would first be better to list all the distinctions this involves."

He could have toted up most of them in his sleep, but they will seem familiar to anyone who substitutes the word "moods" for the "nonspecific emotions" from which Ulrich had formed his second series, although Ulrich deliberately avoided this term. For if one makes a distinction between emotion and mood, it is readily apparent that the "specific emotion" is always directed toward something, originates in a life situation, has a goal, and expresses itself in more or less straightforward behavior, while a mood demonstrates approximately the opposite of all these things: it is encompassing, aimless, widely dispersed, and idle, and no matter how clear it may be, it contains something indeterminate and stands ready to engulf any object without anything happening and without itself changing in the process. So a specific attitude toward something corresponds to the specific emotion, and a general attitude toward everything corresponds to the nonspecific emotion: the one draws us into action, while the other merely allows us to participate from behind a colorful window.

For a moment Ulrich dwelt on this distinction between how specific and nonspecific emotions relate to the world. He said to himself: "I will add this: Whenever an emotion develops toward specificity, it focuses itself, so to speak, it constricts its purposiveness, and it finally ends up both internally and externally in something of a blind alley; it leads to an action or a resolve, and even if it should not cease to exist in one or the other, it continues on, as changed as water leaving a mill. If, on the other hand, it develops toward nonspecificity, it apparently has no energy at all. But while the specifically developed emotion is reminiscent of a creature with grasping arms, the nonspecific emotion changes the world in the same way the sky changes its colors, without desire or self, and in this form objects and actions change like the clouds. The attitude of the nonspecific emotion to the world has in it something magical and—God help me!—in comparison to the specific attitude, something feminine!" This is what Ulrich said to himself, and then something occurred to him that took him far afield: for of course it is chiefly the development toward a specific emotion that brings with it the fragility and instability of the life of the soul. That the moment of feeling can never be sustained, that emotions wilt more quickly than flowers, or transform themselves into paper flowers if one tries to preserve them, that happiness and will, art and conviction, pass away: all this depends on the specificity of the emotion, which always imposes on it a purposiveness and forces it into the pace of life that dissolves or changes it. On the other hand, the emotion that persists in its non-specificity and boundlessness is relatively impervious to change. A comparison occurred to him: "The one dies like an individual, the other lasts like a kind or species." In this arrangement of the emotions there is perhaps repeated in reality, even if very indirectly, a general arrangement of life; he was not able to gauge this but did not stop over it, for he thought he saw the main argument more clearly than he ever had before.

He was now ready to return to his study, but he waited, because he wanted to mull over the entire plan in his head before putting it down on paper. "I spoke of two possibilities of development and two states of one and the same emotion," he reflected, "but then there must also be present at the origin of the emotion, of course, something to initiate the process. And the drives that feed our soul with a life that is still close to animal blood actually demonstrate this bipartite disposition. A drive incites to action, and this appears to be its major task; but it also tunes the soul. If the drive has not yet found a target, its nebulous expanding and stretching become quite apparent; indeed, there will be many people who see precisely this as the sign of an awakening drive—for example, the sex drive—but of course there is a longing of hunger and other drives. So the specific and the nonspecific are present in the drive. I'll add," Ulrich thought, "that the bodily organs that are involved when the external world arouses an affect in us can on other occasions produce this affect themselves if they receive a stimulus from within; and that's all it takes to arrive at a state of ecstasy!"

Then he reflected that according to the results of research, and especially after his discussion of these results in his diaries, it was also to be assumed that the impulse for one emotion can always serve for another emotion, too, and that no emotion, in the process of its shaping and strengthening, ever comes to an entirely specifiable end. But if that was true, then not only would no emotion ever attain its total specificity, but in all probability it would not attain perfect nonspecificity either, and there was neither an entirely specific nor an entirely nonspecific emotion. And in truth it almost always happens that both possibilities combine in a common reality, in which merely the characteristics of one or the other predominate. There is no "mood" that does not also include specific emotions that form and dissolve again; and there is no specific emotion that, at least where it can be said to "radiate," "seize," "operate out of itself," "extend itself," or operate on the world "directly," without an external emotion, does not allow the characteristics of the nonspecific emotion to peer through. There are certainly, however, emotions that closely approximate the one or the other.

Of course the terms "specific" and "nonspecific" involve the disadvantage that even a specific emotion is always insufficiently specified and is in this sense nonspecific; but that should probably be easy to distinguish from significant nonspecificity. "So all that remains is to settle why the particularity of the nonspecific emotion, and the whole development leading up to it, is taken to be less real than its counterpart," Ulrich thought. "Nature contains both. So the different ways they are treated are probably connected with the external development of emotion being more important for us than the inner development, or with the direction of specificity meaning more to us than that of nonspecificity. If this were not so, our life would truly have to be a different one than it is! It is an inescapable peculiarity of European culture that every minute the 'inner world' is proclaimed the best and most profound thing life has to offer, without regard for the fact that this inner world is treated as merely an annex of the outer world. And how this is done is frankly the secret balance sheet of this culture, even though it is an open secret: the external world and the "personality" are set off against each other. The assumption is that the outer world stimulates in a person inner processes that must enable that person to respond in an appropriate fashion; and by mentally setting up this pathway leading from a change in the world through the change in a person to a further change in the world, one derives the peculiar ambiguity that permits us to honor the internal world as the true sphere of human grandeur and yet to presuppose that everything taking place within it has the ultimate task of flowing outward in the form of an orderly external action."

The thought went through Ulrich's mind that it would be rewarding to consider our civilization's attitude toward religion and culture in this sense, but it seemed to him more important to keep to the direction his thoughts had been following. Instead of "inner world," one could simply say "emotions," for they in particular are in the ambiguous position of actually being this inwardness and yet are mostly treated as a shadow of the world outside; and this of course was involved with everything that Ulrich thought he could distinguish as the inner and nonspecific development of emotions. This is already shown in that the expressions we use to describe inner governing processes are almost all derived from external processes; for we obviously transpose the active kind of external happening onto the differently constituted inner events even in representing the latter as an activity, whether we call it an emanation, a switching on or off, a taking hold, or something similar. For these images, derived from the outer world, have become accepted and current for the inner world only because we lack better ones to apprehend it. Even those scientific theories that describe the emotions as an interpenetration or juxtaposition on an equal footing of external and internal actions make a concession to this custom, precisely because they ordinarily speak of acting and overlook pure inwardness's remoteness from acting. And for these reasons alone, it is simply inevitable that the inner development of emotions usually appears to us as a mere annex to their external development, appears indeed to be its repetition and muddying, distinguishing itself from the outer development through less sharply defined forms and hazier connections, and thus evoking the somewhat neglected impression of being an incidental action.

But of course what is at stake is not simply a form of expression or a mental priority; what we "really" feel is itself dependent on reality in hundreds of ways and is therefore also dependent on the specific and external development of emotions to which the development of inner and nonspecific emotions subordinates itself, by which the latter are, as it were, blotted up. "It shouldn't depend on the details," Ulrich resolved, "yet it could probably be shown in every detail not only that the concept we create for ourselves has the task of serviceably integrating its 'subjective' element into our ideas about reality, but also that in feeling itself, both dispositions merge in a holistic process that unites their outer and inner development in very unequal fashion. Simply stated: we are acting beings; for our actions we need the security of thinking; therefore we also need emotions capable of being neutralized—and our feeling has taken on its characteristic form in that we integrate it into our image of reality, and not the other way around, as ecstatics do. Just for that reason, however, we must have within us the possibility of turning our feeling around and experiencing our world differently!"

He was now impatient to write, feeling confident that these ideas had to be subjected to a more intense scrutiny. Once in his study, he turned on the light, as the walls already lay in shadow. Nothing was to be heard of Agathe. He hesitated an instant before beginning.

He was inhibited when he recollected that in his impatience to take shortcuts in laying out and sketching his idea he had used the concepts "inner" and "outer," as well as "individual" and "world," as if the distinction between both agencies of the emotions coincided with these representations. This was of course not so. The peculiar distinction Ulrich had made between the disposition for and the possibility of elaboration into specific and nonspecific emotions, if allowed to prevail, cuts across the other distinctions. The emotions develop in one and the other fashion just as much outwardly and in the world as they do inwardly and in the individual. He pondered over a proper word for this, for he didn't much like the terms "specific" and "nonspecific," although they were indicative. "The original difference in experience is most exposed and yet most expressive in that there is an externalizing of emotions as well as an inwardness both internal and external," he reflected, and was content for a moment, until he found these words, too, as unsatisfactory as all the others, when he went on to try out a dozen. But this did not change his conviction; it only looked to him like a complication in the discussion he was embarking on, the result of language not having been created for this aspect of existence. "If I go over everything once more and find it correct, it won't matter to me if all I end up talking about is our ordinary emotions and our 'other' ones," he concluded.

Smiling, he took down from a shelf a book that had a bookmark in it and wrote at the head of his own words these words of another: "Even if Heaven, like the world, is subjected to a series of changing events, still the Angels have neither concept nor conception of space and time. Although for them, too, everything that happens happens sequentially, in complete harmony with the world, they do not know what time means, because what prevails in Heaven are neither years nor days, but changing states. Where there are years and days, seasons prevail, where there are changes of state, conditions. Since the Angels have no conception of time the way people do, they have no way of specifying time; they do not even know of its division into years, months, weeks, hours, into tomorrow, yesterday, and today. If they should hear a person speak of these things—and God has always linked Angels with people—what they understand by them is states and the determination of states. Man's thinking begins with time, the Angels' with a state; so what for human beings is a natural idea is for the Angels a spiritual one. All movement in the spiritual world is brought about through inner changes in state. When this troubled me, I was raised into the sphere of Heaven to the consciousness of Angels, and led by God through the realms of the firmament and conducted to the constellations of the universe, and all this in my mind, while my body remained in the same place. This is how all the Angels moved from place to place: that is why there are for them no intervals, and consequently no distances either, but only states and changes in state. Every approach is a similarity of inner states, every distancing a dissimilarity; spaces in Heaven are nothing but external states, which correspond to the internal ones. In the spiritual world, everyone will appear visible to the other as soon as he has a yearning desire for the other's presence, for then he is placing himself in the other's state; conversely, in the presence of disinclination he will distance himself from him. In the same way, someone who changes his abode in halls or gardens gets where he is going more quickly if he longs for the place, and more slowly if his longing is less; with astonishment I saw this happen often. And since the Angels are not able to conceive of time, they also have a different idea of eternity than earthly people do; they understand by it an infinite state, not an infinite time."

A few days earlier, Ulrich had accidentally come across this in a selection of the writings of Swedenborg he owned but had never really read; and he had condensed it a little and copied down so much of it because he found it very pleasant to hear this old metaphysician and learned engineer—who made no small impression on Goethe, and even on Kant—talking as confidently about heaven and the angels as if it were Stockholm and its inhabitants. It fit in so well with his own endeavor that the remaining differences, which were by no means insignificant, were brought into relief with uncanny clarity. It gave him great pleasure to seize on these differences and conjure forth in a new fashion from the more cautiously posited concepts of a later century the assertions—dryly unhallucinatory in their premature self-certainty, but with a whimsical effect nevertheless— of a seer.

And so he wrote down what he had thought.

The following four chapters, in corrected fair copy, are alternate versions of the preceding "galley" chapters. (Alternates 47 and 48 have been omitted because the first differs in only minor details from galley chapter 57, and the second closely parallels galley chapter 48.) Musil was working on these during the last two years of his life, up to his sudden death on April 15, 1942.

49

CONVERSATIONS ON LOVE

Man, the speaking animal, is the only one that requires conversation even for his reproduction. And not only because he is always talking does he speak while that is going on too, but apparently his bliss in love is bound root and branch to his loquacity, and in so profoundly mysterious a fashion that it almost calls to mind those ancients according to whose philosophy god, man, and things arose from the "logos," by which they variously understood the Holy Ghost, reason, and speaking. Now not even psychoanalysis and sociology have had anything of consequence to say about this, although both these modern sciences might well compete with Catholicism in intervening in everything human. So one must construct one's own explanation, that in love, conversations play an almost greater role than anything else. Love is the most garrulous of all emotions, and it consists largely of loquaciousness. If the person is young, these conversations that encompass everything are part of the phenomenon of growing up; if he is mature, they form his peacock's fan, which, even though it consists only of quills, unfolds the more vibrantly the later it happens. The reason might lie in the awakening of contemplative thinking through the emotions of love, and in its enduring connection with them; but this would only be putting off the problem for the moment, for even if the word "contemplation" is used almost as often as the word "love," it is not any clearer.

Whether, moreover, what bound Agathe and Ulrich together can be accused of being love or not is not to be decided on these grounds, although they spoke with each other insatiably. What they spoke about, too, turned around love, always and somehow; that is true. But what is true of every emotion is true of love, that its ardor expands more strongly in words the farther off action is; and what persuaded brother and sister, after the initial violent and obscure emotional experiences that had gone before, to give themselves over to conversations, and what seemed to them at times like a magic spell, was above all not knowing how they *could* act. But the timidity before their own emotions that was involved in this, and their curious penetration inward to this emotion from its periphery, sometimes caused these conversations to come out sounding more superficial than the depth that underlay them.

50

DIFFICULTIES WHERE THEY ARE NOT LOOKED FOR

How do things stand with the example, as celebrated as it is happily experienced, of love between two so-called people of different sexes? It is a special case of the commandment to love thy neighbor without knowing what kind of person he is; and a test of the relationship that exists between love and reality.

People make of each other the dolls with which they have already played in dreaming of love.

And what the other thinks and really is has no influence on this at all?

As long as one loves the other, and because one loves the other, everything is enchanting; but this is not true the other way around. Never has a woman loved a man because of his thoughts or opinions, or a man a woman on account of hers. These play only an important secondary role. Moreover, the same is true of thoughts as of anger: if one understands impartially what the other means, not only is anger disarmed, but most of the time, against its expectation, love as well.

But, especially at the beginning, isn't what plays the major role being charmed by the concord of opinions?

When the man hears the woman's voice, he hears himself being repeated by a marvelous submerged orchestra, and women are the most unconscious of ventriloquists; without its coming from their mouths, they hear themselves giving the cleverest answers. Each time it is like a small annunciation: a person emerges from the clouds at the side of another, and everything the one utters seems to the other a heavenly crown, custom fitted to his head! Later, of course, you feel like a drunk who has slept off his stupor.

And then the deeds! Are not the deeds of love—its loyalty, its sacrifices and attentions—its most beautiful demonstration? But deeds, like all mute things, are ambiguous. If one thinks back on one's life as a dynamic chain of actions and events, it amounts to a play in which one has not noticed a single word of the dialogue and whose scenes have the same monotonous climaxes!

So one does not love according to merit and reward, and in antiphony with the immortal spirits mortally in love?

That one is not loved as one deserves is the sorrow of all old maids of both sexes!

It was Agathe who gave this response. The uncannily beautiful where-does-it-come-from of love rose up from past loves in conjunction with the mild frenzy of injustice and even reconciled her to the lack of dignity and seriousness of which she sometimes complained because of her game with Professor Lindner, and which she was always ashamed of whenever she again found herself in Ulrich's vicinity. But Ulrich had begun the conversation, and in the course of it had become interested in pumping her for her memories; for her way of judging these delights was similar to his.

She looked at him and laughed. "Haven't you ever loved a person above everything, and despised yourself for it?"

"I could say no; but I won't indignantly reject it out of hand," Ulrich said. "It could have happened."

"Have you never loved a person," Agathe went on excitedly, "despite the strangest conviction that this person, whether he has a beard or breasts, about whom you thought you knew everything and whom you esteem, and who talks incessantly about you and himself, is really only visiting love? You could leave out his thinking and his merits, give him a different destiny, furnish him with a different beard and different legs: you could almost leave *him* out, and you would still love him! . . . That is, insofar as you love him at all!" she added to soften it.

Her voice had a deep resonance, with a restless glitter in its depths, as from a fire. She sat down guiltily, because in her unintentional eagerness she had sprung up from her chair.

Ulrich, too, felt somewhat guilty on account of this conversation, and smiled. He had not in the least intended to speak of love as one of those contemporary bifurcated emotions that the latest trend calls "ambivalent," which amounts to saying that the soul, as is the case with swindlers, always winks with its left eye while pledging an oath with its right hand. He had only found it amusing that love, to arise and endure, does not depend on anything significant. That is, you love someone in spite of everything, and equally well on account of nothing; and that means either that the whole business is a fantasy or that this fantasy is the whole business, as the world is a whole in which no sparrow falls without the All-Feeling One being aware of it.

"So it doesn't depend on anything at all!" Agathe exclaimed by way of conclusion. "Not on what a person is, not on what he thinks, not on what he wants, and not on what he does."

It was clear to them that they were speaking of the security of the soul, or, since it might be well to avoid such a grand word, of the insecurity, which they—using the term now with modest imprecision and in an overall sense—felt in their souls. And that they were talking of love, in the course of which they reminded each other of its changeability and its art of metamorphosis, happened only because it is one of the most violent and distinctive emotions, and yet it is such a suspicious emotion before the stern throne of sovereign understanding that it causes even this understanding to waver. But here they had already found a beginning when they had scarcely begun strolling in the sunshine of loving one's neighbor; and mindful of the assertion that even in this gracious stupefaction you had no idea whether you really loved people, and whether you were loving real people, or whether, and by means of what qualities, you were being duped by a fantasy and a transformation, Ulrich showed himself assiduous in finding a verbal knot that would give him a handhold on the questionable relationship that exists between emotion and understanding, at least at the present moment and in the spirit of the idle conversation that had just died away.

"This always contains both contradictions; they form a four-horse team," he said. "You love a person because you know him; and because you don't know him. And you understand him because you love him; and don't know him because you love him. And sometimes this reaches such a pitch that it suddenly becomes quite palpable. These are the notorious moments when Venus through Apollo, and Apollo through Venus, gaze at a hollow scarecrow and are mightily amazed that previously they had seen something else there. If love is stronger than this astonishment, a struggle arises between them, and sometimes love—albeit exhausted, despairing, and mortally wounded—emerges the victor. But if love is not so strong, it becomes a struggle between people who think themselves deceived; it comes to insults, crude intrusions of reality, incredible humiliations intended to make up for your having been the simpleton. . . ." He had experienced this stormy weather of love often enough to be able to describe it now quite comfortably.

But Agathe put an end to this. "If you don't mind, I'd like to point out that these marital and extramarital affairs of honor are for the most part much overrated!" she objected, and again tried to find a comfortable position.

"*All* love is overrated! The madman who in his derangement stabs with a knife and runs it through an innocent person who just happens to be standing where his hallucination is—in love he's normal!" Ulrich declared, and laughed.

51

LOVING IS NOT SIMPLE

A comfortable position and lackadaisical sunshine, which caresses without being importunate, facilitated these conversations. They were mostly conducted between two deck chairs that had been not so much moved into the protection and shade of the house as into the shaded light coming from the garden, its freedom modulated by the morning walls. One should not, of course, assume that the chairs were standing there because brother and sister—stimulated by the sterility of their relationship, which in the ordinary sense was simply present but in a higher sense was perhaps threatening—might have had the intention of exchanging their opinions concerning the deceptive nature of love in Schopenhauerian-Hindu fashion, and of defending themselves against the insane seductive workings of its drive to procreation by intellectually dismembering them; what dictated the choice of the half-shadowed, the protective, and the curiously withdrawn had a simpler explanation. The subject matter of the conversation was itself so constituted that in the infinite experience through which the notion of love first emerges distinctly, the most various associative pathways came to light, leading from one question to the next. Thus the two questions of how one loves the neighbor one does not know, and how one loves oneself, whom one knows even less, directed their curiosity to the question encompassing both: namely, how one loves at all; or, put differently, what love "really" is. At first glance this might seem rather precocious, and also an all-too-judicious question for a couple in love; but it gains in mental confusion as soon as one extends it to include millions of loving couples and their variety.

These millions differ not only individually (which is their pride) but also according to their ways of acting, their object, and their relationship. There are times when one cannot speak of loving couples at all but can still speak of love, and other times, when one can talk of loving couples but not of love, in which case things proceed in rather more ordinary fashion. All in all, the word embraces as many contradictions as Sunday in a small country town, where the farm boys go to mass at ten in the morning, visit the brothel in a side street at eleven, and enter the tavern on the main square at noon to eat and drink. Is there any sense in trying to investigate such a word all the way around? But in using it one is acting unconsciously, as if despite all the differences there *were* some inherent common quality! Whether you love a walking stick or honor is six of one and half a dozen of the other, and it would not occur to anybody to name these things in the same breath if one weren't accustomed to so doing every day. Other kinds of games about things that are different and yet one and the same can be addressed with: loving the bottle, loving tobacco, and loving even worse poisons. Spinach and outdoor exercise. Sports or the mind. Truth. Wife, child, dog. Those only added to the list who spoke about: God. Beauty, Fatherland, and money. Nature, friend, profession, and life. Freedom. Success, power, justice, or simply virtue. One loves all these things; in short, there are almost as many things associated with love as there are ways of striving and speaking. But what are the distinctions, and what do these loves have in common?

It might be useful to think of the word "fork." There are eating forks, manure forks, tree-branch forks, gun forks, road forks, and other forks, and what they all have in common is the shaping characteristic of "forkness." This is the decisive experience, what is forked, the gestalt of the fork, in the most disparate things that are called by that name. If you proceed from these things, it turns out that they all belong to the same category; if you proceed from the initial impression of forkness, it turns out that it is filled out and complemented by the impressions of the various specific forks. The common element is therefore a form or gestalt, and the differentiation lies first in the variety of forms it can assume, but then also in the objects having such a form, their purpose, and such things. But while every fork can be directly compared with every other, and is present to the senses, even if only in the form of a chalk line, or mentally, this is not the case with the various shapes of love; and the entire usefulness of the example is limited to the question of whether here, too, corresponding to the forkness of forks, there is in all cases a decisive experience, a loveness, a lovebeing, and a lovekind. But love is not an object of sensory understanding that is to be grasped with a glance, or even with an emotion, but a moral event, in the way that premeditated murder, justice, or scorn is; and this means among other things that a multiply branching and variously supported chain of comparisons is possible among various examples of it, the more distant of which can be quite dissimilar to each other, indeed distinct from each other to the point of being opposite, and yet be connected through an association that echoes from one link to the next. Acting from love can thus go as far as hate; and yet the cause is not the much-invoked "ambivalence," the dichotomy of emotions, but precisely the full totality of life.

Nevertheless, such a word might also have preceded the developing continuation of the conversation. For forks and other such innocent aids aside, sophisticated conversation knows nowadays how to handle the essence and nature of love without faltering, and yet to express itself as grippingly as if this kernel were concealed in all the various appearances of love the way forkness is contained in the manure fork or the salad fork. This leads one to say—and Ulrich and Agathe, too, could have been seduced into this by the general custom—that the important thing in every kind of love is libido, or to say that it is eros. These two words do not have the same history, yet they are comparable, especially in the contemporary view. For when psychoanalysis (because an age that nowhere goes in for intellectual or spiritual depth is riveted to hear that it has a depth psychology) began to become an everyday philosophy and interrupted the middle classes' lack of adventure, everything in sight was called libido, so that in the end one could as little say what this key and skeleton-key idea was *not* as what it was. And much the same is true of eros, except that those who, with the greatest conviction, reduce all physical and spiritual worldly bonds to eros have regarded their eros the same way from the very beginning. It would be futile to translate libido as drive or desire, specifically sexual or presexual drive or desire, or to translate eros, on the other hand, as spiritual, indeed suprasensory, tenderness; you would then have to add a specialized historical treatise. One's boredom with this makes ignorance a pleasure. But this is what determined in advance that the conversation conducted between two deck chairs did not take the direction indicated but found attraction and refreshment instead in the primitive and insufficient process of simply piling up as many examples as possible of what was called love and putting them side by side as in a game: indeed, to behave as ingenuously as possible and not despise even the least judicious examples.

Comfortably chatting, they shared whatever examples occurred to them, and how they occurred to them, whether according to the emotion, according to the object it was directed at, or according to the action in which it expressed itself. But it was also an advantage first to take the procedure in hand and consider whether it merited the name of love in real or metaphorical terms, and to what extent. In this fashion many kinds of material from different areas were brought together.

But spontaneously, the first thing they talked about was emotion; for the entire nature of love appears to be a process of feeling. All the more surprising is the response that emotion is the least part of love. For the completely inexperienced, it would be like sugar and toothache; not quite as sweet, and not quite as painful, and as restless as cattle plagued by horseflies. This comparison might not seem a masterpiece to anyone who is himself tormented by love; and yet the usual description is really not that much different: being torn by doubts and anxieties, pain and longing, and vague desires! Since olden times it seems that this description has not been able to specify the condition any more precisely. But this lack of emotional specificity is not characteristic only of love. Whether one is happy or sad is also not something one experiences as irrevocably and straightforwardly as one distinguishes smooth from rough, nor can other emotions be recognized any better purely by feeling or even touching them. For that reason an observation was appropriate at this point that they might have fleshed out as it deserved, on the unequal disposition and shaping of emotions. This was the term that Ulrich set out as its premise; he might also have said disposition, shaping, and consolidation.

For he introduced it with the natural experience that every emotion involves a convincing certainty of itself that is obviously part of its nucleus; and he added that it must also be assumed, on equally general grounds, that the disparity of emotions began no less with this nucleus. You can hear this in his examples. Love for a friend has a different origin and different traits from love for a girl; love for a

completely faded woman different ones from love for a saintly, reserved woman; and emotions such as (to remain with love) love, ven-
eration, prurience, bondage, or the kinds of love and the kinds of
antipathy that diverge even further from one another are already different in their very roots. If one allows both assumptions, then all
emotions, from beginning to end, would have to be as solid and
transparent as crystals. And yet no emotion is unmistakably what it
appears to be, and neither self-observation nor the actions to which it
gives rise provide any assurance about it. This distinction between
the self-assurance and the uncertainty of emotions is surely not trifling. But if one observes the origin of the emotion in the context of
its physiological as well as its social causes, this difference becomes
quite natural. These causes awaken in general terms, as one might
say, merely the kind of emotion, without determining it in detail; for
corresponding to every drive and every external situation that sets it
in motion is a whole bundle of emotions that might satisfy them. And
whatever of this is initially present can be called the nucleus of the
emotion that is still between being and nonbeing. If one wanted to
describe this nucleus, however it might be constituted, one could not
come up with anything more apt than that it is something that in the
course of its development, and independently of a great deal that
may or may not be relevant, will develop into the emotion it was intended to become. Thus every emotion has, besides its initial disposition, a destiny as well; and therefore, since what it later develops into
is highly dependent on accruing conditions, there is no emotion that
would unerringly be itself from the very beginning; indeed, there
is perhaps not even one that would indisputably and purely be an
emotion. Put another way, it follows from this working together of
disposition and shaping that in the field of the emotions what
predominates are not their pure occurrence and its unequivocal fulfillment, but their progressive approximation and approximate fulfillment. Something similar is also true of everything that requires
emotion in order to be understood.

This was the end of the observation adduced by Ulrich, which contained approximately these explanations in this sequence. Hardly
less brief and exaggerated than the assertion that emotion was the
smallest part of love, it could also be said that because it was an emotion, it was not to be recognized by emotion. This, moreover, shed

some light on the question of why he had called love a moral experience. The three chief terms—disposition, shaping, and consolidation—were, however, the main cruxes connecting the ordered understanding of the phenomenon of emotions: at least according to a particular fundamental view, to which Ulrich not unwillingly turned whenever he had need of such an explanation. But at this stage, because working this out properly had made greater and more profound claims than he was willing to take upon himself, claims that led into the didactic sphere, he broke off what had been begun.

The continuation reached out in two directions. According to the program of the conversation, it ought now to have been the turns of the object and the action of love to be discussed, in order to determine what it was in them that gave rise to their highly dissimilar manifestations and to discover what, ultimately, love "really" is. This was why they had talked about the involvement of actions at the very beginning of the emotion in determining that emotion, which should be all the more repeatable in regard to what happened to it later. But Agathe asked an additional question: it might have been possible—and she had reasons, if not for distrust, at least to be afraid of it—that the explanation her brother had selected was really valid only for a weak emotion, or for an experience that wanted to have nothing to do with strong ones.

Ulrich replied: "Not in the least! It is precisely when it is at its strongest that an emotion is most secure. In the greatest panic, one is paralyzed or screams instead of fleeing or defending oneself. In the greatest happiness there is often a peculiar pain. Great eagerness, too, 'can only harm,' as one says. And in general it can be maintained that at the highest pitch of feeling the emotions fade and disappear as in a dazzling light. It may be that the entire world of emotions that we know is designed for only a middling kind of life and ceases at the highest stages, just as it does not begin at the lowest." An indirect part of this, too, is what you experience when you observe your feelings, especially when you examine them closely: they become indistinct and are hard to distinguish. But what they lose in clarity of strength they need to gain, at least to some degree, through clarity of attentiveness, and they don't do even that. . . . This was Ulrich's reply, and this obliteration of the emotion juxtaposed in self-observation and in its ultimate arousal was not accidental. For in both conditions action is excluded or disturbed; and because the connection between feeling and acting is so close that many consider them a unit, it is not without significance that the two examples are complementary.

But what he avoided saying was precisely what they both knew about it from their own experience, that in actuality a condition of mental effacement and physical helplessness can be combined with the highest stage of the emotion of love. This made him turn the conversation with some violence away from the significance that acting has for feeling, apparently with the intention of again bringing up the division of love according to objects. At first glance, this rather whimsical possibility also seemed better suited to bringing order to ambiguity. For if, to begin with an example, it is blasphemy to label love of God with the same word as love of fishing, this doubtless lies in the differences between the objects this love is aimed at; and the significance of the object can likewise be measured by other examples. What makes the enormous difference in this relationship of loving something is therefore not so much the love as rather the something. Thus there are objects that make love rich and happy; others that make it poor and sickly, as if it were due entirely to them. There are objects that must requite the love if it is to develop all its power and character, and there are others in which any similar demand would be meaningless from the outset. This decisively separates the connection to living beings from the connection to inanimate things; but, even inanimate, the object is the proper adversary of love, and its qualities influence those of love.

The more disproportionate in value this adversary is, the more distorted, not to say passionately twisted, love itself becomes. "Compare," Ulrich admonished, "the healthy love of young people for each other with the ridiculously exaggerated love of the lonely person for a dog, cat, or dickeybird. Observe the passion between man and wife fade away, or become a nuisance like a rejected beggar, if it is not requited, or not fully requited. Don't forget, either, that in unequal associations, such as those between parents and children, or masters and servants, between a man and the object of his ambition or his vice, the relationship of requited love is the most uncertain, and without exception the fatal element. Wherever the governing natural exchange between the condition of love and its adversary is imperfect, love degenerates like unhealthy tissue!" . . . This idea seemed to have something special that attracted him. Ulrich would have expounded on it at length and with numerous examples, but while he was still thinking these over, something unanticipated, which quickened his intended line of thought with expectation like a pleasant fragrance coming across fields, appeared to direct his reflections almost inadvertently toward what in painting is called still life or, according to the contrary but just as fitting procedure of a foreign language, *nature morte*. "It is somehow ridiculous for a person to prize a well-painted lobster," Ulrich continued without transition, "highly polished grapes, and a hare strung up by the legs, always with a pheasant nearby; for human appetite is ridiculous, and painted appetite is even more ridiculous than natural appetite." They both had the feeling that this association reached back in more profound ways than were evident, and belonged to the continuation of what they had omitted to say about themselves.

For in real still lifes—objects, animals, plants, landscapes, and human bodies conjured up within the sphere of art—something other than what they depict comes out: namely, the mysterious, demoniacal quality of painted life. There are famous pictures of this kind, so both knew what they were talking about; it would, however, be better to speak not of specific pictures but of a kind of picture, which, moreover, does not attract imitators but arises without rules from a flourish of creative activity. Agathe wanted to know how this could be recognized. Ulrich gave a sign refusing to indicate any definitive trait, but said slowly, smiling and without hesitation: "The exciting, vague, infinite echo!"

And Agathe understood him. Somehow one has the feeling of being on a beach. Small insects hum. The air bears a hundred meadow scents. Thoughts and feelings stroll busily hand in hand. But before one's eyes lies the unanswering desert of the sea, and what is important on the shore loses itself in the monotonous motion of the endless view. She was thinking how all true still lifes can arouse this happy, insatiable sadness. The longer you look at them, the clearer it becomes that the things they depict seem to stand on the colorful shore of life, their eyes filled with monstrous things, their tongues paralyzed.

Ulrich responded with another paraphrase. "All still lifes really paint the world of the sixth day of creation, when God and the world were still by themselves, with no people!" And to his sister's questioning smile he said: "So what they arouse in people would probably be jealousy, secret inquisitiveness, and grief!"

That was almost an aperçu, and not a bad one; he noted it with displeasure, for he was not fond of these ideas machined like bullets and hastily gilded. But he did nothing to correct it, nor did he ask his sister to do so. For the strange resemblance to their own life was an obstacle that kept both of them from adequately expressing themselves about the uncanny art of the still life or *nature morte*.

This resemblance played a great role in their lives. Without it being necessary to repeat in detail something reaching back to the shared memories of childhood that had been reawakened at their reunion and since then had given a strange cast to all their experiences and most of their conversations, it cannot be passed over in silence that the anesthetized trace of the still life was always to be felt in it. Spontaneously, therefore, and without accepting anything specific that might have guided them, they were led to turn their curiosity toward everything that might be akin to the nature of the still life; and something like the following exchange of words resulted, charging the conversation once more like a flywheel and giving it new energy:

Having to beg for something before an imperturbable countenance that grants no response drives a person into a frenzy of despair, attack, or worthlessness. On the other hand, it is equally unnerving, but unspeakably beautiful, to kneel before an immovable countenance from which life was extinguished a few hours before, leaving behind an aura like a sunset.

This second example is even a commonplace of the emotions, if ever anything could be said to be! The world speaks of the consecration and dignity of death; the poetic theme of the beloved on his bier has existed for hundreds, if not thousands of years; there is a whole body of related, especially lyric, poetry of death. This obviously has something adolescent about it. Who imagines that death bestows upon him the noblest of beloveds for his very own? The person who lacks the courage or the possibility of having a living one!

A short line leads from this poetic immaturity to the horrors of conjuring up spirits and the dead; a second line leads to the abomination of actual necrophilia; perhaps a third to the pathological opposites of exhibitionism and coercion by violence.

These comparisons may be strange, and in part they are extremely unappetizing. But if one does not allow oneself to be deterred but considers them from, as it were, a medical-psychological viewpoint, there is one element they all have in common: an impossibility, an inability, an absence of natural courage or the courage for a natural life.

They also supply the truth—should one already be embarked on daring comparisons—that silence, fainting, and every kind of incompleteness in the adversary is connected with the effect of mental exhaustion.

What is especially repeated in this way, as was mentioned before, is that an adversary who is not on the same level distorts love; it is only necessary to add that it is not infrequently a distorted attitude of the emotion that bids it make a choice at all. And inversely, it would be the responding, living, acting partner who determines the emotions and keeps them in order, without which they degenerate into shadowboxing.

But isn't the strange charm of the still life shadowboxing too? Indeed, almost an ethereal necrophilia?

And yet there is also a similar shadowboxing in the glances of happy lovers as an expression of their highest feelings. They look into each other's eyes, can't tear themselves away, and pine in an infinite emotion that stretches like rubber!

This was more or less how the exchange of words had begun, but at this point its thread was pretty much left hanging, and for quite a while before it was picked up again. For they had both really looked at each other, and this had caused them to lapse into silence.

But if an observation is called for to explain this—and if it is necessary to justify such conversations once again and express their sense—perhaps this much could be said, which at this moment Ulrich understandably left as an unspoken idea: that loving was by no means as simple as nature would have us believe by bestowing on every bungler among her creatures the necessary tools.

52

BREATHS OF A SUMMER DAY

The sun, meanwhile, had risen higher; they had abandoned the chairs like stranded boats in the shallow shade near the house and were lying on a lawn in the garden, beneath the full depth of the summer day. They had been like this for quite some time, and although the circumstances had changed, this change hardly entered their consciousness. Not even the cessation of the conversation had accomplished this; it was left hanging, without a trace of a rift.

A noiseless, streaming snowfall of lusterless blossoms, emanating from a group of trees whose flowering was done, hovered through the sunshine, and the breath that bore it was so gentle that not a leaf stirred. It cast no shadow on the green of the lawn, but this green seemed to darken from within like an eye. Extravagantly leaved by the young summer, the tender trees and bushes standing at the sides or forming the backdrop gave the impression of being amazed spectators who, surprised and spellbound in their gay attire, were participating in this funeral procession and celebration of nature. Spring and fall, speech and nature's silence, and the magic of life and death too, mingled in this picture; hearts seemed to stop, removed from their breasts to join the silent procession through the air. "My heart was taken from out my breast," a mystic had said: Agathe remembered it.

She knew, too, that she herself had read this saying to Ulrich from one of his books.

That had happened here in the garden, not far from the place where they were now. The recollection took shape. Other maxims too that she had recalled to his mind occurred to her: "Are you it, or are you not it? I know not where I am; nor do I wish to know!" "I have transcended all my abilities but for the dark power! I am in love, and know not in whom! My heart is full of love and empty of love at the same time!" Thus echoed in her again the laments of the mystics, into whose hearts God had penetrated as deeply as a thorn that no fingertips can grasp. She had read many such holy laments aloud to Ulrich at that time. Perhaps their rendering now was not exact: memory behaves rather dictatorially with what it wishes to hear; but she understood what was meant, and made a resolve. As it now appeared at this moment of flowery procession, the garden had also once looked mysteriously abandoned and animated at the very hour when the mystical confessions Ulrich had in his library had fallen into her hands. Time stood still, a thousand years weighed as lightly as the opening and closing of an eye; she had attained the Millennium: perhaps God was even allowing his presence to be felt. And while she felt these things one *after* the other—although time was not supposed to exist anymore—and while her brother, so that she should not suffer anxiety during this dream, was *beside* her, although space did not seem to exist any longer either: despite these contradictions, the world seemed filled with transfiguration in all its parts.

What she had experienced since could not strike her as other than conversationally temperate by comparison with what had gone before; but what an expansion and reinforcement it gave to these later things as well, although it had lost the near-body-heat warmth of the immediacy of the first inspiration! Under these circumstances Agathe decided to approach with deliberation the delight that had formerly, in an almost dreamlike way, befallen her in this garden. She did not know why she associated it with the name of the Millennium. It was a word bright with feeling and almost as palpable as an object, yet it remained opaque to the understanding. That was why she could regard the idea as if the Millennium could come to pass at any moment. It is also called the Empire of Love: Agathe knew that too; but only then did it occur to her that both names had been handed down since biblical times and signified the kingdom of God on earth, whose imminent arrival they indicated in a completely real sense. Moreover, Ulrich too, without on that account believing in the Scriptures, sometimes employed these words as casually as his sister, and so she was not at all surprised that she seemed to know exactly how one should behave in the Millennium. "You must keep quite still," her inspiration told her. "You cannot leave room for any kind of desire; not even the desire to question. You must also shed the judiciousness with which you perform tasks. You must deprive the mind of all tools and not allow it to be used as a tool. Knowledge is to be discarded by the mind, and willing: you must cast off reality and the longing to turn to it. You must keep to yourself until head, heart, and limbs are nothing but silence. But if, in this way, you attain the highest selflessness, then finally outer and inner will touch each other as if a wedge that had split the world had popped out!"

Perhaps this had not been premeditated in any clear way. But it seemed to her that if firmly willed, it must be attainable; and she pulled herself together as if she were trying to feign death. But it quickly proved as impossible to completely silence the impulses of thought, senses, and will as it had been in childhood not to commit any sins between confession and communion, and after a few efforts she completely abandoned the attempt. In the process, she discovered that she was only superficially holding fast to her purpose, and that her attention had long since slipped away; at the moment, it was occupied with a quite remote problem, a little monster of disaffection. She asked herself in the most foolish way, reveling in the very foolishness of it: "Was I really ever violent, mean, hateful, and unhappy?" A man without a name came to mind, his name missing because she bore it herself and had carried it away with her. Whenever she thought of him, she felt her name like a scar; but she no longer harbored any hatred for Hagauer, and now repeated her question with the somewhat melancholy obstinacy with which one gazes after a wave that has ebbed away. Where had the desire come from to do him mortal harm? She had almost lost it in her distraction, and appeared to think it was still to be found somewhere nearby. Moreover, Lindner might really be seen as a substitution for this desire for hostility; she asked herself this, too, and thought of him fleetingly. Perhaps she found all the things that had happened to her astonishing, young people always being more disposed to be surprised at how much they have already had to feel than older people, who have become accustomed to the changeability of life's passions and circumstances, like changes in the weather. But what could have so affected Agathe as this: that in the very moment of sudden change in her life, as its passions and conditions took flight, the stone-clear sky reached again into the marvelous river of emotions—in which ignorant youth sees its reflection as both natural and sublime—and lifted from it enigmatically that state out of which she had just awakened.

So her thoughts were still under the spell of the procession of flowers and death; they were, however, no longer moving with it to its rhythms of mute solemnity; Agathe was "thinking flittingly," as it might be called in contrast to the frame of mind in which life lasts "a thousand years" without a wing beating. This difference between two frames of mind was quite clear to her, and she recognized with some amazement how often just this difference, or something closely related to it, had already been touched on in her conversations with Ulrich. Involuntarily she turned toward him and, without losing sight of the spectacle unfolding around them, took a deep breath and asked: "Doesn't it seem to you, too, that in a moment like this, everything else seems feeble by comparison?"

These few words dispersed the cloudy weight of silence and memory. For Ulrich, too, had been looking at the foam of blossoms sweeping by on their aimless journey; and because his thoughts and memories were tuned to the same string as those of his sister, he needed no further introduction to be told what would answer even her unspoken thoughts. He slowly stretched and replied: "I've been wanting to tell you something for a long time—even in the state when we were speaking of the meaning of still lifes, and every day, really—even if it doesn't hit the center of the target: there are, to draw the contrast sharply, two ways of living passionately, and two sorts of passionate people. In one case, you let out a howl of rage or misery or enthusiasm each time like a child, and get rid of your feelings in a trivial swirl of vertigo. In that case, and it is the usual one, emotion is ultimately the everyday intermediary of everyday life; and the more violent and easily aroused it is, the more this kind of life is reminiscent of the restlessness in a cage of wild animals at feeding time, when the meat is carried past the bars, and the satiated fatigue that follows. Don't you think? The other way of being passionate and acting is this: You hold to yourself and give no impetus whatever to the action toward which every emotion is straining. In this case, life becomes like a somewhat ghostly dream in which the emotions rise to the treetops, to the peaks of towers, to the apex of the sky! It's more than likely that that's what we were thinking of when we were pretending to discuss paintings and nothing but paintings."

Agathe propped herself up, curious. "Didn't you once say," she asked, "that there are two fundamentally different possibilities for living and that they resemble different registers of emotion? One would be 'worldly' emotion, which never finds peace or fulfillment; the other . . . I don't know whether you gave it a name, but it would probably have to be the emotion of a 'mystical' feeling that resonates constantly but never achieves 'full reality.' " Although she spoke hesitantly, she had raced ahead too quickly, and finished with some embarrassment.

But Ulrich recognized quite well what he seemed to have said; he swallowed as if he had something too hot in his mouth, and attempted a smile. He said: "If that's what I meant, I'll have to express myself less pretentiously now! So I'll simply use a familiar example and call the two kinds of passionate existence the appetitive and, as its counterpart, the nonappetitive, even if it sounds awkward. For in every person there is a hunger, and it behaves like a greedy animal; yet it is not a hunger but something ripening sweetly, like grapes in the autumn sun, free from greed and satiety. Indeed, in every one of his emotions, the one is like the other."

"In other words, a vegetable—perhaps even a vegetarian—disposition alongside the animal one?" There was a trace of amusement and teasing in this question of Agathe's.

"Almost!" Ulrich replied. "Perhaps the animalistic and the vegetative, understood as the basic opposition of desires, would even strike a philosopher as the most profound discovery! But would that make me want to be one? All I would venture is simply what I have said, and especially what I said last, that both kinds of passionate being have a model, perhaps even their origin, in every emotion. These two aspects can be distinguished in every emotion," he continued. But oddly, he then went on to speak only of what he understood by the appetitive. It urges to action, to motion, to enjoyment; through its effect, emotion is transformed into a work, or into an idea and conviction, or into a disappointment. All these are ways in which it discharges, but they can also be forms of recharging, for in this manner the emotion changes, uses itself up, dissipates in its success and comes to an end; or it encapsulates itself in this success and transforms its vital energy into stored energy that gives up the vital energy later, and occasionally often with multiple interest. "And doesn't this explain that the energetic activity of our everyday feelings and its feebleness, which you were so pleasantly sighing about, don't make any great difference to us, even if it is a profound difference?"

"You may be all too right!" Agathe agreed. "My God, this entire work of the emotions, its worldly wealth, this wanting and rejoicing, activity and unfaithfulness, all only because of the existence of this drive! Including everything you experience and forget, think and passionately desire, and yet forget again. It's as beautiful as a tree full of apples of every color, but it's also formlessly monotonous, like everything that ripens and falls the same way each year!"

Ulrich nodded at his sister's answer, which exuded a breath of impetuousness and renunciation. "The world has the appetitive part of the emotions to thank for all its works and all beauty and progress, but also all the unrest, and ultimately all its senseless running around!" he corroborated. "Do you know, by the way, that 'appetitive' means simply the share that our innate drives have in every emotion? Therefore," he added, "what we have said is that it is the drives that the world has to thank for beauty and progress."

"And its chaotic restlessness," Agathe echoed.

"Usually that's exactly what one says; so it seems to me useful not to ignore the other! For that man should thank for his progress precisely what really belongs on the level of the animal is, at the very least, unexpected." He smiled as he said this. He, too, had propped himself up on his elbow, and he turned completely toward his sister, as if he wished to enlighten her, but he went on speaking hesitantly, like a person who first wants to be instructed by the words he is searching for. "You were right to speak of an animalistic disposition," he said. "Doubtless there are at its core the same few instincts as the animal has. This is quite clear in the major emotions: in hunger, anger, joy, willfulness, or love, the soul's veil barely covers the most naked desire!"

It seemed that he wanted to continue in the same vein. But although the conversation—which had issued from a dream of nature, the sight of the parade of blossoms that still seemed to be drifting through the middle of their minds with a peculiar uneventfulness—did not permit any misconstruing of the fateful question of the relation of brother and sister to each other, it was rather that from beginning to end the conversation was under the influence of this idea and dominated by the surreptitious notion of a "happening without anything happening," and took place in a mood of gentle affliction; although this was the way it was, finally the conversation had led to the opposite of such a pervasive idea and its emotional mood: to the point where Ulrich could not avoid emphasizing the constructive activity of strong drives alongside their disturbing activity. Such a clear indication of the drives, including the instinctive, and of the active person in general—for it signified that too—might well be part of an "Occidental, Western, Faustian life feeling," as it was called in the language of books, in contrast to everything that, according to the same self-fertilizing language, was supposed to be "Oriental" or "Asiatic." He recalled these patronizing vogue words. But it was not his or his sister's intention, nor would it have been in keeping with their habits, to give a misleading significance to an experience that moved them deeply by employing such adventitious, poorly grounded notions; rather, everything they discussed with each other was meant as true and real, even if it may have arisen from walking on clouds.

That was why Ulrich had found it amusing to substitute an explanation of a scientific kind for the caressing fog of the emotions; and in truth he did so just because—even if it appeared to abet the "Faustian"—the mind faithful to nature promised to exclude everything that was excessively fanciful. At least he had sketched out the basis for such an explanation. It was, of course, rather stranger that he had done so only for what he had labeled the appetitive aspect of emotions, but quite ignored how he could apply an analogous idea to the nonappetitive aspect, although at the beginning he had certainly considered them to be of equal importance. This did not come about without a reason. Whether the psychological and biological analysis of this aspect of emotion seemed harder to him, or whether he considered it *in toto* only a bothersome aid—both might have been the case—what chiefly influenced him was something else, of which he had, moreover, shown a glimpse since the moment when Agathe's sigh had betrayed the painful yet joyous opposition between the past restless passions of life and the apparently imperishable ones that were at home in the timeless stillness under the stream of blossoms. For—to repeat what he had already repeated in various ways—not only are two dispositions discernible in every single emotion, through which, and in its own fashion, the emotion can be fleshed out to the point of passion, but there are also two sorts of people, or different periods of destiny within each person, which differ in that one or the other disposition predominates.

He saw a great distinction here. People of the one sort, as already mentioned, reach out briskly for everything and set about everything; they rush over obstacles like a torrent, or foam into a new course; their passions are strong and constantly changing, and the result is a strongly segmented career that leaves nothing behind but its own stormy passage. This was the sort of person Ulrich had had in mind with the concept of the appetitive when he had wanted to make it one major notion of the passionate life; for the other sort of person is, in contrast to this, nothing less than the corresponding opposite of the first kind: the second is timid, pensive, vague; has a hard time making up its mind; is full of dreams and longings, and internalized in its passion. Sometimes—in ideas they were not now discussing—Ulrich also called this sort of person "contemplative," a word that is ordinarily used in another sense and that perhaps has merely the tepid meaning of "thoughtful"; but for him it had more than this ordinary meaning, was indeed equivalent to the previously mentioned Oriental/non-Faustian. Perhaps a major distinction in life was marked in this contemplative aspect, and especially in conjunction with the appetitive as its opposite: this attracted Ulrich more vitally than a didactic rule. But it was also a satisfaction to him, this elementary possibility of explanation, that all such highly composite and demanding notions of life could be reduced to a dual classification found in every emotion.

Of course it was also clear to him that both sorts of people under discussion could signify nothing other than a man "without qualities," in contrast to one who has every quality that a man can show. The one sort could also be called a nihilist, who dreams of God's dreams, in opposition to the activist, who in his impatient mode of conduct is, however, also a kind of God-dreamer and nothing less than a realist, who bestirs himself, clear about the world and active in it. "Why, then, aren't we realists?" Ulrich asked himself. Neither of them was, neither he nor she: their ideas and their conduct had long left no doubt of that; but they *were* nihilists and activists, sometimes one and sometimes the other, whichever happened to come up.

FURTHER SKETCHES

1939–1941

48

A MENTALITY DIRECTED TOWARD THE SIGNIFICANT, AND THE BEGINNING OF A CONVERSATION ON THE SUBJECT

If you speak of the double-sided and disorderly way the human being is constituted, the assumption is that you think you can come up with a better one.

A person who is a believer can do that, but Ulrich was not a believer. On the contrary: he suspected faith of inclining to the over-hasty, and whether the content of this spiritual attitude was an earthly inspiration or a supra-earthly notion, even as a mechanism for the forward movement of the soul it reminded him of the impotent attempts of the domestic chicken to fly. Only Agathe caused him to make an exception; he claimed to envy in her that she was able to believe precipitately and with ardor, and he sometimes felt the femininity of her lack of rational discretion as physically as he did one of those other sexual differentiations, knowledge of which arouses a dazzling bliss. He forgave her this unpredictability even when it really seemed to him unforgivable, as in her association with the ridiculous person of Professor Lindner, about whom there was much that his sister did not tell him. He felt the reticence of her bodily warmth beside him and was reminded of a passionate assertion which had it that no person is beautiful or ugly, good or bad, significant or soul-destroying in himself, but his value always depends on whether one believes in him or is skeptical of him. That was an extravagant observation, full of magnanimity but also undermined by vagueness, which allowed all sorts of inferences; and the hidden question of whether this observation was not ultimately traceable to that billy goat of credulity, this féllow Lindner, of whom he knew little more than his shadow, caused a wave to eddy up jealously in the rapid underground river of his thoughts. But as Ulrich thought about this, he could not recall whether it had been Agathe who had made this observation or he himself; the one seemed as possible as the other. As a result of this heady confusion, the wave of jealousy ebbed over all spiritual and physical distinctions in a delicate foam, and he would have liked to voice what his real reservations were about every predisposition to faith. To believe something and to believe in something are spiritual conditions that derive their power from another condition, which they make use of or squander; but this other condition not only was, as seemed most obvious, the solid condition of knowledge but could, on the contrary, be an even more ephemeral state than that of faith itself: and that everything that moved his sister and him pointed precisely in this direction urged Ulrich to speak out, but his ideas were still far from the prospect of pledging himself to it, and therefore he said nothing, but rather changed the subject before he reached that point.

Even a man of genius bears within himself a standard that could empower him to the judgment that in some totally inexplicable fashion things in the world go backward as well as forward; but who is such a man? Originally Ulrich had not had the slightest desire to think about it, but the problem would not let him go, he had no idea why.

"One must separate genius in general from genius as an individual superlative," he began, but still had not found the right expression. "I sometimes used to think that the only two important species of humans were the geniuses and the blockheads, which don't intermingle very well. But people of the species 'genius,' or people of genius, don't actually need to be geniuses. The genius one gapes at is actually born in the marketplace of the vanities; his splendor is radiated in the mirrors of the stupidity that surround him; it is always connected with something that bestows on it one merit the more, like money or medals: no matter how great his deserts, his appearance is really that of stuffed genius."

Agathe interrupted him, curious about the other: "Fine, but genius itself?"

"If you pull out of the stuffed scarecrow what is just straw, it would probably have to be what's left," Ulrich said, but then bethought himself and added distrustfully: "I'll never really know what genius is, or who should decide!"

"A senate of wise men!" Agathe said, smiling. She knew her brother's often quite idiosyncratic way of thinking; he had plagued her with it in many conversations. Her words were meant to remind him rather hypo-critically of the famous demand of philosophy, which had not been fol-lowed in two thousand years, that the governance of the world ought to be entrusted to an academy of the wisest men.

Ulrich nodded. "That goes back to Plato. And if it could have been brought about, presumably a Platonist would have followed him as leader of the reigning spirit until one day—God knows why—the Ploti-nists would have been seen as the true philosophers. That's the way it is, too, with what passes for genius. And what would the Plotinists have made of the Platonists, and before that the Platonists of them, if not what every truth does with error: mercilessly root it out? God proceeded cautiously when he directed that an elephant bring forth only another elephant, and a cat a cat: but a philosopher produces a blind adherent and a counterphilosopher!"

"So God himself had to decide what genius was!" Agathe exclaimed impatiently, not without feeling a soft, proud shudder at this idea and awareness of its precipitate/childish/vehemence.

"I fear it bores him!" Ulrich said. "At least the Christian God. He's out for hearts, without caring whether they have a lot of understanding or a little. Moreover, I believe that there's a lot to be said for the church's contempt for the genius of laymen."

Agathe waited a bit; then she simply replied: "You used to have a dif-ferent opinion."

"I *could* answer you that the heathen belief that all ideas that move people rested beforehand in the divine spirit must have been quite beautiful; but it's hard to think of divine emanations, since among the things that mean a lot to us there are ideas called guncotton or tires," Ulrich countered at once. But then he seemed to waver and to have grown tired of this jocular tone, and suddenly he revealed to his sister what she wanted to know. He said: "I have always believed, and almost as if it's my nature to, that the spirit, because one feels its power in one-self, also imposes the obligation to make it carry weight in the world. I have believed that to live meaningfully is the only reward, and have wanted never to do anything that was indifferent. And the consequence of this for culture in general may seem an arrogant distortion but is unavoidably this: Only genius is bearable, and average people have to be squeezed to either produce it or allow it to prevail! Mixed in with a thou-sand other things, something of this is also part of the general persua-sion: It's really humiliating for me to have to respond that I never could say what genius was, and don't know now either, although just now I indicated casually that I would ascribe this quality less to a particular individual than to a human modality."

He didn't seem to mean it so seriously, and Agathe carefully kept the conversation going when he fell silent. "Don't you yourself find it pretty easy to speak of an acrobat with genius?" she asked. "It seems that today the difficult, the unusual, and whatever is especially successful ordinarily figure in the notion."

"It began with singers; and if a singer who sings higher than the rest is called a genius, why not someone who jumps higher? By this reasoning you end up with the genius of a pointing dog; and people consider men who won't let themselves be intimidated by anything to be more worthy than a man who can tear his vocal cords out of his throat. Evidently, what's vague here is a twofold use of language: aside from the genius of success, which can be made to cover everything, so that even the stupidest joke can be, 'in its fashion,' a work of genius, there is also the sublimity, dignity, or significance of *what* succeeds: in other words, some kind of ranking of genius." A cheerful expression had replaced the seriousness in Ulrich's eyes, so that Agathe asked what came next, which he seemed to be suppressing.

"It occurs to me that I once discussed the question of genius with our friend Stumm," Ulrich related, "and he insisted on the usefulness of distinguishing between a military and a civilian notion of genius. But to grasp this distinction, I'll probably have to tell you something about the world of the Imperial and Royal military. The companies of engineers,"• he went on, "are there to build fortifications and for similar work, and are made up of soldiers and subalterns and officers who don't have any particular future unless they pass a 'Higher Engineer[/Genius] Course,' after which they land on the 'Engineering[/Genius] Staff.' 'So in the military, the Engineer [/Genius] Staffer stands above the engineer [/genius],' says Stumm von Bordwehr. 'And at the very top, of course, there is the General Staff, because that is absolutely the cleverest thing God has done.' So although Stumm always enjoys playing the antimilitarist, he tried to convince me that the proper usage of 'genius' can really be found only in the military and is graded in steps, while all civilian chatter about genius is regrettably lacking in such order. And the way he twists everything so that you really see to the bottom of truth, it wouldn't be at all a bad idea for us to follow his primer!"

But what Ulrich added to this concerning the dissimilar notions of genius was aimed less at the highest degree of genius than at its basic form, thesignificant, whose doubtfulness seemed to him more painful and confusing. It seemed to him easier to arrive at a judgment about what

---

•The German *Genie* means both "genius" and "engineer."—TRANS.

was exceptionally significant than about the significant in general. The first is merely a step beyond something whose value is already unquestioned, that is, something which is always grounded in a more or less traditional order of spiritual values; the latter, on the other hand, calls for taking the first step into an indefinite and infinite space, which offers almost no prospect of allowing a cogent distinction to be made between what is significant and what is not. So it is natural for language instead to have stuck with the genius of degree and success rather than with the genius value of what succeeds; yet it is also understandable that the custom that has developed of calling any aptitude that is hard to imitate "genius" is connected with a bad conscience, and of course none other than that of a dropped task or a forgotten duty. This scandalized the two of them in a joking and incidental way, but they went on speaking seriously. "This is clearest," Ulrich said to his sister, "when, although it mostly happens only by accident, one becomes conscious of an external sign to which scant attention is paid: namely, our habit of pronouncing the noun *Genie* and its adjective, *genial*, differently, and not in a way to indicate that the adjective derives from the noun."

As happens to everyone who is made aware of a practice to which scant attention is paid, Agathe was somewhat surprised.

"After my conversation with Stumm that time, I looked it up in Grimm's dictionary," Ulrich offered by way of excuse. "The military word *Genie*—in other words, the engineering soldier—came to us, of course, like many military expressions, from the French. In French, the art of the engineer is called *le génie*, and connected with it is *géniecorps*, *arme du génie*, and *École du génie*, as well as the English *engine*, the French *engin*, and the Italian *ingenio macchina*, the artful tool; the whole clan goes back to the late Latin *ingenium*, whose hard g became in its travels a soft g and whose fundamental connotation is dexterity and inventiveness: a summation, like the now rather old and creaky expression, 'arts and crafts,' with which official communications and inscriptions still sometimes bless us. From there a decayed path also leads to the soccer player of genius, indeed even to the hunting dog of genius or the steeplechase horse of genius, but it would be consistent to pronounce adjective and noun the same way. For there is a second *Genie* and *genial*, whose meaning is likewise to be found in every language and does not derive from *genium* but from *genius*, the more-than-human, or at least, in reverence for mind and spirit, the culmination of what is human. I hardly need point out that for centuries these two meanings have been dreadfully confused and mixed up everywhere, in language as in life, and not only in German; but, characteristically, in German most of all, so that not being able to keep genius and ingenious apart can be called a particularly German problem. Moreover, it has in German a history that in one place affects me greatly—"

Agathe had followed this extended explanation, as is usual in such cases, with some mistrust and a readiness for boredom, while waiting for a turn that would free her from this uncertainty. "Would you consider me a linguistic grouch if I were to propose that from now on we both start using the expression 'inspiriting'?" Ulrich asked.

A smile and a movement of her head spontaneously indicated his sister's resistance to this archaic term, which has fallen out of use and now bears the scent of old trunks and costumes.

"It is an archaic word," Ulrich admitted, "but this would be a good occasion to use it! And as I said, I did read up on it. If it doesn't bother you to do this in the street, let me have a look at what else I can tell you about it." With a smile, he pulled a piece of paper from his pocket and deciphered various notes he had made in pencil. "Goethe," he announced. " 'Here I saw regret and penitence pushed to caricature, and because all passion replaces genius, really inspiriting.' In another place: 'Your inspiriting composure often advanced to meet me with magnificent enthusiasm.' Wieland: 'The fruit of inspiriting hours.' Hölderlin: 'The Greeks are still a beautiful, inspiriting, and happy people.' And you'll find a similar 'inspiriting' in Schleiermacher, in his earlier years. But already with Immermann you find 'inspired economy' and 'inspired debauchery.' So there you already have the disconcerting transformation of the notion into the kettle-patching and slovenly, which is how 'inspired' is understood today." He turned the piece of paper this way and that, stuck it back in his pocket, and then took it out once more for assistance. "But its prehistory and preconditions are found earlier," he added. "Kant was already criticizing 'the fashionable tone of a geniuslike freedom in thinking' and speaks with annoyance of 'genius-men' and 'genius-apes.' What annoyed him so much is a respectable piece of German intellectual history. For before him as well as after him people in Germany talked, partly ecstatically, partly disapprovingly, of 'genius urge,' 'genius fever,' 'storm of genius,' 'leaps of genius,' 'calls of genius,' and 'screams of genius,' and even philosophy's fingernails were not always clean, least of all when it believed it could suck the independent truth from its fingers."

"And how does Kant decide what a genius is?" Agathe asked. All she associated with his famous name was that she remembered having heard that he surpassed everything.

"What he emphasized in the nature of genius was the creative element and originality, the 'spirit of originality,' which has remained extraordinarily influential up to the present day," Ulrich replied. "Goethe later was relying on Kant when he defined the geniative with the words: 'to have many objects present and easily relate the most remote ones to each other: this free of egotism and self-complacency.' But that's a view that was very much designed for the achievements of reason, and it leads to the rather gymnastic conception of genius we have succumbed to."

Agathe asked with laughing disbelief: "So now do you know what genius and geniative are?"

Ulrich took the joshing with a shrug of his shoulders. "Anyway, we've found that among Germans, if we don't see the strictly Kantian 'spirit of originality,' we feel that eccentric and conspicuous behavior indicates genius," he said.

49

GENERAL VON STUMM ON GENIUS

The conversation with Stumm that Ulrich mentioned had occurred at a chance meeting and had been brief. The General seemed worried; he did not indicate why, but he began to grumble over the nonsense that in civilian life there were so many geniuses. "What is a genius, really?" he asked. "No one has ever called a general a genius!"

"Except Napoleon," Ulrich interjected.

"Maybe him," Stumm admitted. "But that appears to happen more because his whole evolution was paradoxical!"

Ulrich didn't know what to say to this.

"At your cousin's, I had lots of opportunity to meet people who are designated as geniuses," Stumm declared pensively, and went on: "I believe I can tell you what a genius is: a person who not only enjoys great success but also, in some sense, has to get hold of his subject backward!" And Stumm immediately expounded on this, using the great examples of psychoanalysis and the theory of relativity:

"In the old days it was also often true that you didn't know something," he began in his characteristic fashion. "But you didn't think anything of it, and if it didn't happen during an examination it didn't harm anyone. But suddenly this was turned into the so-called unconscious, and now everyone's unconscious is the size of all the things he doesn't know, and it's much more important to know why you don't know something than what it is you don't know! Humanly speaking, this has, as one says, turned things topsy-turvy, and it's apparently a lot simpler too."

Since Ulrich still did not react, Stumm went on:

"But the man who invented that also established the following law: You will remember that in the regiment one used to admonish the younger men when there had been too much barnyard talk by telling them: 'Don't say it, just do it!' And what's the opposite of that? In some sense, the challenge: If, because you're a civilized human being, you can't do what you want, at least talk it over with a learned man; for he will convince you that everything that exists rests on something that ought not to exist! Of course I can't judge this from a scientific point of view, but in any case you can see from this that the new rules are absolutely the reverse of those that prevailed before, and the man who introduced them is praised today as a top-notch genius!"

Since Ulrich was apparently still not convinced, and Stumm himself did not feel he had got where he wanted, he repeated his argument using "relativity theory," as he conceived of it: "Like me, you learned at school that everything that moves happens in 'space and time,'" was where his thinking started. "But what is it like in practice? Permit me to say something quite ordinary: You are supposed to be with the front of your squadron at a particular place on the map at such and such a time. Or when you get the order, you're supposed to bring your cavalry from a formation to form a new front, which bears no relation at all to the straight lines on the exercise field. It happens in space and time, but it never happens without incident and never works out the way you want. I, at least, received a hundred reprimands so long as I was with the troops, I tell you that candidly. Even at school I always, so to speak, resisted when I had to calculate a mechanical motion in space and time on the blackboard. So I found it a real inspiration of genius the instant I heard that someone had finally discovered that space and time are quite relative concepts, which change at every moment whenever they are put to serious use, although since the creation of the world they have been regarded as the solidest thing there is. That's why this man, and in my view quite rightly, is at least as famous as the other. But it can also be said of him that he's tethered the horse by its tail, which, at least today, is what more or less amounts to the fixed main idea of what a genius is! And that's what I would like to make you see, if you place any value on my experience," Stumm concluded.

Ulrich, in his partiality for him, had conceded that the most important scientific teachings of the present had their eccentric aspects, or at least showed no fear of them. It might not mean much; but if one is so inclined, a sign can be seen in this as well. Fearless showiness, a predisposition for the paradoxical, self-starting ambition, surprise, and revision of everything on the basis of contradictory details that previously had hardly been noticed, all this had doubtless been part of the fashion in thinking for some time, for with their great achievements these things had just begun to crown precisely those fields where one would not have expected it and where one had been accustomed to the steady administration and constant increase of an enormous intellectual estate.

"But why?" Stumm asked. "How did it happen?"

Ulrich shrugged his shoulders. He thought of his own abandoned science, the broaching of its basic questions, their being skewered when their logic was checked out. It had not been much different with other sciences; they felt their edifices shaken through discoveries they had a hard time accommodating. That was the dispensation and the violence of truth. Nevertheless, it still seemed possible to speak of a boredom with everyday, never-ending progress, which up to now, and for the longest time, had been the ideal of real, silent faith amid the racket of all convictions. There was no denying a creeping doubt in all fields about the rightness of the bare, exact process of taking one step before another. That, too, might be a cause. Finally, Ulrich answered: "Perhaps it's simply the same as when you get tired: you need a prospect that refreshes you, or a shove in the back of your knees."

"Why not sit down instead?" Stumm asked.

"I don't know. In any event, after the longish calm flowering of the mind, you prefer to flirt with revolution. Some such thing seems to be in the offing. By way of comparison, you might perhaps think of the prevailing disjointedness in the arts. I don't understand much about politics, but perhaps sometime in the future someone will say that this intellectual restlessness already held signs of a revolution."

"The hell you say!" Stumm exclaimed, arts and revolutionary unrest reminding him of his impressions at Diotima's.

"Perhaps only as a transition to a new stability to come!" Ulrich said soothingly.

That made no difference to Stumm. "Since that tactless business in front of the War Minister I've avoided Diotima's parties," he related. "Don't get me wrong, I have no objection whatever to all those geniuses we've been talking about, who are already preserved in amber—or if I do, it's only that the way they're revered seems to me exaggerated. But I really have it in for the rest of that rabble!" And after a brief but obviously bitter moment he brought himself to ask the question: "Tell me honestly, is genius really so valuable?"

Ulrich had to smile, and disregarding what he had said before, he now mentioned the enormous—he even called it the magically simpleminded—sense of release that one recognized in the solution to any kind of problem that the most talented and even the greatest specialists had vainly striven to find. Genius is the single unconditional human value, it *is* human value, he said. Without the involvement of genius there would not even be the animal group of the higher primates. In his eagerness, he even passionately praised that genius which he was later to call merely the genius of degree and dexterity, to the extent that it was not fundamentally genius by nature.

Stumm nodded with satisfaction. "I know: the invention of fire and the wheel, gunpowder and printing, and so on! In short, from log canoe to logarithms!" But after he had demonstrated his sympathy he went on: "Now let me tell *you* something, and it's from the conversations at Diotima's: 'From Sophocles to Feuermaul!' Some young dolt once shouted that in complete seriousness!"

"What bothers you about Sophocles?"

"Ah! I don't know anything about him. But Feuermaul! And here you are claiming that genius is an unconditional value."

"The touch of genius is the only moment in which that ugly and obdurate pupil of God, man, is beautiful and candid!" Ulrich intensified his statement. "But I did not say that it's easy to decide what's genius and what merely fantasy. I'm just saying that wherever a new value really enters the human game, genius is behind it!"

"How can you know whether something is 'really a new value'?"

Ulrich hesitated, smiling.

"And then, in any case, whether the value really is worth anything!" Stumm added with curiosity and concern.

"You often feel it at first sight," Ulrich said.

"I've been told that people have been mistaken at first sight!"

The conversation faltered. Stumm was perhaps preparing a fundamentally different question.

Ulrich said: "You hear the first bars of Bach or Mozart; you read a page of Goethe or Corneille: and you know that you've touched genius!"

"Maybe with Mozart and Goethe, because with them I already know that; but not with an unknown!" the General protested.

"Do you believe it wouldn't have electrified you even when you were young? The enthusiasm of youth is in itself related to genius!"

"What do you mean, 'in itself'? But if you're really forcing me to answer: maybe an opera diva might have aroused my enthusiasm. And Alexander the Great, Caesar, and Napoleon excited me once too. But 'in itself,' writers or composers of any kind have always left me cold!"

Ulrich beat a retreat, although he felt that he had merely got hold of a good argument from the wrong end. "I meant to say that a young person, as he develops intellectually, sniffs out genius the way a migrating bird senses direction. But apparently that would be confusing things.

For the young person has only the most limited access to what is significant. He has no particular sense of it, but only a sense for what excites him. He's not even looking for genius, but he's searching for himself and for whatever is an appropriate foothold for the shape of his biases. What speaks to him," he declared, "is what's like him, in all the vagueness that goes along with it. It's more or less what he himself believes he can be, and has the same importance in his formation as the mirror, in which he gazes at himself happily, but by no means only out of vanity. That's why it's only to be expected of works of genius that they should have this effect on him; usually it's contemporary things, and among those rather the ones that stimulate moods than those clearly formed by the intellect, just as he prefers mirrors that make his face thin or his shoulders broad to faithful ones."

"That may well be," Stumm agreed pensively. "But do you believe that people get cleverer later on?"

"There's no doubt that the mature person is more capable and has more experience in recognizing what is significant; but his mature personal aims and powers also force him to exclude many things. It's not that he refuses from lack of understanding but that he leaves things aside."

"That's it!" Stumm exclaimed, relieved. "He's not as limited as a young person, but I would say he's more circumscribed! And that has to be too. Whenever people like us associate with immature young people of the kind favored by your cousin, God knows we must be ready for anything and have the good sense not to understand half of what they're saying!"

"You might well criticize them."

"But your cousin says they're geniuses! How do you prove the opposite?"

Ulrich would not have been disinclined to follow up this question as well. "A genius is a person who finds a solution where many have looked for it in vain by doing something nobody before him thought of doing," he defined, in order finally to get on, because he was curious himself.

But Stumm declined. "I can stick to the facts themselves," he commented. "At Frau von Tuzzi's I've met enough critics and professors in person, and every time that one of the geniuses who improve life or art made assertions that were entirely too far out of line, I discreetly sought these experts' advice."

Ulrich allowed himself to be distracted. "And what was the result?"

"Oh, they were always very respectful to me and said: 'You shouldn't bother your head about that, General!' Of course that may be a kind of arrogance they have; for though they nervously praise all new artists,

they nonetheless seem to imagine that these artists, in their own assertions, dangerously contradict each other, indeed that they feel something like blind rage toward each other, and that *summa summarum*
they perhaps don't know what they're doing!"

"And did you also find out what those sun-stricken minds that Diotima cools with laurel think about the critics and professors, to the extent these people don't praise them?" Ulrich asked. "As if the artists
were the ones feeding these beasts of intellect with their flesh, and these
beasts were the ones who would leave a mere struggle over bones as the
final remains of all man's humanity!"

"You've observed them well!" Stumm agreed as a delighted connois-
seur.

"But in the face of so much contradiction, how do you recognize whether you've really got hold of a 'genius' or not?" Ulrich asked
logically.

Stumm's answer was honest, if not compelling: "I don't give a damn,"
he said.

Ulrich looked at him in silence. If he wanted merely to engage in a
rear-guard skirmish and avoid problems that were more difficult than
the circumstances warranted, then it was a mistake for him not to use
this moment "to disengage himself from the enemy," as good tactics
would have dictated. But he himself did not know what mood he was in.
So he finally said: "Nothing gives fake geniuses so much luck with the
masses as the incomprehension that genuine geniuses ordinarily have
for each other, and, following their example, the pseudo-genuine ones;
lamp polishers can't clean Prometheus!" At this conclusion Stumm
looked up at him, uncomprehending but thoughtful. "Don't misunderstand me," he added cautiously. "Remember my eagerness when I was
searching for a great idea for Diotima. I know what intellectual aristocracy is. Nor am I Count Leinsdorf, for whom that's always a kind of
minor nobility. Just now, for example, you brilliantly defined what a genius is. How did it go? It finds a solution by doing something that hadn't
occurred to anyone before! That really says the same thing I've been
saying: the important thing is that a genius gets hold of his subject from
the wrong end. But that's not intellectual aristocracy! And why isn't it
intellectual aristocracy? Because the usual polestar of our age is that
whatever the circumstances, what happens must be meaningful, but
whether you call it genius or intellectual aristocracy, progress or, as you
now often hear people say, a record, just doesn't matter much to our
time!"

"But then why did you mention intellectual aristocracy?" Ulrich
prompted impatiently.

"I can't really say precisely, for that very reason!" Stumm defended himself. "Anyway," he continued, thinking busily, "perhaps you could say in a way that an intellectual aristocracy in particular is not permitted to leave character in peace. Aren't I right?"

"Yes, you're right!" Ulrich encouraged him, made aware for the first time this precise moment, quite incidentally, as it happened, to heed a distinction like the one between genius and dexterity.

"Yes," Stumm repeated thoughtfully. And then he asked: "But what is character? Is it what helps a man develop the ideas that will distinguish him? Or is it what keeps him from having such ideas? For a man who has character doesn't do much flitting around!"

Ulrich decided to shrug his shoulders and smile.

"Presumably it's connected with what one is accustomed to calling *great* ideas," Stumm went on skeptically. "And then intellectual aristocracy would be nothing except the possession of great ideas. But how does one recognize that an idea is great? There are so many geniuses, at least a couple in every profession; indeed, it's a distinctive mark of our time that we have too many geniuses. How is one to understand them all and not overlook any!" His painful familiarity with the question of what a really great idea was had brought him back to its role in genius.

Ulrich shrugged again.

"There are of course some people, and I've met them," Stumm said, "who never miss the smallest genius that can be dug up anywhere!"

Ulrich replied: "Those are the snobs and intellectual pretenders."

The General: "But Diotima is one of these people too."

Ulrich: "Makes no difference. A person into whom everything he finds can be stuffed must be built with no shape of his own, like a sack."

"It's true," the General replied rather reproachfully, "that you've often said that Diotima was a snob. And you've sometimes said it about Arnheim as well. But that made me imagine a snob to be someone who is quite stimulating! I've honestly tried hard to be one myself and not let anything slip past me. It's hard for me to suddenly hear you say that you can't even depend on a snob to understand genius. Because you said before that youth couldn't answer for it, nor age either. And then we discussed how geniuses don't, and critics not at all. Well then, genius will finally have to reveal itself to everyone of its own accord!"

"That will happen in time," Ulrich soothed him, laughing. "Most people believe that time naturally turns up what is significant."

"Yes, one hears that too. But tell me if you can," Stumm asked impatiently. "I can understand that one is cleverer at fifty than one was at twenty. But at eight o'clock in the evening I'm no cleverer than I was at eight in the morning; and that one should be cleverer after nineteen hundred and fourteen years than after eight hundred and fourteen, that I can't see either!" This led them to go on a bit discussing the difficult subject of genius, the only thing, in Ulrich's opinion, that justified mankind, but at the same time the most exciting and confusing, because you never know whether you're looking at genius or at one of its half-baked imitations. What are its distinguishing characteristics? How is it passed on? Could it develop further if it were not constantly being thwarted? Is it, as Stumm had asked, such a desirable thing anyway? These were problems that for Stumm belonged to the beauty of the civilian mind and its scandalous disorder, while Ulrich, on the other hand, compared them with a weather forecast that not only didn't know whether it would be fair tomorrow but didn't know whether it had been fair yesterday either. For the judgment of what constitutes genius changes with the spirit of the times, assuming that anyone is interested in it at all, which by no means need be the mark of greatness of soul or of mind.

Such puzzles would no doubt have been well worth solving, and so it came about in this part of the conversation that Stumm finally, after shaking his head a few times, proffered his observation about the Engineering[/Genius] Staff that Ulrich later repeated to his sister. This explanation, that genius needed a Genius Staff, reminded him somewhat painfully, moreover, of what Ulrich himself had half ironically called the General Secretariat of Precision and Soul, and Stumm did not neglect to remind him that he had last mentioned it in his own and Count Leinsdorf's presence during the unfortunate gathering at Diotima's. "At that time you were demanding something quite similar," he held up to him, "and if I'm not mistaken, it was a department for geniuses and the intellectual aristocracy." Ulrich nodded silently. "For the intellectual aristocracy," Stumm continued, "would ultimately be what ordinary geniuses don't have. No matter how you define them, our geniuses are geniuses and nothing more, nothing but specialists! Am I right? I can really understand why many people say: today there's no such thing as genius!"

Ulrich nodded again. A pause ensued.

"But there's one thing I'd like to know," Stumm asked with that hint of egotism that attaches to a recurrent perplexing thought: "Is it a reproach or a distinction that people never say about a general: he's a genius?"

"Both."

"Both? Why both?"

"I honestly don't know."

Stumm was taken aback but, after thinking it over, said: "You put that brilliantly! The people love an officer as long as they aren't stirred up; and he gets to know the people: the people couldn't care less about geniuses! But by the time he gets to be a general he has to be a specialist, and if he himself is a specialist genius he then falls into the category that there's no such thing as genius. So he never gets, as I would say if I spelled it out, to the point where the use of this wishy-washy term would be appropriate. Do you know, by the way, that I recently heard something really clever? I was at your cousin's, in the most intimate circle, although Arnheim is away, and we were discussing intellectual questions. Then someone pokes me in the ribs and explains Arnheim to me in a whisper: 'He's what you call a genius,' he said. 'More than all the others. A *universal* specialist!' Why don't you say anything?" Ulrich found nothing to say. "The possibilities inherent in this point of view surprised me. Besides, you yourself happen to be such a kind of universal specialist. That's why you shouldn't neglect Arnheim so; because ultimately the Parallel Campaign might get its saving idea from him, and that could be dangerous! I would really much prefer that it came from you."

And although Stumm had (finally) spoken far more than Ulrich, he took his leave with the words: "As always, it's a pleasure talking with you, because you understand all these things de facto much better than everyone else!"

50

GENIUS AS A PROBLEM

Ulrich had related this conversation to his sister.

But even before that he had been speaking of difficulties connected with the notion of genius. What enticed him to do this? He had no intention of claiming to be a genius himself, or of politely inquiring about the conditions that would enable a person to become one. On the contrary, he was convinced that the powerful, exhausted ambition in his time for the vocation of genius was the expression not of intellectual or spiritual greatness but merely of an incongruity. But as all contemporary questions about life become impossibly entangled in an impenetrable thicket, so do the questions surrounding the idea of genius, which in part enticed one's thoughts to penetrate it and in part left them hung up on the difficulties.

After he finished his report, Ulrich had immediately come back to this. Of course, whatever has genius must be significant; for genius is the significant accomplishment that originates under particularly distinctive conditions. But "significant" is not only the lesser but also the more general category. So the first thing was to inquire into this notion again. The words "significant" and "significance" themselves, like all terms that are much used, have different meanings. On the one hand, they are connected with the concepts of thinking and knowing. To say that something signifies or has this significance means that it points to, gives to understand, indicates, or can represent in specific cases, or simply generally, that it is the same as something else, or falls under the same heading and can be known and comprehended as the other. That is, of course, a relationship accessible to reason and involving the nature of reason; and in this manner anything and everything can signify something, as it can also be signified. On the other hand, the term "signifying something" is used as well in the sense of something having significance or being of significance. In this sense, too, nothing is excluded. Not only a thought can be significant, but also an act, a work, a personality, a position, a virtue, and even an individual quality of mind. The distinction between this and the other kind of signifying is that a particular rank and value is ascribed to what is significant. That something is significant means in this sense that it is more significant than other things, or simply that it is unusually significant. What decides this? The ascription gives one to understand that it belongs to a hierarchy, an order of mental powers that is aspired to, even should the attainable measure of order be in many things as undependable as it is strict in others. Does this hierarchy exist?

It is the human spirit itself: named not as a natural concept but as the objective spirit.

Agathe asked what this included; it is a notion that people more scientifically trained than she threw around so much that she ducked.

Ulrich nearly emulated her. He found the word used far too much. At that period it was used so often in scientific and pseudoscientific arguments that it simply revolved around itself. "For heaven's sake! You're becoming profound!" he retorted. The expression had inadvertently slipped from his own lips.

Ordinarily, one understands by "objective spirit" the works of the spirit, the relatively constant share it deposits in the world through the most various signs, in opposition to the subjective spirit as individual quality and individual experience; or one understood by it, and this could not be entirely separated from the first kind, the viable spirit, verifiable, constant in value, in opposition to the inspirations of mood and error. This touched two oppositions whose significance for Ulrich's life had certainly not been simply didactic but—and this he was well aware of and had expressed often enough—had become extremely alluring and worrisome. So what he meant had elements of both.

Perhaps he could also have said to his sister that by "objective spirit" one understands everything that man has thought, dreamed, and desired; but, to do so means not looking at it as components of a spiritual, historical, or other temporal-actual development, and certainly not as something spiritual-suprasensory either, but exclusively as itself, according to its own characteristic content and inner coherence. He could also have said, which appeared to contradict this but in the end came to the same thing, that it should be looked at with the reservation of all the contexts and orderings of which it is at all capable. For what something signifies or is in and of itself he equated with the result that coalesces out of the significances that could accrue to it under all possible conditions.

But one merely needs to put this differently, simply saying that in and of itself, something would be precisely what it never is in and of itself, but rather is in relation to its circumstances; and likewise that its significance is everything that it could signify; so one merely has to turn the expression on its head for the scruple connected with it to immediately become obvious. For of course the usual procedure, on the contrary, is to assume, even if only from a usage of language, that what something is in and of itself, or what it signifies, forms the origin and nucleus of everything that can be expressed about it in mutable relationships. So it was a particular conception of the nature of the notion and of signifying by which Ulrich had let himself be guided; and particularly because it is not unfamiliar, it might also be stated something like this: Whatever may be understood under the nature of the concept of a logical theory is in application, as a concept *of* something, nothing but the countervalue and the stored-up readiness for all possible true statements about that something. This principle, which inverts the procedure of logic, is "empirical," that is, it reminds one, if one were to apply an already coined name to it, of that familiar line of philosophical thought, without, however, being meant in precisely the same sense. Ought Ulrich now to have explained to his companion what empiricism was in its earlier form and what it had become in its more modest, and perhaps improved, modern version? As often happens when an idea gains in correctness, the more finely honed process of thinking renounces false answers but also some more profound questions as well.

What was baptized as empiricism in philosophical language was a doctrine that arbitrarily declared the really astonishing presence and unchangeable sway of laws in nature and in the rules of the intellect to be a deceptive view that originated in habituation to the frequent repetition of the same experiences. The approximate classical formula for this was:

Whatever repeats itself often enough seems to have to be so; and in this exaggerated form, which the eighteenth and nineteenth centuries bestowed upon it, this formula was a repercussion of the long antecedent theological speculation: that is, of the faith placed in God, of being able to explain His works with the aid of whatever one takes into one's head. Notions and ideas demonstrate, when they are dominant, the same inclination to let themselves be worshiped and to broadcast capricious judgments as people do; and that probably led, when empiricism was established in modern times, to the admixture of a rather superficial opposition to totally convinced rationalism, which then, when it came to power itself, bore some of the responsibility for a shallow materialistic nature and societal mentality that at times has become almost popular.

Ulrich smiled when he thought of an example, but did not say why. For it was not reluctantly that one reproached empiricism, which was all too simpleminded and confined to its rules, that according to it the sun rises in the east and sets in the west for no other reason than that up till now it always has. And were he to betray this to his sister and ask her what she thought of it, she would probably answer arbitrarily, without bothering about the arguments and counterarguments, that the sun might one day do it differently. This was why he smiled as he thought of this example; for the relationship between youth and empiricism seemed to him profoundly natural, and youth's inclination to want to experience everything itself, and to expect the most surprising discoveries, moved him to see this as the philosophy appropriate to youth. But from the assertion that awaiting the rising of the sun in the east every day merely has the security of a habit, it is only a step to asserting that all human knowledge is felt only subjectively and at a particular, or is indeed the presumption of a class or race, all of which has gradually become evident in European intellectual history. Apparently one should also add that approximately since the days of our great-grandfathers, a new kind of individuality has made its appearance: this is the type of the empirical man or empiricist, of the person of experience who has become such a familiar open question, the person who knows how to make from a hundred of his own experiences a thousand new ones, which, however, always remain within the same circle of experience, and who has by this means created the gigantic, profitable-in-appearance monotony of the technical age. Empiricism as a philosophy might be taken as the philosophical children's disease of this type of person.

SKETCHES FOR A CONTINUATION OF THE "GALLEY CHAPTERS," 1938 AND LATER

59

NIGHT TALK

In his room he had lit one lamp after the other, as if the stimulating excess of illumination would make the words come more easily, and for a long time he wrote zealously. But after he had accomplished the most important part, he was overcome by the awareness that Agathe had not yet returned, and this became more and more disturbing. Ulrich did not know that she was with Lindner, nor did he know about these visits at all; but since that secret and his diaries were the only things they concealed from each other, he could surmise and also almost understand what she was doing. He did not take it more seriously than it deserved, and was more astonished at it than jealous; then too, he ascribed responsibility for it to his own lack of resolution, insofar as she pursued ways of her own that he could not approve of. It nevertheless inhibited him more and more, and diminished the readiness for belief that was weaving his thoughts together, that in this hour of collectedness he did not even know where she was or why she was late. He decided to interrupt his work and go out, to escape the enervating influence of waiting, but with the intention of soon returning to his labors. As he left the house it occurred to him that going to the theater not only would be the greatest diversion, but would also stimulate him; and so he went, although he was not dressed for it. He chose an inconspicuous seat and at first felt the great pleasure of coming into a performance that was already energetically under way. It justified his coming, for this dynamic mirroring of emotions familiar a hundred times over, by which the theater is accustomed to live under the pretext that this gives it meaning, reminded Ulrich of the value of the task he had left at home and renewed his desire to come to the end of the road that, proceeding from the origin of the emotions, ultimately had to lead to their significance. When he again directed his attention to the goings-on onstage, it occurred to him that most of the actors busily occupied up there, beautifully if meaninglessly imitating passions, bore titles such as Privy Councillor or Professor, for Ulrich was in the Hoftheater, and this raised everything to the level of state comedy. So although he left the theater before the end of the play, he nevertheless returned home with his spirits refreshed.

He again turned on all the lights in his room, and it gave him pleasure to listen to himself writing in the porous stillness of the night. This time, when he had entered the house, all sorts of fleeting signs barely assimilated by his consciousness told him that Agathe had returned; but when he subsequently thought of it and everything was without a sound, he was afraid to look around him. Thus the night became late. He had been once more in the garden, which lay in complete darkness, as inhospitable, indeed as mortally hostile, as deep black ocean; nevertheless, he had groped his way to a bench and persevered there for quite a while. It was difficult, even under these circumstances, to believe that what he was writing was important. But when he was again sitting in the light, he set to work to write to the end, as far as his plan extended this time. He didn't have far to go, but had hardly begun when a soft noise interrupted him. For Agathe, who had been in his room while he was at the theater and had repeated this secret visit while he was in the garden, slipping out upon his return, hesitated a short while outside the door and now softly turned the knob.

∙   ∙   ∙

Agathe's entrance: she is wearing the historical lounging attire, etc. Lets her hand glide over his head, sits with crossed legs on the sofa.

Or: wrapper. Perhaps better. Describe it? Not transparent; on the contrary, heavy material. She was enveloped in a wrapper of old velvet material that reached to her ankles and looked like a completely darkened picture that had once been painted on a gold ground. Like a magician's cape. Her ankles bare, the span of her foot as bare as her hand. Her slippers were of violet silk the color of spindle-tree fruit hanging on its bush in autumn. A collar of some soft weave, whose color hovered between ivory, milk, and dull gilt silver.

She had never worn this wrapper before; Ulrich did not recall it.

Ibidem. When he is near her, Ulrich feels the flowing back into emotion of what is outside and what inside, and the vigorous action of the emotion. Also the sexual propensity, which belongs to a different sphere.

The woman who becomes a guiding image in a different aspect and the woman who is the fulfillment of desire as examples of conceptions of different levels that in life exist side by side.

She settles down on the sofa. Her torso comfortably supported and her legs drawn up beneath her so that only her foot peeks out beneath the hem that forms a wheel. Later she briskly changes position, but at the beginning her posture was thoughtful and her face serious.

"I've read it!" she informed her brother, like a chess player who, after a short pause for reflection, makes his first move.

"It seems to me you shouldn't have," he responded in the same manner.

Agathe burst out laughing. "It was disloyal of you to conceal it from me," she asserted boldly.

If the description of the dress stays, don't have the laughing right after it—

Ulrich listened to her voice and contemplated her beauty. "These reflections make me understand more about myself than many years were able to previously," he said quite calmly.

"And they have nothing to do with me?"

"Yes, it concerns you as well!"

"But why then are you doing it secretly? Why haven't you ever told me about it?

"Why are you secretly visiting that man of tears Lindner?"

"Also to understand myself better. And anyway, he weeps tears of anger."

"Were you there today?"

"Yes." Agathe looked steadily at her brother and noticed the resentment in his eyes.

He strove to control himself and responded as tersely as possible: "I don't like your doing that."

"I don't like doing it myself," Agathe said, continuing after a brief pause: "But I like what you write. The beginning and the end, and what's in between too. I didn't understand everything, but I read it all. I think you could explain a lot of things to me, and because I'm afraid of straining myself, I'll believe a lot without any explanation at all."

(*Post datum.* This is really an example of an inner form of cheerfulness as distinct from outer.)

. . .

She laughed again, and it pealed softly. She seemed to be laughing over nothing and only from joy; and although Ulrich could be quite sensitive to people's laughter when it was aroused by something, for then it sometimes seemed to him just as humdrum an occurrence as sneezing, it immediately enticed him into an impossible task, that of adequately describing this pleasant, unmotivated sound. If, into the bargain, one threw in a little poetic commonplace, the impression could then be compared with that of a small, low-tuned silver bell: a dark bass tone submerged in a soft overflowing sparkle. But while Ulrich was listening to these cheerful sounds spreading out in the quiet room, his eyes also thought they were seeing all its lamps burning that much more quietly / as brightly. Precisely the simplest sensory impressions that populate the world occasionally have surprises in store when it comes to describing them, as if they came from another world.

Influenced by this weakness, Ulrich suddenly felt a confession on his tongue about which he himself had not thought for goodness knew how long. "I once made a devilish bet with our big cousin Tzi, which I will never write down and which I don't think I ever told you about," he began to confess. "He suspected that I would write books, and, as it seems to me, he considered books that did not praise his politics to be deleterious and those that did superfluous, aside from the historical literature and memoirs a diplomat customarily employs. But I swore to him that I would kill myself before I succumbed to the temptation of writing a book; and I really meant it. For what I was able to write would do nothing more than prove that one is able to live differently in some specific fashion; but that I should write a book about it would at the very least be the counterproof that I'm not able to live in that fashion. I didn't expect it would turn out differently."

His sister had listened to him without stirring, without even a muscle in her face twitching. "We can kill each other if it turns into a book," she said. "But it seems to me we have less reason to than before."

Ulrich involuntarily looked her in the eye.

"Rather more reason for the opposite," she went on.

"You can't yet say that (too)," Ulrich objected calmly.

Agathe found that the supporting pillow at her side needed rearranging, which turned her face away from him. "Don't be angry with me," she replied from this posture, "but even though I admire what you write, I still don't quite understand *why* you write. Indeed, sometimes I've found it enormously comical. You carefully dissect according to natural and moral laws the possibility of extending your hand. Why don't you simply reach out?"

"It's ruinous simply to reach out. Did I ever tell you the story of the major's wife?"

Agathe nodded mutely.

"It can't end the way that did!"

The small furrow appeared between Agathe's brows. "The major's wife was a commonplace person," she declared coolly.

"That's right. But whether one discovers a world or goes on a Don Quixote adventure doesn't depend, unfortunately, on the worth of the person in whose honor one embarks on the trip."

"Who knows!" Agathe replied. A moment later she impatiently abandoned her comfortable position and sat down in the ordinary way right in front of her brother, as if she were going to test something. She looked at him (almost grimly) but said nothing. "Well?" Ulrich asked encouragingly, expecting an attack (that was awaiting him).

"Doesn't everything you've written down"—she pointed to the table and the papers lying on it—"answer everything we've been asking ourselves so often and have been so uncertain about?"

"I almost think so."

"I have the feeling that everything we've been discussing back and forth for so long is resolved in these papers. But why didn't you hit on it sooner? I'm even immodest enough to maintain that you've left us both in the dark for quite a while."

"We're still in the dark. You shouldn't overestimate these ideas. And it's been hard for me to open up to you. Sometimes in a dream you have delightful thoughts, but if you carry on with them after you wake up, they're ridiculous."

"Really? But if I've understood you correctly, you're certain that for every emotion there are two worlds and that it depends on us which one we wish to live in!"

"Two *images* of the world! But only one reality! Within it, of course, you can perhaps live in one way or the other. And that is when you apparently have the one or the other reality before you."

"Apparently, but totally? Apparently, and with no gaps? But if everything were living in this other way, wouldn't that be the Millennium?"

Ulrich cautiously confirmed the possibility of this conclusion.

"So the intimation of this other world would also be what brought about belief in a paradise? Don't laugh at me, but it's made me conclude that in this way one would of necessity arrive in paradise just by living according to the other part of one's feelings, as you call it."

"Put correctly, paradise would then have to arrive on earth," Ulrich rectified.

"I'm not laughing at all. I just have to add: as far as one can!" / Or: mysticism as anomalous psychology of normal life: You believe that mysticism is a secret through which we enter another world; but it is only, or even, the secret of living differently in our world."

"Oh? Yes, that's what you wrote. But didn't you even much earlier sometimes call it the concave, submerged world?" Agathe ascertained. "You spoke of an encompassing and an encompassed possibility of feeling as if they were old tales. Of gods and goddesses. Of two branches of development in life. Of moon-nights and day. Of two inseparable twins!"

It is the answer to all our conversations, all our peculiarities.

Agathe was pressing, but Ulrich yielded of his own accord: "You can add anything you like: everything that has truly moved me has its explanation here. The victories that come from acting in the world, and the emotions that go with them, have always been alien to me, even if at times I felt an obligation to them. An apparently inactive state I called love, without loving a woman, was opposed in me to the processes of knowledge that gave me the passion a rider has for his horse / which I called the world of love because I couldn't love in the everyday world! / We always imagined a different life before us."

Agathe interrupted him animatedly. But it was hard for her to find the right words. At the beginning, although soon swept away by what she was saying, there was a little awkwardness in her voice, as when a boy tries to speak in a man's bass voice, or when a girl paints a mustache on her face, as she began: "You know that I'm no shrinking touch-me-not. And I've often reproached myself for my so-called passions, which have always left me completely unmoved. I clearly felt that I was being moved by them only because I hadn't found what could truly move us." Possibly better this way: When she applied the expression "touch-me-not" to herself. She said Ulrich knew that she wasn't one and that she attached no importance to it. But also (that is: he knew) that she found her so-called passions most shameful after the fact. "You scrape yourself like a cow against a tree, just as happily, and suddenly stop in the same bewilderment," she said.

Ulrich: A person is passionate in two senses. A kind of appetitive sense, which reaches out for everything and undertakes everything, and another, which is timid, has a hard time making up its mind to do things, and is full of inexpressible longing. One probably has both within oneself.

Agathe: The man with qualities and the man without qualities! Marvelous, marvelous. If someone understands you properly he has saved his life! What author wouldn't be flattered by such praise! Ulrich responded: It's not immaterial that we are talking about a passionate person in two quite different senses. We've become accustomed to applying the term chiefly to people we really ought to call lustful, to gluttons in every kind of passion, while we rather tend to regard people who are profoundly passionate within themselves as weak in affect, people who ascetically serve some sort of nobler passion of life. That leads to stupid mixups.

Agathe: I'm reproached for acting badly—

Who reproaches you? (a little suspiciously)

Agathe violently twitched her shoulders. "Professor Hagauer. Think of his letters. Indeed, I've often reproached myself for having done what I did with the will—"

"We'll make amends for it," Ulrich intervened.

"What a situation to be in, feeling that you're not a good person and yet not wanting it any other way! You yourself once reproached me about this, and I was insulted—"

Ulrich interrupted her with an apologetic, defensive gesture. Probably (too) from the author, that it's important that they have now recognized that they've got to the center of their difficulties.

Agathe: "Oh, you've often talked about morality. You've set before me at least ten different definitions; every time, listening to you was a totally new experience. But now I'm reproached for being immoral, I'm made to believe it myself, but for all that I'm an absolute marvel of morality!"

Ulrich: And why a marvel?

Agathe: You showed me the way! The only condition I love and seek needs no morality, it *is* morality! Every twitch of the little toe that happens in it is moral. Am I right? (laughs)

Ulrich: Yes, you're right.

Agathe: But first I want to ask you something else . . . Everything we've been talking about half jokingly and half seriously for the last few days: is it all settled?

Ulrich: Of course.

Agathe: To love your neighbor as yourself is an ecstatic demand?

Ulrich: It is the natural morality of mystic ecstasy, which teaches something that never quite fits the ord[inary] activity of our lives.

EARLY-MORNING WALK
Part I

Around Clarisse's mouth laughter was struggling with the difficulties facing her; her mouth kept opening and then pressing itself tightly shut. She had got up too early: Walter was still sleeping; she had hastily thrown on a light dress and gone outside. The singing of birds reached her from the woods through the empty morning stillness. The hemisphere of the sky had not yet filled with warmth. Even the light was still shallowly dispersed. "It only reaches my ankles," Clarisse thought. "The cock of the morning has just been wound up! Everything is before its time!" Clarisse was deeply moved that she was wandering through the world before it was time. It almost made her cry.

Without saying anything about it to Walter or Ulrich, Clarisse had been to the asylum a second time. Since then she had been especially sensitive. She applied everything she had seen or heard during her two visits to herself. Three events especially preoccupied her. The first was that she had been addressed and greeted as the Emperor's son and a man. When this assertion had been repeated, she had quite distinctly felt her resistance to it yield, as if something ordinary that usually stood in the way of this royal quality was vanishing. And she was filled with an inexpressible desire. The second thing that excited her was that Meingast, too, was transforming himself, and was obviously using her and Walter's proximity in the process. Since she had surprised him in the vegetable garden—it might have been a few weeks ago—and terrified him with her truly prophetic shout that she could transform herself too and also be a man, he had been avoiding her company. Since then she had not seen him often, even at meals; he locked himself in with his work or spent the whole day out of the house, and whenever he was hungry he secretly took something to eat from the pantry (without asking). It had been just a short time ago that she had succeeded in talking to him again alone. She had told him: "Walter has forbidden me to talk about how you're undergoing a transformation in our house!" and had blinked her eyes. But even here Meingast kept himself concealed and acted surprised, indeed annoyed. He did not want to let her in on the secret he was busily working on. This seemed to be the explanation. But Clarisse had said to him: "Perhaps I'll steal a march on you!" And she connected that with the first event. There was little reflection in this, and on that account its relation to reality was unclear; but what was clearly palpable was the lustful emergence of a different being from within the foundation of her own.

Clarisse was now convinced that the insane people had found her out (that she had offered to Meingast that she could also be a man). And since then she had one secret more: when an invitation to repeat the interrupted visit did not arrive, either from the secretly resisting General von Stumm or from Ulrich, she had after long hesitation herself called Dr. Friedenthal and announced that she would visit him at the hospital. And the doctor had promptly found time for Clarisse. When she asked him immediately upon her arrival whether mad people did not know a great deal that healthy people could not even guess at, he smiled and shook his head, but gazed deeply into her eyes and answered in a tone of complacency: "The *doctors* of the insane know a lot that healthy people don't even suspect!" And when he had to go on his rounds he had offered to take Clarisse along, and to begin where they had stopped the last time. As if it were already a matter of course, Clarisse again slipped into the white doctor's coat that Friedenthal held for her.

But—and this was the third event that still excited Clarisse after the fact, and even more than the others—she again did not get to see Moosbrugger. For something remarkable happened. They had left the last pavilion and were breathing in the spicy air of the grounds as they walked, during which Friedenthal ventured: "Now it's time for Moosbrugger!" when again a guard came running up with a message. Friedenthal shrugged his shoulders and said: "Strange! It's not going to work out this time either! At this moment the Director and a Commission are with Moosbrugger. I can't take you with me." And after he had assured her on his own initiative that he would invite her to continue her visit at the first opportunity, he left with rapid strides, while the guard conducted Clarisse back to the street.

Clarisse found it striking and extraordinary that her visits had twice come to nothing, and suspected that there was something behind it. She had the impression that she was intentionally not being allowed to see Moosbrugger and that a new excuse was being thought up each time, perhaps even with the purpose of making Moosbrugger disappear before she could get through to him.

But when Clarisse thought this over again, she nearly cried. She had let herself be outsmarted and felt quite ashamed; for she had heard nothing from Friedenthal. But while she was getting so upset, she was also calming down again. A thought occurred to her that often preoccupied her now, that in the course of the history of mankind many great men had been spirited away and tortured by their contemporaries, and that in the madhouse many had even disappeared. "They could neither defend themselves nor explain, because all they felt for their time was scorn!" she thought. And she recalled Nietzsche, whom she idolized, with his great, sad mustache and grown totally mute behind it.

But this gave her an uncanny feeling. What had just now insulted or provoked her, her defeat at the hands of the cunning doctor, was suddenly revealed to her as a sign that the destiny of such a great man might also have been preordained for her. Her eyes sought the direction in which the asylum lay, and she knew that she always felt this direction as something special, even when she wasn't thinking of it.

It was extremely oppressive to feel oneself so at one with madmen, but she told herself that "to put oneself on the level of the uncanny is to decide for genius!"

Meanwhile the sun had come up, and this made the landscape even emptier; it was green and cool, with bloody wisps; the world was still low, and reached up only to Clarisse's ankles on the little rise she was standing on. Here and there a bird's voice shrieked like a lost soul. Her narrow mouth expanded and smiled at the course of the morning. She stood girded round by her smile like the Blessed Virgin on the earth embraced by sin / crescent moon. She mulled over what she should do. She was under the sway of a peculiar mood of sacrifice: far too many things had recently been going through her head. She had repeatedly believed that it was now beginning with her: to do a great deed, something great with all her soul! But she did not know what.

She only felt that something was imminent. She stood in fear of it, but felt a longing for the fearful. It hovered in the emptiness of the morning like a cross above her shoulders. But really it was more an active hurt. A great deed. A transformation. There was that idea again, so laden with associations! But, as it were, empty, like a rising first ball of light. And yet it was something active and aggressive. What it might be and her attempts to imagine it caromed through her head in all directions. The swallows, too, had meanwhile begun to dart back and forth through the air.

Suddenly Clarisse became cheerful again, although the uncanniness did not entirely disappear. It occurred to her that she had got quite far away from her house. She turned around, and began to dance on the way. She stretched her arms straight out and lifted her knee. That was how she traversed the entire last part of her route.

But before she got home, at a bend in the path, she came upon General von Stumm.

Part II

(1) "Good morning, dear lady! How are things?" he called already from a distance of fifteen yards.

"Quite well!" Clarisse replied with a stern face, in a toneless soft voice.

(2) Stumm was in uniform, and his little round legs were ensconced in boots and dun-colored riding breeches with a general's red stripes. At the Ministry he militantly pretended that he sometimes went on long rides in the morning before work, but in reality he went strolling with Clarisse over the banks and meadows that surrounded her house. At this hour Walter was still sleeping, or had to busy himself with his clothes and breakfast in joyless haste so he wouldn't be late to the office; and if Walter peeked out of the window, filled with jealousy he saw the sun sparkling on the buttons and colors of a uniform, alongside which a red or blue summer dress was usually to be seen billowing in the wind, as happens in old paintings to the garments of angels in the exuberance of their descending.

(3) "Shall we go to the ski jump?" Stumm asked cheerfully. The "ski jump" was a small quarry in the hills, and had nothing whatever to do with its name. But Stumm found this name, one that Clarisse had chosen, "exquisite and dynamic." "As if it were winter!" he exclaimed. "It makes me laugh every time. And you would doubtless, my dear lady, call a snowbank a 'summer hill'?"

Clarisse liked being called "my dear lady" and immediately agreed to turn around with him, because once she had become accustomed to the general's company she found it quite agreeable. First, because he was, after all, a general; not "nothing," like Ulrich and Meingast and Walter. She now loved everything that was important in the world. Then, because it had occurred to her that it was really a quite peculiar circumstance to be always carrying a sword around, an odd relation to the world that corresponded to the great and fearful feelings that at times / often preoccupied her. Further, she esteemed the voluble von Stumm because she unconsciously recognized that he did not, like the others, desire her in a way that, when she was not in the mood herself, demeaned her. "There's something strangely pure about him!" she had explained to her jealous husband. But as a final reason, she also needed a person with whom she could talk, for she was oppressed by myriad swarms of inner promptings that she had to keep to herself. And when the General was listening to her, she felt that everything she said and did was good. "You have, my dear lady," the General would often assure her, "something that sets you apart from all women I have had the honor of getting to know. You positively teach me energy, martial courage, and the conquering of Austrian negligence!" He smiled as if it were a joke, but she clearly noticed that he meant some of it seriously.

(4) But the major topic of their conversations was, as is also the rule in love, recollections of their common great experience, the visit to the insane asylum, and so this time Clarisse began to confide to the General that she had since been back a second time.

"With whom?" the General inquired, relieved to have escaped a horrible mission.

"Alone," Clarisse said.

"Good God!" Stumm exclaimed, and stopped, although they had only taken a few steps. "Really alone? You don't let anything give you the creeps! And did you see anything special?" he asked, curious.

"The murderers' house," Clarisse responded with a smile.

This was the designation that Dr. Friedenthal, a good stage director, had used as they had walked across the soundless moss under the trees of the old garden toward a group of small buildings from which horrible cries came echoing toward them with remarkable regularity. Friedenthal, too, had smiled, and had told Clarisse, as Clarisse now told the General, that every inmate of this group of houses had killed at least one person, sometimes a number of people.

"And now they're screaming when it's too late!" Stumm said in a tone of reproachful acquiescence in the way of the world.

But Clarisse did not appreciate his response. She recalled that she, too, had asked what the cries meant. And Friedenthal had told her that they were manic fits; but he said this quite softly and cautiously, as if they were not to intrude. And just at that moment the gigantic guards had suddenly materialized around them and opened the reinforced doors; and Clarisse, repeating this and falling back into the mood, like being at an exciting play, softly whispered the term "manic fits" while looking meaningfully into the General's eyes.

She turned away and walked on a few paces ahead, so that Stumm almost had to run to catch up with her. When he was at her side again, she asked him what he thought about modern painting, but before he could gather his impressions, she surprised him with the information that there was an astonishing correspondence between this painting and an architecture born from the spirit of the madhouse: "The buildings are dice, and the patients live in hollowed-out concrete dice," she explained. "There is a corridor through the middle, and cube-shaped cells left and right, and in each cell there is nothing but one person and the space around him. Even the bench he's sitting on is part of the wall. Of course all edges have been carefully rounded off so he can't hurt himself," she added with precision, for she had observed everything with the greatest attention.

She found no words for what she really wanted to say. Since she had been surrounded by art all her life and had listened to the concerns expressed about art, this island had remained relatively resistant to the changes that had been slowly growing in other areas of her thinking; and especially since her own artistic activity did not spring directly from passion but was merely an appendix of her ambition and a consequence of the circumstances in which she lived, her judgment in this area, despite the illness that had recently made new inroads on her personality, was no more perverse than is common, from time to time, in the development of art. She could, therefore, deal quite comfortably with an idea like "purpose-oriented architecture" or "a manner of building deriving from the mission of an insane asylum," and it was only the peopling of these up-to-date dwellings with the insane that surprised her as a new concept and tickled her like a scent kindled in the nose.

But Stumm von Bordwehr interrupted her with the modest observation that he had always imagined that cells for manics had to be padded.

Clarisse became uncertain, for perhaps the cells had been made of light-colored rubber, and so she cut off his objection. "Maybe in the old days," she said firmly. "In the days of upholstered furniture and tasseled drapes, maybe the cells were upholstered too. But today, when people think objectively and spatially, it's quite impossible. Cultural progress doesn't stop, even in insane asylums!"

But Stumm would rather have heard something about the manics themselves than be diverted by the problem of what connections there might be between them and painting and architecture, so he replied: "Most interesting! But now I'm really anxious to hear what happened in these modern spaces!"

"You'll be surprised," Clarisse said. "As quiet as a cemetery."

"Interesting! I recall that in the courtyard of murderers that we saw, it was that still for a few moments too."

"But this time only a single man had on a striped linen smock," Clarisse went on. "A weak, little old man with blinking eyes." And suddenly she gave a loud laugh. "He dreamed that his wife had deceived him, and when he woke up in the morning he beat her to death with the bootjack!"

Stumm laughed too. "Right when he woke up? That's capital!" he agreed. "He was evidently in a hurry! And the others? Why do you say that he was the only one who had on a smock?"

"Because the others were in black. They were quieter than the dead," Clarisse replied, overcome with seriousness.

"Murderers really don't seem to be merry people," Stumm hazarded.

"Oh, you're thinking of the nutcracker!" Clarisse said.

For a moment the General did not know whom she meant.

"The one with nutcracker teeth who said to me that Vienna is a beautiful city!"

"And what did this lot say to you?" the General asked with a smile.

"But I told you, they were as silent as ghosts!"

"But, my dear lady," Stumm excused himself, "you can't call that manic!"

"They were waiting for their attacks!"

"What do you mean, waiting? It's strange to wait for an attack of mania the way you wait for an inspiring corps commander. And you say that they were dressed in black: ready to be reviewed, in a way? I'm afraid, dear lady, that you must have been mistaken in what you were seeing just then. I most humbly beg your pardon, but I am accustomed to imagining such things with the greatest precision!"

Clarisse, who found it not at all disagreeable that Stumm insisted on precision, for something was weighing her down that was not clear to her either, replied: "Dr. Friedenthal explained it to me that way, and I can only repeat, General, that that's the way it was. There were three men waiting there; all three had on black suits, and their hair and beards were black. One was a doctor, the second a lawyer, and the third a wealthy businessman. They looked like political martyrs about to be shot."

"Why did they look that way?" asked the incredulous Stumm.

"Because they were wearing neither collar nor tie."

"Perhaps they had just arrived?"

"No! Friedenthal said they had been in the asylum a long time," Clarisse asserted warmly. "And yet that's the way they looked, as if they could stand up at any moment and go to the office or visit a patient. That's what was so strange."

"Well, it's all the same to me," Stumm responded, to turn the conversation, and yet with a nobility that was new to him, while at the same time he struck his boots aggressively with his riding crop. "I've seen fools in uniform, and consider more people crazy than one might think I would. But I imagined 'manic' as something more vivid, even if I concede that you can't ask of a person that he be manic all the time. But that all three were so quiet . . . I'm sorry I wasn't there myself, for I think this Dr. Friedenthal is capable of pulling the wool over a person's eyes!"

"When he was speaking they listened quite mutely," Clarisse reported. "You wouldn't have noticed that they were ill at all if you hadn't happened to meet them there. And imagine, as we were leaving, the one who was a doctor stood up and motioned me, with a truly chivalrous gesture, to go first, saying to Friedenthal: 'Doctor, you often bring visitors. You are always showing guests around. Today for a change I'll come with you too.' "

"And then of course those bullies, those toadies of guards, immediately—" the General began heatedly, even though he might have been more touched by the tragedienne than the tragedy.

"No, they didn't grab him," Clarisse interrupted. "It was really with the greatest respect that they kept him from following me. And I assure you, it was all so moving in this polite and silent fashion. As if the world were hung with heavy, precious fabrics, and the words one would like to say have no resonance. It's hard to understand these people. You'd have to live in an asylum yourself for a long time to be able to enter their world!"

"What an exquisite idea! But God preserve us from it!" Stumm responded quickly. "You know, dear lady, that I am indebted to you for a pretty good insight into the value of shaking up the bourgeois spirit by means of illness and murder: but still, there are certain limits!"

With these words they had arrived at the hill that was their goal, and the General paused for breath before undertaking the pathless climb. Clarisse surveyed him with an expression of grateful solicitude and a tender mockery that she rarely showed. "But one of them did have a fit!" she informed him roguishly, the way one hauls out a present that had been concealed.

"Well, so there!" Stumm exclaimed. He could not think of anything else to say. But his mouth remained open as he mindlessly groped around for a word; suddenly he beat against his boots again with his crop. "But of course, the shouts!" he added. "Right at the beginning you spoke of the shouting you heard, and I overlooked that when you were talking about the deathly stillness. You tell a story so magnificently that one forgets everything!"

"As we stood in front of the door from which shouts and a strange moaning alternated," Clarisse began, "Friedenthal asked me once more whether I really wanted to go in. I was so excited I could hardly answer, but the guards paid no attention and began opening the doors. You may imagine, General, that at that moment I was terribly afraid, for I'm really only a woman. I had the feeling: when the door opens, the maniac is going to jump me!"

"One always hears that such mentally ill people have incredible strength," the General said by way of encouragement.

"Yes; but when the door was open and we all stood at the entrance, he paid absolutely no attention to us!"

"Paid no attention?" Stumm asked.

"None at all! He was almost as tall as Ulrich, and perhaps my age. He was standing in the middle of the cell, with his head bent forward and his legs apart. Like this!" Clarisse imitated it.

General: Was he dressed in black too?
Clarisse: No, stark naked.
General: Looks at Clarisse from head to toe.

"Thick strands of saliva were spread all over his young man's brownish-blond beard; the muscles literally jumped out of his scrawniness; he was naked, and his hair, I mean specific hairs—"

"You present everything so vividly one understands it all!" Stumm intervened soothingly.

"—were dully bright, shamelessly bright; he fixed us with them as if they were an eye that looks at you without noticing anything about you!"

Clarisse had reached the top, the General sat at her feet. From the "ski jump" one looked down on vineyards and meadows sloping away, on large and small houses that for a short distance rose in a jumble up the slope from below, and in one place the glance escaped into the charming depth of the hilly plateau that on the far horizon bordered high mountains. But if, like Stumm, you were sitting on a low tree stump, all you saw was an accidental hump of forest arching its back toward the sky, white clouds in the familiar, fatly drifting balls, and Clarisse. She stood with her legs apart in front of the General and mimicked a manic fit. She held one arm bent out at a right angle and stiffly locked to her body; with her head bent forward, she was executing with her torso in an unvarying sequence a jerky motion that formed a shallow forward circle, while she bent one finger after another as if she were counting. And she allowed each of these motions to be accompanied by a pantingly uttered cry, whose force, however, she considerately restrained. "You can't imitate the essential part," she explained. "That's the incredible strain with every motion, which gives an impression as if each time the person is tearing his body from a vise. . . ."

"But that's mora!" the General exclaimed. "You know, that game of chance? Whoever guesses the right number of fingers wins. Except that you can't bend one finger after another but have to show as many as you think of on the spur of the moment. All our peasants on the Italian border play it."

"It really is mora," said Clarisse, who had seen it on her travels. "And he also did it the way *you* described!"

"Well then, mora," Stumm repeated with satisfaction. "But I'd like to know where these insane people get their ideas," he added, and here commenced the strenuous part of the conversation.

Clarisse sat down on the tree stump beside the General, a little apart from him so that she could, if need be, "cast an eye" on him, and each time this happened he had a ridiculous horrible feeling, as if he were being pinched by a stag beetle. She was prepared to explain for his benefit the emotional life of the insane as she herself understood it after much reflection. One of its most important elements—because she connected everything with herself—was the idea that the so-called mentally ill were some kind of geniuses who were spirited away and deprived of their rights, and for some reason that Clarisse had not yet discovered, this was something they were not able to defend themselves against. It was only natural that the General could not concur in this opinion, but this did not surprise either of them. "I am willing to concede that such an idiot might occasionally guess something that the likes of us don't know," he protested. "That's the way you imagine them being: they have a certain aura; but that they should think more than we healthy people— no, please, I beg to differ!"

Clarisse insisted seriously that people who were mentally healthy thought less than those who were mentally unhealthy. "Have you ever strayed off a point, General, from A to B?" she asked Stumm, and he was forced to agree that he had. "Have you ever, then, done it the other way round, from B to A?" she asked further, and Stumm had even less desire to deny it, after considering for a while what it meant, for it is part of a man's pride to think through for himself to the single thing called truth. But Clarisse reasoned: "You see, and that's nothing but cowardice, this neat and orderly reflecting about things. On account of their cowardice men will never amount to anything!"

"I've never heard that before," Stumm asserted dismissively. But he thought it over. Wouldn't that mean . . . ?"

Clarisse moved closer to him with her eyes. "Surely some woman has whispered in your ear: 'You god-man'?"

Stumm could not recall this happening, but he didn't want to admit it, so he merely made a gesture that could just as well mean "unfortunately not" as "I'm sick and tired of hearing it!" In words, he replied: "Many women are very high-strung! But what does that have to do with our conversation? Something of that sort is simply an exaggerated compliment!"

"Do you remember the painter whose sketches the doctor showed us?" Clarisse asked.

"Yes, of course. What he had painted was really magnificent."

"He was dissatisfied with Friedenthal because the doctor doesn't understand anything about art. 'Show it to this gentleman!' he said, pointing to me," Clarisse went on, again suddenly casting her eye on the General. "Do you believe it was merely a compliment that he addressed me as a man?"

"It's just one of those ideas," Stumm said. "Honestly, I've never thought about it. I would assume it's what's called an association, or an analogy, or something like that. He just had some reason or other to take you for a man!"

But does it give you pleasure to be taken for a man?

Pleasure? No. But . . .

Although Stumm was convinced that with these last words he had explained something to Clarisse, he was still surprised by the warmth with which she exclaimed: "Terrific! Then I only need tell you that it has the same cause as in love when there's whispering about god-man! For the world is full of double beings!"

One should not of course believe that it was agreeable to Stumm when Clarisse talked this way, shooting a cleft glance from eyes narrowed to slits; he was thinking, rather, whether it would not be more proper not to conduct such conversations in uniform, but to appear for the next walk in mufti. But on the other hand the good Stumm, who admired Clarisse with great caution, if not concealed terror, had the ambitious desire to understand this young woman who was so passionate, and also to be understood by her, for which reason he quickly discovered a good side to her assertion. He put it this way, that most things involving the world and people were indeed ambivalent, which accorded well with his newly acquired pessimism. He assuaged himself further by assuming that what was meant by god-man and man-woman was no different from what could be said about anybody: that he was a bit of a noble person and a bit of a rascal. Still, he preferred to steer the conversation back to the more natural view, and began to spin out his knowledge of analogies, comparisons, symbolic forms of expression, and the like.

"Please excuse me and permit me, dear lady, to adopt your excitement for a moment and accept the idea that you really are a man," he began, advised by the guardian angel of intuition, and went on in the same fashion: "because then you would be able to imagine what it means for a lady to wear a heavy veil and show only a small part of her face; or, which is almost the same thing, for a ball gown to swirl up from the floor in a dance and expose an ankle: that's how it was just a few years ago, about the time I was a major; and such hints strike one much more strongly, I might almost say more passionately, than if one were to see the lady up to her knee with no obstacle in the way—yes, obstacle is precisely the right word! Because that's how I would also describe what analogies or comparisons or symbols consist of. They present an obstacle to thinking, and in doing so arouse it more strongly than is usually the case. I believe that's what you mean when you say that there's something cowardly about ordinary reflection."

But Clarisse meant nothing of the sort. "People have an obligation to get beyond mere hints!" she asserted.

"Quite remarkable!" Stumm exclaimed, honestly moved. "Old Count Leinsdorf says the same thing you do! Just recently I had a most profound discussion with that distinguished gentleman about metaphors and symbols, and in connection with the patriotic campaign he expressed precisely the opinion you did: that all of us have the obligation to reach out beyond the condition of metaphor to reality!"

"I once wrote him a letter in which I asked him to do something about freeing Moosbrugger," Clarisse said.

You see, even then we already had two acquaintances in common without knowing it!

"And what was his response? For of course he couldn't do it. I mean, even if he could, he couldn't, because he's much too conservative and legalistic a gentleman."

"But you could?" Clarisse asked.

"No; whatever's in the madhouse can stay there. No matter how ambiguous it is. Caution, you know, is the mother of wisdom."

"But what's this?" Clarisse asked, smiling, for she had discovered on the scabbard of the General's sword the woven double eagle, the emblem of the Imperial and Royal Monarchy. "What's this double eagle?"

"What do you mean? What should the double eagle be? It's the double eagle!"

"But what is a double eagle? An eagle with two heads? Only one-headed eagles fly around in the real world! So I'm pointing out to you that you're carrying on your saber the symbol of a double being! I re-

peat, General, enchanting things are all based, it would appear, on primitive nonsense!"

General: Pst! I shouldn't be listening to such things! (smiling)

WALTER AND CLARISSE'S WOODSY ARMISTICE

As they approached her house, she was accompanied by the theatrical
illusion of being a person returning from a distant land. She had given
up her dance but for some reason or other was humming in her head the
melody "There my father Parsifal wore the crown, I his knight, Lohen-
grin my name." When she walked through the door and felt the violent
transition from the morning, whose brightness had already become hard
and warm, into the sleeping twilight of the vestibule, she thought she
was caught in a trap. Under her light weight the steps she climbed emitted a barely audible sound; it echoed like the breath of a sigh, but nothing in the entire house responded. Clarisse cautiously turned the
doorknob of the bedroom: Walter was still sleeping! She was greeted by
light the color of milky coffee penetrating the curtains, and the nursery
odor of the ending night. Walter's lips were sulky like a boy's, and warm;
at the same time his face was simple, indeed impoverished. Much less
was to be seen in it than was normally one's impression. Only a lustful
need for power, otherwise not evident, was now visible. Standing motionless by his bed, Clarisse looked at her husband; he felt his sleep disturbed by her entrance and rolled over on his other side. She lingeringly
enjoyed the superiority of the waking over the sleeping person; she felt
the desire to kiss him or stroke him, or indeed to scare him, but could
not make up her mind. She also did not want to expose herself to the
danger associated with the bedroom, and finding Walter still sleeping
had obviously found her unprepared. She tore off a piece from some
wrapping paper from a purchase, which had been left lying on the table,
and wrote on it in large letters: "I have paid a visit to the sleeper and
await him in the woods."

When Walter awoke shortly afterward and discovered the empty bed
next to his, he dully remembered that something had gone on in the
room while he was sleeping, looked at the clock, discovered the note,
and quickly wiped away the cobwebs of sleep, for he had intended on
this particular day to get up especially early and do some work. Since this
was now no longer possible, he thought it proper, after thinking it over a
bit, to put off the work; and although he saw himself forced to scrape his
own breakfast together, he was soon standing in the best of spirits under

the rays of the morning sun. He assumed that Clarisse was lurking in a hiding place and would materialize from ambush as soon as he entered the woods. He took the usual route, a wide dirt wheelbarrow path, which took about half an hour. It was a half holiday, which is to say one of those days between holidays that do not officially count as holidays; on which account, remarkably enough, precisely those official agencies and the noble professions connected with them took the whole day off, while less responsible private people and businesses worked half the day. Things like this are said to have been sanctioned by history, and the consequence was that on this day Walter was permitted to walk like a private individual in an almost private nature, in which apart from him only a few unsupervised hens were running around. He stretched to see whether he might discover a bright-colored dress either at the edge of the woods or perhaps even coming toward him, but there was nothing to be seen, and although the walk had been lovely at the start, his pleasure in the exercise sank with the increasing heat. His rapid walking soaked his collar and the pores of his face until that unpleasant feeling of damp warmth set in which degrades the human body to a piece of laundry. Walter resolved to get into better shape for the outdoors again; allowed himself the excuse that perhaps he was merely dressed too warmly; was also doubtless anxious lest he might be coming down with something: and his thoughts, which had initially been quite animated, became in this fashion gradually incoherent and finally flopped, as it were, in time with his steps, while the path seemed never to end.

At some point he thought: "As a so-called normal person, one's thoughts are truly hardly less incoherent than a madman's!" And then it occurred to him: "Moreover, one does say that it's insanely hot!" And he smiled weakly that this turn of phrase was apparently not without foundation, since for example the changes a feverish temperature brings about in one's head are really somewhere between the symptoms of ordinary heat and those of mental disturbance. And so, without taking it entirely seriously, it might perhaps also be said of Clarisse that she had always been what one calls a crazy person without her having to be a sick one. Walter would very much have liked to know the answer to this question. Her brother and doctor claimed that there was not the slightest danger. But Walter believed he had known for a long time that Clarisse was already on the other side of a certain boundary. He sometimes had the feeling that she was merely still hovering around him as do departed souls, of whom it is said that they cannot immediately separate themselves from what they had loved. This idea was not unsuited to inflating his pride, for there were not many other people who would have been up to such a ghastly yet beautiful—as he now called it—struggle between love and horror. There were, to be sure, times when he felt irresolute. A sudden push or collapse could carry his wife away into the domain of the completely repellent and ugly, and that would still have been the least of it, for what if, in that case, she did not repel him! No, Walter assumed that she would have to repel him, for the debased mind was ugly! And Clarisse would then have to be put in an institution, for which there was not enough money. That was all quite depressing. Still, there had been times, when her soul was already, so to speak, fluttering in front of the windowpanes, when he had felt himself so bold that he had no desire to think whether he should pull her in to him or rush out to her.

Such thoughts made him forget the sunny, strenuous path, but finally also caused him to leave off thinking altogether, so that while he remained in animated motion he really had no content, or was filled with terribly ordinary contents, which he solemnly pondered; he walked along like a rhythm without notes, and when he bumped into Clarisse he almost stumbled over her. She, too, had at first followed the broad path, and had found at the edge of the woods a small indentation where the spilled sunlight licked the shadows at every breath of wind, like a goddess licking an animal. Here the ground rose gently, and since she was lying on her back, she saw the world within a strange gimlet. Through some kind of kinship of shapes, the uncanny mood that on this day mixed particularly easily with her cheerfulness had again taken hold of her spirits, and gazing long and steadily into the horizontally perverse landscape she began to feel sadness, as if she had to assume the burden of a sorrow or a sin or a destiny. There was an enormous sense of abandonment, of anticipation, and an expectancy of sacrifice abroad in the world, of the kind she had found the first time she had gone out, when the day just "reached her ankles." Her eyes involuntarily sought the place where, behind more distant slopes and not visible to her, the extensive buildings of the asylum for the insane must lie; and when she thought she had located them it calmed her, as it calms the lover to know the direction in which his thoughts can find his beloved. Her thoughts "flew," but not in that direction. "They're now crouching, having fallen quite silent, like huge black birds beside me in the sun," she thought, and the splendid yet melancholy feeling associated with this lasted until Clarisse caught sight of Walter in the distance. Then she had suddenly had enough of her sorrow, hid behind the trees, held her hand in front of her mouth like a funnel, and shouted, as loudly as she could: "Cuckoo!" She then straightened up and ran deeper into the woods, but immediately changed her mind again and threw herself down in the warm forest weeds beside the path Walter would have to use. His countenance then did come along, thinking itself unobserved, expressing nothing but an unconscious, gently animated attentiveness to the obstacles on the path, and this made his face very strange, indeed quite resolutely masculine, to look at. When he was unsuspectingly close, Clarisse stretched out her arm and reached for his foot, and this was the moment when Walter nearly fell and first caught sight of his wife, lying almost under his eyes and directing her smiling glance up at him. Despite some of his concerns, she did not look in the least ugly.

Clarisse laughed. Walter sat down beside her on a tree stump and dried his neck with his handkerchief. "Clarisse . . . !" he began, and continued only after a pause: "I really meant to work today. . . ."

"Meant?" Clarisse mocked. But for once it did not sting. The word whizzed from her tongue and mingled with the cheerful whirring of the flies that zoomed past their ears through the sun like small metal arrows.

Walter replied: "I'll admit that lately I haven't thought working was the right thing to do if you could just as well sniff the new flowers. Work is one-sided; it goes against one's duty to wholeness!"

Since he paused briefly, Clarisse threw a small pine cone that had come to hand up in the air a few times and caught it again.

"Of course I'm also aware of the objections that could be raised against that," Walter asserted.

Clarisse let the pine cone fall to the ground and asked animatedly: "So you're going to begin working again? Today we need an art that has brush strokes and musical intervals *this* big!" She stretched her arms out three feet.

"I don't have to begin that way right off," Walter objected. "Anyway, I still find the whole problematic of the individual artist off-putting. Today we need a problematic of the totality—" But hardly had he uttered the word "problematic" than it seemed to him quite overexcited in the stillness of the woods. He therefore added something new: "But basically it's in no way a demand inimical to life that a person should paint something he loves; in the case of the landscape painter, nature!"

"But a painter also paints his beloved," Clarisse threw in. "One part of the painter loves, the other paints!"

Walter saw his beautiful new idea shrivel up. He was not in the mood to breathe new life into it, but he was still convinced that the idea was important and merely needed careful working out. And the singing of finches, the woodpecker's drumming, the humming of small insects: it didn't move him to work but rather dragged him down into an infinite abyss of indolence.

"We're very much alike, you and I," he said with gratification. "There's hardly another couple like us! Others paint, make music, or write, and I refuse to: basically that's as radical as your eagerness!"

Clarisse turned on her side, raised herself on her elbow, and opened her mouth for a furious response. "I'll set you free yet, all the way!" she said quickly.

Walter looked down at her tenderly. "What do you mean, really, when you say that we have to be saved from our sinful form?" he asked eagerly.

This time Clarisse did not answer. She had the impression that if she were to speak now it would run away too quickly, and although she intended to say something, the woods confused her; for the woods were on her side: that was something that couldn't be expressed properly, although it was clear to see.

Walter probed in the delicious wound. "Did you really talk about that again with Meingast?" he asked in a way that demanded a response, yet hesitantly, indeed fearful that she might have done so although he had forbidden it.

Clarisse lied, for she shook her head; but at the same time she smiled.

"Can you still remember the time we took Meingast's 'sins' on ourselves?" he pursued further. He took her hand. But Clarisse only let him have a finger. It is a remarkable condition when a man has to remind himself with as much reluctance as willingness that nearly everything his beloved bestows on him has previously belonged to another; it may be the sign of a love that is all too strong, or perhaps the sign of a feeble soul, and sometimes Walter actually sought out this condition. He loved the fifteen-to-sixteen-year-old Clarisse, who had never been taken with him completely and unreservedly; loved her almost more than the present Clarisse, and the memory of her caresses, which were perhaps the reflection of Meingast's indecency, stirred him in a peculiar way more profoundly than, by comparison, the cool, unhampered quality of marriage. He found it almost agreeable knowing that Clarisse had a favoring side glance to spare for Ulrich and now entirely once again for the magnificently altered Meingast, and the way in which these men had an unfavorable impact on her imagination magnified his longing for his wife the way the shadows of debauchery and desire under an eye make it appear larger. Of course men in whom jealousy will suffer nothing beside themselves, he-men, will not experience this, but his jealousy was full of love, and when that is the case, then the torture is so precise, so distinct, so alive, that it is almost the vicarious experiencing of desire. Whenever Walter imagined his wife in the act of giving herself to another man he felt more strongly than when he held her in his own arms, and, somewhat disconcerted, he thought by way of excuse: "When I'm painting and I need to see the most subtle curvature of the lines of a face, I don't look at it directly but in a mirror!" It really stung him that he was yielding to such thoughts in the woods, in the healthy world of nature, and the hand that held Clarisse's finger began to tremble. He had to say something, but it could not be what he was thinking. He joked in a strained way: "So now you want to take my sins upon yourself, but how are you going to do that?" He smiled; but Clarisse noticed a slight trembling spreading over his lips. This did not suit her just now; although it is always a marvelous spur to laughter, this image of the way a man who is dragging a much too large bale of useless thoughts along with him tries to stride through the small door to which he is drawn. She sat completely upright, looked at Walter with a mockingly serious glance, shook her head several times, and began reflectively:

"Don't you believe that periods of depression alternate with periods of mania in the world? Urgent, disturbed, fruitful periods of upswing that bring in the new, alternating with sinful periods, despondent, depressed, bad centuries or decades?" Periods in which the world approaches its bright ideal shape and periods where it sinks into its sinful form. Walter looked at her with alarm. "That's how it is; I just can't tell you which years," she continued, adding: "The upswing doesn't have to be beautiful; in fact, it has to shuck off a good deal, which may of course be beautiful. It can look like a disease: I'm convinced that from time to time humanity has to become mentally ill in order to attain the synthesis of a new and higher health!"

Walter refused to understand.

Clarisse talked on: "People who are sensitive, like you and me, feel that! We're now living in a period of decline, and that's why you can't work either. In addition there are sensual ages, and ages that turn away from sensuality. You must prepare yourself for suffering. . . ."

Remarkably, it moved Walter that Clarisse had said "you and me." She had not said that for a long time.

"And of course there are periods of transition," Clarisse went on. "And figures like Saint John, precursors; we may be two precursors."

Now Walter responded: "But you had your way and went to the insane asylum; now we really ought to be of one mind again!"

"You mean that I ought not to go again?" Clarisse interjected, and smiled.

"Don't go again!" Walter pleaded. But he did so without conviction: he felt it himself; his plea was merely meant to cover him.

Clarisse replied: "All 'precursors' complain about the spirit's lack of resolution because they don't yet have complete faith, but no one dares put an end to the irresolution! Even Meingast doesn't dare," she added.

Walter asked: "What is it you'd have to dare?"

"You see, a whole people can't be insane," Clarisse said in an even softer voice. "There is only individual insanity. When everyone is insane, then they are the healthy ones. Isn't that right? Therefore a whole people of the insane is the healthiest of people; you just have to treat them as a people, and not as sick people. And I tell you, the mad think more than the healthy do, and they lead a resolute life of a kind we never have the courage for! To be sure, they are forced to live this life in a sinner's form, or they can't yet do otherwise!"

Walter swallowed and asked: "But what is this sinner's form? You talk about it so much, and a lot about transformation too, about taking sins upon oneself, about double beings and so much else, that I half understand and half don't understand!"

That goes around in circles
 Of course it goes around in circles

Clarisse smiled, and it was her embarrassed and rather excited smile. "That can't be put in a few words," she replied. "The insane are just double beings."

"Well, you said that before. But what does it mean?" Walter probed; he wanted to know how she was feeling, without consideration for her.

Clarisse reflected. "In many depictions, Apollo is man and woman. On the other hand, the Apollo with the arrow was not the Apollo with the lyre, and the Diana of Ephesus wasn't the Diana of Athens. The Greek gods were double beings, and we've forgotten that, but we're double beings too."

Walter said after a while: "You're exaggerating. Of course the god is one thing when he's killing men and another when he's making music."

"That's not natural at all!" Clarisse countered. "You would be the same! You would only be excited in a different way. You're a little different here in the woods and there in your room, but you're not a different person. I could say that you never transform yourself completely into what you do; but I don't want to say too much. We've lost the concepts for these processes. The ancients still had them, the Greeks, the people of Nietzsche!"

"Yes," Walter said, "perhaps; perhaps one could be quite different from the way we are." And then he fell silent. Snapped a twig. They were both now lying on the ground, with their heads turned toward each other. Finally Walter asked:

"What sort of double being am I?"

Clarisse laughed.

He took his twig and tickled her face.

"You are billy goat and eagle," she said, and laughed again.

"I am not a billy goat!" Walter protested sulkily.

"You're a billy goat with eagle's wings!" Clarisse fleshed out her assertion.

"Did you just invent that?" Walter asked.

It had come to her on the spur of the moment, but she could add something to it that she had long known: "Every person has an animal in which he can recognize his fate. Nietzsche had the eagle."

"Perhaps you mean what's called a totem. Do you know that for the Greeks specific animals were still associated with the gods: the wolf, the steer, the goose, the swan, the dog . . ."

"You see!" Clarisse said. "I didn't know that at all, but it's true." And she suddenly added: "Do you know that sick people do disgusting things? Just like the man under my window that time." And she related the story of the old man on the ward who had winked at her and then behaved so indecently.

"A lovely story, that, and moreover in front of the General!" Walter objected heatedly. "You really mustn't go there again!"

"Oh, come on, the General is just afraid of me!" Clarisse defended herself.

"Why should he be afraid?"

"I don't know. But you are too, and Father was afraid, and Meingast is afraid of me too," Clarisse said. "I seem to possess an accursed power, so that men who have something wrong with them are compelled to offer themselves to me. In a word, I tell you, sick people are double beings of god and billy goat!"

"I'm afraid *for* you!" Walter whispered more than spoke, softly and tenderly.

"But the sick ones aren't only double beings of god and goat, but also of child and man, and sadness and gaiety," Clarisse went on without paying attention.

Walter shook his head. "You seem to associate all men with 'goat'!"

"My God, that's true, I do." Clarisse defended it calmly. "I carry the figure of the goat within myself too!"

"The figure!" Walter was a little scornful, but involuntarily; for the constant succession of ideas was making him tired.

"The image, the model, the daimon—call it what you like!"

Walter needed a rest, he wished to stop for a while, and replied: "I will admit that in many respects people are double beings. Recent psychology—"

Clarisse interrupted him vehemently. "Not psychology! You all think much too much!"

"But didn't you claim that the insane think more than we healthy people do?" Walter asked mechanically.

"Then I said it wrong. They think differently. More energetically!" she replied, and went on: "It doesn't make the slightest difference what one thinks; as soon as one acts, what one thought beforehand doesn't matter anymore. That's why I find it right not to go on talking but to go to the insane in their house."

"Just a minute!" Walter begged. "What is *your* double being?"

"I am first of all man and woman."

"But you just said goat too."

"That too. Too! It's not the sort of thing you can measure with ruler and compass."

"No, that you can't!" Walter moaned aloud, covering his eyes with his hands and clenching his hands into fists. As he lay there mute in this posture, Clarisse crept up to him, threw her arms around his shoulders, and kissed him from time to time.

Walter lay motionless.

Clarisse was whispering and murmuring something into his ear. She was telling him that the man under the window had been sent by the goat, and that the goat signified sensuality, which had everywhere separated itself from the rest of mankind. All people creep to each other in bed every night and leave the world where it is: this lower solution to the great powers of desire in people must finally be stopped, and then the goat would become the god! This was what Walter heard her say. And wasn't she right? Yet how did it happen that it pleased him? How did it happen that for a long time nothing else had pleased him? Not the paintings that he had earlier admired; not the masters of music whom he had loved; not the great poems, and not the mighty ideas? And that he now found pleasure in listening to Clarisse telling him something that anyone else would say was fantasy? These were the questions that went through Walter's mind. As long as his life had lain before him, he had felt it to be full of great desire and imagination; since then, Eros had truly separated himself from it. Was there anything he still did body and soul? Was not everything he touched insignificant? Truly, love was gone from his fingertips, the tip of his tongue, his entrails, eyes, and ears, and what remained was merely ashes in the form of life, or, as he now expressed it rather magniloquently, "dung in a polished glass," the "goat"! And beside him, at his ear, was Clarisse: a little bird that had suddenly begun to prophesy this in the woods! He could not find the suggestive, the commanding tone to point out to her where her ideas went too far and where they did not. She was full of images jumbled together; he, too, had been this full of images once, he persuaded himself. And of these great images, one has no idea which ones can be made into reality and which ones cannot. So every person bears within himself a leading ideal figure, Clarisse was now maintaining, but most people settle for living in the form of sin, and Walter found that it might well be said of him that he bore an ideal figure within himself, although he, perhaps even self-penitently, at least voluntarily, lived in ashes. The world also has an ideal figure. He found this image magnificent. Of course it did not explain anything, but what good is explanation? It expressed the will of humanity, striving upward again and again after every defeat. And it suddenly struck Walter that Clarisse had not kissed him voluntarily for at least a year, and that she was now doing it for the first time.

6...

Breaths of a summer day

On the same morning, Agathe, impelled by moody contradictions left over from the previous night, said to her brother: "And why *should* it be possible to live a life in love? There are times when you live no less in anger, in hostility, or even in pride or hardness, and *they* don't claim to be a second world!"

"I'd prefer to say that one lives *for* love," Ulrich replied indolently. "Our other emotions must inspire us to action in order that they last; that's what anchors them in reality."

"But it's usually that way in love too," Agathe objected. She felt as if she were swinging on a high branch that was threatening to break off under her any moment. "But then why does every beginner swear to himself that it will 'last' forever, even if he's beginning for the tenth time?" was her next question.

"Perhaps because it's so inconstant."

"One also swears eternal enmity."

"Perhaps because it's such a violent emotion."

"But there are emotions whose nature it is to last longer than others: loyalty, friendship, obedience, for example."

"I think because they are the expression of stable, indeed even moral, relationships."

"Your answers aren't very consistent!"

The interruptions and continuations of the conversation seemed to nestle in the shallow, lazy breaths of the summer day. Brother and sister lay, a little bleary-eyed and overtired, on garden chairs in the sunshine. After a while Agathe began again:

"Faith in God imposes no action, contains no prescribed relationships to other people, can be totally immoral, and yet it's a lasting emotion."

"Faith and love are related to each other," Ulrich remarked. "Also, unlike all the other emotions, both have available their own manner of thinking: contemplation. That means a great deal; for it is not love and faith themselves that create the image of their world; contemplation does it for them."

"What is contemplation?"

"I can't explain it. Or maybe, in a nutshell, a thinking by intimation. Or, in other words: the way we think when we're happy. The other emotions you named don't have this resource. You could also call it meditating. If you say that faith and love can 'move mountains,' it means that they can entirely take the place of the mind."

"So the thought of the believer and the lover is intimation? The real inner manner of their thinking?"

"Right!" Ulrich confirmed, surprised.

"No reason to praise *me!* You said it yourself yesterday!" his sister informed him. "And just so that I'm sure: contemplation, then, is also the thinking that allows itself to be led not by our actual emotions but by our other ones?"

"If you want to put it that way, yes."

"So that's the way one could think in a world of special people? Yesterday you used the term 'ecstatic society' for it. Do you remember?"

"Yes."

"Good!"

"Why are you laughing now?" Ulrich asked.

"Because Mephistopheles says: 'Truth is proclaimed through the mouths of *two* witnesses!' So two suffice!"

"He's evidently wrong," Ulrich contradicted calmly. "In his day, *délire à deux*, the joint insanity of two people, had not yet been recognized. . . ."

A noiseless stream of weightless drifting blossoms, emanating from a group of trees whose flowering was done, drifted through the sunshine, and the breath that bore it was so gentle that not a leaf stirred. It cast no shadow on the green of the lawn, but this green seemed to darken from within like an eye. Extravagantly and tenderly leaved by the young summer, the trees and bushes standing in the wings or forming the backdrop gave the impression of being amazed spectators who, surprised and spellbound in their gay attire, were participating in this funeral procession and celebration of nature. Spring and fall, speech and nature's silence, life and death, mingled in this picture. Hearts seemed to stop, to have been removed from their breasts, in order to join this silent procession through the air. "My heart was taken from out my breast," a mystic had said. Agathe cautiously abandoned herself to the enthusiasm that once before in this garden had almost led her to believe in the arrival of the Millennium and under the image of which she imagined an ecstatic society. But she did not forget what she had learned since: in this kingdom, you must keep quite still. You cannot leave room for any kind of desire: not even the desire to ask questions. You must also shed the understanding with which you ordinarily perform tasks. You must strip the self of all inner tools. It seemed to her that walls and columns retreated to the side within her, and that the world was entering her eyes the way tears do. But she suddenly discovered that she was only superficially holding fast to this condition, and that her thoughts had long since slipped away from it.

When she encountered them again, her thoughts were considering a quite remote problem, a little monster of disaffection. She was asking herself in the most foolish fashion, and intent on this foolishness: "Was I ever really impetuous and unhappy?" A man without a name came to mind, whose name she bore, indeed had borne away from him, and she repeated her question with the mute, unmoving obstinacy with which one gazes after a wave that has ebbed away. Presumably, young people (whose life span is still short) are more disposed to be amazed at what they have already felt than older people, who have become accustomed to the changeability of life's passions and circumstances; except that the escape of feeling is also the stream in whose motion the stone heavens of mystic emotion are reflected, and for one of these reasons it was probably a supranaturally magnified astonishment that contained the question of where the hatred and violence she had felt against Hagauer had come from. Where was the desire to hurt him? She was close to thinking she had lost it, like an object that must still be somewhere nearby.

So Agathe's thoughts were doubtless still completely under the spell of the procession of flowers and death, but they were not moving with it, and in its mute and solemn way, but making little jumps here and there. It was not "meditating" she was indulging in, but a "thinking," even if a thinking without rigor, a branching off and inner continuation of what had earlier been left unsaid in the fleeting exchange about the constancy of the emotions; without exactly wanting to be, she was still gripped by it, and she recalled an image that Ulrich had suggested on another occasion, and with greater sympathy, about this constancy and inconstancy of the emotions. She was thinking now that nothing was more remote from her than expressing her emotions in "works," and apparently she was thinking for a moment of August Lindner and meant "good works," "works of love," "signs of love's practical orientation," such as he desired of her in vain; but by and large, she meant simply "works" and was thinking of Ulrich, who earlier had always spoken of spiritual work that one had to fashion out of everything, even if it was only a deeper breath. And that one derived a rule or created an idea for everything and felt responsible for the world also remained a matter of indifference to her most profound inclination: her ambition was not tempted to sit in the master's saddle of a hobbyhorse. And finally character was not the refuge of her emotions either, and when she confronted this question she received the answer: "I never used to love what I felt so strongly that I would have wanted to be, so to speak, its cupboard for my entire life!" And it occurred to her that for her emotions, insofar as they had been aroused by men, she had always chosen men whom she did not like with either all her soul or all her body. "How prophetic!" she thought cheerfully. "Even then I weakened the desires, the pull toward reality in my emotions, and kept open the path to the magic kingdom!"

For wasn't that now Ulrich's theory about passion? Either howl like a child with rage and frustration or enthusiasm—and get rid of it! Or abstain entirely from the pull toward the real, the active, and desire of any kind that every emotion contains. What lies in between is the real "kingdom of the emotions"—its works and transformations, its being filled up with reality—as lovely as a storeroom full of apples of every hue, and absurdly monotonous too, like everything that fades and falls the same way with every new year! This was what she was thinking, and she tried to find her way back again to the emotion hovering silently through the world of nature. She kept her mind from turning toward anything in a specific way. She strained to shed all knowledge and desire, all utilitarian use of head and heart and limbs. "You must be unegotistic in this most extreme sense; you have to strive to gain this mysterious 'unmediated' relationship to outer and inner," she said to herself, and collected herself almost as if she wanted to feign death. But this seemed as impossible a task as it had been in childhood not to commit a sin between confession and communion, and finally she abandoned the effort entirely. "What?" she asked herself sulkily. "Is a world in which one desires nothing perhaps not desirable?" At this moment she was honestly suspicious of the world of ecstasy, and she urgently wanted to present this fundamental question that underlies all ascesis to her brother. He, however, seemed not to want to be disturbed by anything as he lay there enjoying his comfortable position and closed the narrow slit between his eyelids completely every time she looked over at him.

So she abandoned her deck chair and stood irresolutely for a while, smiling, looking now at Ulrich, now at the garden. She stretched her legs and adjusted her skirt with small blows of her hand. Each one of these actions had a kind of rustic beauty, simple, healthy, instinctive; and it was this way either by chance or because her most recent thoughts had led her to be cheerful in a robust way. Her hair fell in a scallop at each side of her face, and the background, formed of trees and bushes that, from where she was standing, opened into depth, was a frame that positioned her image before earth and sky. This view, which Ulrich was enjoying, for he was secretly observing his sister, not only was attractive but soon became so much so that it suffered nothing else beside it that it would not have drawn in. Ulrich thought this time of the expression "enhanced accountability" for this enchanting image that was forming, not for the first time, between brother and sister; he extrapolated the term from a word that ages ago, in another charmed circle, had meant much to him: and truly, as there is a diminished sense of accountability, whose bewitched nature had formerly astounded him, and which is ultimately always stamped with the defect of senselessness, what seemed to be reigning here was an increased and intensified fullness of the senses, a high superabundance, indeed a distress, of such a kind that everything about Agathe and which was taking place cast a reflection on her that could not be grasped by sensory designations, and placed her in an aspect for which not only no word existed but also no expression or outlet of any kind. Every fold of her dress was so laden with powers, indeed it almost might be said with value, that it was impossible to imagine a greater happiness, but also no more uncertain adventure, than cautiously to touch this fold with the tips of one's fingers!

She had now half turned away from her brother and was standing motionless, so that he could observe her freely. He knew that experiences of this kind had bound the two of them together for as long as they had known each other. He remembered the morning after his arrival at their father's house, when he had caught sight of her in woman's clothes for the first time; it had been at that time, too, that he had had the strange experience of seeing her standing in a grotto of rays of light, and this in addition: that she was a more beautiful repetition and alteration of his self. There were, moreover, many things connected with this that merely had a different external shape. For the painted circus animals that he had loved more ardently than real ones, the sight of his little sister dressed for a ball, her beauty kindling in him the longing to be her, then even the confectioner's horse that had lately been the object of a bantering conversation, all arose from the same enchantment; and now, when he again returned to the present, which was by no means droll, the most contradictory scruples about coming too close to one another, the staring at and bending over, the heavy figurative quality of many moments, the gliding into an equivocal we-and-the-world feeling, and many other things, demonstrated to him the same forces and weaknesses. Involuntarily he reflected on these things. Common to all these experiences was that they received an emotion of the greatest force from an impossibility, from a failure and stagnation. That they were missing the bridge of action leading to and from the world; and finally, that they ended on a vanishingly narrow borderline between the greatest happiness and pathological behavior. Looked at in an unholy way, they were all somewhat reminiscent of a porcelain still life, and of a blind window, and of a dead-end street, and of the unending smile of wax dolls under glass and light: things that appear to have got stuck on the road between death and resurrection, unable to take a step either forward or backward. In bringing such examples to mind, Ulrich thought that they were also to be understood without mystery and myth. Such images entice our emotions, which are accustomed to act, and our sympathies, which are usually dispersed over many things, in a direction in which no progress is possible; and this might easily give rise to an experience of dammed-up significance that permits no access of any kind, so that it grows and grows in absolutely unbearable fashion. "Externally, nothing new happens anymore, but the one thing is repeated again and again," Ulrich thought. "And internally, it's as if we had henceforth only said, thought, and felt: one thing, one thing, one thing! But it's not entirely like that either!" he interjected to himself. "It's rather like a very slow and monotonous rhythm. And something new arises: bliss! A tormenting bliss one would like to give the slip to but can't! Is it bliss at all?" Ulrich asked himself. "It's an oppressive increase in the emotion that leaves all qualities behind. I could just as easily call it a congestion!"

Agathe did not seem to notice that she was being observed. "And why does my happiness—for it is happiness—search out just such occasions and hiding places?" Ulrich went on to ask again, with one small change. He could not keep from admitting to himself that separated out from the stream, such an emotion could also wash around the love for a dead person, whose countenance belongs with a more profound defenselessness than any living one to the glances which it cannot drive off. And his happening to think that in literature moody, necrophilic art thoughts were not exactly a rarity did not make it any better, but merely led him to reflect that the charming insanity of relating things, which combines all the soul's longing into the representation of a beautiful dead woman, has some kind of connection with the malevolent insanity in which a fetish—a hairband, a shoe—draws all the currents of body and soul to itself. And every "fixed idea" too, even one that is only "overpowering" in the ordinary sense, is accompanied by such an intensified usurpation. There was in this a kinship more or less crippled and not entirely pleasant, and Ulrich would not have been a man had not the twisted, slippery, lurking, lost nature of these relationships filled him with suspicion. To be sure, his spirits were lifted by the idea that there was nothing in the world that did not have some black-sheep kin, for the world of health is composed of the same basic elements as the world of disease: it is only the proportions that differ; but when he cautiously directed his glance at Agathe and allowed it to drink from the sight of her, there still dominated in his feelings, in spite of their miserable sublimity, an uncanny absence of will, a marked displacement or being carried away into the vicinity of sleep, of death, of the image, of the immobile, the imprisoned, the powerless. Ideas drained away, every energetic drive dissipated, the unutterable paralyzed every limb, the world slipped away remote and unheeding, and the unstable armistice on the borderline between the enhanced and the diminished was barely to be borne any longer. But precisely with the entrance of this enormous draining away of power something different began, for their bodies seemed to be losing something of their boundaries, of which they no longer had any need. "It's like the frenzy of the bee swarm that's trying to surround the queen!" Ulrich thought silently.

And finally the unavoidable discovery dawned on him, although he had so far avoided it, that all these strange, individual temptations of the emotions and emotional experiences, which intermingled and hovered within him like the shadows cast by the foliage of a restless tree when the sun is high, could be encompassed and understood at a single glance if he regarded his love for his sister as their origin. For evidently this emotion and this alone was the hero of his breaking down, of his blocked path, and of all the ambiguous adventures and detours associated with this. Even the psychology of the emotions, which he was pursuing on his own in his diaries, now seemed to him merely an attempt to conceal the love between him and his sister in a quixotic edifice of ideas. Did he, then, desire her? He was really astonished that he was confessing this to himself for the first time, and he now clearly saw the possibilities between which he had to make up his mind. Either he really had to believe that he was making ready for an adventure such as had never existed before, an adventure that he needed only to urge on and set out on with no second thoughts . . . Or he had to yield to his emotion, even should this feeling be unnatural, in the natural way, or forbid himself to; and was all he was accomplishing through his irresolution to become inventive in subterfuges? When he asked himself this second, rather contemptible question, he did not fail to ask the third it entailed: What was there to prevent him from doing what he wanted? A biological superstition, a moral one? In short, the judgment of others? Thinking of this, Ulrich felt such a violent boiling up of feeling against these others that he was even more surprised, especially as this sudden stab bore no relation to the gentle emotions with which he believed himself filled.

But in reality what came to the fore was only something that had recently receded into the background. For his attachment to Agathe and his detachment from the world were always two sides of one and the same situation and inclination. Even in those years when he had almost never thought that he had a real sister, the concept of "sister" had had a magic effect on him. No doubt this happens often, and it is usually nothing very different from the soaring youthful form of that need for love which in the later condition of submission seeks out a bird, a cat, or a dog, at times too, probably, humanity or one's neighbor, because between the dust and heat of the struggle to live and life's games this need cannot truly unfold. Sometimes this need for love is already even in youth full of submission, of timidity toward life, and loneliness, and in that case the misty image of the "sister" takes on the shadowboxing grace of the doppelgänger, which transforms the anxiety of being abandoned by the world into the tenderness of lonely togetherness. And sometimes this ecstatic image is nothing but the crassest egotism and selfishness, that is to say an excessive wanting to be loved, which has entered into a jerry-built agreement with sweet selflessness. In all such cases—and Ulrich thought again of the case in which it transforms itself into a fellow human being and then dispenses with its ambiguity, but also with its beauty!—"sister" is a creation originating from the "other" part of emotion, from the uproar of this emotion and the desire to live differently; that's the way Ulrich would understand it now. But it probably is this only in the weak form of longing. But familiar with longing as he was, his mind was no less acquainted with struggle, and if he correctly understood his past, his precipitate turning toward Agathe had initially been a declaration of war against the world; love is, moreover, always the revolt of a couple from the wisdom of the crowd. It could be said that in his case, the revolt had come first; but it could be said just as well that the core of all his criticism of the world was nothing so much as a knowing about love. "So I am—if a hermaphroditic monasticism is conceivable, why shouldn't this be!—in the dubious situation of having been, at bottom, a soldier with monastic inclinations, and ultimately a monk with soldierly inclinations who can't leave off swearing!" he thought cheerfully, but still with astonishment; for he was made aware for perhaps the first time of the profound contradiction between his passion and the entire disposition of his nature. Even as he now looked at Agathe, he thought he perceived his conflict on the sea-bright surface of inwardness spreading out around her, as an evil, metallic reflection. He was so lost in these thoughts that he did not notice that she had for some time been curiously observing his eyes.

Now she stepped up to her brother and mischievously passed her hand downward before his eyes, as if she wished to cut off his peculiar glance. And as if that were not sufficient, she grasped his arm and prepared to pull him up from his chair. Ulrich stood and looked around him the way a person does emerging from sleep. "To think that at this very moment, hundreds of people are fighting for their lives! That ships are sinking, animals are attacking people, thousands of animals are being slaughtered by people!" he said, half like someone looking back with a shudder from a blissful shore, half like a man who is sorry not to be part of it.

"You're certainly sorry not to be part of it?" Agathe then did indeed ask.

His smile denied it, but his words conceded the point: "It's pleasant to think about how pleasant it is when I grasp with my whole hand a thing that I've merely been stroking for some time with the tip of a finger."

His sister put her arm through his. "Come, let's walk around a little!" she proposed. In the hardness of his arm she felt the manly joy at everything savage. She pressed her fingernails against the unyielding muscles, seeking to hurt him. When he complained, she offered the explanation: "In the infinite waters of bliss I'm clutching at the straw of evil! Why should you be the only one?" She repeated her attack. Ulrich placated her with a smile: "What your nails are doing to me is not a straw but a girder!" They were walking meanwhile. Had Agathe demonstrated the ability to guess his thoughts? Were the two of them twin clocks? When emotions are tuned to the same string, is it entirely natural to read emotions from each other's faces? It is at any rate an impressive game, so long as one does not miss the mark and crash. The loveliest assurance of the miracle's enduring now lay in their motion, lay in the garden, which seemed to be sleeping in the sunshine, where the gravel crunched, the breeze freshened from time to time, and their bodies were bright and alert. For surmising oneself bound in feeling to everything the eye could see was as easy as the transparent air, and only when they stopped was it afterward as melancholy as a deep breath to take first steps again through this imagistic landscape. The words they exchanged meanwhile really signified nothing, but merely cradled them as they walked, like the childishly amused conversation a fountain has with itself, babbling gossip about eternity.

But without their needing to say anything, they slowly turned into a path that led them near the boundary of their small garden kingdom, and it was evident that this was not happening for the first time. Where they came in sight of the street, rolling animatedly past beyond the high iron fence that was supported by a stone base, they abandoned the path, taking advantage of the cover of trees and bushes, and paused on a small rise, whose dry earth formed the place where several old trees stood. Here the picture of the resting pair was lost in the play of light and shadow, and there was almost no likelihood of their being discovered from the street, although they were so near it that the unsuspecting pedestrians made that exaggerated outward impression which is peculiar to everything one merely observes without in any way participating in it. The faces seemed like things, indeed even poorer than things, like flat disks, and if words were suddenly carried into the garden they had no sense, only an amplified sound such as hollow, decayed rooms have. But the two observers did not have long to wait before one person or another came still closer to their hiding place: whether it was someone stopping and looking in astonishment at all the green suddenly revealed along his course, or whether it was someone moved to stop by the favorable opportunity of resting something in his hand on the stone base of the fence for a moment, or to tie his shoelace on it, or whether in the short shadows of the fence pillars falling on the path it was two people stopped in conversation, with the others streaming past behind them. And the more accidentally this seemed to happen in single cases, the more clearly the invariable, unconscious, enduring effect of the fence detached itself from the variety and contingency of these manifold actions, invading the individual life like a trap.

They both loved this game of cause and effect, which stood in scornful contrast to the game of souls

They had discovered this place on the days when they, too, had strolled through the streets and talked about the difficulties of loving one's neighbor, and the contradictions of everyone loving everybody;

and the fence, which separated them from the world but connected them with it visually, had seemed to them then the manifest image of the human world, not least of themselves: in short, the image of everything which Ulrich had once summarized in the terse expression "the unseparated and not united." Most of this now seemed quite superfluous and a childish waste of time; as indeed its only mission had been to give them time and to gain from the observing game with the world the conviction that they had something in mind that concerned everyone and did not just spring from a personal need. Now they were much more secure, they knew more about their adventure. All individual questions were froth, beneath which lay the dark mirror of another possible way of life. Their great sympathy with each other and with others, and in general the fulfillment of the promises sunk into the world, promises that constantly emanate the peculiar mirage that life-as-it-is strikes us as fragmented in every way by life-as-it-might-be—this fulfillment was never to be won from details but only from the Totally Different! The fence, however, had still preserved something of its coarse, prompting distinctness, and was at least able to beckon to a leave-taking.

Agathe laid her hand, which had the light, dry warmth of the finest wool, on Ulrich's head, turned it in the direction of the street, let her hand fall to his shoulder, and tickled her brother's ear with her fingernail and no less with the words: "Now let's test our love for our neighbors once more, Teacher! How would it be if today we tried to love one of them like ourselves!"

"I don't love myself!" Ulrich resisted in the same tone. "I even think that all the earlier energy I was so proud of was a running away from myself."

"So what you've sometimes said, that I'm your self-love in the form of a girl, is altogether not terribly flattering."

"Oh, on the contrary! You're another self-love, *the* other!"

"Now, *that* you'll have to explain to me!" Agathe commanded without looking up.

"A good person has good defects and a bad one has bad virtues: so the one has a good self-love and the other a bad one!"

"Obscure!"

"But from a famous author from whom Christendom has learned a great deal, but unfortunately just not that."

"Not much clearer!"

"Half a millennium before Christ, he taught that whoever does not love himself in the right way is not able to love others either. For the right love for oneself is also being naturally good to others. So self-love is not selfishness but being good."

"Did he really say that?"

"Oh, I don't know, perhaps I'm putting the words in his mouth. He also taught that goodwill is not wanting the good but wanting something with goodness. He was a logician and natural philosopher, soldier and mystic, and, significantly, is supposed to have been the greatest teacher, and so it did not even escape him that morality can never be completely detached from mysticism."

"You're an insufferable exercise instructor who shows up in the morning; the cock crows, and one's supposed to hop to it! I'd rather sleep!"

"No, you ought to help me."

They lay on their stomachs on the ground, next to each other. If they raised their heads, they saw the street; if they didn't, they saw between pointed young blades of grass the drying fallen leaves from the high tree.

Agathe asked: "So that's why it's love your neighbor 'as yourself'? It could also be the other way around: Love yourself as your neighbor."

"Yes. And it's easier to love him not only less than oneself but also more. What's almost impossible is to love him and yourself in the same way. Compared with that, loving someone so much that you sacrifice yourself for him is positively a relief," Ulrich replied. For the moment, the conversation had taken on the playful tone that deftly stirred up profound questions, a tone to which they had become accustomed during their walks through the city; but really—and although since then nothing that could be counted as time had passed—they were deliberately imitating themselves, the way one casually immerses oneself again in a game one has outgrown. And Agathe remarked: "So then love your neighbor as yourself also means: don't love your neighbor selflessly!"

"Actually, yes," Ulrich conceded. And without agreeing with her incidental arguments against selfless goodness, which in male human form were courting her soul, he added: "That's even quite important. For the people who talk of *selfless* goodness are teaching something that's better than selfishness and less than goodness."

And Agathe asked: "But when you fall in love the usual way, doesn't that inevitably involve desire *and* selflessness?"

"Yes."

"And it really can't be said of self-love either that one desires oneself, or that one loves oneself selflessly?"

"No," Ulrich said.

"Then what's called self-love may not be any kind of love at all?" Agathe hazarded.

"That's as you take it," her brother replied. "It's more a confiding in oneself, an instinctive caring for oneself—"

"Self-toleration!" Agathe said, quite deliberately making a dissatisfied and slightly disgusted face, although she did not exactly know why.

"Why are we talking about it at all?" Ulrich interjected.

"But we're talking about others!" Agathe answered, and laughter at her brother and herself lit up her face. She had again directed her glance at the fence, drawing her brother's after her; and because their eyes were not focused on a specific distance, the host of vehicles and pedestrians swam past it. "Where shall we begin?" she asked, as if the rest were understood as a matter of course.

"You can't just do it on command!" Ulrich objected.

"No. But we can try to just feel everything in some such way; and we can entrust ourselves to it more and more!"

"That has to happen of itself."

"Let's help it along!" Agathe proposed. "For instance, let's stop talking and do nothing but look at them!"

"That's all right with me," Ulrich agreed.

For a short time they were silent; then something else occurred to Agathe: "To love something in the ordinary sense means to prefer it to something else: so we must try to love one person and at the same time prevent ourselves from preferring him to others," she whispered.

"Keep quiet! You have to be quiet!" Ulrich fended her off.

Now they gazed out for a while again. But soon Agathe propped herself up on her elbow and looked despairingly at her brother. "It's not working! As soon as I tried it, the people outside became like a river full of pale fish. We're dreadful idlers!" she complained.

Ulrich turned toward her, laughing. "You're forgetting that striving for bliss isn't work!"

"I've never done anything in my whole life; now I'd like something to happen! Let's do something good to someone!" Agathe pleaded.

"Even doing good is a notion that doesn't occur at all in real goodness. It's only when the waves break that the ocean disintegrates into droplets!" Ulrich countered. "And what would it mean anyway to do something good in a situation in which you can't do anything but good?" The anticipation, the headiness of a feeling of victory, the confidence of powers that were for the moment at rest, allowed him to be playful with his seriousness.

"So you don't want to do anything?" Agathe asked coolly.

"Of course I do! But the kingdom of love is in every respect the great antireality. That's why the first thing you have to do is cut the arms and legs off your emotions; and then we'll see what can happen in spite of that!"

"You make it sound like a machine," Agathe chided.

"You have to undertake it as a good experimenter," Ulrich contradicted her, unmoved. "You have to try to circumscribe the decisive part."

Agathe now offered serious resistance. "We're not concluding some scientific investigation but, if you'll permit the expression, opening our hearts," she said with somewhat sarcastic sharpness. "And also the point we'd have to start from has not been exactly new for some time, since the Gospels! Exclude hatred, resistance, strife from yourself; just don't believe that they exist! Don't blame, don't get angry, don't hold people responsible, don't defend yourself against anything! Don't struggle anymore; don't think or bargain; forget and unlearn denial! In this way fill every crack, every fissure, between you and them; love, fear, beg, and walk with them; and take everything that happens in time and space, whatever comes and goes, whatever is beautiful or disturbing, not as reality but as a word and metaphor of the Lord. That's how we should go to meet them!"

As usually happened, during this long and passionate and unusually resolute speech her face had taken on a deeper hue. "Splendid! Every word a letter in a great scripture!" Ulrich exclaimed appreciatively. "And we, too, will have to gain courage. But such courage? Is that what you really want?"

Agathe subdued her zeal and denied it mutely and honestly. "Not entirely!" she added by way of explanation, so as not to deny it too much.

"It is the teaching of Him who advised us to offer our left cheek if we have been struck on the right one. And that's probably the mildest transgression that ever was," Ulrich went on reflectively. "But don't misunderstand one thing, that this message too, if carried out, is a psychological exercise! A particular behavior and a particular group of ideas and emotions are bound up in it together and mutually support each other. I mean everything in us that is suffering, enduring, tender, susceptible, protective, and yielding: in short, love. And it's so far from that to everything else, especially to whatever is hard, aggressive, and actively life-shaping, that these other emotions and ideas and the bitter necessities disappear from view entirely. That doesn't mean that they fade from reality; merely that you don't get angry at them, don't deny them, and that you forget knowing about them; so it's like a roof that the wind can get under and that can never stand for long—"

"But one has faith in goodness! It's faith! You're forgetting that!" Agathe interrupted.

"No, I'm not forgetting that, but that came along only later, through Paul. I made a note of his explanation. It runs: 'Faith is the substance of things hoped for, the evidence of things not seen.' And that's a gross, I'd almost say covetous, misunderstanding. The tenet of the kingdom that will come at the end of days would like to have something it can get hold of in place of the bliss that the Son of Man has already experienced on earth."

"It has been promised. Why are you running it down? Is it then worth nothing to be able to believe not merely with all one's soul but utterly, with parasol and clothes?"

"But the breath of the annunciation was not promise and faith but intimation! A condition in which one loves metaphors! A bolder condition than faith! And I'm not the first to notice this. The only thing that's been regarded as truly real for the bringer of salvation has been the experiencing of these foreshadowing metaphors of happy unresistingness and love; the miserable rest, which we call reality, natural, sturdy, dangerous life, has simply mirrored itself in his soul in a completely dematerialized way, like a picture puzzle. And—by Jehovah and Jupiter!—that assumes, first of all, civilization, because no one is so poor that robbers can't be found to murder him; and it assumes a desert in which there are indeed evil spirits, but no lions. Secondly, these high and happy tidings appear to have originated pretty much in ignorance of all contemporary civilizations. It is remote from the multiplicities of culture and the spirit, remote from doubts, but also from choice, remote from sickness but also from almost all discoveries that fight it: in short, it is remote from all the weaknesses, but also from all the advantages of human knowledge and capability, which even in its own time were by no means meager. And incidentally, that's why it also has rather simple notions of good and evil, beautiful and ugly. Now, the moment you make room for such objections and conditions, you'll also have to content yourself with my less simple procedure!"

Agathe argued against it anyway. "You're forgetting one thing," she repeated, "that this teaching claims to come from God; and in that case everything more complex that deviates from it is simply false or indifferent!"

"Quiet!" Ulrich said, placing a finger on his mouth. "You can't talk about God in such a stubbornly physical way, as if He were sitting behind that bush over there the way He did in the year 100!"

"All right, I can't," Agathe conceded. "But let me tell *you* something, too! You yourself, when you're devising bliss on earth, are prepared to renounce science, tendencies in art, luxury, and everything people rush around for every day. Then why do you begrudge it so much to others?"

"You're certainly right," Ulrich conceded. A dry twig had found its way into his hand, and he pensively poked the ground with it. They had slid down a little, so that once again only their heads peeked over the top of the rise, and that only when they lifted them. They lay beside each other on their stomachs like two marksmen who have forgotten what they were lying in wait for; and Agathe, touched by her brother's yielding, threw her arm around his neck and made a concession of her own. "Look, what is it doing?" she exclaimed, pointing with a finger to an ant beside his twig, which had attacked another ant.

"It's murdering," Ulrich ascertained coldly.

"Don't let it!" Agathe pleaded, and in her excitement raised a leg to the sky so that it rose upside down over her knee.

Ulrich proposed: "Try to take it metaphorically. You don't even have to rush to give it a particular significance: just take its own! Then it becomes like a dry breath of air, or the sulfurous smell of decaying foliage in autumn: some kind of volatizing drops of melancholy that make the soul's readiness for dissolution tremble. I can imagine that one could even get over one's own death amicably, but only because one dies just once and therefore regards it as especially important; because the understanding of saints and heroes is pretty lacking in glory in the face of nature's constant small confusions and their dissonances!"

Possibly: Ulrich: Through faith!
            Agathe: Intimation and metaphor won't do it either.
            Ulrich: Exactly!

While he was speaking, Agathe had taken the twig from his fingers and attempted to rescue the ant that had been attacked, with the result that she nearly crushed both, but finally she succeeded in separating them. With diminished vitality, the ants crept toward new adventures.

"Did that make any sense?" Ulrich asked.

"I understand you to mean by that that what we were trying to do by the fence is against nature and reason," Agathe answered.

"Why shouldn't I say it?" Ulrich said. "Anyway, I wanted to say to surprise you: the glory of God does not twitch an eyelid when calamity strikes. Perhaps too: life swallows corpses and filth without a shadow on its smile. And surely this: man is charming as long as no moral demands are made on him." Ulrich stretched out irresponsibly in the sun. For they merely needed to change position slightly, they did not even have to stand up, in order for the world on which they had been eavesdropping to disappear and be replaced by a large lawn, bordered by rustling bushes, that stretched in a gentle incline down to their lovely old house and lay there in the full light of summer. They had given up the ants and offered themselves to the points of the sun's rays, half unawares; from time to time a cool breeze poured over them. "The sun shines on the just and the unjust!" Ulrich offered as benediction, in peaceable mockery.

" 'Love your enemies, for He maketh the sun to rise on the evil and on the good' is the way it goes." Agathe contradicted him as softly as if she were merely confiding it to the air.

"Really? The way I say it, it would be wonderfully natural!"

"But you've got it wrong."

"Are you sure? Where is it from anyway?"

"The Bible, of course. I'll look it up in the house. I want to show you for once that I can be right too!"

He wanted to hold her back, but she was already on her feet beside him and hastened away. Ulrich closed his eyes. Then he opened and closed them again. Without Agathe, the solitude was bereft of everything; as if he were not in it himself. Then the steps returned. Great resounding footsteps in the silence, as in soft snow. Then the indescribable sense of nearness set in, and finally the nearness filled with a cheery laugh, prefacing the words: "It goes: 'Love your enemies, . . . for he maketh his sun to rise on the evil and on the good, and sendeth *rain* on the just and on the unjust'!"

"And where's it from?"

"Nowhere else but the Sermon on the Mount that you seem to know so well, my friend."

"I feel I've been exposed as a bad theologian," Ulrich conceded with a smile, and asked: "Read it aloud!"

Agathe had a heavy Bible in her hands, not an especially old or precious thing, but in any case not a recent edition, and read:

" 'Ye have heard that it hath been said, thou shalt love thy neighbor, and hate thine enemy. But I say unto you, love your enemies, bless them that curse you, do good to them that hate you, and pray for them which despitefully use you, and persecute you; that ye may be the children of your Father which is in heaven: for he maketh the sun to rise on the evil and on the good, and sendeth rain on the just and on the unjust.' "

"Do you know anything else?" Ulrich asked, eager to know.

"Yes," Agathe went on. "It is written: 'Ye have heard that it was said by them of old time, Thou shalt not kill; and whosoever shall kill shall be in danger of the judgment: But I say unto you, that whosoever is angry with his brother without a cause shall be in danger of the judgment: . . . but whosoever shall say, Thou fool, shall be in danger of hell fire.' And then this too, which you know so well: 'But I say unto you, that ye resist not evil: but whosoever shall smite thee on thy right cheek, turn to him the other also. And if any man will sue thee at the law and take away thy coat, let him have thy cloak also. And whosoever shall compel thee to go a mile, go with him twain.' "

"Well, I don't like that!" Ulrich said.

Agathe thumbed through the pages. "Maybe you'll like this: 'And if thy right hand offend thee, cut it off, and cast it from thee: for it is profitable for thee that one of thy members should perish, and not that thy whole body should be cast into hell.' "

Ulrich took the book from her and leafed through it himself. "There are even several variations," he exclaimed. Then he laid the book in the grass, pulled her beside him, and for some time said nothing. At last he replied: "Speaking seriously, I'm like Everyman, or at least like that man; it's natural for me to apply this saying in reverse. If *his* hand offend thee, cut it off, and if you smite someone on the cheek, give him a hook to the heart too, just to make sure."

62

THE CONSTELLATION OF BROTHER AND SISTER;
OR, THE UNSEPARATED AND NOT UNITED

Even in those years when Ulrich had sought his path in life alone and not without bravado, the word "sister" had often been for him heavy with an undefined longing, although at that time he almost never thought that he possessed a real living sister. In this there was a contradiction pointing to disparate origins, which were indicated in many ways that brother and sister ordinarily discounted. Not that they necessarily saw it as false, but it counted as little in relationship to the truth they knew they were approaching as an intruding corner signifies in the sweep of a grandly curving wall.

Without question, such things happen often. In many lives the unreal, invented sister is nothing other than the soaring youthful form of a need for love that later, in the condition of chillier dreams, contents itself with a bird or another animal, or turns toward humanity or one's neighbor. In the life of many others, this sister is adolescent timidity and loneliness, an invented doppelgänger full of shadowboxing charm, which softens the anxieties of loneliness in the tenderness of a lonely togetherness. And of many natures it need merely be said that this image that they cherish so ecstatically is nothing but the crassest egotism and selfishness: an excessive liking to be loved that has entered into a jerry-built agreement with sweet selflessness. But that many men and women bear the image of such a counterpart in their hearts there can be no doubt. It simply represents love and is always the sign of an unsatisfying and tense relation to the world. And it is not only those who are deficient or who are by nature without harmony who have such desires; balanced people have them too.

And so Ulrich began to speak to his sister about an experience he had related to her once already, and repeated the story of the most unforgettable woman who, with the exception of Agathe herself, had ever crossed his path. She was a child-woman, a girl of about twelve, remarkably mature in her behavior, who had ridden in the same trolley car for a short distance with him and a companion, and had charmed him like a mysteriously bygone love poem whose traces are full of never-experienced bliss. Later, the flaming up of his infatuation had sometimes aroused doubts in him, for it was peculiar and admitted dubious inferences about himself. For that reason he did not relate the incident with feeling but spoke of the doubts, even though it was not without feeling that he generalized them. "At that age, a girl quite often has more beautiful legs than she does later," he said. "Their later sturdiness apparently comes from what they need to carry directly above them; in adolescence these legs are long and free and can run, and if their skirts expose the thigh in some activity, the curve already has something gently increasing—oh, the crescent moon occurs to me, toward the end of its tender first virginal moon phase—that's how glorious they look! Later I sometimes investigated the reasons quite seriously. At that age hair has the softest sheen. The face shows its lovely naturalness. The eyes are like some smooth, never-crumpled silk. The mind, destined in future to become petty and covetous, is still a pure flame without much brightness among obscure desires. And what at this age is certainly not yet beautiful—for instance, the childish tummy or the blind expression of the breast—acquires through the clothing, to the extent that it cleverly simulates adulthood, and through the dreamy imprecision of love, everything that a charming stage mask can achieve. So it's quite in order to admire such a creature, and how else should one do so than through a slight attack of love!"

"And it's not at all against nature for a child to be the object of such feelings?" Agathe asked.

"What would be against nature would be a straight-out lustful desire," Ulrich replied. "But a person like that also drags the innocent or, in any event, unready and helpless creature into actions for which it is not destined. He must ignore the immaturity of the developing mind and body, and play the game of his passion with a mute and veiled opponent; no, he not only ignores whatever would get in his way, but brutally sweeps it aside! That's something quite different, with different consequences!"

"But perhaps a touch of the perniciousness of this 'sweeping aside' is already contained in the 'ignoring'?" Agathe objected. She might have been jealous of her brother's tissue of thoughts; at any rate, she resisted. "I don't see any great distinction in whether one pays no attention to what might restrain one, or doesn't feel it!"

Ulrich countered: "You're right and you're not right. I really just told the story because it's a preliminary stage of the love between brother and sister."

"Love between brother and sister?" Agathe asked, and pretended to be astonished, as if she were hearing the term for the first time; but she was digging her nails into Ulrich's arm again, and perhaps she did so too strongly, and her fingers trembled. Ulrich, feeling as if five small warm wounds had opened side by side in his arm, suddenly said: "The person whose strongest stimulation is associated with experiences each of which is, in some way or other, impossible, isn't interested in possible experiences. It may be that imagination is a way of fleeing from life, a refuge and a den of iniquity, as many maintain; I think that the story of the little girl, as well as all the other examples we've talked about, point not to an abnormality or a weakness but to a revulsion against the world and a strong recalcitrance, an excessive and overpassionate desire for love!" He forgot that Agathe could know nothing of the other examples and equivocal comparisons with which his thoughts had previously associated this kind of love; for he now felt himself in the clear again and had overcome, for the time being, the anesthetizing taste, the transformation into the will-less and lifeless, that was part of his experience, so that the automatic reference slipped inadvertently through a gap in his thoughts.

These thoughts were still oriented toward the more general aspect, with which his personal case could be compared as well as contrasted; and if in favor of the inner coherence of these ideas one leaves aside how they succeeded and shaped one another, what remained was a more or less impersonal content that looked something like this: For the articulation of life, hate might be just as important as love. There seem to be as many reasons to love the world as to detest it. Both instincts lie in human nature ready for use, their powers in unequal proportions, which vary in individuals. But there is no way of knowing how pleasure and bitterness balance each other in order to allow us to keep going on with our lives. The opinion we like to hear, that this calls for a preponderance of pleasure, is evidently false. For we also go on with our lives with bitterness, with an excess of unhappiness, hatred, or contempt for life, and proceed as surely as we would with a superabundance of happiness. But it occurred to Ulrich that both are extremes, the life-loving person as well as the person shadowed by animosity, and this is what led him to think of the complicated balance that is the usual one. Belonging to this balance of love and hate, for example, and thereby to the processes and structures with whose help they reach an accommodation, are justice and all other ways of observing moderation; but there belong to it no less the formation of fellowships of two or of vast numbers, combinations that are like feathered nests elaborately girdled with thorns; there belongs to it the certainty of God; and Ulrich knew that in this series the intellectual-sensual structure of the "sister" ultimately also had its place as a most daring expedient. From what weakness of soul this dream drew its nourishment stood hindmost, and foremost stood, as its origin, a really superhuman disparity. And apparently it was for this reason that Ulrich had spoken of revulsion toward the world, for whoever knows the depth of good and evil passion experiences the falling away of every kind of agreement that mediates between them, and he had not spoken the way he did in order to gloss over the passion for his own flesh and blood.

Without accounting for why he was doing so, he now told Agathe a second little story as well, which at the beginning seemed to have no connection at all with the first. "I once came across it, and it is supposed to have actually happened in the time of the Thirty Years' War, when individuals and peoples were thrown about in confusion," he began. "Most of the peasants from one isolated group of farms had been snatched away to serve in the war; none of them returned, and the women managed the farms by themselves, which was tiring and vexatious for them. Then it happened that one of the men who had disappeared returned to the region, and after many adventures came to his wife. I'll say right off that it wasn't the right man but a tramp and deceiver, who had shared camp and march for a few months with the missing and perhaps dead man, and had so successfully absorbed the other man's stories, when homesickness loosened his tongue, that he was able to pretend to be him. He knew the nicknames of wife and cow, and the names and habits of the neighbors, who moreover lived some distance away. He had a beard exactly like the other man's. He had a way of looking, with his two eyes of nondescript color, that one might easily think he wouldn't have done it much differently before; and although his voice sounded strange at first, it could certainly be explained by saying that one was now listening more closely than one had before. In short, the man knew how to imitate his predecessor trait for trait, the way a coarse and unlike portrait at first repeals but becomes more of a likeness the longer one remains alone with it, and finally takes over one's recollection entirely. I can imagine that, from time to time, something like dread must have warned the woman that he was not her husband; but she wanted to have her man again, and perhaps just a man, and so the stranger became more and more established in his role—"

"And how did it end?" Agathe asked.

"I forget. Apparently the man must have been unmasked by some sort of accident. But man in general is never unmasked, his whole life long!"

"You mean: One always only loves the stand-in for the right person? Or do you mean that when a person loves for the second time he doesn't confuse the two, but the image of the new one is in many places only an overpainting of the image of the first one?" Agathe asked, with a charming yawn.

"I intended to say a lot more, and it is much more boring," Ulrich responded. "Try to imagine someone, color-blind, for whom shades of brightness and shadow represent almost the entire world of colors: he can't see a single color and yet can apparently act so that no one notices, for what he can see represents for him what he can't. But what happens in this case in a particular area is what really happens to us all with reality. In our experiences and investigations, reality never appears otherwise than through a glass that partially transmits one's glance and partially reflects back the image of the viewer. If I observe the delicately flushed white of your hand, or feel the refractory inwardness of your flesh in my fingers, I have something real before me, but not in the way in which it *is* real; and just as little when I reduce it to its ultimate atoms and formulas!"

"Then why make such an effort to reduce it to something loathsome!"

"Do you recall what I said about the intellectual portrayal of nature, of its being an image without similarity? There are many quite different ways in which anything can be apprehended as the exact image of something else, but everything that occurs in this image, or results from it, must in just this one specific view always be a depiction of what investigating the original image demonstrates. If this also turns out to be the case where it could not have originally been foreseen, then the image is as justified as it can possibly be. That's a very general and quite unsensory notion of imageability. It presupposes a specific relationship of two areas, and gives to understand that it can be comprehended as a portrayal whenever it covers both areas without exception. In this sense, a mathematical formula can be the image of a natural process, just as much as a portrayal established by external sensory similarity. A theory can in its consequences accord with reality, and the effects of reality with theory. The cylinder in a music box is the portrayal of a way of singing, and an action portrays a fluctuating feeling. In mathematics, where for the sake of unsullied progression of thought one would most like to trust only what can be counted off on one's fingers, one usually speaks only of the precision of coordinates, which has to be possible point for point. But fundamentally, everything can also be regarded as a portrayal that is called correspondence, representability for some purpose, equal value and exchangeability, or equality in respect to something, or undifferentiability, or mutual appropriateness according to some kind of standard. A portrayal, therefore, is something like a relationship of complete correspondence in view of any particular such relationship—"

Agathe interrupted this exposition, which Ulrich was pronouncing listlessly and out of a sense of duty, with the admonition: "You could really get one of our modern painters fired up with all that—"

"Well, why not!" he replied. "Consider what sense there is in talking about fidelity to nature and similarity where the spatial is replaced by a surface, or the motley colors of life by metal or stone. That's why artists aren't entirely wrong to reject these notions of sensory imitation and similarity as photographic and, with the exception of a few traditional laws that go along with their medium and tools, why they recognize only inspiration, or some kind of theory that has been revealed to them; but the customers who are portrayed, who after the execution of these laws see themselves as victims of a miscarriage of justice, mostly aren't. . . ."

Ulrich paused. Although he had intended to speak about the logically strict notion of portrayal only in order to be able to derive from it its free but by no means random consequences, which dominate the various imagistic relationships that occur in life, he was now silent. Observing himself in this attempt left him dissatisfied. He had lately forgotten many things that had formerly been at the tips of his fingers, or to put it better, he had pushed them aside; even the pointed expressions and concepts of his earlier profession, which he had used so often, were no longer viable for him, and in searching for them he not only felt an unpleasant dryness but was also afraid of talking like a bungler.

"You said that a color-blind person isn't missing anything when he looks at the world," Agathe encouraged him.

"Yes. Of course I oughtn't to have put it quite that way," Ulrich responded. "It's still an obscure question altogether. Even if you limit yourself to the intellectual image that the understanding derives from something, in confronting the problem of whether it's true you come up against the greatest difficulties, although the air you ordinarily breathe is always dry and crystalline. However, the images we make for ourselves in life so we can act and feel rightly, or even act and feel energetically, aren't determined just by the understanding; indeed, these images are often quite irrational and, according to rational standards, not at all accurate representations, and yet they must fulfill their purpose in order for us to remain in harmony with reality and with ourselves. They must also be precise and complete according to some kind of key or manual of images, and according to the notion that determines the manner in which they are portrayed, even if this notion leaves room for various methods—"

Agathe interrupted him excitedly. She had suddenly grasped the connection. "So the false peasant was a portrayal of the real one?" she asked.

Ulrich nodded. "Originally, an image always represented its object completely. It bestowed power over it. Whoever cut out the eyes or the heart of an image killed the person portrayed. Whoever secretly got hold of the image of an inaccessible beauty was able to conquer her. The name, too, is part of these images; and so one was able to conjure God with His name, which is equivalent to making Him subservient. As you know, even today one makes off with secret remembrances, or gives oneself a ring with an engraved name, and wears pictures and locks of hair over one's heart as a talisman. In the course of time, something split off; but it has all sunk to the level of superstition, although one part has achieved the tedious dignity of photography, geometry, and such things. But just think of the hypnotized person, who with every sign of satisfaction bites into a potato that for him represents an apple, or think of your childhood dolls, which you loved more passionately the simpler they were and the less they looked like people; so you see that it doesn't depend on externalities, and you're back at the bolt-upright fetish column that represents a god—"

"Couldn't you almost say that the more dissimilar an image is, the greater the passion for it as soon as we've attached ourselves to it?" Agathe asked.

"Yes, absolutely!" Ulrich agreed. "Our reason, our perception, have separated themselves from our emotions in this matter. One could say that the most stirring representations always have something unlike." Smiling, he observed her from the side and added: "When I'm not in your presence I don't see you before me in a way one would like to paint; it's rather as if you had glanced into some water and I was trying vainly to trace your image in the water with my finger. I maintain that it's only indifferent things that one sees properly and truly alike."

"Strange!" his sister replied. "I see you before me precisely! Perhaps because my memory is entirely too precise and dependent!"

"Similarity of portrayal is an approximation of what the understanding finds real and equal; it is a concession to the understanding," Ulrich said agreeably, and went on in a conciliatory way: "But besides that, there are also the images that address themselves to our emotions, and an image in art is, for example, a mixture of both demands. But if, beyond that, you wish to take it to the point where something portrays something else *only* for the emotions, you'll have to think of such examples as a flag flying, which at certain moments is an image of our honor—"

"But there you can only be talking about a symbol, you're no longer talking about images!" Agathe interjected.

"Mental image, simile, metaphor, they shade into one another," Ulrich said. "Even such examples as the image of a disease and the doctor's plan for curing it belong here. They must have imagination's inventive lack of precision, but the precision of executability as well. This flexible boundary between imagining the plan, and the image that endures in the face of reality, is important everywhere in life, but hard to find."

"How different we are!" Agathe repeated thoughtfully.

Ulrich parried the reproach with a smile. "Very much so! I'm speaking of the lack of precision in taking something *for* something, as of a divinity bestowing fruitfulness and life, and I'm trying to impart as much order to it as it will bear; and you don't notice that I've been talking for a long time about the truthful possibility of twins who are doppelgängers, who have two souls, but are one?" He went on spiritedly: "Imagine twins who resemble each other 'interchangeably'; place them before you, each in the same attitude, separated only by a wall indicated by a line to confirm that they are two independent beings. And in an uncanny augmentation, they can repeat themselves in whatever they do, so that you spontaneously assume the same about their inner processes. What's uncanny about this performance? That there's absolutely nothing by which we can distinguish them, and that yet they are two! That in everything we might undertake with them, one is as good as the other, although in the process something like a destiny is being fulfilled! In short, they are the same for us but not for themselves!"

"Why are you playing such gruesome and spooky games with these twins?" Agathe asked.

"Because it's a case that happens often. It's the case of mistaking things, of indifference, of perceiving and acting wholesale, of representability: in other words, a major chapter from the usages of life. I've only prettied it up in order to dramatize something for you. Now let me turn it around: Under what circumstances would the twins be two for us and one for themselves? Is that spooky too?"

Agathe pressed his arm and sighed. Then she admitted: "If it's possible for two people to be the same for the world, it could also be that a

person appears to us doubled— But you're making me speak nonsense!"
she added.

"Imagine two goldfish in a bowl," Ulrich asked.

"No!" Agathe said firmly, but laughing at the same time. "I'm not
going along with any more of this!"

"Please, imagine them! A large bowl in the shape of a ball, as you
sometimes see in someone's living room. You can, incidentally, imagine
the bowl to be as large as the boundaries of our property. And two red-
dish-gold fish, moving their fins slowly up and down like veils. Let's
leave aside whether they are really two or one. For each other, at least,
they will be two, for the time being; their jealousy over feeding and sex
will see to that. They avoid each other, too, whenever they come too
near each other. But I can well imagine that for me they can become
one: I need only concentrate on this motion that slowly draws in upon
itself and unfolds, and then this single shimmering creature becomes
merely a dependent part of this common up-and-down motion. Now I
ask when this might also happen to them—"

"They're goldfish!" Agathe admonished. "Not a group of dancers suffering from supernatural delusions!"

"They are you and I," her brother responded pensively, "and that's
why I would like to try to bring the comparison to a proper conclusion. It
seems to me a soluble problem to imagine how the world glides past in
its separate-but-united motion. It's no different from the world undulat-
ing past from a railway car going around curves, except that it happens
twice over, so that at every one of the double being's moments, the
world occupies two positions, which somehow must coincide in the soul.
That means that the idea of getting from one to the other through some
motion will never be associated with these double beings; the impression of a distance existing between them will not arise; and more such
things. I think I can imagine that one would also manage to be tolerably
comfortable in such a world and could doubtless puzzle out in various
ways the necessary constitution of the mental tools and procedures
needed to make sense of things." Ulrich stopped for a moment and reflected. He had become aware of many objections, and the possibility of
overcoming them also suggested itself. He smiled guiltily. Then he said:
"But if we assume that the constitution of that other world is the same as
ours, the task is much easier! Both hovering creatures will then feel
themselves as one without being bothered by the difference in their perception and without there being any need of a higher geometry or physiology to attain it, as long as you are simply willing to believe that
spiritually they are bound to each other more firmly than they are to the
world. If anything at all important that they share is infinitely stronger

than the difference of their experiences; if it bridges these differences and doesn't even let them reach awareness; if the disturbances reaching them from the world aren't worth being aware of, then it will happen. And a shared suggestion can have this effect; or a sweet indolence and imprecision of the habits of receptiveness, which mix everything up; or a one-sided tension and exaltation that allows only what is desired to get through: one thing, it seems to me, as good as the next—"

Now Agathe laughed at him: "Then why did I have to march through all that precision about the conditions of portrayal?" she asked.

Ulrich shrugged his shoulders. "It's all interconnected," he answered, falling silent.

He himself knew that with all his efforts he had nowhere made a breach, and their variety confused his recollection. He foresaw that they would repeat themselves. But he was tired. And as the world becomes snugly heavy in the evaporating light and draws all its limbs up to itself, so did Agathe's nearness again force its way physically among his thoughts while his mind was giving up. They had both become accustomed to conducting such difficult conversations, and for rather a long time these had already been such a mixture of the pulsating power of the imagination, and the vain utmost effort of the understanding to secure it, that it was nothing new for either of them at one time to hope for a resolution, at another to allow their own words to rock them to sleep much as one listens to the childishly happy conversation of a fountain, babbling to itself happily about eternity. In this condition Ulrich now belatedly thought of something, and again had recourse to his carefully prepared parable. "It's amazingly simple, but at the same time strange, and I don't know how to present it to you convincingly," he said. "You see that cloud over there in a somewhat different position than I do, and also presumably in a different way; and we've discussed how whatever you see and do and what occurs to you will never be the same as what happens to me and what I do. And we've investigated the question of whether, in spite of that, it still might not be possible to be one being to the ultimate degree, and live as two with one soul. We've measured out all sorts of answers with a compass, but I forgot the simplest: that both people could be minded and able to take everything they experience only as a simile! Just consider that for the understanding every simile is equivocal, but for the emotions it's unequivocal. For someone to whom the world is just a simile could also probably, according to his standards, experience as one thing what according to the world's standards is two."

At this moment the idea also hovered before Ulrich that, in an attitude toward life for which being in one place is merely a metaphor for being in another, even that which cannot be experienced—being one person in two bodies wandering about separately—would lose the sting of its impossibility; and he made ready to talk about this further.

But Agathe pointed at the cloud and interrupted him glibly: "Hamlet: 'Do you see yonder cloud that's almost in shape of a camel?' Polonius: 'By th' mass, and 'tis like a camel indeed.' Hamlet: 'Methinks it is like a weasel.' Polonius: 'It is back'd like a weasel.' Hamlet: 'Or like a whale?' Polonius: 'Very like a whale!' " She said this so that it was a caricature of assiduous accord.

Ulrich understood the objection, but it did not prevent him from continuing: "One says of a simile, too, that it is an image. And it could be said just as well of every image that it's a simile. But none is an equation. And just for that reason, the fact that it's part of a world ordered not by equality but by similitude explains the enormous power of representation, the forceful effect that characterizes even quite obscure and unlike copies, which we've already spoken about!" This idea itself burgeoned through its twilight, but he did not complete it. The immediate recollection of what they had said about portrayals combined in it with the image of the twins and with the picture-perfect numbness Agathe had experienced, which had repeated itself before her brother's eyes; and this brew was animated by the distant memory of how often such conversations, when they were at their finest and came from heart and soul, themselves proclaimed an inclination to express themselves only in similes. But today that did not happen, and Agathe again hit the sensitive spot like a marksman as she upset her brother with a remark. "Why, for heaven's sake, are all your words and desires directed at a woman who, oddly enough, is supposed to be your exact second edition?" she exclaimed, innocently offending. She was, nevertheless, a little afraid of the reply, and protected herself with the generalization: "Is it comprehensible that in the whole world the ideal of all lovers is to become one being, without considering that these ungrateful people owe almost all the charm of love to the fact that they are two beings, and of seductively different sexes?" She added sanctimoniously, but with even craftier purpose: "They even sometimes say to one another, as if they wanted to accommodate you, 'You're my doll'!"

But Ulrich accepted the ridicule. He considered it justified, and it was difficult to counter it with a new accommodation. At the moment it was not necessary either. For although brother and sister were speaking quite differently, they were still in agreement. From some undetermined boundary on, they felt as one being: the way that from two people playing piano four-handedly, or reading with two voices a scripture important for their salvation, a single being arises, whose animated, brighter outline is indistinctly set off from a shadowy background. As in a dream, what hovered before them was a melting into one form—just as incomprehensibly, convincingly, and passionately beautifully as it happens that two people exist alongside each other and are secretly the same; and this unity was partly supported and partly upset by ᴄne dubious manipulation that had lately emerged. It can be said of these reflections that it should not be impossible that the effects the emotions can achieve in sleep can be repeated when one is wide awake; perhaps with omissions, certainly in an altered fashion and through different processes, but it could also be expected that it would then happen with greater resistance to dissolving influences. To be sure, they saw themselves sufficiently removed from this, and even the choice of means they preferred distinguished them from each other, to the extent that Ulrich inclined more to accounting for things, and Agathe to spontaneously credulous resolution.

That is why it often happened that the end of a discussion appeared to be further from its goal than its beginning, as was also the case this time in the garden, where the meeting had begun almost as an attempt to stop breathing and had then gone over to suppositions about ways of building variously imagined houses of cards. But it was basically natural that they should feel inhibited about acting according to their all too daring ideas. For how were they to turn into reality something that they themselves planned as pure unreality, and how should it be easy for them to act in one spirit, when it was really an enchanted spirit of inaction? This was why in the midst of this conversation far removed from the world they suddenly had the urgent desire to come into contact with people again.

PART 2

DRAFTS OF CHARACTER AND INCIDENT

ULRICH / ULRICH AND AGATHE / AGATHE

MID 1920S

[Ulrich visits the clinic]

He encountered Moosbrugger towering broadly among the cunning deceivers. It was heroic, the futile struggle of a giant among these people. He seemed through some quality or other to actually deserve the admiration that he found a sham but enjoyed in a naïvely ridiculous way. In the grossest distortions of insanity, there is still a self struggling to find something to hang on to. He was like a heroic ballad in the midst of an age that creates quite different kinds of songs but out of habitual admiration still preserves the old things. Defenseless, admired power, like a club among the arrows of the mind. One could laugh at this person and yet feel that what was comic in him was shattering. / The clouding of this mind was connected with that of the age.

—Do you have a friend? Ulrich asked in a moment when they were unobserved. —I mean, Moosbrugger, don't you have anyone who could get you out of here? There's no other way. Moosbrugger said he did, but he wouldn't be easy to find. What is he? A locksmith. But he's a locksmith who works on cabinets, Moosbrugger grinned rather sheepishly, (he's not easy to find), he works in many places. He'd do it, but Ulrich would have to go to his wife and get his address from her. And he didn't want to impose that on him, this wife was an awful person. Moosbrugger was visibly cutting capers and preening in a courtly way before Ulrich. Ulrich said she would probably give him the information, whether she was awful or not. Yes, she no doubt would; he would have to mention Moosbrugger's name. Before his last wandering, when he was working in Vienna, he had lived with her himself, the heart of the matter now emerged; he, Moosbrugger; but she was a woman with low tastes, a criminal, a quite common sort. . . . Moosbrugger shows all the symptoms of his hatred for women only because he is afraid that Ulrich might have a poor opinion of him when he sees this woman.

So she would tell Ulrich where he could meet her partner.

Ulrich went to see her. Borne by the automatism that accompanies all deeds of daring. He was really not in the least surprised when he entered an apartment that looked like forty others in a building on the outskirts of the city, and encountered in the kitchen a young woman doing chores, who must have been just like the forty other housewives. Nor did the suspicion with which he was greeted in any way differ from the suspicion one often finds in these circles. As soon as he entered he had to say something, and through the general European courtesies he uttered was immediately placed in a quite impersonal relationship. There wasn't a breath of crime in this environment. She was a coarse young woman, and her breasts moved under her blouse like a rabbit under a cloth.

When he brought up the name of Moosbrugger Fräulein Hörnlicher smiled deprecatingly, as if to say: the useless crazy things he gets himself into; but she was willing to help him. Of course it depended on Karl, but she didn't think he'd leave Moosbrugger in the lurch. This all took place in courteous exchanges, as when a businessman who's got himself into a corner begs his solid neighbors for support.

She gave Ulrich the name of a small tavern where he would presumably find Karl. He'd probably have to go several times, since Karl's movements were never entirely predictable. He should tell the tavern keeper who had sent him and whom he wanted to speak to and calmly sit down and wait.

Ulrich was lucky, and found Karl Biziste on his first try. Again an automatic play of limbs and thoughts carried him there; but this time Ulrich was paying attention, and followed with curiosity what seemed to be happening to him rather than to be something he was doing. His emotions were the same as they were the time when he had been arrested. From that moment, when Clarisse's interest had cautiously begun to tickle him like the end of a thread, until now, where events were already being woven into a heavy rope, things had taken their own course, one thing leading to another with a necessity that merely carried him along. It seemed incredibly strange to him that the course of most people's lives is this course of things that so alienated him, while on the contrary for other people it is quite natural to let themselves be borne along by whatever turns up, and thus finally be raised to a solid existence. Ulrich also felt that soon he would no longer be able to turn around, but this made him as curious as when one suddenly notices the inexorable movement of one's own breathing.

And he made yet another observation. When he imagined how much mischief could arise from what he was proposing to do, and that it soon would no longer be in his power to avoid initiating the process. With an evil deed that he felt on his conscience as if it had already been committed, he saw the world he was walking through in a different way. Almost as if he had a vision in his heart. Of God, or a great invention, or a great happiness. Even the starry sky is a social phenomenon, a structure of the shared fantasy of our species, man, and changes when one steps out of its circle.

Moosbrugger—Ulrich told himself—will wreak more havoc if I help him to freedom. There's no denying that sooner or later he will again fall victim to his disposition, and I will bear the responsibility for it. —But when he tried grave self-reproach in order to stop himself, there was something really untruthful in it. About as if one were to take the stance of being able to see clearly through a fog. The sufferings of those victims were really not certain. Had he seen the suffering creatures before him, he would probably have been overcome by a fierce empathy, for he was a person of oscillations, and that also meant of sympathetic oscillations. But as long as this suggestive power of experiencing with the senses was missing, and everything remained only a play of mental forces, these victims remained adherents of a mankind that he would really have liked to abolish, or at least greatly change, and no amount of sympathy diminished the emotional force of this dislike. There are people whom this horrifies; they are under the impress of a very strong moral or social power of suggestion; they speak up and start shouting as soon as they notice even the most remote injustice, and are furious at the badness and coldness of feeling that they frequently find in the world. They demonstrate violent emotions, but in most cases these are the emotions imposed on them by their ideas and principles: that is, an enduring suggestiveness, which like all powers of suggestion has something automatic and mechanical about it, whose path never dips into the realm of living emotions. The person who lives disinterestedly is, in contrast to them, ill-disposed and indifferent toward everything that does not touch his own circle of interests; he not only has the indifference of a mass murderer, in its passive form, when he reads in his morning paper about the accidents and misfortunes of the previous day, but he can also quite easily wish all kinds of misfortune on people he doesn't care about, if they annoy him. Certain phenomena lead one to assume that a forward-marching civilization based on shared works also strengthens the repressed and immured antagonists of these emotions. This was what was going through Ulrich's mind as he walked along. Moosbrugger's victims were abstract, threatened, like all the thousands who are exposed to the dangers of factories, railroads, and automobiles.

When he happened to look around on his way to Herr Biziste, he thought he could see that all the life we have created has been made possible only through our neglecting our duty to care for our more distant neighbor. Otherwise we would never think of putting on the street machines that kill him; indeed, we would never let him go out on the street himself, as is actually the case with cautious parents and their children. Instead of this, however, we live with a statistically predictable annual percentage of murders, which we commit rather than deviate from our manner of living and the line of development we hope to maintain. Ulrich suddenly thought, too, that part of this was a general division of labor in which it is always the task of a particular group of people to heal injuries caused by the indispensable activities of others; but we never restrain a force by demanding that it moderate itself; and finally there are still quite specific institutions, like parliaments, kings, and the like, that serve exclusively as equalizers. Ulrich concluded from this that for him to assist Moosbrugger's escape had no significance, for there were enough other people whose job it was to prevent any injuries that might result, and if they fulfilled their obligations they were bound to succeed, which made his personal deed no worse than an irregularity. This individual, moral prohibition—that he was nevertheless obliged as an individual not to let things go that far—was in this context nothing more than a doubled coefficient of security, which the knowledgeable person could afford to neglect.

The vision of a different order of things hovering far in advance of these specific ideas, an order that was more honest, one might say technically without clichés, accompanied Ulrich even as the adventure enticed him, tired as he was of the indecisive life of a person of today. / Possibly: It was not his good fortune to be effective in the world and to be defined by that. Like Thomas Mann or the good upstanding citizen of this age. Nor was he involved in the struggle *for* something. / Thus this path was not unlike the dive into the water, well known to Ulrich, from a height of thirty feet. On the way down one sees one's own image rushing toward one faster and faster in a watery reflection and can adjust small errors in one's position; but for the rest, one can no longer change anything in what is taking place.

When he had found the tavern, Ulrich did everything as Fräulein Hörnlicher had indicated. He mentioned her name, told the proprietor what he wanted, was asked to sit down and told that he might have to wait quite a while. He inspected the guests, many of whom spoke to the proprietor as they entered and left; felt himself observed, but could not make out a great deal himself. It was an hour at which the patrons were intermingled with workers and petit bourgeois. Finally, he thought he could make out the criminals among the guests by the peculiarly ridiculous elegance of their clothes.

Ulrich had not made out Herr Biziste, who, when he came in, spoke with the proprietor like the others after glancing quickly around the room and, after he had sat down, was looked at in the same way by everyone else around the room, and who was dressed with an equally counterfeit elegance / with a somewhat different elegance. Nor did the owner give Ulrich any sign. Biziste was drinking with several men, then stood up to go, stopped as if idly by Ulrich's table, and asked him dismissively what it was he was after. Ulrich had the tact not to stand, but to look up carelessly and offer Biziste a chair. This was of course presumptuous, but since he could be certain that Biziste was still interested in Moosbrugger, he could permit himself to meet the great man on the same level. He told him that Moosbrugger would be executed within a few weeks if no one helped him. For some reason or other, Ulrich seemed to himself like a spoiled boy who is playing with street urchins and is showing off with fairy tales he has invented. Biziste seemed to disapprove of Ulrich as of an incorrigible blockhead. Still dismissive, he asked Ulrich how he thought this could be done. Ulrich quickly emptied his glass and by a rather vague gesture left it to the proprietor whether he was to bring another glass for himself and his tablemate as well. Then he related that arranging an escape from the observation clinic would not be all that difficult. Herr Biziste was interested in this new milieu that Ulrich described to him. Ulrich became inventive; it amused him to think it out in front of a hardened criminal, and on the spot he made up a specific plan in which only the hour remained unfixed but that otherwise, thanks to Ulrich's exact knowledge of the place, didn't seem at all bad. Three men would be needed, one as a lookout outside the garden wall they had to climb over, so that on their way out they would not fall into the hands of a police patrol or give themselves away to passersby; the other two would be enough to bring Moosbrugger civilian clothes and hold off any guard who might come by until Moosbrugger had changed.

The arrogant irony with which Biziste listened to this plan, as Ulrich spoke faster and faster from nervousness, was striking.

Then Biziste stood up and said: If you come to such and such a place on Wednesday, perhaps we can talk about it some more.

Will you bring along a third person?

Biziste shrugged his shoulders, and Ulrich was dismissed.

• • •

It gave Ulrich a peculiar, bitter pleasure that in the meantime everything else went on inexorably.

On the day Biziste had set, he had gone to the rendezvous but did not meet the third man. Biziste, treating the whole business casually, merely said to him that for a certain sum this third man had declared himself willing. He mentioned a day and time, and revealed that Ulrich would have to go over the wall too, since he was the only one who knew the layout.

All Biziste probably wanted to do was frighten him, and for money a new partner could have been found, but the bizarre situation attracted Ulrich; since one could also break one's neck skiing, why should he not climb over a wall in the night with criminals? Incidentally, he heartily wished the police on this puffed-up Biziste.

He put on his oldest suit, omitted a collar, and topped it off with a sports cap; in this way his silhouette in the shadows of the night was not conspicuously different from that of the other people one might encounter on the remote street along which the wall of the asylum garden ran. Moosbrugger had been alerted; over time, three linen sheets had disappeared in the hospital, to serve as a rope on which he was to let himself down. Ulrich could probably have smuggled in a climber's rope, but he wanted to avoid anything that might betray the assistance supplied, since it was not out of the question that suspicion would fall on him. On this night the window of Moosbrugger's room was dimly lit; Ulrich had got him the stump of a candle so that they would be able to orient themselves in the darkness of the moonless night.

Biziste had climbed onto the back of the second "gentleman," swung himself up on top of the wall, and could be heard jumping down into the leaves on the other side. As Ulrich was about to follow, voices were heard; the "gentleman" stood up so inconsiderately that Ulrich, who had already got a foot up to mount on his back, nearly fell, and the other man strolled, hands in pockets, into the night.

Ulrich's heart was pounding and he felt a need to run, which he controlled with effort; but in order not to attract attention by behaving oddly, he imagined that he ought not to be walking alone, caught up with the "gentleman," and took his arm like that of a drinking companion, which the "gentleman" seemed to find ridiculously overdone.

The voices died away, and the "gentleman" again offered his back; Ulrich grasped the mortar and brick dust, felt the stab of a pulled muscle in his leg, so forcefully had he swung it up in his excitement, hung there, let himself fall into the darkness, and ended in an applauding sound of dead leaves such as he had not heard since his boyhood. He stood up in total darkness, unable to discern the slightest trace of Biziste. He groped right and left, in the hope that another noise would answer his own, but it remained as quiet as it was dark. He had to make up his mind to go in the direction of the building alone, hoping that he would meet up with Biziste on the way.

Again Ulrich's heart pounded; the bushes scratched, as if in his fear he was making only inappropriate movements. Distances, odors, physical contacts, sounds—everything was new, never experienced. He had to stop, collect his will, and tell himself that he had no other recourse than to see this stupid adventure through. He stumbled onto a path and deduced which direction would lead to the building most quickly, but was suddenly overcome by the problem of whether he should walk on the crunching gravel or go on working his way through the bushes.

That damned Biziste ought to have waited for him, but at the same time he longed for him as if he were a stronger brother. If he would not have been ashamed of himself because of the fellow on the other side of the wall, Ulrich would have turned around. But he did not even know what signal he was supposed to give to find out whether all was clear on the other side. He realized that he was a fool, and gained some respect for these rogues. But he was not a man to let himself be defeated so easily; it would have been ridiculous for an intellectual not to be able to cope with this too. Ulrich marched forward straight through the shrubbery; the excitement he was in and the self-control his progress required (entirely without reflection; it was simply moral pains) made him ruthlessly crack, break, and rustle the bushes. To have slunk forward like an Indian seemed to him just then incredibly silly and childish, and this was the moment in which the normal person in him began to reawaken.

When he came to the edge, Biziste, as Ulrich really might have expected from the first, was squatting there observing the building, and he turned a witheringly punitive glance toward his noisy arrival. Moosbrugger's window was dimly lit; Biziste whistled through his teeth. The huge shoulders of the murderer filled the rectangle of the window, the rope fashioned from the sheets rolled down; but Moosbrugger was not skilled in crime and had underestimated the strength of the rescue line required for his enormous weight; hardly had he suspended himself from it when it broke, and the force of his landing exploded the stillness with a muffled detonation. At this moment two guards materialized in the half-light that illuminated the wall.

Two days earlier, two mentally ill prisoners had escaped from another observation clinic, but Ulrich had neither heard nor read about it. And so he had not known that since yesterday security had been generally tightened and old, long-forgotten measures were again being enforced for a while. Among these was the two-man patrol, which, perhaps drawn by the noises Ulrich had made and now alarmed by the muffled fall, stopped, looked around, recognized in the sand a heavy body that with great effort was trying to get up, rushed over, saw a rope hanging from the window, and with all their lung power signaled for help through shrill little whistles. Moosbrugger had dislocated his shoulder and broken an ankle, otherwise it would have been an unhappy encounter for the guards who jumped on him; as it was, he knocked one bleeding into the sand, but when he tried to straighten up to shake off the second, pain deprived him of his footing. The guard hung on his neck and whistled piercingly; the second man, full of pain and rage, pounced on him, and at this moment Biziste sprang out of the bushes. With a powerful blow of his fist, he smashed one guard's whistle between his teeth so that he tumbled off Moosbrugger, but now the other whistled like mad and rushed at Biziste. Such guards are strong men, and Biziste was not exceptionally powerful. If at this instant Ulrich had come forward to help, with his considerable trained strength, they would no doubt have succeeded in rendering both attackers mute and motionless for a while, but Ulrich did not feel the slightest desire to do so. In the tangle before him his sympathies lay quite honestly with the men unexpectedly set upon, who were fighting for their duty, and if he had only followed his emotions, he would have grabbed this Biziste by the collar and given him a solid hook to the chin. But perhaps that was also merely the somewhat comical maternal voice of bourgeois order in him, and as the situation tensed his muscles and nerves, so his mind ebbed, filling him with disgust at contradictions whose resolution was not worth the effort. Another semi-event, Ulrich said to himself. A very painful sensation of the awful ludicrousness of his situation came over him.

Biziste reached for his knife. But before he raised it to thrust, his glance, practiced in weighing risk and advantage, revealed to him the hopelessness of the outcome: Moosbrugger could not stand up without assistance, the noise of the alarmed people on night duty was already coming out of the darkness from the wing of the building, flight was the only recourse. The guard, who would not let him go, screamed, hit by a stab in the arm. Biziste disappeared, leaving Ulrich behind, as Ulrich ascertained with cheerful satisfaction in spite of the quite awkward situation. He had meantime been thinking how he himself might get out of this stupid business. The way over the wall was blocked, for he hadn't the slightest desire to meet Herr Biziste and his friend ever again in his life, nor did he feel like climbing over the wall alone and perhaps being detained by the curious drawn to the scene by the shouts of the guards, who would certainly be chasing after Biziste. He settled on the only thing that occurred to him, a very stupid thing: to run a little farther, quickly find a bench, and pretend to be asleep in case he was found. He raised the collar of his coat so his bare neck could not be seen, took off his cap, and "awoke" with as much surprise as possible when, surrounded by a maze of lights, he was knocked from the bench by an incredible fist and his arms grabbed by six men. He did not know whether he gave a good performance as the righteous person drunk with sleep; it was his good fortune that one of the guards immediately recognized him, upon which he was released with reluctant respect. He was taken for a doctor who was doing studies at the clinic. He now tried to make credible that after a visit he had been walking in the grounds and had fallen asleep here. To this end, he involuntarily looked at his watch, remembered that he had left it at home but could no longer take back the gesture and therefore found it missing; reached into his jacket and pants pockets and immediately found his money missing too, for he had of course also not brought it along; and as stupid as this comedy was, as he told himself, there was an even stupider guard who believed it, or really just one whose servile officiousness and desire to please Ulrich suggested what Ulrich wanted him to believe, so that he immediately called out: The rascals have also robbed the Herr Doktor. Ulrich did not say either yes or no, but only went on like someone who missed his belongings without knowing anything about what had happened and now found out the entire drama backward and in snatches. As an object of respect and the remaining center of interest, he left the clinic in this feigned role as quickly as he could; he was not to enter it again as long as it sheltered Moosbrugger.

For after this attempted flight Moosbrugger was placed under heavy guard, and Ulrich, on the orders of the head of the clinic, was no longer allowed to visit him. Nor did Ulrich have the slightest desire to. Still, the unpleasant uncertainty, whether the doctor . . .

The very unpleasant doubt remained whether, upon investigating the circumstances, they had not come to suspect him, which of course they would not express but were just as little ready to abandon.

In mania, this would be a depressive cycle of short duration.

. . .

LATE 1920s

Her brother's conduct, the restlessness that the visit to Lindner had intensified in her, stimulated Agathe to a degree that remained hidden even from herself. She did not know how it had happened, or when; suddenly her soul was transported out of her body and looked around curiously in the alien world. This world pleased her soul uncommonly. Anything that might have disturbed it was lost in the completeness of its pleasure.

Agathe dreamed.

Her body lay on the bed without stirring, though it was breathing. She looked at it and felt a joy like polished marble at the sight. Then she observed the objects that stood farther back in her room; she recognized them all, but they were not exactly the things that otherwise were hers. For the objects lay outside her in the same way as her body, which she saw resting among them. That gave her a sweet pain!

Why did it hurt? Apparently because there was something deathlike about it; she could not act and could not stir, and her tongue was as if cut off, so that she was also unable to say anything about it. But she felt a great energy. Whatever her senses lit upon she grasped immediately, for everything was visible and shone the way sun, moon, and stars are reflected in water. Agathe said to herself: "You have wounded my body with a rose"—and turned to the bed in order to take refuge in her body.

Then she discovered that it was her brother's body. He, too, was lying in the reflecting glorious light as in a crypt; she saw him not distinctly but more penetratingly than usual, and touched him in the secrecy of the night. She raised him up; he was a heavy burden in her arms, but she nevertheless had the strength to carry and hold him, and this embrace had a supranatural charm. Her brother's body nestled so lovably and indulgently against her that she rested in him; as he in her; nothing stirred in her, not even now the beautiful desire. And because in this suspension they were one and without distinctions, and also without distinctions within themselves, so that her understanding was as if lost and her memory thought of nothing and her will had no activity, she stood in this calm as if facing a sunrise, and melted into it with her earthly details. But while this was happening, joyously, Agathe perceived surrounding her a wild crowd of people who, as it appeared, found themselves around her in great fear. They were running excitedly back and forth, and gesturing warningly and resentfully with increasing din. In the manner of a dream, this was happening quite close to her but without involving her, but only until the noise and fright suddenly intruded violently into her mind. Then Agathe was afraid, and quickly stepped back into her sleeping body; she had no idea at all how everything might have been changed, and for a time left off dreaming.

But after a while she began again. Again she left her body, but this time met her brother immediately. And again her body was lying naked on the bed; they both looked at it, and indeed the hair over the genitals of this unconscious body that had been left behind burned like a small golden fire on a marble tomb. Because there was no "I" or "you" between them, this being three did not surprise her. Ulrich was looking at her softly and earnestly in a way she did not recognize as his. They also looked at their surroundings together, and it was their house in which they found themselves, but although Agathe knew all the objects quite well, she could not have said in which room this was happening, and that again had a peculiar charm, for there was neither right nor left, earlier nor later, but when they looked at something together they were united like water and wine, a union that was more golden or silver, depending on whichever was poured in in greater quantity. Agathe knew immediately: "This is what we have so often talked of, total love," and paid close attention so as not to miss anything. But she still missed how it was happening. She looked at her brother, but he was looking in front of him with a stiff and embarrassed smile. At this moment she heard a voice somewhere, a voice so exceedingly beautiful that it had nothing to compare with earthly things, and it said: "Cast everything you have into the fire, down to your shoes; and when you no longer have anything don't even think of a shroud, but cast yourself naked into the fire!" And while she was listening to this voice and remembering that she knew this sentence, a splendor rose into her eyes and radiated from them, a splendor that took away precise earthly definition even from Ulrich, though she had no impression that anything was missing from him, and her every limb received from it in the manner of its special pleasure great grace and bliss. Involuntarily she took some steps toward her brother. He was coming toward her from the other side in the same way.

Now there was only a narrow chasm between their bodies, and Agathe felt that something must be done. At this place in her dream she began, too, with the greatest effort, to think again. "If he loves something and receives and enjoys it," she said to herself, "then he is no longer he, but his love is my love!" She doubtless sensed that this sentence, the way she had uttered it, was somehow distorted and emasculated, but still she understood it through and through, and it took on a significance that clarified everything. "In the dream," she explained it to herself, "one must not think about things, then everything will happen!" For everything she was thinking she believed to see transpiring, or rather, what happened and partook of the desire of matter also partook of the desire of the spirit, which penetrated it as thought in the profoundest possible way. This seemed to her to give her a great superiority over Ulrich; for while he was now standing there helplessly, without stirring, not only did the same splendor as before rise into her eyes and fill them, but its moist fire suddenly broke out from her breasts and veiled everything that faced her in an indescribable sensation. Her brother was now seized by this fire and began to burn in it, without the fire growing more or less. "Now you see!" Agathe thought. "We've always done it wrong! One always builds a bridge of hard material and always crosses over to the other at a single place: but one must cross the abyss at every place!" She had seized her brother by the hands and tried to draw him to her; but as she pulled, the burning naked male body, without really being changed, dissolved into a bush or a wall of glorious flowers and, in this form, came loosely closer. All intentions and thoughts vanished in Agathe; she lay fainting with desire in her bed, and as the wall strode through her she also believed that she had to wander through large brooks of soft-skinned flowers, and she walked without being able to make the spell vanish. "I am in love!" she thought, as someone finds a moment when he is able to draw breath, for she could hardly still bear this incredible excitement that did not want to end. Since the last transformation she also no longer saw her brother, but he had not disappeared.

And looking for him, she woke up; but she felt that she wanted to go back once more, for her happiness had attained such an intensification that it went on increasing. She was quite confused as she got out of bed: the beginnings of wakefulness were in her mind, and all the rest of her body held the not-yet-ended dream that apparently wanted to have no end.

. . .

Since the dream, there had been in Agathe an intention to lead her brother astray on some mad experiment. It was not clear even to herself. Sometimes the air was like a net in which something invisible had got caught. It spread the web apart but was not able to break through it. All impressions had somewhat too great a weight. When they greeted each other in the morning, the first impression was of a quite sharply sensual delimitation. They emerged from the ocean of sleep onto the islands of "you" and "I." The body's color and shape drifted like a bouquet of flowers on the depths of space. Their glances, their movements, seemed to reach farther than usual; the inhibition that otherwise catches and stops them in the secret mechanism of the world must have grown weaker. But words were often suppressed by the fear that they would be too weak to utter this.

In order to understand such a passion, one must remember the habits of consciousness. Not long ago, for example, a woman wearing glasses not only was considered ridiculous, but really looked it; today is a time in which they make her look enterprising and young: those are habitual attitudes of consciousness; they change but are always present in some connection, forming a scaffolding through which perception enters into consciousness. The image is always present before its component parts are, and is what first gives significance to the meaningless daubings of sense impressions. Polonius's cloud, which appears sometimes as a ship, sometimes as a camel, is not the weakness of a servile courtier but completely characterizes the way God has created us. The play between self and external world is not like the die and the stamping but is reciprocal and capable of extremely fine motions, to the extent that it is freed from the cruder mechanisms of utility. One rarely imagines how far this extends. In truth it reaches from beautiful, ugly, good, and evil, where it still seems natural to everyone that one man's morning cloud should be another man's camel, through bitter and sweet, fragrant and stinking, as far as the apparently most precise and least subjective impressions of colors and forms. Herein lies perhaps the deepest sense of the support that one person seeks in another; but Ulrich and Agathe were like two people who, hand in hand, had stepped out of this circle. What they felt for each other was by no means simply to be called love. Something lay in their relationship to each other that could not be included among the ordinary notions of living together; they had undertaken to live like brother and sister, if one takes this expression in the sense not of an official marriage-bureau document but of a poem; they were neither brother and sister nor man and wife, their desires like white mist in which a fire burns. But that sufficed at times to remove their hold on the world from what they were for each other. The result was that what they were became senselessly strong. Such moments contained a tenderness without goals or limits. And also without names or aid. To do something for someone's sake contains in the doing a thousand connections to the world; to give someone pleasure contains in the giving all considerations that bind us to other people. A passion, on the other hand, is an emotion that, free from all contaminants, can never do enough for itself. It is simultanously the emotion of a powerlessness in the person and that of a movement proceeding from it, which seizes the entire world.

And it is not to be denied that in the company of her brother Agathe tasted the bitter sweetness of a passion. Today one often confuses passion and vice. Cigarette smoking, cocaine, and the vigorously esteemed recurrent need for coitus are, God knows, no passions. Agathe knew that; she knew the substitutes for passion, and recognized passion at the first moment in that not only the self burns, but the world as well; it is as if all things were behind the air just above the tip of a flame. She would have liked to thank the Creator on her knees that she was experiencing it again, although it is just as much a feeling of devastation as of happiness. Agathe felt, too, that this life is like a ship gliding along in infinite seclusion. The sounds on the shore become ever weaker, and objects lose their voice: they no longer say, now you should do this or that with me; movement dies away; the nimble words die away. At times in the mornings there already lay, between the house they were living in and the street, a nothingness that neither Ulrich nor Agathe could penetrate; life's charms lost their power to evoke the ridiculous little decisions that are so vital: putting on a hat, inserting a key, those small touches of the rudder by means of which one moves forward. But the space in the rooms was as if polished, and everything was full of a soft music, which ceased only when one strained to hear it more clearly. And that was why the loving anxiety was there; the silence behind the sound of a word, behind a handshake, a movement, could often suddenly detach itself for a moment from a series of others, divest itself of the chains of temporal and spatial connections and send the sound out onto an infinite deep, above which it rested motionless. Life then stood still. The eye, in sweet torment, could not withdraw itself from the image. It sank into existence as into a wall of flowers. It sank ever deeper and ever more slowly. It reached no bottom; it could not turn around! What might the clocks be doing now? Agathe thought; the idiotic little second hand she remembered, with its precise forward movement around its little circle: with what longing for salvation she now thought of it! And should a glance be absorbed in the other, how painful it was to withdraw it; as if their souls had linked together! It was very nearly comical, this silence. A heavy mountain of soulfulness. Ulrich often struggled to find a word, a jest; it would not matter in the least what one talked about, it only needed to be something indifferent and real that is domesticated in life and has a right to a home. That puts souls back into connection with reality. One can just as well start talking about the lawyer as come up with any clever observation. All it had to be was a betrayal of the moment; the word falls into the silence then, and in the next moment other corpses of words gleam around it, risen up in great crowds like dead fish when one throws poison into the water! Agathe hung on Ulrich's lips while he was searching for such a word, and when his lips could no longer find it and no longer part, she sank back exhausted into the silence that burned her too, like a pallet consisting of nothing but little tips of flame.

Whenever Ulrich resisted: —But we do have a mission, an activity in the world! Agathe answered: —Not I, and you are certainly only imagining yours. We have some idea of what we have to do: be together! What difference does it make what progress is made in the world? Ulrich disagreed, and attempted to convince her ironically of the impossibility of what it was that kept him bound in chains. —There's only one explanation for our inactivity that is to some degree satisfactory: to rest in God and be subsumed in God. You can use another word instead of God: the Primal One, Being, the Unconditional . . . there are a few dozen words, all powerless. They all oppose assurance to the terror at the sweet cessation of being human: you have arrived at the edge of something that is more than being human. Philosophical prejudices then take care of the rest. Agathe replied: —I understand nothing of philosophy. But let's just stop eating! Let's see what comes of that?

Ulrich noticed that in the bright childishness of this proposal there was a fine black line.

—What would come of that? He answered in detail: —First hunger, then exhaustion, then hunger again, raging fantasies about eating, and finally either eating or dying!

—You can't know without having tried it!

—But, Agathe! It's been tried and tested a thousand times!

—By professors! Or by bankrupt speculators. Do you know, dying must be not at all like one says. I nearly died once: it was different.

Ulrich shrugged his shoulders. He had no idea how close together in Agathe the two feelings were, to impulsively ignore all her lost years or, if that failed, to want to stop. She had never, like Ulrich, felt the need of making the world better than it is; she was happy lying around somewhere, while Ulrich was always on the go. This had been a difference between them since childhood, and it remained a difference until death. Ulrich did not so much fear death as regard it as a disgrace that is set as a final price on all striving. Agathe had always been afraid of death when she imagined it, as every young and healthy person does, in the unbearable and incomprehensible form: Now you are, but at some point you will no longer be! But at the same time she had, in her early youth, already become acquainted with the gradual process of separation that is capable of inserting itself into the tiniest span of time, that hurtlingly rapid—

in spite of all its slowness—being turned away from life and becoming tired of and indifferent to it, and striving trustingly into the approaching nothingness that sets in when the body is grievously harmed by an illness without the senses being affected. She had confidence in death. Perhaps it's not so bad, she thought. It's always, in any case, natural and pleasant to stop, in everything one does. But decay, and the rest of those horrible things: for heaven's sake, isn't one used to everything happening to one while one has nothing to do with it? You know, Ulrich—she terminated the conversation—you're like this: if you're given leaves and branches, you always sew them together into a tree; but I would like to see what would happen if we would once, for instance, sew the leaves firmly onto ourselves.

And yet Ulrich, too, felt they had nothing else to do but be together. Whenever Agathe called through the rooms: —Leave the light on!—a quick call, before Ulrich on his way out darkened the room to which Agathe wished to return once more, Ulrich thought: A request, hasty, what more? Oh, what more? No less than Buddha running to catch a tram. An impossible gait! A collapse of absurdity. But still, how lovely Agathe's voice was! What trust lay in the brief request, what happiness that one person can call out something like that to another without being misunderstood. Of course, such a moment was like a piece of earthly thread running among mysterious flowers, but it was at the same time moving, like a woolen thread that one places around one's beloved's neck when one has nothing else to give her. And when they then stepped out into the street and, walking side by side, could not see much of each other but only felt the tender force of unintended contact, they belonged together like an object that stands in an immense space.

It lies in the nature of such experiences that they urge their own telling. Within the tiniest amount of happening they contain an extreme of inner processes that needs to break a path for itself to the outside. And as in music or a poem, at a sickbed or in a church, the circle of what can be uttered in such circumstances is peculiarly circumscribed. Not, as one might believe, through solemnity or some other subjective mood, but through something that has far more the appearance of an objective thing. This can be compared with the remarkable process through which one assimilates intellectual influences in one's youth; there, too, one takes in not every truth that comes along but really only a truth that comes to meet it from one's own mind, a truth that therefore, in a certain sense, has only to be awakened, so that one already knows it in the moment one comes across it. There are at that age the truths that are destined for us and those that aren't; bits of knowledge are true today and false tomorrow, ideas light up or go out—not because we change our minds but because with our thoughts we are still connected to our life as a whole and, fed by the same invisible springs, rise and sink with them. They are true when we feel ourselves rising at the moment of thinking them, and they are false when we feel ourselves falling. There is something inexpressible in ourselves and the world that is increased or diminished in the process. In later years this changes; the disposition of the emotions becomes less flexible, and the understanding becomes that extraordinarily flexible, firm, doughty tool which we know it to be when we refuse to allow ourselves to be swayed by emotion. At this point the world has already divided itself: on the one side into the world of things and dependable sensations of them, of judgments and, as it can also be put, recognized emotions or will; on the other side into the world of subjectivity, that is of caprice, of faith, taste, intimation, prejudices, and all those uncertainties, taking an attitude in regard to which, whatever it may be, there remains a kind of private right of the individual, without any claims to public status. When that happens, individual industry may sniff out and take in everything or nothing; it rarely happens in the steeled soul that in the fire of the impression the walls, too, stretch and move.

But does this attitude really permit one to feel as secure in the world as it might lead one to think? Does not the whole solid world, with all our sensations, buildings, landscapes, deeds, drift on countless tiny clouds? Beneath every perception lies music, poem, feeling. But this feeling is tied down, made invariable, excluded, because we want to perceive things truly, that is, without emotion, in order to let them guide us, instead of our guiding them, which, as one knows, amounts to meaning that we finally, quite suddenly, have really learned to fly instead of merely dreaming about flying, as the millennia before us did. To this emotion imprisoned in objects there corresponds, on the individual side, that spirit of objectivity which has pushed all passion back into a condition where it is no longer perceptible, so that in every person there slumbers a sense of his value, his usefulness, and his significance that cannot be touched, a basic feeling of equilibrium between himself and the world. Yet this equilibrium need only be disturbed at any point, and everywhere the imprisoned little clouds escape. A little fatigue, a little poison, a little excess of excitement, and a person sees and hears things he doesn't want to believe; emotion rises, the world slides out of its middling condition into an abyss or rises up energetically, solitary, like a vision and no longer comprehensible!

Often everything that he and Agathe undertook, or what they saw and experienced, seemed to Ulrich only a simile. This tree and that smile are reality, because they have the quite specific quality of not merely being illusion; but are there not many realities? Was it not just yesterday that we were wearing wigs with long locks, possessed very imperfect machines, but wrote splendid books? And only the day before yesterday that we carried bows and arrows and put on gold hoods at festivals, over cheeks that were painted with the blue of the night sky, and orange-yellow eye sockets? Some kind of vague sympathy for these things still quivers within us today. So much was like today and so much was different, as if it was trying to be one of many hieroglyphic languages. Does not this mean that one should also not set too much store in present things? What is bad today will perhaps in part be good tomorrow, and the beautiful ugly; disregarded thoughts will have become great ideas, and dignified ideas decay to indifference. Every order is somehow absurd and like a wax figure, if one takes it too seriously; every thing is a frozen individual instance of its possibilities. But those are not doubts, rather a dynamic, elastic, undefined quality that feels itself capable of anything.

But it is a peculiarity of these experiences that they are almost always experienced only in a state of nonpossession. Thus the world changes when the impassioned person yearns for God, who does not reveal Himself, or the lover for his distant beloved, who has been snatched from him. Agathe as well as Ulrich had known these things, and to experience them reciprocally when they were together sometimes gave them real difficulty. Involuntarily they pushed the present away, by telling each other for the first time the stories of their past in which this had happened. But these stories again reinforced the miraculousness of their coming together, and ended in the half-light, in a hesitant touching of hands, silences, and the trembling of a current that flowed through their arms.

And sometimes there were violent rebellions.

. . .

Let's make an assumption—[Ulrich] said to himself, for example, in order to exclude it again later—and let's suppose that Agathe would feel loathing at the love of men. In that case, in order to please her as a man, I would have to behave like a woman. I would have to be tender toward her without desiring her. I would have to be good in the same way to all things in order not to frighten her love. I could not lift a chair unfeelingly, in order to move it to some other place in unsentient space; for I may not touch it out of some random idea; whatever I do must *be* something, and it is involved with this spiritual existence, the way an actor lends his body to an idea. Is that ridiculous? No, it's nothing other than festive. For that's the sense of sacred ceremonies, where every gesture has its significance. That is the sense of all things when they emerge again before our eyes for the first time with the morning sun. No, the object is not a means for us. It is a detail, the little nail, a smile, a curly hair of our third sister.° "I" and "you" are only objects too. But we are objects that are engaged in exchanging signals with each other; that is what gives us the miraculous: something is flowing back and forth between us, I cannot look at your eyes as if at some dead object, we are burning at both ends. But if I want to do something for your sake, the thing is not a dead object either. I love it, that means that something is happening between me and it; I don't want to exaggerate, I have no intention of maintaining that the object is alive like me (and has feeling and talks with me), but it does live with me, we always stand in some relationship to each other.

I have said we are sisters. You have nothing against my loving the world, but I must love it like a sister, not like a man or the way a man loves a woman. A little sentimentally; you and it and I give one another presents. I take nothing away from the tenderness that I present you with if I also make a present to the world; on the contrary, every prodigality increases our wealth. We know that each of us has our separate relations to one another that one could not totally reveal even if one wanted to, but these secrets do not arouse any jealousy. Jealousy assumes that one wishes to turn love into a possession. However, I can lie in the grass, pressed to the lap of earth, and you will feel the sweetness of this moment along with me. But I may not regard the earth as an artist or a researcher: then I would be making it my own, and we would form a couple that would exclude you as a third.

What, then, in everyday life really distinguishes the most primitive affect of love from mere sexual desire? Mixed in with the desire to rape is a dread, a tenderness, one might almost say something feminine mixed in with the masculine. And that's the way it is with all emotions; they are peculiarly pitted of their seeds and magnified.

°Ulrich elsewhere defines the three sisters as himself, Agathe, and the Other Condition.—TRANS.

* * *

Morality? Morality is an insult in a condition in which every movement finds its justification in contributing to the honor of that condition.

* * *

But the more vividly Ulrich imagined this assumed sisterly feeling, the more . . .

* * *

To previous page: One could variously call the cardinal sin in this paradise: having, wanting, possessing, knowing. Round about it gather the smaller sins: envying, being offended.

They all come from one's wanting to put oneself and the other in an exclusive relationship. From the self wanting to have its way like a crystal separating from a liquid. Then there is a nodal point, and nothing but nodal points collect around it.

But if we are sisters, then you will want not the man, nor any thing or thought but yours. You do not say: I say. For everything will be said by everything. You do not say: I love. For love is the beloved of all of us, and when it embraces you it smiles at me. . . .

* * *

When Agathe next entered Lindner's house, he seemed to have fled in a hurry a short time before. The inviolable order in hall and rooms had been thrown into disorder, which admittedly did not take much, for quite a few of the objects that were not in their usual places in these rooms were quite upsetting to look at anyway. Hardly had Agathe sat down to wait for Lindner when Peter came rushing through the room; he had no idea that she had come in. He seemed bent on smashing to pieces everything in his path, and his face was bloated, as if everywhere beneath the pink skin tears were hiding, preparing themselves for an eruption.

—Peter? Agathe asked in dismay. —What's the matter?

He wanted to go right by, but suddenly stopped and stuck out his tongue at her with such a comical expression of disgust that she had to laugh.

Agathe had a soft spot for Peter. She understood that it could be no fun for a young man to have Professor Lindner for a father, and when she imagined that Peter perhaps suspected her of being his father's future wife, his antagonistic attitude toward her met with her secret applause. Somehow she felt him to be a hostile ally. Perhaps only because she remembered her own youth as a pious convent-school girl. He had as yet no roots anywhere; was seeking himself, and seeking to grow up; growing up with the same pains and anomalies inside as outside. She understood that so well. What could wisdom, faith, miracles, and principles mean to a young person who is still locked up in himself and not yet opened up by life to assimilate such things! She had a strange sympathy for him; for his being undisciplined and recalcitrant, for his being young, and apparently, too, simply for the badness of his way of thinking. She would gladly have been his playmate, at least here; these surroundings gave her this childish thought, but she sadly noticed that he usually treated her like an old woman.

—Peter! Peter! What's the matter? he aped her. —He'll tell you anyhow. You soul-sister of his!

Agathe laughed even more and caught him by the hand.

—Do you like that? Peter went after her unabashedly. —Do you like me to howl? How old are you anyway? Not so much older than I am, I should think: but he treats you the way he treats the sublime Plato! He had disengaged himself and examined her, looking for an advantage.

—What has he really done to you? Agathe asked.

—What's he done? He's punished me! I'm not at all ashamed in front of you, as you see. Soon he's going to pull down my pants, and you'll be allowed to hold me!

—Peter! For shame! Agathe warned innocently. —Did he really beat you?

—Did he? Peter? Maybe you'd like that?

—Shame on you, Peter!

—Not at all! Why don't you call me Herr Peter? Anyway, what do you think: there! He stretched out his tensed leg and grasped his upper thigh, strengthened from playing soccer. —Have a look for yourself; I could murder him with one hand. He doesn't have as much strength in both legs as I have in one arm. It's not me, it's you who ought to be ashamed, instead of prattling wisdom with him! Do you want to know what he's done to me?

—No, Peter, you can't talk to me that way.

—Why not?

—Because your father's heart is in the right place. And because— But here Agathe could not find the right way to proceed; she was no good at preaching, although the youth was indeed in the wrong, and she suddenly had to laugh again. —So what did he do to you?

—He took away my allowance!

—Wait! Agathe asked. Without stopping to think, she fished out a banknote and handed it to Peter. She herself did not know why she did this; perhaps she thought the first thing to do was to get rid of Peter's anger before she could have an effect on him, perhaps it only gave her pleasure to thwart Lindner's pedagogy. And with the same suddenness she had addressed Peter with the familiar *Du*. Peter looked at her in astonishment. Behind his lovely misted eyes something quite new awoke. —The second thing he imposed on me—he continued, grinning cynically, without thanking her—is also broken: the school of silence! Do you know it? Man learns through silence to remove his speech from all inner and outer irritations and make it the handmaid of his innermost personal considerations!

—You surely said some improper things, said Agathe, falling back on the normal pronoun of address.

—This is how it was! "The first response of man to all interventions and attacks from without happens by means of the vocal cords," he quoted his father. —That's why he's ruined today and my day off from school tomorrow with room arrest, observes total silence toward me, and has forbidden me to speak a single word with anybody in the house. The third thing—he mocked—is control of the instinct for food—

—But, Peter, you must now really tell me—Agathe interrupted him, amused—what did you do to set him off?

The conversation in which he was mocking his father through his future mother had put the youth in the best of spirits. —That's not so simple, Agathe, he replied shamelessly. —There is, you ought to know, something that the old man fears the way the devil fears holy water: jokes. The tickling of jokes and humor, he says, comes from idle fantasy and malice. I always have to swallow them. That's exemplary for one's character. Because, if we look at the joke more closely—

—Enough! Agathe commanded. —What was your forbidden joke about?

—About you! said Peter, his eyes boring into hers in challenge. But at this moment he shrank back, because the doorbell rang, and both recognized from the sound of the ring that it was Professor Lindner. Before Agathe could make any reproaches, Peter pressed his fingernails with painful violence into her hand and stole out of the room.

. . .

There were also violent rebellions.

Agathe owned a piano. She was sitting at it in the twilight, playing. The uncertainty of her frame of mind played along with the notes. Ulrich came in. His voice sounded cold and mute as he greeted her. She interrupted her playing. When the words had died away, her fingers went a few steps further through the boundless land of music.

—Stay where you are! ordered Ulrich, who had stepped back, drawing a pistol from his pocket. —Nothing's going to happen to you. He spoke altogether differently, a stranger. Then he fired at the piano, shooting into the center of its long black flank. The first bullet cut through the dry, tender wood and howled across the strings. A second churned up leaping sounds. As shot followed shot, the keys began to hop. The jubilantly sharp reports of the pistol drove with increasing frenzy into a splintering, screaming, tearing, drumming, and singing uproar. When the magazine was empty, Ulrich let it drop to the carpet—he only noticed it when he futilely tried to get off two more shots. He gave the impression of a madman, pale, his hair hanging down over his forehead; a fit had seized him and carried him far away from himself. Doors slammed in the house, people were listening; slowly, in such impressions, reason again took possession of him.

Agathe had neither lifted her hand nor uttered the slightest sound to prevent the destruction of the expensive piano or flee the danger. She felt no fear, and although the beginning of her brother's outbreak could have seemed insane, this thought did not frighten her. She accepted it as a pleasant end. The strange cries of the wounded instrument aroused in her the idea that she would have to leave the earth in a swarm of fantastically fluttering birds.

Ulrich pulled himself together and asked if she was angry with him; Agathe denied it with radiant eyes. His face again assumed its usual expression. —I don't know—he said—why I did it. I couldn't resist the impulse.

Agathe reflectively tried out a few isolated strings that had survived.

—I feel like a fool . . . , Ulrich pleaded, and cautiously ran his hand through his sister's hair, as if his fingers could find refuge from themselves there. Agathe withdrew them again by the wrist and pushed them away. —What came over you? she asked.

—I have no idea, Ulrich said, making an unconscious motion with his arms as if he wanted to brush off the embrace of something tenacious and kick it away.

Agathe said: If you wished to repeat that, it would turn into a quite ordinary target practice. Suddenly she stood up and laughed. —Now you'll have to have the piano completely rebuilt. What won't that all lead to: orders, explanations, bills . . . ! For that reason alone something like this can't happen again.

—I had to do it, Ulrich explained shyly. —I would just as gladly have shot at a mirror if you'd happened to be looking in it.

—And now you're upset that one can't do such a thing twice. But it was beautiful just as it was. She pushed her arm in his and drew close to him. —The rest of the time you're never willing to do anything unless you know where it will lead!

$$* \quad * \quad *$$

On the same evening, Ulrich had to put in an appearance at a garden party. He could not very well beg off, although he would have done so had not his despair / depression impelled him to go. But he arrived late; it was near midnight. The greater part of the guests had already laid aside their masks. Among the trees of the old grounds torches flamed, rammed into the ground like burning spears or fastened with brackets to the trunks of trees. Gigantic tables had been set up, covered with white cloths. A flickering fire reddened the bark of the trees, the silently swaying canopy of leaves overhead, and the faces of countless people crowded together, which from a little distance seemed to consist only of such red and black spots. It seemed to have been the watchword among the ladies to appear in men's costumes. Ulrich recognized a Frau Maya Sommer as a soldier from the army of Maria Theresa, the painter von Hartbach as a Tyrolean with bare knees, and Frau Clara Kahn, the wife of the famous physician, in a Beardsley costume. He also discovered that even among the younger women of the upper nobility, so far as he knew them by sight, many had chosen a mannish or boyish disguise; there were jockeys and elevator boys, half-mannish Dianas, female Hamlets, and corpulent Turks. The fashion of slacks for women, advocated just recently, seemed, although no one had followed it, to have had some effect upon the imagination nonetheless; for that time, in which women belonged to the world at most from ground level to halfway up their calves, but between there and the neck only to their husbands and lovers, to be seen like that at a party where one might expect to see members of the Imperial House was something unheard of, a revolution, even if only a revolution of caprice, and the precursor of the vulgar customs that the older and stouter ladies were already privileged to predict, while the others noticed nothing but exuberance. Ulrich thought he could excuse himself from greeting the old prince, around whom as master of the house a group of people was in constant attendance, while he barely knew him; he looked for [his valet] Tzi to ask him to do something, but when he could not find him anywhere assumed that the industrious man had already gone home, and sauntered away from the center of activity to the edge of a grove of trees, from which, over an enormous grass lawn, one could catch a glimpse of the castle. This magnificent old castle had had fastened to it long rows of electric lights like footlights, which shone from under cornices or ran up pillars and liquefied, as it were, the forms of the architecture from out of the shadows, as if the stern old master who had devised them was among the guests and a little tipsy beneath a blanched paper hat. Below, one could see the servants running in and out through the dark door openings, while above, the ugly reddish-gray night sky of the city arched forward like an umbrella into the other, pure dark night sky, which one glimpsed, with its stars, whenever one lifted one's eyes. Ulrich did so, and was as if drunk from a combination of disgust and joy. As he let his glance fall, he perceived a nearby figure that had previously escaped his notice.

It was a tall woman in the costume of a Napoleonic colonel, and she was wearing a mask; by which Ulrich recognized immediately that it was Diotima. She acted as if she did not notice him, looking at the shining castle, sunk in thought. —Good evening, cousin! he addressed her. —Don't try to deny it; I recognize you unmistakably because you're the only person still wearing a mask.

—What do you mean? the mask asked.

—Very simple: You feel ashamed. Tell me why so many women showed up in trousers?

Diotima vehemently shrugged her shoulders. —The word went around beforehand. My God, I can understand it: the old ideas are already so worn out. But I really must confess to you that I'm annoyed; it was a tactless idea; you think you've stumbled into a theatrical fancy-dress ball.

—The whole thing is impossible, Ulrich said. —Such parties don't work anymore because their time is past.

—Hmph! Diotima answered perfunctorily. She found the sight of the castle romantic.

—Would the Colonel command where one might find a better opinion? Ulrich asked, with a challenging look at Diotima's body.

—Oh, my dear friend, don't call me Colonel!

There was something new in her voice. Ulrich stepped close to her. She had taken off her mask. He noticed two tears that fell slowly from her eyes. This tall, weeping officer was totally ridiculous, but also very beautiful. He seized her hands and gently asked what the matter was. Diotima could not answer; a sob she was trying to suppress stirred the bright sheen of the white riding breeches that reached far up beneath her flung-back coat. They stood thus in the half-darkness of the light sinking into the lawns. —We can't talk here, Ulrich whispered. —Come with me somewhere else. If you permit, I'll take you to my house. Diotima tried to draw her hand away from his, but when this didn't work she let it be. Ulrich felt by this gesture what he could hardly believe, that his hour with this woman had come. He grasped Diotima respectably around the waist and led her, supporting her tenderly, deeper into the shadows and then around to the exit. / A kiss right here?

Before they again emerged into the light, Diotima had of course dried her tears and mastered her excitement, at least outwardly. —You've never noticed, Ulrich—she said in a low voice—that I've loved you for a long time; like a brother. I don't have anyone I can talk to. Since there were people nearby, Ulrich only murmured: —Come, we'll talk. But in the taxi he did not say a word, and Diotima, anxiously holding her coat closed, moved away from him into the corner. She had made up her mind to confess her woes to him, and when Diotima resolved to do something it was done; although in her whole life she had never been with another man at night than Section Chief Tuzzi, she followed Ulrich because before she had run into him she had made up her mind to have a long talk with him if he was there, and felt / had a great, melancholy longing for such a talk. The excitement of carrying out this firm resolve had an unfortunate physical effect on her; it was literally true that her resolve lay in her stomach like some indigestible food, and when (in addition) the excitement suppressed all the juices that could dissolve it, Diotima felt cold sweat on her forehead and neck as if from nausea. She was diverted from herself only by the impression that arriving at Ulrich's made on her; the small grounds, where the electric bulbs on the tree trunks formed an alley, seemed to her charming as they strolled through; the entry hall with the antlers and the small baroque staircase reminded her of hunting horns, packs of hounds, and horsemen, and— since nighttime reinforces such impressions and conceals their weaknesses—out of admiration for her cousin she could not understand why he had never showed off this house but had, as it always seemed, only made fun of it.

Ulrich laughed, and got something warm to drink. —Looked at more closely, it's a stupid frivolity—he said—but let's not talk about me. Tell me what's been happening to you. Diotima could not utter a word; this had never happened to her before; she sat in her uniform and felt illuminated by the many lights that Ulrich had turned on. It confused her.

—So Arnheim has acted badly? Ulrich tried to help.

Diotima nodded. Then she began. Arnheim was free to do as he pleased. Nothing had ever happened between her and him that would, in the ordinary sense, have imposed any obligations on him or given him any privileges.

—But if I've observed rightly, the situation between you had already gone so far that you were to get a divorce and marry him? Ulrich interjected.

—Oh, marry? the Colonel said. —We might perhaps have got married, if he had behaved himself better; that can come like a ring that one finally slips on loosely, but it ought not to be a band that binds!

—But what did Arnheim do? Do you mean his escapade with Leona?

—Do you know this person?

—Barely.

—Is she beautiful?

—One might call her that.

—Does she have charm? Intelligence? What sort of intelligence does she have?

—But, my dear cousin, she has no intelligence of any kind whatsoever!

Diotima crossed one leg over the other and allowed herself to be handed a cigarette; she had gathered a little courage. —Was it out of protest that you appeared at the party in this outfit? Ulrich asked. —Am I right? Nothing else would have moved you to do such a thing. A kind of Overman in you enticed you, after men failed you: I can't find the right words.

—But, my dear friend, Diotima began, and suddenly behind the smoke of the cigarette tears were again running down her face. —I was the oldest of three daughters. All my youth I had to play the mother; we had no mother; I always had to answer all the questions, know everything, watch over everything. I married Section Chief Tuzzi because he was a good deal older than I and already beginning to lose his hair. I wanted a person I could finally subject myself to, from whose hand my brow would receive grace or displeasure. I am not unfeminine. I am not so proud as you know me. I confess to you that during the early years I felt bliss in Tuzzi's arms, like a little girl that death abducts to God the father. But for . . . years I've had to despise him. He's a vulgar utilitarian. He doesn't see or understand anything about anything else. Do you know what that means!

Diotima had jumped up; her coat remained lying in the chair; her hair hung over her cheeks like a schoolgirl's; her left hand rested now in manly fashion on the pommel of her saber, now in womanly fashion went through her hair; her right arm made large oratorical flourishes; she advanced one leg or closed her legs tightly together, and the round belly in the white riding breeches had—and this lent a remarkably comic effect—not the slightest irregularity such as a man betrays. Ulrich now first noticed that Diotima was slightly drunk. In her doleful mood she had, at the party, tossed off several glasses of hard spirits one after another, and now, after Ulrich, too, had offered her alcohol, the tipsiness had been freshly touched up. But her intoxication was only great enough to erase the inhibitions and fantasies of which she normally consisted, and really only exposed something like her natural nature: not all of it, to be sure, for as soon as Diotima came to speak of Arnheim, she began to talk about her soul.

She had given her entire soul to this man. Did Ulrich believe that in such questions an Austrian has a finer sensibility, more culture?

—No.

—But perhaps he does!— Arnheim was certainly an important person. But he had failed ignominiously. Ignominiously! —I gave him everything, he exploited me, and now I'm miserable!

It was clear that the suprahuman and suggestive love play with Arnheim, rising physically to no more than a kiss but mentally to a boundless, floating duet of souls (a love play that had lasted many weeks, during which Diotima's quarrel with her husband had kept it pure), had so stirred up Diotima's natural fire that, to put it crudely, someone ought to be kicking it out from under the kettle to prevent some kind of accident of exploding nerves. This was what Diotima, consciously or not, wanted from Ulrich. She had sat down on a sofa; her sword lay across her knees, the sulfurous mist of gentle rapture over her eyes, as she said:

—Listen, Ulrich: you're the only person before whom I'm not ashamed. Because you're so bad. Because you're so much worse than I am.

Ulrich was in despair. The circumstances reminded him of the scene with Gerda that had taken place here weeks ago, like this one the result of a preceding overstimulation. But Diotima was no girl overstimulated by forbidden embraces. Her lips were large and open, her body damp and breathing like turned-up garden soil, and under the veil of desire her eyes were like two gates that opened into a dark corridor. But Ulrich was not thinking of Gerda at all; he saw Agathe before him, and wanted to scream with jealousy at the sight of this feminine inability to resist any longer, although he felt his own resistance fading from second to second. His expectation was already a mirror in which he saw the breaking of these eyes, their growing dull, as only death and love can achieve, the parting in a faint of lips between which the last breath steals away, and he could hardly still expect to feel this person sitting there before him collapsing completely and looking at him as he turned away in decay, like a Capuchin monk descending into the catacombs. Apparently his thoughts were already heading in a direction in which he hoped to find salvation, for with all his strength he was fighting his own collapse. He had clenched his fists and was drilling his eyes, from Diotima's viewpoint, into her face in a horrible way. At this moment she felt nothing but fear and approval of him. Then a distorted thought occurred to Ulrich, or he read it from the distortion of the face into which he was looking. Softly and emphatically he replied: —You have no idea how bad I am. I can't love you; I'd have to be able to beat you to love you!

Diotima gazed stupidly into his eyes. Ulrich hoped to wound her pride, her vanity, her reason; but perhaps it was only his natural feelings of animosity against her that had mounted up in him and to which he was giving expression. He went on: —For months I haven't been able to think of anything but beating you until you howl like a little child! And he suddenly seized her by the shoulders, near the neck. The imbecility of sacrifice in her face grew. Beginnings of wanting to say something still twitched in this face, to save the situation through some kind of detached comment. Beginnings of standing up twitched in her thighs, but reversed themselves before reaching their goal. Ulrich had seized her saber and half drawn it from its scabbard. —For God's sake! he felt. —If nothing intervenes I'll hit her over the head with it until she gives no more signs of her damned life! He did not notice that in the meantime a decisive change had been taking place in the Napoleonic colonel. Diotima sighed heavily as if the entire woman that she had been since her twelfth year was escaping from her bosom, and then she leaned over to the side so as to let Ulrich's desire pour itself over her in whatever way he liked.

If her face had not been there, Ulrich would at this moment have laughed out loud. But this face was indescribable the way insanity is, and just as infectious. He threw away the saber and gave her, twice, a rough smack. Diotima had expected it to be different, but the physical concussion nevertheless had its effect. Something started going the way clocks sometimes start when they are roughly treated, and in the ordinary course that events took from that point on something unusual was also mingled, a scream and rattle of the emotions.

Childish words and gestures from long ago mingled with it, and the few hours until morning were filled with a kind of dark, childish, and blissful dream state that freed Diotima from her character and brought her back to the time when one does not yet think about anything and everything is good. When day shone through the panes she was lying on her knees, her uniform was scattered over the floor, her hair had fallen over her face, and her cheeks were full of saliva. She could not recall how she had come to be in this position, and her awakening reason was horrified at her fading ecstasy. There was no sign of Ulrich.

·   ·   ·

[Valerie]

A young person tells himself: I'm in love. For the first time. He tells himself, he doesn't just do it; for there is in him still a little of the childish pride of wanting to possess the world of grownups, the whole world.

He might have previously desired and possessed beautiful women. He might also have been in love before; in various ways: impatiently, boldly, cynically, passionately; and yet the moment may still come when he tells himself for the first time: I'm in love. Ulrich had at the time immediately loosened the bonds that tied him to the woman with whom this happened, so that it was almost like a breaking up. He left from one day to the next; said, We won't write much. Then wrote letters that were like the revelation of a religion, but hesitated to mail them. The more powerfully the new experience grew in him, the less he let any of it show.

He suddenly began to recall this vividly. At that time he had been quite young, an army officer, on leave in the countryside. Perhaps that was what had brought about his shift in mood. He was spiritedly court-ing a woman, older than he, the wife of a cavalry captain, his superior; she had for a long time been favorably inclined toward him, but seemed to be avoiding an adventure with this beardless little man who confused her with his unusual philosophical and passionate speeches, which came from beyond her circle. On a stroll, he suddenly seized her hand; fate had it that the woman left her hand for a moment in his as if powerless, and the next instant a fire blazed from arms to knees and the lightning bolt of love felled both of them, so that they almost fell by the side of the path, to sit on its moss and passionately embrace.

The night that followed was sleepless. Ulrich had said good-bye in the evening and said: tomorrow we run away. Desire aroused and not yet satisfied threw the woman back and forth in her bed, dry as thirst, but at the same time she feared the stream that was to moisten her lips in the morning, because of its overflowing suddenness. The entire night she reproached herself because of the other's youth, and also on account of her husband, for she was a good wife, and in the morning wept tears of relief when she had handed to her Ulrich's letter, in which he took such an abrupt departure amid piled-up protestations.

Valerie had been the name of this good-natured woman, Ulrich remembered, and at that time, in spite of his inexperience, he must have already been clearly aware that she was only the impetus, but not the content, of his sudden experience. For during that sleepless night, shot through with passionate ideas, he had been borne farther and farther away from her, and before morning came, without his rightly knowing why, his resolve was fixed to do something the like of which he had never done before. He took nothing but a rucksack along, traveled a quite short stretch on the train, and then wandered, his first step already in unknown territory, through a completely isolated valley to a tiny shrine hidden high in the mountains, which at this season no one visited and where hardly anyone lived.

What he did there was, if one were to make a story of it to someone, absolutely nothing. It was fall, and in the mountains the early-autumn sun has a power of its own; mornings it lifted him up and bore him to some tree high up on the slopes, from beneath which one looked into the far distance, for in spite of his heavy hiking boots he was really not conscious of walking. In the same self-forgetful way he changed his location several times during the day and read a little in a few books he had with him. Nor was he really thinking, although he felt his mind more deeply agitated than usual, for his thoughts did not shake themselves up as they usually do, so that a new idea is always landing on top of the pyramid of the earlier ones while the ones at the bottom are becoming more and more compacted until finally they fuse with flesh, blood, skull case, and the tendons supporting the muscles, but his insights came like a jet into a full vessel, in endless overflowing and renewal, or they passed in an everlasting progression like clouds through the sky in which nothing changes, not the blue depths and not the soundless swimming of those mother-of-pearl fish. It could happen that an animal came out of the woods, observed Ulrich, and slowly bounded away without anything changing; that a cow grazed nearby, or a person went past, without any more happening than a beat of the pulse, twin to all the others of the stream of life that softly pounds without end against the walls of the understanding.

Ulrich had stumbled into the heart of the world. From there it was as far to his beloved as to the blade of grass beside his feet or to the distant tree on the sky-bare heights across the valley. Strange thought: space, the nibbling in little bites, distance dis-stanced, replaces the warm husk and leaves behind a cadaver; but here in the heart they were no longer themselves, everything was connected with him the way the foot is no farther from the heart than the breast is. Ulrich also no longer felt that the landscape in which he was lying was outside him; nor was it within; that had dissolved or permeated everything. The sudden idea that something might happen to him while he was lying there—a wild animal, a robber, some brute—was almost impossible of accomplishment, as far away as being frightened by one's own thoughts. / Later: Nature itself is hostile. The observer need only go into the water. / And the beloved, the person for whose sake he was experiencing all this, was no closer than some unknown traveler would have been. Sometimes his thoughts strained like eyes to imagine what they might do now, but then he gave it up again, for when he tried to approach her this way it was as if through alien territory that he imagined her in her surroundings, while he was linked to her in subterranean fashion in a quite different way.

. . .

"You're working . . . ?" She did not conceal her disappointment, for with remarkable certainty she felt it as disloyalty whenever Ulrich leafed through books in his hand and his forehead became stiff as bone.

"I have to. I can't bear the uncertainty of what we're going through. And we're not the first people it's happening to either."

"Twin siblings?"

"That's perhaps something especially elect. But I don't believe in such mysteries as being chosen—" He quickly corrected himself. "Hundreds of people have had the experience of believing that they were seeing another world open up before them. Just as we do."

"And what came of it?"

"Books."

"But it can't have been just books?"

"Madness. Superstition. Essays. Morality. And religion. The five things."

"You're in a bad mood."

"I could read to you or talk with you for hours about things from these books. What I began yesterday was an attempt to do that. You can go back as far as you like from this moment in which we're now talking, millennia or as far as human memory can reach, and you will always find described the existence of another world that at times rises up like a deep sea floor when the restless floods of our ordinary life have receded from it.

"Since we've been together I've been comparing as much of this as I could get hold of. All the descriptions state, in odd agreement, that in that condition there is in the world neither measure nor precision, which have made our world of the intellect great, neither purpose nor cause, neither good nor bad, no limit, no greed, and no desire to kill, but only an incomparable excitement and an altered thinking and willing. For as objects and our emotions lose all the limitations that we otherwise impose on them, they flow together in a mysterious swelling and ebbing, a happiness that fills everything, an agitation that is in the true sense boundless, one and multiple in shape as in a dream. One might perhaps add that the ordinary world, with its apparently so real people and things that lord it over everything like fortresses on cliffs, if one looks back at it, together with all its evil and impoverished relationships, appears only as the consequence of a moral error from which we have already withdrawn our organs of sense.

"That describes exactly as much as we ourselves experienced when we looked into each other's eyes for the first time.

"The condition in which one perceives this has been given many names: the condition of love, goodness, turning away from the world, contemplation, seeing, moving away, returning home, willlessness, intuition, union with God, all names that express a vague harmony and characterize an experience that has been described with as much passion as vagueness. Insane peasant women have come to know it, and dogmatic professors of theology; Catholics, Jews, and atheists, people of our time and people of tens of thousands of years ago; and as amazingly similar as the ways are in which they have described it, these descriptions have remained remarkably undeveloped; the greatest intellect has not told us any more about it than the smallest, and it appears that you and I will not learn any more from the experience of millennia than we know by ourselves.

"What does this mean?"

Agathe looked at him questioningly. "Lindner," she said, "when I once asked him about the significance of such experiences—and by the way, he dismisses them—maintains that they go back to the difference between faith and knowledge, and that for the rest, they're neurotic exaggerations—"

"Very good," Ulrich interrupted her. "If you had reminded me of that yesterday, it might perhaps have spared my despair at my lack of results. But we'll come back to Lindner later! Of course that's fibbing; if I believe something, I at least want to have the hope that under favorable circumstances I could also experience it, but not keep stopping after the same first steps all the time.

"No, Agathe, it means something quite different. What would you say if I maintain that it signifies nothing other than the lost paradise. It is a message. A message in a bottle that has been drifting for thousands of years. Paradise is perhaps no fairy tale; it really exists."

Up till then he had spoken with such rational decisiveness that these words had a quite remarkable sound. If he had said: I've done some reconnoitering, come along, we have to go out by the window and then through a dark corridor, and so on, then we'll get there . . . it would not have seemed strange to Agathe to set off immediately.

He really ought to explain it twice: once with yearning, then the way one explains it as prelogical, etc.

But Ulrich merely went on reporting the results of his inquiries.

"From what I've found," he said with the same calm as before, "two things emerge. First, that paradise has been placed where it is unattainable. Even in the first legendary beginnings of the human race it is supposed to have been lost, and what people claim to have experienced of it later is described as ecstasy, trance, madness: in short, as pathological delirium; but it is quite striking that something is simultaneously being denied as illness and considered a paradise: this leads me to suppose that it must also be attainable for healthy and rational people, but on a path that is presumed to be forbidden and dangerous.

"But that then leads me to understand the second point, that this condition of paradise in life, which is supposed to be taboo as a whole, breaks into pieces and is inextricably mingled in with common life, that is, what people consider the highest values.

"In other words: the ideals of humanity. Think about it: they are all unattainable. But not only, as people pretend, because of human frailty but because, were one to fulfill them absolutely, they would become absurd. They are, therefore, the remains of a condition which as a whole is not capable of life, of which our life is not capable.

"One might be tempted to see in this shadowy doppelgänger of another world only a daydream, had it not left behind its still warm traces in countless details of our lives. Religion, art, love, morality . . . these are attempts to follow this other spirit, they project into our lives with enormous power, but they have lost their origin and meaning, and this has made them totally confused and corrupt."

They are bays but not the ocean.

. . .

"And that brings us to Lindner.

"He would go mad if he were to follow the emotions that he has declared to be the decisive ones in his life. That's why he rations them and dilutes them with convictions.

"You want to be good—like a lake without a shore—and its individual drops, which he carefully stores up in himself, are what draw you to him.

"You therefore only have some inkling, and he is convinced (believes) that you feel something is good, feel it like the smell of a field; while he makes a firm distinction between good and evil, but by separating them he mixes them together hopelessly.

"That makes you feel abandoned, even by yourself, because you have an intimation of a togetherness as never before. Your experience is hard to communicate, private, almost unsocial. He ties his soul to experiences that can be repeated and understood, for the unequivocal is repeatable and therefore comprehensible, but the mutuality of the ideals he disseminates is like the shadowy realm that is neither life nor death. He knows the virtue of limitation, you the sin of limitation. You are deprived of power, he is active. His God is nothing but an initial association or the like.

"In a word: You would like to live *in* God, even if only as His worst creature, while he lives *for* Him. But in doing so he is following the same tried-and-true course as everyone else."

. . .

Agathe had found a hairpin. In the period following Bonadea's visit, which Ulrich had not told her about. She was sitting on the sofa and talking with her brother, her hands, full of idle security, supported in the pillows on both sides, when she suddenly felt the small steel object between her fingers. It quite confused her hands before she drew it out. She looked at the pin, which was that of a strange woman, and the blood rose to her cheeks.

It might have been a small occasion for laughter that Agathe, like any jealous woman, hit upon the truth with such uncanny accuracy. But although it would have been easy to explain the discovery in some other fashion, Ulrich made no attempt to do so. Blood had risen to his cheeks too.

Finally, Agathe regained her composure, but her smile was disconcerted.

Ulrich mumbled a confession about Bonadea's assault.

She listened to him restlessly. —I'm not jealous, she said. —I have no right to be. But —

She sought to find this "but"; the demonstration was meant to cover the wildness that rose up in her against another woman taking Ulrich away from her.

Women are peculiarly naïve when they talk about a man's "needs." They have let themselves be persuaded that these needs are inexorable violent forces, a kind of sullied but still grandiose suffering on the part of men, and they seem to know neither that they themselves become just as crazy through long abstinence, nor that after a period of transition it is not much more difficult for men to accustom themselves to it than it is for them; the distinction is, in truth, more a moral than a physiological one, a distinction of the habit of granting or denying oneself one's desires. But for many women, who believe they have grounds for not letting their desires gain control over them, this idea, that the man is not allowed to control himself without doing harm to himself, serves as a welcome opportunity to enclose the suffering man-child in their arms, and Agathe too—put in the role of a rather frigid woman through the taboo against otherwise following toward her brother the unambiguous voice of her heart—unconsciously applied this stratagem in her mind.

—I believe I do understand you—she said—but—but you have hurt me.

When Ulrich tried to ask her pardon and attempted to stroke her hair or her shoulders, she said: —I'm stupid—trembled a little, and moved away.

—If you were reading a poem aloud to me—she tried to explain—and I wasn't able to keep from looking at the latest newspaper the while, you would be disappointed too. That's just the way it hurt. On your account.

Ulrich was silent. The vexation of again experiencing through explanations what had happened sealed his lips.

—Of course I have no right to set rules for you, Agathe repeated. —What is it then that I do give you! But why are you throwing yourself away on such a person! I could imagine your loving a woman I admire. I don't know how to express it, but isn't every caress a person gives someone somehow taken away from everyone else?

She felt that she would want it that way if she were to abandon this dream and have a husband again.

—Inwardly, more than two people can embrace, and everything external is only— She stopped short, but suddenly the comparison occurred to her: —I could imagine that the person who embraces the body is only the butterfly uniting two flowers—

The comparison seemed to her somewhat too poetic. While she voiced it, she felt vividly the warm and ordinary feeling women have: I must give him something and compensate him.

Ulrich shook his head. "I have," he said seriously, "committed a grave error. But it was not the way you think. What you say is beautiful. This bliss that arises from the skin through mechanical stimulation, this sudden being seized and changed by God: to ascribe this to a person who is just the instrument, to give him a privileged place through adoration or hate, is basically as primitive as being angry at the bullet that hits you. But I have too little faith to imagine that one could find such people." Holds her hand—it is a mood borne far away.

When his hand sought pardon on her, Agathe enclosed her brother in her arms and kissed him. And involuntarily, shaken, in a sisterly-comforting way and then no longer able to control it, she opened her lips for the first time on his with that complete, undiminished womanliness that opens up the ripe fruit of love to its core.

· · ·

In the Parallel Campaign everyone declared themselves for Arnheim. Clarisse preferred Meingast.

Ulrich came home embittered. Faced with that powerlessness that *cannot find a single point from which to express its opposition* to the perfecting of an inadequate world.

He felt: They're doing everything I want, it's just that they're doing it badly.

They don't even understand me enough to contradict me; they believe that I'm saying what they're saying, only worse.

Whenever you talk with them you start vomiting from nervousness.

They have goodness, love, soul; chopped into little pieces and mixed in with large chunks of the opposite; this keeps them healthy and makes them idealists, while I end up on the margin of the absurd and the criminal.

Oh, how unbearable they are, these chatterers at Diotima's! But it would be just as nonsensical not to confess *that there are many people who feel it as much as I do and who accomplish better things: Why do I feel so excluded?*

He went through Agathe's room and straight to his study. His face mirrored the strain and silence of a hard struggle.

Believers squabble with God when they get to feel isolated among their fellowmen; *that's when unbelievers get to know Him for the first time*. If it were possible *to run out into the empty, chilly universe*, that would have been the right expression for Ulrich's despair, anger, and unquiet temperament. His flames had inverted themselves and were burning inwardly. It nearly made him suffocate.

Suddenly he stopped. He took paper and pencil, which were lying under the heap of scribbled papers on his desk, and wrote down an idea. Read it through, walked up and down, read it once more, and added something to it.

There is no necessity behind it! This was the first idea, which, still obscure, contained everything. *This world is only one of countless possible experiments?*

Then: In mathematics there are problems that admit of no general solutions but only case-by-case ones. But under certain given conditions these partial solutions are summarized to give relative total solutions. Thus God gives partial solutions; these are the creative people; they contradict one another; *we are condemned again and again to derive from this relative total solutions that don't correspond to anything!*

Finally: *Like molten ore I am poured into the mold* that the world has shaped during my lifetime. For that reason I am never entirely what I think and do. For that reason this self always remains strange to me. *One attempted form in an attempted form of the totality.*

Acting without reflecting: for a man never gets further than when he doesn't know where he's going.

When he read over this last idea, he tore up the piece of paper and went in to Agathe; for then there is only one thing: not to listen to the bad masters, who have erected one of His possible lives as if for eternity, according to God's plan, but to confide oneself to Him humbly and defiantly.

ULRICH-AGATHE JOURNEY

1.

Below lay a narrow stretch of coast with some sand. Boats drawn up on it, seen from above, like blue and green spots of sealing wax. If one looked more closely, oil jugs, nets, men with vertically-striped pants and brown legs; the smell of fish and garlic; patched-up, shaky little houses. The activity on the warm sand was as small and far away as the bustling of beetles. It was framed on both sides by boulders as by stone pegs on which the bay hung, and farther along, as far as the eye could see, the steep coast with its crinkled details simply plunged into the southern sea. If one cautiously clambered down, one could, over the ruins of fallen rocks, venture out a little into the ocean, which filled tubs and troughs among the stones with a warm bath and strange animal comrades.

Ulrich and Agathe felt as if a tremendous din had been raised from them and had flown off. They stood out there in the ocean, swaying white flames, almost sucked up and extinguished by the hot air. It was somewhere in Istria, or the eastern edge of Italy, or on the Tyrrhenian Sea. They hardly knew themselves. They had got on the train and traveled; it seemed to them as if they had been crisscrossing at random / in a way . . . that would prevent them from ever finding their way back.

2.

On their mad journey, Ancona was firmly fixed in their memory. They had arrived dead tired and in need of sleep. They got in early in the forenoon and asked for a room. Ate zabaglione in bed and drank strong coffee, whose heaviness was as if lifted to the skies by the foam of whipped cream. Rested, dreamed. When they had gone to sleep it seemed to them that the white curtains in front of the windows were constantly lifting and sinking in an enchanting current of refreshing air; it was their breathing. When they awoke, they saw through the opening slats ore-blue sea, and the red and yellow sails of the barks entering and leaving the harbor were as shrill as floating whistles.

They understood nothing in this new world; it was all like the words of a poem.

They had left without passports and had a mild fear of some sort of discovery and punishment. When they registered at the hotel they had been taken for a young married couple and offered this lovely room with a wide bed meant for two, a *letto matrimoniale,* which in Germany has fallen into disuse. They had not dared reject it. After the sufferings of the body, the longing for primitive happiness.

Lying in this bed, they noticed an oval window the size of a cabin porthole, high up to the right of the door and near a corner of the room, in a totally incomprehensible place; it had opaque-colored glass, disquietingly like a secret observation post, but surrounded by a casual wreath of painted roses.

In comparison with the enormous tension that had gone before, it was nothing. And afterward there was a conspiratorial happiness in every detail, and at the moment when their resistance wavered and melted Ulrich said: It also makes most sense not to resist; we have to get this behind us so that this tension doesn't debase what we have before us.

And they traveled.

They had stayed three days.

It has to be this way too: charmed by each other again and again. Traversing the scale of the sexual with variations.

For three days they never talked about soul. Only then did they bring it up again.

3.

When they went out on the street for the first time: buzzing of people. Like a flock of sparrows happily dusting themselves in the sand. Curious glances without timidity, which felt themselves at home. At the backs of the brother and sister as they cautiously glided through this crowd lay the room, lay the wakefulness drifting deep over sleep like a cat's paw over water, the blissful exhaustion in which one can ward off nothing, and also not oneself, but hears the world as a pale noise outside the infinitely deep corridors of the ear.

The exhaustion of excessive enjoyment in the body, the consumed marrow. It is shaming and joyful.

4.

They went on. Apparently suitcase nomads. In truth driven by the restlessness of finding a place worth living and dying in.

Much was beautiful and held them enticingly fast. But nowhere did the inner voice say: this is the place.

Finally here. Actually some insignificant chance had brought them here, and they did not notice anything special. Then this voice made itself heard, softly but distinctly.

Perhaps, without knowing it, they had become tired of their random traveling.

5.

Here, where they stayed, a piece of gardenlike nature rose up to the small white hotel, empty at this season, which was concealed on the slope; rose from the narrow beach between the rocky arms of the coast, like a posy of flowers and shrubs pressed against the breast, with narrow paths winding around it in a very gentle, slow climb up to the hotel. A little higher there was nothing but dazzling stone glittering in the sun, between one's feet yellow broom and red thistles that ran from the feet toward the sky, the enormous hard straightness of the plateau's edge, and, if one had climbed up with eyes closed and now opened them: suddenly, like a thunderously opened fan, the motionless sea.

It is probably the size of the arc in the line of the contour, this far-reaching security enclosed by an arm, a security that is more than human? Or only the enormous desert of the dark-blue color, hostile to life? Or that the bowl of the sky never lies so directly over life? Or air and water, of which one never thinks? Otherwise colorless, good-natured messengers, but here where they were at home suddenly rearing up unapproachably like a pair of royal parents.

The legends of almost all peoples report that mankind came from the water and that the soul is a breath of air. Strange: science has determined that the human body consists almost entirely of water. One becomes small. When they got off the train in which they had crisscrossed the dense network of European energies and, still trembling from the motion, had hastened up here, brother and sister stood before the calm of the sea and the sky no differently than they would have stood a hundred thousand years ago. Tears came to Agathe's eyes, and Ulrich lowered his head.

What is this whole exposition for? Can it be retracted? Something's not right here.

.   .   .

Arm on arm, their hands intertwined, they climbed down again in the blue of evening to their new home. In the small dining room the whiteness of the tablecloths sparkled and the glasses stood as soft splendor. Ulrich ordered fish, wine, and fruit, speaking at length and in detail about it with the maître d'hôtel; it did not interfere. The black figures glided around them or stood against the walls. Silverware and teeth functioned. The pair even carried on a conversation so as not to attract notice. Ulrich almost came to speak of the impression they had had up above. As if the people of a hundred thousand years ago had really had a direct revelation: it was like that; if one considers how tremendous the experience of these first myths is, and how little since . . .; it did not interfere; everything that happened was embedded as in the murmuring of a fountain.

Ulrich looked at his sister for a long time; she was now not even beautiful; there was not that either. On an island they had not seen in the daylight a chain of houses shone: that was lovely but far away; the eyes looked at it only fleetingly and then directly in front of themselves again.

They asked for two rooms.

6.

The sea in summer and the high mountains in autumn are the two real tests of the soul. In their silence lies a music greater than anything else on earth; there is a blissful torture in the inability to follow their rhythms, to make the rhythm of word and gesture so broad that it would join with theirs; mankind cannot keep in step with the breath of the gods.

The next morning, Ulrich and Agathe found a tiny pocket of sand up among the rocks beneath the edge of the plateau; when they stumbled onto it they had the feeling as if a creature that lived there had expected them and was looking at them: here no one knows anything about us anymore. They had been following a small, natural path; the coast curved away, they actually convinced themselves that the shining white hotel had disappeared. It was a long, narrow sunlit step of rock, with sand and bits and pieces of stone. They undressed. They felt the need to bend their knees and stretch their arms, naked, unprotected, small as children before the greatness of the sea and the solitude. They did not say this to each other, and were ashamed before each other, but hidden behind the motions of their clothing and of searching for a place to lie down, each tried it for himself.

They were both ashamed because it is so nudist-camp natural and health-conscious, but expected it necessarily had to lead to something else . . .

The silence nailed them to the cross.

They felt that soon they would not be able to stand it anymore, would have to shout, insane as birds.

This was why they were suddenly standing beside each other, with their arms around each other. Skin stuck to skin; timidly this small feeling penetrated the great desert like a tiny succulent flower growing all alone among the stones, and calmed them. They wove the circle of the horizon like a wreath around their hips, and looked at the sky. Stood as on a high balcony, interwoven with each other and with the unutterable like two lovers who, the next instant, will plunge into the emptiness. Plunged. And the emptiness supported them. The instant lasted; did not sink and did not rise. Agathe and Ulrich felt a happiness about which they did not know if it might be grief, and only the conviction inspiring them, that they had been chosen to experience the extraordinary, kept them from weeping.

7.

But they soon discovered . . . if they did not want to, they did not have to leave the hotel at all. A wide glass door led from their room to a small balcony overlooking the sea. Unobserved, they could stand in the doorway, their eyes directed at this never-answering expanse, their arms flung protectively around each other. Blue coolness, on which the living warmth of the day lay like fine gold dust even after midnight, penetrated from the ocean. While their souls were standing erect within them, their bodies found each other like animals seeking warmth. And then the miracle happened to these bodies. Ulrich was suddenly part of Agathe, or she of him.

Agathe looked up, frightened. She looked for Ulrich out there, but found him in the center of her heart. She did see his form leaning out in the night, wrapped in starlight, but it was not his form, only its shining, ephemeral husk; and she saw the stars and the shadows without understanding that they were far away. Her body was light and fleet, it seemed to her that she was floating in the air. A great, miraculous impetus had seized her heart, with such rapidity that she almost thought she felt the gentle jolt. At this moment brother and sister looked at each other confounded.

However much they had been preparing themselves for this every day for weeks, they feared that in this second they had lost their reason. But everything in them was clear. Not a vision. Rather an excessive clarity. And yet they still seemed to have lost and put aside not only their reason but all their capacities; no thoughts stirred in them, they could form no purpose, all words had receded far away, the will lifeless; everything that stirs in the individual was rolled up inertly, like leaves in a burning calm. But this deathlike impotence did not weigh them down; it was as if the lid of a sarcophagus had been rolled off them. Whatever was to be heard during the night sobbed without sound or measure, whatever they looked at was without form or mood and yet contained within itself the joyous delight of all forms and moods. It was really strangely simple: as their powers became circumscribed all boundaries had disappeared, and since they no longer felt any kind of distinctions, neither in themselves nor about objects, they had become one.

They gazed around cautiously. It was almost painful. They were quite confused, far away from themselves, set down in a distance in which they lost themselves. They saw without light and heard without sound. Their soul was as excessively stretched as a hand that loses all its power, their tongue was as if cut off. But this pain was as sweet as a strange, living clarity.

?It was like a pain grating on their sensibilities, and yet could be called more a sweetness than a pain, for there was no vexation in it but a peculiar, quite supranatural comfort.

And they further perceived that the circumscribing powers in them were not lost at all, but in reality inverted, and with them all boundaries had been inverted. They noticed that they had not become mute at all but were speaking, but they were not choosing words but were being chosen by words; no thought stirred in them, but the whole world was full of marvelous thoughts; they thought that they, and things as well, were no longer mutually displacing and repelling hermetic bodies, but opened and allied forms. Their glances, which in their whole lives had followed only the small patterns that objects and people form against the enormous background, had suddenly reversed, and the enormous background played with the patterns of life like an ocean with tiny matches.

Agathe lay half fainting against Ulrich's chest. She felt at this moment embraced by her brother in such a distant, silent, and pure fashion that there was nothing at all like it. Their bodies did not move and were not altered, and yet a sensual happiness flowed through them, the like of which they had never experienced. It was not an idea and not imagined! Wherever they touched each other, whether on their hips, their hands, or a strand of hair, they interpenetrated one another.

They were both convinced at this moment that they were no longer subject to the distinctions of humankind. They had overcome the stage of desire, which expends its energy on an action and a brief intensification, and their fulfillment impinged on them not only in specific places but in all the places of their bodies, as fire does not become less when other fires kindle from it. They were submerged in this fire that fills up everything; swimming in it as in a sea of desire, and flying in it as in a heaven of rapture.

Agathe wept with happiness. Whenever they moved, the recollection that they were still two dropped like a grain of incense into the sweet fire of life and dissolved in it; these were perhaps the happiest moments, where they were not entirely one.

Originally also supposed to come here: . . . I'm in love and don't know with whom . . . I'm neither faithful, nor unfaithful, what am I then.

For they felt, hovering more strongly over this hour than over others a breath of grief and transitoriness, something shadowy and unreal, a being robbed, a cruelty, a fearful tension of uncertain forces against the fear of being transformed once more. Finally, when they felt the condition fade, they separated wordlessly and in utter exhaustion.

The next morning, Ulrich and Agathe had separated without having made plans, and did not see each other the entire day; they could not do otherwise; the emotions of the night were still ebbing away and taking them with them; both felt the need to come to terms with themselves alone, without noticing that this entailed a contradiction of the experience that had overpowered them. Involuntarily they went off far across the countryside in opposite directions, stopped in places at different times, sought a resting place in view of the sea, and thought of each other.

It may be called strange that their love immediately involved the need for separation, but this love was so great that they mistrusted it and desired this test.

Can they still separate? How can it be done?

Now one can dream. Lie under a bush and the bees buzz; or stare into the weaving heat, the thin air. The senses doze off, and in the body memories shine forth again like the stars after sunset. The body is again touched and kissed, and the magic line of demarcation that otherwise still distinguishes the strongest memories from reality is transcended by these soft / dreaming memories. They push time and space aside like a curtain and unite the lovers not only in thought but physically, not with their heavy bodies but with inwardly altered ones consisting entirely of tender mobility. But only when one thinks that during this union, which is more perfect and blissful than bodily union, one has no idea what the other person has just been doing, or what he will be doing the next moment, does the mystery attain its greatest depth. Ulrich assumed that Agathe had remained behind in the hotel. He saw her standing on the white square in front of the white building, speaking with the manager. It was false. Or perhaps she was standing with the young German professor who had arrived and introduced himself, or was talking with Luisina, the chambermaid with the lovely eyes, and laughing at her pert, funny answers. That Agathe was now able to laugh! It destroyed the Condition; a smile was just heavy enough to be borne by it . . . !! When Ulrich turned around, Agathe was suddenly really standing there. Really? She had come across the stones in a great arc; her dress was fluttering in the wind, she cast a dark shadow on the hot ground and was laughing at Ulrich. Blissfully real reality; it hurt as much as when eyes that have been staring into the distance must quickly adapt to nearness.

Agathe sat down beside him. A lizard sat nearby; it silently darted out its tongue, a small, scurrying flame of life, beside their conversation. Ulrich had noticed it some time before. Agathe hadn't. But when Agathe, who was afraid of small animals, caught sight of it, she was frightened and, laughing in embarrassment, scared the little creature away with a stone. And to gather courage she ran after it, clapping her hands and chasing the little beast.

Ulrich, who had been staring at the small creature as at a flickering magic mirror, said to himself: That we were now so different is as sad as that we were born at the same time but will die at different times. With his eyes and ears he followed this strange body, Agathe. But then he suddenly fell deeply once again into and was at the bottom of the experience out of which Agathe had startled him.

He was not able to pin it down clearly, but in this flickering brightness above the stones in which everything was transformed, happiness into grief, and also grief into happiness, the painful moment abruptly took on the secret lust of the hermaphrodite who, separated into two independent beings, finds itself again, whose secret no one who touches it suspects. Yet how glorious it is—Agathe's brother thought—that she is different from me, that she can do things I can't even guess at, which yet also belong to me through our secret empathy. Dreams occurred to him, which he otherwise never recalled but which must have often preoccupied him. Sometimes in a dream he had met the sister of a beloved, although she did not have a sister, and this strange familiar person radiated all the happiness of possession and all the happiness of desire. Or he heard a soft voice speaking. Or saw only the fluttering of a skirt, which most definitely belonged to a stranger, but this stranger was most definitely his beloved. As if a disembodied, completely free attachment was only playing with these people. All at once Ulrich was startled, and thought he saw in the great brightness that the secret of love was precisely this, that lovers are not one.

That belongs to the principles of profane love! Thus really already a game against itself.

"How wonderful it is, Agathe," Ulrich said, "that you can do things I can't guess at."

"Yes," she answered, "the whole world is full of such things. As I was walking across this plateau I felt that I could now walk in every direction."

"But why did you come to me?"

Agathe was silent.

"It is so beautiful to be different from the way one was born," Ulrich continued. "But I was afraid of just that." He told her the dreams that he had remembered, and she knew them too.

"But why are you afraid?" Agathe asked.

"Because it occurred to me that if it is the sense of these dreams—and it might well be that they signify the final memory of it—that our desires aim not at making one person out of two but, on the contrary, at escaping from our prison, our oneness, to become two in a union, but preferably twelve, a thousand, incredibly many, rather, to slip out of ourselves as in a dream, to drink life brewed to the boiling point, to be carried out of ourselves or whatever, for I can't express it very well; then the world contains as much lust as strangeness, as much tenderness as activity, and is not an opium haze but rather an intoxication of the blood, an orgasm of battle, and the only mistake we could make would be to forget the (lustful contact of) lust of strangeness and imagine doing all sorts of things by dividing up the hurricane of love into scanty creeks flowing back and forth between two people—"

He had jumped up.

"But how would one have to be?" Agathe asked pensively and simply. It pained him that she could immediately appropriate his half-loved and half-cursed idea. "One would have to be able to give," she went on, "without taking away. To be such that love does not become less when it's divided. Then that would be possible too.

Not to treat love as a treasure"—she laughed—"the way it's already laid down in language!"

Ulrich was picking up head-sized stones and flinging them from the cliff into the sea, which squirted up a tiny spray; he had not exercised his muscles for a long time.

"But . . . ?" Agathe said. "Isn't what you're saying simply what one reads fairly often, drinking the world in great drafts of desire? To want to be a thousandfold, because once isn't enough?" She was parodying it a little because she suddenly realized that she did not like it.

"No!" Ulrich shouted back. "It's never what others say!" He flung the large stone he was holding in his hand so angrily to the ground that the loose limestone exploded. "We forgot ourselves," he said gently, grasping Agathe under the arm and pulling her away. "It would still have to be a sister and a brother, even if they're divided into a thousand pieces. —Anyway, it's just an idea."

Meanwhile days came when only the surface stirred. On the sparkling damp stones in the sea. A silent being: a fish, flowerlike in the water. Agathe romped after it from stone to stone until it dived under, darting into the darkness like an arrow, and disappeared. Well? Ulrich thought. Agathe was standing out on the rocks, he on the shore; a melody of eventfulness broke off, and a new one must carry on: How will she turn around, how smile back to the shore? Beautifully. Like all perfection. With total charm in her motion is how Agathe did it; the insights of the orchestra of her beauty, though it seemed to be making music without a conductor, were always delightful.

And yet all perfected beauty—an animal, a painting, a woman—is nothing more than the final piece in a circle; an arc is completed, one sees it but would like to know the circle. If it is one of life's familiar circles, for instance that of a great man, then a noble horse or a beautiful woman is like the clasp in a belt, which closes it and for a moment seems to contain the entire phenomenon; in the same way one can be smitten with a lovely farm horse, because in him as in a focusing mirror the entire heavy-footed beauty of the field and its people is repeated. But if there is nothing behind it? Nothing more than is behind the rays of the sun dancing on the stones? If this infinitude of water and sky is pitilessly open? Then one might almost believe that beauty is something that secretly negates, something incomplete and incompletable, a happiness without purpose, without sense. But what if it lacks everything? Then beauty is a torture, something to laugh and cry over, a tickling to make one roll around in the sand, with Apollo's arrow in one's side.

Hatred of beauty. Sense of urgent sexual desire: to destroy beauty.

The brightness of such days was like smoke, which the clarity of the nights wiped away.

Agathe had somewhat less imagination than Ulrich. Because she had not thought as much as he had her emotions were not as volatile as his, but burned like a flame rising straight out of the particular ground on which she happened to be standing. The daring nature of their flight, the conscience made somewhat anxious by the fear of discovery, and finally this hiding place in a flower basket between the porous limestone wall, sea, and sky, at times gave her a high-spirited and childlike cheerfulness. She then treated even their strange experience as an adventure: a forbidden space within herself over whose enclosure one spies, or into which one forces one's way, with beating heart, burning neck, and heavy soles weighed down with clods of damp earth from the path one has hurriedly followed in secret.

In this way very indirect suggestion of repeated coitus.

· · ·

She sometimes had a playful way of allowing herself to be touched, with opened-even-when-closed eyes; of reappearing; a tenderness that was not to be stilled. He secretly observed her, saw this play of love with the body, which has the captivation of a smile and the oppressive quality of a force of nature, for the first time, or was moved by it for the first time. Or there were hours when she did not look at him, was cold, almost angry with him; because she was too agitated; like someone in a boat not daring to move, so it was in her body—afterward, every time. Because the connection does not function. Or afterreactions; at first a blocking and then, for no apparent reason, an afterflood. It was thrilling and charming to let oneself be cradled by these inspirations; they shortened the hours but they forced an optic of nearness and minute observation. Ulrich resisted this. It was a leftover piece of earth drifting in the liquid fire and clouding it; a temptation to explanations such as that Agathe had never learned the proper connection between love and sex. As with most people, the entire power of the sexual had first come together with a spark of inclination at the time she had married Hagauer, who was not yet abhorrent to her. Instead of stumbling into a storm with someone / almost only in the company of / accompanied by someone almost as impersonal as the elements, and only then noticing as a still nameless surprise that this person's legs are not clothed like one's own and that one's soul is beckoning one to change one's hiding place . . .

But such thoughts, too, were like singing in a false key. Ulrich did not allow himself this kind of understanding. Understanding a person one loves cannot involve spying on that person but must come pouring from an overflow of auspicious inspirations. One may only recognize those things that enrich. One makes a gift of qualities in the unshakable security of a predetermined harmony, a separation that has never been—

Especially when ethical magnanimity is stimulated by it. Not the seeing or not seeing of weaknesses, but the large motion in which they float without significance.

An ancient column—thrown down at the time of Venice, Greece, or Rome—lay among the stones and the broom; every groove of its shaft and capital deepened by the ray-sharp graving tool of the midday shadows. Lying next to it belonged to the great hours of love.

Four eyes watching. Nothing but noon, column, four eyes. If the glance of two eyes sees *one* picture, *one* world: why not the glance of four?

When two pairs of eyes look long into each other, one person crosses over to the other on the bridge of glances, and all that remains is a feeling that no longer has a body.

When in a secret hour two pairs of eyes look at an object and come together in it—every object hovering deep down in a feeling, and objects standing only as firmly as they do if this deep ground is hard—then the rigid world begins to move, softly and incessantly. It rises and falls restlessly with the blood. The fraternal twins looked at each other. In the bright light it could not be made out whether they were still breathing or had been lying there for a thousand years like the stones. Whether the stone column was lying there or had risen up in the light without a sound and was floating.

There is a significant difference in the way one looks at people and the way one looks at things. Every time after this when they looked at someone in the hotel: the play of facial expressions of someone with whom one is talking becomes unspeakably alienating if one observes it as an objective process, and not as an ongoing exchange of signals between two souls; we are accustomed to see things lying mutely where they are, and we consider it a disturbing hallucination if they take on a more dynamic relation to us. But it is only we ourselves who are looking at them in such a way that the small changes in their physiognomies are not answered by any alterations in our emotions, and to change this nothing more is needed, basically, than that we not look at the world intellectually but that objects arouse in us our moral emotions instead of our sense-based surveying equipment. At such moments the excitement in which a glimpse brings us something and enriches us becomes so strong that nothing appears real except for a hovering condition, which, beyond the eyes, condenses into objects, and on this side of the eyes condenses into ideas and feelings, without these two sides being separable from each other. Whatever the soul bestows comes forward; whatever loses this power dissipates before one's eyes.

In this flickering silence among the stones there was a panic horror. The world seemed to be only the outer aspect of a specific inner attitude, and interchangeable with it. But world and self were not solid; a scaffolding sunk into soft depths; mutually helping each other out of a formlessness. Agathe said softly to Ulrich: "Are you yourself or are you not? I know nothing of it. I am incognizant of it and I am incognizant of myself."

It was the terror: The world depended on her, and she did not know who she was.

· · ·

Ulrich was silent.

Agathe continued: "I am in love, but I do not know with whom. I am neither faithful nor unfaithful. What am I then? My heart is at once full of love and emptied of love . . . ," she whispered. The horror of a noontime silence seemed to have clutched her heart.

Over and over the great test was the sea. Time and again, when they had climbed down the narrow slope with its many paths, its quantity of laurel, its broom, its figs, and its many bees, and stepped out onto the powerful surface spread out above the ocean, it was like the first great chord sounding after the tuning up of an orchestra. How would one have to be to endure this constantly? Ulrich proposed that they try setting up a tent here. But he did not mean it seriously; it would have frightened him. There were no longer any opponents around, up here they were alone; the rebuffs one receives as long as one must contradict the demands of others and the habits of one's own conscience were used up; in this final battle it was a matter of their resolve. The sea was like a merciless beloved and rival; every minute was an annihilating exploration of conscience. They were afraid of collapsing unconscious before this expanse that swallowed up every resistance.

This monstrously extended sight was not to be borne without its becoming somewhat boring. This being responsible for every slightest motion was—they had to confess—rather empty, if one compared it with the cheerfulness of those hours when they made no such claims on themselves and their bodies played with the soul like a beautiful young animal rolling a ball back and forth.

One day Ulrich said: It's broad and pastoral; there's something of a pastor about it! They laughed. Then they were startled by the scorn that they had inflicted upon themselves.

The hotel had a little bell tower; in the middle of its roof. Around one o'clock this bell rang for lunch. Since they were still almost the only guests, they did not need to respond right away, but the cook was indicating that he was ready. The bright sounds sliced into the stillness like a sharp knife contacting skin, which had shuddered beforehand but at this moment becomes calm. "How lovely it is, really," Ulrich said, as they climbed down on one of these days, "to be driven by necessity. The way one drives geese from behind with a stick, or entices hens from in front with feed. And where everything doesn't happen mysteriously—"
The blue-white trembling air really shuddered like goose pimples if one

stared into it for a long time. At that time memories were beginning to torture Ulrich vividly; he suddenly saw before him every statue and every architectural detail of one of those cities overloaded with such things that he had visited years ago; Nürnberg was before him, and Amiens, although they had never captivated him; some large red book or other that he must have seen years earlier in an exhibit would not go away from before his eyes; a slender tanned boy, perhaps only the counter his imagination had conjured up to Agathe, but in such a way as if he had once really met him but did not know where, preoccupied his mind; ideas that he had had at some time and long forgotten; soundless, shadowy things, things properly forgotten, eddied up in this south of stillness and seized possession of the desolate expanse.

The impatience that from the beginning had been mingled with all this beauty began to rage in Ulrich.

He could be sitting before a stone, lost to the world, sunk in contemplation, and be tortured by this raging impatience. He had come to the end, had assimilated everything into himself and ran the danger of beginning, all alone, to speak aloud in order to recite everything to himself once again. "Yes, you're sitting here," his thoughts said, "and you could tell yourself once again what you're looking at." The stones are of a quite peculiar stone-green, and their image is mirrored in the water. Quite right. Exactly as one says. And the stones are shaped like boxes. . . . But it's all no use, and I'd like to leave. It is so beautiful!

And he remembered: at home, sometimes only years later, and sometimes purely by accident, if one no longer has any idea how everything was, suddenly a light falls from behind, from such past things, and the heart does everything as if in a dream. He longed for the past.

"It's quite simple," he said to Agathe, "and everyone knows it, we're the only ones who don't: the imagination is stimulated only by what one does not yet possess or no longer has; the body wants to have, but the soul does not want to have. Now I understand the tremendous efforts people make to this end. How stupid it is for this ordinary fellow, this art traveler, to compare this flower to a jewel, or that stone over there to a flower: as if the truly intelligent thing to do wouldn't be to transform them for a brief moment into something else. And how stupid all our ideals would be, since every ideal, if one takes it seriously, contradicts some other ideal; thou shalt not kill, therefore perish? Thou shalt not covet thy neighbor's goods, so live in poverty? As if their sense did not lie precisely in the impossibility of carrying them out, which ignites the soul! And how good it is for religion that one can neither see nor comprehend God! But which world? A cold, dark strip between the two fires of the Not-yet and the No-longer!"

"A world to be afraid of oneself in," Agathe said. "You're right." She said this quite seriously, and there was real bitterness in her eyes.

—And if it is so! Ulrich laughed. —It occurs to me for the first time in my life that we would have to be terribly afraid of being tricked if Heaven were not to dangle before us an end of the world that does not exist. Evidently everything absolute, hundred-percent, true, is completely monstrous.

— Between two people as well; you mean between us?

— I now understand so well what visionaries are: food without salt is unbearable, but salt without food is a poison; visionaries are people who want to live from salt alone. Is that right?

Agathe shrugged her shoulders.

— Look at our chambermaid, a cheerful stupid creature smelling of cheap soap. A short time ago I was watching her as she made up the room; she seemed to me as pretty as a freshly washed sky.

It comforted Ulrich to confess this, and a small worm of disgust crawled across Agathe's mouth. Ulrich repeated it; he did not want to drown out this small disharmony with the great peal of the dark bell. "It is a disharmony, isn't it? And any trick will do for the soul to keep itself fruitful. Sometimes it dies from love several times in succession. But"— and now he said something he believed to be a consolation, indeed a new love—"if everything is so sad and a deception, and one can no longer believe in anything: isn't that just when we really need one another? The folk song about the little sister"—he smiled—"quiet, pensive music that nothing can drown out; an accompanying music; a love of lovelessness that softly reaches out its hands . . . ?"

Time is the greatest cynic.

Here sexuality and camaraderie!

A cool, quiet, gray aneroticism?

Agathe was silent. Something had been extinguished. She was inordinately tired. Her heart had suddenly been snatched away from her, and she was tortured by an unbearable fear of a vacuum within, of her unworthiness and her regressive transformation. This is the way ecstatics feel when God withdraws from them and nothing responds any longer to their zealous appeals.

The art traveler, as they called him, was a professor returning from Italian cities, who had the butterfly-net skin and botanizing drum-beating mind of the aspiring art historian. He had stopped over here for a few days to rest before his return and to order his notes. As they were the only guests, he had already introduced himself to the pair on the first day. They chatted briefly after meals, or when they met in the vicinity of the hotel, and there was no denying that although Ulrich made fun of him, at certain moments this man brought them welcome relaxation.

He was strongly convinced of his significance as man and scholar, and from their first encounter, after finding that the couple were not on their honeymoon, he had courted Agathe with great determination. He said to her: You resemble the beautiful ———— in the painting by ————, and all the women who have this expression, which repeats itself in their hair and in the folds of their gowns, have the quality of ———— : As she was telling this to Ulrich Agathe had already forgotten the names, but for a stranger to know what one was was as pleasant as the firm pressure of a masseur, while one knew oneself to be so diffuse that one could barely distinguish oneself from the noontime silence.

This art traveler said: Women's function is to make us dream; they are a stratagem of nature for the fertilization of the masculine mind. He gleamed with self-satisfaction at his paradox, which inverted the sense of fertilization. Ulrich replied: But there are still distinctions in kind among these dreams!

This man asserted that in embracing a "really great female" one must be able to think of Michelangelo's *Creation.* "You pull the blanket of the Sistine ceiling over yourself and underneath it you're naked except for the blue stockings," Ulrich ridiculed. No. He admits that carrying this out calls for tact, but in principle such people could be "twice as big" as others. "In the last analysis, the goal of all ethical life is to unite our actions with the highest that we bear within us!" It was not so easy to contradict this theoretically, although practically speaking it was ridiculous.

—I have discovered—the art historian said—that there are, and in the course of history always have been, two sorts of people. I call them the static and the dynamic. Or, if you prefer, the Imperial and the Faustian. People who are static can feel happiness as something present. They are somehow characterized by balance, equilibrium. What they have done and what they will do blends into what they are doing at the moment, is harmonized, and has a shape like a painting or a melody; has, so to speak, a second dimension, shines in every moment as surface. The Pope, for example, or the Dalai Lama; it is simply unimaginable that they would do something that was not stretched on the frame of their significance. On the other hand, the dynamic people: always tearing themselves loose, merely glancing backward and forward, rolling out of themselves, insensitive people with missions, insatiable, pushy, luckless—whom the static ones conquer over and over in order to keep world history going: in a word, he hinted that he was capable of carrying both strains within himself.

—Tell me—Ulrich asked, as if he were quite serious—are not the dynamic people also those who in love seem not to feel anything because they have either already loved in their imagination or will only love what has slipped away from them again? Couldn't one say that too?

—Quite right! the professor said.

—They are immoral and dreamers, these people, who can never find the right point between future and past—

It's enough to make them throw up.

—Well, I don't think I'd claim that—

—Yes, but you do. They would be capable of committing crazy good or bad deeds because the present means nothing to them.

He really ought to say: they could commit crazy deeds out of impatience.

The art historian did not quite know how to answer this, and found that Ulrich did not understand him.

The restlessness grew. The summer heat increased. The sun burned like a fire to the edge of the earth. The elements filled existence completely, so that there was hardly anyplace left for anything human.

It happened that toward evening, when the burning air already cast light, cooling folds, they went strolling on the steep banks. Yellow bushes of broom sprang up from the embers of the stones and stood there directly before the soul; the mountains gray as donkeys' backs with the washed-out green that the grass growing on the white limestone cast over them; the laurel's hot dark green. The parched glance resting on the laurel sank into cooler and cooler depths. Countless bees hummed;

it fused into a deep metallic tone that shot off little arrows whenever, in a sudden turn, they flew by one's ear. Heroic, tremendous, the approaching line of mountains, in three waves one behind the other, smoothly canted, breaking off steeply.

—Heroic? Ulrich asked. —Or is it only what we have always hated because it was supposed to be heroic? Endlessly portrayed, this painted and engraved, this Greek, this Roman, this Nazarene, classicistic landscape—this virtuous, professorial, idealistic landscape? And ultimately it impresses us only because we've now encountered it in reality? The way one despises an influential man and is nevertheless flattered because one knows him?

But the few things here to which the space belonged respected each other; they kept their distance from each other and did not saturate nature with impressions, as they do in Germany. No mocking helped; as only high in the mountains, where everything earthly keeps diminishing, this landscape was no longer a place of human habitation but a piece of the sky, to whose folds a few species of insects still clung.

And on the other side (of this humility) lay the sea. The great beloved, adorned with the peacock's tail. The beloved with the oval mirror. The opened eye of the beloved. The beloved become God. The pitiless challenge. The eyes still hurt and had to look away, pierced by the shattering spears of light speeding back from the sea. But soon the sun will be lower. It will only be a circumscribed sea of liquid silver, with violets floating on it. And then one *must* look out over the sea! Then one has to look at it. Agathe and Ulrich feared this moment. What can one do to prevail against this monstrous, observing, stimulating, jealous rival? How should they love each other? Sink to their knees? As they had done at first? Spread out their arms? Scream? Can they embrace each other? It is all so ridiculous, as if one were trying to shout angrily at someone while nearby all the bells of a cathedral are pealing! The fearful emptiness again closed in on them from all sides.

So it ends the way it begins!

But at such a moment one can shoot the other, or stab him, since his death cry will be muffled.

Ulrich shook his head. —One must be somewhat limited to find nature beautiful. To be someone like that fellow down there, who would rather talk himself than listen to someone better. One is forcibly reminded by nature of school exercises and bad poems, and one has to be capable of transforming it at the moment of observation into an anointing. Otherwise one collapses. One must always be stupider than nature in order to stand up to it, and must gossip in order not to lose the language.

Fortunately, their skin could not stand the heat. Sweat broke out. It created a diversion and an excuse; they felt themselves relieved of their mission.

But as they were walking back Agathe noticed that she was looking forward to the certainty of meeting the traveling stranger down below in front of the hotel. Ulrich was certainly right, but there was a great consolation in the babbling, insistently pushy company of this person.

Afternoons, in the room, there were fearful moments. Between the extended red-striped awning and the stone railing of the balcony lay a blue, burning band the width of one's hand. The smooth warmth, the severely attenuated brightness, had dislodged everything from the room that was not fixed. Ulrich and Agathe had not brought along anything to read; that had been their plan; they had left behind ideas, normal circumstances, everything having any connection—no matter how sagacious—with the ordinary human way of living: now their souls lay there like two hard-baked bricks from which every drop of water has escaped. This contemplative natural existence had made them unexpectedly dependent on the most primitive elements.

Finally, a day of rain came. The wind lashed. Time became long in a cool way. They straightened up like plants. They kissed each other. The words they exchanged refreshed them. They were happy again. To always be waiting every moment for the next moment is only a habit; dam it up, and time comes forth like a lake. The hours still flow, but they are broader than they are long. Evening falls, but no time has passed.

But then a second rainy day followed; a third. What had seemed a new intensity glided downward as a conclusion. The smallest help, the belief that this weather was a personal dispensation, an extraordinary fate, and the room is full of the strange light from the water, or hollowed out like a die of dark silver. But if no help comes: what can one talk about? One can still smile at the other from far apart—embrace— weaken the other to the point of that fatigue which resembles death, which separates the exhausted like an endless plain; one can call across: I love you, or: You are beautiful, or: I would rather die with you than live without you, or:

What a miracle that you and I, two such separate beings, have been blown together. And one can weep from nervousness when, quite softly, one begins to fall prey to boredom . . .

Fearful violence of repetition, fearful godhead! Attraction of emptiness, always sucking in like the funnel of a whirlpool whose walls yield. Kiss me, and I will bite gently and harder and harder and wilder and wilder, ever more drunken, more greedy for blood, listening into your lips for the plea for mercy, climbing down the ravine of pain until at the end we are hanging in the vertical wall and are afraid of ourselves. Then the deep pantings of breath come to our aid, threatening to abandon the body; the gleam in the eye breaks, the glance rolls from side to side, the grimace of dying begins. Astonishment and a thousandfold ecstasy in each other eddy in this rapture. Within a few minutes concentrated flight through bliss and death, ending, renewed, bodies swinging like howling bells. But at the end one knows: it was only a profound Fall into a world in which it drifts downward on a hundred steps of repetition. Agathe moaned: You will leave me! —No! Darling! Conspirator! Ulrich was searching for expressions of enthusiasm, etc. —No—Agathe softly fended him off—I can't feel anything anymore . . . ! Since it had now been spoken, Ulrich became cold and gave up the effort.

—If we had believed in God—Agathe went on—we would have understood what the mountains and flowers were saying.

—Are you thinking of Lindner? Ulrich probed / What? Lindner . . . ! Ulrich immediately interjected jealously.

It ends in excrement and vomiting like the first time!

—No. I was thinking of the art historian. His thread never breaks. Agathe gave a pained and wan smile. She was lying on the bed; Ulrich had torn open the door to the balcony, the wind flung water in. "What difference does it make," he said harshly. "Think of whomever you want. We have to look around for a third person. Who'll observe us, envy us, or reproach us." He remained standing before her and said slowly: "There is no such thing as love between two people alone!" Agathe propped herself on an elbow and lay there, wide-eyed, as if she were expecting death. —We have yielded to an impulse against order, Ulrich repeated. —A love can grow out of defiance, but it can't consist of defiance. On the contrary, it can only exist when it is integrated into a society. It's not the content of life. But a negation of, an exception to, all life's contents.

But an exception needs whatever it is the exception to. One can't live from a negation alone. —Close the door, Agathe asked. Then she stood up and arranged her dress. —So shall we leave?

Ulrich shrugged his shoulders. —Well, it's all over.

—Don't you remember any more our proviso when we came here?

Ashamed, Ulrich answered: We wanted to find the entrance to paradise!

—And kill ourselves—Agathe said—if we didn't!

Ulrich looked at her calmly. —Do you want to?

Agathe might perhaps have said yes. She did not know why it seemed more honest to slowly shake her head and say no.

—We've lost that resolve too, Ulrich stated.

She stood up in despair. Spoke with her hands on her temples, listening to her own words: I was waiting . . . I was almost decadent and ridiculous . . . Because in spite of the life I've led I was still waiting. I could not name it or describe it. It was like a melody without notes, a picture without form. I knew that one day it will come up to me from outside and will be what treats me tenderly and what will hold no harm for me anymore, either in life or in death. . . .

Ulrich, who had turned violently toward her, cut in, parodying her with a spitefulness that was a torture to himself: —It's a longing, something that's missing: the form is there, only the matter is missing. Then some bank official or professor comes along, and this little beastie slowly fills up the emptiness that was stretched out like an evening sky.

—My love, all movement in life comes from the evil and brutal; goodness dozes off. Is a drop of some fragrance; but every hour is the same hole and yawning child of death, which has to be filled up with heavy ballast. You said before: If we could believe in God! But a game of patience will do as well, a game of chess, a book. Today man has discovered that he can console himself with these things just as well. It just has to be something where board is joined to board in order to span the empty depths.

—But don't we love each other any longer, then? Agathe exclaimed.

Now they are again talking as they had earlier. It is very lovely.

—You can't overlook—Ulrich answered—how much this feeling depends on its surroundings. How it derives its content from imagining a life together, that is, a line between and through other people. From good conscience, because everyone else is so pleased at the way these two love each other, or from bad conscience as well. . . .

—What is it then that we experienced? We mustn't pretend to something untrue: I wasn't a fool for wanting to seek paradise. I could determine it the way one can deduce an invisible planet from certain effects. And what happened? It dissolved into a spiritual and optical illusion and into a physiological mechanism that is repeatable. As with all people!

—It's true, Agathe said. —For the longest time we've been living from what you call evil; from restlessness, small distractions, the hunger and satiety of the body.

—And yet—Ulrich answered, as in an extremely painful vision— when it's forgotten, you'll be waiting again. Days will come where behind many doors someone will beat on a drum. Muffled and insistently: beat, beat. Days, as if you were waiting in a brothel for the creaking of the stairs; it will be some corporal or bank official. Whom fate has sent you. To keep your life in motion. And yet you remain my sister.

—But what is to become of us? Agathe saw nothing before her.

—You must marry or find a lover—I said that before.

—But are we no longer *one* person? she asked sadly.

—One person also has both within himself.

—But if I love *you*? Agathe shouted.

—We must live. Without each other—for each other. Do you want the art historian? Ulrich said this with the coldness of great effort. Agathe dismissed it with a small shrug of her shoulder. —Thank you, Ulrich said. He tried to grasp her slack hand and stroke it. —I'm not so—so firmly convinced either. . . .

Once again, almost the great union. But it seems to Agathe that Ulrich does not have sufficient courage.

They were silent for a while. Agathe opened and closed drawers and began to pack. The storm shook at the doors. Then Agathe turned around and asked her brother calmly and in a different voice:

—But can you imagine that tomorrow or the next day we'll get home and find the rooms the way we left them, and begin to make visits? . . .

Ulrich did not notice with what enormous resistance Agathe struggled against this idea. He could not imagine all that either. But he felt some new kind of tension, even if it was a melancholy task. At this moment he was not paying enough attention to Agathe.

· · ·

Continuation: The day after this dismal conversation Clarisse arrived.

WORKED-OUT SKETCHES FROM THE 1920S
NEW SKETCHES, 1930/31–1933/34

On Kakania

A digression on Kakania. The crucible of the World War is also the birthplace of the poet Feuermaul

It may be assumed that the expression "Crucible of the World War" has, since this object existed, been used often enough, yet always with a certain imprecision as to the question of where it is located. Older people who still have personal memories of those times will probably think of Sarajevo, yet they themselves will feel that this small Bosnian city can only have been the oven vent through which the wind blew in. Educated people will direct their thoughts to political nodal points and world capitals. Those even more highly educated will, moreover, have the names of Essen, Creuzot, Pilsen, and the other centers of the armaments industry confidently in mind. And the most highly educated will add to these something from the geography of oil, potash, and other raw materials, for that's the way one often reads about it. But what follows from all this is merely that the crucible of the World War was no ordinary crucible, for it was located in several places simultaneously.

Perhaps one might say to this that the expression is to be understood only metaphorically. But this is to be assented to so completely that it immediately gives rise to even greater difficulties. For, granting that "crucible" is intended to mean metaphorically approximately the same thing that "origin" or "cause" means nonmetaphorically, while on the one hand one knows that the origin of all things and events is God, on the other it leaves one empty-handed. For "origins" and "causes" are like a person who goes searching for his parents: in the first instance he has two, that is indisputable; but with grandparents it's the square of two, with great-grandparents two to the third, and so on in a powerfully unfolding series, which is totally unassailable but which yields the remarkable result that at the beginning of time there must have been an almost infinite number of people whose purpose was merely to produce a single one of today's individuals. However flattering this may be, and however it may correspond to the significance that the individual feels within himself, today one calculates too precisely for anyone to believe it. Therefore, with heavy heart, one must give up a personal series of ancestors and assume that "starting from someplace" one must have a common descent as a group. And this has a variety of consequences. Such as that people consider themselves in part "brothers," in part "from alien tribes," without a person knowing how to determine where the boundary is, for what is called "nation" and "race" is results and not causes. Another consequence, no less influential even if not as obvious, is that Mr. What's-his-name no longer knows where he has his cause. He consequently feels himself like a snipped thread that the busy needle of life incessantly pulls back and forth because making a button for it was somehow overlooked. A third consequence, just now dawning, is for instance that it has not yet been calculated whether and to what extent there might be two or multiple other Mr. What's-his-names; in the realm of what is hereditarily possible it is entirely conceivable, only one does not know how great the probability is that it could actually happen with oneself; but a dim oppressiveness of the idea that given man's nature today this cannot be entirely excluded lies, as it were, in the air.

And surely it would not even be the worst thing. Count Leinsdorf, speaking with Ulrich for a moment, held forth on the aristocratic institution of chamberlains. "A chamberlain needs to have sixteen noble forebears, and people are upset at that being the height of snobbery; but what, I ask you, do people do themselves? Imitate us with their theories of race, that's what they do," he explained, "and immediately exaggerate it in a fashion that has nothing at all to do with nobility. As far as I'm concerned we can all be descended from the same Adam, a Leinsdorf would still be a Leinsdorf, for it's a damn sight more a matter of education and training than a matter of blood!" His Grace was irritated by the intrusion of populist elements into the Parallel Campaign, which for a variety of reasons had to be countenanced up to a certain point. At that time nationalism was nearly ready to put forth its first bloody blossoms, but no one knew it, for despite its imminent fulfillment it did not seem terrible but only seemed ridiculous: its intellectual aspect consisting for the most part of books pasted together with the well-read busyness of a scholar and the total incoherence of untrained thinking by compilers who lived in some rural backwater as elementary-school teachers or petty customs officials.

. . .

/ Preliminary sketch: continuation after first paragraph above /

Therefore the obvious reservation will probably be put forward that the expression "crucible of the World War" is to be understood merely metaphorically, and this is to be subscribed to so wholeheartedly that it will immediately lead to new difficulties; if on the other hand one maintains that "crucible" signifies the same as causation complex, and such a thing is complicated and extensive in all human endeavors, then it must be contradicted straightaway. For if one pursues causes back in a straight line they lead right back to God as the *Prima Causa* of everything that happens; this is one of the few problems about which centuries of theology have left no doubt. But on the other hand it's like a person going from his father to his father's father, from his father's father to his father and father's father of the father's father, and so on in this series: he will never arrive at a complete notion of his descent. In other words: the causal chain is a warp on a loom; the moment a woof is put in, the causes disappear into a woven texture. In science, research into causes was abandoned long ago, or at least greatly reduced, to be replaced by a functional mode that called for observing relationships. The search for causes belongs to household usage, where the cook's being in love is the cause of the soup's being oversalted. Applied to the World War, this search for a cause and a causer has had the extremely positive negative result that the cause was everywhere and in everyone.

This demonstrates that one can truly say "crucible" just as well as "cause of" or "guilt for" the war; but then one would have to supplement this entire mode of observation with another. For this purpose, let us proceed experimentally from the problem of why the poet Feuermaul should suddenly pop up in the Parallel Campaign, and even why—leaving behind a decisive but merely trivial contribution to its history—he will immediately and permanently drop out of it again. The answer is that this was apparently necessary, that there was absolutely no way of avoiding it—for everything that happens has, as we know, a sufficient cause—but that the reasons for this necessity are themselves, however, completely meaningless or, more properly, were important only for Feuermaul himself, his girlfriend, Professor Drangsal, and her envier, Diotima, and only for a brief period. It would be sheer extravagance were one to relate this. If Feuermaul had not striven to play a role in the Parallel Campaign, someone else would have done so in his place, or if this other person had not shown up, something else would have; in the interweavings of events there is a narrow insert where this or that influences its success with the differences they make; but in the long run, the things represent each other completely, indeed they somehow also represent the characters, with very few exceptions. Arnheim, too, could have been replaced in the same way; perhaps not for Diotima, but probably as the cause of the changes she underwent and, further, the effects that these led to. This view, which today might almost be called a natural one, seems fatalistic but is so only so long as one accepts it as a destiny. But the laws of nature were also a destiny before they were investigated; after that happened, it was even possible to subordinate them to a technology.

/Belongs here: Feuermaul, like all the characters in the story except for Ulrich (and perhaps Leo Fischel), denies the value of technical projects, among others/

As long as this has not happened, one can also say that B., the birthplace of the poet Feuermaul, was also the original crucible of the World War. And that is why it is by no means capricious; what it amounts to, really, is that certain phenomena, which were to be found everywhere in the world and belonged to the crucible that, stretching over the entire planet, was everywhere and nowhere, condensed in B. in a fashion that prematurely brought out its meaning. Instead of B. one could say the whole of Kakania, but B. was one of the special points within it. These phenomena were that in B. the people could not stand each other at all, and on the other hand that the poet Feuermaul, born in their midst, chose as the basic principle of his work the assertion that Man Is Good and one need only turn directly to the goodness that dwells within him. Both signify the same thing.

· · ·

It would have been a lie had one tried to maintain that even the smallest part of what has been described was present in Feuermaul at the time in any real way, or that it was present at any time in such detail. But life is always more detailed than its results: creating, as it were, a vegetarian diet, mountains of leaves, around a tiny pile of . . . The results are a few dispositions of individual conduct.

. . .

1930–1934

While Agathe and Ulrich were living behind closed crystal panels— by no means abstractly and without looking at the world, but looking at it in an unusual, unambiguous light, this world bathed every morning in the hundredfold light of a new day. Every morning cities and villages awaken, and wherever they do it happens, God knows, in more or less the same way; on the other hand, people are conceived and slain in an instant, and small birds fly from one branch to another with the same right to existence that a giant ocean liner expresses as it swims straight between Europe and America. Somehow everything in the world happens uniformly and with statutory monotony, but varied in countless ways, which, depending on the mood in which one observes them, is as much blissful abundance as ridiculous superfluity. And perhaps even the expression "law of nature"—this exalted regency of mechanical laws, which we worship shivering—is still a much too personal expression; laws have something of the personal relationship an accused has with his judge or a subject with his king; there is in them something of the *contrat social* and the beginnings of liberalism too. Nietzsche already noted the more modern view of nature when he wrote: "Nature has a calculable course not because it is ruled by laws but because they are lacking, and every power draws its ultimate consequences at every moment." That is a statement which fits in with the ideas of contemporary physics but was really coined from biological events, and an intimation of such emotions lies over contemporary life. Once, "You can do what you like" meant following your drives; but one was not supposed to do what one liked, and moral laws conceived in sublimity interfered with it. Today everyone feels in some way that these moral laws are a heap of contradictions, and that to follow them would amount to being able to pander to every one of his drives, and he feels a wild, extraordinary freedom. This freedom permits him a path that only leads forward: that, like the orbits of atoms, this chaos must somehow finally yield a specific value, and that with more precise knowledge of how things cohere one would again be able to give life a meaning.

That is more or less the sense of the transition from individualism to the collective view of the world / mission of the world (there is in this no supposition that the value of the individual should cease, only that it be more precisely evaluated).

.   .   .

One day, the General was sitting before the two of them and said in astonishment to Ulrich: "What, you don't read the newspapers?"

Brother and sister blushed as deeply as if the good Stumm had discovered them *in flagrante*, for even though in their condition everything might have been possible, that they might have been able to read the newspapers was not.

"But one must read the newspapers!" said / admonished the General in embarrassment, for he had stumbled upon an incomprehensible fact, and it was discretion that caused him to add reproachfully: There have been big demonstrations against the Parallel Campaign in B.!

Truly, while Ulrich and Agathe had been living behind closed crystal panels—by no means abstractly and without looking at the world, but looking at it in an unusual, unambiguous light—this same world bathed every morning in the hundredfold light of a new day. Every morning cities and villages awaken, and wherever they do it happens, God knows, in more or less the same way; but with the same right to existence that a giant ocean liner expresses when it is under way between two continents, small birds fly from one branch to another, and thus everything happens simultaneously, in a fashion as uniform and simplified as it is uselessly varied in innumerable ways, and in a helpless and blessed abundance reminiscent of the glorious but limited picture books of childhood. Ulrich and Agathe also both felt their book of the world open before them, for the city of B. was none other than the one where they had found each other again after their father had lived and died there.

"And it had to happen precisely in B.!" the General repeated meaningfully.

"You were once stationed in the garrison there," Ulrich affirmed.

"And that's where the poet Feuermaul was born," Stumm added.

"Right!" Ulrich exclaimed. "Behind the theater! That's apparently what gave him his ambition to be a poet. Do you remember that theater? In the '80's or '90s there must have been an architect who plunked down such theatrical jewel boxes in most of the bigger cities, with every available nook and cranny plastered with decoration and ornamental statues. And it was right that Feuermaul came into the world in this spinning-and-weaving city: as the son of a prosperous agent in textiles. I remember that these middlemen, for reasons I don't understand, earned more than the factory owners themselves; and the Feuermauls were already one of the wealthiest families in B. before the father began an even grander life in Hungary with saltpeter or God knows what murderous products. So you've come to ask me about Feuermaul?" Ulrich asked.

"Not really," his friend responded. "I've found out that his father is a great supplier of powder to the Royal Navy. That's a restraint on human goodness that was laid on his son from the beginning. The Resolution will remain an isolated episode, I can guarantee you that!"

But Ulrich was not listening. He had long been deprived of the enjoyment of hearing someone talk in a casual, everyday fashion, and Agathe seemed to feel the same way. "Besides, this old B. is a rotten city," he began to gossip. "On a hill in the middle there's an ugly old fortress whose barbettes served as a prison from the middle of the eighteenth to the nineteenth century and were quite notorious, and the whole city is proud of them!"

"Marymount," the General affirmed politely.

"What a very merry mount!" Agathe exclaimed, becoming irritated at her need for the ordinary when Stumm found the wordplay witty and assured her that he had been garrisoned at B. for two years without having made this connection.

"The true B., of course, is the ring of the factory quarter, the textile and yarn city!" Ulrich went on, and turned to Agathe. "And what big, narrow, dirty boxes of houses with countless window holes, tiny alleys consisting only of yard walls and iron gates, a spreading tangle of bleak, rutted streets!" After the death of his father he had wandered through this area several times. He again saw the high chimneys hung with dirty banners of smoke, and the streets /roadways covered with a film of oil. Then his memory wandered without transition to the farmland, which in fact began right behind the factory walls, with heavy, charged, fruitful loam that in spring the plow turned over black-brown; wandered to the low, long villages lying along their single street, and houses that were painted in not only screaming colors but colors that screamed in an ugly, incomprehensible voice. It was humble and yet alien-mysterious farmland, from which the factories sucked their male and female workers because it lay squeezed between extensive sugar-beet plantations belonging to the great landed estates, which had not left it even the scantest room to thrive. Every morning the factory sirens summoned hordes of peasants from these villages into the city, and in the evening scattered them again over the countryside; but as the years went by, more and more of these Czech country people, fingers and hands turned dark from the oily cotton dust of the factories, stayed behind in the city and caused the Slavic petite bourgeoisie that was already there to grow mightily.

This led to strained relations, for the city was German. It even lay in a German-language enclave, if at its outermost tip, and was proud of its involvement since the thirteenth century in the annals of German history. In the city's German schools one could learn that in the vicinity the Turk Kapistran had preached against the Hussites, at a time when good Austrians could still be born in Naples; that the hereditary bond between the houses of Habsburg and Hungary, which in 1364 laid the groundwork for the Austro-Hungarian monarchy, was forged nowhere else but here; that in the Thirty Years' War the Swedes had besieged this brave town for an entire summer without being able to take it, the Prussians in the Seven Years' War even less so. Of course this made the city just as much part of the proud Hussite memories of the Czechs and the independent historical memories of the Hungarians, and possibly, too, even part of the memories of the Neapolitans, Swedes, and Prussians; and in the non-German schools there was no lack of indications that the city was not German and that the Germans were a pack of thieves who steal even other people's pasts. It was astonishing that nothing was done to stop it, but this was part of Kakania's wise tolerance. There were many such cities, and they all resembled one another. At the highest point they were lorded over by a prison, at the next highest by an episcopal residence, and scattered around in them were some ten cloisters and barracks. If one ranked what were indeed called "the necessities of state," one would not, for the rest, encompass its homogeneity and unity, for Kakania was inspired by a hereditary mistrust, acquired from great historical experiences, of every Either/Or, and always had some glimmering that there were in the world many more contradictions than the one which ultimately led to its demise, and that a contradiction must be decisively resolved. The principle of its government was This-as-well-as-that, or even better, with wisest moderation, Neither/Nor. One was therefore also of the opinion in Kakania that it was not prudent for simple people who have no need of it to learn too much, and they did not regard it as important that economically these people should be immodestly prosperous. One preferred to give to those who already had a great deal, because this no longer carried any risks, and one assumed that if among those other people there was some skill or capacity, it would find a way of making itself known, for resistance is well suited to developing real men.

And so it turned out too: men *did* develop from among the opponents, and the Germans, because property and culture in B. were German, were helped by the state to receive more and more capital and culture. If one walked through the streets of B., one could recognize this in the fact that the beautiful architectural witnesses of the past that had been preserved, of which there were several, stood as a point of pride for the prosperous citizens among many witnesses to the modern period, which did not content themselves with being merely Gothic, Renaissance, or

Baroque but availed themselves of the possibility of being all these things at once. Among the large cities of Kakania, B. was one of the wealthiest, and also displayed this in its architecture, so that even the surroundings, where they were wooded and romantic, got some of the little red turrets, the crenallated slate-blue roofs, and the rings of embrasured-like walls that the prosperous villas had. "And what surroundings!" Ulrich thought and said, hostile to but settled in his home region. This B. lay in a fork between two rivers, but it was a quite broad and imprecise fork, and the rivers were not quite proper rivers either but in many places broad, slow brooks, and in still others standing water that was nevertheless secretly flowing. Nor was the landscape simple, but it consisted, leaving aside the farmland considered above, of three further parts. On one side a broad, yearningly opening plain, which on many evenings was delicately tinged in tender shades of orange and silver; on the second side shaggy, good old German wooded hills with waving tree-tops (although it happened not to be the German side), leading from nearby green to distant blue; on the third side a heroic landscape of Nazarene bareness and almost splendid monotony, with gray-green knolls on which sheep grazed, and plowed brown fields over which hovered something of the murmured singing of peasants' grace at table as it pours out of humble windows.

So while one might boast that this cozy Kakanian region in the middle of which B. lay was hilly as well as flat, no less wooded than sunny, and as heroic as it was humble, there was nevertheless everywhere a little something missing, so that on the whole it was neither this way nor that way. Nor could it ever be decided whether the inhabitants of this town found it beautiful or ugly. If one were to say to one of them that B. was ugly, he would be sure to answer: "But look how pretty Red Mountain is, and Yellow Mountain too . . . and the black fields . . . !" and as he toted up these names, which were so sensual, one had to concede that it was indeed a quite respectable landscape. But if one called it beautiful, an educated B.'er would laugh and say that he was just back from Switzerland or Singapore, and that B. was a lousy hole that couldn't even stand comparison with Bucharest. But this, too, was merely Kakanian, this twilight of the emotions in which they took up their existence, this restless sense of having been all too prematurely laid to rest, in which they felt themselves sheltered and buried. If one puts it this way: for these people everything was simultaneously lack of pleasure and pleasure, one will notice how anticipatorily contemporary it was, for in many respects this most gentle of all states was secretly raging ahead of its time. The people who inhabited B. lived from the production of textiles and yarn, from the sale of textiles and yarn, from the production of and trade in all those things people use who produce or sell textile and yarn, including the production and management of legal disputes, diseases, acquired skills, diversions, and such other things as belong to the needs of a big city. And all the well-off people among them had the quality that there was no beautiful or famous place in the whole world where someone who was from this city would not meet someone else who was also from this city, and when they were home again the consequence of this was that they all bore within themselves as much of the wide world as they did the amazing conviction that everything great ultimately led only to B.

Such a condition, which derives from the production of textiles and yarn, from industriousness, thrift, a civic theater, the concerts of touring celebrities, and from balls and invitations, is not to be conquered with these same means. That might have succeeded in the struggle for political power against a refractory working class, or the struggle against an upper class, or an imperialistic struggle for the world market of the kind other states conducted—in short, being rewarded not according to merit but by a remnant of the animalistic pouncing on prey, a process in which the warmth of life keeps itself alert. But in Kakania, while it was true that a great deal of money was unlawfully earned, there could be no pouncing, and in that country, even if crimes had been permitted, it would have been with strict attention to their being committed only by officially certified criminals. This gave all cities like B. the appearance of a great hall with a low ceiling. A ring of powder arsenals in which the army kept its guns surrounded every fairly large town; big enough, if struck by lightning, to reduce an entire quarter of the city to rubble: but at every powder arsenal provision had been made by means of a sentry and a yellow-and-black sentry pole that no disaster should befall the citizenry. And the police were furnished with sabers as tall as the officers and reaching to the ground, no one knew why anymore, unless it was from moderation, for it was only with their right hand that the police were the instruments of justice; with their left they had to hang on to their swords. Nor did anyone know why on promising building sites in growing cities the state, peering far into the future, constructed military hospitals, warehouses for uniforms, and garrison bakeries, whose giant unwalled rectangles later interfered with development. That is in no way to be taken for militarism, of which old Kakania was thoughtlessly accused; it was only common sense and prudence: for order cannot be otherwise than in order / more properly: it is, so to speak, already by its very nature in order / while, with every other kind of conduct the state engages in, this remains eternally uncertain. This order had become second nature in Kakania in the Franzisco-Josephenian era, indeed it had almost become landscape, and it is quite certain that if the quiet times of peace had lasted longer, the priests, too, would have got swords just as long, as the university professors had got them after the finance authorities and the postal officials, and if a world upheaval with entirely different views had not intervened, the sword would perhaps have developed in Kakania into a spiritual weapon.

When the conversation had proceeded to this point, partly in an exchange of views, partly in the reminiscences that were their silent accompaniment, General Stumm put in: "That, by the way, is something Leinsdorf said already, that the priests really must receive their swords at the next concordat, as a sign that they, too, are performing a function in the state. He then hedged this with the less paradoxical remark that even small daggers might suffice, with mother-of-pearl and a gold handle, of the kind officials used to wear."

"Are you serious?"

"He was," the General replied. "He pointed out to me that in Bohemia during the Thirty Years' War priests rode around in mass-robes of gilt that were leather below—in other words, proper mass-dragoons. He is simply exasperated at the general hostility directed against the state, and recalled that in one of his castle chapels he still has such a garment preserved. Look, you know how he's always talking about the constitution of '61 having given capital and culture the lead here, and that this has led to a big disappointment—"

"How did you actually happen to meet Leinsdorf?" Ulrich interrupted him with a smile.

"Oh, that came about when he was on his way back from one of his estates in Bohemia," Stumm said, without going into greater detail. "Moreover, he has asked you to come see him three times, and you haven't gone. In B. on the way back, his car blundered into the riots and was stopped. On one side of the street stood the Czechs, shouting: 'Down with the Germans!' on the other side the Germans shouted: 'Down with the Czechs!' But when they recognized him they stopped that and asked in chorus in both German and Czech: 'What's going on with the Commission to Ascertain the Desires of the Concerned Sections of the Population, Count?' and some screamed 'Phooey!' at him and others 'Shame!' This stupid Resolution, that one should let oneself be killed for one's own ideas but not other people's, appears to have spread by word of mouth, and because we suppressed it we're now suspected of wanting to be the murderer of nationalities! That's why Leinsdorf said to me: 'You're his friend; why doesn't he come when I call him?' And all I could do was offer: 'If you wish to entrust me with something, I will inform him!'"

Stumm paused.

"And what . . . ?" Ulrich asked.

"Well, you know it's never really easy to understand what he means. First he talked to me about the French Revolution. As is well known, the French Revolution lopped off the heads of many of the nobility, and astonishingly he finds that quite proper, although stones had almost been thrown at him in B. For he says that the ancien régime had its mistakes, and the French Revolution its true ideas. But what ultimately resulted from all the effort? That's what he was asking himself. And then he said the following: Today, for example, the mail is better and quicker; but earlier, while the mail was slow, people wrote better letters. Or: Today clothing is more practical and less ridiculous; but earlier, when it was like a masquerade, far better materials were used. And he concedes that for longer trips he himself uses an automobile because it's faster and more comfortable than a horse-drawn coach, but he maintains that this box with springs on four wheels has deprived traveling of its true nobility. All that's funny, I think, but it's true. Didn't you yourself once say that as mankind progresses one leg always slides backward whenever the other slides forward? Involuntarily, each of us today has something against progress. And Leinsdorf said to me: 'General, earlier our young people spoke of horses and dogs, but today the sons of factory owners talk of horsepower and chassis. So since the constitution of '61, liberalism has shoved the nobility aside, but everything is full of new corruption, and if against expectations the social revolution should ever happen, it will lop the heads off the sons of factory owners, but things won't get any better either!' Isn't that something? You get the impression that something is boiling over in him. With someone else, one might perhaps think that he doesn't know what he wants!"

But in the meantime we've only got as far as the national revolution?

"Do you know what he wants?" Ulrich asked.

"After the business in B., Drangsal tried to have him informed that now one would really have to let oneself be unconditionally swept up in the Ideal of Man, and Feuermaul is supposed to have expressed himself to the effect that it's better as an Austrian not to master the resistance of the nationalities than it is as a German to transform one's country into a field for army maneuvers. To this Leinsdorf's only response was that that wasn't *realpolitik*. He wants a proclamation of power; which is to say, of course it should also be a proclamation of love; that, after all, had been the original idea of the Parallel Campaign. 'We must, General'—

these were his words—'proclaim our unity; that is less contradictory than it seems, but also not as easy!' "

Hearing this, Ulrich forgot himself and gave a rather more serious response. "Tell me," he asked, "doesn't all the talk about the Parallel Campaign ever seem rather childish to you?"

Stumm looked at him with astonishment. "Well, yes," he replied hesitantly. "When I'm talking this way with you, or with Leinsdorf, it does sometimes seem to me that I'm talking like an adolescent, or that you're philosophizing about the immortality of cockchafers; but doesn't that come with the subject? Where it's a question of sublime missions, one never has the feeling of being able / allowed to talk the way one really is.

Agathe laughed.

Stumm laughed along with her. "I'm laughing too, dear lady!" he affirmed in a worldly-wise way, but then seriousness returned to his face and he went on: "But strictly speaking, what the Count means is by no means so wrong. For instance, what do you understand by liberalism?" With these words he again turned to Ulrich, but without waiting for a reply he went on again: "What I mean is that people ought to be left to themselves. And it will also have struck you that that's now going out of fashion. It's given rise to a lot of nonsense. But is that all it is? It seems to me people want something more. They aren't content with themselves. I'm not either; I used to be an amiable person. You didn't really do anything, but you were satisfied with yourself. Work wasn't bad, and after work you played cards or went hunting, and there was in all of that a certain kind of culture. A certain wholeness. Doesn't it seem so to you too? And why isn't it like that anymore today? As far as I can judge from myself, I believe that people feel too clever. If you want to eat a schnitzel, it occurs to you that there are people without one. If someone is after a pretty girl, it suddenly goes through his mind that he really ought to be thinking about settling some conflict or other. That's this insufferable intellectualism that you can't ever shake off today, and that's why there's no going forward anywhere. And without knowing it themselves, people again want something. That means they no longer want a complicated intellect, they don't want a thousand possibilities for living; they want to be satisfied with what they're doing anyway, and for this all they need is to get back some belief or conviction or—well, how to describe what they need to do that? I'd like to hear *your* opinion about all this!"

But that was only self-satisfaction on the part of the animated and excited Stumm, for before Ulrich could even pull a face, he sprang his surprise: "Of course one can just as well call it belief as conviction, but I've thought a lot about it and prefer to call it single-mindedness!"

Stumm paused, with the idea of garnering applause before he unveiled further insights into the workshop of his mind, and then there mingled with the weighty expression on his face another, which was as superior as it was tired of enjoyment. "We used to talk a lot about the problems of order," he reminded his friend, "and so we don't have to stop over them today. So order is to a certain extent a paradoxical notion. Every decent person has a yearning for internal and external order, but on the other hand, you can't bear too much of it; indeed, a perfect order would be, so to speak, the ruination of all progress and pleasure. That is (already) inherent, as it were, in the concept of order. And so you have to ask yourself: what is order after all? And how does it happen that we imagine we're not able to exist without it? And what kind of order is it that we're looking for? A logical, a practical, an individual, a general order, an order of the emotions, of the mind, or of actions? De facto, there's a heap of orders all mixed up: taxes and customs duties are one, religion another, military regulations a third; there's no end of searching them out and enumerating them. I've been preoccupied with this, as you know, and I don't believe that there are many generals in the world who take their profession as seriously as I've had to do this past year. I've helped after my fashion in the search for an encompassing idea, but you yourself ended up proclaiming that to order the spirit one would need an entire global secretariat, and even you'll have to admit that we can't wait for such an ordering. But on the other hand, one can't use that to let everyone do whatever he wants!"

Stumm leaned back and drew breath. The most difficult part had now been said, and he felt the need to excuse himself to Agathe for the gloomy dryness of his behavior, which he did with the words: "You must excuse me, but your brother and I had an old and difficult account to settle; but from now on it will also be more suitable for ladies, for I'm again back to where I was, that people don't have any use for complicated intellect, but would like to believe and be convinced. For if you analyze this, you'll find that the least important thing about the order to which man aspires is whether reason will approve of it or not; there are also totally ungrounded kinds of orders: for instance, the one that's always asserted in the military about one's superior always being right, meaning, of course, so long as *his* superior isn't around. How I puzzled over this as a desecration of the world of ideas when I was a young officer! And what do I see today? Today it's called the principle of the leader—"

"Where did you get that?" Ulrich asked, interrupting the lecture, for he had the distinct suspicion that these ideas were not just taken from a conversation with Leinsdorf.

"Everyone wants strong leadership! And partly from Nietzsche, of course, and his interpreters," Stumm replied nimbly and learnedly. "What's already being called for is a double philosophy and morality: for leader and for led! But as long as we're talking about the military, I must say that the military excels not only in and for itself, as an element of order, but also in always making itself available when all other order fails!"

"The decisive things are happening above and beyond reason, and the greatness of life is rooted in the irrational!" Ulrich brought up, imitating his cousin Diotima from memory.

The General grasped this immediately but did not take offense. "Yes, that's the way she used to talk, your cousin, before she started investigating the proclamations of love in, as it were, too great detail." With this explanation he turned to Agathe.

Agathe was silent, but smiled.

Stumm again turned to Ulrich. "I don't know whether Leinsdorf has perhaps said it to you too; at any rate, it's marvelously right: he maintains that the most important thing about a belief is that one always believe the same thing. That's something like what I'm calling single-mindedness. 'But can civilians do that?' I asked him. 'No,' I said. 'Civilians wear different suits every year, and every few years there are parliamentary elections so they can choose differently every time; the spirit of single-mindedness is much rather to be found in the military!' "

"So you convinced Leinsdorf that a strengthened militarism is the true fulfillment of his aims?"

"God forbid, I didn't say a word! We merely agreed that in the future we would do without Feuermaul because his views are too unusable. And for the rest, Leinsdorf has given me a whole series of assignments for you—"

"That's superfluous!"

"You should quickly get him access to socialist circles—"

"My gardener's son is a zealous member of the party—that I can do!"

"That's just fine! He's only doing it out of conscientiousness, because he once got the idea in his head. The second thing is that you should go see him as soon as possible—"

"But I'm leaving in a few days!"

"Then as soon as you get back—"

"It doesn't look as if I'm ever coming back!"

Stumm von Bordwehr looked at Agathe; Agathe smiled, which encouraged him. "Crazy?" he asked.

Agathe shrugged her shoulders indecisively.

"Well, let me summarize once more—" Stumm said.

"Our friend has had enough philosophy!" Ulrich interrupted him.

"You certainly can't say that about me!" Stumm angrily defended himself. "It's just that we can't wait for philosophy. And I don't want to lie to you: of course whenever I visit Leinsdorf I have orders to influence him in a certain way if it's possible, that you can imagine. And when he says that the most important thing about a belief is that one always believe the same thing, he's thinking above all of religion; but I'm already thinking of single-mindedness, for that's more comprehensive. I don't hesitate to assert that a truly powerful philosophy of life can't wait around for reason; on the contrary, a true philosophy of life must be absolutely directed against reason, otherwise it would not get into the position of being able to force its submission. And the civilian world seeks such a single-mindedness in constant change, but the military has, so to speak, an enduring single-mindedness! Madame," Stumm interrupted his ardor, "you should not believe that I'm a militarist; quite the contrary, the military has always been even a little on the raw side for my taste: but the way the logic of these ideas grabs hold of you is like playing with a large dog: first he bites for fun, and then he gets carried away and goes wild. And I would like to grant your brother, as it were, one last opportunity—"

"And how do you connect that with the proclamation of power and love?" Ulrich asked.

"God, in the meantime I've forgotten," Stumm replied. "But of course these eruptions of nationalism that we're now experiencing in our fatherland are somehow eruptions of the energy of an unhappy love. And also in this area, in the synthesis of power and love, the military is, in a certain sense, exemplary. A person has to have some kind of love for his fatherland, and if he doesn't have it for his fatherland, then he has it for something else. So you just need to grab hold of that something else. As an example that just occurs to me, take the term conscript-volunteer. Who would ever think that a conscript is a volunteer? That's the last thing he is. And yet he was and is, according to the sense of the law. In some such sense people have to be made volunteers again!"

ON THE YOUNG SOCIALIST SCHMEISSER*

Conversations with Schmeisser

It was not the first time that Count Leinsdorf had expressed the opinion
that a practitioner of *realpolitik* had to make use even of socialism in its
search for allies against progress as well as nationalism, for he had repeatedly begged Ulrich to cultivate this connection, since out of political
considerations he did not just now wish to be caught doing it himself. He
advised starting by approaching not the leaders but the young up-and-
comers, those who were not completely corrupted and whose vitality
permitted the hope that through them one might acquire a patriotically
rejuvenating influence over the party. Then Ulrich remembered cheerfully that there lived in his house a young man who never greeted him
but looked away disdainfully whenever they met, which happened rarely
enough. This was Schmeisser, a doctoral student in technical sciences;
his father was a gardener, who had already been living on the property
when Ulrich took it over and who had since, in exchange for free lodging
and occasional gifts, kept the small old grounds in order partly with his
own hands and partly by indicating and supervising any work that became necessary. Ulrich appreciated the fact that this young man, who
lived with his father and earned the money for his studies by tutoring
and doing a little writing, regarded him as one of the idle rich, who was
to be treated with contempt; the experiment of inaction to which he was
subject sometimes made him regard himself in this fashion, and he
found pleasure in challenging his faultfinder when, one day, he stopped
to talk with Schmeisser. It turned out that the student, who, moreover,
seen from closer up, might already be twenty-six years old, had also been
waiting for this moment, and immediately discharged the tension of the
encounter in violent attacks, which ended between an attempt at con-
version and the proffering of personal contempt. Ulrich told him about
the Parallel Campaign, and thought he was doing the right thing by making his assignment out to be as ridiculous as it was while at the same time
indicating the advantages a determined person might be able to draw
from it. He was expecting Schmeisser to fall in with this scheme, which
then with God's help might develop in rather strange directions; this

*Schmeisser (the name means "flinger" or "hurler") is the left-wing counterpart to the
proto-Fascistic Hans Sepp. Peter Lindner seems to represent apolitical, amoral youth.—
TRANS.

young man, however, was no bourgeois romantic and adventurer, but listened with a crafty look around the mouth until Ulrich ran out of things to say. His chest was narrow between broad-boned shoulders, and he wore thick glasses. These really thick glasses were the beautiful part of his face, which had a sallow, fatty, blotchy skin; these thick glasses, made necessary by hard nights over his books and assignments and made stronger by poverty, which had not permitted him to consult a doctor at the first sign that he needed them, had become for Schmeisser's simple emotions an image of self-liberation: when he spied them in the mirror, shining over his pimpled countenance with its saddle nose and sharp proletarian cheeks, it seemed to him like Poverty crowned by Intellect, and this had happened especially often since, against his will, he had come to admire Agathe from afar. Since then he had also hated Ulrich, to whom he had previously paid scant attention, for his athletic build, and Ulrich now read his damnation in these glasses and had the impression of chattering away like a child playing in front of the barrels of two cannons. When he had finished, Schmeisser answered him with lips that could barely separate themselves for satisfaction at what they were saying: "The party has no need of such adventures; we'll arrive at the goal in our own way!"

That was really giving it to the bourgeois!

After this rebuff it was hard for Ulrich to find more to say, but he went straight at his attacker and finally said with a laugh: "If I were the person you take me for, you ought to pour poison in my water pipes, or saw down the trees under which I stroll: why don't you want to do something of that sort in a case where it might really be called for?"

"You have no idea what politics is all about," Schmeisser retorted, "for you are a social-romantic member of the middle class, at most an individual anarchist! Serious revolutionaries aren't interested in bloody revolutions!"

After that, Ulrich often had brief conversations with this revolutionary who didn't want to start revolutions. "I already knew when I was a cavalry lieutenant," he told him, "that in the short or long run mankind is going to be organized according to socialist principles in some form; it is, as it were, the final chance that God has left to it. For the fact that millions of people are oppressed in the most brutal way, in order for thousands of others to fail to do anything worthwhile with the power that derives from this oppression, is not only unjust and criminal but also stupid, inappropriate, and suicidal!"

Schmeisser responded sarcastically: "But you've always settled for knowing that! Haven't you? There's the bourgeois intellectual for you! You've spoken to me a few times about a bank director who's a friend of yours: I assure you, this bank director is my enemy, I'll fight him, I'll show him that his convictions are only pretexts for his profits; but at least he has convictions! He says yes where I say no! But you? In you everything has already dissolved, in you the bourgeois lie has already begun to decompose!"

Ulrich objected peaceably: "It may be that my way of thinking is bourgeois in origin; to some extent it's even probable. But: *Inter faeces et urinam nascimur*—why not our opinions as well? What does that prove against their correctness?"

Every time Ulrich spoke this way, reasoning politely, Schmeisser could not contain himself and exploded anew. "Everything you're saying springs from the moral corruption of bourgeois society!" he would then proclaim, or something similar, for there was nothing he hated more than that form of goodness opposed to reason which is found in amiability; indeed, all form, even that of beauty, was for him an object of suspicion. For this reason he never accepted even one of Ulrich's invitations, but at most let himself be treated to tea and cigarettes, as if in Russian novels. Ulrich loved to provoke him, although these conversations were completely meaningless. Since the year of liberation in '48 and the founding of the German Empire, events that only a minority now personally remembered, politics probably seemed to the majority of educated people more an atavism than an important subject. There was next to no sign that behind these external processes that plodded along out of habit, intellectual processes were already preparing for that deformation, for that propensity for decline, and for the suicidal willingness arising from self-loathing, which undermine a state of affairs and apparently always form the passive precondition to periods of violent political change. Thus his whole life long Ulrich, too, had been accustomed to expect that politics would bring about not what needed to happen but at best what ought to have happened long since. The image it presented to him was mostly that of criminal neglect. The social question too, which formed the whole of Schmeisser's universe, appeared to him not as a question but merely as an omitted answer, though he could list a hundred other such "questions" on which the mental files had been closed and which, as one might say, were waiting in vain for manipulative treatment in the Office of Dispatch. And when he did that, and Schmeisser was in a gentle mood, the latter said: "Just let us first come to power!"

But then Ulrich said: "You're too kind to me, for what I'm asserting isn't true at all. Almost all intellectual people have this prejudice that the practical questions they understand nothing about would be easy to solve, but when they try, of course it turns out that they just haven't thought of everything. On the other hand—here I agree with you—if the politician were to think of everything, he would never get around to acting. Perhaps that's why politics contains as much of the wealth of reality as of the poverty of spirit (lack of ideas)—"

This gave Schmeisser the opportunity for a jubilant interruption, with the words: "People like you never get around to acting because they don't want the truth! The bourgeois so-called mind is in all its works only a procrastination and an excuse!"

"But why don't people like me want?" Ulrich asked. "Why couldn't they want? Wealth, for example, is certainly not what they really desire. I hardly know a prosperous man who doesn't have a small weakness for it, myself included, but I also don't know a single one who loves money for its own sake, except for misers, and greed is a disturbance of personal conduct which is also found in love, in power, and in honor: the pathological nature of greed really proves that giving is more blessed than receiving. By the way, do you believe that giving is more blessed than receiving?" he asked.

"You can raise that question in some aesthete's salon!" was Schmeisser's response.

"But I fear," Ulrich maintained, "that all your efforts will remain pointless as long as you don't know whether giving or receiving is more blessed or how they complement each other!"

Schmeisser crowed: "You no doubt intend to talk mankind into being good? Besides, in the socially organized state, the proper relationship of giving and receiving will be a foregone conclusion!"

"Then I will maintain"—Ulrich completed his sentence with a smile—"that you will just come to grief on something else, for instance that we are capable of cursing someone as a dog even when we love our dog more than our fellowmen!"

A mirror calmed Schmeisser by showing him the image of a young man wearing thick glasses under a stubborn forehead. He gave no answer.

Ulrich had picked out this young man for the General and proposed that they go with the General to visit Meingast, for Schmeisser knew about this prophet, and even if he was a false one, still it was nothing new for Schmeisser to visit the gatherings of opponents; but Ulrich had correctly guessed about his friend Stumm that at various times he was secretly gathering impressions from Clarisse, and through her had also made the acquaintance of the Master, who had made no small impression. But when Ulrich told Agathe about his plan, she didn't want to hear about it.

Ulrich began to jest. —I bet that this Schmeisser is really in love with you—he maintained—and it's no secret that Lindner is. Both are *for*-men. Meingast, too, is a *for*-man. You'll end up winning him over too.

Agathe naturally wanted to know what *for*-men were.

—Lindner is a good person, isn't he? Ulrich asked.

Agathe confirmed it, although for a long time she had not been as enthusiastic on this count as she had been at the beginning.

—But he lives more *for* religion than *in* a religious state?

Agathe didn't contest this at all.

—That's just what a *for*-man is, Ulrich explained. —The extensive activity he bestows upon his faith is perhaps the most important example, but it's just one example of the technique that's always used to make ideals tenable and available for everyday use. So he explained to her in detail his spontaneously invented notion of living *for* and *in* something.

Human life appears to be just long enough so that in it, if one lives *for* something, one can accomplish the trajectory from neophyte to Nestor, patriarch, or pioneer; and in doing so it matters less for human satisfaction *what* one lives for than that one can live *for* something: a Nestor of the German brandy trade and the pioneer of a new worldview enjoy, besides similar honors, the same advantage, which consists in the fact that life, despite its fearful wealth, contains not a single problem that would not be simplified by being brought into contact with a worldview, but would be simplified just as much by being brought into contact with the production of brandy. Such an advantage is precisely what one calls, using a fairly recent term, rationalization, except that what is rationalized is not skilled actions but ideas, and who today would not already be able to survey what that implies? Even in the slightest case this life *for* something is comparable to owning a notebook in which everything is entered and things that have been disposed of are neatly crossed out. Whoever does not do this lives in a disorderly fashion, never finishes things, and is bothered by their comings and goings; whoever, on the other hand, has a notebook resembles the thrifty paterfamilias who saves every nail, every piece of rubber, every scrap of material, because he knows that someday such a stock will come in handy in his household economy. But this solid, civic *for* something, as it was handed down from one's father's generation as the height of worthy endeavor, often too as a hobbyhorse or a secret detail one always keeps one's eye on, represented at that time something which was already somewhat old-fashioned; for a propensity for the broad scale, a yen for developing the living-for-something in mighty associations, had already replaced it.

By this means what Ulrich had begun in jest took on, as he uttered it, more serious significance. The distinction he had hit upon tempted him with its inexhaustible prospects, and became for him at this moment one of those views that make the world fall asunder like a split apple under the knife, exposing what lies within. Agathe objected that one also often says that a person is completely subsumed by something, or lives and breathes it, although it was certain that according to Ulrich's nomenclature such ardent livers and breathers were doing it *for* whatever their affair might be; and Ulrich conceded that it would be more precise to proceed by distinguishing between the notions of "finding oneself in the state of one's ideal" and "finding oneself in the state of working for one's ideal," but in which the second "in" was either unreal and in truth a "for," or the claimed relationship to working *for* it would have to be an unusual and ecstatic one. Language, moreover, has its good reasons not to be so precise about this, since living *for* something is the condition of worldly existence, *in,* on the contrary, always that which one imagines and pretends to live, and the relation of these two states to each other is extremely refractory. People, after all, do secretly know, without, of course, being able to admit it, of the miraculous fact that everything "it's worth living for" would be unreal if not actually absurd the moment one tried to immerse oneself in it completely. Love would never again arise from its lair; in politics, the slightest proof of sincerity would necessarily lead to the mortal destruction of one's opponent; the artist would spurn all contact with less perfect beings, and morality would have to consist not of perforated prescriptions but of taking one back to that childlike condition of love of the good and abhorrence of the bad which takes everything literally. For whoever really abhors crime would not find it too little to hire trained professional devils to torture prisoners as in old paintings of hellfire, and whoever loves virtue with his whole life ought to eat nothing but goodness until his stomach rises into his throat. What's remarkable is that at times things really do go that far, but that such periods of Inquisition or its opposite, gushing over the goodness of man, are in bad odor / bad memories / remain memories.

That is why it is simply to preserve life that mankind has succeeded in inventing, in place of "what it's worth living for," living *for* it or, in other words, putting its idealism in place of its ideal condition. It is a living before something; now, instead of living, one "strives" and is henceforth a being that with all its energies presses on just as much toward fulfillment as it is exonerated from arriving at it. "Living for something" is the permanent principle of the "in." All desires, and not just love, are sad after they are fulfilled; but in the moment in which the activity *for* the desire fully takes the place of the desire, it is canceled out in an ingenious way, for now the inexhaustible system of means and obstacles takes the place of the goal. In this system even a monomaniac does not

live monotonously but constantly has new things to do, and even whoever could not live at all *in* the content of his life—a case that is more
frequent today than one thinks: for example, a professor at an agricul-
tural college who has set the management of stall wastes and dung on
new paths—lives for this content without complaint, and enjoys listening to music or other such experiences, if he is a capable person, always,
as it were, in honor of managing stables. This doing something else "in
honor of something" is, moreover, somewhat further removed from the
"something" than from the "for" and consequently is the method most
frequently applied, because it is as it were the cheapest, of doing in the
name of an ideal all those things that cannot be reconciled with it.

For the advantage of all "for" and "in honor of" consists in the fact
that through serving the ideal, everything which the ideal itself excludes
is again brought to life. The classic example of this was furnished by the
traveling knights of chivalric love, who fell like mad dogs upon every
equal they encountered in honor of a condition in their heart that was as
soft and fragrant as dripping church wax. But the present, too, is not
lacking in small peculiarities of this kind. Thus, for example, it organizes
luxurious festivals for the alleviation of poverty. Or the large number of
strict people who insist on the carrying out of public principles from
which they know themselves exempt. Then, too, the hypocritical admission that the end justifies the means belongs here, for in reality it is the
always active and colorful means for whose sake one usually puts up with
ends that are moral and insipid. And no matter how playful such examples may appear, this objection falls silent before the disturbing observation that civilized life doubtless has a tendency toward the most violent
outbursts, and that these are never more violent than when they take
place in honor of great and sacred, indeed even of tender, emotions!
Are they then felt to be excused? Or is the relationship not rather the
opposite?

Thus, by many interrelated paths, one arrives at the conclusion that
people are not good, beautiful, and truthful, but rather would like to be,
and one has a sense of how the serious problem of why this is so is veiled
by the illuminating pretense that the ideal is, by its very nature, unattainable. This was more or less what Ulrich said, without sparing attacks on
Lindner and what he stood for. Right thinking that was the effortless
result of this. It was certain, he maintained, that Lindner was ten times
more convinced of two-times-two or the rules of morality than he was of
his God, but by working for his conviction about God, he largely evaded
this difficulty. For this purpose he put himself into the condition of *belief,* an attitude in which what he *wanted* to be convinced of was so inge-

niously combined with what he *could* be convinced of that he himself was no longer able to separate them—

Here Agathe noted that all acting is questionable. She reminded herself of the paradoxical assertion that the only people who remain real and good in their hearts are those who do not do many good deeds. This now seemed to her extended, and thus confirmed, by the agreeable possibility that the condition of activity was fundamentally the adulteration of another condition, from which it arose and which it pretended to serve.

Ulrich affirmed this once more. "We have on the one side," he repeated by way of summary, "people who live for and, without taking the word too literally, in something, who are constantly on the move, who strive, weave, till, sow, and harvest, in a word the idealists, for all these idealists of today are really living *for* their ideals. And on the other side are those who would like to live in some fashion *in* their gods, but for these there is not even a name—"

"What is this 'in'?" Agathe asked emphatically.

Ulrich shrugged his shoulders and then gave a few indications. "One could relate 'for' and 'in' to what has been called experiencing in a convex and experiencing in a concave way. Perhaps the psychoanalytic legend that the human soul strives to get back to the tender protection of the intrauterine condition before birth is a misunderstanding of the 'in,' perhaps not. Perhaps 'in' is the presumed descent of all life from God. But perhaps the explanation is also simply to be found in psychology; for every affect bears within it the claim of totality to rule alone and, as it were, form the 'in' in which everything else is immersed; but no affect can maintain itself as primary for long without by that very fact changing, and thus it absolutely yearns for opposing affects in order to renew itself through them, which is pretty much an image of our indispensable 'for'— Enough! One thing is certain: that all sociable life arises from the 'for' and unites mankind in the aim of apparently living *for* something; mankind mercilessly defends these aims; what we see today by way of political developments are all attempts to put other 'for's in place of the lost community of religion. The living 'for something' of the individual person has lagged behind with the paterfamilias and the age of Goethe. The middle-class religion of the future will perhaps be satisfied with bringing the masses together in a belief that might have no content at all but in which the feeling of being *for* it together will be that much more powerful—"

There was no doubt that Ulrich was evading a decision (about the question), for what did Agathe care about political development!

On Agathe

Agathe at Lindner's

During this entire time Agathe was continuing her visits to Lindner.

This made extravagant claims on his Account for Unforeseen Loss of Time, and all too often this overdraft meant a reduction in all his other activities. Moreover, empathy for this young woman also demanded a great deal of time when she was not there:

Thus Lindner had found a soul, but deep tones of discontent were intermingled with it and kept him in a state of constant irritation.

Agathe had simply ignored his forbidding her to visit.

"Does my visiting embarrass you?" she asked the first time she showed up again.

"And what does your brother say to this?" Lindner replied earnestly every time.

"I haven't told him anything about it," Agathe confided in him, "because it might be that he wouldn't like it. You've made me anxious."

Of course one cannot withhold a helping hand from a person seeking help.

But every time they made an appointment Agathe was late. It was no use telling her that unpunctuality was the same as breaking a contract or as lack of conscience. "It indicates that the rest of the time, too, your will is in a slumbering state, and that you're dreamily giving yourself up to things that turn up by chance, instead of breaking away at the right time with collected and focused energy!" Lindner conjectured severely.

"If only it were dreamily!" Agathe replied.

But Lindner declared sharply: "Such a lack of self-control makes one suspect every other kind of undependability!"

"Apparently. I suspect that too," was Agathe's response.

"Don't you have any will?"

"No."

"You're a fantasist and have no discipline!"

"Yes." And after a short pause she added, smiling: "My brother says that I'm a person of fragments; that's lovely, isn't it? Even if it's not clear what it means. One might think of an unfinished volume of unfinished poems."

Lindner was resentfully silent.

"My husband, on the other hand, is now impolitely asserting that I'm pathological, a neuropath or something like that," Agathe went on.

And thereupon Lindner exclaimed sarcastically: "You don't say! How pleased people are today when moral tasks can apparently be reduced to medical ones! But I can't make things that comfortable for you!"

The only pedagogical success that Lindner was able to achieve he owed to the principle that five minutes before the end of each visit, which was always set and agreed upon beforehand, without regard to its delayed start and however much the conversation might absorb him, he began to fall silent and gave Agathe to understand that he now needed to devote his time to other obligations. Agathe not only greeted this rudeness with smiles; she was grateful for it. For such minutes of the conversation, framed on at least one side as if by a metal edge and ticking sharply, also imparted to the remainder of the day something of their incisiveness. After the extravagant conversations with Ulrich, this had the effect of leanness or tightly belted straps.

But when she once said this to Lindner, thinking to be nice to him, it immediately made him miss a quarter of an hour, and the next day he was quite indignant with himself.

In these circumstances he was a strict teacher for Agathe.

But Agathe was an odd pupil. This man, who wanted to do something to help her, although most recently he was having difficulties himself, still gave her confidence and even consolation whenever she was on the point of despairing of making any progress with Ulrich. She then sought Lindner out, and not only because, for whatever external reasons, he was Ulrich's adversary, but also and even more because he revealed as clearly as he did involuntarily the jealousy that came over him at the mere mention of Ulrich's name. It was obviously not personal rivalry, for Agathe was aware that the two men hardly knew each other, but rather a rivalry between intellectual species, the way species of animals have their particular enemies, whom they already recognize when they meet them for the first time and whose slightest approach makes them agitated. And remarkably, she could understand Lindner; for something that might be called jealousy was also among her feelings toward Ulrich, a not being able to keep up, or an offended fatigue, perhaps too, simply put, a feminine jealousy of his masculine pleasure in ideas, and this made her happy to listen, shivering with pleasure, whenever Lindner contested some opinion or other that could be Ulrich's, and this he especially loved to do. She could go along with this the more safely in that she felt closer to Lindner's level than to her brother's, for however militant Lindner appeared, indeed even though he might intimidate her, there always remained working within her a secret mistrust, which was really / sometimes of the kind that women feel against the endeavors of other women.

Agathe still felt her heart beating whenever she sat alone for a moment in Lindner's surroundings, as if she were exposed to the rising of vapors that enchanted her mind. The temptation, the unease she felt at making herself feel at ease, the illusive possibility that it might happen, always evoked in her the story of an abducted girl who, educated among strangers, changed places as it were within herself and became a different woman: this was one of the stories that, reaching back to her childhood and without being especially important to her, had sometimes played a role in the temptations of her life and their excuses. But Ulrich had given her a particular interpretation of these stories, from which otherwise it would be easy to deduce merely a deficient spiritual constitution, and she believed more passionately in his interpretation than he did himself. For in the length and breadth of time, God has created more than this one life that we happen to be leading; it is in no way the true one, it is one of His many hopefully systematic experiments, into which He has placed no compulsion of necessity for those of us who are not blinded by the light of the passing moment, and Ulrich, talking this way about God and the imperfection of the world and the aimless, meaningless facticity of its course, stripping away its false order to reveal the true vision of God that represented the most promising approach to Him, also taught her the meaning of the tentative claim of this way of understanding how one could, in a shadowy figuration alongside oneself, also be another.

So as she attentively observed Lindner's walls, which were equipped (hung) with pictures of divine subjects, Agathe felt that Ulrich was hovering in the vicinity. It occurred to her that she found Raphael, Murillo, and Bernini in individual engravings on the walls, but not Titian, and nothing at all from the Gothic period; on the other hand, there predominated in many of the pictures present-day imitations of that style à la Jesuit Baroque that had sucked up vast quantities of sugar like a puffy omelet. If one followed only these pictures around the walls, the piling up of billowing robes and vacant, uplifted oval faces and sweetish naked bodies was disquieting. Agathe said: There is so much soul in them that the total effect is of a monstrous despiritualization. And look: the heavenward gaze has become such a convention that all the irrepressible human vitality has taken refuge in the less prominent details and hidden itself there. Don't you find these garment hems, shoes, leg positions, arms, robe folds, and clouds loaded down by all the sexuality that isn't openly recognized? This isn't too far removed from fetishism!

Well, Agathe ought to know about this phenomenon of being loaded down. This yearningly leaning out from a balcony into the void. Or it's really the other way around: an infinite pressing inward. With horror, one could see it right here on the borderline between pathological crotchet and exaltation.

Lindner had no inkling of this. But the reproach dismayed him, and he first tried speaking of this beauty in a belittling way. The artist must make use of the material and the fleshly, and clings to it; this leads to a lower order of art. Agathe overestimated it. Art might well propagate the great experiences of mankind but could not turn them into experience.

Agathe then angrily accused him of having too many such pictures. The freedoms that, according to what he said, had to be conceded to the lower humanity in the artist still seemed by that measure to have some meaning even for him. —What? Agathe asked.

Cornered, Lindner gave his views on art. True art is spiritualization of matter. It can represent nakedness only when the superiority of soul over matter speaks from the representation.

Agathe objected that he was mistaken, for it was the superiority not of soul that was speaking, but of convention.

Suddenly he burst out: Or did she think that could justify to a serious person painters' and sculptors' cult of nakedness? —Is the naked human really such a beautiful thing? Something so scandalous! Aren't the transports of aesthetes simply ridiculous, even if one doesn't even try to apply serious moral concepts (to them)?

Agathe: —The naked body is beautiful! . . . This was a lie, for heaven's sake, whose only purpose was to enrage her partner. Agathe had never paid any attention to the beauty of male bodies; women today regard a man's body for the most part only as an armature to support the head. Men are accustomed to pay somewhat more attention to beauty. But let one gather all the naked bodies with which our museums and exhibitions are filled and put them in a single place, and then seek out from among this confusion of white maggots those that are truly beautiful. The first thing one would notice is that the naked body is usually merely naked: naked like a face that for decades has worn a beard and is suddenly shaven. But beautiful? That the world stops in its tracks whenever a truly beautiful person appears reveals beauty to be a mystery; because beauty-love and love are a mystery, it is true for the whole. Likewise that the concept of beauty has been lost (assembly-line art). So she sits there, and Ulrich speaks through her mouth.

But Lindner immediately jumps at the challenge. —Well! he exclaimed. —Oh, of course, the modern cult of the body! It excites the imagination in just one direction and inflames it with claims that life can't fulfill! Even the exaggerated concern with physical culture that the Americans have wished on us is a great danger!

—You're seeing ghosts, Agathe said indifferently.

Lindner to this: —Many pure women, who welcome and participate in such things without a deeper knowledge of life, don't consider that in doing so they are conjuring up spirits that might perhaps destroy their own lives and the lives of those closest to them!

Agathe retorted sharply: —Should one bathe only once every two weeks? Bite off one's nails? Wear flannel and smell of chilblain ointment? . . . It was an attack on these surroundings, but at the same time she felt imprisoned and ridiculously punished for having to argue over such platitudes.

Their conversations often took the form of Agathe's mocking and irritating him so that he would lose his temper and "bark." This was how she was acting now, and Lindner took on the adversary.

—A truly manly soul will regard not only the plastic arts but also the whole institution of the theater with the greatest reservation, and calmly suffer the scorn and mockery of those who are too effeminate to rigorously forbid themselves every tickling of the senses! he asserted, immediately adding novels with the remark that most novels, too, unmistakably breathe the sensual enslavement and overstimulation of their authors and stimulate the reader's lower aspects precisely through the poetic illusion with which they gloss over and cover up everything!

He seemed to assume that Agathe despised him for being inartistic, and was anxious to show his superiority. "It is after all dogma," he exclaimed, "that one must have heard and seen everything in order to be able to talk about it! But how much better it would be if one would be proud of one's lack of culture and let others prattle! One shouldn't convince oneself that it's part of culture to look at filth under electric light."

Agathe looked at him, smiling, without answering. His observations were so dismally obtuse that her eyes misted over. This moist, mocking glance left him uncertain.

—All these observations are not, of course, directed at great and true art! Lindner qualified / assured her / he retreated.

Since Agathe continued her silence, he yielded another step.

"It's not prudery," he defended himself. "Prudery would itself be only a sign of corrupted imagination. But naked beauty evokes the tragic in the inner person and, at the same time, spiritual powers, which the tragic strives to absolve and unbind: do you understand what I'm feeling?" He stopped before her. He was again captivated by her. He looked at her. "That's why one must either conceal nakedness or so associate it with man's higher longings that it isn't enslaving and arousing but calming and liberating." This was what had always been attempted at the high points of art, in the figures of the frieze on the Parthenon, in Raphael's transcendent figures—Michelangelo associates transfigured bodies with the suprasensual world, Titian binds covetousness through a facial expression that does not stem from the world of natural drives.

Agathe stood up. "Just a minute!" she said. "You have a thread in your beard," and she reached up rapidly and seemed to remove something; Lindner could not make out whether it was real or pretended, since he spontaneously and with signs of chaste horror fell back, while she immediately sat down again. He was extremely upset at his clumsy lack of self-control, and attempted to mask it through a blustering tone. He rode around like a Sunday rider on the word "tragic," which suited him so badly. He had said that naked beauty evokes the tragic in the inner man, and now supplemented this by saying that this tragic sense repeats itself in art, whose powers in spite of everything did not suffice for complete spiritualization. This was not very illuminating, but it quite clearly amounted to saying that the soul of man is not a protection against the senses but their powerful echo! Indeed, sensuality acquired its power only in that its false pretenses conquered and usurped man's soul!

"Is that a confession?" Agathe asked dryly, unabashed.

"How so, a confession?" Lindner exclaimed. And he added: "What an arrogant way of looking at things you have! What megalomania! And besides: What do you think of me?" But he fled, quit the field, he actually physically retreated before Agathe.

One discovers nothing so quickly as another's inner insecurity, and pounces on it like a cat on a grubbing beetle: it was really the capricious technique of the girls' boarding school, with its passions between the admired "big ones" and adoring smaller ones, the eternal basic form of spiritual dependency, which Agathe was using against Lindner by appearing to respond understandingly and ardently to his words as often as she fell upon him coldly and frightened him just when he thought he was secure in a shared feeling.

From the corner of the room his voice now boomed like an organ, with an artificially fearless bass; he acted as if *he* were the aggressor by proposing: "Let's talk about this, for once, freely and frankly. Realize how inadequate and unsatisfying the entire process of procreation is as a mere natural process. Even motherhood! Is its physiological mechanism really so indescribably marvelous and perfect? How much horrible suffering it involves, how much senseless and unbearable contingency! So let's just leave the deification of nature to those who don't know what life is, and open our eyes to reality: the process of procreation is ennobled and raised above apathetic servitude only by being endowed with loyalty and responsibility, and subordinated to spiritual ideals!"

Agathe seemed to be reflecting silently. Then she asked relentlessly: "Why are you talking to me about the process of procreation?"

Lindner had to take a deep breath: "Because I am your friend! Schopenhauer has shown us that what we would like to think of as our most intimate experience is the most impersonal of arousals. But the higher emotions are exempted from this deception of the drive to procreate: loyalty, for instance, pure, selfless love, admiration and serving."

"Why?" Agathe asked. "Certain feelings that suit you are supposed to have some supernatural origin, and others to be mere nature?"

Lindner hesitated; he struggled. "I can't marry again," he said softly and hoarsely. "I owe that to my son Peter."

"But who's asking that of you? Now I don't understand you," Agathe replied.

Lindner shrank back. "I meant to say that even if I could do it, I wouldn't," he said defensively. "Moreover, in my opinion friendship between man and wife demands an even more elevated frame of mind than love!" He made another try: "You know my principles, so you must also understand that in accord with them I would like nothing better than to offer to serve you as a brother, even to awaken, so to speak, in the woman the counterweight to the woman: I'd like to reinforce the Mary in the Eve!" He was close to breaking out in a sweat, so strenuous was it to pursue the strict line of his reasoning.

"So you're offering me a kind of eternal friendship," Agathe said quietly. "That's lovely of you. And you surely know that your present was accepted in advance."

She seized his hand, as is appropriate at such a moment, and was a little taken aback at this epidermal piece of strange person that lay in the lap of her hand. Lindner was not able to withdraw his fingers either: it seemed to him that he should, and yet also that he didn't have to. Even Ulrich's lack of resolution sometimes exercised this natural impulse to flirt with her, but Agathe also despaired if she saw that she was doing it successfully herself, for the power of flirtation is united with the notion of bribery, cunning, and compulsion, and no longer with love; and while she was reminded of Ulrich, she looked at this unsteady creature, who was now bobbing up and down inwardly like a cork, in a mood, shot through with evil thoughts, that was close to tears.

"I would like you to open your refractory and taciturn heart to me," Lindner said timorously, warmly, and comically. "Don't think of me as a man. You've missed having a mother!"

"Fine," Agathe responded. "But can you stand it? Would you be prepared to entrust me with your friendship"—she withdrew her hand—"even if I were to tell you that I had stolen and that I had incest on my conscience?" therefore (or) something on account of which one is ruthlessly expelled from the community of others?

Lindner forced himself to smile. "What you're saying is strong, of course; it's even extremely unfeminine to venture such a jest," he scolded. "Honestly! Do you know what you remind me of at such moments? Of a child who's made up its mind to annoy a grownup! But this isn't the moment for that," he added, offended because he was just now reminding himself of it.

But suddenly Agathe had something in her voice that cut through the conversation to the bottom when she asked: "You believe in God; reveal to me: In what way does He answer when you ask Him for advice and a decision about a heavy sin?"

Lindner rejected this question with the appalled severity that a decorous palace employee shows / puts on when asked about the married life of the Royal Couple.

Agathe: God in association with crime, specifically the Augustinian God, the abyss. Maybe really as Augustinian as possible: I see no possibility of being good on my own. I don't understand when I am doing good or evil. Only His grace can tear me away, or something similar. Seems to assume that she had recently been worrying about this. For the moment remains *open*.

Lindner did feel something of the passion of her words, therefore his answer gentle and father-confessorial: I don't know your life, you've only given me a few hints. But I consider it possible that you could act in a way similar to the way a bad person would act. You haven't learned in the small things to take life seriously, and therefore you perhaps won't hit it right when it comes to big decisions. You're probably capable of doing evil and disregarding all standards for no other reason than that it's a matter of indifference to you what the other person feels, but that only because, while you feel the impulse to the good, you don't know how much wisdom and obedience it involves. He seized her hand and asked: "Tell me the truth."

"The truth is more or less what I've already told you," Agathe repeated soberly and emphatically.

"No!"

"Yes." There was something in this simple "yes" that made Lindner suddenly push away her hand.

Agathe said: "You wanted to make me better, didn't you? If I'm like a gold piece twisted out of shape that you'd like to bend back, I'm still a gold piece, aren't I? But you're losing your courage. The challenge (from God?) presented to you in my person collides with your conventional division of actions into light and darkness. And I say to you: to identify God with a human morality is blasphemy!"

The voice in which she exclaimed this had, at least for Lindner, the sound of trumpets, something oddly arousing; he also felt Agathe's wild youthful beauty, and suffered enough as it was, whenever he reproached her, from an unutterable anxiety and insinuation. For his principles, where were his principles? They were round about him, but far off. And in the empty space whose innermost vacuum was now his breast, something stirred that was despicable but as alive as a basket full of puppies. Certainly, the only reason he wanted to strike to the heart of this obdurate young woman was in order to do her a service, but the heart he was aiming at looked like a piece of flower flesh. Since Lindner had become a widower he had lived ascetically and avoided prostitutes and frivolous women on principle, but, to say it straight out, the more ardent he was about saving Agathe, the more grounded his fear became that in the process he would one day experience himself in a state of impermissible arousal. For this reason he often rapidly counted to fifty inwardly, in moments of anger as well as love. But his success was a remarkable one: the more this enabled him to drive his arousal from the point of threatened breach, the more it gathered in his whole body, until his body seemed to shine inside. He chose words of blame, but inwardly they were, ultimately, as soft as dying candles. He himself simply no longer believed what he was saying, for while externally he separated good from evil, inwardly everything was as mixed up together as it had been in Paradise before the Fall. And with a horrifying clarity for which there are no words, he was reminded of that grimly edifying experience which, in his adolescence, had warned him once and for all against the power of the emotions. Lindner felt punished by a bitter self-contempt when he had to think that what at that time had clothed itself with devilish cunning in the appearance of God was now emerging in his mature years as common lust of the flesh, precisely in the way that the Enlightener's shallow view had said it would.

—Get away from me with this lie! he begged.

—The will? Agathe said. —It's not a lie. I've falsified a will.

Lindner seized her by the arm in sudden anger as if she were a pupil and shouted: "Out!"

"No," Agathe replied. "In our struggle against each other we have a secret pact to drive out each other's devils!"

—You are arrogant and vain! Lindner exclaimed. —But behind it lies suffering and disappointment and humiliation! And again he nearly had it right.

But he only nearly had it right, and Agathe suddenly became tired of it (him) and left him standing.

Museum pre-chapter
At the lawyer's

Were their souls two doves in a world of hawks and owls? Ulrich would never have been able to contemplate letting such a view prevail, and he was therefore fond of remarking, and even found a kind of security in doing so, that external events took no account of the ravishments and anxieties of the soul but followed their own logic. Since Hagauer's letters had compelled him to consult a lawyer, Hagauer too had turned to a counselor, and since both attorneys were now exchanging letters, a "case" had begun, independent of personal origins and furnished, as it were, with suprapersonal powers of attorney. This case compelled Ulrich's lawyer to ask for a personal consultation with Agathe and to be surprised when she did not appear and, later, when she still did not appear, to raise serious questions that finally put Ulrich in the extreme position of having to overcome his sister's resistance by painting the unpleasant consequences. When they appeared at their adviser's, this already put the course of events on a certain path. They found before them a secure and adroit man not much older than they, who was accustomed to smiling and preserving a polite composure even in the halls of the court and who, in consulting with his clients, proceeded from the principle that the first thing to do was gain his own picture of all things and people and take care to let himself be influenced as little as possible by the client, who was always undependable and wasted time.

And indeed Agathe did declare afterward that the whole time, she had felt like a "law patient," and this was true to the extent that all her answers to the introductory and basic questions of her lawyer were of a nature to reinforce the latter's doubts. His task was difficult. A departure from "bed and board," the easily arranged "separation," did not suffice for his client's wishes, and a divorce "of the conjugal bond," the true annulment of the Catholic marriage concluded with Hagauer, was, according to the laws of the land, impossible; it could be managed only by a roundabout route through various other countries and their legal interconnections, as well as through complicated acquisitions and renunciations of citizenship, which did open a path that ought to lead safely to the goal but was by no means without difficulty or easily surveyed in advance. So Agathe's lawyer had undertaken to substitute a more valid reason for her all too ordinary grounds for divorce, which she indicated simply as aversion.

"Insurmountable aversion wouldn't be enough; don't you have something else against your husband?" he probed.

Agathe said, curtly, no. There was much she could have reproached Hagauer with, but she became red and pale, for it all belonged in this place as little as she did herself. She was angry with Ulrich.

The lawyer looked at her attentively. "Impolite treatment, frivolous management of property, flagrant neglect of conjugal obligations . . . how about those?" He tried to get her to have an idea. "The surest grounds for divorce, of course, is always marital infidelity!"

Agathe looked at her interlocutor and answered in a clear, composed, low voice: "I have none of those grounds!"

Perhaps she ought to have smiled. Then the man who sat opposite her, in impeccably correct clothes that in no way contradicted his capacity for high spirits, would have been convinced that he had before him a lovely and undefinably captivating woman. But the seriousness of her expression left him no room at all, and his lawyer's brain became dull. He recalled from the files, which contained not only the correspondence of the opposing attorney but also the letters from Hagauer to Ulrich, Hagauer's carefully documented complaints that the desire for a divorce was unjustified and capriciously frivolous, and the thought went through his mind that he would much rather be representing this apparently reasonable and dependable man. Then it occurred to him that somewhere the term "psychopathic woman" occurred, but he rejected it not so much on account of Agathe as because it might have prevented him from taking on this rewarding commission. "Nervous, of course: The kind of nervousness that's capable of anything, not at all uncommon!" he thought, and cautiously began to direct his questioning at the point that had impressed him as most in need of explanation when he had gone over the situation. In the correspondence in the files there were—both in Hagauer's letters to Ulrich and, more significantly, in the correspondence of the opposing lawyer—more or less clear allusions that gave the sense that the two men might know of irregularities which had taken place in the management of the estate, or might even be of a mind to suspect the relations that had since ensued between brother and sister: these results, noted from the point-by-point checklist of Ulrich's brother-in-law's reflections, were intended to be understood as indicating that the pair might well consider whether it would not be better to change their resolve before they went too far in an affair that held all sorts of danger for them. Agathe's new adviser now brought up these unambiguous allusions by turning to Ulrich, as the person more familiar to him, with the politeness of a man who cannot spare another the repetition of a superfluous unpleasantness; but every so often he turned to Agathe and gave her to understand that although it was only a question of pure formality, still she, too, as his client, had to give him some assurance about these objections, which in certain circumstances, when brought unscrupulously out into the open, could weigh so heavily, an assurance on which he could base his further actions.

But Agathe had neither read Hagauer's letters nor informed Ulrich of what she had been doing during the time she had been alone following the "so-called falsifying of the will"—involuntarily, at this moment, he was speaking thus cautiously to himself! This led to a short, embarrassed pause that had a quite peculiar effect. Ulrich sought to bring it to an end by a gesture whose calm superciliousness sought to characterize the lawyer's request as superfluous and already accommodated, but his sister disturbed this plan somewhat by asking the lawyer out of curiosity what her husband really thought he knew. The lawyer looked from one to the other. "My sister will, of course, give you the assurance you desire in any form," Ulrich declared quickly and with the greatest indifference. "I have informed her of the precise content of the letters, but for quite personal reasons she herself has read them only in part." Agathe now smiled in time, having caught her error, and confirmed that this was so. "I was too out of sorts," she asserted calmly.

The attorney reflected for a moment. It went through his mind that this incident could quite well be an unwished-for confirmation of the adversary's assertion that Agathe was under her brother's baleful influence. Of course he did not believe this to be the case, but felt, even so, a slight aversion toward Ulrich. This moved him to answer Agathe with the greatest politeness: "I must sincerely beg your pardon, madame, but my profession compels me to insist on the request that you examine the matter for yourself." And with these words, gently insisting, he handed the file over to her.

Agathe hesitated.

Ulrich said: "You must formally examine it yourself."

The lawyer smiled politely and added: "I beg your pardon, not only formally."

Agathe let her glance dip twice into the pages, pulled a wry face, and slapped the file shut again.

The lawyer was satisfied. "These allusions are meaningless," he assured her. "That's what I assumed from the start. My colleague simply should not have given in to his client's unpleasant irritability. But it would of course be embarrassing if during the civil procedure a criminal indictment should suddenly be entered. If that happens, one would immediately have to respond with a countercomplaint on grounds of slander, or something similar." Seemingly without his wishing it, what he was saying again passed from the unreal to the possible, and it seemed to Ulrich that in these assurances a question was still lurking.

"Of course it would be extremely embarrassing," he confirmed dryly, and thought he would consult, aside from this celebrated divorce lawyer, a proper criminal lawyer, one with whom one could speak more openly in order to address all the possibilities contained in such an unfortunate story. But he did not know how to find such a man. "A battle of this dirty kind is always embarrassing for people who are clean," he added. "But is there something else one can do besides wait?"

The lawyer acted as if he needed to think this over for a moment, smiled, and said that he was sorry, but he must very strongly advise that they go back to his original proposal and show that their adversary had transgressed marital fidelity. The length of time the separation had already lasted gave grounds for assuming the factual basis of such a complaint; there was no lack of investigators who took care of these things dependably and discreetly, and with this, as it were, classical ground for divorce, one would inevitably and most rapidly arrive at their goal, which would be of the greatest advantage in a struggle where one must not leave the adversary any time to develop his intrigues.

Ulrich also seemed to see the necessity of this.

But Agathe, who had completely lost the confidence she had once had in her dealings with lawyers and other persons of the law, said no. Whether she had imagined that one orders a divorce from a lawyer the way one orders a cake from the baker, which is selected and delivered to one's house, or whether it happened that she held it against Ulrich for having put her in a situation where her sense of responsibility for the embarrassments being visited upon the innocent Hagauer was awakened, or whether she simply could not bear the collapse of her world in the continuance of such conferences; enough, she refused vehemently.

She also considered this proposal to be a convenience on the part of the lawyer, and might perhaps have let herself be talked out of it; but Ulrich did not do so, merely excusing her smilingly with the jest that even through a detective she had no desire to find out any more about her husband, and the divorce lawyer suddenly gave a sigh of chivalric defeat, for he wanted to bring the conference to an end. He now assured them that they would try to attain their goal this way, and pushed over to Agathe the power of attorney for her to sign.

Addendum. Possibly: Ulrich asks whether there were any proposals from Hagauer for an amicable settlement, and declares the continuation of the conference in this sense otherwise undesirable.

· · ·

Even as they were descending the steps, Ulrich took Agathe's arm in his, and in that moment they involuntarily stopped.

"We were in reality for an hour!" he said.

Agathe looked at him. Pain closed off the background of her light eyes like a stone wall.

"Are you very depressed?" he asked sympathetically.

"It involves such humiliation that we must withdraw from it," she replied slowly.

"That's very much the question," Ulrich said.

"A real humiliation, like falling with one's mouth in the dust! Something we have forgotten how to imagine lately!" Agathe added in a soft, urgent voice.

"I mean, the question is whether we will be allowed to withdraw from this humiliation," Ulrich responded. "Perhaps there are even greater ones threatening us. I must confess to you that my sense of our situation today is that it's bad. For, granted we give in: perhaps we could claim it had been an error, hastily repair it, cover things up. But it would be up to him to accept it or not, and he isn't going to give you up; indeed, now that he's become suspicious, he won't put down his weapons until you've submitted to him unconditionally. That's simply his sense of order!" Ulrich said, since Agathe did not seem to want to wait for him to finish. "On the other hand, we could of course follow our lawyer's proposal or some similar plan and try to wear him down. But what does that get us? Increased danger, for the enemy will feel himself absolved from all restraint by our attack, and in the best case our success would be that besides the divorce we would have maliciously harmed a person to whom we are profoundly indifferent."

"And the guilt of existence?" Agathe objected passionately, although she violently forced herself to make a jest of it. "What you yourself have often said, that the only woman who remains pure is the one who has her lover's head chopped off?"

"Did I say that? One would have to blow up the planet," Ulrich said calmly, "if one wanted to get rid of all the witnesses to one's mistakes!" And he added seriously: "You're still misjudging the degree of ordinariness, the tangible difficulty, of the situation we're in: one way or the other, we're threatened with disaster and have only the choice of remaining so or—"

"Killing ourselves!" Agathe said curtly and decisively.

"Oh come on! How that echoes in the stones of such a staircase! I hope no one heard it!" he rebuked her angrily, and looked cautiously around. "You're so stupid! It's not even sure that death is better than prison. But we could remove ourselves from the choice by running away."

Agathe looked at him, and in this split second her eyes involuntarily resembled those of a child who has been romping wildly and been picked up.

"To an island in the South Seas," Ulrich said, and smiled. "But perhaps an island in the Adriatic would do as well. Where once a week a boat will bring us what we need."

When they stood below at the gateway, they were benumbed and struck by the shock of the summery street. A whitish fire in which bright shadows lived seemed to be waiting for them. People, animals, curbs, even they themselves lost something of their bodily constraints in the hot rays of light. Agathe had said: "You've never wanted to! For that I mean too little to you?" Ulrich responded: "Oh, let's not talk about it this way! It's harder than the resolve to deny the world. For once we've run away, everything here in the real world, which was imposed on us as ours, will turn really bad, and there's hardly any turning back, although we have no idea whether where we want to go there's solid ground on which people can stand differently from the way they do in dreams. If I still keep thinking about it, it's because I have doubts not about you or myself but about what's possible!"

? But on the other hand it's also quite practical! The lawyer has his instructions, the client is away: either both attorneys will come to an agreement in order to wind it up, or they'll procrastinate.

When they finally do come back, everything is in quite good shape: the automatism of life that protects itself against catastrophes. They were merely on a trip, the lawyers were still procrastinating, etc.

C. 1932

52

THE THREE SISTERS

Ulrich asked: "What is it you want from me: my clothes, my books, my house, my views about the future? What should I give you? I'd like to give you everything I have."

Agathe replied: "Cut off your arm for me, or at least a finger!"

They were in the reception room on the ground floor, whose high, narrow windows, arched at the top, let in the soft new morning light, which mingled with the shade of trees as it fell into its own reflection on the floor. If one looked down at oneself it was like seeing beneath one's feet the discolored sky with its brightness and clouds through a brownish glass. Brother and sister had so retired from the world that there was hardly danger any longer of their being disturbed by a visit.

"You're too modest!" Ulrich went on. "Go ahead, ask for my life! I believe I could discard it for you. But a finger? I must confess: a finger is of no importance to me at all!"

He laughed, his sister along with him; but her face retained the expression of someone who sees another joking about something that is serious to him.

Now Ulrich turned the tables: "When one loves one bestows, one 'keeps nothing for oneself,' one doesn't want to possess anything by oneself: why do you want to possess Lindner for yourself?" he asked.

"But I don't possess him at all!" Agathe retorted.

"You possess your secret emotions for him and your secret thoughts about him. Your error about him!"

"And why don't you cut off an arm?" Agathe challenged.

"We will cut it off," was Ulrich's response. "But for the moment I'm still asking myself what kind of life would result if I really gave up my sense of self, and others did likewise? Everyone would have a self in common with everyone else; not only the feeding bowl and the bed would be shared, but truly the self, so that every one would love his neighbor as himself and no one would be his own neighbor."

Agathe said: "That must somehow be possible."

"Can you imagine sharing a lover with another woman?" Ulrich asked.

"I could," Agathe asserted. "I can even imagine it being quite beautiful! I just can't imagine the other woman."

Ulrich laughed.

Agathe made a parrying gesture. "I have a particular personal dislike of women," she said.

"Of course, of course! And I don't like men!"

Agathe felt his mockery was somewhat insulting because she felt that it was not unjustified, and she did not go on to say what she had intended.

In the resulting pause Ulrich, to encourage her, began to relate something he had recently dreamed up in the distracted condition of shaving. "You know that there were times when aristocratic women," he said, "if a slave pleased them, could have him castrated so that they might have their pleasure of him without endangering the aristocracy of their progeny."

Agathe did not know it, but she gave no sign. On the other hand, she now recalled having once read that among some uncivilized tribes every woman married all her husband's brothers along with him and had to serve them all, and every time she imagined such servile humiliation, an involuntary and yet not quite unwelcome shudder made her shrink. But she did not reveal any of this to her brother either.

". . . whether something like that happened often, or only exceptionally, I don't know, nor does it matter," Ulrich had meanwhile been saying. "For, as I must confess, I was thinking only of the slave. More precisely, I was thinking of the moment when he left his sickbed for the first time and encountered the world again. At first, of course, the will to resist and defend himself, which had been paralyzed at the start of what happened, rouses and thaws out again. But then the awareness must set in that it's too late. Anger wants to rebel, but there follow one after the other the memory of the pain suffered, the cowardly awakening of a fear from which only consciousness was removed, and finally that humility signifying a now irrevocable humiliation, and these emotions now hold down the anger, the way the slave himself was held down while the operation was being performed." Ulrich interrupted this odd recital and searched for words; his eyelids were lowered in meditation. "Physically, he could doubtless still pull himself together," he continued, "but a strange feeling of shame will keep him from doing so, for he must recognize its futility in a way that embraces everything; he is no longer a man, he has been debased to a girl-like existence, to the existence of a towel, a handkerchief, a cup, of some kind of being that, not without affection, is allowed to serve. I would like to know the moment when he is then called for the first time before the lady who tortured him and reads in her eyes what she proposes to do with him. . . ."

Agathe laughed mockingly. "You've been thinking some really strange thoughts, Ulo! And when I think that before he was castrated your slave was perhaps a butcher or a stylish domestic . . ."

Ulrich laughed innocently along with her. "Then I myself would probably find my depiction of the awakening of his soul disturbingly comical," he admitted. He himself was happy that this disreputable emotional report was brought to an end. For without his noticing, various things must have come into his mind that didn't belong there: as if something of the mythological goddesses who consume their devotees, or the Siamese twins, up to masochism or the castration complex, had been drawn with fingernails across the dubious keyboard of contemporary psychology! When he had stopped laughing he immediately made an embittered face.

Agathe laid her hand on his arm. The tiny shadows of a concealed excitement twitched in her gray eyes. "But why did you tell me that?" she asked.

"I don't know," Ulrich said.

"I believe you were thinking of me," she asserted.

"Nonsense!" Ulrich retorted, but after a while he asked: "Do you know that another letter from Hagauer came today?" and so apparently began talking about something else.

The letters from Hagauer that were then arriving became more threatening from one to the next. "I don't understand why, under these circumstances, he doesn't get on the train and come here to confront us," Ulrich went on.

"He won't find the time," Agathe said.

And that was indeed how it was. At the beginning Hagauer had resolved several times to do just that, but every time something intervened, and then he had become rather accustomed to being alone. It seemed to him not a bad thing to live for a while without his wife: man ought not to be too happy or too comfortable—that is a heroic conception of life. So Hagauer confronted his misfortune energetically, and was able to note the compensation that not only time can heal wounds, but lack of time as well. Of course this did not prevent him from continuing to insist that Agathe return; indeed, he could dedicate himself to this question of order with the unruffled mind of a man who has shipped the children of his emotions off to bed. Once again he thoroughly reviewed all the documents, which he preserved in careful order, and evening after evening read through all the personal papers of his deceased father-in-law without finding in a single one any indication of the surprise that had been visited upon him. That a man whom he had always revered as a model could have changed his mind at the last minute, or out of negligence not adapted his will to changed circumstances over the years, seemed the more improbable to Hagauer the more often he untied the ribbons and removed the labeled covers with which he kept his correspondence and other papers in order. He avoided thinking about how, then, the result had come about that finally had come about, and reconciled himself by saying that some error, some carelessness, some guilty or innocent negligence, some lawyer's stratagem, must lie behind it. In this opinion, which permitted him to spare his feelings without wasting his time over it, he contented himself with demanding precise statements and documents, and, when these did not come, calling upon a lawyer for advice; for as an order-loving person, he assumed that in their spiteful endeavor Agathe and Ulrich must obviously have done the same, and he did not want to lag behind them. The lawyer now took over the writing of letters and repeated the demand for an explanation, combining with it the demand that Agathe return: in part because that was the preference of Hagauer, who imputed his wife's conduct to her brother's influence, and in part because it seemed a requisite in this obscure and perhaps shady affair that one should first stick to the established factual basis of "malicious abandonment"; the rest was to be left to the future, and to cautious evaluation of whatever points of attack might develop. From then on Ulrich started reading the antagonistic letters again and did not burn them. But no matter how often since then he had argued with his sister that arming themselves likewise for the legal struggle could not be put off, she would hear nothing of it; indeed, she did not even want to listen to his reports, and finally he had had to undertake the first steps without her, until at last his own lawyer insisted on hearing Agathe himself and receiving his power of attorney from her. This was what Ulrich now informed her of all at once, adding that what he had first, out of consideration, called merely a "communication from Hagauer" was actually a singularly unpleasant legal letter. "It's apparently unavoidable, and without our realizing it it's become high time that we confide to our lawyer, as cautiously and with as much reserve as we can, something about the dangerous business with the will," he finished.

Agathe looked at him for a long time and irresolutely, with a look hooded from within, before she softly answered him with the words: "I did not want that!"

Ulrich made a gesture of excuse and smiled. It was possible to live in the fire of goodness without the necessity of arson, and the criminal trick they had carried out on their father's will had long since become superfluous: but it had happened, and nothing could be done about it without their being exposed. Ulrich understood the connection between resistance and despondency in his sister's answer. Agathe had meanwhile stood up and was moving back and forth among the objects in the room without speaking; she sat down on a chair some distance off and went on looking at her brother in silence. Ulrich knew that she wanted to draw him back into the silence, which was like a bed of rest consisting of tiny points of flame, and a sweet martyrdom demanded his heart back.

As in music or in a poem, by a sickbed or in a church, the circle of what could be uttered was oddly circumscribed, and in their dealings with each other a clear distinction had formed between those conversations that were permissible and those they could not have. But this did not happen through solemnity or any other kind of elevated expectation, but appeared to have its origin outside the personal. They both hesitated. What should the next word be, what should they do? The uncertainty resembled a net in which all unspoken words had been caught: the web was stretched taut, but they were not able to break through it, and in this want of words glances and movements seemed to reach further than usual, and outlines, colors, and surfaces to have an unstoppable weight: A secret inhibition, which usually resides in the arrangement of the world and sets limits to the depth of the senses, had become weaker, or from time to time disappeared entirely. And inevitably the moment came when the house they were in resembled a ship gliding outward on an infinite waste reflecting only this ship: the sounds of the shore grow fainter and fainter, and finally all motion ceases; objects become completely mute and lose the inaudible voices with which they speak to man; before they are even thought, words fall like sick birds from the air and die; life no longer has even the energy to produce the small, nimble resolutions that are as important as they are insignificant: getting up, picking up a hat, opening a door, or saying something. Between the house and the street lay a nothingness that neither Agathe nor Ulrich could cross, but in the room space was polished to an utmost luster, which was intensified and fragile like all highly perfected things, even if the eye did not directly perceive it. This was the anxiety of the lovers, who at the height of their emotion no longer knew which direction led upward and which downward. If they looked at each other, their eyes, in sweet torment, could not draw back from the sight they saw, and sank as in a wall of flowers without striking bottom. "What might the clocks be doing now?" suddenly occurred to Agathe, and reminded her of the small, idiotic second hand of Ulrich's watch, with its precise forward motions along its narrow circle; the watch was in the pocket under the bottommost rib, as if that were where reason's last place of salvation lay, and

Agathe yearned to draw it out. Her glance loosened itself from her brother's: a painful retreat! They both felt that it bordered on the comic, this shared silence under the pressure of a heavy mountain of bliss or powerlessness.

And suddenly Ulrich said, without having previously thought of saying exactly this: "Polonius's cloud, which sometimes appears as a ship, sometimes as a camel, is not the weakness of a servile courtier but characterizes completely the way God has created us!"

Agathe could not know what he meant; but does one always know what a poem means? When it pleases us it opens its lips and causes a smile, and Agathe smiled. She was lovely with her bowed lips, but this gave Ulrich time, and he gradually recalled what it was he had been thinking before he had broken the silence. He had imagined as an example that Agathe was wearing glasses. At that time, a woman with glasses was still regarded as comical and looked quite risible, or pitiable; but a time was already coming when a woman wearing glasses, as is still true today, looked enterprising, indeed positively young. There are firmly inherited habits of consciousness behind this, which change but which in some connection or another are always present and form the pattern through which all perceptions pass before they arrive at consciousness, so that in a certain sense the whole that one thinks one is experiencing is always the cause of what it is that one experiences. And one rarely imagines to oneself how far this extends, that it extends from ugly and beautiful, good and evil, where it still seems natural that one man's morning cloud should be another man's camel, through bitter and sweet or fragrant and noisome, which still have something material about them, to the things themselves with their precise and impersonally attributed qualities, the perception of which is apparently quite independent of intellectual prejudices but in truth is so only in the main. In reality, the relation of the outer to the inner world is not that of a die which impresses its image on a receptive material, but that of a matrix which is deformed in the process, so that its diagram, without its coherence being destroyed, can produce remarkably diverse images. So that Ulrich too, if he was able to think that he was seeing Agathe before him wearing glasses, could think just as well that she loved Lindner or Hagauer, that she was his "sister" or "the being half united with him in twinlike fashion," and it was not a different Agathe each time that was sitting before him but a different sitting there, a different world surrounding her, like a transparent ball dipping into an indescribable light. And it seemed to them both that here lay the deepest sense of the support which they sought in each other and which one person always seeks in another.

They were like two people who, hand in hand, have stepped out of the circle that had firmly enclosed them, without being at home in another one. There was in this something that could not be accounted for in ordinary notions of living together.

C. 1934

48

THE SUN SHINES ON JUST AND UNJUST

The sun shines with one and the same merciful glance on just and unjust; for some reason Ulrich would have found it more comprehensible if it did so with two: one after the other, first on the just and then on the unjust, or vice versa. "Sequentially, man too is living and dead, child and adult, he punishes and pardons; indeed this ability of only being able to do contradictory things in sequence could really be used to define the essence of the individual, for supra-individual entities, like humanity or a people or the population of a village, are able to commit their contradictions not only one after the other, but also simultaneously and all mixed up with each other. So the higher a being stands on the scale of capabilities, the lower he stands on the scale of morality? In any case: you can rely on a tiger, but not on mankind!" This was what Ulrich said.

If his friendship with Stumm had been flourishing, how fruitful such conversations might have been! With Agathe they always ended in a plea to excuse their superfluity and led to new and vain resistance. "There's no sense in talking that way," he conceded, and began from the beginning. "For there are many problems," he instructed, "that make no sense, and they ought always to be suspected of being important ones. There are questions of the kind: Why do I have two ears but only one tongue? Or: Why is man symmetrical only frontally and not hexagonally? Sometimes these questions come straight from the nursery or the madhouse, but sometimes, too, they later achieve scientific respectability." It's different, and yet basically the same, with the problem: Why do people die? We already find in textbooks of logic this model of a reasoned conclusion: "All men are mortal. Caius is a man. Therefore Caius is mortal." But one can also give a scientific answer, and all such answers would leave such a problem in exceptionally rational condition: and yet the irrational way we stare at this problem, Ulrich maintained, an irrational, indeed entirely shameless way of refusing to understand nature, is itself almost morality, philosophy, and literature!

Agathe, by nature easygoing, tolerant, and averse to cloud castles of thought, responded: "Nature has no morality!"

Ulrich said: "Nature has two moralities!"

Agathe said: "I don't care how many it has. It's not a problem. You're only trying to needle and upset me!"

"But it's all the same!" Ulrich answered. "Because since we surely call that good which pleases us and to which we give preference—that's not morality, but it *is* the beginning and end of morality!—wouldn't evil then have to die out in due course, the way snakes or diseases are more or less stamped out and the jungle dies? Why does it survive and thrive so mightily?"

"That's no concern of mine!" Agathe declared, thereby defending her intention of not taking the conversation seriously when it was conducted in this fashion.

But Ulrich replied: "We simply can't do without evil. And what does concern you is even more absurd and profound! For mustn't something exist that is worse than the rest, if only for the reason that we wouldn't know what to do with ourselves if one of our feelings were just as beautiful as any other one, or even if each of our actions were better than its predecessors?"

Agathe looked up, for this was serious. This was the way it often happened now; they were uncertain about where their adventuresome plans were leading them, and avoided talking about it because they did not know how to begin; but suddenly they were to some extent in the midst of it. At that time Ulrich was receiving letters from Professor Schwung, his deceased father's old enemy, entreating him on the head of the revered departed to engage himself in bringing about greater accountability in the world; and he was receiving letters from Professor Hagauer, his embittered brother-in-law, in which his sister and he were sternly suspected of being guilty of profoundly dubious conduct. At first he had answered these letters evasively, then not at all; finally, Agathe even asked him to burn them without opening them. She explained this by saying that it was impossible to read such letters, and in the condition in which they found themselves, that was the truth. But to burn them unread, and not even to listen to what other people were complaining about: how did it happen that this did not move her conscience, although at that time it was so sensitive in every other respect?

That was the time when they were beginning to comprehend what an equivocal role other people played in their feelings. They knew that they were not in accord with the general public; in the thousand kinds of busyness that filled up night and day there was not a single activity in which they could have participated wholeheartedly, and whatever they might venture upon themselves would most certainly have been met with contempt and disdain. There was a remarkable peace in this. Apparently one can (probably) say that a bad conscience, if it is big enough, provides almost a better pillow than a good one: the mind's incidental activity, incessantly expanding with a view to ultimately deriving a good individual conscience from all the wrong that surrounds it and in which it is implicated, is then shut down, leaving a boundless independence in the emotions. At times this caused a tender loneliness, a limitless arrogance, to pour its splendor on the pair's excursions through the world. Alongside their ideas the world could just as easily appear clumsily bloated, like a captive balloon circled by swallows, as it could be humbled to a background as tiny as a forest at the rim of the sky by the intensification of the solipsistic condition of their egos. Their social obligations sounded like a shouting that was reaching them, sometimes rude, sometimes from far away; they were trivial, if not unreal. An enormous arrangement, which is finally nothing but a monstrous absurdity: that was the world. On the other hand, everything they encountered on the plane of ideas had the tensed, tightrope-walking nature of the once-and-never-again, and whenever they talked about it they did so in the awareness that no single word could be used twice without changing its meaning. Likewise, everything that happened to them was connected with the impression of being a discovery that permitted of no repetition, or it happened on precisely the right occasion, as if it had been conjured up by magic.

This gentle mania, which was nothing but an extremely elevated form of the involvement of two people with each other, also unleashed a deepened sympathy, a sinking into togetherness; the change also became apparent in their relation to the world, but in such a manner that along with the arrogance there began to predominate at times a peculiar immersion in the nature and doings of other people, and in the claim this involved to recognition and love. A temperate explanation, such as that this was merely the expression of an overflowing mood, sometimes amicable, sometimes arrogant, did not suffice. For the happy person is no doubt friendly, and with cheerful complaisance wants to let everyone know it, and Ulrich or Agathe, too, felt lifted up at times by such gaiety, like a person being carried on someone's shoulders and waving at everyone: yet this actively outward-striving amicability seemed to them harmless beside the kind that overcame them passively and almost hauntingly at the sight of others as soon as they made room to be ready for what they had called "walking two miles with them." Ulrich might also have wondered that he had often seen himself approaching other people as if they were a generality, with theories and emotions that applied to them all; but now it was happening even in a constrained way on a small individual scale, with that silent insatiability of his which had once made Agathe herself suspect that it was more a longing for empathy on the part of a nature that never involves itself with others than it was the expression of confident benevolence. To be sure, Agathe was now reacting as he did: although she had, for the most part, spent her life without either love or hate, but merely with indifference, she felt the same inclination toward others, quite divorced from any possibility of action, indeed from any idea that might have given comprehensible shape to her almost oppressive empathy.

Ulrich analyzed it: "If you like, you can just as well call it a bifurcated egotism as the start of loving everyone."

Agathe joked: "As love, it's still rather timid at the start."

Ulrich went on: "In truth, it has as little to do with egotism as with its opposite. Those are later concepts, indispensable for decocted souls. In the Eudemian ethics, however, it still runs: Self-love is not selfishness but a higher condition of the self, with the consequence that one loves others, too, in a higher way. Also, more than two thousand years ago the notion was formulated, apparently just for us, and then lost again, a linking of goal and cause into a 'goal-cause' that motivates 'what is loved as it does the lover.' An unreal idea, and yet as if created in order to distinguish the sympathetic awareness of the emotions from the dead truth of reason!"

He touched her hand with his fingertips. Agathe looked around her shyly; they were in one of the busiest streets; there probably weren't many other people roaming around whose concerns reached back to the fourth century B.C. "Don't you think that we're behaving extremely strangely?" Agathe asked. She saw women in the latest fashions, and officers with red, green, yellow, and blue necks and legs; many necks and legs stopped suddenly behind her and turned to look at her or some other woman, expecting an "advance." A ray of light from the heavenly vaults of truth had fallen on all this activity, and it looked somewhat precarious.

"I think so," Ulrich said dryly. "Even if I might have been mistaken."

For he could no longer recall exactly the passage that had once made an impression on him.

Agathe laughed at him. "You're always so truth-loving," she mocked, but secretly she admired him.

But Ulrich knew that what they were commanded to seek had as little to do with truth in the ordinary sense as it did with egotism or altruism, so he replied: "Love of truth is really one of the most contradictory formulations there is. For you can revere truth in God knows how many ways, but the one thing you can't do is love it. If you do, it begins to waver. Love dissolves truth like wine the pearl."

"Do pearls really dissolve in wine?" Agathe asked.

"I have no idea," Ulrich conceded with a sigh. "I'm pretty far gone. I'm already using expressions I can't account for! I meant to say: To the person who loves, truth and deception are equally trivial!"

This observation, that truth is dissolved by love—the opposite of the more fainthearted assertion that love cannot bear the truth!—contains nothing new. The moment a person encounters love not as an experience but as life itself, or at least as a kind of life, he understands that there are several truths about everything. The person who judges without love calls this "opinions" and "subjectivity"; the person who loves denies that with the sage's saying: "We can't know the meaning of even the simplest words if we don't love!" He is not being insensitive to truth, but oversensitive. He finds himself in a kind of enthusiasm of thinking, in which words open up to their very core. The person judging without love calls something an illusion that is merely the consequence of the excited involvement of the emotions. He himself is free of passion, and truth is free of passion; an emotion is injurious to its truth, and to expect to find truth where something is "a matter of the emotions" seems to him just as wrongheaded as demanding justice from wrath. And yet it is precisely the general content of existence and truth that distinguishes love as an experiencing of the world from love as an experience of the individual. In the special world of love, contradictions do not raise each other to nothing and cancel each other out, but raise each other to the heights. They don't adapt to each other, either, but are in advance a part of a higher unity, which, the moment they come into contact, rises from them as a transparent cloud. Therefore, in love as in life itself, every word is an event and none is a complete notion, and no assertion is needed, nor any mere whim.

It is hard to account for this, because the language of love is a secret language, and in its ultimate perfection as silent as an embrace. Ulrich was capable of walking beside Agathe and seeing the reliable line of her profile in sparkling clarity before the swarm of his thoughts; then he perhaps recalled that in every delimitation there resides a tyrannical happiness. This is apparently the basic happiness of all works of art, of all beauty, of whatever is formed by earth at all. But it is perhaps, too, the basic hostility, the armor between all beings. And Agathe looked away from Ulrich into the stream of people and sought to imagine what cannot be imagined, what happiness it would be to do away with all limits. In thought they contradicted each other, but they would also have been able to change sides, since on earlier occasions they had, at times alone, at times together, experienced one side as well as the other. But they did not speak about this at all. They smiled. That was enough. They each guessed what the other meant. And if they guessed wrongly, it was just as good as if it were right. If, on the contrary, they said something that cohered more firmly, they almost felt it as a disturbance. They had already spoken so much about it. A certain indolence, indeed paralysis, of thought was part of their silent insatiability as they now observed people and sought to enclose them within the magic circle that surrounded themselves, just as fluid and fleeting mobility belonged to this thinking. They were like the two halves of the shell of a mussel opening itself to the sea.

And at times they suddenly laughed at each other.

"It's not as simple as one would like to think, loving one's fellow man like oneself!" Ulrich sighed mockingly once again.

Agathe took a deep breath and told him with satisfaction that it was his fault. "You're the one who's always destroying it!" she complained.

"*They're* the ones! Look at them!" Ulrich countered. "Look how they're watching us! They'd say 'Thanks a lot!' to our love!"

And in truth this made them laugh with a kind of abashed shame, for unfortunately nothing is more amusing than raising one's eyes when they are still tender with sentiment. So Agathe laughed beforehand. But then she replied: "And yet what we're looking for can't be far away. Sometimes one feels one's own breath against a veil as warm as a pair of strange lips. This seems to me that close too."

Ulrich added: "And there is a circumstance that could lead one to believe that we're not simply chasing chimeras. For even an enemy can be divined only if you're able to feel what he feels. So there *is* a 'love your neighbor'; it even has a postscript: so you get a cleaner shot at him! And quite generally, you never understand people entirely through knowing and observing them; it also calls for understanding of a kind you have with yourself; you must already have that understanding when you approach them."

"But I usually don't understand them at all," Agathe said, surveying the people.

"You believe in them," Ulrich replied. "At least you want to. You 'lend' them credence. That's what makes them seem worthy of loving."

"No," Agathe said. "I don't believe in them in the least."

"No," Ulrich said. " 'Belief' isn't an accurate expression for it."

"But then what should it really be called," Agathe asked, "when you think you understand people without knowing anything about them, and when you have an irresistible inclination for them, although you can be almost certain that you wouldn't like to know them?"

"One usually lives in the cautious balance between inclination and aversion one keeps ready for one's fellowmen," her brother responded slowly. "If, for whatever reason, the aversion seems to be dormant, then only a desire to yield must remain, a desire that cannot be compared to anything one knows. But it's no longer an attitude that corresponds to reality."

"But you've said so often that it's the possibility of another life!" Agathe reproached him.

"An awareness of the world as it could be is what it is," Ulrich said, "shot through with an awareness of the world as it is!"

"No, that's too little!" Agathe exclaimed.

"But I can't say that I really love these people," Ulrich defended himself. "Or that I love the real people. These people are real when they're in uniform and civilian clothes; that's the norm, so it's *our* attitude that's unreal!"

"But among themselves *they* think of it the same way!" Agathe responded, on the attack. "Because they don't love each other in a real way, or really don't love each other, in exactly the same way you're claiming about our relation to them: their reality consists in part of fantasies, but why should that degrade ours?"

"You're thinking with such strenuous sharpness today!" Ulrich fended her off, laughing.

"I'm so sad," Agathe replied. "Everything is so uncertain. It all seems to shrink to nothing and expand again endlessly. It won't let you do anything, but the inactivity is also unbearable because it really presses in all directions against closed walls."

And in this or similar fashion the preoccupation of brother and sister with their surroundings always broke off. Their involvement remained unarticulated: there was nowhere an accord in opinion or activity in which it could have expressed itself; the feeling grew all the more, the less it found a way of acting that corresponded to it, and the desire to contradict appeared as well: the sun shone on the just and unjust, but Ulrich found that one might better say, on the unseparated and not united, as the real origin of mankind's being evil as well as good.

Agathe concurred in this opinion: "I'm always so sad whenever we have to laugh at ourselves," she asserted, and laughed, because along with everything else an old saying had occurred to her, which sounded quite strange, as idle as it was prophetic. For it proclaimed: "Then the eyes of the soul were opened, and I saw love coming toward me. And I saw the beginning, but its end I did not see, only its progression."

49

SPECIAL MISSION OF A GARDEN FENCE

Another time Agathe asked: "By what right can you speak so glibly of an 'image of the world,' or even of a 'world' of love? Of love as 'life itself'? You're being frivolous!" She felt as if she were swinging back and forth on a high branch that was threatening to break under the exertion at any moment; but she went on to ask: "If one can speak of a cosmic image of love, could one not also finally speak of an image of anger, envy, pride, or hardness?"

"All other emotions last for a shorter period," Ulrich replied. "None of them even claims to last forever."

"But don't you find it somewhat odd of love that it should make that claim?" Agathe asked.

Ulrich countered: "I believe one might well say that it also ought to be possible for other emotions to shape their own images of the world: as it were, one-sided or monochrome ones; but among them love has always enjoyed an obscure advantage and has been accorded a special claim to the power of shaping the world."

During this exchange they sought out a place in their garden where they could look through the fence at the street, with its rich variety of human content, without exposing themselves, as far as possible, to the glances of strangers. This usually led them to a low, sunny rise whose dry soil gave footing to several larches, and where if they lay down they were camouflaged by the play of light and shadow; in this half hiding place they were on the one hand so near the street that the people passing by gave them the peculiar impression of being alive in that merely animalistic way that attaches to all of us when we believe ourselves unobserved and alone with our demeanor, and on the other hand any eyes that were raised could see brother and sister and draw them into the events that they were observing with interest and a reserve for which the fence, a solid barrier but transparent to the glance, served as a positively ideal image.

"Now let's try whether we really love them or not," Agathe proposed, and smiled mockingly or impatiently.

Her brother shrugged his shoulders.

"Stop, O you hastening past, and bestow for a moment your precious soul upon two people who intend to love you!" Ulrich said, pushing it to absurdity.

"You can't bestow yourself for a moment; you have to do it without end!" Agathe corrected him threateningly.

"A park. A mighty fence. Us behind it," Ulrich affirmed. "And what might he be thinking when we called him, after he had involuntarily slowed his steps and before he timidly doubles them? That he's walking by the garden fence of a private madhouse!"

Agathe nodded.

"And we," Ulrich went on, "wouldn't even dare! Don't you absolutely know we won't do it? Our inmost harmony with the world warns us that we're not allowed to do such a thing!"

Agathe said: "If we were to address the brother hastening past, instead of as 'our good friend' or 'dear soul,' as 'dog' or 'criminal,' he probably wouldn't consider us mad but would merely take us for people who 'think differently' and are mad at him!"

Ulrich laughed and was pleased with his sister. "But you see how it is," he declared. "General rudeness is unbearable today. But because it is, goodness too must be false! It's not that rudeness and goodness depend on each other as on a scale, where too much on one side equals too little on the other; they depend on each other like two parts of a body that are healthy and sick together. So nothing is more erroneous," he went on, "than to imagine, as people generally do, that an excess of bad convictions is to blame for a lack of good ones; on the contrary, evil evidently increases through the growth of a false goodness!"

"We've heard that often," Agathe replied with pleasantly dry irony. "But it's apparently not simple to be good in the good way!"

"No, loving is not simple!" Ulrich echoed, laughing.

They lay there looking into the blue heights of the sun; then again through the fence at the street, which, to their eyes dazzled by the sunny sky, was spinning in a hazily excited gray. Silence descended. The feelings of self-confidence that the conversation had raised were slowly transformed into an undercutting, indeed an abduction, of the self. Ulrich related softly: "I've invented a magnificent sham pair of concepts: 'egocentric and allocentric.' The world of love is experienced either egocentrically or allocentrically; but the ordinary world knows only egotism and altruism, a coupled pair that, by comparison, are quarrelsomely rational. Being egocentric means feeling as if one were carrying the center of the world in the center of one's self. Being allocentric means not having a center at all anymore. Participating totally in the world and not laying anything by for oneself. At its highest stage, simply ceasing to be. I could also say: turning the world inward and the self outward. They are the ecstasies of selfishness and selflessness. And although ecstasy appears to be an outgrowth of healthy life, one can evidently say as well that the moral notions of healthy life are a stunted vestige of what were originally ecstatic ones."

Agathe thought: "Moonlit night . . . two miles . . ." And much else drifted through her mind as well. What Ulrich was telling her was one more version of all that; she did not have the impression that she would be losing anything if she did not pay really close attention, although she listened gladly. Then she thought of Lindner's asserting that one had to live *for* something and could not think of oneself, and she asked herself whether that, too, would be "allocentric." Losing oneself in a task, as he demanded? She was skeptical. Pious people have enthusiastically pressed their lips to lepers' sores: a loathsome idea! an "exaggeration that is an affront to life," as Lindner liked to call it. But what he did consider pleasing to God, erecting a hospital, left her cold. Thus it happened that she now plucked her brother by the sleeve and interrupted him with the words: "Our man has shown up again!" For partly out of fun, partly from habit, they had fastened on a particularly unpleasant man to use for their mental experiment. This was a beggar who conducted his business for a while every day in front of their garden fence. He treated the stone base as a bench that was awaiting him; every day he first spread out beside himself a greasy paper with some leftover food on it, with which he casually regaled himself before putting on his business expression and packing away the rest. He was a stocky man with thick, iron-gray hair, had the pasty, spiteful face of an alcoholic, and had defended his location a number of times with great rudeness when other beggars unsuspectingly came near: Ulrich and Agathe hated this parasite who offended against their property—and further refined what was proper to them, their loneliness—hated him with a primitive instinct of possessiveness that made them laugh, because it seemed to them totally illicit; and for just that reason they used this ugly, spiteful guest for their boldest and most dubious conjurations of loving one's neighbor.

Hardly had they caught sight of him than Ulrich said, laughing: "I repeat: If you just, as people say, imagine yourself in this situation or feel any kind of vague sense of social responsibility for him—indeed, even if you only see him as a picturesque, tattered painting—there's already a small percentage of the genuine 'putting oneself in another's place.' Now you have to try it one hundred percent!"

With a smile, Agathe shook her head.

"Imagine you were in accord with this man about everything the way you are with yourself," Ulrich proposed.

Agathe protested. "I've never been in accord with myself!"

"But you will be then," Ulrich said. He took her hand.

Agathe let it happen and looked at the beggar. She became strangely serious and after a while declared: "He's stranger to me than death."

Ulrich enclosed her hand in his more completely and asked again: "Please try!"

After a while Agathe said: "I feel as if I'm hanging on this figure; I myself, and not just my curiosity!" From the tension of concentration, and its focus on a single object, her face had taken on the involuntary expression of a sleepwalker.

Ulrich helped out: "It's like in a dream? Raw-sweet, alien-self, encountering oneself in the shape of another?"

Agathe dismissed this with a smile. "No, it's certainly not as enchantingly sensual as it is in such dreams," she said.

Ulrich's eyes rested on her face. "Try, as it were, to dream him!" he counseled persuadingly. "Cautious hoarders, in our waking state we consist mostly of giving out and taking back; we participate, and in doing so preserve ourselves. But in dreams we have a trembling intimation of how glorious a world is that consists entirely of prodigality!"

"That may be so," Agathe answered hesitantly and distractedly. Her eyes remained fixed on the man. "Thank God," she said slowly after a while, "he's become an ordinary monster again!" The man had got up, gathered his things together, and left. "He was getting uncomfortable!" Ulrich claimed, laughing. When he fell silent, the constant noise of the street rose and mingled with the sunshine in a peculiar feeling of stillness. After a while Ulrich asked pensively: "Isn't it strange that almost every single person knows himself least of all and loves himself most? It's evidently a protective mechanism. And 'Love thy neighbor as thyself' means in this fashion too: love him without knowing him, before you know him, although you know him. I can understand one's taking this merely for an extreme expression, but I doubt that it will satisfy the challenge; for, pursued seriously, it asks: love him without your reason. And so an apparently everyday demand, if taken literally, turns into an ecstatic one!"

Agathe responded: "Truly, the 'monster' was almost beautiful!"

Ulrich said: "I think one not only loves something because it's beautiful, but it's also beautiful because one loves it. Beauty is nothing but a way of saying that something has been loved; the beauty of all art and of the world has its origin in the power of making a love comprehensible."

Agathe thought of the men with whom she had spent her life. The feeling of first being overshadowed by a strange being, and then opening one's eyes in this shadow, is strange. She pictured it to herself. Was it not alien, almost hostile things that fused together in the kiss of two lives? The bodies remained unitedly separated. Thinking of them, you feel the repulsive and ugly with undiminished force. As horror, even. You are also certain that spiritually you have nothing to do with each other. The disparity and separation of the persons involved is painfully clear. If there had been some illusion of a secret accord, a sameness or likeness, this was the moment it vanished like a mist. No, you weren't under the least illusion, Agathe thought to herself. And yet the sense of an independent self is partially extinguished, the self is broken; and amid signs signifying an act of violence no less than a sweet sacrifice, it submits to its new state. All of that causes a "skin rash"? Doubtless the other ways of loving are not able to do as much. Perhaps Agathe had so often felt the inclination to love men she didn't like because this is when this remarkable transformation happens most irrationally. And the remarkable power of attraction that Lindner had lately exercised on her signified nothing else, that she did not doubt. But she hardly knew that this was what she was thinking about; Ulrich, too, had once confessed that he often loved what he didn't like, and she thought she was thinking of him. She recalled that all her life she had believed only in surroundings that rushed past, with the hopeless hope that they could remain the same; she had never been able to change herself by her own volition, and yet now, as a gift, a hovering borne by the forces of summer had taken the place of vexation and disgust. She said to Ulrich gratefully: "You have made me what I am because you love me!"

Their hands, which had been intertwined, had disengaged themselves and were now just touching with their fingertips; these hands awakened to consciousness again, and Ulrich grasped his sister's with his own. "You have changed me completely," he responded. "Perhaps I have had some influence on you, but it was only you who were, so to speak, flowing through me!"

Agathe nestled her hand in the hand that embraced it. "You really don't know me at all!" she said.

"Knowing people is of no consequence to me," Ulrich replied. "The only thing one ought to know about a person is whether he makes our thoughts fruitful. There shouldn't be any other way of knowing people!"

Agathe asked: "But then how am I real?"

"You're not real at all!" Ulrich said with a laugh. "I see you the way I need you, and you make me see what I need. Who can say so casually where the first and fundamental impulse lies? We are a ribbon floating in the air."

Agathe laughed, and asked: "So if I disappoint you it will be your fault?"

"No doubt!" Ulrich said. "For there are heights where it makes no sense to discriminate between 'I have been mistaken in you' and 'I have been mistaken in myself.' For instance, the heights of faith, of love, of magnanimity. Whoever acts from magnanimity, or, as it can also be called, from greatness, doesn't ask about illusion, or about certainty either. There are some things he may even not want to know; he dares the leap over falsehood."

"Couldn't you also be magnanimous toward Professor Lindner?" Agathe asked rather surprisingly, for ordinarily she never spoke of Lindner unless her brother brought up his name. Ulrich knew that she was holding something back. It was not exactly that she was concealing that she had some sort of relationship with Lindner, but she did not say what it was. He more or less guessed it and, with some displeasure, acquiesced in the necessity of allowing Agathe to go her own way. The instant that, for God knows what reasons, such a question sprang from her lips, Agathe had immediately realized once more how ill the term "Professor Lindner" accorded with the term "magnanimity." She felt that in some way or other, magnanimity could not be professed, much as she felt that Lindner was good in some unpleasant way. Ulrich was silent. She sought to look into his face, and when he turned it away as far as he could, she plucked his sleeve. She used his sleeve as a bell rope until Ulrich's laughing countenance again appeared in the doorway of grief and he delivered a small admonishing speech on how the person who in his magnanimity too soon abandons the firm ground of reality can easily become ridiculous. But that not only related to Agathe's readiness for magnanimity in relation to the dubious Lindner, but also directed a scruple at that true and not-to-be-deceived sensibility in which truth and error signify far less than the enduring emanation of the emotions and their power to seize everything for themselves.

49

MUSINGS

Since that scene, Ulrich thought he was being borne forward; but really all that could be said was that something new and incomprehensible had been added, which he perceived, however, as an increase in reality. He was acting perhaps a little like a person who has seen his opinions in print and is ever after convinced of their incontrovertibility; however he might smile at this, he was incapable of changing it. And just as he had been about to draw his conclusions from the millennial book, or perhaps he merely wanted once more to express his astonishment, Agathe had retaliated and cut off the discussion by exclaiming: "We've already spent enough time talking about this!" How Ulrich felt that Agathe was always in the right, even when she wasn't! For although nothing could be less the case than that there had been enough discussion between them—not to mention anything true or decisive—indeed, precisely such a saving event or magic formula for which one might have initially hoped had not materialized; yet he knew, too, that the problems that had dominated his life for the better part of a year were now bunched together dense and compact around him, and not in a rational but in a dynamic fashion. Just as if there would soon be enough talk about them, even if the answer did not happen to come out in words.

He could not even altogether remember what he had thought and said about these problems over the course of time; indeed, he was far from being able to do so. He had doubtless set out to converse about them with all mankind; but it lay, too, in the nature of the reproach itself that nothing one could say about it was joined in a forward-looking way to anything else but that everything was as widely scattered as it was connected. The same movement of the mind, clearly distinguished from the ordinary, arose again and again, and the treasure of the things it reached out to include grew; but no matter what Ulrich might remind himself of, it was always as far from one inspiration to a second as it would have been to a third, and nowhere did a dominant assertion emerge. In this way he recalled, too, that a similar "equally far," of the kind that was now almost burdensomely and depressingly affecting his thoughts, had once existed in the most inspiring way between himself and the whole world around him: an apparent or actual suspension of the spirit of separation, indeed almost of the spirit of space. That had been in the very first years of his manhood, on the island where he had taken refuge from the major's wife but with her image in his heart. He had probably described it in almost the same words too. Everything had been changed in an incomprehensibly visual way through a condition of fullness of love, as if all he had known previously had been a condition of impoverishment. Even pain was happiness. His happiness, too, almost pain. Everything was leaning toward him, suspended. It seemed that all things knew about him, and he about them; that all beings knew about each other, and yet that there was no such thing as knowing at all, but that love, with its attributes of swelling fullness and ripening promise, ruled this island as the one and perfect law. He had later used this often enough as a model, with slight changes, and in recent weeks, too, he might have been able to refresh this description to some extent; it was by no means difficult to go on in it, and the more one did so without thinking, the more fruitful it turned out to be. But it was precisely this indefiniteness that now meant the most to him. For if his thoughts were connected in such a way that nothing of substance could be added to them which they would not have absorbed, the way an arriving person disappears into a crowd, still that only proved their similarity to the emotions by which they had been summoned into Ulrich's life the first time; and this correspondence of an alteration of the sphere of the senses, experienced now a second time through Agathe, which seemed to affect the world with an altered way of thinking—of which it might also be said that it catches the wind in infinite dreams without stirring from the spot and had already exhausted itself once in the process!—this remarkable correspondence, to which Ulrich was only today fully attentive, inspired in him courage and apprehension. He still recalled that on that earlier occasion he had used the expression of having come to the heart of the world. Was there such a thing? Was it really anything more than a circumlocution? Only by excluding his brain was he inclined to mysticism's claim that one must give up one's self; but did he not have to admit to himself just for that reason that he did not know much more about this than he had before?

He walked farther along these expanses, which nowhere seemed to offer access to their depths. Another time he had called this "the right life"; probably not long ago, if he was not mistaken; and certainly if he had been asked earlier what he was up to, even when he was busy with his most precise work he would ordinarily not have found any answer except to say that it was a preliminary study for the right life. Not to think about it was simply impossible. Of course one could not say what it should look like—indeed, not even if there was such a thing—and perhaps it was just one of those ideas that are more a badge of truth than a truth; but a life without meaning, a life that obeyed only the so-called necessities, and their contingency disguised as necessity, in other words a life lived eternally moment to moment—and here again an expression occurred to him that he had once made up: the futility of the centuries!—such a life was for him a simply unbearable idea! But no less unbearable than a life "for something," that sterility of highways shaded by milestones amid unsurveyed expanses. He might call all that a life preceding the discovery of morality. For that, too, was one of his views, that morality is not made by people and does not change with them but is revealed; that it unfolds in seasons and zones and can actually be discovered. This idea, which was as out of fashion as it was current, expressed perhaps nothing but the demand that morality, too, have a morality, or the expectation that it have one hidden away, and that morality was not simply tittle-tattle revolving on itself on a planet circling to the point of implosion. Of course he had never believed that what such a demand contained could be discovered all at once; it merely seemed to him desirable to think of it at times, which is to say at a time that seemed propitious and relatively accommodating, after some thousands of centuries of aimless circling of the question, whether there was not some experience that might be derived from it. But then, what did he really know about it even now? On the whole, nothing more than that this group of problems, too, had in the course of his life been subjected to the same law or fate as the other groups, which closed ranks in all directions without forming a center.

Of course he knew more about it! For instance, that to philosophize as he was doing was considered horribly facile, and at this moment he fervently wished to be able to refute this error. He knew, too, how one goes about such a thing: he had some acquaintance with the history of thought; he could have found in it similar efforts and how they had been contested, with bitterness or mockingly or calmly; he could have ordered his material, arranged it, he could have secured a firm footing and reached beyond himself. For a while he painfully recalled his earlier industriousness, and especially that frame of mind that came to him so naturally that it had once even earned him the derisive appellation of "activist." Was he then no longer the person constantly haunted by the idea that one must work toward the "ordering of the whole"? Had he not, with a certain stubbornness, compared the world to a "laboratory," an "experimental community"; had he never spoken of "mankind's negligent condition of consciousness," which needed to be transformed into will; demanded that one had to "make" history; had he not, finally, even if it had been only ironically, actually called for a "General Secretariat of Precision and Soul"? That was not forgotten, for one cannot suddenly change oneself; it was merely suspended for the moment! There was also no mistaking where the reason lay. Ulrich had never kept accounts on his ideas; but even if he had been able to remember them all at the same time, he knew that it would have been impossible for him to simply take them up, compare them, test them for possible explanations, and so, ultimately, bring forth from the vapors the little tissue-thin metal leaf of truth. It was a peculiarity of this way of thinking that it did not contain any progress toward truth; and although Ulrich basically assumed that such progress might sometime, through a slow and infinite process, be brought about in the totality, this did not console him, for he no longer had the patience to let himself be outlived by whatever it was to which he was contributing something, like an ant. For the longest time his ideas had not stood on the best footing with truth, and this now seemed to him again the question most urgently in need of illumination.

But this brought him back once again to the opposition between truth and love, which for him was nothing new. It occurred to him how often in recent weeks Agathe had laughed at his, for her taste much too pedantic, love of truth; and sometimes it must also have caused her grief! And suddenly he found himself thinking that there is really no more contradictory term than "love of truth." "For one can raise truth up high in God knows how many ways, but love it you can't, because truth dissolves in love," he thought. And this assertion, by no means the same as the fainthearted one that love cannot bear the truth, was for him as familiar and unachievable as everything else. The moment a person encounters love not as an experience but as life itself, or at least as a kind of life, he knows several truths. The person who judges without love calls this opinions, personal views, subjectivity, caprice; but the person who loves knows that he is not insensitive to truth, but oversensitive. He finds himself in a kind of enthusiasm of thinking, where the words open themselves up to their very core. Of course that can be an illusion, the natural consequence of an all too excitedly involved emotion, and Ulrich took that into account. Truth arises when the blood is cold; emotion is to be deducted from it; and to expect to find truth where something is "a matter of feeling" is, according to all experience, just as perverse as demanding justice from wrath. Nevertheless, there was incontestably some general content, a participation in being and truth, that distinguished love "as life itself" from love as individual experience. And Ulrich now reflected on how clearly the difficulties that ordering his life presented to him were always connected with this notion of a superpowerful love that, so to speak, overstepped its bounds. From the lieutenant who sank into the heart of the world to the Ulrich of this past year, with his more or less assertive conviction that there are two fundamentally distinct and badly integrated conditions of life, conditions of the self, indeed perhaps even conditions of the world, the fragments of recollection, so far as he was able to call them to mind, were all in some form connected with the desire for love, tenderness, and gardenlike, struggle-free fields of the soul. In these expanses lay, too, the idea of the "right life"; as empty as it might be in the bright light of reason, it was richly filled by the emotions with half-born shadows.

It was not at all pleasant for him to encounter so unequivocally this preference for love in his thinking; he had really expected that there were more and different things his thinking would have absorbed, and that shocks such as those of the past year would have carried their vibrations in different directions; indeed, it seemed to him really strange that the conqueror, then the engineer of morality, that he had expected himself to be in his energetic years should have finally matured into a mooning seeker of love.

CLARISSE / WALTER / ULRICH

MID 1920S

CLARISSE

Ulrich did not think about Walter and Clarisse. Then one morning he was urgently called to the telephone: Walter. Why didn't he come out to see them; they knew he was back. A lot had changed, they were waiting for his visit.

Ulrich declined with the curt excuse that after his long absence he had a lot of work to do.

To his surprise, Walter appeared soon afterward; he had taken off from work. The manner in which he inquired after Agathe and the experiences of the trip gave the impression of uncertainty or embarrassment; he seemed to know more than he wanted to let on. Finally, the words came out. He had only now realized that it is insanity to doubt the faithfulness of a woman one loves. One has to be able to let oneself be deceived but know how to be deceived in a fruitful way; for example: he had been wrong to be jealous of Ulrich—

—Ah, so he's talking about Clarisse, Ulrich said to himself, suddenly breathing easier.

—Wrong—Walter went on—even if of course he had never thought of it in any terms other than as mental unfaithfulness; but it hurt so much to have to admit the simple bodily empathy.

—Of course, of course. Ulrich nodded.

—Meingast has left, Walter added.

Ulrich looked up; it really didn't interest him, but he had the feeling that this was something new. "Why?"

Simply, it had been time. But for several days afterward Clarisse had been out of sorts in a way that gave grounds for anxiety. A real depression. But that was just it; that was what first made him grasp the whole business. Imagine—Walter said—that you love a woman, and you meet a man you admire, and you see that your wife loves and admires him too; and both of you feel that this man is far superior to you, unreachable—

—That I can't imagine. Ulrich raised his shoulders with a laugh. Walter looked at him with annoyance; both friends felt that they were simulating an old game they had often played with each other.

—Don't pretend, Walter said. —You're not so swellheaded to the point of insensitivity that you believe no one is better than you!

—All right. The formulation is false. Who is objectively superior? Engineer A or Aesthetician B, a master wrestler or a sprinter? Let's drop that. So you're saying that a person becomes emotionally dependent on someone and the beloved does too: then what happens? You would have to play along with her role as well as your own. The man plays the man's role *and* the woman's role; the woman has womanly feelings for the superior man and a more manly inclination for her earlier and still-loved lover. So this gives rise to something hermaphroditic, doesn't it? Assuming that no jealousy is involved. A spiritual intertwining of three people, which appears mysterious, and at times almost mystic? God on six legs.

Ulrich had improvised this reflection and was himself astonished at the conclusion it had involuntarily reached. Walter looked at him in surprise. He did not agree—again there was too much intellect in it—but Ulrich had come surprisingly close to the truth, and Walter admired the rightness of Clarisse's instinct when she had asked that Ulrich be let in on what was going on. He now began to talk a little. —Yes, Clarisse had been swept away by Meingast, and quite rightly, since only a new community of wills and hearts that embraced more than just one couple would be capable of again forging a humanity out of chaos. These ideas had had a powerful effect on her. After Meingast had left she had confessed to Walter: the whole time he had been there—he had really changed in a strange way—she had continually been bothered by the idea that he had taken her and Walter's sins upon himself and overcome them; it only sounds crazy, Walter said defensively, but it isn't at all, for he and Clarisse . . . behind their conflicts one finds everywhere a pathological disorder of the age. She would now like to speak to Ulrich on Moosbrugger's account.

Ulrich was astonished. What brings the two of you to Moosbrugger?

Well. Moosbrugger is of course only a chance encounter. But when one has once come into contact with something like that one can't at the same time just ignore it.

Look, you talked with Clarisse about it yourself a couple of times. Before. How can you forget something like that?

Ulrich shrugged his shoulders, but the next morning went to see Clarisse.

He felt that one of the two things was not to his taste. He had not thought of Moosbrugger for weeks; yet earlier Moosbrugger had for a time been a point of orientation in his thinking! And after he had thought this over for a while he noticed that once again Clarisse had suddenly managed to fasten onto him with this delicate claw, although he had already become indifferent to her, indeed even found her repulsive. He was curious about what it was Clarisse wanted. When he saw her, he knew that he would do something for Moosbrugger in order to get out of the anxious, reproachful, and unsettled state he was in on account of Agathe. When Ulrich came in she was standing at the window, her hands crossed in front of her hips, legs spread apart as if playing ball. It was a habitual stance of hers, from which her smile emerged with paradoxical charm.

—Our destinies are interwoven—she said—yours and mine. Did Walter tell you? she began. Ulrich replied that he had not quite understood what Walter was after. I must see Moosbrugger! Clarisse said. After greeting him she held his hand in hers, moving his index finger downward, as if unintentionally. —I can influence such destinies, she added vaguely.

In the intervening time some quite specific constellation of ideas must have formed in her; one felt it by the way the walls pulsated. With no other person Ulrich knew did everything internal become so physical as with Clarisse, and this, too, doubtless explained her extraordinary ability to impart her excitement to others.

Her brother had already been won over to the idea, Clarisse related. He was a physician. Ulrich could not stand him. Because as a child of the Wagner craze he had been baptized "Wotan" [Siegfried], he believed everyone would think he was Jewish, and emphasized in equal measure his distaste for Jews and music. He had another peculiarity. Since he had grown up among their other friends, he had found himself when young compelled to read Baudelaire, Dostoyevsky, Huysmans, and Peter Altenberg, to whom at that time the spiritual expressiveness of youth was attuned, and when in later years this style eroded and his own nature came to the fore, there arose a quite peculiar mishmash of *fleurs du mal* and provincial hymns to the Alps. He had come to visit his sister today too, and Clarisse said that he was working somewhere in the garden or in the (adjoining) vineyards. Since even his proximity was enough to put Ulrich out of sorts, he responded with some disappointment. But Clarisse seemed to have been expecting this. "We need him," she said, and tried to give this sentence an emphasis from the back of her eyes, as if to mean: it's really too bad he's bothering us, even if we're lucky that Walter isn't here (but it has to be!) —Be reasonable, Ulrich said: —Why do you want to see Moosbrugger?

Clarisse went and shut the door, which was open. Then she asked a question: Do you understand railway accidents? (One never happens because a locomotive engineer deliberately rams his engine into another train.) Well, they all happen because in the confusing network of tracks, switches, signals, and commands, fatigue makes a person lose the power of conscience. He would only have needed to check one more time whether he was doing the right thing . . . isn't that right?

Ulrich shrugged his shoulders.

—So the accident comes about because one allows something to happen, Clarisse went on. She cautiously closed her fangs around Ulrich's hand, smiled in embarrassment, and drilled her glance into his the way one drives a thumbtack into wood. —That's right, Ulrich, I see it in Walter! (You already know what.) (Every time I've yielded we were destroyed. We just didn't know that in doing it we were drinking a drop of the greatest poison in the world.)

—Oh? Ulrich said. —So it's like that again between you?

Clarisse flashed at him from her eyes, pulled out the thumbtack again, and nodded.

—It is and it isn't; I'm already a lot further. What's the extreme opposite of letting things happen; that one yields to . . . impressing? You understand, he wants to impress; nothing else! She did not wait for a response. —To make a mark! she said. Her tiny figure had been striding up and down the room with supple energy, her hands at her back; now she stopped and sought with her eyes to hold fast to Ulrich's, for the words she was now searching for made her mind somewhat unsteady.

—To inscribe himself, I'm saying. Lately I've discovered something else that's really uncanny, it sounds so simple: Half our life is expression. (The) impressions are nothing. A heap of earthworms! When do you understand a piece of music? When you yourself create it inwardly! When do you understand a person? When for a moment you make yourself just like him! In art, in politics, but also in love, we're trying painfully to express ourselves. We re-deem ourselves to the outside. You see—with her hand she described an acute angle lying horizontally, which involuntarily reminded Ulrich of a phallus—like this. That is the expression; the active form of our existence, the pointed form, the— She became quite excited by the effort to make herself understandable to Ulrich. Ulrich must have been rather taken aback, for Clarisse went on to declare: —That's already in the words re-deem and redemption, both, the "deeming" and the active "re-" Now you understand, of course one has to practice it, but ultimately everything will be like an arrow.

· · ·

—Dear Clarisse—Ulrich pleaded—please speak so that I can understand you.

/Continuation: The Dionysiac. The murderer/

At this moment Siegfried came in. Ulrich had not interrupted Clarisse. She had nonetheless retreated and was standing excitedly, as if he were crowding her, against the wall. Ulrich was accustomed to how hard it was for her to find the right words and how she often tried to seize them with her whole body, so that the meaning for which the words were lacking lay in the movement. But this time he was a little astonished. Clarisse, however, was not yet satisfied, there was still something she had to say. —You know, if I'm unfaithful to him—or let's assume anyway that he is to me—then it's like digging into one's own raw flesh. Then you can't do anything that doesn't cut deep. Then you can't talk about that table over there without there being a feeling of bleeding. A smile forced its way through her excitement because Siegfried was listening, but Siegfried was watching her calmly, as if it were a gymnastics exercise. He had taken off his jacket while working, and his hands and shoes were full of dirt. He had been accustomed since Clarisse's marriage to be the confidant of surprising secrets, and used a glance at his watch to urge haste in a businesslike way. Ulrich felt that this last gesture was directed very much at him.

Clarisse quickly changed her dress. The door remained open, and it hardly seemed accidental that he could see her, standing among her skirts like a boy. Siegfried was saying: —The assistant at the clinic was a fellow student. —You don't say, Ulrich said. —What do you really want of him? Siegfried shrugged his shoulders. —Either this Moosbrugger is mentally ill or he's a criminal. That's correct. But if Clarisse imagines that she can help him . . . ? I'm a doctor, and I also have to let the hospital chaplain imagine the same thing. Redeem! she says. Well, why shouldn't she at least see him there? Siegfried went through his calm routine, brushed off his pants and shoes, and washed his hands. Looking at him, it was hard to believe his broad, modishly trimmed mustache. Then they drove to the clinic. Ulrich was in a state in which he would, without resisting, have let far crazier things happen to him.

· · ·

The physician to whom Wotan conducted them was an artist in his profession.

This is something that exists in every profession that depends on working with one's head and consists of unsatisfied emotions.

In earlier decades there were photographers who placed the leg of the person to be immortalized on a cardboard boulder; today they strip him naked and have him emote at the sunset; at that time they were wearing curled beards and flowing neckties, today they are clean-shaven and underline their art's organ of procreation—in precisely the same way a naked African emphasizes her pudenda with a loincloth of mussel shells—by means of glasses. But there were also such artists in the sciences, on the General Staff, and in industry. In such professions they are considered interesting not-just-experts and often, too, as liberators from the narrowness of the craft. In, for instance, the biology of the general doctrine of life, it has been discovered that mechanical, dead, causal explanations and functional laws are inadequate, and that life has to be explained by life or, as they call it, the life force; and in the War they sacrificed entire divisions, or had the population of whole regions shot, because they were generous / thought they owed something to a certain heroic generosity.

With doctors, this romanticism often takes only the harmless form of the family adviser who prescribes marriage, automobile trips, and theater tickets, or advises a neurasthenic who is deeply depressed by his failing business not to pay any attention to the business for a period of two months. It was only psychiatry that occupied a special position, for in science the slighter the success in precision, the greater, generally speaking, is the artistic component, and up until a few years ago psychiatry was by far the most artistic of all modern sciences, with a literature as ingenious as that of theology and a success rate that could not be discerned in the earthly realm here below / was to be as little discerned here below as theology's. Its representatives were therefore often / frequently /, and today to some extent still are, great artists, and Dr. Fried, Wotan's university friend, was one of these. If one asked him about the prospects for a cure he would dismiss it with an ironic or a fatigued gesture, while on the other hand there was always lying on his desk a cleanly prepared and beautifully dyed section of brain on a slide, beside the microscope through which he would look into the incomprehensible astral world of cell tissue, and on his face there was the expression of a man practicing a black art, a notorious but admired craft that brings him into daily contact with the incomprehensible and with depraved desires. His black hair was plastered down demoniacally, as if it would otherwise stand on end; his movements were soft and unnatural, and his eyes those of a cardsharp, hypnotist, master detective, gravedigger, or hangman.

Of the three visitors, he devoted himself from the beginning exclusively to Clarisse. He showed Ulrich the least possible politeness. Since this left Ulrich free to observe him in peace and with annoyance, he soon discovered the man's major points. Clarisse, on the other hand, who from the beginning regarded her desire as fulfilled, was charging ahead too impetuously, and as clinical assistant and instructor, Dr. Fried saw himself compelled to raise obstacles. Clarisse was a woman and not a doctor, and science demands strictly circumscribed limits. Wotan wanted to assume the responsibility of having his sister let in with false documents. But since this was stated openly, the assistant could only smile wearily. —Since we aren't doctors—Ulrich asked—couldn't we be a pair of writers, who for research purposes . . . ? The doctor dismissed this with a gesture: —If you were Zola and Selma Lagerlöf I would be charmed by your visit, which of course I am anyway, but here only scientific interests are recognized. Unless—he made a smiling gesture of yielding—the ambassadors of your countries had made application for you to the administration of the clinic.

—Then I know what we can do, Ulrich said: —We'll invent some charitable motivation. If the lady is not permitted to see the patients, she can at least visit the prisoner. It's no trouble for me to get her the legitimation of a charitable organization and permission of the district court.

—That would be fine. Come here to my official residence; the best time would be after the Chief Physician's rounds. As long as you're in my company nobody would, of course, think of asking to see your credentials. But naturally I have to have a cover for my conscience.

Clarisse, excited by the difficulties that had to be overcome, beamed, and Dr. Fried spoke of his conscience at the last in a highly patronizing way, rather in the tone of a prince giving an order to the lowest of his subjects.

About a week passed.

Clarisse was as excited as a nervous child in the week before Christmas. It gave the impression that she was imparting a symbolic importance to her encounter with Moosbrugger, like the meeting of two rulers.

—I believe I have the strength to help him when I see him, she asserted.

Why don't you take him a sausage instead—Ulrich answered—and cigarettes.

Wotan laughed and proffered a medical joke; but afterward he again gave the impression of being grateful for the greater energy that radiated into his darkness from Clarisse's ideas, like a thunderstorm below the horizon.

Clarisse was tinglingly strengthened when she felt her influence over him.

—If you had first met him a hundred years ago, you would have fallen weeping on his breast, Ulrich remarked.

Wotan of course added that at that time the emotions were not as disturbed as they are today.

—Quite the contrary, Ulrich maintained. —All the weeping and embracing was a sign that people never really possessed these emotions; that's why they were forced. Isn't it true—he turned to Wotan—that this is the same mechanism as in hysteria?

Wotan made a joke about his wife, who he said was hysterical, and all the medical theories he had no idea what to do with. He already had three children.

—When she's playing the piano fortissimo—Walter defended Clarisse—when she's excited and has tears in her eyes: isn't she absolutely right in refusing to get on the streetcar, travel to the clinic, and behave there as if it had been 'just music' and not real tears?

He had, incidentally, excluded himself and did not go along to the clinic.

—She's completely wrong, Ulrich responded. —For Moosbrugger's sentiments toward a sausage are unaffected and healthy, while on the other hand, Clarisse's importunate behavior will only make him regret not being able to plunge a knife into her belly.

—You really think so? Clarisse liked that. She thought it over and said: —It was only the substitute women he was angry at; that's what it was.

—He's an idiot, Ulrich said clearly and calmly. Struggling around Clarisse's mouth were a laugh, a difficulty, and the desire to let Ulrich know that she was reaching an understanding with him. —You're a pessimist! she finally said; and nothing else, except: Nietzsche! Would Ulrich understand this? Would Walter intuit what had just taken place? Her thoughts had squeezed into a very small package, into a sentence and into a word, inserted into the smallest space as miraculously as the burglar's tool that nothing can resist; she was strangely excited. Every evening now she took a volume of Nietzsche to bed with her. "Is there a pessimism of strength?" That was the sentence that had occurred to her; it continues: ". . . an intellectual predilection for what is hard, gruesome, evil, and problematical in existence?" She did not remember it exactly anymore, but an unarticulated essence of these qualities hovered before her, associated with Ulrich, who from—indeed, now this expression popped up—"depths of antimoral inclination," while she constantly had to struggle against the moral inclination to feel sympathy for Walter, made everything look ridiculous and therefore strangely allied with her. She was half fainting as these connections crackled like lightning, half philosophy and half adultery, and all squeezed into a single word as into a hiding place. And like a new avalanche, a sentence rolled down and engulfed her, "the desire for the horrible as the worthy enemy," and fragments from a long quotation swirled around her: "Is insanity perhaps not necessarily the symptom of degeneration? Are there perhaps neuroses of health? What does the synthesis of god and he-goat in the satyr indicate? Out of what experience of the self did the Greeks have to think of the enthusiast and primitive person as satyr? . . ." All that lay in a laugh, a word, and a twisting of the mouth. Walter noticed nothing. Ulrich looked at her with calm merriment—what hardness lay in this unconcern!—and said they should hurry up.

As they were walking to the terminus of the streetcar, she asked Ulrich: "If he's 'only an idiot,' why are you going?" "Oh, for heaven's sake," he replied, "I always do what I don't believe in." He was surprised because Clarisse did not look at him but stared radiantly straight ahead and gave his hand a strong squeeze.

.   .   .

[Clarisse drags Ulrich to a concert of avant-garde music in the studio of some painter friends of hers. This scene is sketched out more fully later.]

From the study of law Walter was driven to music; from music to the theater; from the theater to an art gallery; from the art gallery back to art; from art . . . ? Now he is stuck, no longer has the energy to make another change, is contentedly unhappy, curses us all, and goes punctually to his office. And while he is in his office something may perhaps happen between Clarisse and Ulrich, but if he were to find out about it, it would put him in an enormous uproar, as if the whole ocean of world history were surging. He's as blind as the moon about what goes on behind his back. To Ulrich, on the other hand, all this was far more a matter of indifference. Or: He almost envied him. Clarisse, sitting there hunched over and holding her fingers clenched while the other sounds sifted and shook, he found almost as unpleasant as a caricature of the sensibility of genius, of the revolutionary, the activist; that no emotion, no idea, is worth being the ultimate one, that one should not linger over anything because the sky leads endlessly upward. He is sleepy, but she will not let him rest. But there is something surrounding her! She always has to be doing something. Simply from tension, to get rid of something, to get past the last minute. And Walter? He is the born talented mediocrity; unhappy, but lucky, and everyone likes him; everyone invites him to stick around; with titanic effort he is constantly pulling his feet out of soil where they could take root so beautifully. Ulrich smiled maliciously. —He's really not a weak character at all. It's unbelievably difficult to achieve nothing if you don't have any talent!

And finally he will be happy.

Clarisse would be making a bad exchange.

During the intermission Clarisse sat down beside Ulrich. —I can't take any more, she said. —When I hear music I'd like to either laugh or cry or run away.

—With Meingast? Ulrich asked.

—That was only an experiment. She seized his hand and held it fast. —No, with someone who could make music. Without conscience. A world. I hear that world sometimes.

Ulrich said angrily: "You're primitive, you musicians. What kind of subtle, unheard-of motivation does it take to produce a raging outburst after sinking into oneself in silence! You do it with five notes!

—It's something you don't understand, Uli. Clarisse laughed.

—And it doesn't bother you? Ulrich challenged her scornfully.

—You don't understand it—Clarisse said tenderly—that's just why you're so hard. You don't have a soft conscience. You were never sick.

—I'd cheat on you, Ulrich said.

—Being cheated is meaningless to us. We have to give everything we've got. We can only cheat ourselves. Her fingers snaked around his hand. —Music either is or it isn't.

—You'll run out on me with somebody from the circus, Ulrich said pensively. He stared gloomily into the confusing tangle of people. —You'll be disappointed. For me it's all a tissue of contradictions among which there is no resolution. But perhaps you're right. A few blasts on the trumpet. Fantasized ones. Run to them.

Evening was coming on. Wandering dark-blue clouds were in the sky beyond the studio windows. The tips of a tree reached up from below—houses stood with the backs of their roofs turned upward. —How should they stand otherwise? Ulrich thought, and yet there are moments when the small sorrow that one feels falls into the world as if onto a muffled giant drum. He thought of Agathe and was unspeakably sad. This small creature at his side was rushing forward at an unnatural speed. As if under the pressure of some kind of program. That wasn't the natural way for love to develop. And anyway, there could be no talk of love. He was quite clear about that. And yet he yielded without resistance. He was consoled by a vague thought; something like this: a person is insulted and makes a great invention; that's how the real deeds of the human will come about. Never in a straight line. I love Agathe and am letting myself be seduced by Clarisse. Clarisse believes that the small stir she makes is her will, but mine lies motionless beneath it like the water beneath the waves.

The music, which kindled people's eyes like lights in the darkening room and blew their bodies through each other like smoke, had started up again.

The cleaning woman had already left; Walter was in the middle of his day in the office; Ulrich now chose such hours for his visits, without thinking about the significance of his choice. Yet until a particular Sunday, nothing happened. Walter had received an invitation that called him into town until evening, and half an hour before, after lunch, Ulrich had shown up without suspecting anything and in a bad mood, for the prospect of an afternoon in the presence of his friend had enticed him so little that he really only started out from habit. But when Walter immediately began to say good-bye, Ulrich felt it as a signal. Clarisse had the same thought. They both knew it.

She would play for him, Clarisse said. Clarisse began. From the window Ulrich waved to Walter, who waved back. Keeping his eyes in the room, he leaned farther and farther out, after the vanishing figure. Clarisse suddenly broke off and came to the window too: Walter was no longer to be seen. Clarisse returned to playing. Ulrich now turned his back to her, as if it did not concern him; leaning into the window frame. Clarisse again stopped playing, ran into the hall; Ulrich heard her putting the chain on the door. When she came back he slowly turned around; said nothing; swayed for a moment. She played on. He went up to her and laid his hand on her shoulder. Without turning her head, she pushed his hand away with her shoulder. —Scoundrel! she said; played on. —Strange? he thought. —Does she want to feel force? The idea that urged itself upon him, that he ought to seize her by both shoulders and pull her down off the piano stool, seemed to him as comical as rocking a loose tooth. This constrained him. He went into the middle of the room. Alerted his hearing and sought an opening. But before anything occurred to him his mouth said: "Clarisse!" That had cut loose, detached itself gurgling from his throat, had grown out of his throat like a strange creature. Clarisse obediently stood up and came over to him. Her eyes were wide open. At this moment he understood for the first time that Clarisse was trying artificially, perhaps without knowing it, to evoke the excitement of a tremendous sacrificial act. Since she was standing beside him, the decision had to be made in an instant, but Ulrich was overcome by all the force of these inhibitions; his legs would no longer support him, he could not utter a word, and threw himself on the sofa.

This excitement infecting him really ought to be made more appealing.

At the same instant, Clarisse threw herself on his lap. Her lizard arms slung themselves around his head and neck. She seemed to be tearing at her arms, but without being able to loosen them from the embrace. Heated air came from her mouth and burned words into his face that he could not understand. There were tears in her eyes. Then everything of which he was normally constituted collapsed. He, too, uttered something that had no meaning, but before the eyes of them both; veins shivered and stood out like bars on a cage, their souls went at each other like bulls, and this riot was accompanied by the feeling of a tremendous moral decision. Now neither of them restrained words, faces, hands any longer. Their faces pressed themselves on each other, wet with tears and sweat, as pure flesh; all the words of love that were to be rehearsed tumbled over each other, as if the contents of a marriage had been shaken out upside down; the lascivious, hardened words that come only with long intimacy came first, unmediated, inciting, and yet bringing horror with them. Ulrich had half sat up; everything was so slippery (from their faces to their words) that their gliding into each other no longer made a sound.

. . .

Clarisse tore her hat from the hook and stormed out. He with her. Wordless. Where to? This question was ridiculously lonely in his brain, swept clean by the storm.

Clarisse rushed over paths, across meadows, through hedges, through woods. She was not one of those women who are broken softly, but became hard and angry after the fall. They finally found themselves in a quiet remote corner of the zoo that adjoined the woods. A small rococo summerhouse stood there. Empty. Here she presented herself to him once again. This time with many words and confessions. Driven by the impatience of desire and the fear that people might come by. It was horrible. This time Ulrich became quite cold and hard with remorse. Ulrich left her there. He did not care how she would get home, but rushed off.

When Ulrich got back to the house later, he found Walter there. Clarisse was still angry, and making a gentle show of marital concord. But with a single pouting look she made Ulrich feel that the two of them still belonged together. Only afterward did it occur to him how strange the expression of her eyes had been twice that afternoon: delirious and mad.

In the excitement, Ulrich had agreed to participate in freeing Moosbrugger. Now he fell in with this idea because it had already gone so far. He did not believe in it, and made the preparations convinced that it would not be possible to carry them out.

. . .

Attending physician: Stay in a sanatorium advised; a little rest-and-diet cure. It's not good for the nerves to lie there without any fat—after he had observed Clarisse's body, which had become totally boyish.

To Walter's joyful surprise, Clarisse offered no resistance. (She felt: None of them amount to much: Walter, Ulrich, Meingast.) I have to take it upon myself alone. Her head felt like the peak of a mountain around which clouds gather; she felt a longing for the horizontal, to stretch out, lie down, in a more bracing air than that of the city. Greenness, vine-twistingness, light-dapplingness hovered before her; countryside, like a strong hand compelling sleep.

. . .

She has come through the first phase; now it is a good idea for her to rest and strengthen herself. Moreover, she had the feeling: "I have to do everything by myself."

Wotan had offered to take her; Walter couldn't get away from work; suffered as under a knife when he saw the two of them leave. Suffered as if his heart had been put through a meat grinder / stone crusher.

When Clarisse entered the sanatorium, she inspected it like a general. A feeling of mission and divinity was already mingling again with her depression; she confidently tested the arrangements and the doctors on the question of whether they would be able to shelter and protect the revolution in world ideas that would now be emanating from this place.

So it was also the need to collect herself that had led her there.

The diagnosis put forward for her was general exhaustion and neurasthenia; Clarisse lived quietly and was solicitously cared for. The persistent blows that had shaken her body like a railway journey ceased; she suddenly came to realize that she had been ill, while the ground beneath her feet was becoming firmer and more elastic again; she felt tenderness for her healing body, which was also now "solicitously caring for" her mind, as she ascertained, delighted at this unity of events.

Previously lack of appetite, diarrhea, etc.

But the most recent events suddenly appeared problematical to her.

She got hold of writing materials and proceeded to write down her experiences.

She wrote for a whole day, almost from morning to evening. Without the need for fresh air or food; it struck her that her bodily activities receded almost entirely, and only a certain timidity about the strict house rules of the sanatorium moved her to go to the dining hall. Some time earlier she had read somewhere an article on Francis of Assisi; he showed up again in the notebook she was working on, in whole paragraphs that were repeated with trivial individual changes without this bothering her. The originality of intellectual achievements is judged falsely even today. The traditional idea of the hero still battles for priority with every new idea and new invention, although we have long known from the history of these controversies that every new idea arises in several minds at the same time, but that for some reason the heroic sense finds it more fitting to imagine genius as a bubbling spring instead of a broad current made up of many tributaries and combinations, although the greatest ideas of genius are nothing more than modifications of other ideas of genius, with minor additions. That is why on the one hand "we no longer have any geniuses"—because we think we see the point of origin all too clearly and will not abandon ourselves to believing in the genius of an accomplishment composed of nothing but ideas, emotions, and other elements that, taken singly, we must have unavoidably already encountered here and there. On the other hand, we exaggerate our imaginings about the nature of genius's originality—especially where the testing by facts and by success is lacking; in short, wherever it is a question of nothing less than our soul—in such a senseless and perverted way that we have a great many geniuses whose heads have no more content than the page of a newspaper, but a flashy and original makeup by way of compensation. This makeup—allied with the false belief in the inescapable originality of genius, at odds with the obscure feeling of there being nothing behind it, which climaxes in a total incapacity to take the countless elements of an age and create structures of intellectual life that are nothing more than experiments, yet have the full seriousness of impartiality—belongs to that tepid mood full of doubts about the possibility of genius and the adoration of many ersatz geniuses that prevails today.

In spite of her many weaknesses, Clarisse, for whom genius was a matter of the will, belonged neither to the shrilly got-up people nor to the disheartened ones. She wrote down with great energy what she had read, and in doing so had the right feeling of originality in assimilating this material and feeling it mysteriously becoming part of her inmost being, as in the vividly leaping flames of an immolation. "By accident," she wrote, "while I was already thinking of my departure, memories clashed in my head. That the Sienese (Perugia?) in the year . . . carried a portrait . . . into the church, that Dante . . . names the fountain that is still standing today in the Piazza . . . And that Dante said about the piety of Francis of Assisi, who was canonized shortly afterward: It rose among us like a shining star."

Where she no longer remembered the names she put in periods. There was time for that later. But the words "rose like a shining star" she felt in her body. That she—incidentally—had hit upon the article she had read had come about because she longed for better times; not as an escape, but because—as she felt—something active had to happen.

This Francis of Assisi—she wrote—was the son of prosperous Sienese citizens, a draper, and before that a smart young man about town. People of today like Ulrich, who have access to science, are reminded by his later behavior (after his religious awakening) of certain manic states, and it cannot be denied that they are right in doing so. But what in 1913 is mental illness can in 13 . . . (periodic insanity, hysteria, of course not illnesses with an anatomical course, only those that coexist with health!!) merely have been seen as a one-sided debit of health. *The etiology of certain diseases is not only a personal but also a social phenomenon*— she underlined this sentence. In parentheses she threw in a few additional words: (Hysteria. Freud. Delirium: its forms are different according to the society. Mass psychology offers images that do not differ greatly from the clinical). Then came a sentence that she also underlined: *It is by no means excluded that what today becomes mere inner destruction will one day again have constructive value.*

If the healthy person is a social phenomenon, then so is the sick person.

It went through her mind that Dante and Francis of Assisi were actually one and the same person; it was a tremendous discovery. She did not, however, write it down but undertook to look into this problem later, and the next moment her splendor, too, was extinguished. The decisive thing is—she wrote—that at that time a person, *whom today we would in good conscience put in a sanatorium,* could live, teach, and lead his contemporaries! That the best of his contemporaries saw him as an honor and an illumination! That at that time Siena was a center of culture. But she wrote in the margin: *All people are one person?* Then she went on more calmly: It fascinates me to imagine how things looked then. That age did not have much intelligence. It did not test things; it believed like a good child, without bothering itself about what was improbable. Religion went along with local patriotism; it was not the individual Sienese who would enter into heaven, but one day the whole city of Siena that would be transplanted there as a unit. For one loved heaven by loving the city. (The cheerfulness, the sense of ornament, the broad vistas of small Italian cities!) Religious eccentrics were few; people were proud of their city; what they shared was a common experience. Heaven belonged to this city, how should it be otherwise? The priests were considered not particularly religious people but merely a kind of official; for in all religions God was always something far away and uncertain, but the faith that the Son of God had come to visit, that one still had the writings of those who had seen Him with their own eyes, imparted an enormous vitality, nearness, and security to the experience, which the priests were there to confirm. The officer corps of God.

If in the midst of this one is brushed by God, as Saint Francis was, it is only a new reassurance, which does not disturb the civic cheerfulness of the experience. Because everyone believed, a few could do so in a particular way, and thus intellectual wealth was added to simple, legitimate security. For in sum more energies flow from opposition than from agreement. . . .

Here deep furrows formed on Clarisse's forehead. Nietzsche occurred to her, the enemy of religion: here there were still some difficult things for her to reconcile. —I do not presume to know the enormous history of these emotions—she told herself—but one thing is certain: today the religious experience is no longer the action of all, of a community, but only of individuals. And apparently that is why this experience is sick.

Feeling of solitude in the sea of the spirit, which is in motion in all directions.

/ Note: Mass experience connected with Meingast. /

She stopped writing and walked slowly up and down the room, excitedly rubbing her hands against each other or rubbing her forehead with a finger. It was not from despondency that she fled into past and remote times; it was absolutely clear to her that she, striding up and down in this room, was connected with the Siena of the past. Thoughts of recent days were intermingled with this: she was in some fashion or other not only destined but already actually involved in taking over the mission that recurred over the centuries, like God in every new Host. But she was not thinking of God; remarkably enough, this was the only idea she did not think of, as if it had no role in it at all; perhaps it would have disturbed her, for everything else was as vivid as if she had to get on a train tomorrow to travel there. By the windows great masses of green leaves waved in at her; tree balls; they steeped the whole room in a watery green. This color, "with which at that time my soul was filled," as she said later, played a great role in her as the chief color of these ideas.

This connection to the past, which Ulrich lacks.

Feeling! Pealing of bells. Processions march with banners to the Virgin and gorgeous robes. She was walking in the middle. When they stopped, however, the crowd did not stop. But that was not upsetting.

*   *   *

[Clarisse flees to Italy, where she joins Ulrich on the "Island of Health":]

—In Pompeii—Ulrich said—the cast of a woman has been found sealed in a fraction of a second into the cooling lava like a statue by the gases into which her body dissolved when the terrible stream of fire enveloped her. This nearly naked woman, whose shift had slid up to her back, had been overtaken as she was running and fallen facedown with her arms outstretched, while her small hair-knot, untidily put up, still sat firmly on the back of her head; she was neither ugly nor beautiful, neither voluptuous from living well nor gnawed by poverty, neither twisted by horror nor unwittingly overpowered without fear; but just because of all that, this woman, who many centuries ago jumped out of bed and was thrown on her stomach, has remained as incredibly alive as if at any second she could stand up again and run on. Clarisse understood exactly what he meant. Whenever she scratched her thoughts and emotions in the sand, with some mark or other that was as charged with them as a boat that can hardly stay afloat for the multiplicity of its cargo, and the wind then blew on it for a day, animal tracks ran over it, or rain made pockmarks in it and eroded the sharpness of the outlines the way the cares of life erode a face, but most especially when one had forgotten it completely and only through some chance stumbled on it again and suddenly confronted oneself, confronted an instant compressed and full of emotions and thoughts that had become sunken, faded, small, and barely recognizable, overgrown from left to right but not vanished, with grasses and animals living around it without shyness, when it had become world, earth: then . . . ? Hard to say what then; the island became populated with many Clarisses; they slept on the sand, flew on the light through the air, called from the throats of birds; it was a lust to

touch oneself everywhere, to run into oneself everywhere, an unutterable sensitivity: a giddiness escaped from the eyes of this woman and was
able to infect Ulrich, the way one person's lustful glance can ignite the
greatest lust in another. God knows what it is—Ulrich thought—that
causes lovers to scratch the mystery of their initials into the bark of trees,
so that they grow along with it; that has invented the seal and the coat of
arms, the magic of portraits gazing out of their frames: to end ultimately
in the trace of the photographic plate, which has lost all mystery because
it is already nearly reality again.

But it was not only that. It was also the multiplicity of meaning. Something was a stone and signified Ulrich; but Clarisse knew that it was
more than Ulrich and a stone, that it was everything in Ulrich that was
hard as stone and everything heavy that was oppressing her, and all insight into the world that one acquired, once one had understood that the
stones were like Ulrich. Exactly as if one says: This is Max, but he is a
genius. Or the fork of a branch and a hole in the sand say: this is Clarisse,
but at the same time she is a witch and is riding her heart. Many emotions that are otherwise separate crowd around such a sign, one never
quite knew which ones, but gradually Ulrich also recognized such an
uncertainty in the world in his own feelings. It threw into relief some of
Clarisse's peculiarly invented trains of thought, which he almost learned
to understand.

/ The uncertainty: / For a while Clarisse saw things that one otherwise
does not see. Ulrich could explain that splendidly. Perhaps it was insanity. But a forester out walking sees a different world from the one a botanist or a murderer sees. One sees many invisible things. A woman sees
the material of a dress, a painter a lake of liquid colors in its stead. I see
through the window whether a hat is hard or soft. If I glance into the
street I can likewise see whether it is warm or cold outside, whether
people are happy, sad, healthy, or ailing; in the same way, the taste of a
fruit is sometimes already in the fingertips that touch them. Ulrich remembered: if one looks at something upside down—for instance, behind the lens of a small camera—one notices things one had overlooked.
A waving back and forth of trees or shrubs or heads that to the normal
eye appear motionless. Or one becomes conscious of the peculiar hopping quality of the way people walk. One is astonished at the persistent
restlessness of things. In the same way, there are unperceived double
images in the field of vision, for one eye sees something differently from
the other; afterimages crystallize from still pictures like the most deli-
cate-colored fogs; the brain suppresses, supplements, forms the supposed reality; the ear does not hear the thousand sounds of one's own
body: skin, joints, muscles, the innermost self, broadcast a contrapuntal

composition of innumerable sensations that, mute, blind, and deaf, perform the subterranean dance of the so-called waking state. Ulrich remembered how once, not even very high up in the mountains, he had been overtaken by a snowstorm early in the year; he was on his way to meet some friends who were supposed to be coming down a path, and was surprised at not yet having met up with them, when the weather suddenly changed; the clarity darkened, a howling storm came up, and thick clouds of snow flung sharp icy needles at the solitary wanderer, as if for him it were a matter of life and death. Although after a few minutes Ulrich reached the shelter of an abandoned hut, the wind and the torrents of snow had gone right through him, and the icy cold as well as the exertions of his struggle against the storm and the force of the snow had exhausted him within a very brief period. When the storm passed as quickly as it had come, he of course set out on his way again; he was not the sort of person to let himself be intimidated by such an event, at least his conscious self was totally free of excitement and any kind of overestimation of the danger he had come through; indeed, he felt himself in the highest of spirits. But he still must have been shaken, for he suddenly heard his party coming toward him and cheerfully called to them. But no one answered. He again called out loudly—for it is easy to get off the path in the snow and miss each other—and ran, as well as he could, in the direction indicated, for the snow was deep and he had not been prepared for it, having undertaken the climb without either skis or snowshoes. After some twenty-five paces, at every one of which he sank in up to his hips, exhaustion forced him to stop, but just then he again heard voices in animated conversation, and so near that he absolutely should have seen the speakers, whom there was nothing to conceal. And yet no one was there except the soft, bright-gray snow. Ulrich collected his senses, and the conversation became more distinct. I'm hallucinating, he said to himself. Yet he called out again; without success. He began to fear for himself and checked himself in every way he could think of; spoke loudly and coherently, calculated small sums in his mind, and carried out movements of arms and fingers whose execution demanded total control. All these things worked, without the phenomenon vanishing. He heard whole conversations full of surprising import and a harmonious multiplicity of voices. Then he laughed, found the experience interesting, and began to observe it. But that did not make the phenomenon disappear either; it faded only when he turned around and had already climbed down several hundred yards, while his friends had not taken this way back at all and there was no human soul in the vicinity. So unreliable and extensive is the boundary between insanity and health. It really did not surprise him when in the middle of the night

Clarisse, trembling, woke him up and claimed she was hearing a voice. When he asked her, she said it was not a human voice and not an animal voice, but a "voice of something," and then he, too, suddenly heard a noise that could in no way be ascribed to a material being; and the next instant, while Clarisse was trembling more and more violently and opened her eyes wide like a night bird, something invisible seemed to glide around the room, bumping into the mirror in its glass frame and exerting a disembodied pressure, and in Ulrich, too, fears—not *one* fear, a bundle of fears, a world of fears—poured out in panic, so that he had to bring all his reason to bear in order to resist and to calm Clarisse down.

Dramatize! Make all this present!

But he was reluctant to apply his reason. One could feel strangely happy in this uncertainty that the world assumed in Clarisse's vicinity. The sketchings in the sand and the models made of stones, feathers, and branches now took on meaning for him too, as if here, on this Island of Health, something was trying to come to fulfillment that his life had already touched on several times. The foundation of human life seemed to him a monstrous fear of some kind, indeed really a fear of the indeterminate. He lay on the white sand between the blue of the air and the blue of the water on the small, hot sandy platform of the island between the cold depths of sea and sky. He lay as in snow. If he were to have been blown away then, this is the way it could have happened. Clarisse was romping and playing like a child behind the thistly dunes. He was not afraid. He saw life from above. This island had flown away with him. He understood his past. Hundreds of human orders have come and gone: from the gods to brooch pins, and from psychology to the record player, every one of them an obscure unit, every one an obscure conviction that it was the ultimate, ascendant one, and every one of them mysteriously sinking after a few hundred or a few thousand years and passing into rubble and building site: what else is this but a climbing up out of nothingness, each attempt on a different wall? Like one of those dunes blown by the wind, which for a while forms its own weight and then is blown away again by the wind? What is everything we do other than a nervous fear of being nothing: beginning with our pleasures, which are no pleasures but only a din, a chattering instigated to kill time, because a dark certainty admonishes us that it will in the end annihilate us, all the way to those inventions that outdo each other, the senseless mountains of money that kill the spirit, whether one is suffocated or borne up by them, to the continually changing fashions of the mind, of clothes that change incessantly, to murder, assassination, war, in which a profound mistrust of whatever is stable and created explodes: what is all that but the restlessness of a man shoveling himself down to his knees out of a grave he will never escape, a being that will never entirely climb out of nothingness, who fearfully flings himself into shapes but is, in some secret place that he is hardly aware of himself, vulnerable and nothing?

To here: Role of human experiences that spread not through rational transmission but through contagion. A social (humanity's) experience in two people.

And no way at all of framing this in cycles!

Ulrich remembered the man he had observed with Clarisse and Meingast in the green circle of the lantern. Here on the Island of Health even this distorted human creation, this exhibitionist, this despairing creature, this sexual desire stealing forth in a crouch out of the darkness when a woman passed by, was not basically different from other people. What else but a solitary exhibitionism were Walter's sentimental music, or Meingast's political thoughts about the common will of the many? What is even the success of a statesman standing in the midst of human bustle other than an anesthetizing exercise that has the appearance of a gratification? In love, in art, in greed, in politics, in work, and in play, we seek to articulate our painful secret: A person only half belongs to himself, the other half is expression. / This quotation from Emerson is I think word for word! / In the travail of their souls, all people yearn for expression. The dog sprays a stone with himself and sniffs his excrement: to leave a trace in the world, to erect in the world a monument to oneself, a deed that will still be celebrated after hundreds of years, is the meaning of all heroism. I have done something: that is a trace, a dissimilar but immortal portrait. "I have done something" binds parts of the material world to myself. Even just expressing something already means having one sense more with which to appropriate the world. Even wheedling someone into something the way Walter does has this sense. Ulrich laughed, because it occurred to him that Walter would walk around in despair with the thought: Oh, I could say a thing or two about that . . . ! It is the profound basic feeling of the bourgeois, a feeling that is steadily being silenced and pacified. But on the Island of Health

Ulrich ended by taking back all the ambition of his life. What are even theories, other than wheedling? Discussions. And at the conclusion of such hours Ulrich was no longer thinking of anything but Agathe, the distant, inseparable sister, of whom he did not even know what she was doing. And he sadly recalled her favorite expression: "What can I do for my soul, which lives in me like an unsolved riddle? Which leaves visible man free to make any kind of choice because it cannot govern him in any way?"

Here a settlement of accounts about Ulrich's mood in regard to heroism.

The dog, which after long association with man involuntarily caricatures him so splendidly in many ways.

The feeling of never being allowed to leave here again.

Clarisse meanwhile was playing out her game of signs; sometimes he saw her scurrying over the dunes like a fluttering cloth. "We are playing our story here," she claimed, "on the stage of this island." Basically it was only the exaggerated form of this having to imprint oneself on uncertainty. Formerly, when Clarisse had still been going to the opera with Walter, she had often said: "What is all art! If we could act out our stories!" She was now doing this as well. All lovers ought to do it. All lovers have the feeling that what we are experiencing is something miraculous, we are chosen people; but they ought to play it before a large orchestra and a dark hall—real lovers on the stage, and not people who are paid: not only a new theater would arise but also an entirely new kind of love, which would spread, lighting up human gestures like a fine network of branches, instead of, like today, creeping into the child's darkness. That was what Clarisse said. Please, no child! Instead of accomplishing something, people have children! Sometimes she called the small keepsakes she put in the sand for Ulrich her secret children, or so she called every impression she received, for the impression melted into her like fruit. Between her and things there existed a continual exchanging of signs and understandings, a conspiracy, a heightened thinking / heightened correspondence / a burning, spirited life process. Sometimes this became so intense that Clarisse thought she was being torn out of her slender body and flying like a veil over the island, without rest, until her eyes were transfixed by a small stone or a shell and a credulous astonishment rooted her to the spot, because she had already been here once and always, and had lain quietly as a trace in the sand, while a second Clarisse had flown over the island like a witch.

At times, her person seemed to her only an obstacle, unnaturally inserted in the dynamic exchange between the world that affected her and the world she affected. In its most intense moments, this self seemed to tear apart and disintegrate. / Cf. piano scene. Beethoven—Nietzsche quotation. Even then Clarisse was serious about tearing apart. / Even if she was unfaithful to Walter with this body and this "soul fastened to her skin," it did not mean anything: there were many hours in which the frigid, rejecting Clarisse transformed herself into a vampire, insatiable, as if an obstacle had fallen away and for the first time she could yield to this heretofore forbidden pleasure. She sometimes seemed to plan things to suck Ulrich dry: "There's still one more devil in you I have to exorcise!" she said. He owned a red sport jacket, and she sometimes made him put it on in the middle of the night and did not let up until he turned pale under his tanned skin. Her passion for him, and in general all the emotions she expressed, were not deep—Ulrich felt that distinctly—but somehow at times passed by depth on their precipitous fall into the abyss.

Nor did she entirely trust Ulrich. He did not completely understand the greatness of what she was experiencing. During these days she had of course recognized and seen through everything that had previously been inaccessible to her. Formerly, she had experienced infinite heaviness, the enterprising spirit's fall from almost-attained heights of greatness to the deepest anxiety and anguish. It seems that a person can be driven out from the ordinary real world we all know by processes that take place not in her but above or below the earth, and in the same way the person can intensify them into the incommensurable. On the island she explained it to Ulrich like this: One day everything around Clarisse had been enhanced: colors, smells, straight and crooked lines, noises, her emotions or thoughts, and the ones she aroused in others; what was taking place might have been causal, necessary, mechanical, and psychological, but aside from that it was moved by a secret driving force; it might have happened precisely that way the day before, but today, in some indescribable and fortunate way, it was different. —Oh—Clarisse immediately said to herself—I am freed from the law of necessity, where every thing depends on some other thing. For things depended on her emotions. Or rather, what was at work was a continual activity of the self and of things penetrating and yielding to each other, as if they were on opposite sides of the same elastic membrane. Clarisse discovered that what she was acting from was a veil of emotions, with things on the other side. A little later she received the most terrible confirmation: she perceived everything going on around her just as correctly as before, but it had become totally dissociated and alienated. Her own emotions seemed foreign to her, as if someone else were feeling them, or as if they were drifting around in the world. It was as if she and things were badly fitted to each other. She no longer found any support in the world, did not find the necessary minimum of satisfaction and self-moderation, was no longer able to maintain through inner action the equilibrium with the events of the world, and felt with unspeakable anguish how she was being inexorably squeezed out of the world and could no longer escape suicide (or perhaps madness). Again she was exempted from ordinary necessity and subjected to a secret law; but then she discovered, at the last moment when she could possibly be saved, the law that no one before her had noticed:

We—that is, people lacking Clarisse's insight—imagine that the world is unambiguous, whatever the relationship between the things out there and inner processes may be; and what we call an emotion is a personal matter that is added to our own pleasure or uneasiness but does not otherwise change anything in the world. Not just the way we see red when we get angry—that too, moreover; it is only erroneously that one considers it something that is an occasional exception, without suspecting what deep and general law one has touched upon!—but rather like this: things swim in emotions the way water lilies consist not only of leaves and flowers and white and green but also of "gently lying there." Ordinarily, they are so quiet about this that one does not notice the totality; the emotions have to be calm for the world to be orderly and for merely rational associations to be dominant in it.

But assuming for instance that a person suffers some really serious and annihilating humiliation that would have to lead to his destruction, it does happen that instead of this shame a surpassing pleasure in the humiliation sets in, a holy or smiling feeling about the world, and this is then not merely an emotion like any other or a deliberation, not even the reflection that we might perchance console ourselves that humility is virtuous, but a sinking or rising of the whole person on another level, a "sinking on the rise," and all things change in harmony with this; one might say they remain the same but now find themselves in some other space, or that everything is tinged with another sense. At such moments one recognizes that aside from everyone's world, that solid world that can be investigated and managed by reason, there is a second world, dynamic, singular, visionary, irrational, which is only apparently congruent with the first and which we do not, as people think, merely carry in our hearts or our minds, but which exists externally with precisely the same reality as the prevailing world. It is an uncanny mystery, and like everything mysterious it becomes, whenever one tries to articulate it, easily confused with what is most banal. Clarisse herself had experienced— when she was unfaithful to Walter, and although she had to be, on which account she did not recognize any remorse—how the world became black; however, it was not a real color but a quite indescribable one, and later this "sense color" of the world, as Clarisse called it, became a hard, burnt brown.

Clarisse was very happy on the day when she grasped that her new understanding was the continuation of her efforts on the subject of genius. For what distinguishes the genius from the healthy, ordinary person, other than the secret involvement of the emotions in everything that happens, which in the healthy person is stable and unnoticed but in the genius, on the other hand, is subject to incessant irritations? Moreover, Ulrich too said that there are many possible worlds. Rational, reasonable people adapt themselves to the world, but strong people adapt the world to themselves. As long as the "sense color" of the world, as Clarisse called it, remained stable, equilibrium in the world also had something stable. Its unnoticed stability might even be considered healthy and ordinarily indispensable, the way the body, too, is not permitted to feel all the organs that maintain its equilibrium. Also unhealthy is a labile equilibrium, which tips over at the first chance and falls into the inferior position. Those are the mentally ill, Clarisse told herself, of whom she was afraid. But on top, conquerors in the realm of humanity, are those whose equilibrium is just as vulnerable but full of strength and, constantly disturbed, is constantly inventing new forms of equilibrium.

It is an uncanny balance, and Clarisse had never felt herself as much a creature perched on the razor's edge between annihilation and health as she did now. But whoever has followed the development of Clarisse's thoughts up to this point will already know that she had now come upon the traces of the "secret of redemption." This had entered her life as the mission to liberate the genius that was inhibited by all sorts of relations in herself, Walter, and their surroundings, and it is easy to see that this inhibition comes about because one is forced to yield to the repression the world practices against every person of genius, and is submerged in obscurity; but here, on the other side, it throws the world into relief in a new color. This was for her the significance of the soul color dark red, a marvelous, indescribable, and transparent shade in which air, sand, and vegetation were immersed, so that she moved everywhere as in a red chamber of light.

She once called this the "darkroom," herself surprised by its similarity to a room in which in the midst of acrid vapors one bends tense and excited over the delicate, barely recognizable images that appear on the negative. It was her task to prefigure the redemption, and Ulrich seemed to her to be her apostle, who would after a while leave her and go out into the world, and whose first task would be to liberate Walter and Meingast. From this point on, her progress was much more rapid.

The blows of confused and anarchic ideas that Ulrich received every day, and the movement of these thoughts in an imprudent but clearly palpable direction, had in fact gradually swept him up, and the only thing that still differentiated his life from that of the insane was a consciousness of his situation, which he could interrupt by an effort. But for a long time he did not do so. For while he had always felt only like a guest among rational people and those effectively engaged in life, at least with one part of his being, and as alien or meaningless as a poem would be were he suddenly to start reciting one at the general meeting of a corporation, he felt here in this nothingness of certainty an enhanced security, and lived with precisely this part of his being among the structures of absurdity in the air, but as securely as on solid ground. Happiness is in truth not something rational, which depends once and for all on a specific action or the possession of specific things, but much more a mood of the nerves through which everything becomes happiness or doesn't; to this extent Clarisse was right. And the beauty, goodness, and quality of genius in a woman, the fire she kindles and sustains, is not to be settled by any legal determination of truth but is a mutual delirium. One could maintain, Ulrich told himself, that our entire being—which we basically cannot find a basis for but complacently accept on the whole as God, while, acting from this assumption, it is easy for us to deduce the details—is nothing but the delirium of many; but if order is reason, then every simple fact, if we observe it outside of any order, is already the germ of a madness. For what do facts have to do with our mind? The mind governs itself by them, but they stand there, responsible to no one, like mountain peaks or clouds or the nose on a person's face; there were times when it would have been a pleasure to crush the nose on the face of the lovely Diotima with two fingers; Clarisse's nose sniffed, alert, like the nose of a pointer, and was able to impart all the excitement of the invisible.

.   .   .

But soon he was no longer able to follow Clarisse's idea of order. You scratch a sign in a stone at the spot where you happen to be: that this is art, just as the greatest is, was a feeling one could sympathize with. And Clarisse did not want to possess Ulrich, but—each time in a new leap— live with him. —I don't perceive truly—she said—but I perceive fruit- fully. Her ideas scintillated, things scintillated. One does not gather up one's insights in order to form a self out of them, like a cold snowman, when like her one is growing into ever-new catastrophes; her ideas grew "in the open"; one weakens oneself by scattering everything, but spurs oneself on to new, strange growth. Clarisse began to express her life in poems; on the Island of Health Ulrich found this quite natural. In our poems there is too much rigid reason; the words are burned-out notions, the syntax holds out sticks and ropes as if for the blind, the meaning never gets off the ground everyone has trampled; the awakened soul cannot walk in such iron garments. Clarisse discovered that one would have to choose words that are not ideas; but since there don't seem to be any, she chose instead the word pair. If she said "I," this word was never able to shoot up as vertically as she felt it; but "I-red" is not yet impris- oned by anything, and flew upward. Just as beneficial is freeing words from their grammatical bonds, which are quite impoverished. For exam- ple, Clarisse gave Ulrich three words and asked him to read them in any order he chose. If they were "God," "red," and "goes," he read "God goes red," or "God, red, goes"—that is, his brain immediately either un- derstood them as a sentence or separated them by commas in order to underline that it was *not* making them into a sentence. Clarisse called this the chemistry of words, that they always cohere in groups, and showed how to counter this. Her favorite bit of information was that she worked with exclamation points or underlining. God!! red!!! goes! Such accumulations slow one down, and the word dams up behind them to its full meaning. She also underlined words from one to ten times, and at times a page she had written this way looked like a cryptic musical score. Another means, but one she used less frequently, was repetition; through it the weight of the repeated word became greater than the power of the syntactic bond, and the word began to sink without end. God goes green green green. It was an incredibly difficult problem to ascertain correctly the number of repetitions so that they would express exactly what was meant.

One day, Ulrich showed up with a volume of Goethe's poems, which he happened to have brought along, and proposed taking several words out of each of a number of poems and putting them together, to see what came out. Poems like this came out:

— — — — —

— — — — —

It cannot be overlooked that an obscure, incoherent charm emanates from these constellations, something with the glowing fire of a volcano, as if one were looking into the bowels of the earth. And a few years after Clarisse, a similar play with words actually did become an ominous fashion among the healthy.

Clarisse anticipated remarkable conclusions. Flakes of fire were stolen by poets from the volcano of madness: at some point in primeval times and later, every time a genius revisited earth; these glowing connections of words, not yet constricted to specific meanings, were planted in the soil of ordinary language to form its fertility, "which as we know comes from its volcanic origins." But—so Clarisse concluded—it follows from this that the mind must decay to primal elements again and again in order for life to remain fruitful. This placed in Clarisse's hands the responsibility for a monstrous irresponsibility; she knew that she was really uneducated, but now she was filled with a heroic lack of respect for everything that had been created before her.

Ulrich was able to follow Clarisse's games this far, and youth's lack of respect made it easier for him to dream into the shattered mind these new structures that could be formed: a process that has repeated itself among us several times, around 1900, when people loved the suggestive and sketchy, as after 1910, where in painting people succumbed to the charm of the simplest constructive elements and bid the secrets of the visible world echo by reciting a kind of optical alphabet.

But Clarisse's decline progressed more rapidly than Ulrich could follow. One day, she came with a new discovery. —Life withdraws powers from nature once and for all, forever—she began, making a connection with poems that tear words out of nature in order slowly to make it barren—while life transforms these powers withdrawn from nature into a new condition, "consciousness," from which there is no return. It seemed obvious, and Clarisse was surprised that no one before her had noticed it. This was because people's morality prevented them from noticing certain things. —All physical, chemical, and other such stimuli that strike me—she declared—I transform into consciousness; but never has the reverse been achieved, otherwise I could raise this stone with my will. So consciousness is constantly interfering with the system of nature's powers. Consciousness is the cause of all insignificant, superficial movement, and "redemption" demands that it be destroyed.

. . .

Leo Tolstoy: Consciousness is the greatest moral misfortune that a man can attain.
Fyodor Dostoyevsky: "All consciousness is a disease."
From Gorky's diary.

Clarisse immediately made a further discovery. The vanished forests of the carboniferous era, bubbling, rampant, gigantic, fantastic, are being freed again today under the influence of the sun as psychic forces, and it is through the exploitation of the energy that perished in that earlier time that the enormous spiritual energy of the present age arises.

She says: Before, it was only a game, now it has to get serious; here she becomes uncanny to him.

It was evening. To cool off she and Ulrich went for a walk in the dark. Hundreds of frogs were drumming in a small pond, and the crickets were rasping shrilly, so that the night was as animated as an African village starting a ritual dance. Clarisse asked Ulrich to go into the pond with her and kill himself so that their consciousness would gradually become swamp, coal, and pure energy.

Kill him!

This was a little too much. Ulrich was in danger, if her ideas ran on in this fashion, of having Clarisse slit his throat one of these nights.

Another chapter: she really tries it!

He telegraphed Walter to come immediately, since his attempts to calm Clarisse had failed and he could no longer assume the responsibility.

. . .

A kind of settling of accounts takes place between Walter and Ulrich.

Walter reproaches him: You fell in with this "redemption"; do you want to be a redeemer? (Instead of subjecting Clarisse to being cured by means of society.) Ulrich to this: If I myself really had the redeeming ideas, no one would believe them. If Christ were to return, he wouldn't get through today.

Rather paunchy belly, profound solidarity with Clarisse.

Ulrich: Aren't you jealous?

Walter: If I were, it would be a serious mistake (crime). I can't have that to complain about too; there are deeper values between people (husband and wife) than faithfulness.

Ulrich—who was thinking of Agathe—is depressed, seems ordinary to himself. But sensitive personal reactions while conforming to public norms belong to the uncreative person. Tells himself with a venomous clarity.

Walter sees him lying on the ground. Wrecked person. Takes revenge.

A weak person who sees a strong person on the ground loves him. Not because he now has him in his power. Nor because the envied person is now just as weak as he is. But loving himself in the other. He feels through him an enhancement of his self-love and tortures him from a kind of masochism.

This weak egotist, who has pushed his life hither and yon in trivial arrangements, is in this instance, where everything is the way he wants it to be and has often dreamed it, filled with soft beauty.

It was decided to bring Clarisse back to a new sanatorium; she accepted this without resistance and almost in silence. She was terribly disappointed in Ulrich and realized that she would have to go back into a clinic—"in order to try to get the circulation working once more"; it was so sluggish that even she had not been able to do it the first time.

She settled into her new abode with the confidence of a person returning to a hotel where he is a familiar guest. Walter stayed with her for four days. He felt the blessing of Ulrich's not being along and of being able to control Clarisse alone, but did not admit this to himself. The manner he had adopted toward Ulrich had, he thought, great loftiness, and he also believed he had succeeded in that; but now that it was over, something quite unpleasant made its presence known: that he had been afraid of Ulrich the whole time. His body desired manly satisfaction. He ignored Clarisse's condition and convinced himself that she was not sick but would recover most quickly if, aside from the physical care, she were treated psychologically as an ordinary woman as much as possible. But still he knew that he was only telling himself this. To his astonishment, he found less resistance in Clarisse than he was accustomed to. He suffered. He felt disgusted with himself. In the first night he had got a small cut that hurt: in his pain, and shuddering at his brutality, he thought he was scourging both her and himself. Then his leave was over. It did not occur to him to desert his office. He had to pack his soul with watch in hand.

Clarisse underwent a diet cure that had been prescribed for her, since her nervous overexcitement was regarded as the consequence of her physical deterioration. She was emaciated and as unkempt as a dog that has been wandering around free for weeks. The unaccustomed nourishment, whose effect she began to feel, impressed her. She even put up with Walter, gently, as she did with the cure that forced strange bodies on her and compelled her to gulp down coarse things. Dejectedly she put up with everything in order to acquire in her own mind the attestation of health. "I'm only living on my own credit," she told herself, "no one believes in me. Perhaps it's only a prejudice that I'm alive?" It calmed her, while Walter was there, to fill herself up with matter and take on earthly ballast, as she called it.

But the day Walter left, the Greek was there. He was staying at the sanatorium, perhaps he had been there longer than Clarisse, but now he crossed her path. As Clarisse passed by he was saying to a lady: "A person who has traveled as much as I have finds it absolutely impossible to love a woman." It might even be that he had said: "A person who comes from as far away as I do . . ."; Clarisse immediately understood it as a sign meant for her that this man had been led onto her path. The same evening she wrote him a letter. Its contents ran: I am the only woman you will love. She went into detail. You are a good height for a man—she wrote—but you have a figure like a woman's and feminine hands. You have a "vulture's beak," an aquiline nose from which the useless excess of energy has been drained; it is more beautiful than an aquiline nose. You have large, dark, deep eye sockets, painful caves of vice. You know the world, the overworld, and the underworld. I noticed right away that you wanted to hypnotize me, although your glance was really tired and timid. You guessed that I am your destiny.

I am not here because I am ill. But because, instinctively, I always choose the right means. My blood courses slowly. No one has ever been able to find a fever in me. At worst, some undetectable local contamination; no organically caused stomach illness, however much I suffer the greatest weakness as the result of complete exhaustion of my gastric system. Whatever our doctor may tell you, moreover, I am on the whole healthy, even though I myself might be ill in part. Proof: precisely that energy for absolute isolation and detachment that brought me here. I guessed with unerring accuracy what is needed at the moment, while a typically sick creature cannot become healthy at all, much less make itself healthy. Pay attention to me. This has also made me guess with unerring accuracy what it is you need.

You are the great hermaphrodite everyone is waiting for. Upon you the gods have bestowed male and female in equal measure. You will redeem the radiant world from the dark, unutterable schism of love. Oh, how I understood when you exclaimed that no woman was able to claim you! But I am the great feminine hermaphrodite. Whom no man can satisfy. In solitude I bear being split into two. Which you possess only in your mind, and therefore still only as a longing that we must overcome. With a black shield before it. A divine encounter has brought us here. We cannot evade our destiny and make the world wait a hundred years . . . !

The next day the Greek brought her letter back. Out of discretion he brought it himself. He told her he did not want to give her any occasion to write such things to him. His rejection was noble but firm. His hypnotist's face, cinematically demonic, masculine, would, placed in any random crowd of people, immediately have become the center of attention. But his hands were weak like a woman's; the skin of his head twitched involuntarily at times beneath his thick, carefully parted blue-black hair, and his eyes trembled slightly while Clarisse observed them. Under the influence of the diet cure and new moods, Clarisse had indeed changed physically in the last few days; she had become heavier and coarser, and her piano hands, rough from work, which she was clenching and unclenching in her excitement, aroused in the Levantine a peculiar fear; he was constantly drawn to look at them, felt the impulse to flee, but could not stand up.

Clarisse repeated to him that he could not evade his destiny, and reached out to grab him. He saw the horrible hand coming at him and could not stir. Only when her mouth slid past his eyes to his own did he find the strength to jump up and flee. Clarisse held on to his pants and tried to embrace him. He uttered a soft cry of disgust and fear and reached the door.

Clarisse was overjoyed. She was left with the feeling that this was a man of incredible, rare, and absolutely demonic purity; but the indecencies that she herself had committed also seemed to her tinged with this feeling. Her breathing became broad and free; the satisfaction at following the command of her inner voice past the ultimate constraints stretched her breasts like metal springs. For twenty-four hours she actually forgot everything that had brought her here, mission and suffering; her heart no longer shot arrows at the sky; all those she had fired off previously came back one after the other and drilled through it. Proudly she suffered horrible pains of desire. For the space of twenty-four hours. This frigid young woman, who as long as she had been healthy had never learned the frenzy of sex, received this delirium like an agony that raged through her body with such force that it could not hold still for an instant, but was driven back and forth by the terrible hunger of her nerves, while her delighted mind determined by this violence that the boundless power of all sexual desire, from which she had to redeem the world, had entered into her. The sweetness of this torture, the restless impotence, a need to throw herself in front of this man and weep with gratitude, the happiness she could not forbid herself, were for her a demonstration of how monstrous the demon was with whom she had to take up the struggle. This mentally ill woman who had not yet loved now loved with everything that had been spared in her, like a healthy woman but with desperate intensity, as if, with the utmost possible strength of which this emotion was capable, she wanted to tear it away from the shadows that surrounded and irresistibly reinterpreted it.

Like all women, she waited for the return of the man who had spurned her. Twenty-four hours passed, and then—approximately at the same hour as previously—the Greek actually did knock at Clarisse's door. A power he could not understand led this weak-willed man with the feminine sensibility to return to the situation in which the brutal attack on him had been inconclusively broken off. He came impeccably attired and coiffed, pleading carefully rehearsed excuses, and inwardly reinforced by the reflection that one had to fully enjoy this interesting woman; but when he looked at Clarisse his pupils trembled like the breasts of a girl being fondled for the first time. Clarisse did not beat around the bush. She repeated to him that he was not allowed to duck out, God too had suffered on the Mount of Olives, and went for him. His knees trembled and his hands went up against hers as helplessly as handkerchiefs to fend her off, but Clarisse slung her legs and arms around him and sealed his mouth with the hot phosphate breath of her own. In the extremity of his fear the Greek defended himself by confessing that he was homosexual. The unfortunate man had no idea what to do when she declared that that was precisely why he had to love her.

He was one of those half-sick, half-sociable people who wander through sanatoriums like hotels in which one meets more interesting people than in the ordinary kind. He spoke several languages and had read the books that were on everyone's tongue. A southeastern European elegance, black hair, and indolent dark eyes made him the focus of admiration of all those women who love intellect and the demonic in a man. The story of his life was like a lottery of the numbers of the hotel rooms to which he had been invited. He had never worked in his life, had been set up by his wealthy merchant family, and was in accord with the idea that after the death of his father his younger brother would take charge of their affairs. He did not love women but became their prey out of vanity, and was not resolute enough to follow his preference for men other than occasionally in the circles of big-city prostitution, where they disgusted him. He was really a big fat boy in whom the predilection of that indeterminate age for all vices had never given way to anything subsequent, and who had merely wrapped himself in the protection of a melancholy indolence and irresolution.

This wretched man had never experienced from a woman an attack of the kind Clarisse was now subjecting him to. Without his being able to grasp it from anything specific, she addressed herself to his vanity. "Great hermaphrodite," she said again and again, and there shone from her eyes something that was like the King of the Mountain, for him playful and yet frenzied. —Remarkable woman, the Greek said. —You are the great hermaphrodite—she said—who is not able to love either women or men! And that's just why you've been called to redeem them from the original sin that weakens them!

Of the three men who influenced Clarisse's life, Walter, Meingast, and Ulrich, Meingast, without its ever having become clear to her, was the one who had through his manner made the greatest impression on her by most powerfully stimulating her ambition—if one may so characterize the desire for wings of the uncreative mind banished to an ordinary life. His league of men, from which she was excluded, clanking in her imagination like archangels, had transformed themselves into the idea that the strong and redeemed person (and along with this: redeemed from marriage and love) was homosexual. "God himself is homosexual," she told the Greek. "He penetrates the believer, overpowers him, impregnates him, weakens him, rapes him, treats him like a woman, and demands submission from him, while excluding women from the Church. Impregnated by his God, the believer walks among women as among petty, silly elements he doesn't notice. Love is unfaithfulness to God, adultery; it robs the spirit of its human dignity. The madness of sin and the madness of bliss entice human action into the marriage bed (bed of adultery). O my female king, assume along with me the sins of humanity in order to redeem it by committing them, although we already see through them."

"Crazy—crazy," the Greek murmured, but at the same time Clarisse's ideas made unresisting sense to him and touched a point in his life that had never been treated with such seriousness or such passion. Clarisse roused his indolent soul like a dream raging in deepest darkness but, in doing so, treated him the way an older boy in puberty gets hold of a younger one and fondles him in order to carry out on him the most insane sacrifices of the cult of first love. The Greek's dignity as an interesting man was most violently compromised by this role being forced upon him, but at the same time this role hit upon fantasies buried deep within him, and Clarisse's ruthless visits aroused in him a trembling condition of bondage. Nowhere did he any longer feel safe from her; she invited him on outings in a carriage, during which she molested him behind the driver's back, and his greatest fear was that one day she would do it in the sanatorium in front of everybody, without his being able to defend himself. Finally, he began to tremble as soon as she came near him, but let her do whatever she wanted. *Cette femme est folle*—he said this sentence softly, plaintively, incessantly, in three languages, like a magic charm.

But at last—this peculiar, half-transparent relationship was attracting attention, and he imagined people were already making fun of him—his vanity tore him out of it; weeping almost from weakness, he gathered all his strength to shake this woman off. When they got into the carriage he said, averting his face, that it was the last time. As they were riding, he pointed out a policeman to her, claimed that he was having a relationship with him and that the policeman wanted him to have nothing more to do with Clarisse; he slung his glances around this massive man standing in the street as if he were a rock, but was torn away by the rolling carriage, feeling nevertheless strengthened by his lie, as if someone had sent him some kind of help. But it had the opposite effect on Clarisse. To see the lover of her "female king" affected her as a surprising concretization. In poems she had already characterized herself as a hermaphrodite, and now thought she could distinguish hermaphroditic qualities in her body for the first time. She could hardly expect them to break through to the surface. It's a divine constellation of love, she said.

The Greek was concerned about the coachman and pushed her away. He breathed into her face that this was their last trip. Without looking around, the coachman, apparently sensing that something was going on behind him, whipped the horses on. Suddenly a thunderstorm came up from three sides and surprised them. The air was heavy and filled with an uncanny tension; lightning flashed and thunder came crashing down. "This evening I'm receiving a visit from my lover," the Greek said. "You may not come to me!" "We're leaving tonight!" Clarisse answered. "For Berlin, the city of tremendous energies!" Just then, with a shattering crash, a bolt struck the fields not far from them, and the horses strained in a gallop against the traces. "No!" the Greek shouted, and involuntarily hid himself against Clarisse, who embraced him. "I deem myself a Thessalian witch!" she screamed into the uproar that now broke loose from all sides. Lightning blazes roared, mingled water and earth flew up from the ground, terror shook the air. The Greek was trembling like some poor animal body jolted by an electric charge. Clarisse was jubilant, embraced him with "lightning arms," and enveloped him. That was when he jumped out of the carriage.

When Clarisse got back, long after he did—she had forced the coachman to drive slowly through the storm, and slowly on after the sun had come out again and fields, horses, and the leather of the coach were steaming, while she sang mysterious things—she found in her room a note from the Greek informing her once again that the policeman was in his room, forbidding her to visit, and declaring that he was leaving in the morning. At dinner, Clarisse discovered that his departure was the truth. She wanted to rush to him, but became aware that all the women were observing her. The restlessness in the corridors seemed never to end. Women were passing by every time Clarisse stuck her head out of the door in order to scurry to the Greek's room. These stupid people looked mockingly at Clarisse, instead of comprehending that the policeman was scorning all of them. And for some reason Clarisse suddenly no longer trusted herself to walk upright and innocently to the Greek's door. Finally, it was quiet, and she slipped out barefoot. She scratched softly at the door, but no one answered, although light was coming through the keyhole. Clarisse pressed her lips to the wood and whispered. It remained quiet inside; someone was listening but not answering. The Greek was lying in bed with his "protector" and despised her. / Or: a strange man angrily opens the door. The Greek already gone? / Then she, who had never loved, was overcome by the nameless torment of submissive jealousy. —I am not worthy of him—she whispered—he thinks I'm sick, and, whispering, her lips slid down the door to the dust.

She was befuddled by a heartrending rapture; moaning softly, she pushed against the door in order to crawl to him and kiss his hand, and did not understand that her rapture had been thwarted.

When she awoke in her bed and rang for the chambermaid, she discovered that the Greek had left. She nodded, as if it had been agreed upon between them. —I'm leaving too, Clarisse said. —I'll have to tell the doctor—the girl. Hardly had the girl left the room when Clarisse sprang out of bed and, in a frenzy, dumped her belongings into a suitcase; what did not fit, and the rest of her baggage, she left behind. The girl thought the gentleman had taken the train for Munich. Clarisse fled. "Error is not blindness," she murmured, "error is cowardice! He recognized his mission but did not have enough courage for it." As she slunk out of the building, past his abandoned room, she again encountered the pain and shame of the past night. "He thought I was sick!" Tears streamed down her cheeks. She even did justice to the prison that she was escaping from; she took leave of the walls and the benches outside the door with compassion. People had meant to help her here, the best they could. —They wanted to cure me—Clarisse smiled—but curing is destroying! And when she was sitting in the express, the energy of whose storming bounds permeated her, her resolves became clear.

How can one be mistaken? Only by not seeing. But how can one not see what is there to be seen? By not trusting oneself to see. Clarisse recognized, like a broad field without a boundary, the general law of human progress: Error is cowardice; if people were to stop being cowardly the earth would make a leap forward. / In an analogous way, Ulrich recognizes why there is no radical progress. / Good, the way the train sped on with her without stopping. She knew that she had to catch up with the Greek.

They had all been against her, the sick ones too.

Clarisse took a sleeping compartment. When she got into the carriage she immediately told the conductor: Three gentlemen must be on this train, go and look for them, I absolutely must speak with them! It seemed to her that all her fellow passengers fell under the strong personal influence that emanated from her and were obeying her commands. The waiters in the dining car as well. But nevertheless the conductor had to report that he had not found the Greek, Walter, and Ulrich. After that, with a completely clear sensory impression, she recognized herself in the mirror now as a white she-devil, now as a blood-red madonna.

When she got off the train in Munich the next morning, she went to an elegant hotel, took a room, smoked the whole day, drank brandy and black coffee, and wrote letters and telegrams. Some circumstance or other had led her to assume that the Greek had traveled to Venice, and she issued instructions to him, the hotels, consular offices, and government bureaus. She displayed enormous industriousness. —Hurry up! she said to the page boys, who galloped around for her the whole day. It was a mood like at a fire when the fire trucks rattle up and the sirens wail, or like a mobilization, where horses trot and endless processions of resolute, helmet-enclosed faces march through the streets as if dreaming, the air filled with thrown flowers and heavy with gray tension.

That evening she herself went on to Venice.

In Venice, she registered at a pension frequented by Germans, where she had stayed on her honeymoon; people there dimly recalled the young woman. The same life as in Munich began, with abuse of alcohol and alkaloids, but now she no longer sent off any telegrams or messengers. From the moment she had got to Venice, perhaps because the official emissaries were not already waiting for her at the station with their reports, she had been convinced that the Greek had slipped through her net and fled to his homeland. The task now was to stem the flood and prepare a final assault, without haste and with the strictest measures toward oneself.

It was clear that she would sail to Greece, but first the frenzied desire for the man, a desire that had pushed her almost too far, had to be restrained. Besides coffee and brandy, Clarisse took no meals; she stripped naked and barricaded herself in her room, into which she did not allow even the hotel personnel. Hunger and something else, which she was not able to make out, put her in a state of feverlike confusion that lasted for days, in which impatient sexual arousal gradually faded to a vibrating mood in which all sorts of delusions of the senses were mingled. The abuse of strong substances had undermined her body; she felt it beginning to collapse under her. Constant diarrhea; a cavity appeared in a tooth and bothered her night and day; a small ugly wart began to form on her hand. But all this drove her to exert her mind more and more passionately, like the moment just before the end of a race, when one has to lift one's legs at every step by willpower. She had got hold of brush and paint pots, and from the arm of a chair, the edge of the bed, and an ironing board that she had found outside her door she built herself a scaffolding that she pushed along the wall, and began to paint the walls of her room with large designs. What she crisscrossed on the bare walls was the story of her life; so great was this process of inner purification that Clarisse was convinced that in a hundred years humanity would make a pilgrimage to these sketches and inscriptions in order to see the tremendous works of art with which the greatest of souls had covered her cell.

Perhaps they really were great works for someone who would have had to be in a position to disentangle the wealth of associations that had become tangled up in them. Clarisse created them with enormous tension. She felt herself great and hovering. She was beyond the articulated expression of life that creates words and forms, which are a compromise arranged for everyone, and had again arrived at that magic first encounter with herself, the madness of her first astonishment at those gifts of the gods, word and image. What she created was distorted, was piled up in confusion and yet impoverished, was unrestrained and yet obeyed a rigid compulsion; externally. Internally, it was for the first time the expression of her entire being: without purpose, without reflection, almost without will, becoming literally a second thing, enduring, greater, the transubstantiation of the human being into a piece of eternity: finally, the fulfillment of Clarisse's longing. While she painted she sang: "I am descended from luminous gods."

/ Noted outside the novel: Does greatness never lie in content? In a way of ordering things? /

When they broke into her room, uncomprehending eyes stared at these walls like the eyes of hostile animals. Clarisse had bought a boat ticket and laid out a blanket and a towel twisted into a turban as her imperial attire, which she was going to take on board with her. Then it occurred to her that a person who finds himself on sacred paths is not allowed to have any money with him without falling victim to a ridiculous incongruity, so she gave away her money and jewelry to laughing gondoliers. As she was about to give a speech in the Piazza of St. Mark's to the people assembled for her departure, a man spoke to her and gently brought her back to her pension. But since this man was unwise enough to recommend her to the protection of her hosts, everyone now poured into her room; the *padrona* screamed about the damage, gave orders to seize Clarisse's property, swore in vulgar language when none was to be found, and the staff tittered. A horrendous cruelty stared at Clarisse from every side, that primal hatred of inert matter, one part of which pushes another from the spot unless attraction and understanding mold them together into one. Silently Clarisse took her turban and cloak in order to leave this land and go on board. But at the canal steps the always friendly brown-black chambermaid came after her and begged her to wait, because a gentleman wanted to have the honor of showing her something before she left. Clarisse stopped in silence; she was tired and really no longer had the strength to travel. When the gondola with the man and two strange men appeared she stared gravely into the girl's friendly eyes, which were now almost floating in a moist shimmer, and thought the grievous word: Iscariot. She had no time to reflect on this shattering experience. In the gondola she calmly and seriously kept her eyes on the strange man and had the distinct impression that he was shrinking from her. This satisfied her. They came to the Colleone monument, and now the strange man spoke to her for the first time. "Why don't we go in here," he said, indicating a building beside the church that stood there. "There's something particularly nice to look at." Clarisse suspected the trap being set for her by the official of public security. But this suspicion had no value for her, no causal valency, so to speak. I'm tired and ill, she said to herself. He wants to lure me into the hospital. It's unreasonable of me to go along. But my madness is merely that I fall out of their general order and my causality isn't theirs: only disturbance in a subordinate function, which they overestimate. Their behavior is the crassest lack of ethics / In their causal associations what I do and how I do it is sick; because they don't see the other.

When they entered the building she divided the rest of her jewelry and her towel among the matrons, who accepted them, seized her, and strapped her to a bed. Clarisse began to cry, and the matrons said *"poveretta!"*

After confinement

This time, it was Wotan who went to get her and brought her back; he took her to Dr. Fried's clinic. When she was brought in, the doctor on duty merely looked at her and had her taken to the ward for the distracted.

The very first scream of a madman forced on her the idea of the migration of souls; the ideas of reincarnation, of the attainable Nirvana, were not far away.

"Mother! Mother!" That was the cry of a girl who was covered with horrible wounds. Clarisse longed for her mother on account of the many sins with which her mother had sent her out into the world. Her parents were now sitting around the table at breakfast; there were flowers in the room; Clarisse was covered with all their sins, they felt good; her migration of souls began.

Clarisse's first walk led to the bath, since she had been excited by being brought in. It was a square room with a tile floor and a large pool filled with water and without a raised edge; from the doorway steps led into it. Two wasted bodies fastened longing glances on her and screamed for redemption. They were her best friends, Walter and Ulrich, in sinful form.

During the night the Pope lay beside her. In the shape of a woman. —Church is black night—Clarisse said to herself—now it longs for the woman. There was a dim light, the patients were sleeping, when the Pope fumbled at her blanket and wanted to slip into bed with her. He was longing for his woman; Clarisse had no objection. —The black night longs for redemption, she whispered, as she yielded to the Pope's fingers. The sins of Christendom were extirpated. King Ludwig of Bavaria was lying opposite her, etc. It was a night of crucifixion. Clarisse looked toward her dissolution; she felt free of all guilt, her soul floated weightless and bright as these visions crept to her bed like poems and vanished again without her being able to seize their shapes and hold them fast. The next morning, Nietzsche's soul in the shape of the chief doctor was for her the most glorious sight. Beautiful, kindly, full of profound seriousness, his bushy beard grayed, his eyes seeing as from another world, he nodded to her. She knew it had been he who during the night had bidden her extirpate the sins of Christendom; hot ambition, like the ambition of a schoolgirl, soared in Clarisse.

During the next two weeks she experienced *Faust, Part II*. Three characters represented Antiquity, the Middle Ages, and Modernity. Clarisse trampled them with her feet. That happened in the water chamber. For three days. Cackling screams filled the enclosed room. Through the vapors and tropical fogs of the bath naked women crept like crocodiles and gigantic crabs. Slippery faces screamed into her eyes. Scissor arms grasped at her. Legs twined around her neck. Clarisse screamed and fluttered above the bodies, striking her toenails into the damp, slippery flesh, was pulled down, suffocated beneath bellies and knees, bit into breasts, scratched flabby cheeks bloody, worked herself to the top again, plunged into the water and out, and finally plunged her face into the shaggy wet lap of a large woman and "on the shell of the Triton goddess" roared out a song until hoarseness stifled her voice.

One should not think that insanity has no sense; it merely has the turbid, fuzzy, duplicating lens of the air above this bath, and at times it was quite clear to Clarisse that she was living among the laws of a different but by no means lawless world. Perhaps the idea explicitly governing all these minds was nothing other than the striving to escape the place of interdiction and compulsion, an unarticulated dream of the body rebelling against its poisoned head. While Clarisse was trampling with her feet the less agile in the slippery knot of people, there was in her head a "sinless Nirvana" like the broad white air outside a window, the longing for a painless and unconflicted state of rest, and like a buzzing insect she bumped with her head against the wall that sick bodies erected around her, fluttering aimlessly, driven from one moment's inspiration to the next, while the conviction hovered like a golden halo behind her head, a halo she could not see and could not even imagine but which was nevertheless there, that a profound ethical problem had been laid upon her, that she was the Messiah and the *Übermensch* joined in the same person, and would enter her rest after she had redeemed the others, and she could redeem them only by forcing them down. For three days and three nights she obeyed the irresistible will of the community of the mad, let herself be pushed and pulled and scratched till the blood came, threw herself symbolically on the cross on the tiles of the floor, uttered hoarse, disconnected, incomprehensible words and answered similar words with actions, as if she not only understood them but wanted to stake her life on the communication. They did not ask, they had no need of meaning that dumps words into sentences and sentences into the cellar of the mind; they recognized one another among themselves, and like animals differentiated themselves from the attendants or from anyone who was different, and their ideas produced a chaotic common thread, as during the revolt of a crowd where no one knows or understands anyone else, no one thinks any longer except in fragmented beginnings and endings, but powerful tensions and blows of the oblivious common body unite everyone with one another. After three days and nights, Clarisse was exhausted; her voice was only a bare whisper, her *"über*-strength" had conquered, and she became calm.

She was put to bed and for a few days lay in a state of profound fatigue, interrupted by attacks of tortured, shapeless restlessness. A "disciple," a rosy blond woman of twenty-one, who had regarded her from the first day as a liberator, finally gave her her first redemption. This woman came to her bed and said something or other; for Clarisse it meant: I am taking over the mission. Clarisse later found out that the rosy blonde had, in her stead, exorcised the devil through song in the water chamber day and night. But Clarisse stayed in the big hall, took care of the sick, and "lay in wait for their sins." The communication between her and her confessing charges consisted of sentences like dolls, implausible, wooden little sentences, and God alone knows what they originally meant by them; but if children playing with dolls would have to use concrete words in order to be able to mean the same thing and understand each other, then the magic sleight of hand that pretends a shapeless stick of wood is a living being would never succeed, a trick that excites the soul more than the most passionate lovers are later able to do. Finally, one day, an ordinary woman, who had earlier pounded on Clarisse's back with her fists, spoke to Clarisse, saying this: "Gather your disciples in the coming night and celebrate your Last Supper. What kind of food does the great lord desire? Speak, that it shall be prepared for you. But we intend to leave, and will no longer appear before your eyes!" At the same time another woman, who suffered from catatonia, passionately kissed Clarisse's hands, and her eyes were transfigured by approaching death like a star that in the night outshines all others. Clarisse felt: "It is really not a miracle that I believed I had to fulfill a mission," but in spite of this already more focused feeling, she was uncertain about what it was she had to do. Fortunately, this was the day on which she was transferred to the ward for calm patients.

On Clarisse

1. "Impoverished life"—This is a concept that makes an impression on her, like *décadence*. Her version of the *fin de siècle* mood. Drawn from her experience with Walter.

2. Along with Walter she adores Wagner, but with rising opposition; whenever he has played Wagner his hands are covered by a cold dampness, so this petit-bourgeois heroism comes out at his fingers, this heroic petit-bourgeois posturing. She imagines an Italian music that is driven beyond itself by the cruel cheerfulness of the blue Italian sky (omen!), "the destiny over her": "Her happiness is brief, sudden, unannounced, without pardon." (Omen, but Ulrich at first sees only what is usual for the times.) "The tanned one," "cynical" (omen!). She criticizes how empty Walter's face becomes in so many ways when he is making music.

3. Love is to be understood as fate, innocent and therefore cruel— that's how it hovers before her. She means by this: that's how she would like to be so filled by her own destiny that she would not think at all of the man who had unleashed it. Walter's love is for her only a "finer parasitism, a nesting oneself in an alien soul"; she would like to shake it off.

4. "Being able to forbid oneself something harmful is a sign of vitality"—she will not allow Walter into her bed. "The harmful lures the exhausted person."

5. Later: "Illness itself can be a stimulus to life, but one has to be healthy enough for this stimulus."

6. *Décadence* is for instance the agitated perspective that Wagnerian art compels, "which forces one to change one's position in regard to it at every moment." That is directed squarely at Ulrich, who sees in this changing of positions the energy of the future.

7. But then she disconcerts him with things that he believes too: "What characterizes all literary *décadence?* That life no longer dwells in the whole. The word becomes sovereign and jumps out of the sentence, the sentence reaches out and obscures the sense of the page, the page takes on life at the expense of the whole—the whole is no longer a whole. That's the sign of every decadent style: . . . Anarchy of the atoms, dispersion of the will . . . Life pushed back into the smallest structures . . . the remainder poor in vitality" (Voluntarism. A direct power against what is soft, boyish in Ulrich.)

8. Prophetic: ". . . that in cultures in decline, that everywhere where the power of decision falls into the hands of the masses, what is genuine becomes superfluous, disadvantageous, ignored. Only the actor still evokes great enthusiasm. This means that the golden age for the actor is dawning." Talma: What is supposed to affect one as true can be not true.

9. Against Walter: "The healthy organism does not fight off illness with reasons—one does not contradict a disease—but with inhibition, mistrust, peevishness, disgust, . . . as if there were a great danger slinking around in it."

10. Against Ulrich: "Innocence among oppositions . . . this is almost a definition of modernity. Biologically, modern man represents a contradiction of values, he sits between two stools, in the same breath he says yes and no . . . All of us have, against our knowledge, against our will, values, statements, formulas, and moralities of opposing lineages within us—physiologically regarded, we are false . . . a diagnostic of the modern soul—where would it begin? With a decisive incision into this contradictoriness of instinct . . ."

11. "Everything that is good makes me fruitful. I have no other gratitude . . ."

Clarisse

Nietzsche asks: Is there a pessimism of strength? An intellectual preference for the hardness, the horrible, evil, problematic aspects of existence? (from fullness of existence) Ulrich and Clarisse come together in this intellectual preference. It separates Clarisse from Walter. So that here the problem of adultery starts right off with the intellect. "Depth of the antimoral propensity."

The desire for the terrible as the worthy foe is one of the forebodings that seize her as she reads Nietzsche. Predisposition to her falling sick.

Nietzsche regards dialectic, the contentedness of the theoretically oriented person, as signs of decline, science as a delicate self-defense against truth, an evasion. Here Ulrich distances himself from Nietzsche, for he is enthusiastic about this theoretical person. Indeed, otherwise one would arrive at an imbecilic idolatry of life; but Ulrich runs aground with the ultimate ataraxia [stoical indifference—TRANS.] of the theoretically oriented person.

This could already be initiated in [Part] I and determine the situation in which he encounters Agathe.

What fascinates him so about Nietzsche, and fascinates Clarisse as well, is Nietzsche's intervention on behalf of the artistic person. He writes for artists who have the ancillary disposition of analytic and retrospective capacities, an exceptional kind of artist—therefore really for Ulrich. That Nietzsche says he really does not want to appeal to this kind of artist (but apparently to ones who are less divided) is something Ulrich passes over; that is something which youth reserves to itself as an achievement that *it* will reveal.

Is madness perhaps not necessarily the symptom of the degeneration, the decay, of a superannuated civilization? Are there perhaps . . . neuroses of health? Of the youth and youthfulness of the *Volk?* What does the synthesis of god and he-goat in the satyr show? From what experience of the self, in response to what impulse, was the Greek led to imagine the Dionysian enthusiast and primal man as a satyr? And concerning the origin of the chorus in tragedy: were there perhaps in those centuries in which the Greek body blossomed, and the Greek soul overflowed with life, endemic transports? Visions and hallucinations that imparted themselves to entire communities, whole gatherings of cults? What if the Greeks, precisely in the abundance of their youth, had the will to the tragic and were pessimists? What if it was precisely madness, to employ a term of Plato's, that brought the greatest blessings to Hellas? And if, on the other hand and inversely, what if it was precisely in the periods of their dissolution and weakness that the Greeks became increasingly optimistic, more superficial, more theatrical, also, according to the logic and logicizing of the world, more ardent—that is to say, at once more cheerful and more scientific?

In the Preface addressed to Richard Wagner,° art—and not morality—is already posited as the real metaphysical activity of mankind; in the book itself, the pertinent sentence that the existence of the world is justified only as an aesthetic phenomenon recurs several times.

. . . betrays a spirit that will at some point, at whatever risk, set itself against the moral explication of existence.

The world of ideas in Clarisse's insanity 1

Life is motion. Therefore never-ending. After death, life again dissolves into motion.

Since the motion is never-ending, nothing remains unrevenged. To break out of this chain, the mind must dissolve into harmony before it dies and enters cosmic space. That is the idea of Nirvana, which therefore, accordingly, also issues "unrevenged" from the feeling of guilt; the longing for harmony is the desire to emerge from this condition.

Do you believe in the migration of souls, hell, purgatory? she exclaims. Perhaps some individuals have attained Nirvana in their earthly life, but then they were the final links in a long chain of people—"in their person the ring closed" (Wagner's magic world again comes to life). But everyone else runs around laden with guilt and shame, tortured, reviled, from the first day of their lives onward, sacrifices to a crime committed before their birth.

But there *is* justice. What we call injustice is only the path to eternal justice.

The earth cannot perish before Nirvana has been attained.

She also explains it mathematically: births and deaths balance each other (everyone who is born dies, a tremendous discovery!), therefore the souls of modern people are the souls of ancient people. There are no free souls!

Even Darwinism agrees with this: in human beings, animal instincts are in many people reincarnated animal faces. They are still burdened with the animal soul.

°Musil is referring to Nietzsche's *Birth of Tragedy.*—Trans.

· · ·

Liquidation . . .
Ideas become clearer and more banal. Clearing, boring sky. Only a
deep sadness remains.

The world of ideas in Clarisse's insanity 2

King Ludwig was lying facing her already in Venice.

This is associated with the idea: Between Wagner and Nietzsche
stood the snake. This snake is Ludwig, the "feminine king," who loves
the artist and in doing so robs him of his only dignity. Evidently the reflex of her resistance against her sexual role as a woman for Walter; the
same thing disappointed her in Ulrich, and in the Greek it struck her so
strongly that he was free of it. Therefore a single line of action. Even in
Munich, Walter and Ulrich appeared to her in their "sinful shapes."

Nietzsche, the great friend, turned away horrified from this ignominy,
and from that time on had to follow his solitary path alone. Here she
identifies herself with Nietzsche.

What was done to him and to her is "a sin against the holy spirit." It
must be "reconciled by a human sacrifice." Nietzsche's death—a second
Christ.

Yet neither Christ nor Nietzsche could redeem mankind from evil:
"People remain people."

"Destiny hovers over us, a second reality," is how she expressed her
impotence simultaneously with the thought that in spite of her predecessors she had to suffer.

In between, the thought crosses her mind: "Between Nietzsche and
Wagner stood Jewry!"

The thought later goes on: There are two realities!

"One" is called: "The way I see it"—

The "Other": "The way I don't see it."

They are the same ideas as before, but they no longer have the components of manic redemption.

The world of ideas in Clarisse's insanity 3

In the clinic in Munich she sees a fat blond woman with a masculine voice, a Polish woman. Immediately the thought "Overwoman" springs to her mind. She thinks it over. This person before her is a primitive example. She thinks of Semiramis, Catherine the Great, Elizabeth of Austria. She is helpless because she has no books.

Such women have superhuman strength.

Her thoughts veer off: even before Nietzsche there were Overmen, she discovers: Napoleon, Jesus Christ. Suddenly she thinks: Christ was ignorant. Like her. That's why in our reckoning of time, our epoch, he is one of the most mysterious figures. For she is locked up.

The world of ideas in Clarisse's insanity 4

Sometimes she slips into confused cursing. Men today are horrible idiots, cowards, weaklings, with no backbone, without courage, bravery, or stamina.

They are either brutal or soft. They have lost the skill of using the whip with delicacy. Their dress is unaesthetic. Their manner of thinking cowardly, stupid. Their eyes blue or black (Ulrich and Walter).

If from time to time one comes across a man of chivalric appearance, with steely muscles—he is certainly abnormal, therefore no man either.

Suddenly she realizes: The woman puts on the secret trousers. That's why. She becomes only half natural. She no longer understands how to be a mother. She longs for motherhood. Divine pregnancy is a reminder of Nietzsche. Longingly she imagines the degenerate women on whose physical beauty the "sucking pulls." She would like to feel it.

Later these two words occur again, in another context in which no one understands them. Helplessness of the expression.

Menwomen and womenmen.

.   .   .

Délire à deux: It's a question of two people, one of whom is insane and the other predisposed to insanity. The former usually has some talent, the latter not a great deal of intelligence. Through constant contact, by being constantly bombarded with confused and inchoate ideas, the predisposed person ends up acting like his companion, and gradually the same madness shows up in him. A dependent relationship establishes itself between the two unfortunates; one is the echo of the other:

The impact of confused and inchoate ideas—is not only a danger for the inferior person. Cf. enjoyment of Expressionism and poetry in general.

Being together with Clarisse in Italy often makes Ulrich feel like a hot-air balloon that can be released at any moment. He lives through the essence of Expressionism. He, who is so precise, writes such poems. At that time poetry had not got to that point.

Happiness *is* madness, the not-communicable!

LATE 1920S

Ulrich wanted to see Meingast once more; this eagle, who had floated down from Zarathustra's mountains into the domestic life of Walter and Clarisse, made him curious. Following a sudden inspiration, he invited Schmeisser to go with him; he hoped to summon up in his adversary reasons to soften the latter's opposition to him through the impression made by his friends. He said nothing to Agathe about the expedition; he knew she would not come along.

Meingast had now been whiling away a considerable amount of time with his admirers and adherents Walter and Clarisse, part of whose home consisted of a separate, empty room whose windows looked out on the narrow side of the house. Somewhere the couple had dug up an iron bedstead; a kitchen stool and a tin pail served as bath, and aside from these objects the only other thing in the room, which had no curtains, was an empty dish cupboard, in which there were some books, and a small table of unpainted soft wood. Meingast sat at this table and wrote. That was enough to lend the room, even when he was not in it and Clarisse or Walter glanced in in passing, that ineffable quality of an old cast-off glove that has been worn on a noble and energetic hand. But now, as Meingast was sitting in the room writing, he knew (moreover) that Clarisse was standing beneath his window. Working in such a situation was splendid. Meingast's will formed words on the paper, abandoned them, flowed over the windowsill, and arrived at Clarisse, who, wrapped in the "invisible cloak of an electric northern light," was staring obsessively and absently before her. Meingast did not love Clarisse, but this ambitious pupil whom he paralyzed gave him pleasure. Meingast's pen was driven across the paper by a mysterious power; the nostrils of his sharp, narrow nose quivered like a stallion's, and his beautiful dark eyes glowed. What he had begun under these conditions was one of the most important sections of his new book; but one ought not call this book a book: it was a call, a command, a mobilization order for New People. When Meingast heard a strange male voice beside Clarisse, he interrupted himself and went down.

Ulrich had seen Clarisse right away as he and Schmeisser turned in at the garden gate. She was standing by the fence beside the vegetable garden, with her back to the house, quite stiffly and gazing into the distance, blind to the new arrivals. It did not seem that she was aware of her (frozen) position; her attitude seemed more the involuntary copy of significant ideas with which she was inwardly preoccupied. And so it was. She was thinking: —This time Meingast is transforming himself in our house. He had come to them without saying a word about it, but Clarisse knew that his life contained several of the most remarkable transformations, and was certain that the work he had begun here had something to do with this. The memory of an Indian god, who before every purification settles down somewhere, mingled in Clarisse's mind with the memory that insects choose a specific spot to change into a chrysalis and the memory of the fragrance of espaliered peaches ripening against the sunny wall of a house; the logical result was that Clarisse was standing in the burning sunshine beneath the window of the shadowy cave into which the prophet had withdrawn. The day before, he had explained to her and Walter that *Knecht*° signified, according to its original meaning, youth, boy, page, a man capable of bearing arms, hero; and Clarisse said: —I am his *Knecht!* She didn't need any words, she merely stood fast, motionless, her face blinded, against the arrows of the sun.

When Ulrich called out to her she turned slowly toward the unexpected voice, and he immediately discovered that she was disappointed at his coming. There was no longer any mention of her telling him her childhood stories; she had completely forgotten that. Her eyes, which before he went on his trip had always snatched love for him from the very sight of him, observed him now with that insultingly purposeless indifference that is like an extinguished mountain range after one has seen it in the sunlight. Indeed, this is a petty and also quite common experience, this extinction of light in the eyes when they no longer want

°The English cognate is "knight," but *Knecht* now means farmhand, laborer.—TRANS.

anything from what they are looking at; but it is like a small hole in the veil of life through which nothingness gazes / but it has something of the absolute coldness that is concealed beneath the warm blankets of life, in the absence of the sympathy of empty space.

As Meingast was on his way down, Walter joined him, and it was decided, without making many inquiries of the guests, that they would all walk together to the hill with the pine trees that lay halfway between the house and the edge of the woods. When they reached it, Meingast was charmed. The treetops hovered on their coral-colored trunks as dark-green islands in the burning blue ocean of the sky: hard, insistent colors created room and respect for themselves alongside each other; ideas that are as impossible in words as islands on coral trunks, which one does not trust oneself to think without a cowardly smile, were visible and real. Meingast pointed upward with his finger and spoke with Nietzsche: —A yes, a no; a straight line: formula of my happiness! Clarisse, who had thrown herself down on her back, understood him instantly and answered, with her eyes in the blueness, holding the words firmly between her teeth like a character in the last act where there is a lot of disjointed talking anyway: —Light-showers of the south! Cheerful cruelty! Destiny hovering over one! What need was there to paste sentences together when nature was like an echoing stage; she knew that Meingast would understand her! Walter understood her too. But as always he also understood something more. He saw the feminine softness of his wife lying in the feminine softness of the landscape; for all around, meadows sloped to the valley in soft billows, and aside from the group of pines, a small quarry was the only heroic thing in the midst of a good-natured corporeality that moved him to tears because Clarisse saw nothing of it and knew nothing about herself but had of course chosen just the one place where the landscape was in weighty contradiction to itself. Walter was jealous of Meingast, but he was not jealous in the ordinary way; he was as proud as Clarisse was of their new old friend, who had, after all, returned laden with fame as, in a way, her own messenger whom she had sent out into the world. Ulrich noticed that in this brief time Meingast had acquired enormous influence over Clarisse, and that jealousy of Meingast tortured Walter far more than had his previous jealousy of him, Ulrich, for Walter felt Meingast's superiority, while he had never felt Ulrich's, except physically. At any rate, these three people seemed to be deeply entangled in their affairs; they had already been talking to each other for days, and their guests were as little able to catch up with them as with people who have gone into a jungle. Then too, Meingast did not seem to attach any importance to orienting the newcomers, for without any consideration he went on talking at the point where the discussion might have been broken off hours or days ago.

—Music—he declared—music is a supraspiritual phenomenon. Not the bandmaster's or nickelodeon music, of course, which rules the theater; and also not the music of the erotics, upon which a lightning-bright explication followed as to who such an erotic person was, in a great zigzag from the beginnings of art to the present; but absolute music. Absolute music is suddenly, like a rainbow, from one end to the other, in the world; it is radiantly vaulted, without advance notice; a world on whirring wings, a world of ice, which hovers like a hailstorm in the other world.

Clarisse and Walter listened attentively, flattered. Clarisse, moreover, made note of the chain of ideas "music-ice-hailstorm" in order to use it in the next domestic musical struggle with Walter.

Meingast meanwhile, having worked himself up to a high pitch, explained himself by way of examples from the old Italian still-healthy music. He whistled it for them. He had stepped a little to the side and was standing in the meadow like a totem pole, the describing hand long-limbed, his words an interminable monologue. This really had nothing to do anymore with mere art or an exchange of aesthetic views: Meingast whistled metaphysical examples, absolute shapes, and phenomena of sound that occur only in music and nowhere else in the world. He whistled hovering curves or ineffable images of grief, anger, love, and cheerfulness; challenged the couple to test the extent to which this resembled what in life is understood under the name of music, and expected of Clarisse and Walter that they, pursuing their own feelings, would arrive at the end of a bridge that breaks off in the middle, from which point they would first glimpse the absolute melodic figure as it drifted away in its total ineffability.

Which was also, as it appeared, what happened, diffusing a fixed shudder of happiness over the three of them. —Once it's been pointed out, you yourself feel—said Meingast—that music cannot arise out of us alone. It is the image of itself, and just for that reason not merely an image of your feelings. So it's not an image at all. Not anything that would receive its existence through the existence of something else. It is *itself* simply existence, being, scorning every motivation. And then, with a motion of his hand, Meingast pushed music far behind him, where it became the fragment of something greater, —for—he said—art does not idealize, but realizes. One must, to come to the essential point, break entirely with the view that art lifts up, beautifies, or the like, something within us. It is precisely the other way around. Take greed, greatness, cheerfulness, or whatever you like: it is only the hollow earthly characterization of processes that are far more powerful than their ridiculous trailing thread, which our understanding seizes in order to pull them down to us. In truth, all our feelings are inexpressible. We press them out in drops and think that these drops are our feelings. But they are clouds rushing away! All our experiences are more than we experience of them. I could now simply apply the example of music to this; all our experiences would then be of the essence of music, were it not surrounded by a still greater circle. For—

But here an interruption ensued, for Schmeisser, whose lips had long mated dryly together, could no longer restrain the birth of an objection. He said loudly: —If you derive the birth of morality from the spirit of music, you're forgetting that all the emotions you might care to talk about receive their meaning from middle-class habits and middle-class assumptions!

Meingast turned amicably to the young man. —When, ten years ago, I came to Zürich for the first time—he said slowly—something of that sort would have been considered revolutionary. At that time you would have had great success with your interjection. I may tell you that it was there that I received my first spiritual training, in the left wing of your party, which had members from all the countries of the world. But today it is clear to us that the creative accomplishment of Social Democracy—he emphasized the component "Democracy"—has so far remained zero, and will never get beyond whitewashing the cultural content of liberalism as neorevolutionary!

Schmeisser had no intention of responding to this. It was sufficient that he threw back his hair with a shake of his neck muscles and smiled with sternly closed lips. One could perhaps also say: Oh, don't let *me* bother you! He was thinking that a few lines in *The Shoemaker,* a few juicily pointed sarcastic comments, would be appropriate anytime as warning yet again against bourgeois like these, who never stuck it out for long in the movement. But Ulrich interrupted: —Don't run him through with a quotation from Marx; Herr Meingast would answer with Goethe, and we'd never get home today! But still Schmeisser let himself be carried away, because he had to say something. Since he lacked the will to do battle his answer was too modest. He simply said: —The new culture that socialism has brought into the world is the feeling of solidarity. . . . The response was not immediate; Meingast seemed to be leaving himself time. He replied slowly: —That's correct. But it's precious little. Now Schmeisser lost his patience: —So-called academic learning—he exclaimed—has long since lost its right to be taken seriously as an intellectual center! Poking around among antiquities, pasting together treatises about the poems of some fifth-rate writer, cramming Roman un-Law; that only breeds empty arrogance. The workers' movement, with its definable goals, has long been developing the real intellectual workers, the fighters in the class struggle with their clear aims, who are going to do away with the barbarism of exploitation, and they are the ones who will create the foundations for a culture of the future!

Now it was Meingast's turn to get angry; for years he had not felt as warmly about the culture of the present as he did now, faced with this battler for the future. But with a good-natured motion, Meingast cut off his counterattack. —We are really not at all as far apart as you think, he answered Schmeisser. —I don't think much of academic learning either, and I, too, believe that a new feeling of community, a turning away from the individualism of the most recent age, signifies the most important development under way today. But— And again Meingast stood in the meadow like a totem pole, stretching out the hand that descriptively accompanied his words, and could continue precisely where he had been interrupted: But that had happened before his new doctrine of the will. By "will" one was not, of course, to understand something like the intention of seeking out a specific business because its drawing paper is cheaper, or composing a poem meant to be arrhythmic because up to then all other poems had been rhythmic. Nor was trampling on a superior in order to get ahead a sign of will. On the contrary, that's merely the scum of will, caused by the many obstacles that today stand in the way of will, and is, therefore, broken will. That one applies the word "will" to such things is a sign that its true meaning is no longer felt. Meingast's charter was the unbroken cosmic stream of will. He illustrated its appearance by great men like Napoleon. Compare Shaw's assertion that it is only great men who do anything, and that in vain. The will of such people is uninterrupted activity, an art of burning up like breathing, it must incessantly produce heat and movement, and for such natures standing still and turning back are equivalent to death. But one can illustrate this just as well by the will of primeval mythic times; when the wheel was invented, language, fire, religion: those were breakthroughs with which nothing since can be compared. At most in Homer there are perhaps the last traces of this great simplicity of the will and collected creative energy. Now Meingast brought together with extraordinary force these two discrepant examples: It was no accident that they were talking about a statesman and an artist. —For, if you all remember what I was telling you about music, the aesthetic phenomenon is that which needs nothing in addition to itself; as a phenomenon it is already all that it can possibly be: in other words, purely realized will! Will belongs not to morality but to aesthetics, to unmotivated phenomena. There are three conclusions that can be drawn from this: First, the world can be justified only as an aesthetic phenomenon; every attempt to give it a moral basis has failed up to now, and now we can understand why it must be that way. Second, our statesmen must, as the ancient wisdom of Plato already demanded, learn music again; and Plato drew his impetus for this from the wisdom of the East. Third, systematically executed cruelty is the only means now available for the European peoples, still stupefied by humanitarianism, to find their strength again!

Even though this conversation might at times have been rather opaque to ear and understanding, it was different with eye and feeling; it came tumbling down from a philosophical height where everything is in any case One, and Clarisse felt its onrush. She was enthusiastic. All the emotions in her were stirred up and swam, if one may put it this way, once more in feeling. For a while she had placed herself in the meadow not far from Meingast in order to hear better and to be able to conceal her excitement behind a glance that appeared to be distractedly gazing into the distance. But the inner burning of the world of which Meingast spoke opened her thoughts like nuts bursting with flames. Strange things became clear to her: summer noons, freezing with the fever of light; starry nights, mute as fish with gold scales; experiences without reflection or preparation that sometimes overcame her and remained without response, indeed really without content; tension, whenever she made music, certainly, today, worse than any concert pianist, but to the absolute best of her ability and clearly, with the uncanny feeling that something titanic, nameless experiences, a still-nameless person, greater than the greatest music can encompass, was forcing itself against the limits of her fingers. Now she understood her battles with Walter: they were suddenly moments as when a boat glides over an infinite chasm; in words, perhaps not comprehensible to anyone else. Clarisse's fingers and wrists began barely perceptibly to play along; one saw the young woman translating the prophet's wisdom into her own bodily will. The effect he had on her was related to the essence of a dance, a dancing wandering. Her feet released themselves from the impoverished and hardened present; her soul released itself from the uncertainty of instinct and weakness; the distance reared up; she held a flower with three heads in her hand; to follow after Meingast, following Christ, to redeem Walter, those were the three heads; if they were not, then Clarisse was not thinking it the way one counts or reads, from left to right, but like a rainbow from one end to the other; out of this rainbow arose the smell of the closet in which she kept her traveling clothes, then the three flowers consisted of the three terms *I seek, self-search, self-seeking*—Clarisse had already forgotten what the flower had consisted of before. Walter was a stem, even Meingast was just a stem, from the soles of her feet Clarisse grew taller and taller, it happened with dizzying speed, before one could hold one's breath, and Clarisse threw herself down in the grass, horrified at her enthusiasm for herself. Ulrich, who was already lying there, had misunderstood her movements, and thoughtlessly tickled her with a blade of grass. Clarisse shot out sparks of loathing.

Walter had been observing Clarisse, but something he had to talk about drew him more strongly to Meingast. This was Homer. Homer already a phenomenon of decay? No, decay first set in with Voltaire and Lessing! Meingast was probably the most important person one could encounter today, but what he said about music only showed what a misfortune it was that throughout his life Walter had felt too crippled to put his own views in the form of a book. He could understand Clarisse so well; he had long seen how she was carried away by Meingast; he felt so sorry for her; she was wrong, for despite everything she put the fortissimo of her enthusiasm into unimportant things; this coupling pregnant with destiny made his feelings for her flare up in great flames. While he was walking over to Meingast, Clarisse lay stretched out in the grass, Ulrich at her side not understanding anything at all, only, by lying there, pushing the optical center of gravity of the picture somewhat in his direction; Walter felt totally like an actor walking across a stage; here they were playing out their destiny, their story; in the seconds before he spoke to Meingast he felt lifted out of himself and frozen to icy silence, performer and poet of his self.

Meingast saw him coming. Four paces away like four ages of the world to be strode through. He had recently called Walter's helplessness that of a democracy of feelings, and with that given him the key to his condition, but he had no desire to carry this discussion further, and before Walter reached him he turned to the quarrelsome stranger.

—Perhaps you are a Socialist—Schmeisser answered him—but you are an enemy of democracy!

—Well, thank God you noticed! Meingast turned completely to face him and succeeded in forgetting Walter and Clarisse. —I was, as you heard, a Socialist too. But you say that a new culture will arise by itself out of the workers' movement; and I say to you: on the path that socialism has taken among us, never!

Schmeisser shrugged his shoulders. —The world is certainly not going to be put on a better path by talking about art, love, and the like!

—Who's talking about art? It seems that you haven't understood me in the least. I am of the same opinion as you that the present condition will not last much longer. The culture of bourgeois individualism will perish the way all previous cultures have perished. Of what? I can tell you: Of the increase of all quantities without a corresponding increase of the central quality. Of there being too many people, things, opinions, needs, wills. The firming energies, the perfusing of the community with its mission, its will to get ahead, its community feeling, the connective tissue of public and private institutions: these are not all growing at the same rate; it is rather left far too much to accident and falls further and further behind. The point comes in every culture where this disproportion gets to be too much. From then on, the culture is vulnerable like a weakened organism, and it takes only a push to bring it down. Today the growing complexity of relations and passions can still barely be maintained.

Schmeisser shook his head. —We'll give the push, when the time comes.

—When it comes! It will never come! The materialistic view of history produces passivity! The time will perhaps be here tomorrow. Perhaps it's already here today! You won't take advantage of it, for with democracy you ruin everything! Democracy produces neither thinkers nor doers, but gabblers. Just ask yourself what the characteristic creations of democracy are! Parliament and newspapers! What an idea—Meingast exclaimed—taking over from the whole despised bourgeois world of ideas precisely the most ridiculous one, democracy!

Walter had stood irresolute for a moment and then, since politics repelled him, joined Clarisse and Ulrich. Ulrich was saying: —Such a theory functions only when it is false, but then it's a tremendous machine for happiness! The two of them seem to me like a ticket machine arguing with a candy machine. But he found no echo.

Schmeisser had stood up to Meingast smiling, without responding. He told himself that it made no difference at all what an individual person thought.

Meingast was saying: —A new order, structure, cohesion of energy, is what's needed; that is correct. Pseudohistorical individualism and liberalism have been ruined by mismanagement; that is correct. The masses are coming; that is correct. But their agglomeration must be great, hard, and with the power to do things! And when he had said that he looked probingly at Schmeisser, turned around, plucked a handful of grass, and silently strode away.

Ulrich felt himself superfluous and went off with Schmeisser. Schmeisser did not say a word. —We're each carrying—Ulrich thought to himself—beside each other two glass balloons on our necks. Both transparent, of different colors, and beautifully, hermetically sealed. For heaven's sake don't stumble, so they don't break!

Walter and Clarisse remained behind on their "stage."

· · ·

Addendum: Clarisse notices criminal instincts everywhere (which later lead to war).

The blue parasol of the sky stretched above the green parasol of the pines; the green parasol of the pines stretched over the red coral trunks; at the foot of one of the coral trunks Clarisse was sitting, feeling the large, armadillo-like scales of the bark against her back. Meingast was standing to one side in the meadow. The wind was playing with his leanness as it does around the fence of a steel tower; Clarisse thought: If one could bend one's ear that way one would hear his joints sing. Her heart felt: *I am his younger brother.*

The struggles with Walter, those attempted embraces from which she had to push her way out—chiseling herself out, she called it, although she herself was not made of stone—had left behind in her an excitement that at times chased over her skin in a flash, like a pack of wolves; she had no idea where it had broken out from or where it vanished to. But as she sat there, her knees drawn up, listening to Meingast, who was speaking of men's groups, her panties under her thin dress lying as tight as boy's trousers against her thighs, she felt calmed.

—A league or covenant of men—Meingast was saying—is *armed love* that one can no longer find anywhere today. Today one knows only love for women. A covenant of men demands: loyalty, obedience, standing one for all and all for one; today the manly virtues have been turned into the caricature of a general obligatory military service, but for the Greeks they were still living eros. Male eroticism is not restricted to the sexual; its original form is war, alliance, united energies. Overcoming the fear of death! He stood and spoke into the air.

—When a man loves a woman it is always the start of his becoming a bourgeois: Clarisse completed the thought, convinced. —Tell me, does one have any business wishing for a child in a time like ours?

—Oh God, a child! Meingast warded her off. —Well, yes; only children! You should desire a child. This eroticism of the bourgeoisie, it's all people know today, and the only possibility leading to suffering and sacrifice is by means of a child. And anyway, childbearing is still one of the few great things in life. A certain rehabilitation.

Clarisse slowly shook her head. They had recently begun addressing each other again with the familiar *Du* and had recalled their friendship of long ago, but not in the sensual form it had had before. —If it were only a child of yours! Clarisse said with a smile. —But Walter isn't fit for that.

—Me? That's a really new idea! Besides, I'm going back to Switzerland in a few days. My book is finished.

—I'm coming with you, Clarisse said.

—That's out of the question! My friends are expecting me. There's hard work to be done. We're subject to all sorts of dangers and have to stick together like a phalanx. Meingast said this with a quiet, inward-directed smile. —That's no job for women!

—I'm not a woman! Clarisse exclaimed, and jumped up. (—Didn't you call me "little fellow" when I was fifteen years old?)

The philosopher smiled. Clarisse jumped up and went over to him. —I want to go away with you! she said.

—Love can be revealed in any of the following relations—the philosopher answered—servant to master, friend to friend, child to parents, wife to spouse, soul to God.

Clarisse put her hand on his arm; with a wordless request and awkwardly, but as deeply moving as a dog's faithfulness.

Meingast bent down and whispered something in her ear.

Clarisse whispered back hoarsely: —I'm no woman, Meingast! *I am the hermaphrodite!*

—You? Meingast made no effort to hide a little contempt.

—I'm traveling with you. You'll see. I'll show you the first night. We won't become one, but you will be two. I can leave my body. You will have two bodies.

Meingast shook his head. —Duality of bodies with a certain cancellation of the emphasis on self: a woman can accomplish that. But a woman will never lose herself in a higher community—

—You don't understand me! Clarisse said. —I have the power of transforming myself into a hermaphrodite. I'll be very useful to you in your band of men. You hear that I'm speaking very calmly, but pay attention to what I'm saying: Look at these trees and this round sky above them. Your breath goes further, your heart goes further, health is working in your viscera. But the longer you look, the more the picture sucks you out of yourself. Your body remains standing in its place alone. The world sucks you up, I say. *Your eyes make you a woman.* And if all your feelings could reach the top, for the world you would be dead and your body decayed.

—Am I right? But there are other days. Then all your muscles and thoughts become urgent. Then I'm a man. Then I stand here and raise my arm, and the sky shoots down into my arm. As if I were tearing down a banner, I say to you. I'm not a megalomaniac. My arm, too, tears me away from the place where I'm standing. Whether I dance, fight, weep, or sing: all that's left are my movements, my song, my tears; the world and I are blown up.

—Now do you believe that I belong in the league of men?

Meingast had been listening to Clarisse with an uncertain and almost anxious expression. Now he bent down and kissed her on the forehead. His words inspired Clarisse. —I did not know you! he said. —But it still won't do. A woman's love renders me infertile.

With this, he walked slowly with his high gait through the meadows on the shortest way back to the house. Clarisse did not run after him and did not let any word run after him. She knew that he was leaving. She wanted to wait, to spare him the leave-taking. She was certain that he needed time to come to terms with her proposal, and that a letter would soon call her. Her lips were still murmuring words, like two little sisters talking over an exciting event; she reprimanded them, and closed them.

Addition to hermaphrodite: For the first time again like it used to be, when young girls had secrets. You really know what it means to be married, and you know how Walter is. (Each of these sentences occurs to her as at the beginning.) And I'm sometimes a man. I've never "perished" in a man's arms; I push! I permeate him! I don't belong to anyone; I'm so strong that I could have a friendship with several men at once. A woman loves like an enormous pot that draws all the fire into itself. Clarisse says of herself: To love not like a woman but the way a brave little fox loves a big dog against which it is helpless. Or like a brave dog its master. That's what you love. Or: I'm a soldier, I disarm you, then disarm you just one degree more. Can't move a limb because of so much superior strength. That's the way you love boys. Young people. But I'm a person too, why then just a woman.

But isn't she still—hermaphrodite—a woman too? Perhaps depict it this way: as if a man would think it beautiful.

I go my way, I have my tasks; but you open my dress and fall upon me and draw my helplessness out of me. And I lean on you, unhappy at what you're doing to me but unable to resist. And go on and wear a black crepe on my helmet.

She would like to have intercourse (possibly with Walter too).

It is weakening.

From this the idea: You will weaken me, make me a woman, so that you remain radiant . . . (at times)

We struggle hand to hand and are like the bath after the battle.

Concretely: I have the character and duties of a man. I don't want (this time) a child and don't want love, but I want the deep phenomenon of desire, of purification (salvation) through weakness. I-you like you-me, even if servant and master.

? I'll press one leg against yours and wind the other around your hips, and your eyes will mist over.

I'll be insolent and forget my shyness toward you.

The woman has feminine feelings for the superior man, masculine feelings for the subordinate man. Therefore something hermaphroditic arises, a spiritually intertwined threesome.

Clarisse waited for Meingast's letter; the letter did not arrive. Clarisse became agitated. Ulrich, whom she suddenly thought of again, was away. She did not want to talk to Walter.

One morning, something strange happened. Clarisse was reading the newspaper; Walter had not yet left for the office. Suddenly Clarisse asked: —Wasn't there something in the paper yesterday about a train wreck near Budweis? —Yes, said Walter, who was reading another part of the paper. —How many dead? —Oh, of course I can't remember; I think two or three; it was a small accident. Why are you asking? —Nothing. Reading on for a while, Clarisse said: —Because there's been an accident in America too. Where's Pennsylvania? —I don't know. In America. They went on reading. Clarisse saw strands like railroad tracks fanning out before her, which went on tangling wildly. Had she not seen these strands of tracks weeks or months ago? She reflected. Little trains shot out on the tracks, roared through curves, and collided. Clarisse said: —The engineers never mean for their locomotives to collide. —Of course not, Walter said, without paying attention. Clarisse asked whether her brother Siegfried was coming later that afternoon. Walter answered, he hoped so. He was bothered, it was time for him to be off, and Clarisse was constantly interrupting his reading.

Suddenly Clarisse said: —I want to talk with Siegfried about taking me to see Moosbrugger.

—Who is Moosbrugger?

—You mean you don't remember? Ulrich's friend the murderer.

Now Walter understood whom she meant. She had once talked about this man. —But Ulrich knows him either not at all or only very slightly, he corrected Clarisse.

—Well, in any case—

—You really shouldn't be so eccentric.

Clarisse did not dignify this with a response. Walter leafed through the paper once more and thought he was surprised at not finding any mention of this person; he had assumed that Clarisse had been moved to make her comment because of some article; but he didn't have time for a question or genuine surprise, because he had to find his hat and rush off. Clarisse made an unpleasant face when he kissed her on the forehead; two arrogant long lines ran down alongside her nose, and her chin jutted forward. This very unreal face, which Walter did not notice, might have been grounds for anxiety.

But the strange thing that happened was this. While Clarisse was asking her question, she had recognized that an accident happens not because of evil intent but because in the confused network of tracks, switches, and signals that she saw before her, the human being loses the power of conscience with which he ought to have checked over his task once more; had that happened, he would certainly have done whatever was necessary to avoid the accident. At this moment, where she saw this before her eyes like a child's toy, she felt an enormous power of conscience. So she possessed it. She had to half close her eyes so that Walter would not notice their flashing. For she had recognized instantly that when one said "letting things prevail," it was only another expression for it. She understood that one was forced to let things have their way. But she did not let Walter have his, and would not do so.

That was the moment when Moosbrugger had occurred to her.

Everyone is familiar with what a miracle it is when a long-forgotten name, and one that moreover may be unimportant, suddenly pops up in one's memory. Or a face, with details that one is not at all aware of having seen. Evoked by some accidental stimulus. It is really as if a hole were to open in the sky. Clarisse was by no means wrong when she felt it as a process with two ends, Moosbrugger at one end, and far away, looking at him, herself; although one could of course say that in general this is not correct, because memory outside ourselves is nothing.

But precisely if something is not true in general, but is in particular, then this was something for Clarisse. It now occurred to her that Moosbrugger was a carpenter. And we know who else was a carpenter? Right. So at one end there was the carpenter, and at the other, Clarisse. Clarisse, who was not permitted to let things prevail, who had a black mole on her thigh that fascinated every man. For there was no question that Meingast had run away from her; it had come too suddenly, he had wanted to save himself.

One cannot expect everything to be equally clear in the first moment. Somehow, of course, the carpenter was also connected with Ulrich; when a person whom one has almost forgotten after having loved him

suddenly walks in the door, without, so to speak, being inwardly announced, as Ulrich now did, even though in the company of other people, this is in and of itself something of the kind that makes one have to
hold one's breath for a moment. Nor was it clear what all this had to do
with the hermaphrodite that Clarisse was in order to enter the league of
men; but she would get to that, she felt, and at the root of the emotion
there most certainly was a connection; that could be seen in the manner
of activity among these thoughts, which up there, on the outside, remained isolated for now.

For all these reasons Clarisse considered it her duty to meet Moosbrugger. That certainly wouldn't be difficult. Her brother was a physician and could help her with it. She waited for him, and the time passed
quickly. She considered how little Meingast had meant to her when she
had known him before, and how great he had become since. While he
was present, everything here in the house had been elevated. She had
the feeling that he had simply taken her and Walter's sins upon himself,
and that was what had made everything so easy. Perhaps now, in the next
phase, she would have to take Meingast's sins upon herself.

But what are sins? She used this word perhaps too often, without
thinking enough about it. It is a poisonous Christian word. Clarisse could
not discover what she herself meant, precisely. A butterfly occurred to
her, which suddenly falls motionless to the ground and becomes an ugly
worm with dead wings. Then naturally Walter, who sought the milk of
love at her breast and thereafter became stiff and lazy. Besides, had she
not once known quite clearly that she would redeem this carpenter from
his sins? She had, had she not, once written a letter? It was uncanny to
recall that only so dimly. It obviously signified that something was still to
come.

* * *

No letter came from Meingast, the business with the league of men
remained out of Clarisse's purview; sometimes she forgot it because of
the new things that were happening. She had to think how she might get
into the clinic again in spite of Dr. Friedenthal, who had forbidden her
to return. She realized that it would be difficult. Climb over the wall
surrounding the grounds? she thought; this idea of penetrating the forbidden space like a warrior appealed to her greatly, but since the clinic
was not in open country but in the city, if it was to be done without being
seen it could be risked only at night, and then, once on the grounds, how
was Clarisse to find her way among the many locked buildings? She was

afraid. Although she knew that it would have to be considered out of the question, she was frightened by the image of falling into the hands of a madman among the black trees and being raped or strangled by him. She still had the screams of the maniacs in her ears: at the last station, before she went past the lovely ladies and returned once more to rational life. She often saw before her the naked man standing in the center of a totally empty room that had nothing in it but a low cot and a toilet that were of a piece with the floor. He had a blond beard and light-brown pubic hair. He ignored both the opening of the door and the people looking at him; he stood with his legs spread apart, kept his head lowered like a savage, had thick saliva in his beard, and repeated like a pendulum the same motion again and again, throwing his upper body around in a shallow circle, always with a push, always toward the same side, his arms forming an acute angle to his body, and the only thing that changed was that with every one of these motions another finger jumped up from his clenched fist; it was accompanied by a loud, panting scream, forced out by the requisite monstrous exertion of the whole body. Dr. Friedenthal had explained that this went on for hours, and had allowed Clarisse to look into other cells, where for the moment quiet reigned. But this had been if anything even more horrifying. He showed her the same bare cement room containing nothing but a person whose fit was imminent, and one of these people was sitting there still in his street clothes; only his tie and collar had been removed. It was a lawyer with a lovely full beard and carefully parted hair; he sat there and glanced at the visitors as if he had been on the point of going to court and had sat down on this stone bench only because he was compelled, for God knows what reason, to wait. Clarisse was especially horrified by this person because he looked so natural; but Dr. Friedenthal said that just a few days before, in his first fit, he had killed his wife, and almost all the transient inhabitants of this section were murderers. Clarisse asked herself why she was afraid of them, when it was precisely these patients who were best secured and supervised? She feared them because she did not understand them. There were several others in her memory who affected her the same way. —But that's still no reason for my having to meet them if I'm walking through the grounds at night! she said to herself.

But it was like this. It was almost certain that she would meet them; that was an idea it was impossible to eradicate, for no matter how often Clarisse imagined the process of climbing over the wall and then walking forward through the gloomy, widely spaced trees, sooner or later it came to a gruesome encounter. This was a given fact one had to reckon with, and therefore it was reasonable to ask what it meant. Even as solid a man as the famous old American writer Ralph Waldo Emerson, whom she had read in her adolescence because her friends told her he was marvelous, maintained that it is a general law of nature and man that like is attracted by like. Clarisse remembered a sentence which went, roughly, that everything that comes to a person tends toward him of itself, so that cause and effect only apparently succeed each other but in reality are simply two sides of the same thing, and all cleverness is bad because with every precautionary rule against danger one is put in the power of this danger. All Clarisse had to do, when she remembered this, was to apply it to herself. If it was established that she, even if at first only in some mysterious fashion in her mind, was continually meeting murderers, then she was attracting these murderers. But is like being attracted by like? That meant that she bore within herself the soul of a murderer. One can imagine what it means when such extraordinary thoughts suddenly find solid ground beneath their feet! Meingast had run away from her; she was apparently too strong for him. It was like lightning bolts striking each other! Walter was attracted by her to murder his talent again and again in her, no matter how much she pushed him away. She carried a black medallion at the crease of her hip, and the insane divined it: perhaps such people can see through clothes and came toward her rejoicing. In a confusing way, all the facts fit.

Laughter and difficulties struggled around Clarisse's mouth; it alternately opened and clamped tight. She had got up too early; Walter was still sleeping; she had hastily thrown on a light dress and gone outside. The singing of birds reached her from the woods through the empty morning stillness. The hemisphere of the sky had not yet filled with warmth. Even the light was still shallowly dispersed. —It only reaches as far as my ankles—Clarisse thought—the faucet of the morning has just been opened. Everything was before its time. Clarisse was deeply moved that she was wandering through the world before its time. It almost made her cry. She fervently regretted that during her visit to the madhouse she had seen through Moosbrugger's situation too late. What she had seen being played out before her was worthless devils gambling for a soul. She heard herself being called to turn back there once more, but Dr. Friedenthal blocked her path. She felt quite ashamed, and went on like that for a ways. But at some point a thought took shape that released her from this depression: Many great men had been in insane asylums. And they had been derided by those who had remained in possession of their reason. They had now become incapable of explaining themselves to those for whom earlier they had had only contempt. She remembered the muteness of the late Nietzsche, whom she worshiped. And what had vexed her just now because she had not seen through it in time, how the three devils had intentionally brought her before Moos-brugger in so miserably casual a fashion in order to get the better of her through cunning and paralyze her, indeed that she had really shown her-self to be stupid and weak, now slowly made her understand as a sign that the fate of the great man among the repulsive jailers of the world would be laid upon her too. Her heart was filled by a drifting rain of light and tears. It was uncanny, putting oneself on an equal footing with the insane; but being on the same footing with the uncanny is to cast one's lot for genius! She decided to free Moosbrugger from his jailers. Thoughts regarding how she might do this flitted around in her mind. The swallows had meanwhile begun to flit through the air. In some way it would have to work. Clarisse was so absorbed in these thoughts that she felt the depths like the narrow incline of an abyss. She had to draw in her shoulders and could only cautiously venture a smile. It occurred to her that this would be the "depth of antimoral inclination" that Nietz-sche demanded of his disciples. She was astonished at this, for she had not expected that it was possible to experience it so palpably. It was a path through a "landscape of countermorality."

The landscape of countermorality lies deep beneath that of ordinary life, not deep in yards but many octaves deeper. That is how it seemed to her. Everything great lives in the landscape of countermorality (there). It goes the same ways others go, but without touching them. Against that Clarisse said to herself half aloud: —I am following in Nietzsche's foot-steps. She could also imagine that Moosbrugger had taken Nietzsche's sorrow upon himself and was Nietzsche in the shape of a sinner. But that was not her object at the moment. Now she had to take "the sorrow" upon herself: this is what preoccupied her. She felt it hovering, other-worldly, in the vacancy of the morning. She was carrying something that towered up hugely from her shoulders. But then she thought something over and went home.

When she got there, Walter was not yet up, although he ought to have been on his way to the office already. He slept so badly that he could not get up on time in the morning. Dreams tortured him, leaving behind when he woke up, although he could not remember them, a feeling of being inwardly wiped out. Walter felt like a piece of paper that has been rolled up by an unpleasant warmth, and so dried out that it cracks at the slightest touch. That was the effect of Clarisse, who slept beside him, dressed and undressed beside him, but hardly permitted him to kiss her. His blood stagnated and became restless. It was dammed up like a crowd of people that is stopped at its head, while behind, where people no longer see the cause, they begin to push forward until they're out of control. Walter pulled himself together; he did not want to hurt Clarisse, he understood her, she moved him with her childish resolve, there was nobility in her agonized exaggerating. But perhaps, too, that nervous exaltation which stigmatized everything she did. It seemed to Walter that it was his duty to clear away the obstacles she erected, even with force, if need be. It would be necessary to go through such brutality in order to restore normal intellectual opposition, if opposition there had to be. He felt it in himself; both their minds needed a surgeon: a mental growth had proliferated wildly and needed to be cut out. But he was convinced that a sorrow such as had been laid upon them would not be any less deep or strange than Tristan and Isolde's.

Only his most extreme personal need had prompted him, a few days before, to seek a consultation with Clarisse's brother Siegfried. —You know Clarisse—he had said—that is, of course you don't know her, but you know a lot about her, and perhaps you can just this once, as a doctor, also give some advice. Siegfried gave this advice. It was remarkable how much patronizing he accepted from Walter. Life is full of such relationships, where one person humiliates and brushes aside another, who offers no resistance. Perhaps only healthy life. The world would probably already have perished at the time of the great migrations if people had all defended themselves to the last drop of blood; instead of which the weaker gave in and moved on, preferring to seek other neighbors, whom they in turn could brush aside. This is the model on which human relationships are still carried on, and with time everything works out by itself. In the circle where Walter was thought to be a genius who had not yet found his definitive expression, Siegfried was considered a lout and a blockhead. He had accepted that, never argued against it, and even today, if it should come to an intellectual collision with Walter, Siegfried would be the one to yield and pay homage. But for years he had as good as never been in this situation, for they had grown apart, and the old relations had become quite insignificant in comparison with new ones. Siegfried not only had his practice as a doctor—and the doctor rules differently from the bureaucrat, through his own intellectual power and not that of others, and comes to people who are waiting for his help and accept it obediently—but he also possessed a wife with means, who within a short time had been required to present him with three children and whom he cheated on with other women, if not often at least now and then, when he felt like it. Siegfried was quite logically also in a situation where he could give Walter the advice he demanded. —Clarisse—he diagnosed—is excessively nervous. It was always her way to charge through walls, and now her head has got stuck in a wall. You have to give a good tug, even if she resists. It is against her own advantage if you let her get away with too much. Neurotic people demand a certain strictness. Walter had answered that doctors understand absolutely nothing about spiritual processes, but meanwhile he managed to put Siegfried's advice in a form that was personally agreeable to him: that two people had to suffer in order to accomplish their burdensome destiny of loving each other. As far as the situation itself was concerned, this amounted to the same thing. And he said to Clarisse: —Please, Clarisse, be reasonable!

Clarisse had just got home, had called out: You layabout! to Walter, filled the bath with cold water, and slipped out of her thin dress, when she felt Walter behind her. He was standing there the way he had got out of bed, in a long nightshirt that fell down to his bare feet, and had warm cheeks like a girl's, while Clarisse, in her brief panties and with her skinny arms, looked like a boy. She put her hand on his chest and shoved him back. But Walter reached out for her. With one hand he seized her arm, and with the other sought to grasp her by the crotch and pull her to him. Clarisse tore at the embrace, and when that didn't help shoved her free hand into Walter's face, into his nose and mouth. His face turned red and the blood trembled in his eyes while he struggled with Clarisse. He did not want to let her see that she was hurting him, but when he was in danger of suffocating he had to strike her hand from his face. Quick as lightning, she went at it again, and this time her nails tore two bleeding furrows in his skin. Clarisse was free. Just then Walter again snatched at her, this time with all his strength. He had become angry, and feared nothing in the whole world so much as becoming rational again. Clarisse struck at him. She had lost her shoe and kicked at him. She understood that this time it was for real. Walter was gasping out meaningless sentences. The voices of loneliness, as if a robber had jumped on them. She felt she had the strength of giants. Her clothing tore; Walter seized the shreds; she reached for his neck. She would have liked to kill him. She did not know what she was doing. Naked, slippery, she struggled like a wriggling fish in his arms. She bit Walter, whose strength was not sufficient to overpower her calmly; he swung her this way and that, and painfully sought to block her attacks. Clarisse got tired. Her muscles became numb and slack. There were pauses where she was pressed by Walter's weight against the wall or the floor and could no longer defend herself. Then again there would come a series of defensive movements and ruthless attacks against sensitive parts of the body and face. Then suffocation again, powerlessness, and the heart's beating. Walter was intermittently ashamed. The pain hit him like a ray of light: Reasonable people don't act this way! He thought that Clarisse looked as ugly as a madwoman.

But it had taken so much to get himself this far that the acting man ran on by himself, paying no attention to the feeling man. Clarisse, too, no longer had the feeling that she was being raped by Walter; she had only the feeling that she was not able to insist on her will, and when she was forced to yield she uttered a long, shrill, wild cry, like a locomotive. She herself found this inspiration quite strange. Perhaps her will was escaping in this cry, now that it was of no more use to her. Walter was scared. And while she had to endure his will she had the consolation: Just wait, I'll get my revenge!

The moment this repulsive scene was over, shame crashed down on Walter. Clarisse sat in a corner, naked as she was, with a thunderous face and made no response to his pleas for forgiveness. He had to get dressed; blood and tears flowed through his shaving foam. He had to leave in a hurry. He felt that he could not leave the beloved of all the days since his youth in this condition. He sought to at least move her to get dressed. Clarisse countered that she could just as well remain sitting this way until Judgment Day. In his despair and helplessness, his whole life as a man shrank back; he threw himself on his knees and with hands raised begged her to forgive him, as he had once prayed against blows; he could not think of anything else to do.

—I'll tell Ulrich everything! Clarisse said, slightly reconciled.

Walter begged her to forget it. There was something in his lack of dignity that called for reconciliation: he loved Clarisse; the shame was like a wound from which real, warm blood was flowing. But Clarisse did not forgive him. She could forgive him as little as an emperor who bears the responsibility for a kingdom can forgive; such people are something other than private individuals. She made him swear never to touch her again before she gave him permission. Walter was expected at a meeting; he gave his oath quickly, with the clock in his heart. Then Clarisse gave him the additional task of sending Ulrich over; she agreed to keep silent, but she needed the calming presence of a person she could trust.

.   .   .

During a break at work Walter took a taxi to Ulrich's, to get there as quickly as possible.

Ulrich was at home. His life wearied him. He did not know where Agathe was. Since she had separated herself from him he had had no news of her; he was tortured by worries about what might be happening to her. Everything reminded him of her. How short a time ago he had restrained her from a rash decision. Yet he did not believe she would do it without speaking to him once more.

Perhaps for that very reason: for the intoxication—a real intoxication, an enchantment!—was over. The experiment they had undertaken to shape their relationship had failed irrevocably. Vast regions of emotions and fancies that had endowed many things with a perennial splendor of unknown origin, like an opalizing sky, were now desolate. Ulrich's mind had dried out like soil beneath which the layers that conduct the moisture that nourishes all green things had disappeared. If what he had been forced to wish for was folly—and the exhaustion with which he thought of it admitted of no doubts about that!—then what had been best in his life had always been folly: the shimmer of thinking, the breath of presumption, those tender messengers of a better home that flutter among the things of the world. Nothing remained but to become reasonable; he had to do violence to his nature and apparently submit it to a school that was not only hard but also by definition boring. He did not want to think himself born to be an idler, but would now be one if he did not soon begin to make order out of the consequences of this failure. But when he checked them over, his whole being rebelled against them, and when his being rebelled against them, he longed for Agathe; that happened without exuberance, but still as one yearns for a fellow sufferer when he is the only one with whom one can be intimate.

With distracted politeness, Walter inquired about Ulrich's absence; Ulrich waited with embarrassment for him to ask about Agathe, but fortunately Walter forgot to. He had recently come to realize that it is insanity to doubt the love of a woman whom one loves oneself, he began. Even if one should be disappointed, it was only a matter of letting oneself be disappointed fruitfully, in such a way that the inner lives of all concerned be raised a degree. All feelings that are only negative are unfruitful; on the other hand, there was nothing in which one could not find a core of fruitfulness if one peeled off the layers of world community. For instance: He had often committed the wrong of being jealous of Ulrich.

—Were you really jealous of me? Ulrich asked.

—Yes, Walter confessed, and for an instant, in an unconsciously significant but ridiculously chilling fashion, he bared two teeth. —Of course I never thought of it in any other way than intellectually. Clarisse feels a certain sensual kinship with your body. You understand: it's not that your body attracts her body, or your mind her mind, but your body attracts her mind; you'll have to admit that's not so simple, and that it wasn't always easy for me to behave properly toward you.

—And Meingast?

—Meingast has left—Walter began by saying—but that was different. I admire Meingast myself. Nobody today can compare with him, all in all. There's no way I could forbid Clarisse to love him.

—Yes, you could. First you would have to tell her that Meingast is a woolgatherer—

—Cut it out! Today I need your friendship, not a quarrel!

—Then you could always say to Clarisse that it's not the mission of a great man to draw the nails out of every marriage like a giant magnet; therefore, on the side of the marriage, there has to be something that can't be changed by the superiority of this third person. You're conservative, you'll no doubt be able to work that out. Moreover, it's an absorbing question. Just consider: Today every writer, musician, philosopher, leader, and boss finds people who think he's the greatest thing on earth. The natural consequence, especially for women who are more easily moved, would be that they flock to him as a whole person. Their own personal, bodily philosopher or writer! These words have a right to be taken literally; for where else should one wish to go with soul and body if not to this ultimate refuge? But it's just as certain that this doesn't happen. Today only hysterical women run after great minds. And why?

Walter answered reluctantly. —You said yourself that there are other reasons for living together. Children, the need for a solid place; and then there's a suitability of two people for each other that's greater than the meeting of their minds!

—Those are just excuses! The agreement you're talking about is nothing more than trusting opinions even less than a life of habit that has turned out to be not entirely unbearable. It's just lucky that one doesn't quite trust the person one admires. The confusion through which one is always robbed of vitality by the other has obviously become a means of preserving life. The inclination for each other holds together through a delicate remnant of disinclination against the third person. And altogether, of course, it's nothing but the soul of the pharisee, which, once it's got inside a body, imagines that every other body has secret defects!

—I started out by saying—Walter exclaimed indignantly—that if Clarisse really loved Meingast I could not forbid it.

—Then why don't you permit her to love me? Ulrich asked, laughing.

—Because you don't like me. And you don't like me because when we were children I beat you up a couple of times. As if I had never run into stronger boys who beat me up! That's so absurd, so narrow-minded and petty. I'm not reproaching you; we all have this weakness of not being able to shake off such things, indeed that such idiotic chance happenings actually form the inner building blocks of our personalities, while our knowledge is no more than the breeze that blows around them. Who's stronger, then: you or I? Engineer Short or Art Historian Long? A master wrestler or a sprinter? I think that (the individual) this business has lost a lot of its meaning today. None of us are isolated or individual. To speak in your language: We're instrumentalists who have come together in expectation of playing a marvelous piece, the score for which has not yet been located. So what would happen if Clarisse were to fall in love with me? The idea that one can love only *one* other person is nothing but a legal (civil law) prejudice that has totally overrun us. She would love you, too, and in those circumstances precisely in the way that suits you best, because she would be free of the gnawing anger that you don't have certain qualities which she also considers important. The only condition would be that you would really have to behave toward me as a friend; that doesn't mean you have to understand me, for I don't understand the cells in my brain either, although something far more intimate exists between us than understanding! . . . And you could contradict me with all your emotions and thoughts, but only in a certain way: for there are contradictions that are continuations, for example those within ourselves; we love ourselves along with them.

This seemed to Walter like a bucket being emptied down a flight of steps. What Ulrich said spread out and at some point had to stop; he, meanwhile, paced back and forth in the room but couldn't wait for that to happen. He stopped and said: —I must interrupt you. I don't want to either contradict you or agree with you. I have no idea why you're saying these things; it seems to me that you're talking into the air. Both of us are some thirty years old, everything isn't hovering in the air the way it was when we were nineteen, one is something, one has something, and everything you're saying is infinitely humdrum. But what's horrible is that I've had to promise Clarisse to send you out to see her today. Promise me that you'll speak less unreasonably with her than with me!

—But for that I'd have to first promise that I'll go. Today I don't have the slightest desire to! Excuse me, I don't feel well either.

—But you *must* say yes! It doesn't matter to you, you can put up with it; but for days Clarisse has been in an alarming state. And on top of that I've let myself be guilty of a great mistake, repulsive, I assure you; one is sometimes like an animal. I'm worried about her! For a moment the memory overwhelmed him. He had tears in his eyes and looked at Ulrich angrily through the tears. Ulrich placated him and promised to go.

—Go right now, Walter begged. —I had to leave her all upset. And he hurriedly told Ulrich that Meingast's unexpected departure, which had strangely affected him too, had obviously shaken Clarisse, because since then she was strikingly changed. —You know what she's like—Walter said, a veil of tears again and again running over his eyes—her whole nature keeps her from allowing something she doesn't think right to prevail; letting things happen, which our whole civilization is full of, is for her a cardinal sin! He reported the incident with the newspaper, which he himself suddenly saw in a new light. Then he added softly that after Meingast's departure, Clarisse had confessed to him that while he had been there she had often suffered from obsessive ideas, which all added up to her regarding the entire peculiar progression to greatness that Meingast had gone through, since he had left them long ago as an ordinary young Lothario, as having their basis in his taking upon himself the sins of all the people with whom he came into contact and, it turned out, also the sins of Clarisse and Walter himself.

Ulrich must have looked involuntarily at his childhood friend in inquiry, for Walter instantaneously added a defense. —That only sounds unsettling, he asserted, but it hasn't by any means gone too far. Everyone rises by taking on other people's mistakes and improving them in himself. It was only that Clarisse had an unusually vehement intensity when such problems suddenly got hold of her, and a way of expressing them without making any concessions. —But if you knew her as well as I do, you would find that behind everything that seems strange in her there is an incomparable feeling for the deepest questions of life! Love made him blind, while it made Clarisse transparent for him, all the way to the bottom, where one's thoughts lie, while all distinctions between bright and stupid, healthy and sick minds take place in the shallower layers of what one says and does.

. . .

After the scene with her husband, Clarisse had washed her whole body and run out of the house. The blue line of the edge of the woods attracted her; she wanted to crawl in. And while she was running, the sparkling, shining, drop-spraying of the white water was around her, like a hedgehog with outward-pointing needles. She was pursued by an obsessively irritating need for cleanliness. But when she had reached the woods, she plopped down between the first tree trunks behind the bushes at the edge. From there she looked straight into the small, dark, nostril-like open windows of her house, and this already made her feel much better. The smell of herbs burned in the morning sun; growths tickled her; she was comforted by nature's sticking, hard, hot inconsiderateness. She felt removed from the restrictiveness of her personal bonds. She could think. It had become obvious that Walter was being destroyed by the attraction she radiated; he hardly needed to sink much further than he had today. So it was up to her to make the sacrifice! (Clarisse got up and walked deeper into the woods.) What was it, this sacrifice? Such words pop up like a poem (but she wished to conceal herself with this word, in order to get behind it). The word "sacrifice" followed (first) the same way it followed that she bore within herself the soul of a murderer, and, especially after the scene with her husband, she had to assume that she also concealed in herself the soul of a satyr, a he-goat. Like is, after all, only attracted by like. But whoever *sees* must sacrifice himself: that is the merciless law by which greatness lives. Clarisse began to understand; but at the same time that she realized that she bore within herself the soul of a he-goat, the fright that had rolled into her like a block of ice began to melt, and the excitement caused by the body and inhibited by the soul thawed out in her limbs. It was a marvelous condition. The contact with the bushes pressed deep into her nerves through her skin; the swelling of the moss under her soles, the twittering of the birds, became sensual and covered the interior of the world with something like the flesh of a fruit. —You will all deny me when you recognize me! Clarisse thought. As soon as that was thought, it also came to her that Walter would really have to learn to deny her, for that was the only way he could be freed from her. At this thought she was overcome by an immense sadness. —Everyone will deny me, she said once again. —And only when you have all denied me will you be grown up. Only when you have all grown up will I return to you! she added. That was like the beginnings of splendid poems, whose second lines were already lost in an excess of excitement and beauty. Golgotha Song, she called it. A tension as if she would have to break out in a stream of tears at any moment accompanied this incredible achievement. What she admired most deeply was the incredible compulsion in this storm of freedom. —If I were only a little superstitious and not so hardy— she thought—I would really have to be afraid of myself! Her thoughts went now one way—as if she were only an instrument on which a strange and higher being were playing, her beautiful idol that gave her answers before she had managed to ask the questions, and built up ideas that came to her like the outlines of whole cities, so that she stopped in astonishment—and now another way, so that Clarisse herself seemed quite empty, a feathery light something that had to restrain its steps with effort, for everything upon which her eye fell, or every recollection the ray of memory illuminated, led her hurriedly forward and handed her on to the next thing and the next idea, so that Clarisse's thoughts seemed at times to be running alongside her, and a wild race with her body began, until the young woman in her mental alienation was forced to stop and, exhausted, throw herself into some berry bushes.

She had found a clearing into which the sun shone, and while she felt the warm earth on which she lay, she stretched herself out as if on a cross, and the nails of the sun's rays penetrated her upward-turned hands.

She had left a note for Ulrich in the house, which said nothing but that she was waiting for him in the woods.

After the conversation with Walter, Ulrich had set out and had indeed found the note. He automatically assumed that Clarisse was hiding somewhere and would make her presence known when he entered the woods. Oppressed by the hot morning, he set out (listlessly) on the path that they were accustomed to taking when they went to the woods, and when he did not find Clarisse, he pushed on at random farther into the forest. From everything Walter had said, what most stuck in his mind was the news that Clarisse was preoccupied with Moosbrugger. As far as he was concerned, Moosbrugger could have been long dead and hanged, for he had not thought about him for weeks, which was quite remarkable when he thought that not all that long ago the image of this crude figure of fantasy had been one of the focal points in his life. —One truly feels, as a so-called normal person—he told himself—just as incoherent as someone who is insane. The heat relaxed his collar and the pores of his face, and slowly entered and emerged from his softened skin. Meeting Clarisse aroused no particularly pleasant expectations. What could he say to her? She had always been what one calls crazy without meaning it seriously; if she were now really to become so, she might perhaps be ugly and repellent, that would be simplest; but what if she was not repellent to him? No; Ulrich assumed that she would have to be. The deranged mind is ugly. In this way he suddenly almost tripped over her, for they both had spontaneously followed the direction of a broad path that was the continuation of the one that had led them to the woods. Clarisse, a patch of color among the colorful weeds and concealed from his glance, had seen him coming. She had quickly crawled out into his path and lay there. The many unconscious, manly, and resolute shifts in his face, which believed itself unobserved and was living in no more than vegetative rapport with the obstacles through which it was coming toward her, gave her a marvelous sensation. Ulrich only stopped, surprised, when he discovered her lying almost directly beneath him, her smiling glance lifted up to him. She was not in the least ugly.

—We have to free Moosbrugger, Clarisse declared, after Ulrich had asked her to explain the sudden inspirations he had heard about. —If there's no other way, we have to help him escape! Of course I know you'll help me!

Ulrich shook his head.

—Then come! Clarisse said. —Let's go deeper into the woods, where we'll be alone. She had jumped up. The senselessly raging will that emanated from this small being was like clouds of unfamiliar insects buzzing and swarming among blackberry shoots exhaling their odors in the sun, inhuman but pleasant. —But you're all hot! Clarisse exclaimed. —You'll catch cold among the trees! She took a kerchief from her warm body and swiftly threw it over his head; then she climbed up him, disappearing likewise under the kerchief, and, before he could throw her off, kissed him like a high-spirited little girl. Clarisse stumbled, and fell to a sitting position. —I haven't forgiven you—Ulrich threatened grumblingly— that during the time you were in love with this muddlehead Meingast I simply didn't exist for you! —Oh? Clarisse answered. —You don't understand. Meingast is homosexual. So you didn't understand me at all!

—But what's this chatter about redeeming all about? Ulrich asked severely. —That only blossomed because of him, didn't it?

—Oh, I'll explain that to you. Come! Clarisse assured him.

Ulrich started with what Walter had already told him.

—All right. But that's not the main point. The main point is the bear.
—The bear?

—Yes; the pointed muzzle with the teeth that tear everything to pieces. I arouse the bear in all of you! Clarisse showed with a gesture what she meant, and smiled innocently. —But, Clarisse! —Of course! Clarisse said. —You deny me when I'm being honest! But even Walter believes that every person has an animal in him whom he resembles. From which he has to be redeemed. Nietzsche had his eagle, Walter and Moosbrugger have the bear.

—And I? Ulrich asked, curious.

—I don't know yet.

—And you?

—I'm a he-goat with eagle's wings.

So they wandered through the woods, eating berries now and then, heat and hunger making them as dry as violin wood. Sometimes Clarisse broke off a small dry twig and handed it to Ulrich; he didn't know whether to throw it away or keep it in his hand; as with children, when they do such things, there was something else behind it, for which there was no articulated notion. Now Clarisse stopped in the wilderness, and the light in her eyes shone. She declared: —Moosbrugger has committed a sexual murder, hasn't he? What's that? Desire separated in him from what's human! But isn't that the same in Walter too? And in you?

Moosbrugger has had to pay for it. Isn't one obliged to help him? What do *you* say to that? From the foot of the trees came the smell of darkness, mushrooms, and decay, from above of sunlit fir twigs.

—Will you do that for me? Clarisse asked.

Ulrich again said no, and asked Clarisse to come back to the house.

She meandered along beside him and let her head droop. They had gone quite far from the path. —We're hungry, Clarisse said, and pulled out a piece of old bread she was carrying in her pocket. She gave Ulrich some of it too. It produced a remarkably pleasant-unpleasant feeling, which quieted hunger and tortured thirst. —The mills of time grind dryly—Clarisse poetized—you feel grain after grain falling.

And it occurred to Ulrich without thinking about it much that among these totally meaningless annoyances he felt better than he had in a long time.

Clarisse set about once more to win him over. She would do it herself. She had a plan. She only needed a little money. And he would have to speak to Moosbrugger in her stead, because she wasn't allowed in the clinic anymore.

Ulrich promised. This derring-do fantasy filled up the time. He guarded himself against all consequences. Clarisse laughed.

As they were on the way home, chance had it that they caught up with a man leading a tame bear. Ulrich joked about it, but Clarisse grew serious and seemed to seek protection in the closeness of his body, and her face became deeply absorbed. As they passed the man and the bear, she suddenly called out: —I'll tame every bear! It sounded like an awkward joke. But she suddenly reached for the bear's muzzle, and Ulrich had difficulty pulling her back quickly enough from the startled, growling beast.

· · ·

The next time, Ulrich met Clarisse at the painter's studio of friends of hers, where a circle of people had gathered and was making music. Clarisse did not stand out in these surroundings; the role of odd man out fell to Ulrich instead. He had come reluctantly and felt repugnance among these people, who, contorted, were listening ecstatically. The transitions from charming, gentle, and soft to gloomy, heroic, and tumultuous, which the music went through several times within the space of a quarter hour, musicians don't notice, because for them this progression is synonymous with music and therefore with something of the highest distinction!—but to Ulrich, who at the moment was not at all under the sway of the prejudice that music was something that had to be, this music seemed as badly motivated and unmediated in its progression as the carryings-on of a company of drunks that alternates periodically between sentimentality and fistfights. He had no intention of imagining what the soul of a great musician might be like and passing judgment on it, but what was usually considered great music seemed to him much like a chest with a beautifully carved exterior and full of the contents of the soul, from which one has pulled out all the drawers, so that the contents lie all jumbled together inside. He usually could not understand music as an amalgam of soul and form, because he saw too clearly that the soul of music, aside from rarely encountered pure music, is nothing but the conventional soul of Jack and Jill whipped to a frenzy.

He was, notwithstanding, supporting his head in both hands like the others; he just did not know whether it was because he was thinking of Walter or closing his ears a little. In truth, he was neither keeping his ears entirely closed nor thinking of Walter. He merely wanted to be alone. He did not often reflect about other people; apparently because he also rarely thought about himself as "a person." He usually acted on the opinion that what one thinks, feels, wants, imagines, and creates could, in certain circumstances, signify an enrichment of life; but what one *is* signifies under no circumstances more than a by-product of the process of this production. Musical people, on the other hand, are quite often of the opposite opinion. They do produce something, to which they apply the impersonal name of music, but what they produce consists for the most part, or at least for the part that is most important to them, of themselves, their sensations, emotions, and their shared experience. There is more momentary being and less lasting duration in their music, which among all intellectual activities is closest to that of the actor. This intensification, which he was being forced to witness, aroused Ulrich's antipathy; he sat among these people like an owl among songbirds.

And of course Walter was his exact opposite. Walter thought passionately and a great deal about himself. He took everything he encountered seriously. Because he encountered it; as if that were a merit that can make one thing into another. He was at every moment a complete individual and a complete human being, and because he was, he became nothing. Everybody had found him captivating, brought him happiness, and invited him to remain with them, with the end result that he had become an archivist or curator, had run aground, no longer has the strength to change, curses everyone, is contentedly unhappy, and goes off punctually to his office. And while he is in his office something will perhaps happen between Clarisse and Ulrich that could arouse in the person he is, if he should find out about it, an agitation as if the entire ocean of world history were pouring into it; while Ulrich, on the other hand, was far less agitated. But Clarisse, immediately after she had come in—Walter was not there—had sat down beside Ulrich; with her back bent forward, her knees drawn up, in the darkness, for the lights had not yet been turned on, right after the first beats they heard she had spread her hand over his, as if they belonged together in the most intimate fashion. Ulrich had cautiously freed himself, and that was also a reason for supporting his head with both hands; but Clarisse, when she saw what he was up to, and saw him from the side sitting there just as moved as everyone else, had gently leaned against him, and she had been sitting that way for half an hour now. He was not happy either.

He knew that what he committed over and over was nothing but the opposite error from Walter's. This error gave rise to a dissolution without a center; the person was subsumed in an aura; he ceased to be a thing, with all its limitations, as precious as they were accidental; at the highest degree of intensification he became so indifferent toward himself that the human, as opposed to the suprahuman, had no more significance than the little piece of cork to which is attached a magnet that draws it back and forth through a network of forces. At the last it had been like that for him with Agathe. And now—no, it was a calumny to put these things next to each other—but even between himself and Clarisse something was now "going on," was under way, he had blundered into a realm of effects in which he and Clarisse were being moved toward each other by forces, forces that showed no consideration for whether, on the whole, they felt an inclination for each other or not.

And while Clarisse was leaning on him, Ulrich was thinking about Walter. He saw him before him in a particular way, as he often secretly saw him. Walter was lying at the edge of some woods, wearing short pants and unbecoming black socks, and in these socks had neither the muscular nor the skinny legs of a man, but those of a girl, of a not very pretty girl, with smooth, unlovely legs. His hands crossed behind his head, he was looking at the landscape over which, one day, his immortal works would roll, and he radiated the feeling that talking to him would be an interruption. Ulrich really loved this image. In his youth, Walter had actually looked that way. And Ulrich thought: What has separated us is not the music—for he could quite well imagine a music rising as impersonally and beyond things and each-time-once-only as a trail of smoke that loses itself in the sky—but the difference in the attitude of the individual to music; it is this image that I love because it is left over, a remainder, while he surely loves it for the opposite reason, because it swallows up within itself everything that he might have become, until finally it became precisely Walter. —And really—he thought—all that is nothing but a sign of the times. Today socialism is trying to declare the beloved private self to be a worthless illusion, which should be replaced by social causes and duties. But in this it had long since been preceded by the natural sciences, which dissolved precious private things into nothing but impersonal processes such as warmth, light, weight, and so forth. The object as a matter of importance to private individuals, as a stone that falls on their head or one they can buy in a gold setting, or a flower they smell, does not interest up-to-date people in the least; they treat it as a contingency or even as a "thing in itself," that is, as something that is not there and yet is there, a quite foolish and ghostly personality of a thing. One might well predict that this will change, the way a man who deals daily with millions happens to take with great astonishment a single banknote in his hand; but then object and personality will have become something different. But meanwhile there exists a quite comical juxtaposition. Morally, for instance, one still looks at oneself somewhat as physics looked at bodies three hundred years ago; they "fall" because they have the "quality" of avoiding heights, or they become warm because they contain a fluid: moralists are still attributing such good or bad qualities and fluids to people. Psychologically, on the other hand, one has already gone so far as to dissolve the person into typical bundles of typical averages of behavior. Sociologically, he is treated no differently. But musically, he is again made whole.

Suddenly the light was turned on. The final notes of the music were still swinging back and forth like a branch someone has just jumped off; eyes sparkled; and the silence before everyone started talking set in. Clarisse had promptly moved away from Ulrich, but now new groups formed, and she pulled him into a corner and had something to tell him.

—What is the extreme opposite of letting something prevail? she asked him. And since Ulrich did not respond, she herself gave the answer. —To impose oneself! The tiny figure stood elastically before him, her hands behind her back. But she tried to keep her eyes fixed on Ulrich's, for the words she now had to look for were so difficult that they made her small body stagger. —Inscribe yourself onto something! I say. I thought of that before while we were sitting next to each other. Impressions are nothing; they press you in! Or a heap of earthworms. But when do you understand a piece of music? When you yourself create it inwardly! And when do you understand a person? When you do as he does. You see—with her hand she described an acute angle lying horizontally, which involuntarily reminded Ulrich of a phallus—our entire life is expression! In art, in love, in politics, we seek the active, the pointed form; I've already told you that it's the bear's muzzle! No, I didn't mean that impressions don't mean anything: they're the half of it; it's marvelously in the word "redeem," the active "re" and the "deem"; she became quite excited by the effort of making herself comprehensible to Ulrich.

But just then the music making started up again—it had been only a short intermission—and Ulrich turned away from Clarisse. He looked out at the evening through the large studio window. The eye first had to adjust to the darkness again. Then wandering blue clouds appeared in the sky. The tips of a tree reached up from below. Houses stood with their backs upward. —How should they stand otherwise? Ulrich thought with a smile, and yet there are minutes when everything appears topsy-turvy. He thought of Agathe and was unspeakably depressed. This new, small creature, Clarisse, at his side, was rushing forward at an unnatural speed. That was not a natural process, he was quite clear about that. He considered her crazy. There could be no talk of love. But while behind his back the music seemed to him like a circus, it pleased him to imagine running alongside a circling horse jumping hurdles, with Clarisse standing on it erect and shouting "Aie-ya" and cracking her whip.

1930–1934

On Clarisse—Walter

She comes upon Walter in the "studio"; bare, chilly space. He is half-dressed and has a dressing gown on. The brushes are dry, he is sitting over some sketches. He really should have been at the office already.

He is irritated that Meingast went off without saying good-bye, and Clarisse is secretly excited. Possibly here: He really wanted . . . as long as Meingast was in the house . . .

Already from the doorway Clarisse called out to him: Come, come! We're going to Dr. Friedenthal to ask him to entrust Moosbrugger's care to us.

Walter can't turn his head away from her and looks at her.

Don't ask! Clarisse commands.

Could Walter have any more doubts at this moment that her mind was disturbed? The answer to this question will always be quite dependent on the circumstances. Clarisse looked impetuous and beautiful. The fire in her eyes looked exactly like that of a healthy will. And so what her brother Siegmund had said of her, and had recently repeated when Walter again asked him about it, took hold of Walter: She is excessively nervous, you just have to grab her vigorously.

But for the moment it was Clarisse who was doing the vigorous grabbing: She hopped around Walter incessantly, repeating: Come, come, come! Don't make me have to ask you!

The words seemed to fly around Walter's ears, they confused him. One might have said that he was laying back his ears and digging his feet into the ground the way a horse, a donkey, a calf does, with the obstinacy that is the weak creature's strength of will: but to him it represented itself in the form: Now you'll show her who's master!

"Just come along," Clarisse said, "then you'll see why!"

"No," exclaimed Walter. "You'll tell me right this instant what you're up to!"

"What I'm up to? I'm up to something weird." She had meanwhile begun to gather up in the neighboring room what she needed to go out; now she pulled off her gardening gloves, held them in her hand for a moment, and with a sudden heave flung them among her husband's paint and brush jars. Something fell over, something rolled, something clattered. Clarisse observed the effect on Walter and burst out laughing. Walter got red in the face; he had no desire to hit her but was ashamed of this very lack. Clarisse went on laughing and said: You've been crouching over these jars for a year and a day and haven't produced a thing. I'll show you how it's done. I've told you I'll bring out your genius. I'll make you restless, impatient, daring!" Suddenly she was quiet and said seriously: "It's weird, putting oneself on the same level as the insane, but it's resolving for genius! Do you believe that we'll ever amount to anything the way we've been going along? Among these jars that are all so nicely round and picture frames that are so nicely rectangular? And with music after supper! Why, then, were all gods and goddesses antisocial?"

Antisocial? Walter asked in astonishment.

If you must be precise: uncriminally antisocial. Because they weren't thieves or murderers. But humility, voluntary poverty, and chastity are also the expression of an antisocial mentality. And how otherwise could they have taught mankind how the world is to be improved but have denied the world for themselves?

Now Walter was so constituted that in spite of his initial astonishment he was capable of finding this assertion correct. It reminded him of the question: "Can you imagine Jesus as director of a mine?" A question that would obviously have to be answered simply and naturally "no," if one could not just as well say "official of the Bureau for Monuments" in place of "mine director," and if one didn't feel the accompanying flash of a ridiculously warm spark of ambition. Obviously there was not only a contradiction but a more profound incompatibility separating two world systems between nurturing the middle class and nurturing the divine, but Walter, despite his already long-determined inclination to the middle class, wanted both, or wanted, what is even worse, to renounce neither, and Clarisse possessed what he had once already felt as "calling upon God," the decisiveness of a resolve that shows no consideration for anything. And so it happened that after she had spoken, he felt exactly as she had said, as if he were jammed up to his knees into the life he had created for himself, like a wedge in a block of wood, while she flitted about in front of him as the restless, impatient, daring one who was experimenting with him. As a man of many talents, he knew that genius lay not so much in talent as in willpower. To the person being overtaken by paralysis, which he intuitively understood himself to be, it seemed related to the fermenting, the must, indeed even to the mere foam. He enviously recognized in her the improbable, the zigzag dots of variations around the mean, the creature that at the edge of the crowd half goes along ahead of it and is half lost within it, which lies in the notion of genius. Clarisse was the only person in whom he loved this, who still linked him to it, and because her association with genius was pathological, his fear for her was also a fear for himself. This was how the desire not to listen to her, indeed to show her "the man," as Siegmund, the brother and physician, had advised him to do, arose out of his assent to the words with which she was persuading him and explaining her intention, and out of her powerful charm in pleasing him, which she exercised in an apparently natural way and without any awareness of contradiction.

So after a short pause Walter said rather roughly: "But now be reasonable, Clarisse, stop that nonsense and come over here!" Clarisse had meanwhile taken off her clothes and was in the process of drawing a cold bath. In her short panties and with her thin arms, she looked like a boy. She felt the stale warmth of Walter's body close behind her and immediately understood what he was after. She turned around and put her hand on his chest. But Walter reached out to grab her. With one hand he held her arm, and sought with the other to grasp her by the crotch and pull her to him. Clarisse tore at the embrace, and when that didn't help shoved her free hand into Walter's face, into his nose and mouth. His face turned red and the blood trembled in his eyes while he struggled with Clarisse, but he did not want to let her see that she was hurting him. And when he threatened to suffocate, he had to strike her hand from his face. Quick as lightning she went at it again, and this time her nails tore two bleeding furrows in his skin. Clarisse was free.

They stood this way opposite each other. Neither of them tried to speak. Clarisse was startled by her cruelty, but she was beside herself. Some intervention from above had torn her out of herself; she was totally turned to the outside, a bush full of thorns. She was in ecstasy. None of the thoughts that had preoccupied her for weeks was any longer in her mind; she had even forgotten what she had just been talking about and what it was she wanted. Her whole self was gone, with the exception of what she needed to defend herself. She felt incredibly strong. Just then Walter again snatched at her, this time with all his strength. He had become angry and feared nothing in the whole world so much as becoming rational again. Clarisse struck at him. She was instantly ready to scratch again, to bite, to knee him in the groin or shove her elbow in his mouth, and it was not even anger or dislike that determined this, let alone any rational consideration; rather, in some wild way, this struggle made her like him, even though she was ready to kill him. She wanted to bathe in his blood. She did so with her nails and with the short glances, which, shocked, followed his efforts and the small red gutters that opened up on his face and hands. Walter cursed. He swore at her. Vulgar words, which had no relation to his usual self, came from his mouth. Their pure, undiluted masculinity smelled like brandy, and the need for common, insulting speech suddenly revealed itself to be just as primeval as the need for tenderness. Apparently what was coming out was nothing but a grudge against all the higher ambition that had tortured and humiliated him for decades and was finally raising its head against him once more in Clarisse. Of course he had no time to think about this. But he still felt distinctly that he was not merely on the point of breaking her will because Siegmund had advised him that way, but was also doing it on account of the breaking and snapping itself. In some fashion the ridiculously beautiful motions of a flamingo went through his mind. "We'll see what's left after a bulldog gets hold of it!" was his thought about the flamingo mind, but what he muttered half aloud between his teeth was: "Stupid goose!"

And Clarisse, too, was inspired by the one idea: "He can't be allowed to have his way!" She felt her strength still growing. Her clothes tore, Walter seized the shreds, she seized hold of the neck in front of her. Half naked, slippery as a wriggling fish, she struggled in her husband's arms. Walter, whose strength was not sufficient simply to overpower her, flung her to and fro and painfully sought to block her attacks. She had lost her shoe and kicked at him with her bare foot. They fell. They both appeared to have forgotten the goal of their struggle and its sexual origin, and were fighting only to assert their will. In this utmost, convulsive gathering of their selves they really disappeared. Their perceptions and thoughts gradually took on a totally indefinable texture, as in a blinding light. They almost felt amazement at still being alive / that their selves were still there.

Clarisse especially was worked up to such a pitch that she felt insensitive to the pain inflicted on her, and when she came to herself again this intoxicated her in the conviction that the same spirits that had recently illuminated her were now standing by her in her mission and fighting on her side. So she was all the more horrified when she was forced to notice that with time she was growing fatigued. Walter was stronger and heavier than she; her muscles became numb and lax. There were pauses where his weight pressed her to the ground and she could not defend herself, and the succession of defensive maneuvers and ruthless attacks against sensitive face and body parts, during which she caught her breath, were succeeded more and more frequently by powerlessness and suffocating poundings of her heart. So that what Walter had anticipated happened: nature conquered, Clarisse's body left her mind in the lurch and defended its will no longer. It seemed to her as if she were hearing within herself the cocks crowing on the Mount of Olives: incredibly, God was abandoning her world, something was about to happen that she could not divine. And at moments Walter was already ashamed of himself. Like a bolt of lightning, remorse struck him. It also seemed to him that Clarisse looked horribly distorted. But he had already risked so much that he no longer wanted to stop. To continue anesthetizing himself, he used the excuse that the brutality he was exercising was his right as a husband. Suddenly Clarisse screamed. She made an effort to utter a long, shrill, monotone cry as she saw her will escaping, and in this final, desperate defense it was in her mind that with this cry and what remained of her will she could perhaps slip out of her body. But she no longer had much breath left; the cry did not last long and brought no one rushing in. She was left alone. Walter was alarmed at her cry but then angrily intensified his efforts. She felt nothing. She despised him. Finally, she thought of an expedient: she counted as quickly and as loudly as she could: "One, two, three, four, five. One, two, three, four, five," over and over. Walter found it horrible, but it did not stop him.

And when they separated and straightened up, in a daze she said: "Just wait. I'll have my revenge!"

1936

New ideas about the Clarisse-Walter-Ulrich complex

To make Clarisse human, use the problem of genius. Or instead of genius, one can also say: the will to greatness, to goodness. A miserable Prometheus. Genius in that case about the same thing: a person who is an exception. The person who sees the errors, sees what is out of joint in the world, and has the will not to let the matter drop. In her case she doesn't have the strength.

This defines part of Walter's problem: what has to happen if the strength is lacking?   —island, discussion.

The fact already that she always clung to older men!

The relation to her parents: here she learned to see the world as exception to *her*. —[Part] I, or wherever her early history is recounted.

The whole development of her insanity would then fall—which makes Clarisse more human and motivates the conclusion—under the title: Struggle for Walter as struggle for genius.

In order not to have to speak of Ulrich: she gave him a name, from the beginning. The leader? The Buddha? The Great One? The Eternal One? The Mysterious One? The Redeemer? — Or several names? The Beloved? The Healthy One? The Great Friend?

Clarisse in Rome

Clarisse, however, could not bear to stay in Rome long. Even the square in front of the railway station, with its palm trees, its shops, and the proximity of big hotels, repelled her.

Nevertheless, she walked to the center of the city and checked into a small albergo. In the meantime her impression had changed. The evening sky was orange almost to the zenith; the trees stood black and feathered before it. The air in the Ludovisi quarter, that unique, deliciously light mixture of sea and mountain air, refreshed her. She inhaled the acquaintance of a new strength. Prophecy of fascism. She began to notice the pretentious splendor of the elevated private gardens that rested on walls five to eight yards high above the heads of ordinary pedestrians, and the giant gates and high windows, which in this neighborhood were a feature even of the apartment buildings. Behind a park wall a donkey brayed. —How the donkeys bray here! Clarisse thought. —Differently from home. They don't go "hee-haw," they go "ya"! It was a metallic, persisting trumpet call. She thought she could tell at first glance that there were no philistines in this city. Or there were, but a whirling energy threatened them. As she approached the center, everything was full of energy, rush, and noise: cars raced unexpectedly around corners and crossed the plazas on unpredictable paths; bicyclists cheerfully and at risk of their lives teemed their way through between them; from the bursting trams clusters of young men who were trying to ride hung like grapes, clinging to each other in bold and impossible positions. Clarisse felt that this was a city after her own temperament, she was experiencing such a place for the first time. At night she could not sleep because a small bar had placed its tables in the narrow alley under her windows; people sang popular songs into the early morning and after every verse screamed a cheerfully dissonant refrain. This completely electrified Clarisse. Although it was still relatively early in the year, it was already quite warm, and Clarisse got diarrhea from the heat; it was an enchanting state, as light as elder pith, fledged, and fatiguingly exciting.

Clarisse ordered all the impressions Rome made on her under the color red. When she thought back to her experiences in the sanatorium they had changed from a watery green, a color belonging to the present, the color of the German woods, into this red, which had been the red of the processions in her imagination; but it must be said that Clarisse did not clearly remember the experiences that had driven her to make this journey, but had the clear feeling of running from a green state into one that was glowing red. Unfortunately, it was quite impossible for Clarisse to hit upon the idea that she was suffering from mad delusions. For green states even have their composers, who set them to music; these days sounds are painted, poems form sensory spaces, thoughts are danced: this is a vague kind of associating that has become popular because thinking has lost its authority; it's about one eighth sensible and seven eighths nonsensical, and Clarisse could still regard herself as being very cautious and deliberate. So it was with calm, anticipatory attentiveness that she found herself on the way from a green state into a red one.

On an excursion through Rome's palaces she encountered the marvelous, totally red portrait of Innocent X by Velázquez; the sight shot through her like a bolt of lightning. Now she saw clearly that this burning color of life, red, was at the same time the color of Christianity, which, in Nietzsche's phrase, had given classical Eros poison to drink, the color of ascesis and inculpation of the senses. —Oh my friends—Clarisse thought—you will not catch me! Her heart beat as if she had recognized a mortal danger at the last moment. She had discovered the ambivalent countenance of this city. It was the city of the Pope, and she remembered that Nietzsche had attempted to live here and had fled. She went to the house where he had lived. She took in nothing. The house was "spiritually closed." She walked home smiling, outwitting this city at every step. It was a double city. Here the dark pessimism of Christianity flared up to cardinal red, and here the blackness of insanity had flowed into Nietzsche's red blood. But what she thought was not so important to Clarisse; the main thing was the smiling ambivalence in everything she saw. She went past palaces, excavations, and museums; she had still seen only the least part of them, and her impressions had not sunk to the measure of reality; she had assumed that the most marvelous treasures of the world were here set up side by side, but they were laid out like a bait; she had to remove this beauty from its hook very, very carefully. And everything that is beautiful in youth depends on the things around which people circle having one aspect that is known only to oneself.

In some way or other, the idea had seized Clarisse that she had to take up the mission at which Nietzsche had failed here in a different way, by beginning with the north. Evening had come. Once more she looked out the window of her small room: in the bar below, the first guests were already beginning to shout and sing, and if you leaned your body way out—above their heads, like a northern gargoyle—and craned your neck, you could see the round serrated shape of a gray church standing like a tiara before the still-darker gray of the night.

From what remained of her money she bought a ticket that took her back to one of the small towns through which she had passed on her way down. An unerring feeling told her at the railway station that it was not the right place. She went on by the next train. In this way Clarisse traveled for three days and four nights. On the fourth morning she was traveling along a seacoast and found a place that held her fast. With no money, she went into the hotels. This fact, that she had no money, was quite sudden and very peculiar; she made a rather long speech to the people in the hotels, in order to get them to serve her, and they listened politely but without understanding; then she hit upon the idea, because Walter was not to know where she was staying, of appealing to Ulrich. she sent him a long telegram in German.

Clarisse—Island

That Clarisse appealed to Ulrich was not only due to her needing money and wanting to keep her whereabouts concealed from Walter. Involved as well was an "I mean you," a grasping with rays of feeling across mountains and far distances. Clarisse had come to the conviction that she was in love with Ulrich. That was not quite so simple as such a thing can be. She explained the horrible scene between the two of them that had upset her so, and everything that preceded it, by saying that at the time it had been too soon for Ulrich; it was only now that he was in the right spot in the system of her imaginings (but that is love, when a person finds himself in the right spot in the system of our imaginings), and the energy of the whole was streaming toward him in a way that was unheard of. Wherever his name fell, the earth melted. When she uttered it her tongue was like a wisp of sun in a mild rain. Clarisse explored her new surroundings. They consisted of a small island pitched close to the mainland, bearing an old fort left half open, and a gigantic sandbank that pushed out from this island farther into the sea and that with its trees and bushes formed a large empty second island, belonging to Clarisse alone when she had herself rowed over there. It seemed people did not have much confidence in its stability, for although there was an old hut on it in which to store nets and other fishing gear, this hut, too, was abandoned and decayed, and there were no other signs of settlement or division of possessions. Wind, waves, white sand, sharp grasses, and all sorts of small animals lived here freely together; the resonance of water, earth, and sky was as empty and loud as tin banging on tin.

The inhabited island behind it boasted high, fortified walls overgrown with green; cannons that did not intimidate but, wrapped in sailcloth, looked astonishingly like prehistoric animals; moats, near which were unbelievably large rats; and in the midst of the rats running around in broad daylight there was a small tavern shaped like a cube, with a four-sided pyramid for a roof, under shaggy trees. There Clarisse had taken a room for herself and Ulrich. The house was also the canteen for the fort, and all day long dark-blue soldiers with yellow stripes on their sleeves stood around nearby. One did not have the feeling of people going about life but rather felt an oppression, which emptied the heart, as if before a deportation or something similar. The young men too, strolling with rifles on their arms in front of the cannons wrapped in sails, reinforced this impression: who had put them there? Where, at what distance, was the brain of this madness that expressed itself in a joyless, pedantic automatism preserved in catatonic rigidity?

It was the right island for Ulrich and Clarisse, and Ulrich baptized it the "Island of Health," because every fit of madness seemed bright against its dark background. He had received Clarisse's telegram in the night when he came home and was crossing his garden. In the light of a lamp on the white wall of his house he had torn open the dispatch and read it, because he thought it came from Agathe. It was already the end of May. But the May night was like a belated March night; the stars looked down sharply, withdrawn to their heights, icily crisp out of the unilluminated, infinitely remote canopy of the sky. The telegram's sentences were long and confused, but held together by a rhythm of excitement. When Clarisse turned her back on the small military middle of her island, loneliness stretched before her like the desert of the anchorite. Connected with this idea of retiring from the world was an overloud, unchanging emotional tone full of covetous horror, something like the final purification and trial on the path of the "great one." The adultery to which she had condemned herself would have to be consummated on this island as on a cross, for a cross on which she had to lay herself was what the empty sand over there across the waves, trodden by no one, seemed to her to be. Something of all this came through in the telegram. Ulrich guessed that the great disorder had now really overtaken Clarisse, but that was precisely what suited him.

In their small inn they had a room that contained barely the most indispensable furniture, but a chandelier of Venetian glass hung from the center of the ceiling, and large mirrors in broad glass frames that were painted with flowers hung on the walls. In the mornings they went over to the Island of Health, which hovered in the air like a mirage, and from there they looked back on the inhabited island, which, with its cannons, embrasures, serrations, and little houses and trees, lay there like a round, perfect, exiled word that has lost the connection to its discourse.

Island I

Clarisse arrives while Agathe and Ulrich are still together. Stays 1–3 days in the hotel, during which time she seeks and finds her island. This is when she tells the Moosbrugger story. Invites Ulrich to the island (or Ulrich and Agathe) and Ulrich comes over. Spends half a day with her. Her hut, etc.

So it apparently goes not as far as intercourse but only to Clarisse's readiness. This is the way to utilize the material from the old coitus scene.

Island II

Something like:
(I) Agathe has left only a few lines in a note. Contents?

(II) Shortly thereafter Walter arrives toward evening. Ulrich spontaneously: Did you see Agathe? That did not happen. But that Agathe had been there until just now calms his jealousy. Walter, somewhat paunchy belly.

Ulrich takes him to Clarisse. Clarisse is sitting somewhere on the beach. Ulrich hadn't been paying attention to her. Walter feels profound solidarity with the ill and abandoned.

They enter the fishermen's hut. It looks as if the three of them had lived there. They arrange things for the three of them. Walter doesn't say anything about it; acts as if it is a self-explanatory matter of being chaperon.

(III) How does Clarisse take this? — That also depends on what came before (Island I), which is still undetermined.

Idea: She confesses. If there had been intercourse with Ulrich, that way; but more probably (because of Agathe's proximity) coitus is only to be reduced to hints, a half seduction of Ulrich by Clarisse. So nothing took place, and it also makes the scene stronger if she confesses made-up sins and Ulrich listens. Usable as climax: suddenly or by degrees, the powerful sexual arousal turns into the mystic emotion of transfigured union with God, which is almost unimaginable.

Walter doubtless does not believe, Ulrich makes him a sign, but still there is something credible in it, as if its not being true were merely accidental.

(IV) In order to leave Clarisse alone while she gets undressed, they go outside, then toward the beach. Walter says, because he is jealous: it is madness to doubt a person's faithfulness. There are situations in which one is quite properly uncertain. In the half-light he looks at Ulrich from the side. But you must have the courage to let yourself be deceived. That is the way a bullet must sometimes heal over without being removed. Out of this deception that you encapsulate within yourself something great can arise. It's a matter not only of faithfulness between man and wife but also of other values.

He did not say: greatness, but that's what he was probably thinking. He seemed important to himself, and above all manly, because he wasn't making a scene and forcing Ulrich to confess the truth. Somehow he was grateful to fate for this great trial. Transitionally or combined with:

(V) They sit down by the edge of the melancholy of the evening sea.

She was the star of my life! Walter said.

But Ulrich starts at contact with the word faithfulness. He's not nearly as magnanimous as Walter.

(VI) Walter now picks up on star of my life, develops it.

Now it is sinking into night; what is to become of me? At this moment he has this sense of self-importance they had when they were young. He steps outside himself: I am at a critical juncture. You have no idea what I've had to fight through and suffer this past year. In the last analysis my whole life has been a battle. Fought like a madman / fought day and night with a dagger in my fist. But does it mean anything? I think I have now come so far as really to be the man I wanted to be; but is there any sense in it? Do you believe that the way things are today, we could really carry out anything at all of what we desired as young people?

Ulrich sat there in a dark-blue wool fisherman's sweater; he had lost weight, which only emphasized the breadth of his shoulders and the muscular power of his arms, which, leaning forward, he had rested on his knees—and he wanted most of all to howl at this crepuscular comradeship. He replied gloomily: Don't talk to me about your victories. You were beaten and finally you want to throw up without being embarrassed. You're now in your early thirties, and at forty everyone is through. At fifty everyone sees himself contented in life and soon after that will have all his troubles behind him. The only people who have it good are the ones who seek refuge in conformity! That's the wisdom of life! The best part is reserved for those who are defeated! And nothing is worse than being alone!

He was dejected. His crassness did not prevent Walter from noticing it.

[Visit to the madhouse]

What met her eyes was, in any event, peculiar enough: a game of cards.

Moosbrugger, in dark everyday clothes, was sitting at a table with three men, one of whom was wearing a doctor's white smock, the second a business suit, and the third the rather threadbare cassock of a priest; aside from these four figures around the table, and their wooden chairs, the room was empty, except for the three high windows that looked out over the garden. The four men looked up as Clarisse came toward them, and Friedenthal performed the introductions. Clarisse made the acquaintance of a young intern at the clinic, his mentor, and a doctor who had come to visit, from whom she found out that he had been one of the experts who had declared Moosbrugger sane at his court hearings. The four were playing three-man games, so that one was always sitting watching the others play. The sight of a cozy, ordinary game of cards dashed, for the moment, all Clarisse's ideas. She had been prepared for something horrifying, even if only that she would have been led endlessly farther through such half-empty rooms in order finally to be mysteriously informed that Moosbrugger was once again not to be seen; and after everything she had been through in the last few weeks, and especially today, all she could feel now was an extraordinary sense of oppression. She did not grasp that this card game had been arranged with the others by Dr. Friedenthal in order that Moosbrugger could be observed at leisure; it seemed to her like devils playing with a soul in an ignoble fashion, and she thought she was in empty, icy tracts of hell. To her horror, Moosbrugger stood up straight and gallantly came up to her; Friedenthal introduced him too, and Moosbrugger took her unsteady hand in his paw and made a quick, silent bow, like a big adolescent.

After that was done, Friedenthal asked that they please not disturb themselves and explained that the lady had come from Chicago to study the organization of the clinic and would certainly find that there was no other place in the world where the guests were treated so well.

"Spades were played, not diamonds, Herr Moosbrugger!" said the physician, who had been observing his protégé reflectively. In truth, Moosbrugger had enjoyed Friedenthal's referring to him, in the presence of these strangers, as a guest of the clinic and not as a patient. Savoring this made him misread the cards, but because of the game he overlooked the reproach with a magnanimous smile. Ordinarily he played more carefully than a hawk. It was his ambition to lose to his learned opponents only through the luck of the cards, never by playing worse than they did. But this time he also, after a while, allowed himself to count his tricks in English, which he could do up to thirty even if it interfered with his game, and he had understood that Clarisse came from America. Indeed, a little later he put his cards down entirely, pressed his fists against the table, leaned his strong back so broadly backward that the wood embracing it creaked, and began an involved story about his time in prison. "Take my word for it, gentlemen—" he began, because he knew from experience: if you want to get anywhere with women you have to act as if you aren't even aware of their existence, at least in the beginning; that had brought him success with them every time.

The young asylum physician listened to Moosbrugger's bombastic story with a smile; in the priest's face regret struggled with cheerfulness, while the visiting doctor, who was playing, and who had almost brought Moosbrugger to the gallows, encouraged him from time to time with sarcastic interruptions. The giant's proud but ordinarily basically decent manner of conducting himself had made him a comfortable presence to them. What he said made sense, even if not always in exactly the right places; the spiritual counselor in particular had come to like him sinfully well. When he reminded himself of the brutal crimes of which this man of lamblike piety was capable, he mentally crossed himself in fright, as if he had surprised himself in some reprehensible negligence, humbled himself before the inscrutability of God, and said to himself that such a vexed and complicated affair was best left to God's will. That this will was being manipulated by the two doctors like two levers working against each other, without its being for the moment apparent which was the stronger, was not unbeknownst to the man of the cloth.

A cheerful antagonism prevailed between the two doctors. When Moosbrugger lost the thread of his story for a moment he was interrupted by the older man, the visitor, Dr. Pfeifer, with the words: "Enough talking, Moosbrugger, back to the cards, otherwise the Herr Intern will arrive at his diagnosis too soon!" Moosbrugger immediately replied with subservient eagerness: "If you want to play, Doctor, we can play again!" Clarisse heard this with astonishment. But the younger of the two doctors smiled, unmoved. It was an open secret that he was trying to arrive at an unassailable clinical picture of Moosbrugger's inability to be held accountable for his actions. This doctor was blond and looked ordinary and unsentimental, and the traces of fraternity dueling scars did not exactly make his face any more cultured; but the self-confidence of youth made him advocate the clinical view of Moosbrugger's guilt, and his requisite punishment, with a zeal that scorned the customary detachment. He would not have been able to say precisely in what this clinical view consisted. It was just different. In this view, for example, an ordinary bout of intoxication is a genuine mental disorder that heals by itself; and that Moosbrugger was in part an honorable man, in part a sex murderer, signified, as this view had it, competing drives, for which it was a matter of course that he had to reach a decision according to whether the stronger or the more sustained drive was uppermost at the moment. If others wanted to call that free will or a good or evil moral decision, that was their affair. "Whose deal?" he asked.

It developed that it was his turn to cut and deal the cards. While he was doing this, Dr. Pfeifer turned to Clarisse to ask what interest had brought his "esteemed colleague" here. Dr. Friedenthal raised his hand to ward off the question and advised: "For heaven's sake, don't mention anything about psychiatry: there's no word in the German language this doctor wants to hear less!" This was true, and had the advantage of allowing the unauthorized visitor to appear to the others to be a doctor without Friedenthal having to say so expressly. He smiled contentedly. Dr. Pfeifer left off the banter with a flattered grin. He was a somewhat older little man, whose skull was flat on top and sloped out and down at the back and was festooned with wisps of unkempt hair and beard. The nails on his fingers were oily from cigarettes and cigars, and retained around the edges a narrow rim of dirt, although in medical fashion they appeared to be cut quite short. This could now be clearly seen because in the meantime the players had picked up their cards and were carefully sorting them. "I pass," Moosbrugger declared; "I play," Dr. Pfeifer; "Good," the young doctor; this time the cleric was looking on. The game was languid and ran its uneventful course.

Clarisse, who was standing to one side next to Friedenthal, hidden slightly behind him, raised her mouth to his ear and, indicating Moosbrugger with her glance, whispered: "All he ever had was ersatz women!"

"Shh, for heaven's sake!" Friedenthal whispered back imploringly, and to cover the indiscretion stepped up to the table and asked aloud: "Who's winning?" "I'm losing," Pfeifer declared. "Moosbrugger was lying in wait! Our young colleague won't take any advice from me; there's no way I can convince him that it's a fatal error for doctors to believe sick criminals belong in their hospitals." Moosbrugger grinned. Pfeifer went on joking and picked up the skirmishing with Friedenthal where it had broken off; there was no point going on with the game anyway. "You yourself," he pleaded ironically, "ought to be telling a young Hippocrates like this, when the occasion arises, that trying to cure evil people medically is a utopia and, moreover, nonsense, for evil is not only present in the world but also indispensable for its continuation. We need bad people; we can't declare them all sick."

"You're out of tricks," the calm young doctor said, and put down his cards. This time the cleric, looking on, smiled. Clarisse thought she had understood something. She became warm. But Pfeifer looked loathsome. "It's a nonsensical utopia," he joked. She was at a loss. Presumably it was only the undignified game of devils playing for a soul. Pfeifer had lit a fresh cigar, and Moosbrugger was dealing the cards. For the first time he looked over at Clarisse for a moment, and then he was asked for his response to the others' bids.

This time the intern was odd man out. He seemed to have been waiting for the opportunity, and very slowly pulled his thoughts together in words. "For a scientist," he said, "there is nothing that does not have its basis in a law of nature. So if a person commits a crime without any rational external motive, it must mean he has an inner one. And that's what I have to be on the lookout for. But it's not subtle enough for Dr. Pfeifer." That was all he said. He had turned red, and looked around with amiable annoyance. The cleric and Dr. Friedenthal laughed; Moosbrugger laughed the same way they did and threw a lightning glance at Clarisse. Clarisse said suddenly: "A person can also have unusual rational motives!" The intern looked at her. Pfeifer agreed: "Our colleague is quite right. And you are really betraying a criminal nature just by assuming that there are also rational motives for a crime!" "Oh, nonsense!" the younger man retorted. "You know exactly what I'm talking about." And again to Clarisse: "I'm speaking as a doctor. Splitting words may have a place in philosophy or somewhere else, but I find it repulsive!"

Whenever he was entrusted with preparing a faculty report, he was known for getting angry and upset at the concessions he was expected to make to an unmedical way of thinking and at the unnatural questions to which he was expected to respond. Justice is not a scientific concept any more than the concepts derived from it are, and the doctor associates quite different ideas than does the lawyer with "deserving of punishment," "free will," "use of reason," "derangement of the senses," and all such things that determine the destiny of countless people. Since the lawyer, for whatever reasons, will neither dispense with the doctor nor yield to his judgment, which is understandable, medical experts who testify in court not seldom resemble little children forbidden by an older sister to speak in their natural way, even though at the same time she commands them to do so and then waits for the truth to emerge from their childish mouths. So it was not from any emotional sentimentality but from pure ambition and cutting zeal for his discipline that the young researcher with the dueling scars was inclined to exclude the persons in his report as much as possible from the court's cerebral cortex, and since this had a chance of succeeding only when these persons could be classified quite clearly and distinctly under a recognized category of disease, he was in Moosbrugger's case also collecting everything that pointed to one. But Dr. Pfeifer did exactly the opposite, although he only occasionally came to the clinic to inquire after Moosbrugger, like a sportsman who, once his own match is over, will sit on the rostrum and watch the others. He was recognized as an outstanding expert, even if a rather odd one, on the nature of mentally ill criminals. His practice as a physician could be called at most complaisant, and that only with the accompaniment of disrespectful statements against the value of his discipline. He lived mostly from a modest but steady income from testifying as an expert witness, for he was very popular in the courts on account of his sympathy for the tasks of justice. He was so much the expert (which also earned him Friedenthal's benevolence) that out of sheer scientism he denied his science, indeed denigrated human knowledge in general. Basically, perhaps, he did this only because in this fashion he could abandon himself without restraint to his personal inclinations, which goaded him to treat with great skill every criminal whose mental health was questionable, like a ball that was to be guided through the holes of science to the goal of punishment. All kinds of stories were told about him, and Friedenthal, doubtless fearing that the usual conversation between the two adversaries might well erupt in a quarrel that was better left unheard this time, quickly seized the initiative by turning to Clarisse right after the young doctor and explaining to her what he understood by "splitting words." "According to the opinion of our esteemed guest Dr. Pfeifer," he said with a soothing glance and smile, "no one is capable of deciding whether a person is guilty. We doctors can't because guilt, being held accountable for one's actions, and all those things aren't medical concepts at all, and judges can't because without some knowledge of the important connections between body and mind, there is no way of arriving at a judgment about such questions either. It's only religion that unambiguously demands personal responsibility before God for every sin, so ultimately such questions always become questions of religious conviction." With these last words he had directed his smile at the pastor, hoping by this teasing to give the conversation a harmless turn. The priest did turn slightly red in the face and smiled back in confusion, and Moosbrugger expressed by an unmistakable growl his complete approval of the theory that he belonged before God's tribunal and not psychiatry's. But suddenly Clarisse said: "Perhaps the patient is here because he is standing in for someone else."

She said this so quickly and unexpectedly that it got lost; several astonished glances brushed her, from whose face the color had drained except for two red spots, and then the conversation proceeded on its previous course.

"That's not entirely so," Dr. Pfeifer responded, and laid down his cards. "We can't even talk clearly about what it means to say 'I'm speaking as a doctor,' about which our colleague has such a high opinion. A 'case' that occurred in life is placed before us in the clinic; we compare it with what we know, and the rest, simply everything we don't know, simply our lack of knowledge, is the delinquent's responsibility. Is that the way it is, or isn't it?"

Friedenthal shrugged his shoulders in statesmanlike fashion, but remained silent.

"That's the way it is," Pfeifer repeated. "Despite all the pomp of justice and science, despite all hairsplitting, despite our wigs of split hairs, the whole business finally just comes down to the judge saying: '*I* wouldn't have done that' and to us psychiatrists adding: '*Our* mentally disturbed patients wouldn't have behaved that way'! But the fact that our concepts aren't better sorted out can't be allowed to lead to society's being hurt. Whether the will of an individual person is free or not free, society's will is free as far as what it treats as good and evil. And for myself, I want to be good in society's sense, not in the sense of my private emotions." He relit his dead cigar and brushed the hairs of his beard away from his mouth, which had become moist.

Moosbrugger, too, stroked his mustache, and was beating rhythmically on the tabletop with the edge of his telescoped hand of cards.

"Well, do we want to go on playing, or don't we?" the intern asked patiently.

"Of course we want to go on," Pfeifer responded, and picked up his cards. His eyes met Moosbrugger's. "Moreover, Moosbrugger and I are of the same opinion," he went on, looking at his hand with a worried expression. "How was it, Moosbrugger? The counselor at the trial asked you repeatedly why you put on your Sunday clothes and went to the tavern—"

"And got shaved," Moosbrugger corrected; Moosbrugger was ready to talk about it at any time, as if it was an act of state.

"Calmly got shaved," Pfeifer repeated. " 'You shouldn't have done that!' the counselor told you. Well!" He turned to the rest. "We do exactly the same thing when we say that our mental patients wouldn't have done that. Is this the way to prove anything?" This time, his words were subdued and relaxed and only an echo of his earlier, more passionate protest, because the game had again begun to go around the table.

A patronizing smile could be discerned on Moosbrugger's face for quite some time; it slowly faded in his absorption in the game, the way pleats in a stiff material soften with constant use. So Clarisse was not entirely wrong when she thought she was seeing several devils struggling for a soul, but the relaxed way in which this was happening deceived her, and she was especially confused by the manner in which Moosbrugger was behaving. He apparently did not much like the younger doctor, who wanted to help him; he put up with his efforts only reluctantly and became restless when he felt them. Perhaps he wasn't acting any differently from any simple person who finds it impertinent when someone busies himself about him too earnestly; but he was delighted every time Dr. Pfeifer spoke. Presumably what he was expressing in this case was not exactly delight, for such a condition formed no part of Moosbrugger's demeanor, oriented as it was toward dignity and recognition, and much of what the doctors said among themselves he also found incomprehensible; but if talk there had to be, then it should be like Dr. Pfeifer's. That this was, on the whole, his opinion was unmistakably evident. The collision of the two doctors had made him cheerful; he began to count his tricks again out loud and in English, and in conspicuous repetition threw into the conversation or into the silence from time to time the observation: "If it must be, it must be!" Even the good cleric, who had seen a good deal, shook his head at times, but the scorn heaped on earthly justice had pleased him not a little, and he was also pleased that the scholars of worldly science were not able to agree. He no longer recalled how all these problems that they had been talking about were to be decided according to canon law, but he thought calmly: "Let them carry on, God has the last word," and since this conviction led him not to get involved in the verbal duel, he won the game.

So among these four men there was a quite cordial understanding. It was true that the prize being offered was Moosbrugger's head, but that was not in the least troublesome as long as each person was completely preoccupied with what he had to do first. After all, the men concerned with forging, polishing, and selling knives are not constantly thinking of what it might lead to. Moreover, Moosbrugger, as the only one personally and directly acquainted with the slaying of another person, and whose own execution was in the offing, found that it was not the worst thing that could befall a man of honor. Life is not the highest of values, Schiller says: Moosbrugger had heard that from Dr. Pfeifer, and it pleased him greatly. And so, as he could be touching or a raging animal depending on how his nature was appealed to or manipulated, the others too, as friends and executioners, were stretched over two differing spheres of action that had hardly a single point of contact. But this greatly disturbed Clarisse. She had seen right away that under the guise of cheerfulness something secret was going on, but she had grasped this only as a blurred picture and, confused by the content of the conversation, was just now beginning to understand; but not only did she understand, she saw persistent evidence, ominous and indeed urgent in its uncanniness, that these men were surreptitiously observing Moosbrugger. But Moosbrugger, unsuspecting, was observing her, Clarisse. From time to time he furtively directed his eyes at her and tried to surprise and hold her glance. The visit of this beautiful lady who had come so far—it was only Clarisse's thinness and small size that were just a little too unimpressive—flattered him greatly, in spite of all the deference with which he was generally treated. When he found her extraordinary glance directed at him, he did not doubt for an instant that his bushy-bearded manliness had made her fall in love with him, and now and then a smile arose beneath his mustache that was meant to confirm this conquest, and this, along with the superiority practiced on servant girls, made a quite remarkable impression on Clarisse. An inexpressible helplessness squeezed her heart. She had the notion that Moosbrugger found himself in a trap, and the flesh on her body seemed to her a bait that had been cast before him while the hunters lurked around him.

Quickly making up her mind, she laid her hand on Friedenthal's arm and told him that she had seen enough and felt tired.

"What did you really mean when you said he had always had only 'ersatz women'?" Friedenthal asked after they had left the room.

"Nothing!" Clarisse, still upset at what she had been through, responded with a dismissive gesture.

Friedenthal became melancholy and thought he needed to justify the strange performance. "Basically, of course, none of us are responsible for our actions," he sighed. Clarisse retorted: "He least of all!"

Friedenthal laughed at the "joke." "Were you very much surprised?" he continued, in apparent astonishment. "Some of Moosbrugger's individual traits emerged quite nicely."

Clarisse stopped. "You shouldn't allow that to continue!" she demanded forcefully.

Her companion smiled and devoted himself to dramatizing his state of mind. "What do you expect!" he exclaimed. "For the medical man everything is medicine, and for the lawyer, law! The justice system is in the final analysis a function of the concept of 'compulsion,' which is part of healthy life but is mostly applied without thinking to sick people as well. But in the same way, the concept of 'sickness,' our starting point as doctors, and all its consequences, are also applicable to healthy life. These things can never be reconciled!"

"But there are no such things!" Clarisse exclaimed.

"Oh, but there are," the doctor complained gently. "The human sciences developed at different times and for different purposes, which have nothing to do with each other. So we have the most divergent concepts about the same thing. At most the only place it comes together is in the lexicon. And I bet it's not only the priest and myself but you, too, and, for instance, your brother or your husband and I—each one of us would know only one corner of the contents of every term we would look up in it, and of course each of us would know a different corner! The world hasn't been able to arrange things any better than that!" Friedenthal had leaned over Clarisse, who was standing in a window alcove, and supported his arm against the window bars. Some sort of genuine feeling resonated in his words. He was a doubter. The insecurity of his discipline had opened his eyes to the insecurity of all knowledge. He would have loved to be someone important, but in his best hours had an inkling that for him the paralyzing confusion of everything about which truth existed, did not yet exist, or would never exist, permitted nothing more than a vain and sterile subjectivity. He sighed, and added: "I sometimes feel as if the windows of this building were nothing more than magnifying glasses!"

Clarisse asked seriously: "Can we go to your office for a bit? I can't talk here." Two arrows shot forth from beneath the shield of her eyelids. Friedenthal slowly disengaged his hand from the window and his glance from her eyes. Then he also disengaged his thoughts from the absorption he had revealed, and said, as they walked along the tiled corridor: "This fellow Pfeifer is an extraordinary figure. He lives without friends or girlfriends, but he has the biggest collection of paintings, trial proceedings, and memorabilia connected with the death sentences of the last twenty or thirty years. I saw them once. Extraordinary. Drawers full of his 'victims': polished and brutal faces of men and women, some marked by crime, some quite ordinary-looking, smile up at you from yellowed newspapers and faded photographs, or gaze into their unknown future. Then there are scraps of clothing, rope ends—real gallows ropes—canes, vials of poison. Do you know the museum in Zermatt, where what's left behind by those who've fallen from the surrounding mountains is preserved? It's that kind of impression. He obviously has a tender feeling for these things. You notice it, too, whenever he talks of the 'victims' to whose legal murder, or whatever you want to call it, he himself has contributed. As astute observer might see in this something like a rivalry, the joy of intellectual superiority, sexual cunning. All of course entirely within the bounds of what is permissible and scientifically admissible. But one could indeed say that being preoccupied with danger makes one dangerous—"

"He hunts them?" Clarisse asked in a choked voice.

"Yes; you could almost say he's a hunter in love with his prey."

Clarisse froze; she did not know what was happening to her. Friedenthal had conducted her back along a somewhat different route, and as he was speaking opened the door of a ward they had to traverse, which seemed to contain the most glorious thing she had ever seen. It was a large hall, and she thought she was looking into a living flower bed. They were crossing the ward for hysterical women. These women were standing around singly and in small clusters, and lying in beds. They all appeared to be wearing snow-white clothes and to have loosened and flowing inky-black hair. Clarisse couldn't take in a single detail; the totality resembled something unutterably beautiful and dramatically agitated. "Sisters!" Clarisse felt softly but powerfully in that moment when attention streamed in irregular pulses toward her and Friedenthal; she had the feeling of being able to fly higher with a swarm of wondrous lovebirds than all the excitements of life and art allow. Her companion made only slow forward progress with her, for all sorts of humble enamored souls approached him from every side, or wandered in his path with a strength of erotic gentleness such as Clarisse had never before experienced. Friedenthal directed placating or severe words to them, and with soft movements pushed them away; and meanwhile other women lay in their beds in their white jackets, having spread out their hair darkly over the pillows, women whose bellies and legs under their thin blankets performed the drama of love. Sinning figures. Paired with a partner who remained invisible but was palpably present, against whom they pushed their arms with exaggerated resistance, who exaggeratedly stimulated the swelling of their breasts, from whose mouths they withdrew with superhuman effort and toward whom their bellies vaulted with superhuman effort, while in the midst of this obscene play their eyes shone innocently with the enchanting inert beauty of large, dark flowers.

Clarisse was still deeply confused by this flower bed of love and suffering, by its morbid and yet intoxicating aroma, by its aura, by the gliding-through and not-being-allowed-to-stop, when she was sitting in Friedenthal's office being observed by him with an unflagging smile. Collecting herself and returning from her almost spatially deep distraction, she clung to something she managed to get out in a raw, almost mechanical voice: "Declare him not accountable for his actions!"

Friedenthal looked at her with astonishment. "My dear lady," he asked in a joking tone, "of what concern is that to you?"

Clarisse recoiled because she could not think of an answer. But since nothing occurred to her, she said simply and suddenly: "Because he can't help it!"

Dr. Friedenthal now scrutinized her more closely. "What makes you so sure of that?"

Clarisse energetically withstood his glance and answered haughtily, as if she was not certain whether to condescend to giving him such a response: "But he's here only because he's standing in for someone else!" Annoyed, she shrugged her shoulders, jumped up, and looked out the window. When after a short while she perceived that this did not have any effect, she turned around again and came down a peg. "You can't understand me: he reminds me of someone!" she observed, half attenuating the truth. She did not want to say too much and held back.

"But that's not a scientific reason," Friedenthal drawled.

"I thought you'd do it if I asked you to," she now said simply.

"You're too casual about that." The doctor was reproachful. He leaned back in his armchair like Faust and went on with a glance at his studio: "Have you at all considered whether you are doing the man a favor by wanting him committed instead of punished? It's no fun living within these walls." He shook his head disconsolately.

His visitor replied clearly: "First the executioner must leave him alone!"

"Look," Friedenthal said. "In my opinion, Moosbrugger is probably an epileptic. But he also shows symptoms of paraphrenia systematica and perhaps of dementia paranoides. He just happens to be in every respect a borderline case. His attacks, in which excruciatingly terrifying delusions and sensory disorientation certainly do play a role, can last minutes or weeks, but they often pass over imperceptibly into complete mental clarity, just as they are also capable of arising with no fixed boundaries from this same clarity, and besides, even in the paroxysmal stage consciousness never quite disappears but is only diminished in varying degrees. So something probably could be done for him, but the case is by no means one in which it would be *necessary* for a doctor to exclude his responsibility as a physician!"

"So you'll do something for him?" Clarisse urged.

Friedenthal smiled. "I don't know yet."

"You have to!"

"You're strange," Friedenthal drawled. "But . . . one could weaken."

"You don't have the slightest doubt that the man is sick!" the young woman asserted emphatically.

"Of course not. But it's not my job to judge *that*," the doctor defended himself. "You've already heard: I am to judge whether his free will was excluded during the deed, whether his consciousness was present during the deed, whether he had any insight into his wrongdoing: nothing but metaphysical questions, which put this way have no meaning for me as a physician, but in which I do have to show some consideration for the judge!"

In her excitement Clarisse strode up and down the room like a man.

"Then you oughtn't to let yourself be used like that!" she exclaimed harshly. "If you can't prevail against the judge, it has to be attempted some other way!"

Friedenthal tried another tack to dissuade his visitor from her annoying ideas. "Have you ever really tried to picture to yourself what a horrible raging beast this momentarily calm half-sick man can be?" he asked.

"What's that to us now?" Clarisse retorted, cutting off his effort. "When confronted with a case of pneumonia, you don't ask whether you can help a good person go on living! Your only task now is to prevent yourself from becoming accessory to a murder!"

Friedenthal sadly threw up his hands. "You're crazy!" he said rudely and dejectedly.

"One has to have the courage to be crazy if the world is to be set right again! From time to time there have to be people who refuse to go along with the lies!" Clarisse asserted.

He took this to be a witty joke, which in the rush he had not quite understood. From the start this little person had made an impression on him, especially since, dazzled by General von Stumm, he overestimated her social position; and in any case, many young people these days give a rather confused impression. He found her to be something special, and felt himself restlessly stirred by her spontaneous eagerness as if by something relentlessly, even nobly, radiant. To be sure, he perhaps ought to have seen this radiance as diamondlike, for it also had something of the quality of an overheated stove: something distinctly unpleasant that made one hot and icy. He unobtrusively assessed his visitor: stigmata of a heightened nervousness were doubtless to be perceived in her. But who today did not have such stigmata! Friedenthal's response was no different from the usual one—for when there are hazy notions of what is really meaningful, what is confused always has the same chance to excel that the con artist has in a hazily defined society—and although he was a pretty good observer, he had always managed to regain his composure no matter what Clarisse said. In the last analysis, one can always regard any person as a small-scale swatch of mental illness; that's the job of theory, how one looks at a person at one time psychologically and at another chemically; and since after Clarisse's last words a chasm of silence yawned, Friedenthal again sought "contact" and at the same time sought once more to divert her from her insistent demands. "Did you really like the women we saw?" he asked.

"Oh, enormously!" Clarisse exclaimed. She stood quietly before him, and the hardness was suddenly gone from her face. "I don't know what to tell you," she added softly. "That ward is like a monstrous magnifying glass held over a woman's triumph and suffering!"

Friedenthal smiled with satisfaction. "Well, so now you see," he said. "Now you'll have to concede that the attraction that illness exercises is not alien to me either. But I must observe limits, I have to keep things in their places. Then I wanted to ask you whether you have ever considered that love, too, is a disturbance of the mind. There is hardly anyone who does not conceal something in his most private and proper love life that he reveals only to his guilty partner, some craziness or weakness: why not simply call it perversity and madness? In public you have to take measures against it, but in your inner life you can't always arm yourself against such things with the same rigor. And psychiatrists—psychiatry is ultimately an art too—will celebrate their greatest success when they have a certain sympathy and rapport with the medium in which they are working." He had seized his visitor's hand, and Clarisse ceded to him its outermost fingertips, which she felt lying between his fingers as softly and helplessly as if they had fallen from her like the petals a flower drops. Suddenly she was completely a woman, full of that tender capriciousness in the face of a man's beseeching, and what she had experienced in the morning was forgotten. A soundless sigh parted her lips. It seemed to her that she had never felt this way, or not for the longest time, and evidently at this moment something from the magic of his realm rubbed off on Friedenthal, whom she by no means especially liked. But she pulled herself together and asked sternly: "What have you made up your mind to do?"

"I have to make my rounds now," the doctor replied, "but I would like to see you again. But not here. Can't we meet somewhere else?"

"Perhaps," Clarisse responded. "When you have carried out my request!"

Her lips narrowed, the blood drained from her skin, and this made her cheeks look like two small leather balls; there was too much pressure in her eyes. Friedenthal suddenly felt exploited. It is extraordinary, but when a person sees another as merely a means to an end, it is much easier for him to take on that impenetrable look of someone who is mentally ill, the more natural it seems to him that consideration ought to be shown him. "Every hour here we see souls suffer, but we have to stay within our bounds," he countered. He became circumspect.

Clarisse said: "Good, you don't want to. Let me make you another proposition." She stood before him, small, legs apart, hands behind her back, and looked at him with a bashfully sarcastic, urgent smile: "I'll join the clinic as a nurse!"

The doctor stood up and asked her to talk it over with her brother, who would make clear to her how many necessary prerequisites for such a position she was lacking. As he spoke, the sarcasm that was squeezed into her eyes drained out of them and they filled with tears. "Then I want," she said, almost voiceless from excitement, "to be accepted as a patient! I have a mission!" Because she was afraid of spoiling her chances if she looked directly at the doctor, she looked to one side and up a little, and perhaps her eyes even wandered around. A shudder heated her skin, which swelled up red. Now she looked lovely and in need of tenderness, but it was too late; irritation at her importunity had sobered the doctor and made him reserved. He did not even ask her any more questions, for it seemed politic not to know too much about her out of consideration for the General and Ulrich, who had brought her here, and also in view of the almost forbidden favors he had granted her. And it was only out of old medical habit that from this point on his speech became still gentler and more emphatic as he expressed to Clarisse his regret that there was no way he could meet her second request, and he advised her to confide this wish to her brother too. He even informed her that before that happened he could not allow her to continue her visits to the clinic, much as this would be a loss to him personally.

Clarisse offered no real resistance to what he said. She had already imputed worse to Friedenthal. "He's an impeccable medical bureaucrat," she told herself. That eased her departure: she casually extended her hand to the physician, and her eyes laughed cunningly. She was not at all depressed, and even as she went down the steps was thinking about other possibilities.

FISCHEL / GERDA / HANS SEPP / ULRICH

LATE 1920S

It was Ulrich's bad conscience that drove him to Gerda; since the melancholy scene between them, he had not heard anything from her and did not know how she had come to terms with herself. To his surprise, he found Papa Leo at the Fischels' house; Mama Clementine had gone out with Gerda. Leo Fischel would not let Ulrich go; he had rushed out to the hall himself when he recognized his voice. Ulrich had the impression of changes. Director Fischel seemed to have changed his tailor; his income must have increased and his convictions diminished. Then too, he had usually stayed later at the bank; he had never worked at home after the air there had become so irksome. But today he seemed to have been sitting at his desk, although this "roaring loom of time" had not been used for years; a packet of letters lay on the baize cloth, and the chrome-plated telephone, otherwise used only by the ladies, was standing askew, as if it had just been in use. After Ulrich had sat down, Fischel turned toward him in his desk chair and polished his pince-nez with a handkerchief that he drew from his breast pocket, although earlier he would certainly have objected to such a foppish action, saying that it had been sufficient for a Goethe, a Schiller, and a Beethoven to carry their handkerchiefs in their trouser pocket—whether that was the case or not.

—It's been a long time, said Director Fischel.

—Yes, Ulrich said.

—Did you inherit a great deal? Fischel asked.

—Oh, Ulrich said. —Enough.

—Yes, there are problems.

—But you look splendid. You somehow seem to have got younger.

—Oh, thanks; professionally there have never been any problems. But look— He pointed in a melancholy way to a pile of letters that lay on the desk. You do know Hans Sepp?

—Of course. You took me into your confidence—

—Right! Fischel said.

—Are those love letters?

The telephone rang. Fischel put on his pince-nez, which he had taken off to listen, extracted a paper with notes from his coat, and said: — Buy! Then the inaudible voice at the other end spoke to him for quite a while. From time to time Fischel looked over his spectacles at Ulrich, and once he even said: —Excuse me! Then he said into the instrument: —No, thank you, I don't like the second business! Talk about it? Yes, of course we can talk about it again—and with a short, satisfied pause for reflection, he hung up.

—You see, Fischel said. —That was someone in Amsterdam; much too expensive! Three weeks ago the thing wasn't worth half as much, and in three weeks it won't be worth half what it costs now. But in between there's a deal to be made. A great risk!

—But you didn't want to, Ulrich said.

—Oh, that's not really settled. But a great risk . . . ! But still, let me tell you, that's building in marble, stone on stone! Can you build on the mind, the love, the ideals of a person? He was thinking of his wife and of Gerda. How different it had been at the beginning! The telephone rang again, but this time it was a wrong number.

—You used to put more worth on solid moral values than on a solid purse, Ulrich said. —How often you held it against me that I couldn't follow you in that!

—Oh—he responded—ideals are like air that changes, you don't know how, with closed windows! Twenty-five years ago, who had any notion of anti-Semitism? No, then there were the great perspectives of Humanity! You're too young. But I still managed to hear some of the great parliamentary debates. The last ones! The only thing that's dependable is what you can say with numbers. Believe me, the world would be a lot more reasonable if it were simply left to the free play of supply and demand, instead of being equipped with armored ships, bayonets, diplomats who know nothing about economics, and so-called national ideals.

Ulrich interrupted with the objection that it was precisely heavy industry and the banks whose demands were urging peoples on to armament.

— Well, shouldn't they? Fischel replied. —If the world is the way it is, and runs around in fool's outfits in broad daylight, they shouldn't take account of that? When the military just happens to be convenient for customs dealings, or against strikers? Money, you know, has its own rationale, and it's not to be trifled with. By the way, apropos, have you heard anything new about Arnheim's ore deposits? Again the phone rang; but with his hand on the instrument, Fischel waited for Ulrich's answer. The conversation was brief, and Fischel did not lose the thread of their conversation; since Ulrich knew nothing new about Arnheim, he repeated that money had its own rationale. —Pay attention, he added. —If I were to offer Hans Sepp five hundred marks to move to one of the universities of his revered-above-all Germania (Germany), he would reject them indignantly. If I offered him a thousand, ditto. But if I were to offer him ten thousand—though I never in my life would, even if I had so much money! It almost seemed as if Fischel, horrified at such an idea, had lost the connection, but he was only reflecting, and went on: —One just can't do that, because money has its own rationale. For a man who spends insane amounts, the money won't stick; it will fly from him, make him a spendthrift. That the ten thousand marks refuse to be offered to Hans Sepp proves that this Hans Sepp is not real, is of no value, but an awful, swindling scourge with which God is chastising me.

Again Fischel was interrupted. This time by longer communications. That he was conducting such transactions at home instead of at the office struck Ulrich. Fischel gave three orders to buy and one to sell. In between he had time to think about his wife. —If I were to offer her money so she would divorce me—he asked himself—would Clementine do it? An inner certainty answered: No. Leo Fischel mentally doubled the amount. Ridiculous! said the inner voice. Fischel quadrupled. No, on principle, occurred to him. Then in one swoop he breathlessly increased the sum beyond any human resistance or capability, and angrily stopped. He speedily had to switch his mind to smaller fortunes, which literally shrank in his mind the way the pupils narrow with a sudden change of light; but he did not forget his affairs for an instant, and made no mistakes.

—But now tell me, finally—Ulrich asked, having already become impatient—what kind of letters these are that you wanted to show me. They appear to be love letters. Did you intercept Gerda's love letters?

—I wanted to show you these letters. You should read them. I would just like to know now what *you* would say about them. Fischel handed Ulrich the whole packet and sat back, preoccupied meanwhile with other thoughts, gazing into the air through his pince-nez.

Ulrich glanced at the letters; then he took one out and slowly read it through. Director Fischel asked: —Tell me, Herr Doktor, you used to know this singer Leontine, or Leona, who looks like the late Empress Elizabeth; may God punish me, this woman really has the appetite of a lion!

Ulrich looked up, frowning; he liked the letter, and the interruption bothered him.

—Well, you don't have to answer, Fischel placated him. —I was just asking. You needn't be ashamed. She's no royalty. I met her a little while ago through an acquaintance; we found out that you and she were friends. She eats a lot. Let her eat! Who doesn't like to eat? Fischel laughed.

Ulrich dropped his gaze to the letter again, without responding. Fischel again gazed dreamily into the firmament of the room.

The letter began: —Beloved person! Human goddess! We are condemned to live in an extinguished century. No one has the courage to believe in the reality of myth. You must realize that this applies to you too. You do not have the courage of your nature as goddess. Fear of people holds you back. You are right to consider ordinary human lust as vulgar; indeed, worse than that, as a ridiculous regression from the life of us people of the future into mere atavism! And you are right again when you say that love for a person, animal, or thing is already the beginning of taking possession of it! And we don't even need to mention that possessing is the beginning of despiritualization! But still you have to distinguish: being felt, perhaps also being sensed, is called being mine. I only feel what is mine; I don't hear what is not meant for me! Were this not so, we would be intellectualists. It's perhaps an inescapable tragedy that when we love we are forced to possess with eyes, ears, breath, and thoughts! But consider: I feel that I am not, so long as I am only I myself, I-self. It's only in the things outside me that I first discover myself. That, too, is a truth. I love a flower, a person, because without them I would be nothing. The grand thing about the experience of "mine" is feeling oneself melt away entirely, like a pile of snow under the rays of the sun, drifting upward like a gentle dissipating vapor! The most beautiful thing about "mine" is the ultimate extirpation of the possession of my self! That's the pure sense of "mine," that I possess nothing but am possessed by the entire world. All brooks flow from the heights to the valleys, and you too, O my soul, will not be mine before you have become a drop in the ocean of the world, totally a link in the world brotherhood and world community! This mystery no longer has anything in common with the insipid exaggeration that individual love experiences. In spite of the lust of this age one must have the courage for ardor, for inner fire! Virtue makes action virtuous; actions don't make virtue! Try it! The Beyond reveals itself in fits and starts, and we will not be transported in one jump into the regions of untrammeled life. But moments will come when we who are remote from people will experience moments of grace that are remote from people. Don't throw sensuality and suprasensuality into a pot of what has been! Have the courage to be a goddess! That's German! . . .

—Well? Fischel asked.

Ulrich's face had turned red. He found this letter ridiculous but moving. Did these young people have no inhibitions at all about what was exaggerated, impossible, about the word that will not let itself be redeemed? Words constantly hitched up with new words, and a kernel of truth hazed over with their peculiar web. —So that's what Gerda's like now, he thought. But within this thought he thought a second, unspoken, shaming one; it went something like: —Aren't you insufficiently exaggerated and impossible?

—Well? Fischel repeated.

—Are all the letters like that? Ulrich asked, giving them back to him.

—How do I know which ones you've read! Fischel answered. —They're all like that!

—Then they are quite beautiful, Ulrich said.

—I thought as much! Fischel exploded. —Of course that's why I showed them to you! My wife found them. But no one expects me to have any clever advice in such questions of the soul. So fine! Tell that to my wife!

I would rather talk to Gerda herself about it; there's a lot in the letter that is, of course, quite misguided—

—Misguided? To say the least! But talk to her! And tell Gerda that I can't understand a single word of this jargon, but that I'm ready to pay five thousand marks—no! Better not to say anything! Tell her only that I love her anyway and am ready to forgive her!

The telephone again called Fischel to business. He, who all his life had been only a solid clerk, had begun some time ago to operate on the stock exchange on his own: from time to time and with only small amounts, the scanty savings he possessed and a few stocks belonging to his spouse, Clementine. He could not talk to her about it, but he could be quite satisfied at his success; it was a real recreation from the depressing circumstances at home.

.   .   .

Ulrich is driven to see Gerda. He hadn't spoken to her since the hysterical scene. Conscience impels him. But he finds Gerda very much taken up with Hans Sepp.

Ulrich seeks to be conciliatory with Gerda and to be kind. She pays him back with her involvement with Hans Sepp, which Ulrich perceives as intellectual felony.

Arnheim has become the ideal, the messiah, the savior. The spiritual man of intellect for our time.

Effect of the nabob.

Leo Fischel's belief in progress is part of the problem of culture.

Hans Sepp stimulated by the conflict of the national minorities.

"German-ness" as a vague reaction to the cultural situation.

Ulrich receives a *Stella* shock [Goethe's play—TRANS.] (letters!) for Agathe.

Gerda is "beyond" love. Also against religious mysticism. In future: conflict indicated in letter.

· · ·

Double orientation: Mysticism
                             Antidemocracy

· · ·

Soon after his visit to the Fischels', Ulrich was again driven to see Gerda. He had not seen her since the sad scene that had taken place between them, and felt the desire to speak kindly and reasonably to her. He wanted to suggest that she leave her parents' house for a year or two and undertake something that would give her pleasure, with the aim of forgetting him and Hans Sepp and taking advantage of her youth. But he found her in the company of Hans Sepp. She turned pale when she saw him come in; the thoughts flew out of her head, and even though she looked composed, there was really nothing at all in her that she could compose; she suddenly felt nothing but an emptiness surrounded by the stiff, disciplined, automatic motions of her limbs.

—I don't want to ask your pardon, Gerda—Ulrich began—because that isn't important—

She interrupted him right there. —I behaved ludicrously—she said—I know that; but believe me, it's all over.

—I'll only believe that everything's fine when I know what you're up to and what your plans are.

Hans Sepp was listening with the jealous eyes of one who does not understand.

—What makes you think that Fräulein Fischel has plans? he asked.

Ulrich remembered the letters that Leo Fischel had shown him. Since then he had had a lot of sympathy for this young person in whom mystic feelings raged. But at the same time, seeing him reminded him, God knows why, of a skinny dog that wants to mount a bitch much too big for him. He collected himself and, ignoring his question, asked Hans to explain to him what he wanted. —That is to say, he added, he would like to know what he had in mind to turn his ideas into reality when he was not talking about "human being," "soul," "mystery," "ardor," "contemplation," and the like, but about the future Dr. Hans Sepp, who would be compelled to live in the world.

Ulrich really wanted to know, that was sincerely to be heard in his question; and in addition he had managed to invest it with a Masonic choice of words that astonished Hans, and Gerda's glance rested on Hans with a challenging reproach. Hans scratched his head, because he did not want to be rude and felt embarrassed. —Those aren't my ideas—he finally said—but those of German youth. Ulrich repeated his request to show him how they could be made reality. Hans thought he knew what Ulrich was getting at: whenever Hans courted Gerda with such ideas, the words were like the texture of an orchestra through which, as voice, the sight of Gerda hovered; could one tear that apart and separate it? —You're asking me to make a political treatise out of a piece of music! he said.

Ulrich added: —And the language of politics, of trade, of arithmetic, is the language of the fallen angels, whose wings have long since become as vestigial as, say, our caudal vertebra. It can hardly be articulated in such a language—is that what you mean? But that's exactly why I would like to know what you're thinking of doing. Hans gave him the simplest answer to this: —I don't know! But I'm not alone. And if several thousand people want something that they can't picture, then one day they'll get it, as long as they remain true to themselves!

—Do you believe that too, Gerda? Ulrich asked.

Gerda wavered. —I'm convinced too—she said—that our culture will perish if something isn't done.

Ulrich jumped up. —My dear children! What concern is that of yours? Tell me what you're proposing to do with each other!

Hans set about defending his view. —Don't talk down to us! It's quite certain that this hugger-mugger called culture will perish, and everything else along with it—and nothing will prevail against it but the New Man!

—But Hans overestimates the significance of love between people, Gerda added. —The New will also leave that behind.

Hans was really a melancholy person. An emerging impurity on his skin could put him in a bad mood for days, and that was no rare occurrence, for in his petit-bourgeois family care of the skin did not rank very high. As in many Austrian families, it had stopped at the state it had reached before the middle of the nineteenth century: that is, every Saturday the bathtub or a wash trough would be filled with hot water, and this served for the cleaning of the body that was forgone on all the other days. There were just as few other luxuries in Hans Sepp's family home. His father was a minor government functionary with a small salary and the prospect of an even scantier pension, which in view of his age was imminent, and the principles as well as the conduct of life in his parents' house were distinguished from those at the Fischels' about the way that a cardboard box carefully tied together with knotted bits of string, in which the common people pack their belongings for a journey, differs from a magnificent valise. If he looked around, all that Hans Sepp could claim as a distinction was his German name, and it had taken him a long time before he learned to regard it as more than a gift of fate, on the day that he became acquainted with the view that being German meant being aristocratic. From that day forward he bore a noble name, and it is not necessary to waste words about how nice it is to know that one is personally distinguished; one should rather write a whole book about how one ought to want not to *be* distinguished but to distinguish oneself; but that would turn into a book that would be absolutely and completely unsocial.

The titles Count and Prince pale in comparison with the title Hans Sepp. No one today values belonging to a secret clan whose signs are an ox's head or three stars. On the other hand, to have a German name when one had German sentiments was, among lower-class youth in Austria, a rarity. The friends through whom Hans had been introduced into the movement were named Vybiral and Bartolini. It had about it something of a symbolic cover, the miracle of the manifestation of the Holy Spirit, when one was named Hans and in addition had the family name of Sepp.

Hans Sepp felt himself one of the elect, and in the absence of a bathroom he acquired the ideal of racial purity. But within this ideal there is enclosed the ideal of purity of principles. In this way, even in his early years, Hans Sepp came to fight for all the commandments of morality, which is otherwise the privilege of the incapacity for sinning, and is a position in which one has no desire for any further changes. It is a quite remarkable thing when young people become enthusiastic about virtue: a union of fire and stubbornness.

This union is facilitated if there is the possibility of combining the affirmation with a powerful negation. But in order to arrive at the real significance of such a negation, one must leave aside what is accidental, in this case the racial aspect, which is the form in which it expresses itself though not its sense.

But that was just the smaller and less serious advantage. Far greater is the advantage that a young person who adopts a negative view of the world makes the world into a comfortable nest. It is well-nigh impossible to demonstrate something as notorious as the meager intellectual content of one of those novels that among the German public pass for profound; it is much easier to make this credible by saying that these novels aren't German, or at least it penetrates reality more easily. One should not (on the whole) underestimate the advantage of saying no to everything that is considered great and beautiful. For, first, one almost always hits upon something true, and second, determining it more precisely, and the process of proving it, are in all circumstances extremely difficult and, in terms of having any effect, futile. In Germany there was once the ideal: "Test everything and keep the best"; this ideal ended in filth and scorn; it was the ideal of the dignified life and the cult of the home, which, in a time of obligatory specialization deprived of the aid of interconnections, had the same inner consequence as the purposefulness of a snail: I'll hitch a ride on anything. One must never forget this impotence into which we have put ourselves if one wishes to understand the idealism of maliciousness and evil. When the change of worldview to which every new outfitting of humanity is called stalls and becomes impossible, almost nothing remains but to say no to everything; the lowest point is always a point of rest and balance.

. . .

Closing one's eyes and gently touching one's leg is the simplest picture of the world one can have.

. . .

So there are two main kinds of pessimism. One is the pessimism of *weltschmerz*, which despairs of everything; the other is the contemporary kind, which exempts one's own person from the process. It is quite understandable that when one is young one would rather consider other people bad than oneself. This was the service that the German worldview performed for Hans Sepp. He did not so soon experience the futility of ordering his ideas, he could free himself from everything that oppresses us by calling it "un-German," and he could appear ideal to himself without having to restrain himself from besmirching / scorning the ideals of everyone else.

However, the most remarkable aspect of Hans Sepp was still a third thing. But one should not be deceived by this manner of presentation, taking one thing after another; in reality these reasons were not layers swimming atop one another; any two of them were always dissolved in a third. And what needs to be added to the two reasons named above can perhaps be called, in a correspondingly broad sense, "religious." If one were to have asked Hans Sepp whether, in school, he had believed in the teaching of his catechist, he would have answered indignantly that the German must cut himself loose from Rome and its Jew religion, but it would also not have been possible to win him over to Luther, whom he would have characterized as a pusillanimous compromiser with the Spirit of the World. Hans Sepp's religion did not fit any of the three great European religions; it was a plant of unintelligible ancestry run to seed.

This wild religious nature of nationalism is very peculiar.

Break off: This would be the place to develop the possibility of the Other Condition as something like the component freed by the weathering of religion as well as of liberal heroism.

Perhaps as a supplement to Lindner religious development. But in contrast to Professor August Lindner, God had never once appeared to Hans Sepp. In spite of that, or indeed perhaps just because of it, because he could not bring his vague feelings of faith and love into the solid framework of religion, they were in him especially wild.

. . .

One cannot say whether it is a remnant of bisexuality, the remnant of another primitive stage, or the lost natural tenderness of life, this need to make a community out of people. To feel every action inwardly, that is, a symbol . . .

Of this kind his love for Gerda, which is really less for the woman than for the person.

His misunderstanding of Ulrich, whom he considers a rationalist because he does not understand the difficulty of what Ulrich has an intimation of, and because he makes things easy for himself through community, insolent youthful hordes, etc.

. . .

(Definition after Unger: Symbol. View sees in those events we can not incorporate in any order (e.g., those of the Pentateuch) images to represent the higher world that our consciousness cannot grasp in any other way.)

. . .

Excitement also in the air as the guests left Diotima's house! Gusts of wind ran behind waves of darkness; the streetlamps reeled in their light on one side and let it flow out widely on the other; the leaves in the canopies of the trees pulled and tugged at their thin stems, or suddenly became quite still, as if on command; the clouds played high above the rooftops with the pale fire of the moon like dogs playing with a brown cat; pushed it, jumped over it, and when they retreated, it cowered with arched back, motionless in their midst. Ulrich had fallen in with Gerda and Hans Sepp; all three were surprised that it had already got dark.

Feuermaul had had an effect on Gerda. It seemed to her horribly ruthless that one is an "I," calmly mirrored in the eyes of a "you." She applied it to the whole nation. To universal love. It was a new emotion; how was it to be understood? One is no longer linked with just one other person. That's basically always horrible; one can't stir on account of the other; in spite of love one must feel a lot of resentment. It's also quite unnatural; the only natural thing is getting together to raise a brood, but not for one's whole life, and not because of oneself, or love. Individual love seemed to her like a snowman, hard, cold; on the other hand, if the same thing is spread like a blanket over the whole field . . . she imagined life beneath the pure soft snow cover that hovered before her, warm and protecting every seed. —Strange—Gerda thought—that I happened to think of a snowman! But then she still felt only the other, distant, soft, melting—even if that was not quite the case! —Loving many, many people! she said to herself softly. And it was like: Sleeping with everyone; but with no one so brutally to the very end, but only as in a dream that is never quite clear. Kissing everybody, but the way a child lets itself be stroked. To say something nice to everyone, but not giving anyone the right to forbid her saying it to his enemy as well . . . She felt happy and anxious as she portrayed this to herself, like a tender being that has to slip through rough hands until the hands, fumbling beside it, also learn to be tender.

"A happy-anxious soul": that had been in one of Feuermaul's poems, as if the poet had uttered this expression for no one else but her, the unknown girl. From far away word was dispatched to her, a man who knew nothing about her had sent out this word and still had no idea that the word had already found her; but she knew it, for she bore his word in her breast, which he would never see: That seemed to her like a marriage through magic. Gerda thought over whether she really had a happily anxious soul. She had one that constantly hovered between happiness and fear, without quite making contact with either. Was that the same thing? She was not certain of it, but she felt herself really hovering like a moonbeam in the roaring night, filled with love and free of all misfortune, which rarely happened to her. She squinted over at Ulrich, who was walking mutely beside her; he frightened her and only occasionally gave her a little happiness. Ulrich noticed that she was looking at him; he was angry with her. —The first time some blockhead babbles at you in verses you overflow! he said, smiling; but there was really some pain in this smile. —Didn't you notice that this person is the most vain and selfish creature in the world?

Gerda answered quite seriously. —You're right, he's weak; Stefan George is greater. She named her favorite poet—she knew that Ulrich had an aversion to him as well. She was a little drunk with happiness and felt: —I can love two people who hate each other. At this moment she was all love.

But at this moment Hans Sepp pushed forward from the other side; jealous restlessness impelled him, for Gerda and Ulrich had been speaking softly, and he only half understood; he did not want to be left out.

—Feuermaul is a prattler! he exclaimed angrily.

—Oh, why! Ulrich said.

—Because!

They were just passing beneath a streetlamp. Hans wanted to stop, because his mouth was full of words. But Ulrich did not stop. Hans was dragged on like a screaming child and emptied his words into the darkness. Gerda knew them all. The Beyond, contemplation, Christ, *Edda*, Gautama Buddha, and then the punishment meant for her: Feuermaul, as a Jew, had appropriated these things with his intelligence but inwardly had no idea what they were about. She looked straight ahead, and even at the next streetlamp did not look at Hans. In the darkness she felt his dark mouth wide open at her side. It made her shudder. She did not understand that Hans no longer knew what he was saying. The darkness was terrible for him. He imagined that the two of them were laughing at him. He knew no bounds, and his words poured out as if each were trying to trample the next, the way people do in a panic.

In between, Gerda heard Ulrich speaking quietly and objectively, seeking to divert this storm. —The emotional scribbler—he said—is in himself the most vain and self-seeking person in the world; something like women who have no understanding, only their love. What would happen if these people became you-seeking? . . .

Gerda liked Ulrich's words rather better than Hans's, but they, too, made her cold. With a hasty good-bye, she left the two of them standing there and ran up the steps. Hans gasped for air, hardly touched his hat, and left Ulrich.

But he stopped at the next corner and under cover of darkness looked to see what Ulrich was going to do. Ulrich went home, and Hans began to have regrets. He knew that Gerda's parents would be home late today; Gerda was alone, and he could imagine how much his churlish behavior must be eating at her. He saw light in a window and ran away in order not to go weak. But he only ran around the block, then without stopping went up the steps. He was still excited; his clothes sat on him angrily, the dark-blond hair over his forehead was standing crookedly in the air, and his cheeks had disappeared beneath his cheekbones.

—Forgive me! he begged. —I've behaved badly.

Gerda looked at him without understanding why he was there; her emotions had grown deaf.

—I don't know what I said, Hans went on. —It was probably something ugly. But you're so far gone that you can't even separate Jewish spuriousness and your ideals!

—Ulrich's not a Jew! Gerda said spontaneously. —And I forbid you— she added—to speak that way about Jews! For the first time she dared to say such a thing.

—I was speaking of Feuermaul! Hans corrected her. —But this Jewish poet we heard today might at least be said to have great and honest feelings if his race permitted it, but Ulrich, your father's friend, is ten times worse! Gerda was sitting in an easy chair and looked at Hans doubtingly. Hans was standing in front of her; her behavior unnerved him. —If someone acts—he said—like Feuermaul, as if he had seized hold of the true life, he's a swindler. The Beyond withholds itself; out-of-body contemplation reveals itself only rarely and intermittently. There are whole centuries that know nothing about it. But it is Germanic, nevertheless, never to lose the feeling here below of the Beyond that shimmers through.

—Since I have known you, every second thing you've said has been about out-of-body contemplation—Gerda countered, eager to attack— but you haven't ever, not one single time, really seen anything! Tell me what you've seen! Words!

Hans implored Gerda not to lose her strength! She ought not to be so sensitive, not want to be so clever! She should get away from this Ulrich!

—Where does "sensitive" come from? he exclaimed. —From the senses! It's sensualistic and base!

For heaven's sake, Gerda knew that; but it had never seemed to her so hurdy-gurdy. —If I want, I will also love a Jew, she thought, and thought of Feuermaul. A very gentle smile struggled with the anger in her face. Hans misunderstood it; he thought the tenderness in the resistance was for him. He was so excited by everything that had gone on before that he thought he would break into pieces right then and there. Over Gerda's face there is a breath of the Orient, it occurred to him at this moment, and in the same moment he thought he understood that what he loved most secretly about her was the other-racial, the Jewish; he, with his melancholy, who never felt sure of himself! Hans broke down. He hardly knew what was happening to him; he hid his face against Gerda's legs, and she felt that he was weeping in despair. That tore at her breast like the wild, covetous fingers of a small child; she, too, was suddenly excited, and tears were running down her cheeks without her knowing whether she was weeping over Hans, Feuermaul, herself, or Ulrich. So they gazed into each other's eyes with crumpled faces, when Hans raised his from her lap. He lifted himself half up and reached for her face. Youth's ecstatic desire for words came from his mouth. —There are only three ways back to the Great Truth, he exclaimed. —Suicide, madness, or making ourselves a symbol! She did not understand that. Why suicide or madness? She connected no filled-out notions with these words. —Perhaps Hans doesn't ever know exactly what he means, went through her head. But somehow, if one got free of oneself through suicide or madness, it seemed to be almost as high as being uplifted by some mystic union. Madness, death, and love have always been closely linked in the consciousness of humanity. She did not know why; she did not even think of posing such a question. But the three words, which made no sense as an idea, had somehow come together at this moment in a trembling young person who was holding Gerda's face in his hands as if he were holding in them the deepest import of his life. What they then went on talking about did not matter at all; the great experience was that they said to each other what shook them. Whoever would have heard them wouldn't have understood them; entwined, they pressed forward to God's knee and thought they saw His finger. It was possible, since this scene was being played out in the Fischels' dining room, that this finger pointing the way out of the world and into their own consisted partly of the tasteless self-conscious pictures and furnishings that gave them the feeling of having nothing to do with the universe of the bourgeois.

· · ·

One evening several days after this (the) musical evening in the studio, Gerda appeared at Ulrich's, after having called excitedly on the telephone. With a dramatic swoop she removed her hat from her head and threw it on a chair. To the question of what was up, she answered:
—Now everything's been blown sky-high!
—Has Hans run off?
—Papa's broke! Gerda laughed nervously at her slangy expression. Ulrich recalled that the last time he had been with Director Fischel he had wondered at the kind of telephone conversations the latter had been conducting from his house; but this recollection was not vivid enough to enable him to take Gerda's exclamation with complete seriousness.
—Papa was a gambler—imagine! the excited girl, struggling between merriment and despair, went on to explain. —We all thought he was a solid bank official with no great prospects, but yesterday evening it came out that the whole time he had been making the riskiest stock speculations! You ought to have been there for the blowup! Gerda threw herself on the chair beside her hat and boldly swung one leg over the other. —He came home as if he'd been pulled out of the river. Mama rushed at him with bicarbonate and chamomile, because she thought he was feeling ill. It was eleven-thirty at night; we were already asleep. Then he confessed that in three days he had to come up with lots of money and had no idea where it was to come from. Mama, splendid, offered him her dowry. Mama is always splendid; what would the few thousand crowns have meant to a gambler! But Papa went on to confess that Mama's little fortune had long since been lost along with everything else. What can I tell you? Mama screamed like a dog that's been run over. She had on nothing but her nightgown and slippers. Papa lay in an armchair and moaned. His job of course is also gone once this gets out. I tell you, it was pitiable!
—Shall I speak to your father? Ulrich asked. —I don't understand much about such things. Do you think he might do something to himself?
Gerda shrugged her shoulders. —Today he's trying to convince one of his unsullied business friends to help him. She suddenly turned gloomy. —I hope you don't think that that's why I've come to you? Mama moved out to her brother's today; she wanted to take me with her, but I won't go; I've run away from home—she had become cheerful again. —Do you know that behind the whole thing there's a woman, some sort of chanteuse? Mama found that out, and that was the last straw. Good for Papa! Who would ever have thought him capable of all that! And no, I

don't think he'll kill himself, she went on. —Because when it afterward came out about the woman, today, in the course of the day, he said some remarkable things: he would rather let himself be locked up and afterward earn his bread by hawking pornographic books than go on being Director Fischel with family!

—But what's most important to me—Ulrich asked—what do you intend to do?

—I'm staying with friends, Gerda said saucily. —You don't need to worry!

—With Hans Sepp and his friends! Ulrich exclaimed reproachfully.

—No one's going to bother me there!

Gerda inspected Ulrich's house. Like shadows, the memory of what had once happened here stepped out of the walls. Gerda felt herself to be a poor girl who possessed nothing outside of a few crowns, which in leaving she had, with amazing ease and freedom, taken from her mother's desk. She was sorry for herself. She was inclined to weep over herself as over a tragic figure on the stage. One really ought to do something good for her, she thought, but she hardly expected that Ulrich would take her comfortingly in his arms. Except that if he had, she would not have been such a coward as she had been the first time. But Ulrich said: —You won't let me help you now, Gerda, I see that; you're still much too proud of your new adventure. I can only say that I fear a bad outcome for you. Remember, please, that you always, without hesitation, can call upon me if you need to. He said this reflectively and hesitantly, for he really could have said something else that would have been more kind. Gerda had stood up, fiddled with her hat before the mirror, and smiled at Ulrich. She would have liked to kiss him good-bye, but then it might well not have come to a good-bye; and the stream of tears that was running invisibly behind her eyes bore her like a tenderly tragic music that one cannot interrupt out into the new life which she could still not quite picture to herself.

. . .

Hans Sepp was forced to double-step, kneel down in puddles in the barracks yard, present arms and put them down again until his arms fell off. The corporal torturing him was a green peasant boy, and Hans stared uncomprehendingly into his apoplectic young face, which expressed not only anger, which would have been understandable because he was forced to do extra duty with this recruit, but all the malice of which a person is capable when he lets himself go. If Hans let his glance roam across the breadth of the yard—and a barracks yard has in and of itself something inhuman, some locked-in regularity of the sort the dead world of crystals has—it rested on squatting and stiffly running blue figures painted on all the walls, meant to be assaulted with one's weapon; and this universal goal of being shot at was expressed in the abstract manner of these paintings well enough to drive one to despair. This had already weighed down Hans Sepp's heart in the first hour of his arrival. The people in these pictures painted on the barracks walls had no faces, but instead of faces only a bright area. Nor did they have bodies that the painter had captured in one of those positions such as people and animals, following the play of their needs, assume of themselves, but bodies that consisted of a crude outline filled in with dark-blue paint, capturing for an eternity the attitude of a man running with a weapon in his hand, or a man kneeling and shooting, an eternity in which there will never again be anything so superfluous as the drawing of individual people. This was by no means unreasonable; the technical term for these figures was "target surfaces," and if a person is regarded as a target surface, that is the way he looks; this cannot be explained away (changed). From this one might conclude that one should never be allowed to regard a person as a target surface; but for heaven's sake, if that is the way he looks the minute you lay eyes on him, the temptation to look at him that way is enormous! Hans felt drawn again and again, during the tedium of his punishment drill, by the demonic nature of these pictures, as if he were being tortured by devils; the corporal screamed at him that he was not to gawk around but to look straight ahead; with such raw language he literally seized him by the eyes, and when Hans's glance then fell straight ahead, on the corporal's red face, this face looked warm and human.

Hans had the primitive sensation of having fallen into the hands of a strange tribe and been made a slave. Whenever an officer appeared and glided past on the other side of the yard, an uninvolved, slender silhouette, he seemed to Hans Sepp like one of the inexorable gods of this alien tribe. Hans was treated severely and badly. An official communication from the civil authorities had come to the army at the same time he had, characterizing him as "politically unreliable," and in Kakania that was the term used for individuals hostile to the state. He had no idea who or what had gained him this reputation. Except for his participation in the demonstration against Count Leinsdorf, he had never undertaken anything against the state, and Count Leinsdorf was not the state; since he had become a student, Hans Sepp had spoken only of the community of Germanic peoples, of symbols, and of chastity. But something must have come to the ear of the authorities, and the ear of the authorities is like a piano from which seven of every eight strings have been removed.

Perhaps his reputation had been exaggerated; at any rate, he came to the army with the reputation of being an enemy of war, the military, religion, the Habsburgs, and the Austrian state, suspected of plotting in secret associations and pan-German intrigues directed at "the goal of overthrowing the existing order of the state."

But the situation in the Kakanian military with regard to all these crimes was such that the greatest part of all capable reserve officers could be accused of them without further ado. Almost every German Austrian had the natural sentiment of solidarity with the Germans in the Reich and of being only provisionally separated from it by the sluggish capacity of the historical process, while every non-German Austrian had (making the necessary allowances) twice as much feeling of this kind directed against Kakania; patriotism in Kakania, to the extent that it was not limited to purveyors to the Court, was distinctly a phenomenon of opposition, betraying either a spirit of contradiction or that tepid opposition to life which constantly has need of something finer and higher. The only exception to this was Count Leinsdorf and his friends, who had the "higher" in their blood. But the active officers (of the standing army) were also just as implicated in these reproaches that an unknown authority had raised against Hans Sepp. These officers were for the most part German Austrians, and insofar as they were not, they admired the German army; and since the Kakanian parliament did not appropriate half as many soldiers or warships as the German Reichstag, they all felt that not everything about the pan-Germanic claims could be reprehensible. Then too, they were all antidemocratic and latent revolutionaries. They had been raised from childhood to be the bulwark of patriotism, with the result that this word aroused in them a silent nausea. They had finally got used to leading their soldiers in the Corpus Christi procession and letting the recruits practice "kneel down for prayers" in the barracks yard, but among themselves they called the regimental chaplain Corporal Christ, and for the rank of field bishop, which was associated with a certain fullness of body, these heathens had thought up the army name "skyball."

When they were among themselves, they did not even take it amiss if someone was an enemy of the military, for over a fairly long period of service most of them had become that way themselves, and there were even pacifists in Kakania's army. But this does not mean that later on, in the war, they did not do their duty with as much enthusiasm as their comrades in other countries; on the contrary, one always thinks differently from the way one acts. This fact, of such extraordinary importance for the condition of world civilization as we know it today, is ordinarily understood to mean that thinking is a charming habit of the individual citizen, without damaging which, when it comes to action, one joins in with what is customary and what everyone is doing. This is not quite true, however, for there are people who are totally unoriginal in their thinking; but when *they* act, they often do so in a very personal way, which, because it is more appealing, is superior to their ideas, or, because it is more common, inferior to them, in any case more idiosyncratic. One comes closer to the truth if one does not stop with the object of the action, as opposed to the idea, but recognizes from the beginning that one is dealing with two different kinds of ideas. A person's idea ceases to be only an idea whenever a second person thinks something similar, and between these two something happens, even if it is only being aware of each other, that makes them a pair. Even then the idea is no longer pure possibility but acquires an additional component of ancillary considerations. But this might be a sophism or an artifice. Nevertheless, the fact remains that every powerful idea goes out into the world of reality and permeates it the way energy enters a malleable material and finally rigidifies in it, without entirely losing its effectiveness as an idea. Everywhere, in schools, in lawbooks, in the aspect of houses in the city and fields in the country, in newspaper offices awash in currents of superficiality, in men's trousers and women's hats, in everything where people exercise and receive influence, ideas are encapsulated or dissolved in varying degrees of fixity and content. This is of course no more than a platitude, but we are hardly always aware of its extent, for it really amounts to nothing less than a monstrous, inside-out, third half of the brain. This third half does not think; it emits emotions, habits, experiences, limits, and directions, nothing but unconscious or half-conscious influences, among which individual thinking is as much and as little as a tiny candle flame in the stony darkness of a gigantic warehouse. And not last among these are the ideas held in reserve, which are stored like uniforms for wartime. The moment something extraordinary begins to spread, they climb out of their petrification. Every day bells peal, but when a big fire breaks out or a people is called to arms, one sees for the first time the sort of feelings that have been clanging and churning inside them. Every day the newspapers casually write certain sentences that they habitually use to characterize habitual happenings, but if a revolution threatens or something new is about to happen, it suddenly appears that these words no longer suffice and that in order to ward off or welcome, one must reach back for the oldest hats in the store and the spooks in the closet. The mind enters every great general mobilization, whether for peace or for war, unequipped and laden down with forgotten things.

Hans had fallen into this disproportion between the personal and the general, between living and reserve principles. In other circumstances, people would have been satisfied to find him not very likable, but the official document had raised him out of the midst of private individuals and made him an object of public thought, and had admonished his superiors that they were to apply to him not their uneducated, highly variable personal feelings, but the generally accepted ones that made them vexed and bored and that can at any moment degenerate wildly, like the actions of a drunk or a hysteric who feels quite distinctly that he is stuck inside his frenzy as inside a strange, oversize husk.

But one should not think that Hans was being mistreated, or that impermissible things were being done to him: on the contrary, he was treated strictly according to regulations. All that was missing was that iota of human warmth—no, one cannot call it warmth; but coal, fuel, on hand to be used on a suitable occasion—which even in a barracks still finds a niche. Through the absence of the possibility of any personal sympathy, the right-angled buildings, the monotonous walls with the blue figures, the ruler-straight corridors with the innumerable parallel diagonal lines of guns hanging on them, and the trumpet signals and regulations that divided up the day, all had the effect of the clear, cold crystallizing of a spirit that till then had been alien to Hans Sepp, that spirit of the commonality, of public life, of impersonal community, or whatever it should be called, which had created this building and these forms.

The most crushing thing was that he felt that his whole spirit of contradiction had been blown away. He could, of course, have thought of himself as a missionary being tortured by some Indian tribe. Or he could have expunged the din of the world from his senses and immersed himself in the currents of the transcendental. He could have looked upon his sufferings as a symbol, and so forth. But since a military cap had been clapped on his head, all these thoughts had become like impotent shadows. The sensitive world of the mind paled to a specter, which here, where a thousand people lived together, could not penetrate. His mind was desolate and withered.

Hans Sepp had settled Gerda with the mother of one of his friends. He saw her rarely, and then he was mostly surly from fatigue and despair. Gerda wanted to make herself independent; she did not want anything from him; but she had no way of understanding the events to which he was exposed. Several times she had had the idea of picking him up after his daily duty, as if he were his usual self and was just coming from some kind of event. Lately he had taken to avoiding her. He did not even have the strength to let it bother him. In the pauses during the day, those irregular pauses that fell at the most useless times, he hung around with the other conscripts doing their year of military service, drank brandy and coffee in the canteen, and sat in the disconsolate flood of their conversations and jokes as in a dirty creek, without being able to make up his mind to stand up. Now for the first time he came to hate the soldier class, because he felt himself subjected to its influence. —My mind is now nothing more than the lining of a military coat, he said to himself; but he felt astonishingly tempted to test the new movements in this clothing. It happened that even after duty he stayed with the others and tried out the rather coarse diversions of these half-independent young people.

·   ·   ·

An elegant gentleman had his car stop and called out to Ulrich; with effort Ulrich recognized in the self-confident apparition (that leaned out of the elegant vehicle) Director Leo Fischel. —You're in luck! Fischel called to him. —My secretary's been trying for weeks to get hold of you! She was always told you were away. —He was exaggerating, but this magisterial confidence in his manner was genuinely impressive.

Ulrich said softly: —I thought I'd find you in much different shape.

—What have you been hearing about me? Fischel probed, curious.

—I think pretty much everything. For a long time I've been expecting to hear about you through the newspapers.

—Nonsense! Women always exaggerate. Won't you accompany me home? I'll tell you all about it.

The house had changed, taken on an aura of the top offices of some business enterprise or other, and had become totally unfeminine. But Fischel said nothing specific. He was more concerned with shoring up his reputation with Ulrich. He treated his departure from the bank as a minor incident. —What did you expect? I could have stayed there for ten years without getting anywhere! My leaving was entirely amicable. He had taken on such a self-important manner of speaking that Ulrich felt constrained to express his dry astonishment at it. —But you had ruined yourself so completely—he said inquiringly—that people assumed you had to either shoot yourself or end up in court.

—I'd never shoot myself, I'd poison myself, Leo corrected. —I wouldn't do anyone the favor of dying like an aristocrat or a section chief! But it wasn't at all necessary. Do you know what a "starching," a transitory illiquidity, is? Well! My family made a ridiculous to-do about it that they're very sorry for today!

—By the way, you never said a word—Ulrich exclaimed, having just thought of it—about becoming Leona's friend; I should at least have had the right to know *that!*

—Do you have any idea how this woman behaved toward me? Shameless! Her upbringing!

—I always left Leona the way she is. I suppose that with her natural stupidity she'll end up in a few years as a pensioner in a brothel.

—Far from it! Moreover, I'm not as heartless as you, my friend. I've tried to arouse Leona's reason a little and, so to speak, her economic understanding, as far as they apply to the exploitation of her body. And on the evening when my illiquidity began to make itself palpable to me, I went to her to borrow a few hundred crowns, which I assumed Leona would have laid aside. You ought to have heard this harpy scolding me for being a skinflint, a robber; she even cursed my religion! The one thing she didn't claim was that I had robbed her of her innocence. But you're wrong about Leona's future; do you know who her friend is now, right after me?

He bent over to Ulrich and whispered a name in his ear; he did this more out of respect than because the whispering was necessary.

—What do you say to that? You have to admit she's a beauty.

Ulrich was astounded. The name Fischel had whispered to him was Arnheim.

Ulrich asked after Gerda. Fischel blew his soul's breath out through pursed lips; his face became anxious and betrayed secret worries. He raised his shoulders and slackly let them fall again. —I thought that you might know where she's staying.

—I have a suspicion—Ulrich answered—but I don't know. I assume she's taken a job.

—Job! As what? As governess in a family with small children! Just think, she takes a job as a domestic servant when she could have every luxury! Just yesterday I concluded a deal on a house, top location, with an apartment that's a palace by itself: But no, no, no! Fischel beat his face with his fists; his pain about his daughter was genuine, or at least was the genuine pain that she was preventing him from enjoying his victory completely.

—Why don't you turn to the police? Ulrich asked.

—Oh, please! I can't advertise my family affairs to the world! Besides, I want to, but my wife won't hear of it. I immediately paid my wife back what I had lost of hers; her high-and-mighty brothers aren't going to wear out their mouths about me! And in the last analysis, Gerda is as much her child as mine. In that line I'm not going to do anything without

her agreement. Half the day she rides around in my car and searches her
eyes out. Of course that's absurd; that's not the way to go about it. But
what can one do when one's married to a woman!

—I thought your divorce was under way?

—It was. That is, only verbally. Not yet legally. The lawyers had just
fired the first shots when my situation visibly improved. I don't know
myself what our current relation is; I believe Clementine is waiting for a
discussion. Of course she's still living at her brother's.

—But then why don't you simply hire a private detective to find
Gerda? Ulrich interrupted, having just thought of it.

—Good idea, Fischel replied.

—She can be tracked down through Hans Sepp!

—My wife intends to drive out to Hans Sepp yet again one of these
days and work on him; he's not saying anything.

—Oh, you know what? Hans must be doing his military service now;
don't you remember? He got a six-month postponement on account of
some exams he had to take, which he ended up not taking. He must have
gone in two weeks ago; I can say that precisely because it was very
unusual, since around this time only the medical students are called up.
So your wife will hardly find him. On the other hand, his feet could really be held to the fire through his superiors. You understand, if someone there squeezes him between his fingers, it will really loosen his
tongue!

—Splendid, and thank you! I hope my wife will see that too. For as I
said, without Clementine I don't want to undertake anything in this direction; otherwise I'll immediately be accused again of being a murderer!

Ulrich had to smile. —Freedom seems to have made you anxious, my
dear Fischel.

Fischel had always been easily irritated by Ulrich; now that he had
become an important man, even more so. —You exaggerate freedom—
he said dismissively—and it appears that you've never quite understood
my position. Marriage is often a struggle as to who is the stronger; extraordinarily difficult as long as it involves feelings, ideas, and fantasies!
But not difficult at all as soon as one is successful in life. I have the impression that even Clementine is beginning to realize that. One can
argue for weeks over whether an opinion is correct. But as soon as one is
successful, it is the opinion of a man who might have been mistaken but
who needs this incidental error for his success. In the worst case, it's like
the hobbyhorse of some great artist; and what does one do with the hob-
byhorses of great artists? One loves them; one knows that they're a little
secret. Since Ulrich was laughing freely, Fischel did not want to stop

talking. —Listen to what I'm telling you! Pay close attention! I said that if one has no other ambitions / nothing to do / has nothing / besides feelings and ideas, the quarrel is endless. Ideas and feelings make one petty and neurotic. Unfortunately, that's what happened with me and Clementine. Today I have no time. I don't even know for certain whether Clementine wants to come back to me; I only believe that she does; she's sorry, and sooner or later that will come out of itself, but then most certainly in a simpler and better way than if I were to think out down to the last detail how it has to come about. You could never do business, either, with a plan that is unhealthily pinned down in every detail!

Fischel was almost out of breath, but he felt free. Ulrich had been listening to him seriously, and did not contradict. —I'm quite relieved that everything has taken a turn for the better, he said politely. —Your wife is an excellent woman, and when it will be advantageous for you to have a great house, she will fulfill that task admirably.

—Exactly. That too. Soon we'll be able to celebrate our silver anniversary, and joking aside, if the money is new, the character at least ought to be old. A silver anniversary is worth almost as much as an aristocratic grandmother, which, moreover, she also has.

Ulrich got up to leave, but Fischel was now in high spirits. —But you shouldn't think that Leona managed to clip my wings! I left her to Dr. Arnheim with no envy whatsoever. Do you know the dancer . . . He mentioned an unfamiliar name and pulled a small photo from his wallet. —Well, where should you know her from, she has seldom appeared in public; private dance evenings, distinguished, Beethoven and Debussy, you know, that's now the coming thing. But what I wanted to tell you: you're an athlete, can you manage this? He stepped over to a table and accompanied his words with an echo of arm and leg. —For instance, she lies this way on a table. The upper body flat on the top, her face leaning with one ear on her propped-up arms, and smiling deliciously. But at the same time her legs are spread apart, like this, along the narrow edge of the table, so that it looks like a big T. Or she suddenly stands on her forearms and palms—like this—of course I can't do it. And she has one foot way over her head and almost on the ground, the other against the cabinet up there. I tell you, you couldn't do a tenth of it, in spite of your gymnastics. That's the modern woman. She's lovelier than we, cleverer than we, and I believe that if I tried to box with her I'd soon be clutching my belly. The only thing in which a man is stronger today than a woman is in earning money!

. . .

Who had been responsible for Hans Sepp's receiving his black mark? Remarkably enough, it was Count Leinsdorf. Count Leinsdorf had one day asked Ulrich about this young man, and Ulrich had presented him as a harmless muddlehead; but Count Leinsdorf had recently taken to mistrusting Ulrich, and this information confirmed his conviction that in Hans Sepp he had before him one of those irresponsible elements who are continually preventing anything good from being done in Kakania. Count Leinsdorf had lately become nervous. He had heard through General Director Leo Fischel that a quite distinct group of immature young people that had formed around Hans Sepp had been the real instigator of the demonstration that had caused His Excellency more unpleasantness than might be supposed. For this political procession had created "a quite unfavorable impression upstairs." There was no question that it was completely harmless, and that if one had seriously wanted to prevent such a thing it could be done by a handful of police at any time; but the impression such events make is always much more terrifying than they actually merit, and no true politician dares neglect impressions. Count Leinsdorf had had serious discussions about this with his friend the Commissioner of Police, which had not produced any results, and when Count Leinsdorf afterward learned the name of Hans Sepp, the Commissioner was quite ready to have this lead followed up in order to appease His Excellency. The Commissioner had been convinced from the start that any findings that might have previously escaped his police would be trifling, and was only confirmed in this opinion by the results of the inquiries he had ordered. But still, the preoccupation of a bureaucracy with an individual always leads to the conclusion that this individual is shady and unreliable, that is to say, as measured by the standards of precision and security according to the rules and regulations one applies in a bureaucracy. For this reason the Commissioner found it expedient, when there was room for doubt, not to reproach a man like Count Leinsdorf for imagining things but rather to allow the case of Hans Sepp to be treated according to the model that at the moment nothing could be proved against the suspect, on which account he only remained under suspicion until the matter could be completely cleared up. This complete clearing up was tacitly set for Saint Never-Plus-One's Day, when all the files that are still open rise up from the graves of the archives. That in spite of this it brought suffering on Hans Sepp was a totally impersonal matter, which did not involve trickery of any kind. A buried open file must from time to time be raised from its grave in order to note on it that it is still not possible to close it, and to mark it with a date on which the archivist is again to present it to his supervisor. This is a universal law of bureaucracy, and if it should involve a file that was never intended to be closed, on the pretext that its documentation was not complete, one must pay very close attention, for it can happen that bureaucrats are promoted, transferred, and die, and that a neophyte receiving the file causes, in his excessive zeal, a small supplementary investigation to be added to one of the last investigations that took place years ago, which causes the file to be kept alive for a few weeks until the investigation ends as a report to be inserted in, and disappear with, the file. Through some such process Hans Sepp's file, too, had, without any particular purpose, become current; since Hans Sepp happened to be in the army, his file had to go to the Ministry of Justice, from there to the Ministry of War, and from there to the Commanding Officer, etc., and it is easy to understand how, handed on through the various in and out stamps, presentation stamps, confirmations of action, additions with bureaucratic courtesy, Relinquished, For Report, Not Known in this Office, and such, this file took on a dangerous appearance.

Meanwhile, in desperation, Gerda had run to Ulrich and reported that Hans had to be rescued, because he was not up to the conditions he had fallen into and was already clearly showing alarming signs of cracking up completely. She had still not returned to her parents' house, kept her whereabouts hidden, and was quite proud at having found some piano lessons to give and being able to add a few pennies to the money her friends lent her. At that time Leo Fischel was making the most strenuous efforts to win her back, and so Ulrich intervened as mediator. After long back-and-forth and paternal admonitions, Gerda let herself be talked into considering favorably a promise to move back to her parents' if Papa would declare himself ready and bring about, and Ulrich would support, freeing Hans from his doom. Ulrich spoke with General Director Fischel about it, and General Director Fischel had by then done many a worse thing than was now being asked of him in order to get his daughter back. He turned to Count Leinsdorf. General Director Leo Fischel was actively involved in business relations with Count Leinsdorf; after some commiseration and reflection, His Excellency recommended him to Diotima, who at the moment was on intimate footing with the Ministry of War and, for this reason too more suitable than he was, because this whole affair, especially because of the slightly irregular solution required, was more the province of woman, of the heart, and of feminine tact. In this way Leo Fischel came to Diotima.

Count Leinsdorf had already prepared her for the visit, and she made a powerful impression on Fischel. He had thought that the time when anything intellectual could compel his admiration lay behind him. But it appeared that beautiful women were especially qualified to soften his newly acquired hardness. He had had his first relapse with Leona. Leona had a face of the sort that General Director Fischel's parents would have admired, and this face again came to his mind when he saw Diotima, although there was really no similarity. At that time, the most miserable drawing teacher or photographer would not have been at peace with himself if he had not felt in his hair or his necktie some breath of genius. For this reason Leona, too, was not simply beautiful for Leo but a genius of beauty; that was the special charm through which she had led him astray into risky undertakings. —A pity she had such a mean character, Fischel thought. —Her long fat legs were a long sight lovelier than the desiccated legs of these modern dancers. He did not know whether it was the desiccated legs or the unpleasant character that made him think of his wife, Clementine, but at any rate he remembered with emotion the happy years of his marriage, for then Clementine and he had still believed in the value of genius, and if one considers this in a well-disposed way, it was not so misplaced; the line of Leo Fischel's life, looked at in this light, showed no break, for in the last analysis the belief that there were privileged geniuses was a possible way of justifying ruthless and risky deals. Diotima possessed the quality of awakening such ideas that roam through the far reaches of the soul when one sat opposite her for the first time, and General Director Fischel meanwhile needed only to brush his hands through his sideburns once and set his pince-nez to rights before he began to speak with a sigh. Diotima confirmed this sigh with a motherly smile, and before Fischel even got to what he wanted to say, this woman with a wholly justified reputation for her gift of empathy said: —I have been told the purpose of your visit. It is sad; humanity today suffers grievously from its failure to produce more geniuses, while on the other hand it denies and persecutes every young talent that might perhaps develop into one.

Fischel ventured the question: —You have heard what's happening to my protégé? He's a troublemaker. Well, and what of it? All great people were troublemakers in their youth. I do not, by the way, in the least condone it. But he was also, if you will permit me the observation, a forceps birth; his head was somewhat compressed; he is extremely irritable, and I thought that that might perhaps be a way . . . ?

Diotima raised her eyebrows sadly. —I spoke about it with one of the leading gentlemen of the War Ministry; unfortunately, I must tell you, General Director, that your request is meeting with almost insurmountable difficulties.

Sadly and indignantly Fischel raised his hands. —But one cannot force an intellectual person when it goes against the intellect! The fellow has some ideas about refusing service in wartime, and the gentlemen will end up shooting him on me!

—Yes, Diotima replied. —You are so right! One should not force an intellectual when it goes against the intellect. You are voicing my own opinion. But how is one to make a general understand that?

A pause ensued. Fischel almost thought he should leave, but when he scraped his feet Diotima laid a hand on his arm with mute permission to remain. She seemed to be thinking. Fischel racked his brains to see if he could help her find a good idea. He would have gladly offered her money for the leading gentleman of the War Ministry she had mentioned; but such an idea was at that time absurd. Fischel felt helpless. —A Midas! occurred to him; why, he did not exactly know, and he sought to recollect this ancient legend, without quite being able to. The lenses of his spectacles almost misted over with emotion.

At this moment Diotima brightened. —I believe, General Director, that I perhaps might indeed be able to help you a little. I would in any case be delighted if I could. I can't get over the idea that an intellectual can't be forced against the intellect! Of course, it would be better not to talk too much to the gentlemen of the War Ministry about the nature of this intellect.

Leo Fischel obligingly concurred with this circumspection.

—But this case has also, so to speak, a maternal side—Diotima went on—a feminine, unlogical aspect; I mean, given so-and-so many thousands of soldiers, just one can't be so important. I'll try to make clear to a high officer who is a friend of mine that out of political considerations His Excellency considers it important to have this young man mustered out; the right people should always be put in the right places, and your future son-in-law is not of the slightest use in a barracks, whereas he . . . well, somehow that's the way I see it. Unfortunately, the military is uncommonly resistant to exceptions. But what I hope is that we can at least get the young man a fairly long leave, and then we can think what to do about the rest.

Charmed, Leo Fischel bent over Diotima's hand. This woman had won his complete confidence.

The visit was not without its effect on his way of thinking either. For understandable reasons, he had lately become quite materialistic. His experiences of life had led him to the viewpoint that a right-thinking man had to watch out for himself. Be independent; need nothing from others for which you did not have something they wanted in return: but that is also a Protestant feeling, much as it was for the first colonists in America. Leo Fischel still loved to philosophize, even though his time for it had become much more limited. His affairs now sometimes brought him into contact with the high clergy. He discovered that it is the mistake of all religions to teach virtue as something which is only negative, as abstinence and selflessness; this makes it anachronistic and gives the deals one has to make an aura of something like secret vice. On the other hand, the public religion of efficiency, as he met it in Germany through his business, had seized hold of him. People are glad to help a capable and enterprising person; in other words, he can get credit anywhere: this was a positive formula that allowed one to get somewhere. It taught one to be ready to help without reckoning on gratitude, just as Christian teaching demands, although it did not include the uncertainty of having to rely on noble feeling in someone else, but made use of egotism as the single dependable human quality, which it without doubt is. And money is a tool of genius that makes it possible to calculate and regulate this basic quality. Money is ordered selfishness brought into relation with efficiency. An enormous organization of selfishness according to the hierarchical order of how it is earned. It is a creative umbrella organization built on baseness—emperors and kings have not tamed the passions the way money has. Fischel often wondered what human demiurge might have invented money. If everything were to be accessible to money, and every matter to have its price, which unfortunately is still far from being the case, then any other morality besides the existence of trade would be of no use at all. This was his opinion and his conviction. Even during the time when he had revered the great ideas of humanity, he had always felt a certain aversion to them in the mouth of anybody else. If someone simply says "virtue" or "beauty," there is something as unnatural and affected about it as when an Austrian speaks in the past tense. Now even that had increased. His life was consumed by work, striving for power, efficiency, and the dependence on the greatness of affairs, which he had to observe and exploit. The intellectual and spiritual spheres came to seem to him more and more like clouds having no connection with the earth. But he was no happier. He felt himself somehow weakened. Every amusement seemed to him more superficial than before. He increased his stimuli, with the result that he succeeded only in making himself more distracted. He made fun of his daughter, but secretly he envied her her ideas.

And as Diotima had spoken so naturally and freely of maternal feeling, soul, mind, and goodness, he was constantly thinking: —What a mother this would be for Gerda! (? wife for you) He wept inside to hear the beauty of her speech, and he had great satisfaction in noticing how these great words gave birth to a tiny element of corruption—however elegantly—for she was ultimately fulfilling his request, whatever reasons might have been behind it. In certain cases, when there is a question of some injustice, idealism is almost better than naked calculation; this was the teaching that Fischel drew directly from the impressions of his visit, and that he intended to think about urgently on his further course.

. . .

Hans Sepp had left the barracks and not shown up for duty, although he had been transferred from the hospital back to his company. He knew that his return would entail the most unbearable consequences; being punished like an animal and, still worse—for punishment is solitary—beforehand the dull, set face of the captain and the necessity of having to be interrogated by him. Hans knew that he had made up his mind not to go back. For the first time the holy fire of defiance again flared up in him, and the unbending sense of purity that avoids contamination with the impure flashed through him. This made even more of a torture the memory that he had lost the right to it. He considered his illness incurable and was convinced that he had been sullied for the rest of his life. He had resolved to kill himself; he had left the barracks to completely cut off a return to life; the thought that in a few hours he would have killed himself was the only thing that could to some degree substitute for his self-respect, even if it could not restore it.

In order not to be immediately recognized if they should be looking for him, he had put on civilian clothes. He walked through the city on foot, for he felt incapable of taking a cab; he had a long route before him, as it had seemed to him for some reason a matter of course that he would kill himself only in the open countryside. He actually could have done it on the way, in the middle of the city; presumably, certain ceremonies merely serve to postpone the business a bit, and among these Hans included a last glimpse of nature; but he was not at all one of those people who think about such questions in a situation such as the one he was now in. The famous dark veil that arises when the moisture content of the emotions becomes extreme without precipitating tears lay before his eyes, and the noises of the world echoed softly. Passing cars, the throng of people, housefronts stretching for blocks, all looked like a bas-relief. The tears that Hans Sepp did not want to shed outwardly in public or for other reasons nonetheless fell through him inwardly as if down an incredibly deep, dark shaft onto his own grave, in which he already felt himself lying, which signifies about the same thing as that he was simultaneously sitting beside it and grieving for himself. There is in all this a force that is very cheering, and by the time Hans got to the city line, where the train tracks ran upon which he wanted to throw himself as soon as a train came along, his grief had become attached to and affiliated with so many things that it really felt quite good. The stretch he was on was apparently not well traveled, and Hans had to tell himself that upon arriving he would have immediately thrown himself in front of a train had one happened to be passing by at that instant, but that not knowing the schedule, he could not simply lie down on the tracks and wait. He sat down among the sparse vegetation on the slope at the top of a cut where the railway made a curve, and he could see in both directions. A train passed, but he gave himself time. He observed the incredible increase in speed that takes place when the train shoots, as it were, through one's vicinity, and listened to the din of the wheels in order to be able to picture how he was going to be pounded in it by the next train. This clanging and bawling seemed, in contrast to what he saw, to last for an extraordinary length of time, and Hans turned cold.

The question of what had made him want to end his life by means of a railway train was not at all clear. Hanging had something distorted and spooky. Jumping out a window is a woman's way. He had no poison. To cut his veins he needed a bathtub. On this path of eliminating other possibilities, he pursued methodically the same course he had taken in blind determination with a single step: it satisfied him; his instincts had not yet been affected. To be sure, he had left out death by shooting; he thought of it now for the first time. But Hans did not own a pistol, nor did he know what to do with one, and he did not want to share his last moment with his army rifle. He had to be free of small misfortunes when he exited this life. This reminded him that he had to prepare himself inwardly. He had sinned and contaminated himself: he had to hold on to that. Someone else in his situation might perhaps have hoped for the prospect of recovery; but while recovery might be possible, salvation was irrevocably lost. Involuntarily, Hans pulled out of his coat his little notebook and a pencil; but before he could jot down his idea, he remembered that this was now quite pointless. He idly held notebook and pencil in his hands. His whole mind was directed at the phrase that he had become impure and godless. There was a lot to be said about that. For instance, that Christianity, influenced by Judaism, permitted sin to be redeemed through remorse and penitence, while the pure, Teutonic idea of being healthy and whole permitted of no bargaining or trading. Wholeness is lost once and for all, like virginity; and of course that is precisely where the greatness and challenge of the idea lies. Where today does one find such greatness? Nowhere. Hans was convinced that the world would suffer a great loss from his having to eliminate himself. The size and force of a train was really almost the only possible way of expressing the size and force of such a case. Another one went past. This technological marvel was small and tiny if one compared it to the astronomical construction techniques of the Egyptians and Assyrians, but at all events a train almost succeeded in enabling the present to express itself gothically, yearning outward beyond the limitations of matter. Hans raised his hand and almost irresolutely waved at people, who waved back and shoved their heads out the window in bunches, like the people-grapes on ancient naïve sculptures. This made him feel better, but feeling good, grief, and everything he could think of was simply like smoke, and when it had drifted away the sentence that Hans Sepp had become impure and was not to be saved lay there again, undisturbed; nothing lasting was connected with it, the idea no longer wished to grow. If Hans had been sitting at home before a table with pen and paper, it perhaps might have turned out otherwise; it was just this that gave him the feeling that he was here for no other purpose than to put an end to his existence.

He snapped the pencil in two and tore the notebook into little pieces. That was a major step. Then he climbed down the slope, sat in the grass at the edge of the gravel ballast, and threw the shreds of his intellectual world in front of the next train. The train scattered them. Nothing was to be found of the pencil; the bright paper butterflies, broken on the wheels and sucked up, covered the right-of-way on both sides for five hundred paces. Hans calculated that he was approximately twelve times larger than the notebook. Then he seized his head in both hands and began his final farewell. This pulling everything together was to be devoted to Gerda. He wanted to forgive her and, without leaving her a written word, to die with the all-embracing thought of her on his lips. But even though all kinds of thoughts appeared and disappeared in his mind, his body remained quite empty. It seemed down here in the narrow cut that he could not feel anything and needed to go and sit up above again in order to embrace Gerda once more in his mind. But it seemed silly, it annoyed him to have to crawl up the slope. Gradually the emptiness in his body increased and became hunger. —That's my mind beginning to disintegrate, he told himself. Since his illness, he had lived in constant fear of going insane. He had let train after train go by and had sat down here in the narrow, stupid world of the railway cut without thinking of anything at all. It might already be late afternoon. Then Hans Sepp became aware, as if someone suddenly turned something around in him, that this was his final state, to be succeeded only by its execution. He had the nauseating feeling of an imaginary skin eruption over his whole body. He pulled out his pocket knife and cleaned his nails with it; this was an ill-bred habit he had, which he considered very tidy and elegant; it made him want to cry. Hesitantly he stood up. Everything inside him had receded from him. He was afraid, but he was no longer master of himself; the sole master was the irrevocable resolve that ruled alone in a dark vacuum. Hans looked left and right. One might say that he had already died as he looked in both directions for a train, for this looking was all that was alive in him, this and isolated feelings that drifted past like clumps of grass in a flood. For he no longer knew what to do with himself. He still noticed that his head commanded his legs to leap before the train approached; but his legs were no longer paying attention, they sprang when they wanted to, at the last minute, and Hans's body was struck in the air. He still felt himself plunging down, falling on great sharp knives. Then his world burst into fragments.

.   .   .

Gerda had come back. After Hans's death she had, for the moment, nothing to live for. But if Fischel had expected to find his daughter crushed, he was mistaken. A young lady who obviously had far-reaching plans walked in, wearing the insignia of a Red Cross nurse.

—I'm going to go as a nurse, Papa, Gerda said.

—Not right away, not right away, my child! General Director Fischel answered submissively. —We have to wait and see. No one has any idea what this is going to turn into—

—What should it turn into! I've already seen the young men at the mobilization stations. They're singing. Their wives and fiancées are with them. No one knows how he is going to come back. But if you walk through the city and look in people's eyes, including the people who aren't going to the front yet, it's like a big wedding.

Fischel, concerned, looked at his daughter over his glasses. —I would wish another kind of wedding for you, may God preserve us. A Dutch firm has offered me a shipful of margarine, available at the port of Rotterdam—do you know what that means? Five crowns difference per ton since yesterday! If I don't telegraph right away, tomorrow it will probably be seven crowns. That means prices are going up. If they come back from the campaign with both eyes, the young men will need them both to look out for their money!

—Well—Gerda said—people are talking about increases, but there have always been increases at the beginning. Mama is quite wild too.

—Oh? Fischel asked. —Have you already talked with Mama? What's she up to?

—At the moment, she's in the kitchen—Gerda motioned with her head toward the wall, behind which a hall led to the kitchen—and laying in canned goods like mad. Before that, she cashed in her change, like everyone else. And she fired the kitchen maid; since the manservant has to go in the army anyway, she wants to really cut down on the servants.

Fischel nodded with satisfaction. —She's in favor of the war. She hopes the brutality will cease and people will be purified. But she is also a clever woman and is being prudent. Fischel said this a little mockingly and a little tenderly.

—Oh, Papa. Gerda flared up. —If I had wanted to be the way you are, I would have married a knight in shining armor. You keep misunderstanding me. I'm not letting myself be left by the wayside because my first romantic experience wasn't a good one! You'll manage to get me into a field hospital. When the patients come in from the front they should find real, up-to-date people as nurses, not praying nuns! You have no idea how much love and emotion of a sort we've never experienced before are (to be seen) in the streets today! We've been living like animals, brought down one day by death; it's different now! It's tremendous, I tell you: everyone is a brother; even death isn't an enemy; a person loves his own death for the sake of others; today, for the first time, we understand life!

Fischel had been staring at his daughter with pride and concern. Gerda had got even thinner. Sharp, spinsterish lines cut up her face into an eye segment, a nose-mouth part, and a chin-and-neck section, all of which, whenever Gerda was trying to say something, pulled like horses dragging a load that was too heavy: now one part, now another, never all together, giving the face an overstrained and deeply moving quality. —Now she has a new craze—Fischel thought—and will manage once again not to lead a settled life! In his mind he ran down a list of a dozen men who, now that Hans Sepp was fortunately dead, could be regarded as qualified suitors; but in view of the damned uncertainty that had broken out, there was no predicting what was going to happen to any of them tomorrow. Gerda's blond hair seemed to have become shaggier; she had been neglecting her appearance, but this made her hair look more like Fischel's, and it had lost the presumptuous soft, dark-blond smoothness characteristic of her mother's family. Memories of a brave, unkempt fox terrier and of himself, who had fought his way up and at the moment was standing again before something as yet unseen by man, over which he would go on climbing, mingled in his heart with the brave stupidity of his daughter into a warm togetherness. Leo Fischel straightened up in his chair and laid his hand on the desktop with emphasis. —My child!—he said—I have a strange feeling when I hear you talk this way, while people are shouting hurrah and prices are rising. You say I don't have any idea, but I do, except that I can't say myself what it is. Don't believe that I'm not caught up in this too. Sit down, my child!

Gerda did not want to, she was too impatient; but Fischel repeated his wish more strongly, and she obeyed, sitting hesitantly on the extreme edge of an armchair. —This is the first day you're back; listen to me! Fischel said. —You say I understand nothing about love and killing and such things; that may be. But if nothing happens to you in the hospital, which God forbid, you ought to understand me a little before we part again. I was seven years old when we had the war with Prussia. Then too, for two weeks, all the bells pealed and in the synagogue we prayed to God to annihilate the Prussians, who today are our allies. What do you say to that? What should anyone say to that?

Gerda did not want to answer. She had the prejudice that what was going on now belonged to the enthusiastic young, not the cautious old. And only reluctantly, because her father was looking at her so penetratingly, did she murmur some sort of response. —Over the course of time, people simply learn to understand each other better—was what her answer about the Prussians amounted to. But Leo Fischel snatched up her words spiritedly: —No! People *don't* learn to understand each other better in the course of time; it's just the opposite, I tell you! When you get to know a person and you like him, it may be that you think you understand him; but after you've been around him for twenty-five years you don't understand a word he says! You think, let's say, that he ought to be grateful to you; but no, just at that moment he curses you. Always when you think he has to say yes, he'll say no; and when you think no, he thinks yes. So he can be warm or cold, hard or soft, as it suits him; and do you believe that for your sake he'll be the way you want him to be? It suited your mother as little as it suits this armchair to be a horse, because you're already impatient and want to be off!

Gerda smiled weakly at her father. Since she had come back and seen the new situation, he had made a strong impression on her; she could not help herself. And he loved her, there was no doubting that, and it comforted her.

—But what are we going to do with the things that won't let us understand them? Fischel asked prophetically. —We measure them, we weigh them, we analyze them mentally, and we direct all our keenness to finding in them something that remains constant, something by which we could get hold of them, on which we can rely and which we can count. Those are the laws of nature, my child, and where we have discovered them we can mass-produce things and buy and sell to our heart's content. And now I ask you, how can people relate to one another when they don't understand one another? I tell you, there's only one way! Only when you stimulate or inhibit his desire can you get a person exactly where you want him. Whoever wants to build solidly must make use of force and basic desires. Then a person suddenly becomes unambiguous, predictable, dependable, and your experience with him is repeated everywhere in the same fashion. You can't rely on goodness. You can rely on bad qualities. God is wonderful, my child; he has given us our bad qualities so that we can achieve some semblance of order.

—But in that case the order of the world would be nothing but baseness jumping through hoops! Gerda flared up.

—You're clever! Perhaps so. But who can know? At any rate, I don't point a bayonet at a person's chest to have him do what *he* thinks is right. Are you following the newspapers? I'm still getting foreign papers, although it's beginning to be difficult. Here and abroad they're saying the same things. Get the screws on them. Tighten the screws on them. Cold-bloodedly continue the tight-screw policy. Don't hesitate to apply the "strong method" of breaking windows. That's the way they're talking here, and abroad it's not much different. I believe they've already introduced martial law, and if we should get into the war zone we'll be threatened with the gallows. That's the strong method. I can understand that it makes an impression on you. It's clean, precise, and abhors chatter. It qualifies the nation for great things by treating each individual person who is part of it like a dog! Leo Fischel smiled.

Gerda shook her tousled head decisively, but in a slow, friendly way.

—You must be clear about this, Fischel added. —When the industrialists' association supplied a bourgeois workers' opposition party with an election fund, or when my former bank made money available for something, they weren't doing anything different. And a deal only comes about at all if I either force another person to meet me halfway, because otherwise it will hurt him, or if I give him the impression that there's a good deal to be made; then I mostly outsmart him, and that's also a form of my power over him. But how delicate and adaptable this power is! It's creative and flexible. Money gives measure to a man. It's *ordered* selfishness. It's the most splendid organization of selfishness, a creative super-organization, constructed on a real notion of bearish speculation!

Gerda had been listening to her father, but her own thoughts buzzed in her mind. She answered: —Papa, I didn't understand everything, but you're surely right. Of course, you're looking at things as a rationalist, and for me it's precisely the irrational (what goes beyond all calculation) in what's going on now that's fascinating!

—What does irrational mean? General Director Fischel protested. —By that you mean illogical and incalculable and wild, the way one sometimes is in dreams? To that I can only say that buying and selling is like war; you have to calculate and you can calculate, but even there what is decisive in the last analysis is will, courage, the individual, or, as you call it, the irrational. No, my child—he concluded—money is self-ishness brought into relation with enterprise and efficiency. All of you are trying another way to regulate selfishness. It's not new, I acknowl-edge it, it's related. But wait and see how it works! For centuries capital-ism has been a proven way of organizing human powers according to the ability to make money; where its influence is suppressed, you will find that arbitrariness, backroom deals, kowtowing for advantage, and adven-turism will spring up. As far as I'm concerned, you can do away with money if you like, but you won't abolish the superior power of whoever is holding the advantages in his hand. Except that you'll put someone who doesn't know what to do with them in the place of someone who did! For you're mistaken if you believe that money is the cause of our selfishness; it's the consequence.

—But I don't believe that at all, Papa, Gerda said modestly. —I'm only telling you that's what's going on now—

—And furthermore—Fischel interrupted her—it's the most reason-able consequence!

—What's going on now—Gerda went on with her sentence—rises above reason. The way a poem or love rises above the commerce of the world.

—You're a deep girl! Fischel embraced her and released her. He liked Gerda's youthful ardor. —My fortune! he called her mentally, and fol-lowed her with a tender glance. A discussion with a person one loves and understands is bracing. He had not philosophized this way for a long time; it was a remarkable period. In conversation with this child Fischel had achieved some clarity about himself. He wanted to buy. Not a ship; at least five ships. He summoned his secretary. —We can't do this our-selves—he told him—it wouldn't look good, but let's do it through an intermediary. But for Leo Fischel this was not the main thing. The main thing was that he had gained a feeling of connection with events and yet a feeling of isolation, too. In spite of the ups and downs going on around him, he had created order within himself.

1936

Note: Development of a Man of Action (Leo Fischel)

Title: Return to an abandoned world / Leo Fischel as messenger from the world / Encounter with a messenger from an abandoned world / News from a lost world

Walking through the train, Ulrich saw a familiar face, stopped, and realized that it was Leo Fischel, who was sitting in a compartment by himself, leafing through a stack of flimsy papers he held in his hand. With his pince-nez far down on his nose, and his reddish-blond mutton-chop sideburns, he looked like an English lord of the 1860s. Ulrich was so in need of contact with everyday life that he greeted his old acquaintance, whom he had not seen for months, almost joyfully.

Fischel asked him where he was coming from.

"From the south," Ulrich responded vaguely.

"We haven't seen you for quite a while," Fischel said with concern. "You've been having trouble, haven't you?"

"How so?"

"I just mean in general. In your position with the campaign, I'm thinking."

"I never had a connection with the campaign that could be called a position," Ulrich objected with some heat.

"You just disappeared one day," Fischel said. "Nobody knew where you were. That led me to think that you were having problems."

"Except for that error, you're very well informed: how come?" Ulrich laughed.

"I was looking for you like a needle in a haystack. Hard times, bad stories, my friend," Fischel replied with a sigh. "The General didn't know where you were, your cousin didn't know where you were, and you weren't having your mail forwarded, I was told. Did you get a letter from Gerda?"

"Get it? No. Perhaps I'll find it waiting for me at home. Has something happened to Gerda?"

Director Fischel did not answer; the conductor was passing by, and he motioned him in to give him some telegrams, requesting that he send them off at the next stop.

Ulrich now first noticed that Fischel was traveling first class, which he would not have expected of him.

"Since when are you seeing my cousin and the General?" he asked.

Fischel looked at him reflectively. Obviously he did not understand the question right away. "Oh," he then said, "I think you hadn't even left yet. Your cousin consulted me on a matter of business, and through her I met the General, whom I wanted at that time to request something of on account of Hans Sepp. You know, don't you, that Hans shot and killed himself?"

Ulrich gave an involuntary start.

"It even got into some of the newspapers," Fischel confirmed. "He was called up for his military service and a few weeks later shot himself."

"But why?"

"God knows! Frankly speaking, he could just as well have done it sooner. He could always have shot himself. He was a fool. But in the final analysis, I liked him. You won't believe it, but I even liked his anti-Semitism and his diatribes against bank directors."

"Was there anything between him and Gerda?"

"Bitter quarrels," Fischel confirmed. "But it wasn't that alone. Listen: I've missed you. I searched for you. When I'm talking with you I have the feeling I'm talking not with a reasonable person but with a philosopher. Whatever you say—please permit an old friend to say this—is never to the point, never has hands and feet, but it has head and heart! So what do you say about Hans Sepp's having shot himself?"

"Is that why you were searching for me?"

"No, not because of that. On account of business and the General and Arnheim, who are friends of yours. The man before you is no longer with Lloyd's Bank but has gone into business for himself. It's a handful, let me tell you! I've had a lot of trouble, but now, thank goodness, things are going splendidly—"

"If I'm not mistaken, what you call trouble is losing your job?"

"Yes; thank goodness I lost my job at Lloyd's; otherwise today I would still be a head clerk with the title of Director and would remain one until I was put out to pasture. When I was forced to give that up, my wife began divorce proceedings against me—"

"Honestly! You really do have a lot of news to tell!"

"Hmph!" Fischel went. "We no longer live in the old apartment. While the divorce is going on, my wife has moved in with her brother"—he took out a business card—"and this is my address. I hope you'll pay me a visit soon." On the card Ulrich read several ambiguous titles, such as "Import/Export" and "Trans-European Goods and Currency Exchange Company," and a prestigious address. "You have no idea how one rises all by oneself," Fischel explained to him, "once all those weights like family and job responsibilities, the wife's fancy relations, and responsibility for the leading minds of humanity are taken off one's shoulders! In a few weeks I became an influential man. And a well-off man, to boot. Perhaps the day after tomorrow I'll have nothing again, but I may have even more!"

"What are you now, actually?"

"It's not easy to explain casually to an outsider. I conduct transactions. Transactions of goods, transactions of currency, political transactions, art transactions. In every case the important thing is to get out at the right moment; then you can never lose." As in the old days, it seemed to give Leo Fischel pleasure to accompany his activity with "philosophy," and Ulrich listened to him with curiosity.

> —Philosophy of money
> of the free man, among others—

Then Ulrich: "But with all that, it's also important for me to know what Gerda said about Hans's suicide."

"She claims I murdered him! But they had broken up definitively well before!"

RACHEL

And while Ulrich was letting the notion of remorse surface in his reflections, in order to dissolve it immediately again in the deep play of thought, his little friend Rachel was suffering this word in all its tortures, dissolved by nothing but the palliative effect of tears and the cautious return of temptation after the remorse had gone on for a while. One will recall that Diotima's intense little maid, ejected from her parents' house because of a misstep, who had landed in the golden aura of virtue surrounding her mistress, had, in the weakest of a series of increasingly weak moments, submitted to the attacks of the black Moorish boy. It happened and made her very unhappy. But this unhappiness aspired to repeat itself as often as the scanty opportunities that Diotima's house offered would allow. On the second or third day after every unhappiness a remarkable change occurred, which can be compared to a flower that, bent over by the rain, raises its little head again. Can be compared to fine weather that, way up above, peeks from a remote corner of the sky through a rainy day; finds friendly little spots of blue; forms a blue lake; becomes a blue sky; is veiled by a light haze of the overwhelming brightness of a day of happiness; is tinged with brown; lets down one hot veil of haze after another and finally towers, torrid and trembling, from earth to sky, filled with the zigzags and cries of birds, filled with the listless droop of tree and leaf, filled with the craziness of not-yet-discharged tensions that cause man and beast to roam madly about.

On the last day before the remorse, the head of the Moor always twitched through the house like a rolling head of cabbage, and little Rachel would have loved to creep on it like a caterpillar with a sweet tooth. But then remorse set in. As if a pistol had been fired and a shimmering glass ball been turned into a powder of glassy sand. Rachel felt sand between her teeth, in her nose, her heart; nothing but sand. The world was dark; not dark like a Moor, but nauseatingly dark, like a pigsty. Rachel, having disappointed the confidence placed in her, seemed to herself besmirched through and through. Grief placed a deep drill in the vicinity of her navel. A raging fear of being pregnant blinded her thoughts. One could go on in this fashion—every limb in Rachel ached individually with remorse—but the main thing was not in these details but seized hold of the whole person, driving her before the wind like a cloud of dust raised by a broom. The knowledge that a misstep that has happened cannot be rectified by anything in the world made the world something of a hurricane in which one can find no support to stand up. The peacefulness of death seemed to Rachel like a dark feather bed, which it must be delightful to roll on. She had been torn out of her world, abandoned to a feeling whose intensity was unlike anything in Diotima's house. She could not get at this feeling with an idea, any more than comfortings can get at a toothache, while it actually seemed to her, on the other hand, that there was only one remedy, to pull little Rachel entirely out of the world like a bad tooth.

Had she been cleverer, she would have been able to assert that remorse is a basic disturbance of equilibrium, which one can restore in the most various ways. But God helped her out with his old, proven home remedy by again giving her, after a few days, the desire to sin.

We, however, cannot of course be as indulgent as the great Lord, to whom earthly matters offer little that is new or important. We must ask whether in a condition in which there is no sin there can be any remorse. And since this question has already been answered in the negative, except for a few borderline cases, a second question immediately arises: from which ocean did the little drop of hell's fire fall into Rachel's heart, if it may not be said to have originated in the ocean whose clouds Ulrich had discovered? Every such question was suited to plunge Ulrich out of the sky on which he wanted to set foot purely theoretically. There are so many lovely things on earth that have nothing to do with divine, seraphic love, and most decidedly there are among them things that forbid anything and everything to be expected from their rediscovery. This question was later to be of the greatest significance for Ulrich and Agathe.

LATE 1920S

The weeks since Rachel had left Diotima's house had passed with an improbability that a different person would hardly have accepted calmly. But Rachel had been shown the door of her parents' house as a sinner, and at the conclusion of that fall had landed, straight as an arrow, in paradise, at Diotima's; now Diotima had thrown her out, but such an enchantingly refined man as Ulrich had been standing there and had caught her: how could she not believe that life is the way it is described in the novels she loved to read? Whoever is destined to be a hero fate throws into the air in daredevil ways over and over, but it always catches him again in its strong arms. Rachel placed blind confidence in fate, and during this entire time had really done nothing but wait for its next intervention, when it might perhaps unveil its intentions. She had not become pregnant; so the experience with Soliman seemed to have been only a passing incident. She ate in a small pub, together with coachmen, out-of-work servant girls, workers who had business in the neighborhood, and those undefinable transients who flood a large city. The place she had chosen for herself, at a specific table, was reserved for her every day; she wore better clothes than the other women who frequented the pub; the way she used her knife and fork was different from what one was accustomed to seeing here; in this place Rachel enjoyed a secret respect, which she was acutely aware of even though not many people wanted to show it, and she assumed that she was taken for a countess or the mistress of a prince, who for some reason was compelled for a time to conceal her class. It happened that men with dubious diamonds on their fingers and with slicked-down hair, who sometimes turned up among the respectable guests, arranged to sit at Rachel's table and directed seductively sinuous compliments to her; but Rachel knew how to refuse these with dignity and without unfriendliness, for although the compliments pleased her as much as the buzzing and creeping of insects and caterpillars and snakes on a luxuriant summer day, she still sensed that she could not let herself go in this direction without running the risk of losing her freedom. She most liked to converse with older people, who knew something of life and told stories of its dangers, disappointments, and events. In this way she picked up knowledge that, broken into crumbs, came to her the way food sinks down to a fish lying quietly at the bottom of its tank. Adventurous things were going on in the world. People were now said to be flying faster than birds. Building houses entirely without bricks. The anarchists wanted to assassinate the Emperor. A great revolution was imminent, and then the coachmen would sit inside the coaches and the rich people would be in harness, instead of the horses. In a tenement block in the vicinity, a woman had, in the night, poured petroleum on her husband and lit him; it was unimaginable! In America, blind people were given glass eyes with which they could really see again, but it still cost lots of money and was only for billionaires. These were the gripping things Rachel heard, of course not all at once, as she sat and ate. When afterward she stepped out into the street, nothing of such monstrosities was to be seen: everything flowed on in its well-ordered way or stood there exactly as it had the day before; but was not the air boiling in these summer days, was not the asphalt secretly yielding underfoot, without Rachel having to picture clearly that the sun had softened it? On the church roofs the saints stretched out their arms and lifted their eyes in a way that made one think that everywhere there must be something special to be seen. The policemen wiped away the sweat of their exertions in the midst of the commotion that roared around them. Vehicles going at high speed braked violently as an old lady crossing the street was almost run over because she was not paying attention to anything. When Rachel got back to her little room, she felt her curiosity sated by this light nourishment; she took out her undergarments to mend them, or altered a dress or read a novel—for with astonishment at the way the world was run, she had discovered the institution of the lending library—her landlady came in and chatted with her deferentially, because Rachel had money without having to work and without one's being able to discern any misconduct; and so the day passed, with no time to miss anything in the least, and poured its contents, filled to the brim with exciting things, into the dreams of the night.

To be sure, Ulrich had forgotten to send money promptly, or to ask Rachel to come to him, and she had already begun to use up the small savings from her work. But she was not concerned, for Ulrich had promised to protect her for the present, and to go to him to remind him seemed to her quite improper. In all the fairy tales she knew, there was something one was forbidden to say or do; and it would have been exactly that had she gone to Ulrich and told him she was out of money. This is not in any way to imply that she expressly thought that her manner of life seemed like a fairy tale, or that she believed in fairy tales at all. On the contrary, that was the way the reality that she had never known differently was constituted, even if it had never been as beautiful as it was now. There are people to whom this is permitted, and people to whom it is forbidden; the ones sink from step to step and end in utter misery, while the others become rich and happy—and leave behind lots of children. Rachel had never been told to which of the two groups she belonged; she had never revealed to the two people who might have explained the difference to her that she was dreaming, but had worked industriously, except for the two unintentional missteps that had had such serious consequences. And one day her landlady actually reported that while she was out to eat, a fine lady had asked for her and announced that she would return in an hour. Anxiously, Rachel gave a description of Diotima; but the lady who was looking for her was most decidedly not tall, the landlady asserted, and not stout either, not even if by stout one did not mean fat. The lady who was looking for Rachel was most decidedly, rather, to be called small and skinny.

And indeed the lady was slender and small, and returned within a half hour. She said "Dear Fräulein" to Rachel, mentioned Ulrich's name, and pulled from her purse a tightly folded, rather considerable sum of money, which she gave to Rachel on behalf of their friend. Then she began to tell an involved and exciting story, and Rachel had never in her life been so enthralled by a conversation. There was a man, the lady said, who was being pursued by his enemies because he had nobly sacrificed himself for them. Really not nobly; for he had to do it, it was his inner law, every person has an animal which he inwardly resembles. —You, for example, Fräulein—the lady said—have either a gazelle or a queen snake in you—it can't always be determined at first glance.

If it had been the cook in Diotima's kitchen who had said that, it would have made either no impression on Rachel or an unfavorable one; but it was said by someone who with every word radiated the certainty of a well-bred lady, the gift of command that would make any doubt appear to be an offense against respect. It was therefore firmly established in Rachel's mind that there was some link between herself and a gazelle or a queen snake, a link that at the moment was over her head, but that could doubtless be explained in some fashion, for one sometimes does hear such things. Rachel felt herself charged with this piece of news like a candy box one can't get open.

The man who had sacrificed himself, the lady continued, had within himself a bear, that is to say, the soul of a murderer, and that meant that he had taken murder upon himself, all murder: the murder of unborn and handicapped children, the cowardly murder that people commit against their talents, and murder on the street by vehicles, bicyclists, and trams. Clarisse asked Rachel—for of course it was Clarisse who was speaking—whether she had ever heard the name Moosbrugger. Now, Rachel had, although she later forgot him again, loved and feared Moosbrugger like a robber captain, at the time when he had horrified all the newspapers, and he had often been the topic of conversation at Diotima's; so she asked right away whether it concerned him.

Clarisse nodded. —He is innocent!

For the first time Rachel heard from an authority what she had earlier often thought herself.

—We have freed him, Clarisse went on. —We, the responsible people, who know more than the others do. But now we must hide him. Clarisse smiled, and so peculiarly and yet with such rapturous friendliness that Rachel's heart, intending to fall into her panties, got stuck on the way, somewhere in the neighborhood of her stomach. —Hide where? she stammered, pale.

—The police will be looking for him—Clarisse declared—so it has to

be where no one would think of looking for him. The best thing would
be if you would pretend he was your husband. He would have to wear a
wooden leg, that's easy to pretend, or something, and you would get a
little shop with living quarters attached, so it would look as if you were
supporting your invalid husband who can't leave the house. The whole
thing would be for only a few weeks, and I could offer you more money
than you need.

—But why don't you take him in yourself? Rachel dared to counter.

—My husband isn't in on it and would never allow it, Clarisse answered, adding the lie that the proposal she had made came from Ulrich.

—But I'm afraid of him! Rachel exclaimed.

—That's as it should be, Clarisse said. —But, my dear Fräulein, everything great is terrible. Many great men have been in the insane asylum. It *is* uncanny to put oneself on a level with someone who is a
murderer; but to put oneself on a level with the uncanny is to resolve to
be great!

—But does he want to? Rachel asked. —Does he know me? He won't
do anything to me?

—He knows that we want to save him. Look, his whole life he's known
only substitute women; you understand what I mean. He'll be happy at
having a real woman to protect him and take him in; and he won't lay a
finger on you if you don't let him. I'll back you up on that all the way! He
knows that I have the power to compel him, if I want!

—No, no! was all Rachel could get out; from everything Clarisse was
saying she could hear only the shape of the voice and language, a friendliness and a sisterly equality that she could not resist. A lady had never
spoken to her this way, and yet there was nothing artificial or false in it;
Clarisse's face was on a level with hers and not up in the air like Diotima's; she saw her features working, especially two long furrows that
constantly formed by the nose and ran down by the mouth; Clarisse was
visibly struggling together with her for the solution.

—Consider, Fräulein— Clarisse went on to say—that he who recognizes must sacrifice himself. You recognized right away that Moosbrugger only appears to be a murderer. Therefore you must sacrifice
yourself. You must draw what is murderous out of him, and then what's
behind it, which corresponds to your own nature, will come out. For like
is attracted only by like; that's the merciless law of greatness!

—But when will it be?

—Tomorrow. I'll come in the late afternoon and get you. By that time
everything will be arranged.

—If a third person could live with us, I'd do it, Rachel said.

—I'll drop in every day—Clarisse said—and watch over things; the living arrangement is only for show. Then too, it wouldn't do to be ungrateful to Ulrich if he needs you to do him a favor.

That clinched the matter. Clarisse had confidently used his Christian name. It appeared to Rachel as though her cowardice were unworthy of her benefactor. The portrayal our inner being gives us of what we ought to do is extraordinarily deceitful and capricious. Suddenly the whole thing seemed to Rachel a joke, a game, a trifle. She would have a shop and a room; if she wanted, she could bar the door between them. Then too, there would be two exits, the way there are in rooms on the stage. The whole proposal was only a formality, and it was really exaggerated of her to make difficulties, even though she was horribly afraid of Moosbrugger. She had to get over this cowardice. And what had the lady said? What corresponds to your own nature will come out in him. If he really was not so fearsome, then she would have what she had earlier passionately wished for.

. . .

The shop and the adjoining room and the two exits came to nothing. Clarisse had appeared and declared that at the last minute the rent had posed an obstacle; since time was pressing, they had to take what was available, and fate perhaps depended on a matter of minutes. She had found another room. Had Rachel already packed up her things, and was she ready? The taxi was waiting downstairs. Unfortunately, it was not a nice room. And above all it was not yet furnished. But Clarisse had hastily had the most necessary items brought over. Now it was only a matter of getting Moosbrugger settled quickly. Everything else could be taken care of tomorrow. Today everything was only provisional. Clarisse reported the greater part of this when they were in the taxi. The words were dizzying. Rachel had no time to think. The taxi meter, half lit by a tiny light, advanced incessantly; with every revolution of the wheels Rachel heard the ticking of the meter, like a jug that has sprung a leak and drips unceasingly; in the darkness of the old cab Clarisse pressed a sum of money into her hand, and Rachel had to concentrate on stuffing it into her purse; in the process, the paper expanded, individual notes sailed away and had to be pursued and caught; laughing, Clarisse helped her find them, and this took up the rest of the long ride.

The taxi stopped in a remote alley in front of an old tumbledown "court," one of those deep plots of land where, from a narrow frontage on the alley, low wings run to the back, with workshops, stables, chickens, children, and the small dwellings of large families opening directly onto the courtyard or, one story higher, onto an open gallery connecting everything from the outside. Clarisse helped Rachel drag her things and seemed anxious to avoid the superintendent; they bumped into wagons standing in the dark, into tools that lay around everywhere, and into the well, but they arrived undamaged at Rachel's new dwelling. Clarisse had a candle in her pocket and with its aid found a large oil lamp she had remembered to sneak from her parents' attic. It was a tall piece worked in metal, incorporating all the latest advances the petroleum age had made just before it was irrevocably shunted aside by electrical illumination, and it filled the entire room, because it lacked a shade, with moderate light. Clarisse was very proud of it, but she had to hurry, since she had had the taxi wait at the next corner in order to fetch Moosbrugger.

As soon as she was alone and looked around in her new surroundings, tears filled Rachel's eyes. Except for the dirty walls, the thick white light of the lamp was almost the only thing in the room. But her fright had made Rachel misjudge; on closer inspection she found against one wall a narrow iron bed, on which there was something like bedclothes; in a corner, a pile of blankets was heaped up in disorder, no doubt meant to be the second sleeping place; blankets were also hanging in front of the windows and the door that led outside, and formed before a small and extremely plain table a kind of carpet, on which a roughly finished chair stood. Sighing, Rachel sat down on it and drew out her money in order to count and sort it. But now she again got a fright, this time over the size, indeed the excess, of the amount Clarisse, throwing caution to the winds, had thrust at her in the taxi. She smoothed the banknotes and concealed them in a small purse, which she wore on her breast. If she had known that she was sitting at the table at which Meingast had created his great work, and that the narrow iron bed had also been his, she might perhaps have understood a little more. But as it was, she simply sighed once more, already made easier about the future, and even discovered an old fireplace, a spirit stove, and odds and ends of dishes before Clarisse returned with Moosbrugger.

This moment was like the terrifying moment when one is called in by the dentist, which Rachel had experienced only once, and she stood up obediently as the two entered.

Moosbrugger allowed himself to be led into the room the way a great artist is introduced to a circle of people who have been waiting for him. He pretended not to notice Rachel, and first inspected the new room; only then, after he had found fault with nothing, did he direct his glance at the girl and nod by way of greeting. Clarisse seemed to have no more to say to him; she pushed him, her tiny hand against his gigantic arm, toward the table and merely smiled, the way a person does who during a risky enterprise has to tense every muscle and is meanwhile trying to smile, so that the delicate facial muscles have to pull themselves together sharply in order to force their way between the pressure of all the other muscles. She maintained this expression while she placed a bag of groceries on the table and explained to the other two that she could not stay a minute longer but had to rush home. She promised to come back the next morning around ten and would then take care of anything else they might need.

So now Rachel was alone with the revered man. She covered the table with a pillowcase, since she could not find a tablecloth, and spread out on a large platter the cold cuts Clarisse had brought. These duties greatly eased her embarrassment. Then, placing the meal on the table, she said in carefully chosen German: "You will most certainly be hungry"; she had thought out this sentence ahead of time. Moosbrugger had stood up, and with a gallant gesture of his big paw offered her his place, for it turned out that there was only the one chair. —Oh, no thank you— Rachel said—I don't want much; I'll sit over there. She took two slices from the platter Moosbrugger offered her and sat down on the bed.

Moosbrugger had taken a horrifying long folding knife from his pocket and used it while eating. In the days of his flight he had eaten irregularly and badly, and had developed a great hunger. Rachel took advantage of the opportunity to study him; more properly, she had to, for as soon as she turned in the direction of the table, this man completely filled her field of vision; more, his appearance overflowed her eyes, spilling over their rims in every direction, and Rachel could not properly let her glance roam around; it was, for instance, quite a long distance across the whole extent of his chest, or from the edge of the table to his thick mustache, and also from his chin to the top of his powerful skull, and one could linger in the reddish-blond hairs of his mighty fists as in underbrush. In the meantime, all the ideas and some of the fantasies of which Moosbrugger had once been the object came back to Rachel. Above all, she sought to bring to mind how many women would envy the situation in which she found herself. For her, Moosbrugger was a great and famous man, which corresponded to the truth if one leaves aside the different degrees of public notoriety that are made but are by no means clear or precise. She did not at all overlook the fearfulness of the notoriety, which had been acquired by cruel, indeed even treacherous deeds, for she was trembling with fear, although she was also burning with excitement. But like all people, she admired the energy in this cruelty, and like all impulsive people she assumed that in contact with her, this herculean strength would not be dangerous but could be turned toward the good, so that her fear seemed to her only a petty external habit, while her soul became braver and braver the longer she was together with Moosbrugger. And indeed, whoever lives in the proper relation to criminals lives as securely among them as among other people.

Moosbrugger had not found it proper to be bothered by the girl's glances during such an important an occasion as eating. But when he had finished he leaned back, snapped his knife shut, stroked the crumbs from his mustache, and said: —Well, little Fräulein, now a glass of schnapps wouldn't be—

Rachel hastened to assure him that there were no alcoholic drinks in the house, adding the lie that Clarisse had charged her not to provide any.

Moosbrugger hadn't meant it that seriously. He was not a drinker, indeed he himself took care not to drink, out of fear of its unpredictable effects. But he hadn't seen a drop for months, and after the substantial meal had thought it wouldn't be a bad idea to try one on this dull evening. He was angry at her refusal. These women had him really locked up. But he did not show it, and undertook to carry on the conversation in the most civilized manner.

—So here we are, man and wife, in a way, for the time being, little Fräulein, he began. —What should I call you? He used the natural *Du* of simple people; Rachel did not find this unpleasant, but just as naturally she stayed with the formal *Sie*. —My name is Rachel or Rèle, whichever you like.

—Oo-la-la, Rèle, my compliments! He pronounced the French name twice over, with pleasure. —And Rachel was the loveliest daughter of Laban. He laughed gallantly.

—Tell me how you beat the masons! Rachel asked. She dared not ask about anything more exciting.

Moosbrugger turned away and rolled a cigarette. He was insulted. In his circles such a question was regarded as an unwarranted intimacy after so short an acquaintance. He smoked several cigarettes in succession. He was bored. Insignificant, importunate women meant nothing to him. He became sleepy. In prison and the asylum he had become accustomed to going to bed early.

Rachel was upset that he was smoking so inconsiderately. She also had the feeling of having done something wrong, without knowing what.

Moosbrugger stood up, stretched his legs, and yawned.

—Do you want to go to sleep? Rachel asked.

—What else is there to do? Moosbrugger said. He inspected the bed; then, remembering the commandments of chivalry, turned to the corner where the bedding lay.

—Sleep in the bed; you need rest, Rachel said.

—No, you can sleep in the bed. Indolently, he removed his coat. Rachel was embarrassed when Moosbrugger took off his pants. But then he lay down on the blankets as he was, and pulled one of them over himself. Rachel waited awhile, then blew out the lamp and undressed in the dark.

During the night she again grew afraid; she imagined that if she were to fall asleep it might happen that she would never wake up again. But soon she did sleep, and when she awoke, morning was shining into the room. Moosbrugger lay covered up in the corner like a huge mountain. Everything was still quiet in the house. Rachel took advantage of it to fetch water from the well. She also cleaned her shoes and Moosbrugger's out in the courtyard. When she softly slipped in the door again, Moosbrugger said good morning to her.

—Would you like coffee, tea, or hot chocolate? she asked him. Moosbrugger was astonished. He said coffee, but did not find the decision an easy one. Then too, he liked Rachel better in the daylight than he had last evening; there was something delicate and refined in her appearance. He took care getting dressed, and turned away from the wall only when he was finished.

—Were you angry at me last evening? Rachel asked, noticing his good humor.

—Oh, women always want to know everything, but if you like I'll tell you the story about the masons. That will show you what people are like; they're all the same. And what have you been doing up to now?

—I was in a very elegant house, where I was treated like a daughter.

—Well, and what got you turned out?

—Oh! said Rachel, not at all resolved to tell the truth. —You know, the master in this house is a very high diplomat, and there was this business with a Moorish prince—

—Are you pregnant? Moosbrugger asked suspiciously.

—For shame! Rachel exclaimed indignantly. —You're taking too many liberties in speaking to me that way! Would the lady have entrusted you to me?

Moosbrugger definitely liked her. She was something finer, you could see and hear that. When he thought over the females he knew, he had never had anything so fine. —Well, all right, he said. —I didn't mean to insult you. The story with the masons went like this:

He told it minutely and with dignity, together with all the scheming and corruption that a man like himself encounters before the court, and because she had mentioned an acquaintance with a Moorish prince, he felt he had to match it, so he also told her about his march to Constantinople.

—Do the Turks have more than one wife? Rachel asked.

—Only the rich ones. But that's why the Turks aren't worth anything, he answered with a gallant smile. —Even one wife will ruin a man!

—Have you had bad experiences with women? Rachel asked, her blood twitching in circles like the tail of a cat lying in ambush.

Moosbrugger looked at her inquiringly, and became serious. —All my life I've had only bad experiences. If I were to write down my life, a lot of people would be surprised!

—You ought to! Rachel proposed enthusiastically.

—Writing is much too uncomfortable for me! Moosbrugger said proudly, and stretched his shoulders. —But you're an educated girl. Perhaps I'll tell you something. Then you can write it.

—I've never written a book, Rachel replied modestly; but she felt as if she had been offered Section Chief Tuzzi's job. And this man before her was no idle gossip; he had shown that he could put meaning into his words.

Thus the time passed in animated conversation, and it got to be ten o'clock, but Clarisse did not appear.

Moosbrugger pulled his large, fat, chrome-plated watch from his vest and determined that it was ten thirty-five.

When they next looked, it was seven minutes before eleven.

—She's not coming; I thought as much, Moosbrugger said.

—But she has to come! Rachel said.

The conversation ran down. They had got up early and had not left the room. Being cooped up made them tired. Moosbrugger stood and stretched. Rachel finally declared herself ready to go and get something to eat without waiting any longer. But first Moosbrugger had to put on the green eyeshade and strap on the wooden leg, in case during Rachel's absence a stranger should come in; wooden leg and eyeshade were a legacy of Clarisse's. It was no simple matter to get his leg, which was bent back to the thigh and on whose knee the wooden leg was strapped, through a pant leg; Moosbrugger had to place his arm around Rachel's neck, and he took the opportunity to draw her gently toward himself.

He hobbled around the room alone for more than a quarter of an hour; it was nauseatingly tedious; then Rachel cooked, but she did not know much about cooking, and the meal was not exactly cheerful. Gradually, Moosbrugger became fed up with this seclusion, but realized that it would be a long time before he could give it up. He wanted to sleep a bit to make the time pass, yawned like a lion, and sat on the bed to un-buckle the damn leg, which was driving the blood to his head. Rachel had to help him. And as he again laid his arm around her shoulder, he thought that after all she really was his wife for the time being. Surely she had never expected anything else of him and had made fun of him yesterday when he went straight off to sleep. As the wooden leg fell to the ground, with the arm that was around her shoulder he pulled Rachel back on the bed and drew her up on it a little, until her head rested on a pillow. Rachel did not resist. His large mustache descended on her mouth. But her small mouth came to meet it. Went into this mustache as into a forest, as it were, and sought the mouth in it. When the man pushed himself up on her, Rachel lay with her face almost under his chest and had to move her head to one side in order to be able to breathe; it seemed to her as if she were being buried by soil that was trembling volcanically. The really great bodily arousals are brought about by the imagination; Rachel saw in Moosbrugger not a hero with-out his peer on earth—for comparison and reflection would then have killed the power of imagination—but simply a hero, a notion that is less definite but blends with the time and place in which it appears and with the person who arouses admiration. Where there are heroes the world is still soft and glowing, and the web of creation unbroken. The adventur-ous room with the covered windows suddenly took on the appearance of the cave of a big robber who has withdrawn from the world. Rachel felt her breast lying under an enormous pressure; the scurrying quality that was part of her nature was pinned down for the moment by an overpow-ering force and compelled to be patient; her upper body could move as little as if it had fallen under the iron wheels of a truck, and this position would have been torture had not all the spontaneity and independence of which her body was capable gathered in her hips, where a giant was struggling with clouds and which despite their helplessness were em-bracing him again and again, and were just as strong in their way as he was in his. A desire such as Rachel had never felt in her life, indeed had never suspected, pressed upon her mind and from there opened up her entire person: she wanted to conceive and bear a hero. Her lips re-mained open in astonishment, her limbs lay where they were when Moosbrugger got up, and her eyes remained for a long time misted over with a bluish-yellow mist, the way chanterelles do when one breaks them. She did not get up until it was time to light the lamp and think of the evening meal; till then she had waited, with a kind of emptiness of mind, for a continuation that she was not able to picture to herself but did not think of at all as simply a repetition.

For Moosbrugger, the matter was finished until further notice. People who on occasion commit sexual crimes are, as one knows, ordinarily anything but flamboyant lovers, since their crimes, to the extent that they do not spring from external influences, express nothing but the irregularity of their desire. Moosbrugger felt nothing more than boredom while Rachel lay demolished on the bed. So what had given their being together a certain tension was now, in his opinion, over and done with before one had thought of it.

Clarisse did not come; she did not come the next day either; she did not come at all.

Moosbrugger smoked cigarettes and yawned. Several times Rachel put her hand around his neck and her hand in his hair; he shook her off. He pulled her onto his lap, and then immediately set her on her feet again because he had changed his mind. What he felt beside boredom was that he had been insulted. These women had fetched him out of school like a boy and taken him home; he had sometimes observed this picture and thought that such sonny boys could never develop into real men. But he realized that for the time being he had to go along with it; he did not dare venture out on the street as long as the zeal of the police was still fresh, and to visit Biziste or other friends would not be a good idea at all. He had Rachel bring him the newspapers and looked for what was being said about him; but this time he was not at all pleased with his press: the papers dismissed his escape in three to five lines. He knew that Rachel was just as downcast as he was at Clarisse's not showing up; but he still laid on her the resentment that was building in him, even if he did not regard Rachel as its cause, since she was Clarisse's representative. Rachel committed the error of continuing to refuse to provide alcohol, though if she had done so, that would have been a mistake as well. Moosbrugger was silent after such refusals, but the insults to which he was exposed formed, together with the stale boredom and his longing for a tavern, a tangle of revulsion whose spindle was the skinny girl who moved around him the entire day. He spoke only when he had to and disregarded all Rachel's attempts to bring the conversation back to the level of the first morning. Tortured in addition by her own cares, Rachel was very unhappy.

A few days later they had their first scene. After supper and a period of yawning, Moosbrugger pulled over the little purse from which Rachel paid for their daily needs, and tried to fish out a coin with his thick fingers. Rachel, who immediately saw what he was up to, could not get her purse away from him in time; she ran around the table and fell on his arm. —No! she exclaimed. —You mustn't go to the tavern! You'll be— But she did not get to finish her sentence, for Moosbrugger's arm shoved her away so violently that she lost her balance and had to make strenuous efforts not to fall. Moosbrugger put on his hat and left the room, as unapproachable as a huge stone figure.

In desperation, Rachel thought over what she should do. She decided to do battle against Moosbrugger's indiscretion. She reproached herself with letting herself be frightened by the change in his behavior, which in the loneliness of reflection seemed to her understandable. As the weaker person, it was easy for her to be the cleverer, but she had to bend every effort to make clear to him that in this case she really was more clever; and if he saw that, then he might possibly accommodate himself to his situation; for Rachel understood quite well that it was no situation for a hero to be in. But when Moosbrugger came home he was drunk. The room filled with a bad smell, his shadow danced on the walls, Rachel was dispirited, and her words chased after this shadow with sharp reproaches she did not intend. Moosbrugger had landed on the bed and was beckoning her with his finger. —No, never again! Rachel screamed. Moosbrugger pulled from his pocket a bottle he had brought along. He had left the tavern at eleven, only one third filled with schnapps; the second third was filled with a bad conscience, and the third third with anger at having left. Rachel committed the strategic error of rushing at him in order to tear the bottle away. The next moment, she thought her head was bursting; the lamp revolved, and her body lost all connection to the world; Moosbrugger had warded off her attack with a powerful slap of his paw to her face, and when Rachel came to, she was lying far away from him on the floor; something was dripping out between her teeth, and her upper lip and nose seemed to have grown painfully together. She saw how Moosbrugger was still staring at the bottle, which he then rudely smashed on the floor; after which he stood up and blew out the lamp.

Whether deliberately or merely in his stupor, Moosbrugger had taken the bed, and Rachel crept weeping onto the pile of blankets, near which she had fallen. The pain in her face and body did not let her sleep, but she did not dare light the lamp to make poultices for herself. She was cold, humiliation filled her mind with a hazy restlessness that closely resembled feverish fantasies, and the spilled schnapps covered the floor with a nauseating, paralyzing haze. All night she thought over as well as she could what had to be done. She had to find Clarisse, but she had no idea where Clarisse lived. She wanted to run away, but then she told herself that she would be betraying Clarisse's confidence if she left Moosbrugger in the lurch before Clarisse returned; she had taken money for this. It also occurred to her that she could go find Ulrich, but she was ashamed and put that off for later. She had never been beaten before, but aside from the pain it wasn't so bad; it simply expressed the fact that she was weaker than this giant whom she loved, that her entreaties did not penetrate to his ear, and that she had to be circumspect; he did not mean to harm her, she realized that quite well, and the most unpleasant thing remained the fear that her chastisement would be repeated, an idea that robbed her breast of courage and made her totally miserable.

So day came before she reached any conclusions. Moosbrugger got up, and stumbling with inner emptiness, she had to follow his example. A glance in the mirror showed that her nose and mouth were badly swollen in a discolored, greenish-yellow, half-extinguished face; the magic of this night had made Rachel ugly and unprepossessing. Neither she nor Moosbrugger said anything. Moosbrugger had a fuzzy head; in his sleep he had smelled the schnapps and woken up with the feeling of not having drunk enough. When he saw Rachel's swollen face, he had an inkling of what had happened the day before; a dim recollection that she had provoked him kept him from asking her about it. But he really would have liked to ask her; he just did not know how to go about it. And Rachel waited for a kind word from him the way any girl in love waits; when he let himself be served in silence, she became more and more sulky. Moosbrugger would have liked most of all to go straight back to the bar, but he was afraid of this girl, who would again make a scene, and he could not go on beating her every time. Her eyes, swollen with weeping, repelled him even more than her swollen mouth, which was visible every time she moistened the cloth she was holding to it. It was indeed his fault, he said to himself, what's right is right, but to have this around first thing in the morning was too much. Rachel's tender back and her slender arms, which she exposed as she washed, the devil take them, he didn't like them, they looked like chicken bones.

He summed it all up by finding himself in a really stupid situation that he had to stick out as honorably as he could. In the evenings he went to the tavern; he had made up his mind to risk it in this part of town where no one knew him, and Rachel no longer dared to refuse him the money or reproach him for it. Not even when he began to play cards and needed more. There was pretty good company in the bar; in this way, Moosbrugger thought, you can stick it out if you sleep a lot during the day. But Rachel did not sleep during the day, and bothered him like a bat. A few times he caught her in his arms. A few times, too, he made an attempt to begin a better life and to talk with her as the little Fräulein whom she indeed was. But then it came out that Rachel could do no more. She answered evasively and monosyllabically. Whenever Moosbrugger opened his mouth she froze, without meaning to, for she would have liked to talk with him; but he had poured something alien into her,

violence, and the well that is the source of everything worth saying had
frozen over. So there remained nothing for Moosbrugger to do but turn
to the wall.

But there was one occasion when she always spoke up, and that was
when Moosbrugger returned from the tavern. If he was not drunk he did
not respond, or merely growled incomprehensible answers, and Rachel
pursued him into sleep with reproaches about his heedlessness. He had
beaten her in the tension, the very unpleasant tension, that ruled in him
as long as he had been tempted to leave the house but could not make
up his mind to do so; now that this was no longer a problem, he was
tender and well-mannered, and Rachel, sensing that she was not in any
danger, became bolder and bolder. He stayed out longer from one day
to the next, in the hope of returning only after she had gone to sleep. But
Rachel had developed a strange habit of sleeping. When he left the
house after dark she instantly fell asleep, and when he returned she
woke up, and with an assurance as if it were only the continuation of her
dream, she began to quarrel with him. Her poor soul, condemned to be
unable to resolve her situation through reflection and thought, allowed
itself to be borne upward by the drunken powers of sleep.

—Such a scrawny little chicken! Moosbrugger thought about her, and
the insult that such a meager chicken was allowed to scratch around him,
day in, day out, gnawed at him. But Rachel, as if she knew what he
thought about her without his having said it aloud, and in almost telepathic (somnambulent) concord with the silent man who groped his way
through the room in the night, felt an obsessive desire to cackle and
argue. And when Moosbrugger came home drunk, which was not exactly seldom, his stumbling and tottering was like a large ship dancing on
the same waves as the girl's small, excited sentences. And if one of these
sentences struck too close to home, the powerfully drunken Christian
Moosbrugger grabbed at her. As mentioned, it was never again the impulsive rage it had been the first time, when he had nearly crushed Rachel with a sweep of his hand, but he wanted to make this screeching,
rebellious child shut up, and with cautiously measured force, the way a
drunk carefully calculates his step over the curb, he let his hand fall on
her. When Rachel was beaten she became still for a moment. A boundless astonishment came over her, as at a totally unexpected, conclusive
answer. Since leaving her parents' house she had not been religious; the
way she had grown up, she thought religion was something for coarse
people: but if Elohim, or better yet an evil spirit, had suddenly sat on a
bench in the park among the dressed-up people, that was exactly how it
seemed to her when she was beaten. She was drawn to observe this evil
spirit closely once more and sought to set it in motion. Then she would

open her mouth again and say something about which she knew just as surely that it would irritate Moosbrugger as that if he would follow it it would be what he needed for his salvation. Then Moosbrugger would hit her with the back of his hand, or shove her to the wall. And Rachel, although again astonished, would find another expression, as sharp and penetrating as a knitting needle. And then of course Moosbrugger would have to increase the size of his gift. This giant, not wanting to kill her, beats her wildly on her back, her buttocks, tears her shift, throws her by the hair to the ground, or with a kick sends her flying into the corner; but he does all this with as much care in his wildness as his drunken condition permits, so that no bones will be broken. Rachel is amazed at the evil spirit of force and brutality that demolishes all words. When Moosbrugger shoves her she becomes completely weightless. No will can prevail against his strength. The will returns only when the pain stops. And as long as the pain is there she howls, and is herself astonished at the way she screams at the walls. And Moosbrugger would like to seize his head and, raising it from his fists, smash his own head against the ground, if that would only get this damned nothing of a person to shut up!

On the days after such evenings it seemed to Rachel as if she herself had been drunk. Her reason told her that she had to put an end to this. She went looking for Ulrich. But she was told he was away, and no one knew where he was or when he would return. On her way back she thought she noticed that everything in the world was secretly contrived for beatings. It was just a thought that went through her mind. Parents their child. The state its convicts. The military its soldiers. The rich the poor. The coachman his horse. People went walking with big dogs on leashes. Everyone would rather intimidate another person than come to an understanding with him. What had happened to her was no different from what it would have been if she had thrust her hand into pure lye instead of the diluted lye that is used everywhere for laundering. She had to get out! Her mind was confused. She resolved that in the evening, when Moosbrugger was out of the house, she would flee with everything she still possessed. It would be enough to last her for a few weeks by herself. She put on an innocent face when she entered the room, so as not to make Moosbrugger suspicious. But although it was only six o'clock and still daylight, she did not find him there. An instant suspicion made her inspect the room. Almost all her clothes were missing. The lamp and some of the blankets were gone. If thieves hadn't broken in during his absence, Moosbrugger himself must have thrown it all together and pawned it.

Rachel packed up what was left. But then she did not know where to go, as evening was falling. She decided to stick it out one more night and hold her tongue when Moosbrugger came back sodden drunk, as was to be expected from these preparations. Then in the morning she intended to disappear without a trace. She lay down on the bed, and even though Moosbrugger had also taken the pillow, for the first time she slept soundly the whole night.

Despite her deep sleep, in the morning she immediately knew, even before she opened her eyes, that Moosbrugger had not come home. She looked around, wanting quickly to take the opportunity to make herself ready. But she was sad; she feared that in his rashness Moosbrugger had fallen into the hands of the police, and that grieved her. Involuntarily she hesitated while she tied up her bundle. In truth, Moosbrugger had for quite a while had something in mind. He had noticed that Rachel kept her money on her breast, and wanted to take it from her. But he shrank from reaching for it. He was afraid of those two girlish things between which it lay; he didn't know why. Perhaps because they were so unmasculine. So he fell back on his other plan. It was the more natural one. It lifted Moosbrugger up and set him down again. But if it worked out the way he wanted, it would give him travel money and he could let himself be borne away. He really liked living with Rachel. She had her oddities, which dully persecuted him; but each time he fell into a rage or caught her for love, he unloaded a part of his unease, and this made the water level of his plan rise fairly slowly. He felt reasonably secure with Rachel; indeed, that was what it was, a really ordered life, when he went out in the evenings, drank something, and then had his quarrel with her. It removed, so to speak, the bullet from the magazine every evening. Both were lucky that he beat Rachel, as it were, in small installments. But just because life with her was so healthy, she did not greatly arouse his fantasies, and he nourished his secret plan to disappear into the world; he wanted to begin by getting totally drunk. When it got to be nine in the morning Rachel went for a newspaper to see if there was any bad news in it. She found it immediately. During the night a woman had been torn to pieces by a drunk or a madman; the murderer had been seized, and the establishment of his identity was imminent. Rachel knew that it was none other than Moosbrugger. Tears started to her eyes. She did not know why, for she felt cheerful and relieved. And should it occur to Clarisse to free Moosbrugger again, Rachel would tell the police about her. But she had to cry all day long, as if it were part of herself that would go to the gallows.

Narrative Drafts

Mid to Late 1920s

The Redeemer
(C. 1924/25)

I.
A dreadful chapter
The dream

Around midnight, no matter what the night, the heavy wooden door of the entryway was closed and two iron bars thick as arms were shoved in behind it; until then, a sleepy maid with the look of a peasant about her waited for late guests. A quarter of an hour later a policeman came by on his long, slow rounds, overseeing the closing time of inns. Around 1:00 a.m. the swelling three-step of a patrol from the nearby supply barracks emerged from the fog, echoed past, and faded away again. Then for a long time there was nothing but the cold, damp silence of November nights; only around three did the first carts come in from the country. They broke over the pavement with a heavy noise; wrapped in their coverings, deaf from the clatter and the morning cold, the corpses of the drivers swayed behind the horses.

Was it like that or wasn't it, when on this night, shortly before the closing hour, the couple asked about a room? The maid, unhurried, first shut and barred the door, and then without asking any questions went on ahead. First there was a stone staircase, then a long, windowless corridor, and suddenly two unexpected corners; a staircase with five stone steps hollowed out by many feet, and another corridor, whose loosened tiles wobbled under their soles. At its end, without the visitors being put off by it, a ladder with a few rungs led up to a small attic space onto which three doors opened, doors that stood low and brown around the hole in the floor.

"Are the other rooms taken?" The old woman shook her head while, by the light of her candle, she opened one of the rooms. Then she stood with her light raised and allowed the guests to enter. It might not have happened often that she heard the rustle of silk petticoats in this room; and the tattoo of high heels, which in fright gave way to every shadow on the tile floor, seemed stupid to her; obtuse and obstinate, she looked the lady, who now had to brush past her, straight in the face. The lady nodded patronizingly in her embarrassment; she might be forty, or somewhat older. The maid took the money for the room, extinguished the last light in the corridor, and went to bed in her room.

After that there was no sound in the whole house. The light of the candle had not yet found time to creep into all the corners of the wretched room. The strange man stood by the window like a flat shadow, while the lady, with uncertain expectations, had sat down on the edge of the bed. She had to wait an agonizingly long time; the stranger did not stir from his place. If up till now things had gone as quickly as the beginning of a dream, now every motion was mired in a stubborn resistance that did not let go of a single limb. He felt that this woman was expecting something from him. Opening her stays—that was like opening the doors of a room. A table was standing in the middle. At it sat the man, the son. He observed it secretly, hostilely, and fearfully, full of arrogance. He would have liked to throw a grenade, or tear the wallpaper to tatters. With the greatest effort he finally succeeded in at least wresting a sentence from the stubborn resistance. "Did you really notice me right away when I looked at you?"

Oh, it worked. She could not control her impatience any longer. She had let herself be led astray, but no one should think she was a bad woman. So in order to save her honor she had to find him still magical. The blood that had risen to her throat in fear and vexation now rushed pell-mell down to her hips.

At this moment he felt that it would be quite impossible to take a bird in his hand, and this naked skin was to be pressed against his naked and unprotected skin? His breast was to be filled with warmth from her breast? He sought to draw things out with jokes. They were tortured and fearful. He said, "Isn't it true that fat women lace their feet too. Along with their shoes. And above the knot the flesh spills over a little, and there is a little unpleasant smell there. A little smell that exists nowhere else in the world."

She said to herself: "He must be a writer; now I understand his odd behavior. Later I will play the elegant lady with him." She resolutely began to undress; she owed it to her honor.

He became anxious; now he knew for certain: I can never take this leap into another human being, let myself into an utterly alien existence. Since he did not move, she stopped; she was suddenly bad-tempered; she too became fearful. What if she had fallen victim to an unconscionable man? She did not know him. The woman, who had not revealed her name, began to have regrets. She still waited. But something told her: it will get better once we've gone further.

He felt all that. The idea "Open up!" tortured him. Like a child's toy. That's what she wants. But over and over again there is some new wall of disappointment with no way through, and then she will get angry with me.

And the second torture was: She's pursuing me. She's just unrolling herself. Always right in front of me. What's she talking about so incessantly? I'm supposed to fall like a dog all over the round, rolling ball of her life. Otherwise she'll do something to me. His eyes darted back and forth in the darkness like fish.

Now she was sitting before him in only shoes and stockings. Her hips rolled down in three swelling folds. She began to tremble.

She had taken off all her clothes because he had spoken about her. That seemed certain to her. And she felt that she was wronging him; did he not have to mistrust her, since he knew nothing more about her than that she had followed him? She wanted to tell him that Leopold was, of course, a good person. . . . Again silence intervened.

Then he heard himself saying the nonsensical sentence: Whoever loves is young. At the same moment he felt her arms around his neck. To save herself she had to find him enchanting. "Beloved, beloved! Leave your eyes, you look so suffering and noble!"

Then with the strength of despair he lifted up his burden and heard himself asking: "Would you rather make Kung Fu-tse, or do you prefer rollies?" She took these for technical terms from men's talk. She did not want to expose her ignorance. She made herself cozy with them. What does your Kung Fu-tse do? The tip of his tongue touched her lips. This ancient manner of understanding between people, such foreheads always sitting above such lips, was familiar to her. The stranger knew so much. She slowly flattened out her tongue and pushed it forward. Then she quickly drew it back and smiled roguishly; when she was still a child she knew herself to be already famous for her roguish smile. And she said without thinking, moved perhaps by some unconscious association of sounds: "I'd like rollies. My husband will be gone for a week."

At this moment he bit off her tongue. It seemed to him to be a long time before his teeth got all the way through. Then he felt it thick in his mouth. The storm of a great deed whirled up in him, but the unfortunate woman was a white, bleeding mass, beating all around her in a corner of the room, circling around a high, hoarse, screeching note, around the reeling root of a sound.

In those places where the woman and his reaction to her is described: Is this a woman at all? Or is it the being pushed from the experience into a jackal's den of the imagination, condensation of all the hatefulness of the world in the infantilely special person with skirts and ringlets, rage against the most lovable thing on earth?

It is probably unnecessary to say that this is not a true experience but a dream, for no decent person would think such a thing in a waking state.

The place of this dream lay on one of the major traffic arteries that radiate out from the center of Vienna. Even though from that time on, when world metropolises full of enormous rushing around came into being, Vienna was still only a big city, traffic in the peak hours filled this tube of streets with a dizzying stream of life, which can best be compared with swill being poured into a trough. Dark lumps of cars shot around in a no-longer-transparent fluid of voices, metals, air, stones, and wood, in a pleasantly tart smell of haste, through the standing throng of interests running in and out at the opening of a thousand stores, and the constitutive stream of pedestrians hastening toward some distant goal pushed forward. This is the city person's drink that invigorates the nerves. At the place of this dream fifty cars a minute came by on average, at a speed of twenty miles an hour, and six hundred pedestrians. If the eye, or at least the mind, took all that in, then the stimulus had to traverse a path of 1,800 feet per second, leaving aside smell, hearing, aroused desire, and everything else, and observing only the mad film.

An unnatural spread.

But the place itself did not appear on this film; only the fence around its grounds did. If one were propelled on past this garden fence, there lay behind it well-tended grounds, and among trees one saw a small white house with broad wings and looked into the noble stillness of a scholar's home. Between it and the nature in front of the fence the un-nature of trees, muffled sound, and pure air intervened; as indeed the un-nature of various ideals and antiquities also lie between life and the thinking of a scholar (and only a quite complicated connection makes it possible for life to afford scholars).

The scholar who had unfortunately had this dream had a great many friends among men and women, and was a quite pleasant, handsome, and well-to-do young man. In order not to expose him, and for various reasons, let us assume that his name was simply Anders [literally, "different": an earlier name for Ulrich—TRANS.].

Here it could also go on:
One of his women friends happened to be with him at the moment and was called . . . and because of the moral songs she sang. She looked like a beautiful woman from an illustrated magazine of 1870. Her beauty was like a lion's skin stuffed by a furrier. She spelled out this beauty from an invisible book and underlined the teasing as well as the tragic qualities of love with gestures like the emphases of an eight-year-old schoolgirl reciting Schiller.

It would not be appropriate to inquire further into the meaning of his horrible dream, but on the other hand we cannot avoid mentioning Christian Moosbrugger, for Moosbrugger doubtless had something to do with its source. Who was Christian Moosbrugger?

What distinguished him from other good-natured and right-thinking carpenters was merely that he was to be executed on account of several sex murders.

In one of the newspaper reports, a collection of which lay in front of Anders (while he held an unopened letter in his hand), it was said of Moosbrugger that he was good-natured. All the other reports described him in similar fashion, but the thing about his smile, for instance, was wrong, and in general the business about his self-important smile, his good nature, and his monstrous deeds was by no means a simple affair.

There was no doubt that he was, at times, mentally ill. But since the bestial crimes that he committed in this condition were presented in the newspapers in the most extreme detail, and thirstily sucked up by their readers, his mental illness must have somehow partaken of the general mental health. He had cut up a woman, a prostitute of the lowest class, with a knife in the most horrifying manner, and the newspapers fully and pitilessly described the delights, to be sure incomprehensible to us, of a wound reaching from the back part of the neck to the middle of the front part; further, two stab wounds to the breast, which bored through the heart, two more in the left side of the back, and the cutting off of the breasts. In spite of (the most vivid retching of) their loathing, the reporters and editors could not look away before adding up thirty-five stab wounds to the belly, which, moreover, was slit open by a wound running to the sacrum and continuing on up the back in a swarm of wounds, while the neck bore traces of strangulation.

Perhaps one ought not repeat this at all, for it is dubious whether the novelist will be allowed the protection of the duties of his calling enjoyed by the newspapers, which, like those men who prowl in the dark of night with shielded lanterns and seamen's boots, have to climb into all those things in which mankind, upon waking, is accustomed to proclaim its interest. But ultimately it cannot be said anywhere but in a less serious place than the newspapers how remarkable it is that no sooner were Moosbrugger's abominable excesses made known to thousands of people, who lose no opportunity to scold the public's desire for sensation, than they were immediately felt by these very people to be "at last something interesting again": by capable officials in a hurry to get to the office, by their fourteen-year-old sons, and by their spouses immersed in a cloud of household cares. People of course sighed over such a monster, but inwardly he preoccupied them more than their professions did. Indeed, it might happen that on going to bed the very correct Section Chief Tuzzi, or the second in command of the Nature Cure Association, said to his sleepy wife: What would you do if I were a Moosbrugger now?

C. 1932

49

ULRICH'S DIARY

Often Ulrich thought that everything he was experiencing with Agathe was reciprocal hypnotic suggestion and conceivable only under the influence of the idea that they had been chosen by some unusual destiny. At one time this destiny represented itself to them under the sign of the Siamese twins, at another under that of the Millennium, the love of the seraphs, or the myths of the "concave" experiencing of the world. These conversations were no longer repeated, but they had in the past assumed the more potent shadow of real events, of which mention was made earlier. One might call it merely half a conviction, if one is of the opinion that the kind of thinking involved in conviction is one that has to be entirely certain of its subject; but there is also a total conviction that arises simply from the absence of all objections, because an emotional mood that is strong and one-sidedly motivated keeps all doubt away from conscious awareness: there were times when Ulrich already felt almost convinced of something without even knowing what it was. But if he then asked himself—for he had to assume that he was suffering from delusions—what it was that he and Agathe must have reciprocally imagined at the beginning, their wondrous feeling for each other or the no less remarkable alteration in their thinking in which this feeling expressed itself, that could not be determined either; for both had appeared at the very beginning, and taken singly, one was as unfounded as the other.

This sometimes made him think of the idea of a hypnotic suggestion, and then he felt the uncanny anxiety that steals up on the independent will which sees itself treacherously attacked and shackled from within. "What am I to understand by this? How is one to explain this vulgar notion of hypnosis, which I use as facilely as everyone else, without understanding it? I was reading about it today," Ulrich noted on a piece of paper. "The language of animals consists of affective expressions that evoke the same affects in their companions. Warning call, feeding call, mating call. I might add that these utterances activate and permeate not only the same affect but also quite directly the action associated with it. The terror call, the mating call, goes right through them! Your word is in me and moves me: if the animal were a person it would feel a mysterious, incorporeal union! But this affective suggestibility is also supposed to be still completely intact in people, in spite of the highly developed language of reason. Affect is contagious: panic, yawning. It easily evokes the ideas appropriate to it: a cheerful person spreads cheerfulness. It also encroaches on unsuitable vehicles: this occurs in all gradations, from the silliness of a love token to the complete frenzy of love, whose brainstorms are worthy of the madhouse. But affect also knows how to exclude what is inappropriate, and in both ways evokes in people that persistent unified attitude that gives the state of hypnotic suggestion the power of fixed ideas. Hypnosis is only a special case of these general relations. I like this explanation, and I'll adopt it. A singular, persistent, unified attitude, but one that blocks us off from the totality of life: that is our condition!"

Ulrich was now beginning to write many such pages. They formed a sort of diary, with whose aid he sought to preserve the mental clarity he felt was threatened. But immediately after he had put the first of his notes on paper, he thought of a second: "What I have called magnanimity may also be connected with hypnotic suggestion. By passing over what is not part of it, and seizing hold of what furthers it, it is magnanimous." When that was done, his observations did not, of course, seem nearly as remarkable as they had before he had written them down, and he made another effort to look for an indisputable milestone of the condition in which he found himself together with his sister. He found it once more in the realization that thinking and feeling were changed in the same sense, and they not only corresponded with each other to a remarkable degree but also stood in contrast to the ordinary condition as something one-sided, indeed almost insoluble and addictive, an inevitable synthesis of aspirations and insights of all kinds. When their conversations were in the right mood—and the susceptibility to this was extremely great—the impression they gave was never that one word was forcing another, or one action dragging the next along after it, but that something was aroused in the mind to which the answer followed as the next-higher step. Every movement of the mind became the discovery of a new, even finer movement; they furthered each other reciprocally, and in this manner gave rise to the impression of an intensification that did not end, and of a discussion that rose without falling. It seemed that the last word could never be spoken, for every end was a beginning, and every final result the start of a new opening, so that every second shone like the rising sun but at the same time carried with it the peaceful passing of the setting sun. "If I were a believer, I would find in this the confirmation of the unfathomable assertion that His nearness is for us as inexpressible a raising up as our oppressive helplessness allows us to feel!" Ulrich wrote.

He recalled having read with his senses on fire, in those early years when he was entering upon his intellectual life, the description of similar feelings in all sorts of books that he never read through to the end because impatience and a will that urged him to assert his own power prevented him, although he was moved by them, indeed for just that reason. Then too, he had not lived as was to have been expected, and when he now happened to pick up several of these books again, which was something he did gladly, meeting the old witnesses once more made it seem as if he were quietly entering a door in his house that he had once arrogantly slammed shut. His life seemed to lie unrealized behind him, or perhaps even before him. Intentions not carried out can be like rejected lovers in dreams, who have remained beautiful over many years while the astonished wanderer returning home sees himself devastated: in the exquisite expansion of the power of one's dreams, one thinks these lovers make one grow young again, and this was the mood, divided between enterprise and doubt, between the tips of flame and ashes, in which Ulrich now most frequently found himself. He read a great deal. Agathe, too, read a great deal. She was already content that the passion for reading, which had accompanied her in all the circumstances of her life, no longer served as mere distraction but had a purpose, and she kept up with her brother like a girl whose blowing dress leaves her no time to think about the path she's taking. It happened that brother and sister got up in the night, after just having gone to bed, and met each other anew with their books, or that they prevented each other from going to bed at all, in spite of the late hour. About this Ulrich wrote: "It seems to be the only passion we permit ourselves. Even when we are tired we don't want to part. Agathe says: 'Aren't we brother and sister?' That means: Siamese twins; for otherwise it would be meaningless. Even when we're too tired to talk she won't go to bed, because we can't sleep beside each other. I promise to sit beside her until she falls asleep, but she doesn't want to undress and get into bed; not out of shame but because she would be doing something before I did. We put on bathrobes. A few times we've even fallen asleep leaning on each other. She was warm with the fervor of her mind. I had, to support her, wrapped my arm around her body and didn't even realize it. She has fewer ideas than I do, but a higher temperature. She must have a very warm skin. In the morning we are pale with fatigue, and sleep for part of the day. Incidentally, we don't derive the slightest intellectual progress from this reading. We burn in the books like the wick in oil. We assimilate them really without any effect other than our burning. . . ."

Ulrich added: "The young person listens with only half an ear to the voice of those books which become his destiny: he flees them in order to raise his own voice! For he is not seeking truth; he is seeking himself. That's the way it was with me too. Large-scale conclusion: There are always new people and always the old events, merely mixed in new combinations! Moral fragility of the age. They are essentially like our reading, a burning for its own sake. When was the last time I told myself that? Shortly before Agathe's arrival. Ultimate cause of this phenomenon? The absence of system, principles, a goal, and also absence of the possibility of intensifying life and any logical consequence in it. I hope to be able to write down some things that have occurred to me about this. It's part of the 'General Secretariat.' But the strange thing about my present condition is that I am further away than ever from such active participation in intellectual work. That's Agathe's influence. She radiates immobility. Nevertheless, this incoherent state has peculiar weight. It is pregnant with meaning. What characterizes it, I would say, is the great amount of rapture it contains; although this notion is of course as vague as all the rest. Temporizing restriction, which I allow myself to be guilty of! *Our* condition is that other life which has always hovered before me. Agathe is working toward it, but I ask myself: can it be carried out as actual life? Not long ago she, too, asked me about that. . . ."

But Agathe, when she had done so, had merely lowered her book and asked: "Can you love two people who are enemies?" She added by way of explanation: "I sometimes read something in a book that contradicts what I have read in another book, but I love both passages. Then I think of how both of us, you and I, contradict each other about lots of things. Isn't that what it depends on? Or is conscience not involved?"

Ulrich immediately recalled that in the irresponsible state of mind in which she had altered the will, she had asked him something similar. This led to a remarkable depth and undermining beneath the present situation, for the main current of his thoughts led Agathe's statement without reflection back to Lindner. He knew that she was seeing him; she had, to be sure, never told him so, but also made no efforts to conceal it.

The response to this open manner of concealment was Ulrich's diary. Agathe was not supposed to know anything about it.

When he wrote in it, he suffered from the feeling of having committed an act of disloyalty. Or it reinforced and liberated him, for the chilling state of the wrong secretly committed destroyed the intellectual magic spell that was feared as much as it was desired.

That is why in response to Agathe's question Ulrich smiled but gave no other answer.

But now Agathe had suddenly asked: "Do you have mistresses?" This was the first time that she was again addressing such a question to him. "You should, of course," she added, "but you told me yourself that you don't love them!" And then she asked: "Do you have another friend besides me?"

She said this casually, as if she were no longer expecting an answer, but also in an easy and playful way, as if a tiny quantity of a very precious substance were lying in the palm of her hand and she was preoccupied with it.

Late at night Ulrich wrote down in his diary the answer he had given.

50

An entry

It was only one of life's small challenges that she asked me this question, and what it means is: But you and I are *still* living outside of the "condition"! One might just as well exclaim: "Give me some water, please!" or: "Stop! Leave the light burning!" It is the request of a moment, something hasty, unconsidered, and nothing more. I say "nothing more," but still I know that it's nothing less than if a goddess were running to catch a bus! A most unmystic gait, an implosion of absurdity! Such small experiences demonstrate how much our Other Condition assumes a single, specific state of mind, and capsizes in an instant if one disturbs its equilibrium.

And yet it is such moments that make one really happy. How beautiful Agathe's voice is! What trust lies in such a tiny request, popping up in the midst of a high and solemn context! It's touching, the way a bouquet of expensive flowers snagged with a wool thread off the beloved's dress is touching, or a protruding piece of wire for which the hands of the bouquet maker were too weak. At such moments one knows exactly that one is overestimating oneself, and yet everything that is more than oneself, all the thoughts of mankind, seem like a spiderweb; the body is the finger that tears it at every moment and to which a wisp still clings.

I just said: The hands of the bouquet maker and abandoned myself to the seesaw feeling of a simile, as if this woman could never be old and fat. That's moonshine of the wrong sort! And that's why I gave Agathe a methodical lecture rather than a direct answer. But I was really only describing the life that hovers before me. I'd like to repeat that and, if I can, improve on it.

In the center stands something I have called motivation. In ordinary life we act not according to motivation but according to necessity, in a concatenation of cause and effect; of course something of ourselves is always involved in this concatenation, which makes us think we are free. This freedom of will is man's ability to do voluntarily what he wishes involuntarily. But motivation has nothing to do with wishing; it cannot be divided according to the opposition of freedom and compulsion: it is the highest freedom and the most profound compulsion. I chose the word because I couldn't find a better one; it's probably related to the painter's term "motif." When a landscape painter goes out in the morning with the intention of finding a motif he will usually find it, that is, he will find something that fulfills his intention; yet it would be more accurate to say: something that fits in with his intention—the way a word, unless it happens to be too big, fits in every mouth. For something that fulfills is rare, it overfills immediately, spilling over the intention and seizing hold of the entire person. The painter who originally intended to paint "something," even though "from his own point of view," now paints to paint, he paints for the salvation of his soul, and only in such moments does he really have a motif before him; at all other times he merely talks himself into thinking he does. Something has come over him that crushes intention and will. When I say it has nothing at all to do with them, I am of course exaggerating. But one must exaggerate when one is looking at the region that one's soul calls home. There are surely all sorts of transitions, but they are like those of the spectrum: you go through innumerable gradations from green to red, but when you are there you are all there, and there is no longer the slightest trace of green.

Agathe said the gradation is the same as when one more or less lets things happen, does some things from inclination, and finally when one acts from love.

At any rate, there is something similar in speaking, too. One can clearly make a distinction between a thought that is only thinking and a thought that moves the entire person. In between are all sorts of transitions. I said to Agathe: Let's only talk about what moves the entire person!

But when I'm alone I think how murky that is. A scientific idea can also move me. But that isn't the kind of moving that matters. On the other hand, an affect, too, can move me totally, and yet afterward I am merely confounded. The truer something is, the more it is turned away from us in a peculiar way, no matter how much it may concern us. I've asked myself about this remarkable connection a thousand times. One might think that the less "objective" something is, the more "subjective," the more it would have to be turned toward us in the same way, but that is false; subjectivity turns its back on our inner being in just the same way that objectivity does. One is subjective in questions where one thinks one way today and another tomorrow, either because one doesn't know enough or because the object itself depends on the whim of the emotions: but what Agathe and I would like to say to each other is not the provisional or incidental expression of a conviction that on some better occasion could be raised to the status of truth, but could equally well be recognized as error, and nothing is more alien to our condition than the irresponsibility and sloppiness of such witty brainstorms, for between us everything is governed by a strict law, even if we can't articulate it. The boundary between subjectivity and objectivity crosses without touching the boundary along which we are moving.

Or should I perhaps rather restrict myself to the uprooted subjectivity of the arguments one carries on as an adolescent with one's friends? to their mixture of personal sensitivity and impartiality, their conversions and apostasies? These are the preliminary stage of politics and history and of humanitarianism, with their vague wishy-washiness. They move the entire self, they are connected with its passions and seek to lend them the dignity of a spiritual law and the appearance of an infallible system. What they mean to us lies in their indications of how we ought to be. And all right, even when Agathe tells me something, it's always as if her words go through *me* and not merely through the sphere of thoughts to which they are addressed. But what happens between us doesn't appear to have great significance. It is so quiet. It avoids knowledge. "Milky" and "opalizing" are the words that occur to me: what happens between us is like a movement in a shimmering but not very transparent liquid, which is always moved along with it as a whole. What happens is almost entirely a matter of indifference: everything goes through life's center. Or comes from it to us. Happens with the remarkable feeling that everything we have ever done and could do is also involved. If I try to describe it as concretely as possible, I would have to say: Agathe gives me some answer or other or does something, and right away it takes on for me as much significance as it has for her, indeed apparently the same significance, or one like it. Perhaps in reality I don't understand her rightly at all, but I complement her in the direction of her inner motion. Because we are in the same state of excitement, we are evidently guessing at what can intensify it and have to follow along unresistingly. When two people find themselves in anger or in love, they intensify each other in similar fashion. But the uniqueness of the excitement, and the significance that everything assumes in this state of excitement, is precisely what is extraordinary.

If I could say that we are accompanied by the feeling of living in harmony with God, it would be simple; but how can one describe without presuppositions what it is that constantly excites us? "In harmony" is right, but with what cannot be said. We are accompanied by the feeling that we have reached the middle of our being, the secret center, where life's centrifugal force is preserved, where the incessant twisting of experience ceases, where the conveyor belt of stamping and ejecting that makes the soul resemble a machine stops, where motion is rest; that we have arrived at the axis of the spinning top. These are symbolic expressions, and I absolutely hate these symbols, because they are so ready to hand and spread out endlessly without yielding anything. Let me see if I

can attempt it once again, and as rationally as possible: the state of excitement in which we live is that of correctness. This word, which used
this way is as unusual as it is sensible, calms me somewhat. The feeling of
correctness contains contentment and satiation. Conviction and the
bringing of things to the still point are part of it; it is the profound state
into which one falls after attaining one's goal. If I continue to represent
it to myself this way and ask myself: what is the goal that is attained? I
don't know. Yet it's really not quite right, either, to speak of a state of the
attained goal; it's at least just as true that this state is accompanied by an
enduring impression of intensification. But it is an intensification without progression. It is also a state of the highest happiness, although it
does not lead beyond a weak smile. At every second we feel ourselves
swept away, yet externally and internally we hold ourselves rather inert;
the motion never ceases, but it oscillates in the smallest space. Also involved is a profound collectedness combined with a broad dispersion
and the awareness of animated activity, with a breakthrough by means of
a process we do not sufficiently understand. Thus my intention to limit
myself to the most neutral description immediately results again in surprising contradictions. But what presents itself so disjointedly to the
mind is, as experience, of great simplicity. It is simply there; so to be
properly understood it would also have to be simple!*

There is also between Agathe and me not the slightest discrepancy in
the opinion that the question: "How should I live?," which we have both
taken upon ourselves, is to be answered: *This* is the way we should live!

And sometimes I think it's crazy.

51

END OF THE ENTRY

I now see the task more clearly. Something in human life makes happiness short, so much so that happiness and brevity apparently go together
like siblings. This makes all the great and happy hours of our existence

---

*This dilemma, that the state of highest happiness is a state of inertness and passivity
instead of leading to the simplicity of experience (= action), is one that Musil returns to
again and again, both philosophically and in terms of how to work it into the fabric of the
novel.—TRANS.

disjointed—a time that drifts *in* time in fragments—and gives to all other hours their necessary, emergency coherence. This "something" causes us to lead a life that does not touch us inwardly. It causes us to gobble people as easily as to build cathedrals. It is the reason why all that happens is always only "pseudoreality," what is real merely in an external sense. It bears the guilt for our being deceived by all our passions. It evokes the ever-recurring futility of youth and the senseless eternal upheaval of the ages. It explains why activity is merely the result of the instinct for activity rather than a person's decision, why our actions complete themselves as insistently as if they belonged more to each other than to us, and why our experiences can fly in the air but not in our will. This "something" has the same significance as our not quite knowing what to do with all the spirit we produce; it also causes us to not love ourselves and is the reason we may well find ourselves talented but, all things considered, see no purpose in it.

This "something" is: that over and over again we leave the condition of significance in order to enter the state of what is in and of itself meaningless in order to bring some significance to it. We leave the condition of the meaningful and enter the state of the necessary and makeshift; we leave the condition of life to step into the world of the dead. But now that I have written this down, I notice that what I am saying is a tautology and apparently meaningless. Yet before I wrote, what was in my head was: "Agathe gives me some answer or other, a sign; it makes me happy"; and then the thought: "We do not step out of the world of the intellect in order to put intellect in an unintellectual world." And it seemed to me that this thought was complete, and that the "stepping out" characterizes exactly what I mean. And I only need to put myself back in that state for it still to seem to me to be so.

I must ask myself how a stranger might understand me. When I say "significance," he would certainly understand: what is significant. When I say "intellect," he would first of all understand: stimulation, active thinking, receptivity, and the exercise of will. And it would seem to him a matter of course that one must step out of the world of the intellect and carry its significance into life; indeed, he would consider such a striving for "intellectualization" as the worthiest fulfillment of human tasks. How can I express that "intellectualization" is already original sin, and "not to leave the world of the intellect" a commandment that knows no gradations but is fulfilled either entirely or not at all?

Meanwhile a better explanation has occurred to me. The state of excitement in which we find ourselves, Agathe and I, doesn't urge us to actions or to truths, which means that it doesn't break anything off from the edge, but flows back into itself again through that which it evokes.

This is of course only a description of the *form* of what happens. But when I describe in this way *what* I experience, I am able to grasp the changed, indeed quite different, role that my conduct, my action, has: What I do is no longer the discharge of my tension in the final form of a state in which I have found myself, but a channel and relay station on the way back to significance!

To be sure, I almost said: "Way back to an intensification of my tension"—but then one of those contradictions occurred to me which our condition exhibits, namely that it demonstrates no progression and therefore can't very well demonstrate intensification either. Accordingly, I thought I ought to say "way back to myself"—how imprecise all this is!—but the condition is not in the least egotistic but full of a love turned toward the world. And so I simply wrote "significance" again, and the word is good and natural in its context, without my having so far succeeded in getting at its content.

But as uncertain as all this is, a life has always hovered before me whose centerpiece this would be. In all the other ways I've lived, I always had the obscure feeling of having seen it, forgotten it, and not found it again. It robbed me of satisfaction in everything that was mere calculating and thinking, but it also made me come home after every adventure and from every passion with the stale feeling of having missed the mark, until finally I lost almost all desire to have an effect in the world. That happened because I did not want to let anything compel me to leave the sphere of significance. Now I can also say what "motif" is. Motif is what leads me from significance to significance. Something happens, or something is said, and that increases the meaning of two human lives and unites them through its meaning, and what happens, which physical or legal concept it represents, is quite unimportant, plays absolutely no role in it.

But can I imagine what that means in its fullest extent, can I even imagine what it means in its smallest? I must try. A person does something . . . no, I can't duck it: Professor Lindner does something! He arouses Agathe's inclination. I feel this event, want to spoil it and negate it — and the moment I yield to my dislike, I step out of the sphere of significance. What *I* feel can never become a motif for Agathe. My breast may be full of vexation or anger, my head an arsenal of sharp and ready objections—my heart is empty! My condition is then suddenly negative! My state is no longer positive! There's another marvelous pair of notions I've got hold of! What makes me think of the characterizations "positive" and "negative"? I unexpectedly recall a day when I was also sitting with some paper in front of me and trying to write—at the time it was to be a letter to Agathe. And gradually it comes to mind: a condition of "do" and a condition of "don't" as the two component elements of every morality, the "do" prevailing during its rise, the "don't" during the satiety of its reign—is not this relationship between "challenge" and "prohibition" the same as what I am now calling positive and negative? The connection between Agathe and me characterized by everything being challenge and nothing prohibition? I recall speaking at that time of Agathe's passionate, affirming goodness, which in an age in which things of that sort are no longer understood looks like a primitive vice. I said: It's like returning home after the longest time and drinking water from the well of one's village! And challenge of course does not mean that we demand but means that everything we do demands the utmost from us.

Not leaving the sphere of the significant would therefore be the same as a life in pure positiveness? The thought that it is also the same as "living essentially" alarms me, although it was to be expected. For what else should "essentially" signify? The word probably comes from mysticism or metaphysics, and characterizes the opposition to all earthly happenings that are without peace and full of doubts; but since we have separated ourselves from Heaven, it lives on on earth as the longing to find among thousands of moral convictions the one that gives life a meaning that does not change. Endless conversations between Agathe and me on the subject! Her youthful desire for moral instruction alongside the defiance in which she wanted to kill Hagauer and has at least really injured him in a material way! And the same search for conviction everywhere in the world; the intimation that man can't live without morality, and the deep disquiet at how his own emotions undermine every one of them! Where is the possibility of a "whole" life, a "complete" conviction, a love that is without any admixture of not-love, without a shred of self-seeking and selfishness? What that means is: only living positively. And it means: not wanting to admit any happening without "significance" whenever I speak of a "never-ending condition," in contrast to the "eternally futile moment-to-moment quality" of our usual way of acting, or of the alliance of every momentary state with a "lasting state" of the emotions, which restores our "responsibility." I could go on repeating such expressions for pages, expressions that characterized what we meant from one side or another. We summarized it as "living essentially," always somewhat embarrassed by the term's bombastic-transcendental overtones, but we had no other that would have been simpler to use. So it is no small surprise for me to suddenly find almost in my hands what I was seeking in the clouds!

Of course it is part of the peculiarity of our condition that every new observation assimilates all the earlier ones, so that there is no hierarchy among them; they seem, rather, to be infinitely entangled. I could just as well go on to call our condition magnanimous, which in fact I did some days ago, as I could characterize it as creative, for creating and creation are possible only in an attitude that is positive through and through, and so that, too, would be in accord; ultimately such a life, in which every moment is to be as significant as possible, is also that "life in the sense of the maximal challenge" which I sometimes imagined as the spiritual complement to the laconic resolve of true science. But whether maximal, magnanimous, creative, or significant, essential or whole, how do I account for my feelings for Professor Lindner being what they are? That's the problem I am drawn back to, the crux of the experiment, the crossroads! It occurs to me that I have deprived him of the possibility of having part of Agathe. Why? Because having part of, indeed even understanding, is never possible through "putting oneself in the place of the other," but is possible only if both mutually take part in something greater. It's impossible for me to feel my sister's headaches; but I find myself transported with her in a state in which there is no pain, or where pain has the hovering wings of bliss!

I have doubts about this, I see the exaggeration in it. But perhaps that's only because I'm not capable of ecstasy?

Toward Lindner I would have to conduct myself as if I were somehow united with him in God. Even a smaller whole, like "nation" or some other confraternity, would suffice. At least it would suffice to prescribe my conduct. Even an idea in common would be enough. It merely has to be something new and dynamic that is not merely Lindner and I. So the answer to Agathe's question, what a contradiction signifies between two books both of which one loves, is: it never signifies a calculation or a balance, but signifies a third, dynamic thing, which envelops both aspects in itself. And that's how the life was that was always before my eyes, even if rarely clearly: the people united, I united with people through something that makes us renounce our hundred dislikes. The contradictions and hostilities that exist between us cannot be denied, but one can also imagine them "suspended," the way the strong current of a liquid picks up and suspends whatever it encounters in its path. There would then not be certain feelings among people, but there would be others. All impossible feelings could be summarized as neutral and negative; as petty, gnawing, constricting, base, but also as indifferent or merely rooted in connections that were necessary. So what remains would be great, increasing, demanding, encumbered, affirming, rising: in my hurry I can't describe it adequately, but it lay in the depths of my body like a dream, and isn't what I ultimately wanted simply to love life and everyone in it? I, with my arms, my muscles, trained to the point of malignity, basically nothing but crazy for love and lacking love? Is this the secret formula of my life?

I can conceive of that when I fantasize and think of the world and people, but not when I think of Lindner, that specific, ridiculous person, the man Agathe will perhaps see again tomorrow in order to discuss with him what she does not discuss with me. So what's left? That there are two groups of emotions which can be separated to some extent, which I would now again like to characterize only as positive and negative conditions, without placing a value on them, but merely according to a peculiarity of their appearance; although I love one of these two overall conditions from the depths (that also means: well hidden) of my soul. And the reality is left that I now find myself almost constantly in this condition, and Agathe too! Perhaps this is a great experiment that fate intends with me. Perhaps everything I have attempted was there only so that I could experience this. But I also fear that there's a vicious circle lurking in everything that I think I have understood up to now. For I don't want—if I now go back to my original motif—to leave the state of "significance," and if I try to tell myself what significance is, all I come back to again and again is the state I'm in, which is that I don't want to leave a specific state! So I don't believe I'm looking at the truth, but what I experience is certainly not simply subjective, either; it reaches out for the truth with a thousand arms. For that reason it could truly seem to me to be a hypnotic suggestion. All my emotions happen to be remarkably homogeneous or harmonized, and the resistive ones are excluded, and such a condition of the emotions, which regulates action in a unified way, is precisely what is regarded as the centerpiece of a hypnosis. But can something be hypnotic whose premonition, whose first traces, I can follow back through almost my entire life?

So there remains . . . ? It isn't imagination and it isn't reality; even if it is not hypnotic suggestion, I would almost have to conclude that it is the beginning of suprareality.

SKETCHES AND NOTES ABOUT THE NOVEL

1920–1929

Preface:

This novel takes place before 1914, a time that young people will no longer know at all. And the novel does not describe this time the way it really was, so that one could learn about it from this book. But it describes the time as it is mirrored in a person outside the mainstream. Then what does this novel have to do with people of today? Why don't I write a novel about today instead? This has to be established, as best it can.

But that it concerns an (invented) story should also become part of the manner of its telling. The path of history is to be applied not only in the novel but to it.

From the perspective of the book, the portrayal of the time has to be abridged. But I'm not capable of that. The Parallel Campaign, for instance, ought to connect with the Eucharistic Congress and other things about which I know too little. Absolute necessity of creating the technique from this error!

Preface

Ulrich considers himself a person who has a message to bring the world. Fragments are to be found here.

Later he judges [. . .]: In one's lifetime one must have presented a good front and the like if one wants to have even a posthumous effect. He is not bad, just gives up.

That is also his development in the novel. *He does not write his book but is present in all the events.*

The narrator is, in a way, his friend.

Present Ulrich not as the "true-strong" person but as an important statement that has gone astray.

Mood: This is the tragedy of the failed person (more properly: the person who in questions of emotion and understanding is always aware of a further possibility. For he is not simply a failure) who is always alone, in contradiction with everything, and cannot change anything. All the rest is logically consistent.

Preface

People will find the excuse—because they don't want to explore the idea—that what is offered here is as much essay as novel.

Query: Why is it that people today don't pay attention to ideas in art, while in other respects they demonstrate an absolutely ridiculous interest in "doctrines"?

1st section before Agathe

An athletic young man—very intellectual—attempts normal life—has ideas that don't seem to fit in—suspicious of the transparent humbug with ideals—tries to find a way out by means of functional morality—is himself morally indifferent—but unhappy about it—is arrogant toward his time but always looking for a way out of his arrogance—and from this an emotion crystallizes: swimming through a space—jagged stage sets loom up—Ulrich was good. As a child. He simply saw that this "good" could not become the desiccated commonly accepted one. If among his ideas there are some that are right, then he is a precursor. But apparently evil develops the way he doesn't imagine it à la journalism. He is interested in evil and despises the common.

Preface

I dedicate this novel to German youth. Not the youth of today—intellectual vacuum after the war—quite amusing frauds—but the youth that will come after a time and that will have to begin exactly where we stopped before the war, etc. (On this also rests my justification for writing a prewar novel today!)

Preface

"Superfluous," "wandering" discussions: that's a reproach that's often been made against me, in which it was perhaps graciously conceded that I *could* tell a story. But these discussions are for me the most important thing!

I could have depicted many things more realistically. For instance,

Hans Sepp and National Socialist politics. But there is already enough of the ridiculous in the book, and I then would not have been able to counterbalance it, which was what I was trying to do.

Preface

Where one speaks of relative originality:

The phenomenon that a relatively or entirely original writer—completely inaccessible to the average critic—who in desperation analyzes him only in isolated, dependent particles—as has happened to me.

Preface

Why Vienna instead of an invented metropolis. Because it would have been more effort to invent one than a "crossed-out" Vienna.

Manner of representation to be frequently used

Assemble a composite person, but with cards faceup! From settled ideas and a few obsessive linkages of ideas, e.g., the way Hagauer is. All the intellectual characters this way: Arnheim, Diotima, etc. Whatever is added that is human and personal, particularly to those characters who are "only people," is accidental; moreover, from the psychological point of view also characteristic, frequently repellent, like Arnheim's predilection for the behind, or wishy-washy psychology like Schnitzler's.

events
depictions°
conversations } are the only bearers of the narration
interweavings

°of the nature of the person, of changes in the physical and moral landscape

Theories, half ironic, chiefly in the
agitations of the unsympathetic and
half-sympathetic figures

Journey with Agathe

Trip across. Seasickness. Burgeoning awareness of a fearful passion for each other because they see each other in this state, bear it, feel it appropriate, with mouths agape, vomiting. The whole ship an orgy.

Ancona. Exhaustion. Taken for a married couple, room with double bed; they don't want to reject it; fear almost amounting to a feeling of persecution, sweetness.

Only the terrible things about Rome. The smoothed and polished, the ravinelike streets with green window shutters. The being tortured from before.

That was the first trip. On the second, with Clarisse, he recalls it. In Venice, where Clarisse is confined on the way back, meeting with Gustav [the model for Walter—TRANS.]. Rather fat paunch, deep devotion to Clarisse. Forced back to Vienna; meeting with Agathe, beginning of the spy story. The inner city entwined around St. Stephen's Cathedral like a ball of tangled yarn. Yellow-gray darkness. Air like down.

On the trip: They really don't do anything at all; they only suffer the fear that they could be accused, and the desire.

Someplace or other, memory from Esslingen. Second floor of the museum. He is sitting at the window; it mirrors nothing, reflects the room. But if one bends closer, then from all sides the blackness plunges in, and then the church, the jagged black houses with their caps of snow.

First trip. It's boringly different; we're traveling as man and wife. Nothing else; everything only in the hesitation that they have to overcome inwardly to do so. They are traveling without passports. Morning in Budapest. Conference with a lawyer. The square before the Parliament: something breaks under their feet like thin sheets of ice; gusts of wind sweep the square clean of people, mere existence makes itself palpable as an exertion. Impatience to get on the train. Just ten minutes before departure, resistance against order. Reacting to some kind of feeling, they buy second-class tickets; some pleasant thought or other of black leather. Tip, alone. Everywhere they are taken for a young married couple. It's boring, Agathe lies down to nap. It turns fine; white plain like a sea, forests buried in snow, heavy pillows of snow on the branches of the firs. Achilles [earlier name for Ulrich—TRANS.] wakes Agathe up; this white and black, perhaps a white and mysteriously bottle-green landscape rushes through their eyes—lovely, she says, presses his hand—and melts into sleep; he stares at the strange countryside, sees in the darkness of the compartment Agathe's shoulders and hips as she lies on her side, like hills, mysterious. . . .

Morning near Fiume. Through the opened window damp, warm air. Speckled flanks of the bowl of the valley they are descending into.

In Fiume rain, storm. Somebody in the train says that the steamer left already this morning; someone else: it will still be there. Going across the harbor square the storm turns their umbrella inside out—laughter on the flagstones, the rain soaks their clothes so that they are wading in their shoes.

Walk in the sunshine, palm trees, a street like a ribbon tied in bows.

What is an execution compared to an operation?

He drives back with someone else, who is horrified. When they get to where the pavement begins, the carriage jolts so that they don't continue talking. Trees are torn past, sometimes the glance is flung through a hole into sand, pines. . . .

The man: walks, looks around. Achilles feels an inexpressible link to him. Dostoyevskian. Laughs at it. Yields voluntarily.

At his execution, Moosbrugger is simply embarrassed. Execution like a fire-brigade drill. The solemn flourishes at the end don't move Ulrich. On his way out he nods vaguely and politely. Feels that it is perhaps out of place. Only when he looks into the face of his driver does he notice a difference of brightness and warmth in the surroundings as opposed to before. This face seems to him quite hard, he sees every single hair of the beard stubble. A man who was there to do a journalistic study, whom he had invited to share his carriage and forgotten, gets in with him. Out of some vague feeling he remains sitting on the right. Country road, then extended city street. Pubs, people in black skirts and shirtsleeves. Ulrich feels a vague, scornful hatred for these people.

Study for Conclusion

Ulrich, to begin with without irony:

Reversal of a feeling about life with hard, bright, challenging . . . into soft, dark, smeared . . . What was so important to one a moment ago becomes completely indifferent.

One has the feeling that this passivity is not entirely without activity, but this activity is something quite different from the disputatious passivity of before. Ulrich remembers having felt something similar in [chapter] 30. He was dissatisfied with himself and (1) his house made him shudder. He recalled once more his feeling of the "ahistorical," the world new with every day. In addition: accidental and essential qualities, possibly being broken in spirit from strength; one's being is still strength, but the object being seized is always simply larger.

(1) I was born, abandoned into this world; from one protective darkness into another. Mother? Ulrich had not had a mother. The world my mother? He stood up and stretched his muscles.

[Fragment]

I did not answer my father's letter. An odd destiny had led me into the same aristocratic circles to which he owed his rise in life, the naïve lack of dignity of which irritated me; I had resolved to look around in these circles as in a room into which one had stumbled by some secret chance, and if in doing so I would have had to have the least thought of a resemblance, this would have been impossible for me. It was no doubt for this reason that I refrained from giving my father the satisfaction of having his wish fulfilled. He took it amiss, and I received no more letters from him, so that not long after, I was completely surprised by a message reporting his demise. I cannot say I was shaken; we had little fondness for each other. Also, I was totally lacking in the feeling for that continuity which, it is claimed, binds ancestors and posterity; the inheritance of certain dispositions and qualities, while certainly present, did not seem to me any more important than that the most disparate melodies can be constructed from the same notes, and the generally prevailing demand for pious respect is a con game; at least that's how most unconstrained young people feel it, although later they deny it. Besides, I was in a great hurry to complete the arrangements for my trip.

I remember that while I was overseeing the packing, the barbaric ideas of patriarchy that are dinned into shrinking children went through my head; the hand that strikes out at the father grows from the grave, the disobedient child is afflicted with its parents' tears when they are dead, and many such techniques from the wild primitive era of mankind. Primal epochs come to life again in the nursery, where nannies let themselves go. Somewhat later I was overcome by the desolate feeling that the entire atmosphere surrounding the ultimate questions and their philosophy, which I had involuntarily been seeking in my memory, are of a pronounced banality. Just as when you look up at the starry sky for the space of five minutes. We know nothing, and what we feel is warmed-over cabbage. I did not even know whether I ought to give myself over to my distaste or whether I should set it straight; the beginnings of both were in me. Whatever the philosophers may have contributed, no matter how enormous it might be as an intellectual accomplishment, from the human point of view we have remained in these questions undeniably limited and boring. Of course my own ideas shared in this too, except that it suddenly seemed to me incredibly remarkable that one lives with this quite contentedly. The well-known feeling of extraterritoriality rose up in me: even if I do not presume to be able to order things and thoughts any better, in the order that they have found for themselves they are for me immensely alien. And I gradually noticed that I had fallen into a quite specific stream of ideas and emotions that I had almost forgotten.

The thought of my father, whom I did not esteem, was unpleasant for me, the way a plant might feel whose roots have been burned by acid. I remembered once having said to someone: The founders of empires have no ancestors! That, too, was now unpleasant to me, because it sounded so childishly arrogant, if I had meant just then that everyone ought to be such a founder of kingdoms. That person was my

Or: I had hardly begun to look around in my new circle when I received a telegram from my father that reported . . . I was now completely master of my life. When I stepped out onto the square in front of the railroad station . . .

August 16, 1929, evening

The man without qualities thought through consistently
First considerations

Don't give him a name. Explain briefly in Part I. It's not hard to say what a man without qualities looks like: like most other people.

There is only at times a shimmer in him, as in a solution that is trying to crystallize but always drops back.

Clarisse says and sees: You look like Satan. Colossal energy, etc.

Walter says: Your appearance is falling apart, etc. More or less what could be said about him.

Arnheim and Diotima are troubled. Arnheim says: The "cousin."

It's only for the police that he has qualities. For General Stumm: The old comrade.

For Count Leinsdorf he is something definite (true).

For Bonadea he is splendid, mean, etc.

I say: the or a man without qualities (and this is without overvaluing him, as would be the case with a "hero" Ulrich) is an object to be depicted. I constantly ask myself: what would a man without qualities say, think, do, in such a situation.

The ideas are such as present themselves to any clever person today. They could also be different; it doesn't amount to the formation of a will or a conviction, beyond a given point or a paranoid system.

By this means one gains relations to the characters, the situative dialogue.

Of course they are all without qualities, but in Ulrich it is somehow visible.

He is tall, etc., sympathetic but also unsympathetic.

The other people, on the other hand, have their stories told properly.

Possibly: Everything about the man without qualities in the present tense, everything else that is narrated in the imperfect.

Characterize Ulrich as unsympathetically as myself.

Arnheim calls him: The young doctor.

Diotima: My learned cousin (with ironic undertone).

Bring out more strongly the leave from life: resolve to commit suicide (instead of that, then the war); don't give reasons. They were neither concrete ones nor a disdain for life; on the contrary, although he found life abominable he made an effort to love it, felt himself somehow obligated to.

Ocean trip: the way it was. To hang on to it, grab hold of it as concretely as possible.

For the first time as man and wife beside each other in this weakness afterward. Their bodies are as insubstantial as silk ribbons. Nothing happens. Only afterward the timorous walking among the loud people.

Railroad journey: their muscles are tossed back and forth, back and forth. Their bodies sway. The weak smile that was yesterday's day pales. Here and there a glance. Or a closing of the eyes. Need for the schedule, for a sturdy compartment conversation. But between silence, fatigue, gliding through a strange landscape, and even boredom, still a hanging on to the possession of something different.

First attempt to strip naked. Above rocks on an inaccessible rock terrace. Even undressing has no effect. Here the charming play of clothes in the room has no force. The naked body like a line. If at least it were burned by the sun.

Union. Like two one-celled animals. Consciously—in a pause when the moon is gone—sexuality as concentration on a goal and a way. There must be this penetration. (Conversation) The moon is there again and the penetration begins. Until they release each other fatigued and satiated. Lying on their beds like flour dust in human shape. Happy, confused; but all human content was blown away. Can that be repeated? Only if an intellectual system is involved, such as *unio mystica* or the like. This system might perhaps be possible. Tragedy: an unborn world.

Normal desire in Ulrich. Also in Agathe. But repressed again and again until the longing for ordinary obstacles like rivals etc. comes.

Diotima-Arnheim: Sitting knee-to-knee holding hands. Diotima's knees make a motion to open. She presses them together. She stands up, Arnheim kisses the curled hair on her neck. (He is unaware of this nestling up from behind.) The kiss down her back, through her legs, comes out at her breasts.

Diotima-Ulrich afterward. Diotima just looks at him, upset. Everything in her is destroyed. He has put her feelings back on track again.

Meingast. Is democracy a system that picks out leaders? No.

Does it further the intellectual and spiritual? No.

It drags down whatever is outstanding, while raising the general level only a tiny bit.

. . .

My view of, or task I would set for, literature: partial solution, contribution to the solution, investigation, or the like. I feel exempted from having to give an unequivocal response. I have, after all, also postulated the morality of individual cases, etc.

A justified objection: That was from the period before the war. There was no way of shaking up the totality. It went further too: everyone had this feeling. Whether one wanted it that way or not, there was a firm system of coordinates. A floating ball, which one pushed and turned every which way. One's interest exhausted itself in the variations. The tacit assumption was probably not the solidity of the environment but one's lack of concern for it, without one's being aware of it.

Disposition to understanding the way I am in, for instance, Martha [Musil's wife—TRANS.]: because she paid no attention to the totality in any event.

This situation has now changed. The whole person has been flung into uncertainty. Discussions are of no use to him, he needs the solidity that has been lost. Hence the desire for resolution, for yes and no. In this sense, a person with as little substance as Brecht is exemplary through the form of his behavior. He moves people because he demonstrates their own experience to them. One has to understand this completely.

Therefore the didactic element in the book must be strengthened. A practical formula must be advanced.

Not further thought out: apparently this gives the practical-theoretical opposition, the original spy concept, new content.

LATE 1920S

a. Loving fear

It was spring. The air like a net. Behind it something that stretched the weave. But was not able to break through. They [Ulrich and Agathe—TRANS.] both knew it but no longer trusted themselves to talk about it. They knew, in the moment when they would seek words for it . . . it would be dead. Fear made them tender. Their eyes and hands (often) brushed each other, a trembling around the lips sought its reflection, one second seemed to separate itself from the ranks of the others and sink into the depths.

The second time, such a movement was a massive mountain of bliss.

The third time, very nearly comical.

Then the loving fear came over them.

They looked for a jest, a cynical word; just something unimportant but real; something that is at home in life and has a right to a home. It makes no difference what one talks about. Every word falls into the silence, and the next moment the corpses of other words are shining in a circle around it, the way masses of dead fish rise to the surface when one casts poison into the water. The order of words in a real connection destroys the deep reflective luster with which, unspoken, they lie above the unutterable, and one could just as well speak about lawyers as philosophy.

b.

Agathe is playing the piano.

Ulrich comes in, a book in his hand; it is Emerson, whom he loves. He heard only at the last moment that Agathe was making music. What he hates: music as subterfuge, music as intoxicant deadening the life-forming will. He becomes gloomy, wants to turn around, but nevertheless reads aloud to Agathe the place he wanted to show her.

Can be applied to the description of the nature of an idea:

" 'In common hours, society sits cold and statuesque. We all stand waiting, empty—knowing, possibly, that we can be full, surrounded by mighty symbols which are not symbols to us, but prose and trivial toys. Then cometh the god and converts the statues into fiery men, and by a flash of his eye burns up the veil which shrouded all things, and the meaning of the very furniture, of cup and saucer, of chair and clock and tester, is manifest. The facts which loomed so large in the fogs of yesterday—property, climate, breeding, personal beauty, and the like—have strangely changed their proportions. All that we reckoned solid shakes and rattles. . . .' "

His voice sounds despondently "cold and silent" as he reads with lost confidence. Agathe has interrupted her playing; when the words, too, have died away, her fingers take a few acoustic steps through the boundless land of music, stop, and she listens. "Lovely," she says, but does not know what she means.

To her surprise Ulrich says: "Yes; it can drive one mad." Agathe, who knows that Ulrich does not like it when she plays music, abandons the instrument.

—Pay attention! Ulrich says, having stepped back and drawn a pistol from his pocket. He fires at the piano, shooting into the center of its long black flank. The bullet cuts through the dry, tender wood and howls across the strings. A second churns up jumping sounds. The keys begin to hop. The jubilantly sharp reports of the pistol drive with increasing frenzy into a splintering, screaming, tearing, drumming, and singing uproar. He does not know why he is shooting. Certainly not because of anger at the piano, or to express anything at all symbolically. When the magazine is empty Ulrich lets it drop to the carpet, and his cheeks are still hollowed out from tension.

Agathe had neither lifted her hand nor uttered the slightest sound to prevent the destruction of the expensive instrument. She felt no fear, and although the way her brother began must have been quite incomprehensible to her, the thought that he had gone mad did not seem terrifying to her, caught up as she was by the pathos of the shots and the strange wounded cries of the struck instrument.

When her brother then asked whether she was angry at him, she denied it with radiant eyes.—I ought to feel like a fool—Ulrich said, somewhat ashamed—but if I tried to repeat that, it would turn into ordinary target practice, and its never being repeatable was perhaps the stimulus.

—Always, when one has done something, Agathe said.

Ulrich looked at her in astonishment and said nothing.

c.

It was only the next day that Ulrich referred to the incident again. "Now you won't be able to play the piano for a while," he tried saying by way of excuse; where the piano had stood there was emptiness in the room. "Why did you say yesterday that these books could drive one mad?" Agathe asked. "Before your mad idea. Are they very beautiful?"

"Just because they're beautiful. It's perhaps good that you can't make music now." What followed was a long conversation. —It's all like blowing bubbles, Ulrich said. Beautiful? With his hands he spontaneously formed in the air an iridescent ball—"completely self-contained and round, like a globe, and the next instant vanished without trace. I've been working again for a while—"

. . .

(But it is also possible to take everything theoretical out of the description of the Other Condition and apply it as fiction in an ironic way as depiction of the age. Then all that would remain here would be those remarks that have the character of events.)

. . .

Agathe: *Depict a deep depression.*
It is as if a secret drawer within her had been turned upside down and contents never before seen had come to light. Everything is obscured. Little reflection; really an inability to reflect. The idea: I must kill myself, is present only in the form of this sentence, unspoken, yet its presence eerily known; it fills the dark vacuum more and more completely.
The condition is uncanny. Much less free of the fear of death than were many of the healthy moments in which Agathe had often thought of death. And much less beautiful: dull, colorless. But the idea now has a fearful attraction.
She begins to put her affairs in order: there really aren't any. Ulrich is right, when he struggles and works, that yields content; *he is marvelous the way he is—she thinks.*
Then: He'll get over it. *I'm not leaving behind anyone who will weep over me.*

Sadness at living. The flowing of the blood is a weeping. Everything done badly, without energy, half; like a small parrot among coarse sparrows. Incapable of the simple emotions. She had been afraid of her father; the same fear that had recurred often in her life: not being able to defend herself, because the defense leads to things that one finds just as meaningless. She never knew love, and the suggestion that this was now the most important thing; this child's idea, this rapture of so many women, is a matter of indifference to her.

But *The sovereignty of the resolve.* Whoever is able to do this is free and owes no one an accounting. The world becomes quite calm. In spite of its rush. The strange loneliness! With which one is born.

. . .

All objects in the room become friends for the first time; have seriously found their place.

A long time ago she had obtained a capsule with cyanide; it was her solace in many hours. Pours it for the first time into a glass; the carafe with water beside it. Describe how it is done. Possibly the confidence that this world, in which Agathe feels herself so imperfect, is not the only one.

At the last moment, Ulrich enters.

Agathe would have had to say farewell, become sentimental, offer explanations. Or jump up and run away from him. She looks at him helplessly, and he notices the disturbance in her face. The spark jumps over to him. —Today you have no courage. He was still trying to jest. —I, at least, shot up a piano. —Let's kill ourselves . . . , Agathe said. *We are miserable creatures who bear within ourselves the law of another world,* without being able to carry it out! We love what is forbidden and will not defend ourselves.

Ulrich threw himself down beside her and embraced her. *We will not let ourselves be killed by anything before we have tried it!*

What? Agathe looked at him, trembling.

God has . . . Ulrich smiled . . . The lost paradise! We don't need to ask ourselves whether what we propose will stand every test: *everything is fleeting and fluid. Whoever is not like us will not understand us. Because one understands nothing of what one sees and does, but only what one is.* Do you understand me, my soul?

And if it fails, we'll kill ourselves?

We'll kill ourselves! Voices were singing in them like a chorus of heavenly storms: *Do what you feel!!*

Next chapter

If they had done what they were feeling, in an hour everything would have been over. But as it is, they travel.

1930–1934

Nations chapter

This chapter, as reminder of the world, inserted in the progression of the extremely personal chapters. Also works as antidote to the other life that Ulrich has devised.

Basic idea: presenting and ironizing "making everyone dance to the same tune." (But deeper basic idea: Age of empiricism.)

Extremes appeal more to the average person than does the strict truth.

· · ·

Sketch for crisis and decision chapter

Preceded by: Ulrich-Bonadea

Ulrich stays behind; like a dog that has killed a chicken. Leaves the room briefly; Agathe comes in; she's had enough of Lindner; Peter preceded her. Her thoughts and their result. This should be followed by a—not written—conversation to the effect that disavowal produced by the result justifies the crisis.

On the real and urgent level, Ulrich has to go on an errand. Agathe's attempt at suicide. Saved by Ulrich. Final resolve.

What is the resolve based on? What Agathe's attempted suicide?

Ulrich really ought to answer—in the sense of Schleiermacher's moral indifference of the religious person—that the Other Condition offers no precepts for everyday life. You can marry, live as you wish, etc. Utopias, too, have not produced any practicable results. That's also something like the race of genius inside the race of stupidity. That also means: against the total solution and system. Against the sense of community. Adventure of rejecting life. But without going into the theory.

After the eruption he concedes: intimation and God, even if dubious. His real justification is fear of the sweetness of the three sisters [Agathe, Ulrich himself, and the Other Condition—TRANS.], and so they decide to go away, and coitus is unarticulated. So, at least for the time being, he half abandons image and the like.

Agathe wants a decision the way youth does.

Ulrich: I have decided. Suicide year.

Agathe: Mysticism that could not ally itself with religion allies itself with Ulrich.

Decision to be: instrument of an unknown goal.

Agathe: There is really no good and evil, but only faith or doubt. Let's get away from all that.

Lacking faith, leave it to intimations. Ulrich rejects believing but follows intimations.

Agathe's depression: One main argument: The lawyer proposed she should have herself declared ill. She did the will on account of Ulrich, and now everything threatens to fall on top of her. Lindner, too, she only treated badly.

She is for action (youth), but it also looks like this: Whatever one can object to about others, and also about God and the Other Condition, is a matter of indifference to her; she wants to live with Ulrich, thinks it's very bad of her but wants to anyway, and if that won't work, then all that remains is badness and the end.

On Agathe's depression: According to Adler, the person inclined toward God is the person deficient in a sense of community—according to Schleiermacher, the morally indifferent person, therefore evil. Woman, too, is a criminal. True sympathy for no one but Ulrich. I have to love you because I cannot love the others. God and antisocial. Her love for Ulrich has from the beginning mobilized hatred and hostility against the world.

Note: this mood has the quality of magnanimity; she has to (can) remember what Ulrich has said about it. It contains the continuation into life.

It *has* to happen with (undescribed) Clarisse! That's why not with Bonadea! Disturbance, interruption at the last minute. Ulrich knows that he has already given in.

. . .

In this mood, God is the hypostasized need to believe. But it is not given her to see God. The mood is really a fulfillment of the Other Condition, but still schematically.

Differently: When Ulrich comes in again she recalls his aversion to defectiveness. Impels her to do it quickly, but also inhibits her.

Ulrich: experimental year. Is there enough for both of them?

We will not kill ourselves until we have tried everything.

Addendum: Belief can only be an hour old. But then it is an intimation.

Missing: Ulrich's depression and possible grounds for suicide.

49 now 50

CRISIS AND DECISION

Main point here: suicide attempt.

Content: Agathe hurt, feminine. Silly weeping, mindless weeping; but a fountain of the body, the body claiming its right. You have hurt me. As excuse: reading poems and newspapers. Insight: What is it then that I should give you? I could perhaps consent to it with a woman I love. Inwardly more than two people can be in love. Ulrich depicts what that would be like and confesses that he is too fainthearted for it. Ulrich develops the idea. Suddenly Agathe kisses him, and the kiss becomes sensual.

Between this chapter and the preceding there must be a brief separation, Ulrich's leaving the house or just the room. During this time Agathe's mood suddenly changes.

Description of a deep depression and the happiness of such a resolve.

(Clarisse's exaltation in 46 or 47 corresponds to this deep depression.)

Tentative résumé: Always did everything badly, beginning with father, and one can't defend oneself because the defense is still worse (more stupid).

Ulrich manages to prevent her. Used *as motives* for the resolve:

It is our destiny: perhaps we love what is forbidden. But we will not kill ourselves before we have attempted the utmost. Promise!

The world is fleeting and fluid: Do what you want!

We stand powerless before a perfected imperfected world. Other people also have everything that's in us, but they've shunted it aside without noticing. They remain healthy and idealistic; we skirt the edge of crime.

Loneliness: people who believe quarrel with God, unbelievers are getting to know him for the first time. There is no necessity in this. This world is only one of . . . experiments. God bestows partial solutions, creative people do the same, they contradict one another, out of this the world forms a relative whole that doesn't correspond to any solution. Into the mold of this world I am poured like molten ore: that's why I never entirely am what I do and think: an attempted form within an attempted form of the totality. One can't listen to the bad teachers, who according to God's plan have constructed one of His lives for eternity, but must humbly and stubbornly entrust oneself to God himself. Act without reflection, for a man never gets further than when he doesn't know where he's going. (That is Agathe's influence! Ironic, but already anticipated by Count Leinsdorf.) / narratively: Perhaps Ulrich reflects about this in a pause, so that there are no reflections at the end /

Over all a breath of *Stella* morality [Goethe's play—TRANS.]. Otherwise he would have said literally the same things to Stumm and others. To be described more as mood and state than as idea. If they had now carried out what they were feeling, in an hour everything would have been over. But this way . . .

Poison as support. Confidence that this world, in which she feels incomplete, is not the only one—

On the suicidal mood: This sadness was like a deep ditch with slippery sides that had her going back and forth, while she heard Ulrich above, invisible and inaccessible, talking with other people.

When Agathe returned home, this took place at twilight, she looked around for Ulrich, but he had (after Bonadea's departure) left the house (for a while) in order to forget what had happened as much as he possibly could. She sat down in his study, laid her hat and gloves beside her on the sofa, and abandoned herself to the slow fall of darkness, which suited her mood. It was her intention not to visit Lindner so soon again, and she wanted to ask Ulrich's forgiveness for her ill nature.

Just then her fingers came in contact among the pillows with a hard, gently curved, pronged object, and when she held it up to the light she recognized it as a small comb of the kind women wear in their hair. Bonadea had lost it. It quite confused Agathe's hands as they held it. She looked at it with parted lips, and the blood drained from her face. If the word "thunderstruck" means that all thoughts are struck out and the small house of the skull stands empty with opened drawers and doors, then Agathe was thunderstruck. Tears rose to her eyes without brimming over.

She waited vacantly—with few thoughts, which hardly tried to stir in her—for her brother. Among them was the thought that now everything was over, and the opposite one, that what she had stumbled upon was only natural and that she ought to have believed in it at any time; she appeared unable to grasp what lay between these thoughts until Ulrich should come.

When he came in, he immediately noticed the presence of someone else in the darkness and went up to his sister, who was the only person it could be, in order to greet her gently and ruefully. But Agathe asked him in such a voice not to come near her, but rather to turn on the light, that he turned on his heel. When light came on she held out the little comb to him with outstretched arm, and he read in her eyes what she did not say. Ulrich could have denied it; it probably would not have been credible to explain her find through disorder, as something left behind from earlier times, and yet it would perhaps have deflected and softened the immediate effect: but he was overcome with remorse and made no attempt at denial.

Agathe got hold of herself and listened to him with a dismayed smile.

"Are you jealous of Bonadea?" he asked her, and wanted to stroke her face in order to turn the incident into a jest. But before it touched her, Agathe grabbed his hand and held it fast. "I have no right to be," she said. At the same moment tears began streaming from her eyes. Ulrich's eyes, too, nearly misted over—"You know how such things happen."

Ulrich stays behind. Satiated like a beast of prey / Better: As he tells himself: like a dog that has torn a chicken to pieces and that on the one hand is oppressed by conscience, on the other contentedly suffused with having satisfied a basic instinct / Possibly: Remorse is nothing other than the collapse of a dominant affect brought about by the one competing with it / So he is predisposed to remorse.

Second part

Finally they sat together for a while, held each other by the hands and did not trust themselves to either say or do anything. It had become quite dark. Agathe felt a temptation to undress without saying a word. Perhaps the darkness also enticed Ulrich to creep over to her or do something similar. Both resisted this energy of the sex drive that forms types of actions (or something similar). But Agathe asked herself: Why doesn't anything happen? / Why not . . . ? Something from the paradise conversation, so to speak: why doesn't he try it!

And when nothing happened she asked her brother: Don't you want to turn the light on now?

Ulrich hesitated. But then out of fear he turned on the light.

And then it appeared that he had forgotten something he had to take care of himself. It was evident that he had to take care of it, it would take at most forty-five minutes, and Agathe herself persuaded him to do it. He had promised someone important some information, and it couldn't be done over the phone. Thus even in this hour normal life intervened, and normal life was what it was, and after they had separated both became melancholy.

Ulrich became so melancholy that he nearly turned around, but continued on; Agathe, on the other hand, became more melancholy than she had ever been in her life. In contrast to all the other times, this melancholy seemed to her positively unnatural; she shrank back and even felt an inquisitive astonishment. Unnaturalness was a special kind of peculiarity. As far as this melancholy left any room at all for anything else; as it were like a shimmer at its margin. Profound melancholy, moreover, is not black, but dark green or dark blue, and has the softness of velvet; it is not so much annihilation as rather a rare, positive quality. This deep happiness in melancholy, which Agathe felt immediately, apparently has its origin in the relationship of single-mindedness and enthusiasm, that happiness is associated with the exclusive dominance of every individual emotion at being freed from all contradictions and irresolution, not in a cold, pedantic, impersonal way, as through reason, but magnanimously. All great courage and bad temper have the quality of magnanimity. Without having to think for a moment Agathe remembered where she kept her poison and stood up to get it. The possibility of ending life and its ambivalences liberates the joy that dwells within it. Agathe's melancholy became cheerful in a way she found barely comprehensible as she emptied the poison, as the directions prescribed, into a glass of water / when she put the poison in front of her on a table. She fetched a glass and a bottle of water and put them beside it. In the most natural way her future split into the two possibilities of killing herself or attaining the Millennium, and since the latter had not worked, there remained only the former.

It was time to take leave. Agathe was much too young to be able to part from life totally without pathos, and to understand her properly it cannot be passed over in silence that her resolve was not, affectively speaking, sufficiently fixed: her despair was not without remedy, it was not collapse after every attempt had been made, there was always for her, even if at the moment it seemed obscured, still a second way. Initially, her departure from the world was animated, like leaving on a trip. For the first time, all the people she had encountered in the world appeared to her as something that was quite in order, now that she was not to have anything more to do with it.

It seemed to her peaceful and lovely to look back at life. And besides, entire generations disappear in a flash. She was not the only person who had not really known what to do with her beauty. She thought of the year 2000, would have liked to have known how things would look then. Then she remembered faces from the sixteenth century she must have seen portrayed in some collection. Splendid faces with strong foreheads and far more powerful features than one sees today. One could understand that all these people had once played a role. But for that you doubtless need fellow players: a profession, a task, and an animating life. But this ambition to have a role was completely alien to her. She had never wanted to be any of the things one could be. The world of men had always been foreign to her. She had despised the world of women. At times, she had brought the curiosity of her body, the desire of the flesh, in contact with others the way one eats and drinks. But it had always happened without any deeper responsibility, and so her life had led only from the desert of the nursery where it had started into a vague kind of happening with no borders. Thus everything ended in impotence.

To be sure, this impotence was not without a core: It was not only this world that God . . . World one of many possible ones . . . The best in us a breathlike (mass) that flies eternally like a bird from its branch . . . There was always a vision contained within her dislike of the world's authority. Indeed, more than a vision; she had almost got hold of it already: one comes to oneself when . . . vanishes. It is more than a seizure, this obscure twinkling . . . But it seemed to her not to make much sense to go over it again. All these experiences mixed up together echoed along with it, but they were not . . . before. They have something schematic *and* . . . real. It had not been given to her to see God clearly, as little as anything!

Without God, all that remained of her was the bad that she had done. She was uselessly besmirched and felt repugnant to herself. Everything, too, that she had just gone over had become clear to her only in Ulrich's company, become more than a nervous playing of games. She spontaneously felt warmly grateful to her brother. At this moment she loved him madly.

And then it occurred to her: everything he had said, everything he still might say, he had debased!

She had to do it before he came back. She looked at her watch. What a delicate thing its tiny hand was. She pushed the watch away. A gloominess came over her . . . fear of death . . . dull, horribly painful, repugnant. But the thought that it had to happen—she had no idea how it had come in . . . horrible appeal. She found she had very little reflection left . . . inability . . . nothing but the idea . . . kill, and this only in the form of this sentence . . . emptiness.

She wanted to put her affairs in order; she had none. I'm not leaving anyone behind . . . not even Ulrich . . . She pitied herself. The pulse in her wrist flowed like weeping.

Ulrich was to be envied, when he struggled and worked. Possibly: He is marvelous just as he is!

But the sovereignty of her resolve calmed her. She, too, had an advantage. Whoever is able to do this . . . She felt the marvelous isolation with which she had been born.

And when she had emptied the powder into the glass the possibility of turning back was gone, for now she had committed her talisman (like the bee, which can sting only once).

Suddenly she heard Ulrich's steps, sooner than expected. She could have quickly downed the glass. But when she heard him she also wanted to see him once more. After that she could have jumped up and . . . downed the glass. She could have said something peremptory and withdrawn from life that way. But she looked at him helplessly, and he saw the devastation in her face. He saw the glass; he did not ask. He did not understand; the spark of excitement jumped over to him instantaneously. He took the glass and asked: "Is there enough for us both?" Agathe tore it from his hand.

With the exclamation . . . ? . . . ? I've never loved anything besides you! "he clasped her in his arms."

Or: not a word, [but] an action, an event! He collapses or the like. Horrified at what he has brought about!

Better: Ulrich's aversion against defectiveness. Suicide. But finally:

one cannot make amends for anything but can only make them better. That's why remorse is passionate. For both. Suddenly one of them is struck by this idea and laughs.

I have decided. Experimental year . . . kill myself.

That is the resolution that is now impetuously carried out.

But that would also mean, more or less: journey to God.

Perhaps in place of the rejected jealousy chapter

The period of mobilization. Agathe had, in spite of it, had a carpenter called in. He might be a little under thirty, is tall and really built like a mechanic, that is, slender, with broad shoulders, dry; long, well-formed hands of great strength, and sinewy wrists. His face is open and intelligent, his hair dark blond and quite natural. His overalls become him. He speaks dialect but without roughness.

Agathe in the next room with him. Ulrich—lost in thought—has left. He doesn't want to be bothered by anything anymore. But then he turned around and crossed a garden terrace back into the house and into his room, without Agathe noticing.

He eavesdrops on the next room. The expression of both voices strikes him. The man's voice is explaining something: articulately, quietly, and with a certain superiority. Ulrich doesn't understand what it's about but guesses from his prior knowledge and the sound of wood that it has something to do with a rolltop desk of Agathe's. It is opened and closed. The young workman demands Agathe's assent to a more comprehensive repair than she would like, and she makes uncertain objections. Ulrich knows and understands all that. It must have something to do with a mystery of the old rolltop mechanism.

And suddenly it breaks loose from reality. For the conversation would have run exactly the same course if it had been a love transaction. The persuading, the easy superiority, the positing-as-necessary or it's-not-such-a-big-thing in the man's voice. As if it were for him a sexual improvisation. And then that beloved voice! Resisting, intimidated, unsure. She would like to and doesn't want to. She yields, but here and there still stands firm. She says in an undertone: "yes . . . yes . . . but . . ." She's known for quite a while that she will yield. How Ulrich loves this restrained, brave voice and the woman who fears everything as she does darkness and yet who does everything! He would not have been able to bring himself to rush in with a gun and take revenge, or even call them to account.

Then a sigh of submission even comes over Agathe's lips, and the cracking of wood is deceptively heard.

And in spite of this being-happy-for-Agathe that Ulrich has dreamed through, he goes off to the war. But by no means with conviction.

1930–1938/39

QUESTIONS FOR VOLUME TWO

Exposition of Volume Two of *The Man Without Qualities*

When I think of the reviews of Volume One [Musil is here referring to Chapters 1–123, which were published in 1930/31; Chapters 1–38 of Part III appeared in 1932/33—TRANS.], I note again and again as something they have in common the question as to what will or might happen in the second volume. The answer to this is simple: nothing or the beginning of the World War. Note the title of the major portion of the first volume: Pseudoreality Prevails. This means that in general today the personal givens of events are definite and delineated, but that what is general about them, or their significance, is indefinite, faded, and equivocal, and repeats itself unintelligibly. The person awakened to awareness of the current situation has the feeling that the same things are happening to him over and over again, without there being a light to guide him out of this disorderly circle. I believe that this characterizes a major idea of the first volume, around which large parts of the material could be ordered. Above all, there is a continuity in that volume that permits the present period to be already grasped in the past one, and even the technical problem of the book could be characterized as the attempt to make a story at all possible in the first place.

I add that what I have just referred to in other terms as the unequivocal nature of the event (of life) is by no means a philosophical demand but one that in an animal would already be satisfied, while in a person it can apparently be lost.

This makes comprehensible that the major problem of the second volume is the search for what is definitely signified or, to use another expression, the search for the ethically complete action or, as I might call it ironically, the search for 100 percent being and acting.

The more general investigations of the first volume permit me to concentrate here more on the moral problems or, according to an old expression, on the question of the right life. I attempt to show what I call "the hole in European morality" (as in billiards, where sooner or later the ball gets stuck in such a hole), because it interferes with right action: it is, in a word, the false treatment that the mystic experience has been subjected to.

But here I would like to stop burdening your desire for information with the impossible problem of philosophical window dressing and conclude: Ulrich, who has traveled to his father's funeral, encounters in the house cleared out by death his almost unknown and unremembered sister. They fall in love, not so much with each other as with the idea of being siblings. I greatly regret that this problem has a certain higher banality, but on the other hand, this proves that it is the expression of broad currents. My representation is aimed at the needs leading to this expression. I contrast the two theses, one can love only one's Siamese-twin sister, and man is good. This means (the relation of brother and sister to each other is at first purely spiritual) Ulrich returns after a period filled with their being together in intense intimacy; his sister follows him, and they begin a provisional living together according to principles revealed to them, but they are disturbed by the attention of society, which is deeply touched by this act of brotherly and sisterly devotion. General Stumm reports on the state of the Parallel Campaign, which is fed up with the spirit and longs for deeds. Diotima, whose relation with Arnheim is cooling, busies herself with sexual science and again devotes more attention to her husband, Section Chief Tuzzi.

Feeling has never had freedom of association.

Fundamental idea: The first part turns out to be too overloaded, even if consideration did have to be given to the problems brought up in Volume One. On the other hand, there was no way around them. What had been analyzed must somehow be summarized. Cf., e.g., the desire for a solution (Brecht) noted as justified in [a cross-reference—TRANS.]. This coincides with Ulrich having in any event to build his life anew after the journey with Agathe, during which the "reserve idea" of his life has collapsed. So the connection to the ideas of Volume One and their new context is indicated from his point of view also. This, whatever may happen in between, is the content of the second half.

Fundamental idea: The coinciding of the contemporary intellectual situation with the situation at the time of Aristotle. Then people wanted to unite understanding of nature with religious feeling, causality with love. In Aristotle there was a split; that's when analytical investigation arose. However much of a model the fourth century B.C. has been, this problem has not been admitted. In a certain sense, all philosophies, from scholasticism to Kant, have been, with their systems, interludes.

That is the historical situation.

What prevails today is what Ulrich wants: every age must have a guiding idea about what it's here for, a balance between theory and ethics, God, etc. The age of empiricism still does not have this. Hence Walter's inconsistent demands.

Fundamental idea: This furnishes Ulrich's relationship to the social sphere. Criminality out of a sense of opposition follows from this. Aims at the period after Bolshevism. Against total solutions.

Ulrich is, finally, one who desires community while rejecting the given possibilities.

Fundamental idea: War. All lines lead to the war.

Fundamental idea: Ulrich has sought to isolate: feeling—Other Condition. Now tries: deed—Moosbrugger. (*An idea:* he arranges things but is then drawn as a spectator only out of curiosity.) Corresponding to the way he thinks. Finally, orgy of the contemporary horrible blending of qualities into the cultural type.

Fundamental idea: Keep putting depiction of the time up front. Ulrich's problems and those of the secondary figures are problems of the time!

. . .

Comprehensive structural idea:
The immanent depiction of the period that led to the catastrophe must be the real substance of the story, the context to which it can always retreat as well as the thought that is implicit in everything.

All the problems, like search for order and conviction, role of the Other Condition, situation of the scientific person, etc., are also problems of the time and are to be regularly presented as such.

Especially the Parallel Campaign is to be presented this way.

Clarisse is an aggressive, Walter a conservative embodiment of the changing times.

Diotima, Arnheim: impotence of the idea of culture, of its accompanying ideology.

This age desires deeds, exactly like the present time, because ideology, or the relation of ideology to the other elements, has failed.

There is today no lack of men of action, but of human deeds.

Man without qualities against deed: The man who is not satisfied by any of the available solutions. (I'm thinking of deed vs. intellect in National Socialism. Of the desire of youth today to find a resolution, etc. "Resolution": a synonym for deed. Likewise: "conviction." This is what lends significance to Hans Sepp and his circle.)

The conception of life as partial solution and the like as anachronistic. Derives from the prewar period, where the totality seemed relatively immutable even for the person who did not believe in it. Today all of existence has been thrown into disorder; discussions, contributions, articles, and tinkerings are of no use, people want resolution, yes or no. The didactic element in the book is to be strengthened, a practical formula to be advanced. The opposition: practical-theoretical, the original idea of espionage, gains new importance through this.

Supplement: Up to now the answer has been Walter's. Perhaps like this: Ulrich repeats this response from time to time, but no one believes him or even takes it seriously.

Germany's enthusiasm for National Socialism is proof that a firm mental and spiritual mind-set is what is most important to people. The war was the first attempt.

Politics is only to be understood as education for action; what sovereignty, then, do thinking, feeling, etc., have. National Socialism = dominance of the political more than = part of collectivism.

I probably really ought to make "the idea of the inductive age" the central argument. Induction calls for pre-assumptions, but these may only be employed heuristically and not regarded as immutable. Democracy's error was the absence of any deductive basis; it was an induction that did not correspond to the motivating mental and spiritual mind-set.

God, thought's strong approach to Him, was an episode.

From today's vantage point the problem is: the (warlike) man capable of defense is to be preserved, but war is to be avoided. Or: The man without qualities, but without decadence.

What has so far been missing in Volume Two is intellectual humor. The Stumm chapters are no substitute for the theory of the Other Condition and the love between brother and sister being treated without humor. First attempt now in the Monster chapter (kiss). Occurred to me as paradigm: The duel is a remnant of courtship rivalry, therefore our conceptions of honor are too. My principles are now nothing more than such an aperçu: this awareness must still be added to its serious treatment!

What is the basic theme of the whole second volume? Really, perhaps, the utopia of the Other Condition. The utopia of the Other Condition is replaced by that of the inductive way of thinking.

Professor Lindner's view of the world: Example of a person who lives "For" and fears the "In"— Augustinian Christianity (therefore future) and incapability of believing— Lindner's bearing arms corresponds to the wearing of swords in the B[rünn] chapter (Ulrich can be aware of the allusion)— His being energetic is not merely German, intended as a profound, irrational trait of the time— The contradictions of the time in the form: One would like to be this way and one would like to be different, and therefore feels oneself a whole man—the most vain time: from lack of metaphysical decisiveness— Credulity in the form of the "For"— His impression of liberalism. This expression of a particular constellation. It needs a strict new pulling together— *Since God speaks to him about "For" and "In"* it's not an Ulrich-Agathe problem but a general one— Religion is an institution for people and not for saints— The remarkable phenomenon of emotions not remaining fresh. Dogmatizing and constant reactualizing: aims at God as empiricism, transformation of the intimation that can be experienced into faith that is not experienced (along with: Do and Don't do, affirmative actions) and distinction between good and goody-good. (The first comes from morality, the second from God)— Acquisition of a bureaucratic language of the emotions.

Ulrich's relation to politics really reduces to the following: like all people who objectively or subjectively have their own mission, he wants to be disturbed by politics as little as possible. He did not expect that what was important to him could be endangered by it. That in any case even in the existing state of affairs there is already a certain degree of implicit challenge, in other words that it could also get a lot worse, did not cross his mind. For him a politician was a specialist who dedicates himself to the by no means easy task of combining and representing various interests. He would also have been prepared to subordinate himself to a bearable degree and assume some sacrifice.

Ulrich was not unaware that the element of power is part of the concept of politics; he had often considered the question whether anything good could come about without the "supporting" involvement of evil. Politics is command. Astonishingly, his own teacher Nietzsche: Will to power! But Nietzsche had sublimated it into the intellectual. Power stands in contradiction to the principles / condition essential for life / of the mind. Here two claims to power compete. Power in the political way disappeared from his field of view, as did power in the manner of war. It might exist, but basically it is as primitive as boys fighting.

He now becomes aware of this naïveté.

The marasmus of democracy advanced to meet this. The tacit assumption of parliamentarianism was that progress would emerge from all the chatter, that it would yield an increasingly close approach to the truth. It did not look that way. The press, etc. The horrendous notion of "worldviews." The politicizing of the mind through letting only what is acceptable prevail. Beyond that the fiction of the unity of culture, a fiction that had grown thin and brittle. (Represented by the *monarchy.*

Democracy had not yet been stripped of its skin.) Whatever was good in this life was done by individuals.

Today there are only dishonorably acquired convictions.

N.B.: If Ulrich looks away from his Other Condition adventure: The relation of power to mind will always be there, but it can take on sublimated forms (and will perhaps do so, after it has run through a series of collective attempts that are now just beginning).

If Ulrich imagined this practically: One would have to begin with the schools, no, one has no idea where *not* to begin! That is the individual's feeling of being abandoned, etc., which leads Ulrich to his experiment and to crime.

"If Europe doesn't join together, in the foreseeable future European culture will be destroyed by the yellow race." "Unless Japan harnesses all its energies, then . . ." etc. This could be reduced to the formula: they would rather destroy their own culture themselves! It's comical, this hot, sudden, and doubtless momentarily not disreputable passion for one's culture.

Incidentally, behind this also lies the experience that dependent countries are treated ruthlessly. Just like dependent people.

It's the feeling for one's own well-worn groove. Progress would be something shared and unifying.

They defend culture instead of having it.

The person with culture is alone all over the world.

There are only the two views: Culture! Then everything that happens is perverse. Or: Power! or similar struggle between animal species. Between chosen peoples. A vision that could be great in certain circumstances but is completely unfounded, since the peoples involved have no goal beyond self-assertion.

Differently: A spirit rules without having been completely developed. Then someone comes along and imposes something different. In other words, perhaps: The totality is changed by an individual / produces him, many say. It seems to people to be absurdity, insanity, criminality. After a short time they adapt to it. Carrot–stick, the notorious lack of character and despicableness of people, what is it really? And spirit is always only a decorative frill in a room, the room can be laid out for it. That's why mind and spirit are never constant but change with the change in power.

A useful pendant to government bureaucracy.

Connected with this: Nietzsche predicted it. The mind lives more or less the way a woman does: it subjects itself to power, is thrown down, resisting, and then finds pleasure in the process. And prettifies, makes reproaches, persuades in matters of detail. Offers pleasure. What need was it leaning on there?

Ulrich-Agathe is really an attempt at anarchy in love. Which ends negatively even there. That's the deeper link between the love story and the war. (Also its connection to the Moosbrugger problem.) But what remains in the end? That there is a sphere of ideals and a sphere of reality? Guidelines and the like? How profoundly unsatisfying! Isn't there a better answer?

Utopia of Precision: Ideal of the three treatises is characterized as the most important expression of a state of mind that is extremely sharp-sighted toward what is nearest and blind toward the whole. A laconic frame of mind. The less something is written about, the more productive one is. Presumably, therefore, one should conduct all human business in the manner of the exact sciences. That is the ideal of the precise life. It means that one's lifework ought also to consist only of three poems or three treatises, in which one concentrates oneself in the extreme; for the rest, one ought to keep silent, do what is essential, and remain without emotion wherever one does not have creative feeling. One should be "moral" only in the exceptional cases and standardize everything else, like pencils or screws. In other words, morality is reduced to the moments of genius, and for the rest treated merely reasonably.

It is determined that this (utopian) person as man of action is already present today; but precise people don't bother about the utopias plotted out inside them.

In connection with this, the nature of utopias is described as an experiment in which the possible alteration of one element of life, and its effects, are observed. A possibility released from its inhibiting bond to reality and developed.

The Utopia of Precision yields a person in whom a paradoxical combination of precision and vagueness occurs. Aside from the temperament of precision, everything else in him is vague. He places little value in morality, since his imagination is directed toward changes; and, as demonstrated, his passions disappear and in their place something like the primitive fire of goodness appears.

More developed version: Inductive attitude also toward his own affects and principles.

Addendum: It should be noted about "vagueness" that what occurs in its place is not a vacuum but simply the rational morality of a social, technical sobriety that jumps in. (The present version relies rather too much on the Other Condition.)

But that implicitly assumes that the "nongenius" relationships could be regulated through reason. This is contested, and to a great degree properly so; the motor of social action is affect. We therefore have to see to what extent that is satisfactorily taken into consideration in what comes later.

Provisional summation

We have hit upon Ulrich's three utopias: The utopia of inductive thinking or

> of the given social condition;
> the utopia of life in love;
> the utopia of the Other Condition.

Of these, the utopia of inductive thinking is in a certain sense the worst! That would be the standpoint to be adopted from a literary point of view (which justifies the other two utopias). But this demonstration, or the representation that goes along with it, is only completed with the end (war). An apparent interim summary: the museum chapter. The journey into the Millennium places the other two utopias in the foreground and disposes of them as much as possible. But a good deal about the utopia of inductive thinking occurs in the Stumm, Parallel Campaign, Lindner, Schmeisser, and Moosbrugger chapters. So it is not necessary to master the utopia of inductive thinking down to the last detail around the diary chapters, but it probably is necessary to be familiar with its important general characteristics.

War and the age. Notes

Individualism is coming to an end
This is of no concern to Ulrich
But the right thing to do would be
to rescue something from it.

I am struck in my notes on Moór [Gyulia Moór, *On Eternal Peace: Outline of a Philosophy of Pacifism and Anarchism* (Leipzig, 1930)— TRANS.] how the just-concluded Kellogg Treaty is immediately being interpreted by France according to its needs of the moment.

States are really such that they not only take account of aesthetic needs but also actually obey them, while interpreting the ideas involved the way passionate people do. (Hans Sepp would therefore be only an overt instance.) What is it that plays the role of the affect in this. Evidently the affects arising for statesmen through responsibility. In this regard, responsibility is as much a national egotism as is the individual and party egotism of the politician who is dependent on his people.

A goal, a striving, determine the emotions, and the emotions the argumentation.

States are intellectually inferior.

A question: How can one lose wars? (Stumm: That's something we know something about!) Earlier: How could an absolute ruler miscalculate so badly as often happened? False intelligence, also lack of talent, will have played a role. But for the most part it was probably always a not-being-able-to-retreat, and the human quality that it is easier to assume the burden of a great remote danger than a smaller but closer one. Before one discards a city, rather than taking upon oneself a war that can cost one a province. Then the collective boastfulness; so great that no single person could achieve it, and there is no escaping it. Patriotism as affect instead of reason: the state is not conducted like a business but as an ethical "good." Yet they are also manly affects!

But that doubtless happens as it should. What is striking is only that the moral nature of the state has remained far less developed than that of the individual.

The outstanding personalities of history are criminals: Ulrich's plans to become a Napoleon. But for the most part, criminal here means: anti-philistine, someone unconstrained. But they really *were* criminals: murderers, oath breakers, liars, tricksters, in a word: on principle, the historical personality can be credited with any iniquity: the mature person is confronted with this idea. And has less sympathy for it. An effeminacy?

In a criminal, affects outweigh the inhibitions (except when caused by environment or degeneration, weakness and such). But don't they in a man of action too? Revision of the reflections that are occasionally given to Moosbrugger? Clarisse?

The world calls for strongly affective, strong-willed leaders.

But compare it to the individual person: will and intelligence must be strong. Beginning miscreants later become self-possessed. I must have a note about this (cf. men of action and human deeds).

The valuation of historical personalities and deeds is a functional one.

Here, in distinction to historical and private morality, is an example of functional evaluation. Absolutely the paradigm, for translated into the private sphere the historical is positively disgusting.

1930–1942

Concluding portion

Overall problem: war.

Pseudorealities lead to war. The Parallel Campaign leads to war!

War as: How a great event comes about.

All lines lead to the war. Everyone welcomes it in his fashion.

The religious element in the outbreak of the war.

Deed, emotion, and Other Condition join as one.

Someone remarks: that was what the Parallel Campaign had always been looking for. It has found its great idea.

Arises (like crime) from all those things that people ordinarily allow to dissipate in small irregularities.

Ulrich recognizes: either real working together (Walter's inductive piety) or Other Condition, or from time to time *this* has to happen.

Agathe says (repeatedly): We were the last romantics of love.

Ulrich possibly: the genius's needs and way of life are different from those of the masses. Perhaps better: . . . from the *condition* of genius and the condition of masses.

Individualist with the awareness of the impossibility of this viewpoint.

Doesn't go to Switzerland because he has no confidence in any idea at all.

Regards it as his suicide.

The collectivity needs a stable mental attitude. Its first attempt.

Ulrich: It's the same thing we did: flight (from peace).

Ulrich at the end: knowing, working, being effective without illusions.

Something like a religious shudder.

The fixed and stable is disavowed.

Other Condition—normal condition will never be resolved.

Most profound hostility toward all these people; at the same time one rushes around with them and wants to embrace the first person who comes along.

The individual will sinks, a new age of multipolar relations emerges before the eye of the mind.

Ulrich sees what a fascinating moment it was that never quite happened between himself and Agathe. Ultimate refuge sex and war, but sex lasts for one night, the war evidently for a month, etc.

Arnheim: The individual is the one who is fooled.

Agathe: We go on living as if nothing were happening. Ulrich: Timidity before this robustness.

The priests: God's Officer Corps.

Overpowered by a ridiculous feeling for his homeland. Strives to regret, do penance, let himself be swept up. At the same time mocked.

Te deum laudamus.

National romanticism, displacement into scapegoats and love-goats.

Nations have no intentions. Good people can make a cruel nation. Nations have a mind that is not legally accountable. More properly: they have no mind at all. Comparison with the insane. They don't want to. But they have at each other.

Also a solution to: loving a person and not being able to love him.

. . .

Anarchism couldn't prove itself even in love! Ulrich stands and acts under this impression.

In general the mob chapters, and within them especially Ulrich, depend on the as yet undetermined outcome of the Utopia of Inductive Thinking. But apparently it will amount to: struggling (mentally) and not despairing. Intimation reduced to belief, belief in an inductive God, unprovable but credible. As an adventure that keeps the affects in motion. Main idea. Circulation of the emotions without mysticism. Discovery of God in Köhler's fashion [Wolfgang Köhler, founder of gestalt psychology—TRANS.], or on the basis of other ideas: God's becoming material. Intimation, Other Condition: someone else, who is better suited, might perhaps take these up. How one could force this on people: unimaginable. Either leave what is hated to the age. Or work toward it, that is for it: write a book, therefore suicide, therefore go to war.

Once again the uppermost problem: To be advanced more concretely than both "Pseudorealities," therefore externalized: collapse of the culture (and of the idea of culture). This is in fact what the summer of 1914 initiated.

Now it turns out that this was the great idea the Parallel Campaign was searching for, and what happens is the unfathomable flight from culture. Stumm might say that he is fleeing. All states claim to stand for something spiritual, which they don't define and summarily call culture. It turns out to be utopian in my assessments too. And that's what people no longer have confidence in.

In a certain sense, the entire problem of reality and morality is also the problem of drives. Of their running their instinctive course without result, their causing mischief; they must be controlled in order to prevent murder, usury, etc. But the counterproblem of being controlled is weakness of the drives, the paling of life, and how this is to be compensated for cannot be clearly imagined.

Studies for chapters (1932/33–1941)

Study for the closing session, and then Ulrich—Agathe

Beginning: No one wants to host the closing session of the Parallel Campaign. Finally, Count Leinsdorf: it ought to be ceremonial, not simply a leaving in the lurch, decides to host it himself. Again the hall, etc., as at the last meeting; but this time without the secretaries. And he delivers the concluding address.

Beforehand people gather (ceremoniously) in another room. This provides the opportunity (or also short conversations as they hasten away) of having the other characters pass by in review.

Reconciliation scene between Tuzzi and Diotima. Tuzzi: Now reason wins out. Does he mean that against pacifism? He means: Now the situation is clearing up, perhaps: the situation that up to now has unconsciously hidden behind pacifism. And most profoundly: Reason belongs to the realm of evil. Morality and reason are the opposites of goodness. (Ulrich, too, might possibly say that, coming up to them.)

Then what dominates is: We are in the right; according to the rules of reason and morality we are the ones attacked: perhaps Count Leinsdorf's address. Everyone: We are defending what is ours (homeland, culture).

Arnheim: The world is perhaps perishing or entering a long hell— But perhaps Arnheim is no longer present.

Who?: The world would then perish not through its immoral but through its moral citizens.

Agathe: We go on living as if it were nothing.

Ulrich: No. Suicide. I'm going to war.

Agathe: If anything happens to you: poison.

The shadowing presence of death suddenly becomes visible. One's personal death, without one's having got anything straightened out, and ignoring which life stumbles on and continues unfolding its diversions. In the mob mood, moreover, everyone believes in giving up diversions for a long time. Isn't the final result for Ulrich something like ascesis? The Other Condition has miscarried, and diversions belong to the mutation of emotions? So that would once again be in opposition to the healthy life. An end of utopias.

Buildings—breathlike mass, condensation on surfaces that present themselves . . .

Freed from connections, every impulse momentarily deforms the individual.

The individual, who comes about only through expression, forms himself in the forms of society. He is violated and thus acquires surface.

He is formed by the back-formations of what he has created. If one takes away these back-formations, what remains is something indefinite, unshaped. The walls of the streets radiate ideologies.

GENERAL REFLECTIONS
(C. 1930–1942)

For the beginning

The stories being written today are all very fine, significant, profound, useful distillations and full of spirit. But they have no introductions.

Therefore I have decided to write this story in such a way that in spite of its length it needs an introduction.

It is said that a story needs an introduction only if the writer has not been able to shape it successfully. Splendid! Literature's progress, which expresses itself today in the absence of introductions, proves that writers are very sure of their subjects and their audience. For of course the audience is involved too; the writer has to open his mouth, and the audience must already know what it is he wants to say; if he then says it a little differently and in an unexpected way, he has legitimized himself as creative. So authors and public are generally on good terms today, and the need for an introduction indicates an exceptional case.

A small variation. I would not, however, want to be understood to mean that in my view the greatness of the genius is expressed in the greatness of the variation. On the contrary—the age of fools.

But we also do not want to overlook the fact that in writing introductions a relationship with the audience can be expressed that is *too* good; looked at historically, this is even the way it has been most of the time. The author appears in his window in shirtsleeves and smiles down at the street; he is certain that people will obligingly look up to his popular face if he says a few words personally. It is enough for me to say that I have been spoiled far too little by success to hit upon such an idea. My need for an introduction does not indicate a particularly good relation with the public, and although, as is already apparent, I will make abundant use of the custom of talking about myself in this preface, I hope to be speaking not about an individual person but about a public matter.

Preface, first continuation

Many will ask: What viewpoint is the author taking, and with what results? I can't give a satisfactory account of myself. I take the matter neither from all sides (which in the novel is impossible) nor from one side, but from various congruent sides. But one must not confuse the unfinished state of something with the author's skepticism. I expound my subject even though I know it is only a part of the truth, and I would expound it in just the same way if I knew it was false, because certain errors are way stations of the truth. Given a specific task, I am doing what I can.

This book has a passion that in the area of belles lettres today is somewhat out of place, the passion for rightness/precision. (Polgar [Alfred Polgar, writer and friend of Musil—TRANS.]: Spare us brief stories. In saying that he writes a long one.)

The story of this novel amounts to this, that the story that ought to be told in it is not told.

Possibly: Adduce as well the principle of partial solutions, which is vital to the way I have set up my task. For instance *Törless, Unions*. The basis of many misunderstandings. The public prefers writers who go for the whole.

The term "essayism" is impossibly chosen if one thinks for instance of Carlyle.

Readers are accustomed to demanding that you tell them about life and not about the reflection of life in the heads of literature and people. But that is justified with certainty only insofar as this reflection is merely an impoverished and conventionalized copy of life. I am trying to offer them originals, so they have to suspend their prejudice too.

Mastering unreality is a program, so point to Volume Two, but as a way of concluding it is almost absurd.

Volume One closes approximately at the high point of an arch; on the other side it has no support. What moves me to publication (aside from Rowohlt [Musil's publisher—TRANS.]) is what I have always done; today the structure of a work of fiction is more important than its course. One must learn to understand that side again, then one will have books.

Behind the problems of the day the constitutive problems, which are not, however, the so-called eternal problems.

This is not a skeptic speaking but a person who considers the problem difficult and who has the impression that it is being worked at unmethodically.

Perhaps a preface at the end? A deferred preface.

A depiction of the time? Yes and no. A representation of constitutive relations. Not current; but one level further down. Not skin, but joints.

The problems don't have the form in which they appear? No. The problems don't seem modern. The problems of the present *aren't* modern!

In the chapters on surface and precision I have sought to indicate how that works.

At bottom is the way the mind and spirit of an age are constituted. Here the opposition between empirical thinking and thinking with the emotions.

A glance at life teaches us that it is different. I am by neither talent nor inclination a "naturalist."

There is a lot of talk here about an emotion that today apparently has no place in our lives. If the visitors at a racetrack move in an instant from dissatisfaction with the way the race is conducted to plundering the cash receipts, and a hundred policemen hardly suffice to restore order, what then should . . .

What would it mean, further, in a time in which new forms of states
. . . with power and older forms . . . with power.

Here, too, you will find wit and idea somewhat less responsive than
they might be, badly informed, not up-to-date, at least three months behind. The significance lies less in the examples than in the teaching (ex-
empla docent).

For example, the democracy of the spirit has already advanced as far
as Emil Ludwig, while I am still depicting Arnheim-Rathenau. The
schools as far as Minister of Education Grimm (the age of the great in-
dividualists is past), while I'm still with Kerschensteiner. The literature
industry with looking for Bruckner. Sports at Schäfer's radiant report
that in the list of celebrities in the *Bord* he was far ahead of Jeritza.*
—All this has not escaped me entirely. But I am slow. And I have intentionally remained with my old examples—here or somewhere ought to
come, however, that I do not intend to be historically accurate—because
I believe that investigating my examples will necessarily lead to the same
result. (By doing this I lose effects but win anatomically, or something
similar.)

Nevertheless, in what they yield these examples are not complete either. What ultimately emerges are major lines or only preferred lines, an
ideal scaffolding from which the Gobelins hang, if I may call these stories such on account of their flat technique.

Think of Grimm's speech. This is the way the world is moved, and,
moreover, the struggle of power interests becomes ever purer. But your
criticism, your problem, is directed almost exclusively at democracy.
How do you defend this? You represent as purely as possible the interests of the spirit and intellect, and can't help it that democracy, too, has
partially taken them up in its program and makes fine phrases out of
them. The things you're saying are prolegomena for every party, except
of course for a party that is after fundamental change in a spirit that has
remained unchanged for millennia. You are incessantly in motion be-

*Musil kept up with people and events. He had modeled those in the novel on ones of
an earlier day and is ruminating on the possible effect of the march of time on his novel.—
TRANS.

neath and behind the parties or, as people used to say, above them. You're engaged in trying to find what's independent.

The request that I write an announcement meets with such obstacles in the case of a book with . . . pages, . . . chapters, . . . characters, and thirty-three times as many lines, of which not a single one is intentionally empty, that I prefer to say what this book is *not*.

It is not the Great Austrian Novel people have been awaiting for ages, although . . .

It is not a depiction of the time, in which Herr . . . recognizes his spitting image.

It is just as little a depiction of a society.

It does not contain the *problems* we're suffering from, but . . .

It is not the work of a writer, insofar as   has the task (to repeat, what . . .) but as far as   constructive variation.

One might add: Since the latter lies in the spirit of the totality, this book is idealistic, analytic, possibly synthesizing.

It is not a satire, but a positive construal.

It is not a confession, but a satire.

It is not the book of a psychologist.

It is not the book of a thinker (since it places the ideational elements in an order that—)

It is not the book of a singer who . . .

It is not the book of a successful
                    unsuccessful author.

It is not an easy and not a difficult book, for that depends entirely on the reader.

Without having to go on in this fashion, I think that after this I can say that anyone who wants to know what this book is would do best to read it himself / not rely on my judgment or that of others, but read it himself.

Testament. Notes

The unnecessary expansiveness. A function of the understanding.

Irony is: presenting a cleric in such a way that along with him you have also captured a Bolshevist. Presenting a blockhead so that the author suddenly feels: that's partly me too. This kind of irony, constructive irony, is fairly unknown in Germany today. It is the connection among things, a connection from which it emerges naked. One thinks of irony as ridicule and jeering.

Mysticism: One can only advise every reader: lie down in the woods on a lovely or even a windy day, then you'll know it all yourself. It is not to be assumed that I have never lain in the woods.

The hardest thing to bear: the current misery. But I have to do my work, which has no currency, I must at least carry on with it, after having begun it beforehand.

People expect that in the second volume Ulrich will do something. People know what's to be done. How to do it: I won't give the German Communist Party, etc., any tips. Active spirit and spirit of action.

Why the problem is not an out-of-the-way one.

The practical (political-social) usefulness of such a book. (Avant garde.)

Wilhelm Meister was also well-to-do.

People want Ulrich to *do* something. But I'm concerned with the *meaning* of the action. Today these are confused with each other. Of course Bolshevism, for example, has to occur; but (a) not through books, (b) books have other tasks. Similarity with the war situation and the Ministry of War Information.

. . .

Quotes from Kerschenstein are used too. Arnheim. Lazarsfeld. Förster.

Psychoanalysis!

Frame of mind directed against the present. Therefore, too, against narration, action . . .

That I conclude unfavorably, and precisely in this volume make the greatest demands on the reader, without making it easier for him by means of recapitulation in what happens later.

Also unfavorable structurally.

(There must be something about well-to-do people that lets them admire Thomas Mann. And about my readers that they are people without influence.)

The religious today "represses" (that must be some kind of historical process). This book is religious with the assumptions of the unbeliever.

Always: An intellectual adventure, an intellectual expedition and voyage of exploration. Partial solutions are only one way of expressing this. Here really and truly in a different condition of life. That's not why I'm describing it, but because it touches on a basic phenomenon of our morality. Perhaps a writer can't say "basic phenomenon," but it has to be deeper than the superficial phenomenon. Then it is independent of developments.

One tells a story for the sake of telling, for the significance of the story, for the sake of the significance: three steps.

Afterword: This book had to be broken off before its climax because of lack of money, and it is uncertain whether it will be continued.

For the afterword (and interim preface)

"An affect can induce a violent external action, and internally too the person involved can appear to be quite agitated, and yet it can be a matter of a very superficial affect with little energy" (Kurt Lewin, "Researches on the Psychology of Actions and Affects I," *Psychologische Forschung* VII, no. 1/2 [1941—TRANS.], p. 309). A sentence such as this has been made possible only by psychology's having become literary. But do we writers have a preliminary activity to fulfill? If we did, then in external nature our messiah would have been something like the geographer or botanist! The problem first arises, of course, with the novel. In the epic, and also in the truly epic novel, the character derives from the action. That is, the characters were embedded far more immovably in the action because the action, too, was far more of a piece. So how do I come to insert even a digression on psychology? In ten years it can be superseded and thereby outdated. But the weightiness of the step, the responsibility of the turning toward God, compels the greatest conscientiousness. As does the nature of the adventure in the inductive picture of the world. And that of the "final" love story. And that of the hesitation.

Kitsch: Inadmissibly simplifying the task of life in every situation. (Hence, too, the affiliation of certain kinds of politics with kitsch.)

Quite presumptuously: I ask to be read twice, in parts and as a whole.

One of my principles: it does not matter what, but how, one depicts.
In the psychology chapters that's taken to the point of abuse.
Hence the observation belongs (where?) that today one does not describe the automobile as a miracle but says: car, brand Y, type X.

Moreover, in art one can also do the opposite of everything.

What is brief in relation to the whole, because the appropriate length becomes evident, can be considered long, indeed perhaps endless, if presented by itself. And the tempo is determined only as the sequence unfolds.

. . .

About the chapters on the psychology of the emotions: this is not psychology (in its ultimate intention), but description of the world.

During my work on it and under my hand this book has become a historical novel; it takes place twenty-five years ago! It has always been a contemporary novel developed out of the past, but now the span and tension are very great; but still, what lies beneath the surface, which is one of the chief objects of representation, does not need to be laid significantly deeper.

If I should be reproached with going in for too much reflection, then—without my wanting to go into the relationship between thinking and narrating—today there is too little reflection.

There are too many people in the world who say exactly what must be thought and done for me not to be seduced by the opposite. Strict freedom.

It appears that much is superfluous, present only for its own sake, in the first volume. It is my view that narrated episodes *can* be superfluous and present only for their own sake, but not ideas. In a composition I place unpretentiousness above the so-called wealth of ideas, and in the case of this book there should be nothing superfluous. The statements about the joining together of emotions and ideas which this partial volume contains permit me to establish that like this: The chief effect of a novel ought to be directed at the emotions. Ideas are not to be included in a novel for their own sake. And, a particular difficulty, they cannot be developed in the novel the way a thinker would develop them; they are "components" of a gestalt. And if this book succeeds, it will be a gestalt, and the objections that it resembles a treatise, etc., will then be incomprehensible. The wealth of ideas is a part of the wealth of emotions.

Noted to be mentioned:
Anachronisms in general, and particularly that the representation of the psychology of the emotions stands between that time and today.

Satire getting ahead of itself, procession, possibly Lindner.
Excuse for theory: today we have to explain what we describe.
Where?
Too heavy. Unsolved task of mediating instances.

For an expert, on the other hand, too unfocused!

H. F. Amiel quotes von Csokor: "There is no rest for the spirit except in the absolute, no rest for the feeling except in the infinite, no rest for the soul other than in the divine!" This book is just as opposed to such responses as it is to materialism.

From a book that was a world success (S. Salminen, *Katrina,* from the Swedish, Insel Verlag S. 334–335): ". . . She pulled away from him to the wall, but when he folded her in his arms she did not resist. Only her soft, timid giggling sounded through the dark room. When Gustave saw Serafia with the other village girls on the street, he looked at her full of disquiet. No, no, it had all been in a dream, it had never ever happened. The whole night had been unreal. Yet a few days later, when, late at night, he was passing by Larsson's farm, the unreal came to life again and everything real became strange. He left the road, went across the yard, opened the door and stepped into the room." (A rather idiotic, misshapen creature with lovely eyes, exciting mouth, and voluptuous breast.)

If I could just accustom myself to this a little, I could write such passages too. It's the inception of a double world, of a double person—narrated. But I don't want to. Any talented person can carry on this tradition. And so I have rather attempted the unenjoyable. Someone, sometime, must tie the final knot in this endless thread.

This is, provisionally, still a matter of analyzing peaceful times, but the analysis of pathological times has its foundation here (and some aspects of this will come out in what follows).

What is boring for one person goes by too quickly for another; the expanse of a book is a relation between its actual fullness of detail and the interests of the time.

· · ·

Because a specific section, an adventure, needs to be narrated extensively should not make one forget that Ulrich was by nature energetic and a man with fighting instincts.

[Quoted by Musil in French—TRANS.]: "This feeling is regarded by the Germans as a virtue, as an emanation of the godhead, as something mystical. It is not vibrant, impetuous, jealous, tyrannical, as in the heart of an Italian girl: it is deep and resembles illuminism." Stendhal, *De l'amour* (p. 149)(chapter 48), quoting an author of 1809 (*Voyage en Autriche par M. Cadet-Gassicourt*). (Invented? I don't know.): So this book of mine is a little German?

That I cannot say what this book is, but rather what it is not . . .

A novel's major effect should be on the emotions. Ideas can't be present in it for their own sake. Nor can they—this is a particular difficulty—be developed the way a thinker would; they are "parts" of a *Gestalt*. And if this book succeeds, it will be *Gestalt*, and the objections that it resembles a treatise and the like will then be foolish. The richness of ideas is part of the richness of feelings.

Ulrich's afterword, conclusion

Idea from mid-January 1942.

Thought about the world's political situation. The great yellow-white problem. The coming new epoch in cultural history. China's possible role. On a smaller scale, the quarrel between Russia and the West. Hexner's question, how do you imagine it happening in reality, can't be put off. Even the man without qualities can't ignore it. But that would be a volume of historical, philosophical, etc., essays, or the last of the volumes of aphorisms.

Moreover, influenced by my renewed interest in Dostoyevsky. Hastily noted the impression in a note for my style. I would like to write an essay about his "journalism." About its interpretation by Zdanow, about Pan-Slavism, the Pushkin speech, etc. Before the current background it yields ideas about Russia that I have not even attempted to think through.

This is not to be taken up in the second part of Volume Two, although it is quite pertinent to it.

In this fashion concluding somehow and (instead of or after "A Kind of Conclusion") write an Afterword, concluding word, of Ulrich's.

The Ulrich of today grown older, who experiences the Second World War, and on the basis of these experiences writes an epilogue to his story and my book. This makes possible the union of my plans concerning the aphorisms with this book. It also makes it possible to consider the story and its value for current and future reality.

To be harmonized: the romantic or even Pirandellesque irony of the character above the author.

The story of the characters, considered historically.

Important: the argument with Lao-tsu, which makes Ulrich, but also my task, comprehensible, carried out afterward by Ulrich. Abdul Hasan Summun and Sufism. The story of Agathe and Ulrich would have been more impressive told as a story about him!

TRANSLATOR'S AFTERWORD

Musil's idiosyncratic prose style is unique in German. It is a medium intended to directly engage the reader's emotions as well as his thoughts in a search for the right life in the midst of a crumbling social order. Musil's use of language is virtuosic, and language itself is one of his subjects: it is our vehicle for relating to ourselves and the world and for shaping and expressing both our moral sense and our culture. But language is unstable: "No word means the same thing twice," Agathe says in one place and the author in another.

Language, then, is much more than the vehicle of *The Man Without Qualities;* it is the lever that has the potential to raise up new worlds. This view of language has its roots in Nietzsche, who broke up the classical German sentence along with the attitudes behind it, and close parallels in Musil's Austrian contemporaries Wittgenstein, Freud, Rilke, Kafka, and Karl Kraus. Musil's language is radically experimental: analytical and essayistic, but at the same time permeated with powerful feelings, it is a vividly metaphorical language designed to fuse "precision and soul" and to make the reader feel the fusion. It is a unique achievement. This translator often found himself comparing the style of the novel with the ways in which color, form, and light are variously used in Impressionistic, Expressionistic, and Abstract painting in an attempt to create in the viewer an actual *sense impression* (including the medium of the paint itself), which is seen as somehow closer to truth than a writer simply "telling a story" would be.

Musil's writing is striking and challenging, not comfortable, and in the Modernist vein makes few concessions to the reader, who is expected to do some work. A translator usually looks around in his own language for a model on which to base his translation, so that readers will be able to relate the foreign work to something they are familiar with. Leishman and Spender did this in modeling the translation of

Rilke's *Duino Elegies* on the august tradition of the English elegy, with the result that Rilke's great cycle was domesticated (in every sense) in English. Unfortunately, Rilke, Musil's favorite poet, was doing something far more radical, disruptive, and astonishing with language than the Leishman-Spender model could encompass. But with Musil—all of Musil—one looks in vain in English for any equivalent. Lacking a model, the translator has to stick more closely than he otherwise might to the original, every nuance of which was weighed with great precision by the author. The translator's intention was to have the writing startle the reader in English in the same way it startles a reader in German.

Musil was an experimental writer who was trained as a scientist (behavioral psychologist, mathematician, and engineer) and widely read in psychology and philosophy, so that his impressive literary style is not based on a literary formation. He often writes on a level of semi-abstraction that is meaningful and focused in German but that only produces indigestion in English, the most ruthlessly concrete of languages.

While the novel is analytic and largely essayistic, Musil devoted enormous attention to his characters. He puts himself into their minds: what would this person see in this particular situation, how would he feel, she respond, how would they talk at this moment? These characters speak in their individual voices of background, social class, and profession as well as of personality and mood, and all their perceptions are encapsulated within their individual languages, their idiolects, without the characters themselves being aware of it (as Musil makes the reader aware). Stumm talks like a general in the Austrian army he struggles to transcend; Fischel talks like a self-made businessman; Rachel talks like an uneducated servant girl with delicate feelings who yearns for "higher things." Count Leinsdorf, the feudal aristocrat as influential politician, looks at the modern world through medieval eyes. The sex murderer Moosbrugger has a quite astonishing relation to language, one of the most subtle ventriloquistic effects in the entire novel. This is a function of his entire presentation, but for example the spin on Moosbrugger's ingenious distinction between *Weib* (a loose woman) and *Frau* (a woman one can respect) is beyond translation, rooted as it is in both his sick imagination and the cultural values of his time; and when he refers to Rachel's breasts as *Dinger* (those things), he is indicating his own inability—which also has cultural overtones—to confront the female body.

The narrator's essayistic language (that is, when he is speaking in his own voice), again differs from the characters', as the characters' language differs from individual to individual. The conflicts and misunderstandings on the level of language render vividly the ways in which the conflicted and dying culture of the old Austrian Empire, "Kakania," had become in every sense a Babel.

As a writer, Musil was an obsessive perfectionist and polisher, and his words have a poetic concision and a freight of nuances that must be the despair of any translator. His sentences are rhythmic but often syntactically convoluted, reflecting the old Austrian culture, itself a huge catalog of infinitely nuanced gradations, that this novel memorializes with wit and wonder. It is simply not possible to render all these subtleties in English. There is also the problem of anachronism: although the novel opens in 1913, Musil began working on it in earnest only after World War I, and he was still writing when he died, in exile, in the middle of World War II. So *The Man Without Qualities* is only ostensibly limited by its given year of 1913–1914. Writing after the collapse of the Austrian Empire in 1918 and through the Nazi period and World War II, Musil took subtle but full advantage of anachronisms of reference and language in order to broaden his canvas.

A great help in translating was the discovery that Musil read his writing over aloud. Once the complex rhythms of this prose were understood as spoken rhythms, in spite of the analytic and metaphoric incisiveness, it was possible to more closely approximate the original, whose hallmark in the polished sections is the cadence of clauses set off by semicolons. (Musil is the master of the semicolon!) Paying close attention to the rhythm of Musil's German helped capture both the music and the unremitting sense of urgency that mark the original.

The material in Part 2 of "From the Posthumous Papers" presented different problems. It consists largely of unpolished drafts and fragments encompassing a wide range, from Musil's cryptic notes to himself to fairly worked out scenes. Care had to be taken not to "brush up" inadequacies and inconsistencies but to keep a sense of the relative finish of the different passages, while at the same time making these fragments comprehensible to the reader.

There were the mundane and not quite minor problems that always bedevil the translator, exemplified in Musil's extraordinarily plastic use of the pronoun *es* (it), which darts in all sorts of directions, often in flagrant disregard of the rules governing its use. Musil is fond of the term *unheimlich,* which is difficult to render in English; something that gives you a shiver is *unheimlich,* hence uncanny, haunted, haunting, spooky, weird—none of which, however, capture the immediacy of the German word in its literary use. (It also has a casual and vague colloquial usage.) Musil's most noticeable tic is the overuse of the phrase *in diesem Augenblick* (at this moment), although it follows logically from his insistence on presenting his characters as living in a succession of particular moments, and this succession of moments consequently becomes at least the de facto organizing principle of the novel. There is also his use of the pronoun *man,* which was carefully kept, for the most part, as "one" in English, although its usual translation would be "you" or "we" or a passive construction. Musil uses *man* as a distancing device, to keep his narrator detached from the plane of the characters. This narrator remains as the experimental moralist above the characters, including his protagonist, Ulrich.

I am grateful to many people for their assistance with the swarm of questions that arose in the course of my work. I would like to thank Dagmar Leupold for her patience in helping disentangle many impenetrabilities of Musil's language. I also owe a debt to the cordial and tireless faculty and staff of the Musil Research Institute at the University of Saarbrücken for their help with textual cruxes, as well as to Musil's German editor, Professor Adolf Frisé, for elucidating some places in the German edition that were not clear to me. Not least, I would like to thank my colleagues in the German, psychology, and philosophy departments at the Graduate School of the City University of New York, whom I have often pestered in tracking down a word, terminology, or notion in their disciplines that Musil had appropriated for his purposes.

BURTON PIKE